SIXTEEN SHORT NOVELS

SIXTEEN SHORT NOVELS

An Anthology

Selected and
with an introduction by
WILFRID SHEED

E. P. DUTTON   NEW YORK

BOMC offers recordings and compact discs, cassettes
and records. For information and catalog write to
BOMR, Camp Hill, PA 17012.

Published in the United States by E. P. Dutton, a division of New American Library,
2 Park Avenue, New York, N.Y. 10016

Library of Congress Catalog Number: 85-72562

Contents

CONTENTS

Ground Rules
and Acknowledgments

In choosing these particular titles, I have tried where possible to avoid the over-anthologized: partly because these can easily be found elsewhere, and partly to break a monopoly. There must be veterans of the paperback racks who believe that *The Bear* by William Faulkner, Thomas Mann's *Death in Venice* and Henry James's *The Aspern Papers* are the only short novels ever written. Yet even sticking to these three authors, one could rustle up a fresh anthology of extraordinary quality—and not simply of *Great Writers' Second-Bests*. Collections tend to repeat each other, until their repetitions become classics, while those left out seem to dwindle with each omission.

This exclusionary principle has been broken at least once here, by *Notes from Underground,* which simply barreled its way in, and been bent more often than that. But such masterworks as Tolstoy's *Death of Ivan Illych* and Nathanael West's *Miss Lonelyhearts* have been reluctantly omitted on grounds of super-availability. Contrariwise, an equal number of fine but largely unknown (to me) entries from Japan, Africa, Latin America, *et al.,* have also had to wait till next time simply because my editor Joe Kanon's shoehorn could not ease them in. In short, it's a vast field still crying out for exploration, and no anthology is the last word on it.

Several friends and colleagues must be thanked for suggestions, especially the omnilibrous (to off-rhyme with omnivorous) Clifton Fadiman, Berton Roueché, Ted Hoagland, Burt Pike, and Sea Captain Paul Schiffman. Al Silverman was merely indispensable—let's leave it at that. Alice van Straalen was, if such be possible, even more so. Alice not only found most of the editions we used (and most of the ones we didn't), but read and discussed every one of them with a professional skill and originality that made the final selection a pleasure rather than a chore. I salute her now as a full partner in crime.

WILFRID SHEED

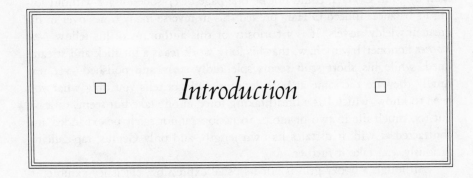

Introduction

E. M. Forster defined "the Novel" as a "prose fiction of a certain length." Quite so. This would make "the short novel" "a prose fiction of a certain *other* length." Except that, whereas the novel can, like a heavyweight boxer, grow to infinity, the short novel is pre-eminently a story that knows when to stop.

For various dingy economic reasons, the short novel has been in eclipse lately; but this doesn't mean it isn't being written. All that's happened is that the author now doesn't stop when he ought to but continues to pad and stretch until out waddles another of those fat, blowsy models in vogue, like Gibson girls, at the moment. Fillet a best-seller and you will often find the delicate bones of a short novel.

Thus a form which the greatest masters have found essential for certain effects has gone into hiding within the flab and folds of the overweight, over-dressed potboiler. People who buy their books by the pound probably deserve what they get. But if one stops for a moment to compare written fiction with the very best plays and movies, one hits on a curiosity—to wit, that these artifacts almost invariably fall within the rubber boundaries we've set for short novels (20,000–50,000 words). Which means that this is the optimum scale for such drama as can be taken at one sitting, a scale that literature can hardly afford to forfeit. In fact if a filmmaker wishes to tackle a long novel he is best advised to boil it down to a short one first, not only in length but in scope. (I understand how stage directions, etc., can distort word count but scope doesn't lie.) As somebody once said, or should have, they might have got away with the War or the Peace but not with both.

Some of the selections in this volume are there partly to demonstrate the short novel's efficiency, before we go on to higher things. The unsung *An-*

drea, by John O'Hara, could not be one page or episode longer without losing its balance. Indeed O'Hara proved this in reverse many times over in his great unwieldy novels. It is a curiosity of this author, as of his fellow *New Yorker* fictioner Irwin Shaw, that his long work reads a bit slick and streamlined, while his short stuff seems splendidly spare and polished—yet texturally they are the same at both lengths. O'Hara tells you only what you need to know, which has a breathtaking force in one take but seems to leave out too much life in two or more. So fiction cannot safely be expanded and contracted at will: it dictates its own length, and only Genius, tap-dancing furiously, can take it further.

Although a boozy grin is not its usual expression, efficiency exhibits itself also, in strange ways, in John Steinbeck's *Tortilla Flat.* Samuel Coleridge once said (as a metaphor for poetry) that a palace is more than a house but it must at least be a house, and *Tortilla Flat* is a very fine house of fiction: people can live in it and die, enter, look around and leave. Within a small frame, Steinbeck contrives to animate a whole landscape, like a Brueghel painting, with such vividness and bold colors that the reader feels he could write stories about it himself, forever and ever. One wonders by the end why anyone *needs* more pages than this: which, coming from the author of such marathons as *East of Eden,* seems like a saturnine joke.

Andrea and *Tortilla Flat* are two extremes of efficiency and can be used here as bookends marked "personal" and "public," within which our other specimens can be ranged right to left. *Andrea* is a hermetically private story. We hear one side of a relationship and trust it, perhaps because the speaker is a lawyer (O'Hara left nothing to chance) and then we witness the other side with a start. Surprise endings are rare in the best fiction: they only work when one feels "but of course. I knew that." Rereading is the test: usually the story seems dead and used up once you know the surprise. But with *Andrea* the male reader at least may get a queasy feeling the second time round that some weakness in himself has made him too gullible, too willing to accept a man's version of a love affair. This goes considerably beyond the accomplishment of my first choice, Scott Fitzgerald's *The Rich Boy,* which tells the same kind of story with the cards face up and which leaves the reader as smugly detached as it found him.

Tortilla Flat is, of course, a public story. Its characters have no insides to speak of, and there isn't a narrator in sight, although the latter's voice actually fills the ear with reverberant chatter in the manner of a stage illusionist, like the late Ruth Draper, who fills the theater with voices and street sounds while chatting quietly to herself. Other stories at the public end of our line include Edith Wharton's *The Old Maid,* in which the stage is almost empty, but a whole society, Old New York, waits in the wings watching and judging: the characters twitch to the silent demands of this invisible presence, or try vainly to rebel against it, but in either case are broken. Society kills, in the

Gospel of Wharton—although she was excessively "Society" herself, prefer-
ring to be on the side of the killers (compare Evelyn Waugh). In *Old Maid,*
Wharton uses, incomparably well, a technique which has since been vulgarized beyond recognition by the movies: namely, the bland exterior followed by the harsh close-up. In the early going, we see how Society looks,
then, from a single case, we see how it works: the Old Maid of the title is
making only one of the million artful sacrifices that keep the surface smooth.

Wharton also dabbles here with the notion dear to modern philosophy
that you are what you pretend to be. The Old Maid has become like the hero
of Kurt Vonnegut's *Mother Night,* identical with her role, impressed on it
like the face on a coin. What began as an act is finally her very substance. Yet
this crippling role was the best deal she could strike with convention and
have any life at all. The haunting thing about this story is that it is not exactly sad, in fact it has a curious vivacity: it is merely hopeless.

Tortilla Flat is conversely a dream of triumphant anarchy—but by necessity only a dream. The *paisans* who romp through the incessant sunshine of
Steinbeck's Monterey are like gypsies observed by a small boy: carefree, colorful, fun-loving. The author knows better, of course, that up close they are as
warmhearted as condors and only unintentionally funny, but he observes the
author's right to keep his distance and fashion us an idyll. The headlong,
higgledy-piggledy rush of events in *Tortilla* leaves us feeling that we have
seen more than we have. This is one of many ways of stretching the short
novel, which in the right hands can be almost any size that it likes. Incidentally for revisionists who wonder if anything good could come out of Steinbeck, Edmund Wilson makes an interesting point: he believed that Steinbeck
was at heart a marine biologist who wrote very well about people in clusters
going blindly about their biological business, but not so well without his
microscope. For which reason, he names *Tortilla Flat* perhaps Steinbeck's best
work.

A final example of a story that bursts its narrative seams is *Mario and the
Magician,* by Thomas Mann. I once tried to teach Mann's unteachable *Death
in Venice,* only to be stopped in my tracks by a student who said, "I don't dig
stories about fags." I generally have a weakness for the literal mind; it is, like
Coleridge's good house, the least that can be asked of criticism. But in this
case, it hadn't occurred to me that I'd been reading a story about fags. Mann
was much too grand for that; nothing less than the Human Condition was
worth his time. *Death in Venice* was written shortly before World War I, and
although one couldn't precisely say that it is "about" that either, the malaise
in the air, the plague that frees and even obliges the hero to pursue his fantasy makes a nice metaphor for the coming of war.

In *Mario and the Magician* (1929) the malaise is pettier and more specific: the rudeness on the beach, the meaningless little scenes—the new
plague is mean and squalid and we know its name. In real life, Mussolini has

risen and Hitler is coiled to pounce in Mann's own Germany. This is no time to be subtle, so Mann is appropriately blunter and more, by his pure standards, journalistic, than usual. Mario clearly represents the new dictators, whom Mann's lofty narrator sees right away to be shabby, gimcrack magicians who know how to dazzle and control provincials, but not people like himself. The story's horror, which the narrator cannot quite bring himself to face, is that by the end he is dazzled and controlled too, as many intellectuals would soon be by Hitler and his fellow clown. Later he can neither understand nor believe it; but by exaggerating the nightmare quality of Mario's magic show he reveals inadvertently that something unspeakable happened to him that night: he was violated; "the citadel of his integrity," as Lawrence of Arabia called it, was stormed. Thus Mann anticipates the voice of the World War II collaborator: whining, dissociating himself, mumbling "you had to be there."

Short novels are written for a variety of reasons, not the least of them pure accident. Some are short stories that just grew; others are novels that wouldn't. Henry James was the patron saint of the latter, scrupulously spotting when his novels had run down and mercifully killing them. As for the former, the process is a good deal woollier and less surgical, at least as described by Mark Twain. It seems that *Pudd'nhead Wilson* started out as a very short story about Siamese twins, but that these were soon joined by a whole raft of other characters, who in turn took to elbowing each other, to the point where our desperate author decided to clear the sprawl by literally drowning some of them. "I was going to drown some more but I gave up the idea, partly because I believed . . . it would arouse attention." So he settled for flattening them out until "they were not even worth drowning" and keeping them around as props.

In the end *Pudd'nhead* may have reached its final slightly ungainly size not only because even a flat Twain character has to be reckoned with and the gang wound up requiring at least two stories in one, but because the mishmash was presided over by two Twains, the younger of them still skylarking like Huck Finn and the older one beginning to hate mankind too much to laugh. The two selves are most clearly to be found in the chapter headings, Pudd'nhead Wilson's diary entries, where Twain is sometimes at his feckless funniest ("cauliflower is nothing but cabbage with a college education"), and sometimes just mechanically, misanthropically cynical. A third, more serene fellow may even be spotted betwixt and between the Twains, trying to make them meet; but whether two or three, they cannot be crammed into the pleasant and rather ordinary skull of the character Pudd'nhead Wilson.

In the story itself the blend is more artful. The villain is a textbook psychopath, although the textbook hadn't been written yet: a scoundrel with no conscience except when caught, at which point his grief is fearsome; also a reflexive liar and the object of much twentieth-century study and handwring-ing. Yet Twain handles him as pure entertainment, a stage villain less harbin-ger than throwback. As with *Andrea,* the tension between the facts and the telling is the story's generator. Twain, the black-hearted comedian, was never to combine his gifts, or curses, so well again.

Many short novels mark turning points in their author's careers, or simply beginnings. It is a form ideally designed for feeling one's way, either in or out of a phase. Chekhov's *Ward No. 6,* for instance, pretty much marks the end of his great short-story period and the dawn of his playwriting. How better to celebrate than with a short novel? In passing he also gives a poisoned-kiss farewell to an older love, the craft of medicine. "People," he writes in *Ward No. 6,* "who have official, professional relations with someone else's suf-fering—judges, authorities, physicians, for example—become so inured in the course of time, from force of habit, that even should they want to be sympa-thetic, they are incapable of any but a formal concern for their clients. In this respect they are no different from the peasant who slaughters [animals] without noticing the blood." Chekhov must have felt he'd escaped this pro-fession with his life.

After *Ward No. 6,* where might one have expected such a writer to go next? Very likely, one would have guessed Novel. The psychological horror story at the core of *Ward No. 6* reminded me, if not Chekhov, of Dos-toevsky's efforts (Russian writers are not as alike as they look at this dis-tance), and the picture of bureaucracy's mincing, insinuating role in modern life cries out for more canvas. And yet, if I may use another sporting meta-phor, a sprinter running a mile does it very differently from a long-distance man, the former setting a fast pace and just hoping to finish, while the latter has to remind himself he hasn't got all day; there is something about *Ward No. 6* which suggests that Chekhov is not prepared to go an inch further than he has to.

So plays it was—which as we have seen are just the right length for a short novelist. *Ward No. 6* turns out to have been a felicitous warm-up for the theater. Having started with short comic sketches, a strange place for a Russian to start, Chekhov reaches maximum extension and is ready for his extraordinary last act.

In this he differed drastically from Dostoevsky, who could run all day, even with a natural short novel like *Crime and Punishment. Notes from Under-ground* marks a multiple turning point. Young Fyodor had been something of a literary dandy, whose first published work was a translation of Balzac's *Eugénie Grandet,* a novel of great technical virtuosity and an excellent book to go to school to. The dandy may be said to have died in front of a tsarist firing squad (Tsar Nicholas I was a tease who thought fake firing squads were a grand way to cow dissidents), but the Europeanized skill survived, looking for a place to go. Like a sophisticate who has found Jesus, Dostoevsky had trouble finding a suitable form at first. In this phase he wrote two books best described simply as notebooks, storehouses of raw thought and experience, and began, with his brother, to edit magazines. And it was in this unlikely capacity that he found himself writing *Notes from Underground.*

This must be the only short novel that ever started out as a book review. The target was an inane popular book called *What Is to be Done?*, by one N. G. Chernyshevsky, remembered today solely because Dostoevsky attacked it. N. G., as we'll call him, preached that as man grew wiser he must automatically grow better. Fyodor, perhaps remembering his firing squad, found this hilarious: what about willfulness and boredom? he asks N.G. for openers. What happens to the man who is tired of being good? Let me tell you a story.

The rest of the argument can be retired to the attic after the grotesqueries of our century. But it served its purpose. Dostoevsky was able to spew out all the polemic in his editorial heart, while his real genius couldn't help refining the review into fiction. The narrator is a tireless and familiar café arguer, but there's something funny about him. Even though he is writing for his own eyes only, he is constantly apologizing, retracting, bowing and scraping as it were to himself. He offers himself in a series of anecdotes as the embodiment of man's willfulness that forever frustrates the Rule of Reason: but what he turns out to be is an embodiment of cowardice, a Great Clown who consistently misreads his own actions and is afraid even of offending himself. Either way the Rule of Reason gets clobbered. But Dostoevsky ends with a significant point that wasn't in the original indictment. The new urban man, it seems, lives his life so indirectly, through books and dreams and hearsay, that when he bumps perforce into reality itself he finds it distasteful and almost unrecognizable and quite beyond his capacity to cope. Thus the bookish Dostoevsky, with all his European and Romantic charms, dismisses his old muse and girds himself for the direct, overpowering Russian reality that will thunder through the great novels.

Of Camus's *The Fall* it is safe to say it could not have been written if Dostoevsky hadn't been there already. The narrator, who must first bore and madden before he can mesmerize, is a Russian import that suited the French all too well. But Camus has his own "fine Arabian" (as Fats Waller would say) reasons for using him. Recurrently Camus used to tell his Dominican priest friends that his real dream was to be the twentieth-century Saint Augustine, the great penitent miraculously reborn in North Africa—as soon as his affairs of the heart were straightened out. Of course, these were not going to get straightened out overnight ("Give me chastity but not yet."—Saint Augustine) but if by God's grace they did, he would need a good confession. And in fact his next book was planned as an autobiography, which he also dragged his feet on, perhaps not knowing whether it would be a confession or a crow of triumph.

So, as if to mark time, he wrote this mock confession that can also be read as a trial run for the real thing. Because Camus had split with his left-wing intellectual friends he dragged them in, too—one might as well use a book for as many purposes as possible, including, pre-eminently in this case, swatting one's enemies. Camus had broken with the Paris café even as Dostoevsky had, in favor of something cruder and more genuine.

But the real subject is himself, a man at peace only in the theater and on the soccer field, Camus's own favorite haunts. His original sin, and his old radical friends' sin, is simply loving humanity for one's own greater glory. His spokesman Jean-Baptiste (what better name for a trial run?) Clemence gets an almost sensual pleasure from doing good; and then reverberant waves of softer pleasure from the world's approval of his goodness. To escape this sin, Clemence twists and plunges through a sewer of other sins. But as he emerges bespattered through the manhole of Amsterdam he finds that his real sin is mediocrity, he is no better than Everyman.

He has even, he claims, fashioned this confession to fit his listener: it isn't his own at all. Unfortunately this elegant twist brings with it a tiresome technical difficulty: because, for this particular end game to work, the sins have to have been kept general enough for Everyman to have done them, so the episodes lack particularity and hence life. We don't get to meet anybody, because we're supposed to fill them in for ourselves.

As fiction kept bursting in on Dostoevsky, it keeps leaking out of Camus—and not just in *The Fall*. The talky ending of the fictionally superb *The Stranger* shows that Camus, like his patron saint, couldn't wait to get up in the pulpit. Yet even from there, his parables have the sensual "felt" quality of his straight fiction, and if *The Fall* can loosely be described as "the short novel as sermon" it is a rare sermon you can live through as intensely as this, remembering even the sights and smells. I have my own special fondness for it because it also demonstrates that a love affair with one's own mind can be quite as poignant as a great romance, especially when it seems to end, like this one, with a breakup.

William Faulkner's motive for writing *Old Man* is as wayward and unexpected as one might expect from the crafty woodsman. It seems his early novel *The Wild Palms* needed a booster shot, "something to lift it like counterpoint. So I wrote on the *Old Man* story until *The Wild Palms* story rose back to pitch." Then he dropped the Old Man until it was needed once again, to carry its sagging partner across the finish line.

A story composed like that might be expected to have trouble standing up by itself: counterpoint heard in isolation can be pretty bewildering. But one doesn't read Faulkner for form. Here as elsewhere, he seems to be playing a different game from other writers. Every now and then in *Old Man* he throws in a bit of a plot, like a man giving the rudder a twitch with his big toe, but otherwise the whole ensemble of author and story simply seems to rush forward like the "Old Man," the river itself. Faulkner on the Mississippi is Faulkner at his purest: prose and the river. Only in such a flood of sensation could one put up with characters simply called "the convict" and "the woman" and "the *fat* convict" (my italics). But when Old Man Faulkner is rolling along, the characters become mere flotsam like the dead cows and deer that float past the convict's skiff.

This is the short novel as pastoral epic, and it is the one instance in this anthology where the novel form is principally useful as a frame and not as an innate shape. I quite like the plot, mind you, but it could easily be dispatched in a few pages. What it needs is a great river to bob along on, in order to reduce the characters to pinpoints, and to render them priceless at the same time—a trick worked less successfully by Faulkner's sentimental rival Hemingway in *The Old Man and the Sea*. But enough river is enough and another ten pages of it in *Old Man* could easily have left a reader waterlogged.

Which brings us of course to Joseph Conrad. Conrad, as was his wont, became testy after a while about his identification with the sea, possibly because the British have a rollicking niche for sea writers in which the somber Pole wouldn't have wished to be found dead. But *Youth* was written before all that fuss, when his love of the sea was as hearty as anyone's and he was still delighted to be writing English stories of any kind at all. "This could have occurred nowhere but in England," he starts off exuberantly, "where men and sea interpenetrate." His two grand passions, England and water, seem to effervesce into a sort of briny rebirth—and where better than a short novel for such a ceremony?

It would probably be a mistake to call Conrad himself lighthearted even at this point, but *Youth* is a magnificent testament to remembered lightheartedness. The author was only 41, young at writing but old at sailing, and he could still call on the joy of youth at his desk as he had at the tiller: but the story is actually told by an older man, the ubiquitous Marlow, who knows that outside the story lies darkness.

But the story shines the brighter for it. Marlow becomes his young self again (a relief for those who didn't think he had one), and as long as the bottle lasts, he relives the giddiness and cruelty, the passion for adventure and the regal isolation of youth, from other people's feelings or interests, along with youth's paradoxically acute observation of their characters. The result is a sort of nautical *Candide,* in which every misfortune is greeted by our hero with glad cries of welcome. The rustbucket he sails in, the *Judea,* is a veritable Buster Keaton of boats, moving doggedly through a sea of troubles—fires, floods, explosions—while our hero raves on inwardly about the excitement of it all. I hesitate to use the word in this august connection, but *Youth* strikes me as very funny. I also have the word of a sea-captain friend of mine that *Youth* is perhaps the best piece of writing about that particular business, down to the smallest tremor of the winches, that you are likely to find anywhere.

As a landlubber who quickly gets his fill of seas, rivers and navigable waterways, I find Conrad's aquatic interests just a good excuse for his prose, which was never fresher or more thrillingly exact than here. In later years, sitting up through the night with the likes of Henry James and Ford Madox Ford, and then for agonized hours sitting just by himself, he *thought* his way bloodily into being a better novelist, on land or sea. But in *Youth* he seems to be waving good-bye to something for good. *Landfalls and Departures* is not only one of his titles but a throbbing obsession. His sea treasury was still good for years at this stage, but the boy who had been there sails away in this short trim novel while the old man at the dock watches, shrugs and shivers.

With Henry James, we move emphatically back indoors: even his exteriors sound like drawing rooms. I have grouped him and Willa Cather together, not because they are soulmates (far from it) but because of an observation by the ever helpful Edmund Wilson, to wit, "Miss Cather seems to suffer from a disability like that of Henry James: it is almost impossible for her to describe an emotion or an action except at secondhand." Wilson himself felt that one had almost a moral duty to court raw experience, the seedier the nobler, as his diaries show, and he is merciless to writers who shirk this. So he is temperamentally unsympathetic to James's famous indirection.

In fact James showed again and again that the overheard story, the *half* overheard story can reverberate more powerfully than many a slice of life. However, an unmixed diet of indirectness could drive even such an admirer as Graham Greene to mutter "you can't be ambiguous in bed," so I have chosen stories from both James and Cather where, however seemingly secondhand, the emotions seem most likely to be their own.

If we use the English formulation "James I, James II, and the Old Pretender," *The Lesson of the Master* could be called late I or early II, another of those handy bridges that short novels form. James had settled into, and was busily furnishing, his role of "artist person," a creature of monastic dedication observing life through the barred windows of his art. In *The Lesson of the Master* he makes rather startling fun of this new self before disappearing into it for good. He suggests that these high-minded eunuchs of Art may even miss the point of such life as forces its way through the bars, owing to their fever of introspection. But of course one cannot be sure. The worldly old Master (one thinks of Robert Browning, who fascinated James and turns up for certain in *The Private Life,* another novella) may have sacrificed even more in *not* choosing the monastic path. James, who was himself to set some sort of record as a London dinner guest, is as usual in two minds. But one senses that he was slightly more likely to look one in the eye on the subject of art than of love.

Willa Cather's case seems simpler. As a lesbian she was forced by convention to write forever around her emotions, while calling them something else. *A Lost Lady* should have been sensual enough even for Wilson, but Cather had to fuzz it with male surrogates. *My Mortal Enemy* comes as close as she could get to her subject, and in this case the fact that she couldn't get closer is a strength—and a classic confirmation of Hemingway's mystagogical dictum that if you know something and leave it out you strengthen a story, but if you don't know it, you leave a hole. Curiously enough, Cather felt frustrated at not being allowed to identify her *Mortal Enemy;* yet surely if she had, one would have said, "Oh, is *that* all" and forgotten the whole matter. The unanswered question is part and parcel of the impact.

Two very different offshoots of *The Lesson of the Master* show how snugly indirection fits into a small frame. Philip Roth's *Ghost Writer* is a superb imitation of James and none the less so for being about a pair of Jewish-American writers. A good story should be doing more than one thing, and Roth is able to settle his affairs with his contemporaries in a mode of Victorian reticence that is a million miles from his original beat in Newark. But again, the force would evaporate if we or the hero knew exactly what was going on. If the voice upstairs really is Anne Frank, that's that. The game stops while we decide whether this is a good idea or not. If she's just pretending, then we have to know much more: if she's not, probably we know too much already. But our observer is sleepy and unJameseanly muddled with lust. And the next morning a whole fresh set of clues awaits us for breakfast: not to be answered but to be mixed in with the others. The clues are the story. Any solution is a diminution. Again, shortness is all. A reader can only stand on his tiptoes for so long.

In John Fowles's *The Ebony Tower* the partition between the hero and life is the hero himself. David Williams has a very good view from his ebony tower of criticism and abstraction—he sees two girls lying naked on the lawn and eventually hears their stories; nothing is kept from him, nothing needs to be. Because he cannot descend. Fowles, to be sure, stands James on his head by making his scurvy, life-loving master the real artist and the pure young man a second-rater, but James on his head is still James, viewed from a slightly different angle.

"Faut couper les racines," says the old rogue in the story: one must cut the roots. Fowles suggests that his own inspiration came from a medieval Celtic legend called *Eliduc.* But to read it is to come against a stone wall. What on earth did he get out of it? *Eliduc* is a bare little narrative of courtly love that a scurvier generation might have entitled "I love my wife, but oh you kid." There is no telling what will set an author off: but why this clanking tale of

love thwarted and rewarded should have put Mr. Fowles in the mood to write *The Ebony Tower* is a secret between him and his muse. However, the attribution does serve to deflect the eye from Fowles's other roots, whatever they may be.

Of Brian Moore's *Catholics* it may be enough to say that it started the train of thought for which this volume constitutes the terminal. Moore had written some wonderful early novels based on his Belfast and Canadian origins but then, like many a writer, seemed to find himself slightly at sea in Hollywood, where the novelist's left hand tends to be doodling with screenplays and treatments, to the distraction of both hands. And even if the writer is innocent of film, novels require a time and concentration that war with the whole atmosphere of moviemaking; a serious fictioner would feel like a truck horse lumbering alone down a fast track.

The short novel has come to the rescue of several writers in this predicament, including James M. Cain and Nathanael West, but never more resoundingly than with Brian Moore. Because he used the form for a complete escape: if a book can be called the opposite of a place, *Catholics* is the opposite of Hollywood: the cold monastery stones, the placid faces and movements of the monks, the primacy of the spiritual. It must have been intoxicating to write a story in which the life-or-death struggle centers not on what the public presumably wants this year but on the survival of the Latin Mass. Moore as he writes it seems himself like a man on spiritual retreat, regaining his strength in a monastery, even if he has to build it himself. For the reader the miracle is to watch a writer coming back to life in a place associated by nonbelievers with death.

But *Catholics* is a small book, and small books can get lost. Hence this volume and I hope many others.

As to the last selection, *The Blacking Factory* by Wilfrid Sheed, there is absolutely no excuse for it—except to say that there is probably not a writer in or out of this book (you don't have to be good to be pushy) who wouldn't have done the same for himself. Let this rank abuse of editorial privilege serve as a last specimen of the randomness that often attends the birth of these little fellows. The first chapter of my novella appeared (in somewhat different form, as they say) in *Vogue* in 1958. Ten years later, it collided in my memory with a scrap of information I'd been carrying for years: that Colonel McCormick, the isolationist, anglophobe tsar of the *Chicago Tribune,* had once gone to school in England. What on earth can they have done to him over there? thought I. And then I realized I had already written the start of my answer. Since I didn't want any more answers, I quit when I had polished off the Colonel's schooling—only to find that I needed to run up another novella *(Pennsylvania Gothic)* to go with it and help make the publishing weight.

Unfortunately, some readers groping among the few famous names they knew assumed I was writing about William F. Buckley. Far from it: Buckley's English school days must surely have been a purple triumph for that sensitive lad. The notion of moving my man from print into radio came not from anyone special but from intermittent exposure to radio cranks of all sorts who constitute a vast underworld that, quite unknown to those aboveground, claims the allegiance of millions. I did not even need to borrow Buckley's accent, which I believe is more a family heirloom than an English souvenir, because far riper off-English accents than his crash on my transatlantic ears constantly. I may even have been using my own.

So we have it: fifteen short novels and one horrible example. And let the reader be warned. I have at least another fifteen up my sleeve that I am prepared to unleash on the slightest provocation. *Caveat lector* and enjoy your dinner.

JOHN O'HARA

Andrea

Nearly everything she said was truthful, but because she laughed so much her friends often believed she was joking and remained her friends. She had beautiful teeth, even and strong all the way back, and some of her friends had been known to remark that it was such a pleasure to look at her teeth that it actually did not matter much what she said. There were, of course, a few people who were not deceived by her laughter or diverted by the display of her teeth, and those people hated her. "How can you hate someone like Andrea Cooper?" her more constant friends would say. "There's no one around that brightens up a room the way she does." But Andrea had left many wounded souls along her merry way, and there were men among them as well as women.

Throughout her lifetime Andrea's popularity had always been more immediate and durable with boys and with men. It was said of her that her frankness, her honesty, appealed to the males. It was certainly true that if she had ever been ill at ease with the opposite sex, it did not show. One of the first things I noticed about her when I began to notice her at all was her quick decision, at a party or on the club verandah, to join the young men in preference to the girls. If there were two or three young men standing together she would go up to one of them and tug his sleeve. "Andrea's here," she would say, and she would be sure of her welcome. In those days a lot of girls were borrowing a line from a movie called *Young Man of Manhattan,* in which Ginger Rogers (or maybe it was Toby Wing) said, "Cigarette me, big boy." I never heard Andrea say just those words, but then I did not often hear Andrea use a line that was not her own.

She was then about sixteen years old, maybe fifteen but not seventeen. Her mother and father had come to town the year before, leaving Andrea and her brother in school in California while Mr. and Mrs. Cooper found a suitable place to live. Mrs. Cooper had inherited the second largest department store from her grandmother, and Mr. Cooper, who had been working in a bank in Santa Barbara, was going to try his hand at managing the store. Everyone agreed that King's needed new blood and that Mr. Cooper could not do any worse than the previous managers. With his banking experience he might even put King's back on its feet again. Much to everyone's surprise he did just that, although the results were slow in coming. Mr. and Mrs. Cooper were young, still in their thirties, and young for their age. He possessed a California affability that could have affected people either way, but in his case it worked favorably on the other business men. Mrs. Cooper, a native Pennsylvanian who had grown up on the West Coast, was a rather diffident woman who let her husband do most of the talking. She was obviously devoted to him, had no designs on other women's husbands, and the Coopers fitted in much more quickly than most newcomers to the town. In their first year in town they won the mixed doubles in the club tennis tournament, knocking off a much younger couple who had two legs on the cup and were believed to be invincible.

They had Andrea finish out the year in a Santa Barbara school before transferring her to one in New England, and what with one thing and another, I did not get a good look at Andrea until after her mother and father had been living in town for the better part of two years. *"Who is that?"* I said, when I first saw her. She was obviously too young for me; I was already halfway through law school and had been having an affair with a married woman in West Philadelphia. Nevertheless my first reaction on seeing Andrea, with a golden band in her pale blond hair, those teeth, her breasts as firm as fists under her sequined white dress, was of civic pride. This radiant creature had come to live in my home town, and I had seen nothing like her at the Philadelphia parties. It may have been that she was overdressed for her age, but as someone said, she would have looked good in a sweatshirt.

I cut in on her at that first dance, and she flattered me by knowing who I was. "Hello, Judge," she said. "Thanks for rescuing me."

"What do you mean, *judge?*" I said.

"Isn't that what you're going to be?"

"It's a long way off if I am," I said. "But how did you know?"

"I made a point of knowing," she said.

"You mean it was love at first sight?"

"No, I didn't say that. I just said I make a point of knowing *if* they're at all attractive," she said.

"Score one for the common people," I said. "You build me up and then knock me down."

"Didn't knock you down," she said. "How could I? You saved my life. That horny man you cut in on, he's older than my father."

"Peter Hofman," I said.

"He didn't want to dance, he wanted to wrestle."

"That's the price you pay," I said. "You're the belle of the ball. Peter Hofman is always out to show us young fellows that he's the best dancer, the greatest lover."

"I've seen his wife, *and* his children. He ought to keep them in hiding. They're not much of an ad for him."

The music stopped. "Are you thirsty?" I said.

"No, but if you are, go ahead. You want to go out to the smoking-room."

"Not necessarily."

"I'm not supposed to go there," she said. "My parents issued strict orders."

"Do you always obey your parents?"

"Of course, especially when they're in the same room and keeping an eye on me."

"Oh, I haven't seen them," I said. "They're here?"

"They're probably in the smoking-room. Daddy probably having a ginger ale and Mother the same. But I'm sure that's where they are. You go on, I won't mind."

"No, I can get a drink any time."

"Then how would you like to take me out on the porch and give me a cigarette? I've also been told not to smoke, although they know I do smoke. But it's unbecoming, very unbecoming for a young girl to smoke."

"They're pretty strict with you," I said, as we moved toward the verandah.

"They have to be," she said. "Otherwise there's no telling what I'd do. I might be out in the car, wrestling with Mr. Hofman."

"Would you wrestle very hard?"

"If it was Mr. Hofman I'd kick him, you know where," she said.

"Where it would do the most good, but not for old Peter," I said. "I have a car out there."

"Then we won't have to freeze on the porch," she said.

"I've even got a pint of prescription liquor."

"You think of everything, don't you? Unfortunately, they'll smell it on my breath when I kiss them goodnight. Then they won't let me go to the other dances. I'm not supposed to drink till I'm eighteen."

We got in my car, an Essex speedster in which you practically sat on the floor, and I lit her cigarette. "I'll never get used to the weather in the East," she said. "Maybe I'll never get used to the East, period."

"Did you have a heavy beau in California?"

"About your weight, I guess," she said.

"A hundred and seventy-four," I said.

"No, it isn't just him. There's something different about Easterners.

Even Mother, brought up in California, she's different than Daddy, the way they look at things. She was born here, but she left when she was a little girl. Do you know who's like us? The Swedes. So it isn't just the climate."

"How are you like the Swedes?" I said. "Have you known many Swedes?"

"My heavy beau was from a Swedish family. They all moved to Southern California from Minnesota. His father and his uncles and aunts, and cousins. I must know a hundred or more. And they're always picked out as typical Southern Californians. People used to think I was one of them, when I went to their parties. But my mother's family were from the North of Ireland, and Daddy's people came from Iowa."

"Aren't there a lot of Swedes in Iowa? They spilled over from Minnesota."

"I didn't know that. Then I may *be* part Swedish. I've never been to Iowa."

"You do look rather Swedish," I said. "I've been there, on the North Cape cruise. You could be taken for a Swede."

"They like to have a good time, and so do I," she said. "I'd give anything for a drink."

"No, you don't want to miss the other parties."

She looked at me, frowning and studying me as though I were some strange specimen that she was having trouble identifying.

"What?" I said.

"I'm not sure," she said, still studying me.

"About what?"

"You. Do you care whether I miss the other parties?"

"I don't, but you do," I said. "I won't even *be* here, but two of the parties are bound to be good, and there's the Assembly."

"I can't go to the Assembly. I'm too young."

"Well, there are the other two. You wouldn't want to miss them. Markel's for one, and Sherbo for the other."

"I suppose they're orchestras," she said.

"You'll soon find out," I said.

"We have Arnheim's. I don't know the Eastern orchestras unless they're on records. It's nice of you to care whether I miss the parties, it really is. Is it because you like me, or what? I mean—me especially?"

"Yes. And I think you'd be a good addition to the parties. You're what we call new talent."

"Thank you," she said. She was thinking. "You're not at all what I expected."

"No?"

"Maybe because you're older. Maybe because you're so Easternish. Both,

I guess. Why do you wear those pumps? I thought you only wore them with tails."

"I always wear them, I always have."

"And the kind of a collar. Daddy always wears those collars that open at the neck. Wings?"

"I'll wear a wing collar with tails, but not with a Tuck."

"Daddy says Tux. You say Tuck. I'll have to tell my brother these things. He's not here for Christmas, but next year he's entered in Andover. What do you think of Andover?"

"Good."

"Where did you go?"

"I went to a small church school called St. Bartholomew's."

"Oh, come on. A small church school. I've heard about St. Bartholomew's. Then where did you go? Yale?"

"Williams," I said.

"And now you're at the U. of Penn," she said.

"Jesus, don't call it the U. of Penn. Penn, or the U. of P., but not the U. of Penn. Ugh."

"So sorry. When my brother comes here next summer, will you help him out? Show him things?"

"I'm afraid I won't be here next summer," I said. "I have a job in Philadelphia. Anyway, the kind of things you're thinking of, he'll learn them at Andover."

"I'd like him to know them before he goes to Andover."

"How old is this boy?"

"Fourteen."

"Hell, he has plenty of time," I said. "And he might resent my telling him things."

"No he wouldn't. I'd see to that. He listens to me. He adores me, he really does."

"Well, you are rather adorable."

"If you think I am now, wait'll you see me in a bathing suit."

"I can hardly wait," I said.

"You *should* be making passes at me," she said.

"Oh, I don't know."

"Mr. Hofman would be making passes at me," she said.

"Not after you kicked him."

"But you're not afraid I'd kick you."

"No. But you couldn't kick anybody in this car."

"Then why haven't you made a pass at me?"

"Do you really want to know?"

"Yes," she said.

"Because you're a virgin."

"That's never stopped anyone else from making passes at me."

"It stops me."

"Oh, you have to go all the way?" she said. "How do you know I wouldn't go all the way?"

"It would be almost physically impossible in this car."

"You don't approve of necking? Heavy necking?"

"Do you?"

"Morally, I don't. But I've done it."

"But you've managed to stay a virgin. You must have given that Swedish boy a bad time."

"He didn't think so," she said. "He didn't expect me to go all the way. The night before I came East I would have, but he didn't know that."

"Then you were lucky," I said.

"Yes, but I didn't think so at the time. Now I do, but then. I was sure he didn't love me."

"And now you're sure he did?"

"No, and I don't love him any more. We don't even write to each other. I was really glad to get out of California. Not so much glad to get out of California as to be moving back East. Everything is new and different here."

"Maybe not as different as you think," I said.

"Have you ever been there?"

"No," I said.

"Then how can you tell?"

"There are differences but I don't think they matter so much when you come right down to it," I said.

"Oh, are *you* ever wrong!" she said. "If you went to California you'd find out. I wish I could fall in love here, but I feel like such a stranger."

"That's not why you haven't fallen in love. Use your head. When you're ready to fall in love, the geography isn't going to make any difference. It's the person, not the location."

"It must be the location. I've been ready to fall in love ever since I got here, but the people are so different."

"Don't rush things."

"Why not? I want to rush things."

"Then you probably will, and you won't be a virgin much longer."

"That would suit me," she said.

"Even if you weren't in love?"

"I've thought about that. And I've come to the conclusion that I am not going to wait till I'm in love."

"You're just going to give the fair white body to some guy with a dimple in his chin?"

"Oh, no. I hate dimples in chins."

"Well, then one of us lucky guys without a dimple in our chins."

"You're razzing me, but I'm serious."

"You'd better be, about this. You might have a little accident."

"Not me. I'm not that naïve," she said. "You know, I haven't even called you by your first name. I know it's Philip. But do you know why I'm so relaxed with you? Telling you so much?"

"No, why?"

"Because when you said I oughtn't to take a drink and miss those parties, that was the first time since I came East that anyone was really human. And the funny thing is, you didn't seem very human. You and that collar and those pumps. Studying to be a lawyer. Cold as an icicle. And you're not really."

"No, I'm not."

"Where do you live in Philadelphia? At a fraternity house?"

"No, I share an apartment with two friends of mine. Why, were you thinking of paying me a visit?"

"Naturally. Why else would I ask?"

"We have a thing in the Commonwealth of Pennsylvania called statutory rape."

"It wouldn't be rape if I went there of my own accord," she said.

"Yes, I'm afraid it would. Your father and mother aren't the kind of people that would have me arrested, but frankly you're a bit young for me."

"Look, is this young?" She pulled down the straps of her evening dress and bared her breasts.

"Cut that out," I said.

"Kiss them," she said.

"God damn it, I said cut that out."

"You're a son of a *bitch,*" she said. She replaced the straps, and began to weep. I said nothing for a while, then passed her my handkerchief. She took a deep breath and said, "I guess we ought to be going back."

"All right with me," I said.

"You have every right to be cross with me," she said.

"Well, God damn it."

"I *want* somebody."

"I want *you,*" I said. "But for God's sake."

"I know, I know."

"No, you don't know, Andrea. You really don't."

"Yes I do. I honestly do, Philip. Honestly and truly, I know everything you could say to me."

"I doubt that but let's forget about it."

She shook her head. "I won't and you won't. Is your number in the telephone book, in Philadelphia?"

"Yes. I could say no, but if you looked you'd find it."

"Right," she said. "What's a good time to call you?"

"After four o'clock, and any evening."

"Next week?"

"Yes," I said.

"You'd be better for me than some guy with a dimple in his chin," she said. She was smiling now, and I put my arms around her and kissed her.

"That's better," she said. "You could love me, you know. I know it, if you don't."

"Oh, I know it now," I said.

We went back to the clubhouse, and several of my friends looked at me in mock disapproval and said things about robbing the cradle. But I told them to grow up, and I think I deceived them by not dancing again with Andrea. I had never been much of a parked-car Romeo, and my reputation for good conduct was paying off. The next week, on a Tuesday afternoon, Andrea came to our apartment on Walnut Street, and I committed statutory rape. Six years later, the week before she was to be married, she came to another apartment I had on Spring Garden Street; and ten years after that, when she had been divorced a second time, she was still the only woman I could not do without.

She had a way of turning up just as I was beginning to convince myself that I ought to put an end to my bachelorhood. Two or three times as much as a year would pass without my hearing from her except for a message scribbled on a Christmas card. In Philadelphia, and I suppose in any other city, a busy man who likes his work is not uncomfortably conscious of the passage of time. I had all the legal practice I could handle, and I was making a good deal of money. From my office on South Broad Street I would alternate between clubs for lunch on working days, and on Sundays I would join a group of men who foregathered to eat and drink and play shuffleboard. My evenings were as socially active or filled with work as I wished to make them, and it did not matter to me that I was sometimes called a selfish pig and a stuffed shirt. Some of the wives who called me a selfish pig for not marrying a suitable divorcée or widow were also pleased to have me as an extra man. And as for my being a stuffed shirt, the epithet was most often conferred upon me by the other lawyers who had not done their homework as thoroughly as I. I was an upstate carpetbagger as well, but some of the men who called me that were also known to have remarked that it was too bad I was single and could not run for high public office. There were moments when bachelorhood seemed less desirable than matrimony, but I found that such spells of weakening usually coincided with the end of a long period of silence on the part of Andrea. Days would come when I became so obsessed with the need of her presence that only habit and routine kept me from chucking my practice and seeking her out. But then I would hear from her, remarkably soon and even on the very same day, and we would be together for a while. Only once did we discuss marriage. I proposed to her, and she said, "No, never to you, Phil. It would be pure hell for both of us. I'd rather keep coming back to you than keep running away from you every few months. That's the difference. I actually consider myself faithful to you all these years. And as far as that goes, I consider you faithful to me." There was no more to be said, unless I cared to admit that my fine legal mind had not summarized our situation as precisely as hers.

We had good times together. Between us there were no sexual inhibitions, and almost no twinge of jealousy. She would tell me about the problems she was having in breaking in a new man and she would talk freely and coolly about her husbands and lovers, one after another doomed to failure. "It makes me so cross when you say they call you a selfish pig," she once said. "You were never that with me, never for an instant. But they weren't with us back in that little car of yours. Oh, I love you, Phil. Andrea Cooper Et Cetera loves you."

"And I love Andrea Cooper—without the et cetera," I said.

"Yes," she said. "We have a love. Love, love, love, love, love. Now tell me something about your latest. How is she peculiar?"

"Not very peculiar," I said.

"You're holding out on me," she said.

"Well, one peculiarity," I said. "She likes to drive around with nothing on under her fur coat."

"Oh, yes, I've heard of that. That's fairly common. What does she do in the summertime? A raincoat?"

"I should imagine so," I said.

"My theory is that they want to be raped, but don't want to be, if you know what I mean. They're teasers, I think."

"Yes, that fits in. She's a teaser."

"Is she good at it?"

"Yes, I must say she is. She can be very aggravating."

"But satisfactory?"

"Eventually," I said.

"Is she living with her husband? I assume she's married."

"Oh, yes."

"Does he know about the fur coat business?" she said.

"He doesn't know anything about anything, from what I gather."

"You know what we are, you and I?"

"Among other things, what?" I said.

"What do they call those things? Safety valves. I wonder how many people there are that owe their sanity to us."

"Well, yes, but I owe my sanity to you."

"Oh, that goes without saying, you and I. But I was thinking of the other people."

"But what happens to them when you ditch them? In my case I don't think it matters too much. The women's peculiarities are rather minor things. Some like the phonograph playing, some don't. Some like to be hurt, others don't. But with men, there's the danger of violence."

"Yes," she said. "There is with women, too, but not as much as with men." She was silent.

"What?" I said.

"I was thinking of Stanley Broman. He's a man I had an affair with two years ago, until I broke it off. He's been calling me up late at night. If the Gibbsville operators ever listen in on those calls they must have a lovely opinion of me."

"Get an unlisted number, or turn off your phone," I said.

"I've done both. But what happens next? I'm afraid he may turn up some night."

"Tell him you're getting married again."

"I did, and that was a mistake. He said he was going to do everything to stop it."

"But you're not getting married again, are you?" I said.

"No. At least I have no plans to," she said.

"Then how can he stop what you have no intention of doing?" I said.

"I'm not worried about that. I just don't want to have him come near me again."

"What do you want me to do?" I said.

"I don't know. I was hoping you'd think of something," she said.

"Well, give me all the details and I'll bring in a private detective."

"I don't want to get you mixed up in anything," she said.

"I won't have to be," I said. "My man isn't a movie private eye. He's a member of the bar, a full-fledged attorney-at-law. Name is John MacIlreddy. Actually he was once a cop and studied law at night school. We use him for all sorts of things. Tell me about Mr. Broman."

"Well, he's a promoter. He has an office on Fifth Avenue and a house in Great Neck, Long Island. In his late forties. Married. Two or three children."

"What does he promote?"

"Various things. Sporting events, like prizefighting. Automobile races. I met him one night in the Stork Club, when he came to the table where I was having supper with some characters. You wouldn't know them, but Stanley did. 'The hell with the rest of you,' he said. 'I'm smitten by this lady,' meaning me. 'Well, I'm not smitten by you,' I said, 'so why don't you go back to your table.' But the others were amused, or impressed, or as I later found out, somewhat terrified by Stanley, and he stayed."

"Why were they terrified?" I said.

"Not really terrified, but afraid of him. Apparently he got into fights, and made scenes, and he certainly was mixed up with some very shady characters. In any event, he believed in the direct approach. He pulled a chair up beside me and began talking very dirty and invited me to go to his hotel with him. I stood as much of it as I could, then I excused myself to go to the ladies' room and never went back to the table. When I got outside on Fifty-whatever-it-is Street, he was waiting for me. Sitting in the first taxi. I was actually halfway in the taxi before I realized he was there. He grabbed my hand and pulled me in the rest of the way. Obviously the taxi driver knew him. In fact, he was part owner of a fleet of taxicabs. He's in all sorts of things. Loads of money. Spends a lot on clothes, and was probably a very handsome Jew when he was younger. Oh, let's face it, he had sex appeal. 'I'm gonna take you to your hotel and I'm gonna leave you there,' he said. 'But I just didn't want you to think you were outsmarting me.' And that's exactly what he did. He dropped me at the Barclay, where I was staying, and went on his way.

"The next morning, when they brought my breakfast, there were two dozen yellow roses. How he found that out, I don't know. But they're my favorites, as you know. I opened the envelope to look at the card, and there was this thin little diamond bracelet. No big diamonds, but it was narrow and beautiful. On the card was written, 'Think it over,' and it was signed with his initials. I looked him up in the phone book to know where to return the bracelet, but no Stanley Broman. Then I called up one of the people I'd been to the Stork Club with and found out that he was at the Waldorf. So I sent the bracelet back by messenger. Within half an hour he was on the phone. 'All I wanted you to do was think it over,' he said. 'That didn't take long,' I said. Oh, what's the use of telling you inch by inch? He was waiting for me in the Barclay lobby when I came down to go out for lunch. 'Lady, I told you I was smitten and I am,' he said. 'If necessary I'll move to Gibbsville P A.' I couldn't have dinner with him that night, but I did the next. He took me to the Colony and the theater and El Morocco, behaved like his idea of the perfect gentleman, and left me at the Barclay."

"And then you had an affair with him," I said. "How long did that last?"

"Oh, maybe six months. He never came to Gibbsville. I was firm about that. But he used to send a private plane to take me to New York, and sometimes I'd stay a week at a time. His friends were unbelievable. The women were almost worse then the men. They all looked like whores that had struck it rich, and did they ever hate me! Where did I get this, where did I get that? If it wasn't a personal question, but how much did this cost? What infuriated them most was knowing that Stanley wasn't keeping me. He paid for the plane and I stayed in his suite at the Waldorf, but my clothes were my own and I refused his expensive presents. After all, I have some very nice things I got from you and other people."

"The affair lasted six months, then what? Why did you give him the air?" I said.

"Because my bloomers got warm for someone else, to put it delicately," she said.

"But you don't get rid of people like him that easily," I said.

"I found that out. 'Who is this guy? I'll kill him,' he said, And I said I'd like to see him try. The new man was half a head taller and—and Stanley isn't small—and does boxing every day to keep in shape. Doesn't drink, doesn't smoke. He played football at Holy Cross University, and he could probably go out and play now. He's a lawyer, too, although actually he's a politician."

"Where?"

"In Brooklyn. Not really Brooklyn. Queens, sort of a part of Brooklyn, but closer to Great Neck, where Stanley lives when he goes home. Stanley knew right away who he was, and stopped making threats or trying to see me."

"You told him about Stanley?" I said.

"No. I didn't have to, and the affair with Jack Spellacy didn't last long enough to get to the exchange-of-confidences stage. However, it did last long enough to get rid of Stanley. Till about two months ago, when the phone calls began. He called up one night and said he was sending the plane next day. They called me from the airport, and I sent the plane back to New York."

"And the calls have persisted. It's odd that a man like that hasn't showed up in Gibbsville. I'll have to look into that," I said. "In fact, I'll do it right now."

"At this hour? All the offices are closed," she said.

"Watch me spring into action," I said. I telephoned the office of the Philadelphia *Bulletin* and was put through to George Taylor, the financial vice-president, with whom I occasionally had lunch. "George, I'd like to know what you have on a man named Stanley Broman. He's a New Yorker. A promoter. Will you see if you have any clippings on him?" George Taylor promised to call me back or to have someone in the *Bulletin* "morgue" give me the information. I hung up and waited.

"You're marvelous," said Andrea.

"I impress you, do I?" I said.

"This is the first time I've ever seen you in action. That kind of action."

"I know a lot of people," I said. "You never know when they'll come in handy. I have no friends, but I never have had."

"That's your fault. You could have. Or maybe you couldn't. No, I think you've learned to get along without them. I have no *women* friends. That's why you and I have love, love, love."

The telephone rang. It was a man in the *Bulletin* office. He said he had quite a batch of clippings on Stanley Broman. Did I want him to read them all? It was against the rules to take them out of the building, although in my case they might make an exception. "Just read the headlines and I'll tell you which ones interest me," I said.

He read a dozen or so before he came to one in particular. "Hold it," I said. "Read the whole article, please." He did so, and I asked him to read several others pertaining to the same topic. I thanked him and we hung up. "As I suspected," I said.

"I have never in my life seen you look so smug," she said. "What is it?"

"Good news for you," I said. "Your Mr. Broman will never bother you in Gibbsville. At least that's a reasonable assumption. He faces a lawsuit if he sets foot in our glorious Commonwealth. Under the statute of limitations, as it applies to this case, you're safe for four more years. Apparently he owes a lot of people a lot of money. I know the lawyer who represented him here, and I could find out all there is to know, but that won't be necessary, or desirable, from your point of view."

"You're absolutely clever," she said. "You spotted that right away."

"There had to be some very good reason why a man like that stayed away from Gibbsville. I suggest you say nothing to him about this. What he doesn't know won't hurt us. You'll have to put up with the telephone calls, but at least you can rest easy about his appearing in person. He'll get over you in four years. His kind of ego can't endure defeat, and pretty soon he'll be able to convince himself that you're not worth bothering about. However, I'm glad we found out about the lawsuit. If it weren't for that I might have recommended your taking out a pistol license."

"How can I thank you?" she said.

"In various ways. And you do."

"We just won't say that we love each other."

"We say it all the time," I said. "But we have sense enough to know that our way is the best way for us. When I'm eighty and you're seventy I'll propose to you again."

"And I'll accept your proposal. I would now, but you don't want that hanging over you."

"It would be interesting to announce our engagement now, and say that the wedding will take place in the spring of 1986. I can just see it in the Evening Chat column in the *Bulletin*. Actually, you know, in my business I project myself into the future every day. Bond issues maturing at such and such a date. Wills. Trust funds. Ninety-nine-year leases. Then on the other hand, we're always having title searches that go back to 1681. In case you've forgotten, that was the year William Penn was granted his charter."

"Oh, I knew that all along," she said.

"In a pig's ass you did," I said.

"You can be so *vulgar*," she said. "Thank God."

That was shortly after the end of World Ward II. She vanished again and I did not see or hear from her until about a year later. My secretary said that Mrs. Andrea Cooper—she had adopted her maiden name—wished to speak to me. Ruth, of course, knew that any call from Andrea had top priority.

"Have you been listening to the radio?" said Andrea.

"Naturally," I said. "I come to the office every day to listen to the radio. We get such good reception here. Why are you so breathless?"

"I just heard over the radio that Stanley Broman's been murdered. Is there anything I ought to do?"

"Well, obviously you didn't do it, so if I were you I'd open a small bottle of champagne. Who gets the medal for this public-spirited act?"

"They don't know. They found him in his car, in the meadows near Newark, New Jersey. The car was on fire, and he was shot and stabbed. Shot *and* stabbed."

"They really wanted to get rid of him, didn't they?"

"Is there anything I ought to do? Am I liable to get mixed up in it? I don't *want* to get mixed up in it, especially now."

"Romance in the air?"

"Very much so. I'm on the verge of marrying my doctor."

"With what *he* must know about you, it must be true love," I said. "No, you have nothing to worry about. You didn't write the late Mr. Broman any letters, did you? You've never been much for letters."

"No, he never put anything in writing if he could help it, either."

"Then I would say that the New Jersey gangsters have given you a very nice wedding present. I'll admit now that I was always a trifle apprehensive about Broman. Just a trifle."

"Don't think *I* wasn't."

"Are you coming to see me before you go to the altar with your doctor?"

"I will if you want me to," she said.

"I always want you to," I said.

"Then I'll come down this afternoon. He's dead, but he frightens me, that man. I have to be back here tomorrow. Is that all right?"

"Of course it's all right," I said.

She was remarkable. She was thirty-three years old, give or take a few months, yet when she arrived at my apartment she was fresh and unstained and—radiant. I always went back to that word to describe her to myself. She almost never wore a hat and she was not wearing one now. Her hair was cut in a longish page-boy style, and I said to her, "Tell me something. Do you dye your hair?"

"I have it touched," she said. "But I'm a light blonde and you damn well know it. What kind of a greeting is that? *Do I dye my hair?*"

"We're very hostile today. I was only curious," I said.

"I drove a hundred miles to see you. I expect a nicer welcome than that. Would it be too much to offer me a drink?"

"You can have anything but a Martini. I won't give you a Martini when you're in this mood."

"I don't want a Martini. Give me a bourbon with ice, no water. Please."

"My question abut your hair was in the nature of a compliment. I have a favorite word for you. Radiant. In addition, I was thinking that you had driven ninety-four miles—not a hundred, by the way—and not a hair was out of place."

"I ran a comb through it in the elevator."

I handed her the drink. "Which doctor is it you're going to marry? One of the newer ones?"

"Not so new," she said. "He came there after you left, but he's been there about ten years. Sam Young."

"I know the name, but I've never met him. You know how often I get back there. Maybe once in five years, since Mother died."

"Yes, people have been known to say that the old town isn't good enough for you," she said.

"They're right. It isn't," I said. "The last time anything interesting happened there was when you arrived."

"Are you trying to get me back in a good mood?"

"Trying as hard as I can," I said. "We only have tonight, and then it may be years before we see each other again."

"Oh, I want to sleep with you. You needn't worry about that," she said.

"Well, I was worrying about it," I said.

"I'll always sleep wth you," she said. "You were my first, and maybe you'll be my last. Who knows?"

"Why are you marrying Dr. Young?"

"First of all, because he's nice, and if you're going to live in Gibbsville it's better to be married."

"But why go on living in Gibbsville?"

She stretched out on the sofa. "Yes, why? It's home, with Mother and Daddy there, and my kid brother married and raising a family. I've lost all contact with my friends in California. I've been married and divorced twice, and I don't think those marriages did me any great harm, but I can't go on getting married and divorced. Stability. I need some stability, and I'd never get it if I moved away from Gibbsville. Look at what happened to me in New York. I fell in love with a gangster."

"You're dramatizing that," I said. "You didn't fall in love with him, and he wasn't a real gangster."

"Yes he was. I saw enough of him to find that out. He was a gangster. Maybe he didn't go around with a machine-gun in his hand, but they don't do that any more."

"Someone did, or he wouldn't be lying in the Jersey meadows," I said.

"He was a modern gangster. He made his money in the black market during the war. Not nylons and things like that. He used to call himself a steel executive. Rubber. Steel. Building materials."

"You knew a lot more than I thought you did."

"He thought I was a dizzy blonde that didn't know what was going on. And maybe I was. But I couldn't help but overhear some of his conversations."

"Now I see why you were so worried. You're afraid you might be called on to testify. That's doubtful. If he lived, and there was some kind of Congressional investigation, they'd have the F.B.I. visit you. It's still a possibility, but very remote."

"That's what I want to know," she said. "What do I do if they come and start asking me a lot of questions?"

"The first thing you do is ask for their credentials. I mean that. The F.B.I. men have a kind of wallet, with their picture in it. Take your time about examining it. If you have any reason to be doubtful, tell the man that you're going to call their office to check. If he's a phony, he'll give you an argument. If not, and if you're satisfied that he's the real thing, give him all the information he asks for. Sometimes there are two of them. Make them both identify themselves. One man can put on a convincing act, but when there are two of them it's not so easy. Your instinct will warn you. But once you're satisfied, tell them everything. You can trust them. Above all, don't lie to them. You may just happen to lie about something they know all about, in which case you make everything you say suspect."

"Can't I simply say I don't want to talk to them?" she said.

"Yes. But if you do, be sure and call me right away," I said. "By the way, does Dr. Young know about me, you and me?"

"Nobody knows about you and me," she said.

"Still?" I said.

"I've never told anyone. Maybe you have, but I haven't. They all want to know who my first was, and I tell them it was a boy in California. For some reason they don't seem to mind that. California is so far away. So is my virginity."

"You're feeling a little better now," I said.

"Well, for Christ's sake, starting out with 'Do you dye your hair?' What did you expect? By the way, *you're* getting a bit grey."

"I'm getting grey in your service," I said.

"Yes, I guess that's true," she said. "What I said about Gibbsville and stability—as long as I have you, I have *some* stability. I wouldn't want to live any place that was too far from you."

"I'll never be farther away than the telephone and the airplane. You're announcing your impending nuptials. Well, I have an announcement of my own, just for you. I am never going to get married."

"When you're eighty and I'm seventy?"

"Then, yes, but not before. When I was still in my thirties, I could have adjusted to marriage. But now I'm only seven years from fifty, and my habits are frozen. The first time I ever danced with you, you called me Judge. I was in law school."

"The night I did my strip tease," she said.

I nodded. "And they're even better now than they were then."

"By an inch and a half," she said.

"I wish I could say the same for my own measurements," I said. "Anyway, I remember telling you that a judgeship was a long way off for me. Now it isn't, and that's my ambition, my goal. It always has been. By the time I'm fifty I'll have enough money for one man."

"Don't forget us when we're married," she said.

"I won't. There'll be enough for the two of us," I said. "Do you want to hear about my ambition, or don't you?"

"Yes, dear. I promise not to interrupt any more."

"There are two things I can't discuss with anyone but you. My sex life and my ambition. Naturally I'd like to be an associate justice of the U.S. Supreme Court, but that's out of the question. They don't appoint my kind of lawyer to the Supreme Court any more. I've handled too many cases for large corporations. But I've been sounded out on running for a state job, which I won't do. Before they sound you out they study your qualifications, so mine must be all right. I'm being over-modest. They're damn good. Too good for the job they want me for. However, they did come to me, spontaneously, and they'll come again. And again. Then I'll tell them that I'll run if unopposed."

"You mean if nobody runs against you?"

"Yes. You can't be permanently appointed, you have to be elected. But you can be unopposed. I'm a hell of a good lawyer, you know, with a hell of a good record. The public doesn't know much about me, but the other lawyers do. I've never lost a case in the U.S. Supreme Court, and only two in the state court. And I'm not getting any dumber."

"Just think of you sitting up there in those black robes. I'll go and make faces at you."

"I'll have you held in contempt," I said.

"You do, and I'll tell your guilty secret. What kind of rape was that?"

"Statutory," I said.

"I knew it wasn't statuary. I was anything but statuary. Well, I'll be proud of you. I really will. I am anyway. I can't tell people I've been your girl all these years, but I'm secretly proud. And you're getting grey hairs. And I also notice you're wearing your Phi Beta Kappa key. I never knew you were one."

"I was wearing the key the first night I danced with you," I said.

"Maybe you were, but I didn't know what it was. I never knew what it was till my brother made it. But you must have stopped wearing it."

"Vests are coming back," I said.

"That's not why you're wearing it. You're running for judge. Don't try to fool me, Phil."

"That would be a great mistake, I guess. Besides, I never wanted to fool you."

"We must never try to fool each other," she said. "Let there be two people in the world that don't."

"How about your mother and father?" I said. "You've always had great admiration for them."

"Have I? Not in recent years. Not since I've been able to think for myself, instead of being a yes-man to them. He's cruel, my father. He dominates her in every little thing. For instance, she never wanted to leave California, but he did. He didn't want to be stuck in the bank in Santa Barbara. He wanted to be the manager of King's department store."

"He's done very well, though," I said.

"The store has, I have to admit that. But Mother has aged terribly. She hates the climate, she doesn't like the people. Consequently, she comes to see me every day, not because she wants to see me but because she knows where I keep the vodka. 'Oh, I think I'll have a little cocktail,' she says. Then you ought to see what she pours herself. Right up to the top. One cube of ice, the rest straight vodka. Her little cocktail. Then she has another little cocktail. I tried watering the vodka, but she noticed it right away. Insisted that I get a different brand and offered to pay for it. My mother has become a quiet lush. My brother's no help. He says he's very sorry, but he doesn't want Mother coming to his house and criticizing the way his wife is bringing up their kids. Mother knows she's not welcome there, so I get her every afternoon."

"What if you and the doctor have children?"

"We won't. He's sterile. I didn't say impotent. He can get it up all right, but he's sterile. And I doubt if I could have children now. Three abortions since I was nineteen."

"Beginning with mine," I said.

"Yes, and each of my husbands. The last one the doctor didn't want to do it, but I told him if he didn't do it I'd have to go to some butcher. That was Sam Young. So you see he knew me pretty well before he knew me at all, so to speak."

"A moment ago you spoke of stability," I said. "You said you stayed in Gibbsville because it offered stability, and you mentioned your parents. Then a bit later you gave me a quite unhappy picture of them. He's cruel, she's an alcoholic. What kind of stability do you call that?"

"It's stability. It isn't happiness, but it's stability. What kind of a lawyer's trick is this, going back to things I said before?"

"It's a lawyer's trick, all right," I said. "I'm doing it for a reason. I want to find out why you're marrying your doctor. Does he represent stability?"

"Yes," she said.

"You don't love him."

"No."

"What do you like about him, besides the dream of stability?"

"Are you going to try to argue me out of marrying him?" she said.

"I know better than that," I said.

"Then what are you trying to do?" she said. "You can't make me a better offer."

"No, I can't. But I've always seemed to take the role of uncle, or big brother, with you. You don't remember this, but that first night we sat in my car together—"

"You told me not to take a drink or my parents wouldn't let me go to the other dances."

"You do remember," I said.

"I ought to. That's what got us in the hay together. But I don't see what you're trying to do now."

"It would help if you answered my question, what do you like about the doctor?"

"Well, he's a man. All man. He was married before and his wife died of leukemia, the year he went into private practice. Then he went into the Navy for three years, and after that he came back to Gibbsville, reopened his practice. When I got the flu I sent for him, having already been his patient once before. The abortion. He annoyed me by throwing in a piece of advice that I hadn't asked for. It was part medical and part moral. He said that a woman with my record of abortions ought to have periodic checkups for T.B., and I told him to mind his own business. We became friends, and lovers. He had other women, but I was it, he said."

"What makes either of you think you'll make a good doctor's wife?"

"You *are* trying to talk me out of it," she said.

"All right, maybe I am. Three abortions aren't good for you, but neither are four marriages."

"This will be my third marriage!"

"Which will last two years, then there'll be a fourth. And quite possibly a fifth."

"You're jealous! You pretend you're not, but you are. You don't show it because I go away. You want me to go away so I won't see how jealous you are!"

I waited, and went on. "And there might even be a sixth."

She threw her glass at me, a heavy piece of Steuben. It missed me and broke against the paneling of the wall behind me. The dent in the woodwork was half an inch deep. I got up and stood over the largest piece of glass, which lay on the carpet. I was being dramatic while trying to think of the right thing to say. I was also frightened. Retroactively I could hear the thud of the glass on the woodwork, and imagine what it would have done to my skull. Looking down at the broken glass I was avoiding looking at her, and I did not see her coming toward me. When she touched me I reacted out of fear; I sprang away from her.

"Phil! Phil! I could have killed you!" She put her arms around my waist and held on to me, and then for only the second time in our life together she began to cry. I put my arms around her and held on to her, and she kissed me time after time, on the lips, on my neck, my hands, passionately but without passion. Now, having retroactively heard the glass smashing against the wall, I could retroactively see it passing over my shoulder, and though I was safe I was impotent with the effects of fear. I could feel impotence in my genitals and age in my soul. She stopped kissing me and looked at me. The tears streaked down her cheeks but she had stopped crying. "Are you all right?" she said.

"I want to sit down," I said.

"You're pale," she said.

"Odd," I said.

She held my hand on her bosom and drew me to the sofa, and I sat down. She sat on the edge of the sofa, waiting for whatever was next, act or words. "Think I'll have a cigarette," I said. I was recovering rapidly, but I had to know what to do. It had to be right, or I had lost her forever; that much I knew. It was like that moment in a jury trial when you are addressing the twelve good men and true, and something tells you to stop, or to go on, you're not sure which but you are sure that in two seconds you will have them or have lost them, regardless of whatever else you do or have done, say or have said.

I hesitated, and I guess she read into my hesitation some other emotion than the vestige of fear. Deep disappointment, disillusionment perhaps. She got the cigarette for me and put it in my mouth and lit it. "I would rather die than hurt you," she said. "Than hurt you in any way. If that glass had hit you I'd have jumped out your window. See my hand?" Her hands were shaking. She got up and used the letter-opener and pencil tray from my desk to sweep up the broken glass fragments. She took them and the larger pieces of glass to the kitchen. "I put them in the garbage pail," she said. She was standing in the middle of the room. "Do you want me to go?"

"No," I said.

"What do you want me to do? Shall I fix you a drink?"

"No thanks," I said.

"Please tell me what to do. I can't think," she said.

"Why don't you just come here and sit down?" I said.

She sat beside me and gently put her head on my shoulder and I put my arm around her. We stayed that way for a full two minutes, which can be a long time of silence for two such people as she and I; I suddenly older, she as suddenly younger. "I feel as though I'd thrown something at God," she said.

"I'm not God. I'm not even a very minor god," I said. "I'm not even a good first baseman or I'd have caught the damn thing. Would you mind if we just stayed here and didn't go out for dinner?"

"Oh, I don't *want* to go out for dinner. I'd be almost sure to burst into tears, and embarrass you. Would you like me to show you what a good cook I am?"

"I know what a good cook you are. Let's sit here a while and later on you can make one of your omelettes. Do you want to listen to some records?"

"No thanks," she said. "When you're ready, we'll talk. You have something you want to say, and so have I."

"I haven't much to say, but what there is is fairly important," I said. "I'm all right now but I have to tell you, I'm a different man from five or ten minutes ago. I never thought so before, but I'm a middle-aged man. I don't want to exaggerate anything, but there it is. And you know it. That's why you somehow got me confused with God, because I happen to know you don't believe in God."

"No, I don't. I stopped believing in God when I changed my mind about my father."

"And I suppose I took their place. Father. God. And perennial lover."

"I guess that's right," she said.

"An all-purpose man in your life," I said.

"And what have I been to you? Perennial mistress and what else? Not your mother, or the Virgin Mary."

"Well, there've been hundreds of times when I was a child at your breast."

"You're feeling better now, aren't you?"

"I told you, I'm all right," I said. "But you have to know that when that glass went whizzing by me, my reflexes were slow and one of the slow reflexes was fear. I wasn't afraid till after it was over. A young man's reflexes protect him. I didn't move. I played first base when I was in school but tonight I was rigid. With a kind of anticipatory fear, I guess."

"I threw the glass without any warning," she said.

"A prep school pitcher does the same thing, trying to pick a runner off first base. No signal. No warning. Or a first baseman misses the signal that the pitcher's going to throw to him."

"What has all this stuff about baseball got to do with us?"

"I'm trying to explain what's happened to me. I'll be brief, if you like. In a word, I got old."

"All right, if you insist. You're forty-three years old. I never have any trouble remembering your age."

"But let me go on, Andrea. This is important. I'm forty-three, but *you* suddenly *lost* a batch of years. Your reaction was very young, and you practically said so when you said it was like throwing something at God."

"I'll agree with that, too. It was childish."

"Young-girlish, not childish," I said.

"I've decided not to marry Sam Young," she said.

Her statement was so out of order that in a courtroom I would have requested a recess. For the truth was I had been leading up to a repudiation of my earlier opposition to her marriage. It was frustrating and confusing to have her brush aside my speech before it was made.

"You've decided *not* to marry him?" I said.

"It wouldn't work out. Not even for two years," she said. "It would be very bad for both of us. For him and me, that is."

"What convinced you of that?" I said.

"Something you said, of course," she said. "You asked me why either of us, Sam or I, thought I'd make a good doctor's wife. Actually, we never talked about that. I mean about the doctor's-wife part of it. We've always talked about ourselves and each other, but being a doctor's wife is something special. He must have thought about it, but he avoided bringing it up. I'd make a terrible doctor's wife. He'd lose every patient he has."

"Would he? Why?"

"Because he would, that's why. I'm not cut out for that kind of a life. My mother could have done it, but not me."

"What about all that business of living in Gibbsville and stability and so on?"

"I can always find good reasons for doing something I want to do," she said. "Even now I can think of a good reason for throwing a glass at you. You taunted me, you went too far. You should know better than to make me angry. I'm a very impulsive girl. If I'd hit you, I *would* have jumped out the window. That would have been great, you with your head bashed in, and me lying on the sidewalk in Rittenhouse Square. And all because you needled me when I was tired from a long drive."

"Yes, of course, of course," I said. "Is this final, your decision not to marry Young?"

"Absolutely," she said. "Just as final as my decision not to marry you."

"I was coming to that," I said. "Just thinking out loud, as the advertising people say. Just as a trial balloon, how would it be if you and I got married and kept it secret—don't interrupt me, please—and thereby prevented you from a hasty marriage to someone else?"

"We're not married now, and I prevented myself from a hasty marriage, as you call it."

"So you did. But you're quite liable to find yourself in the same situation again, and marry the man."

"You're quite liable to get another glass thrown at you," she said.

"Not so soon," I said. "Let's speculate as to the advantages for you. I don't know how close you ever came to marrying that gangster. Not very close, I guess. He had that wife in Great Neck or wherever it was, and Jews generally, even gangster Jews, don't go rushing to the divorce courts. But you're impulsive, by your own admission, and the record speaks for itself. Two marriages, two divorces. Both of your ex-husbands married again and I believe they've stayed married?"

"Yes," she said.

"And you were about to marry a widower until you suddenly, impulsively changed your mind. Doesn't all this seem to indicate that it'd be to your advantage to have a legal husband to protect you from your own impulses? Don't start throwing things. I'm asking you to consider the matter."

"I'm considering it. What's the advantage for you?"

"For me? Well, I could say that I was looking ahead to the time when I become a judge. Stability and all that. I'll never marry anyone but you, that's a certainty. But I'd like to be sure of having you, when that time comes."

"You're just so God damn jealous."

"You've probably put your finger on it. Our hidden motives we won't admit to, even to ourselves sometimes."

"The answer is no," she said. "I'm not giving up Sam Young to marry you."

"There would be financial advantages, too," I said. "What do you live on now? It's mostly your stock in King's store, isn't it?"

"Mostly," she said. "I had alimony from my first husband, but that stopped when I married again. I got no alimony from my second husband. I was the guilty party there. Yes, my income is from the store."

"I happen to know something about economic conditions in the coal region. They're not getting any better. I don't know much about King's, but how long do you think they can compete against Stewart's, which is bigger and older, and the new Sears? King's is in the middle there. And no matter how efficient your father may be, the economic facts of life are running against him. Sears has the big buying power and lower prices. Stewart's has four other stores besides Gibbsville, and third-generation charge accounts. They make money with their charge accounts, because they're not the old-time charge accounts. Stewart's is really in the same business as a loan com-

pany. Selling on the installment plan, and collecting their pound of flesh by
financing the retail purchases."

"I've head Daddy talk about that, but it's too deep for me," she said.

"You ought to try to understand it, because it's going to affect you. I
don't want to frighten you, but if King's had two or three bad years they'd
have to go out of business. I assume that Dr. Young makes pretty good
money."

"About twenty thousand a year. He told me."

"And you?"

"Last year, around ten."

"Is that all?" I said.

She nodded. "Daddy told me to expect less this year."

"You spend it all, of course," I said.

"Oh, do I! I'm continually overdrawn. But I work, you know."

"I didn't know," I said.

"Before Easter I help out in ladies' ready-to-wear. Four weeks. And before Christmas in the toy department or wherever they send me. I get a hundred dollars a week, which just about covers what I owe Daddy."

"I'll *bet* it does," I said.

"Not entirely. He gives me the rest as a Christmas present."

"Encouraging bad habits," I said.

"That's exactly what he says."

"Does he worry about you?"

"Not about me. He'd wet his drawers if he knew his little daughter's ex-
boy friend was killed by gangsters, but he wouldn't be worrying for me. For
himself and Bud, my brother, Bud. I love Bud, but I hate what my father's
doing to him. When Bud graduated from Colgate my father gave him a present of a trip abroad, and Bud came back thinking he'd get a job on a newspaper, in hopes of becoming a foreign correspondent. My father talked him into
taking a quote temporary unquote job in the store. It was a job anyone could
have done, not a Phi Beta Kappa with a knack for languages. What Daddy
really wanted was a doubles partner, and Bud had been captain of the Colgate
tennis team. So Bud gave in, and got himself married, and then the war came
and he quit his job to go to O.C.S. and they sent him to England with the
O.S.S. because he knew German. After the war he wanted to live over there,
but he already had one child and his wife was producing another. Well,
Daddy began working on him again, a year at a time. You can imagine what
happened. Bud could have lived abroad with a wife and one child, on his income. But with a wife and three he had to have more than that. Kids are expensive, so are young American wives. The sad thing, but funny, ironical, is
that now Daddy plays golf, and Bud doesn't even get to the semi-finals in the
singles any more."

"Let's hope your father doesn't turn the store over to him just before it folds up," I said.

"He would if he thought of it."

"You don't want to marry me for my money?" I said.

"No."

"Or to keep yourself out of trouble?" I said.

"No."

"Or to possibly be of some help to your brother if the store goes out of business?" I said.

"No."

"Or because you know that eventually you will marry me," I said.

"You're more sure of that than I am," she said.

"Only if we both live long enough. I'm not talking about when I'm eighty. I honestly believe we'll be married before that, and unless I'm very wrong, you believe it too."

"You don't know what it's like to be married, Phil. I do. It takes a long time to get used to living with someone, and we both like our privacy. We both like to come and go as we please. You can't do that, and you can't have your privacy, when you're someone's wife. Maybe I was cut out to be an old maid. Not the usual kind of old maid that looks under beds. But an old maid with plenty of memories. I'm not going to marry you just so you'll have a wife in reserve for when you're a judge."

"All right," I said.

"I'm going to get you some supper. Do you mind if I unpack first?"

"Did you bring a bag?"

She laughed, "No, I'm kidding. I didn't even bring a toothbrush. I know you always have extras, and I count on wearing your pajamas. You have your bath and I'll have your supper ready by the time you're out of the shower. Then we can have a quiet evening at home. The kind that makes you think you'd like to be married to me."

I took a shower and put on pajamas and dressing-gown. She had set the table and lighted the candles in my small diningroom. We had the omelette and toast and a bottle of Rhine wine that she found in the refrigerator. "Do you still get your own breakfast every morning?" she said.

"Coffee," I said. "I usually stop at the drug store at Broad and Locust and have bacon and eggs."

"And lunch at your club. When you're having dinner alone what do you do?"

"One of the other clubs, or I can have it sent in from the hotel across the way. But usually at the Racquet Club. Why?"

"That's the life you like, you see? You could afford a much larger apartment and a full-time servant, but you prefer this. I do too, really. The differ-

ence being that I do my own cooking, make my own bed and so on. Once a
week I have a woman come in to give the place a good cleaning. Are you
simply dying to give me a present?"

"Yes."

"They're going to raise my rent from seventy-five to a hundred dollars a
month. I could get a cheaper apartment but I don't want to, and so I've been
wondering where I could economize, to make up the difference. I figured out
that I could save ten dollars a month by going to the hairdresser twice a
month instead of once a week. But then what? I went over all my bills and I
was amazed to discover that I spend about fifty cents a day on perfume. It
comes to that, about fifty cents a day. Fifteen dollars a month. Now if you
would like to leave a standing order with your drug store to send me a bottle
of perfume once a month, I could go on staying in my apartment and smelling nice, too."

"Write down the name of the perfume or I'll forget it," I said.

"It's a hundred and eighty dollars a year," she said.

"I'll be able to swing it," I said.

"In case I should happen to impulsively marry someone else, I'll tell the
drug store to stop sending it to me."

"It would be a waste of time to offer you money, wouldn't it?" I
said.

"Don't try *too* hard," she said. "Actually, the way I feel about it is, if I
really need more money, I can get a job. Me, that never wears a hat, I have a
standing offer to work in a millinery shop. There's a new little fairy on Market Street near the Y.M.C.A. who thinks I'm just *perfectly adorable*, and he'll
pay me two hundred dollars a month, five days from ten to four. He calls me
Butch, or did till I told him I knew what it meant in fairy talk."

"What does it mean?"

"It means a bull-dike."

"Well, you're certainly not that," I said.

"No, that's the least of my problems. I've had my palm scratched by several women, but that's as far as they ever got. Actually, you know, I think
I'm under-sexed. I can go awfully long without it, and the man always has to
be somewhat unusual. I know a girl at home that gets tight and she frankly
admitted to me that it might just as well be a broom-handle, for all the difference it makes. She doesn't give a damn about the preliminaries, or giving the
man any pleasure."

"Do you call me somewhat unusual?"

"I should say I do. Anybody that's put up with me all these years. I'm
sure I know you better than anyone else does, but how well is that? Sometimes when I leave you after spending the night with you, I say to myself,
'What does he really think of me? Or does he think of me at all?' I know that
we have love, love, love, but sometimes I think I'm just a lay, lay, lay, al-

though I know better. I don't think I could live without knowing that you were somewhere on the same earth."

"How are you going to break it to the doctor?" I said.

"I don't know," she said. "We hadn't set an actual date. Vaguely sometime in the next few months. What I'll probably do is wait till he says something about a definite date, and then I'll put him off. Then the next time he brings it up again, I'll put him off again. On the other hand, I might just tell him tomorrow. I don't know."

"The fair thing to do would be to tell him tomorrow," I said.

"Yes, that would be the fair thing. So I may. On the other hand, what has fairness got to do with it?"

"That's entirely up to you and how you feel about him."

"If I went out with someone else a few times, he might get the message."

"I should think so," I said. "As a doctor's wife in Gibbsville you'd be expected to give up dates with other men."

"If I were going to marry him, I wouldn't have dates with other men, but since I'm not going to marry him, I think I'll have a few dates and let him tell me that that has to stop. Then I'll say I'm sorry, but it isn't going to stop, and that will give him a good out. Result—no wedding bells, but no hard feelings. I like him, and I don't want to lose him as a friend. Also, I want him to go on being my doctor."

"It sounds to me as though Dr. Young might turn into a Gibbsville version of me," I said.

"No, but he might turn into a Gibbsville version of Dr. Young. You see, I can tell you about him but I could never tell him abut you. It always comes down to that. I never tell them about you. You're private and personal to me. There's probably some very good psychological reason for that, but offhand I wouldn't know what it is."

"If I were just a little older I might say that you were ashamed of me," I said.

"I see what you mean, yes, but not a woman that's had two husbands and liable to have six," she said. "I wonder, Phil, if we saw each other oftener, would we always spend so much time talking about what's kept us together?"

"No, not if we saw each other oftener."

"We meet, and we're like a child studying its own belly-button," she said. "I was twelve years old before I understood that, either. I still don't understand why men have nipples, but they *would* look very strange without them, now that I've got used to them. Have you got a lot of work to do?"

"It doesn't have to be done tonight," I said.

"If I weren't here, it would be, though."

"Yes," I said.

"Well, let me do the dishes and put things away, and I'll have a bath and get into a pair of your pajamas. Then we can go to bed early and get a good night's sleep and I'll get your breakfast in the morning. You won't have to go to the drug store."

"That seems like a very sensible program," I said. We even made sensible love that night, and at seven-thirty in the morning she brought me a cup of coffee. She was already dressed in a sweater and the skirt of her Glen plaid suit. "Couldn't you sleep?" I said.

"As if I'd been pole-axed, till about six o'clock," she said.

I put my hand under her skirt and felt her leg. She stood still. "Do you think that's wise?" she said.

"What do you think?" I said.

"Whatever you want. All this can come off in no time," she said.

"Are you trying to spare me because I suddenly got old?"

"Well, something like that," she said. "But if you keep doing that, I'm not going to give a damn how old you are."

"Let's see how quickly you can take that stuff off," I said.

"Before you can change your mind, that's how quickly," she said.

"Remember a tune by Vincent Youmans? 'Day will break and you'll awake'?"

"No singing before breakfast," she said. "Supposed to be very bad luck."

"If you don't believe in God you can't believe in foolish superstitions," I said.

She lay on top of me. "Stop being so bossy so early in the morning. If there's anything I hate it's a bossy old man."

"If there's anything I love it's you," I said.

"I know," she said. "That—I know."

I remembered to place the order for her perfume, and for seven or eight months the only communication I had with her—if it could be called that—was the monthly bill from the drug store. Then my firm took a case involving some mineral rights near Gibbsville and I volunteered to confer with one of the principals, a boyhood chum of mine. We were not at all sure that we wanted to go into court with the case, and someone had to explain the delay. Accordingly, I drove up to Gibbsville and spent the day with my friend. "It was damn nice of you to come," he said. "But I wish they'd told me it was going to be you. Mary and I could have had some of the old crowd in for dinner."

"That's just what I didn't want," I said. "I'll have a little look around, and I may even drive back tonight."

My look around consisted of finding Andrea's telephone number and a visit, on foot, to her apartment. She was pleased but not overjoyed to see me. "Am I wrong, or am I getting a cool reception?" I said.

"No, you're right," she said.

"Did I louse up other plans?"

"I had to get out of something else," she said.

"Dr. Young?"

"Oh, no. Not that kind of thing. It's my brother. If it isn't my brother it's my mother, and in between it's my father. The store is in trouble, and my mother is hitting the bottle and Bud's had a fight with Daddy. The last time I saw you you told me some things about the store. I wish you'd told me more."

"I didn't know more. I was only conjecturing," I said.

"My father is turning out to be a crook. At least that's what Bud thinks."

"Whose money is he stealing?" I said.

"Ours. Mother's and Bud's and mine, among others. I don't want to talk about it," she said.

"I do. It's obviously what's uppermost in your mind, and as long as it is, there's no use talking about anything else."

"All right," she said. "It's complicated, and it's nothing he can be arrested for. But it's crooked. As I understand it, from Bud, Daddy is deliberately letting the store go to hell. They've had an offer to sell it to a chain of stores, with Daddy to be manager if they sold. But Daddy hasn't got any stock in the company. It's all Mother's and Bud's and mine and some cousins'. Bud is our advisor. Before that we always did exactly what Daddy said, but Bud found out that the chain store people had offered some ridiculously low price for King's, and Daddy was trying to persuade us to accept it. He had Mother all but talked into it."

"I begin to get the picture," I said.

"Oh, there's a lot more, but that's the gist of it. Bud wants us to fire Daddy, but Daddy has a contract with the company that we all voted for without reading it. Twenty-five thousand dollars a year for life, a share in the profits, et cetera. Can you imagine anybody being such a son of a bitch? According to Bud, Daddy gets some kind of a bonus if the chain stores buy King's. That's why he's so eager to have us sell. That, and an agreement that he'll be the new manager. Daddy has cut down the inventory so that the chain stores won't have to pay for goods on the shelves, and there *are* no goods on the shelves. Customers ask for things, and we're out of them. The chain store of course can buy everything cheaper than we can."

"You're learning something about business," I said.

"I wish I had earlier. I'm working. I have a job in a hat store on Market Street."

"The new little fairy?" I said.

"Oh, did I tell you about that? I guess I did."

"You probably have a case against your father if you wanted to sue him."

"Bud would, but Mother won't, and she can outvote everybody else. Such a hypocrite, my father. He'd never allow us to take a discount at the store unless we were actually on the payroll. Things like that. But he has a Cadillac that the company paid for and his expense account is something you wouldn't believe, according to Bud. He never spends a cent of his own money if he can help it. Mother paid all of Bud's expenses through college, and their house is in his name, although she paid for it. That's enough. Who are you suing? Anybody I know?"

"This isn't that kind of case. It has to do with mineral rights. Mighty dull stuff at this stage of the game," I said.

"How long are you going to be in town?" she said.

"That depends on you. I may go back tonight," I said.

"You can stay, but you have to be out of here before daylight. You can't be seen leaving at eight or nine o'clock in the morning. And you'd be recognized. This building is full of people you used to know. In fact, you may have made a mistake coming here in the first place, but I wasn't thinking very clearly when you phoned."

"I take it you've had your dinner," I said.

"Yes, I was just putting the dishes away when you arrived," she said.

She took a cigarette out of a box and tapped it, a gesture which was not habitual with her. "Listen, are you sore at me?" I said. "And if so, what for?"

"No, I'm not sore at you, but if you stay here tonight I'm going to be more careful. The last time, you knocked me up. That morning when I was all dressed and ready to give you your breakfast. I was unprepared, but I took a chance. Bingo! That's twice you've got me pregnant."

"Why didn't you let me know?" I said.

"What for? You couldn't come and hold my hand."

"Don't tell me Dr. Young performed the abortion," I said.

"Well, he did, and that solved the problem of whether to tell him I wasn't going to marry him. Neatly. 'By the way, Doctor, I'm not going to marry you, and while I'm here will you take care of this little problem?' "

"You didn't say that," I said.

"No, it wasn't as easy as that. He took it rather big. It wasn't any fun at all for either of us. And right about then Bud began telling me what was going on at the store. So you see I'm not sore at just you, I'm sour on the world, and have been for months. The only person I can let down my hair with is my boss. The little fairy. He's the most sympathetic man, woman, or child I've ever known."

"You told him about your abortion?"

"After it was all over and I went to work for him, he asked me one day if I was having love-trouble, and he was so kind that I burst into tears and told him everything but names. He's like a mother hen. Makes me sit down and rest between customers. Takes me to the movies, and dinner at the hotel. Next month we're going to New York together on a buying trip. He's the only bright spot in these last few months, I must say."

"What's his name?"

"His real name is John W. Metz, from Swedish Haven. But he calls himself Jacques. The name of the shop is Jacques, no last name. He studied to be a schoolteacher, but they expelled him in his second year in spite of having good marks and everything. He had a very hard time getting a job. In fact, at one time he worked as a stock-boy at King's, and that was how he got interested in millinery. His father wouldn't have anything to do with him, but he had a sister that helped him get started in business. He's a very good businessman, too. That's the Pennsylvania Dutch, I guess. He reads everything. Books. *The New Yorker. Time. The Wall Street Journal!* You should see his apartment. There's nothing else like it in Gibbsville. It's on the third floor of the building the shop's in, and when you get inside you can't believe you're not in New York or Paris. Très moderne, ness pa? I *love* him."

"Why, I think you do," I said.

She shook her head. "He has boy friends. One's a politician, a really quite horrible man, looks as if he ought to be a priest. He's not, though. He even has the nerve to bring his wife to the shop and sit there while she tries on hats. The only good thing is he can keep Jack out of the clutches of the law. Once in a while they have parties on Saturday night that get a bit raucous. Not that it's a residential neighborhood any more, but they do get noisy."

"I'm very sorry about the pregnancy," I said.

"It was worse on Sam than on anyone else. The blow to his pride, to start with. As I said, he took it big. But just as bad was the fact that he didn't want to do the abortion. He'd warned me once before, and this time he asked me please to go to someone else. He recommended two other doctors. But I said I was frightened. He even tried to get me to have the baby. Even if the father was a married man, I ought to have the baby. And he said frankly he was just as frightened as I was. I said that if anything happened to me, they'd never be able to trace it to him. *I'd* never tell on him. So, there in his office, without a nurse or anyone to assist him, he did it. Nothing went wrong then, but he'd warned me about these fits of depression, and he was certainly right. On top of which, came all this business about the store."

"I feel left out," I said.

"My troubles aren't your troubles," she said.

"I have no troubles to compare with yours," I said. "And besides, you're wrong. Your troubles are my troubles, as far as my wanting to share them is concerned. Apart from the fact that I was the one that got you pregnant.

Apart from the fact that I'm not married and would gladly have married you.
Dr. Young was right, there."

"Don't *you* start telling me I should have had the baby. It's a little late
for that," she said. "It's easy to say now."

"There's never been a moment in the last fifteen years when I wouldn't
have married you if you'd said the word."

"Oh, that's a lie, Phil. That's such a lie that it should have stuck in your
throat."

"There were times when I was more ready than others, but I *don't* lie to
you. What it comes down to is that you preferred dying to marrying me."

"That's something you just thought up to put me in the wrong. You
love to argue, and twist what I say," she said.

"Half true. I love to argue with you, and I suppose I enjoy the give-and-
take. But I play fair, and I don't reinforce my arguments with untruths. From
force of habit a lawyer is probably more aware of truth and untruth than anyone else."

"Oh, lawyers are no more honest than other people," she said.

"I didn't say anything about honesty. I only said we were more aware,
from force of habit, of the truth. We can distort it, in various ways, but we're
accustomed to speaking for the record and extremely conscious of such
things as perjured testimony, and disbarment proceedings, and so on. Honesty, ethics—that's another matter."

"Oh, shut up," she said.

"Very well," I said. "We're also pretty good at controlling our tempers."

"I said, shut up."

"If we're not going to talk, there's no point in my staying here."

"There's no point anyway," she said. "What you really came here for
you're not going to get."

"You haven't even got a very high opinion of yourself, have you? I came
here to see you. Sex isn't the only thing that's kept us together all these
years." I stood up. "I'll leave you with this thought, my girl. What if I'd
come to Gibbsville and not telephoned you? Sex or no sex. Goodnight, and
I'm very sorry."

Never in a million years would she have called me back after I closed the
door, and knowing that, I took my time in making my departure. But she let
me go, and the walk back to the hotel was a dreary one. There were not many
people on the street; it was just after the dinner hour for most of them. But
at one time I had known the ownership of every house in the ten blocks to
the hotel, and I had been inside a good many of them, played in their back
yards. In a couple of days all my old friends would know that I had been in
town on business, and some of them would be hurt or annoyed because I had
not looked them up. But I had reconciled myself to that before leaving Philadelphia; what I did not like was this furtive walk from Andrea's apartment to

the hotel. I wanted to drive back to the city, but I was too tired p̶
and my visit to Andrea had not revived me. At the hotel I asked to h
ner in my room and was told that room service was not available af
o'clock, and so I had to throw my weight around with the manager, whom I
did not know but who knew who I was. He assured me that *of course* in my
case I could have dinner in my room. When it arrived the soup was tepid and
the chicken and vegetables were not even as warm as that. "Be sure and put
the tray out in the hall, will you?" said the waiter. No "please" and no
"thank-you" for the tip. And no "goodnight." I got out some transcripts of
testimony in old mineral rights cases, and wished I was back in Rittenhouse
Square. At six o'clock in the morning—I must say I slept well—I asked the
telephone operator if I could have a cup of coffee in my room. He, probably a
bellboy, said the kitchen wasn't open yet but if a cup of coffee was all I
wanted, he himself would bring me that and a cinnamon bun. In five minutes he was at my door, with a thermos of hot coffee and a bun. I gave him
five dollars, but I almost kissed him too. "You know this is a five?" he said.

"I know it's a five," I said.

He laughed. "This don't even go on your bill," he said. "They got no
way to charge you till the checker comes on in the kitchen. But thanks."

"Not at all. Virtue must not go unrewarded," I said.

"Didn't you used to be here in town?" he said.

"I was born here," I said.

"You's smart to get out. There's nothin' here no more. Nothin'. You
used to have the house out Lantenengo, between Fifteenth and Sixteenth?"

"That's right," I said.

"Delivered groceries there, many a time," he said. "I remember that
kitchen. A big coal stove, you could of put a thirty-pound turkey in that
oven. You had a colored woman for a cook. I used to sit there and get
warm."

"You must have worked for Frank Snodgrass."

"For Frank Snodgrass is right. Christ, all them old stores went out of
business. The out-of-town chains. I tell you, there's nothin' here. Nothin'."

"I'm afraid you're right," I said.

"Well, I gotta start wakin' them up. Thanks for the fin."

I had no idea who he was, I don't think I had ever seen him before. He
probably had been the Snodgrass delivery man during my years at prep school
and college. But he remembered Rhoda Hume, our cook, and our Buckeye
range, and as far as I was concerned he was right about Gibbsville. For him
and for me there was nothin' there, nothin'.

I wrote a note to Andrea. "It is now 7:30 A.M. and I am about to leave.
Too early to telephone you. I have finished my business here and will not be
coming back. If you need me, or if I can do anything for you, you know
where to reach me. I am going abroad next month for about seven weeks,

but will leave word with my secretary to forward any messages from you. Love, Phil." I posted the note on my way out of the hotel.

For almost twenty years, now, our love affair had consisted of brief meetings and absences that varied in length. On my part, and I am sure on hers, there had been no deceitfulness; no broken promises of fidelity since there had been no promises. A certain amount, probably a greal deal, of honesty ensued as an accompaniment of the freedom we granted ourselves. I was able, for instance, to admit to myself without shame that it was very pleasant to have a love affair with a stunning young woman who came and went and did nothing to disarrange my comfortable bachelorhood. If I occasionally accused myself of selfishness, I defended myself on the ground that she had more than once refused to marry me. Equally true, I could defensively argue, was the fact that I was a convenience for her. In her somewhat raffish life I was the one consistently dependable man to give her the emotional security that she seemed to reject by her conduct with the others. So much so that morally I was probably bad for her. She could always turn to steadfast me, and she always did.

But it was her nature to pass herself around among men, and she would have done so whether I was in her background or not. It was therefore a spurious twinge of conscience that I sometimes allowed myself. Long ago she had told me the complete details of her love affair with the boy in California, and though I was the first male with whom she experienced true copulation, she and the boy had gone from fellatio to coitus interruptus, which she was pleased to call heavy necking. It also pleased her (and my masculinity) to regard me as the taker of her virginity, but the distinction was to at least some extent honorary. We had something besides the sexual relationship, and had had it from the start. But, circumstances permitting, we had always had intercourse at some point during our sporadic reunions. It was customary, and we had always taken it for granted. As usual, I had taken it for granted when I visited her in her apartment, and my dissatisfaction with our meeting was two-fold: I had not gone to bed with her, as I had been looking forward to doing, and our conversation had not brought out a physical reason, meaning the after-effects of her latest abortion, for her coolness. I was inclined to believe that she had not been to bed with anyone since the abortion, and I tended to substantiate my belief with her account of her fondness for her pansy employer. I had known a Philadelphia girl who, after a bad abortion, took up with a band of homosexuals and became one herself, never to return to heterosexuality. At the moment I had no such fears for Andrea, but I did not give the matter much thought. I was more deeply concerned with my overall relationship with her, and disturbed by the appearance of a coolness that was without precedent. We had had quarrels aplenty, but coolness never. As I drove back to Philadelphia I tried to correlate the new coolness with the angry outburst in which she had thrown the glass at me. It was possible that a deep-seated resentment of me had existed that far back, despite the fact that we went on that night to make love with tenderness and consideration. Although I cared for no one else in the world, I realized that I did not know her, and in self-preservation I began to make preparations for the contingency of life without her.

That, however, was not easy. I said I began to make preparations, but no specific preparations occurred to me. How do you go about making plans to live without something you never really had? If she had been really my mistress, I most likely would have had some possessions of hers in my apartment, to put in a box and send back to her. But I did not have so much as a douche bag, a toothbrush, to get rid of. The only thing of that sort that I could do would be to tell the drug store to stop sending her that monthly bottle of perfume, and I briefly considered that move to remind her that she had banished me. But in addition to its being ridiculously petty, such a move would have been effective as a reminder just once. Oddly enough, though, I had hit upon a most significant detail. A couple of days after I got back from the Gibbsville fiasco, the drug store, one of the last of the old-time ethical pharmacies, sent me a letter to notify me that at the request of Mrs. Cooper, they were discontinuing monthly delivery of the perfume. So she had put me out of her life.

Fortunately for my state of mind, I had made my plans for the trip abroad, which was to combine pleasure and business. My passage had been booked in both directions, my hotel reservations made, and the exact time of my business appointments in London, Paris, Brussels, and Berlin was set. On the social side, I had accepted invitations for the two weekends I would be in England, as well as for the weekend that I would be in France, and it was a safe guess that my overseas acquaintances would wish to entertain for me as the representative of clients. My schedule was tight, but for once I welcomed the restrictions on my free time. I would not have to brood about that little bitch.

I began brooding about her the moment the *Queen Mary* sounded its horn and backed into the channel in the North River. The sound of the horn went right to my guts and standing alone on the boat deck I ignored the Manhattan skyline and stared out toward the Jersey meadows, where her lover had been done in, and I tried to guess the precise direction of a straight line to Gibbsville, Pennsylvania, where at this moment she would be in all likelihood having lunch at the Y.M.C.A. cafeteria. People like her, in jobs like hers, all had lunch at the "Y" cafeteria. I would be having mine shortly in the Verandah Grill of the *Queen Mary,* with a Boston lawyer and his wife who were on their way to a world convention of breeders of Dandie Dinmonts at Edinburgh. I had a feeling that I was going to see a lot of Mr. and Mrs. Wallen, and I was right. She introduced me to her sister, another Dandie Dinmont fancier, and the four of us played bridge all the way to Southampton. By skill, luck, and intense concentration on the cards, I won sixty-five dollars.

The whole trip was like that, more or less. In Brussels, where my business acquaintance was a fat bachelor, I was provided with a tall young blonde who could have worn any item of Andrea's clothes. She was very pleasing to the eye and to the senses, and was under strict orders to accept no money from me. But I gave her fifty dollars anyhow so that she would not think the less kindly of gentlemen from Philadelphia. She knew of Philadelphia as the home town of Grace Kelly, of the cinema, and of Eddie Fisher, a singer. No, I had never met Miss Kelly or Fisher, and I had to assure the young woman that it was not so much because I was a *snopp* as that Philadelphia was a large city, about twice as many people as Brussels, which she manifestly did not believe. She was a very competent professional, kept busy by the delegates to the Benelux Customs Union, and was moderately pleased when I told her that she reminded me very much of a young woman I knew in the United States. "Your mistress?" she said, and I said yes, and let it go at that. She had guessed immediately that I was not married, and could not explain her guess other than to say that she had never yet been wrong. Intuition. I could not reasonably argue with that; intuitively I had guessed that she was a high-class whore.

She was my only physical contact with her sex throughout my trip, and just what I wanted. I wanted no involvement with a non-professional, no polite wooing for the privilege of the bed. Twice I had conversations with my secretary on the overseas telephone, and she would not have failed to report a message from Andrea. The distance and the time that had intervened since my Gibbsville fiasco now seemed very great indeed. I attributed that notion to my realizing, retroactively, that Andrea intended the rupture to be permanent. If that were the case, three weeks and three thousand miles were only the beginning, and if so, I would do well to make a more serious effort to dismiss her from my thoughts. That I had never done, neither on this trip nor in the past, when she had stayed away from me for a year at a time.

Going home, in the *Queen Elizabeth,* I played bridge with other men for higher stakes than I had played for with the Wallens. I hate to lose at anything, particularly at bridge, and I suggested the ten-cents-a-point game because it was the only way I knew to divert me from the excitement I had begun to feel as soon as I boarded the ship. I drank a little more than I usually do; not enough to have a noticeable effect on my bridge game, but enough to make me ready for sleep when our nightly game was over. There was nothing—meaning no one, meaning Andrea—waiting for me at home, and yet the excitement demanded some attention. Several nights I went to bed quite sozzled, the result of nightcaps following the bridge games. On totting up the score on the night before we were to land, I was delighted to find that I had won more than a thousand tax-free dollars, and I was gratified to discover that the bridge and the whiskey had had the desired palliative effect. One disturbing note: as he paid up, one of my bridge-game companions said, "For a man that put away as much Scotch as you did, you played awfully good bridge." He was a New Yorker, a member of my New York club, and I was glad he was not Philadelphian. At home no one had ever had occasion to comment on my intake of whiskey. I had actually never been a heavy drinker by the standards of the men whom I saw every day. Yet the bridge companion had seen fit to comment on the quantity of my drinking and not on the effect on me.

The next day one of our clients sent a company limousine to meet me at the pier and transport me to Philadelphia, and I was home in time for lunch at the club. Lunch at a club was the antithesis of the kind of excitement that I had been subduing on the ship. I took my seat at the large, common table, and the man next to me said, "I missed you the last couple days," and the man on the other side of me asked me if I had had a good trip. That was par for the course, and I was home again, back in the old routine. From the club I walked to my office, spent an hour with my secretary and another hour with my partners. By quitting time it was hard to believe that I had been in New York that morning, and the most surprising thing of all was that as I slipped back into my routine, I almost believed that Andrea was where she had always been as a sort of offstage character in the comedy-drama of my life. Everything else was the same; why not she? But she refused to stay put in the customary role.

The next few weeks were busy ones for me. After all, I had spent about $7,000 of other people's money, and they were entitled to their conferences and my reports and opinions. I found that it was taking as long to report on the trip as the trip itself had taken, and one day I happened to notice on my calendar that four months had passed since my visit to Gibbsville. It did not seem possible. Meanwhile the mineral rights case had been turned over to Whitman, one of our junior partners, and it was trudging along as such cases tend to do. It could and might go on for years. Two teams of accountants were working on the basically same set of figures and coming out with wildly disparate results, a normal condition when the accountants are on opposite sides of the fence. At a senior partners' weekly meeting, during which we regularly go through the list of our cases, I said, "What about Southern Anthracite? Any progress there?"

Joe Sloan, one of the senior partners, said, "Slow as molasses, Phil. You wouldn't like to have another go at it?"

"Isn't Whitman doing all he can?" I said.

"No criticism of Whitman, but he's young. If we want to goose them, one of us will have to go. It must be six months since you went up to Gibbsville—"

"It's four," I said.

"Well, do you want to wait another two months and then go up? This thing may drag along and drag along till nobody gets any money out of it but the accountants. I was thinking that we could have our accountants do a pressure job, work overtime if necessary, and finish up well ahead of their accountants. Then if you went up to Gibbsville with the final figures you could get both litigants together and say, 'Here it is, let's sit down and work this out.' They won't take our figures as gospel, but they'll have a basis to work on. And I'm afraid you're elected, Phil. You're the only one they'll all listen to. I'd like to get this case finalized. I hate to see all that money going to the accountants, and not to us."

"Joe, you're just greedy," I said.

"I know I am. My one besetting sin," he said.

"I'll think it over and let you know tomorrow," I said.

If Joe Sloan's one besetting sin was greed—which it was not—mine was curiosity. I agreed to go to Gibbsville, and arranged to have a little article printed in the Gibbsville papers to the effect that the Southern Anthracite mineral rights dispute might be reaching its final stages ("Settlement Looms," the paper said) with the arrival of the noted Philadelphia attorney, meaning me, for several days of conferences. The dispute was of sufficient local interest to warrant its being printed on the front page, where Andrea would not miss it. This time everybody in town would know I was coming.

Before departing I received hasty invitations from the Lantenengo Bar Association, the Gibbsville Chamber of Commerce, and the Gibbsville Rotary Club to say a few words. With my judicial ambition in mind, I accepted the Bar Association invitation. They promised that their meeting would be informal, one of their regular monthly dinners, and that they were not asking me to prepare a speech. Anything I cared to say. Off the record. Intra-professional. No questions relating to the Southern Anthracite case or the subject of mineral rights. Just a hastily planned get-together in tribute to one of the county's most distinguished sons.

In theory, I was only the attorney for one party to the mineral rights dispute, but obviously during the first all-day conference I was in command. Whenever anyone was speaking, he would address me, and I slowly assumed the position of arbiter. I had Whitman with me to dig the appropriate papers out of his attaché case, and until late afternoon I did not say a word. Then, shortly after five o'clock, I said, "Gentlemen, this thing has gone on long enough. Here we are, eight men who are reasonable men, men of good will and personal integrity, here to serve the best interests of the people we represent. If that were not the case, I would not do what I am about to do." I paused and looked at each man, excluding Whitman. Across the table was a shyster who should have been disbarred years ago; a johnny-come-lately to the coal industry who had once been a bootlegger; a weak sister of a fellow whose family name was as old as the mining of hard coal; a man from Wilkes-Barre who had been in a lot of trouble for violations of the safety regulations. On our side of the table, besides Whitman and me, were our clients. I reached in my inside coat pocket and drew out a sheet of paper. "This is a memorandum that we prepared in my office. It is confidential, but I am going to read it to you." I then recited, or intoned, an almost day-to-day list of the expenses of the dispute between the two parties: accountants' fees, accountants' expenses, our disbursements, and so on and so on. I gave them five minutes of $125 for this, $54 for that, and finished up by saying, "That comes to sixty-two thousand, nine hundred and twelve dollars and twenty-seven cents. Sixty-two thousand, nine hundred and twelve dollars and twenty-seven cents. That's a lot of coal, gentlemen. A lot of coal. But you haven't even heard the half of it. You may have noticed that I did not mention legal fees. I don't know what our fee will be, but I doubt if it will be less than the accountants' fees. Let's say it will be the same. Sixty-three thousand dollars. That comes to, in round numbers, one hundred and twenty-six thousand dollars. That's *our* side of it. Let's say that your side of it matches that figure. That means that two hundred and fifty-two thousand dollars has been spent by both sides so far. *So far!* At the rate we're going, we could go well over the half-a-million-dollar mark. A half a million dollars is a lot of coal, a lot of coal. You could build a breaker for that kind of money. You could buy fifty trucks. But that's not all. If we go into court, the legal expenses on both sides will be staggering. Staggering. And even *that* isn't all, because I assure you gentlemen, if our side loses, we are going to appeal, and if our side wins, your side will probably appeal." I paused, to let the financial points sink in, and then I continued: "We have all had a tough day. I suggest we adjourn until ten o'clock tomorrow morning." I then, in my capacity as unofficial arbiter, stood up to give the signal for the others to stand up. They did so. If they had not done so, my argument would have been futile, but I had been silent all day and studying the opposition's shyster. They all got up automatically, and the meeting broke up then and there.

"That was masterful," Whitman whispered to me as he was putting his papers back in the attaché case.

"Maybe it was, but I hope you don't think it was the argument that did it. It was the timing and the psychology. Let's get out of here quick," I said.

I had won the case and I knew it. The details would be worked out later. I felt like one of those football players who, having scored a touchdown, leave the ball on the ground for the umpire to pick up. "Tomorrow you take over," I said to Whitman.

"You're not going to be there?" said Whitman.

"That's part of the psychology," I said. "I'll be at the hotel if you need me, but I have no intention of facing that shyster Spockman. He'll spend the night thinking up arguments against me, but they're not going to be any good if I'm not there. You go to the meeting as though we'd all agreed to behave sensibly, and I think you'll find that Spockman will be the only hold-out. Care to join me for a drink?"

"No sir, I have to call Mr. Sloan, but thanks."

"I'll be at the Gibbsville Club, then there's a Bar Association dinner that I'm going to. Look in if you feel like it," I said. "It's at the hotel."

I saw some old friends at the Gibbsville Club, where I had retained my non-resident membership. I stayed there until it was time to go to the Bar Association dinner, at which I arrived in a very very cheerful mood. Some-how the rumor had spread that I had conducted a highly successful meeting in the mineral rights case, and I was compelled several times to say that con-gratulations were premature; but I was a lawyer among lawyers, and they were aware, and pleased, that I had outsmarted Mr. Spockman. He, of course, stayed away from the dinner.

When it came my turn to speak, I played it safe. I was not drunk, but I had had a lot to drink, and this seemed to be a good opportunity to dispel the notion that I was a stuffed shirt. I therefore confined my remarks to profes-sional jokes and anecdotes about old-time members of the county bench and bar. I turned the meeting into a social evening, and when it was over I was told repeatedly that it was the liveliest session they had had in years. About a dozen of us repaired to the taproom to reminisce. At midnight I grew weary of their adulation and obsequiousness, and said goodnight.

There were two identical telephone messages under my door. I checked the number in the telephone book, and it was Andrea, who had not left her name. "Please call 625-1181," and the calls had been received during the time I was at the Gibbsville Club. I called her, and I woke her up. Her speech was slow, heavy with sleep, and I had trouble making her understand that it was I who was calling. "I took a sleeping pill," she said, obviously with an effort.

"Go back to sleep," I said.

"All right," she said and hung up. She was no good to me that night, and I took a bottle of Scotch out of my bag and poured a nightcap. She was no damn good to me, full of sleeping pills and dead to the world.

In a way, to be perfectly truthful, I was relieved. I had come to Gibbs-ville on the early morning train, had gone almost immediately to the morn-ing meeting, lunched with Whitman and our clients, returned to the afternoon meeting, and built up to the climax of the meeting which was my speech to Spockman and the others. Then instead of slowing down, I had kept going at the Gibbsville Club and the Bar Association dinner. More than eighteen hours of more or less intense effort. I was annoyed but at the same time grateful that for that night there would be no more demands on my physical and mental resources. I got into bed without finishing my nightcap, and fell asleep with the light on.

From another world came the ringing of my telephone. It rang several times, stopped, and then was rung again with renewed vigor. "For Christ's sake," I said, and answered it. It was my old friend the night man who had delivered groceries for Snodgrass. "There's a lady to see you, sir."

"To *see* me? You mean downstairs?"

"Yes sir, she says you sent for her and she won't go away," he said. In a lower tone, barely audible, he added: "It's somebody you know."

"All right, send her up," I said.

I had time to splash some cold water on my face and run a comb through my hair, but I was unsteady and drowsy when the rap came on the fireproof door. Behind her stood the night man, waiting to see if I was going to let her in. "Hello, come in," I said, and the door closed behind her.

"You did send for me, didn't you?" she said.

"No, I didn't, but you're here," I said.

"Did I imagine it? You did call me, didn't you?"

"Yes, but you were full of sleeping pills, you said."

"One. Not pills, just one."

"I might as well be," I said. "My sleeping pill was Scotch."

"So I see," she said, looking at the unfinished nightcap.

"Do you want some?" I said. "Did I hear three o'clock strike?"

"You could have. It's after four, now."

"Then I didn't hear three o'clock strike. I was really pounding away. Do you want a drink of Scotch? And tap water? It's all I can offer you at this hour."

"And you're not offering that very graciously. No thanks," she said. "Go on back to bed," she said. "I woke up thinking you'd sent for me, but if you didn't—the hell with it."

"How'd you get here?"

"On my Flexible-Flyer," she said. "What do you mean, how did I get here? I have a car. It sits out in front of my apartment all night, case some traveling salesman gets horny. *How* did I *get* here!"

I was coming to, and I knew it by the fact that desire for her was growing in me. I closed the windows, and put on my dressing-gown. "I'm not going to pull a knife on you," I said. "There's no use watching me that way."

"*I'm* not going to pull a knife on *you*, either."

"Well, why don't you take off your coat?"

"Because it's still cold in here," she said.

I turned up the thermostat. "Take off your coat," I said.

"Are we going to go to bed?" she said.

"That's always up to you," I said.

"No, it isn't," she said. "That's what I came here for, but that was when I thought you'd sent for me. However, you deny that. You *didn't* send for me, and I was laboring under a misapprehension."

"If I ask you now, politely and unequivocally, will you go to bed with me?"

"Are either one of us going to get any pleasure out of it?" she said. "I don't think I'll be any good."

"Well, then let's talk," I said. "Frankly, I thought I was never going to see you again."

"I thought I was going to have to struggle along without you, too," she said.

"And you seem to have," I said. "Are you still working at the hat store?"

"Thank *God* I am. Otherwise I would be waiting for horny salesmen to call me at night," she said. "You heard about King's?"

"No."

"Bankruptcy, or receivership. Anyway, it's going out of business. Daddy flew the coop, taking all the cash with him. Mother is living with Bud, my brother. She rented her house, furnished, and that's all she has to live on. Fortunately, she doesn't have to spend much money on food. Just give her a bottle of vodka every day and she's happy and contented."

"That must be pretty tough on your brother. What is he living on?"

"He's a substitute teacher in the high school, and his wife's family are giving them something. There are so many people around here having financial difficulties, it's becoming quite the thing. I hate this hotel. It's always filled up with people from out-of-town, squeezing the last dollar out of Gibbsville."

"What about the hat store?"

"It's amazing. Women can always scrape up twelve-ninety-five for a hat."

"And your fairy friend, your boss?"

"One of the few prosperous men in town," she said.

"And you still love him dearly?" I said.

"Of course I do," she said. "If he was a man, I'd marry him. And he says the same thing about me."

"What about the doctor?"

"He comes to see me once in a while. We go out to dinner together."

"And?"

"Oh, sure," she said.

"Then you might marry him after all," I said.

"No. We don't even discuss marriage any more. We have dinner together. Sex. And he goes home. He's seriously considering going back in the Navy again. If they'll take him back as a lieutenant commander, and let him take a two-year course in urology, he'll go. He's in the reserve, and apparently they need doctors."

"He's willing to give up twenty thousand a year?"

"It's less than that now, and he wouldn't have to pay rent and a secretary and all that. It makes a lot of sense."

She stood up and took off her coat and folded it on the back of a chair. Then she kicked off her shoes and lay beside me on the bed. "Rather crowded in here," she said. She put her arms around me and kissed me on the mouth. "We're getting there," she said.

"I missed you," I said.

She nodded. "Yes," she said. She got up and took off her clothes and got back into bed with me. "Don't you think it'd be polite if you took yours off too?"

"It wouldn't be polite, exactly. I'm getting a paunch. But it'd be more comfortable."

"Well, then be comfortable," she said. She watched me. "You're not *getting* a paunch, you have one. What is it? The booze?"

"It's the booze," I said.

"Is that my fault?"

"If I want to put the blame on someone else, yes," I said.

"Don't become a drunkard on account of me," she said.

"I don't intend to become a drunkard," I said.

"You'd better be careful, then," she said.

"I'm careful," I said.

"No," she said. "You got drunk tonight, didn't you?"

"How did you know?"

"You didn't even finish your last drink," she said. She began to make love to me, startlingly like the Belgian girl, the girl in Brussels who had made me think of her. "Maybe if we went to sleep for a little while," she said.

"No," I said. "Unless you want to."

"Suddenly you lost interest," she said.

"It'll come back," I said.

"Oh, I know that," she said. She sat up. "There's something on your mind. Either that, or you're too tired. Which is it?"

I could not lie to her, so I told her about the Belgian girl.

"Well, it almost had to be something like that," she said. "Now we can forget about her—or, if you want to think about her, turn out the light."

"I don't want to think about her," I said.

"That's good. Don't think about me, either. The hell with thinking. It's me, Phil. Your girl." She nestled down, and slowly we returned to our old selves and now everything was all right.

"That was good," she said. "It's still good. With you it's never over so soon. There's always something left. Something nice. I don't know. Something nice. You have it for me, and I guess I have it for you."

"It'd be too obvious to call it love," I said.

"It obviously isn't love, either," she said. "Love quits on you. At least it always has on me. I guess you're my steady. How many years is it?"

"Oh—twenty."

"Then it certainly isn't love," she said. "Although it certainly is."

"We don't have to have a name for it," I said.

"Phil and Andrea, Incorporated," she said.

"Or as the French say, Société Anonyme," I said.

"I don't quite get it," she said.

"Americans say incorporated, the British say limited. The French say société anonyme, using the initials s.a. You probably thought they stood for sex appeal."

"You've lost me," she said.

"Well, the next time you look at a bottle of perfume—speaking of which, you sorehead."

She smiled. "Yes, that was sorehead. Now you can tell them to start sending it again. What was that horrid noise?"

"It sounded like a bus."

"That's exactly what it was. It's getting daylight," she said. "You have time for a few hours' sleep. And I have time to get out of here before everybody in Gibbsville sees me. Will you take me to dinner tonight, or come to my apartment?"

"Whatever you like."

"Come to my apartment. Société anonyme."

"All right, fine," I said.

I lay in bed and watched her get dressed, an operation that was almost as fascinating as watching her undress. "Shall I open the windows?" she said.

"If you don't mind," I said.

"Of course I don't mind. We have to have a clear head," she said. She kissed me on the forehead and went to the window and opened it. Then she went to the other window and opened it, and I don't know what happened because I was not watching. But when I did look she was not there, and I did not believe that until I heard a most awful scream. Then I believed it, and it is all I have left to believe.

EDITH WHARTON

The Old Maid

□ **I** □

In the old New York of the 'fifties a few families ruled, in simplicity and affluence. Of these were the Ralstons.

The sturdy English and the rubicund and heavier Dutch had mingled to produce a prosperous, prudent and yet lavish society. To "do things handsomely" had always been a fundamental principle in this cautious world, built up on the fortunes of bankers, India merchants, ship-builders and ship-chandlers. Those well-fed slow-moving people, who seemed irritable and dyspeptic to European eyes only because the caprices of the climate had stripped them of superfluous flesh, and strung their nerves a little tighter, lived in a genteel monotony of which the surface was never stirred by the dumb dramas now and then enacted underground. Sensitive souls in those days were like muted key-boards, on which Fate played without a sound.

In this compact society, built of solidly welded blocks, one of the largest areas was filled by the Ralstons and their ramifications. The Ralstons were of middle-class English stock. They had not come to the colonies to die for a creed but to live for a bank-account. The result had been beyond their hopes, and their religion was tinged by their success. An edulcorated Church of England which, under the conciliatory name of the "Episcopal Church of the United States of America," left out the coarser allusions in the Marriage Service, slid over the comminatory passages in the Athanasian Creed, and thought it more respectful to say "Our Father *who*" than *"which"* in the Lord's Prayer, was exactly suited to the spirit of compromise whereon the Ralstons had built themselves up. There was in all the tribe the same instinctive recoil from new religions as from unaccounted-for people. Institutional to the core, they represented the conservative element that holds new societies together as seaplants bind the seashore.

Compared with the Ralstons, even such traditionalists as the Lovells, the

Halseys or the Vandergraves appeared careless, indifferent to money, almost reckless in their impulses and indecisions. Old John Frederick Ralston, the stout founder of the race, had perceived the difference, and emphasized it to his son, Frederick John, in whom he had scented a faint leaning toward the untried and unprofitable.

"You let the Lannings and the Dagonets and the Spenders take risks and fly kites. It's the county-family blood in 'em: we've nothing to do with that. Look how they're petering out already—the men, I mean. Let your boys marry their girls, if you like (they're wholesome and handsome); though I'd sooner see my grandsons take a Lovell or a Vandergrave or any of our own kind. But don't let your sons go mooning around after their young fellows, horse-racing, and running down south to those d——d Springs, and gambling at New Orleans, and all the rest of it. That's how you'll build up the family, and keep the weather out. The way we've always done it."

Frederick John listened, obeyed, married a Halsey, and passively followed in his father's steps. He belonged to the cautious generation of New York gentlemen who revered Hamilton and served Jefferson, who longed to lay out New York like Washington, and who laid it out instead like a gridiron, lest they should be thought "undemocratic" by people they secretly looked down upon. Shop-keepers to the marrow, they put in their windows the wares there was most demand for, keeping their private opinions for the back-shop, where through lack of use, they gradually lost substance and colour.

The fourth generation of Ralstons had nothing left in the way of convictions save an acute sense of honour in private and business matters: on the life of the community and the state they took their daily views from the newspapers, and the newspapers they already despised. The Ralstons had done little to shape the destiny of their country, except to finance the Cause when it had become safe to do so. They were related to many of the great men who had built the Republic; but no Ralston had so far committed himself as to be great. As old John Frederick said, it was safer to be satisfied with three per cent: they regarded heroism as a form of gambling. Yet by merely being so numerous and so similar they had come to have a weight in the community. People said: "The Ralstons" when they wished to invoke a precedent. This attribution of authority had gradually convinced the third generation of its collective importance, and the fourth, to which Delia Ralston's husband belonged, had the ease and simplicity of a ruling class.

Within the limits of their universal caution, the Ralstons fulfilled their obligations as rich and respected citizens. They figured on the boards of all the old-established charities, gave handsomely to thriving institutions, had the best cooks in New York, and when they travelled abroad ordered statuary of the American sculptors in Rome whose reputation was already established. The first Ralston who had brought home a statue had been regarded as a wild fellow; but when it became known that the sculptor had executed several orders for the British aristocracy it was felt in the family that this too was a three per cent investment.

Two marriages with the Dutch Vandergraves had consolidated these qualities of thrift and handsome living, and the carefully built-up Ralston character was now so congenital that Delia Ralston sometimes asked herself whether, were she to turn her own little boy loose in a wilderness, he would not create a small New York there, and be on all its boards of directors.

Delia Lovell had married James Ralston at twenty. The marriage, which had taken place in the month of September, 1840, had been solemnized, as was then the custom, in the drawing-room of the bride's country home, at what is now the corner of Avenue A and Ninety-first Street, overlooking the Sound. Thence her husband had driven her (in Grandmamma Lovell's canary-coloured coach with a fringed hammer-cloth) through spreading suburbs and untidy elm-shaded streets to one of the new houses in Gramercy Park, which the pioneers of the younger set were just beginning to affect; and there, at five-and-twenty, she was established, the mother of two children, the possessor of a generous allowance of pin-money, and, by common consent, one of the handsomest and most popular "young matrons" (as they were called) of her day.

She was thinking placidly and gratefully of these things as she sat one afternoon in her handsome bedroom in Gramercy Park. She was too near to the primitive Ralstons to have as clear a view of them as, for instance, the son in question might one day command: she lived under them as unthinkingly as one lives under the laws of one's country. Yet that tremor of the muted key-board, that secret questioning which sometimes beat in her like wings, would now and then so divide her from them that for a fleeting moment she could survey them in their relation to other things. The moment was always fleeting; she dropped back from it quickly, breathless and a little pale, to her children, her house-keeping, her new dresses and her kindly Jim.

She thought of him today with a smile of tenderness, remembering how he had told her to spare no expense on her new bonnet. Though she was twenty-five, and twice a mother, her image was still surprisingly fresh. The plumpness then thought seemly in a young wife stretched the grey silk across her bosom, and caused her heavy gold watch-chain—after it left the anchorage of the brooch of St. Peter's in mosaic that fastened her low-cut Cluny collar—to dangle perilously in the void above a tiny waist buckled into a velvet waist-band. But the shoulders above sloped youthfully under her Cashmere scarf, and every movement was as quick as a girl's.

Mrs. Jim Ralston approvingly examined the rosy-cheeked oval set in the blonde ruffles of the bonnet on which, in compliance with her husband's instructions, she had spared no expense. It was a cabriolet of white velvet tied with wide satin ribbons and plumed with a crystal-spangled marabout—a wedding bonnet ordered for the marriage of her cousin, Charlotte Lovell, which was to take place that week at St. Mark's-in-the-Bouwerie. Charlotte was making a match exactly like Delia's own: marrying a Ralston, of the Waverly Place branch, than which nothing could be safer, sounder or more—well, usual. Delia did not know why the word had occurred to her, for it could hardly be postulated, even of the young women of her own narrow clan, that they "usually" married Ralstons; but the soundness, safeness, suitability of the arrangement, did make it typical of the kind of alliance which a nice girl in the nicest set would serenely and blushingly forecast for herself.

Yes—and afterward?

Well—what? And what did this new question mean? Afterward: why, of course, there was the startled puzzled surrender to the incomprehensible exigencies of the young man to whom one had at most yielded a rosy cheek in return for an engagement ring; there was the large double-bed; the terror of seeing him shaving calmly the next morning, in his shirt-sleeves, through the dressing-room door: the evasions, insinuations, resigned smiles and Bible texts of one's Mamma; the reminder of the phrase "to obey" in the glittering blur of the Marriage Service; a week or a month of flushed distress, confusion, embarrassed pleasure; then the growth of habit, the insidious lulling of the matter-of-course, the dreamless double slumbers in the big white bed, the early morning discussions and consultations through that dressing-room door which had once seemed to open into a fiery pit scorching the brow of innocence.

And then, the babies; the babies who were supposed to "make up for everything," and didn't—though they were such darlings, and one had no definite notion as to what it was that one had missed, and that they were to make up for.

Yes: Charlotte's fate would be just like hers. Joe Ralston was so like his second cousin Jim (Delia's James), that Delia could see no reason why life in the squat brick house in Waverly Place should not exactly resemble life in the tall brown-stone house in Gramercy Park. Only Charlotte's bedroom would certainly not be as pretty as hers.

She glanced complacently at the French wall-paper that reproduced a watered silk, with a "valanced" border, and tassels between the loops. The mahogany bedstead, covered with a white embroidered counterpane, was symmetrically reflected in the mirror of a wardrobe which matched it. Coloured lithographs of the "Four Seasons" by Léopold Robert surmounted groups of family daguerreotypes in deeply-recessed gilt frames. The ormolu clock represented a shepherdess sitting on a fallen trunk, a basket of flowers at her feet. A shepherd, stealing up, surprised her with a kiss, while her little dog barked at him from a clump of roses. One knew the profession of the lovers by their crooks and the shape of their hats. This frivolous time-piece had been a wedding-gift from Delia's aunt, Mrs. Manson Mingott, a dashing widow who lived in Paris and was received at the Tuileries. It had been entrusted by Mrs. Mingott to young Clement Spender, who had come back from Italy for a short holiday just after Delia's marriage: the marriage which might never have been, if Clem Splender could have supported a wife, or if he had consented to give up painting and Rome for New York and the law. The young man (who looked, already, so odd and foreign and sarcastic) had laughingly assured the bride that her aunt's gift was "the newest thing in the Palais Royal"; and the family, who admired Mrs. Mason Mingott's taste though they disapproved of her "foreignness," had criticized Delia's putting the clock in her bedroom instead of displaying it on the drawing-room mantel. But she liked, when she woke in the morning to see the bold shepherd stealing his kiss.

Charlotte would certainly not have such a pretty clock in her bedroom; but then she had not been used to pretty things. Her father, who had died at thirty of lung-fever, was one of the "poor Lovells." His widow, burdened with a young family, and living all the year round "up the River," could not do much for her eldest girl; and Charlotte had entered society in her mother's turned garments and shod with satin sandals handed down from a defunct aunt who had "opened a ball" with General Washington. The old-fashioned Ralston furniture, which Delia already saw herself banishing, would seem sumptuous to Chatty; very likely she would think Delia's gay French time-piece somewhat frivolous, or even not "quite nice." Poor Charlotte had become so serious, so prudish almost, since she had given up balls and taken to visiting the poor! Delia remembered, with ever-recurring wonder, the abrupt change in her: the precise moment at which it had been privately agreed in the family that, after all, Charlotte Lovell was going to be an old maid.

They had not thought so when she came out. Though her mother could not afford to give her more than one new tarlatan dress, and though nearly everything in her appearance was regrettable, from the too bright red of her hair to the too pale brown of her eyes—not to mention the rounds of brick-rose on her cheek-bones, which almost (preposterous thought!) make her look as if she painted—yet these defects were redeemed by a slim waist, a light foot and a gay laugh; and when her hair was well oiled and brushed for an evening party, so that it looked almost brown, and lay smoothly along her delicate cheeks under a wreath of red and white camellias, several eligible young men (Joe Ralston among them) were known to have called her pretty.

Then came her illness. She caught cold on a moonlight sleighing-party, the brick-rose circles deepened, and she began to cough. There was a report that she was "going like her father," and she was hurried off to a remote village in Georgia, where she lived alone for a year with an old family governess. When she came back everyone felt at once that there was a change in her. She was pale, and thinner than ever, but with an exquisitely transparent cheek, darker eyes and redder hair; and the oddness of her appearance was increased by plain dresses of Quakerish cut. She had left off trinkets and watch-chains, always wore the same grey cloak and small close bonnet, and displayed a sudden zeal for visiting the indigent. The family explained that during her year in the south she had been shocked by the hopeless degradation of the "poor whites" and their children, and that this revelation of misery had made it impossible for her to return to the light-hearted life of her young friends. Everyone agreed, with significant glances, that this unnatural state of mind would "pass off in time": and meanwhile old Mrs. Lovell, Chatty's grandmother, who understood her perhaps better than the others, gave her a little money for her paupers, and lent her a room in the Lovell stables (at the back of the old lady's Mercer Street house) where she gathered about her, in what would afterward have been called a "day-nursery," some of the destitute children of the neighbourhood. There was even, among them, the baby girl whose origin had excited such intense curiosity two or three years earlier, when a veiled lady in a handsome cloak had brought it to the hovel of Cyrus Washington, the Negro handy-man whose wife Jessamine took in Dr. Lanskell's washing. Dr. Lanskell, the chief medical practitioner of the day, was presumably versed in the secret history of every household from the Battery to Union Square; but, though beset by inquisitive patients, he had invariably declared himself unable to identify Jessamine's "veiled lady," or to hazard a guess as to the origin of the hundred dollar bill pinned to the baby's bib.

The hundred dollars were never renewed, the lady never reappeared, but the baby lived healthily and happily with Jessamine's piccaninnies, and as soon as it could toddle was brought to Chatty Lovell's day-nursery, where it appeared (like its fellow paupers) in little garments cut down from her old dresses, and socks knitted by her untiring hands. Delia, absorbed in her own babies, had nevertheless dropped in once or twice at the nursery, and had come away wishing that Chatty's maternal instinct might find its normal outlet in marriage. The married cousin confusedly felt that her own affection for her handsome children was a mild and measured sentiment compared with Chatty's fierce passion for the waifs in Grandmamma Lovell's stable.

And then, to the general surprise, Charlotte Lovell engaged herself to Joe Ralston. It was known that Joe had "admired her" the year she came out. She was a graceful dancer, and Joe, who was tall and nimble, had footed it with her through many a reel and *Schottische*. By the end of the winter all the match-makers were predicting that something would come of it: but when Delia sounded her cousin, the girl's evasive answer and burning brow seemed to imply that her suitor had changed his mind, and no further questions could be asked. Now it was clear that there had, in fact, been an old romance between them, probably followed by that exciting incident, a "misunderstanding"; but at last all was well, and the bells of St. Mark's were preparing to ring in happier days for Charlotte. "Ah, when she has her first baby," the Ralston mothers chorused . . .

* * *

"Chatty!" Delia exclaimed, pushing back her chair as she saw her cousin's image reflected in the glass over her shoulder.

Charlotte Lovell had paused in the doorway. "They told me you were here—so I ran up."

"Of course, darling. How handsome you do look in your poplin! I always said you needed rich materials. I'm so thankful to see you out of grey cashmere." Delia, lifting her hands, removed the white bonnet from her dark polished head, and shook it gently to make the crystals glitter.

"I hope you like it? It's for your wedding," she laughed.

Charlotte Lovell stood motionless. In her mother's old dove-coloured poplin, freshly banded with narrow rows of crimson velvet ribbon, an ermine tippet crossed on her bosom, and a new beaver bonnet with a falling feather, she had already something of the assurance and majesty of a married woman.

"And you know your hair certainly *is* darker, darling," Delia added, still hopefully surveying her.

"Darker? It's grey," Charlotte suddenly broke out in her deep voice. She pushed back one of the pommaded bands that framed her face, and showed a white lock on her temple. "You needn't save up your bonnet; I'm not going to be married," she added, with a smile that showed her small white teeth in a fleeting glare.

Delia had just enough presence of mind to lay down the bonnet, marabout-up, before she flung herself on her cousin.

"Not going to be married? Charlotte, are you perfectly crazy?"

"Why is it crazy to do what I think right?"

"But people said you were going to marry him the year you came out. And no one understood what happened then. And now—how can it possibly be right? You simply *can't!*" Delia incoherently cried.

"Oh—people!" said Charlotte Lovell wearily.

Her married cousin looked at her with a start. Something thrilled in her voice that Delia had never heard in it, or in any other human voice, before. Its echo seemed to set their familiar world rocking, and the Axminster carpet actually heaved under Delia's shrinking slippers.

Charlotte Lovell stood staring ahead of her with strained lids. In the pale brown of her eyes Delia noticed the green specks that floated there when she was angry or excited.

"Charlotte—where on earth have you come from?" she questioned, drawing the girl down to the sofa.

"Come from?"

"Yes. You look as if you had seen a ghost—an army of ghosts."

The same snarling smile drew up Charlotte's lip. "I've seen Joe," she said.

"Well?—Oh, Chatty," Delia exclaimed abruptly illuminated, "you don't mean to say that you're going to let any little thing in Joe's past—? Not that I've ever heard the least hint; never. But even if there were ..." She drew a deep breath, and bravely proceeded to extremities. "Even if you've heard that he's been ... that he's had a child—of course he would have provided for it before ..."

The girl shook her head. "I know: you needn't go on. 'Men will be men'; but it's not that."

"Tell me what it is."

Charlotte Lovell looked about the sunny prosperous room as if it were the image of her world, and that world were a prison she must break out of. She lowered her head. "I want—to get away," she panted.

"Get away? From Joe?"

"From his ideas—the Ralston ideas."

Delia bridled—after all, she was a Ralston! "The Ralston ideas? I haven't found them—so unbearably unpleasant to live with," she smiled a little tartly.

"No. But it was different with you: they didn't ask you to give up things."

"What things?" What in the world (Delia wondered) had poor Charlotte that any one could want her to give up? She had always been in the position of taking rather than of having to surrender. "Can't you explain to me, dear?" Delia urged.

"My poor children—he says I'm to give them up," cried the girl in a stricken whisper.

"Give them up? Give up helping them?"

"Seeing them—looking after them. Give them up altogether. He got his mother to explain to me. After—after we have children ... he's afraid ... afraid our children might catch things ... He'll give me money, of course, to pay some one ... a hired person, to look after them. He thought that handsome," Charlotte broke out with a sob. She flung off her bonnet and smothered her prostrate weeping in the cushions.

Delia sat perplexed. Of all unforeseen complications this was surely the least imaginable. And with all the acquired Ralston that was in her she could not help seeing the force of Joe's objection, could almost find herself agreeing with him. No one in New York had forgotten the death of the poor Henry van der Luydens' only child, who had caught small-pox at the circus to which an unprincipled nurse had surreptitiously taken him. After such a warning as that, parents felt justified in every precaution against contagion. And poor people were so ignorant and careless, and their children, of course, so perpetually exposed to everything catching. No, Joe Ralston was certainly right, and Charlotte almost insanely unreasonable. But it would be useless to tell her so now. Instinctively, Delia temporized.

"After all," she whispered to the prone ear, "if it's only after you have children—you may not have any—for some time."

"Oh, yes, I shall!" came back in anguish from the cushions.

Delia smiled with matronly superiority. "Really, Chatty, I don't quite see how you can know. You don't understand."

Charlotte Lovell lifted herself up. Her collar of Brussels lace had come undone and hung in a wisp on her crumpled bodice, and through the disorder of her hair the white lock glimmered haggardly. In her pale brown eyes the little green specks floated like leaves in a trout-pool.

"Poor girl," Delia thought, "how old and ugly she looks! More than ever like an old maid; and she doesn't seem to realize in the least that she'll never have another chance."

"You must try to be sensible, Chatty dear. After all, one's own babies have the first claim."

"That's just it." The girl seized her fiercely by the wrists. "How can I give up my own baby?"

"Your—your—?" Delia's world again began to waver under her. "Which of the poor little waifs, dearest, do you call your own baby?" she questioned patiently.

Charlotte looked her straight in the eyes. "I call my own baby my own baby."

"Your own—? Take care—you're hurting my wrists, Chatty!" Delia freed herself, forcing a smile. "Your own—?"

"My own little girl. The one that Jessamine and Cyrus—"

"Oh—" Delia Ralston gasped.

The two cousins sat silent, facing each other; but Delia looked away. It came over her with a shudder of repugnance that such things, even if they had to be said, should not have been spoken in her bedroom, so near the spotless nursery across the passage. Mechanically she smoothed the organ-like folds of her silk skirt, which her cousin's embrace had tumbled. Then she looked again at Charlotte's eyes, and her own melted.

"Oh, poor Chatty—my poor Chatty!" She held out her arms to her cousin.

□ **II** □

The shepherd continued to steal his kiss from the shepherdess, and the clock in the fallen trunk continued to tick out the minutes.

Delia, petrified, sat unconscious of their passing, her cousin clasped to her. She was dumb with the horror and amazement of learning that her own blood ran in the veins of the anonymous foundling, the "hundred dollar baby" about whom New York had so long furtively jested and conjectured. It was her first contact with the nether side of the smooth social surface, and she sickened at the thought that such things were, and that she, Delia Ralston, should be hearing of them in her own house, and from the lips of the victim! For Chatty of course was a victim—but whose? She had spoken no name, and Delia could put no question: the horror of it sealed her lips. Her mind had instantly raced back over Chatty's past; but she saw no masculine figure in it but Joe Ralston's. And to connect Joe with the episode was obviously unthinkable. Some one in the south, then—? But no: Charlotte had been ill when she left—and in a flash Delia understood the real nature of that illness, and of the girl's disappearance. But from such speculations too her mind recoiled, and instinctively she fastened on something she could still grasp: Joe Ralston's attitude about Chatty's paupers. Of course Joe could not let his wife risk bringing contagion into their home—that was safe ground to dwell on. Her own Jim would have felt in the same way; and she would certainly have agreed with him.

Her eyes travelled back to the clock. She always thought of Clem Spender when she looked at the clock, and suddenly she wondered—if things had been different—what *he* would have said if she had made such an appeal to him as Charlotte had made to Joe. The thing was hard to imagine; yet in a flash of mental readjustment Delia saw herself as Clem's wife, she saw her children as his, she pictured herself asking him to let her go on caring for the poor waifs in the Mercer Street stable, and she distinctly heard his laugh and his light answer: "Why on earth did you ask, you little goose? Do you take me for such a Pharisee as that?"

Yes, that was Clem Spender all over—tolerant, reckless, indifferent to consequences, always doing the kind thing at the moment, and too often leaving others to pay the score. "There's something cheap about Clem," Jim had once said in his heavy way. Delia Ralston roused herself and pressed her cousin closer. "Chatty, tell me," she whispered.

"There's nothing more."

"I mean, about yourself . . . this thing . . . this . . ." Clem Spender's voice was still in her ears. "You loved some one," she breathed.

"Yes, that's over—. Now it's only the child . . . And I could love Joe—in another way." Chatty Lovell straightened herself, wan and frowning.

"I need the money—I must have it for my baby. Or else they'll send it to an Institution." She paused. "But that's not all. I want to marry—to be a wife, like all of you. I should have loved Joe's children—our children. Life doesn't stop . . ."

"No; I suppose not. But you speak as if . . . as if . . . the person who took advantage of you . . ."

"No one took advantage of me. I was lonely and unhappy. I met some one who was lonely and unhappy. People don't all have your luck. We were both too poor to marry each other . . . and mother would never have consented. And so one day . . . one day before he said goodbye . . ."

"He said goodbye?"

"Yes. He was going to leave the country."

"He left the country—knowing?"

"How was he to know? He doesn't live here. He'd just come back—come back to see his family—for a few weeks . . ." She broke off, her thin lips pressed together upon her secret.

There was silence. Blindly Delia stared at the bold shepherd.

"Come back from where?" she asked at length in a low tone.

"Oh, what does it matter? You wouldn't understand," Charlotte broke off, in the very words her married cousin had compassionately addressed to her virginity.

A slow blush rose to Delia's cheek: she felt oddly humiliated by the rebuke conveyed in that contemptuous retort. She seemed to herself shy, ineffectual, as incapable as an ignorant girl of dealing with the abominations that Charlotte was thrusting on her. But suddenly some fierce feminine intuition struggled and woke in her. She forced her eyes upon her cousin's.

"You won't tell me who it was?"

"What's the use? I haven't told anybody."

"Then why have you come to me?"

Charlotte's stony face broke up in weeping. "It's for my baby . . . my baby . . ."

Delia did not heed her. "How can I help you if I don't know?" she insisted in a harsh dry voice: her heart-beats were so violent that they seemed to send up throttling hands to her throat.

Charlotte made no answer.

"Come back from where?" Delia doggedly repeated; and at that, with a long wail, the girl flung her hands up, screening her eyes. "He always thought you'd wait for him," she sobbed out, "and then, when he found you hadn't . . . and that you were marrying Jim . . . He heard it just as he was sailing . . . He didn't know it till Mrs. Mingott asked him to bring the clock back for your wedding . . ."

"Stop—stop," Delia cried, springing to her feet. She had provoked the avowal, and now that it had come she felt that it had been gratuitously and indecently thrust upon her. Was this New York, *her* New York, her safe friendly hypocritical New York, was this James Ralston's house, and this his wife listening to such revelations of dishonour?

Charlotte Lovell stood up in her turn. "I knew it—I knew it! You think worse of my baby now, instead of better ... Oh, why did you make me tell you? I knew you'd never understand. I'd always cared for him, ever since I came out; that was why I wouldn't marry any one else. But I knew there was no hope for me ... he never looked at anybody but you. And then, when he came back four years ago, and there was no *you* for him any more, he began to notice me, to be kind, to talk to me about his life and his painting ..." She drew a deep breath, and her voice cleared. "That's over—all over. It's as if I couldn't either hate him or love him. There's only the child now—my child. He doesn't even know of it—why should he? It's none of his business; it's nobody's business but mine. But surely you must see that I can't give up my baby."

Delia Ralston stood speechless, looking away from her cousin in a growing horror. She had lost all sense of reality, all feeling of safety and self-reliance. Her impulse was to close her ears to the other's appeal as a child buries its head from midnight terrors. At last she drew herself up, and spoke with dry lips.

"But what do you mean to do? Why have you come to me? Why have you told me all this?"

"Because he loved you!" Charlotte Lovell stammered out; and the two women stood and faced each other.

Slowly the tears rose to Delia's eyes and rolled down her cheeks, moistening her parched lips. Through the tears she saw her cousin's haggard countenance waver and droop like a drowning face under water. Things half-guessed, obscurely felt, surged up from unsuspected depths in her. It was almost as if, for a moment, this other woman were telling her of her own secret past, putting into crude words all the trembling silences of her own heart.

The worst of it was, as Charlotte said, that they must act now; there was not a day to lose. Chatty was right—it was impossible that she should marry Joe if to do so meant giving up the child. But, in any case, how could she marry him without telling him the truth? And was it conceivable that, after hearing it, he should repudiate her? All these questions spun agonizingly through Delia's brain, and through them glimmered the persistent vision of the child—Clem Spender's child—growing up on charity in a Negro hovel, or herded in one of the plague-houses they called Asylums. No: the child came first—she felt it in every fibre of her body. But what should she do, of whom take counsel, how advise the wretched creature who had come to her in Clement's name? Delia glanced about her desperately, and then turned back to her cousin.

"You must give me time. I must think. You ought not to marry him—and yet all the arrangements are made; and the wedding presents ... There would be a scandal ... it would kill Granny Lovell ..."

Charlotte answered in a low voice: "There *is* no time. I must decide now."

Delia pressed her hands against her breast. "I tell you I must think. I wish you would go home.—Or, no: stay here: your mother mustn't see your eyes. Jim's not coming home till late; you can wait in this room till I come back." She had opened the wardrobe and was reaching up for a plain bonnet and heavy veil.

"Stay here? But where are you going?"

"I don't know. I want to walk—to get the air. I think I want to be alone." Feverishly, Delia unfolded her Paisley shawl, tied on bonnet and veil, thrust her mittened hands into her muff. Charlotte, without moving, stared at her dumbly from the sofa.

"You'll wait," Delia insisted, on the threshold.

"Yes: I'll wait."

Delia shut the door and hurried down the stairs.

□ III □

She had spoken the truth in saying that she did not know where she was going. She simply wanted to get away from Charlotte's unbearable face, and from the immediate atmosphere of her tragedy. Outside, in the open, perhaps it would be easier to think.

As she skirted the park-rails she saw her rosy children playing, under their nurse's eyes, with the pampered progeny of other square-dwellers. The little girl had on her new plaid velvet bonnet and white tippet, and the boy his Highland cap and broad-cloth spencer. How happy and jolly they looked! The nurse spied her, but she shook her head, waved at the group and hurried on.

She walked and walked through the familiar streets decked with bright winter sunshine. It was early afternoon, an hour when the gentlemen had just returned to their offices, and there were few pedestrians in Irving Place and Union Square. Delia crossed the Square to Broadway.

The Lovell house in Mercer Street was a sturdy old-fashioned brick dwelling. A large stable adjoined it, opening on an alley such as Delia, on her honey-moon trip to England, had heard called a "mews." She turned into the alley, entered the stable court, and pushed open a door. In a shabby white-washed room a dozen children, gathered about a stove, were playing with broken toys. The Irishwoman who had charge of them was cutting out small garments on a broken-legged deal table. She raised a friendly face, recognizing

Delia as the lady who had once or twice been to see the children with Miss Charlotte.

Delia paused, embarrassed.

"I—I came to ask if you need any new toys," she stammered.

"That we do, ma'am. And many another thing too, though Miss Charlotte tells me I'm not to beg of the ladies that comes to see our poor darlin's."

"Oh, you may beg of me, Bridget," Mrs. Ralston answered, smiling. "Let me see your babies—it's so long since I've been here."

The children had stopped playing and, huddled against their nurse, gazed up open-mouthed at the rich rustling lady. One little girl with pale brown eyes and scarlet cheeks was dressed in a plaid alpaca frock trimmed with imitation coral buttons that Delia remembered. Those buttons had been on Charlotte's "best dress" the year she came out. Delia stopped and took up the child. Its curly hair was brown, the exact color of the eyes—thank heaven! But the eyes had the same little green spangles floating in their transparency. Delia sat down, and the little girl, standing on her knee, gravely fingered her watch-chain.

"Oh, ma'am—maybe her shoes'll soil your skirt. The floor here ain't none too clean."

Delia shook her head, and pressed the child against her. She had forgotten the other gazing babies and their wardress. The little creature on her knee was made of different stuff—it had not needed the plaid alpaca and coral buttons to single her out. Her brown curls grew in points on her high forehead, exactly as Clement Spender's did. Delia laid a burning cheek against the forehead.

"Baby want my lovely yellow chain?"

Baby did.

Delia unfastened the gold chain and hung it about the child's neck. The other babies clapped and crowed, but the little girl, gravely dimpling, continued to finger the links in silence.

"Oh, ma'am, you can't leave that fine chain on little Teeny. When she has to go back to those blacks . . ."

"What is her name?"

"Teena they call her, I believe. It don't seem a Christian name, har'ly."

Delia was silent.

"What I say is, her cheeks is too red. And she coughs too easy. Always one cold and another. Here, Teeny, leave the lady go."

Delia stood up, loosening the tender arms.

"She doesn't want to leave go of you, ma'am. Miss Chatty ain't been in today, and the little thing's kinder lonesome without her. She don't play like the other children, somehow . . . Teeny, you look at that lovely chain you've got . . . there, there now . . ."

"Goodbye, Clementina," Delia whispered below her breath. She kissed the pale brown eyes, the curly crown, and dropped her veil on rushing tears. In the stable-yard she dried them on her large embroidered handkerchief, and stood hesitating. Then with a decided step she turned toward home.

The house was as she had left it, except that the children had come in; she heard them romping in the nursery as she went down the passage to her bedroom. Charlotte Lovell was seated on the sofa, upright and rigid, as Delia had left her.

"Chatty—Chatty, I've thought it out. Listen. Whatever happens, the baby shan't stay with those people. I mean to keep her."

Charlotte stood up, tall and white. The eyes in her thin face had grown so dark that they seemed like spectral hollows in a skull. She opened her lips to speak, and then, snatching at her handkerchief, pressed it to her mouth, and sank down again. A red trickle dripped through the handkerchief onto her poplin skirt.

"Charlotte—Charlotte," Delia screamed, on her knees beside her cousin. Charlotte's head slid back against the cushions and the trickle ceased. She closed her eyes, and Delia, seizing a vinaigrette from the dressing-table, held it to her pinched nostrils. The room was filled with an acrid aromatic scent.

Charlotte's lids lifted. "Don't be frightened. I still spit blood some-times—not often. My lung is nearly healed. But it's the terror—"

"No, no: there's to be no terror. I tell you I've thought it all out. Jim is going to let me take the baby."

The girl raised herself haggardly. "Jim? Have you told him? Is that where you've been?"

"No, darling. I've only been to see the baby."

"Oh," Charlotte moaned, leaning back again. Delia took her own hand-kerchief, and wiped away the tears that were raining down her cousin's cheeks.

"You mustn't cry, Chatty; you must be brave. Your little girl and his—how could you think? But you must give me time: I must manage it in my own way . . . Only trust me . . ."

Charlotte's lips stirred faintly.

"The tears . . . don't dry them, Delia . . . I like to feel them . . ."

The two cousins continued to lean against each other without speaking. The ormolu clock ticked out the measure of their mute communion in min-utes, quarters, a half-hour, then an hour: the day declined and darkened, the shadows lengthened across the garlands of the Axminster and the broad white bed. There was a knock.

"The children's waiting to say their grace before supper, ma'am."

"Yes, Eliza. Let them say it to you. I'll come later." As the nurse's steps receded Charlotte Lovell disengaged herself from Delia's embrace.

"Now I can go," she said.

"You're not too weak, dear? I can send for a coach to take you home."

"No, no; it would frighten mother. And I shall like walking now, in the darkness. Sometimes the world used to seem all one awful glare to me. There were days when I thought the sun would never set. And then there was the moon at night." She laid her hands on her cousin's shoulders. "Now it's different. Bye and bye I shan't hate the light."

The two women kissed each other, and Delia whispered: "Tomorrow."

□ **IV** □

The Ralstons gave up old customs reluctantly, but once they had adopted a new one they found it impossible to understand why everyone else did not immediately do likewise.

When Delia, who came of the laxer Lovells, and was naturally inclined to novelty, had first proposed to her husband to dine at six o'clock instead of two, his malleable young face had become as relentless as that of the old original Ralston in his grim Colonial portrait. But after a two days' resistance he had come round to his wife's view, and now smiled contemptuously at the obstinacy of those who clung to a heavy mid-day meal and high tea.

"There's nothing I hate like narrow-mindedness. Let people eat when they like, for all I care; it's their narrow-mindedness that I can't stand."

Delia was thinking of this as she sat in the drawing-room (her mother would have called it the parlour) waiting for her husband's return. She had just had time to smooth her glossy braids, and slip on the black-and-white striped moiré with cherry pipings which was his favourite dress. The drawing-room, with its Nottingham lace curtains looped back under florid gilt cornices, its marble centre-table on a carved rosewood foot, and its old-fashioned mahogany armchairs covered with one of the new French silk damasks in a tart shade of apple-green, was one for any young wife to be proud of. The rosewood what-nots on each side of the folding doors that led into the dining-room were adorned with tropical shells, feld-spar vases, an alabaster model of the Leaning Tower of Pisa, a pair of obelisks made of scraps of porphyry and serpentine picked up by the young couple in the Roman Forum, a bust of Clytie in chalk-white biscuit de Sèvres, and four old-fashioned figures of the Seasons in Chelsea ware, that had to be left among the newer ornaments because they had belonged to great-grandmamma Ralston. On the walls hung large dark steel-engravings of Cole's "Voyage of Life," and between the windows stood the lifesize statue of "A Captive Maiden" executed for Jim

Ralston's father by the celebrated Harriet Hosmer, immortalized in Hawthorne's novel of the Marble Faun. On the table lay handsomely tooled copies of Turner's Rivers of France, Drake's Culprit Fay, Crabbe's Tales, and the Book of Beauty containing portraits of the British peeresses who had participated in the Earl of Eglinton's tournament.

As Delia sat there, before the hard-coal fire in its arched opening of black marble, her citron-wood work-table at her side, and one of the new French lamps shedding a pleasant light on the centre-table from under a crystal-fringed shade, she asked herself how she could have passed, in such a short time, so completely out of her usual circle of impressions and convictions—so much farther than ever before beyond the Ralston horizon. Here it was, closing in on her again, as if the very plaster ornaments of the ceiling, the forms of the furniture, the cut of her dress, had been built out of Ralston prejudices, and turned to adamant by the touch of Ralston hands.

She must have been mad, she thought, to have committed herself so far to Charlotte; yet, turn about as she would in the every-tightening circle of the problem, she could still find no other issue. Somehow, it lay with her to save Clem Spender's baby.

She heard the sound of the latch-key (her heart had never beat so high at it), and the putting down of a tall hat on the hall console—or of two tall hats, was it? The drawing-room door opened, and two high-stocked and ample-coated young men came in: two Jim Ralstons, so to speak. Delia had never before noticed how much her husband and his cousin Joe were alike; it made her feel how justified she was in always thinking of the Ralstons collectively.

She would not have been young and tender, and a happy wife, if she had not thought Joe but an indifferent copy of her Jim; yet, allowing for defects in the reproduction, there remained a striking likeness between the two tall athletic figures, the short sanguine faces with straight noses, straight whiskers, straight brows, candid blue eyes and sweet selfish smiles. Only, at the present moment, Joe looked like Jim with a tooth-ache.

"Look here, my dear: here's a young man who's asked to take pot-luck with us." Jim smiled, with the confidence of a well-nourished husband who knows that he can always bring a friend home.

"How nice of you, Joe!—Do you suppose he can put up with oyster soup and a stuffed goose?" Delia beamed upon her husband.

"I knew it! I told you so, my dear chap! He said you wouldn't like it—that you'd be fussed about the dinner. Wait till you're married, Joseph Ralston—." Jim brought down a genial paw on his cousin's bottle-green shoulder, and Joe grimaced as if the tooth had stabbed him.

"It's excessively kind of you, cousin Delia, to take me in this evening. The fact is—"

"Dinner first, my boy, if you don't mind! A bottle of Burgundy will brush away the blue devils. Your arm to your cousin, please; I'll just go and see that the wine is brought up."

Oyster soup, broiled bass, stuffed goose, apple fritters and green peppers, followed by one of Grandmamma Ralston's famous caramel custards: through all her mental anquish, Delia was faintly aware of a secret pride in her achievement. Certainly it would serve to confirm the rumour that Jim Ralston could always bring a friend home to dine without notice. The Ralston and Lovell wines rounded off the effect, and even Joe's drawn face had mellowed by the time the Lovell Madeira started westward. Delia marked the change when the two young men rejoined her in the drawing-room.

"And now, my dear fellow, you'd better tell her the whole story," Jim counselled, pushing an armchair toward his cousin.

The young woman, bent above her wool-work, listened with lowered lids and flushed cheeks. As a married woman—as a mother—Joe hoped she would think him justified in speaking to her frankly: he had her husband's authority to do so.

"Oh, go ahead, go ahead," chafed the exuberant after-dinner Jim from the hearth-rug.

Delia listened, considered, let the bridegroom flounder on through his embarrassed exposition. Her needle hung like a sword of Damocles above the canvas; she saw at once that Joe depended on her trying to win Charlotte over to his way of thinking. But he was very much in love: at a word from Delia, she understood that he would yield, and Charlotte gain her point, save the child, and marry him . . .

How easy it was, after all! A friendly welcome, a good dinner, a ripe wine, and the memory of Charlotte's eyes—so much the more expressive for all that they had looked upon. A secret envy stabbed the wife who had lacked this last enlightenment.

How easy it was—and yet it must not be! Whatever happened, she could not let Charlotte Lovell marry Joe Ralston. All the traditions of honour and probity in which she had been brought up forbade her to connive at such a plan. She could conceive—had already conceived—of high-handed measures, swift and adroit defiances of precedent, subtle revolts against the heartlessness of the social routine. But a lie she could never connive at. The idea of Charlotte's marrying Joe Ralston—her own Jim's cousin—without revealing her past to him, seemed to Delia as dishonourable as it would have seemed to any Ralston. And to tell him the truth would at once put an end to the marriage; of that even Chatty was aware. Social tolerance was not dealt in the same measure to men and to women, and neither Delia nor Charlotte had ever wondered why: like all the young women of their class they simply bowed to the ineluctable.

No; there was no escape from the dilemma. As clearly as it was Delia's duty to save Clem Spender's child, so clearly, also, she seemed destined to sacrifice his mistress. As the thought pressed on her she remembered Charlotte's wistful cry: "I want to be married, like all of you," and her heart tightened. But yet it must not be.

"I make every allowance" (Joe was droning on) "for my sweet girl's ignorance and inexperience—for her lovely purity. How could a man wish his future wife to be—to be otherwise? You're with me, Jim? And Delia? I've told her, you understand, that she shall always have a special sum set apart for her poor children—in addition to her pin-money; on that she may absolutely count. God! I'm willing to draw up a deed, a settlement, before a lawyer, if she says so. I admire, I appreciate her generosity. But I ask you, Delia, as a mother—mind you, now, I want your frank opinion. If you think I can stretch a point—can let her go on giving her personal care to these children until . . . until . . ." A flush of pride suffused the potential father's brow . . . "till nearer duties claim her, why, I'm more than ready . . . if you'll tell her so. I undertake," Joe proclaimed, suddenly tingling with the memory of his last glass, "to make it right with my mother, whose prejudices, of course, while I respect them, I can never allow to—to come between me and my own convictions." He sprang to his feet, and beamed on his dauntless double in the chimney-mirror. "My convictions," he flung back at it.

"Hear, hear!" cried Jim emotionally.

Delia's needle gave the canvas a sharp prick, and she pushed her work aside.

"I think I understand you both, Joe. Certainly, in Charlotte's place, I could never give up those children."

"There you are, my dear fellow!" Jim triumphed, as proud of this vicarious courage as of the perfection of the dinner.

"Never," said Delia. "Especially, I mean, the foundlings—there are two, I think. Those children always die if they are sent to asylums. That is what is haunting Chatty."

"Poor innocents! How I love her for loving them! That there should be such scoundrels upon this earth unpunished—. Delia, will you tell her that I'll do whatever—"

"Gently, old man, gently," Jim admonished him, with a flash of Ralston caution.

"Well, that is to say, whatever—in reason—"

Delia lifted an arresting hand. "I'll tell her, Joe: she will be grateful. But it's of no use—"

"No use? What more—?"

"Nothing more: except this. Charlotte has had a return of her old illness. She coughed blood here today. You must not marry her."

There: it was done. She stood up, trembling in every bone, and feeling herself pale to the lips. Had she done right? Had she done wrong? And would she ever know?

Poor Joe turned on her a face as wan as hers: he clutched the back of his armchair, his head drooping forward like an old man's. His lips moved, but made no sound.

"My God!" Jim stammered. "But you know you've got to buck up, old boy."

"I'm—I'm so sorry for you, Joe. She'll tell you herself tomorrow," Delia faltered, while her husband continued to proffer heavy consolations.

"Take it like a man, old chap. Think of yourself—your future. Can't be, you know. Delia's right: she always *is*. Better get it over—better face the music now than later."

"Now than later," Joe echoed with a tortured grin; and it occurred to Delia that never before in the course of his easy good-natured life had he had—any more than her Jim—to give up anything his heart was set on. Even the vocabulary of renunciation, and its conventional gestures, were unfamiliar to him.

"But I don't understand. I can't give her up," he declared, blinking away a boyish tear.

"Think of the children, my dear fellow; it's your duty," Jim insisted, checking a glance of pride at Delia's wholesome comeliness.

In the long conversation that followed between the cousins—argument, counter-argument, sage counsel and hopeless protest—Delia took but an occasional part. She knew well enough what the end would be. The bridegroom who had feared that his bride might bring home contagion from her visits to the poor would not knowingly implant disease in his race. Nor was that all. Too many sad instances of mothers prematurely fading, and leaving their husbands alone with a young flock to rear, must be pressing upon Joe's memory. Ralstons, Lovells, Lannings, Archers, van der Luydens—which one of them had not some grave to care for in a distant cemetery: graves of young relatives "in a decline," sent abroad to be cured by balmy Italy? The protestant grave-yards of Rome and Pisa were full of New York names; the vision of that familiar pilgrimage with a dying wife was one to turn the most ardent Ralston cold. And all the while, as she listened with bent head, Delia kept repeating to herself: "This is easy; but how am I going to tell Charlotte?"

When poor Joe, late that evening, wrung her hand with a stammerd farewell, she called him back abruptly from the threshold.

"You must let me see her first, please; you must wait till she sends for you—" and she winced a little at the alacrity of his acceptance. But no amount of rhetorical bolstering-up could make it easy for a young man to face what lay ahead of Joe; and her final glance at him was one of compassion ...

* * *

The front door closed upon Joe, and she was roused by her husband's touch on her shoulder.

"I never admired you more, darling. My wise Delia!"

Her head bent back, she took his kiss, and then drew apart. The sparkle in his eyes she understood to be as much an invitation to her bloom as a tribute to her sagacity.

She held him at arm's length. "What should you have done, Jim, if I'd had to tell you about myself what I've just told Joe about Chatty?"

A slight frown showed that he thought the question negligible, and hardly in her usual taste. "Come," his strong arm entreated her.

She continued to stand away from him, with grave eyes. "Poor Chatty! Nothing left now—"

His own eyes grew grave, in instant sympathy. At such moments he was still the sentimental boy whom she could manage.

"Ah, poor Chatty, indeed!" He groped for the readiest panacea. "Lucky, now, after all, that she has those paupers, isn't it? I suppose a woman *must* have children to love—somebody else's if not her own." It was evident that the thought of the remedy had already relieved his pain.

"Yes," Delia agreed, "I see no other comfort for her. I'm sure Joe will feel that too. Between us, darling—" and now she let him have her hands— "between us, you and I must see to it that she keeps her babies."

"Her babies?" He smiled at the possessive pronoun. "Of course, poor girl! Unless indeed she's sent to Italy?"

"Oh, she won't be that—where's the money to come from? And, besides, she'd never leave Aunt Lovell. But I thought, dear, if I might tell her tomorrow—you see, I'm not exactly looking forward to my talk with her—if I might tell her that you would let me look after the baby she's most worried about, the poor little foundling girl who has no name and no home—if I might put aside a fixed sum from my pin-money . . ."

Their hands flowed together, she lifted her flushing face to his. Manly tears were in his eyes; ah, how he triumphed in her health, her wisdom, her generosity!

"Not a penny from your pin-money—never!"

She feigned discouragement and wonder. "Think, dear—if I'd had to give you up!"

"Not a penny from your pin-money, I say—but as much more as you need, to help poor Chatty's pauper. There—will that content you?"

"Dearest! When I think of our own, upstairs!" They held each other, awed by that evocation.

□   V   □

Charlotte Lovell, at the sound of her cousin's step, lifted a fevered face from the pillow.

The bedroom, dim and close, smelt of eau de Cologne and fresh linen. Delia, blinking in from the bright winter sun, had to feel her way through a twilight obstructed by dark mahogany.

"I want to see your face, Chatty: unless your head aches too much?"

Charlotte signed "No," and Delia drew back the heavy window curtains and let in a ray of light. In it she saw the girl's head, livid against the bed-linen, the brick-rose circles again visible under darkly shadowed lids. Just so, she remembered, poor cousin So-and-so had looked the week before she sailed for Italy!

"Delia!" Charlotte breathed.

Delia drew near the bed, and stood looking down at her cousin with new eyes. Yes: it had been easy enough, the night before, to dispose of Chatty's future as if it were her own. But now?

"Darling—"

"Oh, begin, please," the girl interrupted, "or I shall know that what's coming is too dreadful!"

"Chatty, dearest, if I promised you too much—"

"Jim won't let you take my child? I knew it! Shall I always go on dreaming things that can never be?"

Delia, her tears running down, knelt by the bed and gave her fresh hand into the other's burning clutch.

"Don't think that, dear: think only of what you'd like best . . ."

"Like best?" The girl sat up sharply against her pillows, alive to the hot fingertips.

"You can't marry Joe, dear—can you—and keep little Tina?" Delia continued.

"Not keep her with me, no: but somewhere I could slip off to see her— oh, I had hoped such follies!"

"Give up follies, Charlotte. Keep her where? See your own child in secret? Always in dread of disgrace? Of wrong to your other children? Have you ever thought of that?"

"Oh, my poor head won't think! You're trying to tell me that I must give her up?"

"No, dear; but that you must not marry Joe."

Charlotte sank back on the pillow, her eyes half-closed. "I tell you I must make my child a home. Delia, you're too blest to understand!"

"Think yourself blest too, Chatty. You shan't give up your baby. She shall live with you: you shall take care of her—for me."

"For you?"

"I promised you I'd take her, didn't I? But not that you should marry Joe. Only that I would make a home for your baby. Well, that's done; you two shall be always together."

Charlotte clung to her and sobbed. "But Joe—I can't tell him, I can't!" She put back Delia suddenly. "You haven't told him of my—of my baby? I couldn't bear to hurt him as much as that."

"I told him that you coughed blood yesterday. He'll see you presently: he's dreadfully unhappy. He has been given to understand that, in view of your bad health, the engagement is broken by your wish—and he accepts your decision; but if he weakens, or if you weaken, I can do nothing for you or for little Tina. For heaven's sake remember that!"

Delia released her hold, and Charlotte leaned back silent, with closed eyes and narrowed lips. Almost like a corpse she lay there. On a chair near the bed hung the poplin with red velvet ribbons which had been made over in honour of her betrothal. A pair of new slippers of bronze kid peeped from beneath it. Poor Chatty! She had hardly had time to be pretty . . .

Delia sat by the bed motionless, her eyes on her cousin's closed face. They followed the course of a tear that forced a way between Charlotte's tight lids, hung on the lashes, glittered slowly down the cheeks. As the tear reached the narrowed lips they spoke.

"Shall I live with her somewhere, do you mean? Just she and I together?"

"Just you and she."

"In a little house?"

"In a little house . . ."

"You're sure, Delia?"

"Sure, my dearest."

Charlotte once more raised herself on her elbow and sent a hand groping under the pillow. She drew out a narrow ribbon on which hung a diamond ring.

"I had taken it off already," she said simply, and handed it to Delia.

□ VI □

You could always have told, every one agreed afterward, that Charlotte Lovell was meant to be an old maid. Even before her illness it had been manifest:

there was something prim about her in spite of her fiery hair. Lucky enough
for her, poor girl, considering her wretched health in her youth: Mrs. James
Ralston's contemporaries, for instance, remembered Charlotte as a mere
ghost, coughing her lungs out—that, of course, had been the reason for her
breaking her engagement with Joe Ralston.

True, she had recovered very rapidly, in spite of the peculiar treatment
she was given. The Lovells, as every one knew, couldn't afford to send her to
Italy; the previous experiment in Georgia had been unsuccessful; and so she
was packed off to a farm-house on the Hudson—a little place on the James
Ralstons' property—where she lived for five or six years with an Irish ser-
vant-woman and a foundling baby. The story of the foundling was another
queer episode in Charlotte's history. From the time of her first illness, when
she was only twenty-two or three, she had developed an almost morbid tenderness for children, especially for the children of the poor. It was said—Dr.
Lanskell was understood to have said—that the baffled instinct of motherhood was peculiarly intense in cases where lung-disease prevented marriage.
And so, when it was decided that Chatty must break her engagement to Joe
Ralston and go to live in the country, the doctor had told her family that the
only hope of saving her lay in not separating her entirely from her pauper
children, but in letting her choose one of them, the youngest and most piti-
able, and devote herself to its care. So the James Ralstons had lent her their
little farm-house, and Mrs. Jim, with her extraordinary gift of taking things
in at a glance, had at once arranged everything, and even pledged herself to
look after the baby if Charlotte died.

Charlotte did not die. She lived to grow robust and middle-aged, energetic and even tyrannical. And as the transformation in her character took
place she became more and more like the typical old maid: precise, methodical, absorbed in trifles, and attaching an exaggerated importance to the smallest social and domestic observances. Such was her reputation as a vigilant
house-wife that, when poor Jim Ralston was killed by a fall from his horse,
and left Delia, still young, with a boy and girl to bring up, it seemed perfectly
natural that the heart-broken widow should take her cousin to live with her
and share her task. But Delia Ralston never did things quite like other people. When she took Charlotte she took Charlotte's foundling too: a dark-
haired child with pale brown eyes, and the odd incisive manner of children
who had lived too much with their elders. The little girl was called Tina Lovell: it was vaguely supposed that Charlotte had adopted her. She grew up on
terms of affectionate equality with her young Ralston cousins, and almost as
much so—it might be said—with the two women who mothered her. But,
impelled by an instinct of imitation which no one took the trouble to correct, she always called Delia Ralston "Mamma" and Charlotte Lovell "Aunt
Chatty." She was a brilliant and engaging creature, and people marvelled at
poor Chatty's luck in having chosen so interesting a specimen among her

foundlings (for she was by this time supposed to have had a whole asylum-full to choose from).

The agreeable elderly bachelor, Sillerton Jackson, returning from a prolonged sojourn in Paris (where he was understood to have been made much of by the highest personages) was immensely struck by Tina's charms when he saw her at her coming-out ball, and asked Delia's permission to come some evening and dine alone with her and her young people. He complimented the widow on the rosy beauty of her own young Delia; but the mother's keen eye perceived that all the while he was watching Tina, and after dinner he confided to the older ladies that there was something "very French" in the girl's way of doing her hair, and that in the capital of all the Elegances she would have been pronounced extremely stylish.

"Oh—" Delia deprecated, beamingly, while Charotte Lovell sat bent over her work with pinched lips; but Tina, who had been laughing with her cousins at the other end of the room, was around upon her elders in a flash.

"I heard what Mr. Sillerton said! Yes, I did, Mamma: he says I do my hair stylishly. Didn't I always tell you so? I *know* it's more becoming to let it curl as it wants to than to plaster it down with bandoline like Aunty's—"

"Tina, Tina—you always think people are admiring you!" Miss Lovell protested.

"Why shouldn't I, when they do?" the girl laughingly challenged; and, turning her mocking eyes on Sillerton Jackson: "Do tell Aunt Charlotte not to be so dreadfully old-maidish!"

Delia saw the blood rise to Charlotte Lovell's face. It no longer painted two brick-rose circles on her thin cheekbones, but diffused a harsh flush over her whole countenance, from the collar fastened with an old-fashioned garnet brooch to the pepper-and-salt hair (with no trace of red left in it) flattened down over her hollow temples.

That evening, when they went up to bed, Delia called Tina into her room.

"You ought not to speak to your Aunt Charlotte as you did this evening, dear. It's disrespectful—you must see that it hurts her."

The girl overflowed with compunction. "Oh, I'm so sorry! Because I said she was an old maid? But she *is*, isn't she, Mamma? In her inmost soul, I mean. I don't believe she's ever been young—ever thought of fun or admiration or falling in love—do you? That's why she never understands me, and you always do, you darling dear Mamma." With one of her light movements, Tina was in the widow's arms.

"Child, child," Delia softly scolded, kissing the dark curls planted in five points on the girl's forehead.

There was a soft foot-fall in the passage, and Charlotte Lovell stood in the door. Delia, without moving, sent her a glance of welcome over Tina's shoulder.

"Come in, Charlotte, I'm scolding Tina for behaving like a spoilt baby before Sillerton Jackson. What will he think of her?"

"Just what she deserves, probably," Charlotte returned with a cold smile. Tina went toward her, and her thin lips touched the girl's proffered forehead just where Delia's warm kiss had rested. "Goodnight, child," she said in her dry tone of dismissal.

The door closed on the two women, and Delia signed to Charlotte to take the armchair opposite to her own.

"Not so near the fire," Miss Lovell answered. She chose a straight-backed seat, and sat down with folded hands. Delia's eyes rested absently on the thin ringless fingers: she wondered why Charlotte never wore her mother's jewels.

"I overhead what you were saying to Tina, Delia. You were scolding her because she called me an old maid."

It was Delia's turn to colour. "I scolded her for being disrespectful, dear; if you heard what I said you can't think that I was too severe."

"Not too severe; no. I've never thought you too severe with Tina; on the contrary."

"You think I spoil her?"

"Sometimes."

Delia felt an unreasoning resentment. "What was it I said that you object to?"

Charlotte returned her glance steadily. "I would rather she thought me an old maid than—"

"Oh—" Delia murmured. With one of her quick leaps of intuition she had entered into the other's soul, and once more measured its shuddering loneliness.

"What else," Charlotte inexorably pursued, "*can* she possibly be allowed to think me—ever?"

"I see . . . I see . . ." the widow faltered.

"A ridiculous narrow-minded old maid—nothing else," Charlotte Lovell insisted, getting to her feet, "or I shall never feel safe with her."

"Goodnight, my dear," Delia said compassionately. There were moments when she almost hated Charlotte for being Tina's mother, and others, such as this, when her heart was wrung by the tragic spectacle of that unavowed bond.

Charlotte seemed to have divined her thought.

"Oh, but don't pity me! She's mine," she murmured, going.

□ VII □

Delia Ralston sometimes felt that the real events of her life did not begin until both her children had contracted—so safely and suitably—their irreproachable New York alliances. The boy had married first, choosing a Vandergrave in whose father's bank at Albany he was to have an immediate junior partnership; and young Delia (as her mother had foreseen she would) had selected John Junius, the safest and soundest of the many young Halseys, and followed him to his parents' house the year after her brother's marriage.

After young Delia had left the house in Gramercy Park it was inevitable that Tina should take the centre front of its narrow stage. Tina had reached the marriageable age, she was admired and sought after; but what hope was there of her finding a husband? The two watchful women did not propound this question to each other; but Delia Ralston, brooding over it day by day, and taking it up with her when she mounted at night to her bedroom, knew that Charlotte Lovell, at the same hour, carried the same problem with her to the floor above.

The two cousins, during their eight years of life together, had seldom openly disagreed. Indeed, it might almost have been said that there was nothing open in their relation. Delia would have had it otherwise: after they had once looked so deeply into each other's souls it seemed unnatural that a veil should fall between them. But she understood that Tina's ignorance of her origin must at all costs be preserved, and that Charlotte Lovell, abrupt, passionate and inarticulate, knew of no other security than to wall herself up in perpetual silence.

So far had she carried this self-imposed reticence that Mrs. Ralston was surprised at her suddenly asking, soon after young Delia's marriage, to be allowed to move down into the small bedroom next to Tina's that had been left vacant by the bride's departure.

"But you'll be so much less comfortable there, Chatty. Have you thought of that? Or is it on account of the stairs?"

"No; it's not the stairs," Charlotte answered with her usual bluntness. How could she avail herself of the pretext Delia offered her, when Delia knew that she still ran up and down the three flights like a girl? "It's because I should be next to Tina," she said, in a low voice that jarred like an untuned string.

"Oh—very well. As you please." Mrs. Ralston could not tell why she felt suddenly irritated by the request, unless it were that she had already amused herself with the idea of fitting up the vacant room as a sitting-room for Tina. She had meant to do it in pink and pale green, like an opening flower.

"Of course, if there is any reason—" Charlotte suggested, as if reading her thought.

"None whatever; except that—well, I'd meant to surprise Tina by doing the room up as a sort of little boudoir where she could have her books and things, and see her girl friends."

"You're too kind, Delia; but Tina mustn't have boudoirs," Miss Lovell answered ironically, the green specks showing in her eyes.

"Very well: as you please," Delia repeated, in the same irritated tone. "I'll have your things brought down tomorrow."

Charlotte paused in the doorway. "You're sure there's no other reason?"

"Other reason? Why should there be?" The two women looked at each other almost with hostility, and Charlotte turned to go.

The talk once over, Delia was annoyed with herself for having yielded to Charlotte's wish. Why must it always be she who gave in, she who, after all, was the mistress of the house, and to whom both Charlotte and Tina might almost be said to owe their very existence, or at least all that made it worth having? Yet whenever any question arose about the girl it was invariably Charlotte who gained her point, Delia who yielded: it seemed as if Charlotte, in her mute obstinate way, were determined to take every advantage of the dependence that made it impossible for a woman of Delia's nature to oppose her.

In truth, Delia had looked forward more than she knew to the quiet talks with Tina to which the little boudoir would have lent itself. While her own daughter inhabited the room, Mrs. Ralston had been in the habit of spending an hour there every evening, chatting with the two girls while they undressed, and listening to their comments on the incidents of the day. She always knew before-hand exactly what her own girl would say; but Tina's views and opinions were a perpetual delicious shock to her. Not that they were strange or unfamiliar; there were moments when they seemed to well straight up from the dumb depths of Delia's own past. Only they expressed feelings she had never uttered, ideas she had hardly avowed to herself: Tina sometimes said things which Delia Ralston, in far-off self-communions, had imagined herself saying to Clement Spender.

And now there would be an end to these evenings talks: if Charlotte had asked to be lodged next to her daughter, might it not conceivably be because she wished them to end? It had never before occurred to Delia that her influence over Tina might be resented; now the discovery flashed a light far down into the abyss which had always divided the two women. But a moment later Delia reproached herself for attributing feelings of jealousy to her cousin. Was it not rather to herself that she should have ascribed them? Charlotte, as Tina's mother, had every right to wish to be near her, near her in all senses of the word; what claim had Delia to oppose to that natural privilege? The next morning she gave the order that Charlotte's things should be taken down to the room next to Tina's.

That evening, when bedtime came, Charlotte and Tina went upstairs together; but Delia lingered in the drawing-room, on the pretext of having letters to write. In truth, she dreaded to pass the threshold where, evening after evening, the fresh laughter of the two girls used to waylay her while Charlotte Lovell already slept her old-maid sleep on the floor above. A pang went through Delia at the thought that henceforth she would be cut off from this means of keeping her hold on Tina.

An hour later, when she mounted the stairs in her turn, she was guiltily conscious of moving as noiselessly as she could along the heavy carpet of the corridor, and of pausing longer than was necessary over the putting out of the gas-jet on the landing. As she lingered she strained her ears for the sound of voices from the adjoining doors behind which Charlotte and Tina slept; she would have been secretly hurt at hearing talk and laughter from within. But none came, nor was there any light beneath the doors. Evidently Charlotte, in her hard methodical way, had said goodnight to her daughter, and gone straight to bed as usual. Perhaps she had never approved of Tina's vigils, of the long undressing punctuated with mirth and confidences; she might have asked for the room next to her daughter's simply because she did not want the girl to miss her "beauty sleep."

Whenever Delia tried to explore the secret of her cousin's actions she returned from the adventure humiliated and abashed by the base motives she found herself attributing to Charlotte. How was it that she, Delia Ralston, whose happiness had been open and avowed to the world, so often found herself envying poor Charlotte the secret of her scanted motherhood? She hated herself for this movement of envy whenever she detected it, and tried to atone for it by a softened manner and a more anxious regard for Charlotte's feelings; but the attempt was not always successful, and Delia sometimes wondered if Charlotte did not resent any show of sympathy as an indirect glance at her misfortune. The worst of suffering such as hers was that it left one sore to the gentlest touch . . .

Delia, slowly undressing before the same lace-draped toilet-glass which had reflected her bridal image, was turning over these thoughts when she heard a light knock. She opened the door, and there stood Tina, in a dressing-gown, her dark curls falling over her shoulders.

With a happy heart-beat Delia held out her arms.

"I had to say goodnight, Mamma," the girl whispered.

"Of course, dear." Delia pressed a long kiss on her lifted forehead. "Run off now, or you might disturb your aunt. You know she sleeps badly, and you must be as quiet as a mouse now she's next to you."

"Yes, I know," Tina acquiesced, with a grave glance that was almost of complicity.

She asked no further question, she did not linger: lifting Delia's hand she held it a moment against her cheek, and then stole out as noiselessly as she had come.

□   VIII   □

"But you must see," Charlotte Lovell insisted, laying aside the *Evening Post,* "that Tina has changed. You do see that?"

The two women were sitting alone by the drawing-room fire in Gramercy Park. Tina had gone to dine with her cousin, young Mrs. John Junius Halsey, and was to be taken afterward to a ball at the Vandergraves', from which the John Juniuses had promised to see her home. Mrs. Ralston and Charlotte, their early dinner finished, had the long evening to themselves. Their custom, on such occasions, was for Charlotte to read the news aloud to her cousin, while the latter embroidered; but tonight, all through Charlotte's conscientious progress from column to column, without a slip or an omission, Delia had felt her, for some special reason, alert to take advantage of her daughter's absence.

To gain time before answering, Mrs. Ralston bent over a stitch in her delicate white embroidery.

"Tina changed? Since when?" she questioned.

The answer flashed out instantly. "Since Lanning Halsey had been coming here so much."

"Lanning? I used to think he came for Delia," Mrs. Ralston mused, speaking at random to gain still more time.

"It's natural you should suppose that every one came for Delia," Charlotte rejoined dryly; "but as Lanning continues to seek every chance of being with Tina—"

Mrs. Ralston raised her head and stole a swift glance at her cousin. She had in truth noticed that Tina had changed, as a flower changes at the mysterious moment when the unopened petals flush from within. The girl had grown handsomer, shyer, more silent, at times more irrelevantly gay. But Delia had not associated these variations of mood with the presence of Lanning Halsey, one of the numerous youths who had haunted the house before young Delia's marriage. There had, indeed, been a moment when Mrs. Ralston's eye had been fixed, with a certain apprehension, on the handsome Lanning. Among all the sturdy and stolid Halsey cousins he was the only one to whom a prudent mother might have hesitated to entrust her daughter; it would have been hard to say why, except that he was handsomer and more conversable then the rest, chronically unpunctual, and totally unperturbed by the fact. Clem Spender had been like that; and what if young Delia—?

But young Delia's mother was speedily reassured. The girl, herself arch and appetizing, took no interest in the corresponding graces except when backed by more solid qualities. A Ralston to the core, she demanded the Ralston virtues, and chose the Halsey most worthy of a Ralston bride.

Mrs. Ralston felt that Charlotte was waiting for her to speak. "It will be hard to get used to the idea of Tina's marrying," she said gently. "I don't know what we two old women shall do, alone in this empty house—for it will be an empty house then. But I suppose we ought to face the idea."

"I *do* face it," said Charlotte Lovell gravely.

"And you dislike Lanning? I mean, as a husband for Tina?"

Miss Lovell folded the evening paper, and stretched out a thin hand for her knitting. She glanced across the citron-wood work-table at her cousin. "Tina must not be too difficult—" she began.

"Oh—" Delia protested, reddening.

"Let us call things by their names," the other evenly pursued. "That's my way, when I speak at all. Usually, as you know, I say nothing."

The widow made a sign of assent, and Charlotte went on: "It's better so. But I've always known a time would come when we should have to talk this thing out."

"Talk this thing out? You and I? What thing?"

"Tina's future."

There was a silence. Delia Ralston, who always responded instantly to the least appeal to her sincerity, breathed a deep sigh of relief. At last the ice in Charlotte's breast was breaking up!

"My dear," Delia murured, "you know how much Tina's happiness concerns me. If you disapprove of Lanning Halsey as a husband, have you any other candidate in mind?"

Miss Lovell smiled one of her faint hard smiles. "I am not aware that there is a queue at the door. Nor do I disapprove of Lanning Halsey as a husband. Personally, I find him very agreeable; I understand his attraction for Tina."

"Ah—Tina *is* attracted?"

"Yes."

Mrs. Ralston pushed aside her work and thoughtfully considered her cousin's sharp-lined face. Never had Charlotte Lovell more completely presented the typical image of the old maid than as she sat there, upright on her straight-backed chair, with narrowed elbows and clicking needles, and imperturbably discussed her daughter's marriage.

"I don't understand, Chatty. Whatever Lanning's faults are—and I don't believe they're grave—I share your liking for him. After all—" Mrs. Ralston paused— "What is it that people find so reprehensible in him? Chiefly, as far as I can hear, that he can't decide on the choice of a profession. The New York view about that is rather narrow, as we know. Young men may have other tastes . . . artistic . . . literary . . . they may even have difficulty in deciding . . ."

Both women coloured slightly, and Delia guessed that the same reminiscence which shook her own bosom also throbbed under Charlotte's strait bodice.

Charlotte spoke. "Yes: I understand that. But hesitancy about a profession may cause hesitancy about . . . other decisions . . ."

"What do you mean? Surely not that Lanning—?"

"Lanning has not asked Tina to marry him."

Charlotte paused. The steady click of her needles punctuated the silence as once, years before, it had been punctuated by the tick of the Parisian clock on Delia's mantel. As Delia's memory fled back to that scene she felt its mysterious tension in the air.

Charlotte spoke. "Lanning is not hesitating any longer: he has decided *not* to marry Tina. But he has also decided—not to give up seeing her."

Delia flushed abruptly; she was irritated and bewildered by Charlotte's oracular phrases, doled out between parsimonious lips.

"You don't mean that he has offered himself and then drawn back? I can't think him capable of such an insult to Tina."

"He has not insulted Tina. He has simply told her that he can't afford to marry. Until he chooses a profession his father will allow him only a few hundred dollars a years; and that may be suppressed if—if he marries against his parents' wishes."

It was Delia's turn to be silent. The past was too overwhelmingly resuscitated in Charlotte's words. Clement Spender stood before her, irresolute, impecunious, persuasive. Ah, if only she had let herself be persuaded!

"I'm very sorry that this should have happened to Tina. But as Lanning appears to have behaved honourably, and withdrawn without raising false expectations, we must hope . . . we must hope . . ." Delia paused, not knowing what they must hope.

Charlotte Lovell laid down her knitting. "You know as well as I do, Delia, that every young man who is inclined to fall in love with Tina will find as good reasons for not marrying her."

"Then you think Lanning's excuses are a pretext?"

"Naturally. The first of many that will be found by his successors—for of course he will have successors. Tina—attracts."

"Ah," Delia murmured.

Here they were at last face to face with the problem which, through all the years of silence and evasiveness, had lain as close to the surface as a corpse too hastily buried! Delia drew another deep breath, which again was almost one of relief. She had always known that it would be difficult, almost impossible, to find a husband for Tina; and much as she desired Tina's happiness, some inmost selfishness whispered how much less lonely and purposeless the close of her own life would be should the girl be forced to share it. But how say this to Tina's mother?

"I hope you exaggerate, Charlotte. There may be disinterested characters ... But, in any case, surely Tina need not be unhappy here, with us who love her so dearly."

"Tina an old maid? Never!" Charlotte Lovell rose abruptly, her closed hand crashing down on the slender work-table. "My child shall have her life ... her own life ... whatever it costs me ..."

Delia's ready sympathy welled up. "I understand your feeling. I should want also ... hard as it will be to let her go. But surely there is no hurry—no reason for looking so far ahead. The child is not twenty. Wait."

Charlotte stood before her, motionless, perpendicular. At such moments she made Delia think of lava struggling through granite: there seemed no issue for the fires within.

"Wait? But if *she* doesn't wait?"

"But if he has withdrawn—what do you mean?"

"He has given up marrying her—but not seeing her."

Delia sprang up in her turn, flushed and trembling.

"Charlotte! Do you know what you're insinuating?"

"Yes: I know."

"But it's too outrageous. No decent girl—"

The words died on Delia's lips. Charlotte Lovell held her eyes inexorably. "Girls are not always what you call decent," she declared.

Mrs. Ralston turned slowly back to her seat. Her tambour frame had fallen to the floor; she stooped heavily to pick it up. Charlotte's gaunt figure hung over her, relentless as doom.

"I can't imagine, Charlotte, what is gained by saying such things—even by hinting them. Surely you trust your own child."

Charlotte laughed. "My mother trusted me," she said.

"How dare you—how dare you?" Delia began: but her eyes fell, and she felt a tremor of weakness in her throat.

"Oh, I dare anything for Tina, even to judging her as she is," Tina's mother murmured.

"As she is? She's perfect!"

"Let us say then that she must pay for my imperfections. All I want is that she shouldn't pay too heavily."

Mrs. Ralston sat silent. It seemed to her that Charlotte spoke with the voice of all the dark destinies coiled under the safe surface of life; and that to such a voice there was no answer but an awed acquiescence.

"Poor Tina!" she breathed.

"Oh, I don't intend that she shall suffer! It's not for that I've waited . . . waited. Only I've made mistakes: mistakes that I understand now, and must remedy. You've been too good to us—and we must go."

"Go?" Delia gasped.

"Yes. Don't think me ungrateful. You saved my child once—do you suppose I can forget? But now it's my turn—it's I who must save her. And it's only by taking her away from everything here—from everything she's known till now—that I can do it. She's lived too long among unrealities: and she's like me. They won't content her."

"Unrealities?" Delia echoed vaguely.

"Unrealities for her. Young men who make love to her and can't marry her. Happy households where she's welcomed till she's suspected of designs on a brother or a husband—or else exposed to their insults. How could we ever have imagined, either of us, that the child could escape disaster? I thought only of her present happiness—of all the advantages, for both of us, of being with you. But this affair with young Halsey has opened my eyes. I must take Tina away. We must go and live somewhere where we're not known, where we shall be among plain people, leading plain lives. Somewhere where she can find a husband, and make herself a home."

Charlotte paused. She had spoken in a rapid monotonous tone, as if by rote; but now her voice broke and she repeated painfully: "I'm not ungrateful."

"Oh, don't let's speak of gratitude! What place has it between you and me?"

Delia had risen and began to move uneasily about the room. She longed to plead with Charlotte, to implore her not to be in haste, to picture to her the cruelty of severing Tina from all her habits and associations, of carrying her inexplicably away to lead "a plain life among plain people." What chance was there, indeed, that a creature so radiant would tamely submit to such a fate or find an acceptable husband in such conditions? The change might only precipitate a tragedy. Delia's experience was too limited for her to picture exactly what might happen to a girl like Tina, suddenly cut off from all that sweetened life for her; but vague visions of revolt and flight—of a "fall" deeper and more irretrievable than Charlotte's—flashed through her agonized imagination.

"It's too cruel—it's too cruel," she cried, speaking to herself rather than to Charlotte.

Charlotte, instead of answering, glanced abruptly at the clock.

"Do you know what time it is? Past midnight. I mustn't keep you sitting up for my foolish girl."

Delia's heart contracted. She saw that Charlotte wished to cut the conversation short, and to do so by reminding her that only Tina's mother had a right to decide what Tina's future should be. At that moment, though Delia had just protested that there could be no question of gratitude between them, Charlotte Lovell seemed to her a monster of ingratitude, and it was on the tip of her tongue to cry out: "Have all the years then given me no share in Tina?" But at the same instant she had put herself once more in Charlotte's place, and was feeling the mother's fierce terrors for her child. It was natural enough that Charlotte should resent the faintest attempt to usurp in private the authority she could never assert in public. With a pang of compassion Delia realized that she herself was literally the one being on earth before whom Charlotte could act the mother. "Poor thing—ah, let her!" she murmured inwardly.

"But why should you sit up for Tina? She has the key, and Delia is to bring her home."

Charlotte Lovell did not immediately answer. She rolled up her knitting, looked severely at one of the candelabra on the mantelpiece, and crossed over to straighten it. Then she picked up her work-bag.

"Yes, as you say—why should any one sit up for her?" She moved about the room, putting out the lamps, covering the fire, assuring herself that the windows were bolted, while Delia passively watched her. Then the two cousins lit their bedroom candles and walked upstairs through the darkened house. Charlotte seemed determined to make no further allusion to the subject of their talk. On the landing she paused, bending her head toward Delia's nightly kiss.

"I hope they've kept up your fire," she said, with her capable housekeeping air; and on Delia's hasty reassurance the two murmured a simultaneous "Goodnight," and Charlotte turned down the passage to her room.

□ IX □

Delia's fire had been kept up, and her dressing-gown was warming on an arm-chair near the hearth. But she neither undressed nor yet seated herself. Her conversation with Charlotte had filled her with a deep unrest.

For a few moments she stood in the middle of the floor, looking slowly about her. Nothing had ever been changed in the room which, even as a bride, she had planned to modernize. All her dreams of renovation had faded long ago. Some deep central indifference had gradually made her regard herself as a third person, living the life meant for another woman, a woman totally unrelated to the vivid Delia Lovell who had entered that house so full of plans and visions. The fault, she knew, was not her husband's. With a little managing and a little wheedling she would have gained every point as easily as she had gained the capital one of taking the foundling baby under her wing. The difficulty was that, after that victory, nothing else seemed worth trying for. The first sight of little Tina had somehow decentralized Delia Ralston's whole life, making her indifferent to everything else, except indeed the welfare of her own husband and children. Ahead of her she saw only a future full of duties, and these she had gaily and faithfully accomplished. But her own life was over; she felt as detached as a cloistered nun.

The change in her was too deep not to be visible. The Ralstons openly gloried in dear Delia's conformity. Each acquiescence passed for a concession, and the family doctrine was fortified by such fresh proofs of its durability. Now, as Delia glanced about her at the Léopold Robert lithographs, the family daguerreotypes, the rosewood and mahogany, she understood that she was looking at the walls of her own grave.

The change had come on the day when Charlotte Lovell, cowering on that very lounge, had made her terrible avowal. Then for the first time Delia, with a kind of fearful exaltation, had heard the blind forces of life groping and crying underfoot. But on that day also she had known herself excluded from them, doomed to dwell among shadows. Life had passed her by, and left her with the Ralstons.

Very well, then! She would make the best of herself, and of the Ralstons. The vow was immediate and unflinching: and for nearly twenty years she had gone on observing it. Once only had she been not a Ralston but herself; once only had it seemed worth while. And now perhaps the same challenge had sounded again; again, for a moment, it might be worth while to live. Not for the sake of Clement Spender—poor Clement, married years ago to a plain determined cousin, who had hunted him down in Rome, and enclosing him in an unrelenting domesticity, had obliged all New York on the grand tour to buy his pictures with a resigned grimace. No, not for Clement Spender, hardly for Charlotte or even for Tina; but for her own sake, hers, Delia Ralston's, for the sake of her one missed vision, her forfeited reality, she would once more break down the Ralston barriers and reach out into the world.

A faint sound through the silent house disturbed her meditation. Listening, she heard Charlotte Lovell's door open and her stiff petticoats rustle toward the landing. A light glanced under the door and vanished: Charlotte had passed Delia's threshold on her way downstairs.

Without moving, Delia continued to listen. Perhaps the careful Charlotte had gone down to make sure that the front door was not bolted, or that she had really covered up the fire. If that were her object, her step would presently be heard returning. But no step sounded; and it became gradually evident that Charlotte had gone down to wait for her daughter. Why?

Delia's bedroom was at the front of the house. She stole across the heavy carpet, drew aside the curtains and cautiously folded back the inner shutters. Below her lay the empty square, white with moonlight, its tree-trunks patterned on a fresh sprinkling of snow. The houses opposite slept in darkness; not a footfall broke the white surface, not a wheel-track marred the brilliant street. Overhead a heaven full of stars swam in the moonlight.

Of the households around Gramercy Park Delia knew that only two others had gone to the ball: the Petrus Vandergraves and their cousins the young Parmly Ralstons. The Lucius Lannings had just entered on their three years of mourning for Mrs. Lucius's mother (it was hard on their daughter Kate, just eighteen, who would be unable to "come out" till she was twenty-one); young Mrs. Marcy Mingott was "expecting her third," and consequently secluded from the public eye for nearly a year; and the other denizens of the square belonged to the undifferentiated and uninvited.

Delia pressed her forehead against the pane. Before long carriages would turn the corner, the sleeping square ring with hoof-beats, fresh laughter and young farewells mount from the door-steps. But why was Charlotte waiting for her daughter downstairs in the darkness?

The Parisian clock struck one. Delia came back into the room, raked the fire, picked up a shawl, and wrapped in it, returned to her vigil. Ah, how old she must have grown that she should feel the cold at such a moment! It reminded her of what the future held for her: neuralgia, rheumatism, stiffness, accumulating infirmities. And never had she kept a moonlight watch with a lover's arms to warm her . . .

The square still lay silent. Yet the ball must surely be ending: the gayest dances did not last long after one in the morning, and the drive from University Place to Gramercy Park was a short one. Delia leaned in the embrasure and listened.

Hoof-beats, muffled by the snow, sounded in Irving Place, and the Petrus Vandergraves' family coach drew up before the opposite house. The Vandergrave girls and their brother sprang out and mounted the steps; then the coach stopped again a few doors farther on, and the Parmly Ralstons, brought home by their cousins, descended at their own door. The next carriage that rounded the corner must therefore be the John Juniuses', bringing Tina.

The gilt clock struck half-past one. Delia wondered, knowing that young Delia, out of regard for John Junius's business hours, never stayed late at evening parties. Doubtless Tina had delayed her; Mrs. Ralston felt a little annoyed with Tina's thoughtlessness in keeping her cousin up. But the feeling was swept away by an immediate wave of sympathy. "We must go away somewhere, and lead plain lives among plain people." If Charlotte carried out her threat—and Delia knew she would hardly have spoken unless her resolve had been taken—it might be that at that very moment poor Tina was dancing her last *valse*.

Another quarter of an hour passed; then, just as the cold was finding a way through Delia's shawl, she saw two people turn into the deserted square from Irving Place. One was a young man in opera hat and ample cloak. To his arm clung a figure so closely wrapped and muffled that, until the corner light fell on it, Delia hesitated. After that, she wondered that she had not at once recognized Tina's dancing step, and her manner of tilting her head a little sideways to look up at the person she was talking to.

Tina—Tina and Lanning Halsey, walking home alone in the small hours from the Vandergrave ball! Delia's first thought was an accident: the carriage might have broken down, or else her daughter been taken ill and obliged to return home. But no; in the latter case she would have sent the carriage on with Tina. And if there had been an accident of any sort the young people would have been hastening to apprise Mrs. Ralston; instead of which, through the bitter brilliant night, they sauntered like lovers in a midsummer glade, and Tina's thin slippers might have been falling on daisies instead of snow.

Delia began to tremble like a girl. In a flash she had the answer to a question which had long been the subject of her secret conjectures. How did lovers like Charlotte and Clement Spender contrive to meet? What Latmian solitude hid their clandestine joys? In the exposed compact little society to which they all belonged, how was it possible—literally—for such encounters to take place? Delia would never have dared to put the question to Charlotte; there were moments when she almost preferred not to know, not even to hazard a guess. But now, at a glance, she understood. How often Charlotte Lovell, staying alone in town with her infirm grandmother, must have walked home from evening parties with Clement Spender, how often have let herself and him into the darkened house in Mercer Street, where there was no one to spy upon their coming but a deaf old lady and her aged servants, all securely sleeping overhead! Delia, at the thought, saw the grim drawing-room which had been their moonlit forest, the drawing-room into which old Mrs. Lovell no longer descended, with its swathed chandelier and hard Empire sofas, and the eyeless marble caryatids of the mantel; she pictured the shaft of moonlight falling across the swans and garlands of the faded carpet, and in that icy light two young figures in each other's arms.

Yes: it must have been some such memory that had roused Charlotte's suspicions, excited her fears, sent her down in the darkness to confront the culprits. Delia shivered at the irony of the confrontation. If Tina had but known! But to Tina, of course, Charlotte was still what she had long since resolved to be: the image of prudish spinsterhood. And Delia could imagine how quietly and decently the scene below stairs would presently be enacted: no astonishment, no reproaches, no insinuations, but a smiling and resolute ignoring of excuses.

"What, Tina? You walked home with Lanning? You imprudent child—in this wet snow! Ah, I see: Delia was worried about the baby, and ran off early, promising to send back the carriage—and it never came? Well, my dear, I congratulate you on finding Lanning to see you home ... Yes—I sat up because I couldn't for the life of me remember whether you'd taken the latch-key—was there ever such a flighty old aunt? But don't tell your Mamma, dear, or she'd scold me for being so forgetful, and for staying downstairs in the cold ... You're quite sure you have the key? Ah, Lanning has it? Thank you, Lanning; so kind! Goodnight—or one really ought to say, good morning."

As Delia reached this point in her mute representation of Charlotte's monologue the front door slammed below, and young Lanning Halsey walked slowly away across the square. Delia saw him pause on the opposite pavement, look up at the house-front, and then turn lingeringly away. His dismissal had taken exactly as long as Delia had calculated it would. A moment later she saw a passing light under her door, heard the starched rustle of Charlotte's petticoats, and knew that mother and daughter had reached their rooms.

Slowly, with stiff motions, she began to undress, blew out her candles, and knelt by her bedside, her face hidden.

□ X □

Lying awake till morning, Delia lived over every detail of the fateful day when she had assumed the charge of Charlotte's child. At the time she had been hardly more than a child herself, and there had been no one for her to turn to, no one to fortify her resolution, or to advise her how to put it into effect. Since then, the accumulated experiences of twenty years ought to have prepared her for emergencies, and taught her to advise others instead of seeking their guidance. But these years of experience weighed on her like chains binding her down to her narrow plot of life; independent action struck her as more dangerous, less conceivable than when she had first ventured on it. There seemed to be so many more people to "consider" now ("consider" was the Ralston word): her children, their children, the families into which they had married. What would the Halseys say, and what the Ralstons? Had she then become a Ralston through and through?

A few hours later she sat in old Dr. Lanskell's library, her eyes on his sooty Smyrna rug. For some years now Dr. Lanskell had no longer practised: at most, he continued to go to a few old patients, and to give consultations in "difficult" cases. But he remained a power in his former kingdom, a sort of lay Pope or medical Elder to whom the patients he had once healed of physical ills often returned for moral medicine. People were agreed that Dr. Lanskell's judgments was sound: but what secretly drew them to him was the fact that, in the most totem-ridden of communities, he was known not to be afraid of anything.

Now, as Delia sat and watched his massive silver-headed figure moving ponderously about the room, between rows of medical books in calf bindings and the Dying Gladiators and Young Augustuses of grateful patients, she already felt the reassurance given by his mere bodily presence.

"You see, when I first took Tina I didn't perhaps consider sufficiently—"

The Doctor halted behind his desk and brought his fist down on it with a genial thump. "Thank goodness you didn't! There are considerers enough in this town without you, Delia Lovell."

She looked up quickly. "Why do you call me Delia Lovell?"

"Well, because today I rather suspect you *are,*" he rejoined astutely; and she met this with a wistful laugh.

"Perhaps, if I hadn't been, once before—I mean, if I'd always been a prudent deliberate Ralston it would have been kinder to Tina in the end."

Dr. Lanskell sank his gouty bulk into the armchair behind his desk, and beamed at her through ironic spectacles. "I hate in-the-end kindnesses: they're about as nourishing as the third day of cold mutton."

She pondered. "Of course I realize that if I adopt Tina—"

"Yes?"

"Well, people will say . . ." A deep blush rose to her throat, covered her cheeks and brow, and ran like fire under her decently-parted hair.

He nodded: "Yes."

"Or else—" the blush darkened—"that she's Jim's—"

Again Dr. Lanskell nodded. "That's what they're more likely to think: and what's the harm if they do? I know Jim: he asked you no questions when you took the child—but he knew whose she was."

She raised astonished eyes. "He knew—?"

"Yes: he came to me. And—well—in the baby's interest I violated professional secrecy. That's how Tina got a home. You're not going to denounce me, are you?"

"Oh, Dr. Lanskell—" Her eyes filled with painful tears. "Jim knew? And didn't tell me?"

"No. People didn't tell each other things much in those days, did they? But he admired you enormously for what you did. And if you assume—as I suppose you do—that he's now in a world of completer enlightenment, why not take it for granted that he'll admire you still more for what you're going to do? Presumably," the Doctor concluded sardonically, "people realize in heaven that it's a devilish sight harder, on earth, to do a brave thing at forty-five than at twenty-five."

"Ah, that's what I was thinking this morning," she confessed.

"Well you're going to prove the contrary this afternoon." He looked at his watch, stood up and laid a fatherly hand on her shoulder. "Let people think what they choose and send young Delia to me if she gives you any trouble. Your boy won't, you know, nor John Junius either; it must have been a woman who invented that third-and-fourth generation idea . . ."

An elderly maid-servant looked in, and Delia rose; but on the threshold she halted.

"I have an idea it's Charlotte I may have to send to you."

"Charlotte?"

She'll hate what I'm going to do, you know."

Dr. Lanskell lifted his silver eyebrows. "Yes: poor Charlotte? I suppose she's jealous? That's where the truth of the third-and-fourth generation business comes in, after all. Somebody always has to foot the bill."

"Ah—if only Tina doesn't!"

"Well—that's just what Charlotte will come to recognize in time. So your course is clear."

He guided her out through the dining-room, where some poor people and one or two old patients were already waiting.

Delia's course, in truth, seemed clear enough till, that afternoon, she summoned Charlotte alone to her bedroom. Tina was lying down with a headache: it was in those days the accepted state of young ladies in sentimental dilemmas, and greatly simplified the communion of their elders.

Delia and Charlotte had exchanged only conventional phrases over their midday meal; but Delia still had the sense that her cousin's decision was final. The events of the previous evening had no doubt confirmed Charlotte's view that the time had come for such a decision.

Miss Lovell, closing the bedroom door with her dry deliberateness, advanced toward the chintz lounge between the windows.

"You wanted to see me, Delia?"

"Yes—Oh, don't sit there," Mrs. Ralston exclaimed uncontrollably.

Charlotte stared: was it possible that she did not remember the sobs of anguish she had once smothered in those very cushions?

"Not—?"

"No, come nearer to me. Sometimes I think I'm a little deaf," Delia nervously explained, pushing a chair up to her own.

"Ah." Charlotte seated herself. "I hadn't remarked it. But if you are, it may have saved you from hearing at what hour of the morning Tina came back from the Vandergraves' last night. She would never forgive herself—inconsiderate as she is—if she thought she'd waked you."

"She didn't wake me," Delia answered. Inwardly she thought: "Charlotte's mind is made up; I shan't be able to move her."

"I suppose Tina enjoyed herself very much at the ball?" she continued.

"Well, she's paying for it with a headache. Such excitements are not meant for her, I've already told you—"

"Yes," Mrs. Ralston interrupted. "It's to continue our talk of last night that I've asked you to come up."

"To continue it?" The brick-red circles appeared on Charlotte's dried cheeks. "Is it worth while? I think I ought to tell you at once that my mind's make up. I suppose you'll admit that I know what's best for Tina."

"Yes of course. But won't you at least allow me a share in your decision?"

"A share?"

Delia leaned forward, laying a warm hand on her cousin's interlocked fingers. "Charlotte, once in this room, years ago, you asked me to help you—you believed I could. Won't you believe it again?"

Charlotte's lips grew rigid. "I believe the time has come for me to help myself."

"At the cost of Tina's happiness?"

"No: but to spare her greater unhappiness."

"But, Charlotte, Tina's happiness is all I want."

"Oh, I know. You've done all you could do for my child."

"No; not all." Delia rose, and stood before her cousin with a kind of solemnity. "But now I'm going to." It was as if she had pronounced a vow.

Charlotte Lovell looked up at her with a glitter of apprehension in her hunted eyes.

"If you mean that you're going to use your influence with the Halseys—I'm very grateful to you; I shall always be grateful. But I don't want a compulsory marriage for my child."

Delia flushed at the other's incomprehension. It seemed to her that her tremendous purpose must be written on her face. "I'm going to adopt Tina—give her my name," she announced.

Charlotte Lovell stared at her stonily. "Adopt her—adopt her?"

"Don't you see, dear, the difference it will make? There's my mother's money—the Lovell money; it's not much, to be sure; but Jim always wanted it to go back to the Lovells. And my Delia and her brother are so handsomely provided for. There's no reason why my little fortune shouldn't go to Tina. And why she shouldn't be known as Tina Ralston." Delia paused. "I believe—I think I know that Jim would have approved of that too."

"*Approved?*"

"Yes. Can't you see that when he let me take the child he must have foreseen and accepted whatever—whatever might eventually come of it?"

Charlotte stood up also. "Thank you, Delia. But nothing more must come of it, except our leaving you: our leaving you now. I'm sure that's what Jim would have approved."

Mrs. Ralston drew back a step or two. Charlotte's cold resolution benumbed her courage, and she could find no immediate reply.

"Ah, then it's easier for you to sacrifice Tina's happiness than your pride?" she exclaimed.

"My pride? I've no right to any pride, except in my child. And that I'll never sacrifice."

"No one asks you to. You're not reasonable. You're cruel. All I want is to be allowed to help Tina, and you speak as if I were interfering with your rights."

"My rights?" Charlotte echoed the words with a desolate laugh. "What are they? I have no rights, either before the law or in the heart of my own child."

"How can you say such things? You know how Tina loves you."

"Yes; compassionately—as I used to love my old-maid aunts. There were two of them—you remember? Like withered babies! We children used to be warned never to say anything that might shock Aunt Josie or Aunt Nonie; exactly as I heard you telling Tina the other night—"

"Oh—" Delia murmured.

Charlotte Lovell continued to stand before her, haggard, rigid, unrelenting. "No, it's gone on long enough. I mean to tell her everything; and to take her away."

"To tell her about her birth?"

"I was never ashamed of it," Charlotte panted.

"You do sacrifice her, then—sacrifice her to your desire for mastery?"

The two women faced each other, both with weapons spent. Delia, through the tremor of her own indignation, saw her antagonist slowly waver, step backward, sink down with a broken murmur on the lounge. Charlotte hid her face in the cushions, clenching them with violent hands. The same fierce maternal passion that had once flung her down upon those same cushions was now bowing her still lower, in the throes of a bitterer renunciation. Delia seemed to hear the old cry: "But how can I give up my baby?" Her own momentary resentment melted, and she bent over the mother's labouring shoulders.

"Chatty—it won't be like giving her up this time. Can't we just go on loving her together?"

Charlotte did not answer. For a long time she lay silent, immovable, her face hidden: she seemed to fear to turn it to the face bent down to her. But presently Delia was aware of a gradual relaxing of the stretched muscles, and saw that one of her cousin's arms was faintly stirring and grouping. She lowered her hand to the seeking fingers, and it was caught and pressed to Charlotte's lips.

□ XI □

Tina Lovell—now Miss Clementina Ralston—was to be married in July to Lanning Halsey. The engagement had been announced only in the previous April; and the female elders of the tribe had begun by crying out against the indelicacy of so brief a betrothal. It was unanimously agreed in the New York of those times that "young people should be given the chance to get to know each other"; though the greater number of the couples constituting New York society had played together as children, and been born of parents as long and as familiarly acquainted, yet some mysterious law of decorum required that the newly affianced should always be regarded as being also newly known to each other. In the southern states things were differently conducted: headlong engagements, even runaway marriages, were not uncommon in their annals; but such rashness was less consonant with the sluggish blood of New York, where the pace of life was still set with a Dutch deliberateness.

In a case as unusual as Tina Ralston's, however, it was no great surprise to any one that tradition should have been disregarded. In the first place, everybody knew that she was no more Tina Ralston than you or I; unless, indeed, one were to credit the rumours about poor Jim's unsuspected "past," and his widow's magnanimity. But the opinion of the majority was against this. People were reluctant to charge a dead man with an offense from which he could not clear himself; and the Ralstons unanimously declared that, thoroughly as they disapproved of Mrs. James Ralston's action, they were convinced that she would not have adopted Tina if her doing so could have been construed as "casting a slur" on her late husband.

No: the girl was perhaps a Lovell—though even that idea was not generally held—but she was certainly not a Ralston. Her brown eyes and flighty ways too obviously excluded her from the clan for any formal excommunication to be needful. In fact, most people believed that—as Dr. Lanksell had always affirmed—her origin was really undiscoverable, that she represented one of the unsolved mysteries which occasionally perplex and irritate well-regulated societies, and that her adoption by Delia Ralston was simply one more proof of the Lovell clannishness, since the child had been taken in by Mrs. Ralston only because her cousin Charlotte was so attached to it. To say that Mrs. Ralson's son and daughter were pleased with the idea of Tina's adoption would be an exaggeration; but they abstained from comment, minimizing the effect of their mother's whim by a dignified silence. It was the old New York way for families thus to screen the eccentricities of an individual member, and where there was "money enough to go round" the heirs would have been thought vulgarly grasping to protest at the alienation of a small sum from the general inheritance.

Nevertheless, Delia Ralston, from the moment of Tina's adoption, was perfectly aware of a different attitude on the part of both her children. They dealt with her patiently, almost parentally, as with a minor in whom one juvenile lapse has been condoned, but who must be subjected, in consequence, to a stricter vigilance; and society treated her in the same indulgent but guarded manner.

She had (it was Sillerton Jackson who first phrased it) an undoubted way of "carrying things off"; since that dauntless woman, Mrs. Manson Mingott, had broken her husband's will, nothing so like her attitude had been seen in New York. But Mrs. Ralston's method was different, and less easy to analyze. What Mrs. Manson Mingott had accomplished by dint of epigram, invective, insistency and runnings to and fro, the other achieved without raising her voice or seeming to take a step from the beaten path. When she had persuaded Jim Ralston to take in the foundling baby, it had been done in the turn of a hand, one didn't know when or how; and the next day he and she were as untroubled and beaming as usual. And now, this adoption—! Well, she had pursued the same method; as Sillerton Jackson said, she behaved as if her adopting Tina had always been an understood thing, as if she wondered that people should wonder. And in face of her wonder theirs seemed foolish, and they gradually desisted.

In reality, behind Delia's assurance there was a tumult of doubts and uncertainties. But she had once learned that one can do almost anything (perhaps even murder) if one does not attempt to explain it; and the lesson had never been forgotten. She had never explained the taking over of the foundling baby; nor was she now going to explain its adoption. She was just going about her business as if nothing had happened that needed to be accounted for; and a long inheritance of moral modesty helped her to keep her questionings to herself.

These questionings were in fact less concerned with public opinion than with Charlotte Lovell's private thoughts. Charlotte, after her first moment of tragic resistance, had shown herself pathetically, almost painfully, grateful. That she had reason to be, Tina's attitude abundantly revealed. Tina, during the first days after her return from the Vandergrave ball, had shown a closed and darkened face that terribly reminded Delia of the ghastliness of Charlotte

Lovell's sudden reflection, years before, in Delia's own bedroom mirror. The first chapter of the mother's history was already written in the daughter's eyes; and the Spender blood in Tina might well precipitate the sequence. During those few days of silent observation Delia discovered, with terror and compassion, the justification of Charlotte's fears. The girl had nearly been lost to them both: at all costs such a risk must not be renewed.

The Halseys, on the whole, had behaved admirably. Lanning wished to marry dear Delia Ralston's protégée—who was shortly, it was understood, to take her adopted mother's name, and inherit her fortune. To what better could a Halsey aspire than one more alliance with a Ralston? The families had always intermarried. The Halsey parents gave their blessing with a precipitation which showed that they too had their anxieties, and that the relief of seeing Lanning "settled" would more than compensate for the conceivable drawbacks of the marriage; though, once it was decided on, they would not admit even to themselves that such drawbacks existed. Old New York always thought away whatever interfered with the perfect propriety of its arrangements.

Charlotte Lovell of course perceived and recognized all this. She accepted the situation—in her private hours with Delia—as one more in the long list of mercies bestowed on an undeserving sinner. And one phrase of hers perhaps gave the clue to her acceptance: "Now at least she'll never suspect the truth." It had come to be the poor creature's ruling purpose that her child should never guess the tie between them . . .

But Delia's chief support was the sight of Tina. The older woman, whose whole life had been shaped and coloured by the faint reflection of a rejected happiness, hung dazzled in the light of bliss accepted. Sometimes, as she watched Tina's changing face, she felt as though her own blood were beating in it, as though she could read every thought and emotion feeding those tumultuous currents. Tina's love was a stormy affair, with continual ups and downs of rapture and depression, arrogance and self-abasement; Delia saw displayed before her, with an artless frankness, all the visions, cravings and imaginings of her own stifled youth.

What the girl really thought of her adoption it was not easy to discover. She had been given, at fourteen, the current version of her origin, and had accepted it as carelessly as a happy child accepts some remote and inconceivable fact which does not alter the familiar order of things. And she accepted her adoption in the same spirit. She knew that the name of Ralston had been given to her to facilitate her marriage with Lanning Halsey; and Delia had the impression that all irrelevant questionings were submerged in an overwhelming gratitude. "I've always thought of you as my Mamma; and now, you dearest, you really are," Tina had whispered, her cheek against Delia's; and Delia had laughed back: "Well, if the lawyers can make me so!" But there the matter dropped, swept away on the current of Tina's bliss. They were all, in those days, Delia, Charlotte, even the gallant Lanning, rather like straws whirling about on a sunlit torrent.

The golden flood bore them onward, nearer and nearer to the enchanted date; and Delia, deep in bridal preparations, wondered at the comparative indifference with which she had ordered and inspected her own daughter's twelve-dozen-of-everything. There had been nothing to quicken the pulse in young Delia's placid bridal; but as Tina's wedding approached imagination burgeoned like the year. The wedding was to be celebrated at Lovell Place, the old house on the Sound where Delia Lovell had herself been married, and where, since her mother's death, she spent her summers. Although the neighbourhood was already overspread with a net-work of mean streets, the old house, with its thin colonnaded verandah, still looked across an uncurtailed lawn and leafy shrubberies to the narrows of Hell Gate; and the drawing-rooms kept their frail slender settees, their Sheraton consoles and cabinets. It had been thought useless to discard them for more fashionable furniture, since the growth of the city made it certain that the place must eventually be sold.

Tina, like Mrs. Ralston, was to have a "house-wedding," though Episcopalian society was beginning to disapprove of such ceremonies, which were regarded as the despised *pis-aller* of Baptists, Methodists, Unitarians and the other altarless sects. In Tina's case, however, both Delia and Charlotte felt that the greater privacy of a marriage in the house made up for its more secular character; and the Halseys favoured their decision. The ladies accordingly settled themselves at Lovell Place before the end of June, and every morning young Lanning Halsey's cat-boat was seen beating across the bay, and furling its sail at the anchorage below the lawn.

There had never been a fairer June in any one's memory. The damask roses and mignonette below the verandah had never sent such a breath of summer through the tall French windows; the gnarled orange-trees brought out from the old arcaded orange-house had never been so thickly blossomed; the very haycocks on the lawn gave out whiffs of Araby.

The evening before the wedding Delia Ralston sat on the verandah watching the moon rise across the Sound. She was tired with the multitude of last preparations, and sad at the thought of Tina's going. On the following evening the house would be empty: till death came, she and Charlotte would sit alone together beside the evening lamp. Such repinings were foolish—they were, she reminded herself, "not like her." But too many memories stirred and murmured in her: her heart was haunted. As she closed the door on the silent drawing-room—already transformed into a chapel, with its lace-hung altar, the tall alabaster vases awaiting their white roses and June lilies, the strip of red carpet dividing the rows of chairs from door to chancel—she felt that it had perhaps been a mistake to come back to Lovell Place for the wedding. She saw herself again, in her high-waisted "India mull" embroidered with daisies, her flat satin sandals, her Brussels veil—saw again her reflection in the shallow pier-glass as she had left that same room on Jim Ralston's triumphant arm, and the one terrified glance she had exchanged with her own image before she took her stand under the bell of white roses in the hall, and smiled upon the congratulating company. Ah, what a different image the pier-glass would reflect tomorrow!

Charlotte Lovell's brisk step sounded indoors, and she came out and joined Mrs. Ralston.

"I've been to the kitchen to tell Melissa Grimes that she'd better count on at least two hundred plates of ice-cream."

"Two hundred? Yes—I suppose she had, with all the Philadelphia connection coming." Delia pondered. "How about the doylies?" she enquired.

"With your aunt Cecilia Vandergrave's we shall manage beautifully."

"Yes—Thank you, Charlotte, for taking all this trouble."

"Oh—" Charlotte protested, with her flitting sneer; and Delia perceived the irony of thanking a mother for occupying herself with the details of her own daughter's wedding.

"Do sit down, Chatty," she murmured, feeling herself redden at her blunder.

Charlotte, with a sigh of fatigue, sat down on the nearest chair.

"We shall have a beautiful day tomorrow," she said, pensively surveying the placid heaven.

"Yes. Where is Tina?"

"She was very tired. I've sent her upstairs to lie down."

This seemed so eminently suitable that Delia made no immediate answer. After an interval she said: "We shall miss her."

Charlotte's reply was an inarticulate murmur.

The two cousins remained silent, Charlotte as usual bolt upright, her thin hands clutched on the arms of her old-fashioned rush-bottomed seat, Delia somewhat heavily sunk into the depths of a high-backed armchair. The two had exchanged their last remarks on the preparations for the morrow; nothing more remained to be said as to the number of guests, the brewing of the punch, the arrangements for the robing of the clergy, and the disposal of the presents in the best spare-room.

Only one subject had not yet been touched upon, and Delia, as she watched her cousin's profile grimly cut upon the melting twilight, waited for Charlotte to speak. But Charlotte remained silent.

"I have been thinking," Delia at length began, a slight tremor in her voice, "that I ought presently—?"

She fancied she saw Charlotte's hand tighten on the knobs of the chair-arms.

"You ought presently—?"

"Well, before Tina goes to bed, perhaps go up for a few minutes—"

Charlotte remained silent, visibly resolved on making no effort to assist her.

"Tomorrow," Delia continued, "we shall be in such a rush from the earliest moment that I don't see how, in the midst of all the interruptions and excitement, I can possibly—"

"Possibly?" Charlotte monotonously echoed.

Delia felt her blush deepening through the dusk. "Well, I suppose you agree with me, don't you, that a word ought to be said to the child as to the new duties and responsibilities that—well—what is usual, in fact, at such a time?" she falteringly ended.

"Yes, I have thought of that," Charlotte answered. She said no more, but Delia divined in her tone the stirring of that obscure opposition which, at the crucial moments of Tina's life, seemed automatically to declare itself. She could not understand why Charlotte should, at such times, grow so enigmatic and inaccessible, and in the present case she saw no reason why this change of mood should interfere with what she deemed to be her own duty. Tina must long for her guiding hand into the new life as much as she herself yearned for the exchange of half-confidences which would be her real farewell to her adopted daughter. Her heart beating a little more quickly than usual, she rose and walked through the open window into the shadowy drawing-room. The moon, between the columns of the verandah, sent a broad band of light across the rows of chairs, irradiated the lace-decked altar with its empty candlesticks and vases, and outlined with silver Delia's heavy reflection in the pier-glass.

She crossed the room toward the hall.

"Delia!" Charlotte's voice sounded behind her. Delia turned, and the two women scrutinized each other in the revealing light. Charlotte's face looked as it had looked on the dreadful day when Delia had suddenly seen it in the looking-glass above her shoulder.

"You were going up now to speak to Tina?" Charlotte asked.

"I—yes. It's nearly nine. I thought . . ."

"Yes; I understand." Miss Lovell made a visible effort at self-control. "Please understand me too, Delia, if I ask you—not to."

Delia looked at her cousin with a vague sense of apprehension. What new mystery did this strange request conceal? But no—such a doubt as flitted across her mind was inadmissible. She was too sure of her Tina!

"I confess I don't understand, Charlotte. You surely feel that, on the night before her wedding, a girl ought to have a mother's counsel, a mother's . . ."

"Yes; I feel that." Charlotte Lovell took a hurried breath. "But the question is: *which of us is her mother?*"

Delia drew back involuntarily. "Which of us—?" she stammered.

"Yes. Oh, don't imagine it's the first time I've asked myself the question!

There—I mean to be calm; quite calm. I don't intend to go back to the past. I've accepted—accepted everything—gratefully. Only tonight—just tonight ..."

Delia felt the rush of pity which always prevailed over every other sensation in her rare interchanges of truth with Charlotte Lovell. Her throat filled with tears, and she remained silent.

"Just tonight," Charlotte concluded, *"I'm* her mother."

"Charlotte! You're not going to tell her so—not now?" broke involuntarily from Delia.

Charlotte gave a faint laugh. "If I did, should you hate it as much as all that?"

"Hate it? What a word, between us!"

"Between us? But it's the word that's been between us since the beginning—the very beginning! Since the day when you discovered that Clement Spender hadn't quite broken his heart because he wasn't good enough for you; since you found your revenge and your triumph in keeping me at your mercy, and in taking his child from me!" Charlotte's words flamed up as if from the depth of the infernal fires; then the blaze dropped, her head sank forward, and she stood before Delia dumb and stricken.

Delia's first movement was one of an indignant recoil. Where she had felt only tenderness, compassion, the impulse of help and befriend, these darknesses had been smouldering in the other's breast! It was as if a poisonous smoke had swept over some pure summer landscape ...

Usually such feelings were quickly followed by a reaction of sympathy. But now she felt none. An utter weariness possessed her.

"Yes," she said slowly, "I sometimes believe you really have hated me from the very first; hated me for everything I've tried to do for you."

Charlotte raised her head sharply. "To do for me? But everything you've done has been done for Clement Spender!"

Delia stared at her with a kind of terror. "You are horrible, Charlotte. Upon my honour, I haven't thought of Clement Spender for years."

"Ah, but you have—you have! You've always thought of him in thinking of Tina—of him and nobody else! A woman never stops thinking of the man she loves. She thinks of him years afterward, in all sorts of unconscious ways, in thinking of all sorts of things—books, pictures, sunsets, a flower or a ribbon—or a clock on the mantelpiece," Charlotte broke off with her sneering laugh. "That was what I gambled on, you see—that's why I came to you that day. I knew I was giving Tina another mother."

Again the poisonous smoke seemed to envelop Delia: that she and Charlotte, two spent old women, should be standing before Tina's bridal altar and talking to each other of hatred, seemed unimaginably hideous and degrading.

"You wicked woman—you *are* wicked!" she exclaimed.

Then the evil mist cleared away, and through it she saw the baffled pitiful figure of the mother who was not a mother, and who, for every benefit accepted, felt herself robbed of a privilege. She moved nearer to Charlotte and laid a hand on her arm.

"Not here! Don't let us talk like this here."

The other drew away from her. "Wherever you please, then. I'm not particular!"

"But tonight, Charlotte—the night before Tina's wedding? Isn't every place in this house full of her? How could we go on saying cruel things to each other anywhere?" Charlotte was silent, and Delia continued in a steadier voice: "Nothing you say can really hurt me—for long; and I don't want to hurt you—I never did."

"You tell me that—and you've left nothing undone to divide me from my daughter! Do you suppose it's been easy, all these years, to hear her call you 'mother'? Oh, I know, I know—it was agreed that she must never guess . . . but if you hadn't perpetually come between us she'd have had no one but me, she'd have felt about me as a child feels about its mother, she'd have *had* to love me better than any one else. With all your forbearances and your generosities you've ended by robbing me of my child. And I've put up with it all for her sake—because I knew I had to. But tonight—tonight she belongs to me. Tonight I can't bear that she should call you 'mother'."

Delia Ralston made no immediate reply. It seemed to her that for the first time she had sounded the deepest depths of maternal passion, and she stood awed of the echoes it gave back.

"How you must love her—to say such things to me," she murmured; then, with a final effort: "Yes, you're right. I won't go up to her. It's you who must go."

Charlotte started toward her impulsively; but with a hand lifted as if in defense, Delia moved across the room and out again to the verandah. As she sank down in her chair she heard the drawing-room door open and close, and the sound of Charlotte's feet on the stairs.

Delia sat alone in the night. The last drop of her magnanimity had been spent, and she tried to avert her shuddering mind from Charlotte. What was happening at this moment upstars? With what dark revelations were Tina's bridal dreams to be defaced? Well, that was not matter for conjecture either. She, Delia Ralston, had played her part, done her utmost: there remained nothing now but to try to lift her spirit above the embittering sense of failure.

There was a strange element of truth in some of the things that Charlotte had said. With what divination her maternal passion had endowed her! Her jealousy seemed to have a million feelers. Yes; it was true that the sweetness and peace of Tina's bridal eve had been filled, for Delia, with visions of her own unrealized past. Softly, imperceptibly, it had reconciled her to the memory of what she had missed. All these last days she had been living the girl's life, she had been Tina, and Tina had been her own girlish self, the far-off Delia Lovell. Now for the first time, without shame, without self-reproach, without a pang or a scruple, Delia could yield to that vision of requited love from which her imagination had always turned away. She had made her choice in youth, and she had accepted it in maturity; and here in this bridal joy, so mysteriously her own, was the compensation for all she had missed and yet never renounced.

Delia understood now that Charlotte had guessed all this, and that the knowledge had filled her with a fierce resentment. Charlotte had said long ago that Clement Spender had never really belonged to her; now she had perceived that it was the same with Clement Spender's child. As the truth stole upon Delia her heart melted with the old compassion for Charlotte. She saw that it was a terrible, a sacrilegious thing to interfere with another's destiny, to lay the tenderest touch upon any human being's right to love and suffer after his own fashion. Delia had twice intervened in Charlotte Lovell's life: it was natural that Charlotte should be her enemy. If only she did not revenge herself by wounding Tina!

The adopted mother's thoughts reverted painfully to the little white room upstairs. She had meant her half-hour with Tina to leave the girl with thoughts as fragrant as the flowers she was to find beside her when she woke. And now—.

Delia started up from her musing. There was a step on the stair—Charlotte coming down through the silent house. Delia rose with a vague impulse of escape: she felt that she could not face her cousin's eyes. She turned the corner of the verandah, hoping to find the shutters of the dining-room unlatched, and to slip away unnoticed to her room; but in a moment Charlotte was beside her.

"Delia!"

"Ah, it's you? I was going up to bed." For the life of her Delia could not keep an edge of hardness from her voice.

"Yes: it's late. You must be very tired." Charlotte paused; her own voice was strained and painful.

"I *am* tired," Delia acknowledged.

In the moonlit hush the mother went up to her, laying a timid touch on her arm.

"Not till you've seen Tina."

Delia stiffened. "Tina? But it's late! Isn't she sleeping? I thought you'd stay with her until—"

"I don't know if she's sleeping," Charlotte paused. "I haven't been in—but there's a light under her door."

"You haven't been in?"

"No: I just stood in the passage, and tried—"

"Tried—?"

"To think of something ... something to say to her without ... without her guessing ..." A sob stopped her, but she pressed on with a final effort. "It's no use. You were right: there's nothing I can say. You're her real mother. Go to her. It's not your fault—or mine."

"Oh—" Delia cried.

Charlotte clung to her in inarticulate abasement. "You said I was wicked—I'm not wicked. After all, she was mine when she was little!"

Delia put an arm about her shoulder.

"Hush, dear! We'll go to her together."

The other yielded automatically to her touch, and side by side the two women mounted the stairs, Charlotte timing her impetuous step to Delia's stiffened movements. They walked down the passage to Tina's door; but there Charlotte Lovell paused and shook her head.

"No—you," she whispered, and turned away.

Tina lay in bed, her arms folded under her head, her happy eyes reflecting the silver space of sky which filled the window. She smiled at Delia through her dream.

"I knew you'd come."

Delia sat down beside her, and their clasped hands lay down upon the coverlet. They did not say much, after all; or else their communion had no need of words. Delia never knew how long she sat by the child's side: she abandoned herself to the spell of the moonlit hour.

But suddenly she thought of Charlotte, alone behind the shut door of her own room, watching, struggling, listening. Delia must not, for her own pleasure, prolong that tragic vigil. She bent down to kiss Tina goodnight; then she paused on the threshold and turned back.

"Darling! Just one thing more."

"Yes?" Tina murmured through her dream.

"I want you to promise me—"

"Everything, everything, you darling mother!"

"Well, then, that when you go away tomorrow—at the very last moment, you understand—"

"Yes?"

"After you've said goodbye to me, and to everybody else—just as Lanning helps you into the carriage—"

"Yes?"

"That you'll give your last kiss to Aunt Charlotte. Don't forget—the very last."

JOHN STEINBECK

Tortilla Flat

PREFACE

This is the story of Danny and of Danny's friends and of Danny's house. It is a story of how these three became one thing, so that in Tortilla Flat if you speak of Danny's house you do not mean a structure of wood flaked with old whitewash, overgrown with an ancient untrimmed rose of Castile. No, when you speak of Danny's house you are understood to mean a unit of which the parts are men, from which came sweetness and joy, philanthropy and, in the end, a mystic sorrow. For Danny's house was not unlike the Round Table, and Danny's friends were not unlike the knights of it. And this is the story of how that group came into being, of how it flourished and grew to be an organization beautiful and wise. This story deals with the adventuring of Danny's friends, with the good they did, with their thoughts and their endeavors. In the end, this story tells how the talisman was lost and how the group disintegrated.

In Monterey, that old city on the coast of California, these things are well known, and they are repeated and sometimes elaborated. It is well that this cycle be put down on paper so that in a future time scholars, hearing the legends, may not say as they say of Arthur and of Roland and of Robin Hood— "There was no Danny nor any group of Danny's friends, nor any house. Danny is a nature god and his friends primitive symbols of the wind, the sky, the sun." This history is designed now and ever to keep the sneers from the lips of sour scholars.

Monterey sits on the slope of a hill, with a blue bay below it and with a forest of tall dark pine trees at its back. The lower parts of the town are inhabited by Americans, Italians, catchers and canners of fish. But on the hill where the forest and the town intermingle, where the streets are innocent of asphalt and the corners free of street lights, the old inhabitants of Monterey are embattled as the Ancient Britons are embattled in Wales. These are the paisanos.

They live in old wooden houses set in weedy yards, and the pine trees from the forest are about the houses. The paisanos are clean of commercialism, free of the complicated systems of American business, and, having nothing that can be stolen, exploited, or mortgaged, that system has not attacked them very vigorously.

What is a paisano? He is a mixture of Spanish, Indian, Mexican, and assorted Caucasian bloods. His ancestors have lived in California for a hundred or two years. He speaks English with a paisano accent and Spanish with a paisano accent. When questioned concerning his race, he indignantly claims pure Spanish blood and rolls up his sleeve to show that the soft inside of his arm is nearly white. His color, like that of a well-browned meerschaum pipe, he ascribes to sunburn. He is a paisano, and he lives in the uphill district above the town of Monterey called Tortilla Flat, although it isn't a flat at all.

Danny was a paisano, and he grew up in Tortilla Flat and everyone liked him, but he did not stand out particularly from the screeching children of Tortilla Flat. He was related to nearly everyone in the Flat by blood or romance. His grandfather was an important man who owned two small houses in Tortilla Flat and was respected for his wealth. If the growing Danny preferred to sleep in the forest, to work on ranches, and to wrest his food and wine from an unwilling world, it was not because he did not have influential relatives. Danny was small and dark and intent. At twenty-five his legs were bent to the exact curves of a horse's sides.

Now when Danny was twenty-five years old, the war with Germany was declared. Danny and his friend Pilon (Pilon, by the way, is something thrown in when a trade is conducted—a boot) had two gallons of wine when they heard about the war. Big Joe Portagee saw the glitter of the bottles among the pines and he joined Danny and Pilon.

As the wine went down in the bottles, patriotism arose in the three men. And when the wine was gone they went down the hill arm in arm for comradeship and safety, and they walked into Monterey. In front of an enlistment station they cheered loudly for America and dared Germany to do her worst. They howled menaces at the German Empire until the enlistment sergeant awakened and put on his uniform and came into the street to silence them. He remained to enlist them.

The sergeant lined them up in front of his desk. They passed everything but the sobriety test and then the sergeant began his questions with Pilon.

"What branch do you want to go in?"

"I don' give a god-damn," said Pilon jauntily.

"I guess we need men like you in the infantry." And Pilon was written so.

He turned then to Big Joe, and the Portagee was getting sober. "Where do you want to go?"

"I want to go home," Big Joe said miserably.

The sergeant put him in the infantry too. Finally he confronted Danny, who was sleeping on his feet. "Where do you want to go?"

"Huh?"

"I say, what branch?"

"What do you mean, 'branch'?"

"What can you do?"

"Me? I can do anything."

"What did you do before?"

"Me? I'm a mule skinner."

"Oh, you are? How many mules can you drive?"

Danny leaned forward, vaguely and professionally. "How many you got?"

"About thirty thousand," said the sergeant.

Danny waved his hand. "String 'em up!" he said.

And so Danny went to Texas and broke mules for the duration of the war. And Pilon marched about Oregon with the infantry, and Big Joe, as shall be later made clear, went to jail.

□ **I** □

How Danny, home from the wars, found himself an heir,
and how he swore to protect the helpless.

When Danny came home from the army he learned that he was an heir and an owner of property. The *viejo,* that is the grandfather, had died, leaving Danny the two small houses on Tortilla Flat.

When Danny heard about it he was a little weighed down with the responsibility of ownership. Before he ever went to look at his property he bought a gallon of red wine and drank most of it himself. The weight of responsibility left him then, and his very worst nature came to the surface. He shouted; he broke a few chairs in a poolroom on Alvarado Street; he had two short but glorious fights. No one paid much attention to Danny. At last his wavering bowlegs took him toward the wharf where, at this early hour in the morning, the Italian fishermen were walking down in rubber boots to go out to sea.

Race antipathy overcame Danny's good sense. He menaced the fishermen. "Sicilian bastards," he called them, and "Scum from the prison island," and Dogs of dogs of dogs." He cried, *"Chinga tu madre, Piojo."* He thumbed his nose and made obscene gestures below his waist. The fishermen only grinned and shifted their oars and said, "Hello, Danny. When'd you get home? Come around tonight. We got new wine."

Danny was outraged. He screamed, *"Pon un condo a la cabeza."*

They called, "Good-by, Danny. See you tonight." And they climbed into their little boats and rowed out to the lampara launches and started their engines and chugged away.

Danny was insulted. He walked back up Alvarado Street, breaking windows as he went, and in the second block a policeman took him in hand. Danny's great respect for the law caused him to go quietly. If he had not just been discharged from the army after the victory over Germany, he would have been sentenced to six months. As it was, the judge gave him only thirty days.

And so for one month Danny sat on his cot in the Monterey city jail. Sometimes he drew obscene pictures on the walls, and sometimes he thought over his army career. Time hung heavy on Danny's hands there in his cell in the city jail. Now and then a drunk was put in for the night, but for the most part crime in Monterey was stagnant, and Danny was lonely. The bedbugs bothered him a little at first, but as they got used to the taste of him and he grew accustomed to their bites, they got along peacefully.

He started playing a satiric game. He caught a bedbug, squashed it against the wall, drew a circle around it with a pencil and named it "Mayor Clough." Then he caught others and named them after the City Council. In a little while he had one wall decorated with squashed bedbugs, each named for a local dignitary. He drew ears and tails on them, gave them big noses and mustaches. Tito Ralph, the jailer, was scandalized; but he made no complaint because Danny had not included either the justice of the peace who had sentenced him or any of the police force. He had a vast respect for the law.

One night when the jail was lonely, Tito Ralph came into Danny's cell bearing two bottles of wine. An hour later he went out for more wine, and Danny went with him. It was cheerless in the jail. They stayed at Torrelli's, where they bought the wine, until Torrelli threw them out. After that Danny went up among the pines and fell asleep, while Tito Ralph staggered back and reported his escape.

When the brilliant sun awakened Danny about noon, he determined to hide all day to escape pursuit. He ran and dodged behind bushes. He peered out of the undergrowth like a hunted fox. And, at evening, the rules having been satisfied, he came out and went about his business.

Danny's business was fairly direct. He went to the back door of a restaurant. "Got any old bread I can give my dog?" he asked the cook. And while that gullible man was wrapping up the food, Danny stole two slices of ham, four eggs, a lamb chop, and a fly swatter.

"I will pay you sometime," he said.

"No need to pay for scraps. I throw them away if you don't take them."

Danny felt better about the theft then. If that was the way they felt, on the surface he was guiltless. He went back to Torrelli's, traded the four eggs, the lamb chop, and the fly swatter for a water glass of grappa and retired toward the woods to cook his supper.

The night was dark and damp. The fog hung like limp gauze among the black pines that guard the landward limits of Monterey. Danny put his head down and hurried for the shelter of the woods. Ahead of him he made out another hurrying figure; and as he narrowed the distance, he recognized the scuttling walk of his old friend Pilon. Danny was a generous man, but he recalled that he had sold all his food except the two slices of ham and the bag of stale bread.

"I will pass Pilon by," he decided. "He walks like a man who is full of roast turkey and things like that."

Then suddenly Danny noticed that Pilon clutched his coat lovingly across his bosom.

"Ai, Pilon, *amigo!*" Danny cried.

Pilon scuttled on faster. Danny broke into a trot. "Pilon, my little friend! Where goest thou so fast?"

Pilon resigned himself to the inevitable and waited. Danny approached warily, but his tone was enthusiastic. "I looked for thee, dearest of little angelic friends, for see, I have here two great steaks from God's own pig, and a sack of sweet white bread. Share my bounty, Pilon, little dumpling."

Pilon shrugged his shoulders. "As you say," he muttered savagely. They walked on together into the woods. Pilon was puzzled. At length he stopped and faced his friend. "Danny," he asked sadly, "how knewest thou I had a bottle of brandy under my coat?"

"Brandy?" Danny cried. "Thou hast brandy? Perhaps it is for some sick old mother," he said naïvely. "Perhaps thou keepest it for Our Lord Jesus when He comes again. Who am I, thy friend, to judge the destination of this brandy? I am not even sure thou hast it. Besides I am not thirsty. I would not touch this brandy. Thou art welcome to this big roast of pork I have, but as for thy brandy, that is thine own."

Pilon answered him sternly, "Danny, I do not mind sharing my brandy with you, half and half. It is my duty to see you do not drink it all."

Danny dropped the subject then. "Here in the clearing I will cook this pig, and you will toast the sugar cakes in this bag here. Put thy brandy here, Pilon. It is better there, where we can see it, and each other."

They built a fire and broiled the ham and ate the stale bread. The brandy receded quickly down the bottle. After they had eaten, they huddled near the fire and sipped delicately at the bottle like effete bees. And the fog came down upon them and grayed their coats with moisture. The wind sighed sadly in the pines about them.

And after a time a loneliness fell upon Danny and Pilon. Danny thought of his lost friends.

"Where is Arthur Morales?" Danny asked, turning his palms up and thrusting his arms forward. "Dead in France," he answered himself, turning the palms down and dropping his arms in despair. "Dead for his country. Dead in a foreign land. Strangers walk near his grave and they do not know Arthur Morales lies there." He raised his hands palms upward again, "Where is Pablo, that good man?"

"In jail," said Pilon. "Pablo stole a goose and hid in the brush; and that goose bit Pablo and Pablo cried out and so was caught. Now he lies in jail for six months."

Danny sighed and changed the subject, for he realized that he had prodigally used up the only acquaintance in any way fit for oratory. But the loneliness was still on him and demanded an outlet. "Here we sit," he began at last.

"—broken-hearted," Pilon added rhythmically.

"No, this is not a poem," Danny said. "Here we sit, homeless. We gave our lives for our country, and now we have no roof over our head."

"We never did have," Pilon added helpfully.

Danny drank dreamily until Pilon touched his elbow and took the bottle. "That reminds me," Danny said, "of a story of a man who owned two whorehouses—" His mouth dropped open. "Pilon!" he creid "Pilon! my little fat duck of a baby friend. I had forgotten! I am an heir! I own two houses."

"Whorehouses?" Pilon asked hopefully. "Thou art a drunken liar," he continued.

"No, Pilon, I tell the truth. The *viejo* died. I am the heir. I, the favorite grandson."

"Thou art the only grandson," said the realist Pilon. "Where are these houses?"

"You know the *viejo's* house on Tortilla Flat, Pilon?"

"Here in Monterey?"

"Yes, here in Tortilla Flat."

"Are they any good, these houses?"

Danny sank back, exhausted with emotion. "I do not know. I forgot I owned them."

Pilon sat silent and absorbed. His face grew mournful. He threw a handful of pine needles on the fire, watched the flames climb frantically among them and die. For a long time he looked into Danny's face with deep anxiety, and then Pilon sighed noisily, and again he sighed. "Now it is over," he said sadly. "Now the great times are done. Thy friends will mourn, but nothing will come of their mourning."

Danny put down the bottle, and Pilon picked it up and set it in his own lap.

"Now what is over?" Danny demanded. "What do you mean?"

"It is not the first time," Pilon went on. "When one is poor, one thinks, 'If I had money I would share it with my good friends.' But let that money come and charity flies away. So it is with thee, my once-friend. Thou art lifted above thy friends. Thou art a man of property. Thou wilt forget thy friends who shared everything with thee, even their brandy."

His words upset Danny. "Not I," he cried, "I will never forget thee, Pilon."

"So you think now," said Pilon coldly. "But when you have two houses to sleep in, then you will see. Pilon will be a poor paisano, while you eat with the mayor."

Danny arose unsteadily and held himself upright against a tree. "Pilon, I swear, what I have is thine. While I have a house, thou hast a house. Give me a drink."

"I must see this to believe it," Pilon said in a discouraged voice. "It would be a world wonder if it were so. Men would come a thousand miles to look upon it. And besides, the bottle is empty."

□ **II** □

How Pilon was lured by greed of position to forsake Danny's hospitality.

The lawyer left them at the gate of the second house and climbed into his Ford and stuttered down the hill into Monterey.

Danny and Pilon stood in front of the paintless picket fence and looked with admiration at the property, a low house streaked with old whitewash, uncurtained windows blank and blind. But a great pink rose of Castile was on the porch, and grandfather geraniums grew among the weeds in the front yard.

"This is the best of the two," said Pilon. "It is bigger than the other."

Danny held a new skeleton key in his hand. He tiptoed over the rickety porch and unlocked the front door. The main room was just as it had been when the *viejo* had lived there. The red rose calendar for 1906, the silk banner on the wall, with Fighting Bob Evans looking between the superstructures of a battleship, the bunch of red paper roses tacked up, the strings of dusty red peppers and garlic, the stove, the battered rocking chairs.

Pilon looked in the door. "Three rooms," he said breathlessly, "and a bed and a stove. We will be happy here, Danny."

Danny moved cautiously into the house. He had bitter memories of the *viejo*. Pilon darted ahead of him and into the kitchen. "A sink with a faucet," he cried. He turned the handle. "No water, Danny, you must have the company turn on the water."

They stood and smiled at each other. Pilon noticed that the worry of property was settling on Danny's face. No more in life would that face be free of care. No more would Danny break windows now that he had windows of his own to break. Pilon had been right—he had been raised among his fellows. His shoulders had straightened to withstand the complexity of life. But one cry of pain escaped him before he left for all time his old and simple existence.

"Pilon," he said sadly, "I wish you owned it and I could come to live with you."

While Danny went to Monterey to have the water turned on, Pilon wandered into the weed-tangled back yard. Fruit trees were there, bony and black with age, and gnarled and broken from neglect. A few tent-like chicken coops lay among the weeds. A pile of rusty barrel hoops, a heap of ashes, and a sodden mattress. Pilon looked over the fence into Mrs. Morales' chicken yard, and after a moment of consideration he opened a few small holes in the fence for the hens. "They will like to make nests in the tall weeds," he thought kindly. He considered how he could make a figure-four trap in case the roosters came in too and bothered the hens and kept them from the nests. "We will live happily," he thought again.

Danny came back indignant from Monterey. "That company wants a deposit," he said.

"Deposit?"

"Yes. They want three dollars before they will turn on the water."

"Three dollars," Pilon said severely, "is three gallons of wine. And when that is gone, we will borrow a bucket of water from Mrs. Morales, next door."

"But we haven't three dollars for wine."

"I know," Pilon said. "Maybe we can borrow a little wine from Mrs. Morales."

The afternoon passed. "Tomorrow we will settle down," Danny announced. "Tomorrow we will clean and scrub. And you, Pilon, will cut the weeds and throw the trash in the gulch."

"The weeds?" Pilon cried in horror. "Not *those* weeds." He explained his theory of Mrs. Morales' chickens.

Danny agreed immediately. "My friend," he said, "I am glad that you have come to live with me. Now, while I collect a little wood, you must get something for dinner."

Pilon, remembering his brandy, thought this unfair. "I am getting in debt to him," he thought bitterly. "My freedom will be cut off. Soon I shall be a slave because of this Jew's house." But he did go out to look for some dinner.

Two blocks away, near the edge of the pine wood, he came upon a half-grown Plymouth Rock rooster scratching in the road. It had come to that adolescent age when its voice cracked, when its legs and neck and breast were naked. Perhaps because he had been thinking of Mrs. Morales' hens in a charitable vein, this little rooster engaged Pilon's sympathy. He walked slowly on toward the dark pine woods, and the chicken ran ahead of him.

Pilon mused, "Poor little bare fowl. How cold it must be for you in the early morning, when the dew falls and the air grows cold with the dawn. The good God is not always so good to little beasts." And he thought, "Here you play in the street, little chicken. Some day an automobile will run over you; and if it kills you, that will be the best thing that can happen. It may only break your leg or your wing. Then all of your life you will drag along in misery. Life is too hard for you, little bird."

He moved slowly and cautiously. Now and then the chicken tried to double back, but always there was Pilon in the place it chose to go. At last it disappeared into the pine forest, and Pilon sauntered after it.

To the glory of his soul be it said that no cry of pain came from that thicket. That chicken, which Pilon had prophesied might live painfully, died peacefully, or at least quietly. And this is no little tribute to Pilon's technique.

Ten minutes later he emerged from the woods and walked back toward Danny's house. The little rooster, picked and dismembered, was distributed in his pockets. If there was one rule of conduct more strong than any other to Pilon, it was this: Never under any circumstances bring feathers, head or feet home, for without these a chicken cannot be identified.

In the evening they had a fire of cones in the airtight stove. The flames growled in the chimney. Danny and Pilon, well fed, warm, and happy, sat in the rocking chairs and gently teetered back and forth. At dinner they had used a piece of candle, but now only the light from the stove cracks dispelled the darkness of the room. To make it perfect, rain began to patter on the roof. Only a little leaked through, and that in places where no one wanted to sit anyway.

"It is good, this," Pilon said. "Think of the nights when we slept in the cold. This is the way to live."

"Yes, and it is strange," Danny said. "For years I had no house. Now I have two. I cannot sleep in two houses."

Pilon hated waste. "This very thing has been bothering me. Why don't you rent the other house?" he suggested.

Danny's feet crashed down on the floor. "Pilon," he cried. "Why didn't I think of it?" The idea grew more familiar. "But who will rent it, Pilon?"

"I will rent it," said Pilon. "I will pay ten dollars a month in rent."

"Fifteen," Danny insisted. "It's a good house. It is worth fifteen."

Pilon agreed, grumbling. But he would have agreed to much more, for he saw the elevation that came to a man who lived in his own house; and Pilon longed to feel that elevation.

"It is agreed, then," Danny concluded. "You will rent my house. Oh, I will be a good landlord, Pilon. I will not bother you."

Pilon, except for his year in the army, had never possessed fifteen dollars in his life. But, he thought, it would be a month before the rent was due, and who could tell what might happen in a month.

They teetered contentedly by the fire. After a while Danny went out for a few moments and returned with some apples. "The rain would have spoiled them anyway," he apologized.

Pilon, not to be oudone, got up and lighted the candle; he went into the bedroom and in a moment returned with a wash bowl and pitcher, two red glass vases, and a bouquet of ostrich plumes. "It is not good to have so many breakable things around," he said. "When they are broken you become sad. It is much better never to have had them."He picked the paper roses from the wall. "A compliment for Señora Torrelli," he explained as he went out the door.

Shortly afterward he returned, wet through from the rain, but tri-umphant in manner, for he had a gallon jug of red wine in his hand.

They argued bitterly later, but neither cared who won, for they were tired with the excitements of the day. The wine made them drowsy, and they went to sleep on the floor. The fire died down; the stove cricked as it cooled. The candle tipped over and expired in its own grease, with little blue protest-ing flares. The house was dark and quiet and peaceful.

□   III   □

*How the poison of possessions wrought with Pilon, and
how evil temporarily triumphed in him.*

The next day Pilon went to live in the other house. It was exactly like Danny's house, only smaller. It had its pink rose of Castile over the porch, its weed-grown yard, its ancient, barren fruit trees, its red geraniums—and Mrs. Soto's chicken yard was next door.

Danny became a great man, having a house to rent, and Pilon went up the social scale by renting a house.

It is impossible to say whether Danny expected any rent, or whether Pilon expected to pay any. If they did, both were disappointed. Danny never asked for it, and Pilon never offered it.

The two friends were often together. Let Pilon come by a jug of wine or a piece of meat and Danny was sure to drop in to visit. And, if Danny were lucky or astute in the same way, Pilon spent a riotous night with him. Poor Pilon would have paid the money if he ever had any, but he never did have—not long enough to locate Danny. Pilon was an honest man. It worried him sometimes to think of Danny's goodness and his own poverty.

One night he had a dollar, acquired in a manner so astounding that he tried to forget it immediately for fear the memory might make him mad. A man in front of the San Carlos hotel had put the dollar in his hand, saying, "Run down and get four bottles of ginger ale. The hotel is out." Such things were almost miracles, Pilon thought. One should take them on faith, not worry and question them. He took the dollar up the road to give to Danny, but on the way he bought a gallon of wine, and with the wine he lured two plump girls into his house.

Danny, walking by, heard the noise and joyfully went in. Pilon fell into his arms and placed everything at Danny's disposal. And later, after Danny had helped to dispose of one of the girls and half of the wine, there was a really fine fight. Danny lost a tooth, and Pilon had his shirt torn off. The girls stood shrieking by and kicked whichever man happened to be down. At last Danny got up off the floor and butted one of the girls in the stomach, and she went out the door croaking like a frog. The other girl stole two cooking pots and followed her.

For a little while Danny and Pilon wept over the perfidy of women.

"Thou knowest not what bitches women are," Danny said wisely.

"I do know," said Pilon.

"Thou knowest not."

"I do know."

"Liar."

There was another fight, but not a very good one.

After that Pilon felt better about the unpaid rent. Had he not been host to his landlord?

A number of months passed. Pilon began again to worry about the rent. And as time went by the worry grew intolerable. At last in desperation he worked a whole day cleaning squids for Chin Kee and made two dollars. In the evening he tied his red handkerchief around his neck, put on his father's revered hat, and started up the hill to pay Danny the two dollars on account.

But on the way he bought two gallons of wine. "It is better so," he thought. "If I give him hard money, it does not express how warmly I feel toward my friend. But a present, now. And I will tell him the two gallons cost five dollars." This was silly, and Pilon knew it, but he indulged himself. No one in Monterey better knew the price of wine than Danny.

Pilon was proceeding happily. His mind was made up; his nose pointed straight toward Danny's house. His feet moved, not quickly, but steadily in the proper direction. Under each arm he carried a paper bag, and a gallon of wine was in each bag.

It was purple dusk, that sweet time when the day's sleeping is over, and the evening of pleasure and conversation has not begun. The pine trees were very black against the sky, and all objects on the ground were obscured with dark; but the sky was as mournfully bright as memory. The gulls flew lazily home to the sea rocks after a day's visit to the fish canneries of Monterey.

Pilon was a lover of beauty and a mystic. He raised his face into the sky and his soul arose out of him into the sun's afterglow. That not too perfect Pilon, who plotted and fought, who drank and cursed, trudged slowly on; but a wistful and shining Pilon went up to the sea gulls where they bathed on sensitive wings in the evening. That Pilon was beautiful, and his thoughts were unstained with selfishness and lust. And his thoughts are good to know.

"Our Father is in the evening," he thought. "These birds are flying across the forehead of the Father. Dear birds, dear sea gulls, how I love you all. Your slow wings stroke my heart as the hand of a gentle master strokes the full stomach of a sleeping dog, as the hand of Christ stroked the heads of little children. Dear birds," he thought, "fly to our Lady of Sweet Sorrows with my open heart." And then he said the loveliest words he knew, *"Ave Maria, gratia plena—"*

The feet of the bad Pilon had stopped moving. In truth the bad Pilon for the moment had ceased to exist. (Hear this, recording angel!) There was, nor is, nor ever has been a purer soul than Pilon's at that moment. Galvez' bad bulldog came to Pilon's deserted legs standing alone in the dark. And Galvez' bulldog sniffed and went away without biting the legs.

A soul washed and saved is a soul doubly in danger, for everything in the world conspires against such a soul. "Even the straws under my knees," says Saint Augustine, "shout to distract me from prayer."

Pilon's soul was not even proof against his own memories; for as he watched the birds, he remembered that Mrs. Pastano used sea gulls sometimes in her tamales, and that memory made him hungry, and hunger tumbled his soul out of the sky. Pilon moved on, once more a cunning mixture of good and evil. Galvez' bad bulldog turned snarling and stalked back, sorry now that he had let go such a perfect chance at Pilon's legs.

Pilon hunched his arms to ease the weight of the bottles.

It is a fact verified and recorded in many histories that the soul capable of the greatest good is also capable of the greatest evil. Who is there more impious than a backsliding priest? Who more carnal than a recent virgin? This, however, may be a matter of appearance.

Pilon, just back from Heaven, was, although he did not know it, singularly receptive of every bitter wind, toward every evil influence that crowded the night about him. True, his feet still moved toward Danny's house, but there was neither intention nor conviction in them. They awaited the littlest signal to turn about. Already Pilon was thinking how stupendously drunk he could get on two gallons of wine, and more, how long he could stay drunk.

It was almost dark now. The dirt road was no longer visible, nor the ditches on either side. No moral conclusion is drawn from the fact that at this moment, when Pilon's impulses were balanced as precariously as a feather, between generosity and selfishness, at this very moment Pablo Sanchez happened to be sitting in the ditch at the side of the road, wishing he had a cigarette and a glass of wine.

Ah, the prayers of the millions, how they must fight and destroy each other on their way to the throne of God.

Pablo first heard footsteps, then saw a blurred figure, and then recognized Pilon. "Ai, *amigo*," he called enthusiastically. "What great burden is it thou carriest?"

Pilon stopped dead and faced the ditch. "I thought you were in jail," he said severely. "I heard about a goose."

"So I was, Pilon," Pablo said jocularly. "But I was not well received. The judge said the sentence did me no good, and the police said I ate more than the allowance for three men. And so," he finished proudly, "I am on parole."

Pilon was saved from selfishness. True, he did not take the wine to Danny's house, but instantly he invited Pablo to share it at the rented house. If two generous paths branch from the highroad of life and only one can be followed, who is to judge which is best?

Pilon and Pablo entered the little house joyfully. Pilon lighted a candle and produced two fruit jars for glasses.

"Health!" said Pablo.

"*Salud!*" said Pilon.

And in a few moments, "*Salud!*" said Pablo.

"Mud in your eye!" said Pilon.

They rested a little while. "*Su servidor,*" said Pilon.

"Down the rat-hole," said Pablo.

Two gallons is a great deal of wine, even for two paisanos. Spiritually the jugs may be graduated thus: Just below the shoulder of the first bottle, serious and concentrated conversation. Two inches farther down, sweetly sad memory. Three inches more, thoughts of old and satisfactory loves. An inch, thoughts of bitter loves. Bottom of the first jug, general and undirected sadness. Shoulder of the second jug, black, unholy despondency. Two fingers down a song of death or longing. A thumb, every other song each one knows. The graduations stop here, for the trail splits and there is no certainty. From this point on anything can happen.

But let us go back to the first mark, which says serious and concentrated conversation, for it was at that place that Pilon made his coup. "Pablo," he said, "dost thou never get tired of sleeping in ditches, wet and homeless, friendless and alone?"

"No," said Pablo.

Pilon mellowed his voice persuasively. "So *I* thought, my friend, when I was a dirty gutter-dog. I too was content, for I did not know how sweet a little house is, and a roof, and a garden. Ah, Pablo, this is indeed living."

"It's pretty nice," Pablo agreed.

Pilon pounced. "See, Pablo, how would you like to rent part of my house? There would never be the cold ground for you any more. Never the hard sand under the wharf with crabs getting in your shoes. How would you like to live here with me?"

"Sure," said Pablo.

"Look, you will pay only fifteen dollars a month! And you may use all the house except my bed, and all the garden. Think of it, Pablo! And if someone should write you a letter, he will have some place to send it to."

"Sure," said Pablo. "That's swell."

Pilon sighed with relief. He had not realized how the debt to Danny rode on his shoulders. The fact that he was fairly sure Pablo would never pay any rent did not mitigate his triumph. If Danny should ever ask for money, Pilon could say, "I will pay when Pablo pays."

They moved on to the next graduation, and Pilon remembered how happy he had been when he was a little boy. "No care then, Pablo. I knew not sin. I was very happy."

"We have never been happy since," Pablo agreed sadly.

□ **IV** □

How Jesus Maria Corcoran, a good man, became an unwilling vehicle of evil.

Life passed smoothly on for Pilon and Pablo. In the morning when the sun was up clear of the pine trees, when the blue bay rippled and sparkled below them, they arose slowly and thoughtfully from their beds.

It is a time of quiet joy, the sunny morning. When the glittery dew is on the mallow weeds, each leaf holds a jewel which is beautiful if not valuable. This is no time for hurry or for bustle. Thoughts are slow and deep and golden in the morning.

Pablo and Pilon in their blue jeans and blue shirts walked in comradeship into the gulch behind the house, and after a little time they returned to sit in the sun on the front porch, to listen to the fish horns on the streets of Monterey, to discuss in wandering, sleepy tones the doings of Tortilla Flat; for there are a thousand climaxes on Tortilla Flat for every day the world wheels through.

They were at peace there on the porch. Only their toes wriggled on the warm boards when the flies landed on them.

"If all the dew were diamonds," Pablo said, "we would be very rich. We would be drunk all our lives."

But Pilon, on whom the curse of realism lay uneasily, added, "Everybody would have too many diamonds. There would be no price for them, but wine always costs money. If only it would rain wine for a day, now, and we had a tank to catch it in."

"But good wine," interjected Pablo. "Not rotgut swill like the last you got."

"I didn't pay for it," said Pilon. "Someone hid it in the grass by the dance hall. What can you expect of wine you find?"

They sat and waved their hands listlessly at the flies. "Cornelia Ruiz cut up the black Mexican yesterday," Pilon observed.

Pablo raised his eyes in mild interest, "Fight?" he asked.

"Oh, no, the black one did not know Cornelia got a new man yesterday, and he tried to come in. So Cornelia cut him."

"He should have known," Pablo said virtuously.

"Well, he was down in the town when Cornelia got her new man. The black one just tried to go in through the window when she locked the door."

"The black one is a fool," said Pablo. "Is he dead?"

"Oh, no. She just cut him up a little bit on the arms. Cornelia was not angry. She just didn't want the black one to come in."

"Cornelia is not a very steady woman," said Pablo. "But still she has masses sung for her father, ten years dead."

"He will need them," Pilon observed. "He was a bad man and never went to jail for it, and he never went to confession. When old Ruiz was dying the priest came to give him solace, and Ruiz confessed. Cornelia says the priest was white as buckskin when he came out of the sickroom. But afterward that priest said he didn't believe half what Ruiz confessed."

Pablo, with a cat-like stroke, killed a fly that landed on his knee. "Ruiz was always a liar," he said. "That soul will need plenty of masses. But do you think a mass has virtue when the money for that mass comes out of men's pockets while they sleep in wine at Cornelia's house?"

"A mass is a mass," said Pilon. "Where you get two-bits is of no interest to the man who sells you a glass of wine. And where a mass comes from is of no interest to God. He just likes them, the same as you like wine. Father Murphy used to go fishing all the time, and for months the Holy Sacrament tasted like mackerel, but that did not make it less holy. These things are for priests to explain. They are nothing for us to worry about. I wonder where we could get some eggs to eat. It would be good to eat an egg now."

Pablo tilted his hat down over his eyes to keep the sun from bothering him. "Charlie Meeler told me that Danny is with Rosa Martin, that Portagee girl."

Pilon sat upright in alarm. "Maybe that girl will want to marry Danny. Those Portagees always want to marry, and they love money. Maybe when they are married Danny will bother us about the rent. That Rosa will want new dresses. All women do. I know them."

Pablo too looked annoyed. "Maybe if we went and talked to Danny—" he suggested.

"Maybe Danny has some eggs," said Pilon. "Those chickens of Mrs. Morales are good layers."

They put on their shoes and walked slowly toward Danny's house.

Pilon stooped and picked up a beer bottle cap and cursed and threw it down. "Some evil man has left it there to deceive people," he said.

"I tried it last night," said Pablo. He looked into a yard where the green corn was ripe and made a mental note of its ripeness.

They found Danny sitting on his front porch, behind the rose bush, wriggling his toes to keep the flies off.

"Ai, *amigos*," he greeted them listlessly.

They sat down beside him and took off their hats and their shoes. Danny took out a sack of tobacco and some papers and passed them to Pilon. Pilon looked mildly shocked, but made no comment.

"Cornelia Ruiz cut up the black Mexican," he said.

"I heard about it," said Danny.

Pablo spoke acidly. "These women, there is no virtue in them any more."

"It is dangerous to lie with them," said Pilon. "I have heard that there is one young Portagee girl here on the Flat who can give a man something to remember her by, if he goes to the trouble to get it."

Pablo made disapproving clucking noises with his tongue. He spread his hands in front of him. "What is a man to do?" he asked. "Is there no one to trust?"

They watched Danny's face and saw no alarm appear there.

"This girl's name is Rosa," said Pilon. "I would not say her last name."

"Oh, you mean Rosa Martin," Danny observed with very little interest.

"Well, what can you expect of a Portagee?"

Pablo and Pilon sighed with relief.

"How are Mrs. Morales' chickens getting along?" Pilon asked casually.

"Danny shook his head sadly. "Every one of those chickens is dead. Mrs. Morales put some some string beans in jars, and the jars blew up, and she fed the beans to the chickens, and those chickens all died, every one."

"Where are those chickens now?" Pablo demanded.

Danny waved two fingers back and forth in negation. "Someone told Mrs. Morales not to eat those chickens or she would be sick, but we scraped the insides good and sold them to the butcher."

"Has anybody died?" Pablo asked.

"No, I guess those chickens would have been all right."

"Perhaps you bought a little wine with the money from those chickens?" Pilon suggested.

Danny smiled cynically at him. "Mrs. Morales did, and I went to her house last night. That is a pretty woman in some lights, and not so old either."

The alarm came back to Pablo and Pilon.

"My Cousin Weelie says she is fifty years old," Pilon said excitedly.

Danny spread his hands. "What is it how old in years she is?" he observed philosophically. "She is lively, that one. She owns her house and has two hundred dollars in the bank." Then Danny became a little embarrassed. "I would like to make a present to Mrs. Morales."

Pilon and Pablo regarded their feet and tried by strenuous mental effort to ward off what was coming. But their effort had no value.

"If I had a little money," said Danny, "I would buy her a box of big candy." He looked meaningly at his tenants, but neither one answered him. "I would need only a dollar to two," he suggested.

"Chin Kee is drying squids," Pilon observed. "Perhaps you could cut squids for half a day."

Danny spoke pointedly. "It would not look well for a man who owns two houses to cut squids. But perhaps if a little rent were ever paid—"

Pilon arose angrily. "Always the rent," he cried. "You would force us into the streets—into the gutters, while you sleep in your soft bed. Come, Pablo," Pilon said angrily, "we will get money for this miser, this Jew."

The two of them stalked off.

"Where will we get money?" Pablo asked.

"I don't know," said Pilon. "Maybe he won't ask again." But the inhuman demand had cut deep into their mental peace. "We will call him 'Old Jew' when we see him," said Pilon. "We have been his friends for years. When he was in need, we fed him. When he was cold, we clothed him."

"When was that?" Pablo asked.

"Well, we would have, if he needed anything and we had it. That is the kind of friends we were to him. And now he crushes our friendship into the ground for a box of big candy to give to an old fat woman."

"Candy is not good for people," said Pablo.

So much emotion had exhausted Pilon. He sat down in the ditch beside the road and put his chin in his hands and was disconsolate.

Pablo sat down too, but he only did it to rest, for his friendship with Danny was not as old and beautiful as Pilon's was.

The bottom of the ditch was choked with dry grass and bushes. Pilon, staring downward in his sorrow and resentment, saw a human arm sticking out from under a bush. And then, beside the arm, a half-full gallon bottle of wine. He clutched Pablo's arm and pointed.

Pablo stared. "Maybe he is dead, Pilon."

Pilon had got his breath and his fine clear vision again. "If he is dead, the wine will do him no good. He can't be buried with it."

The arm stirred, swept back the bushes, and disclosed the frowsy face and red stubble beard of Jesus Maria Corcoran. "Ai, Pilon. Ai, Pablo," he said hazily. *"Que tomas?"*

Pilon leaped down the bank on him. *"Amigo,* Jesus Maria! you are not well!"

Jesus Maria smiled sweetly. "Just drunk," he murmured. He rose to his knees. "Come have a drink, my friends. Drink deep. There is plenty more."

Pilon tilted the bottle over his elbow. He swallowed four times and over a pint left the jug. Then Pablo took the bottle from him, and Pablo played with it as a cat plays with a feather. He polished the mouth with his sleeve. He smelled the wine. He took three or four preliminary sips and let a few drops run all around his mouth, to tantalize himself. At last, *"Madre de Dios, que vino!"* he said. He raised the jug and the red wine gurgled happily down his throat.

Pilon's hand was out long before Pablo had to breathe again. Pilon turned a soft and admiring countenance to his friend Jesus Maria. "Hast thou discovered a treasure in the woods?" he asked. "Has some great man died and named thee in his will, my little friend?"

Jesus Maria was a humanitarian, and kindness was always in him. He cleared his throat and spat. "Give me a drink," he said. "My thoat is dry. I will tell you how it was." He drank dreamily, like a man who has so much wine that he can take his time in drinking it, can even spill a little without remorse. "I was sleeping on the beach two nights ago," he said. "Out on the beach near Seaside. In the night the little waves washed a rowboat to the shore. Oh, a nice little rowboat, and the oars were there. I got in and rowed it down to Monterey. It was easily worth twenty dollars, but trade was slow, and I only got seven."

"Thou hast money left?" Pilon put in excitedly.

"I am telling you how it was," Jesus Maria said with some dignity. "I bought two gallons of wine and brought them up here to the woods, and then I went to walk with Arabella Gross. For her I bought one pair of silk drawers in Monterey. She liked them—so soft they were, and so pink. And then I bought a pint of whisky for Arabella, and then after a while we met some soldiers and she went away with them."

"Oh, the thief of a good man's money!" Pilon cried in horror.

"No, said Jesus Maria dreamily. "It was time she went anyway. And then I came here and went to sleep."

"Then thou hast no more money?"

"I don't know," said Jesus Maria. "I will see. "He fished in his pocket and brought out three crumpled dollar bills and a dime. "Tonight," he said. "I will buy for Arabella Gross one of those little things that goes around higher up."

"You mean the little silk pockets on a string?"

"Yes," said Jesus Maria, "and not so little as you might think either." He coughed to clear his throat.

Instantly Pilon was filled with solicitude. "It is the night air," he said. "It is not good to sleep out in the open. Come, Pablo, we will take him to our house and cure this cold of his. The malady of the lungs has a good start, but we will cure it."

What are you talking about?" said Jesus Maria. "I'm all right."

"So you think," said Pilon. "So Rudolfo Kelling thought. And you yourself went to his funeral a month ago. So Angelina Vasquez thought. She died last week."

Jesus Maria was frightened. "What do you think is the matter?"

"It is sleeping in this night air," Pilon said sagely. "Your lungs will not stand it."

Pablo wrapped the wine jug in a big weed, so disguising it that anyone passing would have been consumed with curiosity until he knew what that weed contained.

Pilon walked beside Jesus Maria, touching him now and then under the elbow to remind him that he was not a well man. They took him to their house and laid him on a cot, and although the day was warm, they covered him with an old comforter. Pablo spoke movingly of those poor ones who writhed and suffered with tuberculosis. And then Pilon pitched his voice to sweetness. He spoke with reverence of the joy of living in a little house. When the night was far gone, and all the talk and wine were gone, and outside the deadly mists clung to the ground like the ghosts of giant leeches, then one did not go out to lie in the sickly damp of a gulch. No, one got into a deep, soft, warm bed and slept like a little child.

Jesus Maria went to sleep at this point, Pilon and Pablo had to wake him up and give him a drink. Then Pilon spoke movingly of the mornings when one lay in one's warm nest until the sun was high enough to be of some use. One did not go shivering about in the dawn, beating one's hands to keep them from freezing.

As last Pilon and Pablo moved in on Jesus Maria as two silent hunting Airedales converge on their prey. They rented the use of their house to Jesus for fifteen dollars a month. He accepted happily. They shook hands all around. The jug came out of its weed. Pilon drank deeply, for he knew his hardest task was before him. He said it very gently and casually, while Jesus Maria was drinking out of the bottle.

"And you will pay only three dollars on account now."

Jesus Maria put down the bottle and looked at him in horror. "No," he exploded. "I made a promise to Arabella Gross to buy one of those little things. I will pay the rent when it is time."

Pilon knew he had blundered. "When you lay on that beach at Seaside, God floated the little rowboat to you. Do you think the good God did it so you could buy silk drawers for a cannery slut? No! God did it so you would not die from sleeping on the ground in the cold. Do you think God is interested in Arabella's breasts? And besides, we will take a two-dollar deposit," he want on. "For one dollar you can get one of those things big enough to hold the udders of a cow."

Still Jesus Maria protested.

"I will tell you," Pilon went on, "unless we pay Danny two dollars we shall all be turned into the street, and it will be your fault. You will have it on your soul that we sleep in ditches."

Under so many shots, coming from so many directions, Jesus Maria Corcoran succumbed. He passed two of the crumpled bills to Pilon.

And now the tense feeling went out of the room, and peace and quiet and a warm deep comradeship took its place. Pilon relaxed. Pablo took the comforter back to his own bed, and conversation sprang up.

"We must take this money to Danny."

Their first appetite over, they were sipping the wine out of fruit jars now.

"What is this great need Danny has for two dollars?" Jesus Maria asked.

Pilon grew confidential. His hands came into play like twin moths, restrained only by his wrists and arms from flying out the door. "Danny, our friend, is taking up with Mrs. Morales. Oh, don't think Danny is a fool. Mrs. Morales has two hundred dollars in the bank. Danny wants to buy a box of big candy for Mrs. Morales."

"Candy is not good for people," Pablo observed. "It makes their teeth ache."

"That is up to Danny," said Jesus Maria. "If he wants to ache Mrs. Morales' teeth, that is his business. What do we care for Mrs. Morales' teeth?"

A cloud of anxiety had settled on Pilon's face. "But," he interposed sternly, "if our friend Danny takes big candy to Mrs. Morales, he will eat some too. So it is the teeth of our friend that will ache."

Pablo shook his head anxiously. "It would be a bad thing if Danny's friends, on whom he depends, should bring about the aching of his teeth."

"What shall we do then?" asked Jesus Maria, although he and everyone else knew exactly what they would do. They waited politely, each one for another, to make the inevitable suggestion. The silence ran on. Pilon and Pablo felt that the suggestion should not come from them, since, by some lines of reasoning, they might be considered interested parties. Jesus Maria kept silence in duty to his hosts, but when their silence made him aware of what was required of him, he came instantly into the breach.

"A gallon of wine makes a nice present for a lady," he suggested in a musing tone.

Pilon and Pablo were astonished at his brilliance. "We can tell Danny it would be better for his teeth to get wine."

"But maybe Danny will pay no heed to our warning. If you give money to that Danny, you can't tell what he will do with it. He might buy candy anway, and then all of our time and worry are wasted."

They had made of Jesus Maria their feeder of lines, their opener of uneasy situations. "Maybe if we buy the wine ourselves and then give it to Danny there is no danger," he suggested.

"That is the thing," cried Pilon. "Now you have it."

Jesus Maria smiled modestly at being given credit for this. He felt that sooner or later this principle would have been promulgated by someone in the room.

Pablo poured the last little bit of wine into the fruit jars and they drank tiredly after their effort. It was a matter of pride to them that the idea had been arrived at so logically, and in such a philanthropic cause.

"Now I am hungry," said Pablo.

Pilon got up and went to the door and looked at the sun. "It is after noon," he said. "Pablo and I will go to Torrelli's to get the wine, while you, Jesus Maria, go into Monterey for something to eat. Maybe Mrs. Bruno, on the wharf, will give you a fish. Maybe you can get a little bread some place."

"I would rather go with you," said Jesus Maria, for he suspected that another sequence, just as logical, and just as inevitable, was beginning to grow in the heads of his friends.

"No, Jesus Maria," they said firmly. "It is now two o'clock, or about that. In an hour it will be three o'clock. Then we will meet you here and have something to eat. And maybe a little glass of wine to go with it."

Jesus Maria started for Monterey very reluctantly, but Pablo and Pilon walked happily down the hill toward Torrelli's house.

□   V   □

How Saint Francis turned the tide and put a gentle punishment
on Pilon and Pablo and Jesus Maria.

The afternoon came down as imperceptibly as age comes to a happy man. A little gold entered into the sunlight. The bay became bluer and dimpled with shore-wind ripples. Those lonely fishermen who believe that the fish bite at high tide left their rocks, and their places were taken by others, who were convinced that the fish bite at low tide.

At three o'clock the wind veered around and blew softly in from the bay, bringing all manner of fine kelp odors. The menders of nets in the vacant lots of Monterey put down their spindles and rolled cigarettes. Through the streets of the town, fat ladies, in whose eyes lay the weariness and the wisdom one sees so often in the eyes of pigs, were trundled in overpowered motorcars toward tea and gin fizzes at the Hotel del Monte. On Alvarado Street, Hugo Machado, the tailor, put a sign in his shop door, "Back in Five Minutes," and went home for the day. The pines waved slowly and voluptuously. The hens in a hundred hen yards complained in placid voices of their evil lot.

Pilon and Pablo sat under a pink rose of Castile in Torrelli's yard and quietly drank wine and let the afternoon grow on them as gradually as hair grows.

"It is just as well that we do not take two gallons of wine to Danny," said Pilon. "He is a man who knows little restraint in drinking."

Pablo agreed. "Danny looks healthy," he said, "but it is just such people that you hear of dying every day. Look at Rudolfo Kelling. Look at Angelina Vasquez."

Pilon's realism arose mildly to the surface. "Rudolfo fell into the quarry above Pacific Grove," he observed in mild reproof. "Angelina ate a bad can of fish. But," he continued kindly, "I know what you mean. And there are plenty of people who die through abuse of wine."

All Monterey began to make gradual instinctive preparations against the night. Mrs. Guttierez cut little chiles into her enchilada sauce. Rupert Hogan, the seller of spirits, added water to his gin and put it away to be served after midnight. And he shook a little pepper into his early evening whisky. At El Paseo dancing pavilion, Bullet Rosendale opened a carton of pretzels and arranged them like coarse brown lace on the big courtesy plates. The Palace Drug Company wound up its awnings. A little group of men who had spent the afternoon in front of the post office, greeting their friends, moved toward the station to see the Del Monte Express from San Francisco come in. The sea gulls arose glutted from the fish cannery beaches and flew toward the sea rocks. Lines of pelicans pounded doggedly over the water wherever they go to spend the night. On the purse-seine fishing boats the Italian men folded their nets over the big rollers. Little Miss Alma Alvarez, who was ninety years old, took her daily bouquet of pink geraniums to the Virgin on the outer wall of the church of San Carlos. In the neighboring and Methodist village of Pacific Grove the W.C.T.U. met for tea and discussion, listened while a little lady described the vice and prostitution of Monterey with energy and color. She thought a committee should visit these resorts to see exactly how terrible conditions really were. They had gone over the situation so often, and they needed new facts.

The sun went westering and took on an orange blush. Under the rose bush in Torrelli's yard Pablo and Pilon finished the first gallon of wine. Torrelli came out of his house and passed out of the yard without seeing his erstwhile customers. They waited until he was out of sight on the way to Monterey; whereupon Pablo and Pilon went into the house and, with conscious knowlege of their art, cozened their supper out of Mrs. Torrelli. They slapped her on the buttocks and called her a "Butter Duck" and took little courteous liberties with her person, and finally left her, flattered and slightly tousled.

Now it was evening in Monterey, and the lights went on. The windows glowed softly. The Monterey Theater began to spell "Children of Hell—Children of Hell" over and over with its lights. A small but fanatic group of men who believe that the fish bite in the evening took their places on the cold sea rocks. A little fog drifted through the streets and hung about the chimneys, and a fine smell of burning pine wood filled the air.

Pablo and Pilon went back to their rose bush and sat on the ground, but they were not as contented as they had been. "It is cool here," said Pilon, and he took a drink of wine to warm himself.

"We should go to our own house where it is warm," said Pablo.

"But there is no wood for the stove."

"Well," said Pablo, "if you will take the wine, I will meet you at the corner of the street." And he did, in about half an hour.

Pilon waited patiently, for he knew there are some things even one's friends cannot help with. While he waited, Pilon kept a watchful eye aimed down the street in the direction Torrelli had taken, for Torrelli was a forceful man to whom explanations, no matter how carefully considered nor how beautifully phrased, were as chaff. Moreover, Torrelli had, Pilon knew, the Italian's exaggerated and wholly quixotic ideal of marital relations. But Pilon watched in vain. No Torrelli came brutally home. In a little while Pablo joined him, and Pilon noticed with admiration and satisfaction that he carried an armful of pine sticks from Torrelli's wood pile.

Pablo made no comment on his recent adventure until they arrived at their house. Then he echoed Danny's words, "A lively one, that Butter Duck."

Pilon nodded his head in the dark and spoke with a quiet philosophy. "It is seldom that one finds all things at one market—wine, food, love, and firewood. We must remember Torrelli, Pablo, my friend. There is a man to know. We must take him a little present sometime."

Pilon built a roaring fire in the cast-iron stove. The two friends drew their chairs close and held their fruit jars to the heat to warm the wine a little. This night the light was holy, for Pablo had bought a candle to burn for San Francisco. Something had distracted his attention before that sacred plan had been consummated. Now the little wax taper burned beautifully in an abalone shell, and it threw the shadows of Pablo and Pilon on the wall and made them dance.

"I wonder where that Jesus Maria has gone," Pilon observed.

"He promised he would come back long ago," said Pablo. "I do not know whether that is a man to trust or not."

"Perhaps some little thing happened to detain him, Pablo. Jesus Maria, with that red beard and that kind heart, is nearly always in some kind of trouble with ladies."

"His is a grasshopper brain," said Pablo. "He sings and plays and jumps. There is no seriousness in him."

They had no great time to wait. They had barely started their second fruit jar of wine when Jesus Maria staggered in. He held each side of the door to steady himself. His shirt was torn and his face was bloody. One eye showed dark and ominous in the dancing candlelight.

Pablo and Pilon rushed to him. "Our friend! He is hurt. He has fallen from a cliff. He has been run over by a train!" There was not the slightest tone of satire, but Jesus Maria knew it for the most deadly kind of satire. He glared at them out of the eye which still had some volition in such matters.

"Both thy mothers were udderless cows," he remarked.

They fell back from him in horror at the vulgarity of the curse. "Our friend is wandering in his mind."

"The bone of his head has been broken."

"Pour him a little wine, Pablo."

Jesus Maria sat morosely by the fire and caressed his fruit jar, while his friends waited patiently for an explanation of the tragedy. But Jesus Maria seemed content to leave his friends in ignorance of the mishap. Although Pilon cleared his throat several times, and although Pablo looked at Jesus Maria with eyes which offered sympathy and understanding, Jesus Maria sat sullenly and glared at the stove and at the wine and at the blessed candle, until at length his discourteous reticence drove Pilon to an equal discourtesy. Afterward he did not see how he could have done it.

"Those soldiers again?" he asked.

"Yes," Jesus Maria growled. "This time they came too soon."

"There must have been twenty of them to have used thee so," Pablo observed, for the good of his friend's spirit. "Everyone knows thou art a bad man in a fight."

And Jesus Maria did look a little happier then.

"They were four," he said. "Arabella Gross helped too. She hit me on the head with a rock."

Pilon felt a wave of moral resentment rising within him. "I would not remind thee," he said severely, "how thy friends warned thee against this cannery slob." He wondered whether he had warned Jesus Maria, and seemed to remember that he had.

"These cheap white girls are vicious, my friend," Pablo boke in. "But did you give her that little thing that goes around?"

Jesus Maria reached into his pocket and brought out a crumpled pink rayon brassiere. "The time had not come," he said. "I was just getting to that point; and besides, we had not come into the woods yet."

Pilon sniffed the air and shook his head, but not without a certain sad tolerance. "Thou hast been drinking whisky."

Jesus Maria nodded.

"Where did this whisky come from?"

"From those soldiers," said Jesus Maria. "They had it under a culvert. Arabella knew it was there, and she told me. But those soldiers saw us with the bottle."

The story was gradually taking shape. Pilon liked it this way. It ruined a story to have it all come out quickly. The good story lay in half-told things which must be filled in out of the hearer's own experience. He took the pink brassiere from Jesus Maria's lap and ran his fingers over it, and his eyes went to musing. But in a moment they shone with a joyous light.

"I know," he cried. "We'll give this thing to Danny as a gift to Mrs. Morales."

Everyone except Jesus Maria applauded the idea, and he felt himself hopelessly outnumbered. Pablo, with a delicate understanding of the defeat, filled up Jesus Maria's fruit jar.

When a little time had passed, all three men began to smile. Pilon told a very funny story of a thing that had happened to his father. Good spirits returned to the company. They sang. Jesus Maria did a shuffling dance to prove he was not badly hurt. The wine went down and down in the jug, but before it was gone the three friends grew sleepy. Pilon and Pablo staggered off to bed, and Jesus Maria lay comfortably on the floor, beside the stove.

The fire died down. The house was filled with the deep sounds of slumber. In the front room only one thing moved. The blessed candle darted its little spear-pointed flame up and down with incredible rapidity.

Later, this little candle gave Pilon and Pablo and Jesus Maria some ethical things to think about. Simple small rod of wax with a string through it. Such a thing, you would say, is answerable to certain physical laws, and to none other. Its conduct, you would think, was guaranteed by certain principles of heat and combustion. You light the wick; the wax is caught and drawn up the wick; the candle burns a number of hours, goes out, and that is all. The incident is finished. In a little while the candle is forgotten, and then, of course, it has never existed.

Have you forgotten that this candle was blessed? That in a moment of conscience of perhaps pure religious exaltation, it was designed by Pablo for San Francisco? Here is the principle which takes the waxen rod outside the jurisdiction of physics.

The candle aimed its spear of light at heaven, like an artist who consumes himself to become divine. The candle grew shorter and shorter. A wind sprang up outside and sifted through the cracks in the wall. The candle sagged sideways. A silken calendar, bearing the face of a lovely girl looking out of the heart of an American Beauty rose, floated out a little distance from the wall. It came into the spear of flame. The fire licked up the silk and raced toward the ceiling. A loose piece of wallpaper caught fire and fell flaming into a bundle of newspapers.

In the sky, saints and martyrs looked on with set and unforgiving faces. The candle was blessed. It belonged to Saint Francis. Saint Francis will have a big candle in its place tonight.

If it were possible to judge depth of sleep, it would be said with justice that Pablo, whose culpable action was responsible for the fire, slept even more soundly than his two friends. But since there is no gauge, it can only be said that he slept very very soundly.

The flames ran up the walls and found little holes in the roof, and leaked through into the night. The house filled with the roar of fire. Jesus Maria turned over uneasily and began, in his sleep, to take off his coat. Then a flaming shingle dropped in his face. He leaped up with a cry, and stood shocked at the fire that raged about him.

"Pilon!" he shrieked. "Pablo!" He ran into the other room, pulled his friends out of bed and pushed them out of the house. Pilon still grasped the pink brassiere in his fingers.

They stood outside the burning house and looked in the open fire-curtained door. They could see the jug standing on the table with a good two inches of wine in it.

Pilon sensed the savage incipient heroism of Jesus Maria. "Do not do it," he shouted. "It must be lost in the fire as a punishment on us for leaving it."

The cry of sirens came to them, and the roar of trucks climbing the hill in second gear from the fire house in Monterey. The big red fire vehicles drew near and their searchlights played among the pine trunks.

Pilon turned hastily to Jesus Maria, "Run and tell Danny his house is burning. Run quickly, Jesus Maria."

"Why don't you go?"

"Listen," said Pilon. "Danny does not know you are one who rents his house. He may be a little bit angry with Pablo and me."

Jesus Maria grasped this logic and raced toward Danny's house. The house was dark. "Danny," Jesus Maria cried. "Danny, your house is on fire!" There was no answer. "Danny!" he cried again.

A window went up in Mrs. Morales' house next door. Danny sounded irritable. "What the hell do you want?"

"Your other house is on fire, the one Pablo and Pilon live in."

For a moment Danny did not answer. Then he demanded, "Is the fire department there?"

"Yes," cried Jesus Maria.

The whole sky was lighted up by now. The crackling of burning timbers could be heard. "Well," said Danny, "if the fire department can't do anything about it, what does Pilon expect me to do?"

Jesus Maria heard the window bang shut, and he turned and trotted back towards the fire. It was a bad time to call Danny, he knew, but then how could one tell? If Danny had missed the fire, he might have been angry. Jesus Maria was glad he had told him about it anyway. Now the responsibility lay on Mrs. Morales.

It was a little house, there was plenty of draft, the walls were perfectly dry. Perhaps not since old Chinatown had burned had there been such a quick and thorough fire. The men of the fire department took a look at the blazing walls and then began wetting the brush and the trees and the neighboring houses. In less than an hour the house was completely gone. Only then did the hoses play on the heap of ashes to put out the coals and the sparks.

Pilon and Pablo and Jesus Maria stood shoulder to shoulder and watched the whole thing. Half the population of Monterey and all the population of Tortilla Flat except Danny and Mrs. Morales stood happily about and watched the fire. At last, when it was all over, when only a cloud of steam arose from the black heap, Pilon turned silently away.

"Where goest thou?" Pablo called.

"I go," said Pilon, "to the woods to have out my sleep. I counsel you to come too. It will be well if Danny does not see us for a little while." They nodded gravely and followed him into the pine forest. "It is a lesson to us," said Pilon. "By this we learn never to leave wine in a house overnight."

"Next time," Pablo said hopelessly, "you will take it outside and someone will steal it."

□   VI   □

How three sinful men, through contrition, attained peace.
How Danny's Friends swore comradeship.

When the sun was clear of the pines, and the ground was warm, and the
night's dew was drying on the geranium leaves, Danny came out on his
porch to sit in the sunshine and to muse warmly of certain happenings. He
slipped off his shoes and wriggled his toes on the sun-warmed boards of the
porch. He had walked down earlier in the morning and viewed the square
black ashes and twisted plumbing which had been his other house. He had
indulged in a little conventional anger against careless friends, had mourned
for a moment over that transitory quality of earthly property which made
spiritual property so much more valuable. He had thought over the ruin of
his status as a man with a house to rent; and, all this clutter of necessary and
decent emotion having been satisfied and swept away, he had finally slipped
into his true emotion, one of relief that at least one of his burdens was removed.

"If it were still there, I would be covetous of the rent," he thought. "My
friends have been cool toward me because they owed me money. Now we can
be free and happy again."

But Danny knew he must discipline his friends a little, or they would
consider him soft. Therefore, as he sat on his porch, warding off flies with a
moving hand which conveyed more warning than threat to the flies, he went
over the things he must say to his friends before he allowed them back into
the corral of his affection. He must show them that he was not a man to be
imposed upon. But he yearned to get it over and to be once more that Danny
whom everyone loved, that Danny whom people sought out when they had a
gallon of wine or a piece of meat. As the owner of two houses he had been
considered rich, and he had missed a great many tidbits.

Pilon and Pablo and Jesus Maria Corcoran slept a long time on the pine
needles in the forest. It had been a night of terrible excitement, and they were
tired. But at length the sun shone into their faces with noonday ardor and
the ants walked on them, and two blue jays stood on the ground near by,
calling them all manner of sharp names.

What finished their sleep, though, was a picnic party which settled just
on the other side of the bush from them and opened a big lunch basket from
which moving smells drifted to Pilon and Pablo and Jesus Maria. They awakened; they sat up; and then the enormity of their situation burst upon them.

"How did the fire start?" asked Pablo plaintively, and no one knew.

"Perhaps," said Jesus Maria, "we had better go to another town for a while—to Watsonville or to Salinas; those are nice towns."

Pilon pulled the brassiere from his pocket and ran his fingers over its pink smoothness. And he held it to the sunlight and looked through it.

"That would only delay matters," he decided. "I think it would be better to go to Danny and confess our fault, like little children to a father. Then he can't say anything without being sorry. And besides, have we not this present for Mrs. Morales?"

His friends nodded agreement. Pilon's eyes strayed through the thick brush to the picnic party, and particularly to that huge lunch basket from which came the penetrating odors of deviled eggs. Pilon's nose wrinkled a little, like a rabbit's. He smiled in a quiet reverie. "I am going to walk, my friends. In a little while I will meet you at the quarry. Do not bring the basket if you can help it."

They watched sadly as Pilon got up and walked away, through the trees, in a direction at right angles to the picnic and the basket. Pablo and Jesus Maria were not surprised, a few moments later, to hear a dog bark, a rooster crow, high shrill laughter, the snarl of a wildcat, a little short scream and a cry for help; but the picnic party was surprised and fascinated. The two men and two women left their basket and trotted away toward these versatile sounds.

Pablo and Jesus Maria obeyed Pilon. They did not take the basket, but always afterward their hats and their shirts were stained with deviled eggs.

At about three o'clock in the afternoon the three penitents walked slowly toward Danny's house. Their arms were loaded with offerings of reconciliation: oranges and apples and bananas, bottles of olives and pickles, sandwiches of pressed ham, egg sandwiches, bottles of soda pop, a paper carton of potato salad, and a copy of the *Saturday Evening Post*.

Danny saw them coming, and he stood up and tried to remember the things he had to say. They lined up in front of him and hung their heads.

"Dogs of dogs," Danny called them, and "Thieves of decent folks' other house," and "Spawn of cuttlefish." He named their mothers cows and their fathers ancient sheep.

Pilon opened the bag he held and exposed the ham sandwiches. And Danny said he had no more trust in friends, that his faith had been frostbitten and his friendship trampled upon. And then he began to have a little trouble remembering, for Pablo had taken two deviled eggs out of his bosom. But Danny went back to the grand generation and criticized the virtue of its women and the potency of its men.

Pilon pulled the pink brassiere from his pocket and let it dangle listlessly from his fingers.

Danny forgot everything then. He sat down on the porch and his friends sat down and the packages came open. They ate to a point of discomfort. It was an hour later, when they reclined at ease on the porch, giving attention to little besides digestion, when Danny asked casually, as about some far-off object, "How did the fire start?"

"We don't know," Pilon explained. "We went to sleep, and then it started. Perhaps we have enemies."

"Perhaps," said Pablo devoutly, "perhaps God had a finger in it."

"Who can say what makes the good God act the way He does?" added Jesus Maria.

When Pilon handed over the brassiere and explained how it was a present for Mrs. Morales, Danny was reticent. He eyed the brassiere with some skepticism. His friends, he felt, were flattering Mrs. Morales. "That is not a woman to give presents to," he said finally. "Too often we are tied to women by the silk stockings we give them." He could not explain to his friends the coolness that had come to his relationship with Mrs. Morales since he was the owner of only one house; nor could he, in courtesy to Mrs. Morales, describe his own pleasure at that coolness. "I will put this little thing away," he said. "Some day it may be of use to someone."

When the evening came, and it was dark, they went into the house and built a fire of cones in the airtight stove. Danny, in proof of his forgiveness, brought out a quart of grappa and shared its fire with his friends.

They settled easily into the new life. "It is too bad Mrs. Morales' chickens are all dead," Pilon observed.

But even here was no bar to happiness. "She is going to buy two dozen new ones on Monday," said Danny.

Pilon smiled contentedly. "Those hens of Mrs. Soto's were no good," he said. "I told Mrs. Soto they needed oyster shells, but she paid no attention to me."

They drank the quart of grappa, and there was just enough to promote the sweetness of comradeship.

"It is good to have friends," said Danny. "How lonely it is in the world if there are no friends to sit with one and to share one's grappa."

"Or one's sandwiches," Pilon added quickly.

Pablo was not quite over his remorse, for he suspected the true state of celestial politics which had caused the burning of the house. "In all the world there are few friends like thee, Danny. It is not given to many to have such solace."

Before Danny sank completely under the waves of his friends, he sounded one warning. "I want all of you to keep out of my bed," he ordered. "That is one thing I must have to myself."

Although no one had mentioned it, each of the four knew they were all going to live in Danny's house.

Pilon sighed with pleasure. Gone was the worry of the rent; gone the responsibility of owing money. No longer was he a tenant, but a guest. In his mind he gave thanks for the burning of the other house.

"We will all be happy here, Danny," he said. "In the evenings we will sit by the fire and our friends will come in to visit. And sometimes maybe we will have a glass of wine to drink for friendship's sake."

Then Jesus Maria, in a frenzy of gratefulness, made a rash promise. It was the grappa that did it, and the night of the fire, and all the deviled eggs. He felt that he had received great gifts, and he wanted to distribute a gift. "It shall be our burden and our duty to see that there is always food in the house of Danny," he declaimed. "Never shall our friend go hungry."

Pilon and Pablo looked up in alarm, but the thing was said; a beautiful and generous thing. No man could with impunity destroy it. Even Jesus Maria understood, after it was said, the magnitude of his statement. They could only hope that Danny would forget it.

"For," Pilon mused to himself, "if this promise were enforced, it would be worse then rent. It would be slavery."

"We swear it, Danny!" he said.

They sat about the stove with tears in their eyes, and their love for one another was almost unbearable.

Pablo wiped his wet eyes with the back of his hand, and he echoed Pilon's remark. "We shall be very happy living here," he said.

□ **VII** □

How Danny's Friends became a force for Good. How they
succored the poor Pirate.

A great many people saw the Pirate every day, and some laughed at him, and some pitied him; but no one knew him very well, and no one interfered with him. He was a huge, broad man, with a tremendous black and bushy beard. He wore jeans and a blue shirt, and he had no hat. In town he wore shoes. There was a shrinking in the Pirate's eyes when he confronted any grown person, the secret look of an animal that would like to run away if it dared turn its back long enough. Because of this expression, the paisanos of Monterey knew that his head had not grown up with the rest of his body. They called him the Pirate because of his beard. Every day people saw him wheeling his barrow of pitchwood about the streets until he sold the load. And always in a cluster at his heels walked his five dogs.

Enrique was rather houndish in appearance, although his tail was bushy. Pajarito was brown and curly, and these were the only two things you see about him. Rudolph was a dog of whom passers-by said, "He is an American dog." Fluff was a Pug and Señor Alec Thompson seemed to be a kind of an Airedale. They walked in a squad behind the Pirate, very respectful toward him, and very solicitous for his happiness. When he sat down to rest from wheeling his barrow, they all tried to sit on his lap and have their ears scratched.

Some people had seen the Pirate early in the morning on Alvarado Street; some had seen him cutting pitchwood; some knew he sold kindling; but no one except Pilon knew everything the Pirate did. Pilon knew everybody and everything about everybody.

The Pirate lived in a deserted chicken house in the yard of a deserted house on Tortilla Flat. He would have thought it presumptuous to live in the house itself. The dogs lived around and on top of him, and the Pirate liked this, for his dogs kept him warm on the coldest nights. If his feet were cold, he had only to put them against the belly of Señor Alec Thompson. The chicken house was so low that the Pirate had to crawl in on his hands and knees.

Early every morning, well before daylight, the Pirate crawled out of his chicken house, and the dogs followed him, roughing their coats and sneezing in the cold air. Then the party went down to Monterey and worked along an alley. Four or five restaurants had their back doors on this alley. The Pirate entered each one, into a restaurant kitchen, warm and smelling of food. Grumbling cooks put packages of scraps in his hands at each place. They didn't know why they did it.

When the Pirate had visited each back door and had his arms full of parcels, he walked back up the hill to Munroe Street and entered a vacant lot, and the dogs excitedly swarmed about him. Then he opened the parcels and fed the dogs. For himself he took bread or a piece of meat out of each package, but he did not pick the best for himself. The dogs sat down about him, licking their lips nervously and shifting their feet while they waited for food. They never fought over it, and that was a surprising thing. The Pirate's dogs never fought each other, but they fought everything else that wandered the streets of Monterey on four legs. It was a fine thing to see the pack of five, hunting fox-terriers and Pomeranians like rabbits.

Daylight had come by the time the meal was over. The Pirate sat on the ground and watched the sky turn blue with the morning. Below him he saw the schooners put out to sea with deckloads of lumber. He heard the bell buoy ringing sweetly off China Point. The dogs sat about him and gnawed at the bones. The Pirate seemed to be listening to the day rather than seeing it, for while his eyes did not move about, there was an air of attentiveness in him. His big hands strayed to the dogs and his fingers worked soothingly in the coarse hair. After about half an hour the Pirate went to the corner of the vacant lot, threw the covering sacks from his wheelbarrow, and dug up his ax out of the ground where he buried it every evening. Then up the hill he pushed the barrow, and into the woods, until he found a dead tree, full of pitch. By noon he had a load of fine kindling; and then, still followed by his dogs, he walked the streets until he had sold the load for twenty-five cents.

It was possible to observe all this, but what he did with the quarter, no one could tell. He never spent it. In the night, guarded from danger by his dogs, he went into the woods and hid the day's quarter with hundreds of others. Somewhere he had a great hoard of money.

Pilon, that acute man, from whom no details of the life of his fellows escaped, and who was doubly delighted to come upon those secrets that nestled deep in the brains of his acquaintances, discovered the Pirate's hoard by a logical process. Pilon reasoned thus: "Every day that Pirate has a quarter. If it is two dimes and a nickel, he takes it to a store and gets a twenty-five cent piece. He never spends any money at all. Therefore, he must be hiding it."

Pilon tired to compute the amount of the treasure. For years the Pirate had been living in this way. Six days a week he cut pitchwood, and on Sundays he went to church. His clothes he got from the back doors of houses, his food at the back doors of restaurants. Pilon puzzled with the great numbers for a while, and then gave it up. "The Pirate must have at least a hundred dollars," he thought.

For a long time Pilon had considered these things. But it was only after the foolish and enthusiastic promise to feed Danny that the thought of the Pirate's hoard gained any personal significance to Pilon.

Before he approached the subject at all, Pilon put his mind through a long and stunning preparation. He felt very sorry for the Pirate. "Poor little half-formed one," he said to himself. "God did not give him all the brain he should have. That poor little Pirate cannot look after himself. For see, he lives in filth in an old chicken house. He feeds upon scraps fit only for his dogs. His clothes are thin and ragged. And because his brain is not a good one, he hides his money."

Now, with his groundwork of pity laid, Pilon moved on to his solution. "Would it not be a thing of merit," he thought, "to do those things for him which he cannot do for himself? To buy him warm clothes, to feed him food fit for a human? But," he reminded himself, "I have no money to do these things, although they lie squirming in my heart. How can these charitable things be accomplished?"

Now he was getting somewhere. Like the cat, which during a long hour closes in on a sparrow, Pilon was ready for his pounce. "I have it!" his brain cried. "It is like this: The Pirate has money, but he has not the brain to use it.

I have the brain! I will offer my brain to his use. I will give freely of my mind. That shall be my charity toward this poor little half-made man."

It was one of the finest structures Pilon had ever built. The urge of the artist to show his work to an audience came upon him. "I will tell it to Pablo," he thought. But he wondered whether he would dare do such a thing. Was Pablo strictly honest? Would he not want to divert some of this money to his own ends? Pilon decided not to take the chance, right then, anyway.

It is astounding to find that the belly of every black and evil thing is as white as snow. And it is saddening to discover how the concealed parts of angels are leprous. Honor and peace to Pilon, for he had discovered how to uncover and to disclose to the world the good that lay in every evil thing. Nor was he blind, as so many saints are, to the evil of good things. It must be admitted with sadness that Pilon had neither the stupidity, the self-righteousness, nor the greediness for reward ever to become a saint. Enough for Pilon to do good and to be rewarded by the glow of human brotherhood accomplished.

That very night he paid a visit to the chicken house where the Pirate lived with his dogs. Danny, Pablo, and Jesus Maria, sitting by the stove, saw him go and said nothing. For, they thought delicately, either a vapor of love had been wafted to Pilon or else he knew where he could get a little wine. In either case it was none of their business until he told them about it.

It was well after dark, but Pilon had a candle in his pocket, for it might be a good thing to watch the expression on the Pirate's face while he talked. And Pilon had a big round sugar cookie in a bag, that Susie Francisco, who worked in a bakery, had given him in return for a formula for getting the love of Charlie Guzman. Charlie was a Postal Telegraph messenger and rode a motorcycle; and Susie had a man's cap to put on backward in case Charlie should ever ask her to ride with him. Pilon thought the Pirate might like the sugar cookie.

The night was very dark. Pilon picked his way along a narrow street bordered with vacant lots and with weedgrown, neglected gardens.

Galvez' bad bulldog came snarling out of Galvez' yard, and Pilon spoke soothing compliments to him. "Nice dog," he said gently, and "Pretty dog," both of them palpable lies. They impressed the bulldog, however, for he retired into Galvez' yard.

Pilon came at last to the vacant property where the Pirate lived. And now he knew he must be careful, for the Pirate's dogs, if they suspected ill of anyone toward their master, were known to become defending furies. As Pilon stepped into the yard, he heard deep and threatening growls from the chicken house.

"Pirate," he called, "it is thy good friend Pilon, come to talk with thee."

There was silence. The dogs stopped growling.

"Pirate, it is only Pilon."

A deep surly voice answered him, "Go away. I am sleeping now. The dogs are sleeping. It is dark, Pilon. Go to bed."

"I have a candle in my pocket," Pilon called. "It will make a light as bright as day in thy dark house. I have a big sugar cookie for thee too."

A faint scuffling sounded in the chicken house. "Come then," the Pirate said. "I will tell the dogs it is all right."

As he advanced through the weeds, Pilon could hear the Pirate talking softly to his dogs, explaining to them that it was only Pilon, who would do no harm. Pilon bent over in front of the dark doorway and scratched a match and lighted his candle.

The Pirate was seated on the dirt floor, and his dogs were all about him. Enrique growled and had to be reassured again. "That one is not so wise as the others," the Pirate said pleasantly. His eyes were the pleased eyes of an amused child. When he smiled his big white teeth glistened in the candle-light.

Pilon held out the bag. "It is a fine cake for you," he said.

The Pirate took the bag and looked into it; then he smiled delightedly and brought out the cookie. The dogs all grinned and faced him, and moved their feet and licked their lips. The Pirate broke his cookie into seven pieces. The first he gave to Pilon, who was his guest. "Now, Enrique," he said. "Now Fluff. Now Señor Alec Thompson." Each dog received his piece and gulped it and looked for more. Last, the Pirate ate his and held up his hands to the dogs. "No more, you see," he told them. Immediately the dogs lay down about him.

Pilon sat on the floor and stood the candle on the ground in front of him. The Pirate questioned him self-consciously with his eyes. Pilon sat silently, to let many questions pass through the Pirate's head. At length he said, "Thou art a worry to thy friends."

The Pirate's eyes filled with astonishment. "I? To my friends? What friends?"

Pilon softened his voice. "Thou hast many friends who think of thee. They do not come to see thee because thou art proud. They think it might hurt thy pride to have them see thee living in this chicken house, clothed in rags, eating garbage with thy dogs. But these friends of thine worry for fear the bad life may make thee ill."

The Pirate was following his words with breathless astonishment, and his brain tried to realize these new things he was hearing. It did not occur to him to doubt them, since Pilon was saying them. "I have all these friends?" he said in wonder. "And I did not know it. And I am a worry to those friends. I did not know, Pilon. I would not have worried them if I had known." He swallowed to clear his throat of emotion. "You see, Pilon, the dogs like it here. And I like it because of them. I did not think I was a worry to my friends." Tears came into the Pirate's eyes.

"Nevertheless," Pilon said, "thy mode of living keeps all thy friends uneasy."

The Pirate looked down at the ground and tried to think clearly, but as always, when he attempted to cope with a problem, his brain grew gray and no help came from it, but only a feeling of helplessness. He looked to his dogs for protection, but they had gone back to sleep, for it was none of their business. And then he looked earnestly into Pilon's eyes. "You must tell me what to do, Pilon. I did not know these things."

It was too easy. Pilon was a little ashamed that it should be so easy. He hesitated; nearly gave it up; but then he knew he would be angry with himself if he did. "Thy friends are poor," he said. "They would like to help thee, but they have no money. If thou hast money hidden, bring it out into the open. Buy thyself some clothes. Eat food that is not cast out by other people. Bring thy money out of its hiding place, Pirate."

Pilon had been looking closely at the Pirate's face while he spoke. He saw the eyes droop with suspicion and then with sullenness. In a moment Pilon knew two things certainly; first, that the Pirate had money hidden; and second, that it was not going to be easy to get at it. He was pleased at the latter fact. The Pirate had become a problem in tactics such as Pilon enjoyed.

Now the Pirate was looking at him again, and in his eyes was cunning, and on top of that, a studied ingenuousness. "I have no money anywhere," he said.

"But every day, my friend, I have seen thee get a quarter for thy wood, and never have I seen thee spend it."

This time the Pirate's brain came to his rescue. "I give it to a poor old woman," he said. "I have no money anywhere." And with his tone he closed a door tightly on the subject.

"So it must be guile," Pilon thought. So those gifts, that in him were so sharpened, must be called into play. He stood up and lifted his candle. "I only thought to tell thee how thy friends worry," he said critically. "If thou wilt not try to help, I can do nothing for thee."

The sweetness came back into the Pirate's eyes. "Tell them I am healthy," he begged. "Tell my friends to come and see me. I will not be too proud. I will be glad to see them any time. Will thou tell them for me, Pilon?"

"I will tell them," Pilon said ungraciously. "But thy friends will not be pleased when they see thou dost nothing to relieve their minds." Pilon blew out his candle and went away into the darkness. He knew that the Pirate would never tell where his hoard was. It must be found by stealth, taken by force, and then all the good things given to the Pirate. It was the only way.

And so Pilon set himself to watch the Pirate. He followed him into the forest when he went to cut kindlings. He lay in wait outside the chicken house at night. He talked to him long and earnestly, and nothing came of it. The treasure was as far from discovery as ever. Either it lay buried in the chicken house or it was hidden deep in the forest and was only visited at night.

The long and fruitless vigils wore out the patience of Pilon. He knew he must have help and advice. And who could better give it than those comrades, Danny, Pablo, and Jesus Maria? Who could be so stealthy, so guileful? Who could melt to kindness with more ease?

Pilon took them into his confidence; but first he prepared them, as he had prepared himself: The Pirate's poverty, his helplessness, and finally—the solution. When he came to the solution, his friends were in a philanthropic frenzy. They applauded him. Their faces shone with kindness. Pablo thought there might be well over a hundred dollars in the hoard.

When their joy had settled to a working enthusiasm, they came to plans.

"We must watch him," Pablo said.

"But I have watched him," Pilon argued. "It must be that he creeps off in the night, and then one cannot follow too close, for his dogs guard him like devils. It is not going to be so easy."

"You've used every argument?" Danny asked.

"Yes. Every one."

In the end it was Jesus Maria, that humane man, who found the way out. "It is difficult while he lives in that chicken house," he said. "But suppose he lived here, with us? Either his silence would break under our kindness, or else it would be easier to know when he goes out at night."

The friends gave a good deal of thought to this suggestion. "Sometimes the things he gets out of restaurants are nearly new," mused Pablo. "I have seen him with a steak out of which only a little was missing."

"It might be as much as two hundred dollars," said Pilon.

Danny offered an objection. "But those dogs—he would bring his dogs with him."

"They are good dogs," said Pilon. "They obey him exactly. You may draw a line around a corner and say, 'Keep thy dogs within this line.' He will tell them, and those dogs will stay."

"I saw the Pirate one morning, and he had nearly half a cake, just a little bit damp with coffee," said Pablo.

The question settled itself. The house resolved itself into a committee, and the committee visited the Pirate.

It was a crowded place, that chicken house, when they all got inside. The Pirate tried to disguise his happiness with a gruff tone.

"The weather has been bad," he said socially. And, "You wouldn't believe, maybe, that I found a tick as big as a pigeon's egg on Rudolph's neck."

And he spoke disparagingly of his home, as a host should. "It is too small," he said. "It is not a fit place for one's friends to come. But it is warm and snug, especially for the dogs."

Then Pilon spoke. He told the Pirate that worry was killing his friends; but if he would go to live with them, then they could sleep again, with their minds at ease.

It was a very great shock to the Pirate. He looked at his hands. And he looked to his dogs for comfort, but they would not meet his glance. At last he wiped the happiness from his eyes with the back of his hand, and he wiped his hand on his big black beard.

"And the dogs?" he asked softly. "You want the dogs too? Are you friends of the dogs?"

Pilon nodded. "Yes, the dogs too. There will be a whole corner set aside for the dogs."

The Pirate had a great deal of pride. He was afraid he might not conduct himself well. "Go away now," he said pleadingly. "Go home now. Tomorrow I will come."

His friends knew how he felt. They crawled out of the door and left him alone.

"He will be happy with us, that one," said Jesus Maria.

"Poor little lonely man," Danny added. "If I had known, I would have asked him long ago, even if he had no treasure."

A flame of joy burned in all of them.

They settled soon into the new relationship. Danny, with a piece of blue chalk, drew a segment of a circle, enclosing a corner of the living room, and that was where the dogs must stay when they were in the house. The Pirate slept in that corner too, with the dogs.

The house was beginning to be a little crowded, with five men and five dogs; but from the first Danny and his friends realized that their invitation to the Pirate had been inspired by that weary and anxious angel who guarded their destinies and protected them from evil.

Every morning, long before his friends were awake, the Pirate arose from his corner, and, followed by his dogs, he made the rounds of the restaurants and the wharves. He was one of those for whom everyone feels a kindliness. His packages grew larger. The paisanos received his bounty and made use of it: fresh fish, half pies, untouched loaves of stale bread, meat that required only a little soda to take the green out. They began really to live.

And their acceptance of his gifts touched the Pirate more deeply than anything they could have done for him. There was a light of worship in his eyes as he watched them eat the food he brought.

In the evening, when they sat about the stove and discussed the doings of Tortilla Flat with the lazy voices of fed gods, the Pirate's eyes darted from mouth to mouth, and his own lips moved, whispering again the words his friends said. The dogs pressed in about him jealously.

These were his friends, he told himself in the night, when the house was dark, when the dogs snuggled close to him so that all might be warm. These men loved him so much that it worried them to have him live alone. The Pirate had often to repeat this to himself, for it was an astounding thing, an unbelievable thing. His wheelbarrow stood in Danny's yard now, and every day he cut his pitchwood and sold it. But so afraid was the Pirate that he might miss some word his friends said in the evening, might not be there to absorb some stream of the warm companionship, that he had not visited his hoard for several days to put the new coins there.

His friends were kind to him. They treated him with a sweet courtesy; but always there was some eye open and upon him. When he wheeled his barrow into the woods, one of the friends walked with him, and sat on a log while he worked. When he went into the gulch, the last thing at night, Danny or Pablo or Pilon or Jesus Maria kept him company. And in the night he must have been very quiet to have crept out without a shadow behind him.

For a week the friends merely watched the Pirate. But at last the inactivity tired them. Direct action was out of the question, they knew. And so one evening the subject of desirability of hiding one's money came up for discussion.

Pilon began it. "I had an uncle, a regular miser, and he hid his gold in the woods. And one time he went to look at it, and it was gone. Someone had found it and stolen it. He was an old man, then, and all his money was gone, and he hanged himself." Pilon noticed with some satisfaction the look of apprehension that came upon the Pirate's face.

Danny noticed it too; and he continued, "The *viejo*, my grandfather, who owned this house, also buried money. I do not know how much, but he was reputed a rich man, so there must have been three or four hundred dollars. The *viejo* dug a deep hole and put his money in it, and then he covered it up, and then he strewed pine needles over the ground until he thought no one could see that anything had been done there. But when he went back, the hole was open, and the money was gone."

The Pirate's lips followed the words. A look of terror had come into his face. His fingers picked among the neck hairs of Señor Alec Thompson. The friends exchanged a glance and dropped the subject for the time being. They turned to the love life of Cornelia Ruiz.

In the night the Pirate crept out of the house, and the dogs crept after him; and Pilon crept after all of them. The Pirate went swiftly into the forest, leaping with sure feet over logs and brush. Pilon floundered behind him. But when they had gone at least two miles, Pilon was winded, and torn by vines.

He paused to rest a moment; and then he realized that all sounds ahead of him had ceased. He waited and listened and crept about, but the Pirate had disappeared.

After two hours Pilon went back again, slowly and tiredly. There was the Pirate in the house, fast asleep among his dogs. The dogs lifted their heads when Pilon entered, and Pilon thought they smiled satirically at him for a moment.

A conference took place in the gulch the next morning.

"It is not possible to follow him," Pilon reported. "He vanished. He sees in the dark. He knows every tree in the forest. We must find some other way."

"Perhaps one is not enough," Pablo suggested. "If all of us should follow him, then one might not lose track of him."

"We will talk again tonight," said Jesus Maria, "only worse. A lady I know is going to give me a little wine," he added modestly. "Maybe if the Pirate has a little wine in him, he will not disappear so easily." So it was left.

Jesus Maria's lady gave him a whole gallon of wine. What could compare with the Pirate's delight that evening when a fruit jar of wine was put into his hand, when he sat with his friends and sipped his wine and listened to the talk? Such joy had come rarely into the Pirate's life. He wished he might clasp these dear people to his breast and tell them how much he loved them. But that was not a thing he could do, for they might think he was drunk. He wished he could do some tremendous thing to show them his love.

"We spoke last night of burying money," said Pilon. "Today I remembered a cousin of mine, a clever man. If anyone in the world could hide money where it would never be found, he could do it. So he took his money and hid it. Perhaps you have seen him, that poor little one who crawls about the wharf and begs fish heads to make soup of. That is my cousin. Someone stole his buried money."

The worry came back into the Pirate's face.

Story topped story, and in each one all manner of evil dogged the footsteps of those who hid their money.

"It is better to keep one's money close, to spend some now and then, to give a little to one's friends," Danny finished.

They had been watching the Pirate narrowly, and in the middle of the worst story they had seen the worry go from his face, and a smile of relief take its place. Now he sipped his wine and his eyes glittered with joy.

The friends were in despair. All their plans had failed. They were sick at heart. After all their goodness and their charity, this had happened. The Pirate had in some way escaped the good they had intended to confer upon him. They finished their wine and went moodily to bed.

Few things could happen in the night without Pilon's knowledge. His ears remained open while the rest of him slept. He heard the stealthy exit of the Pirate and his dogs from the house. He leaped to awaken his friends, and in a moment the four were following the Pirate in the direction of the forest. It was very dark when they entered the pine forest. The four friends ran into trees, tripped on berry vines; but for a long time they could hear the Pirate marching on ahead of them. They followed as far as Pilon had followed the night before, and then, suddenly, silence, and the whispering forest and the vague night wind. They combed the woods and the brush patches, but the Pirate had disappeared again.

At last, cold and disconsolate, they came together and trudged wearily back toward Monterey. The dawn came before they got back. The sun was already shining on the bay. The smoke of the morning fires arose to them out of Monterey.

The Pirate walked out on the porch to greet them, and his face was happy. They passed him sullenly and filed into the living room. There on the table lay a large canvas bag.

The Pirate followed them in. "I lied to thee, Pilon," he said. "I told thee I had no money, for I was afraid. I did not know about my friends then. You have told how hidden money is so often stolen, and I am afraid again. Only last night did a way out come to me. My money will be safe with my friends. No one can steal it if my friends guard it for me. You would not believe it, but the last two nights someone followed me into the forest to steal my money."

Terrible as the blow was, Pilon, that clever man, tried to escape it. "Before this money is put into our hands, maybe you would like to take some out," he suggested smoothly.

The Pirate shook his head. "No: I cannot do that. It is promised. I have nearly a thousand two-bitses. When I have a thousand I will buy a gold candlestick for San Francisco de Assisi.

"Once I had a nice dog, and that dog was sick; and I promised a gold candlestick of one thousand days if that dog would get well. And," he spread his great hands, "that dog got well."

"Is it one of these dogs?" Pilon demanded.

"No," said the Pirate. "A truck ran over him a little later."

So it was over, all hope of diverting the money. Danny and Pablo morosely lifted the heavy bag of silver quarters, took it in the other room, and put it under the pillow of Danny's bed. In time they would take a certain pleasure in the knowledge that this money lay under the pillow, but now their defeat was bitter. There was nothing in the world they could do about it. Their chance had come, and it had gone.

The Pirate stood before them, and there were tears of happiness in his eyes, for he had proved his love for his friends.

"To think," he said, "all those years I lay in that chicken house, and I did not know any pleasure. But now," he added, "oh, now I am very happy."

□   VIII   □

How Danny's Friends sought mystic treasure on Saint Andrew's Eve.
How Pilon found it and later how a pair of
serge pants changed ownership twice.

If he had been a hero, the Portagee would have spent a miserable time in the army. The fact that he was Big Joe Portagee, with a decent training in the Monterey jail, not only saved him the misery of patriotism thwarted, but solidified his conviction that as a man's days are rightly devoted half to sleeping and half to waking, so a man's years are rightly spent half in jail and half out. Of the duration of the war, Joe Portagee spent considerably more time in jail than out.

In civilian life one is punished for things one does; but army codes add a new principle to this—they punish a man for things he does not do. Joe Portagee never did figure this out. He didn't clean his rifle; he didn't shave; and once or twice, on leave, he didn't come back. Coupled with these shortcomings was a propensity Big Joe had for genial argument when he was taken to task.

Ordinarily he spent half his time in jail; of two years in the army, he spent eighteen months in jail. And he was far from satisfied with prison life in the army. In the Monterey jail he was accustomed to ease and companionship. In the army he found only work. In Monterey only one charge was ever brought against him: Drunk and Disorderly Conduct. The charges in the army bewildered him so completely that the effect on his mind was probably permanent.

When the war was over, and all the troops were disbanded, Big Joe still had six months' sentence to serve. The charge had been: "Being drunk on duty. Striking a sergeant with a kerosene can. Denying his identity (he couldn't remember it, so he denied everything). Stealing two gallons of cooked beans. And going A.W.O.L. on the Major's horse."

If the Armistice had not already been signed, Big Joe would probably have been shot. He came home to Monterey long after the other veterans had arrived and had eaten up all the sweets of victory.

When Big Joe swung down from the train, he was dressed in an army overcoat and tunic and a pair of blue serge trousers.

The town hadn't changed much, except for prohibition; and prohibition hadn't changed Torrelli's. Joe traded his overcoat for a gallon of wine and went out to find his friends.

True friends he found none that night, but in Monterey he found no lack of those vile and false harpies and pimps who are ever ready to lead men into the pit. Joe, who was not very moral, had no revulsion for the pit; he liked it.

Before very many hours had passed, his wine was gone, and he had no money; and then the harpies tried to get Joe out of the pit, and he wouldn't go. He was comfortable there.

When they tried to eject him by force, Big Joe, with a just and terrible resentment, broke all the furniture and all the windows, sent half-clothed girls screaming into the night; and then, as an afterthought, set fire to the house. It was not a safe thing to lead Joe into temptation; he had no resistance to it at all.

A policeman finally interfered and took him in hand. The Portagee sighed happily. He was home again.

After a short and juryless trial, in which he was sentenced to thirty days, Joe lay luxuriously on his leather cot and slept heavily for one-tenth of his sentence.

The Portagee liked the Monterey jail. It was a place to meet people. If he stayed there long enough, all his friends were in and out. The time passed quickly. He was a little sad when he had to go, but his sadness was tempered with the knowledge that it was very easy to get back again.

He would have liked to go into the pit again, but he had no money and no wine. He combed the streets for his old friends, Pilon and Danny and Pablo, and could not find them. The police sergeant said he hadn't booked them for a long time.

"They must be dead," said the Portagee.

He wandered sadly to Torrelli's, but Torrelli was not friendly toward men who had neither money nor barterable property, and he gave Big Joe little solace; but Torrelli did say that Danny had inherited a house on Tortilla Flat, and that all his friends lived there with him.

Affection and a desire to see his friends came to Big Joe. In the evening he wandered up toward Tortilla Flat to find Danny and Pilon. It was dusk as he walked up the street, and on the way he met Pilon, hurrying by in a businesslike way.

"Ai, Pilon. I was just coming to see you."

"Hello, Joe Portagee." Pilon was brusque. "Where you been?"

"In the army," said Joe.

Pilon's mind was not on the meeting. "I have to go on."

"I will go with you," said Joe.

Pilon stopped and surveyed him. "Don't you remember what night it is?" he asked.

"No. What is it?"

"It is Saint Andrew's Eve."

Then the Portagee knew; for this was the night when every paisano who wasn't in jail wandered restlessly through the forest. This was the night when all buried treasure sent up a faint phosphorescent glow through the ground. There was plenty of treasure in the woods too. Monterey had been invaded many times in two hundred years, and each time valuables had been hidden in the earth.

The night was clear. Pilon had emerged from his hard daily shell, as he did now and then. He was the idealist tonight, the giver of gifts. This night he was engaged in a mission of kindness.

"You may come with me, Big Joe Portagee, but if we find any treasure I must decide what to do with it. If you do not agree, you can go by yourself and look for your own treasure."

Big Joe was not an expert at directing his own efforts. "I will go with you, Pilon," he said. "I don't care about the treasure."

The night came down as they walked into the forest. Their feet found the pine-needle beds. Now Pilon knew it for a perfect night. A high fog covered the sky, and behind it the moon shone, so that the forest was filled with a gauze-like light. There was none of the sharp outline we think of as reality. The tree trunks were not black columns of wood, but soft and unsubstantial shadows. The patches of brush were formless and shifting in the queer light. Ghosts could walk freely tonight, without fear of the disbelief of men; for this night was haunted, and it would be an insensitive man who did not know it.

Now and then Pilon and Big Joe passed other searchers who wandered restlessly, zigzagging among the pines. Their heads were down, and they moved silently and passed no greeting. Who could say whether all of them were really living men? Joe and Pilon knew that some were shades of those old folk who had buried the treasures; and who, on Saint Andrew's Eve, wandered back to the earth to see that their gold was undisturbed. Pilon wore his saint's medallion, hung around his neck, outside his clothes; so he had no fear of the spirits. Big Joe walked with his fingers crossed in the Holy Sign. Although they might be frightened, they knew they had protection more than adequate to cope with the unearthly night.

The wind rose as they walked, and drove the fog across the pale moon like a thin wash of gray water color. The moving fog gave shifting form to the forest, so that every tree crept stealthily along and the bushes moved soundlessly, like great dark cats. The treetops in the wind talked huskily, told fortunes and foretold deaths. Pilon knew it was not good to listen to the talking of the trees. No good ever came of knowing the future; and besides, this whispering was unholy. He turned the attention of his ears from the trees' talking.

He began a zigzag path through the forest, and Big Joe walked beside him like a great alert dog. Lone silent men passed them and went on without a greeting; and the dead passed them noiselessly, and went on without a greeting.

The fog siren began its screaming on the Point, far below them; and it wailed its sorrow for all the good ships that had drowned on the iron reef, and for all those others that would sometime die there.

Pilon shuddered and felt cold, although the night was warm. He whispered a Hail Mary under his breath.

They passed a gray man who walked with his head down and who gave them no greeting.

An hour went by, and still Pilon and Big Joe wandered as restlessly as the dead who crowded the night.

Suddenly Pilon stopped. His hand found Big Joe's arm. "Do you see?" he whispered.

"Where?"

"Right ahead there."

"Yes—I think so."

It seemed to Pilon that he could see a soft pillar of blue light that shone out of the ground ten yards ahead of him.

"Big Joe," he whispered, "find two sticks about three or four feet long. I do not want to look away. I might lose it."

He stood like a pointing dog while Big Joe scurried off to find the sticks. Pilon heard him break two small dead limbs from a pine tree. And he heard the snaps as Big Joe broke the twigs from his sticks. And still Pilon stared at the pale shaft of nebulous light. So faint it was that sometimes it seemed to disappear altogether. Sometimes he was not sure he saw it at all. He did not move his eyes when Big Joe put the sticks in his hands. Pilon crossed the sticks at right angles and advanced slowly, holding the cross in front of him. As he came close, the light seemed to fade away, but he saw where it had come from, a perfectly round depression in the pine needles.

Pilon laid his cross over the depression, and he said, "All that lies here is mine by discovery. Go away, all evil spirits. Go away, spirits of men who buried this treasure, *In Nomen Patris et Filius et Spiritu Sancti,*" and then he heaved a great sigh and sat down on the ground.

"We have found it, oh my friend, Big Joe," he cried. "For many years I have looked, and now I have found it."

"Let's dig," said Big Joe.

But Pilon shook his head impatiently. "When all the spirits are free? When even to be here is dangerous? You are a fool, Big Joe. We will sit here until morning; and then we will mark the place, and tomorrow night we will dig. No one else can see the light now that we have covered it with the cross. Tomorrow night there will be no danger."

The night seemed more fearful now that they sat in the pine needles, but the cross sent out a warmth of holiness and safety, like a little bonfire on the ground. Like a fire, however, it only warmed the front of them. Their backs were to the cold and evil things that wandered about in the forest.

Pilon got up and drew a big circle around the whole place, and he was inside when he closed the circle. "Let no evil thing cross this line, in the Name of the Most Holy Jesus," he chanted. Then he sat down again. Both he and Big Joe felt better. They could hear the muffled footsteps of the weary, wandering ghosts; they could see the little lights that glowed from the transparent forms as they walked by; but their protecting line was impregnable. Nothing bad from this world or from any other world could cross into the circle.

"What are you going to do with the money?" Big Joe asked.

Pilon looked at him in contempt. "You have never looked for treasure, Big Joe Portagee, for you do not know how to go about it. I cannot keep this treasure for myself. If I go after it intending to keep it, then the treasure will dig itself down and down like a clam in the sand, and I shall never find it. No, that is not the way. I am digging this treasure for Danny."

All the idealism in Pilon came out then. He told Big Joe how good Danny was to his friends.

"And we do nothing for him," he said. "We pay no rent. Sometimes we get drunk and break the furniture. We fight with Danny when we are angry with him, and we call him names. Oh, we are very bad, Big Joe. And so all of us, Pablo and Jesus Maria and the Pirate and I talked and planned. We are all in the woods tonight, looking for treasure. And the treasure is to be for Danny. He is so good, Big Joe. He is so kind; and we are so bad. But if we take a great sack of treasure to him, then he will be glad. It is because my heart is clean of selfishness that I can find this treasure."

"Won't you keep any of it?" Big Joe asked, incredulous. "Not even for a gallon of wine?"

Pilon had no speck of the Bad Pilon in him this night. "No, not one scrap of gold! Not one little brown penny! It is all for Danny, every bit."

Joe was disappointed. "I walked all this way and I won't even get a glass of wine for it," he mourned.

"When Danny has the money," Pilon said delicately, "it may be that he will buy a little wine. Of course I shall not suggest it, for this treasure is Danny's. But I think maybe he might buy a little wine. And then if you were good to him, you might get a glass."

Big Joe was comforted, for he had known Danny a long time. He thought it possible that Danny might buy a great deal of wine.

The night passed on over them. The moon went down and left the forest in muffled darkness. The fog siren screamed and screamed. During the whole night Pilon remained unspotted. He preached a little to Big Joe as recent converts are likely to do.

"It is worth while to be kind and generous," he said. "Not only do such actions pile up a house of joy in Heaven; but there is, too, a quick reward here on earth. One feels a golden warmth glowing like a hot enchilada in one's stomach. The Spirit of God clothes one in a coat as soft as camel's hair. I have not always been a good man, Big Joe Portagee. I confess it freely."

Big Joe knew it perfectly well.

"I have been bad," Pilon continued ecstatically. He was enjoying himself thoroughly. "I have lied and stolen. I have been lecherous. I have committed adultery and taken God's name in vain."

"Me too," said Big Joe happily.

"And what was the result, Big Joe Portagee? I have had a mean feeling. I have known I would go to Hell. But now I see that the sinner is never so bad that he cannot be forgiven. Although I have not yet been to confession, I can feel that the change in me is pleasing to God, for His grace is upon me. If you too would change your ways, Big Joe, if you would give up drunkenness and fighting and those girls down at Dora Williams' House, you too might feel as I do."

But Big Joe had gone to sleep. He never stayed awake very long when he was not moving about.

The grace was not quite so sharp to Pilon when he could not tell Big Joe about it, but he sat and watched the treasure place while the sky grayed and the dawn came behind the fog. He saw the pine trees take shape and emerge out of obscurity. The wind died down and the little blue rabbits came out of the brush and hopped about on the pine needles. Pilon was heavy-eyed but happy.

When it was light he stirred Big Joe Portagee with his foot. "It is time to go to Danny's house. The day has come." Pilon threw the cross away, for it was no longer needed, and he erased the circle. "Now," he said, "we must make no mark, but we must remember this by trees and rocks."

"Why don't we dig now?" Big Joe asked.

"And everybody in Tortilla Flat would come to help us," Pilon said sarcastically.

They looked hard at the surroundings, saying, "Now there are three trees together on the right, and two on the left. That patch of brush is down there, and here is a rock." At last they walked away from the treasure, memorizing the way as they went.

At Danny's house they found tired friends. "Did you find any?" the friends demanded.

"No," said Pilon quickly, to forestall Joe's confession.

"Well, Pablo thought he saw the light, but it disappeared before he got to it. And the Pirate saw the ghost of an old woman, and she had his dog with her."

The Pirate broke into a smile, "That old women told me my dog was happy now," he said.

"Here is Big Joe Portagee, back from the army," announced Pilon.

"Hello, Joe."

"You got a nice place, here," said the Portagee, and let himself down easily into a chair.

"You keep out of my bed," said Danny, for he knew that Joe Portagee had come to stay. The way he sat in a chair and crossed his knees had an appearance of permanence.

The Pirate went out and took his wheelbarrow and started into the forest to cut his kindlings; but the other five men lay down in the sunshine that broke though the fog, and in a little while they were asleep.

It was midafternoon before any of them awakened. At last they stretched their arms and sat up and looked listlessly down at the bay below, where a brown oil tanker moved slowly out to sea. The Pirate had left the bags on the table, and the friends opened them and brought out the food the Pirate had collected.

Big Joe walked down the path toward the sagging gate. "See you later," he called to Pilon.

Pilon anxiously watched him until he saw that Big Joe was headed down the hill to Monterey, not up toward the pine forest. The four friends sat down and dreamily watched the evening come.

At dusk Joe Portagee returned. He and Pilon conferred in the yard, out of earshot of the house.

"We will borrow tools from Mrs. Morales," Pilon said. "A shovel and a pickax stand by her chicken house."

When it was quite dark they started. "We go to see some girls, friends of Joe Portagee's," Pilon explained. They crept into Mrs. Morales' yard and borrowed the tools. And then, from the weeds beside the road, Big Joe lifted out a gallon jug of wine.

"Thou has sold the treasure," Pilon cried fiercely. "Thou art a traitor, oh dog of a dog."

Big Joe quieted him firmly. "I did not tell where the treasure was," he said with some dignity. "I told like this, 'We found a treasure,' I said, 'but it is for Danny. When Danny has it, I will borrow a dollar and pay for the wine.'"

Pilon was overwhelmed. "And they believed, and let you take the wine?" he demanded.

"Well—" Big Joe hesitated. "I left something to prove I would bring the dollar."

Pilon turned like lightning and took him by the throat. "What did you leave?"

"Only one little blanket, Pilon," Joe Portagee wailed. "Only one."

Pilon shook at him, but Big Joe was so heavy that Pilon only succeeded in shaking himself. "What blanket?" he cried. "Say what blanket it was you stole."

Big Joe blubbered. "Only one of Danny's. Only one. He has two. I took only the little tiny one. Do not hurt me, Pilon. The other one was bigger. Danny will get it back when we find the treasure."

Pilon whirled him around and kicked him with accuracy and fire. "Pig," he said, "dirty thieving cow. You will get the blanket back or I will beat you to ribbons."

Big Joe tried to placate him. "I thought how we are working for Danny," he whispered. "I thought, 'Danny will be so glad, he can buy a hundred new blankets.'"

"Be still," said Pilon. "You will get that same blanket back or I will beat you with a rock." He took up the jug and uncorked it and drank a little to soothe his frayed sensibilities; morever, he drove the cork back and refused the Portagee even a drop. "For this theft you must do all the digging. Pick up those tools and come with me."

Big Joe whined like a puppy and obeyed. He could not stand against the righteous fury of Pilon.

They tried to find the treasure for a long time. It was late when Pilon pointed to three trees in a row. "There!" he said.

They searched about until they found the depression in the ground. There was a little moonlight to guide them, for this night the sky was free of fog.

Now that he was not going to dig, Pilon developed a new theory for uncovering the treasure. "Sometimes the money is in sacks," he said, "and the sacks are rotted. If you dig straight down you might lose some." He drew a generous circle around the hollow. "Now, dig a deep trench around, and then you will come *up* on the treasure."

"Aren't you going to dig?" Big Joe asked.

Pilon broke into a fury. "Am I a thief of blankets?" he cried. "Do I steal from the bed of my friend who shelters me?"

"Well, I ain't going to do all the digging," Big Joe said.

Pilon picked up one of the pine limbs that only the night before had served as part of the cross. He advanced ominously toward Big Joe Portagee. "Thief," he snarled. "Dirty pig of an untrue friend. Take up that shovel."

Big Joe's courage flowed away, and he stooped for the shovel on the ground. If Joe Portagee's conscience had not been bad, he might have remonstrated; but his fear of Pilon, armed with a righteous cause and a stick of pine wood, was great.

Big Joe abhorred the whole principle of shoveling. The line of the moving shovel was unattractive. The end to be gained, that of taking dirt from one place and putting it in another, was, to one who held the larger vision, silly and gainless. A whole lifetime of shoveling could accomplish practically nothing. Big Joe's reaction was a little more simple than this. He didn't like to shovel. He had joined the army to fight and had done nothing but dig.

But Pilon stood over him, and the trench stretched around the treasure place. It did no good to profess sickness, hunger, or weakness. Pilon was inexorable, and Joe's crime of the blanket was held against him. Although he whined, complained, held up his hands to show how they were hurt, Pilon stood over him and forced the digging.

Midnight came, and the trench was three feet down. The roosters of Monterey crowed. The moon sank behind the trees. At last Pilon gave the word to move in on the treasure. The bursts of dirt came slowly now; Big Joe was exhausted. Just before daylight his shovel struck something hard.

"Ai," he cried. "We have it, Pilon."

The find was large and square. Frantically they dug at it in the dark, and they could not see it.

"Careful," Pilon cautioned. "Do not hurt it."

The daylight came before they had it out. Pilon felt metal and leaned down in the gray light to see. It was a goodsized square of concrete. On the top was a round brown plate. Pilon spelled out the words on it:

UNITED STATES GEODETIC SURVEY
+ 1915 +
ELEVATION 600 FEET

Pilon sat down in the pit and his shoulders sagged in defeat.

"No treasure?" Big Joe asked plaintively.

Pilon did not answer him. The Portagee inspected the cement post and his brow wrinkled with thought. He turned to the sorrowing Pilon. "Maybe we can take this good piece of metal and sell it."

Pilon peered up out of his dejection. "Johnny Pom-pom found one," he said with a quietness of great disappointment. "Johnny Pom-pom took the metal piece and tried to sell it. It is a year in jail to dig one of these up," Pilon mourned. "A year in jail and two thousand dollars fine." In his pain Pilon wanted only to get away from this tragic place. He stood up, found a weed in which to wrap the wine bottle, and started down the hill.

Big Joe trotted after him solicitously. "Where are we going?" he asked.

"I don't know," said Pilon.

The day was bright when they arrived at the beach, but even there Pilon did not stop. He trudged along the hard sand by the water's edge until Monterey was far behind and only the sand dunes of Seaside and the rippling waves of the bay were there to see his sorrow. At last he sat in the dry sand, with the sun warming him. Big Joe sat beside him, and he felt that in some way he was responsible for Pilon's silent pain.

Pilon took the jug out of its weed and uncorked it and drank deeply, and because sorrow is the mother of a general compassion, he passed Joe's wine to the miscreant Joe.

"How we build," Pilon cried. "How our dreams lead us. I had thought how we would carry bags of gold to Danny. I could see how his face would look. He would be surprised. For a long time he would not believe it." He took the bottle from Joe Portagee and drank colossally. "All this is gone, blown away in the night."

The sun was warming the beach now. In spite of his disappointment Pilon felt a traitorous comfort stealing over him, a treacherous impulse to discover some good points in the situation.

Big Joe, in his quiet way, was drinking more than his share of the wine. Pilon took it indignantly and drank again and again.

"But after all," he said philosophically, "maybe if we had found gold, it might not have been good for Danny. He has always been a poor man. Riches might make him crazy."

Big Joe nodded solemnly. The wine went down and down in the bottle.

"Happiness is better than riches," said Pilon. "If we try to make Danny happy, it will be a better thing than to give him money."

Big Joe nodded again and took off his shoes. "Make him happy. That's the stuff."

Pilon turned sadly upon him. "You are only a pig and not fit to live with men," he said gently. "You who stole Danny's blanket should be kept in a sty and fed potato peelings."

They were getting very sleepy in the warm sun. The little waves whispered along the beach. Pilon took off his shoes.

"Even Stephen," said Big Joe, and they drained the jug to the last drop.

The beach was swaying gently, heaving and falling with a movement like a ground-swell.

"You aren't a bad man," Pilon said. But Big Joe Portagee was already asleep. Pilon took off his coat and laid it over his face. In a few moments he too was sleeping sweetly.

The sun wheeled over the sky. The tide spread up the beach and then retreated. A squad of scampering kildeers inspected the sleeping men. A wandering dog sniffed them. Two elderly ladies, collecting seashells, saw the bodies and hurried past let these men should awaken in passion, pursue and criminally assault them. It was a shame, they agreed, that the police did nothing to control such matters. "They are drunk," one said.

And the other stared back up the beach at the sleeping men. "Drunken beasts," she agreed.

When at last the sun went behind the pines of the hill in back of Monterey, Pilon awakened. His mouth was as dry as alum; his head ached and he was stiff from the hard sand. Big Joe snored on.

"Joe," Pilon cried, but the Portagee was beyond call. Pilon rested on his elbow and stared out to sea. "A little wine would be good for my dry mouth," he thought. He tipped up the jug and got not a single drop to soothe his dry tongue. Then he turned out his pockets in the hope that while he slept some miracle had taken place there; but none had. There was a broken pocketknife for which he had been refused a glass of wine at least twenty times. There was a fishhook in a cork, a piece of dirty string, a dog's tooth, and several keys that fit nothing Pilon knew of. In the whole lot was not a thing Torrelli would consider as worth having, even in a moment of insanity.

Pilon looked speculatively at Big Joe. "Poor fellow," he thought. "When Joe Portagee wakes up he will feel as dry as I do. He will like it if I have a little wine for him." He pushed Big Joe roughly several times; and when the Portagee only mumbled, and then snored again, Pilon looked through his pockets. He found a brass pants' button, a little metal disk which said "Good Eats at the Dutchman," four or five headless matches, and a little piece of chewing tobacco.

Pilon sat back on his heels. So it was no use. He must wither here on the beach while his throat called lustily for wine.

He noticed the serge trousers the Portagee was wearing and stroked them with his fingers. "Nice cloth," he thought. "Why should this dirty Portagee wear such good cloth when all his friends go about in jeans?" The he remembered how badly the pants fitted Big Joe, how tight the waist was even with two fly-buttons undone, how the cuffs missed the shoe tops by inches. "Someone of a decent size would be happy in those pants."

Pilon remembered Big Joe's crime against Danny, and he became an avenging angel. How did this big black Portagee dare to insult Danny so! "When he wakes up I will beat him! But," the more subtle Pilon argued, "his crime was theft. Would it not teach him a lesson to know how it feels to have something stolen? What good is punishment unless something is learned?" It was a triumphant position for Pilon. If, with one action, he could avenge Danny, discipline Big Joe, teach an ethical lesson, and get a little wine, who in the world could criticize him?

He pushed the Portagee vigorously, and Big Joe brushed at him as though he were a fly. Pilon deftly removed the trousers, rolled them up, and sauntered away into the sand dunes.

Torrelli was out, but Mrs. Torrelli opened the door to Pilon. He was mysterious in his manner, but at last he held up the pants for her inspection.

She shook her head decisively.

"But look," said Pilon, "you are seeing only the spots and the dirt. Look at this fine cloth underneath. Think, señora! You have cleaned the spots off and pressed the trousers! Torrelli comes in! He is silent; he is glum. And then you bring him these fine pants! See how his eyes grow bright! See how happy he is! He takes you on his lap! Look how he smiles at you, señora! Is so much happiness too high at one gallon of red wine?"

"The seat of the pants is thin," she said.

He held them up to the light. "Can you see through them? No! The stiffness, the discomfort is taken out of them. They are in prime condition."

"No," she said firmly.

"You are cruel to your husband, señora. You deny him happiness. I should not be surprised to see him going to other women, who are not so heartless. For a quart, then?"

Finally her resistance was beaten down and she gave him the quart. Pilon drank it off immediately. "You try to break down the price of pleasure," he warned her. "I should have half a gallon."

Mrs. Torrelli was hard as stone. Not a drop more could Pilon get. He sat there brooding in the kitchen. "Jewess, that's what she is. She cheats me out of Big Joe's pants."

Pilon thought sadly of his friend out there on the beach. What could he do? If he came into town he would be arrested. And what had this harpy done to deserve the pants? She had tried to buy Pilon's friend's pants for a miserable quart of miserable wine. Pilon felt himself dissolving into anger at her.

"I am going away in a moment," he told Mrs. Torrelli. The pants were hung in a little alcove off the kitchen.

"Good-by," said Mrs. Torrelli over her shoulder. She went into her little pantry to prepare dinner.

On his way out Pilon passed the alcove and lifted down not only the pants, but Danny's blanket.

Pilon walked back down the beach, toward the place where he had left Big Joe. He could see a bonfire burning brightly on the sand, and as he drew nearer, a number of small dark figures passed in front of the flame. It was very dark now; he guided himself by the fire. As he came close, he saw that it was a Girl Scout wienie bake. He approached warily.

For a while he could not see Big Joe, but at last he discovered him, lying half covered with sand, speechless with cold and agony. Pilon walked firmly up to him and held up the pants.

"Take them, Big Joe, and be glad you have them back."

Joe's teeth were chattering. "Who stole my pants, Pilon? I have been lying here for hours, and I could not go away because of those girls."

Pilon obligingly stood between Big Joe and the little girls who were running about the bonfire. The Portagee brushed the cold damp sand from his legs and put on his pants. They walked side by side along the dark beach toward Monterey, where the lights hung, necklace above necklace against the hill. The sand dunes crouched along the back of the beach like tired hounds, resting; and the waves gently practiced at striking and hissed a little. The night was cold and aloof, and its warm life was withdrawn, so that it was full of bitter warnings to man that he is alone in the world, and alone among his fellows; that he has no comfort owing him from anywhere.

Pilon was still brooding, and Joe Portagee sensed the depth of his feeling. At last Pilon turned his head toward his friend. "We learn by this that it is great foolishness to trust a women," he said.

"Did some woman take my pants?" Big Joe demanded excitedly. "Who was it? I'll kick the hell out of her!"

But Pilon shook his head as sadly as old Jehovah, who, resting on the seventh day, sees that his world is tiresome. "She is punished," Pilon said. "You might say she punished herself, and that is the best way. She had thy pants; she bought them with greed; and now she has them not."

These things were beyond Big Joe. They were mysteries it was better to let alone; and this was as Pilon wished it. Big Joe said humbly, "Thanks for getting my pants back, Pilon." But Pilon was so sunk in philosophy that even thanks were valueless.

"It was nothing," he said. "In the whole matter only the lesson we learn has any value."

They climbed up from the beach and passed the great silver tower of the gas works.

Big Joe Portagee was happy to be with Pilon. "Here is one who takes care of his friends," he thought. "Even when they sleep he is alert to see that no harm comes to them." He resolved to do something nice for Pilon sometime.

□   IX   □

*How Danny was ensnared by a vacuum-cleaner and how
Danny's Friends rescued him.*

Dolores Engracia Ramirez lived in her own little house on the upper edge of Tortilla Flat. She did housework for some of the ladies in Monterey, and she belonged to the Native Daughters of the Golden West. She was not pretty, this lean-faced paisana, but there was in her figure a certain voluptuousness of movement; there was in her voice a throatiness some men found indicative. Her eyes could burn behind a mist with a sleepy passion which those men to whom the flesh is important found attractive and downright inviting.

In her brusque moments she was not desirable, but an amorous combination came about within her often enough so that she was called Sweets Ramirez on Tortilla Flat.

It was a pleasant thing to see her when the beast in her was prowling. How she leaned over her front gate! How her voice purred drowsily! How her hips moved gently about, now pressing against the fence, now swelling back like a summer beach-wave, and then pressing the fence again! Who in the world could put so much husky meaning into *"Ai, amigo, a'onde vas?"*

It is true that ordinarily her voice was shrill, her face hard and sharp as a hatchet, her figure lumpy, and her intentions selfish. The softer self came into possession only once or twice a week, and then, ordinarily, in the evening.

When Sweets heard that Danny was an heir, she was glad for him. She dreamed of being his lady, as did every other female on Tortilla Flat. In the evenings she leaned over the front gate waiting for the time when he would pass by and fall into her trap. But for a long time her baited trap caught nothing but poor Indians and paisanos who owned no houses, and whose clothes were sometimes fugitive from better wardrobes.

Sweets was not content. Her house was up the hill from Danny's house, in a direction he did not often take. Sweets could not go looking for him. She was a lady, and her conduct was governed by very strict rules of propriety. If Danny should walk by, now, if they should talk, like the old friends they were, if he should come in for a social glass of wine; and then, if nature proved too strong, and her feminine resistance too weak, there was no grave breach of propriety. But it was unthinkable to leave her web on the front gate.

For many months of evenings she waited in vain, and took such gifts as walked by in jeans. But there are only a limited number of pathways on Tortilla Flat. It was inevitable that Danny should, sooner or later, pass the gate of Dolores Engracia Ramirez; and so he did.

In all the time they had known each other, there had never been an occasion when it was more to Sweets' advantage to have him walk by; for Danny had only that morning found a keg of copper shingle nails, lost by the Central Supply Company. He had judged them jetsam because no member of the company was anywhere near. Danny removed the copper nails from the keg and put them in a sack. Then, borrowing the Pirate's wheelbarrow, and the Pirate to push it, he took his salvage to the Western Supply Company, where he sold the copper for three dollars. The keg he gave to the Pirate.

"You can keep things in it," he said. That made the Pirate very happy.

And now Danny came down the hill, aimed with a fine accuracy toward the house of Torrelli, and the three dollars there in his pocket.

Dolores' voice sounded as huskily sweet as the drone of a bumblebee. *"Ai, amigo, a'onde vas?"*

Danny stopped. A revolution took place in his plans. "How are you, Sweets?"

"What difference is it how I am? None of my friends are interested," she said archly. And her hips floated in a graceful and circular undulation.

"What do you mean?" he demanded.

"Well, does my friend Danny ever come to see me?"

"I am here to see thee now," he said gallantly.

She opened the gate a little. "Wilt thou come in for a tiny glass of wine in friendship's name?" Danny went into her house. "What hast thou been doing in the forest?" she cooed.

Then he made an error. He told vaingloriously of his transaction up the hill, and he boasted of his three dollars.

"Of course I have only enough wine to fill two thimbles," she said.

They sat in Sweets' kitchen and drank a glass of wine. In a little while Danny assaulted her virtue with true gallantry and vigor. He found to his amazement a resistance out of all proportion to her size and reputation. The ugly beast of lust was awakened in him. He was angry. Only when he was leaving was the way made clear to him.

The husky voice said, "Maybe you would like to come and see me this evening, Danny." Sweets' eyes swam in a mist of drowsy invitation. "One has neighbors," she suggested with delicacy.

Then he understood. "I will come back," he promised.

It was midafternoon. Danny walked down the street, reaimed at Torrelli's; and the beast in him had changed. From a savage and snarling wolf it had become a great, shaggy, sentimental bear. "I will take wine to that nice Sweets," he thought.

On the way down, whom should he meet but Pablo, and Pablo had two sticks of gum. He gave one to Danny and fell into step. "Where goest thou?"

"It is no time for friendship," Danny said tartly. "First I go to buy a little wine to take to a lady. You may come with me, and have one glass only. I am tired of buying wine for ladies only to have my friends drink it all up."

Pablo agreed that such a practice was unendurable. For himself, he didn't want Danny's wine, but only his companionship.

They went to Torrelli's. They had a glass of wine out of the new bought gallon. Danny confessed that it was shabby treatment to give his friend only one little glass. Over Pablo's passionate protest they had another. Ladies, Danny thought, should not drink too much wine. They were apt to become silly; and besides, it dulled some of those senses one liked to find alert in a lady. They had a few more glasses. Half a gallon of wine was a bountiful present, especially as Danny was about to go down to buy another present. They measured down half a gallon and drank what was over. Then Danny hid the jug in the weeds in a ditch.

"I would like you to come with me to buy the present, Pablo," he said.

Pablo knew the reason for the invitation. Half of it was a desire for Pablo's company, and half was fear of leaving the wine while Pablo was at large. They walked with studied dignity and straightness down the hill to Monterey.

Mr. Simon, of Simon's Investment, Jewelry, and Loan Company, welcomed them into his store. The name of the store defined the outward limits of the merchandise the company sold; for there were saxophones, radios, rifles, knives, fishing-rods, and old coins on the counter; all secondhand, but all really better than new because they were just well broken-in.

"Something you would like to see?" Mr. Simon asked.

"Yes," said Danny.

The proprietor named over a tentative list and then stopped in the middle of a word, for he saw that Danny was looking at a large aluminum vacuum-cleaner. The dust-bag was blue and yellow checks. The electric cord was long and black and slick. Mr. Simon went to it and rubbed it with his hand and stood off and admired it. "Something in a vacuum-cleaner?" he asked.

"How much?"

"For this one, fourteen dollars." It was not a price so much as an endeavor to find out how much Danny had. And Danny wanted it, for it was large and shiny. No woman of Tortilla Flat had one. In this moment he forgot there was no electricity on Tortilla Flat. He laid his two dollars on the counter and waited while the explosion took place; the fury, the rage, the sadness, the poverty, the ruin, the cheating. The polish was invoked, the color of the bag, the extra long cord, the value of the metal alone. And when it was all over, Danny went out carrying the vacuum-cleaner.

Often as a *pasatiempo* in the afternoon, Sweets brought out the vacuum-cleaner and leaned it against a chair. While her friends looked on, she pushed it back and forth to show how easily it rolled. And she made a humming with her voice to imitate a motor.

"My friend is a rich man," she said. "I think pretty soon there will be wires full of electricity coming right into the house, and then zip and zip and zip! And you have the house clean!"

Her friends tried to belittle the present, saying, "It is too bad you can't run this machine." And, "I have always held that a broom and dust-pan, *properly* used, are more thorough."

But their envy could do nothing against the vacuum. Through its possession Sweets climbed to the peak of the social scale of Tortilla Flat. People who did not remember her name referred to her as "that one with the sweeping-machine." Often when her enemies passed the house, Sweets could be seen through the window, pushing the cleaner back and forth, while a loud humming came from her throat. Indeed, after she had swept her house every day, she pushed the cleaner about on the theory that of course it would clean better with electricity but one could not have everything.

She excited envy in many houses. Her manner became dignified and gracious, and she held her chin high as befitted one who had a sweeping-machine. In her conversation she included it. "Ramon passed this morning while I was pushing the sweeping-machine"; "Louise Meater cut her hand this morning, not three hours after I had been pushing the sweeping-machine."

But in her elevation she did not neglect Danny. Her voice growled with emotion when he was about. She swayed like a pine tree in the wind. And he spent every evening at the house of Sweets.

At first his friends ignored his absence, for it is the right of every man to have these little affairs. But as the weeks went on, and as a rather violent domestic life began to make Danny listless and pale, his friends became convinced that Sweets' gratitude for the sweeping-machine was not to Danny's best physical interests. They were jealous of a situation that was holding his attention so long.

Pilon and Pablo and Jesus Maria Corcoran in turn assaulted the nest of his affections during his absence; but Sweets, while she was sensible of the compliment, remained true to the man who had raised her position to such a gratifying level. She tried to keep their friendship for a future time of need, for she knew how fickle fortune is; but she stoutly refused to share with Danny's friends that which was dedicated for the time being to Danny.

Wherefore the friends, in despair, organized a group, formed for and dedicated to her destruction.

It may be that Danny, deep in his soul, was beginning to tire of Sweets' affection and the duty of attendance it demanded. If such a change were taking place, he did not admit it to himself.

At three o'clock one afternoon Pilon and Pablo and Jesus Maria, followed vaguely by Big Joe Portagee, returned triumphant from three-quarters of a day of strenuous effort. Their campaign had called into play and taxed to the limit the pitiless logic of Pilon, the artistic ingenuousness of Pablo, and the gentleness and humanity of Jesus Maria Corcoran. Big Joe had contributed nothing.

But now, like four hunters, they returned from the chase more happy because their victory had been a difficult one. And in Monterey a poor puzzled Italian came gradually to the conviction that he had been swindled.

Pilon carried a gallon jug of wine concealed in a bundle of ivy. They marched joyfully into Danny's house, and Pilon set the gallon on the table.

Danny, awakened out of a sound sleep, smiled quietly, got up from bed, and laid out the fruit jars. He poured the wine. His four friends fell into chairs, for it had been an exhausting day.

They drank quietly in the late afternoon, that time of curious intermission. Nearly everyone in Tortilla Flat stops then and considers those things that have taken place in the day just past, and thinks over the possibilities of the evening. There are many things to discuss in an afternoon.

"Cornelia Ruiz got a new man this morning," Pilon observed. "He has a bald head. His name is Kilpatrick. Cornelia says her other man didn't come home three nights last week. She didn't like that."

"Cornelia is a woman who changes her mind too quickly," said Danny. He thought complacently of his own sure establishment, built on the rock of the vacuum-cleaner.

"Cornelia's father was worse," said Pablo. "He could not tell the truth. Once he borrowed a dollar from me. I have told Cornelia about it, and she does nothing."

"Two of one blood. 'Know the breed and know the dog,'" Pilon quoted virtuously.

Danny poured the jars full of wine again, and the gallon was exhausted. He looked ruefully at it.

Jesus Maria, that lover of the humanities, spoke up quietly. "I saw Susie Francisco, Pilon. She said the recipe worked fine. She has been out riding with Charlie Guzman on his motorcycle three times. The first two times she gave him the love medicine it made him sick. She thought it was no good. But now Susie says you can have some cookies any time."

"What was in that potion?" Pablo asked.

Pilon became secretive. "I cannot tell all of it. I guess it must have been the poison oak in it that made Charlie Guzman sick."

The gallon of wine had gone too quickly. Each of the six friends was conscious of a thirst so sharp that it was a pain of desire. Pilon looked at his friends with drooped eyes, and they looked back at him. The conspiracy was ready.

Pilon cleared his throat. "What hast thou done, Danny, to set the whole town laughing at thee?"

Danny looked worried. "What do you mean?"

Pilon chuckled. "It is said by many that you bought a sweeping-machine for a lady, and that machine will not work unless wires are put into the house. Those wires cost a great deal of money. Some people find this present very funny."

Danny grew uncomfortable. "That lady likes the sweeping-machine," he said defensively.

"Why not?" Pablo agreed. "She has told some people that you have promised to put wires into her house so the sweeping-machine will work."

Danny looked even more perturbed. "Did she say that?"

"So I was told."

"Well, I will not," Danny cried.

"If I did not think it funny, I should be angry to hear my friend laughed at," Pilon observed.

"What will you do when she asks for those wires?" Jesus Maria asked.

"I will tell her 'no,'" said Danny.

Pilon laughed. "I wish I could be there. It is not such a simple thing to tell that lady 'no.' "

Danny felt that his friends were turning against him. "What shall I do?" he asked helplessly.

Pilon gave the matter his grave consideration and brought his realism to bear on the subject. "If that lady did not have the sweeping-machine, she would not want those wires," he said.

The friends nodded in agreement. "Therefore," Pilon continued, "the thing to do is to remove the sweeping-machine."

"Oh, she wouldn't let me take it," Danny protested.

"Then we will help you," said Pilon. "I will take the machine, and in return you can take the lady a present of a gallon of wine. She will not even know where the sweeping-machine has gone."

"Some neighbor will see you take it."

"Oh, no," said Pilon. "You stay here, Danny. I will get the machine."

Danny sighed with relief that his problem was assumed by his good friends.

There were few things going on in Tortilla Flat that Pilon did not know. His mind made sharp little notes of everything that his eyes saw or his ears heard. He knew that Sweets went to the store at four-thirty every afternoon. He depended upon this almost invariable habit to put his plan into effect.

"It is better that you do not know anything about it," he told Danny.

In the yard Pilon had a gunny sack in readiness. With his knife he cut a generous branch from the rose bush and pushed it into the sack.

At Sweets' house he found her absent, as he had expected and hoped she would be. "It is really Danny's machine," he told himself.

It was a moment's work to enter the house, to put the vacuum-cleaner in the sack, and to arrange the rose branch artistically in the sack's mouth.

As he came out of the yard, he met Sweets. Pilon took off his hat politely. "I stepped in to pass the time," he said.

"Will you stop now, Pilon?"

"No, I have business down in Monterey. It is late."

"Where do you go with this rose bush?"

"A man in Monterey is to buy it. A very fine rose bush. See how strong it is."

"Stop in some other time, Pilon."

He heard no cry of anger as he walked sedately down the street. "Perhaps she will not miss it for a while," he thought.

Half the problem was solved, but half was yet to be approached. "What can Danny do with this sweeping-machine?" Pilon asked himself. "If he has it, Sweets will know he has taken it. Can I throw it away? No, for it is valuable. The thing to do would be to get rid of it and still to reap the benefit of its value."

Now the whole problem was solved. Pilon headed down the hill toward Torrelli's house.

It was a large and shining vacuum-cleaner. When Pilon came again up the hill, he had a gallon of wine in each hand.

The friends received him in silence when he entered Danny's house. He set one jug on the table and the other on the floor.

"I have brought you a present to take to the lady," he told Danny. "And here is a little wine for us."

They gathered happily, for their thirst was a raging fire. When the first gallon was far gone, Pilon held his glass to the candlelight and looked through it. "Things that happen are of no importance," he said. "But from everything that happens, there is a lesson to be learned. By this we learn that a present, especially to a lady, should have no quality that will require a further present. Also we learn that it is sinful to give presents of too great value, for they may excite greed."

The first gallon was gone. The friends looked at Danny to see how he felt about it. He had been very quiet, but now he saw that his friends were waiting on him.

"That lady was lively," he said judiciously. "That lady had a very sympathetic nature. But God damn it!" he said, "I'm sick of it!" He went to the second jug and drew the cork.

The Pirate, sitting in the corner among his dogs, smiled to himself and whispered in admiration, " 'God damn it, I'm sick of it.' " That, thought the Pirate, was very fine.

They had not more than half finished the second jug, indeed they had sung only two songs, when young Johnny Pom-pom came in. "I was at Torrelli's," Johnny said. "Oh, that Torrelli is mad! He is shouting! He is beating on the table with his fists."

The friends looked up with mild interest. "Something has happened. It is probable Torrelli deserves it."

"Often he has refused his good customers a little glass of wine."

"What is the matter with Torrelli?" Pablo asked.

Johnny Pom-pom accepted a jar of wine. "Torrelli says he bought a sweeping-machine from Pilon, and when he hooked it up to his light wire, it would not work. So he looked on the inside, and it had no motor. He says he will kill Pilon."

Pilon looked shocked. "I did not know this machine was at fault," he said. "But did I not say Torrelli deserved what was the matter with him? That machine was worth three or four gallons of wine, but that miser Torrelli would give no more than two."

Danny still felt a glow of gratitude toward Pilon. He smacked his lips on his wine. "This stuff of Torrelli's is getting worse and worse," he said. "At its best it is swill the pigs leave, but lately it is so bad that Charlie Marsh even would not drink it."

They all felt a little bit revenged on Torrelli then.

"I think," said Danny, "that we will buy our wine some place else, if Torrelli does not look out."

□   X   □

*How the Friends solaced a Corporal and in return received
a lesson in paternal ethics.*

Jesus Maria Corcoran was a pathway for the humanities. Suffering he tried to relieve; sorrow he tried to assuage; happiness he shared. No hard nor haunted Jesus Maria existed. His heart was free for the use of anyone who had a use for it. His resources and wits were at the disposal of anyone who had less of either than had Jesus Maria.

He it was who carried José de la Nariz four miles when José's leg was broken. When Mrs. Palochico lost the goat of her heart, the good goat of milk and cheese, it was Jesus Maria who traced that goat to Big Joe Portagee and halted the murder and made Big Joe give it back. It was Jesus Maria who once picked Charlie Marsh out of a ditch where he lay in his own filth, a deed which required not only a warm heart, but a strong stomach.

Together with his capacity for doing good, Jesus Maria had a gift for coming in contact with situations where good wanted doing.

Such was his reputation that Pilon had once said, "If that Jesus Maria had gone into the Church, Monterey would have had a saint for the calendar, I tell you."

Out of some deep pouch in his soul Jesus Maria drew kindness that renewed itself by withdrawal.

It was Jesus Maria's practice to go to the post office every day, first because there he could see many people whom he knew, and second because on that windy post office corner he could look at the legs of a great many girls. It must not be supposed that in this latter interest there was any vulgarity. As soon criticize a man who goes to art galleries or to concerts. Jesus Maria liked to look at girls' legs.

One day when he had leaned against the post office for two hours with very little success, he was witness to a pitiful scene. A policeman came along the sidewalk leading a young boy of about sixteen, and the boy carried a little baby wrapped in a piece of gray blanket.

The policeman was saying, "I don't care if I can't understand you. You can't sit in the gutter all day. We'll find out about you."

And the boy, in Spanish with a peculiar inflection, said, "But señor, I do nothing wrong. Why do you take me away?"

The policeman saw Jesus Maria. "Hey, paisano," he called. "What's this *cholo* talking about?"

Jesus Maria stepped out and addressed the boy. "Can I be of service to you?"

The boy broke into a relieved flood. "I came here to work. Some Mexican men said there would be work here, and there was none. I was sitting down resting when this man came to me and dragged me away."

Jesus Maria nodded and turned back to the policeman. "Has he done some crime, this little one?"

"No, But he's been sitting in the gutter on Alvarado Street for about three hours."

"He is a friend of mine," Jesus Maria said, " I will take care of him."

"Well, keep him out of the gutter."

Jesus Maria and his new friend walked up the hill. "I will take you to the house where I live. There you will have something to eat. What baby is this?"

"It is my baby," said the boy. "I am a *caporál,* and he is my baby. He is sick now; but when he grows up, he is going to be a *generál.*"

"What is he sick from, Señor Caporál?"

"I don't know. He is just sick." He showed the baby's face, and it looked very ill indeed.

The sympathies of Jesus Maria mounted. "The house where I live is owned by my friend Danny, and there is a good man, Señor Caporál. There is one to appeal to when trouble is upon one. Look, we will go there, and that Danny will give us shelter. My friend Mrs. Palochico has a goat. We will borrow a little milk for the baby."

The corporal's face for the first time wore a smile of comfort. "It is good to have friends," he said. "In Torreón I have many friends who would make themselves beggars to help me." He boasted a little to Jesus Maria. "I have rich friends, but of course they do not know my need."

Pilon pushed open the gate of Danny's yard, and they entered together. Danny and Pablo and Big Joe were sitting in the living room, waiting for the daily miracle of food. Jesus Maria pushed the boy into the room.

"Here is a young solider, a *caporál,*" he explained. "He has a baby here with him, and that baby is sick."

The friends arose with alacrity. The corporal threw back the gray blanket from the baby's face.

"He is sick, all right," Danny said. "Maybe we should get a doctor."

But the soldier shook his head. "No doctors. I do not like doctors. This baby does not cry, and he will not eat much. Maybe when he rests, then he will be well again."

At this moment Pilon entered and inspected the child. "This baby is sick," he said.

Pilon immediately took control. Jesus Maria he sent to Mrs. Palochico's house to borrow goat milk, Big Joe and Pablo to get an apple box, pad it with dry grass, and line it with a sheepskin coat. Danny offered his bed, but it was refused. The corporal stood in the living room and smiled gently on these good people. At last the baby lay in its box, but its eyes were listless and it refused the milk.

The Pirate came in, bearing a bag of mackerels. The friends cooked the fish and had their dinner. The baby would not even eat mackerel. Every now and then one of the friends jumped up and ran to look at the baby. When supper was over, they sat about the stove and prepared for a quiet evening.

The corporal had been silent, had given no account of himself. The friends were a little hurt at this, but they knew he would tell them in time. Pilon, to whom knowledge was as gold to be mined, made a few tentative drills into the corporal's reticence.

"It is not often that one sees a young soldier with a baby," he suggested delicately.

The corporal grinned with pride.

Pablo added, "This baby was probably found in the garden of love. And that is the best kind of babies, for only good things are in it."

"We too have been soldiers," said Danny. "When we die, we will go to the grave on a gun carriage, and a firing squad will shoot over us."

They waited to see whether the corporal would improve upon the opportunity they had offered. The corporal looked his appreciation. "You have been good to me," he said. "You have been as good and kind as my friends in Torreón would be. This is my baby, the baby of my wife."

"And where is your wife?" Pilon asked.

The corporal lost his smile. "She is in Mexico," he said. Then he grew vivacious again. "I met a man, and he told me a curious thing. He said we can make of babies what we will. He said, 'You tell the baby often what you want him to do, and when he grows up he will do that.' Over and over I tell this baby, 'You will be a *generál.*' Do you think it will be so?"

The friends nodded politely. "It may be," said Pilon. "I have not heard of this practice."

"I say twenty times a day, 'Manuel, you will be a *generál* some day. You will have big epaulets and a sash. Your sword will be gold. You will ride a palomino horse. What a life for you, Manuel!" The man said he surely will be a *generál* if I say it so."

Danny got up and went to the apple box. "You will be a *generál*," he said to the baby. "When you grow up you will be a great *generál*."

The others trooped over to see whether the formula had had any effect.

The Pirate whispered, "You will be a *generál*," and he wondered whether the same method would work on a dog.

"This baby is sick all right," Danny said. "We must keep him warm."

They went back to their seats.

"Your wife is in Mexico—" Pilon suggested.

The corporal wrinkled his brows and thought for a while, and then he smiled brilliantly. "I will tell you. It is not a thing to tell to strangers, but you are my friends. I was a soldier in Chihuahua, and I was diligent and clean and kept oil in my rifle, so that I became a *caporál*. And then I was married to a beautiful girl. I do not say that it was not because of the chevrons that she married me. But she was very beautiful and young. Her eyes were bright, she had good white teeth, and her hair was long and shining. So pretty soon this baby was born."

"That is good," said Danny. "I should like to be you. There is nothing so good as a baby."

"Yes," said the corporal, "I was glad. And we went in to the baptism, and I wore a sash, although the book of the army did not mention it. And when we came out of that church, a *capitán* with epaulets and a sash and a silver sword saw my wife. Pretty soon my wife went away. Then I went to that *capitán* and I said, 'Give me back my wife,' and he said, 'You do not value your life, to talk this way to your superior.'" The corporal spread his hands and lifted his shoulders in a gesture of caged resignation.

"Oh, that thief!" cried Jesus Maria.

"You gathered your friends. You killed that *capitán*," Pablo anticipated.

The corporal looked self-conscious. "No. There was nothing to do. The first night, someone shot at me through the window. The second day a field gun went off by mistake and it came so close to me that the wind knocked me down. So I went away from there, and I took the baby with me."

There was fierceness in the faces of the friends, and their eyes were dangerous. The Pirate, in his corner, snarled, and all the dogs growled.

"We should have been there," Pilon cried. "We would have made that *capitán* wish he had never lived. My grandfather suffered at the hands of a priest, and he tied that priest naked to a post in a corral and turned a little calf in with him. Oh, there are ways."

"I was only a *caporál*," said the boy. "I had to run away." Tears of shame were in his eyes. "There is no help for a *caporál* when a *capitán* is against him; so I ran away, with the baby Manuel. In Fresno I met this wise man, and he told me I could make Manuel be what I wished. I tell that baby twenty times every day, 'You will be a *generál*. You will wear epaulets and carry a golden sword.' "

Here was drama that made the experiments of Cornelia Ruiz seem uninteresting and vain. Here was a situation which demanded the action of the friends. But its scene was so remote that action was impossible. They looked in admiration at the corporal. He was so young to have had such an adventure!

"I wish," Danny said wickedly, "that we were in Torreón now. Pilon would make a plan for us. It is too bad we cannot go there."

Big Joe Portagee had stayed awake, a tribute to the fascination of the corporal's story. He went to the apple box and looked in. "You going to be a general," he said. And then "Look! This baby is moving funny." The friends crowded around. The spasm had already started. The little feet kicked down and then drew up. The hands clawed about helplessly, and then the baby scrabbled and shuddered.

"A doctor," Danny cried. "We must have a doctor." But he and everyone knew it was no use. Approaching death wears a cloak no one ever mistakes. While they watched, the baby stiffened and the struggle ended. The mouth dropped open, and the baby was dead. In kindness Danny covered the apple box with a piece of blanket. The corporal stood very straight and stared before him, so shocked that he could not speak nor think.

Jesus Maria laid a hand on his shoulder and led him to a chair. "You are so young," he said. "You will have many more babies."

The corporal moaned, "Now he is dead. Now he will never be a *generál* with that sash and that sword."

There were tears in the eyes of the friends. In the corner all the dogs whined miserably. The Pirate buried his big head in the fur of Señor Alec Thompson.

In a soft tone, almost a benediction, Pilon said, "Now you yourself must kill the *capitán*. We honor you for a noble plan of revenge, but that is over and you must take your own vengeance, and we will help you, if we can."

The corporal turned dull eyes to him. "Revenge?" he asked. "Kill the *capitán*? What do you mean?"

"Why, it was plain what your plan was," Pilon said. "This baby would grow up, and he would be a *generál;* and in time he would find that *capitán*, and he would kill him slowly. It was a good plan. The long waiting, and then the stroke. We, your friends, honor you for it."

The corporal was looking bewilderedly at Pilon. "What is this?" he demanded. "I have nothing to do with this *capitán*. He is the *capitán*."

The friends sat forward.

Pilon cried, "Then what was this plan to make the baby a *generál?* Why was that?"

The corporal was a little embarrassed then. "It is the duty of a father to do well by his child. I wanted Manuel to have more good things than I had."

"Is that all?" Danny cried.

"Well," said the corporal, "my wife was so pretty, and she was not any *puta,* either. She was a good woman, and that *capitán* took her. He had little epaulets, and a little sash, and his sword was only of a silver color. Consider," said the corporal, and he spread out his hands, "if that *capitán,* with the little epaulets and the little sash, could take my wife, imagine what a *generál* with a big sash and a gold sword could take!"

There was a long silence while Danny and Pilon and Pablo and Jesus Maria and the Pirate and Big Joe Portagee digested the principle. And when it was digested, they waited for Danny to speak.

"It is to be pitied," said Danny at last, "that so few parents have the well-being of their children at heart. Now we are more sorry than ever that the baby is gone, for with such a father, what a happy life he has missed."

All of the friends nodded solemnly.

"What will you do now?" asked Jesus Maria, the discoverer.

"I will go back to Mexico," said the corporal. "I am a soldier in my heart. It may be, if I keep oiling my rifle, I myself may be an officer some day. Who can tell?"

The six friends looked at him admiringly. They were proud to have known such a man.

□ **XI** □

How, under the most adverse circumstances, love came to Big Joe Portagee.

For Big Joe Portagee, to feel love was to do something about it. And this is the history of one of his love affairs.

It had been raining in Monterey; from the tall pines the water dripped all day. The paisanos of Tortilla Flat did not come out of their houses, but from every chimney a blue column of pinewood smoke drifted so that the air smelled clean and fresh and perfumed.

At five o'clock in the afternoon the rain stopped for a few moments, and Big Joe Portagee, who had been under a rowboat on the beach most of the day, came out and started up the hill toward Danny's house. He was cold and hungry.

When he came to the very edge of Tortilla Flat, the skies opened and the rain poured down. In an instant Big Joe was soaked through. He ran into the nearest house to get out of the rain, and that house was inhabited by Tia Ignacia.

The lady was about forty-five, a widow of long standing and some success. Ordinarily she was taciturn and harsh, for there was in her veins more Indian blood than is considered decent in Tortilla Flat.

When Big Joe entered she had just opened a gallon of red wine and was preparing to pour out a glass for her stomach's sake. Her attempt to push the jug under a chair was unsuccessful. Big Joe stood in her doorway, dripping water on the floor.

"Come in and get dry," said Tia Ignacia. Big Joe, watching the bottle as a terrier watches a bug, entered the room. The rain roared down on the roof. Tia Ignacia poked up a blaze in her airtight stove.

"Would you care for a glass of wine?"

"Yes," said Big Joe. Before he had finished his first glass, Big Joe's eyes had refastened themselves on the jug. He drank three glasses before he consented to say a word, and before the wolfishness went out of his eyes.

Tia Ignacia had given her new jug of wine up for lost. She drank with him as the only means to preserve a little of it to her own use. It was only when the fourth glass of wine was in his hands that Big Joe relaxed and began to enjoy himself.

"This is not Torrelli's wine," he said.

"No, I get it from an Italian lady who is my friend." She poured out another glass.

The early evening came. Tia Ignacia lighted a kerosene lamp and put some wood in the fire. As long as the wine must go, it must go, she thought. Her eyes dwelt on the huge frame of Big Joe Portagee with critical appraisal. A little flush warmed her chest.

"You have been working out in the rain, poor man," she said. "Here, take off your coat and let it dry."

Big Joe rarely told a lie. His mind didn't work quickly enough. "I been on the beach under a rowboat, asleep," he said.

"But you are all wet, poor fellow." She inspected him for some response to her kindness, but on Big Joe's face nothing showed except gratification at being out of the rain and drinking wine. He put out his glass to be filled again. Having eaten nothing all day, the wine was having a profound effect on him.

Tia Ignacia addressed herself anew to the problem. "It is not good to sit in a wet coat. You will be ill with cold. Come, let me help you to take off your coat."

Big Joe wedged himself comfortably into his chair. "I'm all right," he said stubbornly.

Tia Ignacia poured herself another glass. The fire made a rushing sound to counteract with comfort the drumming of water on the roof.

Big Joe made absolutely no move to be friendly, to be gallant, even to recognize the presence of his hostess. He drank his wine in big swallows. He smiled stupidly at the stove. He rocked himself a little in the chair.

Anger and despair arose in Tia Ignacia. "This pig," she thought, "this big and dirty animal. It would be better for me if I brought some cow in the house out of the rain. Another man would say some little friendly word at least."

Big Joe stuck out his glass to be filled again.

Now Tia Ignacia strove heroically. "In a little warm house there is happiness on such a night," she said. "When the rain is dripping and the stove burns sweetly, then is a time for people to feel friendly. Don't you feel friendly?"

"Sure," said Big Joe.

"Perhaps the light is too bright in your eyes," she said coyly. "Would you like me to blow out the light?"

"It don't bother me none," said Big Joe, "if you want to save oil, go ahead."

She blew down the lamp chimney, and the room leaped to darkness. Then she went back to her chair and waited for his gallantry to awaken. She could hear the gentle rocking of his chair. A little light came from the cracks of the stove and struck the shiny corners of the furniture. The room was nearly luminous with warmth. Tia Ignacia heard his chair stop rocking and braced herself to repel him. Nothing happened.

"To think," she said, "you might be out in this storm, shivering in a shed or lying on the cold sand under a boat. But no; you are sitting in a good chair, drinking good wine, in the company of a lady who is your friend."

There was no answer from Big Joe. She could neither hear him nor see him. Tia Ignacia drank off her glass. She threw virtue to the winds. "My friend Cornelia Ruiz has told me that some of her best friends came to her out of the rain and cold. She comforted them, and they were her good friends."

The sound of a little crash came from the direction of Big Joe. She knew he had dropped his glass, but no movement followed the crash. "Perhaps he is ill," she thought. "Maybe he has fainted." She jumped up, lighted a match, and set it to the lamp wick. And then she turned to her guest.

Big Joe was mountainously asleep. His feet stuck out ahead of him. His head was back and his mouth wide open. While she looked, amazed and shocked, a tremendous rattling snore came from his mouth. Big Joe simply could not be warm and comfortable without going to sleep.

It was a moment before Tia Ignacia could move all her crowding emotions into line. She inherited a great deal of Indian blood. She did not cry out. No, shivering with rage although she was, she walked to her wood basket, picked out a likely stick, weighed it, put it down, and picked out another one. And then she turned slowly on Big Joe Portagee. The first blow caught him on the shoulder and knocked him out of the chair.

"Pig!" Tia Ignacia screamed. "Big dirty garbage! Out in the mud with you!"

Joe rolled over on the floor. The next blow made a muddy indentation on the seat of his pants. Big Joe was waking up rapidly now.

"Huh?" he said. "What's the matter? What you doing?"

"I'll show you," she screamed. She flung open her door and ran back to him. Big Joe staggered to his feet under the beating. The stick hammered at his back and shoulders and head. He ran out of the door, protecting his head with his hands.

"Don't," he pleaded. "Now don't do that. What's the matter?"

The fury followed him like a hornet, down the garden path and into the muddy street. Her rage was terrible. She followed him along the street, still beating him.

"Hey," he cried. "Now don't." He grabbed her and held her while her arms struggled violently to be free to continue the beating.

"Oh, great garbage pig!" she cried. "Oh, cow!"

He could not let her go without more beating, so he held her tightly; and as he stood here, love came to Big Joe Portagee. It sang in his head; it roared through his body like a great freshet; it shook him as a tropical storm shakes a forest of palms. He held her tightly for a moment, until her anger relaxed.

In the night, in Monterey, a policeman patrols the streets on a motorcycle to see that good things come to no evil. Jake Lake rode about now, his slicker shining dully, like basalt. He was unhappy and uncomfortable. It was not so bad on the paved streets, but part of his route lay through the mud paths of Tortilla Flat, and there the yellow mud splashed nastily. His little light flashed about. The motor coughed with effort.

All of a sudden Jake Lake cried out in astonishment and stopped his motor. "What the devil! Say, what the hell is this?"

Big Joe twisted his neck. "Oh, is that you, Jake? Say, Jake as long as you're going to take us to jail anyway, can't you just wait a minute?"

The policeman turned his motor around. "You get out of the street," he said. "Somebody'll come along and run over you."

His motor roared in the mud, and the flicker of his little headlight disappeared around the corner. The rain pattered gently among the trees of Tortilla Flat.

□ **XII** □

*How Danny's Friends assisted the Pirate to keep a vow, and
how as a reward for merit the Pirate's dogs saw a holy vision.*

Every afternoon the Pirate pushed his empty wheelbarrow up the hill and
into Danny's yard. He leaned it against the fence and covered it with a sack;
then he buried his ax in the ground, for, as everyone knows, it makes steel
much harder to be buried. Last, he went into the house, reached into a Bull
Durham bag which hung around his neck on a string, took out the day's
quarter dollar, and gave it to Danny. Then Danny and the Pirate and any
other of the friends who happened to be in the house went solemnly into the
bedroom, stepping over the bedding that littered the floor. While the paisanos looked on, Danny reached under his pillow, brought out the canvas
bag, and deposited the new quarter. This practice had continued for a long
time.

The bag of money had become the symbolic center of the friendship, the
point of trust about which the fraternity revolved. They were proud of the
money, proud that they had never tampered with it. About the guradianship
of the Pirate's money there had grown a structure of self-respect and not a
little complacency. It is a fine thing for a man to be trusted. This money had
long ceased, in the minds of the friends, to be currency. It is true that for a
time they had dreamed of how much wine it would buy, but after a while
they lost the conception of it as legal tender. The hoard was aimed at a gold
candlestick, and this potential candlestick was the property of San Francisco
de Assisi. It is far worse to defraud a saint than it is to take liberties with the
law.

One evening, by that quick and accurate telegraph no one understands,
news came in that a Coast Guard cutter had gone on the rocks near Carmel.
Big Joe Portagee was away on business of his own, but Danny and Pablo and
Pilon and Jesus Maria and the Pirate and his dogs joyfully started over the
ridge; for if there was anything they loved, it was to pick up usable articles on
the beach. This they thought the most exciting thing in the world. Although
they arrived a little late, they made up for lost time. All night the friends
scurried about the beach, and they accumulated a good pile of flotsam, a five-
pound can of butter, several cases of canned goods, a water-soaked Bowditch,
two pea jackets, a water barrel from a lifeboat, and a machine gun. When
daylight came they had a goodly pile under guard.

They accepted a lump sum of five dollars for the lot from one of the
spectators, for it was out of the question to carry all those heavy things over
six miles of steep hillside to Tortilla Flat.

Because he had not cut his day's wood, the Pirate received a quarter from Danny, and he put it in his Bull Durham bag. Then they started tiredly, but with a warm and expectant happiness, straight over the hills to Monterey.

It was afternoon when they got back to Danny's house. The Pirate ritualistically opened his bag and gave the quarter to Danny. The whole squad trooped into the other room. Danny reached under the pillow—and his hand came out empty. He threw the pillow back, threw the mattress back, and then he turned slowly to his friends, and his eyes had become as fierce as a tiger's eyes. He looked from face to face, and on every one saw horror and indignation that could not be simulated.

"Well," he said, "—well." The Pirate began to cry, Danny put his arm around his shoulder. "Do not cry, little friend," he said ominously. "Thou wilt have thy money again."

The paisanos went silently out of the room. Danny walked out into the yard and found a heavy pine stick three feet long, and swung it experimentally. Pablo went into the kitchen and returned bearing an ancient can-opener with a vicious blade. Jesus Maria from under the house pulled out a broken pick handle. The Pirate watched them bewilderedly. They all came back to the house and sat quietly down.

The Pirate aimed down the hill with his thumb. "Him?" he asked.

Danny nodded slowly. His eyes were veiled, and deadly. His chin stuck out, and, as he sat in the chair, his whole body weaved a little, like a rattlesnake aiming to strike.

The Pirate went into the yard and dug up his ax.

For a long time they sat in the house. No words were spoken, but a wave of cold fury washed and crouched in the room. The feeling in the house was the feeling of a rock when the fuse is burning in toward the dynamite.

The afternoon waned; the sun went behind the hill. The whole of Tortilla Flat seemed hushed and expectant.

They heard his footsteps on the street and their hands tightened on their sticks. Joe Portagee walked uncertainly up on the porch and in the front door. He had a gallon of wine in his hand. His eyes went uneasily from face to face, but the friends sat still and did not look directly at him.

"Hello," said Big Joe.

"Hello," said Danny, He stood up and stretched lazily. He did not look at Big Joe; he did not walk directly toward him, but at an angle, as though to pass him. When he was abreast, he struck with the speed of a striking snake. Fair on the back of Big Joe's head the stick crashed, and Big Joe went down, completely out.

Danny thoughtfully took a string of rawhide from his pocket and tied the Portagee's thumbs together. "Now water," he said.

Pablo threw a bucket of water in Big Joe's face. He turned his head and stretched his neck like a chicken, and then he opened his eyes and looked dazedly at his friends. They did not speak to him at all. Danny measured his distance carefully, like a golfer addressing the ball. His stick smashed on Big Joe's shoulder; then the friends went about the business in a cold and methodical manner. Jesus Maria took the legs, Danny the shoulders and chest. Big Joe howled and rolled on the floor. They covered his body from the neck down. Each blow found a new space and welted it. The shrieks were deafening. The Pirate stood helplessly by, holding his ax.

At last, when the whole front of the body was one bruise they stopped. Pablo knelt at Big Joe's head with his can-opener. Pilon took off the Portagee's shoes and picked up his stick again.

Then Big Joe squalled with fear. "It's buried out by the front gate," he cried. "For the love of Christ, don't kill me!"

Danny and Pilon went out the front door and in a few minutes they came back, carrying the canvas bag. "How much did you take out?" Danny asked. There was no inflection in his voice at all.

"Only four, honest to God. I only took four, and I'll work and put them back."

Danny leaned down, took him by the shoulder, and rolled him over on his face. Then the friends went over his back with the same deadly precision. The cries grew weaker but the work only stopped when Big Joe was beaten into unconsciousness. Then Pilon tore off the blue shirt and exposed the pulpy raw back. With the can-opener he cross-hatched the skin so deftly that a little blood ran from each line. Pablo brought the salt to him and helped him to rub it in all over the torn back. At last Danny threw a blanket over the unconscious man.

"I think he will be honest now," said Danny.

"We should count the money," Pilon observed. "We have not counted it for a long time." They opened Big Joe's gallon of wine and poured the fruit jars full, for they were tired from their work and their emotions were exhausted.

Then they counted the quarters out in piles of ten, and excitedly counted again. "Pirate," Danny cried, "there are seven over a thousand! Thy time is done! The day is come for thee to buy thy candlestick for San Francisco!"

The day had been too full for the Pirate. He went into the corner with his dogs, and he put his head down on Fluff and burst into hysterical sobs. The dogs moved uneasily about, and they licked his ears and pushed at his head with their noses; but Fluff, sensible of the honor of being chosen, lay quietly and nuzzled the thick hair on the Pirate's neck.

Danny put all the money back in the bag, and the bag under his pillow again.

Now Big Joe came to and groaned, for the salt was working into his back. The paisanos paid no attention to him until at last Jesus Maria, that prey to the humanities, untied Big Joe's thumbs and gave him a jar of wine. "Even the enemies of our Savior gave him a little comfort," he excused himself.

The action broke up the punishment. The friends gathered tenderly about Big Joe. They laid him on Danny's bed and washed the salt out of his wounds. They put cold cloths on his head and kept his jar full of wine. Big Joe moaned whenever they touched him. His morals were probably untouched, but it would have been safe to prophesy that never again would he steal from the paisanos of Danny's house.

The Pirate's hysteria was over. He drank his wine and his face shone with pleasure while he listened to Danny make plans for him.

"If we take all this money into town, to the bank, they will think we have stolen it from a slot machine. We must take this money to Father Ramon and tell him about it. Then we will buy the gold candlestick, and he will bless it, and the Pirate will go into the church. Maybe Father Ramon will say a word about him on Sunday. The Pirate must be there to hear."

Pilon looked distastefully at the Pirate's dirty, ragged clothes. "Tomorrow," he said sternly, "you must take the seven extra two-bitses and buy some decent clothes. For ordinary times these may be all right, but on such an occasion as this you cannot go into the church looking like a gutter rat. It will not be a compliment to your friends."

The Pirate beamed at him. "Tomorrow I will do it," he promised.

The next morning, true to his promise, he went down to Monterey. He shopped carefully and bargained with an astuteness that seemed to belie the fact that he had bought nothing in over two years. He came back to Danny's house in triumph, bearing a huge silk handkerchief in purple and green and also a broad belt studded profusely with colored glass jewels. His friends admired his purchases.

"But what are you going to wear?" Danny asked despairingly. "Two toes are out of your shoes where you cut holes to ease your bunions. You have only ragged overalls and no hat."

"We will have to lend him clothes," said Jesus Maria, "I have a coat and vest. Pilon has his father's good hat. You, Danny, have a shirt, and Big Joe has those fine blue pants."

"But then we can't go," Pilon protested.

"It is not our candlestick," said Jesus Maria. "Father Ramon is not likely to say anything nice about us."

That afternoon they convoyed the treasure to the priest's house. He listened to the story of the sick dog, and his eyes softened. "—And then, Father," said the Pirate, "there was that good little dog, and his nose was dry, and his eyes were like the glass of bottles out of the sea, and he groaned because he hurt inside. And then, Father, I promised the gold candlestick of one thousand days to San Francisco. He is really my patron, Father. And then there was a miracle! For that dog wagged his tail three times, and right away he started to get well. It was a miracle from San Francisco, Father, wasn't it?"

The priest nodded his head gravely. "Yes" he said. "It was a miracle sent by our good Saint Francis. I will buy the candlestick for thee."

The Pirate was very glad, for it is no little thing to have one's prayer answered with a true miracle. If it were noised about, the Pirate would have a higher station on Tortilla Flat. Already his friends looked at him with a new respect. They thought no more of his intelligence than they had before, but they knew now that his meager wits were supplemented with all the power of Heaven and all the strength of the saints.

They walked back up to Danny's house, and the dogs walked behind them. The Pirate felt that he had been washed in a golden fluid of beatitude. Little chills and fevers of pleasure chased one another through his body. The paisanos were glad they had guarded his money, for even they took a little holiness from the act. Pilon was relieved that he had not stolen the money in the first place. What terrible things might not have happened if he had taken the two-bits belonging to a saint! All of the friends were as subdued as though they were in church.

The five dollars from the salvage had lain like fire in Danny's pocket, but now he knew what to do with it. He and Pilon went to the market and bought seven pounds of hamburger and a bag of onions and bread and a big paper of candy. Pablo and Jesus Maria went to Torrelli's for two gallons of wine, and not a drop did they drink on the way home either.

That night when the fire was lighted and two candles burned on the table, the friends feasted themselves to repletion. It was a party in the Pirate's honor. He behaved himself with a great deal of dignity. He smiled and smiled when he should have been grave, though. But he couldn't help that.

After they had eaten enormously, they sat back and sipped wine out of the fruit jars. "Our little friend," they called the Pirate.

Jesus Maria asked, "How did you feel when it happened? When you promised the candlestick and the dog began to get well, how did you feel? Did you see any holy vision?"

The Pirate tried to remember. "I don't think so—Maybe I saw a little vision—maybe I saw San Francisco in the air and he was shining like the sun—"

"Wouldn't you remember that?" Pilon demanded.

"Yes—I think I remember—San Francisco looked on me—and he smiled, like the good saint he is. Then I knew the miracle was done. He said, 'Be good to little doggies, you dirty man.'"

"He called you that?"

"Well, I was, and he is not a saint to be telling lies."

"I don't think you remember that at all," said Pablo.

"Well—maybe not. I think I do, though." The Pirate was drunk with happiness from the honor and the attention.

"My grandmother saw the Holy Virgin," said Jesus Maria. "She was sick to death, and I myself heard her cry out. She said, 'Ohee. I see the Mother of God. Ohee. My dear Mary, full of grace.' "

"It is given to some to see these things," said Danny. "My father was not a very good man, but he sometimes saw saints, and sometimes he saw bad things. It depended on whether he was good or bad when he saw them. Have you ever seen any other visions, Pirate?"

"No," said the Pirate. "I would be afraid to see any more."

It was a decorous party for a long time. The friends knew that they were not alone this night. Through the walls and the windows and the roof they could feel the eyes of the holy saints looking down upon them.

"On Sunday your candlestick will be there," said Pilon. "We cannot go, for you will be wearing our clothes. I do not say Father Ramon will mention you by name, but maybe he will say something about the candlestick. You must try to remember what he says, Pirate, so you can tell us."

Then Pilon grew stern. "Today, my little friend, there were dogs all over Father Ramon's house. That was all right for today, but you must remember not to take them to the church on Sunday. It is not fitting that dogs should be in the church. Leave the dogs at home."

The Pirate looked disappointed. "They want to go," he cried. "How can I leave them? Where can I leave them?"

Pablo was shocked. "In this affair so far thou hast conducted thyself with merit, little Pirate. Right at the last do you wish to commit sacrilege?"

"No," said the Pirate humbly.

"Then leave thy dogs here, and we will take care of them. It will be a sacrilege to take them into the church."

It was curious how soberly they drank that night. It was three hours before they sang even an obscene song. And it was late before their thoughts strayed to light women. And by the time their minds turned to fighting they were almost too sleepy to fight. This evening was a great good marker in their lives.

On Sunday morning the preparation was violent. They washed the Pirate and inspected his ears and his nostrils. Big Joe, wrapped in a blanket, watched the Pirate put on his blue serge trousers. Pilon brought out his father's hat. They persuaded the Pirate not to wear his jewel-studded belt outside his coat, and showed him how he could leave his coat open so that the jewels flashed now and then. The item of shoes give the most trouble. Big Joe had the only shoes big enough for the Pirate, and his were worse even than the Pirate's. The difficulty lay in the holes cut for the comfort of bunions, where the toes showed through. Pilon solved it finally with a little soot from the inside of the stove. Well rubbed into the skin, the soot made it quite difficult to see the bunion holes.

At last he was ready; Pilon's father's hat rakishly on his head, Danny's shirt, Big Joe's pants, the huge handkerchief around his neck, and, at intervals, the flashing of the jeweled belt. He walked, for the friends to inspect him, and they looked on critically.

"Pick up your feet, Pirate."

"Don't drag your heels."

"Stop picking at your handkerchief."

"Those people who see you will think you are not in the habit of good clothes."

At last the Pirate turned to his friends. "If those dogs could only come with me," he complained. "I would tell them they must not come in the church."

But the paisanos were firm. "No," said Danny. "They might get in some way. We will keep them here in the house for you."

"They won't like it," said the Pirate helplessly. "They will be lonely, maybe." He turned to the dogs in the corner. "You must stay here," he said. "It would not be good for you to go to church. Stay with my friends until I come back again." And then he slipped out and closed the door behind him. Instantly a wild clamor of barking and howling broke out in the house. Only his faith in the judgment of his friends prevented the Pirate's relenting.

As he walked down the street, he felt naked and unprotected without his dogs. It was as though one of his senses were gone. He was frightened to be out alone. Anyone might attack him. But he walked bravely on, through the town and out to the Church of San Carlos.

Now, before the service began, the swinging doors were open. The Pirate dipped Holy Water out of the marble font, crossed himself, genuflected before the Virgin, went into the church, did his duty to the altar, and sat down. The long church was rather dark, but the high altar was on fire with candles. And in front of the images at the sides, the votive lights were burning. The old and sweet incense perfumed the church.

For a time the Pirate sat looking at the altar, but it was too remote, too holy to think about very much, too unapproachable by a poor man. His eyes sought something warmer, something that would not frighten him. And there, in front of the figure of Saint Francis, was a beautiful golden candlestick, and in it a tall candle was burning.

The Pirate sighed with excitement. And although the people came in and the swinging doors were shut, and the service began and the Pirate went through the form, he could not stop looking at his saint and at the candlestick. It was so beautiful. He could not believe that he, the Pirate, had given it. He searched the face of the saint to see whether Saint Francis liked the candlestick. He was sure the image smiled a little now and then, the recurring smile of one who thinks of pleasant things.

At last the sermon began. "There is a new beauty in the church," Father Ramon said. "One of the children of the church has given a golden candlestick to the glory of Saint Francis." He told the story of the dog, then, told it rather badly on purpose. His eyes searched the faces of the parishioners until he saw little smiles appear there. "It is not a thing to be considered funny," he said. "Saint Francis loved the beasts so much that he preached to them." Then Father Ramon told the story of the bad wolf of Gubbio and he told of the wild turtle doves and of the sister larks. The Pirate looked at him in wonder as the sermon went on.

Suddenly a rushing sound came from the door. A furious barking and scratching broke out. The doors swung wildly and in rushed Fluff and Rudolph, Enrique, Pajarito, and Señor Alec Thompson. They raised their noses, and then darted in a struggling squad to the Pirate. They leaped upon him with little cries and whinings. They swarmed over him.

The priest stopped talking and looked sternly down toward the commotion. The Pirate looked back helplessly, in agony. So it was in vain, and the sacrilege was committed.

Then Father Ramon laughed, and the congregation laughed. "Take the dogs outside," he said. "Let them wait until we are through."

The Pirate, with embarrassed, apologetic gestures, conducted his dogs outside. "It is wrong," he said to them. "I am angry with you. Oh, I am ashamed of you." The dogs cringed to the ground and whined piteously. "I know what you did," said the Pirate. "You bit my friends, you broke a window, and you came. Now stay here and wait, oh, wicked dogs; oh, dogs of sacrilege."

He left them stricken with grief and repentance and went back into the church. The people, still laughing, turned and looked at him, until he sank into his seat and tried to efface himself.

"Do not be ashamed," Father Ramon said. "It is no sin to be loved by your dogs, and no sin to love them. See how Saint Francis loved the beasts." Then he told more stories of that good saint.

The embarrassment left the Pirate. His lips moved. "Oh," he thought, "if the dogs could only hear this. They would be glad if they could know all this." When the sermon was over, his ears still rang with the stories. Automatically he followed the ritual, but he did not hear the service. And when it was over, he rushed for the door. He was first out of the church. The dogs, still sad and diffident, crowded about him.

"Come," he cried. "I have some things to tell you."

He started at a trot up the hill toward the pine forest, and the dogs galloped and bounced about him. He came at last to the shelter of the woods, and still he went on, until he found a long aisle among the pines, where the branches met overhead, where the tree trunks were near together. For a moment he looked helplessly about.

"I want it to be the way it was," he said. "If only you could have been there and heard the father say it." He laid one big stone on top of another. "Now here is the image," he told the dogs. He stuck a little stick in the ground. "Right here is the candlestick, with a candle in it."

It was dusky in the glade, and the air was sweet with pine resin. The trees whispered softly in the breeze. The Pirate said with authority, "Now Enrique, you sit here. And you, Rudolph, here. I want Fluff here because he is the littlest. Pajarito, thou great fool, sit here and make no trouble. Señor Alec Thompson, you may not lie down."

Thus he arranged them in two rows, two in the front line and three in the back.

"I want to tell you how it was," he said. "You are forgiven for breaking into the church. Father Ramon said it was no sacrilege this time. Now, attention, I have things to tell."

The dogs sat in their places and watched him earnestly. Señor Alec Thompson flapped his tail, until the Pirate turned to him. "Here is no place for that," he said. "Saint Francis would not mind, but I do not like you to wag your tail while you listen. Now, I am going to tell you about Saint Francis."

That day his memory was inspired. The sun found interstices in the foliage and threw brilliant patterns on the pine-needle carpet. The dogs sat patiently, their eyes on the Pirate's lips. He told everything the priest had told, all the stories, all the observations. Hardly a word was out of its place.

When he was done, he regarded the dogs solemnly. "Saint Francis did all that," he said.

The trees hushed their whispering. The forest was silent and enchanted.

Suddenly there was a tiny sound behind the Pirate. All the dogs looked up. The Pirate was afraid to turn his head. A long moment passed.

And then the moment was over. The dogs lowered their eyes. The treetops stirred to life again and the sunlight patterns moved bewilderingly.

The Pirate was so happy that his heart pained him. "Did you see him?" he cried. "Was it San Francisco? Oh! What good dogs you must be to see a vision."

The dogs leaped up at his tone. Their mouths opened and their tails threshed joyfully.

□ XIII □

*How Danny's Friends threw themselves to the aid of a
distressed lady.*

Señora Teresina Cortez and her eight children and her ancient mother lived
in a pleasant cottage on the edge of the deep gulch that defines the southern
frontier of Tortilla Flat. Teresina was a good figure of a mature woman, nearing thirty. Her mother, that ancient, dried, toothless one, relict of a past generation, was nearly fifty. It was long since any one had remembered that her
name was Angelica.

During the week work was ready to this *vieja's* hand, for it was her duty
to feed, punish, cajole, dress, and bed down seven of the eight children. Teresina was busy with the eighth, and with making certain preparations for the
ninth.

On Sunday, however, the *vieja,* clad in black satin more ancient even
than she, hatted in a grim and durable affair of black straw, on which were
fastened two true cherries of enameled plaster, threw duty to the wind and
went firmly to church, where she sat as motionless as the saints in their
niches. Once a month, in the afternoon, she went to confession. It would be
interesting to know what sins she confessed, and where she found the time to
commit them, for in Teresina's house there were creepers, crawlers, stumblers,
shriekers, cat-killers, fallers-out-of-trees; and each one of these charges could
be trusted to be ravenous every two hours.

Is it any wonder that the *vieja* had a remote soul and nerves of steel? Any
other kind would have gone screaming out of her body like little skyrockets.

Teresina was a mildly puzzled woman, as far as her mind was concerned.
Her body was one of those perfect retorts for the distillation of children. The
first baby, conceived when she was fourteen, had been a shock to her; such a
shock, that she delivered it in the ball park at night, wrapped it in newspaper,
and left it for the night watchman to find. This is a secret. Even now Teresina
might get into trouble if it were known.

When she was sixteen, Mr. Alfred Cortez married her and gave her his
name and the two foundations of her family, Alfredo and Ernie. Mr. Cortez
gave her that name gladly. He was only using it temporarily anyway. His
name, before he came to Monterey and after he left, was Guggliemo. He
went away after Ernie was born. Perhaps he foresaw that being married to
Teresina was not going to be a quiet life.

The regularity with which she became a mother always astonished Teresina. It occurred sometimes that she could not remember who the father of
the impending baby was; and occasionally she almost grew convinced that no

lover was necessary. In the time when she had been under quarantine as a diphtheria carrier she conceived just the same. However, when a question became too complicated for her mind to unravel, she usually laid that problem in the arms of the Mother of Jesus, who, she knew, had more knowledge of, interest in, and time for such things than she.

Teresina went often to confession. She was the despair of Father Ramon. Indeed he had seen that while her knees, her hands, and her lips did penance for an old sin, her modest and provocative eyes, flashing under drawn lashes, laid the foundation for a new one.

During the time I have been telling this, Teresina's ninth child was born, and for the moment she was unengaged. The *vieja* received another charge; Alfredo entered his third year in the first grade, Ernie his second, and Panchito went to school for the first time.

At about this time in California it became the stylish thing for school nurses to visit the classes and to catechize the children on intimate details of their home life. In the first grade, Alfredo was called to the principal's office, for it was thought that he looked thin.

The visiting nurse, trained in child psychology, said kindly, "Freddie, do you get enough to eat?"

"Sure," said Alfredo.

"Well, now. Tell me what you have for breakfast."

"Tortillas and beans," said Alfredo.

The nurse nodded her head dismally to the principal. "What do you have when you go home for lunch?"

"I don't go home."

"Don't you eat at noon?"

"Sure. I bring some beans wrapped up in a tortilla."

Actual alarm showed in the nurse's eyes, but she controlled herself. "At night what do you have to eat?"

"Tortillas and beans."

Her psychology deserted her. "Do you mean to stand there and tell me you eat nothing but tortillas and beans?"

Alfredo was astonished. "Jesus Christ," he said, "what more do you want?"

In due course the school doctor listened to the nurse's horrified report. One day he drove up to Teresina's house to look into the matter. As he walked through the yard the creepers, the crawlers, and the stumblers were shrieking one terrible symphony. The doctor stood in the open kitchen door. With his own eyes he saw the *vieja* go to the stove, dip a great spoon into a kettle, and sow the floor with boiled beans. Instantly the noise ceased. Creepers, crawlers, and stumblers went to work with silent industry, moving from bean to bean, pausing only to eat them. The *vieja* went back to her chair for a few moments of peace. Under the bed, under the chairs, under the stove the children crawled with the intentness of little bugs. The doctor stayed two hours, for his scientific interest was piqued. He went away shaking his head.

He shook his head incredulously while he made his report. "I gave them every test I know of," he said, "teeth, skin, blood, skeletons, eyes, co-ordination. Gentlemen, they are living on what constitutes a slow poison, and they have from birth. Gentlemen, I tell you I have never seen healthier children in my life!" His emotion overcame him. "The little beasts," he cried. "I never saw such teeth in my life. I *never* saw such teeth!"

You will wonder how Teresina procured food for her family. When the bean threshers have passed, you will see, where they have stopped, big piles of bean chaff. If you will spread a blanket on the ground, and, on a windy afternoon, toss the chaff in the air over the blanket, you will understand that the threshers are not infallible. For an afternoon of work you may collect twenty or more pounds of beans.

In the autumn the *vieja* and those children who could walk went into the fields and winnowed the chaff. The landowners did not mind, for she did no harm. It was a bad year when the *vieja* did not collect three or four hundred pounds of beans.

When you have four hundred pounds of beans in the house, you need have no fear of starvation. Other things, delicacies such as sugar, tomatoes, peppers, coffee, fish, or meat, may come sometimes miraculously, through the intercession of the Virgin, sometimes through industy or cleverness; but your beans are there, and you are safe. Beans are a roof over your stomach. Beans are a warm cloak against economic cold.

Only one thing could threaten the lives and happiness of the family of the Señora Teresina Cortez; that was a failure of the bean crop.

When the beans are ripe, the little bushes are pulled and gathered into piles, to dry crisp for the threshers. Then is the time to pray that the rain may hold off. When the little piles of beans lie in lines, yellow against the dark fields, you will see the farmers watching the sky, scowling with dread at every cloud that sails over; for if a rain comes, the bean piles must be turned over to dry again. And if more rain falls before they are dry, they must be turned again. If a third shower falls, mildew and rot set in, and the crop is lost.

When the beans were drying, it was the *vieja*'s custom to burn a candle to the Virgin.

In the year of which I speak, the beans were piled and the candle had been burned. At Teresina's house, the gunny sacks were laid out in readiness.

The threshing machines were oiled and cleaned.

A shower fell.

Extra hands rushed to the fields and turned the sodden hummocks of beans. The *vieja* burned another candle.

More rain fell.

Then the *vieja* bought two candles with a little gold piece she had kept for many years. The field hands turned over the beans to the sun again; and then came a downpour of cold streaking rain. Not a bean was harvested in all Monterey County. The soggy lumps were turned under by the plows.

Oh, then distress entered the house of Señora Teresina Cortez. The staff of life was broken; the little roof destroyed. Gone was that eternal verity, beans. At night the children cried with terror at the approaching starvation. They were not told, but they knew. The *vieja* sat in church, as always, but her lips drew back in a sneer when she looked at the Virgin. "You took my candles," she thought. "Ohee, yes. Greedy you are for candles. Oh, thoughtless one." And sullenly she transferred her allegiance to Santa Clara. She told Santa Clara of the injustice that had been done. She permitted herself a little malicious thought at the Virgin birth. "You know, sometimes Teresina can't remember either," she told Santa Clara viciously.

It has been said that Jesus Maria Corcoran was a great-hearted man. He had also that gift some humanitarians possess of being inevitably drawn toward those spheres where his instinct was needed. How many times had he not come upon young ladies when they needed comforting. Toward any pain or sorrow he was irresistibly drawn. He had not been to Teresina's house for many months. If there is no mystical attraction between pain and humanitarianism, how did it happen that he went there to call on the very day when the last of the old year's beans was put in the pot?

He sat in Teresina's kitchen, gently brushing children off his legs. And he looked at Teresina with polite and pained eyes while she told of the calamity. He watched, fascinated, when she turned the last bean sack inside out to show that not one single bean was left. He nodded sympathetically when she pointed out the children, so soon to be skeletons, so soon to die of starvation.

Then the *vieja* told bitterly how she had been tricked by the Virgin. But upon this point Jesus Maria was not sympathetic.

"What do you know, old one?" he said sternly. "Maybe the Blessed Virgin had business some place else."

"But four candles I burned," the *vieja* insisted shrilly.

Jesus Maria regarded her coldly. "What are four candles to Her?" he said. "I have seen one church where She had hundreds. She is no miser of candles."

But his mind burned with Teresina's trouble. That evening he talked mightily and piteously to the friends at Danny's house. Out of his great heart he drew a compelling oratory, a passionate plea for those little children who had no beans. And so telling was his speech that the fire in his heart ignited the hearts of his friends. They leaped up. Their eyes glowed.

"The children shall not starve," they cried. "It shall be our trust!"

"We live in luxury," Pilon said.

"We shall give of our substance," Danny agreed. "And if they needed a house, they could live here."

"Tomorrow we shall start," Pablo exclaimed. "No more laziness! To work! There are things to be done!"

Jesus Maria felt the gratification of a leader with followers.

Theirs was no idle boast. Fish they collected. The vegetable patch of the Hotel Del Monte they raided. It was a glorious game. Theft robbed of the stigma of theft, crime altruistically committed—what is more gratifying?

The Pirate raised the price of kindlings to thirty cents and went to three new restaurants every morning. Big Joe stole Mrs. Palochico's goat over and over again, and each time it went home.

Now food began to accumulate in the house of Teresina. Boxes of lettuce lay on her porch, spoiled mackerel filled the neighborhood with a strong odor. And still the flame of charity burned in the friends.

If you could see the complaint book at the Monterey Police Department, you would notice that during this time there was a minor crime wave in Monterey. The police car hurried from place to place. Here a chicken was taken, there a whole patch of pumpkins. Paladini Company reported the loss of two one-hundred-pound cases of abalone steaks.

Teresina's house was growing crowded. The kitchen was stacked high with food. The back porch overflowed with vegetables. Odors like those of a packing house permeated Tortilla Flat. Breathlessly the friends dashed about at their larcenies, and long they talked and planned with Teresina.

At first Teresina was maddened with joy at so much food, and her head was turned by the compliment. After a week of it, she was not so sure. The baby was down with colic. Ernie had some kind of bowel trouble, Alfredo's face was flushed. The creepers and crawlers cried all the time. Teresina was ashamed to tell the friends what she must tell them. It took her several days to get her courage up; and during that time there arrived fifty pounds of celery and a crate of cantaloupes. At last she had to tell them. The neighbors were beginning to look at her with lifted brows.

She asked all of Danny's friends into her kitchen, and then she informed them of the trouble, modestly and carefully, that their feelings might not be hurt.

"Green things and fruit are not good for children," she explained. "Milk is constipating to a baby after it is weaned." She pointed to the flushed and irritable children. See, they were all sick. They were not getting the proper food.

"What is the proper food?" Pilon demanded.

"Beans," she said. "There you have something to trust, something that will not go right through you."

The friends went silently away. They pretended to themselves to be disheartened but they knew that the first fire of their enthusiasm had been lacking for several days.

At Danny's house they held a conference.

This must not be told in some circles, for the charge might be serious.

Long after midnight four dark forms who shall be nameless moved like shadows through the town. Four indistinct shapes crept up on the Western Warehouse Company platform. The watchman said, afterward, that he heard sounds, investigated, and saw nothing. He could not say how the thing was done, how a lock was broken and the door forced. Only four men know that the watchman was sound asleep, and they will never tell on him.

A little later the four shadows left the warehouse, and now they were bent under tremendous loads. Pantings and snortings came from the shadows.

At three o'clock in the morning Teresina was awakened by hearing her back door open. "Who is there?" she cried.

There was no answer, but she heard four great thumps that shook the house. She lighted a candle and went to the kitchen in her bare feet. There, against the wall, stood four one-hundred-pound sacks of pink beans.

Teresina rushed in and awakened the *vieja*. "A miracle!" she cried. "Come look in the kitchen."

The *vieja* regarded with shame the plump full sacks. "Oh, miserable dirty sinner am I," she moaned. "Oh, Holy Mother, look with pity on an old fool. Every month thou shalt have a candle, as long as I live."

At Danny's house four friends were lying happily in their blankets. What pillow can one have like a good conscience? They slept well into the afternoon, for their work was done.

And Teresina discovered, by a method she had found to be infallible, that she was going to have a baby. As she poured a quart of the new beans into the kettle, she wondered idly which one of Danny's friends was responsible.

□ XIV □

*Of the good life at Danny's house, of a gift pig, of the pain of Tall Bob,
and of the thwarted love of the Viejo Ravanno.*

Clocks and watches were not used by the paisanos of Tortilla Flat. Now and then one of the friends acquired a watch in some extraordinary manner, but he kept it only long enough to trade it for something he really wanted. Watches were in good repute at Danny's house, but only as media of exchange. For practical purposes, there was the great golden watch of the sun. It was better than a watch, and safer, for there was no way of diverting it to Torrelli.

In the summer when the hands of a clock point to seven, it is a nice time to get up, but in winter the same time is of no value whatever. How much better is the sun! When he clears the pine tops and clings to the front porch, be it summer or winter, that is the sensible time to get up. That is a time when one's hands do not quiver nor one's belly quake with emptiness.

The Pirate and his dogs slept in the living room, secure and warm in their corner. Pilon and Pablo and Jesus Maria and Danny and Big Joe Portagee slept in the bedroom. For all his kindness, his generosity, Danny never allowed his bed to be occupied by anyone but himself. Big Joe tried it twice, and was smacked across the soles of the feet with a stick; so that even he learned the inviolable quality of Danny's bed.

The friends slept on the floor, and their bedding was unusual. Pablo had three sheepskins stitched together. Jesus Maria retired by putting his arms through the sleeves of one old overcoat and his legs through the sleeves of another. Pilon wrapped himself in a big strip of carpet. Most of the time Big Joe simply curled up like a dog and slept in his clothes. Big Joe, while he had no ability to keep any possession for very long, had a well-developed genius for trading everything that came into his hands for some little measure of wine. Thus they slept, noisily sometimes, but always comfortably. On one cold night Big Joe tried to borrow a dog for his feet, and got well bitten, for the Pirate's dogs were not lendable.

No curtains covered the windows, but a generous Nature had obscured the glass with cobwebs, with dust, and with the neat marks of raindrops. "It would be nice to clean that window with soap and water," Danny said one time.

Pilon's sharp mind leaped to the problem with energy, but it was too easy for him. It did not require a decent quota of his powers. "More light would get in," he said. "We would not spend so much time out in the air if it were light in here. And at night, when the air is poisonous, we have no need for light."

Danny retired from the field, for if one little mention brought such clear and quick refutation of his project, what crushing logic would insistence bring forth? The window remained as it was; and as time passed, as fly after fly went to feed the spider family with his blood and left his huskish body in the webs against the glass, as dust adhered to dust, the bedroom took on a pleasant obscurity which made it possible to sleep in a dusky light even at noonday.

They slept peacefully, the friends; but when the sun struck the window in the morning and, failing to get in, turned the dust to silver and shone on the iridescence of the blue-bottle flies, then the friends awakened and stretched and looked about for their shoes. They knew the front porch was warm when the sun was on the window.

They did not awaken quickly, nor fling about nor shock their system with any sudden movement. No, they arose from slumber as gently as a soap bubble floats out from its pipe. Down into the gulch they trudged, still only half awake. Gradually their wills coagulated. They built a fire and boiled some tea and drank it from the fruit jars, and at last they settled in the sun on the front porch. The flaming flies made halos about their heads. Life took shape about them, the shape of yesterday and of tomorrow.

Discussion began slowly, for each man treasured the little sleep he still possessed. From this time until well after noon, intellectual comradeship came into being. Then roofs were lifted, houses peered into, motives inspected, adventures recounted. Ordinarily their thoughts went first to Cornelia Ruiz, for it was a rare day and night during which Cornelia had not some curious and interesting adventure. And it was an unusual adventure from which no moral lesson could be drawn.

The sun glistened in the pine needles. The earth smelled dry and good. The rose of Castile perfumed the world with its flowers. This was one of the best of times for the friends of Danny. The struggle for existence was remote. They sat in judgment on their fellows, judging not for morals, but for interest. Anyone having a good thing to tell saved it for recounting at this time. The big brown butterflies came to the rose and sat on the flowers and waved their wings slowly, as though they pumped honey out by wing power.

"I saw Albert Rasmussen," said Danny. "He came from Cornelia's house. What trouble that Cornelia has. Every day some trouble."

"It is her way of life," said Pablo. "I am not one to cast stones, but sometimes I think Cornelia is a little too lively. Two things only occur to Cornelia, love and fighting."

"Well," said Pilon. "What do you want?"

"She never has any peace," Jesus Maria said sadly.

She doesn't want any," said Pilon. "Give peace to that Cornelia, and she will die. Love and fighting. That is good, what you said, Pablo. Love and fighting, and a little wine. Then you are always young, always happy. What happened to Cornelia yesterday?"

Danny looked in triumph at Pilon. It was an unusual thing for Pilon not to know everything that happened. And now Danny could tell by the hurt and piqued look on Pilon's face that he did not know this one.

"All of you know Cornelia," he began. "Sometimes men take presents to Cornelia, a chicken or a rabbit or a cabbage. Just little things, and Cornelia likes those things. Well, yesterday Emilio Murietta took to Cornelia a little pig, only so long; a nice little pink pig. Emilio found that pig in the gulch. The sow chased him when he picked it up, but he ran fast, and he came to Cornelia's house with that pig.

"This Emilio is a great talker. He said to Cornelia, 'There is nothing nicer to have than a pig. He will eat anything. He is a nice pet. You get to love that little pig. But then that pig grows up and his character changes. That pig becomes mean and evil-tempered, so that you do not love him any more. Then one day that pig bites you, and you are angry. And so you kill that pig and eat him.'"

The friends nodded gravely, and Pilon said, "In some ways Emilio is not a dull man. See how many satisfactions he has made with his pig—affection, love, revenge, and food. I must go to talk with Emilio sometime." But the friends could see that Pilon was jealous of a rival logician.

"Go on with this pig," said Pablo.

"Well," said Danny, "Cornelia took that little pig, and she was nice to Emilio. She said that when the time came, and she was angry at that pig, Emilio could have some of it to eat. Well, then Emilio went away. Cornelia made a little box for that pig to sleep in, by the stove.

"Some ladies come in to see her then, and Cornelia let them hold the little pig and pet it. After a while Sweets Ramirez stepped on that pig's tail. Oh! It squealed like a steam whistle. The front door was open. That big sow she came in for her little pig again. All the tables and all the dishes were smashed. All the chairs, they were broken. And that big sow bit Sweets Ramirez and pulled off Cornelia's skirt, and then, when those ladies were in the kitchen and the door locked, the sow went away, and that little pig went too. Now Cornelia is furious. She says she will beat Emilio."

"There it is," said Pablo. "That is the way life goes, never the way you planned. It was that way when Tall Bob Smoke went to kill himself."

The faces of the friends swung appreciatively toward Pablo.

"You will know Bob Smoke," Pablo began. "He looks the way a vaquero should look, long legs, thin body; but he cannot ride very well. At the rodeo he is often in the dust. Now this Bob is one who wants to be admired. When there is a parade he likes to carry the flag. When there is a fight he wants to be referee. At the show he is always the first to say 'Down in front!' Yes, there is a man who wants to be a great man, and to have people see him, and admire him. And something you do not know, perhaps, he wants people to love him too.

"Poor unfortunate one, he is a man born to be laughed at. Some people pity him, but most of them just laugh at him. And laughter stabs that Tall Bob Smoke.

"Maybe you remember that time in the parade when he carried the flag. Very straight Bob sat, on a big white horse. Right in front of the place where the judges sat that big stupid horse fainted from the heat. Bob went flying right over that horse's head, and the flag sailed through the air like a spear and stuck in the ground, upside down.

"That is how it is with him. Whenever he tries to be a great man, something happens and everybody laughs. You remember when he was poundmaster he tried all afternoon to lasso a dog. Everybody in town came to see. He threw the rope and the dog squatted down and the rope slipped off and the dog ran away. Oh, the people laughed. Bob was so ashamed that he thought, 'I will kill myself, and then people will be sad. They will be sorry they laughed.' And then he thought, 'But I will be dead. I will not know how sorry they are.' So he made this plan, 'I will wait until I hear someone coming to my room. I will point a pistol at my head. Then that friend will argue with me. He will make me promise not to shoot myself. The people will be sorry then that they drove me to kill myself.' That is the way he thought it.

"So he walked home to his little house, and everybody he passed called out, 'Did you catch the dog, Bob?' He was very sad when he got home. He took a pistol and put cartridges in it, and then he sat down and waited for someone to come.

"He planned how it would be, and he practiced it with a pistol. The friend would say, 'Ai, what you doing? Don't shoot yourself, poor fellow.' Then Bob would say how he didn't want to live any more because everyone was so mean.

"He thought about it over and over, but no one came. And the next day he waited, and no one came. But that next night Charlie Meeler came. Bob heard him on the porch and put the pistol to his head. And he cocked it to make it look more real. 'Now he will argue with me, and I will let him persuade me,' Bob thought.

"Charlie Meeler opened the door. He saw Bob holding that pistol to his head. But he did not shout; no, Charlie Meeler jumped and grabbed that gun and that gun went off and shot away the end of Bob's nose. And then the people laughed even more. There were pieces in the paper about it. The whole town laughed.

"You have all seen Bob's nose, with the end shot off. The people laughed; but it was a hard kind of laughing, and they felt bad to laugh. And ever since then they let Tall Bob carry the flag in every parade there is. And the city bought him a net to catch dogs with.

"But he is not a happy man, with his nose like that." Pablo fell silent and picked up a stick from the porch and whipped his leg a little.

"I remember his nose, how it was," said Danny. "He is not a bad one, that Bob. The Pirate can tell you when he gets back. Sometimes the Pirate puts all his dogs in Bob's wagon and then the people think Bob has caught them, and the people say, 'There is a poundman for you.' It is not so easy to catch dogs when it is your business to catch dogs."

Jesus Maria had been brooding, with his head back against the wall. He observed, "It is worse than whipping to be laughed at. Old Tomas, the rag sucker, was laughed right into his grave. And afterward the people were sorry they laughed.

"And," said Jesus Maria, "there is another kind of laughing too. That story of Tall Bob is funny; but when you open your mouth to laugh, something like a hand squeezes your heart. I know about old Mr. Ravanno who hanged himself last year. And there is a funny story too, but it is not pleasant to laugh at."

"I heard something about it," said Pilon, "but I do not know that story."

"Well," said Jesus Maria. "I will tell you that story, and you will see if you can laugh. When I was a little boy, I played games with Petey Ravanno. A good quick little boy, that Petey, but always in trouble. He had two brothers and four sisters, and there was his father, Old Pete. All that family is gone now. One brother is in San Quentin, the other was killed by a Japanese gardener for stealing a wagonload of watermelons. And the girls, well, you know how girls are; they went away. Susy is in Old Jenny's house in Salinas right now.

"So there was only Petey and the old man left. Petey grew up, and always he was in trouble. He went to reform school for a while, then he came back. Every Saturday he was drunk, and every time he went to jail until Monday. His father was a kind of a friendly man. He got drunk every week with Petey. Nearly always they were in jail together. Old man Ravanno was lonely when Petey was not there with him. He liked that boy Petey. Whatever Petey did, that old man did, even when he was sixty years old.

"Maybe you remember that Gracie Montez?" Jesus Maria asked. "She was not a very good girl. When she was only twelve years old the fleet came to Monterey, and Gracie had her first baby, so young as that. She was pretty, you see, and quick, and her tongue was sharp. Always she seemed to run away from men, and men ran fast after her. And sometimes they caught her. But you could not get close to her. Always that Gracie seemed to have something nice that she did not give to you, something in back of her eyes that said, 'If I really wanted to, I would be different to you from any woman you ever knew.'

"I know about that," said Jesus Maria, "for I ran after Gracie too. And Petey ran after her. Only Petey was different." Jesus Maria looked sharply into his friends' eyes to emphasize his point.

"Petey wanted what Gracie had so much that he grew thin, and his eyes were as wide and pained as the eyes of one who smokes marihuana. Petey could not eat, and he was sick. Old Man Ravanno went over and talked to Gracie. He said, 'If you are not nice to Petey, he will die.' But she only laughed. She was not a very good one. And then her little sister 'Tonia came into the room. 'Tonia was fourteen years old. The old man looked at her and his breath stopped. 'Tonia was like Gracie, with that funny thing that she kept away from men. Old Man Ravanno could not help it. He said, 'Come to me, little girl.' But 'Tonia was not a little girl. She knew. So she laughed and ran out of the room.

"Old man Ravanno went home then. Petey said, 'Something is the matter with thee, my father.'

" 'No, Petey,' the old man said, 'only I worry that you do not get this Gracie, so you can be well again.'

"Hot-blooded, all those Ravannos were!

"And then what do you think?" Jesus Maria continued. "Petey went to cut squids for Chin Kee, and he made presents to Gracie, big bottles of Agua Florida and ribbons and garters. He paid to have her picture taken, with colors on the picture too.

"Gracie took all the presents and she ran away from him and laughed. You should have heard how she laughed. It made you want to choke her and pet her at the same time. It made you want to cut her open and get that thing that was inside of her. I know how it was. I ran after her, and Petey told me too. But it made Petey crazy. He could not sleep any more. He said to me, 'If that Gracie will marry me in the church, then she will not dare to run away any more, because she will be married, and it will be a sin to run away.' So he asked her. She laughed that high laugh that made you want to choke her.

"Oh! Petey was crazy. He went home and put a rope over a rafter and he stood on a box and put the rope around his neck and then he kicked out the box. Well, Petey's father came in then. He cut the rope and called the doctor. But it was two hours before Petey opened his eyes, and it was four days before he could talk."

Jesus Maria paused. He saw with pride that his friends were leaning in toward the story. "That was the way of it," he said.

"But Gracie Montez married that Petey Ravanno," Pilon cried excitedly. "I know her. She is a good woman. She never misses mass, and she goes once a month to confession."

"So it is now," Jesus Maria agreed. "Old Man Ravanno was angry. He ran to Gracie's house, and he cried, 'See how you murder my boy with your foolishness. He tried to kill himself for you, dung-heap chicken.'

"Gracie was afraid, but she was pleased too, because it is not many women who can make a man go so far. She went to see Petey where he was in bed with a crooked neck. After a little while they were married.

"It turned out the way Petey thought it would, too. When the church told her to be a good wife, she was a good wife. She didn't laugh to men any more. And she didn't run away so they chased her. Petey went on cutting squids, and pretty soon Chin Kee let him empty the squid boxes. And not long after that he was the mayordomo of the squid yard. You see," said Jesus Maria, "there is a good story. It would be a story for a priest to tell, if it stopped there."

"Oh, yes," said Pilon gravely. "There are things to be learned in this story."

The friends nodded appreciatively, for they liked a story with a meaning.

"I knew a girl in Texas like that," said Danny. "Only she didn't change. They called her the wife of the second platoon. 'Mrs. Second Platoon,' they said."

Pablo held up his hand. "There is more to this story," he said. "Let Jesus Maria tell the rest."

"Yes, there is more. And it is not such a good story, in the ending. There was the *viejo,* over sixty. And Petey and Gracie went to live in another house. The Viejo Ravanno was lonely, for he had always been with Petey. He didn't know how to take up his time. He just sat and looked sad, until one day he saw 'Tonia again. 'Tonia was fifteen, and she was prettier, even, than Gracie. Half the soldiers from the Presidio followed her around like little dogs.

"Now as it had been with Petey, so it was with the old man. His desire made him ache all over. He could not eat or sleep. His cheeks sunk in, and his eyes stared like the eyes of a marihuana smoker. He carried candy to 'Tonia, and she grabbed the candy out of his hands and laughed at him. He said, 'Come to me, little dear one, for I am thy friend.' She laughed again.

"Then the *viejo* told Petey about it. And Petey laughed too. 'You old fool,' Petey said. 'You've had enough women in your life. Don't run after babies.' But it did no good. Old Man Ravanno grew sick with longing. They are hot-blooded, those Ravannos. He hid in the grass and watched her pass by. His heart ached in his breast.

"He needed money to buy presents, so he got a job in the Standard Service Station. He raked the gravel and watered the flowers at that station. He put water in the radiators and cleaned the windshields. With every cent he bought presents for 'Tonia, candy and ribbons and dresses. He paid to have her picture taken with colors.

"She only laughed more, and the *viejo* was nearly crazy. So he thought, 'If marriage in the church made Gracie a good woman, it will make 'Tonia a good woman too.' He asked her to marry him. Then she laughed more than ever. She flung up her skirts to worry him. Oh, she was a devil, that 'Tonia."

"He was a fool," said Pilon smugly. "Old men should not run after babies. They should sit in the sun."

Jesus Maria went on irritably. "Those Ravannos are different," he said, "so hot-blooded."

"Well, it was not a decent thing," said Pilon. "It was a shame on Petey."

Pablo turned to him. "Let Jesus Maria go on. It is his story, Pilon, not thine. Sometime we will listen to thee."

Jesus Maria looked gratefully to Pablo. "I was telling.

"The *viejo* could not stand it any more. But he was not a man to invent anything. He was not like Pilon. He could not think of anything new. The Viejo Ravanno thought like this: 'Gracie married Petey because he hanged himself. I will hang myself, and maybe 'Tonia will marry me.' And then he thought, 'If no one finds me soon enough, I will be dead. Someone must find me.'

"You must know," said Jesus Maria, "at that service station there is a tool house. Early in the morning the *viejo* went down and unlocked the tool house and raked the gravel and watered the flowers before the station opened. The other men came to work at eight o'clock. So, one morning, the *viejo* went into the tool house and put up a rope. Then he waited until it was eight o'clock. He saw the men coming. He put the rope around his neck and stepped off a work bench. And just when he did that, the door of the tool shed blew shut."

Broad smiles broke out on the faces of the friends. Sometimes, they thought, life was very, very humorous.

"Those men did not miss him right away," Jesus Maria went on. "They said, 'He is probably drunk, that old one.' It was an hour later when they opened the door of that tool shed." He looked around.

The smiles were still on the faces of the friends, but they were changed smiles. "You see," Jesus Maria said, "it is funny. But it squeezes in you too."

"What did 'Tonia say?" Pilon demanded. "Did she read a lesson and change her living?"

"No. She did not. Petey told her, and she laughed. Petey laughed too. But he was ashamed. 'Tonia said, 'What an old fool he was,' and 'Tonia looked at Petey that way she had.

"Then Petey, said, 'It is good to have a little sister like thee. Some night I will walk in the woods with thee.' Then 'Tonia laughed again and ran away a little. And she said, 'Do you think I am as pretty as Gracie?' So Petey followed her into the house."

Pilon complained, "It is not a good story. There are too many meanings and too many lessons in it. Some of those lessons are opposite. There is not a story to take into your head. It proves nothing."

"I like it," said Pablo. "I like it because it hasn't any meaning you can see, and still it does seem to mean something, I can't tell what."

The sun had turned across noon, and the air was hot.

"I wonder what the Pirate will bring to eat," said Danny.

"There is a mackerel run in the bay," Pablo observed.

Pilon's eyes brightened. "I have a plan that I thought out," he said.

"When I was a little boy, we lived by the railroad. Every day when the train went by, my brothers and I threw rocks at the engine, and the firemen threw coal at us. Sometimes we picked up a big bucketful of coal and took it in to our mother. Now I thought maybe we could take rocks down on the pier. When the boats come near, we will call names, we will throw rocks. How can those fishermen get back at us? Can they throw oars, or nets? No! They can only throw mackerel."

Danny stood up joyfully. "Now there is a plan!" he cried. "How this little Pilon of ours is our friend! What would we do without our Pilon? Come, I know where there is a great pile of rocks."

"I like mackerel better than any other fish," said Pablo.

□ XV □

How Danny brooded and became mad.
How the devil in the shape of Torrelli assaulted Danny's House.

There is a changeless quality about Monterey. Nearly every day in the morning the sun shines in the windows on the west sides of the streets; and, in the afternoons, on the east sides of the streets. Every day the red bus clangs back and forth between Monterey and Pacific Grove. Every day the canneries send a stink of reducing fish into the air. Every afternoon the wind blows in from the bay and sways the pines on the hills. The rock fishermen sit on the rocks holding their poles, and their faces are graven with patience and with cynicism.

On Tortilla Flat, above Monterey, the routine is changeless too; for there is only a given number of adventures that Cornelia Ruiz can have with her slowly changing procession of sweethearts. She has been known to take again a man long since discarded.

In Danny's house there was even less change. The friends had sunk into a routine which might have been monotonous for anyone but a paisano—up in the morning, to sit in the sun and wonder what the Pirate would bring. The Pirate still cut pitchwood and sold it in the streets of Monterey, but now he bought food with the quarter he earned every day. Occasionally the friends procured some wine, and then there was singing and fighting.

Time is more complex near the sea than in any other place, for in addition to the circling of the sun and the turning of the seasons, the waves beat out the passage of time on the rocks and the tides rise and fall as a great clepsydra.

Danny began to feel the beating of time. He looked at his friends and saw how with them every day was the same. When he got out of his bed in the night and stepped over the sleeping paisanos, he was angry with them for being there. Gradually, sitting on the front porch, in the sun, Danny began to dream of the days of his freedom. He had slept in the woods in summer, and in the warm hay of barns when the winter cold was in. The weight of property was not upon him. He remembered that the name of Danny was a name of storm. Oh, the fights! The flights through the woods with an outraged chicken under his arm! The hiding places in the gulch when an outraged husband proclaimed feud! Storm and violence, sweet violence! When Danny thought of the old lost time, he could taste again how good the stolen food was, and he longed for that old time again. Since his inheritance had lifted him, he had not fought often. He had been drunk, but not adventurously so. Always the weight of the house was upon him; always the responsibility to his friends.

Danny began to mope on the front porch, so that his friends thought him ill.

"Tea made from yerba buena will be good," Pilon suggested. "If you will go to bed, Danny, we will put hot rocks to your feet."

It was not coddling Danny wanted, it was freedom. For a month he brooded, stared at the ground, looked with sullen eyes at his ubiquitous friends, kicked the friendly dogs out of his way.

In the end he gave up to his longing. One night he ran away. He went into the pine woods and disappeared.

When in the morning the friends awakened and found him missing, Pilon said, "It is some lady. He is in love."

They left it there, for every man has a right to love. The friends went on living as they had. But when a week passed with no sign of Danny, they began to worry. In a body they went to the woods to look for him.

"Love is nice," said Pilon. "We cannot blame any man for following a girl, but a week is a week. It must be a lively girl to keep Danny away for a week."

Pablo said, "A little love is like a little wine. Too much of either will make a man sick. Maybe Danny is already sick. Maybe this girl is too lively."

Jesus Maria was worried too. "It is not like the Danny we know to be gone so long. Some bad thing has happened."

The Pirate took his dogs into the woods. The friends advised the dogs, "Find Danny. He may be sick, somewhere he may be dead, that good Danny who lets you sleep in his house."

The Pirate whispered to them, "Oh, evil, ungrateful dogs, find our friend." But the dogs waved their tails happily and sought out a rabbit and went kyoodling after it.

The paisanos ranged all day through the woods, calling Danny's name, looking in places they themselves might have chosen to sleep in, the good hollows between the roots of trees, the thick needle beds, encircled by bushes. They knew where a man would sleep, but they found no sign of Danny.

"Perhaps he is mad," Pilon suggested. "Some secret worry may have turned his wit."

In the evening they went back to Danny's house and opened the door and went in. Instantly they became intense. A thief had been busy. Danny's blankets were gone. All the food was stolen. Two pots were missing.

Pilon looked quickly as Big Joe Portagee, and then he shook his head. "No, you were with us. You didn't do it."

"Danny did it," Pablo said excitedly. "Truly he is mad. He is running through the woods like an animal."

Great care and worry settled on Danny's house. "We must find him," the friends assured one another. "Some harm will fall upon our friend in his craziness. We must search through the whole world until we find him."

They threw off their laziness. Every day they looked for him, and they began to hear curious rumors. "Yes, Danny was here last night. Oh, that drunk one! Oh, that thief! For see, Danny knocked down the *viejo* with a fence picket and he stole a bottle of grappa. What kind of friends are these who let their friend do such things?"

"Yes, we saw Danny. His eye was closed, and he was singing. 'Come into the woods and we will dance, little girls,' but we would not go. We were afraid. That Danny did not look very quiet."

At the wharf they found more evidence of their friend. "He was here," the fishermen said. "He wanted to fight everybody. Benito broke an oar on Danny's head. Then Danny broke some windows, and then a policeman took him to jail."

Hot on the path of their wayward friend, they continued. "McNear brought him in last night," the sergeant said. "Some way he got loose before morning. When we catch him, we'll give him six months."

The friends were tired of the chase. They went home, and to their horror they found that the new sack of potatoes that Pilon had found only that morning was gone.

"Now it is too much," Pilon cried. "Danny is crazy, and he is in danger. Some terrible thing will happen to him if we do not save him."

"We will search," said Jesus Maria.

"We will look behind every tree and every shed," Pablo guaranteed.

"Under the boats on the beach," Big Joe suggested.

"The dogs will help," the Pirate said.

Pilon shook his head. "That is not the way. Every time we come to a place after Danny has gone. We must wait in some place where he will come. We must act as wise men, not as fools."

"But where will he come?"

The light struck all of them at once. "Torrelli's! Sooner or later Danny will go to Torrelli's. We must go there to catch him, to restrain him in the madness that has fallen upon him."

"Yes," they agreed. "We must save Danny."

In a body they visited Torrelli, and Torrelli would not let them in. "Ask me," he cried through the door, "have I seen Danny? Danny brought three blankets and two cooking pots, and I gave him a gallon of wine. What did that devil do then? My wife he insulted and me he called bad names. My baby he spanked, my dog he kicked! He stole the hammock from my porch." Torrelli gasped with emotion. "I chased him to get my hammock back, and when I returned, he was with my wife! Seducer, thief, drunkard! That is your friend Danny! I myself will see that he goes to penitentiary."

The eyes of the friends glinted. "Oh Corsican pig," Pilon said evenly. "You speak of our friend. Our friend is not well."

Torrelli locked the door. They could hear the bolt slide, but Pilon continued to speak through the door. "Oh, Jew," he said, "if thou wert a little more charitable with thy wine, these things would not happen. See that thou keepest that cold frog which is thy tongue from dirtying our friend. See thou treatest him gently, for his friends are many. We will tear thy stomach out if thou art not nice to him."

Torrelli made no sound inside the locked house, but he trembled with rage and fear at the ferocity of the tones. He was relieved when he heard the footsteps of the friends receding up the path.

That night, after the friends had gone to bed, they heard a stealthy step in the kitchen. They knew it was Danny, but he escaped before they could catch him. They wandered about in the dark, calling disconsolately, "Come, Danny, our little sugar friend, we need thee with us."

There was no reply, but a thrown rock struck Big Joe in the stomach and doubled him up on the ground. Oh, how the friends were dismayed, and how their hearts were heavy!

"Danny is running to his death," they said sadly. "Our little friend is in need, and we cannot help him."

It was difficult to keep house now, for Danny had stolen nearly everything in it. A chair turned up at a bootlegger's. All the food was taken, and once, when they were searching for Danny in the woods, he stole the airtight stove; but it was heavy, he abandoned it in the gulch. Money there was none, for Danny stole the Pirate's wheelbarrow and traded it to Joe Ortiz for a bottle of whiskey. Now all peace had gone from Danny's house, and there was only worry and sadness.

"Where is our happiness gone?" Pablo mourned. "Somewhere we have sinned. It is a judgment. We should go to confession."

No more did they discuss the marital parade of Cornelia Ruiz. Gone were the moralities, lost were the humanities. Truly the good life lay in ruins. And into the desolation came the rumors.

"Danny committed partial rape last night."

"Danny has been milking Mrs. Palochico's goat."

"Danny was in a fight with some soldiers the night before last."

Sad as they were at this moral decay, the friends were not a little jealous of the good time Danny was having.

"If he is not crazy, he will be punished," said Pilon. "Be sure of that. Danny is sinning in a way which, sin for sin, beats any record I ever heard of. Oh, the penances when he wants to be decent again! In a few weeks Danny has piled up more sins than Old Ruiz did in a lifetime."

That night Danny, unhindered by the friendly dogs, crept into the house as silently as the moving shadow of a limb under a street light, and wantonly he stole Pilon's shoes. In the morning it did not take Pilon long to understand what had happened. He went firmly to the porch and sat down in the sun and regarded his feet.

"Now he has gone too far," Pilon said. "Pranks he has played, and we were patient. But now he turns to crime. This is not the Danny we know. This is another man, a bad man, We must capture this bad man."

Pablo looked complacently down at his shoes. "Maybe this is only a prank too," he suggested.

"No," Pilon said severely. "This is crime. They were not very good shoes, but it is a crime against friendship to take them. And that is the worst kind of crime. If Danny will steal the shoes of his friends, there is no crime he will stop at."

The friends nodded in agreement. "Yes, we must catch him," said Jesus Maria of the humanities. "We know he is sick. We will tie him to his bed and try to cure him of the sickness. We must try to wipe the darkness from his brain."

"But now," said Pablo, "before we catch him, we must remember to put our shoes under our pillows when we sleep."

The house was in a state of siege. All about it raged Danny, and Danny was having a wonderful time.

Seldom did the face of Torrelli show any emotions but suspicion and anger. In his capacity as bootlegger, and in his dealings with the people of Tortilla Flat, those two emotions were often called into his heart, and their line was written on his face. Moreover, Torrelli had never visited anyone. He had only to stay at home to have everyone visit him. Consequently, when Torrelli walked up the road toward Danny's house in the morning, his face suffused with a ferocious smile of pleasure and anticipation, the children ran into their yards and peeked through the pickets at him; the dogs caressed their stomachs with their tails and fled with backward, fearful looks; men, meeting him, stepped out of his path and clenched their fists to repel a madman.

This morning the fog covered the sky. The sun, after a number of unsuccessful skirmishes, gave up and retired behind the gray folds. The pine trees dripped dusty dew on the ground; and in the faces of the few people who were about, the day was reflected with somber looks and gray skins. There were no hearty greetings. There was none of that human idealism which blandly hopes this day will be better than all other days.

Old Roca, seeing Torrelli smiling, went home and told his wife, "That one has just killed and eaten his children. You will see!"

Torrelli was happy, for in his pocket there was a folded, precious paper. His fingers sought his coat again and again, and pressed until a little crackling sound assured Torrelli that the paper was still there. As he walked through the gray morning, he muttered to himself.

"Nest of snakes," he said. "I will wipe out this pestilence of Danny's friends. No more will I give wine for goods, and have the goods stolen again. Each man alone is not so bad, but the nest of them! Madonna, look down how I will cast them out into the street! The toads, the lice, the stinging flies! When they sleep in the woods again, they will not be so proud.

"I would have them know that Torrelli has triumphed. They thought to cheat me, despoil my house of furniture and my wife of virtue! They will see that Torrelli, the great sufferer, can strike back. Oh, yes, they will see!"

Thus he muttered as he walked, and his fingers crackled the paper in his pocket. The trees dripped mournful drops into the dust. The seagulls circled in the air, screaming tragically. Torrelli moved like gray Fate on Danny's house.

In Danny's house there was gloom. The friends could not sit on the porch in the sunshine, for there was no sunshine. No one can produce a better reason for gloom. They had brought back the stolen stove from the gulch and set it up. They clustered to it now, and Johnny Pom-pom, who had come to call, told the news he had.

"Tito Ralph," he said, "is no longer the jailer down at the city jail. No, this morning the police judge sent him away."

"I liked Tito Ralph," said Pilon. "When a man was in jail, Tito Ralph would bring him a little wine. And he knew more stories than a hundred other men. Why did he lose his job, Johnny Pom-pom?"

"That is what I came to tell. Tito Ralph, you know, was often in jail, and he was a good prisoner. He knew how a jail should be run. After a while he knew more about the jail than anyone. Then Daddy Marks, the old jailer, died, and Tito Ralph took his place. Never has there been such a good jailer as Tito Ralph. Everything he did just right. But he has one little fault. When he drinks wine, he forgets he is the jailer. He escapes, and they have to catch him."

The friends nodded. "I know," said Pablo. "I have heard he is hard to catch too. He hides."

"Yes," continued Johnny Pom-pom, "except for that, he is the best jailer they ever had. Well, this is the thing that I came to tell. Last night Danny had enough wine for ten men, and he drank it. Then he drew pictures on windows. He was very rich, he bought eggs to throw at a Chinaman. And one of those eggs missed the Chinaman and hit a policeman. So, Danny was in jail.

"But he was rich. He sent Tito Ralph out to get some wine, and then some more wine. There were four men in the jail. They all drank wine. And at last that fault of Tito Ralph's came out. So he escaped, and all the others escaped with him. They caught Tito Ralph this morning and told him he could not be jailer any more. He was so sad that he broke a window, and now he is in jail again."

"But Danny," Pilon cried. "What about Danny?"

"Oh, Danny," said Johnny Pom-pom, "he escaped too. They did not catch him."

The friends sighed in dismay.

"Danny is getting bad," Pilon said seriously. "He will not come to a good end. I wonder where he got the money."

It was at this moment that the triumphant Torrelli opened the gate and strode up the path. The Pirate's dogs got up nervously from their corner and moved toward the door, snarling. The friends looked up and questioned one another with their eyes. Big Joe picked up the pick handle that had so lately been used on him. The heavy confident step of Torrelli pounded on the porch. The door flew open, and there stood Torrelli, smiling. He did not bluster at them. No, he approached as delicately as a house cat. He patted them kindly, as a house cat pats a cockroach.

"Oh, my friends," he said gently, at their looks of alarm. "My dear good friends and customers. My heart is torn that I must be a carrier of bad news to those whom I love."

Pilon leaped up. "It is Danny. He is sick, he is hurt. Tell us."

Torrelli shook his head daintily. "No, my little ones, it is not Danny. My heart bleeds, but I must tell you that you cannot live here any more." His eyes gloated at the amazement his words wrought. Every mouth dropped open, every eye went blank with astonishment.

"That is foolish," Pablo cried. "Why can't we live here any more?"

Torrelli's hand went lovingly into his breast pocket, and his fingers brought out the precious paper and waved it in the air. "Imagine my suffering," Torrelli went on. "Danny does not own this house any more."

"What!" they cried. "What do you mean? How does not Danny own his house any more? Speak, O Corsican pig."

Torrelli giggled, a thing so terrible that the paisanos stepped back from him. "Because," he said, "the house belongs to me. Danny came to me and sold me his house for twenty-five dollars last night." Fiendishly he watched the thoughts crowd on their faces.

"It is a lie," their faces said. "Danny would not do such a thing." And then, "But Danny has been doing many bad things lately. He has been stealing from us. Maybe he has sold the house over our heads."

"It is a lie," Pilon cried aloud. "It is a dirty wop lie."

Torrelli smiled on and waved the paper. "Here I have proof," he said. "Here is the paper Danny signed. It is what we of business call a bill of sale."

Pablo came to him furiously. "You got him drunk. He did not know what he did."

Torrelli opened the paper a little bit. "The law will not be interested in that," he said. "And so, my dear little friends, it is my terrible duty to tell you that you must leave my house. I have plans for it." His face lost its smile then, and all the cruelty came back into it. "If you are not out by noon, I will send a policeman."

Pilon moved gently toward him. Oh, beware, Torrelli, when Pilon moves smiling on you! Run, hide yourself in some iron room and weld up the door. "I do not understand these things," Pilon said gently. "Of course I am sad that Danny should do a thing like this."

Torrelli giggled again.

"I never had a house to sell," Pilon continued. "Danny signed this paper, is that it?"

"Yes," Torrelli mimicked him, "Danny signed this paper. That is it."

Pilon blundered on, stupidly. "That is the thing that proves you own this house?"

"Yes, O little fool. This is the paper that proves it."

Pilon looked puzzled. "I thought you must take it down and have some record made."

Torrelli laughed scornfully. Oh, beware, Torrelli! Do you not see how quietly these snakes are moving? There is Jesus Maria in front of the door. There is Pablo by the kitchen door. See Big Joe's knuckles white on the pick handle.

Torrelli said, "You know nothing of business, little hobos and tramps. When I leave here I shall take this paper down and—"

It happened so quickly that the last words belched out explosively. His feet flew up in the air. He landed with a great thump on the floor and clawed at the air with his fat hands. He heard the stove lid clang.

"Thieves," he screamed. The blood pressed up his neck and into his face. "Thieves, oh, rats and dogs, give me my paper!"

Pilon, standing in front of him, looked amazed.

"Paper?" he asked politely. "What is this paper you speak of so passionately?"

"My bill of sale, my ownership. Oh, the police will hear of this!"

"I do not recall a paper," said Pilon. "Pablo, do you know what is this paper he talks about?"

"Paper?" said Pablo. "Does he mean a newspaper or a cigarette paper?"

Pilon continued with the roll. "Johnny Pom-pom?"

"He is dreaming, maybe, that one," said Johnny Pom-pom.

"Jesus Maria? Do you know of a paper?"

"I think he is drunk," Jesus Maria said in a scandalized voice. "It is too early in the morning to be drunk."

"Joe Portagee?"

"I wasn't here," Joe insisted. "I just came in now."

"Pirate?"

"He don't have no paper," the Pirate turned to his dogs, "do he?"

Pilon turned back to the apoplectic Torrelli. "You are mistaken, my friend. It is possible that I might have been wrong about this paper, but you can see for yourself that no one but you saw this paper. Do you blame me when I think that maybe there was no paper? Maybe you should go to bed and rest a little."

Torrelli was too stunned to shout any more. They turned him about and helped him out of the door and sped him on his way, sunk in the awfulness of his defeat.

And then they looked at the sky, and were glad; for the sun had fought again, and this time won a pathway through the fog. The friends did not go back into the house. They sat happily down on the front porch.

"Twenty-five dollars," said Pilon. "I wonder what he did with the money."

The sun, once its first skirmish was won, drove the fog headlong from the sky. The porch boards warmed up, and the flies sang in the light. Exhaustion had settled on the friends.

"It was a close thing," Pablo said wearily. "Danny should not do such things."

"We will get all our wine from Torrelli to make it up to him," said Jesus Maria.

A bird hopped into the rose bush and flirted its tail. Mrs. Morales' new chickens sang a casual hymn to the sun. The dogs, in the front yard, thoughtfully scratched all over and gnawed their tails.

At the sound of footsteps from the road, the friends looked up, and then stood up with welcoming smiles. Danny and Tito Ralph walked in the gate, and each of them carried two heavy bags. Jesus Maria darted into the house and brought out the fruit jars. The friends noticed that Danny looked a little tired when he set his jugs on the porch.

"It is hot climbing that hill," Danny said.

"Tito Ralph," cried Johnny Pom-pom, "I heard you were put in jail."

"I escaped again," Tito Ralph said wanly. "I still had the keys."

The fruit jars gurgled full. A great sigh escaped from the men, a sigh of relief that everything was over.

Pilon took a big drink. "Danny," he said, "that pig Torrelli came up here this morning with lies. He had a paper he said you signed."

Danny looked startled. "Where is that paper?" he demanded.

"Well," Pilon continued. "We knew it was a lie, so we burned that paper. You didn't sign it, did you?"

"No," said Danny, and he drained his jar.

"It would be nice to have something to eat," observed Jesus Maria.

Danny smiled sweetly. "I forgot. In one of those bags are three chickens and some bread."

So great was Pilon's pleasure and relief that he stood up and made a little speech. "Where is there a friend like our friend?" he exclaimed. "He takes us into his house out of the cold. He shares his good food with us, and his wine. Ohee, the good man, the dear friend."

Danny was embarrassed. He looked at the floor. "It is nothing," he murmured. "It has no merit."

But Pilon's joy was so great that it encompassed the world, and even the evil things of the world. "We must do something nice some time for Torrelli," he said.

□   # XVI   □

Of the sadness of Danny. How through sacrifice Danny's
Friends gave a party. How Danny was Translated.

When Danny came back to his house and to his friends after his amok, he was not conscience-stricken, but he was very tired. The rough fingers of violent experience had harped upon his soul. He began to live listlessly, arising from bed only to sit on the porch, under the rose of Castile; arising from the porch only to eat; arising from the table only to go to bed. The talk flowed about him and he listened, but he did not care. Cornelia Ruiz had a quick and superb run of husbands, and no emotion was aroused in Danny. When Big Joe got in his bed one evening, so apathetic was Danny that Pilon and Pablo had to beat Big Joe for him. When Sammy Rasper, celebrating a belated New Year with a shotgun and a gallon of whisky, killed a cow and went to jail, Danny could not even be drawn into a discussion of the ethics of the case, although the arguments raged about him and although his judgment was passionately appealed to.

After a while it came about that the friends began to worry about Danny. "He is changed," said Pilon. "He is old."

Jesus Maria suggested, "This Danny has crowded the good times of a life into a little three weeks. He is sick of fun."

In vain the friends tried to draw him from the cavern of his apathy. In the mornings, on the porch, they told their funniest stories. They reported details of the love life of Tortilla Flat so penetratingly that they would have been of interest to a dissection class. Pilon winnowed the Flat for news and brought home every seedling of interest to Danny; but there was age in Danny's eyes and weariness.

"Thou art not well," Jesus Maria insisted in vain. "There is some bitter secret in thine heart."

"No," said Danny.

It was noticed that he let flies crawl on his feet a long time, and that when he did slap them off there was no art in his stroke. Gradually the high spirits, the ready laughter went out of Danny's house and tumbled into the dark pool of Danny's quietness.

Oh, it was a pity to see him, that Danny who had fought for lost causes, or any other kind; that Danny who could drink glass for glass with any man in the world; that Danny who responded to the look of love like an aroused tiger. Now he sat on his front porch in the sunlight, his blue-jeaned knees drawn up against his chest, his arms hanging over, his hands dangling from limp wrists, his head bent forward as though by a heavy black thought. His eyes had no light of desire nor displeasure nor joy nor pain.

Poor Danny, how has life left thee! Here thou sittest like the first man before the world grew up around him; and like the last man, after the world has eroded away. But see, Danny! Thou art not alone. Thy friends are caught in this state of thine. They look at thee from their eye-corners. They wait like expectant little dogs for the first waking movement of their master. One joyful word from thee, Danny, one joyful look, and they will bark and chase their tails. Thy life is not thine own to govern, Danny, for it controls other lives. See how thy friends suffer! Spring to life, Danny, that thy friends may live again!

This, in effect, although not in words so beautiful, was what Pilon said. Pilon held out a jar of wine to Danny. "Come on," he said. "Get up off your can."

Danny took the jar and drained it. And then he settled back and tried to find again his emotional Nirvana.

"Do you hurt any place?" Pilon asked.

"No," said Danny.

Pilon poured him another jar of wine and watched his face while the wine disappeared. The eyes lost their lackluster. Somewhere in the depths, the old Danny stirred to life for a moment. He killed a fly with a stroke that would have done justice to a master.

Slowly a smile spread over Pilon's face. And later he gathered all the friends, Pablo and Jesus Maria and Big Joe and the Pirate and Johnny Pompom and Tito Ralph.

Pilon led them all into the gulch behind the house. "I gave Danny the last of the wine, and it did him good. What Danny needs is lots of wine, and maybe a party. Where can we get wine?"

Their minds combed the possibilities of Monterey like rat terriers in a barn, but there were no rats. These friends were urged on by altruism more pure than most men can conceive. They loved Danny.

Jesus Maria said, finally, "Chin Kee is packing squids."

Their minds bolted, turned with curiosity and looked at the thing, crept stealthily back and sniffed it. It was several moments before their shocked imaginations could become used to the thing. "But after all, why not?" they argued silently. "One day would not be so bad—only one day."

Their faces showed the progress of the battle and how they were defeating their fears in the interest of Danny's welfare.

"We will do it," Pilon said. "Tomorrow we will all go down and cut squid, and tomorrow night we will give a party for Danny."

When Danny awakened the next morning, the house was deserted. He got up from his bed and looked through the silent rooms. But Danny was not a man to brood very long. He gave it up as a problem, and then as a thought. He went to the front porch and listlessly sat down.

Is it premonition, Danny? Do you fear the fate that is closing in on you? Are there no pleasures left? No. Danny is as sunk in himself as he had been for a week.

Not so Tortilla Flat. Early the rumor flew about. "Danny's friends are cutting squids for Chin Kee." It was a portent, like the overthrow of government, or even of the solar system. It was spoken of in the street, called over back fences to ladies who were just then hurrying to tell it. "All of Danny's friends are down cutting squids."

The morning was electric with the news. There must be some reason, some secret. Mothers instructed their children and sent them running toward Chin Kee's squid yard. Young matrons waited anxiously behind their curtains for later news. And news came.

"Pablo has cut his hand with a squid knife."

"Chin Kee has kicked the Pirate's dogs."

Riot.

"The dogs are back."

"Pilon looks grim."

A few small bets were laid. For months nothing so exciting had happened. During one whole morning not a single person spoke of Cornelia Ruiz. It was not until the noon hour that the real news leaked out, but then it came with a rush.

"They are going to give a big party for Danny."

"Everyone is going."

Instructions began to emerge from the squid yard. Mrs. Morales dusted her phonograph and picked out her loudest records. Some spark flared, and Tortilla Flat was tinder. Seven friends, indeed, to give a party for Danny! It is as though to say Danny had only seven friends! Mrs. Soto descended upon her chicken yard with a cleaver. Mrs. Palochico poured a bag of sugar into her largest cooking pot to make dulces. A delegation of girls went into the Woolworth store in Monterey and bought the complete stock of colored crepe paper. Guitars and accordions cried experimentally through the Flat.

News! More news from the squid yard. They are going to make it. They are firm. They will have at least fourteen dollars. See that fourteen gallons of wine are ready.

Torrelli was overwhelmed with business. Everyone wanted to buy a gallon to take to Danny's house. Torrelli himself, caught in the fury of the movement, said to his wife, "Maybe we will go to Danny's house. I will take a few gallons for my friends."

As the afternoon passed, waves of excitement poured over the Flat. Dresses unworn in a lifetime were unpacked and hung to air. Shawls the moths had yearned for during two hundred years hung from porch railings and exuded the odor of moth balls.

And Danny? He sat like a half-melted man. He moved only when the sun moved. If he realized that every inhabitant of Tortilla Flat had passed his gate that afternoon, he gave no sign. Poor Danny! At least two dozen pairs of eyes watched his front gate. At about four o'clock he stood up, stretched, and sauntered out of his yard, toward Monterey.

Why, they hardly waited until he was out of sight. Oh, the twisting and stringing of green and yellow and red crepe paper! Oh, the candles shaved, and the shavings thrown on the floor! Oh, the mad children who skated the wax in evenly!

Food appeared. Basins of rice, pots of steaming chicken, dumplings to startle you! And the wine came, gallons and gallons of it. Martinez dug up a keg of potato whisky from his manure pile and carried it to Danny's house.

At five-thirty the friends marched up the hill, tired and bloody, but triumphant. So must the Old Guard have looked when they returned to Paris after Austerlitz. They saw the house, bristling with color. They laughed, and their weariness fell from them. They were so happy that tears came into their eyes.

Mama Chipo walked into the yard followed by her two sons who carried a washtub of salsa pura between them. Paulito, that rich scamp, rushed the fire under a big kettle of beans and chili. Shouts, songs broken off, shrieks of women, the general turmoil of excited children.

A carful of apprehensive policemen drove up from Monterey. "Oh, it is only a party. Sure, we'll have a glass of wine. Don't kill anybody."

Where is Danny? Lonely as smoke on a clear cold night, he drifts through Monterey in the evening. To the post office he goes, to the station, to the pool rooms on Alvarado Street, to the wharf where the black water mourns among the piles. What is it, Danny? What makes you feel this way? Danny didn't know. There was an ache in his heart like the farewell to a dear woman; there was vague sorrow in him like the despair of autumn. He walked past the restaurants he used to smell with interest, and no appetite was aroused in him. He walked by Madam Zuca's great establishment, and exchanged no obscene jests with the girls in the windows. Back to the wharf he went. He leaned over the rail and looked into the deep, deep water. Do you know, Danny, how the wine of your life is pouring into the fruit jars of the gods? Do you see the procession of your days in the oily water among the piles? He remained motionless, staring down.

They were worried about him at Danny's house, when it began to get dark. The friends left the party and trotted down the hill into Monterey. They asked, "Have you seen Danny?"

"Yes, Danny walked by here an hour ago. He walked slow."

Pilon and Pablo hunted together. They traced their friend over the route he had followed, and at last they saw him, on the end of the dark pier. He was lighted by a dim electric wharf light. They hurried out to him.

Pablo did not mention it then, but ever afterward it was his custom, when Danny was mentioned, to describe what he saw as he and Pilon walked out on the wharf toward Danny. "There he stood," Pablo always said. "I could just see him, leaning on the rail. I looked at him, and then I saw something else. At first it looked like a black cloud in the air over Danny's head. And then I saw it was a big black bird, as big as a man. It hung in the air like a hawk over a rabbit hole. I crossed myself and said two Hail Marys. The bird was gone when we came to Danny."

Pilon did not see it. Moreover, Pilon did not remember Pablo crossing himself and saying the Hail Marys. But he never interfered with the story, for it was Pablo's story.

They walked rapidly toward Danny; the wharf boards drummed hollowly under their feet. Danny did not turn. They took him by the arms and turned him about.

"Danny! What is wrong?"

"Nothing. I'm all right."

"Are you sick, Danny?"

"No."

"Then what is it that makes you so sad?"

"I don't know," said Danny. "I just feel this way. I don't want to do anything."

"Maybe a doctor could do something for you, Danny."

"I tell you I am not sick."

"Then look," Pilon cried. "We are having a party for you at your house. Everybody in Tortilla Flat is there, and music and wine and chicken! There are maybe twenty or thirty gallons of wine. And bright paper hanging up. Don't you want to come?"

Danny breathed deeply. For a moment he turned back to the deep black water. Perhaps he whispered to the gods a promise or a defiance.

He swung around again to his friends. His eyes were feverish.

"You're goddam right I want to go. Hurry up. I am thirsty. Any girls there?"

"Lots of girls. All the girls."

"Come on, then. Hurry up."

He led them, running up the hill. Long before they arrived they could hear the sweetness of the music through the pines, and the shrill notes of excited happy voices. The three belated ones arrived at a dead run. Danny lifted his head and howled like a coyote. Jars of wine were held out to him. He took a gulp from each one.

That was a party for you! Always afterward when a man spoke of a party with enthusiasm, someone was sure to say with reverence, "Did you go to that party at Danny's house?" And, unless the first speaker were a newcomer, he had been there. That was a party for you! No one ever tried to give a better one. Such a thing was unthinkable, for within two days Danny's party was lifted out of possible comparison with all other parties that ever were. What man came out of that night without some glorious cuts and bruises? Never had there been so many fights; not fights between two men, but roaring battles that raged through whole clots of men, each one for himself.

Oh, the laughter of women! Thin and high and brittle as spun glass. Oh, the ladylike shrieks of protest from the gulch. Father Ramon was absolutely astounded and incredulous at the confessions the next week. The whole happy soul of Tortilla Flat tore itself from restraint and arose into the air, one ecstatic unit. They danced so hard that the floor gave way in one corner. The accordions played so loudly that always afterward they were windbroken, like foundered horses.

And Danny—just as this party knew no comparison, so Danny defied emulation as a celebrant. In the future let some squirt say with excitement,

"Did you see me? Did you see me ask that nigger wench for a dance? Did you see us go 'round and 'round like a tom cats?" and some old, wise, and baleful eye would be turned on him. Some voice, sated with having known the limit of possibilities, would ask quietly, "Did you see Danny the night of the party?"

Sometime a historian may write a cold, dry, fungus-like history of The Party. He may refer to the moment when Danny defied and attacked the whole party, men, women and children, with a table-leg. He may conclude, "A dying organism is often observed to be capable of extraordinary endurance and strength." Referring to Danny's superhuman amorous activity that night, this same historian may write with unshaking hand: "When any living organism is attacked, its whole function seems to aim toward reproduction."

But I say, and the people of Tortilla Flat would say, "To hell with it. That Danny was a man for you!" No one kept actual count, and afterward, naturally, no lady would willingly admit that she had been ignored; so that the reputed prowess of Danny may be somewhat overstated. One tenth of it would be an overstatement for anyone in the world.

Where Danny went, a magnificent madness followed. It is passionately averred in Tortilla Flat that Danny alone drank three gallons of wine. It must be remembered, however, that Danny is now a god. In a few years it may be thirty gallons. In twenty years it may be plainly remembered that the clouds flamed and spelled DANNY in tremendous letters; that the moon dripped blood; that the wolf of the world bayed prophetically from the mountains of the Milky Way.

Gradually a few of those whose stuff was less stern than Danny's began to wilt, to sag, to creep out from under foot. Those who were left, feeling the lack, shouted the louder, fought the more viciously, danced the harder. In Monterey the motors of the fire trucks were kept running, and the firemen, in their red tin hats and raincoats, silently sat in their places and waited.

The night passed quickly, and still Danny roared through the party.

What happened is attested by many witnesses, both men and women. And although their value as witnesses is sometimes attacked on the ground that they had drunk thirty gallons of wine and a keg of potato whisky, those people are sullenly sure of the major points. It took some weeks to get the story into line; some said one thing, some another. But gradually the account clarified into the reasonable form it now has and always will have.

Danny, say the people of Tortilla Flat, had been rapidly changing his form. He had grown huge and terrible. His eyes flared like the headlights of an automobile. There was something fearsome about him. There he stood, in the room of his own house. He held the pine table-leg in his right hand, and even it had grown. Danny challenged the world.

"Who will fight?" he cried. "Is there no one left in the world who is not afraid?" The people were afraid; that table-leg, so hideous and so alive, had become a terror to them all. Danny swung it back and forth. The accordions wheezed to silence. The dancing stopped. The room grew chill, and a silence seemed to roar in the air like an ocean.

"No one?" Danny cried again. "Am I alone in the world? Will no one fight with me?" The men shuddered before his terrible eyes, and watched, fascinated, the slashing path of the table-leg through the air. And no one answered the challenge.

Danny drew himself up. It is said that his head just missed touching the ceiling. "Then I will go out to The One who can fight. I will find The Enemy who is worthy of Danny!" He stalked to the door, staggering a little as he went. The terrified people made a broad path for him. He bent to get out of the door. The people stood still and listened.

Outside the house they heard his roaring challenge. They heard the table-leg whistle like a meteor through the air. They heard his footsteps charging down the yard. And then, behind the house, in the gulch, they heard an answering challenge so fearful and so chill that their spines wilted like nasturtium stems under frost. Even now, when the people speak of Danny's Opponent, they lower their voices and look furtively about. They heard Danny charge to the fray. They heard his last shrill cry of defiance, and then a thump. And then silence.

For a long moment the people waited, holding their breaths lest the harsh rush of air from their lungs should obscure some sound. But they listened in vain. The night was hushed, and the gray dawn was coming.

Pilon broke the silence. "Something is wrong," he said. And Pilon it was who first rushed out of the door. Brave man, no terror could restrain him. The people followed him. Back of the house they went, where Danny's footsteps had sounded, and there was no Danny. They came to the edge of the gulch, where a sharp zigzag path led down to the bottom of that ancient watercourse wherein no stream had flowed for many generations. The following people saw Pilon dart down the path. They went after him, slowly. And they found Pilon at the bottom of the gulch, leaning over a broken and twisted Danny. He had fallen forty feet. Pilon lighted a match. "I think he is alive," he shrieked. "Run for a doctor. Run for Father Ramon."

The people scattered. Within fifteen minutes four doctors were awakened, dragged from their beds by frantic paisanos. They were not allowed that slow deliberateness by which doctors love to show that they are no slaves to emotion. No! They were hustled, rushed, pushed, their instrument cases were shoved into their hands by men hopelessly incapable of saying what they wanted. Father Ramon, dragged from his bed, came panting up the hill, uncertain whether it was a devil to drive out, a newborn baby to baptize before it died, or a lynching to attend. Meanwhile Pilon and Pablo and Jesus Maria carried Danny up the hill and laid him on his bed. They stood candles all about him. Danny was breathing heavily.

First the doctors arrived. They glanced suspiciously at one another, considered precedence; but the moment of delay brought threatening looks into the eyes of the people. It did not take long to look Danny over. They were all through by the time Father Ramon arrived.

I shall not go into the bedroom with Father Ramon, for Pilon and Pablo and Jesus Maria and Big Joe and Johnny Pom-pom and Tito Ralph and the Pirate and the dogs were there; and they were Danny's family. The door was, and is, closed. For after all there is pride in men, and some things cannot decently be pried into.

But in the big room, crowded to suffocation with the people of Tortilla Flat, there was tenseness and a waiting silence. Priests and doctors have developed a subtle means of communication. When Father Ramon came out of the bedroom his face had not changed, but at sight of him the women broke into a high and terrible wail. The men shifted their feet like horses in a box stall, and then went outside into the dawning. And the bedroom door remained closed.

□   **XVII**   □

How Danny's sorrowing Friends defied the conventions.
How the Talismanic Bond was burned. How each Friend
departed alone.

Death is a personal matter, arousing sorrow, despair, fervor, or dry-hearted philosophy. Funerals, on the other hand, are social functions. Imagine going to a funeral without first polishing the automobile. Imagine standing at a graveside not dressed in your best dark suit and your best black shoes, polished delightfully. Imagine sending flowers to a funeral with no attached card to prove you had done the correct thing. In no social institution is the codified ritual of behavior more rigid than in funerals. Imagine the indignation if the minister altered his sermon or experimented with facial expression. Consider the shock if, at the funeral parlors, any chairs were used but those little folding yellow torture chairs with the hard seats. No, dying, a man may be loved, hated, mourned, missed; but once dead he becomes the chief ornament of a complicated and formal social celebration.

Danny was dead, two days dead; and already he had ceased to be Danny. Although the faces of the people were recently and mournfully veiled with gloom, there was excitement in their hearts. The government has promised a military funeral to all of its ex-soldier sons who wish it. Danny was the first of Tortilla Flat to go, and Tortilla Flat was ready critically to test the government promises. Already news had been sent to the Presidio and Danny's body had been embalmed at government expense. Already a caisson was newly painted and waiting in the artillery shed with a neat new flag folded on top of it. Already orders of the day for Friday were made out:

> TEN TO ELEVEN A.M., FUNERAL. ESCORT, SQUADRON A,
> 11TH CAVALRY, 11TH CAVALRY BAND, AND FIRING
> SQUAD.

Were these not things to set every woman in Tortilla Flat window shopping at the National Dollar Store in Monterey? During the day dark children walked the streets of Monterey, begging flowers from the gardens for Danny's funeral. And at night the same children visited the same gardens to augment their bouquets.

At the party, the finest clothes had been worn. During the two-day interval, those clothes had to be cleaned, washed, starched, mended, and ironed. The activity was frantic. The excitement was decently intense.

On the evening of the second day, Danny's friends were gathered in Danny's house. The shock and the wine had worn off; and now they were horror-stricken, for in all Tortilla Flat they, who had loved Danny most, who had received the most from his hands, they, the paisanos, were the only ones who could not attend Danny's funeral. Through the murk of the headaches they had been conscious of this appalling tragedy, but only on this evening had the situation become so concrete that it must be faced. Ordinarily their clothes were unspeakable. The party had aged their jeans and blue shirts by years. Where was the trouser knee unburst? Where the shirt unripped? If anyone else had died, they could have borrowed clothes; but there was no person in Tortilla Flat who was not going to wear his good clothes to the funeral. Only Cocky Riordan was not going, but Cocky was in quarantine for smallpox, and so were his clothes. Money might be begged or stolen to buy one good suit, but money for six suits was simply impossible to get.

You may say, did they not love Danny enough to go to his funeral in rags? Would you go in rags when your neighbors were dressed in finery? Would not the disrespect to Danny be more if they went in rags than if they did not go at all?

The despair that lay on their hearts was incalculable. They cursed their fate. Through the front door they could see Galvez parading by. Galvez had bought a new suit for the funeral, and he had it on twenty-four hours in advance. The friends sat, chin in hand, crushed by their ill fortune. Every possibility had been discussed.

Pilon, for once in his life, descended to absurdity. "We might go out tonight and each one steal a suit," he suggested. He knew that was silly, for every suit would be laid on a chair beside a bed that night. It would be death to steal a suit.

"The Salvation Army sometimes gives suits," said Jesus Maria.

"I have been there," Pablo said. "They have fourteen dresses this time, but no suits."

On every side Fate was against them. Tito Ralph came in with his new green handkerchief sticking out of his breast pocket, but the hostility he aroused made him back apologetically out of the room.

"If we had a week, we could cut squids," Pilon said heroically. "The funeral is tomorrow. We must look in the eye at this thing. Of course we can go to the funeral all right."

"How?" the friends demanded.

"We can go on the sidewalk, while the band and the people march in the street. It is all grass around the cemetery fence. We can lie there in the grass and see everything."

The friends looked at Pilon gratefully. They knew how his sharp wits had been digging over possibilities. But it was only half, less than half, to see the funeral. Being seen at the funeral was the more important half. This was the best that could be done.

"In this we learn a lesson," said Pilon. "We must take it to heart that we should always have a good suit of clothes laid by. We can never tell what may happen."

There they left it, but they felt that they had failed. All through the night they wandered in the town. What yard then was not plundered of its finest blooms? What flowering tree remained standing? In the morning the hole in the cemetery that was to receive Danny's body was almost hidden by a mound of the finest flowers from the best gardens in Monterey.

It is not always that Nature arranges her effects with good taste. Truly, it rained before Waterloo; forty feet of snow fell in the path of the Donner Party. But Friday turned out a nice day. The sun arose as though this were a day for a picnic. The gulls flew in across a smiling bay to the sardine canneries. The rock fishermen took their places on the rocks for the ebbing tide. The Palace Drug Company ran down its awnings to protect the red hot-water bottles in its windows from the chemical action of the sun. Mr. Machado, the tailor, put a sign in his window, Back in Ten Minutes, and went home to dress for the funeral. Three purse seiners came in, loaded with sardines. Louie Duarte painted his boat, and changed its name from Lolita to The Three Cousins. Jake Lake, the cop, arrested a roadster from Del Monte and turned it loose and bought a cigar.

It is a puzzle. How can life go on its stupid course on such a day? How can Mamie Jackson hose off her front sidewalk? How can George W. Merk write his fourth and angriest letter to the water company? How can Charlie Marsh be as dirtily drunk as usual? It is sacrilege. It is outrage.

Danny's friends awakened sadly and got up off the floor. Danny's bed was empty. It was like the riderless charger of an officer which follows its master to his grave. Even Big Joe Portagee had cast no covetous glance at Danny's bed. The sun shone enthusiastically through the window and cast the delicate shadows of spider webs on the floor.

"Danny was glad on mornings like this," said Pilon.

After their trip to the gulch the friends sat for a while on the front porch and celebrated the memory of their friend. Loyally they remembered and proclaimed Danny's virtues. Loyally they forgot his faults.

"And strong," said Pablo. "He was as strong as a mule! He could lift a bale of hay."

They told little stories of Danny, of his goodness, his courage, his piety.

All too soon it was time to go to the church, to stand across the street in their ragged clothes. They blushed inwardly when luckier people went into the church, dressed so beautifully, smelling so prodigally of Agua Florida. The friends could hear the music and the shrill drone of the service. From their vantage point they saw the cavalry arrive, and the band with muffled drums, and the firing squad, and the caisson with its three pairs of horses, and a cavalryman on the near horse of each pair. The mournful clop-clop of shod horses on asphalt put despair in the hearts of the friends. Helplessly they watched the casket carried out and laid on the caisson, and the flag draped over it. The officer blew his whistle, raised his hand and threw it forward. The squadron moved, the firing squad dropped its rifles. The drums thundered their heartbreaking, slow rhythm. The band played its sodden march. The caisson moved. The people walked majestically behind, men straight and stern, women daintily holding their skirts up out of the indelible trail of the cavalry. Everyone was there, Cornelia Ruiz, Mrs. Morales, Galvez, Torrelli and his plump wife, Mrs. Palochico, Tito Ralph the traitor, Sweets Ramirez, Mr. Machado, everyone who amounted to anything on Tortilla Flat, and everyone else, was there.

Is it any wonder that the friends could not stand the shame and misery of it? For a little while they slunk along the sidewalk, bolstered with heroism.

Jesus Maria broke down first. He sobbed with shame, for his father had been a rich and respected prize-fighter. Jesus Maria put down his head and bolted; and the five other friends followed, and the five dogs bounded behind them.

Before the procession was in sight, Danny's friends were lying in the tall grass that edged the cemetery. The service was short and military. The casket was lowered; the rifles cracked; the bugle sang taps, and at the sound Enrique and Fluff, Pajarito and Rudolph and Señor Alec Thompson laid back their heads and howled. The Pirate was proud of them then!

It was over too soon; the friends walked hurriedly away so that the people would not see them.

They had to pass Torrelli's deserted house anyway, on the way home. Pilon went in through a window and brought out two gallons of wine. And then they walked slowly back to Danny's quiet house. Ceremoniously they filled the fruit jars and drank.

"Danny liked wine," they said. "Danny was happy when he had a little wine."

The afternoon passed, and the evening came. Each man, as he sipped his wine, roved through the past. At seven o'clock a shamed Tito Ralph came in with a box of cigars he had won on a punch board. The friends lighted the cigars and spat, and opened the second gallon. Pablo tried a few notes of the song "Tuli Pan," to see whether his voice was gone for good.

"Cornelia Ruiz was alone today," Pilon said speculatively.

"Maybe it would be all right to sing a few sad songs," said Jesus Maria.

"But Danny did not like sad songs," Pablo insisted. "He liked the quick ones, about lively women."

They all nodded gravely. "Yes, Danny was a great one for women."

Pablo tried the second verse to "Tuli Pan," and Pilon helped a little, and the others joined in toward the end.

When the song was done, Pilon puffed at his cigar, but it had gone out. "Tito Ralph," he said, "why don't you get your guitar so we can sing a little better?" He lighted his cigar and flipped the match.

The little burning stick landed on an old newspaper against the wall. Each man started up to stamp it out; and each man was struck with a celestial thought, and settled back. They found one another's eyes and smiled the wise smiles of the deathless and hopeless ones. In a reverie they watched the flame flicker and nearly die, and sprout to life again. They saw it bloom on the paper. Thus do the gods speak with tiny causes. And the men smiled on as the paper burned and the dry wooden wall caught.

Thus must it be, O wise friends of Danny. The cord that bound you together is cut. The magnet that drew you has lost its virtue. Some stranger will own the house, some joyless relative of Danny's. Better that this symbol of holy friendship, this good house of parties and fights, of love and comfort, should die as Danny died, in one last glorious, hopeless assault on the gods.

They sat and smiled. And the flame climbed like a snake to the ceiling and broke through the roof and roared. Only then did the friends get up from the chairs and walk like dreaming men out of the door.

Pilon, who profited by every lesson, took what was left of the wine with him.

The sirens screamed from Monterey. The trucks roared up the hill in second gear. The searchlights played among the trees. When the Department arrived, the house was one great blunt spear of flame. The hoses wet the trees and brush to keep the flames from spreading.

Among the crowding people of Tortilla Flat, Danny's friends stood entranced and watched until at last the house was a mound of black, steaming cinders. Then the fire trucks turned and coasted away down the hill.

The people of the Flat melted into the darkness. Danny's friends still stood looking at the smoking ruin. They looked at one another strangely, and then back to the burned house. And after a while they turned and walked slowly away, and no two walked together.

THOMAS MANN

Mario and the Magician

TRANSLATED BY H. T. LOWE-PORTER

The atmosphere of Torre di Venere remains unpleasant in the memory. From the first moment the air of the place made us uneasy, we felt irritable, on edge; then at the end came the shocking business of Cipolla, that dreadful being who seemed to incorporate, in so fateful and so humanly impressive a way, all the peculiar evilness of the situation as a whole. Looking back, we had the feeling that the horrible end of the affair had been preordained and lay in the nature of things; that the children had to be present at it was an added impropriety, due to the false colours in which the weird creature presented himself. Luckily for them, they did not know where the comedy left off and the tragedy began; and we let them remain in their happy belief that the whole thing had been a play up till the end.

Torre di Venere lies some fifteen kilometres from Portoclemente, one of the most popular summer resorts on the Tyrrhenian Sea. Portoclemente is urban and elegant and full to overflowing for months on end. Its gay and busy main street of shops and hotels runs down to a wide sandy beach covered with tents and pennanted sand-castles and sunburnt humanity, where at all times a lively social bustle reigns, and much noise. But this same spacious and inviting fine-sanded beach, this same border of pine grove and near, presiding mountains, continues all the way along the coast. No wonder then that some competition of a quiet kind should have sprung up further on. Torre di Venere—the tower that gave the town its name is gone long since, one looks for it in vain—is an offshoot of the larger resort, and for some years remained an idyll for the few, a refuge for more unworldly spirits. But the usual history of such places repeated itself: peace has had to retire further along the coast, to Marina Petriera and dear knows where else. We all know how the world at once seeks peace and puts her to flight—rushing upon her in the fond idea that they two will wed, and where she is, there it can be at

home. It will even set up its Vanity Fair in a spot and be capable of thinking
that peace is still by its side. Thus Torre—though its atmosphere so far is
more modest and contemplative than that of Portoclemente—has been quite
taken up, by both Italians and foreigners. It is no longer the thing to go to
Portoclemente—though still so much the thing that it is as noisy and
crowded as ever. One goes next door, so to speak: to Torre. So much more
refined, even, and cheaper to boot. And the attractiveness of these qualities
persists, though the qualities themselves long ago ceased to be evident. Torre
has got a Grand Hotel. Numerous pensions have sprung up, some modest,
some pretentious. The people who own or rent the villas and pinetas overlooking the sea no longer have it all their own way on the beach. In July and
August it looks just like the beach at Portoclemente: it swarms with a
screaming, squabbling, merrymaking crowd, and the sun, blazing down like
mad, peels the skin off their necks. Garish little flat-bottomed boats rock on
the glittering blue, manned by children, whose mothers hover afar and fill the
air with anxious cries of Nino! and Sandro! and Bice! and Maria! Pedlars step
across the legs of recumbent sun-bathers, selling flowers and corals, oysters,
lemonade, and *cornetti al burro,* and crying their wares in the breathy, full-
throated southern voice.

Such was the scene that greeted our arrival in Torre: pleasant enough,
but after all, we thought, we had come too soon. It was the middle of August, the Italian season was still at its height, scarcely the moment for strangers to learn to love the special charms of the place. What an afternoon crowd
in the cafés on the front! For instance, in the Esquisito, where we sometimes
sat and were served by Mario, that very Mario of whom I shall have presently
to tell. It is well-nigh impossible to find a table; and the various orchestras
contend together in the midst of one's conversation with bewildering effect.
Of course, it is in the afternoon that people come over from Portoclemente.
The excursion is a favourite one for the restless denizens of that pleasure resort, and a Fiat motor-bus plies to and from, coating inch-thick with dust the
oleander and laurel hedges along the highroad—a notable if repulsive sight.

Yes, decidedly one should go to Torre in September, when the great
public has left. Or else in May, before the water is warm enough to tempt the
Southerner to bathe. Even in the before and after seasons Torre is not empty,
but life is less national and more subdued. English, French, and German prevail under the tent-awnings and in the pension dining-rooms; whereas in August—in the Grand Hotel, at least, where, in default of private addresses, we
had engaged rooms—the stranger finds the field so occupied by Florentine
and Roman society that he feels quite isolated and even temporarily *déclassé.*

We had, rather to our annoyance, this experience on the evening we arrived, when we went in to dinner and were shown to our table by the waiter
in charge. As a table, it had nothing against it, save that we had already fixed
our eyes upon those on the veranda beyond, built out over the water, where

little red-shaded lamps glowed—and there were still some tables empty, though it was as full as the dining-room within. The children went into raptures at the festive sight, and without more ado we announced our intention to take our meals by preference in the veranda. Our words, it appeared, were prompted by ignorance; for we were informed, with somewhat embarrassed politeness, that the cosy nook outside was reserved for the clients of the hotel: *ai nostri clienti.* Their clients? But we were their clients. We were not tourists or trippers, but boarders for a stay of some three or four weeks. However, we forbore to press for an explanation of the difference between the likes of us and that clientèle to whom it was vouchsafed to eat out there in the glow of the red lamps, and took our dinner by the prosaic common light of the dining-room chandelier—a thoroughly ordinary and monotonous hotel bill of fare, be it said. In Pensione Eleonora, a few steps landward, the table, as we were to discover, was much better.

And thither it was that we moved, three or four days later, before we had had time to settle in properly at the Grand Hotel. Not on account of the veranda and the lamps. The children, straightway on the best of terms with waiters and pages, absorbed in the joys of life on the beach, promptly forgot those colourful seductions. But now there arose, between ourselves and the veranda clientèle—or perhaps more correctly with the compliant management—one of those little unpleasantnesses which can quite spoil the pleasure of a holiday. Among the guests were some high Roman aristocracy, a Principe X and his family. These grand folk occupied rooms close to our own, and the Principessa, a great and a passionately maternal lady, was thrown into a panic by the vestiges of a whooping-cough which our little ones had lately got over, but which now and then still faintly troubled the unshatterable slumbers of our youngest-born. The nature of this illness is not clear, leaving some play for the imagination. So we took no offence at our elegant neighbour for clinging to the widely held view that whooping-cough is acoustically contagious and quite simply fearing lest her children yield to the bad example set by ours. In the fullness of her feminine self-confidence she protested to the management, which then, in the person of the proverbial frock-coated manager, hastened to represent to us, with many expressions of regret, that under the circumstances they were obliged to transfer us to the annexe. We did our best to assure him that the disease was in its very last stages, that it was actually over, and presented no danger of infection to anybody. All that we gained was permission to bring the case before the hotel physician—not one chosen by us—by whose verdict we must then abide. We agreed, convinced that thus we should at once pacify the Princess and escape the trouble of moving. The doctor appeared, and behaved like a faithful and honest servant of science. He examined the child and gave his opinion: the disease was quite over, no danger of contagion was present. We drew a long breath and considered the incident closed—until the manager announced that despite the doctor's verdict it would still be necessary for us to give up our rooms and retire to the *dépendance*. Byzantinism like this outraged us. It is not likely that the Principessa was responsible for the wilful breach of faith. Very likely the fawning management had not even dared to tell her what the physician said. Anyhow, we made it clear to his understanding that we preferred to leave the hotel altogether and at once—and packed our trunks. We could do so with a light heart, having already set up casual friendly relations with Casa Eleonora. We had noticed its pleasant exterior and formed the acquaintance of its proprietor, Signora Angiolieri, and her husband: she slender and black-haired, Tuscan in type, probably at the beginning of the thirties, with the dead ivory complexion of the southern woman, he quiet and bald and carefully dressed. They owned a larger establishment in Florence and presided only in summer and early autumn over the branch in Torre di Venere. But earlier, before her marriage, our new landlady had been companion, fellow-traveller, wardrobe mistress, yes, friend, of Eleanora Duse and manifestly regarded that period as the crown of her career. Even at our first visit she spoke of it with animation. Numerous photographs of the great actress, with affectionate inscriptions, were displayed about the drawing-room, and other souvenirs of their life together adorned the little tables and étagères. This cult of a so interesting past was calculated, of course, to heighten the advantages of the signora's present business. Nevertheless our pleasure and interest were quite genuine as we were conducted through the house by its owner and listened to her sonorous and staccato Tuscan voice relating anecdotes of that immortal mistress, depicting her suffering saintliness, her genius, her profound delicacy of feeling.

Thither, then, we moved our effects, to the dismay of the staff of the Grand Hotel, who, like all Italians, were very good to children. Our new quarters were retired and pleasant, we were within easy reach of the sea through the avenue of young plane trees that ran down to the esplanade. In the clean, cool dining-room Signora Angiolieri daily served the soup with her own hands, the service was attentive and good, the table capital. We even discovered some Viennese acquaintances, and enjoyed chatting with them after luncheon, in front of the house. They, in their turn, were the means of our finding others—in short, all seemed for the best, and we were heartily glad of the change we had made. Nothing was now wanting to a holiday of the most gratifying kind.

And yet no proper gratification ensued. Perhaps the stupid occasion of our change of quarters pursued us to the new ones we had found. Personally, I admit that I do not easily forget these collisions with ordinary humanity, the naïve misuse of power, the injustice, the sycophantic corruption. I dwelt upon the incident too much, it irritated me in retrospect—quite futilely, of course, since such phenomena are only all too natural and all too much the rule. And we had not broken off relations with the Grand Hotel. The children were as friendly as ever there, the porter mended their toys, and we sometimes took tea in the garden. We even saw the Principessa. She would come out, with her firm and delicate tread, her lips emphatically corallined, to look after her children, playing under the supervision of their English governess. She did not dream that we were anywhere near, for so soon as she appeared in the offing we sternly forbade our little one even to clear his throat.

The heat—if I may bring it in evidence—was extreme. It was African. The power of the sun, directly one left the border of the indigo-blue wave, was so frightful, so relentless, that the mere thought of the few steps between the beach and luncheon was a burden, clad though one might be only in pyjamas. Do you care for that sort of thing? Weeks on end? Yes, of course, it is proper to the south, it is classic weather, the sun of Homer, the climate wherein human culture came to flower—and all the rest of it. But after a while it is too much for me, I reach a point where I begin to find it dull. The burning void of the sky, day after day, weighs one down; the high coloration, the enormous naïveté of the unrefracted light—they do, I dare say, induce light-heartedness, a carefree mood born of immunity from downpours and other meteorological caprices. But slowly, slowly, there makes itself felt a lack: the deeper, more complex needs of the northern soul remain unsatisfied. You are left barren—even, it may be, in time, a little contemptuous. True, without that stupid business of the whooping-cough I might not have been feeling these things. I was annoyed, very likely I wanted to feel them and so half-unconsciously seized upon an idea lying ready to hand to induce, or if not to induce, at least to justify and strengthen, my attitude. Up to this point, then, if you like, let us grant some ill will on our part. But the sea; and the mornings spent extended upon the fine sand in face of its eternal splendours—no, the sea could not conceivably induce such feelings. Yet it was none the less true that, despite all previous experience, we were not at home on the beach, we were not happy.

It was too soon, too soon. The beach, as I have said, was still in the hands of the middle-class native. It is a pleasing breed to look at, and among the young we saw much shapeliness and charm. Still, we were necessarily surrounded by a great deal of very average humanity—a middle-class mob, which, you will admit, is not more charming under this sun than under one's own native sky. The voices these women have! It was sometimes hard to believe that we were in the land which is the western cradle of the art of song. *"Fuggièro!"* I can still hear that cry, as for twenty mornings long I heard it close behind me, breathy, full-throated, hideously stressed, with a harsh open *e*, uttered in accents of mechanical despair. *"Fuggièro! Rispondi almeno!"* Answer when I call you! The *sp* in *rispondi* was pronounced like *shp*, as Germans pronounce it; and this, on top of what I felt already, vexed my sensitive soul. The cry was addressed to a repulsive youngster whose sunburn had made disgusting raw sores on his shoulders. He outdid anything I have ever seen for

ill-breeding, refractoriness, and temper and was a great coward to boot, putting the whole beach in an uproar, one day, because of his outrageous sensi-
tiveness to the slightest pain. A sand-crab had pinched his toe in the water,
and the minute injury made him set up a cry of heroic proportions—the
shout of an antique hero in his agony—that pierced one to the marrow and
called up visions of some frightful tragedy. Evidently he considered himself
not only wounded, but poisoned as well; he crawled out on the sand and lay
in apparently intolerable anguish, groaning *"Ohi!"* and *"Ohimè!"* and threshing about with arms and legs to ward off his mother's tragic appeals and the
questions of the bystanders. An audience gathered round. A doctor was
fetched—the same who had pronounced objective judgment on our whooping-cough—and here again acquitted himself like a man of science. Good-naturedly he reassured the boy, telling him that he was not hurt at all, he
should simply go into the water again to relieve the smart. Instead of which,
Fuggièro was borne off the beach, followed by a concourse of people. But he
did not fail to appear next morning, nor did he leave off spoiling our children's sand-castles. Of course, always by accident. In short, a perfect terror.

And this twelve-year-old lad was prominent among the influences that,
imperceptibly at first, combined to spoil our holiday and render it unwhole-
some. Somehow or other, there was a stiffness, a lack of innocent enjoyment.
These people stood on their dignity—just why, and in what spirit, it was not
easy at first to tell. They displayed much self-respectingness; towards each
other and towards the foreigner their bearing was that of a person newly
conscious of a sense of honour. And wherefore? Gradually we realized the political implications and understood that we were in the presence of a national
ideal. The beach, in fact, was alive with patriotic children—a phenomenon as
unnatural as it was depressing. Children are a human species and a society
apart, a nation of their own, so to speak. On the basis of their common form
of life, they find each other out with the greatest ease, no matter how different their small vocabularies. Ours soon played with natives and foreigners
alike. Yet they were plainly both puzzled and disappointed at times. There
were wounded sensibilities, displays of assertiveness—or rather hardly assertiveness, for it was too self-conscious and too didactic to deserve the name.
There were quarrels over flags, disputes about authority and precedence.
Grown-ups joined in, not so much to pacify as to render judgment and enun-
ciate principles. Phrases were dropped about the greatness and dignity of
Italy, solemn phrases that spoilt the fun. We saw our two little ones retreat,
puzzled and hurt, and were put to it to explain the situation. These people,
we told them, were just passing through a certain stage, something rather
like an illness, perhaps; not very pleasant, but probably unavoidable.

We had only our own carelessness to thank that we came to blows in the
end with this "stage"—which, after all, we had seen and sized up long before
now. Yes, it came to another "cross-purposes," so evidently the earlier ones

had not been sheer accident. In a word, we became an offence to the public morals. Our small daughter—eight years old, but in physical development a good year younger and thin as a chicken—had had a good long bathe and gone playing in the warm sun in her wet costume. We told her that she might take off her bathing-suit, which was stiff with sand, rinse it in the sea, and put it on again, after which she must take care to keep it cleaner. Off goes the costume and she runs down naked to the sea, rinses her little jersey, and comes back. Ought we to have foreseen the outburst of anger and resentment which her conduct, and thus our conduct, called forth? Without delivering a homily on the subject, I may say that in the last decade our attitude towards the nude body and our feelings regarding it have undergone, all over the world, a fundamental change. There are things we "never think about" any more, and among them is the freedom we had permitted to this by no means provocative little childish body. But in these parts it was taken as a challenge. The patriotic children hooted. Fuggièro whistled on his fingers. The sudden buzz of conversation among the grown people in our neighbourhood boded no good. A gentleman in city togs, with a not very apropos bowler hat on the back of his head, was assuring his outraged womenfolk that he proposed to take punitive measures; he stepped up to us, and a philippic descended on our unworthy heads, in which all the emotionalism of the sense-loving south spoke in the service of morality and discipline. The offence against decency of which we had been guilty was, he said, the more to be condemned because it was also a gross ingratitude and an insulting breach of his country's hospitality. We had criminally injured not only the letter and spirit of the public bathing regulations, but also the honour of Italy; he, the gentleman in the city togs, knew how to defend that honour and proposed to see to it that our offence against the national dignity should not go unpunished.

We did our best, bowing respectfully, to give ear to this eloquence. To contradict the man, overheated as he was, would probably be to fall from one error into another. On the tips of our tongues we had various answers: as, that the word "hospitality," in its strictest sense, was not quite the right one, taking all the circumstances into consideration. We were not literally the guests of Italy, but of Signora Angiolieri, who had assumed the rôle of dispenser of hospitality some years ago on laying down that of familiar friend to Eleonora Duse. We longed to say that surely this beautiful country had not sunk so low as to be reduced to a state of hypersensitive prudishness. But we confined ourselves to assuring the gentleman that any lack of respect, any provocation on our parts, had been the furthest from our thoughts. And as a mitigating circumstance we pointed out the tender age and physical slightness of the little culprit. In vain. Our protests were waved away, he did not believe in them; our defence would not hold water. We must be made an example of. The authorities were notified, by telephone, I believe, and their representative appeared on the beach. He said the case was *"molto grave."* We had to go with him to the Municipio up in the Piazza, where a higher official confirmed the previous verdict of *"molto grave,"* launched into a stream of the usual didactic phrases—the selfsame tune and words as the man in the bowler hat—and levied a fine and ransom of fifty lire. We felt that the adventure must willy-nilly be worth to us this much of a contribution to the economy of the Italian government; paid, and left. Ought we not at this point to have left Torre as well?

If we only had! We should thus have escaped that fatal Cipolla. But circumstances combined to prevent us from making up our minds to a change. A certain poet says that it is indolence that makes us endure uncomfortable situations. The *aperçu* may serve as an explanation for our inaction. Anyhow, one dislikes voiding the field immediately upon such an event. Especially if sympathy from other quarters encourages one to defy it. And in the Villa Eleonora they pronounced as with one voice upon the injustice of our punishment. Some Italian after-dinner acquaintances found that the episode put their country in a very bad light, and proposed taking the man in the bowler hat to task, as one fellow-citizen to another. But the next day he and his party had vanished from the beach. Not on our account, of course. Though it might be that the consciousness of his impending departure had added energy to his rebuke; in any case his going was a relief. And, futhermore, we stayed because our stay had by now become remarkable in our own eyes, which is worth something in itself, quite apart from the comfort or discomfort involved. Shall we strike sail, avoid a certain experience so soon as it seems not expressly calculated to increase our enjoyment or our self-esteem? Shall we go away whenever life looks like turning in the slightest uncanny, or not quite normal, or even rather painful and mortifying? No, surely not. Rather stay and look matters in the face, brave them out; perhaps precisely in so doing lies a lesson for us to learn. We stayed on and reaped as the awful reward of our constancy the unholy and staggering experience with Cipolla.

I have not mentioned that the after season had begun, almost on the very day we were disciplined by the city authorities. The worshipful gentleman in the bowler hat, our denouncer, was not the only person to leave the resort. There was a regular exodus, on every hand you saw luggage-carts on their way to the station. The beach denationalized itself. Life in Torre, in the cafés and the pinetas, became more homelike and more European. Very likely we might even have eaten at a table in the glass veranda, but we refrained, being content at Signora Angiolieri's—as content, that is, as our evil star would let us be. But at the same time with this turn for the better came a change in the weather: almost to an hour it showed itself in harmony with the holiday calendar of the general public. The sky was overcast; not that it grew any cooler, but the unclouded heat of the entire eighteen days since our arrival, and probably long before that, gave place to a stifling sirocco air, while from time to time a little ineffectual rain sprinkled the velvety surface of the beach. Add to which, that two-thirds of our intended stay at Torre had passed. The colourless, lazy sea, with sluggish jellyfish floating in its shallows, was at least a change. And it would have been silly to feel retrospective longings after a sun that had caused us so many sighs when it burned down in all its arrogant power.

At this juncture, then, it was that Cipolla announced himself. Cavaliere Cipolla he was called on the posters that appeared one day stuck up everywhere, even in the dining-room of Pensione Eleonora. A travelling virtuoso, an entertainer, *"forzatore, illusionista, prestidigatore,"* as he called himself, who proposed to wait upon the highly respectable population of Torre di Venere with a display of extraordinary phenomena of a mysterious and staggering kind. A conjuror! The bare announcement was enough to turn our children's heads. They had never seen anything of the sort, and now our present holiday was to afford them this new excitement. From that moment on they besieged us with prayers to take tickets for the performance. We had doubts, from the first, on the score of the lateness of the hour, nine o'clock; but gave way, in the idea that we might see a little of what Cipolla had to offer, probably no great matter, and then go home. Besides, of course, the children could sleep late next day. We bought four tickets of Signora Angiolieri herself, she having taken a number of the stalls on commission to sell them to her guests. She could not vouch for the man's performance, and we had no great expectations. But we were conscious of a need for diversion, and the children's violent curiosity proved catching.

The Cavaliere's performance was to take place in a hall where during the season there had been a cinema with a weekly programme. We had never been there. You reached it by following the main street under the wall of the *"palazzo,"* a ruin with a "For sale" sign, that suggested a castle and had obviously been built in lordlier days. In the same street were the chemist, the hairdresser, and all the better shops; it led, so to speak, from the feudal past the bourgeois into the proletarian, for it ended off between two rows of poor fishing-huts, where old women sat mending nets before the doors. And here, among the proletariat, was the hall, not much more, actually, than a wooden shed, though a large one, with a turreted entrance, plastered on either side with layers of gay placards. Some while after dinner, then, on the appointed evening, we wended our way thither in the dark, the children dressed in their best and blissful with the sense of so much irregularity. It was sultry, as it had been for days; there was heat lightning now and then, and a little rain; we proceeded under umbrellas. It took us a quarter of an hour.

Our tickets were collected at the entrance, our places we had to find ourselves. They were in the third row left, and as we sat down we saw that, late though the hour was for the performance, it was to be interpreted with even more laxity. Only very slowly did an audience—who seemed to be relied upon to come late—begin to fill the stalls. These comprised the whole auditorium; there were no boxes. This tardiness gave us some concern. The children's cheeks were already flushed as much with fatigue as with excitement. But even when we entered, the standing-room at the back and in the side aisles was already well occupied. There stood the manhood of Torre di Venere, all and sundry, fisherfolk, rough-and-ready youths with bare forearms crossed over their striped jerseys. We were well pleased with the presence of this native assemblage, which always adds colour and animation to occasions like the present; and the children were frankly delighted. For they had friends among these people—acquaintances picked up on afternoon strolls to the further ends of the beach. We would be turning homeward, at the hour when the sun dropped into the sea, spent with the huge effort it had made and gilding with reddish gold the oncoming surf; and we would come upon bare-legged fisherfolk standing in rows, bracing and hauling with long-drawn cries as they drew in the nets and harvested in dripping baskets their catch, often so scanty, of *frutta di mare*. The children looked on, helped to pull, brought out their little stock of Italian words, made friends. So now they exchanged nods with the "standing-room" clientèle; there was Guiscardo, there Antonio, they knew them by name and waved and called across in half-whispers, getting answering nods and smiles that displayed rows of healthy white teeth. Look, there is even Mario, Mario from the Esquisito, who brings us the chocolate. He wants to see the conjuror, too, and he must have come early, for he is almost in front; but he does not see us, he is not paying attention; that is a way he has, even though he is a waiter. So we wave instead to the man who lets out the little boats on the beach; he is there too, standing at the back.

It had got to a quarter past nine, it got to almost half past. It was natural that we should be nervous. When would the children get to bed? It had been a mistake to bring them, for now it would be very hard to suggest breaking off their enjoyment before it had got well under way. The stalls had filled in time; all Torre, apparently, was there: the guests of the Grand Hotel, the guests of Villa Eleonora, familiar faces from the beach. We heard English and German and the sort of French that Rumanians speak with Italians. Madame Angiolieri herself sat two rows behind us, with her quiet, bald-headed spouse, who kept stroking his moustache with the two middle fingers of his right hand. Everybody had come late, but nobody too late. Cipolla made us wait for him.

He made us wait. That is probably the way to put it. He heightened the suspense by his delay in appearing. And we could see the point of this, too—only not when it was carried to extremes. Towards half past nine the audience began to clap—an amiable way of expressing justifiable impatience, evincing as it does an eagerness to applaud. For the little ones, this was a joy in itself—all children love to clap. From the popular sphere came loud cries of

"*Pronti!*" "*Cominciamo!*" And lo, it seemed now as easy to begin as before it had been hard. A gong sounded, greeted by the standing rows with a many-voiced "Ah-h!" and the curtains parted. They revealed a platform furnished more like a schoolroom than like the theatre of a conjuring performance—largely because of the blackboard in the left foreground. There was a common yellow hat-stand, a few ordinary straw-bottomed chairs, and further back a little round table holding a water carafe and glass, also a tray with a liqueur glass and a flask of pale yellow liquid. We had still a few seconds of time to let these things sink in. Then, with no darkening of the house, Cavaliere Cipolla made his entry.

He came forward with a rapid step that expressed his eagerness to appear before his public and gave rise to the illusion that he had already come a long way to put himself at their service—whereas, of course, he had only been standing in the wings. His costume supported the fiction. A man of an age hard to determine, but by no means young; with a sharp, ravaged face, piercing eyes, compressed lips, small black waxed moustache, and a so-called imperial in the curve between mouth and chin. He was dressed for the street with a sort of complicated evening elegance, in a wide black pelerine with velvet collar and satin lining; which, in the hampered state of his arms, he held together in front with his white-gloved hands. He had a white scarf round his neck; a top hat with a curving brim sat far back on his head. Perhaps more than anywhere else the eighteenth century is still alive in Italy, and with it the charlatan and mountebank type so characteristic of the period. Only there, at any rate, does one still encounter really well-preserved specimens. Cipolla had in his whole appearance much of the historic type; his very clothes helped to conjure up the traditional figure with its blatantly, fantastically foppish air. His pretentious costume sat upon him, or rather hung upon him, most curiously, being in one place drawn too tight, in another a mass of awkward folds. There was something not quite in order about his figure, both front and back—that was plain later on. But I must emphasize the fact that there was not a trace of personal jocularity or clownishness in his pose, manner, or behaviour. On the contrary, there was complete seriousness, an absence of any humorous appeal; occasionally even a cross-grained pride, along with that curious, self-satisfied air so characteristic of the deformed. None of all this, however, prevented his appearance from being greeted with laughter from more than one quarter of the hall.

All the eagerness had left his manner. The swift entry had been merely an expression of energy, not of zeal. Standing at the footlights he negligently drew off his gloves, to display long yellow hands, one of them adorned with a seal ring with a lapis-lazuli in a high setting. As he stood there, his small hard eyes, with flabby pouches beneath them, roved appraisingly about the hall, not quickly, rather in a considered examination, pausing here and there upon a face with his lips clipped together, not speaking a word. Then with a dis-

play of skill as surprising as it was casual, he rolled his gloves into a ball and
tossed them across a considerable distance into the glass on the table. Next
from an inner pocket he drew forth a packet of cigarettes; you could see by
the wrapper that they were the cheapest sort the government sells. With his
fingertips he pulled out a cigarette and lighted it, without looking, from a
quick-firing benzine lighter. He drew the smoke deep into his lungs and let it
out again, tapping his foot, with both lips drawn in an arrogant grimace and
the grey smoke streaming out between broken and saw-edged teeth.

With a keenness equal to his own his audience eyed him. The youths at
the rear scowled as they peered at this cocksure creature to search out his secret weaknesses. He betrayed none. In fetching out and putting back the cigarettes his clothes got in his way. He had to turn back his pelerine, and in so
doing revealed a riding-whip with a silver claw-handle that hung by a leather
thong from his left forearm and looked decidedly out of place. You could see
that he had on not evening clothes but a frock-coat, and under this, as he
lifted it to get at his pocket, could be seen a striped sash worn about the
body. Somebody behind me whispered that this sash went with his title of
Cavaliere. I give the information for what it may be worth—personally, I
never heard that the title carried such insignia with it. Perhaps the sash was
sheer pose, like the way he stood there, without a word, casually and arro-
gantly puffing smoke into his audience's face.

People laughed, as I said. The merriment had become almost general
when somebody in the "standing seats," in a loud, dry voice, remarked:
"Buona sera."

Cipolla cocked his head. "Who was that?" asked he, as though he had
been dared. "Who was that just spoke? Well? First so bold and now so modest? *Paura,* eh?" He spoke with a rather high, asthmatic voice, which yet had
a metallic quality. He waited.

"That was me," a youth at the rear broke into the stillness, seeing himself thus challenged. He was not far from us, a handsome fellow in a woollen
shirt, with his coat hanging over one shoulder. He wore his curly, wiry hair
in a high, dishevelled mop, the style affected by the youth of the awakened
Fatherland; it gave him an African appearance that rather spoiled his looks.
"Bè! That was me. It was your business to say it first, but I was trying to be
friendly."

More laughter. The chap had a tongue in his head. *"Ha sciolto la scilin-
guágnolo,"* I heard near me. After all, the retort was deserved.

"Ah, bravo!" answered Cipolla. "I like you, *giovanotto.* Trust me, I've had
my eye on you for some time. People like you are just in my line. I can use
them. And you are the pick of the lot, that's plain to see. You do what you
like. Or is it possible you have ever not done what you liked—or even,
maybe, what you didn't like? What somebody else liked, in short? Hark ye,
my friend, that might be a pleasant change for you, to divide up the willing

and the doing and stop tackling both jobs at once. Division of labour, *sistema americano, sa'!* For instance, suppose you were to show your tongue to this select and honourable audience here—your whole tongue, right down to the roots?"

"No, I won't," said the youth, hostilely. "Sticking out your tongue shows a bad bringing-up."

"Nothing of the sort," retorted Cipolla. "You would only be *doing* it. With all due respect to your bringing-up, I suggest that before I count ten, you will perform a right turn and stick out your tongue at the company here further than you knew yourself that you could stick it out."

He gazed at the youth, and his piercing eyes seemed to sink deeper into their sockets, *"Uno!"* said he. He had let his riding-whip slide down his arm and made it whistle once through the air. The boy faced about and put out his tongue, so long, so extendedly, that you could see it was the very uttermost in tongue which he had to offer. Then turned back, stony-faced, to his former position.

"That was me," mocked Cipolla, with a jerk of his head towards the youth. *"Bè!* That was me." Leaving the audience to enjoy its sensations, he turned towards the little round table, lifted the bottle, poured out a small glass of what was obviously cognac, and tipped it up with a practised hand.

The children laughed with all their hearts. They had understood practically nothing of what had been said, but it pleased them hugely that something so funny should happen, straightaway, between that queer man up there and somebody out of the audience. They had no preconception of what an "evening" would be like and were quite ready to find this a priceless beginning. As for us, we exchanged a glance and I remember that involuntarily I made with my lips the sound that Cipolla's whip had made when it cut the air. For the rest, it was plain that people did not know what to make of a preposterous beginning like this to a sleight-of-hand performance. They could not see why the *giovanotto,* who after all in a way had been their spokesman, should suddenly have turned on them to vent his incivility. They felt that he had behaved like a silly ass and withdrew their countenances from him in favour of the artist, who now came back from his refreshment table and addressed them as follows:

"Ladies and gentlemen," said he, in his wheezing, metallic voice, "you saw just now that I was rather sensitive on the score of the rebuke this hopeful young linguist saw fit to give me"—*"questo linguista di belle speranze"* was what he said, and we all laughed at the pun. "I am a man who sets some store by himself, you may take it from me. And I see no point in being wished a good-evening unless it is done courteously and in all seriousness. For anything else there is no occasion. When a man wishes me a good-evening he wishes himself one, for the audience will have one only if I do. So this lady-killer of Torre di Venere" (another thrust) "did well to testify that I have one tonight and that I can dispense with any wishes of his in the matter. I can boast of having good evenings almost without exception. One not so good does come my way now and again, but very seldom. My calling is hard and my health not of the best. I have a little physical defect which prevented me from doing my bit in the war for the greater glory of the Fatherland. It is perforce with my mental and spiritual parts that I conquer life—which after all only means conquering oneself. And I flatter myself that my achievements have aroused interest and respect among the educated public. The leading newspapers have lauded me, the *Corriere della Sera* did me the courtesy of calling me a phenomenon, and in Rome the brother of the *Duce* honoured me by his presence at one of my evenings. I should not have thought that in a relatively less important place" (laughter here, at the expense of poor little Torre) "I should have to give up the small personal habits which brilliant and elevated audiences had been ready to overlook. Nor did I think I had to stand being heckled by a person who seems to have been rather spoilt by the favours of the fair sex." All this of course at the expense of the youth whom Cipolla never tired of presenting in the guise of *donnaiuolo* and rustic Don Juan. His persistent thin-skinnedness and animosity were in striking contrast to the self-confidence and the worldly success he boasted of. One might have assumed that the *giovanotto* was merely the chosen butt of Cipolla's customary professional sallies, had not the very pointed witticisms betrayed a genuine antagonism. No one looking at the physical parts of the two men need have been at a loss for the explanation, even if the deformed man had not constantly played on the other's supposed success with the fair sex. "Well," Cipolla went on, "before beginning our entertainment this evening, perhaps you will permit me to make myself comfortable."

And he went towards the hat-stand to take off his things.

"*Parla benissimo,*" asserted somebody in our neighbourhood. So far, the man had done nothing; but what he had said was accepted as an achievement, by means of that he had made an impression. Among southern peoples speech is a constituent part of the pleasure of living, it enjoys far livelier social esteem than in the north. That national cement, the mother tongue, is paid symbolic honours down here, and there is something blithely symbolical in the pleasure people take in their respect for its forms and phonetics. They enjoy speaking, they enjoy listening; and they listen with discrimination. For the way a man speaks serves as a measure of his personal rank; carelessness and clumsiness are greeted with scorn, elegance and mastery are rewarded with social éclat. Wherefore the small man too, where it is a question of getting his effect, chooses his phrase nicely and turns it with care. On this count, then, at least, Cipolla had won his audience; though he by no means belonged to the class of men which the Italian, in a singular mixture of moral and aesthetic judgments, labels "*simpatico.*"

After removing his hat, scarf, and mantle he came to the front of the stage, settling his coat, pulling down his cuffs with their large cuff-buttons, adjusting his absurd sash. He had very ugly hair; the top of his head, that is, was almost bald, while a narrow, black-varnished frizz of curls ran from front to back as though stuck on; the side hair, likewise blackened, was brushed forward to the corners of the eyes—it was, in short, the hairdressing of an old-fashioned circus-director, fantastic, but entirely suited to his outmoded personal type and worn with so much assurance as to take the edge off the public's sense of humour. The little physical defect of which he had warned us was now all too visible, though the nature of it was even now not very clear: the chest was too high, as is usual in such cases; but the corresponding malformation of the back did not sit between the shoulders, it took the form of a sort of hips or buttocks hump, which did not indeed hinder his movements but gave him a grotesque and dipping stride at every step he took. However, by mentioning his deformity beforehand he had broken the shock of it, and a delicate propriety of feeling appeared to reign throughout the hall.

"At your service," said Cipolla. "With your kind permission, we will begin the evening with some arithmetical tests."

Arithmetic? That did not sound much like sleight-of-hand. We began to have our suspicions that the man was sailing under a false flag, only we did not yet know which was the right one. I felt sorry on the children's account; but for the moment they were content simply to be there.

The numerical test which Cipolla now introduced was as simple as it was baffling. He began by fastening a piece of paper to the upper right-hand corner of the blackboard; then lifting it up, he wrote something underneath. He talked all the while, relieving the dryness of his offering by a constant flow of words, and showed himself a practised speaker, never at a loss for conversational turns of phrase. It was in keeping with the nature of his performance, and at the same time vastly entertained the children, that he went on to eliminate the gap between stage and audience, which had already been bridged over by the curious skirmish with the fisher lad: he had representatives from the audience mount the stage, and himself descended the wooden steps to seek personal contact with his public. And again, with individuals, he fell into his former taunting tone. I do not know how far that was a deliberate feature of his system; he preserved a serious, even a peevish air, but his audience, at least the more popular section, seemed convinced that that was all part of the game. So then, after he had written something and covered the writing by the paper, he desired that two persons should come up on the platform and help to perform the calculations. They would not be difficult, even for people not clever at figures. As usual, nobody volunteered, and Cipolla took care not to molest the more select portion of his audience. He kept to the populace. Turning to two sturdy young louts standing behind us, he beckoned them to the front, encouraging and scolding by turns. They should not stand there gaping, he said, unwilling to oblige the company. Actually, he got them in motion; with clumsy tread they came down the middle aisle, climbed the steps, and stood in front of the blackboard, grinning sheepishly at their comrades' shouts and applause. Cipolla joked with them for a few minutes, praised their heroic firmness of limb and the size of their hands, so well calculated to do this service for the public. Then he handed one of them the chalk and told him to write down the numbers as they were called out. But now the creature declared that he could not write! *"Non so scrivere,"* said he in his gruff voice, and his companion added that neither did he.

God knows whether they told the truth or whether they wanted to make game of Cipolla. Anyhow, the latter was far from sharing the general merriment which their confession aroused. He was insulted and disgusted. He sat there on a straw-bottomed chair in the centre of the stage with his legs crossed, smoking a fresh cigarette out of his cheap packet; obviously it tasted the better for the cognac he had indulged in while the yokels were stumping up the steps. Again he inhaled the smoke and let it stream out between curling lips. Swinging his leg, with his gaze sternly averted from the two shamelessly chuckling creatures and from the audience as well, he stared into space as one who withdraws himself and his dignity from the contemplation of an utterly despicable phenomenon.

"Scandalous," said he, in a sort of icy snarl. "Go back to your places! In Italy everybody can write—in all her greatness there is no room for ignorance and unenlightenment. To accuse her of them, in the hearing of this international company, is a cheap joke, in which you yourselves cut a very poor figure and humiliate the government and the whole country as well. If it is true that Torre di Venere is indeed the last refuge of such ignorance, then I must blush to have visited the place—being, as I already was, aware of its inferiority to Rome in more than one respect—"

Here Cipolla was interrupted by the youth with the Nubian coiffure and his jacket across his shoulder. His fighting spirit, as we now saw, had only abdicated temporarily, and he now flung himself into the breach in defence of his native heath. "That will do," said he loudly. "That's enough jokes about Torre. We all come from the place and we won't stand strangers making fun of it. These two chaps are our friends. Maybe they are no scholars, but even so they may be straighter than some folks in the room who are so free with their boasts about Rome, though they did not build it either."

That was capital. The young man had certainly cut his eye-teeth. And this sort of spectacle was good fun, even though it still further delayed the regular performance. It is always fascinating to listen to an altercation. Some people it simply amuses, they take a sort of kill-joy pleasure in not being principals. Others feel upset and uneasy, and my sympathies are with these latter, although on the present occasion I was under the impression that all this was part of the show—the analphabetic yokels no less than the *giovanotto* with the jacket. The children listened well pleased. They understood not at all, but the sound of the voices made them hold their breath. So this was a "magic evening"—at least it was the kind they have in Italy. They expressly found it "lovely."

Cipolla stood up and with two of his scooping strides was at the foot-lights.

"Well, well, see who's here!" said he with grim cordiality. "An old acquaintance! A young man with his heart at the end of his tongue" (he used the word *linguaccia,* which means a coated tongue, and gave rise to much hilarity). "That will do, my friends," he turned to the yokels. "I do not need you now, I have business with this deserving young man here, *con questo torregiano di Venere,* this tower of Venus, who no doubt expects the gratitude of the fair as a reward for his prowess—"

"*Ah, non scherziamo!* We're talking earnest," cried out the youth. His eyes flashed, and he actually made as though to pull off his jacket and proceed to direct methods of settlement.

Cipolla did not take him too seriously. We had exchanged apprehensive glances; but he was dealing with a fellow-countryman and had his native soil beneath his feet. He kept quite cool and showed complete mastery of the situation. He looked at his audience, smiled, and made a sideways motion of the head towards the young cockerel as though calling the public to witness how the man's bumptiousness only served to betray the simplicity of his mind. And then, for the second time, something strange happened, which set Cipolla's calm superiority in an uncanny light, and in some mysterious and irritating way turned all the explosiveness latent in the air into matter for laughter.

Cipolla drew still nearer to the fellow, looking him in the eye with a peculiar gaze. He even came half-way down the steps that led into the auditorium on our left, so that he stood directly in front of the trouble-maker, on slightly higher ground. The riding-whip hung from his arm.

"My son, you do not feel much like joking," he said. "It is only too natural, for anyone can see that you are not feeling too well. Even your tongue, which leaves something to be desired on the score of cleanliness, indicates acute disorder of the gastric system. An evening entertainment is no place for people in your state; you yourself, I can tell, were of several minds whether you would not do better to put on a flannel bandage and go to bed. It was not good judgment to drink so much of that very sour white wine this afternoon. Now you have such a colic you would like to double up with the pain. Go ahead, don't be embarrassed. There is a distinct relief that comes from bending over, in cases of intestinal cramp."

He spoke thus, word for word, with quiet impressiveness and a kind of stern sympathy, and his eyes, plunged the while deep in the young man's, seemed to grow very tired and at the same time burning above their enlarged tear-ducts—they were the strangest eyes, you could tell that not manly pride alone was preventing the young adversary from withdrawing his gaze. And presently, indeed, all trace of its former arrogance was gone from the bronzed young face. He looked open-mouthed at the Cavaliere and the open mouth was drawn in a rueful smile.

"Double over," repeated Cipolla. "What else can you do? With a colic like that you *must* bend. Surely you will not struggle against the performance of a perfectly natural action just because somebody suggests it to you?"

Slowly the youth lifted his forearms, folded and squeezed them across his body; it turned a little sideways, then bent, lower and lower, the feet shifted, the knees turned inward, until he had become a picture of writhing pain, until he all but grovelled upon the ground. Cipolla let him stand for some seconds thus, then made a short cut through the air with his whip and went with his scooping stride back to the little table, where he poured himself out a cognac.

"*Il boit beaucoup,*" asserted a lady behind us. Was that the only thing that struck her? We could not tell how far the audience grasped the situation. The fellow was standing upright again, with a sheepish grin—he looked as though he scarcely knew how it had all happened. The scene had been followed with tense interest and applauded at the end; there were shouts of "*Bravo, Cipolla!*" and "*Bravo, giovanotto!*" Apparently the issue of the duel was not looked upon as a personal defeat for the young man. Rather the audience encouraged him as one does an actor who succeeds in an unsympathetic rôle. Certainly his way of screwing himself up with cramp had been highly picturesque, its appeal was directly calculated to impress the gallery—in short, a fine dramatic performance. But I am not sure how far the audience were moved by that natural tactfulness in which the south excels, or how far it penetrated into the nature of what was going on.

The Cavaliere, refreshed, had lighted another cigarette. The numerical tests might now proceed. A young man was easily found in the back row who was willing to write down on the blackboard the numbers as they were dictated to him. Him too we knew; the whole entertainment had taken on an intimate character through our acquaintance with so many of the actors. This was the man who worked at the greengrocer's in the main street; he had served us several times, with neatness and dispatch. He wielded the chalk with clerkly confidence, while Cipolla descended to our level and walked with his deformed gait through the audience, collecting numbers as they were given, in two, three, and four places, and calling them out to the grocer's assistant, who wrote them down in a column. In all this, everything on both sides was calculated to amuse, with its jokes and its oratorical asides. The artist could not fail to hit on foreigners, who were not ready with their figures, and with them he was elaborately patient and chivalrous, to the great amusement of the natives, whom he reduced to confusion in their turn, by

making them translate numbers that were given in English or French. Some
people gave dates concerned with great events in Italian history. Cipolla took
them up at once and made patriotic comments. Somebody shouted "Number
one!" The Cavaliere, incensed at this as at every attempt to make game of
him, retorted over his shoulder that he could not take less than two-place figures. Whereupon another joker cried out "Number two!" and was greeted
with the applause and laughter which every reference to natural functions is
sure to win among southerners.

When fifteen numbers stood in a long straggling row on the board, Cipolla called for a general adding-match. Ready reckoners might add in their
heads, but pencil and paper were not forbidden. Cipolla, while the work went
on, sat on his chair near the blackboard, smoked and grimaced, with the
complacent, pompous air cripples so often have. The five-place addition was
soon done. Somebody announced the answer, somebody else confirmed it, a
third had arrived at a slightly different result, but the fourth agreed with the
first and second. Cipolla got up, tapped some ash from his coat, and lifted the
paper at the upper right-hand corner of the board to display the writing. The
correct answer, a sum close on a million, stood there; he had written it down
beforehand.

Astonishment, and loud applause. The children were overwhelmed.
How had he done that, they wanted to know. We told them it was a trick,
not easily explainable offhand. In short, the man was a conjuror. This was
what a sleight-of-hand evening was like, so now they knew. First the fisherman had cramp, and then the right answer was written down beforehand—it
was all simply glorious, and we saw with dismay that despite the hot eyes and
the hand of the clock at almost half past ten, it would be very hard to get
them away. There would be tears. And yet it was plain that this magician did
not "magick"—at least not in the accepted sense, of manual dexterity—and
that the entertainment was not at all suitable for children. Again, I do not
know, either, what the audience really thought. Obviously there was grave
doubt whether its answers had been given of "free choice"; here and there an
individual might have answered of his own motion, but on the whole Cipolla
certainly selected his people and thus kept the whole procedure in his own
hands and directed it towards the given result. Even so, one had to admire
the quickness of his calculations, however much one felt disinclined to admire anything else about the performance. Then his patriotism, his irritable
sense of dignity—the Cavaliere's own countrymen might feel in their element
with all that and continue in a laughing mood; but the combination certainly gave us outsiders food for thought.

Cipolla himself saw to it—though without giving them a name—that
the nature of his powers should be clear beyond a doubt to even the least-in-
structed person. He alluded to them, of course, in his talk—and he talked
without stopping—but only in vague, boastful, self-advertising phrases. He

went on awhile with experiments on the same lines as the first, merely making them more complicated by introducing operations in multiplying, subtracting, and dividing; then he simplified them to the last degree in order to bring out the method. He simply had numbers "guessed" which were previously written under the paper; and the guess was nearly always right. One guesser admitted that he had had in mind to give a certain number, when Cipolla's whip went whistling through the air, and a quite different one slipped out, which proved to be the "right" one. Cipolla's shoulders shook. He pretended admiration for the powers of the people he questioned. But in all his compliments there was something fleering and derogatory; the victims could scarcely have relished them much, although they smiled, and although they might easily have set down some part of the applause to their own credit. Moreover, I had not the impression that the artist was popular with his public. A certain ill will and reluctance were in the air, but courtesy kept such feeling in check, as did Cipolla's competency and his stern self-confidence. Even the riding-whip, I think, did much to keep rebellion from being overt.

From tricks with numbers he passed to tricks with cards. There were two packs, which he drew out of his pockets, and so much I still remember, that the basis of the tricks he played with them was as follows: from the first pack he drew three cards and thrust them without looking at them inside his coat. Another person then drew three out of the second pack, and these turned out to be the same as the first three—not invariably all the three, for it did happen that only two were the same. But in the majority of cases Cipolla triumphed, showing his three cards with a little bow in acknowledgment of the applause with which his audience conceded his possession of strange powers—strange whether for good or evil. A young man in the front row, to our right, an Italian, with proud, finely chiselled features, rose up and said that he intended to assert his own will in his choice and consciously to resist any influence, of whatever sort. Under these circumstances, what did Cipolla think would be the result? "You will," answered the Cavaliere, "make my task somewhat more difficult thereby. As for the result, your resistance will not alter it in the least. Freedom exists, and also the will exists; but freedom of the will does not exist, for a will that aims at its own freedom aims at the unknown. You are free to draw or not to draw. But if you draw, you will draw the right cards—the more certainly, the more wilfully obstinate your behaviour."

One must admit that he could not have chosen his words better, to trouble the waters and confuse the mind. The refractory youth hesitated before drawing. Then he pulled out a card and at once demanded to see if it was among the chosen three. "But why?" queried Cipolla. "Why do things by halves?" Then, as the other defiantly insisted, *"E servito,"* said the juggler, with a gesture of exaggerated servility; and held out the three cards fanwise, without looking at them himself. The left-hand card was the one drawn.

Amid general applause, the apostle of freedom sat down. How far Cipolla employed small tricks and manual dexterity to help out his natural talents, the deuce only knew. But even without them the result would have been the same: the curiosity of the entire audience was unbounded and universal, everybody both enjoyed the amazing character of the entertainment and unanimously conceded the professional skill of the performer. *"Lavora bene,"* we heard, here and there in our neighbourhood; it signified the triumph of objective judgment over antipathy and repressed resentment.

After his last, incomplete, yet so much the more telling success, Cipolla had at once fortified himself with another cognac. Truly he did "drink a lot," and the fact made a bad impression. But obviously he needed the liquor and the cigarettes for the replenishment of his energy, upon which, as he himself said, heavy demands were made in all directions. Certainly in the intervals he looked very ill, exhausted and hollow-eyed. Then the little glassful would redress the balance, and the flow of lively, self-confident chatter run on, while the smoke he inhaled gushed out grey from his lungs. I clearly recall that he passed from the card-tricks to parlour games—the kind based on certain powers which in human nature are higher or else lower than human reason: on intuition and "magnetic" transmission; in short, upon a low type of manifestation. What I do not remember is the precise order things came in. And I will not bore you with a description of these experiments; everybody knows them, everybody has at one time or another taken part in this finding of hidden articles, this blind carrying out of a series of acts, directed by a force that proceeds from organism to organism by unexplored paths. Everybody has had his little glimpse into the equivocal, impure, inexplicable nature of the occult, has been conscious of both curiosity and contempt, has shaken his head over the human tendency of those who deal in it to help themselves out with humbuggery, though, after all, the humbuggery is no disproof whatever of the genuineness of the other elements in the dubious amalgam. I can only say here that each single circumstance gains in weight and the whole greatly in impressiveness when it is a man like Cipolla who is the chief actor and guiding spirit in the sinister business. He sat smoking at the rear of the stage, his back to the audience while they conferred. The object passed from hand to hand which it was his task to find, with which he was to perform some action agreed upon beforehand. Then he would start to move zigzag through the hall, with his head thrown back and one hand outstretched, the other clasped in that of a guide who was in the secret but enjoined to keep himself perfectly passive, with his thoughts directed upon the agreed goal. Cipolla moved with the bearing typical in these experiments; now groping upon a false start, now with a quick forward thrust, now pausing as though to listen and by sudden inspiration correcting his course. The rôles seemed reversed, the stream of influence was moving in the contrary direction, as the artist himself pointed out, in his ceaseless flow of discourse. The suffering, receptive, performing part was now his, the will he had before imposed on others was shut out, he acted in obedience to a voiceless common will which was in the air. But he made it perfectly clear that it all came to the same thing. The capacity for self-surrender, he said, for becoming a tool, for the most unconditional and utter self-abnegation, was but the reverse side of that other power to will and to command. Commanding and obeying formed together one single principle, one indissoluble unity; he who knew how to obey knew also how to command, and conversely; the one idea was comprehended in the other, as people and leader were comprehended in one another. But that which was *done,* the highly exacting and exhausting performance, was in every case his, the leader's and mover's, in whom the will became obedience, the obedience will, whose person was the cradle and womb of both, and who thus suffered enormous hardship. Repeatedly he emphasized the fact that his lot was a hard one—presumably to account for his need of stimulant and his frequent recourse to the little glass.

Thus he groped his way forward, like a blind seer, led and sustained by the mysterious common will. He drew a pin set with a stone out of its hiding-place in an Englishwoman's shoe, carried it, halting and pressing on by turns, to another lady—Signora Angiolieri—and handed it to her on bended knee, with the words it had been agreed he was to utter. "I present you with this in token of my respect," was the sentence. Their sense was obvious, but the words themselves not easy to hit upon, for the reason that they had been agreed on in French; the language complication seemed to us a little malicious, implying as it did a conflict between the audience's natural interest in the success of the miracle, and their desire to witness the humiliation of this presumptuous man. It was a strange sight: Cipolla on his knees before the signora, wrestling, amid efforts at speech, after knowledge of the preordained words. "I must say something," he said, "and I feel clearly what it is I must say. But I also feel that if it passed my lips it would be wrong. Be careful not to help me unintentionally!" he cried out, though very likely that was precisely what he was hoping for. *"Pensez très fort,"* he cried all at once, in bad French, and then burst out with the required words—in Italian, indeed, but with the final substantive pronounced in the sister tongue, in which he was probably far from fluent: he said *vénération* instead of *venerazione,* with an impossible nasal. And this partial success, after the complete success before it, the finding of the pin, the presentation of it on his knees to the right person—was almost more impressive than if he had got the sentence exactly right, and evoked bursts of admiring applause.

Cipolla got up from his knees and wiped the perspiration from his brow. You understand that this experiment with the pin was a single case, which I describe because it sticks in my memory. But he changed his method several times and improvised a number of variations suggested by his contact with his audience; a good deal of time thus went by. He seemed to get particular inspiration from the person of our landlady; she drew him on to the most extraordinary displays of clairvoyance. "It does not escape me, madame," he said to her, "that there is something unusual about you, some special and honourable distinction. He who has eyes to see descries about your lovely brow an aureola—if I mistake not, it once was stronger than now—a slowly paling radiance ... hush, not a word! Don't help me. Beside you sits your husband—yes?" He turned towards the silent Signor Angiolieri. "You are the husband of this lady, and your happiness is complete. But in the midst of this happiness memories rise ... the past, signora, so it seems to me, plays an important part in your present. You knew a king ... has not a king crossed your path in bygone days?"

"No," breathed the dispenser of our midday soup, her golden-brown eyes gleaming in the noble pallor of her face.

"No? No, not a king; I meant that generally, I did not mean literally a king. Not a king, not a prince, and a prince after all, a king of a loftier realm; it was a great artist, at whose side you once—you would contradict me, and yet I am not wholly wrong. Well, then! It was a woman, a great, a world-renowned woman artist, whose friendship you enjoyed in your tender years, whose sacred memory overshadows and transfigures your whole existence. Her name? Need I utter it, whose fame has long been bound up with the Fatherland's, immortal as its own? Eleonora Duse," he finished, softly and with much solemnity.

The little woman bowed her head, overcome. The applause was like a patriotic demonstration. Nearly everyone there knew about Signora Angiolieri's wonderful past; they were all able to confirm the Cavaliere's intuition—not least the present guests of Casa Eleonora. But we wondered how much of the truth he had learned as the result of professional inquiries made on his arrival. Yet I see no reason at all to cast doubt, on rational grounds, upon powers which, before our very eyes, became fatal to their possessor.

At this point there was an intermission. Our lord and master withdrew. Now I confess that almost ever since the beginning of my tale I have looked forward with dread to this moment in it. The thoughts of men are mostly not hard to read; in this case they are very easy. You are sure to ask why we did not choose this moment to go away—and I must continue to owe you an answer. I do not know why. I cannot defend myself. By this time it was certainly eleven, probably later. The children were asleep. The last series of tests had been too long, nature had had her way. They were sleeping in our laps, the little one on mine, the boy on his mother's. That was, in a way, a consolation; but at the same time it was also ground for compassion and a clear leading to take them home to bed. And I give you my word that we wanted to obey this touching admonition, we seriously wanted to. We roused the poor things and told them it was now high time to go. But they were no sooner conscious than they began to resist and implore—you know how horrified children are at the thought of leaving before the end of a thing. No cajoling has any effect, you have to use force. It was so lovely, they wailed. How did we know what was coming next? Surely we could not leave until after the intermission; they liked a little nap now and again—only not go home, only not go to bed, while the beautiful evening was still going on!

We yielded, but only for the moment, of course—so far as we knew—only for a little while, just a few minutes longer. I cannot excuse our staying, scarcely can I even understand it. Did we think, having once said A, we had to say B—having once brought the children hither we had to let them stay? No, it is not good enough. Were we ourselves so highly entertained? Yes, and no. Our feelings for Cavaliere Cipolla were of a very mixed kind, but so were the feelings of the whole audience, if I mistake not, and nobody left. Were we under the sway of a fascination which emanated from this man who took so strange a way to earn his bread; a fascination which he gave out independently of the programme and even between the tricks and which paralysed our resolve? Again, sheer curiosity may account for something. One was curious to know how such an evening turned out; Cipolla in his remarks having all along hinted that he had tricks in his bag stranger than any he had yet produced.

But all that is not it—or at least it is not all of it. More correct it would be to answer the first question with another. Why had we not left Torre di Venere itself before now? To me the two questions are one and the same, and in order to get out of the impasse I might simply say that I had answered it already. For, as things had been in Torre in general; queer, uncomfortable, troublesome, tense, oppressive, so precisely they were here in this hall tonight. Yes, more than precisely. For it seemed to be the fountainhead of all the uncanniness and all the strained feelings which had oppressed the atmosphere of our holiday. This man whose return to the stage we were awaiting was the personification of all that; and, as we had not gone away in general, so to speak, it would have been inconsistent to do it in the particular case. You may call this an explanation, you may call it inertia, as you see fit. Any argument more to the purpose I simply do not know how to adduce.

Well, there was an interval of ten minutes, which grew into nearly twenty. The children remained awake. They were enchanted by our compliance, and filled the break to their own satisfaction by renewing relations with the popular sphere, with Antonio, Guiscardo, and the canoe man. They put their hands to their mouths and called messages across, appealing to us for the Italian words. "Hope you have a good catch tomorrow, a whole netful!" They called to Mario, Esquisito Mario: *"Mario, una cioccolata e biscotti!"* And this time he heeded and answered with a smile: *"Subito, signorini!"* Later we had reason to recall this kindly, if rather absent and pensive smile.

Thus the interval passed, the gong sounded. The audience, which had scattered in conversation, took their places again, the children sat up straight in their chairs with their hands in their laps. The curtain had not been dropped. Cipolla came forward again, with his dipping stride, and began to introduce the second half of the programme with a lecture.

Let me state once for all that this self-confident cripple was the most powerful hypnotist I have ever seen in my life. It was pretty plain now that he threw dust in the public eye and advertised himself as a prestidigitator on account of police regulations which would have prevented him from making his living by the exercise of his powers. Perhaps this eye-wash is the usual thing in Italy; it may be permitted or even connived at by the authorities. Certainly the man had from the beginning made little concealment of the actual nature of his operations; and this second half of the programme was quite frankly and exclusively devoted to one sort of experiment. While he still practised some rhetorical circumlocutions, the tests themselves were one long series of attacks upon the will-power, the loss or compulsion of volition. Comic, exciting, amazing by turns, by midnight they were still in full swing; we ran the gamut of all the phenomena this natural-unnatural field has to show, from the unimpressive at one end of the scale to the monstrous at the other. The audience laughed and applauded as they followed the grotesque details; shook their heads, clapped their knees, fell very frankly under the spell of this stern, self-assured personality. At the same time I saw signs that they were not quite complacent, not quite unconscious of the peculiar ignominy which lay, for the individual and for the general, in Cipolla's triumphs.

Two main features were constant in all the experiments: the liquor glass and the claw-handled riding-whip. The first was always invoked to add fuel to his demoniac fires; without it, apparently, they might have burned out. On this score we might even have felt pity for the man; but the whistle of his scourge, the insulting symbol of his domination, before which we all cowered, drowned out every sensation save a dazed and outbraved submission to his power. Did he then lay claim to our sympathy to boot? I was struck by a remark he made—it suggested no less. At the climax of his experiments, by stroking and breathing upon a certain young man who had offered himself as a subject and already proved himself a particularly susceptible one, he had not only put him into the condition known as deep trance and extended his insensible body by neck and feet across the backs of two chairs, but had actually sat down on the rigid form as on a bench, without making it yield. The sight of this unholy figure in a frock-coat squatted on the stiff body was horrible and incredible; the audience, convinced that the victim of this scientific diversion must be suffering, expressed its sympathy. *"Ah, poveretto!"* Poor soul, poor soul! *"Poor soul!"* Cipolla mocked them, with some bitterness. "Ladies and gentlemen, you are barking up the wrong tree. *Sono io il poveretto.* I am the person who is suffering, I am the one to be pitied." We pocketed the information. Very good. Maybe the experiment was at his expense, maybe it was he who had suffered the cramp when the *giovanotto* over there had made the faces. But appearances were all against it; and one does not feel like saying *poveretto* to a man who is suffering to bring about the humiliation of others.

I have got ahead of my story and lost sight of the sequence of events. To this day my mind is full of the Cavaliere's feats of endurance; only I do not recall them in their order—which does not matter. So much I do know: that the longer and more circumstantial tests, which got the most applause, impressed me less than some of the small ones which passed quickly over. I remember the young man whose body Cipolla converted into a board, only because of the accompanying remarks which I have quoted. An elderly lady in a cane-seated chair was lulled by Cipolla in the delusion that she was on a voyage to India and gave a voluble account of her adventures by land and sea. But I found this phenomenon less impressive than one which followed immediately after the intermission. A tall, well-built, soldierly man was unable to lift his arm, after the hunchback had told him that he could not and given a cut through the air with his whip. I can still see the face of that stately, mustachioed colonel smiling and clenching his teeth as he struggled to regain his lost freedom of action. A staggering performance! He seemed to be exerting his will, and in vain; the trouble, however, was probably simply that he could not will. There was involved here that recoil of the will upon itself which paralyses choice—as our tyrant had previously explained to the Roman gentleman.

Still less can I forget the touching scene, at once comic and horrible, with Signora Angiolieri. The Cavaliere, probably in his first bold survey of the room, had spied out her ethereal lack of resistance to his power. For actually he bewitched her, literally drew her out of her seat, out of her row, and away with him whither he willed. And in order to enhance his effect, he bade Signor Angiolieri call upon his wife by her name, to throw, as it were, all the weight of his existence and his rights in her into the scale, to rouse by the voice of her husband everything in his spouse's soul which could shield her virtue against the evil assaults of magic. And how vain it all was! Cipolla was standing at some distance from the couple, when he made a single cut with his whip through the air. It caused our landlady to shudder violently and turn her face towards him. "Sofronia!" cried Signor Angiolieri—we had not known that Signora Angiolieri's name was Sofronia. And he did well to call, everybody saw that there was no time to lose. His wife kept her face turned in the direction of the diabolical Cavaliere, who with his ten long yellow fingers was making passes at his victim, moving backwards as he did so, step by step. Then Signora Angiolieri, her pale face gleaming, rose up from her seat, turned right round, and began to glide after him. Fatal and forbidding sight! Her face as though moonstruck, stiff-armed, her lovely hands lifted a little at the wrists, the feet as it were together, she seemed to float slowly out of her row and after the tempter. "Call her, sir, keep on calling," prompted the redoubtable man. And Signor Angiolieri, in a weak voice, called; "Sofronia!" Ah, again and again he called; as his wife went further off he even curved one hand round his lips and beckoned with the other as he called. But the poor voice of love and duty echoed unheard, in vain, behind the lost one's back; the signora swayed along, moonstruck, deaf, enslaved; she glided into the middle aisle and down it towards the fingering hunchback, towards the door. We were convinced, we were driven to the conviction, that she would have followed her master, had he so willed it, to the ends of the earth.

"*Accidente!*" cried out Signor Angiolieri, in genuine affright, springing up as the exit was reached. But at the same moment the Cavaliere put aside, as it were, the triumphal crown and broke off. "Enough, signora, I thank you," he said, and offered his arm to lead her back to her husband. "Signor," he greeted the latter, "here is your wife. Unharmed, with my compliments, I give her into your hands. Cherish with all the strength of your manhood a treasure which is so wholly yours, and let your zeal be quickened by knowing that there are powers stronger than reason or virtue, and not always so magnanimously ready to relinquish their prey!"

Poor Signor Angiolieri, so quiet, so bald! He did not look as though he would know how to defend his happiness, even against powers much less demoniac than these which were now adding mockery to frightfulness. Solemnly and pompously the Cavaliere retired to the stage, amid applause to which his eloquence gave double strength. It was this particular episode, I feel sure, that set the seal upon his ascendancy. For now he made them dance, yes, literally; and the dancing lent a dissolute, abandoned, topsy-turvy air to the scene, a drunken abdication of the critical spirit which had so long resisted the spell of this man. Yes, he had had to fight to get the upper hand— for instance against the animosity of the young Roman gentleman, whose rebellious spirit threatened to serve others as a rallying-point. But it was precisely upon the importance of example that the Cavaliere was so strong. He had the wit to make his attack at the weakest point and to choose as his first victim that feeble, ecstatic youth whom he had previously made into a board. The master had but to look at him, when this young man would fling himself back as though struck by lightning, place his hands rigidly at his sides, and fall into a state of military somnambulism, in which it was plain to any eye that he was open to the most absurd suggestion that might be made to him. He seemed quite content in his abject state, quite pleased to be relieved of the burden of voluntary choice. Again and again he offered himself as a subject and gloried in the model facility he had in losing consciousness. So now he mounted the platform, and a single cut of the whip was enough to make him dance to the Cavaliere's orders, in a kind of complacent ecstasy, eyes closed, head nodding, lank limbs flying in all directions.

It looked unmistakably like enjoyment, and other recruits were not long in coming forward: two other young men, one humbly and one well dressed, were soon jigging alongside the first. But now the gentleman from Rome bobbed up again, asking defiantly if the Cavaliere would engage to make him dance too, even against his will.

"Even against your will," answered Cipolla, in unforgettable accents. That frightful *"anche se non vuole"* still rings in my ears. The struggle began. After Cipolla had taken another little glass and lighted a fresh cigarette he stationed the Roman at a point in the middle aisle and himself took up a position some distance behind him, making his whip whistle through the air as he gave the order: *"Balla!"* His opponent did not stir. *"Balla!"* repeated the Cavaliere incisively, and snapped his whip. You saw the young man move his neck round in his collar; at the same time one hand lifted slightly at the wrist, one ankle turned outward. But that was all, for the time at least; merely a tendency to twitch, now sternly repressed, now seeming about to get the upper hand. It escaped nobody that here a heroic obstinacy, a fixed resolve to resist, must needs be conquered; we were beholding a gallant effort to strike out and save the honour of the human race. He twitched but danced not; and the struggle was so prolonged that the Cavaliere had to divide his attention between it and the stage, turning now and then to make his riding-whip whistle in the direction of the dancers, as it were to keep them in leash. At the same time he advised the audience that no fatigue was involved in such activities, however long they went on, since it was not the automatons up there who danced, but himself. Then once more his eye would bore itself into the back of the Roman's neck and lay siege to the strength of purpose which defied him.

One saw it waver, that strength of purpose, beneath the repeated summons and whip-crackings. Saw with an objective interest which yet was not quite free from traces of sympathetic emotion—from pity, even from a cruel kind of pleasure. If I understand what was going on, it was the negative character of the young man's fighting position which was his undoing. It is likely that *not* willing is not a practicable state of mind: *not* to want to do something may be in the long run a mental content impossible to subsist on. Between not willing a certain thing and not willing at all—in other words, yielding to another person's will—there may lie too small a space for the idea of freedom to squeeze into. Again, there were the Cavaliere's persuasive words, woven in among the whip-crackings and commands, as he mingled effects that were his own secret with others of a bewilderingly psychological kind. *"Balla!"* said he. "Who wants to torture himself like that? Is forcing yourself your idea of freedom? *Una ballatina!* Why, your arms and legs are aching for it. What a relief to give way to them—there, you are dancing already! That is no struggle any more, it is a pleasure!" And so it was. The jerk-ing and twitching of the refractory youth's limbs had at last got the upper hand; he lifted his arms, then his knees, his joints quite suddenly relaxed, he flung his legs and danced, and amid bursts of applause the Cavaliere led him to join the row of puppets on the stage. Up there we could see his face as he "enjoyed" himself; it was clothed in a broad grin and the eyes were half-shut. In a way, it was consoling to see that he was having a better time than he had had in the hour of his pride.

His "fall" was, I may say, an epoch. The ice was completely broken, Ci-polla's triumph had reached its height. The Circe's wand, that whistling leather whip with the claw handle, held absolute sway. At one time—it must have been well after midnight—not only were there eight or ten persons dancing on the little stage, but in the hall below a varied animation reigned, and a long-toothed Anglo-Saxoness in a pince-nez left her seat of her own motion to perform a tarantella in the centre aisle. Cipolla was lounging in a cane-seated chair at the left of the stage, gulping down the smoke of a ciga-rette and breathing it impudently out through his bad teeth. He tapped his foot and shrugged his shoulders, looking down upon the abandoned scene in the hall; now and then he snapped his whip backwards at a laggard upon the stage. The children were awake at the moment. With shame I speak of them. For it was not good to be here, least of all for them; that we had not taken them away can only be explained by saying that we had caught the general devil-may-careness of the hour. By that time it was all one. Anyhow, thank goodness, they lacked understanding for the disreputable side of the enter-tainment, and in their innocence were perpetually charmed by the unheard-of indulgence which permitted them to be present at such a thing as a magi-cian's "evening." Whole quarter-hours at a time they drowsed on our laps, waking refreshed and rosy-cheeked, with sleep-drunken eyes, to laugh to bursting at the leaps and jumps the magician made those people up there make. They had not thought it would be so jolly; they joined with their clumsy little hands in every round of applause. And jumped for joy upon their chairs, as was their wont, when Cipolla beckoned to their friend Mario from the Esquisito, beckoned to him just like a picture in a book, holding his hand in front of his nose and bending and straightening the forefinger by turns.

Mario obeyed. I can see him now going up the stairs to Cipolla, who continued to beckon him, in that droll, picture-book sort of way. He hesi-tated for a moment at first; that, too, I recall quite clearly. During the whole evening he had lounged against a wooden pillar at the side entrance, with his arms folded, or else with his hands thrust into his jacket pockets. He was on our left, near the youth with the militant hair, and had followed the perform-ance attentively, so far as we had seen, if with no particular animation and God knows how much comprehension. He could not much relish being summoned thus, at the end of the evening. But it was only too easy to see why he obeyed. After all, obedience was his calling in life; and then, how should a simple lad like him find it within his human capacity to refuse compliance to a man so throned and crowned as Cipolla at that hour? Willy-nilly he left his column and with a word of thanks to those making way for him he mounted the steps with a doubtful smile on his full lips.

Picture a thickset youth of twenty years, with clipt hair, a low forehead, and heavy-lidded eyes in an indefinite grey, shot with green and yellow. These things I knew from having spoken with him, as we often had. There was a saddle of freckles on the flat nose, the whole upper half of the face retreated behind the lower, and that again was dominated by thick lips that parted to show the salivated teeth. These thick lips and the veiled look of the eyes lent the whole face a primitive melancholy—it was that which had drawn us to him from the first. In it was not the faintest trace of brutality—indeed, his hands would have given the lie to such an idea, being unusually slender and delicate even for a southerner. They were hands by which one liked being served.

We knew him humanly without knowing him personally, if I may make that distinction. We saw him nearly every day, and felt a certain kindness for his dreamy ways, which might at times be actual inattentiveness, suddenly transformed into a redeeming zeal to serve. His mien was serious, only the children could bring a smile to his face. It was not sulky, but uningratiating, without intentional effort to please—or, rather, it seemed to give up being pleasant in the conviction that it could not succeed. We should have remembered Mario in any case, as one of those homely recollections of travel which often stick in the mind better than more important ones. But of his circumstances we knew no more than that his father was a petty clerk in the Municipio and his mother took in washing.

His white waiter's-coat became him better than the faded striped suit he wore, with a gay coloured scarf instead of a collar, the ends tucked into his jacket. He neared Cipolla, who however did not leave off that motion of his finger before his nose, so that Mario had to come still closer, right up to the chair-seat and the master's legs. Whereupon the latter spread out his elbows and seized the lad, turning him so that we had a view of his face. Then gazed him briskly up and down, with a careless, commanding eye.

"Well, *ragazzo mio*, how comes it we make acquaintance so late in the day? But believe me, I made yours long ago. Yes, yes, I've had you in my eye this long while and known what good stuff you were made of. How could I go and forget you again? Well, I've had a good deal to think about. . . . Now tell me, what is your name? The first name, that's all I want."

"My name is Mario," the young man answered, in a low voice.

"Ah, Mario. Very good. Yes, yes, there is such a name, quite a common name, a classic name too, one of those which preserve the heroic traditions of the Fatherland. *Bravo! Salve!*" And he flung up his arm slantingly above his crooked shoulder, palm outward, in the Roman salute. He may have been slightly tipsy by now, and no wonder; but he spoke as before, clearly, fluently, and with emphasis. Though about this time there had crept into his voice a gross, autocratic note, and a kind of arrogance was in his sprawl.

"Well, now, Mario *mio*," he went on, "it's a good thing you came this evening, and that's a pretty scarf you've got on; it is becoming to your style of beauty. It must stand you in good stead with the girls, the pretty pretty girls of Torre—"

From the row of youths, close by the place where Mario had been standing, sounded a laugh. It came from the youth with the militant hair. He stood there, his jacket over his shoulder, and laughed outright, rudely and scornfully.

Mario gave a start. I think it was a shrug, but he may have started and then hastened to cover the movement by shrugging his shoulders, as much as to say that the neckerchief and the fair sex were matters of equal indifference to him.

The Cavaliere gave a downward glance.

"We needn't trouble about him," he said. "He is jealous, because your scarf is so popular with the girls, maybe partly because you and I are so friendly up here. Perhaps he'd like me to put him in mind of his colic—I could do it free of charge. Tell me, Mario. You've come here this evening for a bit of fun—and in the daytime you work in an ironmonger's shop?"

"In a café," corrected the youth.

"Oh, in a café. That's where Cipolla nearly came a cropper! What you are is a cup-bearer, a Ganymede—I like that, it is another classical allusion—*Salvietta!*" Again the Cavaliere saluted, to the huge gratification of his audience.

Mario smiled too. "But before that," he interpolated, in the interest of accuracy, "I worked for a while in a shop in Portoclemente." He seemed visited by a natural desire to assist the prophecy by dredging out its essential features.

"There, didn't I say so? In an ironmonger's shop?"

"They kept combs and brushes," Mario got round it.

"Didn't I say that you were not always a Ganymede? Not always at the sign of the serviette? Even when Cipolla makes a mistake, it is a kind that makes you believe in him. Now tell me: Do you believe in me?"

An indefinite gesture.

"A half-way answer," commented the Cavaliere. "Probably it is not easy to win your confidence. Even for me, I can see, it is not so easy. I see in your features a reserve, a sadness, *un tratto di malinconia* ... tell me" (he seized Mario's hand persuasively) "have you troubles?"

"*Nossignore,*" answered Mario, promptly and decidedly.

"You *have* troubles," insisted the Cavaliere, bearing down the denial by the weight of his authority. "Can't I see? Trying to pull the wool over Cipolla's eyes, are you? Of course, about the girls—it is a girl, isn't it? You have love troubles?"

Mario gave a vigorous head-shake. And again the *giovanotto's* brutal laugh rang out. The Cavaliere gave heed. His eyes were roving about somewhere in the air; but he cocked an ear to the sound, then swung his whip backwards, as he had once or twice before in his conversation with Mario, that none of his puppets might flag in their zeal. The gesture had nearly cost him his new prey: Mario gave a sudden start in the direction of the steps. But Cipolla had him in his clutch.

"Not so fast," said he. "That would be fine, wouldn't it? So you want to skip, do you, Ganymede, right in the middle of the fun, or, rather, when it is just beginning? Stay with me, I'll show you something nice. I'll convince you. You have no reason to worry, I promise you. This girl—you know her and others know her too—what's her name? Wait! I read the name in your eyes, it is on the tip of my tongue and yours too—"

"Silvestra!" shouted the *giovanotto* from below.

The Cavaliere's face did not change.

"Aren't there the forward people?" he asked, not looking down, more as in undisturbed converse with Mario. "Aren't there the young fighting-cocks that crow in season and out? Takes the word out of your mouth, the conceited fool, and seems to think he has some special right to it. Let him be. But Silvestra, your Silvestra—ah, what a girl that is! What a prize! Brings your heart into your mouth to see her walk or laugh or breathe, she is so lovely. And her round arms when she washes, and tosses her head back to get the hair out of her eyes! An angel from paradise!"

Mario stared at him, his head thrust forward. He seemed to have forgotten the audience, forgotten where he was. The red rings round his eyes had got larger, they looked as though they were painted on. His thick lips parted.

"And she makes you suffer, this angel," went on Cipolla, "or, rather, you make yourself suffer for her—there is a difference, my lad, a most important difference, let me tell you. There are misunderstandings in love, maybe nowhere else in the world are there so many. I know what you are thinking: what does this Cipolla, with his little physical defect, know about love? Wrong, all wrong, he knows a lot. He has a wide and powerful understanding of its workings, and it pays to listen to his advice. But let's leave Cipolla out, cut him out altogether and think only of Silvestra, your peerless Silvestra! What! Is she to give any young gamecock the preference, so that he can laugh while you cry? To prefer him to a chap like you, so full of feeling and so sympathetic? Not very likely, is it? It is impossible—we know better, Cipolla and she. If I were to put myself in her place and choose between the two of you, a tarry lout like that—a codfish, a sea-urchin—and a Mario, a knight of the serviette, who moves among gentlefolk and hands round refreshments with an air—my word, but my heart would speak in no uncertain tones—it knows to whom I gave it long ago. It is time that he should see and understand, my chosen one! It is time that you see me and recognize me, Mario, my beloved! Tell me, who am I?"

It was grisly, the way the betrayer made himself irresistible, wreathed and coquetted with his crooked shoulder, languished with the puffy eyes, and showed his splintered teeth in a sickly smile. And alas, at his beguiling words, what was come of our Mario? It is hard for me to tell, hard as it was for me to see; for here was nothing less than an utter abandonment of the inmost soul, a public exposure of timid and deluded passion and rapture. He put his hands across his mouth, his shoulders rose and fell with his pantings. He could not, it was plain, trust his eyes and ears for joy, and the one thing he forgot was precisely that he could not trust them. "Silvestra!" he breathed, from the very depths of his vanquished heart.

"Kiss me!" said the hunchback. "Trust me, I love thee. Kiss me here." And with the tip of his index finger, hand, arm, and little finger outspread, he pointed to his cheek, near the mouth. And Mario bent and kissed him.

It had grown very still in the room. That was a monstrous moment, grotesque and thrilling, the moment of Mario's bliss. In that evil span of time, crowded with a sense of the illusiveness of all joy, one sound became audible, and that not quite at once, but on the instant of the melancholy and ribald meeting between Mario's lips and the repulsive flesh which thrust itself forward for his caress. It was the sound of a laugh, from the *giovanotto* on our left. It broke into the dramatic suspense of the moment, coarse, mocking, and yet—or I must have been grossly mistaken—with an undertone of compassion for the poor bewildered, victimized creature. It had a faint ring of that *"Poveretto"* which Cipolla had declared was wasted on the wrong person, when he claimed the pity for his own.

The laugh still rang in the air when the recipient of the caress gave his whip a little swish, low down, close to his chair-leg, and Mario started up and flung himself back. He stood in that posture staring, his hands one over the other on those desecrated lips. Then he beat his temples with his clenched fists, over and over; turned and staggered down the steps, while the audience applauded, and Cipolla sat there with his hands in his lap, his shoulders shaking. Once below, and even while in full retreat, Mario hurled himself round with legs flung wide apart; one arm flew up, and two flat shattering detonations crashed through applause and laughter.

There was instant silence. Even the dancers came to a full stop and stared about, struck dumb. Cipolla bounded from his seat. He stood with his arms spread out, slanting as though to ward everybody off, as though next moment he would cry out: "Stop, Keep back! Silence! What was that?" Then, in that instant, he sank back in his seat, his head rolling on his chest; in the next

he had fallen sideways to the floor, where he lay motionless, a huddled heap
of clothing, with limbs awry.

The commotion was indescribable. Ladies hid their faces, shuddering, on
the breasts of their escorts. There were shouts for a doctor, for the police.
People flung themselves on Mario in a mob, to disarm him, to take away the
weapon that hung from his fingers—that small, dull-metal, scarcely pistol-
shaped tool with hardly any barrel—in how strange and unexpected a direction had fate levelled it!

And now—now finally, at last—we took the children and led them towards the exit, past the pair of *carabinieri* just entering. Was that the end,
they wanted to know, that they might go in peace? Yes, we assured them,
that was the end. An end of horror, a fatal end. And yet a liberation—for I
could not, and I cannot, but find it so!

MARK TWAIN

Pudd'nhead Wilson

A WHISPER TO THE READER

There is no character, howsoever good and fine, but it can be destroyed by ridicule, howsoever poor and witless. Observe the ass, for instance: his character is about perfect, he is the choicest spirit among all the humbler animals, yet see what ridicule has brought him to. Instead of feeling complimented when we are called an ass, we are left in doubt.
—PUDD'NHEAD WILSON'S CALENDAR.

A person who is ignorant of legal matters is always liable to make mistakes when he tries to photograph a court scene with his pen; and so I was not willing to let the law chapters in this book go to press without first subjecting them to rigid and exhausting revision and correction by a trained barrister—if that is what they are called. These chapters are right now in every detail, for they were rewritten under the immediate eye of William Hicks, who studied law part of a while in southwest Missouri thirty-five years ago and then came over here to Florence for his health and is still helping for exercise and board in Macaroni Vermicelli's horse-feed shed which is up the back alley as you turn around the corner out of the Piazza del Duomo just beyond the house where that stone that Dante used to sit on six hundred years ago is let into the wall when he let on to be watching them build Giotto's campanile and yet always got tired looking as soon as Beatrice passed along on her way to get a chunk of chestnut cake to defend herself with in case of a Ghibelline outbreak before she got to school, at the same old stand where they sell the same old cake to this day and it is just as light and good as it was then, too, and this is not flattery, far from it. He was a little rusty on his law, but he rubbed up for this book, and those two or three legal chapters are right and straight now. He told me so himself.

Given under my hand this second day of January, 1893, at the Villa Vi-

viani, village of Settignano, three miles back of Florence, on the hills—the
same certainly affording the most charming view to be found on this planet,
and with it the most dreamlike and enchanting sunsets to be found in any
planet or even in any solar system—and given, too, in the swell room of the
house, with the busts of Cerretani senators and other grandees of this line
looking approvingly down upon me as they used to look down upon Dante,
and mutely asking me to adopt them into my family, which I do with pleasure, for my remotest ancestors are but spring chickens compared with these
robed and stately antiques, and it will be a great and satisfying lift for me,
that six hundred years will.

MARK TWAIN.

□   I   □

PUDD'NHEAD WINS HIS NAME

Tell the truth or trump—but get the trick.
—PUDD'NHEAD WILSON'S CALENDAR.

The scene of this chronicle is the town of Dawson's Landing, on the Missouri
side of the Mississippi, half a day's journey, per steamboat, below St. Louis.

In 1830 it was a snug little collection of modest one and two-story frame
dwellings whose whitewashed exteriors were almost concealed from sight by
climbing tangles of rose vines, honeysuckles, and morning-glories. Each of
these pretty homes had a garden in front fenced with white palings, and opu-
lently stocked with hollyhocks, marigolds, touch-me-nots, prince's-feathers,
and other old-fashioned flowers; while on the window-sills of the houses
stood wooden boxes containing moss-rose plants and terra-cotta pots in
which grew a breed of geranium whose spread of intensely red blossoms accented the prevailing pink tint of the rose-clad house-front like an explosion
of flame. When there was room on the ledge outside of the pots and boxes
for a cat, the cat was there—in sunny weather—stretched at full length, asleep
and blissful, with her furry belly to the sun and a paw curved over her nose.
Then that house was complete, and its contentment and peace were made
manifest to the world by this symbol, whose testimony is infallible. A home
without a cat—and a well-fed, well-petted and properly revered cat—may be a
perfect home, perhaps, but how can it prove title?

All along the streets, on both sides, at the outer edge of the brick sidewalks, stood locust-trees with trunks protected by wooden boxing, and these furnished shade for summer and a sweet fragrance in spring when the clusters of buds came forth. The main street, one block back from the river, and running parallel with it, was the sole business street. It was six blocks long, and in each block two or three brick stores three stories high towered above interjected bunches of little frame shops. Swinging signs creaked in the wind, the street's whole length. The candy-striped pole, which indicates nobility proud and ancient along the palace-bordered canals of Venice, indicated merely the humble barber shop along the main street of Dawson's Landing. On a chief corner stood a lofty unpainted pole wreathed from top to bottom with tin pots and pans and cups, the chief tinmonger's noisy notice to the world (when the wind blew) that his shop was on hand for business at that corner.

The hamlet's front was washed by the clear waters of the great river; its body stretched itself rearward up a gentle incline; its most rearward border fringed itself out and scattered its houses about the baseline of the hills; the hills rose high, inclosing the town in a half-moon curve, clothed with forests from foot to summit.

Steamboats passed up and down every hour or so. Those belonging to the little Cairo line and the little Memphis line always stopped; the big Orleans liners stopped for hails only, or to land passengers or freight; and this was the case also with the great flotilla of "transients." These latter came out of a dozen rivers—the Illinois, the Missouri, the Upper Mississippi, the Ohio, the Monongahela, the Tennessee, the Red River, the White River, and so on; and were bound every whither and stocked with every imaginable comfort or necessity which the Mississippi's communities could want, from the frosty Falls of St. Anthony down through nine climates to torrid New Orleans.

Dawson's Landing was a slaveholding town, with a rich slave-worked grain and pork country back of it. The town was sleepy and comfortable and contented. It was fifty years old, and was growing slowly—very slowly, in fact, but still it was growing.

The chief citizen was York Leicester Driscoll, about forty years old, judge of the county court. He was very proud of his old Virginian ancestry, and in his hospitalities and his rather formal and stately manners he kept up its traditions. He was fine and just and generous. To be a gentleman—a gentleman without stain or blemish—was his only religion, and to it he was always faithful. He was respected, esteemed, and beloved by all the community. He was well off, and was gradually adding to his store. He and his wife were very nearly happy, but not quite, for they had no children. The longing for the treasure of a child had grown stronger and stronger as the years slipped away, but the blessing never came—and was never to come.

With this pair lived the Judge's widowed sister, Mrs. Rachel Pratt, and she also was childless—childless, and sorrowful for that reason, and not to be

comforted. The women were good and commonplace people, and did their
duty and had their reward in clear consciences and the community's approba-
tion. They were Presbyterians, the Judge was a free-thinker.

Pembroke Howard, lawyer and bachelor, aged about forty, was another
old Virginian grandee with proved descent from the First Families. He was a
fine, brave, majestic creature, a gentleman according to the nicest requirements of the Virginia rule, a devoted Presbyterian, an authority on the
"code," and a man always courteously ready to stand up before you in the
field if any act or word of his had seemed doubtful or suspicious to you, and
explain it with any weapon you might prefer from brad-awls to artillery. He
was very popular with the people, and was the Judge's dearest friend.

Then there was Colonel Cecil Burleigh Essex, another F. F. V. of formidable caliber—however, with him we have no concern.

Percy Northumberland Driscoll, brother to the Judge, and younger than
he by five years, was a married man, and had had children around his hearthstone; but they were attacked in detail by measles, croup, and scarlet fever,
and this had given the doctor a chance with his effective antediluvian
methods; so the cradles were empty. He was a prosperous man, with a good
head for speculations, and his fortune was growing. On the 1st of February,
1830, two boy babes were born in his house; one to him, the other to one of
his slave girls, Roxana by name. Roxana was twenty years old. She was up
and around the same day, with her hands full, for she was tending both
babies.

Mrs. Percy Driscoll died within the week. Roxy remained in charge of
the children. She had her own way, for Mr. Driscoll soon absorbed himself in
his speculations and left her to her own devices.

In that same month of February, Dawson's Landing gained a new citizen. This was Mr. David Wilson, a young fellow of Scotch parentage. He had
wandered to this remote region from his birthplace in the interior of the state
of New York, to seek his fortune. He was twenty-five years old, college-bred,
and had finished a post-college course in an Eastern law school a couple of
years before.

He was a homely, freckled, sandy-haired young fellow, with an intelligent blue eye that had frankness and comradeship in it and a covert twinkle
of a pleasant sort. But for an unfortunate remark of his, he would no doubt
have entered at once upon a successful career at Dawson's Landing. But he
made his fatal remark the first day he spent in the village, and it "gaged" him.
He had just made the acquaintance of a group of citizens when an invisible
dog began to yelp and snarl and howl and make himself very comprehensively disagreeable, whereupon young Wilson said, much as one who is thinking aloud:

"I wish I owned half of that dog."

"Why?" somebody asked.

"Because I would kill my half."

The group searched his face with curiosity, with anxiety even, but found no light there, no expression that they could read. They fell away from him as from something uncanny, and went into privacy to discuss him. One said:

" 'Pears to be a fool."

" 'Pears?" said another. *"Is,* I reckon you better say."

"Said he wished he owned *half* of the dog, the idiot," said a third. "What did he reckon would become of the other half if he killed his half? Do you reckon he thought it would live?"

"Why, he must have thought it, unless he *is* the downrightest fool in the world; because if he hadn't thought it, he would have wanted to own the whole dog, knowing that if he killed his half and the other half died, he would be responsible for that half just the same as if he had killed that half instead of his own. Don't it look that way to you, gents?"

"Yes, it does. If he owned one half of the general dog, it would be so; if he owned one end of the dog and another person owned the other end, it would be so, just the same; particularly in the first case, because if you kill one half of a general dog, there ain't any man that can tell whose half it was, but if he owned one end of the dog, maybe he could kill his end of it and—"

"No, he couldn't, either; he couldn't and not be responsible if the other end died, which it would. In my opinion the man ain't in his right mind."

"In my opinion he hain't *got* any mind."

No. 3 said: "Well, he's a lummox, anyway."

"That's what he is," said No. 4, "he's a labrick—just a Simon-pure labrick, if ever there was one."

"Yes, sir, he's a damn fool, that's the way I put him up," said No. 5. "Anybody can think different that wants to, but those are my sentiments."

"I'm with you, gentlemen," said No. 6. "Perfect jackass—yes, and it ain't going too far to say he is a pudd'nhead. If he ain't a pudd'nhead, I ain't no judge, that's all."

Mr. Wilson stood elected. The incident was told all over the town, and gravely discussed by everybody. Within a week he had lost his first name; Pudd'nhead took its place. In time he came to be liked, and well liked, too; but by that time the nickname had got well stuck on, and it stayed. That first day's verdict made him a fool, and he was not able to get it set aside, or even modified. The nickname soon ceased to carry any harsh or unfriendly feeling with it, but it held its place, and was to continue to hold its place for twenty long years.

□ **II** □

DRISCOLL SPARES HIS SLAVES

*Adam was but human—this explains it all. He did not want the apple
for the apple's sake, he wanted it only because it was forbidden. The mistake was in not forbidding the serpent: then he would have eaten the serpent.*

—PUDD'NHEAD WILSON'S CALENDAR.

Pudd'nhead Wilson had a trifle of money when he arrived, and he bought a
small house on the extreme western verge of the town. Between it and Judge
Driscoll's house there was only a grassy yard, with a paling fence dividing the
properties in the middle. He hired a small office down in the town and hung
out a tin sign with these words on it:

DAVID WILSON
ATTORNEY AND COUNSELOR-AT-LAW
SURVEYING, CONVEYANCING, ETC.

But his deadly remark had ruined his chance—at least in the law. No clients came. He took down his sign after a while and put it up on his own
house with the law features knocked out of it. It offered his services now in
the humble capacities of land-surveyor and expert accountant. Now and then
he got a job of surveying to do, and now and then a merchant got him to
straighten out his books. With Scotch patience and pluck he resolved to live
down his reputation and work his way into the legal field yet. Poor fellow! he
could not foresee that it was going to take him such a weary long time to do
it.

He had a rich abundance of idle time, but it never hung heavy on his
hands, for he interested himself in every new thing that was born into the
universe of ideas, and studied it and experimented upon it at his house. One
of his pet fads was palmistry. To another one he gave no name, neither would
he explain to anybody what its purpose was, but merely said it was an amusement. In fact, he had found that his fads added to his reputation as a
pudd'nhead; therefore he was growing chary of being too communicative
about them. The fad without a name was one which dealt with people's finger-marks. He carried in his coat pocket a shallow box with grooves in it, and
in the grooves strips of glass five inches long and three inches wide. Along
the lower edge of each strip was pasted a slip of white paper. He asked people
to pass their hands through their hair (thus collecting upon them a thin
coating of the natural oil) and then make a thumb-mark on a glass strip, fol-

lowing it with the mark of the ball of each finger in succession. Under this row of faint grease-prints he would write a record on the strip of white paper—thus:

JOHN SMITH, *right hand*—

and add the day of the month and the year, then take Smith's left hand on another glass strip, and add name and date and the words "left hand." The strips were now returned to the grooved box, and took their place among what Wilson called his "records."

He often studied his records, examining and poring over them with absorbing interest until far into the night; but what he found there—if he found anything—he revealed to no one. Sometimes he copied on paper the involved and delicate pattern left by the ball of a finger, and then vastly enlarged it with a pantograph so that he could examine its web of curving lines with ease and convenience.

One sweltering afternoon—it was the first day of July, 1830—he was at work over a set of tangled account-books in his workroom, which looked westward over a stretch of vacant lots, when a conversation outside disturbed him. It was carried on in yells, which showed that the people engaged in it were not close together:

"Say, Roxy, how does yo' baby come on?" This from the distant voice.

"Fust-rate; how does *you* come on, Jasper?" This yell was from close by.

"Oh, I's middlin'; hain't got noth'n' to complain of. I's gwine to come a-court'n' you bimeby, Roxy."

"*You* is, you black mudcat! Yah—yah—yah! I got somep'n' better to do den 'sociat'n' wid niggers as black as you is. Is ole Miss Cooper's Nancy done give you de mitten?" Roxy followed this sally with another discharge of carefree laughter.

"You's jealous, Roxy, dat's what's de matter wid *you,* you hussy—yah—yah—yah! Dat's de time I got you!"

"You, yes, *you* got me, hain't you. 'Clah to goodness if dat conceit o' yo'n strikes in, Jasper, it gwine to kill you sho'. If you b'longed to me I'd sell you down de river 'fo' you git too fur gone. Fust time I runs acrost yo' marster, I's gwine to tell him so."

This idle and aimless jabber went on and on, both parties enjoying the friendly duel and each well satisfied with his own share of the wit exchanged—for wit they considered it.

Wilson stepped to the window to observe the combatants; he could not work while their chatter continued. Over in the vacant lots was Jasper, young, coal-black, and of magnificent build, sitting on a wheelbarrow in the pelting sun—at work, supposably, whereas he was in fact only preparing for it by taking an hour's rest before beginning. In front of Wilson's porch stood Roxy, with a local handmade baby-wagon, in which sat her two charges—one at each end and facing each other. From Roxy's manner of speech, a stranger would have expected her to be black, but she was not. Only one-sixteenth of her was black, and that sixteenth did not show. She was of majestic form and stature, her attitudes were imposing and statuesque, and her gestures and movements distinguished by a noble and stately grace. Her complexion was very fair, with the rosy glow of vigorous health in the cheeks, her face was full of character and expression, her eyes were brown and liquid, and she had a heavy suit of fine soft hair which was also brown, but the fact was not apparent because her head was bound about with a checkered handkerchief and the hair was concealed under it. Her face was shapely, intelligent, and comely—even beautiful. She had an easy, independent carriage—when she was among her own caste—and a high and "sassy" way, withal; but of course she was meek and humble enough where white people were.

To all intents and purposes Roxy was as white as anybody, but the one-sixteenth of her which was black outvoted the other fifteen parts and made her a negro. She was a slave, and salable as such. Her child was thirty-one parts white, and he, too, was a slave, and by a fiction of law and custom a negro. He had blue eyes and flaxen curls like his white comrade, but even the father of the white child was able to tell the children apart—little as he had commerce with them—by their clothes; for the white babe wore ruffled soft muslin and a coral necklace, while the other wore merely a coarse tow-linen shirt which barely reached to its knees, and no jewelry.

The white child's name was Thomas à Becket Driscoll, the other's name was Valet de Chambre; no surname—slaves hadn't the privilege. Roxana had heard that phrase somewhere, the fine sound of it had pleased her ear, and as she had supposed it was a name, she loaded it onto her darling. It soon got shortened to "Chambers," of course.

Wilson knew Roxy by sight, and when the duel of wit began to play out, he stepped outside to gather in a record or two. Jasper went to work energetically, at once, perceiving that his leisure was observed. Wilson inspected the children and asked:

"How old are they, Roxy?"

"Bofe de same age, sir—five months. Bawn de fust o' Feb'uary."

"They're handsome little chaps. One's just as handsome as the other, too."

A delighted smile exposed the girl's white teeth, and she said:

"Bless yo' soul, Misto Wilson, it's pow'ful nice o' you to say dat, 'ca'se one of 'em ain't on'y a nigger. Mighty prime little nigger, I al'ays says, but dat's 'ca'se it's mine, o' course."

"How do you tell them apart, Roxy, when they haven't any clothes on?"

Roxy laughed a laugh proportioned to her size, and said:

"Oh, I kin tell 'em 'part, Misto Wilson, but I bet Marse Percy couldn't, not to save his life."

Wilson chatted along for a while, and presently got Roxy's finger-prints for his collection—right hand and left—on a couple of his glass strips; then labeled and dated them, and took the "records" of both children, and labeled and dated them also.

Two months later, on the 3d of September, he took this trio of finger-marks again. He liked to have a "series," two or three "takings" at intervals during the period of childhood, these to be followed by others at intervals of several years.

The next day—that is to say, on the 4th of September—something occurred which profoundly impressed Roxana. Mr. Driscoll missed another small sum of money—which is a way of saying that this was not a new thing, but had happened before. In truth, it had happened three times before. Driscoll's patience was exhausted. He was a fairly humane man toward slaves and other animals; he was an exceedingly humane man toward the erring of his own race. Theft he could not abide, and plainly there was a thief in his house. Necessarily the thief must be one of his negroes. Sharp measures must be taken. He called his servants before him. There were three of these, besides Roxy; a man, woman, and a boy twelve years old. They were not related. Mr. Driscoll said:

"You have all been warned before. It has done no good. This time I will teach you a lesson. I will sell the thief. Which of you is the guilty one?"

They all shuddered at the threat, for here they had a good home, and a new one was likely to be a change for the worse. The denial was general. None had stolen anything—not money, anyway—a little sugar, or cake, or honey, or something like that, that "Marse Percy wouldn't mind or miss," but not money—never a cent of money. They were eloquent in their protestations, but Mr. Driscoll was not moved by them. He answered each in turn with a stern "Name the thief!"

The truth was, all were guilty but Roxana; she suspected that the others were guilty, but she did not know them to be so. She was horrified to think how near she had come to being guilty herself; she had been saved in the nick of time by a revival in the colored Methodist church, a fortnight before, at which time and place she "got religion." The very next day after that gracious experience, while her change of style was fresh upon her and she was vain of her purified condition, her master left a couple of dollars lying unprotected on his desk, and she happened upon that temptation when she was polishing around with a dust-rag. She looked at the money awhile with a steadily rising resentment, then she burst out with:

"Dad blame dat revival, I wisht it had 'a' be'n put off till to-morrow!"

Then she covered the tempter with a book, and another member of the kitchen cabinet got it. She made this sacrifice as a matter of religious etiquette; as a thing necessary just now, but by no means to be wrested into a precedent; no, a week or two would limber up her piety, then she would be rational again, and the next two dollars that got left out in the cold would find a comforter—and she could name the comforter.

Was she bad? Was she worse than the general run of her race? No. They had an unfair show in the battle of life, and they held it no sin to take military advantage of the enemy—in a small way; in a small way, but not in a large one. They would smouch provisions from the pantry whenever they got a chance; or a brass thimble, or a cake of wax, or an emery-bag, or a paper of needles, or a silver spoon, or a dollar bill, or small articles of clothing, or any other property of light value; and so far were they from considering such reprisals sinful, that they would go to church and shout and pray their loudest and sincerest with their plunder in their pockets. A farm smokehouse had to be kept heavily padlocked, for even the colored deacon himself could not resist a ham when Providence showed him in a dream, or otherwise, where such a thing hung lonesome and longed for some one to love. But with a hundred hanging before him the deacon would not take two—that is, on the same night. On frosty nights the humane negro prowler would warm the end of a plank and put it up under the cold claws of chickens roosting in a tree; a drowsy hen would step onto the comfortable board, softly clucking her gratitude, and the prowler would dump her into his bag, and later into his stomach, perfectly sure that in taking this trifle from the man who daily robbed him of an inestimable treasure—his liberty—he was not committing any sin that God would remember against him in the Last Great Day.

"Name the thief!"

For the fourth time Mr. Driscoll had said it, and always in the same hard tone. And now he added these words of awful import:

"I give you one minute"—he took out his watch. "If at the end of that time you have not confessed, I will not only sell all four of you, *but* I will sell you DOWN THE RIVER!"

It was equivalent to condemning them to hell! No Missouri negro doubted this. Roxy reeled in her tracks and the color vanished out of her face; the others dropped to their knees as if they had been shot; tears gushed from their eyes, their supplicating hands went up, and three answers came in the one instant:

"I done it!"

"I done it!"

"I done it!—have mercy, master—Lord have mercy on us po' niggers!"

"Very good," said the master, putting up his watch. "I will sell you *here* though you don't deserve it. You ought to be sold down the river."

The culprits flung themselves prone, in an ecstasy of gratitude, and kissed his feet, declaring that they would never forget his goodness and never cease to pray for him as long as they lived. They were sincere, for like a god he had stretched forth his mighty hand and closed the gates of hell against them. He knew, himself, that he had done a noble and gracious thing, and was privately well pleased with his magnanimity; and that night he set the incident down in his diary, so that his son might read it in after years, and be thereby moved to deeds of gentleness and humanity himself.

□ **III** □

ROXY PLAYS A SHREWD TRICK

Whoever has lived long enough to find out what life is, knows how deep a debt of gratitude we owe to Adam, the first great benefactor of our race. He brought death into the world.
—PUDD'NHEAD WILSON'S CALENDAR.

Percy Driscoll slept well the night he saved his house-minions from going down the river, but no wink of sleep visited Roxy's eyes. A profound terror had taken possession of her. Her child could grow up and be sold down the river! The thought crazed her with horror. If she dozed and lost herself for a moment, the next moment she was on her feet flying to her child's cradle to see if it was still there. Then she would gather it to her heart and pour out her love upon it in a frenzy of kisses, moaning, crying, and saying, "Dey sha'n't, oh, dey *sha'n't!*—yo' po' mammy will kill you fust!"

Once, when she was tucking it back in its cradle again, the other child nestled in its sleep and attracted her attention. She went and stood over it a long time communing with herself:

"What has my po' baby done, dat he couldn't have yo' luck? He hain't done noth'n'. God was good to you; why warn't he good to him? Dey can't sell *you* down de river. I hates yo' pappy; he hain't got no heart—for niggers he hain't, anyways. I hates him, en I could kill him!" She paused awhile, thinking; then she burst into wild sobbings again, and turned away, saying, "Oh, I got to kill my chile, dey ain't no yuther way—killin' *him* wouldn't save de chile fum goin' down de river. Oh, I got to do it, yo' po' mammy's got to kill you to save you, honey"—she gathered her baby to her bosom now, and began to smother it with caresses—"Mammy's got to kill you— how *kin* I do it! But yo' mammy ain't gwine to desert you—no, no; *dah,* don't cry—she gwine *wid* you, she gwine to kill herself, too. Come along, honey, come along wid mammy; we gwine to jump in de river, den de troubles o' dis worl' is all over—dey don't sell po' niggers down the river over *yonder.*"

She started toward the door, crooning to the child and hushing it; midway she stopped suddenly. She had caught sight of her new Sunday gown—a cheap curtain-calico thing, a conflagration of gaudy colors and fantastic figures. She surveyed it wistfully, longingly.

"Hain't ever wore it yet," she said, "en it's jist lovely." Then she nodded her head in response to a pleasant idea, and added, "No, I ain't gwine to be fished out, wid everybody lookin' at me, in dis mis'able ole linsey-woolsey."

She put down the child and made the change. She looked in the glass and was astonished at her beauty. She resolved to make her death-toilet perfect. She took off her handkerchief-turban and dressed her glossy wealth of hair "like white folks"; she added some odds and ends of rather lurid ribbon and a spray of atrocious artificial flowers; finally she threw over her shoulders a fluffy thing called a "cloud" in that day, which was of a blazing red complexion. Then she was ready for the tomb.

She gathered up her baby once more; but when her eye fell upon its miserably short little gray tow-linen shirt and noted the contrast between its pauper shabbiness and her own volcanic irruption of infernal splendors, her mother-heart was touched, and she was ashamed.

"No, dolling, mammy ain't gwine to treat you so. De angels is gwine to 'mire you jist as much as dey does yo' mammy. Ain't gwine to have 'em putt'n' dey han's up 'fo' dey eyes en sayin' to David en Goliah en dem yuther prophets, 'Dat chile is dress' to indelicate fo' dis place.' "

By this time she had stripped off the shirt. Now she clothed the naked little creature in one of Thomas à Becket's snowy long baby gowns, with its bright blue bows and dainty flummery of ruffles.

"Dah—now you's fixed." She propped the child in a chair and stood off to inspect it. Straightway her eyes began to widen with astonishment and admiration, and she clapped her hands and cried out, "Why, it do beat all!—I *never* knowed you was so lovely. Marse Tommy ain't a bit puttier—not a single bit."

She stepped over and glanced at the other infant; she flung a glance back at her own; then one more at the heir of the house. Now a strange light dawned in her eyes, and in a moment she was lost in thought. She seemed in a trance; when she came out of it she muttered, "When I 'uz a-washin' 'em in de tub, yistiddy, his own pappy asked me which of 'em was his'n."

She began to move about like one in a dream. She undressed Thomas à Becket, stripping him of everything, and put the tow-linen shirt on him. She put his coral necklace on her own child's neck. Then she placed the children side by side, and after earnest inspection she muttered:

"Now who would b'lieve clo'es could do de like o' dat? Dog my cats if it ain't all *I* kin do to tell t'other fum which, let alone his pappy."

She put her cub in Tommy's elegant cradle and said:

"You's young Marse *Tom* fum dis out, en I got to practise and git used to 'memberin' to call you dat, honey, or I's gwine to make a mistake some time en git us bofe into trouble. Dah—now you lay still en don't fret no mo', Marse Tom—oh, thank de good Lord in heaven, you's saved, you's saved!— dey ain't no man kin ever sell mammy's po' little honey down de river now!"

She put the heir of the house in her own child's unpainted pine cradle, and said, contemplating its slumbering form uneasily:

"I's sorry for you, honey; I's sorry, God knows I is,—but what *kin* I do, what *could* I do? Yo' pappy would sell him to somebody, some time, en den he'd go down de river, sho', en I couldn't, couldn't, *couldn't* stan' it."

She flung herself on her bed and began to think and toss, toss and think. By and by she sat suddenly upright, for a comforting thought had flown through her worried mind:

" 'Tain't no sin—*white* folks has done it! It ain't no sin, glory to goodness it ain't no sin! *Dey's* done it—yes, en dey was de biggest quality in de whole bilin', too—*kings!*"

She began to muse; she was trying to gather out of her memory the dim particulars of some tale she had heard some time or other. At last she said:

"Now I's got it; now I 'member. It was dat ole nigger preacher dat tole it, de time he come over here fum Illinois en preached in de nigger church. He said dey ain't nobody kin save his own self—can't do it by faith, can't do it by works, can't do it no way at all. Free grace is de *on'y* way, en dat don't come fum nobody but jis' de Lord; en *he* kin give it to anybody he please, saint or sinner—*he* don't kyer. He do jis' as he's a mineter. He s'lect out anybody dat suit him, en put another one in his place, en make de fust one happy forever an leave t'other one to burn wid Satan. De preacher said it was jist like dey done in Englan' one time, long time ago. De queen she lef' her baby layin' aroun' one day, en went out callin'; en one o' de niggers roun' 'bout de place dat was 'mos' white, she come in en see de chile layin' aroun', en tuck en put her own chile's clo'es on de queen's chile, en put de queen's chile's clo'es on her own chile, and den lef' her own chile layin' aroun' en tuck en toted de queen's chile home to de nigger quarter, en nobody ever foun' it out, en her child was de king bimeby, en sole de queen's child down de river one time when dey had to settle up de estate. Dah, now—de preacher said it his own self, en it ain't no sin, 'ca'se white folks done it. *Dey* done it—yes, *dey* done it; en not on'y jis' common white folks nuther, but de biggest quality dey is in de whole bilin'. Oh, I's *so* glad I 'member 'bout dat!"

She got up right-hearted and happy, and went to the cradles and spent what was left of the night "practising." She would give her own child a light pat and say humbly, "Lay still, Marse Tom," then give the real Tom a pat and say with severity, "Lay *still*, Chambers!—does you want me to take somep'n' *to* you?"

As she progressed with her practice, she was surprised to see how steadily and surely the awe which had kept her tongue reverent and her manner humble toward her young master was transferring itself to her speech and manner toward the usurper, and how similarly handy she was becoming in transferring her motherly curtness of speech and peremptoriness of manner to the unlucky heir of the ancient house of Driscoll.

She took occasional rests from practising, and absorbed herself in calculating her chances.

"Dey'll sell dese niggers to-day fo' stealin' de money, den dey'll buy some mo' dat don't know de chillen—so *dat's* all right. When I takes de chillen out to git de air, de minute I's roun' de corner I's gwine to gaum dey mouths all roun' wid jam, den dey can't *nobody* notice dey's changed. Yes, I gwineter do dat till I's safe, if it's a year.

"Dey ain't but one man dat I's afeard of, en dat's dat Pudd'nhead Wilson. Dey calls him a pudd'nhead, en says he's a fool. My lan', dat man ain't no mo' fool den I is! He's de smartes' man in dis town, less'n it's Jedge Driscoll or maybe Pem Howard. Blame dat man, he worries me wid dem ornery glasses o' his'n; I b'lieve he's a witch. But nemmine, I's gwine to happen aroun' dah one o' dese days en let on dat I reckon he wants to print de chillen's fingers ag'in; en if *he* don't notice dey's changed, I bound dey ain't nobody gwine to notice it, en den I's safe, sho'. But I reckon I'll take along a hoss-shoe to keep off de witch work."

The new negroes gave Roxy no trouble, of course. The master gave her none, for one of his speculations was in jeopardy, and his mind was so occupied that he hardly saw the children when he looked at them, and all Roxy had to do was to get them both into a gale of laughter when he came about; then their faces were mainly cavities exposing gums, and he was gone again before the spasm passed and the little creatures resumed a human aspect.

Within a few days the fate of the speculation became so dubious that Mr. Percy went away with his brother the Judge, to see what could be done with it. It was a land speculation, as usual, and it had gotten complicated with a lawsuit. The men were gone seven weeks. Before they got back Roxy had paid her visit to Wilson, and was satisfied. Wilson took the finger-prints, labeled them with the names and the date—October the first—put them carefully away and continued his chat with Roxy, who seemed very anxious that he should admire the great advance in flesh and beauty which the babies had made since he took their finger-prints a month before. He complimented their improvement to her contentment; and as they were without any disguise of jam or other stain, she trembled all the while and was miserably frightened lest at any moment he—

But he didn't. He discovered nothing; and she went home jubilant, and dropped all concern about the matter permanently out of her mind.

□ IV □

THE WAYS OF THE CHANGELINGS

Adam and Eve had many advantages, but the principal one was, that they escaped teething.
—PUDD'NHEAD WILSON'S CALENDAR.

There is this trouble about special providences—namely, there is so often a doubt as to which party was intended to be the beneficiary. In the case of the children, the bears, and the prophet, the bears got more real satisfaction out of the episode than the prophet did, because they got the children.
—PUDD'NHEAD WILSON'S CALENDAR.

This history must henceforth accommodate itself to the change which Roxana has consummated, and call the real heir "Chambers" and the usurping little slave "Thomas à Becket"—shortening this latter name to "Tom," for daily use, as the people about him did.

"Tom" was a bad baby from the very beginning of his usurpation. He would cry for nothing; he would burst into storms of devilish temper without notice, and let go scream after scream and squall after squall, then climax the thing with "holding his breath"—that frightful specialty of the teething nursling, in the throes of which the creature exhausts its lungs, then is convulsed with noiseless squirmings and twistings and kickings in the effort to get its breath, while the lips turn blue and the mouth stands wide and rigid, offering for inspection one wee tooth set in the lower rim of a hoop of red gums; and when the appalling stillness has endured until one is sure the lost breath will never return, a nurse comes flying, and dashes water in the child's face, and—presto! the lungs fill, and instantly discharge a shriek, or a yell, or a howl which bursts the listening ear and surprises the owner of it into saying words which would not go well with a halo if he had one. The baby Tom would claw anybody who came within reach of his nails, and pound anybody he could reach with his rattle. He would scream for water until he got it, and then throw cup and all on the floor and scream for more. He was indulged in all his caprices, howsoever troublesome and exasperating they might be; he was allowed to eat anything he wanted, particularly things that would give him the stomach-ache.

When he got to be old enough to begin to toddle about and say broken words and get an idea of what his hands were for, he was a more consummate pest than ever. Roxy got no rest while he was awake. He would call for anything and everything he saw, simply saying, "Awnt it!" (want it) which was a command. When it was brought, he said in a frenzy, and motioning it away with his hands, "Don't awnt it! Don't awnt it!" and the moment it was gone he set up frantic yells of "Awnt it! awnt it! awnt it!" and Roxy had to give wings to her heels to get that thing back to him again before he could get time to carry out his intention of going into convulsions about it.

What he preferred above all other things was the tongs. This was because his "father" had forbidden him to have them lest he break windows and furniture with them. The moment Roxy's back was turned he would toddle to the presence of the tongs and say, "Like it!" and cock his eye to one side to see if Roxy was observing; then, "Awnt it!" and cock his eye again: then, "Hab it!" with another furtive glance; and finally, "Take it!"—and the prize was his. The next moment the heavy implement was raised aloft; the next, there was a crash and a squall, and the cat was off on three legs to meet an engagement; Roxy would arrive just as the lamp or a window went to irremediable smash.

Tom got all the petting, Chambers got none. Tom got all the delicacies, Chambers got mush and milk, and clabber without sugar. In consequence, Tom was a sickly child and Chambers wasn't. Tom was "fractious," as Roxy called it, and overbearing; Chambers was meek and docile.

With all her splendid common sense and practical every-day ability, Roxy was a doting fool of a mother. She was this toward her child—and she was also more than this; by the fiction created by herself, he was become her master; the necessity of recognizing this relation outwardly and of perfecting herself in the forms required to express the recognition, had moved her to such diligence and faithfulness in practising these forms that this exercise soon concreted itself into habit; it became automatic and unconscious; then a natural result followed; deceptions intended solely for others gradually grew practically into self-deceptions as well; the most reverence became real reverence, the mock obsequiousness real obsequiousness, the mock homage real homage; the little counterfeit rift of separation between imitation slave and imitation master widened and widened, and became an abyss, and a very real one—and on one side of it stood Roxy, the dupe of her own deceptions, and on the other stood her child, no longer a usurper to her, but her accepted and recognized master. He was her darling, her master, and her deity all in one, and in her worship of him she forgot who she was and what he had been.

In babyhood Tom cuffed and banged and scratched Chambers unrebuked, and Chambers early learned that between meekly bearing it and resenting it, the advantage all lay with the former policy. The few times that his persecutions had moved him beyond control and made him fight back had cost him very dear at headquarters; not at the hands of Roxy, for if she ever went beyond scolding him sharply for "forgitt'n' who his young marster was," she at least never extended her punishment beyond a box on the ear. No, Percy Driscoll was the person. He told Chambers that under no provocation whatever was he privileged to lift his hand against his little master. Chambers overstepped the line three times, and got three such convincing canings from the man who was his father and didn't know it, that he took Tom's cruelties in all humility after that, and made no more experiments.

Outside the house the two boys were together all through their boyhood. Chambers was strong beyond his years, and a good fighter; strong because he was coarsely fed and hard-worked about the house, and a good fighter because Tom furnished him plenty of practice—on white boys whom he hated and was afraid of. Chambers was his constant body-guard, to and from school; he was present on the playground at recess to protect his charge. He fought himself into such a formidable reputation, by and by, that Tom could have changed clothes with him, and "ridden in peace," like Sir Kay in Launcelot's armor.

He was good at games of skill, too. Tom staked him with marbles to play "keeps" with, and then took all the winnings away from him. In the winter season Chambers was on hand, in Tom's worn-out clothes, with "holy" red mittens, and "holy" shoes, and pants "holy" at the knees and seat, to drag a sled up the hill for Tom, warmly clad, to ride down on; but he never got a ride himself. He built snow men and snow fortifications under Tom's directions. He was Tom's patient target when Tom wanted to do some snowballing, but the target couldn't fire back. Chambers carried Tom's skates to the river and strapped them on him, then trotted around after him on the ice, so as to be on hand when wanted; but he wasn't ever asked to try the skates himself.

In summer the pet pastime of the boys of Dawson's Landing was to steal apples, peaches, and melons from the farmers' fruit-wagons—mainly on account of the risk they ran of getting their heads laid open with the butt of the farmer's whip. Tom was a distinguished adept at these thefts—by proxy. Chambers did his stealing, and got the peach-stones, apple-cores, and melon-rinds for his share.

Tom always made Chambers go in swimming with him, and stay by him as a protection. When Tom had had enough, he would slip out and tie knots in Chambers's shirt, dip the knots in the water to make them hard to undo, then dress himself and sit by and laugh while the naked shiverer tugged at the stubborn knots with his teeth.

Tom did his humble comrade these various ill turns partly out of native viciousness, and party because he hated him for his superiorities of physique and pluck, and for his manifold clevernesses. Tom couldn't dive, for it gave him splitting headaches. Chambers could dive without inconvenience, and was fond of doing it. He excited so much admiration, one day, among a crowd of white boys, by throwing back somersaults from the stern of a canoe, that it wearied Tom's spirit, and at last he shoved the canoe underneath Chambers while he was in the air—so he came down on his head in the canoe-bottom; and while he lay unconscious, several of Tom's ancient adversaries saw that their long-desired opportunity was come, and they gave the false heir such a drubbing that with Chambers's best help he was hardly able to drag himself home afterward.

When the boys were fifteen and upward, Tom was "showing off" in the river one day, when he was taken with a cramp, and shouted for help. It was a common trick with the boys—particularly if a stranger was present—to pretend a cramp and howl for help; then when the stranger came tearing hand over hand to the rescue, the howler would go on struggling and howling till he was close at hand, then replace the howl with a sarcastic smile and swim blandly away, while the town boys assailed the dupe with a volley of jeers and laughter. Tom had never tried this joke as yet, but was supposed to be trying it now, so the boys held warily back; but Chambers believed his master was in earnest, therefore he swam out, and arrived in time, unfortunately, and saved his life.

This was the last feather. Tom had managed to endure everything else, but to have to remain publicly and permanently under such an obligation as this to a nigger, and to this nigger of all niggers—this was too much. He heaped insults upon Chambers for "pretending" to think he was in earnest in calling for help, and said that anybody but a blockheaded nigger would have known he was funning and left him alone.

Tom's enemies were in strong force here, so they came out with their opinions quite freely. They laughed at him, and called him coward, liar, sneak, and other sorts of pet names, and told him they meant to call Chambers by a new name after this, and make it common in the town—"Tom Driscoll's niggerpappy"—to signify that he had had a second birth into this life, and that Chambers was the author of his new being. Tom grew frantic under these taunts, and shouted:

"Knock their heads off, Chambers! knock their heads off! What do you stand there with your hands in your pockets for?"

Chambers expostulated, and said, "But, Marse Tom, dey's too many of 'em—dey's—"

"Do you hear me?"

"Please, Marse Tom, don't make me! Dey's so many of 'em dat—"

Tom sprang at him and drove his pocket-knife into him two or three times before the boys could snatch him away and give the wounded lad a chance to escape. He was considerably hurt, but not seriously. If the blade had been a little longer his career would have ended there.

Tom had long ago taught Roxy "her place." It had been many a day now since she had ventured a caress or a fondling epithet in his quarter. Such things, from a "nigger," were repulsive to him, and she had been warned to keep her distance and remember who she was. She saw her darling gradually cease from being her son, she saw *that* detail perish utterly; all that was left was master—master, pure and simple, and it was not a gentle mastership, either. She saw herself sink from the sublime height of motherhood to the somber depths of unmodified slavery. The abyss of separation between her and her boy was complete. She was merely his chattel now, his convenience, his dog, his cringing and helpless slave, the humble and unresisting victim of his capricious temper and vicious nature.

Sometimes she could not go to sleep, even when worn out with fatigue, because her rage boiled so high over the day's experiences with her boy. She would mumble and mutter to herself:

"He struck me, en I warn't no way to blame—struck me in de face, right before folks. En he's al'ays callin' me nigger-wench, en hussy, en all dem mean names, when I's doin' de very bes' I kin. Oh, Lord, I done so much for him—I lift' him away up to what he is—en dis is what I get for it."

Sometimes when some outrage of peculiar offensiveness stung her to the heart, she would plan schemes of vengeance and revel in the fancied spectacle of his exposure to the world as an imposter and a slave; but in the midst of these joys fear would strike her; she had made him too strong; she could prove nothing, and—heavens, she might get sold down the river for her pains! So her schemes always went for nothing, and she laid them aside in impotent rage against the fates, and against herself for playing the fool on that fatal September day in not providing herself with a witness for use in the day when such a thing might be needed for the appeasing of her vengeance-hungry heart.

And yet the moment Tom happened to be good to her, and kind—and this occurred every now and then—all her sore places were healed, and she was happy; happy and proud, for this was her son, her nigger son, lording it among the whites and securely avenging their crimes against her race.

There were two grand funerals in Dawson's Landing that fall—the fall of 1845. One was that of Colonel Cecil Burleigh Essex, the other that of Percy Driscoll.

On his death-bed Driscoll set Roxy free and delivered his idolized ostensible son solemnly into the keeping of his brother the Judge, and his wife. Those childless people were glad to get him. Childless people are not difficult to please.

Judge Driscoll had gone privately to his brother, a month before, and bought Chambers. He had heard that Tom had been trying to get his father to sell the boy down the river, and he wanted to prevent the scandal—for public sentiment did not approve of that way of treating family servants for light cause or for no cause.

Percy Driscoll had worn himself out in trying to save his great speculative landed estate, and had died without succeeding. He was hardly in his grave before the boom collapsed and left his hitherto envied young devil of an heir a pauper. But that was nothing; his uncle told him he should be his heir and have all his fortune when he died; so Tom was comforted.

Roxy had no home now; so she resolved to go around and say good-by to her friends and then clear out and see the world—that is to say, she would go chambermaiding on a steamboat, the darling ambition of her race and sex.

Her last call was on the black giant, Jasper. She found him chopping Pudd'nhead Wilson's winter provision of wood.

Wilson was chatting with him when Roxy arrived. He asked her how she could bear to go off chambermaiding and leave her boys; and chaffingly offered to copy off a series of their finger-prints, reaching up to their twelfth year, for her to remember them by; but she sobered in a moment, wondering if he suspected anything; then she said she believed she didn't want them. Wilson said to himself, "The drop of black blood in her is superstitious; she thinks there's some deviltry, some witch business about my glass mystery somewhere; she used to come here with an old horseshoe in her hand; it could have been an accident, but I doubt it."

□ V □

THE TWINS THRILL DAWSON'S LANDING

Training is everything. The peach was once a bitter almond; cauliflower is nothing but cabbage with a college education.
—PUDD'NHEAD WILSON'S CALENDAR.

Remark of Dr. Baldwin's, concerning upstarts: We don't care to eat toadstools that think they are truffles.
—PUDD'NHEAD WILSON'S CALENDAR.

Mrs. York Driscoll enjoyed two years of bliss with that prize, Tom—bliss that was troubled a little at times, it is true, but bliss nevertheless; then she died, and her husband and his childless sister, Mrs. Pratt, continued the bliss business at the old stand. Tom was petted and indulged and spoiled to his entire content—or nearly that. This went on till he was nineteen, then he was sent to Yale. He went handsomely equipped with "conditions," but otherwise he was not an object of distinction there. He remained at Yale two years, and then threw up the struggle. He came home with his manners a good deal improved; he had lost his surliness and brusqueness, and was rather pleasantly soft and smooth now: he was furtively, and sometimes openly, ironical of speech, and given to gently touching people on the raw, but he did it with a good-natured semiconscious air that carried it off safely, and kept him from getting into trouble. He was as indolent as ever and showed no very strenuous desire to hunt up an occupation. People argued from this that he preferred to be supported by his uncle until his uncle's shoes should become vacant. He brought back one or two new habits with him, one of which he rather openly practised—tippling—but concealed another, which was gambling. It would not do to gamble where his uncle could hear of it; he knew that quite well.

Tom's Eastern polish was not popular among the young people. They could have endured it, perhaps, if Tom had stopped there; but he wore gloves, and that they couldn't stand, and wouldn't; so he was mainly without society. He brought home with him a suit of clothes of such exquisite style and cut and fashion—Eastern fashion, city fashion—that it filled everybody with anguish and was regarded as a peculiarly wanton affront. He enjoyed the feeling which he was exciting, and paraded the town serene and happy all day; but the young fellows set a tailor to work that night, and when Tom started out on his parade next morning he found the old deformed negro bell-ringer straddling along in his wake tricked out in a flamboyant curtain-calico exaggeration of his finery, and imitating his fancy Eastern graces as well as he could.

Tom surrendered, and after that clothed himself in the local fashion. But the dull country-town was tiresome to him since his acquaintanceship with livelier regions, and it grew daily more and more so. He began to make little trips to St. Louis for refreshment. There he found companionship to suit him, and pleasures to his taste, along with more freedom, in some particulars, than he could have at home. So, during the next two years his visits to the city grew in frequency and his tarryings there grew steadily longer in duration.

He was getting into deep waters. He was taking chances, privately, which might get him into trouble some day—in fact, *did*.

Judge Driscoll had retired from the bench and from all business activities in 1850, and had now been comfortably idle three years. He was president of the Free-thinkers' Society, and Pudd'nhead Wilson was the other member. The society's weekly discussions were now the old lawyer's main interest in life. Pudd'nhead was still toiling in obscurity at the bottom of the ladder, under the blight of that unlucky remark which he had let fall twenty-three years before about the dog.

Judge Driscoll was his friend, and claimed that he had a mind above the average, but that was regarded as one of the Judge's whims, and it failed to modify the public opinion. Or, rather, that was one of the reasons why it

failed, but there was another and better one. If the Judge had stopped with
bare assertion, it would have had a good deal of effect; but he made the mistake of trying to prove his position. For some years Wilson had been privately at work on a whimsical almanac, for his amusement—a calendar, with
a little dab of ostensible philosophy, usually in ironical form, appended to
each date; and the Judge thought that these quips and fancies of Wilson's
were neatly turned and cute; so he carried a handful of them around one day,
and read them to some of the chief citizens. But irony was not for those people; their mental vision was not focused for it. They read those playful trifles
in the solidest earnest, and decided without hesitancy that if there had ever
been any doubt that Dave Wilson was a pudd'nhead—which there hadn't—
this revelation removed that doubt for good and all. That is just the way in
this world; an enemy can partly ruin a man, but it takes a good-natured inju-
dicious friend to complete the thing and make it perfect. After this the Judge
felt tenderer than ever toward Wilson, and surer than ever that his calendar
had merit.

Judge Driscoll could be a free-thinker and still hold his place in society,
because he was the person of most consequence in the community, and
therefore could venture to go his own way and follow out his own notions.
The other member of his pet organization was allowed the like liberty because he was a cipher in the estimation of the public, and nobody attached
any importance to what he thought or did. He was liked, he was welcome
enough all around, but he simply didn't count for anything.

The widow Cooper—affectionately called "Aunt Patsy" by everybody—
lived in a snug and comely cottage with her daughter Rowena, who was nineteen, romantic, amiable, and very pretty, but otherwise of no consequence.
Rowena had a couple of young brothers—also of no consequence.

The widow had a large spare room which she let to a lodger, with board,
when she could find one, but this room had been empty for a year now, to
her sorrow. Her income was only sufficient for the family support, and she
needed the lodging-money for trifling luxuries. But now, at last, on a flaming
June day, she found herself happy; her tedious wait was ended; her year-worn
advertisement had been answered; and not by a village applicant, oh, no!—
this letter was from away off yonder in the dim great world of the north; it
was from St. Louis. She sat on her porch gazing out with unseeing eyes upon
the shining reaches of the mighty Mississippi, her thoughts steeped in her
good fortune. Indeed, it was specially good fortune, for she was to have two
lodgers instead of one.

She had read the letter to the family, and Rowena had danced away to
see to the cleaning and airing of the room by the slave woman Nancy, and
the boys had rushed abroad in the town to spread the great news, for it was
matter of public interest, and the public would wonder and not be pleased if

not informed. Presently Rowena returned, all ablush with joyous excitement, and begged for a rereading of the letter. It was framed thus:

HONORED MADAM: My brother and I have seen your advertisement, by chance, and beg leave to take the room you offer. We are twenty-four years of age and twins. We are Italians by birth, but have lived long in the various countries of Europe, and several years in the United States. Our names are Luigi and Angelo Capello. You desire but one guest; but, dear Madam, if you will allow us to pay for two, we will not incommode you. We shall be down Thursday.

"Italians! How romantic! Just think, ma—there's never been one in this town, and everybody will be dying to see them and they're all *ours!* Think of that!"

"Yes, I reckon they'll make a grand stir."

"Oh, indeed they will. The whole town will be on its head! Think—they've been in Europe and everywhere! There's never been a traveler in this town before. Ma, I shouldn't wonder if they've seen kings!"

"Well, a body can't tell; but they'll make stir enough, without that."

"Yes, that's of course. Luigi—Angelo. They're lovely names; and so grand and foreign—not like Jones and Robinson and such. Thursday they are coming, and this is only Tuesday; it's a cruel long time to wait. Here comes Judge Driscoll in at the gate. He's heard about it. I'll go and open the door."

The Judge was full of congratulations and curiosity. The letter was read and discussed. Soon Justice Robinson arrived with more congratulations, and there was a new reading and a new discussion. This was the beginning. Neighbor after neighbor, of both sexes, followed, and the procession drifted in and out all day and evening, and all Wednesday and Thursday. The letter was read and reread until it was nearly worn out; everybody admired its courtly and gracious tone, and smooth and practised style, everybody was sympathetic and excited, and the Coopers were steeped in happiness all the while.

The boats were very uncertain in low water in these primitive times. This time the Thursday boat had not arrived at ten at night—so the people had waited at the landing all day for nothing; they were driven to their homes by a heavy storm without having had a view of the illustrious foreigners.

Eleven o'clock came; and the Cooper house was the only one in town that still had lights burning. The rain and thunder were booming yet, and the anxious family were still waiting, still hoping. At last there was a kncok at the door and the family jumped to open it. Two negro men entered, each carrying a trunk, and proceeded up-stairs toward the guest-room. Then entered the twins—the handsomest, the best dressed, the most distinguished-looking pair of young fellows the West had ever seen. One was a little fairer than the other, but otherwise they were exact duplicates.

□ **VI** □

SWIMMING IN GLORY

Let us endeavor so to live that when we come to die even the undertaker will be sorry.

—PUDD'NHEAD WILSON'S CALENDAR.

Habit is habit, and not to be flung out of the window by any man, but coaxed down-stairs a step at a time.

—PUDD'NHEAD WILSON'S CALENDAR.

At breakfast in the morning the twins' charm of manner and easy and polished bearing made speedy conquest of the family's good graces. All constraint and formality quickly disappeared, and the friendliest feeling succeeded. Aunt Patsy called them by their Christian names almost from the beginning. She was full of the keenest curiosity about them, and showed it; they responded by talking about themselves, which pleased her greatly. It presently appeared that in their early youth they had known poverty and hardship. As the talk wandered along the old lady watched for the right place to drop in a question or two concerning that matter, and when she found it she said to the blond twin who was now doing the biographies in his turn while the brunette one rested:

"If it ain't asking what I ought not to ask, Mr. Angelo, how did you come to be so friendless and in such trouble when you were little? Do you mind telling? But don't if you do."

"Oh, we don't mind it at all, madam; in our case it was merely misfortune, and nobody's fault. Our parents were well to do, there in Italy, and we were their only child. We were of the old Florentine nobility"—Rowena's heart gave a great bound, her nostrils expanded, and a fine light played in her eyes—"and when the war broke out my father was on the losing side and had to fly for his life. His estates were confiscated, his personal property seized, and there we were, in Germany, strangers, friendless, and, in fact, paupers. My brother and I were ten years old, and well educated for that age, very studious, very fond of our books, and well grounded in the German, French, Spanish, and English languages. Also, we were marvelous musical prodigies—if you will allow me to say it, it being only the truth.

"Our father survived his misfortunes only a month, our mother soon followed him, and we were alone in the world. Our parents could have made themselves comfortable by exhibiting us as a show, and they had many and large offers; but the thought revolted their pride, and they said they would starve and die first. But what they wouldn't consent to do we had to do without the formality of consent. We were seized for the debts occasioned by their illness and their funerals, and placed among the attractions of a cheap museum in Berlin to earn the liquidation money. It took us two years to get out of that slavery. We traveled all about Germany receiving no wages, and not even our keep. We had to be exhibited for nothing, and beg our bread.

"Well, madam, the rest is not of much consequence. When we escaped from that slavery at twelve years of age, we were in some respects men. Experience had taught us some valuable things; among other, how to take care of ourselves, how to avoid and defeat sharks and sharpers, and how to conduct our own business for our own profit and without other people's help. We traveled everywhere—years and years—picking up smatterings of strange tongues, familiarizing ourselves with strange sights and strange customs, accumulating an education of a wide and varied and curious sort. It was a pleasant life. We went to Venice—to London, Paris, Russia, India, China, Japan—"

At this point Nancy, the slave woman, thrust her head in at the door and exclaimed:

"Ole Missus, de house is plum' jam full o' people, en dey's jes' a-spi'lin' to see de gen'lmen!" She indicated the twins with a nod of her head, and tucked it back out of sight again.

It was a proud occasion for the widow, and she promised herself high satisfaction in showing off her fine foreign birds before her neighbors and friends—simple folk who had hardly ever seen a foreigner of any kind, and never one of any distinction or style. Yet her feeling was moderate indeed when contrasted with Rowena's. Rowena was in the clouds, she walked on air; this was to be the greatest day, the most romantic episode, in the colorless history of that dull country-town. She was to be familiarly near the source of its glory and feel the full flood of it pour over her and about her; the other girls could only gaze and envy, not partake.

The widow was ready, Rowena was ready, so also were the foreigners.

The party moved along the hall, the twins in advance, and entered the open parlor door, whence issued a low hum of conversation. The twins took a position near the door, the widow stood at Luigi's side, Rowena stood beside Angelo, and the march-past and the introductions began. The widow was all smiles and contentment. She received the procession and passed it on to Rowena.

"Good mornin', Sister Cooper"—handshake.

"Good morning, Brother Higgins—Count Luigi Capello, Mr. Higgins"—handshake, followed by a devouring stare and "I'm glad to see ye," on the part of Higgins, and a courteous inclination of the head and a pleasant "Most happy!" on the part of Count Luigi.

"Good mornin', Roweny"—handshake.

"Good morning, Mr. Higgins—present you to Count Angelo Capello." Handshake, admiring stare, "Glad to see ye," courteous nod, smily "Most happy!" and Higgins passes on.

None of these visitors was at ease, but, being honest people, they didn't pretend to be. None of them had ever seen a person bearing a title of nobility before, and none had been expecting to see one now, consequently the title came upon them as a kind of pile-driving surprise and caught them unprepared. A few tried to rise to the emergency, and got out an awkward "My lord," or "Your lordship," or something of that sort, but the great majority were overwhelmed by the unaccustomed word and its dim and awful associations with gilded courts and stately ceremony and anointed kingship, so they only fumbled through the handshake and passed on speechless. Now and then, as happens at all receptions everywhere, a more than ordinarily friendly soul blocked the procession and kept it waiting while he inquired how the brothers liked the village, and how long they were going to stay, and if their families were well, and dragged in the weather, and hoped it would get cooler soon, and all that sort of thing, so as to be able to say, when they got home, "I had quite a long talk with them"; but nobody did or said anything of a regrettable kind, and so the great affair went through to the end in a creditable and satisfactory fashion.

General conversation followed, and the twins drifted about from group to group, talking easily and fluently and winning approval, compelling admiration and achieving favor from all. The widow followed their conquering march with a proud eye, and every now and then Rowena said to herself with deep satisfaction, "And to think they are ours—all ours!"

There were no idle moments for mother or daughter. Eager inquiries concerning the twins were pouring into their enchanted ears all the time; each was the constant center of a group of breathless listeners; each recognized that she knew now for the first time the real meaning of that great word Glory, and perceived the stupendous value of it, and understood why men in all ages had been willing to throw away meaner happinesses, treasure, life itself, to get a taste of its sublime and supreme joy. Napoleon and all his kind stood accounted for—and justified.

When Rowena had at last done all her duty by the people in the parlor, she went up-stairs to satisfy the longings of an overflow-meeting there, for the parlor was not big enough to hold all the comers. Again she was besieged by eager questioners and again she swam in sunset seas of glory. When the forenoon was nearly gone, she recognized with a pang that this most splendid episode of her life was almost over, that nothing could prolong it, that nothing quite its equal could ever fall to her fortune again. But never mind, it was sufficient unto itself, the grand occasion had moved on an ascending scale from the start, and was a noble and memorable success. If the twins could but do some crowning act now to climax it, something unusual, something startling, something to concentrate upon themselves the company's loftiest admiration, something in the nature of an electric surprise—

Here a prodigious slam-banging broke out below, and everybody rushed down to see. It was the twins knocking out a classic four-handed piece on the piano in great style. Rowena was satisfied—satisfied down to the bottom of her heart.

The young strangers were kept long at the piano. The villagers were astonished and enchanted with the magnificence of their performance, and could not bear to have them stop. All the music that they had ever heard before seemed spiritless prentice-work and barren of grace or charm when compared with these intoxicating floods of melodious sound. They realized that for once in their lives they were hearing masters.

□ VII □

THE UNKNOWN NYMPH

One of the most striking differences between a cat and a lie is that a cat has only nine lives.

—PUDD'NHEAD WILSON'S CALENDAR.

The company broke up reluctantly, and drifted toward their several homes, chatting with vivacity, and all agreeing that it would be many a long day before Dawson's Landing would see the equal of this one again. The twins had accepted several invitations while the reception was in progress, and had also volunteered to play some duets at an amateur entertainment for the benefit of a local charity. Society was eager to receive them to its bosom. Judge Driscoll had the good fortune to secure them for an immediate drive, and to be the first to display them in public. They entered his buggy with him, and were paraded down the main street, everybody flocking to the windows and sidewalks to see.

The Judge showed the strangers the new graveyard, and the jail, and where the richest man lived, and the Free-masons' hall, and the Methodist church, and the Presbyterian church, and where the Baptist church was going to be when they got some money to build it with, and showed them the town hall and the slaughter-house, and got out the independent fire company in uniform and had them put out an imaginary fire; then he let them inspect the muskets of the militia company, and poured out an exhaustless stream of enthusiasm over all these splendors, and seemed very well satisfied with the responses he got, for the twins admired his admiration, and paid him back the best they could, though they could have done better if some fifteen or sixteen hundred thousand previous experiences of this sort in various countries had not already rubbed off a considerable part of the novelty of it.

The Judge laid himself out hospitably to make them have a good time, and if there was a defect anywhere it was not his fault. He told them a good many humorous anecdotes, and always forgot the nub, but they were always able to furnish it, for these yarns were of a pretty early vintage, and they had had many a rejuvenating pull at them before. And he told them all about his several dignities, and how he had held this and that and the other place of honor or profit, and had once been to the legislature, and was now president of the Society of Free-thinkers. He said the society had been in existence four years, and already had two members, and was firmly established. He would call for the brothers in the evening if they would like to attend a meeting of it.

Accordingly he called for them, and on the way he told them all about Pudd'nhead Wilson, in order that they might get a favorable impression of him in advance and be prepared to like him. This scheme succeeded—the favorable impression was achieved. Later it was confirmed and solidified when Wilson proposed that out of courtesy to the strangers the usual topics be put aside and the hour be devoted to conversation upon ordinary subjects and the cultivation of friendly relations and good-fellowship—a proposition which was put to vote and carried.

The hour passed quickly away in lively talk, and when it was ended the lonesome and neglected Wilson was richer by two friends than he had been when it began. He invited the twins to look in at his lodgings, presently, after disposing of an intervening engagement, and they accepted with pleasure.

Toward the middle of the evening they found themselves on the road to his house. Pudd'nhead was at home waiting for them and putting in his time puzzling over a thing which had come under his notice that morning. The matter was this: He happened to be up very early—at dawn, in fact; and he crossed the hall which divided his cottage through the center, and entered a room to get something there. The window of the room had no curtains, for that side of the house had long been unoccupied, and through this window he caught sight of something which surprised and interested him. It was a young woman—a young woman where properly no young woman belonged; for she was in Judge Driscoll's house, and in the bedroom over the Judge's private study or sitting-room. This was young Tom Driscoll's bedroom. He and the Judge, the Judge's widowed sister, Mrs. Pratt, and three negro servants were the only people who belonged in the house. Who, then, might this young lady be? The two houses were separated by an ordinary yard, with a low fence running back through its middle from the street in front to the lane in the rear. The distance was not great, and Wilson was able to see the girl very well, the window-shades of the room she was in being up, and the window also. The girl had on a neat and trim summer dress, patterned in broad stripes of pink and white, and her bonnet was equipped with a pink veil. She was practising steps, gaits, and attitudes, apparently; she was doing the thing gracefully, and was very much absorbed in her work. Who could she be, and how come she to be in young Tom Driscoll's room?

Wilson had quickly chosen a position from which he could watch the girl without running much risk of being seen by her, and he remained there hoping she would raise her veil and betray her face. But she disappointed him. After a matter of twenty minutes she disappeared, and although he stayed at his post half an hour longer, she came no more.

Toward noon he dropped in at the Judge's and talked with Mrs. Pratt about the great event of the day, the levee of the distinguished foreigners at Aunt Patsy Cooper's. He asked after her nephew Tom, and she said he was on his way home, and that she was expecting him to arrive a little before night; and added that she and the Judge were gratified to gather from his letters that he was conducting himself very nicely and creditably—at which Wilson winked to himself privately. Wilson did not ask if there was a new-comer in the house, but he asked questions that would have brought light-throwing answers to that matter if Mrs. Pratt had had any light to throw; so he went away satisfied that he knew of things that were going on in her house of which she herself was not aware.

He was now waiting for the twins, and still puzzling over the problem of who that girl might be, and how she happened to be in that young fellow's room at daybreak in the morning.

□ **VIII** □

MARSE TOM TRAMPLES HIS CHANCE

The holy passion of Friendship is of so sweet and steady and loyal and enduring a nature that it will last through a whole lifetime, if not asked to lend money.

—PUDD'NHEAD WILSON'S CALENDAR.

Consider well the proportions of things. It is better to be a young June-bug than an old bird of paradise.

—PUDD'NHEAD WILSON'S CALENDAR.

It is necessary now to hunt up Roxy.

At the time she was set free and went away chambermaiding, she was thirty-five. She got a berth as second chambermaid on a Cincinnati boat in the New Orleans trade, the *Grand Mogul*. A couple of trips made her wonted and easy-going at the work, and infatuated her with the stir and adventure and independence of steamboat life. Then she was promoted and became head chambermaid. She was a favorite with the officers, and exceedingly proud of their joking and friendly ways with her.

During eight years she served three parts of the year on that boat, and the winters on a Vicksburg packet. But now for two months she had had rheumatism in her arms, and was obliged to let the wash-tub alone. So she resigned. But she was well fixed—rich, as she would have described it; for she had lived a steady life, and had banked four dollars every month in New Orleans as a provision for her old age. She said in the start that she had "put shoes on one bar'footed nigger to tromple on her with," and that one mistake like that was enough; she would be independent of the human race thenceforth forevermore if hard work and economy could accomplish it. When the boat touched the levee at New Orleans she bade good-by to her comrades on the *Grand Mogul* and moved her kit ashore.

But she was back in an hour. The bank had gone to smash and carried her four hundred dollars with it. She was a pauper, and homeless. Also disabled bodily, at least for the present. The officers were full of sympathy for her in her trouble, and made up a little purse for her. She resolved to go to her birthplace; she had friends there among the negroes, and the unfortunate always help the unfortunate, she was well aware of that; those lowly comrades of her youth would not let her starve.

She took the little local packet at Cairo, and now she was on the homestretch. Time had worn away her bitterness against her son, and she was able to think of him with serenity. She put the vile side of him out of her mind, and dwelt only on recollections of his occasional acts of kindness to her. She gilded and otherwise decorated these, and made them very pleasant to contemplate. She began to long to see him. She would go and fawn upon him, slave-like—for this would have to be her attitude, of course—and maybe she would find that time had modified him, and that he would be glad to see his long-forgotten old nurse and treat her gently. That would be lovely; that would make her forget her woes and her poverty.

Her poverty! That thought inspired her to add another castle to her dream; maybe he would give her a trifle now and then—maybe a dollar, once a month, say; any little thing like that would help, oh, ever so much.

By the time she reached Dawson's Landing she was her old self again; her blues were gone, she was in high feather. She would get along, surely; there were many kitchens where the servants would share their meals with her, and also steal sugar and apples and other dainties for her to carry home—or give her a chance to pilfer them herself, which would answer just as well. And there was the church. She was a more rabid and devoted Methodist than ever, and her piety was no sham, but was strong and sincere. Yes, with plenty of creature comforts and her old place in the amen-corner in her possession again, she would be perfectly happy and at peace thenceforward to the end.

She went to Judge Driscoll's kitchen first of all. She was received there in great form and with vast enthusiasm. Her wonderful travels, and the strange countries she had seen and the adventures she had had, made her a marvel, and a heroine of romance. The negroes hung enchanted upon the great story of her experiences, interrupting her all along with eager questions, with laughter, exclamations of delight and expressions of applause; and she was obliged to confess to herself that if there was anything better in this world than steamboating, it was the glory to be got by telling about it. The audience loaded her stomach with their dinners, and then stole the pantry bare to load up her basket.

Tom was in St. Louis. The servants said he had spent the best part of his time there during the previous two years. Roxy came every day, and had many talks about the family and its affairs. Once she asked why Tom was away so much. The ostensible "Chambers" said:

"De fac' is, ole marster kin git along better when young marster's away den he kin when he's in de town; yes, en he love him better, too; so he gives him fifty dollahs a month—"

"No, is dat so? Chambers, you's a-jokin', ain't you?"

" 'Clah to goodness I ain't, mammy; Marse Tom tole so his own self. But nemmine, 't ain't enough."

"My lan', what de reason 't ain't enough?"

"Well, I's gwine to tell you, if you gimme a chanst, mammy. De reason it ain't enough is 'ca'se Marse Tom gambles."

Roxy threw up her hands in astonishment and Chambers went on:

"Ole marster found it out, 'ca'se he had to pay two hundred dollahs for Marse Tom's gamblin' debts, en dat's true, mammy, jes as dead certain as you's bawn."

"Two—hund'd—dollahs! Why, what is you talkin' 'bout? Two—hund'd—dollahs. Sakes alive, it's mos' enough to buy a tol'able good second-hand nigger wid. En you ain't lyin', honey?—You wouldn't lie to yo' ole mammy?"

"It's God's own truth, jes as I tell you—two hund'd dollahs—I wisht I may never stir outen my tracks if it ain't so. En, oh, my lan', ole Marse was jes a-hoppin'! He was b'ilin' mad, I tell you! He tuck 'n' dissenhurrit him."

He licked his chops with relish after that stately word. Roxy struggled with it a moment, then gave it up and said:

"Dissen*whiched* him?"

"Dissenhurrit him."

"What's dat? What do you mean?"

"Means he bu'sted de will."

"Bu's—ted de will! He wouldn't *ever* treat him so! Take it back, you mis'able imitation nigger dat I bore in sorrow en tribbilation."

Roxy's pet castle—an occasional dollar from Tom's pocket—was tumbling to ruin before her eyes. She could not abide such a disaster as that; she couldn't endure the thought of it. Her remark amused Chambers:

"Yah-yah-yah! jes listen to dat! If I's imitation, what is you? Bofe of us is imitation *white*—dat's what we is—en pow'ful good imitation, too—yah-yah-yah!—we don't 'mount to noth'n' as imitation niggers; and as for—"

"Shet up yo' foolin', 'fo' I knock you side de head, en tell me 'bout de will. Tell me 'tain't bu'sted—do, honey, en I'll never forgit you."

"Well, *'tain't*—'ca'se dey's a new one made, an Marse Tom's all right ag'in. But what is you in sich a sweat 'bout it for, mammy? 'Tain't none o' your business I don't reckon."

" 'Tain't none o' my business? Whose business is it den, I'd like to know? Wuz I his mother tell he was fifteen years old, or wusn't I?—you answer me dat. En you speck I could see him turned out po' en ornery on de worl' en never care noth'n' 'bout it? I reckon if you'd ever be'n a mother yo'self, Valet de Chambers, you wouldn't talk sich foolishness as dat."

"Well, den, ole Marse forgive him en fixed up de will ag'in—do dat satisfy you?"

Yes, she was satisfied now, and quite happy and sentimental over it. She kept coming daily, and at last she was told that Tom had come home. She began to tremble with emotion, and straightway sent to beg him to let his "po' ole nigger mammy have jes one sight of him en die for joy."

Tom was stretched at his lazy ease on a sofa when Chambers brought the petition. Time had not modified his ancient detestation of the humble drudge and protection of his boyhood; it was still bitter and uncompromising. He sat up and bent a severe gaze upon the fair face of the young fellow whose name he was unconsciously using and whose family rights he was enjoying. He maintained the gaze until the victim of it had become satisfactorily pallid with terror, then he said:

"What does the old rip want with me?"

The petition was meekly repeated.

"Who gave you permission to come and disturb me with the social attentions of niggers?"

Tom had risen. The other young man was trembling now, visibly. He saw what was coming, and bent his head sideways, and put up his left arm to shield it. Tom rained cuffs upon the head and its shield, saying no word; the victim received each blow with a beseeching "Please, Marse Tom!—oh, please, Marse Tom!" Seven blows—then Tom said, "Face the door—march!" He followed behind with one, two, three solid kicks. The last one helped the pure-white slave over the door-sill, and he limped away mopping his eyes with his old ragged sleeve. Tom shouted after him, "Send her in!"

Then he flung himself panting on the sofa again, and rasped out the remark, "He arrived just at the right moment; I was full to the brim with bitter thinkings, and nobody to take it out of. How refreshing it was! I feel better."

Tom's mother entered now, closing the door behind her, and approached her son with all the wheedling and supplicating servilities that fear and interest can impart to the words and attitudes of the born slave. She stopped a yard from her boy and made two or three admiring exclamations over his manly stature and general handsomeness, and Tom put an arm under his head and hoisted a leg over the sofa-back in order to look properly indifferent.

"My lan', how you is growed, honey! 'Clah to goodness, I wouldn't 'a' knowed you, Marse Tom! 'deed I wouldn't! Look at me good; does you 'member old Roxy?—does you know yo' old nigger mammy, honey? Well, now, I kin lay down en die in peace, 'ca'se I's seed—"

"Cut it short, —— it, cut it short! What is it you want?"

"You heah dat? Jes de same old Marse Tom, al'ays so gay and funnin' wid de old mammy. I 'uz jes as shore—"

"Cut it short, I tell you, and get along! What do you want?"

This was a bitter disappointment. Roxy had for so many days nourished and fondled and petted her notion that Tom would be glad to see his old nurse, and would make her proud and happy to the marrow with a cordial word or two, that it took two rebuffs to convince her that he was not funning, and that her beautiful dream was a fond and foolish vanity, a shabby and pitiful mistake. She was hurt to the heart, and so ashamed that for a moment she did not quite know what to do or how to act. Then her breast began to heave, the tears came, and in her forlornness she was moved to try that other dream of hers—an appeal to her boy's charity; and so, upon the impulse, and without reflection, she offered her supplication:

"Oh, Marse Tom, de po' ole mammy is in sich hard luck dese days; en she's kinder crippled in de arms en can't work, en if you could gimme a dollah—on'y jes one little dol—"

Tom was on his feet so suddenly that the supplicant was startled into a jump herself.

"A dollar!—give you a dollar! I've a notion to strangle you! Is *that* your errand here? Clear out! and be quick about it!"

Roxy backed slowly toward the door. When she was half-way she stopped, and said mournfully:

"Marse Tom, I nussed you when you was a little baby, en I raised you all by myself tell you was 'most a young man; en now you is young en rich, en I is po' en gitt'n ole, en I come heah b'lievin' dat you would he'p de ole mammy 'long down de little road dat's lef' twix' her en de grave, en—"

Tom relished this tune less than any that had preceded it, for it began to wake up a sort of echo in his conscience; so he interrupted and said with decision, though without asperity, that he was not in a situation to help her, and wasn't going to do it.

"Ain't you ever gwine to he'p me, Marse Tom?"

"No! Now go away and don't bother me any more."

Roxy's head was down, in an attitude of humility. But now the fires of her old wrongs flamed up in her breast and began to burn fiercely. She raised her head slowly, till it was well up, and at the same time her great frame unconsciously assumed an erect and masterful attitude, with all the majesty and grace of her vanished youth in it. She raised her finger and punctuated with it:

"You has said de word. You has had yo' chance, en you has trompled it under yo' foot. When you git another one, you'll git down on yo' knees en *beg* for it!"

A cold chill went to Tom's heart, he didn't know why; for he did not reflect that such words, from such an incongruous source, and so solemnly delivered, could not easily fail of that effect. However, he did the natural thing; he replied with bluster and mockery:

"*You'll* give me a chance—*you!* Perhaps I'd better get down on my knees now! But in case I don't—just for argument's sake—what's going to happen, pray?"

"Dis is what is gwine to happen. I's gwine as straight to yo' uncle as I kin walk, en tell him every las' thing I knows 'bout you."

Tom's cheek blenched, and she saw it. Disturbing thoughts began to chase each other through his head. "How can she know? And yet she must have found out—she looks it. I've had the will back only three months, and am already deep in debt again, and moving heaven and earth to save myself from exposure and destruction, with a reasonably fair show of getting the thing covered up if I'm let alone, and now this fiend has gone and found me out somehow or other. I wonder how much she knows? Oh, oh, oh, it's enough to break a body's heart! But I've got to humor her—there's no other way."

Then he worked up a rather sickly sample of a gay laugh and a hollow chipperness of manner, and said:

"Well, well, Roxy dear, old friends like you and me mustn't quarrel. Here's your dollar—now tell me what you know."

He held out the wildcat bill; she stood as she was, and made no movement. It was her turn to scorn persuasive foolery now, and she did not waste it. She said, with a grim implacability in voice and manner which made Tom almost realize that even a former slave can remember for ten minutes insults and injuries returned for compliments and flatteries received, and can also enjoy taking revenge for them when the opportunity offers:

"What does I know? I'll tell you what I knows, I knows enough to bu'st dat will to flinders—en more, mind you, *more!*"

Tom was aghast.

"More?" he said. "What do you call more? Where's there any room for more?"

Roxy laughed a mocking laugh, and said scoffingly, with a toss of her head, and her hands on her hips:

"Yes!—oh, I reckon! *Co'se* you'd like to know—wid yo' po' little old rag dollah. What you reckon I's gwine to tell *you* for?—you ain't got no money. I's gwine to tell yo' uncle—en I'll do it dis minute, too—he'll gimme *five* dollahs for de news, en mighty glad, too."

She swung herself around disdainfully, and started away. Tom was in a panic. He seized her skirts, and implored her to wait. She turned and said, loftily:

"Look-a-heah, what 'uz it I tole you?"

"You—you—I don't remember anything. What was it you told me?"

"I tole you dat de next time I give you a chance you'd git down on yo' knees en beg for it."

Tom was stupefied for a moment. He was panting with excitement. Then he said:

"Oh, Roxy, you wouldn't require your young master to do such a horrible thing. You can't mean it."

"I'll let you know mighty quick whether I means it or not! You call me names, en as good as spit on me when I comes here po' en ornery en 'umble, to praise you for bein' growed up so fine en handsome, en tell you how I used to nuss you en tend you en watch you when you 'uz sick en hadn't no mother but me in de whole worl', en beg you to give de po' ole nigger a dollah for to git her som'n' to eat, en you call me names—*names*, dad blame you! Yassir, I gives you jes one chance mo', and dat's *now*, en it las' on'y a half a second—yo hear?"

Tom slumped to his knees and began to beg, saying:

"You see, I'm begging, and it's honest begging, too! Now tell me, Roxy, tell me!"

The heir of two centuries of unatoned insult and outrage looked down on him and seemed to drink in deep draughts of satisfaction. Then she said:

"Fine nice young white gen'l'man kneelin' down to a nigger wench! I's wanted to see dat jes once befo' I's called. Now, Gabr'el, blow de hawn, I's ready.... Git up!"

Tom did it. He said, humbly:

"Now, Roxy, don't punish me any more. I deserved what I've got, but be good and let me off with that. Don't go to uncle. Tell me—I'll give you the five dollars."

"Yes, I bet you will; en you won't stop dah, nuther. But I ain't gwine to tell you heah—"

"Good gracious, no!"

"Is you 'feared o' de ha'nted house?"

"N-no."

"Well, den, you come to de ha'nted house, 'bout ten or 'leven to-night, en climb up de ladder, 'ca'se de sta'rsteps is broke down, en you'll find me. I's a-roostin' in de ha'nted house 'ca'se I can't 'ford to roos' nowhers' else." She started toward the door, but stopped and said, "Gimme de dollah bill!" He gave it to her. She examined it and said, "H'm—like enough de bank's bu'sted." She started again, but halted again. "Has you got any whisky?"

"Yes, a little."

"Fetch it!"

He ran to his room overhead and brought down a bottle which was two-thirds full. She tilted it up and took a drink. Her eyes sparkled with satisfaction and she tucked the bottle under her shawl, saying, "It's prime. I'll take it along."

Tom humbly held the door for her, and she marched out as grim and erect as a grenadier.

☐ IX ☐

TOM PRACTISES SYCOPHANCY

Why is it that we rejoice at a birth and grieve at a funeral? Is it because we are not the person involved?
                                        —PUDD'NHEAD WILSON'S CALENDAR.

It is easy to find fault, if one has that disposition. There was once a man who, not being able to find any other fault with his coal, complained that there were too many prehistoric toads in it.
                                        —PUDD'NHEAD WILSON'S CALENDAR.

Tom flung himself on the sofa, and put his throbbing head in his hands, and rested his elbows on his knees. He rocked himself back and forth and moaned.

"I've knelt to a nigger wench!" he muttered. "I thought I had struck the deepest depths of degradation before, but oh, dear, it was nothing to this. . . . Well, there is one consolation, such as it is—I've struck bottom this time; there's nothing lower."

But that was a hasty conclusion.

At ten that night he climbed the ladder in the haunted house, pale, weak, and wretched. Roxy was standing in the door of one of the rooms, waiting, for she had heard him.

This was a two-story log house which had acquired the reputation a few years before of being haunted, and that was the end of its usefulness. Nobody would live in it afterward, or go near it by night, and most people even gave it a wide berth in the daytime. As it had no competition, it was called *the* haunted house. It was getting crazy and ruinous now from long neglect. It stood three hundred yards beyond Pudd'nhead Wilson's house, with nothing between but vacancy. It was the last house in the town at that end.

Tom followed Roxy into the room. She had a pile of clean straw in the corner for a bed, some cheap but well-kept clothing was hanging on the wall, there was a tin lantern freckling the floor with little spots of light, and there were various soap and candle boxes scattered about, which served for chairs. The two sat down. Roxy said:

"Now den, I'll tell you straight off, en I'll begin to k'leck de money later on; I ain't in no hurry. What does you reckon I's gwine to tell you?"

"Well, you—you—oh, Roxy, don't make it too hard for me! Come right out and tell me you've found out somehow what a shape I'm in on account of dissipation and foolishness."

"Disposition en foolishness! *No,* sir, dat ain't it. Dat jist ain't nothin' at all, 'longside o' what *I* knows."

Tom stared at her, and said:

"Why, Roxy, what do you mean?"

She rose, and gloomed above him like a Fate.

"I mean dis—en it's de Lord's truth. You ain't no more kin to ole Marse Driscoll den I is!—*dat's* what I means!" and her eyes flamed with triumph.

"What!"

"Yassir, en *dat* ain't all. You's a *nigger!*—*bawn* a nigger an a *slave!*—en you's a nigger en a slave dis minute; en if I opens my mouf ole Marse Driscoll 'll sell you down de river befo' you is two days older den what you is now!"

"It's a thundering lie, you miserable old blatherskite!"

"It ain't no lie, nuther. It's jes de truth, en nothin' *but* de truth, so he'p me. Yessir—you's my *son*—"

"You devil!"

"En dat po' boy dat you's be'n a-kicken' en a-cuffin' to-day is Percy Driscoll's son en yo' *marster*—"

"You beast!"

"En *his* name's Tom Driscoll, en *yo'* name's Valet de Chambers, en you ain't *got* no fambly name, beca'se niggers don't *have* 'em!"

Tom sprang up and seized a billet of wood and raised it; but his mother only laughed at him, and said:

"Set down, you pup! Does you think you kin skyer me? It ain't in you, nor de likes of you. I reckon you'd shoot me in de back, maybe, if you got a chance, for dat's jist yo' style—*I* knows you, throo en throo—but I don't mind gitt'n killed, beca'se all dis is down in writin' en it's in safe hands, too, en de man dat's got it knows whah to look for de right man when I gits killed. Oh, bless yo' soul, if you puts yo' mother up for as big a fool as *you* is, you's pow'ful mistaken, I kin tell you! Now den, you set still en behave yo'self; en don't you git up ag'in till I tell you!"

Tom fretted and chaffed awhile in a whirlwind of disorganizing sensations and emotions, and finally said, with something like settled conviction:

"The whole thing is moonshine; now then, go ahead and do your worst; I'm done with you."

Roxy made no answer. She took the lantern and started toward the door. Tom was in a cold panic in a moment.

"Come back, come back!" he wailed. "I didn't mean it, Roxy; I take it all back, and I'll never say it again! Please come back, Roxy!"

The woman stood a moment, then she said gravely:

"Dat's one thing you's got to stop, Valet de Chambers. You can't call me *Roxy,* same as if you was my equal. Chillen don't speak to dey mammies like dat. You'll call me ma or mammy, dat's what you'll call me—leastways when dey ain't nobody aroun'. *Say* it!"

It cost Tom a struggle, but he got it out.

"Dat's all right. Don't you ever forgit it ag'in, if you knows what's good for you. Now den, you has said you wouldn't ever call it lies en moonshine ag'in. I'll tell you dis, for a warnin': if you ever does say it ag'in, it's de *las'* time you'll ever say it to me; I'll tramp as straight to de Judge as I kin walk, en tell him who you is, en *prove* it. Does you b'lieve me when I says dat?"

"Oh," groaned Tom, "I more than believe it; I *know* it."

Roxy knew her conquest was complete. She could have proved nothing to anybody, and her threat about the writings was a lie; but she knew the person she was dealing with, and had made both statements without any doubt as to the effect they would produce.

She went and sat down on her candle-box, and the pride and pomp of her victorious attitude made it a throne. She said:

"Now den, Chambers, we's gwine to talk business, en dey ain't gwine to be no mo' foolishness. In de fust place, you gits fifty dollahs a month; you's gwine to han' over half of it to yo' ma. Plank it out!"

But Tom had only six dollars in the world. He gave her that, and promised to start fair on next month's pension.

"Chambers, how much is you in debt?"

Tom shuddered, and said:

"Nearly three hundred dollars."

"How is you gwine to pay it?"

Tom groaned out—"Oh, I don't know; don't ask me such awful questions."

But she stuck to her point until she wearied a confession out of him: he had been prowling about in disguise, stealing small valuables from private houses; in fact, had made a good deal of a raid on his fellow-villagers a fortnight before, when he was supposed to be in St. Louis; but he doubted if he had sent away enough stuff to realize the required amount, and was afraid to make a further venture in the present excited state of the town. His mother approved of his conduct, and offered to help, but this frightened him. He tremblingly ventured to say that if she would retire from the town he should feel better and safer, and could hold his head higher—and was going on to make an argument, but she interrupted and surprised him pleasantly by saying she was ready; it didn't make any difference to her where she stayed, so that she got her share of the pension regularly. She said she would not go far, and would call at the haunted house once a month for her money. Then she said:

"I don't hate you so much now, but I've hated you a many a year—and anybody would. Didn't I change you off, en give you a good fambly en a good name, en made you a white gen'l'man en rich, wid store clothes on—en what did I git for it? You despised me all de time, en was al'ays sayin' mean hard things to me befo' folks, en wouldn't ever let me forgit I's a nigger—en—en—"

She fell to sobbing, and broke down. Tom said:

"But you know I didn't know you were my mother; and besides—"

"Well, nemmine 'bout dat, now; let it go. I's gwine to fo'git it." Then she added fiercely, "En don't ever make me remember it ag'in, or you'll be sorry, *I* tell you."

When they were parting, Tom said, in the most persuasive way he could command:

"Ma, would you mind telling me who was my father?"

He had supposed he was asking an embarrassing question. He was mistaken. Roxy drew herself up with a proud toss of her head, and said:

"Does I mine tellin' you? No, dat I don't! You ain't got no 'casion to be shame' o' yo' father, *I* kin tell you. He wuz the highest quality in dis whole town—ole Virginny stock. Fust famblies, he wuz. Jes as good stock as de Driscolls en de Howards, de bes' day dey ever seed." She put on a little prouder air, if possible, and added impressively: "Does you 'member Cunnel Cecil Burleigh Essex, dat died de same year yo' young Marse Tom Driscoll's pappy died, en all de Masons en Odd Fellers en Churches turned out en give him de bigges' funeral dis town ever seed? Dat's de man."

Under the inspiration of her soaring complacency the departed graces of her earlier days returned to her, and her bearing took to itself a dignity and state that might have passed for queenly if her surroundings had been a little more in keeping with it.

"Dey ain't another nigger in dis town dat's as high-bawn as you is. Now den, go 'long! En jes you hold yo' head up as high as you want to—you has de right, en dat I kin swah."

□   X   □

THE NYMPH REVEALED

*All say, "How hard it is that we have to die"—a strange complaint to
come from the mouths of people who have had to live.*
                                                —PUDD'NHEAD WILSON'S CALENDAR.

When angry, count four; when very angry, swear.
                                                —PUDD'NHEAD WILSON'S CALENDAR.

Every now and then, after Tom went to bed, he had sudden wakings out of
his sleep, and his first thought was, "Oh, joy, it was all a dream!" Then he
laid himself heavily down again, with a groan and the muttered words, "A
nigger! I am a nigger! Oh, I wish I was dead!"

He woke at dawn with one more repetition of this horror, and then he
resolved to meddle no more with that treacherous sleep. He began to think.
Sufficiently bitter thinkings they were. They wandered along something after
this fashion:

"Why were niggers *and* whites made? What crime did the uncreated
first nigger commit that the curse of birth was decreed for him? And why is
this awful difference made between white and black? . . . How hard the nigger's fate seems, this morning!—yet until last night such a thought never entered my head."

He sighed and groaned an hour or more away. Then "Chambers" came
humbly in to say that breakfast was nearly ready. "Tom" blushed scarlet to
see this aristocratic white youth cringe to him, a nigger, and call him
"Young Marster." He said roughly:

"Get out of my sight!" and when the youth was gone, he muttered, "He
has done me no harm, poor wretch, but he is an eyesore to me now, for he is
Driscoll the young gentleman, and I am a—oh, I wish I was dead!"

A gigantic eruption, like that of Krakatoa a few years ago, with the accompanying earthquakes, tidal waves, and clouds of volcanic dust, changes
the face of the surrounding landscape beyond recognition, bringing down the
high lands, elevating the low, making fair lakes where deserts had been, and
deserts where green prairies had smiled before. The tremendous catastrophe
which had befallen Tom had changed his moral landscape in much the same
way. Some of his low places he found lifted to ideals, some of his ideals had
sunk to the valleys, and lay there with the sackcloth and ashes of pumice-
stone and sulphur on their ruined heads.

For days he wandered in lonely places, thinking, thinking, thinking—

trying to get his bearings. It was new work. If he met a friend, he found that the habit of a lifetime had in some mysterious way vanished—his arm hung limp, instead of involuntarily extending the hand for a shake. It was the "nigger" in him asserting its humility, and he blushed and was abashed. And the "nigger" in him was surprised when the white friend put out his hand for a shake with him. He found the "nigger" in him involuntarily giving the road, on the sidewalk, to the white rowdy and loafer. When Rowena, the dearest thing his heart knew, the idol of his secret worship, invited him in, the "nigger" in him made an embarrassed excuse and was afraid to enter and sit with the dread white folks on equal terms. The "nigger" in him went shrinking and skulking here and there and yonder, and fancying it saw suspicion and maybe detection in all faces, tones, and gestures. So strange and un-characteristic was Tom's conduct that people noticed it, and turned to look after him when he passed on; and when he glanced back—as he could not help doing, in spite of his best resistance—and caught that puzzled expres-sion in a person's face, it gave him a sick feeling, and he took himself out of view as quickly as he could. He presently came to have a hunted sense and a hunted look, and then he fled away to the hilltops and the solitudes. He said to himself that the curse of Ham was upon him.

He dreaded his meals; the "nigger" in him was ashamed to sit at the white folks' table, and feared discovery all the time; and once when Judge Driscoll said, "What's the matter with you? You look as meek as a nigger," he felt as secret murderers are said to feel when the accuser says, "Thou art the man." Tom said he was not well, and left the table.

His ostensible "aunt's" solicitudes and endearments were become a ter-ror to him, and he avoided them.

And all the time, hatred of his ostensible "uncle" was steadily growing in his heart; for he said to himself, "He is white; and I am his chattel, his property, his goods, and he can sell me, just as he could his dog."

For as much as a week after this, Tom imagined that his character had undergone a pretty radical change. But that was because he did not know himself.

In several ways his opinions were totally changed, and would never go back to what they were before, but the main structure of his character was not changed, and could not be changed. One or two very important features of it were altered, and in time effects would result from this, if opportunity offered—effects of a quite serious nature, too. Under the influence of a great mental and moral upheaval his character and habits had taken on the appear-ance of complete change, but after a while with the subsidence of the storm both began to settle toward their former places. He dropped gradually back into his old frivolous and easy-going ways and conditions of feeling and manner of speech, and no familiar of his could have detected anything in him that differentiated him from the weak and careless Tom of other days.

The theft-raid which he had made upon the village turned out better than he had ventured to hope. It produced the sum necessary to pay his gaming debts, and saved him from exposure to his uncle and another smashing of the will. He and his mother learned to like each other fairly well. She couldn't love him, as yet, because there "warn't nothing *to* him," as she expressed it, but her nature needed something or somebody to rule over, and he was better than nothing. Her strong character and aggressive and commanding ways compelled Tom's admiration in spite of the fact that he got more illustrations of them than he needed for his comfort. However, as a rule her conversation was made up of racy tattle about the privacies of the chief families of the town (for she went harvesting among their kitchens every time she came to the village), and Tom enjoyed this. It was just in his line. She always collected her half of his pension punctually, and he was always at the haunted house to have a chat with her on these occasions. Every now and then she paid him a visit there on between-days also.

Occasionally he would run up to St. Louis for a few weeks, and at last temptation caught him again. He won a lot of money, but lost it, and with it a deal more besides, which he promised to raise as soon as possible.

For this purpose he projected a new raid on his town. He never meddled with any other town, for he was afraid to venture into the houses whose ins and outs he did not know and the habits of whose households he was not acquainted with. He arrived at the haunted house in disguise on the Wednesday before the advent of the twins—after writing his aunt Pratt that he would not arrive until two days after—and lay in hiding there with his mother until toward daylight Friday morning, when he went to his uncle's house and entered by the back way with his own key, and slipped up to his room, where he could have the use of mirror and toilet articles. He had a suit of girl's clothes with him in a bundle as a disguise for his raid, and was wearing a suit of his mother's clothing, with black gloves and veil. By dawn he was tricked out for his raid, but he caught a glimpse of Pudd'nhead Wilson through the window over the way, and knew that Pudd'nhead had caught a glimpse of him. So he entertained Wilson with some airs and graces and attitudes for a while, then stepped out of sight and resumed the other disguise, and by and by went down and out the back way, and started down-town to reconnoiter the scene of his intended labors.

But he was ill at ease. He had changed back to Roxy's dress, with the stoop of age added to the disguise, so that Wilson would not bother himself about a humble old woman leaving a neighbor's house by the back way in the early morning, in case he was still spying. But supposing Wilson had seen him leave, and had thought it suspicious, and had also followed him? The thought made Tom cold. He gave up the raid for the day, and hurried back to the haunted house by the obscurest route he knew. His mother was gone; but she came back by and by, with the news of the grand reception at Patsy

Cooper's, and soon persuaded him that the opportunity was like a special providence, it was so inviting and perfect. So he went raiding, after all, and made a nice success of it while everybody was gone to Patsy Cooper's. Success gave him nerve and even actual intrepidity; insomuch, indeed, that after he had conveyed his harvest to his mother in a back alley, he went to the reception himself, and added several of the valuables of that house to his takings.

After this long digression we have now arrived once more at the point where Pudd'nhead Wilson, while waiting for the arrival of the twins on that same Friday evening, sat puzzling over the strange apparition of that morning—a girl in young Tom Driscoll's bedroom; fretting, and guessing, and puzzling over it, and wondering who the shameless creature might be.

□ XI □

PUDD'NHEAD'S STARTLING DISCOVERY

There are three infallible ways of pleasing an author, and the three form a rising scale of compliment: 1, to tell him you have read one of his books; 2, to tell him you have read all of his books; 3, to ask him to let you read the manuscript of his forthcoming book. No. 1 admits you to his respect; No. 2 admits you to his admiration; No. 3 carries you clear into his heart.
                                    —PUDD'NHEAD WILSON'S CALENDAR.

As to the Adjective: when in doubt, strike out.
                                    —PUDD'NHEAD WILSON'S CALENDAR.

The twins arrived presently, and talk began. It flowed along chattily and sociably, and under its influence the new friendship gathered ease and strength. Wilson got out his Calendar, by request, and read a passage or two from it, which the twins praised quite cordially. This pleased the author so much that he complied gladly when they asked him to lend them a batch of the work to read at home. In the course of their wide travels they had found out that there are three sure ways of pleasing an author; they were now working the best of the three.

There was an interruption, now. Young Tom Driscoll appeared, and joined the party. He pretended to be seeing the distinguished strangers for the first time when they rose to shake hands; but this was only a blind, as he had already had a glimpse of them, at the reception, while robbing the house.

The twins made mental note that he was smooth-faced and rather handsome, and smooth and undulatory in his movements—graceful, in fact. Angelo thought he had a good eye; Luigi thought that there was something veiled and sly about it. Angelo thought he had a pleasant free-and-easy way of talking; Luigi thought it was more so than was agreeable. Angelo thought he was a sufficiently nice young man; Luigi reserved his decision. Tom's first contribution to the conversation was a question which he had put to Wilson a hundred times before. It was always cheerily and good-naturedly put, and always inflicted a little pang, for it touched a secret sore; but this time the pang was sharp, since strangers were present.

"Well, how does the law come on? Had a case yet?"

Wilson bit his lip, but answered, "No—not yet," with as much indifference as he could assume. Judge Driscoll had generously left the law feature out of the Wilson biography which he had furnished to the twins. Young Tom laughed pleasantly, and said:

"Wilson's a lawyer, gentlemen, but he doesn't practise now."

The sarcasm bit, but Wilson kept himself under control, and said without passion:

"I don't practise, it is true. It is true that I have never had a case, and have had to earn a poor living for twenty years as an expert accountant in a town where I can't get hold of a set of books to untangle as often as I should like. But it is also true that I did fit myself well for the practice of the law. By the time I was your age, Tom, I had chosen a profession, and was soon competent to enter upon it." Tom winced. "I never got a chance to try my hand at it, and I may never get a chance; and yet if I ever do get it I shall be found ready, for I have kept up my law studies all these years."

"That's it; that's good grit! I like to see it. I've a notion to throw all my business your way. My business and your law practice ought to make a pretty gay team, Dave," and the young fellow laughed again.

"If you will throw—" Wilson had thought of the girl in Tom's bedroom, and was going to say, "If you will throw the surreptitious and disreputable part of your business my way, it may amount to something"; but thought better of it and said, "However, this matter doesn't fit well in a general conversation."

"All right, we'll change the subject; I guess you were about to give me another dig, anyway, so I'm willing to change. How's the Awful Mystery flourishing these days? Wilson's got a scheme for driving plain window-glass out of the market by decorating it with greasy finger-marks, and getting rich by selling it at famine prices to the crowned heads over in Europe to outfit their palaces with. Fetch it out, Dave."

Wilson brought three of his glass strips, and said:

"I get the subject to pass the fingers of his right hand through his hair,

so as to get a little coating of the natural oil on them, and then press the balls
of them on the glass. A fine and delicate print of the lines in the skin results,
and is permanent, if it doesn't come in contact with something able to rub it
off. You begin, Tom."

"Why, I think you took my finger-marks once or twice before."

"Yes, but you were a little boy the last time, only about twelve years
old."

"That's so. Of course I've changed entirely since then, and variety is
what the crowned heads want, I guess."

He passed his fingers through his crop of short hair, and pressed them
one at a time on the glass. Angelo made a print of his fingers on another
glass, and Luigi followed with the third. Wilson marked the glasses with
names and date, and put them away. Tom gave one of his little laughs, and
said:

"I thought I wouldn't say anything, but if variety is what you are after,
you have wasted a piece of glass. The hand-print of one twin is the same as
the hand-print of the fellow twin."

"Well, it's done now, and I like to have them both, anyway," said Wilson, returning to his place.

"But look here, Dave," said Tom, "you used to tell people's fortunes,
too, when you took their finger-marks. Dave's just an all-round genius—a genius of the first water, gentlemen; a great scientist running to seed here in
this village, a prophet with the kind of honor that prophets generally get at
home—for here they don't give shucks for his scientifics, and they call his
skull a notion factory—hey, Dave, ain't it so? But never mind; he'll make his
mark some day—finger-mark, you know, he-he! But really, you want to let
him take a shy at your palms once; it's worth twice the price of admission or
your money's returned at the door. Why, he'll read your wrinkles as easy as a
book, and not only tell you fifty or sixty things that's going to happen to
you, but fifty or sixty thousand that ain't. Come, Dave, show the gentlemen what an inspired Jack-at-all-science we've got in this town, and don't
know it."

Wilson winced under this nagging and not very courteous chaff, and the
twins suffered with him and for him. They rightly judged, now, that the best
way to relieve him would be to take the thing in earnest and treat it with
respect, ignoring Tom's rather overdone raillery; so Luigi said:

"We have seen something of palmistry in our wanderings, and know
very well what astonishing things it can do. If it isn't a science, and one of
the greatest of them, too, I don't know what its other name ought to be. In
the Orient—"

Tom looked surprised and incredulous. He said:

"That juggling a science? But really, you ain't serious, are you?"

"Yes, entirely so. Four years ago we had our hands read out to us as if our palms had been covered with print."

"Well, do you mean to say there was actually anything in it?" asked Tom, his incredulity beginning to weaken a little.

"There was this much in it," said Angelo; "what was told us of our characters was minutely exact—we could not have bettered it ourselves. Next, two or three memorable things that had happened to us were laid bare— things which no one present but ourselves could have known about."

"Why, it's rank sorcery!" exclaimed Tom, who was now becoming very much interested. "And how did they make out with what was going to happen to you in the future?"

"On the whole, quite fairly," said Luigi. "Two or three of the most striking things foretold have happened since; much the most striking one of all happened within that same year. Some of the minor prophecies have come true; some of the minor and some of the major ones have not been fulfilled yet, and of course may never be: still, I should be more surprised if they failed to arrive than if they didn't."

Tom was entirely sobered, and profoundly impressed. He said, apologetically:

"Dave, I wasn't meaning to belittle that science; I was only chaffing— chattering, I reckon I'd better say. I wish you would look at their palms. Come, won't you?"

"Why, certainly, if you want me to; but you know I've had no chance to become an expert, and don't claim to be one. When a past event is somewhat prominently recorded in the palm I can generally detect that, but minor ones often escape me—not always, of course, but often—but I haven't much confidence in myself when it comes to reading the future. I am talking as if palmistry was a daily study with me, but that is not so. I haven't examined half a dozen hands in the last half-dozen years; you see, the people got to joking about it, and I stopped to let the talk die down. I'll tell you what we'll do, Count Luigi: I'll make a try at your past, and if I have any success there—no, on the whole, I'll let the future alone; that's really the affair of an expert."

He took Luigi's hand. Tom said:

"Wait—don't look yet, Dave! Count Luigi, here's paper and pencil. Set down that thing that you said was the most striking one that was foretold to you, and happened less than a year afterward, and give it to me so I can see if Dave finds it in your hand."

Luigi wrote a line privately, and folded up the piece of paper, and handed it to Tom, saying:

"I'll tell you when to look at it, if he finds it."

Wilson began to study Luigi's palm, tracing life lines, heart lines, head lines, and so on, and noting carefully their relations with the cobweb of finer and more delicate marks and lines that enmeshed them on all sides; he felt of the fleshy cushion at the base of the thumb, and noted its shape; he felt of the fleshy side of the hand between the wrist and the base of the little finger, and noted its shape also; he painstakingly examined the fingers, observing their form, proportions, and natural manner of disposing themselves when in repose. All this process was watched by the three spectators with absorbing interest, their heads bent together over Luigi's palm, and nobody disturbing the stillness with a word. Wilson now entered upon a close survey of the palm again, and his revelations began.

He mapped out Luigi's character and disposition, his tastes, aversions, proclivities, ambitions, and eccentricities in a way which sometimes made Luigi wince and the others laugh, but both twins declared that the chart was artistically drawn and was correct.

Next, Wilson took up Luigi's history. He proceeded cautiously and with hesitation, now, moving his finger slowly along the great lines of the palm, and now and then halting it at a "star" or some such landmark, and examining that neighborhood minutely. He proclaimed one or two past events, Luigi confirmed his correctness, and the search went on. Presently Wilson glanced up suddenly with a surprised expression—

"Here is record of an incident which you would perhaps not wish me to—"

"Bring it out," said Luigi, good-naturedly; "I promise you it sha'n't embarrass me."

But Wilson still hesitated, and did not seem quite to know what to do. Then he said:

"I think it is too delicate a matter to—to—I believe I would rather write it or whisper it to you, and let you decide for yourself whether you want it talked out or not."

"That will answer," said Luigi; "write it."

Wilson wrote something on a slip of paper and handed it to Luigi, who read it to himself and said to Tom:

"Unfold your slip and read it, Mr. Driscoll."

Tom read:

"It was prophesied that I would kill a man. It came true before the year was out."

Tom added, "Great Scott!"

Luigi handed Wilson's paper to Tom, and said:

"Now read this one."

Tom read:

"You have killed some one, but whether man, woman, or child, I do not make out."

"Caesar's ghost!" commented Tom, with astonishment. "It beats anything that was ever heard of! Why, a man's own hand is his deadliest enemy!

Just think of that—a man's own hand keeps a record of the deepest and fatalest secrets of his life, and is treacherously ready to expose him to any black-magic stranger that comes along. But what do you let a person look at your hand for, with that awful thing printed in it?"

"Oh," said Luigi, reposefully, "I don't mind it. I killed the man for good reasons, and I don't regret it."

"What were the reasons?"

"Well, he needed killing."

"I'll tell you why he did it, since he won't say himself," said Angelo, warmly. "He did it to save my life, that's what he did it for. So it was a noble act, and not a thing to be hid in the dark."

"So it was, so it was," said Wilson; "to do such a thing to save a brother's life is a great and fine action."

"Now come," said Luigi, "it is very pleasant to hear you say these things, but for unselfishness, or heroism, or magnanimity, the circumstances won't stand scrutiny. You overlook one detail; suppose I hadn't saved Angelo's life, what would have become of mine? If I had let the man kill him, wouldn't he have killed me, too? I saved my own life, you see."

"Yes; that is your way of talking," said Angelo, "but I know you—I don't believe you thought of yourself at all. I keep that weapon yet that Luigi killed the man with, and I'll show it to you sometime. That incident makes it interesting, and it had a history before it came into Luigi's hands which adds to its interest. It was given to Luigi by a great Indian prince, the Gaekwar of Baroda, and it had been in his family two or three centuries. It killed a good many disagreeable people who troubled that hearthstone at one time or another. It isn't much to look at, except that it isn't shaped like other knives, or dirks, or whatever it may be called—here, I'll draw it for you." He took a sheet of paper and made a rapid sketch. "There it is—a broad and murderous blade, with edges like a razor for sharpness. The devices engraved on it are the ciphers or names of its long line of possessors—I had Luigi's name added in Roman letters myself with our coat of arms, as you see. You notice what a curious handle the thing has. It is solid ivory, polished like a mirror, and is four or five inches long—round, and is thick as a large man's wrist, with the end squared off flat, for your thumb to rest on; for you grasp it, with your thumb resting on the blunt end—so—and lift it aloft and strike downward. The Gaekwar showed us how the thing was done when he gave it to Luigi, and before that night was ended Luigi had used the knife, and the Gaekwar was a man short by reason of it. The sheath is magnificently ornamented with gems of great value. You will find the sheath more worth looking at than the knife itself, of course."

Tom said to himself:

"It's lucky I came here. I would have sold that knife for a song; I supposed the jewels were glass."

"But go on; don't stop," said Wilson. "Our curiosity is up now, to hear about the homicide. Tell us about that."

"Well, briefly, the knife was to blame for that, all around. A native servant slipped into our room in the palace in the night, to kill us and steal the knife on account of the fortune incrusted on its sheath, without a doubt. Luigi had it under his pillow; we were in bed together. There was a dim night light burning. I was alseep, but Luigi was awake, and he thought he detected a vague form nearing the bed. He slipped the knife out of the sheath and was ready, and unembarrassed by hampering bedclothes, for the weather was hot, and we hadn't any. Suddenly that native rose at the bedside, and bent over me with his right hand lifted and a dirk in it aimed at my throat; but Luigi grabbed his wrist, pulled him downward, and drove his own knife into the man's neck. That is the whole story."

Wilson and Tom drew deep breaths, and after some general chat about the tragedy, Pudd'nhead said, taking Tom's hand:

"Now, Tom, I've never had a look at your palms, as it happens; perhaps you've got some little questionable privacies that need—hel-lo!"

Tom had snatched away his hand, and was looking a good deal confused.

"Why, he's blushing!" said Luigi.

Tom darted an ugly look at him, and said, sharply:

"Well, if I am, it ain't because I'm a murderer!" Luigi's dark face flushed, but before he could speak or move, Tom added with anxious haste: "Oh, I beg a thousand pardons. I didn't mean that; it was out before I thought, and I'm very, very sorry—you must forgive me!"

Wilson came to the rescue, and smoothed things down as well as he could; and in fact was entirely successful as far as the twins were concerned, for they felt sorrier for the affront put upon him by his guest's outburst of ill manners than for the insult offered to Luigi. But the success was not so pronounced with the offender. Tom tried to seem at his ease, and he went through the motions fairly well, but at bottom he felt resentful toward all the three witnesses of his exhibition; in fact, he felt so annoyed at them for having witnessed it and noticed it that he almost forgot to feel annoyed at himself for placing it before them. However, something presently happened which made him almost comfortable, and brought him nearly back to a state of charity and friendliness. This was a little spat between the twins; not much of a spat, but still a spat; and before they got far with it they were in a decided condition of irritation with each other. Tom was charmed; so pleased, indeed, that he cautiously did what he could to increase the irritation while pretending to be actuated by more respectable motives. By his help the fire got warmed up to the blazing-point, and he might have had the happiness of seeing the flames show up, in another moment, but for the interruption of a knock on the door—an interruption which fretted him as much as it gratified Wilson. Wilson opened the door. The visitor was a good-natured, ignorant, energetic, middle-aged Irishman named John Buckstone, who was a great politician in a small way, and always took a large share in public matters of every sort. One of the town's chief excitements, just now, was over the matter of rum. There was a strong rum party and a strong anti-rum party. Buckstone was training with the rum party, and he had been sent to hunt up the twins and invite them to attend a mass-meeting of that faction. He delivered his errand, and said the clans were already gathering in the big hall over the market-house. Luigi accepted the invitation cordially, Angelo less cordially, since he disliked crowds, and did not drink the powerful intoxicants of America. In fact, he was even a teetotaler sometimes—when it was judicious to be one.

The twins left with Buckstone, and Tom Driscoll joined company with them uninvited.

In the distance one could see a long wavering line of torches drifting down the main street, and could hear the throbbing of the bass drum, the clash of cymbals, the squeaking of a fife or two, and the faint roar of remote hurrahs. The tail end of this procession was climbing the market-house stairs when the twins arrived in its neighborhood; when they reached the hall it was full of people, torches, smoke, noise, and enthusiasm. They were conducted to the platform by Buckstone—Tom Driscoll still following—and were delivered to the chairman in the midst of a prodigious explosion of welcome. When the noise had moderated a little, the chair proposed that "our illustrious guests be at once elected, by complimentary acclamation, to membership of our ever-glorious organization, the paradise of the free and the perdition of the slave."

This eloquent discharge opened the flood-gates of enthusiasm again, and the election was carried with thundering unanimity. Then arose a storm of cries:

"Wet them down! Wet them down! Give them a drink!"

Glasses of whisky were handed to the twins, Luigi waved his aloft, then brought it to his lips; but Angelo set his down. There was another storm of cries:

"What's the matter with the other one?" "What is the blond one going back on us for?" "Explain! Explain!"

The chairman inquired, and then reported:

"We have made an unfortunate mistake, gentlemen. I find that the Count Angelo Capello is opposed to our creed—is a teetotaler, in fact, and was not intending to apply for membership with us. He desires that we reconsider the vote by which he was elected. What is the pleasure of the house?"

There was a general burst of laughter, plentifully accented with whistlings and cat-calls, but the energetic use of the gavel presently restored something like order. Then a man spoke from the crowd, and said that while he was very sorry that the mistake had been made, it would not be possible to rectify it at the present meeting. According to the by-laws it must go over to the next regular meeting for action. He would not offer a motion, as none was required. He desired to apologize to the gentleman in the name of the house, and begged to assure him that as far as it might lie in the power of the Sons of Liberty, his temporary membership in the order would be made pleasant to him.

This speech was received with great applause, mixed with cries of:

"That's the talk!" "He's a good fellow, anyway, if he *is* a teetotaler!" "Drink his health!" "Give him a rouser, and no heeltaps!"

Glasses were handed around, and everybody on the platform drank Angelo's health, while the house bellowed forth in song:

> *For he's a jolly good fel-low,*
> *For he's a jolly good fel-low,*
> *For he's a jolly good fe-el-low,—*
> *Which nobody can deny.*

Tom Driscoll drank. It was his second glass, for he had drunk Angelo's the moment that Angelo had set it down. The two drinks made him very merry—almost idiotically so—and he began to take a most lively and prominent part in the proceedings, particularly in the music and cat-calls and side remarks.

The chairman was still standing at the front, the twins at his side. The extraordinarily close resemblance of the brothers to each other suggested a witticism to Tom Driscoll, and just as the chairman began a speech he skipped forward and said with an air of tipsy confidence to the audience:

"Boys, I move that he keeps still and lets this human philopena snip you out a speech."

The descriptive aptness of the phrase caught the house, and a mighty burst of laughter followed.

Luigi's southern blood leaped to the boiling-point in a moment under the sharp humiliation of this insult delivered in the presence of four hundred strangers. It was not in the young man's nature to let the matter pass, or to delay the squaring of the account. He took a couple of strides and halted behind the unsuspecting joker. Then he drew back and delivered a kick of such titanic vigor that it lifted Tom clear over the footlights and landed him on the heads of the front row of the Sons of Liberty.

Even a sober person does not like to have a human being emptied on him when he is not doing any harm; a person who is not sober cannot endure such an attention at all. The nest of Sons of Liberty that Driscoll landed in had not a sober bird in it; in fact, there was probably not an entirely sober one in the auditorium. Driscoll was promptly and indignantly flung onto the heads of Sons of the next row, and these Sons passed him on toward the rear, and then immediately began to pummel the front-row Sons who had passed him to them. This course was strictly followed by bench after bench as Driscoll traveled in his tumultuous and airy flight toward the door; so he left behind him an ever-lengthening wake of raging and plunging and fighting and swearing humanity. Down went group after group of torches, and presently above the deafening clatter of the gavel, roar of angry voices, and crash of succumbing benches, rose the paralyzing cry of "FIRE!"

The fighting ceased instantly; the cursing ceased; for one distinctly defined moment there was a dead hush, a motionless calm, where the tempest had been; then with one impulse the multitude awoke to life and energy again, and went surging and struggling and swaying, this way and that, its outer edges melting away through windows and doors and gradually lessening the pressure and relieving the mass.

The fire-boys were never on hand so suddenly before; for there was no distance to go, this time, their quarters being in the rear end of the market-house. There was an engine company and a hook-and-ladder company. Half of each was composed of rummies and the other half of anti-rummies, after the moral and political share-and-share-alike fashion of the frontier town of the period. Enough anti-rummies were loafing in quarters to man the engine and the ladders. In two minutes they had their red shirts and helmets on—they never stirred officially in unofficial costume—and as the mass-meeting overhead smashed through the long row of windows and poured out upon the roof of the arcade, the deliverers were ready for them with a powerful stream of water which washed some of them off the roof and nearly drowned the rest. But water was preferable to fire, and still the stampede from the windows continued, and still the pitiless drenching assailed it until the building was empty; then the fire-boys mounted to the hall and flooded it with water enough to annihilate forty times as much fire as there was there; for a village fire company does not often get a chance to show off, and so when it does get a chance it makes the most of it. Such citizens of that village as were of a thoughtful and judicious temperament did not insure against fire; they insured against the fire company.

☐   **XII**   ☐

THE SHAME OF JUDGE DRISCOLL

Courage is resistance to fear, mastery of fear—not absence of fear. Except a creature be part coward it is not a compliment to say it is brave; it is merely a loose misapplication of the word. Consider the flea!—incomparably the bravest of all the creatures of God, if ignorance of fear were courage. Whether you are asleep or awake he will attack you, caring nothing for the fact that in bulk and strength you are to him as are the massed armies of the earth to a sucking child; he lives both day and night and all days and nights in the very lap of peril and the immediate presence of death, and yet is no more afraid than is the man who walks the streets of a city that was threatened by an earthquake ten centuries before. When we speak of Clive, Nelson, and Putnam as men who "didn't know what fear was," we ought always to add the flea—and put him at the head of the procession.

—PUDD'NHEAD WILSON'S CALENDAR.

Judge Driscoll was in bed and asleep by ten o'clock on Friday night, and he was up and gone a-fishing before daylight in the morning with his friend Pembroke Howard. These two had been boys together in Virginia when that state still ranked as the chief and most imposing member of the Union, and they still coupled the proud and affectionate adjective "old" with her name when they spoke of her. In Missouri a recognized superiority attached to any person who hailed from Old Virginia; and this superiority was exalted to supremacy when a person of such nativity could also prove descent from the First Families of that great commonwealth. The Howards and Driscolls were of this aristocracy. In their eyes it was a nobility. It had its unwritten laws, and they were as clearly defined and as strict as any that could be found among the printed statutes of the land. The F. F. V. was born a gentleman; his highest duty in life was to watch over that great inheritance and keep it unsmirched. He must keep his honor spotless. Those laws were his chart; his course was marked out on it; if he swerved from it by so much as half a point of the compass it meant shipwreck to his honor; that is to say, degradation from his rank as a gentleman. These laws required certain things of him which his religion might forbid: then his religion must yield—the laws could not be relaxed to accommodate religions or anything else. Honor stood first; and the laws defined what it was and wherein it differed in certain details from honor as defined by church creeds and by the social laws and customs of some of the minor divisions of the globe that had got crowded out when the sacred boundaries of Virginia were staked out.

If Judge Driscoll was the recognized first citizen of Dawson's Landing, Pembroke Howard was easily its recognized second citizen. He was called "the great lawyer"—an earned title. He and Driscoll were of the same age—a year or two past sixty.

Although Driscoll was a free-thinker and Howard a strong and determined Presbyterian, their warm intimacy suffered no impairment in consequence. They were men whose opinions were their own property and not subject to revision and amendment, suggestion or criticism, by anybody, even their friends.

The day's fishing finished, they came floating down-stream in their skiff, talking national politics and other high matters, and presently met a skiff coming up from town, with a man in it who said:

"I reckon you know one of the new twins gave your nephew a kicking last night, Judge?"

"Did *what?*"

"Gave him a kicking."

The old Judge's lips paled, and his eyes began to flame. He choked with anger for a moment, then he got out what he was trying to say:

"Well—well—go on! give me the details."

The man did it. At the finish the Judge was silent a minute, turning over in his mind the shameful picture of Tom's flight over the footlights; then he said, as if musing aloud—"H'm—I don't understand it. I was alseep at home. He didn't wake me. Thought he was competent to manage his affair without my help, I reckon." His face lit up with pride and pleasure at that thought, and he said with a cheery complacency, "I like that—it's the true old blood—hey, Pembroke?"

Howard smiled an iron smile, and nodded his head approvingly. Then the news-bringer spoke again:

"But Tom beat the twin on the trial."

The Judge looked at the man wonderingly, and said:

"The trial? What trial?"

"Why, Tom had him up before Judge Robinson for assault and battery."

The old man shrank suddenly together like one who had received a death-stroke. Howard sprang for him as he sank forward in a swoon, and took him in his arms, and bedded him on his back in the boat. He sprinkled water in his face, and said to the startled visitor:

"Go, now—don't let him come to and find you here. You see what an effect your heedless speech has had; you ought to have been more considerate than to blurt out such a cruel piece of slander as that."

"I'm right down sorry I did it now, Mr. Howard, and I wouldn't have done it if I had thought: but it ain't slander; it's perfectly true, just as I told him."

He rowed away. Presently the old Judge came out of his faint and looked up piteously into the sympathetic face that was bent over him.

"Say it ain't true, Pembroke; tell me it ain't true!" he said in a weak voice.

There was nothing weak in the deep organ-tones that responded:

"You know it's a lie as well as I do, old friend. He is of the best blood of the Old Dominion."

"God bless you for saying it!" said the old gentleman, fervently. "Ah, Pembroke, it was such a blow!"

Howard stayed by his friend, and saw him home, and entered the house with him. It was dark, and past suppertime, but the Judge was not thinking of supper; he was eager to hear the slander refuted from headquarters, and as eager to have Howard hear it, too. Tom was sent for, and he came immediately. He was bruised and lame, and was not a happy-looking object. His uncle made him sit down, and said:

"We have been hearing about your adventure, Tom, with a handsome lie added to it for embellishment. Now pulverize that lie to dust! What measures have you taken? How does the thing stand?"

Tom answered guilelessly: "It don't stand at all; it's all over. I had him up in court and beat him. Pudd'nhead Wilson defended him—first case he ever had, and lost it. The judge fined the miserable hound five dollars for the assault."

Howard and the Judge sprang to their feet with the opening sentence—why, neither knew; then they stood gazing vacantly at each other. Howard stood a moment, then sat mournfully down without saying anything. The Judge's wrath began to kindle, and he burst out:

"You cur! You scum! You vermin! Do you mean to tell me that blood of my race has suffered a blow and crawled to a court of law about it? Answer me!"

Tom's head dropped, and he answered with an eloquent silence. His uncle stared at him with a mixed expression of amazement and shame and incredulity that was sorrowful to see. At last he said:

"Which of the twins was it?"

"Count Luigi."

"You have challenged him?"

"N—no," hesitated Tom, turning pale.

"You will challenge him to-night. Howard will carry it."

Tom began to turn sick, and to show it. He turned his hat round and round in his hand, his uncle glowering blacker and blacker upon him as the heavy seconds drifted by; then at last he began to stammer, and said piteously:

"Oh, please don't ask me to do it, uncle! He is a murderous devil—I never could—I—I'm afraid of him!"

Old Driscoll's mouth opened and closed three times before he could get it to perform its office; then he stormed out:

"A coward in my family! A Driscoll a coward! Oh, what have I done to deserve this infamy!" He tottered to his secretary in the corner repeating that lament again and again in heartbreaking tones, and got out of a drawer a paper, which he slowly tore to bits, scattering the bits absently in his track as he walked up and down the room, still grieving and lamenting. At last he said:

"There it is, shreds and fragments once more—my will. Once more you have forced me to disinherit you, you base son of a most noble father! Leave my sight! Go—before I spit on you!"

The young man did not tarry. Then the Judge turned to Howard:

"You will be my second, old friend?"

"Of course."

"There is pen and paper. Draft the cartel, and lose no time."

"The Count shall have it in his hands in fifteen minutes," said Howard.

Tom was very heavy-hearted. His appetite was gone with his property and his self-respect. He went out the back way and wandered down the obscure lane grieving, and wondering if any course of future conduct, however discreet and carefully perfected and watched over, could win back his uncle's favor and persuade him to reconstruct once more that generous will which had just gone to ruin before his eyes. He finally concluded that it could. He said to himself that he had accomplished this sort of triumph once already, and that what had been done once could be done again. He would set about it. He would bend every energy to the task, and he would score that triumph once more, cost what it might to his convenience, limit as it might his frivolous and liberty-loving life.

"To begin," he said to himself, "I'll square up with the proceeds of my raid, and then gambling has got to be stopped—and stopped short off. It's the worst vice I've got—from my standpoint, anyway, because it's the one he can most easily find out, through the impatience of my creditors. He thought it expensive to have to pay two hundred dollars to them for me once. Expensive—*that!* Why, it cost me the whole of his fortune—but of course he never thought of that; some people can't think of any but their own side of a case. If he had known how deep I am in, now, the will would have gone to pot without waiting for a duel to help. Three hundred dollars! It's a pile! But he'll never hear of it, I'm thankful to say. The minute I've cleared it off, I'm safe; and I'll never touch a card again. Anyway, I won't while he lives, I make oath to that. I'm entering on my last reform—I know it—yes, and I'll win; but after that if I ever slip again I'm gone."

☐ XIII ☐

TOM STARES AT RUIN

When I reflect upon the number of disagreeable people who I know have gone to a better world, I am moved to lead a different life.
                                        —PUDD'NHEAD WILSON'S CALENDAR.

October. This is one of the peculiarly dangerous months to speculate in stocks in. The others are July, January, September, April, November, May, March, June, December, August, and February.
                                        —PUDD'NHEAD WILSON'S CALENDAR.

Thus mournfully communing with himself Tom moped along the lane past Pudd'nhead Wilson's house, and still on and on between fences inclosing vacant country on each hand till he neared the haunted house, then he came moping back again, with many sighs and heavy with trouble. He sorely wanted cheerful company. Rowena! His heart gave a bound at the thought, but the next thought quieted it—the detested twins would be there.

He was on the inhabited side of Wilson's house, and now as he approached it he noticed that the sitting-room was lighted. This would do; others made him feel unwelcome sometimes, but Wilson never failed in courtesy toward him, and a kindly courtesy does at least save one's feelings, even if it is not professing to stand for a welcome. Wilson heard footsteps at his threshold, then the clearing of a throat.

"It's that fickle-tempered, dissipated young goose—poor devil, he finds friends pretty scarce to-day, likely, after the disgrace of carrying a personal-assault case into a law-court."

A dejected knock. "Come in!"

Tom entered, and dropped into a chair, without saying anything. Wilson said kindly:

"Why, my boy, you look desolate. Don't take it so hard. Try and forget you have been kicked."

"Oh, dear," said Tom, wretchedly, "it's not that, Pudd'nhead—it's not that. It's a thousand times worse than that—oh, yes, a million times worse."

"Why, Tom, what do you mean? Has Rowena—"

"Flung me? No, but the old man has."

Wilson said to himself, "Aha!" and thought of the mysterious girl in the bedroom. "The Driscolls have been making discoveries!" Then he said aloud, gravely:

"Tom, there are some kinds of dissipation which—"

"Oh, shucks, this hasn't got anything to do with dissipation. He wanted me to challenge that derned Italian savage, and I wouldn't do it."

"Yes, of course, he would do that," said Wilson in a meditative matter-of-course way, "but the thing that puzzzled me was, why he didn't look to that last night, for one thing, and why he let you carry such a matter into a court of law at all, either before the duel or after it. It's no place for it. It was not like him. I couldn't understand it. How did it happen?"

"It happened because he didn't know anything about it. He was asleep when I got home last night."

"And you didn't wake him? Tom, is that possible?"

Tom was not getting much comfort here. He fidgeted a moment, then said:

"I didn't choose to tell him—that's all. He was going a-fishing before dawn, with Pembroke Howard, and if I got the twins into the common cala-boose—and I thought sure I could—I never dreamed of their slipping out on a paltry fine for such an outrageous offense—well, once in the calaboose they would be disgraced, and uncle wouldn't want any duels with that sort of characters, and wouldn't allow any."

"Tom, I am ashamed of you! I don't see how you could treat your good old uncle so. I am a better friend of his than you are; for if I had known the circumstances I would have kept that case out of court until I got word to him and let him have a gentleman's chance."

"You would?" exclaimed Tom, with lively surprise. "And it your first case! And you know perfectly well there never would have *been* any case if he had got that chance, don't you? And you'd have finished your days a pauper nobody, instead of being an actually launched and recognized lawyer to-day. And you would really have done that, would you?"

"Certainly."

Tom looked at him a moment or two, then shook his head sorrowfully and said:

"I believe you—upon my word I do. I don't know why I do, but I do. Pudd'nhead Wilson, I think you're the biggest fool I ever saw."

"Thank you."

"Don't mention it."

"Well, he has been requiring you to fight the Italian and you have refused. You degenerate remnant of an honorable line! I'm thoroughly ashamed of you, Tom!"

"Oh, that's nothing! I don't care for anything, now that the will's torn up again."

"Tom, tell me squarely—didn't he find any fault with you for anything but those two things—carrying the case into court and refusing to fight?"

He watched the young fellow's face narrowly, but it was entirely repose-ful, and so also was the voice that answered:

"No, he didn't find any other fault with me. If he had had any to find, he would have begun yesterday, for he was just in the humor for it. He drove that jack-pair around town and showed them the sights, and when he came home he couldn't find his father's old silver watch that don't keep time and he thinks so much of, and couldn't remember what he did with it three or four days ago when he saw it last, and so when I arrived he was all in a sweat about it, and when I suggested that it probably wasn't lost but stolen, it put him in a regular passion and he said I was a fool—which convinced me, without any trouble, that that was just what he was afraid *had* happened, himself, but did not want to believe it, because lost things stand a better chance of being found again than stolen ones."

"Whe-ew!" whistled Wilson, "score another on the list."

"Another what?"

"Another theft!"

"Theft?"

"Yes, theft. That watch isn't lost, it's stolen. There's been another raid on the town—and just the same old mysterious sort of thing that has happened once before, as you remember."

"You don't mean it!"

"It's as sure as you are born! Have you missed anything yourself?"

"No. That is, I did miss a silver pencil-case that Aunt Mary Pratt gave me last birthday—"

"You'll find it stolen—that's what you'll find."

"No, I sha'n't; for when I suggested theft about the watch and got such a rap, I went and examined my room, and the pencil-case was missing, but it was only mislaid, and I found it again."

"You are sure you missed nothing else?"

"Well, nothing of consequence. I missed a small plain gold ring worth two or three dollars, but that will turn up. I'll look again."

"In my opinion you'll not find it. There's been a raid, I tell you. Come *in!*"

Mr. Justice Robinson entered, followed by Buckstone and the town constable, Jim Blake. They sat down, and after some wandering and aimless weather conversation Wilson said:

"By the way, we've just added another to the list of thefts, maybe two. Judge Driscoll's old silver watch is gone, and Tom here has missed a gold ring."

"Well, it is a bad business," said the Justice, "and gets worse the further it goes. The Hankses, the Dobsons, the Pilligrews, the Ortons, the Grangers, the Hales, the Fullers, the Holcombs, in fact everybody that lives around about Patsy Cooper's has been robbed of little things like trinkets and tea-spoons and such-like small valuables that are easily carried off. It's perfectly plain that the thief took advantage of the reception at Patsy Cooper's when all the neighbors were in her house and all their niggers hanging around her fence for a look at the show, to raid the vacant houses undisturbed. Patsy is miserable about it; miserable on account of the neighbors, and particularly miserable on account of her foreigners, of course; so miserable on their account that she hasn't any room to worry about her own little losses."

"It's the same old raider," said Wilson. "I suppose there isn't any doubt about that."

"Constable Blake doesn't think so."

"No, you're wrong there," said Blake; "the other times it was a man; there was plenty of signs of that, as we know, in the profession, though we never got hands on him; but this time it's a woman."

Wilson thought of the mysterious girl straight off. She was always in his mind now. But she failed him again. Blake continued:

"She's a stoop-shouldered old woman with a covered basket on her arm, in a black veil, dressing in mourning. I saw her going aboard the ferry-boat yesterday. Lives in Illinois, I reckon; but I don't care where she lives, I'm going to get her—she can make herself sure of that."

"What makes you think she's the thief?"

"Well, there ain't any other, for one thing; and for another, some of the nigger draymen that happened to be driving along saw her coming out of or going into houses, and told me so—and it just happens that they was *robbed* houses, every time."

It was granted that this was plenty good enough circumstantial evidence. A pensive silence followed, which lasted some moments, then Wilson said:

"There's one good thing, anyway. She can't either pawn or sell Count Luigi's costly Indian dagger."

"My!" said Tom, "is *that* gone?"

"Yes."

"Well, that was a haul! But why can't she pawn it or sell it?"

"Because when the twins went home from the Sons of Liberty meeting last night, news of the raid was sifting in from everywhere, and Aunt Patsy was in distress to know if they had lost anything. They found that the dagger was gone, and they notified the police and pawnbrokers everywhere. It was a great haul, yes, but the old woman won't get anything out of it, because she'll get caught."

"Did they offer a reward?" asked Buckstone.

"Yes; five hundred dollars for the knife, and five hundred dollars for the thief."

"What a leather-headed idea!" exclaimed the constable. "The thief da'sn't go near them, nor send anybody. Whoever goes is going to get himself nabbed, for there ain't any pawnbroker that's going to lose the chance to—"

If anybody had noticed Tom's face at that time, the gray-green color of it might have provoked curiosity; but nobody did. He said to himself: "I'm gone! I never can square up; the rest of the plunder won't pawn or sell for half the bill. Oh, I know it—I'm gone, I'm gone—and this time it's for good. Oh, this is awful—I don't know what to do, nor which way to turn!"

"Softly, softly," said Wilson to Blake. "I planned their scheme for them at midnight last night, and it was all finished up shipshape by two this morning. They'll get their dagger back, and then I'll explain to you how the thing was done."

There were strong signs of a general curiosity, and Buckstone said:

"Well, you have whetted us up pretty sharp, Wilson, and I'm free to say that if you don't mind telling us in confidence—"

"Oh, I'd as soon tell as not, Buckstone, but as long as the twins and I agreed to say nothing about it, we must let it stand so. But you can take my word for it you won't be kept waiting three days. Somebody will apply for that reward pretty promptly, and I'll show you the thief and the dagger both very soon afterward."

The constable was disappointed, and also perplexed. He said:

"It may all be—yes, and I hope it will, but I'm blamed if I can see my way through it. It's too many for yours truly."

The subject seemed about talked out. Nobody seemed to have anything further to offer. After a silence the justice of the peace informed Wilson that he and Buckstone and the constable had come as a committee, on the part of the Democratic party, to ask him to run for mayor—for the little town was about to become a city and the first charter election was approaching. It was the first attention which Wilson had ever received at the hands of any party; it was a sufficiently humble one, but it was a recognition of his début into the town's life and activities at last; it was a step upward, and he was deeply gratified. He accepted, and the committee departed, followed by young Tom.

□ XIV □

ROXANA INSISTS UPON REFORM

The true Southern watermelon is a boon apart, and not to be mentioned
with commoner things. It is chief of this world's luxuries, king by the
grace of God over all the fruits of the earth. When one has tasted it, he
knows what the angels eat. It was not a Southern watermelon that Eve
took; we know it because she repented.

—PUDD'NHEAD WILSON'S CALENDAR.

About the time that Wilson was bowing the committee out, Pembroke
Howard was entering the next house to report. He found the old Judge sitting grim and straight in his chair, waiting.

"Well, Howard—the news?"

"The best in the world."

"Accepts, does he?" and the light of battle gleamed joyously in the
Judge's eye.

"Accepts? Why, he jumped at it."

"Did, did he? Now that's fine—that's very fine. I like that. When is it to
be?"

"Now! Straight off! To-night! An admirable fellow—admirable!"

"Admirable? He's a darling! Why, it's an honor as well as a pleasure to
stand up before such a man. Come—off with you! Go and arrange everything—and give him my heartiest compliments. A rare fellow, indeed; an admirable fellow, as you have said!"

Howard hurried away, saying:

"I'll have him in the vacant stretch between Wilson's and the haunted
house within the hour, and I'll bring my own pistols."

Judge Driscoll began to walk the floor in a state of pleased excitement;
but presently he stopped, and began to think—began to think of Tom. Twice
he moved toward the secretary, and twice he turned away again; but finally he
said:

"This may be my last night in the world—I must not take the chance.
He is worthless and unworthy, but it is largely my fault. He was intrusted to
me by my brother on his dying bed, and I have indulged him to his hurt,
instead of training him up severely, and making a man of him. I have violated my trust, and I must not add the sin of desertion to that. I have forgiven him once already, and would subject him to a long and hard trial
before forgiving him again, if I could live; but I must not run that risk. No,
I must restore the will. But if I survive the duel, I will hide it away, and he

will not know, and I will not tell him until he reforms, and I see that his reformation is going to be permanent."

He redrew the will, and his ostensible nephew was heir to a fortune again. As he was finishing his task, Tom, wearied with another brooding tramp, entered the house and went tiptoeing past the sitting-room door. He glanced in, and hurried on, for the sight of his uncle had nothing but terrors for him to-night. But his uncle was writing! That was unusual at this late hour. What could he be writing? A chill of anxiety settled down upon Tom's heart. Did that writing concern him? He was afraid so. He reflected that when ill luck begins, it does not come in sprinkles, but in showers. He said he would get a glimpse of that document or know the reason why. He heard someone coming and stepped out of sight and hearing. It was Pembroke Howard. What could be hatching?

Howard said, with great satisfaction:

"Everything's right and ready. He's gone to the battle-ground with his second and the surgeon—also with his brother. I've arranged it all with Wilson—Wilson's his second. We are to have three shots apiece."

"Good! How is the moon?"

"Bright as day, nearly. Perfect, for the distance—fifteen yards. No wind—not a breath; hot and still."

"All good; all first-rate. Here, Pembroke, read this, and witness it."

Pembroke read and witnessed the will, then gave the old man's hand a hearty shake and said:

"Now that's right, York—but I knew you would do it. You couldn't leave that poor chap to fight along without means or profession, with certain defeat before him, and I knew you wouldn't, for his father's sake if not for his own."

"For his dead father's sake I couldn't, I know; for poor Percy—but you know what Percy was to me. But mind—Tom is not to know of this unless I fall to-night."

"I understand. I'll keep the secret."

The Judge put the will away, and the two started for the battle-ground. In another minute the will was in Tom's hands. His misery vanished, his feelings underwent a tremendous revulsion. He put the will carefully back in its place, and spread his mouth and swung his hat once, twice, three times around his head, in imitation of three rousing huzzas, no sound issuing from his lips. He fell to communing with himself excitedly and joyously, but every now and then he let off another volley of dumb hurrahs.

He said to himself: "I've got the fortune again, but I'll not let on that I know about it. And this time I'm going to hang onto it. I take no more risks. I'll gamble no more, I'll drink no more, because—well, because I'll not go where there is any of that sort of thing going on, again. It's the sure way, and the only sure way; I might have thought of that sooner—well, yes, if I had wanted to. But now—dear me, I've had a scare this time, and I'll take no more chances. Not a single chance more. Land! I persuaded myself this evening that I could fetch him around without any great amount of effort, but I've been getting more and more heavy-hearted and doubtful straight along, ever since. If he tells me about this thing, all right; but if he doesn't, I sha'n't let on. I—well, I'd like to tell Pudd'nhead Wilson, but—no, I'll think about that; perhaps I won't." He whirled off another dead huzza, and said, "I'm reformed, and this time I'll stay so, sure!"

He was about to close with a final grand silent demonstration, when he suddenly recollected that Wilson had put it out of his power to pawn or sell the Indian knife, and that he was once more in awful peril of exposure by his creditors for that reason. His joy collapsed utterly, and he turned away and moped toward the door moaning and lamenting over the bitterness of his luck. He dragged himself upstairs, and brooded in his room a long time disconsolate and forlorn, with Luigi's Indian knife for a text. At last he sighed and said:

"When I supposed these stones were glass and this ivory bone, the thing hadn't any interest for me because it hadn't any value, and couldn't help me out of my trouble. But now—why, now it is full of interest; yes, and of a sort to break a body's heart. It's a bag of gold that has turned to dirt and ashes in my hands. It could save me, and save me so easily, and yet I've got to go to ruin. It's like drowning with a life-preserver in my reach. All the hard luck comes to me, and all the good luck goes to other people—Pudd'nhead Wilson, for instance; even his career has got a sort of a little start at last, and what has he done to deserve it, I should like to know? Yes, he has opened his own road, but he isn't content with that, but must block mine. It's a sordid, selfish world, and I wish I was out of it." He allowed the light of the candle to play upon the jewels of the sheath, but the flashings and sparklings had no charm for his eye; they were only just so many pangs to his heart. "I must not say anything to Roxy about this thing," he said, "she is too daring. She would be for digging these stones out and selling them, and then—why, she would be arrested and the stones traced, and then—" The thought made him quake, and he hid the knife away, trembling all over and glancing furtively about, like a criminal who fancies that the accuser is already at hand.

Should he try to sleep? Oh, no, sleep was not for him; his trouble was too haunting, too afflicting for that. He must have somebody to mourn with. He would carry his despair to Roxy.

He had heard several distant gunshots, but that sort of thing was not uncommon, and they had made no impression upon him. He went out at the back door, and turned westward. He passed Wilson's house and proceeded along the lane, and presently saw several figures approaching Wilson's place through the vacant lots. These were the duelists returning from the fight; he thought he recognized them, but as he had no desire for white people's company, he stooped down behind the fence until they were out of his way.

Roxy was feeling fine. She said:

"Whah was you, child? Warn't you in it?"

"In what?"

"In de duel."

"Duel? Has there been a duel?"

" 'Cos dey has. De old Jedge has be'n havin' a duel wid one o' dem twins."

"Great Scott!" Then he added to himself: "That's what made him re-make the will; he thought he might get killed, and it softened him toward me. And that's what he and Howard were so busy about. . . . Oh dear, if the twin had only killed him, I should be out of my—"

"What is you mumblin' 'bout, Chambers? Whah was you? Didn't you know dey was gwyne to be a duel?"

"No, I didn't. The old man tried to get me to fight one with Count Luigi, but he didn't succeed, so I reckon he concluded to patch up the family honor himself."

He laughed at the idea, and went rambling on with a detailed account of his talk with the Judge, and how shocked and ashamed the Judge was to find that he had a coward in his family. He glanced up at last and got a shock himself. Roxana's bosom was heaving with suppressed passion, and she was glowering down upon him with measureless contempt written in her face.

"En you refuse' to fight a man dat kicked you, 'stid o' jumpin' at de chance! En you ain't got no mo' feelin' den to come en tell me, dat fetched sich a po' low-down ornery rabbit into de worl'! Pah! it makes me sick! It's de nigger in you, dat's what it is. Thirty-one parts o' you is white, en on'y one part nigger, en dat po' little one part is yo' *soul*. 'Tain't wuth savin'; 'tain't wuth totin' out on a shovel en throwin' in de gutter. You has disgraced yo' birth. What would yo' pa think o' you? It's enough to make him turn in his grave."

The last three sentences stung Tom into a fury, and he said to himself that if his father were only alive and in reach of assassination his mother would soon find that he had a very clear notion of the size of his indebtedness to that man, and was willing to pay it up in full, and would do it too, even at risk of his life; but he kept his thought to himself; that was safest in his mother's present state.

"Whatever has come o' yo' Essex blood? Dat's what I can't understan'. En it ain't on'y jist Essex blood dat's in you, not by a long sight—'deed it ain't! My great-great-great-gran'father en yo' great-great-great-great-gran'father was Ole Cap'n John Smith, de highest blood dat Old Virginny ever turned out, en *his* great-great-gran'mother or somers along back dah, was

Pocahontas de Injun queen, en her husbun' was a nigger king outen Africa—en yit here you is, a-slinkin' outen a duel en disgracin' our whole line like a ornery low-down hound! Yes, it's de nigger in you!"

She sat down on her candle-box and fell into a reverie. Tom did not disturb her; he sometimes lacked prudence, but it was not in circumstances of this kind. Roxana's storm went gradually down, but it died hard, and even when it seemed to be quite gone, it would now and then break out in a distant rumble, so to speak, in the form of muttered ejaculations. One of these was, "Ain't nigger enough in him to show in his finger-nails, en dat takes mighty little—yit dey's enough to paint his soul."

Presently she muttered: "Yassir, enough to paint a whole thimbleful of 'em." At last her ramblings ceased altogether, and her countenance began to clear—a welcome sign to Tom, who had learned her moods, and knew she was on the threshold of good humor, now. He noticed that from time to time she unconsciously carried her finger to the end of her nose. He looked closer and said:

"Why, mammy, the end of your nose is skinned. How did that come?"

She sent out the sort of whole-hearted peal of laughter which God has vouchsafed in its perfection to none but the happy angels in heaven and the bruised and broken black slave on the earth, and said:

"Dad fetch dat duel, I be'n in it myself."

"Gracious, did a bullet do that?"

"Yassir, you bet it did!"

"Well, I declare! Why, how did that happen?"

"Happened dis-away. I 'uz a-sett'n' here kinder dozin' in de dark, en *chebang!* goes a gun, right out dah. I skips along out towards t'other end o' de house to see what's gwyne on, en stops by de ole winder on de side towards Pudd'nhead Wilson's house dat ain't got no sash in it—but dey ain't none of 'em got any sashes, fur as dat's concerned—en I stood dah in de dark en look out, en dar in de moonlight, right down under me, 'uz one o' de twins a-cussin'—not much, but jist a-cussin' soft—it 'uz de brown one dat 'uz cussin', ca'se he 'uz hit in de shoulder. En Dr. Claypool he 'uz a-workin' at him, en Pudd'nhead Wilson he 'uz a-he'pin', en ole Jedge Driscoll en Pem Howard 'uz a-standin' out yonder a little piece waitin' for 'em to get ready ag'in. En treckly dey squared off en give de word, en *bang-bang* went de pistols, en de twin he say, 'Ouch!'—hit him on de han' dis time—en I hear dat same bullet go *spat!* ag'in de logs under de winder; en de nex' time dey shoot, de twin say, 'Ouch!' ag'in, en I done it too, 'ca'se de bullet glance on his cheek-bone en skip up here en glance on de side o' de winder en whiz right acrost my face en tuck de hide off'n my nose—why, if I'd 'a' be'n jist a inch or a inch en a half furder 'twould 'a' tuck de whole nose en disfiggered me. Here's de bullet; I hunted her up."

"Did you stand there all the time?"

"Dat's a question to ask, ain't it! What else would I do? Does I git a chance to see a duel every day?"

"Why, you were right in range! Weren't you afraid?'

The woman gave a sniff of scorn.

" 'Fraid! De Smith-Pocahontases ain't 'fraid o' nothin', let alone bullets."

"They've got pluck enough, I suppose; what they lack is judgment. *I* wouldn't have stood there."

"Nobody's accusin' you!"

"Did anybody else get hurt?"

"Yes, we all got hit 'cep' de blon' twin en de doctor en de seconds. De Jedge didn't git hurt, but I hear Pudd'nhead say de bullet snip some o' his ha'r off."

"George!" said Tom to himself, "to come so near being out of my trouble, and miss it by an inch. Oh dear, dear, he will live to find me out and sell me to some nigger-trader yet—yes, and he would do it in a minute." Then he said aloud, in a grave tone:

"Mother, we are in an awful fix."

Roxana caught her breath with a spasm, and said:

"Chile! What you hit a body so sudden for, like dat? What's be'n en gone en happen?"

"Well, there's one thing I didn't tell you. When I wouldn't fight, he tore up the will again, and—"

Roxana's face turned a dead white, and she said:

"Now you's *done!*— done forever! Dat's de end. Bofe un us is gwyne to starve to—"

"Wait and hear me through, can't you! I reckon that when he resolved to fight, himself, he thought he might get killed and not have a chance to forgive me any more in this life, so he made the will again, and I've seen it, and it's all right. But—"

"Oh, thank goodness, den we's safe ag'in—safe! en so what did you want to come here en talk sich dreadful—"

"Hold *on,* I tell you, and let me finish. The swag I gathered won't half square me up, and the first thing we know, my creditors—well, you know what'll happen."

Roxana dropped her chin, and told her son to leave her alone—she must think this matter out. Presently she said impressively:

"You got to go mighty keerful now, I tell you! En here's what you got to do. He didn't git killed, en if you gives him de least reason, he'll bust de will ag'in, en dat's de *las'* time, now you hear me! So—you's got to show him what you kin do in de nex' few days. You's got to be pison good, en let him see it; you got to do everything dat'll make him b'lieve in you, en you got to sweeten aroun' old Aunt Pratt, too—she's pow'ful strong wid de Jedge, en de bes' frien' you got. Nex', you'll go 'long away to Sent Louis, en dat'll *keep* him in yo' favor. Den you go en make a bargain wid dem people. You tell 'em he ain't gwyne to live long—en dat's de fac', too—en tell 'em you'll pay 'em intrust, en big intrust, too—ten per—what you call it?"

"Ten per cent a month?"

"Dat's it. Den you take and sell yo' truck aroun', a little at a time, en pay de intrust. How long will it las'?"

"I think there's enough to pay the interest five or six months."

"Den you's all right. If he don't die in six months, dat don't make no diff'rence—Providence 'll provide. You's gwyne to be safe—if you behaves." She bent an austere eye on him and added, "En you *is* gwyne to behave—does you know dat?"

He laughed and said he was going to try, anyway. She did not unbend. She said gravely:

"Tryin' ain't de thing. You's gwyne to *do* it. You ain't gwyne to steal a pin—'ca'se it ain't safe no mo'; en you ain't gwyne into no bad company— not even once, you understand; en you ain't gwyne to drink a drop—nary single drop; en you ain't gwyne to gamble one single gamble—not one! Dis ain't what you's gwyne to *try* to do, it's what you's gwyne to *do*. En I'll tell you how I knows it. Dis is how. I's gwyne to foller along to Sent Louis my own self, en you's gwyne to come to me every day o' yo' life, en I'll look you over; en if you fails in one single one o' dem things—jist *one*—I take my oath I'll come straight down to dis town en tell de Jedge you's a nigger en a slave—en *prove* it!" She paused to let her words sink home. Then she added, "Chambers, does you b'lieve me when I says dat?"

Tom was sober enough now. There was no levity in his voice when he answered:

"Yes, mother, I know, now, that I am reformed—and permanently. Permanently—and beyond the reach of any human temptation."

"Den g' long home en begin!"

☐ **XV** ☐

THE ROBBER ROBBED

Nothing so needs reforming as other people's habits.
—PUDD'NHEAD WILSON'S CALENDAR.

*Behold, the fool saith, "Put not all thine eggs in the one basket"—which
is but a manner of saying, "Scatter your money and your attention"; but
the wise man saith, "Put all your eggs in the one basket and—WATCH
THAT BASKET."*
—PUDD'NHEAD WILSON'S CALENDAR.

What a time of it Dawson's Landing was having! All its life it had been
asleep but now it hardly got a chance for a nod, so swiftly did big events and
crashing surprises come along in one another's wake: Friday morning, first
glimpse of Real Nobility, also grand reception at Aunt Patsy Cooper's, also
great robber raid; Friday evening dramatic kicking of the heir of the chief citizen in presence of four hundred people; Saturday morning, emergence as
practising lawyer of the long-submerged Pudd'nhead Wilson; Saturday night,
duel between chief citizen and titled stranger.

The people took more pride in the duel than in all the other events put
together, perhaps. It was a glory to their town to have such a thing happen
there. In their eyes the principals had reached the summit of human honor.
Everybody paid homage to their names; their praises were in all mouths. Even
the duelists' subordinates came in for a handsome share of the public appro-
bation: wherefore Pudd'nhead Wilson was suddenly become a man of consequence. When asked to run for the mayoralty Saturday night he was
risking defeat, but Sunday morning found him a made man and his success
assured.

The twins were prodigiously great, now; the town took them to its
bosom with enthusiasm. Day after day, and night after night, they went dining and visiting from house to house, making friends, enlarging and solidi-
fying their popularity, and charming and surprising all with their musical
prodigies, and now and then heightening the effects with samples of what
they could do in other directions, out of their stock of rare and curious accomplishments. They were so pleased that they gave the regulation thirty
days' notice, the required preparation for citizenship, and resolved to finish
their days in this pleasant place. That was the climax. The delighted community rose as one man and applauded; and when the twins were asked to stand

for seats in the forthcoming aldermanic board, and consented, the public contentment was rounded and complete.

Tom Driscoll was not happy over these things; they sunk deep, and hurt all the way down. He hated the one twin for kicking him, and the other one for being the kicker's brother.

Now and then the people wondered why nothing was heard of the raider, or of the stolen knife or the other plunder, but nobody was able to throw any light on that matter. Nearly a week had drifted by, and still the thing remained a vexed mystery.

On Saturday Constable Blake and Pudd'nhead Wilson met on the street, and Tom Driscoll joined them in time to open their conversation for them. He said to Blake: "You are not looking well, Blake; you seem to be annoyed about something. Has anything gone wrong in the detective business? I believe you fairly and justifiably claim to have a pretty good reputation in that line, isn't it so?"—which made Blake feel good, and look it; but Tom added, "for a country detective"—which made Blake feel the other way, and not only look it, but betray it in his voice:

"Yes, sir, I *have* got a reputation; and it's as good as anybody's in the profession, too, country or no country."

"Oh, I beg pardon; I didn't mean any offense. What I started out to ask was only about the old woman that raided the town—the stoop-shouldered old woman, you know, that you said you were going to catch; and I knew you would, too, because you have the reputation of never boasting, and—well, you—you've caught the old woman?"

"D—— the old woman!"

"Why, sho! you don't mean to say you haven't caught her?"

"No; I haven't caught her. If anybody could have caught her, I could; but nobody couldn't, I don't care who he is."

"I am sorry, real sorry—for your sake; because, when it gets around that a detective has expressed himself so confidently, and then—"

"Don't you worry, that's all—don't you worry; and as for the town, the town needn't worry, either. She's my meat—make yourself easy about that. I'm on her track; I've got clues that—"

"That's good! Now if you could get an old veteran detective down from St. Louis to help you find out what the clues mean, and where they lead to, and then—"

"I'm plenty veteran enough myself, and I don't need anybody's help. I'll have her inside of a we—inside of a month. That I'll swear to!"

Tom said carelessly:

"I suppose that will answer—yes, that will answer. But I reckon she is pretty old, and the old people don't often outlive the cautious pace of the professional detective when he has got his clues together and is out on his still-hunt."

Blake's dull face flushed under this gibe, but before he could set his retort in order Tom had turned to Wilson, and was saying, with placid indifference of manner and voice:

"Who got the reward, Pudd'nhead?"

Wilson winced slightly, and saw that his own turn was come.

"What reward?"

"Why, the reward for the thief, and the other one for the knife."

Wilson answered—and rather uncomfortably, to judge by his hesitating
fashion of delivering himself:

"Well, the—well, in fact, nobody has claimed it yet."

Tom seemed surprised.

"Why, is that so?"

Wilson showed a trifle of irritation when he replied:

"Yes, it's so. And what of it?"

"Oh, nothing. Only I thought you had struck out a new idea, and invented a scheme that was going to revolutionize the time-worn and ineffectual methods of the—" He stopped, and turned to Blake, who was happy
now that another had taken his place on the gridiron: "Blake, didn't you understand him to intimate that it wouldn't be necessary for you to hunt the
old woman down?"

"B'George, he said he'd have thief and swag both inside of three days—
he did, by hokey! and that's just about a week ago. Why, I said at the time
that no thief and no thief's pal was going to try to pawn or sell a thing where
he knowed the pawnbroker could get both rewards by taking *him* into camp
with the swag. It was the blessedest idea that ever *I* struck!"

"You'd change your mind," said Wilson, with irritated bluntness, "if
you knew the entire scheme instead of only part of it."

"Well," said the constable, pensively, "I had the idea that it wouldn't
work, and up to now I'm right anyway."

"Very well, then, let it stand at that, and give it a further show. It has
worked at least as well as your own methods, you perceive."

The constable hadn't anything handy to hit back with, so he discharged
a discontented sniff, and said nothing.

After the night that Wilson had partly revealed his scheme at his house,
Tom had tried for several days to guess out the secret of the rest of it, but had
failed. Then it occurred to him to give Roxana's smarter head a chance at it.
He made up a supposititious case, and laid it before her. She thought it over,
and delivered her verdict upon it. Tom said to himself, "She's hit it, sure!"
He thought he would test that verdict, now, and watch Wilson's face; so he
said reflectively:

"Wilson, you're not a fool—a fact of recent discovery. Whatever your
scheme was, it had sense in it, Blake's opinion to the contrary notwithstanding. I don't ask you to reveal it, but I will suppose a case—a case which will

answer as a starting-point for the real thing I am going to come at, and that's all I want. You offered five hundred dollars for the knife, and five hundred for the thief. We will suppose, for argument's sake, that the first reward is *advertised* and the second offered by *private letter* to pawnbrokers and—"

Blake slapped his thigh, and cried out:

"By Jackson, he's got you, Pudd'nhead! Now why couldn't I or *any* fool have thought of that?"

Wilson said to himself, "Anybody with a reasonably good head would have thought of it. I am not surprised that Blake didn't detect it; I am only surprised that Tom did. There is more to him than I supposed." He said nothing aloud, and Tom went on:

"Very well. The thief would not suspect that there was a trap, and he would bring or send the knife, and say he bought it for a song, or found it in the road, or something like that, and try to collect the reward, and be arrested—wouldn't he?"

"Yes," said Wilson.

"I think so," said Tom. "There can't be any doubt of it. Have you ever seen that knife?"

"No."

"Has any friend of yours?"

"Not that I know of."

"Well, I begin to think I understand why your scheme failed."

"What do you mean, Tom? What are you driving at?" asked Wilson, with a dawning sense of discomfort.

"Why, that there *isn't* any such knife."

"Look here, Wilson," said Blake, "Tom Driscoll's right, for a thousand dollars—if I had it."

Wilson's blood warmed a little, and he wondered if he had been played upon by those strangers; it certainly had something of that look. But what could they gain by it? He threw out that suggestion. Tom replied:

"Gain? Oh, nothing that you would value, maybe. But they are strangers making their way in a new community. Is it nothing to them to appear as pets of an Oriental prince—at no expense? Is it nothing to them to be able to dazzle this poor little town with thousand-dollar rewards—at no expense? Wilson, there isn't any such knife, or your scheme would have fetched it to light. Or if there is any such knife, they've got it yet. I believe, myself, that they've seen such a knife, for Angelo pictured it out with his pencil too swiftly and handily for him to have been inventing it, and of course I can't swear that they've never had it; but this I'll go bail for—if they had it when they came to this town, they've got it yet."

Blake said:

"It looks mighty reasonable, the way Tom puts it; it most certainly does."

Tom responded, turning to leave:

"You find the old woman, Blake, and if she can't furnish the knife, go and search the twins!"

Tom sauntered away. Wilson felt a good deal depressed. He hardly knew what to think. He was loath to withdraw his faith from the twins, and was resolved not to do it on the present indecisive evidence; but—well, he would think, and then decide how to act.

"Blake, what do you think of this matter?"

"Well, Pudd'nhead, I'm bound to say I put it up the way Tom does. They hadn't the knife; or if they had it, they've got it yet."

The men parted. Wilson said to himself:

"I believe they had it; if it had been stolen, the scheme would have restored it, that is certain. And so I believe they've got it yet."

Tom had no purpose in his mind when he encountered those two men. When he began his talk he hoped to be able to gall them a little and get a trifle of malicious entertainment out of it. But when he left, he left in great spirits, for he perceived that just by pure luck and no troublesome labor he had accomplished several delightful things: he had touched both men on a raw spot and seen them squirm; he had modified Wilson's sweetness for the twins with one small bitter taste that he wouldn't be able to get out of his mouth right away; and, best of all, he had taken the hated twins down a peg with the community; for Blake would gossip around freely, after the manner of detectives, and within a week the town would be laughing at them in its sleeve for offering a gaudy reward for a bauble which they either never possessed or hadn't lost. Tom was very well satisfied with himself.

Tom's behavior at home had been perfect during the entire week. His uncle and aunt had seen nothing like it before. They could find no fault with him anywhere.

Saturday evening he said to the Judge:

"I've had something preying on my mind, uncle, and as I am going away, and might never see you again, I can't bear it any longer. I made you believe I was afraid to fight that Italian adventurer. I had to get out of it on some pretext or other, and maybe I chose badly, being taken unawares, but no honorable person could consent to meet him in the field, knowing what I know about him."

"Indeed? What was that?"

"Count Luigi is a confessed assassin."

"Incredible!"

"It is perfectly true. Wilson detected it in his hand, by palmistry, and charged him with it, and cornered him up so close that he had to confess; but both twins begged us on their knees to keep the secret, and swore they would lead straight lives here; and it was all so pitiful that we gave our word of honor never to expose them while they kept that promise. You would have done it yourself, uncle."

"You are right, my boy; I would. A man's secret is still his own property, and sacred, when it has been surprised out of him like that. You did well, and I am proud of you." Then he added mournfully, "But I wish I could have been saved the shame of meeting an assassin on the field of honor."

"It couldn't be helped, uncle. If I had known you were going to challenge him I should have felt obliged to sacrifice my pledged word in order to stop it, but Wilson couldn't be expected to do otherwise than keep silent."

"Oh, no; Wilson did right, and is in no way to blame. Tom, Tom, you have lifted a heavy load from my heart; I was stung to the very soul when I seemed to have discovered that I had a coward in my family."

"You may imagine what it cost *me* to assume such a part, uncle."

"Oh, I know it, poor boy, I know it. And I can understand how much it has cost you to remain under that unjust stigma to this time. But it is all right now, and no harm is done. You have restored my comfort of mind, and with it your own; and both of us had suffered enough."

The old man sat awhile plunged in thought; then he looked up with a satisfied light in his eye, and said: "That this assassin should have put the affront upon me of letting me meet him on the field of honor as if he were a gentleman is a matter which I will presently settle—but not now. I will not shoot him until after election. I see a way to ruin them both before; I will attend to that first. Neither of them shall be elected, that I promise. You are sure that the fact that he is an assassin has not got abroad?"

"Perfectly certain of it, sir."

"It will be a good card. I will fling a hint at it from the stump on the polling day. It will sweep the ground from under both of them."

"There's not a doubt of it. It will finish them."

"That and outside work among the voters will, to a certainty. I want you to come down here by-and-by and work privately among the rag, tag, and bobtail. You shall spend money among them; I will furnish it."

Another point scored against the detested twins! Really it was a great day for Tom. He was encouraged to chance a parting shot, at the same target, and did it.

"You know that wonderful Indian knife that the twins have been making such a to-do about? Well, there's no track or trace of it yet; so the town is beginning to sneer and gossip and laugh. Half the people believe they never had any such knife, the other half believe they had it and have got it still. I've heard twenty people talking like that to-day."

Yes, Tom's blemishless week had restored him to the favor of his aunt and uncle.

His mother was satisfied with him, too. Privately, she believed she was coming to love him, but she did not say so. She told him to go along to St. Louis, now, and she would get ready and follow. Then she smashed her whisky bottle and said:

"Dah now! I's a-gwyne to make you walk as straight as a string, Chambers, en so I's bown' you ain't gwyne to git no bad example out o' yo' mammy. I tole you you couldn't go into no bad comp'ny. Well, you'se gwyne into my comp'ny, en I's gwyne to fill de bill. Now, den, trot along, trot along!"

Tom went aboard one of the big transient boats that night with his heavy satchel of miscellaneous plunder, and slept the sleep of the unjust, which is serener and sounder than the other kind, as we know by the hanging-eve history of a million rascals. But when he got up in the morning, luck was against him again: A brother thief had robbed him while he slept, and gone ashore at some intermediate landing.

□   **XVI**   □

SOLD DOWN THE RIVER

If you pick up a starving dog and make him prosperous, he will not bite you. This is the principal difference between a dog and a man.
                                    —PUDD'NHEAD WILSON'S CALENDAR.

We know all about the habits of the ant, we know all about the habits of the bee, but we know nothing at all about the habits of the oyster. It seems almost certain that we have been choosing the wrong time for studying the oyster.
                                    —PUDD'NHEAD WILSON'S CALENDAR.

When Roxana arrived, she found her son in such despair and misery that her heart was touched and her motherhood rose up strong in her. He was ruined past hope, now; his destruction would be immediate and sure, and he would be an outcast and friendless. That was reason enough for a mother to love a child; so she loved him, and told him so. It made him wince, secretly—for she was a "nigger." That he was one himself was far from reconciling him to that despised race.

Roxana poured out endearments upon him, to which he responded uncomfortably, but as well as he could. And she tried to comfort him, but that was not possible. These intimacies quickly became horrible to him, and within the hour he began to try to get up courage enough to tell her so, and require that they be discontinued or very considerably modified. But he was afraid of her; and besides, there came a lull, now, for she had begun to think. She was trying to invent a saving plan. Finally she started up, and said she had found a way out. Tom was almost suffocated by the joy of this sudden good news. Roxana said:

"Here is de plan, en she'll win, sure. I's a nigger, en nobody ain't gwyne to doubt it dat hears me talk. I's wuth six hund'd dollahs. Take en sell me, en pay off dese gamblers."

Tom was dazed. He was not sure he had heard aright. He was dumb for a moment; then he said:

"Do you mean that you would be sold into slavery to save me?"

"Ain't you my chile? En does you know anything dat a mother won't do for her chile? Dey ain't nothin' a white mother won't do for her chile. Who made 'em so? De Lord done it. En who made de niggers? De Lord made 'em. In de inside, mothers is all de same. De good Lord he made 'em so. I's gwyne to be sole into slavery, en in a year you's gwyne to buy yo' ole mammy free ag'in. I'll show you how. Dat's de plan."

Tom's hopes began to rise, and his spirits along with them. He said:

"It's lovely of you, mammy—it's just—"

"Say it ag'in! En keep on sayin' it! It's all de pay a body kin want in dis worl', en it's mo' den enough. Laws bless you, honey, when I's slavin' aroun', en dey 'buses me, if I know you's a-sayin' dat, 'way off yonder somers, it'll heal up all de sore places, en I kin stan' 'em."

"I *do* say it again, mammy, and I'll keep on saying it, too. But how am I going to sell you? You're free, you know."

"Much diff'rence dat make! White folks ain't partic'lar. De law kin sell me now if dey tell me to leave de state in six months en I don't go. You draw up a paper—bill o' sale—en put it 'way off yonder, down in de middle o' Kaintuck somers, en sign some names to it, en say you'll sell me cheap 'ca'se you's hard up; you'll find you ain't gwyne to have no trouble. You take me up de country a piece, en sell me on a farm; den people ain't gwyne to ask no questions if I's a bargain."

Tom forged a bill of sale and sold his mother to an Arkansas cotton-planter for a trifle over six hundred dollars. He did not want to commit this treachery, but luck threw the man in his way, and this saved him the necessity of going up country to hunt up a purchaser, with the added risk of having to answer a lot of questions, whereas this planter was so pleased with Roxy that he asked next to none at all. Besides, the planter insisted that Roxy wouldn't know where she was, at first, and that by the time she found out she would already have become contented.

So Tom argued with himself that it was an immense advantage to Roxy to have a master who was as pleased with her, as this planter manifestly was. In almost no time his flowing reasonings carried him to the point of even half believing he was doing Roxy a splendid surreptitious service in selling her "down the river." And then he kept diligently saying to himself all the time: "It's for only a year. In a year I buy her free again; she'll keep that in mind, and it'll reconcile her." Yes, the little deception could do no harm, and everything would come out right and pleasant in the end, anyway. By agreement, the conversation in Roxy's presence was all about the man's "up-country" farm, and how pleasant a place it was, and how happy the slaves were there; so poor Roxy was entirely deceived; and easily, for she was not dreaming that her own son could be guilty of treason to a mother who, in voluntarily going into slavery—slavery of any kind, mild or severe, or of any duration, brief or long—was making a sacrifice for him compared with which death would have been a poor and commonplace one. She lavished tears and loving caresses upon him privately, and then went away with her owner—went away broken-hearted, and yet proud of what she was doing, and glad that it was in her power to do it.

Tom squared his accounts, and resolved to keep to the very letter of his reform, and never to put that will in jeopardy again. He had three hundred dollars left. According to his mother's plan he was to put that safely away, and add her half of his pension to it monthly. In one year this fund would buy her free again.

For a whole week he was not able to sleep well, so much the villainy which he had played upon his trusting mother preyed upon his rag of a conscience; but after that he began to get comfortable again, and was presently able to sleep like any other miscreant.

The boat bore Roxy away from St. Louis at four in the afternoon, and she stood on the lower guard abaft the paddle-box and watched Tom through a blur of tears until he melted into the throng of people and disappeared; then she looked no more, but sat there on a coil of cable crying till far into the night. When she went to her foul steerage bunk at last, between the clashing engines, it was not to sleep, but only to wait for the morning and, waiting, grieve.

It had been imagined that she "would not know," and would think she was traveling up-stream. She! Why, she had been steamboating for years. At dawn she got up and went listlessly and sat down on the cable-coil again. She passed many a snag whose "break" could have told her a thing to break her heart, for it showed a current moving in the same direction that the boat was going; but her thoughts were elsewhere, and she did not notice. But at last the roar of a bigger and nearer break than usual brought her out of her torpor, and she looked up, and her practised eye fell upon that telltale rush of water. For one moment her petrified gaze fixed itself there. Then her head dropped upon her breast, and she said:

"Oh, de good Lord God have mercy on po' sinful me—*I's sole down de river!*"

□ XVII □

THE JUDGE UTTERS DIRE PROPHECY

Even popularity can be overdone. In Rome, along at first, you are full of regrets that Michelangelo died; but by and by you only regret that you didn't see him do it.
—PUDD'NHEAD WILSON'S CALENDAR.

July 4. Statistics show that we lose more fools on this day than in all the other days of the year put together. This proves, by the number left in stock, that one Fourth of July per year is now inadequate, the country has grown so.
—PUDD'NHEAD WILSON'S CALENDAR.

The summer weeks dragged by, and then the political campaign opened—opened in pretty warm fashion, and waxed hotter and hotter daily. The twins threw themselves into it with their whole heart, for their self-love was engaged. Their popularity, so general at first, had suffered afterward; mainly because they had been *too* popular, and so a natural reaction had followed. Besides, it had been diligently whispered around that it was curious—indeed, *very* curious—that that wonderful knife of theirs did not turn up—*if* it was so valuable, or *if* it had ever existed. And with the whisperings went chucklings and nudgings and winks, and such things have an effect. The twins considered that success in the election would reinstate them, and that defeat would work them irreparable damage. Therefore they worked hard, but not harder than Judge Driscoll and Tom worked against them in the closing days of the canvass. Tom's conduct had remained so letter-perfect during two whole months, now, that his uncle not only trusted him with money with which to persuade voters, but trusted him to go and get it himself out of the safe in the private sitting-room.

The closing speech of the campaign was made by Judge Driscoll, and he made it against both of the foreigners. It was disastrously effective. He poured out rivers of ridicule upon them, and forced the big mass-meeting to laugh and applaud. He scoffed at them as adventurers, mountebanks, side-show riffraff, dime-museum freaks; he assailed their showy titles with mea-sureless derision; he said they were back-alley barbers disguised as nobilities, peanut-peddlers masquerading as gentlemen, organ-grinders bereft of their brother monkey. At last he stopped and stood still. He waited until the place had become absolutely silent and expectant, then he delivered his deadliest shot; delivered it with ice-cold seriousness and deliberation, with a significant emphasis upon the closing words: he said that he believed that the reward offered for the lost knife was humbug and buncombe, and that its owner would know where to find it whenever he should have occasion *to assassinate somebody*.

Then he stepped from the stand, leaving a startled and impressive hush behind him instead of the customary explosion of cheers and party cries.

The strange remark flew far and wide over the town and made an ex-traordinary sensation. Everybody was asking, "What could he mean by that?"

And everybody went on asking that question, but in vain; for the Judge only said he knew what he was talking about, and stopped there; Tom said he hadn't any idea what his uncle meant, and Wilson, whenever he was asked what he thought it meant, parried the question by asking the questioner that *he* thought it meant.

Wilson was elected, the twins were defeated—crushed, in fact, and left forlorn and substantially friendless. Tom went back to St. Louis happy.

Dawson's Landing had a week of repose, now, and it needed it. But it was in an expectant state, for the air was full of rumors of a new deal. Judge Driscoll's election labors had prostrated him, but it was said that as soon as he was well enough to entertain a challenge he would get one from Count Luigi.

The brothers withdrew entirely from society, and nursed their humilia-tion in privacy. They avoided the people, and went out for exercise only late at night, when the streets were deserted.

□ XVIII □

ROXANA COMMANDS

Gratitude and treachery are merely the two extremities of the same procession. You have seen all of it that is worth staying for when the band and the gaudy officials have gone by.
—PUDD'NHEAD WILSON'S CALENDAR.

Thanksgiving Day. *Let all give humble, hearty, and sincere thanks, now, but the turkeys. In the island of Fiji they do not use turkeys; they use plumbers. It does not become you and me to sneer at Fiji.*
—PUDD'NHEAD WILSON'S CALENDAR.

The Friday after the election was a rainy one in St. Louis. It rained all day long, and rained hard, apparently trying its best to wash that soot-blackened town white, but of course not succeeding. Toward midnight Tom Driscoll arrived at his lodgings from the theater in the heavy downpour, and closed his umbrella and let himself in; but when he would have shut the door, he found that there was another person entering—doubtless another lodger; this person closed the door and tramped up-stairs behind Tom. Tom found his door in the dark, and entered it and turned up the gas. When he faced about, lightly whistling, he saw the back of a man. The man was closing and locking his door for him. His whistle faded out and he felt uneasy. The man turned around, a wreck of shabby old clothes, sodden with rain and all a-drip, and showed a black face under an old slouch hat. Tom was frightened. He tried to order the man out, but the words refused to come, and the other man got the start. He said, in a low voice:

"Keep still—I's yo' mother!"

Tom sunk in a heap on a chair, and gasped out:

"It was mean of me, and base—I know it; but I meant it for the best, I did indeed—I can swear it."

Roxana stood awhile looking mutely down on him while he writhed in shame and went on incoherently babbling self-accusations mixed with pitiful attempts at explanation and palliation of his crime; then she seated herself and took off her hat, and her unkempt masses of long brown hair tumbled down about her shoulders.

"It ain't no fault o' yo'n dat dat ain't gray," she said sadly, noticing the hair.

"I know it, I know it! I'm a scoundrel. But I swear I meant it for the best. It was a mistake, of course, but I thought it was for the best, I truly did."

Roxy began to cry softly, and presently words began to find their way out between her sobs. They were uttered lamentingly, rather than angrily:

"Sell a pusson down de river—*down de river!*—for de bes'! I wouldn't treat a dog so! I is all broke down en wore out, now, en so I reckon it ain't in me to storm aroun' no mo', like I used to when I 'uz trompled on en 'bused. I don't know—but maybe it's so. Leastways, I's suffered so much dat mournin' seem to come mo' handy to me now den stormin'."

These words should have touched Tom Driscoll, but, if they did, that effect was obliterated by a stronger one—one which removed the heavy weight of fear which lay upon him, and gave his crushed spirit a most grateful rebound, and filled all his small soul with a deep sense of relief. But he kept prudently still, and ventured no comment. There was a voiceless interval of some duration, now, in which no sounds were heard but the beating of the rain upon the panes, the sighing and complaining of the winds, and now and then a muffled sob from Roxana. The sobs became more and more infrequent, and at last ceased. Then the refugee began to talk again.

"Shet down dat light a little. More. More yit. A pusson dat is hunted don't like de light. Dah—dat'll do. I kin see whah you is, en dat's enough. I's gwyne to tell you de tale, en cut it jes as short as I kin, en den I'll tell you what you's got to do. Dat man dat bought me ain't a bad man; he's good enough, as planters goes; en if he could 'a' had his way I'd 'a' be'n a houseservant in his fambly en be'n comfortable: but his wife she was a Yank, en not right down goodlookin', en she riz up agin me straight off; so den dey sent me out to de quarter 'mongst de common fiel' han's. Dat woman warn't satisfied even wid dat, but she worked up de overseer agin me, she 'uz dat jealous en hateful; so de overseer he had me out befo' day in de mawnin's en worked me de whole long day as long as dey 'uz any light to see by; en many's de lashin's I got 'ca'se I couldn't come up to de work o' de stronges'. Dat overseer wuz a Yank, too, outen New Englan', en anybody down South kin tell you what dat means. *Dey* knows how to work a nigger to death, en dey knows how to whale 'em, too—whale 'em till dey backs is welted like a washboard. 'Long at fust my marster say de good word for me to de overseer, but dat 'uz bad for me; for de mistis she fine it out, en arter dat I jis ketched it at every turn—dey warn't no mercy for me no mo'."

Tom's heart was fired—with fury against the planter's wife; and he said to himself, "But for that meddlesome fool, everything would have gone all right." He added a deep and bitter curse against her.

The expression of this sentiment was fiercely written in his face, and stood thus revealed to Roxana by a white glare of lightning which turned the somber dusk of the room into dazzling day at that moment. She was pleased—pleased and grateful; for did not that expression show that her child was capable of grieving for his mother's wrongs and of feeling resentment toward her persecutors?—a thing which she had been doubting. But her flash of happiness was only a flash, and went out again and left her spirit dark; for she said to herself, "He sole me down de river—he can't feel for a body long: dis 'll pass en go." Then she took up her tale again.

" 'Bout ten days ago I 'uz sayin' to myself dat I couldn't las' many mo' weeks I 'uz so wore out wid de awful work en de lashin's, en so downhearted en misable. En I didn't care no mo', nuther—life warn't wuth noth'n' to me, if I got to go on like dat. Well, when a body is in a frame o' mine like dat, what do a body care what a body do? Dey was a little sickly nigger wench 'bout ten year ole dat 'uz good to me, en hadn't no mammy, po' thing, en I loved her en she loved me; en she come out whah I 'uz workin', en she had a roasted tater, en tried to slip it to me—robbin' herself, you see, 'ca'se she knowed de overseer didn't gimme enough to eat—en he ketched her at it, en give her a lick acrost de back wid his stick, which 'uz as thick as a broom-handle, en she drop' screamin' on de groun', en squirmin' en wallerin' aroun' in de dust like a spider dat's got crippled. I couldn't stan' it. All de hell-fire dat 'uz ever in my heart flame' up, en I snatch de stick outen his han' en laid him flat. He laid dah moanin' en cussin', en all out of his head, you know, en de niggers 'uz plumb sk'yerd to death. Dey gathered roun' him to he'p him, en I jumped on his hoss en took out for de river as tight as I could go. I knowed what dey would do wid me. Soon as he got well he would start in en work me to death if marster let him; en if dey didn't do that, dey'd sell me furder down de river, en dat's de same thing. So I 'lowed to drown myself en git out o' my troubles. It 'uz git'n' towards dark. I 'uz at de river in two minutes. Den I see a canoe, en I says dey ain't no use to drown myself tell I got to; so I ties de hoss in de edge o' de timber en shove out down de river, keepin' in under de shelter o' de bluff bank en prayin' for de dark to shet down quick. I had a pow'ful good start, 'ca'se de big house 'uz three mile back f'om de river en on'y de work-mules to ride dah on, en on'y niggers to ride 'em en *dey* warn't gwyne to hurry—dey'd gimme all de chance dey could. Befo' a body could go to de house en back it would be long pas' dark, en dey couldn't track de hoss en fine out which way I went tell mawnin', en de niggers would tell 'em all de lies dey could 'bout it.

"Well, de dark come, en I went on a-spinning' down de river. I paddled mo'n two hours, den I warn't worried no mo', so I quit paddlin', en floated down de current, considerin' what I 'uz gwyne to do if I didn't have to drown myself. I made up some plans, en floated along, turnin' 'em over in my mine. Well, when it 'uz a little pas' midnight, as I reckoned, en I had come fifteen or twenty mile, I see de lights of a steamboat layin' at de bank, whah dey warn't no town en no wood-yard, en putty soon I ketched de shape o' de chimbly-tops agin de stars, en de good gracious me, I 'most jumped out o' my skin for joy! It 'uz *Gran' Mogul*—I 'uz chambermaid on her for eight seasons

in de Cincinnati en Orleans trade. I slid 'long pas'—don't see nobody stirrin'
nowhah—hear 'em a-hammerin' away in de engine-room, den I knowed what
de matter was—some o' de machinery's broke. I got asho' below de boat en
turn' de canoe loose, den I goes 'long up, en dey 'uz jes one plank out, en I
step' 'board de boat. It 'uz pow'ful hot, deck-han's en roustabouts 'uz
sprawled aroun' asleep on de fo'cas'l', de second mate, Jim Bangs, he sot dah
on de bitts wid his head down, asleep—'ca'se dat's de way de second mate
stan' de cap'n's watch!— en de ole watchman, Billy Hatch, he 'uz a-noddin'
on de companionway;—en I knowed 'em all; 'en, lan', but dey did look good!
I says to myself, I wished old marster'd come along *now* en try to take me—
bless yo' heart, I's 'mong frien's, I is. So I tromped right along 'mongst 'em,
en went up on de b'iler-deck en 'way back aft to de ladies' cabin guard, en sot
down dah in de same cheer dat I'd sot in 'mos' a hund'd million times, I
reckon; en it 'uz jist home ag'in, I tell you!

"In 'bout an hour I heard de ready-bell jingle, en den de racket begin.
Putty soon I hear de gong strike. 'Set her back on de outside,' I says to myself—'I reckon I knows dat music!' I hear de gong ag'in. 'Come ahead on de
inside,' I says. Gong ag'in. 'Stop de outside.' Gong ag'in. 'Come ahead on de
outside—now we's pinted for Sent Louis, en I's outer de woods en ain't got
to drown myself at all.' I knowed de *Mogul* 'uz in de Sent Louis trade now,
you see. It 'uz jes fair daylight when we passed our plantation, en I seed a
gang o' niggers en white folks huntin' up en down de sho', en troublin' dey-
selves a good deal 'bout me; but I warn't troublin' myself none 'bout dem.

" 'Bout dat time Sally Jackson, dat used to be my second chambermaid
en 'uz head chambermaid now, she come out on de guard, en 'uz pow'ful
glad to see me, en so 'uz all de officers; en I tole 'em I'd got kidnapped en sole
down de river, en dey made me up twenty dollahs en give it to me, en Sally
she rigged me out wid good clo'es, en when I got here I went straight to
whah you used to wuz, en den I come to dis house, en day say you's away but
'spected back every day; so I didn't dast to go down de river to Dawson's,
'ca'se I might miss you.

"Well, las' Monday I 'uz pass'n' by one o' dem places in Fourth Street
whah deh sticks up runaway-nigger bills, en he'ps to ketch 'em, en I seed my
marster! I 'mos' flopped down on de groun', I felt so gone. He had his back
to me, en 'uz talkin' to de man en givin' him some bills—nigger-bills, I
reckon, en I's de nigger. He's offerin' a reward—dat's it. Ain't I right, don't
you reckon?"

Tom had been gradually sinking into a state of ghastly terror, and he
said to himself, now: "I'm lost, no matter what turn things take! This man
has said to me that he thinks there was something suspicious about that sale.
He said he had a letter from a passenger on the *Grand Mogul* saying that
Roxy came here on that boat and that everybody on board knew all about the
case; so he says that her coming here instead of flying to a free state looks bad

for me, and that if I don't find her for him, and that pretty soon, he will make trouble for me. I never believed that story; I couldn't believe she would be so dead to all motherly instincts as to come here, knowing the risk she would run of getting me into irremediable trouble. And after all, here she is! And I stupidly swore I would help him find her, thinking it was a perfectly safe thing to promise. If I venture to deliver her up, she—she—but how can I help myself? I've got to do that or pay the money, and where's the money to come from? I—I—well, I should think that if he would swear to treat her kindly hereafter—and she says, herself, that he is a good man—and if he would swear to never allow her to be overworked, or ill fed, or—"

A flash of lightning exposed Tom's pallid face, drawn and rigid with these worrying thoughts. Roxana spoke up sharply now, and there was apprehension in her voice:

"Turn up dat light! I want to see yo' face better. Dah now—lemme look at you. Chambers, you's as white as yo' shirt! Has you seen dat man? Has he be'n to see you?"

"Ye-s."

"When?"

"Monday noon."

"Monday noon! Was he on my track?"

"He—well, he thought he was. That is, he hoped he was. This is the bill you saw." He took it out of his pocket.

"Read it to me!"

She was panting with excitement, and there was a dusky glow in her eyes that Tom could not translate with certainty, but there seemed to be something threatening about it. The handbill had the usual rude woodcut of a turbaned negro woman running, with the customary bundle on a stick over her shoulder, and the heading in bold type, "$100 REWARD." Tom read the bill aloud—at least the part that described Roxana and named the master and his St. Louis address and the address of the Fourth Street agency; but he left out the item that applicants for the reward might also apply to Mr. Thomas Driscoll.

"Gimme de bill!"

Tom had folded it and was putting it in his pocket. He felt a chilly streak creeping down his back, but said as careless as he could:

"The bill? Why, it isn't any use to you, you can't read it. What do you want with it?"

"Gimme de bill!" Tom gave it to her, but with a reluctance which he could not entirely disguise. "Did you read it *all* to me?"

"Certainly I did."

"Hole up yo' han' en swah to it."

Tom did it. Roxana put the bill carefully away in her pocket, with her eyes fixed upon Tom's face all the while; then she said:

"Yo's lying!"

"What would I want to lie about it for?"

"I don't know—but you is. Dat's my opinion, anyways. But nemmine 'bout dat. When I seed dat man I 'uz dat sk'yerd dat I could sca'cely wabble home. Den I give a nigger man a dollar for dese clo'es, en I ain't be'n in a house sence, night ner day, till now. I blackened my face en laid hid in de cellar of a ole house dat's burnt down, daytimes, en robbed de sugar hogs-heads en grain-sacks on de wharf, nights, to git somethin' to eat, en never dast to try to buy noth'n', en I's mos' starved. En I never dast come near dis place till dis rainy night, when dey ain't no people roun' sca'cely. But to-night I be'n a-stannin' in de dark alley ever sence night come, waitin' for you to go by. En here I is."

She fell to thinking. Presently she said:

"You seed dat man at noon, las' Monday?"

"Yes."

"I seed him de middle o' dat arternoon. He hunted you up, didn't he?"

"Yes."

"Did he give you de bill dat time?"

"No, he hadn't got it printed yet."

Roxana darted a suspicious glance at him.

"Did you he'p him fix up de bill?"

Tom cursed himself for making that stupid blunder, and tried to rectify it by saying he remembered, now, that it *was* at noon Monday that the man gave him the bill. Roxana said:

"You's lyin' ag'in, sho." Then she straightened up and raised her finger:

"Now den! I's gwyne to ask you a question, en I wants to know how you's gwyne to get aroun' it. You knowed he 'uz arter me; en if you run off, 'stid o' stayin' here to he'p him, he'd know dey 'uz somethin' wrong 'bout dis business, en den he would inquire 'bout you, en dat would take him to yo' uncle, en yo' uncle would read de bill en see dat you be'n sellin' a free nigger down de river, en you know *him,* I reckon! He'd t'ar up de will en kick you outen de house. Now, den, you answer me dis question: Hain't you tole dat man dat I would be sho' to come here, and den you would fix it so he could set a trap en ketch me?"

Tom recognized that neither lies nor argument could help him any longer—he was in a vise, with the screw turned on, and out of it there was no budging. His face began to take on an ugly look, and presently he said, with a snarl:

"Well, what could I do? You see, yourself, that I was in his grip and couldn't get out."

Roxy scorched him with a scornful gaze awhile, then she said:

"What could you do? You could be Judas to yo' own mother to save yo' wuthless hide! Would anybody b'lieve it? No—a dog couldn't! You is de low-downest orneriest hound dat was ever pup'd into dis worl'—en I's 'sponsible for it!"—and she spat on him.

He made no effort to resent this. Roxy reflected a moment, then she said:

"Now I'll tell you what you's gwyne to do. You's gwyne to give dat man de money dat you's got laid up, en make him wait till you kin go to de Jedge en git de res' en buy me free ag'in."

"Thunder! what are you thinking of? Go and ask him for three hundred dollars and odd? What would I tell him I want with it, pray?"

Roxy's answer was delivered in a serene and level voice:

"You'll tell him you's sole me to pay you' gamblin' debts en dat you lied to me en was a villain, en dat I 'quires you to git dat money en buy me back ag'in."

"Why, you've gone stark mad! He would tear the will to shreds in a minute—don't you know that?"

"Yes, I does."

"Then you don't believe I'm idiot enough to go to him, do you?"

"I don't b'lieve nothin' 'bout it—I *knows* you's a-goin'. I knows it 'ca'se you knows dat if you don't raise dat money I'll go to him myself, en den he'll sell *you* down de river, en you kin see how you like it!"

Tom rose, trembling and excited, and there was an evil light in his eye. He strode to the door and said he must get out of this suffocating place for a moment and clear his brain in the fresh air so that he could determine what to do. The door wouldn't open. Roxy smiled grimly, and said:

"I's got de key, honey—set down. You needn't cle'r up yo' brain none to find out what you gwyne to do. I knows what you's gwyne to do." Tom sat down and began to pass his hands through his hair with a helpless and desperate air. Roxy said, "Is dat man in dis house?"

Tom glanced up with a surprised expression, and asked:

"What gave you such an idea?"

"You done it. Gwyne out to cle'r yo' brain! In de fust place you ain't got none to cle'r, en in de second place yo' ornery eye tole on you. You's de lowdownest hound dat ever—but I done tole you dat befo'. Now den, dis is Friday. You kin fix it up wid dat man, en tell him you's gwyne away to git de res' o' de money, en dat you'll be back wid it nex' Tuesday, or maybe Wednesday. You understan'?"

Tom answered sullenly:

"Yes."

"En when you gits de new bill o' sale dat sells me to my own self, take en send it in de mail to Mr. Pudd'nhead Wilson, en write on de back dat he's to keep it tell I come. You understan'?"

"Yes."

"Dat's all den. Take yo' umbreller, en put on yo' hat."

"Why?"

"Beca'se you's gwyne to see me home to de wharf. You see dis knife? I's toted it aroun' sence de day I seed dat man en bought dese clo'es en it. If he ketch me, I's gwyne to kill myself wid it. Now start along, en go sof', en lead de way; en if you gives a sign in dis house, or if anybody comes up to you in de street, I's gwyne to jam it right into you. Chambers, does you b'lieve me when I says dat?"

"It's no use to bother me with that question. I know your word's good."

"Yes, it's diff'rent from yo'n! Shet de light out en move along—here's de key."

They were not followed. Tom trembled every time a late straggler brushed by them on the street, and half expected to feel the cold steel in his back. Roxy was right at his heels and always in reach. After tramping a mile they reached a wide vacancy on the deserted wharves, and in this dark and rainy desert they parted.

As Tom trudged home his mind was full of dreary thoughts and wild plans; but at last he said to himself, wearily:

"There is but the one way out. I must follow her plan. But with a variation—I will not ask for the money and ruin myself; I will *rob* the old skinflint."

□ XIX □

THE PROPHECY REALIZED

Few things are harder to put up with than the annoyance of a good example.

—PUDD'NHEAD WILSON'S CALENDAR.

It were not best that we should all think alike; it is difference of opinion that makes horse-races.

—PUDD'NHEAD WILSON'S CALENDAR.

Dawson's Landing was comfortably finishing its season of dull repose and waiting patiently for the duel. Count Luigi was waiting, too; but not patiently, rumor said. Sunday came, and Luigi insisted on having his challenge conveyed. Wilson carried it. Judge Driscoll declined to fight with an assassin—"that is," he added significantly, "in the field of honor."

Elsewhere, of course, he would be ready. Wilson tried to convince him that if he had been present himself when Angelo told about the homicide committed by Luigi, he would not have considered the act discreditable to Luigi; but the obstinate old man was not to be moved.

Wilson went back to his principal and reported the failure of his mission. Luigi was incensed, and asked how it could be that the old gentleman, who was by no means dull-witted, held his trifling nephew's evidence and inferences to be of more value than Wilson's. But Wilson laughed, and said:

"That is quite simple; that is easily explicable. I am not his doll—his baby—his infatuation: his nephew is. The Judge and his late wife never had any children. The Judge and his wife were past middle age when this treasure fell into their lap. One must make allowances for a parental instinct that has been starving for twenty-five or thirty years. It is famished, it is crazed with hunger by that time, and will be entirely satisifed with anything that comes handy; its taste is atrophied, it can't tell mudcat from shad. A devil born to a young couple is measurably recognizable by them as a devil before long, but a devil adopted by an old couple is an angel to them, and remains so, through thick and thin. Tom is this old man's angel; he is infatuated with him. Tom can persuade him into things which other people can't—not all things; I don't mean that, but a good many—particularly one class of things: the things that create or abolish personal partialities or prejudices in the old man's mind. The old man liked both of you. Tom conceived a hatred for you. That was enough; it turned the old man around at once. The oldest and strongest friendship must go to the ground when one of these late-adopted darlings throws a brick at it."

"It's a curious philosophy," said Luigi.

"It ain't a philosophy at all—it's a fact. And there is something pathetic and beautiful about it, too. I think there is nothing more pathetic than to see one of these poor old childless couples taking a menagerie of yelping little worthless dogs to their hearts; and then adding some cursing and squawking parrots and a jackass-voiced macaw; and next a couple of hundred screeching song-birds, and presently some fetid guinea-pigs and rabbits; and a howling colony of cats. It is all a groping and ignorant effort to construct out of base metal and brass filings, so to speak, something to take the place of that golden treasure denied them by Nature, a child. But this is a digression. The unwritten law of this region requires you to kill Judge Driscoll on sight, and he and the community will expect that attention at your hands—though of course your own death by his bullet will answer every purpose. Look out for him! You are heeled—that is, fixed?"

"Yes; he shall have his opportunity. If he attacks me I will respond."

As Wilson was leaving, he said:

"The Judge is still a little used up by his campaign work, and will not get out for a day or so; but when he does get out, you want to be on the alert."

About eleven at night the twins went out for exercise, and started on a long stroll in the veiled moonlight.

Tom Driscoll had landed at Hackett's Store, two miles below Dawson's, just about half an hour earlier, the only passenger for that lonely spot, and had walked up the shore road and entered Judge Driscoll's house without having encountered any one either on the road or under the roof.

He pulled down his window-blinds and lighted his candle. He laid off his coat and hat and began his preparations. He unlocked his trunk and got his suit of girl's clothes out from under the male attire in it, and laid it by. Then he blacked his face with burnt cork and put the cork in his pocket. His plan was, to slip down to his uncle's private sitting-room below, pass into the bedroom, steal the safe-key from the old gentleman's clothes, and then go back and rob the safe. He took up his candle to start. His courage and confidence were high, up to this point, but both began to waver a little, now. Suppose he should make a noise, by some accident, and get caught—say, in the act of opening the safe? Perhaps it would be well to go armed. He took the Indian knife from its hiding-place, and felt a pleasant return of his wandering courage. He slipped stealthily down the narrow stair, his hair rising and his pulses halting at the slightest creak. When he was half-way down, he was disturbed to perceive that the landing below was touched by a faint glow of light. What could that mean? Was his uncle still up? No, that was not likely; he must have left his night taper there when he went to bed. Tom crept on down, pausing at every step to listen. He found the door standing open, and glanced in. What he saw pleased him beyond measure. His uncle was alseep on the sofa; on a small table at the head of the sofa a lamp was burning low, and by it stood the old man's small tin cash-box, closed. Near the box was a pile of bank-notes and a piece of paper covered with figures in pencil. The safe-door was not open. Evidently the sleeper had wearied himself with work upon his finances, and was taking a rest.

Tom set his candle on the stairs, and began to make his way toward the pile of notes, stooping low as he went. When he was passing his uncle, the old man stirred in his sleep, and Tom stopped instantly—stopped, and softly drew the knife from its sheath, with his heart thumping, and his eyes fastened upon his benefactor's face. After a moment or two he ventured forward again—one step—reached for his prize and seized it, dropping the knife-sheath. Then he felt the old man's strong grip upon him, and a wild cry of "Help! help!" rang in his ear. Without hesitation he drove the knife home—and was free. Some of the notes escaped from his left hand and fell in the blood on the floor. He dropped the knife and snatched them up and started to fly; transferred them to his left hand, and seized the knife again, in his fright and confusion, but remembered himself and flung it from him, as being a dangerous witness to carry away with him.

He jumped for the stair-foot, and closed the door behind him; and as he snatched his candle and fled upward, the stillness of the night was broken by the sound of urgent footsteps approaching the house. In another moment he was in his room and the twins were standing aghast over the body of the murdered man!

Tom put on his coat, buttoned his hat under it, threw on his suit of girl's clothes, dropped the veil, blew out his light, locked the room door by which he had just entered, taking the key, passed through his other door into the back hall, locked that door and kept the key, then worked his way along in the dark and descended the back stairs. He was not expecting to meet anybody, for all interest was centered in the other part of the house, now; his calculation proved correct. By the time he was passing through the back yard, Mrs. Pratt, her servants, and a dozen half-dressed neighbors had joined the twins and the dead, and accessions were still arriving at the front door.

As Tom, quaking as with a palsy, passed out at the gate, three women came flying from the house on the opposite side of the lane. They rushed by him and in at the gate, asking him what the trouble was there, but not waiting for an answer. Tom said to himself, "Those old maids waited to dress—they did the same thing the night Stevens' house burned down next door." In a few minutes he was in the haunted house. He lighted a candle and took off his girl clothes. There was blood on him all down his left side, and his right hand was red with the stains of the blood-stained notes which he had crushed in it; but otherwise he was free from this sort of evidence. He cleansed his hand on the straw, and cleaned most of the smut from his face. Then he burned his male and female attire to ashes, scattered the ashes, and put on a disguise proper for a tramp. He blew out his light, went below, and was soon loafing down the river road with the intent to borrow and use one of Roxy's devices. He found a canoe and paddled off down-stream, setting the canoe adrift as dawn approached, and making his way by land to the next village, where he kept out of sight till a transient steamer came along, and then took deck-passage for St. Louis. He was ill at ease until Dawson's Landing was behind him; then he said to himself, "All the detectives on earth couldn't trace me now; there's not a vestige of a clue left in the world; that homicide will take its place with the permanent mysteries, and people won't get done trying to guess out the secret of it for fifty years."

In St. Louis, next morning, he read this brief telegram in the papers—dated at Dawson's Landing:

> Judge Driscoll, an old and respected citizen, was assassinated here about midnight by a profligate Italian nobleman or barber on account of a quarrel growing out of the recent election. The assassin will probably be lynched.

"One of the twins!" soliloquized Tom. "How lucky! It is the knife that has done him this grace. We never know when fortune is trying to favor us. I actually cursed Pudd'nhead Wilson in my heart for putting it out of my power to sell that knife. I take it back, now."

Tom was now rich and independent. He arranged with the planter, and mailed to Wilson the new bill of sale which sold Roxana to herself; then he telegraphed his Aunt Pratt:

> Have seen the awful news in the papers and am almost prostrated with grief. Shall start by packet to-day. Try to bear up till I come.

When Wilson reached the house of mourning and had gathered such details as Mrs. Pratt and the rest of the crowd could tell him, he took command as mayor, and gave orders that nothing should be touched, but everything left as it was until Justice Robinson should arrive and take the proper measures as coroner. He cleared everybody out of the room but the twins and himself. The sheriff soon arrived and took the twins away to jail. Wilson told them to keep heart, and promised to do his best in their defense when the case should come to trial. Justice Robinson came presently, and with him Constable Blake. They examined the room thoroughly. They found the knife and the sheath. Wilson noticed that there were finger-prints on the knife-handle. That pleased him, for the twins had required the earliest comers to make a scrutiny of their hands and clothes, and neither these people nor Wilson himself had found any blood-stains upon them. Could there be a possibility that the twins had spoken the truth when they said they found the man dead when they ran into the house in answer to the cry for help? He thought of that mysterious girl at once. But this was not the sort of work for a girl to be engaged in. No matter; Tom Driscoll's room must be examined.

After the coroner's jury had viewed the body and its surroundings, Wilson suggested a search up-stairs, and he went along. The jury forced an entrance to Tom's room, but found nothing, of course.

The coroner's jury found that the homicide was committed by Luigi, and that Angelo was accessory to it.

The town was bitter against the unfortunates, and for the first few days after the murder they were in constant danger of being lynched. The grand jury presently indicted Luigi for murder in the first degree, and Angelo as accessory before the fact. The twins were transferred from the city jail to the county prison to await trial.

Wilson examined the finger-marks on the knife-handle and said to himself, "Neither of the twins made those marks." Then manifestly there was another person concerned, either in his own interest or as hired assassin.

But who could it be? That, he must try to find out. The safe was not open, the cash-box was closed, and had three thousand dollars in it. Then robbery was not the motive, and revenge was. Where had the murdered man an enemy except Luigi? There was but that one person in the world with a deep grudge against him.

The mysterious girl! The girl was a great trial to Wilson. If the motive had been robbery, the girl might answer; but there wasn't any girl that would want to take this old man's life for revenge. He had no quarrels with girls; he was a gentleman.

Wilson had perfect tracings of the finger-marks of the knife-handle; and among his glass records he had a great array of the finger-prints of women and girls, collected during the last fifteen or eighteen years; but he scanned them in vain, they successfully withstood every test; among them were no duplicates of the prints on the knife.

The presence of the knife on the stage of the murder was a worrying circumstance for Wilson. A week previously he had as good as admitted to himself that he believed Luigi had possessed such a knife, and that he still possessed it notwithstanding his pretense that it had been stolen. And now here was the knife, and with it the twins. Half the town had said the twins were humbugging when they claimed that they had lost their knife, and now these people were joyful, and said, "I told you so!"

If their finger-prints had been on the handle—but it was useless to bother any further about that; the finger-prints on the handle were *not* theirs—that he knew perfectly.

Wilson refused to suspect Tom; for first, Tom couldn't murder anybody—he hadn't character enough; secondly, if he could murder a person he wouldn't select his doting benefactor and nearest relative; thirdly, self-interest was in the way; for while the uncle lived, Tom was sure of a free support and a chance to get the destroyed will revived again, but with the uncle gone, that chance was gone, too. It was true the will had really been revived, as was now discovered, but Tom could not have been aware of it, or he would have spoken of it, in his native talky, unsecretive way. Finally, Tom was in St. Louis when the murder was done, and got the news out of the morning journals, as was shown by his telegram to his aunt. These speculations were unemphasized sensations rather than articulated thoughts, for Wilson would have laughed at the idea of seriously connecting Tom with the murder.

Wilson regarded the case of the twins as desperate—in fact, about hopeless. For he argued that if a confederate was not found, an enlightened Missouri jury would hang them, sure; if a confederate was found, that would not improve the matter, but simply furnish one more person for the sheriff to hang. Nothing could save the twins but the discovery of a person who did the murder on his sole personal account—an undertaking which had all the aspect of the impossible. Still, the person who made the finger-prints must be sought. The twins might have no case *with* him, but they certainly would have none without him.

So Wilson mooned around, thinking, thinking, guessing, guessing, day and night, and arriving nowhere. Whenever he ran across a girl or a woman he was not acquainted with, he got her finger-prints, on one pretext or an-

other; and they always cost him a sigh when he got home, for they never tal-
lied with the finger-marks on the knife-handle.

As to the mysterious girl, Tom swore he knew no such girl, and did not
remember ever seeing a girl wearing a dress like the one described by Wilson.
He admitted that he did not always lock his room, and that sometimes the
servants forgot to lock the house doors; still, in his opinion the girl must
have made but few visits or she would have been discovered. When Wilson
tried to connect her with the stealing-raid, and thought she might have been
the old woman's confederate, if not the very thief herself disguised as an old
woman, Tom seemed struck, and also much interested, and said he would
keep a sharp eye out for this person or persons, although he was afraid that
she or they would be too smart to venture again into a town where everybody
would now be on the watch for a good while to come.

Everybody was pitying Tom, he looked so quiet and sorrowful, and
seemed to feel his great loss so deeply. He was playing a part, but it was not
all a part. The picture of his alleged uncle, as he had last seen him, was before
him in the dark pretty frequently, when he was awake, and called again in his
dreams, when he was asleep. He wouldn't go into the room where the tragedy had happened. This charmed the doting Mrs. Pratt, who realized now,
"as she had never done before," she said, what a sensitive and delicate nature
her darling had, and how he adored his poor uncle.

□   XX   □

THE MURDERER CHUCKLES

*Even the clearest and most perfect circumstantial evidence is likely to be at
fault, after all, and therefore ought to be received with great caution.
Take the case of any pencil, sharpened by any woman: if you have witnesses, you will find she did it with a knife; but if you take simply the
aspect of the pencil, you will say she did it with her teeth.*
—PUDD'NHEAD WILSON'S CALENDAR.

The weeks dragged along, no friend visiting the jailed twins but their counsel
and Aunt Patsy Cooper, and the day of trial came at last—the heaviest day in
Wilson's life; for with all his tireless diligence he had discovered no sign or
trace of the missing confederate. "Confederate" was the term he had long ago

privately accepted for that person—not as being unquestionably the right term, but as being at least possibly the right one, though he was never able to understand why the twins did not vanish and escape, as the confederate had done, instead of remaining by the murdered man and getting caught there.

The court-house was crowded, of course, and would remain so to the finish, for not only in the town itself, but in the country for miles around, the trial was the one topic of conversation among the people. Mrs. Pratt, in deep mourning, and Tom with a weed on his hat, had seats near Pembroke Howard, the public prosecutor, and back of them sat a great array of friends of the family. The twins had but one friend present to keep their counsel in countenance, their poor old sorrowing landlady. She sat near Wilson, and looked her friendliest. In the "nigger corner" sat Chambers; also Roxy, with good clothes on, and her bill of sale in her pocket. It was her most precious possession, and she never parted with it, day or night. Tom had allowed her thirty-five dollars a month ever since he came into his property, and had said that he and she ought to be grateful to the twins for making them rich; but had roused such a temper in her by this speech that he did not repeat the argument afterward. She said the old Judge had treated her child a thousand times better than he deserved, and had never done her an unkindness in his life; so she hated these outlandish devils for killing him, and shouldn't ever sleep satisfied till she saw them hanged for it. She was here to watch the trial, now, and was going to lift up just one "hooraw" over it if the County Judge put her in jail a year for it. She gave her turbaned head a toss and said, "Whan dat verdic' comes, I's gwyne to lif' dat *roof*, now, I *tell* you."

Pembroke Howard briefly sketched the State's case. He said he would show by a chain of circumstantial evidence without break or fault in it anywhere, that the principal prisoner at the bar committed the murder; that the motive was partly revenge, and partly a desire to take his own life out of jeopardy, and that his brother, by his presence, was a consenting accessory to the crime; a crime which was the basest known to the calendar of human misdeeds—assassination; that it was conceived by the blackest of hearts and consummated by the cowardliest of hands; a crime which had broken a loving sister's heart, blighted the happiness of a young nephew who was as dear as a son, brought inconsolable grief to many friends, and sorrow and loss to the whole community. The utmost penalty of the outraged law would be exacted, and upon the accused, now present at the bar, that penalty would unquestionably be executed. He would reserve further remark until his closing speech.

He was strongly moved, and so also was the whole house; Mrs. Pratt and several other women were weeping when he sat down, and many an eye that was full of hate was riveted upon the unhappy prisoners.

Witness after witness was called by the State, and questioned at length; but the cross-questioning was brief. Wilson knew they could furnish nothing valuable for his side. People were sorry for Pudd'nhead; his budding career would get hurt by this trial.

Several witnesses swore they heard Judge Driscoll say in his public speech that the twins would be able to find their lost knife again when they needed it to assassinate somebody with. This was not news, but now it was seen to have been sorrowfully prophetic, and a profound sensation quivered through the hushed court-room when those dismal words were repeated.

The public prosecutor rose and said that it was within his knowledge, through a conversation held with Judge Driscoll on the last day of his life, that counsel for the defense had brought him a challenge from the person charged at this bar with murder; that he had refused to fight with a confessed assassin—"that is, on the field of honor," but had added significantly, that he would be ready for him elsewhere. Presumably, the person here charged with murder was warned that he must kill or be killed the first time he should meet Judge Driscoll. If counsel for the defense chose to let the statement stand so, he would not call him to the witness-stand. Mr. Wilson said he would offer no denial [Murmurs in the house—"It is geting worse and worse for Wilson's case."]

Mrs. Pratt testifed that she heard no outcry, and did not know what woke her up, unless it was the sound of rapid footsteps approaching the front door. She jumped up and ran out in the hall just as she was, and heard the footsteps flying up the front steps and then following behind her as she ran to the sitting-room. There she found the accused standing over her murdered brother. [Here she broke down and sobbed. Sensation in the court.] Resuming, she said the persons entering behind her were Mr. Rogers and Mr. Buckstone.

Cross-examined by Wilson, she said the twins proclaimed their innocence; declared that they had been taking a walk, and had hurried to the house in response to a cry for help which was so loud and strong that they had heard it at a considerable distance; that they begged her and the gentlemen just mentioned to examine their hands and clothes—which was done, and no blood-stains found.

Confirmatory evidence followed from Rogers and Buckstone.

The finding of the knife was verified, the advertisement minutely describing it and offering a reward for it was put in evidence, and its exact correspondence with that description proved. Then followed a few minor details, and the case for the State was closed.

Wilson said that he had three witnesses, the Misses Clarkson, who would testify that they met a veiled young woman leaving Judge Driscoll's premises by the back gate a few minutes after the cries for help were heard, and that their evidence, taken with certain circumstantial evidence which he would call the court's attention to, would in his opinion convince the court that there was still one person concerned in this crime who had not yet been found, and also that a stay of proceedings ought to be granted, in justice to his clients, until that person should be discovered. As it was late, he would ask leave to defer the examination of his three witnesses until the next morning.

The crowd poured out of the place and went flocking away in excited groups and couples, talking the events of the session over with vivacity and consuming interest, and everybody seemed to have had a satisfactory and enjoyable day except the accused, their counsel, and their old-lady friend. There was no cheer among these, and no substantial hope.

In parting with the twins Aunt Patsy did attempt a good night with a gay pretense of hope and cheer in it, but broke down without finishing.

Absolutely secure as Tom considered himself to be, the opening solemnities of the trial had nevertheless oppressed him with a vague uneasiness, his being a nature sensitive to even the smallest alarms; but from the moment that the poverty and weakness of Wilson's case lay exposed to the court, he was comfortable once more, even jubilant. He left the court-room sarcastically sorry for Wilson. "The Clarksons met an unknown woman in the back lane," he said to himself—"*that* is his case! I'll give him a century to find her in—a couple of them if he likes. A woman who doesn't exist any longer, and the clothes that gave her her sex burnt up and the ashes thrown away—oh, certainly, he'll find *her* easy enough!" This reflection set him to admiring, for the hundredth time, the shrewd ingenuities by which he had insured himself against detection—more, against even suspicion.

"Nearly always in cases like this there is some little detail or other overlooked, some wee little track or trace left behind, and detection follows; but here there's not even the faintest suggestion of a trace left. No more than a bird leaves when it flies through the air—yes, through the night, you may say. The man that can track a bird through the air in the dark and find that bird is the man to track me out and find the Judge's assassin—no other need apply. And that is the job that has been laid out for poor Pudd'nhead Wilson, of all people in the world! Lord, it will be pathetically funny to see him grubbing and groping after that woman that don't exist, and the right person sitting under his very nose all the time!" The more he thought the situation over, the more the humor of it struck him. Finally he said, "I'll never let him hear the last of that woman. Every time I catch him in company, to his dying day, I'll ask him in the guileless affectionate way that used to gravel him so when I inquired how his unborn law business was coming along, 'Got on her track yet—hey, Pudd'nhead?' " He wanted to laugh, but that would not have answered; there were people about, and he was mourning for his uncle. He made up his mind that it would be good entertainment to look in on Wilson that night and watch him worry over his barren law case and goad him with an exasperating word or two of sympathy and commiseration now and then.

Wilson wanted no supper, he had no appetite. He got out all the finger-prints of girls and women in his collection of records and pored gloomily over them an hour or more, trying to convince himself that that troublesome girl's marks were there somewhere and had been overlooked. But it was not so. He drew back his chair, clasped his hands over his head, and gave himself up to dull and arid musings.

Tom Driscoll dropped in, an hour after dark, and said with a pleasant laugh as he took a seat:

"Hello, we've gone back to the amusements of our days of neglect and obscurity for consolation, have we?" and he took up one of the glass strips and held it against the light to inspect it. "Come, cheer up, old man; there's no use in losing your grip and going back to this child's-play merely because this big sunspot is drifting across your shiny new disk. It'll pass, and you'll be all right again,"—and he laid the glass down. "Did you think you could win always?"

"Oh, no," said Wilson, with a sigh, "I didn't expect that, but I can't believe Luigi killed your uncle, and I feel very sorry for him. It makes me blue. And you would feel as I do, Tom, if you were not prejudiced against those young fellows."

"I don't know about that," and Tom's countenance darkened, for his memory reverted to his kicking; "I owe them no good will, considering the brunette one's treatment of me that night. Prejudice or no prejudice, Pudd'nhead, I don't like them, and when they get their deserts you're not going to find me sitting on the mourner's bench."

He took up another strip of glass, and exclaimed:

"Why, here's old Roxy's label! Are you going to ornament the royal palaces with nigger pawmarks, too? By the date here, I was seven months old when this was done, and she was nursing me and her little nigger cub. There's a line straight across her thumb-print. How comes that?" and Tom held out the piece of glass to Wilson.

"That is common," said the bored man, wearily. "Scar of a cut or a scratch, usually"—and he took the strip of glass indifferently, and raised it toward the lamp.

All the blood sunk suddenly out of his face; his hand quaked, and he gazed at the polished surface before him with the glassy stare of a corpse.

"Great Heavens, what's the matter with you, Wilson? Are you going to faint?"

Tom sprang for a glass of water and offered it, but Wilson shrank shuddering from him and said:

"No, no!—take it away!" His breast was rising and falling, and he moved his head about in a dull and wandering way, like a person who has been stunned. Presently he said, "I shall feel better when I get to bed; I have been overwrought to-day; yes, and overworked for many days."

"Then I'll leave you and let you get to your rest. Good night, old man."

But as Tom went out he couldn't deny himself a small parting gibe: "Don't take it so hard; a body can't win every time; you'll hang somebody yet."

Wilson muttered to himself, "It is no lie to say I am sorry I have to begin with you, miserable dog though you are!"

He braced himself up with a glass of cold whisky, and went to work again. He did not compare the new finger-marks unintentionally left by Tom a few minutes before on Roxy's glass with the tracings of the marks left on the knife-handle, there being no need of that (for his trained eye), but busied himself with another matter, muttering from time to time, "Idiot that I was!—nothing but a *girl* would do me—a man in girl's clothes never occurred to me." First, he hunted out the plate containing the finger-prints made by Tom when he was twelve years old, and laid it by itself; then he brought forth the marks made by Tom's baby fingers when he was a suckling of seven months, and placed these two plates with the one containing this subject's newly (and unconsciously) made record.

"Now the series is complete," he said with satisfaction, and sat down to inspect these things and enjoy them.

But his enjoyment was brief. He stared a considerable time at the three strips, and seemed stupefied with astonishment. At last he put them down and said, "I can't make it out at all—hang it, the baby's don't tally with the others!"

He walked the floor for half an hour puzzling over his enigma, then he hunted out two other glass plates.

He sat down and puzzled over these things a good while, but kept muttering, "It's no use; I can't understand it. They don't tally right, and yet I'll swear the names and dates are right, and so of course they *ought* to tally. I never labeled one of these things carelessly in my life. There is a most extraordinary mystery here."

He was tired out, now, and his brains were beginning to clog. He said he would sleep himself fresh, and then see what he could do with this riddle. He slept through a troubled and unrestful hour, then unconsciousness began to shred away, and presently he rose drowsily to a sitting posture. "Now what was that dream?" he said, trying to recall it; "what was that dream?—it seemed to unravel the puz—"

He landed in the middle of the floor at a bound, without finishing the sentence, and ran and turned up his lights and seized his "records." He took a single swift glance at them and cried out:

"It's so! Heavens, what a revelation! And for twenty-three years no man has ever suspected it!"

□ XXI □

DOOM

He is useless on top of the ground; he ought to be under it, inspiring the cabbages.

—PUDD'NHEAD WILSON'S CALENDAR.

April 1. *This is the day upon which we are reminded of what we are on the other three hundred and sixty-four.*

—PUDD'NHEAD WILSON'S CALENDAR.

Wilson put on enough clothes for business purposes and went to work under a high pressure of steam. He was awake all over. All sense of weariness had been swept away by the invigorating refreshment of the great and hopeful discovery which he had made. He made fine and accurate reproductions of a number of his "records," and then enlarged them on a scale of ten to one with his pantograph. He did these pantograph enlargements on sheets of white cardboard, and made each individual line of the bewildering maze of whorls or curves or loops which constituted the "pattern" or a "record" stand out bold and black by reinforcing it with ink. To the untrained eye the collection of delicate originals made by the human finger on the glass plates looked about alike; but when enlarged ten times they resembled the markings of a block of wood that has been sawed across the grain, and the dullest eye could detect at a glance, and at a distance of many feet, that no two of the patterns were alike. When Wilson had at last finished his tedious and difficult work, he arranged its results according to a plan in which a progressive order and sequence was a principal feature; then he added to the batch several pantograph enlargements which he had made from time to time in bygone years.

The night was spent and the day well advanced, now. By the time he had snatched a trifle of breakfast it was nine o'clock, and the court was ready to begin its sitting. He was in his place twelve minutes later with his "records."

Tom Driscoll caught a slight glimpse of the records, and nudged his nearest friend and said, with a wink, "Pudd'nhead's got a rare eye to business—thinks that as long as he can't win his case it's at least a noble good chance to advertise his palace-window decorations without any expense." Wilson was informed that his witnesses had been delayed, but would arrive presently; but he rose and said he should probably not have occasion to make use of their testimony. [An amused murmur ran through the room—"It's a clean backdown! he gives up without hitting a lick!"] Wilson continued—"I have other testimony—and better. [This compelled interest, and evoked murmurs of surprise that had a detectable ingredient of disappointment in them.] If I seem to be springing this evidence upon the court, I offer as my justification for this, that I did not discover its existence until late last night, and have been engaged in examining and classifying it ever since, until half an hour ago. I shall offer it presently; but first I wish to say a few preliminary words.

"May it please the court, the claim given the front place, the claim most persistently urged, the claim most strenuously and I may even say aggressively and defiantly insisted upon by the prosecution, is this—that the person whose hand left the blood-stained finger-prints upon the handle of the Indian knife is the person who committed the murder." Wilson paused, during several moments, to give impressiveness to what he was about to say, and then added tranquilly, *"We grant that claim."*

It was an electrical surprise. No one was prepared for such an admission. A buzz of astonishment rose on all sides, and people were heard to intimate that the overworked lawyer had lost his mind. Even the veteran judge, accustomed as he was to legal ambushes and masked batteries in criminal procedure, was not sure that his ears were not deceiving him, and asked counsel what it was he had said. Howard's impassive face betrayed no sign, but his attitude and bearing lost something of their careless confidence for a moment. Wilson resumed:

"We not only grant that claim, but we welcome it and strongly indorse it. Leaving that matter for the present, we will now proceed to consider other points in the case which we propose to establish by evidence, and shall include that one in the chain in its proper place."

He had made up his mind to try a few hardy guesses, in mapping out his theory of the origin and motive of the murder—guesses designed to fill up gaps in it—guesses which could help if they hit, and would probably do no harm if they didn't.

"To my mind, certain circumstances of the case before the court seem to suggest a motive for the homicide quite different from the one insisted on by the State. It is my conviction that the motive was not revenge, but robbery. It has been urged that the presence of the accused brothers in that fatal room, just after notification that one of them must take the life of Judge Driscoll or lose his own the moment the parties should meet, clearly signifies that the natural instinct of self-preservation moved my clients to go there secretly and save Count Luigi by destroying his adversary.

"Then why did they stay there, after the deed was done? Mrs. Pratt had time, although she did not hear the cry for help, but woke up some moments later, to run to that room—and there she found these men standing and making no effort to escape. If they were guilty, they ought to have been running out of the house at the same time that she was running to that room. If

they had had such a strong instinct toward self-preservation as to move them
to kill that unarmed man, what had become of it now, when it should have
been more alert than ever? Would any of us have remained there? Let us not
slander our intelligence to that degree.

"Much stress has been laid upon the fact that the accused offered a very
large reward for the knife with which this murder was done; that no thief
came forward to claim that extraordinary reward; that the latter fact was good
circumstantial evidence that the claim that the knife had been stolen was a
vanity and a fraud; that these details taken in connection with the memorable
and apparently prophetic speech of the deceased concerning that knife, and
the final discovery of that very knife in the fatal room where no living person
was found present with the slaughtered man but the owner of the knife and
his brother, form an indestructible chain of evidence which fixes the crime
upon those unfortunate strangers.

"But I shall presently ask to be sworn, and shall testify that there was a
large reward offered for the *thief,* also; that it was offered secretly and not advertised; that this fact was indiscreetly mentioned—or at least tacitly admitted—in what was supposed to be safe circumstances, but may *not* have been.
The thief may have been present himself. [Tom Driscoll had been looking at
the speaker, but dropped his eyes at this point.] In that case he would retain
the knife in his possession, not daring to offer it for sale, or for pledge in a
pawnshop. [There was a nodding of heads among the audience by way of admission that this was not a bad stroke.] I shall prove to the satisfaction of the
jury that there *was* a person in Judge Driscoll's room several minutes before
the accused entered it. [This produced a strong sensation; the last drowsy-
head in the court-room roused up now, and made preparation to listen.] If it
shall seem necessary, I will prove by the Misses Clarkson that they met a
veiled person—ostensibly a woman—coming out of the back gate a few minutes after the cry for help was heard. This person was not a woman, but a
man dressed in woman's clothes." Another sensation. Wilson had his eye on
Tom when he hazarded this guess, to see what effect it would produce. He
was satisfied with the result, and said to himself, "It was a success—he's hit!"

"The object of that person in that house was robbery, not murder. It is
true that the safe was not open, but there was an ordinary tin cash-box on the
table, with three thousand dollars in it. It is easily supposable that the thief
was concealed in the house; that he knew of this box, and of its owner's habit
of counting its contents and arranging his accounts at night—if he had that
habit, which I do not assert, of course;—that he tried to take the box while
its owner slept, but made a noise and was seized, and had to use the knife to
save himself from capture; and that he fled without his booty because he
heard help coming.

"I have now done with my theory, and will proceed to the evidences by
which I propose to try to prove its soundness." Wilson took up several of his

strips of glass. When the audience recognized these familiar mementoes of Pudd'nhead's old-time childish "puttering" and folly, the tense and funereal interest vanished out of their faces, and the house burst into volleys of relieving and refreshing laughter, and Tom chirked and joined in the fun himself; but Wilson was apparently not disturbed. He arranged his records on the table before him, and said:

"I beg the indulgence of the court while I make a few remarks in explanation of some evidence which I am about to introduce, and which I shall presently ask to be allowed to verify under oath on the witness-stand. Every human being carries with him from his cradle to his grave certain physical marks which do not change their character, and by which he can always be identified—and that without shade of doubt or question. These marks are his signature, his physiological autograph, so to speak, and this autograph cannot be counterfeited, nor can he disguise it or hide it away, nor can it become illegible by the wear and mutations of time. This signature is not his face— age can change that beyond recognition; it is not his hair, for that can fall out; it is not his height, for duplicates of that exist; it is not his form, for duplicates of that exist also, whereas this signature is each man's very own— there is no duplicate of it among the swarming populations of the globe! [The audience were interested once more.]

"This autograph consists of the delicate lines or corrugations with which Nature marks the insides of the hands and the soles of the feet. If you will look at the balls of your fingers—you that have very sharp eyesight—you will observe that these dainty curving lines lie close together, like those that indicate the borders of oceans in maps, and that they form various clearly defined patterns, such as arches, circles, long curves, whorls, etc., and that these patterns differ on the different fingers. [Every man in the room had his hand up to the light, now, and his head canted to one side, and was minutely scrutinizing the balls of his fingers; there were whispered ejaculations of "Why, it's so—I never noticed that before!"] The patterns on the right hand are not the same as those on the left. [Ejaculations of "Why, that's so, too!"] Taken finger for finger, your patterns differ from your neighbor's. [Comparisons were made all over the house—even the judge and jury were absorbed in this curious work.] The patterns of a twin's right hand are not the same as those on his left. One twin's patterns are never the same as his fellow-twin's patterns—the jury will find that the patterns upon the finger-balls of the accused follow this rule. [An examination of the twins' hands was begun at once.] You have often heard of twins who were so exactly alike that when dressed alike their own parents could not tell them apart. Yet there was never a twin born into this world that did not carry from birth to death a sure identifier in this mysterious and marvelous natal autograph. That once known to you, his fellow-twin could never personate him and deceive you."

Wilson stopped and stood silent. Inattention dies a quick and sure death when a speaker does that. The stillness gives warning that something is coming. All palms and finger-balls went down, now, all slouching forms straightened, all heads came up, all eyes were fastened upon Wilson's face. He waited yet one, two, three moments, to let his pause complete and perfect its spell upon the house; then, when through the profound hush he could hear the ticking of the clock on the wall, he put out his hand and took the Indian knife by the blade and held it aloft where all could see the sinister spots upon its ivory handle; then he said, in a level and passionless voice:

"Upon this haft stands the assassin's natal autograph, written in the blood of that helpless and unoffending old man who loved you and whom you all loved. There is but one man in the whole earth whose hand can duplicate that crimson sign"—he paused and raised his eyes to the pendulum swinging back and forth—"and please God we will produce that man in this room before the clock strikes noon!"

Stunned, distraught, unconscious of its own movement, the house half rose, as if expecting to see the murderer appear at the door, and a breeze of muttered ejaculations swept the place. "Order in the court!— sit down!" This from the sheriff. He was obeyed, and quiet reigned again. Wilson stole a glance at Tom, and said to himself, "He is flying signals of distress, now; even people who despise him are pitying him; they think this is a hard ordeal for a young fellow who has lost his benefactor by so cruel a stroke—and they are right." He resumed his speech.

"For more than twenty years I have amused my compulsory leisure with collecting these curious physical signatures in this town. At my house I have hundreds upon hundreds of them. Each and every one is labeled with name and date; not labeled the next day or even the next hour, but in the very minute that the impression was taken. When I go upon the witness-stand I will repeat under oath the things which I am now saying. I have the finger-prints of the court, the sheriff, and every member of the jury. There is hardly a person in this room, white or black, whose natal signature I cannot produce, and not one of them can so disguise himself that I cannot pick him out from a multitude of his fellow-creatures and unerringly identify him by his hands. And if he and I should live to be a hundred I could still do it. [The interest of the audience was steadily deepening now.]

"I have studied some of these signatures so much that I know them as well as the bank cashier knows the autograph of his oldest customer. While I turn my back now, I beg that several persons will be so good as to pass their fingers through their hair, and then press them upon one of the panes of the window near the jury, and that among them the accused may set *their* finger-marks. Also, I beg that these experimenters, or others, will set their finger-marks upon another pane, and add again the marks of the accused, but not placing them in the same order or relation to the other signatures as before—for, by one chance in a million, a person might happen upon the right marks by pure guesswork *once,* therefore I wish to be tested twice."

He turned his back, and the two panes were quickly covered with delicately lined oval spots, but visible only to such persons as could get a dark background for them—the foliage of a tree, outside, for instance. Then, upon call, Wilson went to the window, made his examination, and said:

"This is Count Luigi's right hand; this one, three signatures below, is his left. Here is Count Angelo's right; down here is his left. Now for the other pane: here and here are Count Luigi's, here and here are his brother's." He faced about. "Am I right?"

A deafening explosion of applause was the answer. The Bench said:

"This certainly approaches the miraculous!"

Wilson turned to the window again and remarked, pointing with his finger:

"This is the signature of Mr. Justice Robinson [Applause.] This, of Constable Blake. [Applause.] This, of John Mason, juryman. [Applause.] This, of the sheriff. [Applause.] I cannot name the others, but I have them all at home, named and dated, and could identify them all by my fingerprint records."

He moved to his place through a storm of applause—which the sheriff stopped, and also made the people sit down, for they were all standing and struggling to see, of course. Court, jury, sheriff, and everybody had been too absorbed in observing Wilson's performance to attend to the audience earlier.

"Now, then," said Wilson, "I have here the natal autographs of two children—thrown up to ten times the natural size by the pantograph, so that any one who can see at all can tell the markings apart at a glance. We will call the children *A* and *B.* Here are *A's* finger-marks, taken at the age of five months. Here they are again, taken at seven months. [Tom started.] They are alike, you see. Here are *B's* at five months, and also at seven months. They, too, exactly copy each other, but the patterns are quite different from *A's,* you observe. I shall refer to these again presently, but we will turn them face down, now.

"Here, thrown up ten sizes, are the natal autographs of the two persons who are here before you accused of murdering Judge Driscoll. I made these pantographic copies last night, and will so swear when I go upon the witness-stand. I ask the jury to compare them with the finger-marks of the accused upon the window-panes, and tell the court if they are the same."

He passed a powerful magnifying-glass to the foreman.

One juryman after another took the cardboard and the glass and made the comparison. Then the foreman said to the judge:

"Your honor, we are all agreed that they are identical."

Wilson said to the foreman:

"Please turn that cardboard face down, and take this one, and compare it searchingly by the magnifier, with the fatal signature upon the knife-handle, and report your finding to the court."

Again the jury made minute examinations, and again reported:

"We find them to be exactly identical, your honor."

Wilson turned toward the counsel for the prosecution, and there was a clearly recognizable note of warning in his voice when he said:

"May it please the court, the State has claimed, strenuously and persistently, that the blood-stained finger-prints upon that knife-handle were left there by the assassin of Judge Driscoll. You have heard us grant that claim, and welcome it." He turned to the jury: "Compare the finger-prints of the accused with the finger-prints left by the assassin—and report."

The comparison began. As it proceeded, all movement and all sound ceased, and the deep silence of an absorbed and waiting suspense settled upon the house; and when at last the words came—

"They do not even resemble," a thunder-crash of applause followed and the house sprang to its feet, but was quickly repressed by official force and brought to order again. Tom was altering his position every few minutes, now, but none of his changes brought repose nor any small trifle of comfort. When the house's attention was become fixed once more, Wilson said gravely, indicating the twins with a gesture:

"These men are innocent—I have no further concern with them. [Another outbreak of applause began, but was promptly checked.] We will now proceed to find the guilty. [Tom's eyes were starting from their sockets—yes, it was a cruel day for the bereaved youth, everybody thought.] We will return to the infant autographs of *A* and *B*. I will ask the jury to take these large pantograph facsimiles of *A's* marked five months and seven months. Do they tally?"

The foreman responded:

"Perfectly."

"Now examine this pantograph, taken at eight months, and also marked *A*. Does it tally with the other two?"

The surprised response was:

"No—they differ widely!"

"You are quite right. Now take these two pantographs of *B's* autograph, marked five months and seven months. Do they tally with each other?"

"Yes—perfectly."

"Take this third pantograph marked *B*, eight months. Does it tally with *B's* other two?"

"By no means!"

"Do you know how to account for those strange discrepancies? I will tell you. For a purpose unknown to us, but probably a selfish one, somebody changed those children in the cradle."

This produced a vast sensation, naturally; Roxana was astonished at this admirable guess, but not disturbed by it. To guess the exchange was one thing, to guess who did it quite another. Pudd'nhead Wilson could do wonderful things, no doubt, but he couldn't do impossible ones. Safe? She was perfectly safe. She smiled privately.

"Between the ages of seven months and eight months those children were changed in the cradle"—he made one of his effect-collecting pauses, and added—"and the person who did it is in this house!"

Roxy's pulses stood still! The house was thrilled as with an electric shock, and the people half rose as if to seek a glimpse of the person who had made that exchange. Tom was growing limp; the life seemed oozing out of him. Wilson resumed:

"*A* was put into *B's* cradle in the nursery; *B* was transferred to the kitchen and became a negro and a slave [Sensation—confusion of angry ejaculations)—but within a quarter of an hour he will stand before you white and free! [Burst of applause, checked by the officers.] From seven months onward until now, *A* has still been a usurper, and in my finger-record he bears *B's* name. Here is his pantograph at the age of twelve. Compare it with the assassin's signature upon the knife-handle. Do they tally?"

The foreman answered:

"To the minutest detail!"

Wilson said, solemnly:

"The murderer of your friend and mine—York Driscoll—of the generous hand and the kindly spirit—sits in among you. Valet de Chambre, negro and slave—falsely called Thomas à Becket Driscoll—make upon the window the finger-prints that will hang you!"

Tom turned his ashen face imploringly toward the speaker, made some impotent movement with his white lips, then slid limp and lifeless to the floor.

Wilson broke the awed silence with the words:

"There is no need. He has confessed."

Roxy flung herself upon her knees, covered her face with her hands, and out through her sobs the words struggled:

"De Lord have mercy on me, po' misable sinner dat I is!"

The clock struck twelve.

The court rose; the new prisoner, handcuffed, was removed.

CONCLUSION

It is often the case that the man who can't tell a lie thinks he is the best judge of one.
                                    —PUDD'NHEAD WILSON'S CALENDAR.

October 12, the Discovery. *It was wonderful to find America, but it would have been more wonderful to miss it.*
                                    —PUDD'NHEAD WILSON'S CALENDAR.

The town sat up all night to discuss the amazing events of the day and swap guesses as to when Tom's trial would begin. Troop after troop of citizens came to serenade Wilson, and require a speech, and shout themselves hoarse over every sentence that fell from his lips—for all his sentences were golden, now, all were marvelous. His long fight against hard luck and prejudice was ended; he was a made man for good.

And as each of these roaring gangs of enthusiasts marched away, some remorseful member of it was quite sure to raise his voice and say:

"And this is the man the likes of us have called a pudd'nhead for more than twenty years. He has resigned from that position, friends."

"Yes, but it isn't vacant—we're elected."

The twins were heroes of romance, now, and with rehabilitated reputations. But they were weary of Western adventure, and straightway returned to Europe.

Roxy's heart was broken. The young fellow upon whom she had inflicted twenty-three years of slavery continued the false heir's pension of thirty-five dollars a month to her, but her hurts were too deep for money to heal; the spirit in her eye was quenched, her martial bearing departed with it, and the voice of her laughter ceased in the land. In her church and its affairs she found her only solace.

The real heir suddenly found himself rich and free, but in a most embarrassing situation. He could neither read nor write, and his speech was the basest dialect of the negro quarter. His gait, his attitudes, his gestures, his bearing, his laugh—all were vulgar and uncouth; his manners were the manners of a slave. Money and fine clothes could not mend these defects or cover them up; they only made them the more glaring and the more pathetic. The poor fellow could not endure the terrors of the white man's parlor, and felt at home and at peace nowhere but in the kitchen. The family pew was a misery to him, yet he could nevermore enter into the solacing refuge of the "nigger gallery"—that was closed to him for good and all. But we cannot follow his curious fate further—that would be a long story.

The false heir made a full confession and was sentenced to imprisonment for life. But now a complication came up. The Percy Driscoll estate was in such a crippled shape when its owner died that it could pay only sixty per cent of its great indebtedness, and was settled at that rate. But the creditors came forward, now, and complained that inasmuch as through an error for which *they* were in no way to blame the false heir was not inventoried at that time with the rest of the property, great wrong and loss had thereby been inflicted upon them. They rightly claimed that "Tom" was lawfully their property and had been so for eight years; that they had already lost sufficiently in being deprived of his services during that long period, and ought not to be required to add anything to that loss; that if he had been delivered up to them in the first place, they would have sold him and he could not have murdered Judge Driscoll; therefore it was not he that had really committed the murder, the guilt lay with the erroneous inventory. Everybody saw that there was reason in this. Everybody granted that if "Tom" were white and free it would be unquestionably right to punish him—it would be no loss to anybody; but to shut up a valuable slave for life—that was quite another matter.

As soon as the Governor understood the case, he pardoned Tom at once, and the creditors sold him down the river.

ANTON CHEKHOV

Ward No. 6

I

In the hospital courtyard stands a rather small annex, enclosed by a whole forest of burdocks, nettles, and wild hemp. Its roof is rusted, its chimney half collapsed, the porch steps are rotted and overgrown with grass, and only traces remain of the stucco. The front faces the hospital; the back overlooks a field, isolated by the gray, nail-studded hospital wall. These nails, their tips pointed upward, the wall, and the annex itself have that unique, melancholy, accursed look peculiar to our hospital and prison edifices.

If you are not afraid of being stung by the nettles, let us go up the narrow path leading to the building and see what is happening inside. Opening the first door, we walk into the entry. Here, along the walls and around the stove, are piled mounds of hospital rubbish. Mattresses, old, torn bathrobes, trousers, blue-striped shirts, utterly useless, worn-out shoes—all this trash is piled in heaps, rumpled and entangled, rotting and emitting a suffocating stench.

On top of the trash, a pipe invariably clenched in his teeth, lies the watchman, Nikita, an old, retired soldier with faded chevrons. He has a red nose and a harsh, weary face with overhanging brows which give him the expression of a steppe sheep dog; he is short in stature, lean and sinewy in appearance, but his bearing is authoritative and his fists hardy. He is one of those simple, positive, diligent, and dense people who love order above anything in the world and are therefore convinced that *they* have to be beaten. He hits faces, chests, backs—whatever he can reach—and is convinced that there would otherwise be no order at all.

Next, you walk into a large, wide room which occupies the entire building, not counting the entry. The walls are covered with dirty blue paint, the ceiling is smoke-blackened as in a chimneyless peasant's hut—it obviously becomes stifling when the stove smokes here in winter. The windows are disfigured by iron bars on the inside. The floor is gray and splintery. It stinks of sour cabbage, smoldering wicks, bugs, and ammonia, and in the first instant, this stench gives you the impression that you are entering a bear pit.

About the room stand beds, screwed to the floor. Sitting and lying on them are men in dark blue hospital bathrobes and, as in the old days, night-caps. These are the lunatics.

There are five in all. Only one is of noble birth; the rest are commoners. The nearest to the door, a tall, spare man with shining red mustaches and tear-swollen eyes, sits holding his head and staring. He grieves day and night, shaking his head, sighing, and smiling bitterly; he rarely takes part in conver-sations and usually does not reply to questions. He eats and drinks mechani-cally whenever served. Judging from his tortured, racking cough, his emaciation, and his flushed cheeks, he is tubercular.

Next to him is a small, lively, very active old man with a pointed little beard and dark hair as curly as a Negro's. He spends the day walking around the ward from window to window or sitting on his bed, his legs folded Turk-ish-style, whistling indefatigably like a bullfinch, singing softly, and giggling. At night he manifests the same childish gaiety and lively character when he gets up to pray, that is, to beat his fists on his chest and dig at the doors with his fingers. This is the Jew, Moiseika, a fool, who lost his mind twenty years ago when his hat workshop burned down.

Of all the inmates of Ward No. 6, he alone is allowed to go out of the building and even out of the hospital courtyard into the street. He has proba-bly enjoyed this privilege for a long time, as an old inmate of the hospital and a gentle, harmless fool, a town joke, long a familiar sight in the streets, sur-rounded by little boys and dogs. In his shabby bathrobe, ridiculous nightcap and slippers, sometimes stockingless and even trouserless, he walks through the streets, stopping at house gates and shops, begging a kopeck. In one place they give him kvass,* in another—bread, in a third—a kopeck, so that he usually returns to the annex sated and rich. Everything Moiseika brings back is confiscated by Nikita for his own use. This the soldier does roughly, ar-dently, turning Moiseika's pockets inside out and calling God to witness that he will never let the Jew out in the street again, and that disorder is the worst thing in the world.

Moiseika loves to be of service. He brings his companions water, covers them up while they sleep, promises to bring each a little kopeck from the street and to make each one a new hat; he even spoonfeeds his neighbor on the left, a paralytic. He does not act this way out of compassion or any con-cept of human fellowship, but parroting and involuntarily subordinating himself to his neighbor on the right, Gromov.

Ivan Dmitrich Gromov, a man of thirty-three, of noble birth, formerly a court process server and provincial secretary, suffers from paranoia. He either

* A thin, sour fermented beverage made from rye or barley.

lies in bed, crumpled into a ball, or paces from corner to corner as if for the exercise; very rarely does he sit. He is always excited, agitated, and tense with some sort of troubled, undefined anticipation. The slightest rustle in the entry or cry in the courtyard is enough for him to raise his head and begin listening: is it not someone coming for him? Someone searching for him? And at this he displays intense anxiety and horror.

I like his broad face with its prominent cheekbones, perpetually pale and unhappy, reflecting like a mirror the agonizing, protracted fear in his soul. His grimaces are strange and sickly, but the sharp traits carved on his face by profound, sincere suffering are rational and intelligent, and his eyes have a warm, healthy glow. I like him, too: polite, obliging, and unusually delicate in his behavior toward everyone except Nikita. When anyone drops a button or a spoon, he quickly jumps out of bed to pick it up. Every day he greets his comrades with a good morning, and on going to bed he wishes them good night.

In addition to grimaces and constant tension, his madness shows itself in the following way. From time to time in the evening, he wraps his bathrobe tightly around himself and, his whole body trembling and his teeth chattering, begins to dart rapidly from corner to corner and between the beds. He acts as if he had a high fever. From the way he stops suddenly and glances at his companions, it is clear that he wants to say something very important, but apparently concluding that they will neither listen nor understand, he impatiently shakes his head and resumes his pacing.

Soon, however, the urge to speak dominates all other considerations, and he unleashes his feelings, talking heatedly and passionately. His speech is disorganized, feverish, broken, and not always intelligible, as in a delirium—but something exceptionally fine is nevertheless perceptible in his words and voice. When he talks, you recognize both the lunatic and the man in him. His mad harangue is hard to reproduce on paper. He talks about human villainy, about violence crushing truth, about the splendid life there will be on earth in time, about window bars, reminding him every minute of the denseness and cruelty of the violators. It is a disorderly, disconnected potpourri put together out of the old refrains.

□ **II** □

Twelve—or fifteen—years ago, an official named Gromov, a solid and wealthy man, lived in his own house on the main street of a town. He had two sons: Sergei and Ivan. When still a fourth form student, Sergei caught galloping consumption and died, and this death seemed to be the prelude to a whole series of misfortunes which suddenly befell the Gromov family. A week after Sergei's burial, the aged father was taken to court for fraud and embezzlement and died soon after of typhus in a prison hospital. The house and all the household goods were seized and auctioned, and Ivan Dmitrich and his mother were left without means.

During his father's lifetime, Ivan Dmitrich was allotted sixty to seventy rubles a month while living in St. Petersburg as a university student, and had no conception whatsoever of need; now he was obliged to transform his life abruptly. He had to give ill-paid lessons from morning till night and work as a scribe and still go hungry because all his earnings went to his mother for her subsistence. Ivan Dmitrich could not withstand this sort of life; he lost heart, languished, and quitting the university, went home. Here, in the small town, he obtained a position as a teacher in the district school through his connections, but failed to get along with his colleagues, was disliked by his pupils, and soon resigned. His mother died. For half a year he went jobless, living on bread and water alone, then entered the court staff as a process server. He held this job until he was cashiered because of ill health.

Even in his youthful student days he had never looked healthy. Always pale, thin, subject to colds, he ate little; slept badly. One glass of wine made his head whirl and gave him hysterics. He was always drawn to people, but thanks to his irascible character and mistrustfulness, never became close to anyone and had no friends. The townspeople he always referred to with contempt, saying that he found their coarse ignorance and sluggish animal life nasty and repelling. He spoke in a tenor, loudly, heatedly, and invariably either with exasperation and indignation or with enthusiasm and wonder—and always sincerely. No matter what you talked to him about, he always came back to the same theme: the town is oppressive and boring to live in; the society has no elevated interests: it leads a dingy, unreflecting life which it diversifies with violence, coarse debauchery, and hypocrisy; the scoundrels are well-fed and well-dressed, while the honest sustain themselves on crumbs; there is need for schools, a local paper with an honest viewpoint, a theater, public readings, and a fraternity of intellectual forces; society needs to realize what it is and take alarm. In judging people, he laid the colors on heavily, black and white only, recognizing no shades whatsoever; for him, humanity was divided into the honest and the scoundrels; there was no middle ground. He always spoke passionately, with enthusiasm, of women and love, but he had never been in love.

In spite of the sharpness of his judgments and his restlessness, he was well liked in town and behind his back was affectionately spoken of as Vanya. His innate delicacy, complaisance, respectability, and moral purity, his worn frock coat, sickly appearance, and family misfortunes inspired a pleasant, warm, melancholy feeling; moreover, he was well-educated and well-read; in the townspeople's opinion, he knew everything, and he was a kind of local walking encyclopedia.

He read a great deal. He used to sit in the club, nervously plucking at his beard and leafing through magazines and books; it was obvious from his face that he was not reading, but gulping with barely time to digest. One must conclude that reading was one of his morbid habits because he threw himself with the same avidity on everything which fell under his hands, even last year's newspapers and calendars. At home he always read lying down.

□ **III** □

One fall morning, the collar of his overcoat turned up, splashing through the mud, Ivan Dmitrich was making his way through alleys and back ways to some tradesman or other to collect a fine. He was in a gloomy mood, as always in the morning. In one of the alleys he met two convicts in chains, escorted by four guards with rifles. Ivan Dmitrich had often encountered convicts before, and they invariably aroused feelings of pity and awkwardness in him; this encounter awakened a peculiar, strange feeling. For some reason he suddenly felt that he, too, could be clapped in irons and led through the mud to prison in just the same way. As he passed the post office on his return, he met a police inspector he knew who greeted him and accompanied him a few paces down the street; for some reason this seemed suspicious to Ivan Dmitrich. The prisoners and the soldiers with their rifles stayed on his mind all day at home, and an inexplicable inner anxiety kept him from reading and concentrating. That evening he did not light the lamp and that night he did sleep, but kept thinking about how he could be arrested, clapped in irons, and put in prison. He knew of no crime in his past and knew he would never kill, burn, or steal in the future; but was it so hard, then, to commit a crime accidentally, involuntarily, and was calumny inconceivable, or even judicial error? It is certainly not for nothing that ageless popular experience teaches that no one is immune to poverty and prison. Besides, a judicial error can easily happen under current judicial procedures, and there is nothing exceptional about it. People who have official, professional relations with someone else's suffering—judges, authorities, physicians, for example— become so inured in the course of time, from force of habit, that even should they want to be sympathetic, they are incapable of any but a formal concern for their clients. In this respect they are no different from the peasant who slaughters sheep and cattle in his backyard without noticing the blood. Having this formal, heartless relationship toward the individual, a judge needs just one thing to deprive an innocent man of all his property rights and sentence him to hard labor: time. Just time for the observation of formalities of some sort, for which the judge earns his wages, and then—it is all over. Try to find justice or protection then in this dirty little town, twenty versts from the railroad line! Yes, and is it not absurd to think of justice when society accepts every kind of violence as a rational and expedient necessity, while every act of mercy, such as an exculpatory decree, provokes an explosion of dissatisfied, vindictive feelings?

That morning Ivan Dmitrich got out of bed in terror with cold sweat on his forehead, now absolutely certain he could be arrested any moment. "If yesterday's gloomy ideas have not left me by now," he thought, "it means they have a measure of truth. They certainly could not enter my mind for no reason."

A policeman walked slowly past the window: it was not for nothing. Over there, two men stopped near the house and stood in silence. Why were they silent?

Thus the days and nights of torment began for Ivan Dmitrich. All the people passing by his window or entering the courtyard looked like spies and detectives. At noon the district police inspector usually drove down the street with his pair of horses on his way from his estate on the outskirts of town to the police administration, but each time it seemed to Ivan Dmitrich that he was driving too fast and had a singular expression; obviously he was hurrying to announce that a very important criminal had appeared in town. Ivan Dmitrich trembled at every ring and knock at the gate; he was anguished when someone new visited the landlady; on meeting policemen and gendarmes, he would smile and whistle to show his indifference. He spent night after night without sleeping, awaiting arrest, but he snored loudly and sighed to make the landlady believe he was asleep: you see, if he is awake it means the gnawing of his conscience is tormenting him—what damning evidence! Reality and common sense told him that all these fears were psychopathic nonsense; that, taking a broader view, there is really nothing frightening about arrest and imprisonment if your conscience is at peace; but the more sensibly and logically he reasoned, the stronger and more tormenting his inner anxiety became. He was like the hermit who wanted to clear a place for himself in a virgin forest: the more vigorously he wielded his ax, the thicker and stronger the forest grew. Realizing in the end that it was useless, Ivan Dmitrich completely stopped reasoning and abandoned himself entirely to fear and despair.

He began to avoid people and seek seclusion. His job, distasteful to him before, now became unbearable. He was afraid they would trick him, put a bribe in his pocket without his noticing, and then convict him; or that he himself would accidentally make an error tantamount to fraud in state fiscal papers, or would lose other people's money. Strangely, never before had his thinking been so supple and inventive as now, when he thought up a thousand different reasons for being seriously afraid of losing his freedom and honor. But in return, his interest in the outside world, and particularly in books, decreased significantly, and his memory began to fail notably.

When the snow melted in the spring, two half-rotted corpses were discovered in the ravine near the cemetery—an old woman and a young boy, with the marks of a violent death. These corpses and the unknown murderers were the only topic discussed in town. So they would not think he was the killer, Ivan Dmitrich walked through the streets and smiled, but when he met acquaintances, he turned pale, blushed, and vehemently asserted that there was no crime more reprehensible than the murder of the weak and defenseless. But this lie soon wearied him, and after some thought, he decided that in his position the best thing was to hide in the landlady's cellar. He sat in the cellar the whole day, then that night and the following day, became thoroughly chilled, and after waiting for darkness, stole secretly, like a thief, to his own room. He stood in the middle of the room, immobile, listening, until daybreak. The stokers came to the landlady's early in the morning, before sunrise. Ivan Dmitrich knew perfectly well they had come to start the fire in the kitchen, but fear whispered to him that it was the police, disguised as stokers. He quietly left the apartment, and seized by terror, ran hatless and coatless down the street. Barking, dogs chased after him; a peasant shouted somewhere behind him; the wind whistled in his ears, and it seemed to Ivan Dmitrich that all the violence of the world had gathered behind his back and was hunting him down.

They caught him, brought him home, and sent the landlady for a doctor. Dr. Andrei Yefimich, of whom more later, prescribed cold compresses for his head and cherry-laurel drops, sadly shook his head and left, telling the landlady he would not come again as it was not right to keep people from going out of their minds. Because Ivan Dmitrich could not afford to be treated at home, they soon sent him to the hospital and put him in the ward for venereal diseases. He did not sleep at night, was capricious, disturbed the other patients, and soon, on Andrei Yefimich's orders, was transferred to Ward No. 6.

Within a year Ivan Dmitrich had already been completely forgotten in the town, and his books, which the landlady had piled in the storeroom under the eaves, had been pilfered by little boys.

□ **IV** □

The neighbor on Ivan Dmitrich's left, as I have already said, is the Jew, Moiseika; on his right is a fat-swollen, almost round peasant with a dull, completely blank face. This is an immobile, gluttonous, slovenly animal, who long ago lost the capacity to think and feel. He continuously gives off a sharp, suffocating stench.

When cleaning up after him, Nikita beats him mercilessly with all his strength, not sparing his fists; what is awful is not that this stupefied animal is beaten—one can get used to that—but that it does not respond to blows by sound, movement, or an expression of the eyes, but just rocks slightly like a heavy barrel.

The fifth and last inmate of Ward No. 6 is a former mail sorter at the post office, a small thin blond with a kindly but somewhat cunning face. Judging from his wise, peaceful eyes with their clear, merry gaze, he has a very important and agreeable secret. He keeps something under his pillow and mattress that he never shows to anyone, not from fear of its being taken away or stolen, but from modesty. Sometimes he goes up to the window and, turning his back on his comrades, puts something on his chest and crooks his head to look at it; if you approach him at that moment, he become flustered and snatches the object off his chest. But his secret is not hard to guess.

"Congratulate me," he often says to Ivan Dmitrich; "I was recommended for the Stanislas, second grade, with a star. The second grade with a star is only given to foreigners, but they wanted to make an exception for me for some reason," he smiles, shrugging his shoulders in bewilderment. "That, I confess, I hadn't expected!"

"I don't understand any of this," Ivan Dmitrich declares morosely.

"But you know what I'll get sooner or later?" the former mail sorter continues with a sly wink. "I'll undoubtedly receive the Swedish 'polar star.' That's a medal worth angling for. A white cross and black ribbon. It's very handsome."

There is probably no place on earth where life is as monotonous as in the annex. In the mornings, the patients, except for the paralytic and the fat peasant, wash in the entry in a big tub and dry themselves with the tails of their bathrobes; after that they drink tea brought by Nikita from the main building in tin mugs; each is entitled to one mugful. At noon they eat kasha* and sour cabbage soup; in the evening they sup on the kasha left over from dinner. In the intervals they lie, sleep, look out the window, and pace the room. And so on every day. And the former mail sorter keeps talking about the very same medals.

* A porridge usually made of barley or oats.

New faces are rarely seen in Ward No. 6. The doctor stopped admitting new lunatics long ago, and amateurs of visits to insane asylums are few in the world. Once every two months Semon Lazarich, the barber, comes to the annex. Of how he shears the lunatics, and how Nikita helps him do it, and what pandemonium overtakes the patients every time the drunken smiling barber appears, we shall not speak.

Aside from the barber, no one casts a glance in the annex. The patients are condemned to seeing only Nikita day after day.

However, not long ago, a rather strange rumor began circulating among the hospital corps.

The rumor reported that the doctor had started to visit Ward No. 6.

□ V □

A strange rumor!

Dr. Andrei Yefimich Ragin was a remarkable man in his way. They say he was religious in his early youth and prepared himself for a clerical career, and that, after graduating from preparatory school in 1863, he had intended to enter a theological academy. However, his father, a doctor of medicine and a surgeon, is supposed to have sneered and laughed at him, and declared categorically that he would disown him if he became a priest. How much is true, I do not know, but Andrei Yefimich himself confessed more than once that he had never felt any calling for medicine nor for the specialized sciences in general.

However that may be, after graduating from the medical faculty, he did not take the habit. He gave no sign of piety and looked as little like a priest at the beginning of his medical career as now.

His outward appearance is heavy, coarse, virile; his face, beard, dull hair, and strong clumsy build evoke an innkeeper on the highway: well-fattened, intemperate, and gruff. His face is harsh, covered with blue veins; his eyes small; his nose red. In relation to his height and the breadth of his shoulders, his hands and feet are huge, as if one blow would knock you out. But his conduct is gentle and his bearing cautious, ingratiating; on encountering someone in a narrow corridor, he is always the first to stop to make room and to say—not, as you would expect, in a bass voice, but in a thin, soft tenor— "My fault!" He has a small tumor on his neck which keeps him from wearing stiff, starched collars, and he therefore always goes around in a soft linen or cotton shirt. On the whole, he does not dress like a doctor. He has been wearing out the same suit for ten years, and his new clothes, which he usually buys in a Jewish shop, look as worn and rumpled on him as the old ones; he receives patients, eats dinner, and goes out in the same frock coat; not, however, from parsimony, but from a complete lack of attention to his outward appearance.

When Andrei Yefimich arrived in town to assume his responsibilities, the "charitable institution" was in a terrible state. It was hard to breathe for the stench in the wards, corridors, and hospital courtyard. The hospital attendants, the nurses, and their children slept in the wards with the patients. They complained that one could not live for the cockroaches, bugs, and mice. Erysipelas had not been eliminated in the surgical section. There were only two scalpels in the entire hospital and not one thermometer; they stored potatoes in the bathrooms. The superintendent, the housekeeper, and the assistant physician robbed the patients, and the previous doctor, Andrei Yefimich's predecessor, was said to have engaged in the clandestine sale of hospital alcohol and to have organized a whole harem for himself among the nurses and women patients. These disorders were very well known in town and even exaggerated, but were taken calmly; some justified them on the grounds that the only people confined in the hospital were commoners and peasants who could not be dissatisfied since they lived much worse at home; and in any case you could hardly feed them on woodcocks! Others said in justification that the town was unable to support a good hospital without the villagers' help, and thank God it's there, poor as it is! But the recently formed village council opened no infirmaries either in or near the town on the grounds that the town already had a hospital.

After looking the hospital over, Andrei Yefimich came to the conclusion that the institution was immoral and exceedingly harmful to the health of the patients. In his opinion, the wisest thing to do was to release the patients and close the hospital. But he reasoned that his will alone was not enough to accomplish this, and that it would be useless. Drive physical and moral uncleanliness from one spot and it will move to another; one must wait for it to clear up by itself. Moreover, people had opened the hospital and tolerated it among themselves, which meant that they needed it; prejudices and all life's filth and foulness were needed because they would be transformed into something useful with the passage of time, just as manure becomes rich soil. There is nothing on earth so fine that it has not had some filth at its origin.

After taking up his duties, Andrei Yefimich seemed to accept disorder fairly indifferently. He asked only that the hospital attendants and nurses not sleep in the wards, and he installed two cupboards of instruments; the superintendent, the housekeeper, the assistant physician, and the surgical erysipelas remained in their places.

Andrei Yefimich loves reason and honesty intensely, but has insufficient character and belief in his rights to build a reasonable and honest life around him. He is positively incapable of commanding, forbidding, insisting. It is as though he had vowed never to raise his voice or use the imperative mood. Saying "fetch" or "bring" is difficult for him; when he wants to eat, he clears his throat haltingly and says to the cook: "If I might have tea ..." or: "If I might have dinner." To tell the superintendent to stop stealing or to turn him out, or even to abolish this unnecessary, parasitic job, is completely beyond his strength. When Andrei Yefimich is cheated or flattered or brought a deliberately falsified account to sign, he reddens like a lobster and feels guilty, but signs the account just the same; when the patients complain to him of hunger or the nurses' callousness, he is flustered and mutters guiltily: "Fine, fine, I'll look into that later ... There's probably a misunderstanding ..."

Andrei Yefimich worked very hard in the beginning. He received patients from morning until dinnertime daily, performed operations, and even took care of the maternity practice. The ladies said he was attentive and diagnosed illnesses exceptionally well, particularly women's and children's. But in the course of time he became visibly bored with the monotony and obvious uselessness of his work. You receive thirty patients today and tomorrow— look—thirty-five of them have crowded in, and the day after, forty, and so on, day after day, year after year, while the mortality rate of the town remains undiminished and the sick never stop coming. Rendering real assistance to forty outpatients between morning and dinnertime is a physical impossibility, inevitably resulting in a swindle. To receive twelve thousand outpatients in a year means, by simple calculation, the swindling of twelve thousand people. Putting the seriously ill in wards and taking care of them according to scientific principles is also impossible because while the principles exist, scientific means do not. To abandon philosophy and pedantically follow the rules as other doctors do, you need cleanliness and ventilation first of all, not filth; healthy nourishment, not soup made of reeking sour cabbage, and good assistants, not thieves.

Yes, and furthermore, why keep people from dying if death is the normal, legitimate end for everyone? What difference does it make if some peddler or official lives an extra five or ten years? If one sees the purpose of medicine in the alleviation of sufferings by medication, the question necessarily arises: Why alleviate them? Firstly, suffering is said to lead man to perfection, and secondly, if humanity does, in fact, learn to alleviate its sufferings with drops and pills, it will completely cast aside religion and philosophy, in which it has found until now not just a defense against all kinds of ills, but even happiness. Pushkin underwent terrible torments before his death; poor Heine lay paralyzed for several years; why should an Andrei Yefimich or a Matrona Savshina be spared illness, when their lives are null and would be utterly empty and like an amoeba's were it not for suffering?

Crushed by these arguments, Andrei Yefimich lost courage and stopped going to the hospital every day.

□   VI   □

His life goes like this. He usually gets up at eight in the morning, dresses, and has tea. Then he either sits in his study and reads or goes to the hospital. In the narrow dark little corridor of the hospital sit the ambulatory patients, waiting to be received. Past them, their shoes pounding on the brick floor, run the attendants and nurses; gaunt patients walk by in bathrobes; corpses and used dishes with their refuse are carried through; children cry; a sharp draft blows. Andrei Yefimich knows such surroundings are a torment for the fever-stricken, the tubercular, and for impressionable patients in general, but what can you do? In the receiving room he meets his assistant, Sergei Sergeich, a fat little man with a shaven, cleanly scrubbed, bloated face and mild, facile manners, wearing an amply cut new suit and looking more like a senator than a doctor. He has a large practice in town, wears a white tie, and considers himself more competent than the doctor, who has no practice at all. In one corner of the reception room is a big image in a case with a heavy incense lamp; nearby is a candle-stand on a white cloth; on the walls hang portraits of prelates, a vew of the Sviatogorsky Monastery, and wreaths of dried cornflowers. Sergei Sergeich is pious and loves pomp. The image was installed at his expense; on his orders, one of the patients reads the hymns of praise aloud in the reception room on Sundays, and after the reading, Sergei Sergeich himself walks through all the wards with a censer and thurifies them with incense.

The patients are numerous, but time short, and therefore the examination is limited to a brief questioning and the handing out of some medicament or other, such as a volatile salve or castor oil. Andrei Yefimich sits, his cheek propped on his fist, lost in thought, and poses questions mechanically. Sergei Sergeich sits there too, rubbing his hands, and interfering now and then.

"We are sick and endure want," he says, "because we pray badly to the All-Merciful Lord. Yes!"

Andrei Yefimich performs no operations during receiving hours; he has been out of practice for a long time, and the sight of blood affects him unpleasantly. When he has to open a child's mouth to look at his throat, if the child screams and shields himself with his little hands, Andrei Yefimich's head spins from the noise and tears start in his eyes. He hastens to prescribe some medication and gestures for the woman to take the child away as quickly as possible.

In receiving, he soon wearies of the timidity of the patients and their digressions, of the proximity of the pompous Sergei Sergeich, of the portraits on the walls, and of his own questions, which he has been asking unchanged for already more than twenty years. And he goes away after seeing five or six patients, leaving the rest to his assistant.

With the agreeable thought that, thank God, he has not had any private practice for a long time and no one will bother him, Andrei Yefimich sits down at the desk in his study and begins reading as soon as he reaches home. He reads a great deal and always with much pleasure. Half his salary is spent on purchasing books, and of the six rooms of his apartment three are crammed with books and old magazines. He favors works of history and philosophy; as for medicine, he subscribes only to *The Physician,* which he always begins reading from the back. His reading invariably continues without interruption for several hours, and without tiring him. He does not read as quickly nor as impetuously as Ivan Dmitrich used to, but slowly, with absorption, often stopping at places pleasing or puzzling to him. There is always a small decanter of vodka near the book, and a salted cucumber or a pickled apple placed directly on the tablecloth. Every half hour, without removing his eyes from his book, he pours himself a glass of vodka and drains it, then, without looking, gropes for the cucumber and bites off a morsel.

At three o'clock he cautiously approaches the kitchen door, coughs, and says: "Darushka, if I might have dinner . . ."

After a rather poor, slipshod dinner, Andrei Yefimich walks around his rooms, arms folded on his chest, and thinks. Four o'clock strikes, then five, and still he walks and thinks. From time to time the kitchen door creaks and from behind it appears the red, sleepy face of Darushka.

"Andrei Yefimich, isn't it time for your beer?" she asks anxiously.

"No, it's not time yet . . ." he answers. "I'll wait a bit . . . a bit . . ."

Toward evening the postmaster, Mikhail Averyanich, usually calls, the only person in the entire town whose company is not a burden to Andrei Yefimich. Mikhail Averyanich, a former cavalry officer, had once been a very rich landowner, but had ruined himself and been forced to enter the postal service in his old age. He has a sound, healthy appearance, luxuriant gray side-whiskers, good manners, and a loud, pleasant voice. He is kind and sensitive, but irascible. When anyone at the post office protests, disagrees, or simply starts to argue, Mikhail Averyanich turns purple, trembles from head to toe, and shouts in a thunderous voice: "Shut up!" As a result, the postal division long ago acquired the reputation of being an awesome institution to visit. Mikhail Averyanich esteems and likes Andrei Yefimich for his culture and nobility of spirit; with the rest of the inhabitants he behaves haughtily, as toward his inferiors.

"And here I am!" he says, coming into Andrei Yefimich's apartment. "Greetings, my dear! Perhaps you're already tired of me, ah?"

"On the contrary, I'm delighted," the doctor answered him. "I'm always delighted to see you."

The friends sit down on the sofa in the study annd smoke in silence for a while.

"Darushka, if we might have some beer!" says Andrei Yefimich.

The first bottle they drink in silence, the doctor lost in thought; Mikhail Averyanich with the merry lively look of a man with something very interesting to tell. The doctor always starts the conversation.

"What a pity," he says slowly and softly, nodding his head and not looking at his companion's eyes (he never looks anyone in the eyes); "what a great pity, honored Mikhail Averyanich, that there are simply no people in our town who could and would enjoy holding an intelligent and interesting conversation. It's a great privation for us. Even the intelligentsia doesn't rise above vulgarity; its level of development, I assure you, is not a bit higher than in the lowest class."

"Absolutely true. I agree."

"As you yourself know," the doctor continues softly, after a pause, "everything in the world is insignificant and uninteresting except the high spiritual manifestations of the human mind. The mind marks a sharp division between animal and man, suggests the divinity of the latter, and to some degree even compensates him for immortality, which does not exist. As a consequence, the mind serves as the only possible source of pleasure. We, however, neither see nor hear minds around us—meaning that we are deprived of pleasure. True, we have books, but that is not at all the same as a live conversation and exchange. If you will excuse a not completely successful comparison: books are notes, and conversation singing."

"Absolutely true."

A silence falls. Darushka comes out of the kitchen and, propping her face on her fist with an expression of dense sorrow, stays near the door to listen.

"Eh!" sighs Mikhail Averyanich. "What can you expect from today's minds!"

And he tells how healthily, merrily, and interestingly he used to live, how intelligent the intelligentsia in Russia had been, and how highly it had valued an understanding of honor and friendship. They used to lend each other money without promissory notes, and considered it disgraceful not to extend a helping hand to a companion in need. And what campaigns there were! What adventures, skirmishes; what comrades, what women! And the Caucasus—what a marvelous land! There was the wife of one of the battalion commanders, a strange woman, who used to put on an officer's uniform and drive out in the mountains at night alone, without escort. They say she had a romance with some prince or other in a native village.

"Heavenly Tsaritsa, Little Mother . . ." sighs Darushka.

"And how we used to drink! And eat! And what desperate liberals we were!"

Andrei Yefimich listens without hearing; he is lost in thought, sipping his beer.

"I often dream of intelligent people and conversation with them," he says unexpectedly, interrupting Mikhail Averyanich. "My father gave me an excellent education, but under the influence of the ideas of the sixties, forced me to become a physician. It seems to me that if I hadn't listened to him then, I'd find myself in the very center of an intellectual movement now. I'd probably have been a member of some faculty or other. Of course the intellect is transitory and not eternal, but you already know why I maintain an inclination toward it. Life is an exasperating trap. When a thoughtful person reaches manhood and arrives at a mature understanding, he involuntarily feels caught in a trap from which there is no exit. Indeed, he is brought to life from nothingness against his will, by chance . . . Why? If he tries to learn the meaning and aim of his own existence, he is either told nothing or told nonsense; he knocks—no one opens; death overtakes him—also against his will. And so, just as people in prison, linked by common misfortune, feel better in a group, in life you don't notice the trap when people inclined to analysis and deduction get together and pass the time in the exchange of proud, free ideas. In this sense, the mind is an irreplaceable source of pleasure."

"Absolutely true."

Not looking his friend in the eyes, softly, with pauses, Andrei Yefimich continues to talk about intelligent people and conversation with them, while Mikhail Averyanich listens to him attentively and agrees: "Absolutely true."

"Then you don't believe in the immortality of the soul?" the postmaster asks suddenly.

"No, respected Mikhail Averyanich, I don't believe in it and haven't any basis for believing."

"I confess I, too, have doubts. But, however, on the other hand, I have a feeling as though I would never die. Aiee, I think to myself, old fogey, it's time to die! But in my soul a kind of little voice says: 'Don't believe it, you won't die!' . . ."

A little after nine, Mikhail Averyanich leaves. Putting on his fur coat in the entry, he says with a sigh: "Still, what a desert fate brought us to! What's most annoying is that we'll have to die here. Eh! . . ."

□ **VII** □

After showing his friend out, Andrei Yefimich sits at his desk and resumes
his reading. The silence of the evening and then the night is unbroken by a
single sound, and time seems to stop and fade away along with the doctor
over his book, as if nothing exists except this book and the lamp with the
green globe. Little by little, the doctor's coarse peasant face is illuminated by
a smile of emotion and excitement before the progress of the human mind.
Oh, why isn't man immortal? he reflects. Why have brain centers and nerves,
why have vision, speech, internal sensations, genius, if all this is condemned
to disappear into the ground, and in the final end to grow cold along with
the earth's crust and then hover with the earth around the sun senselessly and
aimlessly for millions of years? To grow cold and then hover, it is absolutely
unnecessary to draw man with his lofty, almost divine mind out of nothingness and then, like a joke, turn him into clay.

The transmutation of matter! But how cowardly to comfort oneself with
this substitute immortality! The unconscious processes which take place in
nature are beneath even human stupidity, for in stupidity there is still consciousness and will, while in these processes there is absolutely nothing. Only
a coward who has less dignity than fear of death can comfort himself that in
time his body will be reborn in grass, rock, a toad . . . Seeing his own immortality in the transmutation of matter is as strange as predicting a brilliant future for the violin case after a precious violin has been smashed and rendered
worthless.

When the clock strikes, Andrei Yefimich leans back in his armchair and
closes his eyes to think awhile. And unintentionally, under the influence of
the fine thoughts gleaned from his book, he casts a glance over his past and
present. The past is repellent; best not to recall it. And the present is the same
as the past. He knows that at the same time that his thoughts are hovering
with the cooled earth around the sun, in a large building next to his apartment, people are languishing in sickness and filth. Perhaps someone is awake,
waging war with the bugs; someone else is catching erysipelas or groaning
because of tightly wound bandages; perhaps the patients are playing cards
with the nurses and drinking vodka. Twelve thousand people are swindled a
year; the whole hospital business is founded, just as it was twenty years ago,
on theft, scandal, slander, nepotism, on crude charlatanism and, as before, the
hospital is an immoral institution, exceedingly harmful to the health of the
inmates. He knows that in Ward No. 6, Nikita thrashes the patients behind
bars, and that Moiseika goes around town every day to collect alms.

On the other hand, he knows very well that medicine has undergone a
fantastic transformation in the last twenty-five years. When he was studying

at the university, he felt that the fate of alchemy and metaphysics would soon overtake medicine; now, when he reads at night, medicine moves him and arouses his wonder, and even enthusiasm. In truth, what unexpected brilliance, what a revolution! Thanks to antiseptics, they perform operations the great Pirogov used to consider impossible, even *in spe.** Ordinary village physicians take the decision of making a resection of the knee joint; for a hundred abdominal operations, there is only one mortality, while gallstones are considered such a trifle that nothing is even written about them. There is a complete cure for syphilis. And what of the theory of heredity, hypnotism, the discoveries of Pasteur and Koch, statistical hygienics, and our Russian village doctors? Psychiatry with its current classification of diseases, methods of diagnosis and treatment—this, in comparison with what used to be, is a whole Mount Elbrus. They don't pour cold water over the heads of the insane now or envelop them in hot plasters; they are treated humanely and, according to the newspapers, balls and spectacles are even organized for them. Andrei Yefimich knows that according to current views and tastes, an abomination such as Ward No. 6 is possible only two hundred versts away from the railroad line, in a small town where the mayor and all the councilmen are semiliterate commoners who regard the doctor as a sacrificial priest to be trusted without criticism, even if he pours molten lead down people's thoats; in another place, the public and the newspaper would have scattered this little Bastille to bits long ago.

"And what then?" Andrei Yefimich asked himself, opening his eyes. "What of it, then? There's antiseptics and Koch and Pasteur, but the essence of the work hasn't changed a bit. Illness and mortality exist just the same. They organize spectacles and balls for the insane, but still don't let them free. Meaning it's all rubbish and bustle, and the difference between the best Viennese clinic and my hospital is, in effect, nonexistent."

But dejection and a feeling resembling envy prevent him from being indifferent. It must be from tiredness. His heavy head sinks toward the book; he cradles his face in his hands and thinks: "I serve a pernicious business and receive a salary from people I swindle; I'm dishonest. But, of course, I'm nothing by myself, I'm only a part of an inevitable social evil: all provincial officials are harmful and receive salaries for nothing ... Meaning it's not I who am guilty in my dishonesty, but the times ... If I had been born two hundred years later, I would be another person."

When three o'clock struck, he put out the lamp and went to his bedroom. He had no desire to sleep.

* In the future.

□   **VIII**   □

Two years ago, in a generous mood, the village council decided to hand out three hundred rubles annually to contribute to the strengthening of the medical staff in the town hospital until the opening of a village hospital, and the district physician, Yevgeny Fedorich Khobotov, was hired by the town as Andrei Yefimich's assistant. He is still a young man—not yet thirty—tall, dark, with wide cheekbones and small eyes; his ancestors were probably of another race. He arrived in town without a kopeck, bringing only a small trunk and a homely young woman whom he called his cook. This woman had a newborn child. Yevgeny Fedorich goes around in high boots and a forage cap with a visor, and wears a short fur coat in winter. He is friendly with the assistant, Sergei Sergeich, and the paymaster, but for some reason calls the rest of the staff "aristocrats" and avoids them. There is only one book in his entire apartment—*The Latest Prescriptions of the Viennese Clinic for 1881*. He always brings this book with him when he visits a patient. In the evenings, he plays billiards in the club; cards he does not like. He is a great enthusiast of the use in conversation of expressions such as "trumpery," "flummery with sauce," "don't cloud things over," and so forth.

Twice a week he visits the hospital, goes through the wards, and receives patients. The complete absence of antiseptics and the practice of blood cupping disturb him, but he does not introduce any improvements for fear of insulting Andrei Yefimich. He considers his colleague Andrei Yefimich an old fraud, suspects him of large means, and secretly envies him. He would eagerly take his place.

□   **IX**   □

On a spring evening at the end of March, when all the snow had melted on the ground and the starlings were singing in the hospital garden, the doctor came out to escort his friend the postmaster to the gates. At that moment, the Jew Moiseika walked into the courtyard with his spoils. He was hatless, wore galoshes on his bare legs, and held a small sack with alms in his hands.

"Give a little kopeck!" he said, trembling with cold and smiling, to the doctor.

Andrei Yefimich, who had never been able to refuse, gave him a ten-ko-peck piece.

"How awful this is," he thought, glancing at Moiseika's bare legs with their thick red ankles. "After all, it's wet."

And moved by a feeling akin to pity and aversion, glancing from the Jew's bald pate to his ankles, the doctor followed him into the annex. At the doctor's entrance, Nikita jumped up from a pile of rubbish and drew himself to attention.

"Good day, Nikita," Andrei Yefimich said softly. "If this Jew might be issued boots, what? or he'll catch cold."

"At your orders, Your Honor. I'll notify the superintendent."

"Please do. Ask him in my name. Say I requested it."

The door to the ward was open. Ivan Dmitrich, who was lying in bed and had raised himself on his elbow, listened anxiously to the unfamiliar voice and suddenly recognized the doctor. Trembling with anger, he jumped up with a red, spiteful face; his eyes protruding, he ran out into the middle of the ward.

"The doctor has come!" he shouted and burst out laughing. "At last! Gentlemen, I congratulate you, the doctor is honoring us with his visit! Cursed vermin!" he shrieked and in a rage such as they had never seen in the ward, he stamped his foot. "Kill this vermin! No, killing isn't enough! Drown him in the toilet!"

Hearing this, Andrei Yefimich glanced from the entry into the ward and asked softly: "What for?"

"What for?" shouted Ivan Dmitrich, going to him with a threatening look and feverishly wrapping himself in his bathrobe. "What for? Thief!" he pronounced with revulsion, moving his lips as though about to spit. "Charlatan! Hangman."

"Calm yourself," said Andrei Yefimich, smiling guiltily. "I assure you I never stole anything; for the rest, you are probably greatly exaggerating. I see you are angry with me. Calm yourself, I beg you, if you can, and tell me coolly: why are you angry?"

"Why do you keep me here?"

"Because you're sick."

"Yes, I'm sick. But look, dozens, hundreds of lunatics are walking around in freedom because your ignorance is incapable of distinguishing them from the sane. Why then should I and these unfortunates be forced to sit here like scapegoats for the rest? You, the assistant, the superintendent, and all your hospital riffraff are morally immeasurably inferior to every one of us; then why should we sit here and not you? Where's the logic?"

"Morals and logic do not enter into it. Everything depends on chance. Whoever is locked up, sits there; and whoever is not, walks around; that's all.

There is neither morality nor logic in the fact that I'm a doctor and you're mentally ill, but just an empty hazard."

"I don't understand this bosh ..." Ivan Dmitrich said dully and sat down on his bed.

Moiseika, whom Nikita had hesitated to search in the doctor's presence, was laying out bits of bread, paper, and little bones on his bed and, still trembling with cold, quickly chanting something in Hebrew. He probably imagined he had opened his shop.

"Release me," said Ivan Dmitrich, and his voice quavered.

"I can't."

"But why? Why?"

"Because it's not in my power. Think, what use would it be to you if I released you? You leave. The townspeople or the police will stop you and bring you back here."

"Yes, yes, it's true ..." said Ivan Dmitrich and rubbed his forehead. "It's horrible! But what can I do then? What?"

Ivan Dmitrich's voice and his intelligent young face with its grimaces pleased Andrei Yefimich. He wanted to treat the young man kindly and soothe him. He sat down beside him on the bed, thought a moment, and said: "You're asking me what to do? The best thing in your position—run away from here. But, unfortunately, it's useless. They'll arrest you. When society fences itself off from criminals, from the mentally ill and generally disconcerting people, it is invincible. You have one thing left: to soothe yourself with the thought that your presence here is indispensable."

"No one needs it."

"Once prisons and insane asylums exist, there must be someone to sit in them. If not you—then I; if not I—then some third person. Wait a bit till, in the distant future, prisons and insane asylums will have ceased to exist; then there will be no bars on the windows, no bathrobes. Such a time will come, of course, sooner or later."

Ivan Dmitrich smiled derisively.

"You're joking," he said, squinting. "People like you and your helper Nikita have no concern with the future, but you may be sure, my dear sir, that better times will come! If I express myself vulgarly, you may laugh; but the dawn of a new life is beginning to glow, truth will triumph—it'll be our turn to celebrate! I won't last that long, I'll expire, but, on the other hand, someone's great-grandsons will last out. I greet them with all my heart and I'm glad, glad for them! Forward! May God help you, friends!"

Ivan Dmitrich arose with shining eyes, and stretching his arms toward the window, continued with emotion in his voice: "From behind these bars I bless you! Yes, long live the truth! I'm glad!"

"I find no particular reason to be glad," said Andrei Yefimich, who found Ivan Dmitrich's gesture theatrical, but at the same time very pleasing. "Prisons and insane asylums won't exist, and the truth, as you like to put it, will triumph, but you see, the essence of things will not change, the laws of nature will remain exactly the same. People will suffer, grow old, and die, just as now. Whatever magnificent dawn illuminated your life, just the same, in the final end, they'd nail you in a coffin and throw you in a pit."

"And immortality?"

"Eh, nonsense!"

"You don't believe in it; well, I do. In Dostoevsky or in Voltaire, someone says if there were no God, people would have invented him. But I deeply believe that if there is no immortality, the great human mind will contrive it, sooner or later."

"Well said," Andrei Yefimich commented, smiling with pleasure. "It's good that you believe. With such faith, one can be well off even walled in. Did you have an education somewhere, if I may ask?"

"Yes, I attended the university, but didn't finish."

"You are a reasoning and meditative man. You can find consolation in yourself in any surroundings. Free and profound thought which strives toward an understanding of life, and a complete contempt for the foolish bustle of the world—those are two blessings higher than any man has ever known. And you can possess them even if you live behind three sets of bars. Diogenes lived in a barrel, yet was happier than all the earthly tsars."

"Your Diogenes was a blockhead," Ivan Dmitrich remarked morosely. "What's this you're telling me about Diogenes and about some kind of understanding?" He suddenly became angry and jumped up. "I love life, love it passionately! I have a persecution complex, a constantly tormenting fear, but there are minutes when a thirst for life seizes me, and then I am afraid of going out of my mind. I want terribly to live, terribly!"

He walked through the ward in agitation and said, lowering his voice: "When I dream, phantoms visit me. People of some sort come toward me; I hear voices, music, and it seems to me that I am walking through a kind of woods, along the seashore, and I long passionately for the bustle, the worries ... Tell me, well, what's new over there?" asked Ivan Dmitrich. "What's happening?"

"You want to hear about the town or things in general?"

"Well, first tell me about the town, and then things in general."

"Well? In town it's tediously boring ... There's nobody to exchange a word with, nobody to listen to. No new people. However, not long ago a young doctor arrived: Khobotov."

"He arrived after I was already here. An oaf, eh?"

"Yes, an uncultured man. It's strange, you know ... Everything considered, there's no intellectual stagnation in our cities, there's movement—

meaning, there must be genuine people there, but for some reason they invariably send us people the like of which you've never seen. Unfortunate town!"

"Yes, unfortunate town!" sighed Ivan Dmitrich, and he started laughing. "And how are things in general? What are they writing in the papers and magazines?"

It was already dark in the ward. The doctor rose and standing, began to describe what was being written abroad and in Russia, and what trend of thought was discernible now. Ivan Dmitrich listened attentively and posed questions, but suddenly, as if he had remembered something horrible, he seized his head and lay down on the bed with his back to the doctor.

"What's wrong with you?" asked Andrei Yefimich.

"You won't hear another word from me," Ivan Dmitrich said roughly. "Leave me alone!"

"Why?"

"I tell you: leave me! What the hell!"

Andrei Yefimich shrugged his shoulders, sighed, and went out. As he crossed the entry, he said: "If it might be cleaned up here, Nikita . . . Terribly strong odor!"

"At your orders, Your Honor."

"What a pleasant young man!" thought Andrei Yefimich as he went home to his apartment. "In all the time I've been living here, he seems to be the first one can talk to. He can reason and is interested in just the right things."

Reading, and then going to bed, he continued to think about Ivan Dmitrich, and on waking up the next morning, he remembered that he had met an intelligent and interesting person the day before, and decided to visit him again as soon as possible.

□ **X** □

Ivan Dmitrich was lying in the very same position as yesterday, his head clutched in his hands and his legs folded under. His face was not visible.

"Greetings, my friend," said Andrei Yefimich. "You're not asleep?"

"First of all, I'm no friend to you," Ivan Dmitrich answered into his pillow, "and secondly, you're exerting yourself in vain: you won't get a single word out of me."

"Strange . . ." Andrei Yefimich muttered, disconcerted. "Yesterday we were chatting so peacefully, but suddenly you took offense at something and immediately broke off . . . I probably expressed something awkwardly or, perhaps, uttered a thought not in accord with your convictions . . ."

"So you want me to believe that!" said Ivan Dmitrich, raising himself slightly and looking at the doctor derisively and anxiously; his eyes were red. "You can go spy and probe somewhere else, but there's nothing for you here. I already understood yesterday what you came for."

"A strange fantasy!" smiled the doctor. "Meaning you think I'm a spy?"

"Yes, I think so . . . Spy or doctor, through whom they're testing me—it's all the same."

"Ah, truly, what a—forgive me—odd fellow you are!" The doctor sat down on a stool near the bed and shook his head reproachfully. "But let us say you're right," he said. "Let us say I treacherously trip you on a word in order to hand you over to the police. They arrest you and then try you. But would you be worse off in court and in prison than here? And if they sent you to a settlement and even to hard labor, would it be worse than being locked up in this annex? I think it's no worse . . . What are you afraid of then?"

Evidently these words had an effect on Ivan Dmitrich. He sat down peacefully.

It was after four in the afternoon—the time when Andrei Yefimich is usually pacing around his apartment and Darushka is asking him if it is not time for his beer. In the courtyard, the weather was still and clear.

"I went out for a walk after dinner, and here I came to call, as you see," said the doctor. "It's really spring."

"What month is it now? March?" asked Ivan Dmitrich.

"Yes, the end of March."

"Muddy in the courtyard?"

"No, not very. You can already walk on the paths in the garden."

"It would be nice to drive somewhere out of town now in an open carriage," said Ivan Dmitrich, rubbing his red eyes as if only half awake; "and then return home to a warm, comfortable study and . . . have one's headache treated by a decent doctor . . . It's been so long since I lived like a human being. It's foul here! Unbearably foul!"

After yesterday's excitement he was exhausted and limp and spoke unwillingly. His fingers trembled and his face showed that he was suffering from an acute headache.

"There is no difference whatsoever between a warm, cozy study and this ward," said Andrei Yefimich. "Man's peace and contentment are not outside but within himself."

"How is that?"

"The ordinary man awaits the good or the bad from the outside, that is, from a carriage and a study, while the reasoning man—from his own self."

"Go preach that philosophy in Greece where it's warm and smells of oranges; it doesn't fit the climate here. Who was it I was talking to about Diogenes? You, wasn't it?"

"Yes, yesterday, to me."

"Diogenes didn't need a study and a warm place to live; it was hot without that there. Lie down in a barrel and eat oranges and olives. But take him to Russia to live and he'd be begging for a room inside in May, not just in December. He'd probably be doubled up from the cold."

"No. It's possible to not feel the cold, as with any other discomfort in general. Marcus Aurelius said, 'Pain is the living image of pain: make an effort to change this image, thrust it away, stop complaining, and the pain will disappear.' It's true. A sage or simply a reasoning, meditative man is distinguished precisely by his contempt for suffering; he is always content and never surprised by anything."

"Meaning I am an idiot since I suffer, am discontented, and am surprised at human villainy."

"You're wrong there. If you will reflect more often, you'll understand how insignificant all the exterior things which agitate us are. One must strive for an understanding of life, for in that lies the true blessing."

"Understanding . . ." frowned Ivan Dmitrich. "External, internal . . . I'm sorry, I don't understand it. All I know," he said, standing up and looking angrily at the doctor; "all I know is that God created me out of warm blood and nerves, yes! And organic tissue, if it's viable, must react to every irritation. And I react! I answer pain with a cry and tears; villainy with displeasure; foulness with revulsion. In my opinion this is reality and what is called life. The lower the organism, the less sensitive it is, and the more feebly it responds to irritation; the higher it is, the more responsively and energetically it reacts to reality. How could one deny that? A doctor, and he doesn't know such simple things! In order to despise suffering, to be always content, and to be surprised at nothing, you must reach this state here," and Ivan Dmitrich pointed to the bloated, fat-swollen peasant, "or inure yourself through suffering until you become completely insensitive to it, that is, in other words, until you stop living. I'm sorry, I'm no sage and no philosopher," Ivan Dmitrich continued with irritation, "and I don't understand any of this. I'm not in condition to argue."

"On the contrary you are arguing splendidly."

"The Stoics, whom you parody, were remarkable people, but their teaching became inert a good two thousand years ago, hasn't moved an inch forward since, and won't move because it's not practical and not part of life. Its success was limited to the minority which spends its life in the study and savoring of every kind of learning; the majority did not understand it. A doctrine which teaches indifference to wealth and the comforts of life, contempt for suffering and death, is absolutely incomprehensible to the large majority, because this majority has never known either wealth or comfort in life; and to despise suffering would mean to despise one's own life, for man's whole existence consists of the sensations of hunger, cold, insult, deprivation, and a Hamletlike fear of death. The whole of life lies in these sensations: one may be oppressed by it, hate it, but not despise it. Yes, so, I repeat, the Stoics' teachings can never have a future, they progress, as you see, from the beginning of the century to today, the struggle, sensibility to pain, a capacity for responding to irritation . . ."

Ivan Dmitrich suddenly lost the thread of his thoughts, stopped, and rubbed his forehead with vexation.

"I was about to say something important, then lost myself," he said. "Where was I? Yes! Here's what I'm saying: one of the Stoics sold himself into slavery in order to ransom someone close to him. There you see, meaning, the Stoic reacted to irritation too, because for such a magnanimous deed as self-destruction for someone close, one must have indignation, a compassionate heart. If I hadn't forgotten everything I'd ever learned here in confinement, I could recall something else. And take Christ? Christ responded to reality by crying, smiling, grieving, growing angry; even feeling melancholy; He didn't go to meet sufferings with a smile and didn't have contempt for death, but prayed in the Garden of Gethsemane that this cup would pass Him by."

Ivan Dmitrich laughed and sat down.

"Let us assume that man's peace and contentment is not outside him, but within himself," he continued. "Let us assume it's necessary to despise suffering and be surprised at nothing. But what basis do you yourself have for preaching this? Are you a sage? A philosopher?"

"No, I'm no philosopher, but everyone should preach this because it's common sense."

"No, I want to know why you consider yourself competent in the matter of understanding, contempt for suffering, and so on? Have you ever suffered? Do you have a knowledge of suffering? Allow me: were you whipped as a child?"

"No, my parents were averse to physical punishment."

"While my father flogged me cruelly. My father was a stern, hemorrhoidal functionary with a long nose and yellow neck. But let's talk about you. Throughout your whole life no one laid a finger on you, no one frightened you or hit you; you're strong as an ox. You grew up under your father's wing and studied at his expense, and then immediately got hold of a sinecure. For more than twenty years you've been living in a rent-free apartment with heat, light, a maid, and having in addition the right to work however and as much as you please, or even to do nothing at all. By nature you're a soft, lazy man, and you therefore tried to arrange your life so that nothing would bother you or force you to budge. You handed the work over to your assistant and such swine, while you yourself sat in warmth and tranquillity, amassed money, passed the time reading books, amusing yourself with reflections about diverse exalted nonsense and (Ivan Dmitrich glanced at the doctor's red nose) with drinking. In short, you haven't seen life, you don't know it at all, and you're acquainted with reality in theory only. Yet you despise suffering and are surprised at nothing for a very simple reason: all this hustle-bustle, external and internal, this contempt for life, suffering, and death; understanding, true blessing—all this is the most convenient philosophy for a Russian sluggard. For example, you see a peasant beating his wife. Why meddle? Let him beat her, they'll both die sooner or later just the same; and moreover, the one who beats wrongs himself, not the person he's beating. Getting drunk is stupid, unseemly, but if you drink—you die, and if you don't drink—you die. A woman comes with a toothache ... Well, so what? Pain is an image of pain and furthermore, you can't live without sickness in this world; we all die, and therefore off with the woman, don't disturb my thinking and drinking vodka. A young man asks for advice on what to do, how to live; someone else would have reflected a bit before answering, but here there's a ready answer: strive for understanding or for the true blessing. But what is this fantastic 'true blessing'? There's no answer, naturally. We're kept behind bars, left to rot, tortured, but this is splendid and rational because between this ward and a warm, cozy study there is no difference whatsoever. A comfortable philosophy: there's nothing to be done, your conscience is clear and you feel you're a sage ... No sir, this is no philosophy, no thought, no breadth of vision, but laziness, sham, sluggish stupefaction ... Yes!" Ivan Dmitrich became angry again. "You despise suffering, but never fear, pinch your finger in the door and you'll start howling at the top of your voice!"

"But perhaps I wouldn't howl," said Andrei Yefimich, smiling benignly.

"Yes, I bet! Look, if paralysis hit you, or, let's say, some fool and upstart used his position and rank to insult you publicly, and you knew he would go unpunished for it—well, then you would understand what it is to send other people off to understanding and the true blessing."

"That's original," said Andrei Yefimich, smiling with pleasure and rubbing his hands. "I'm pleasantly struck by your inclination to deduction, and the character sketch you just made of me is simply brilliant. I confess that talking with you gives me great pleasure. Well, I heard you through, now please hear me out ..."

□ **XI** □

This conversation continued for about an hour more and evidently made a deep impression on Andrei Yefimich. He began going to the annex every day. He went there in the mornings and after dinner, and often the evening darkness found him in conversation with Ivan Dmitrich. At first Ivan Dmitrich was wary of him, suspected him of evil intentions, and frankly expressed his hostility; then he became accustomed to him and his abrupt attitude turned into condescending irony.

Soon rumors about Dr. Andrei Yefimich's visits to Ward No. 6 began going around the hospital. No one—not the assistant nor Nikita nor the nurses—could understand why he went there, spent hours there; what he talked about, and why he wrote no prescriptions. His conduct seemed strange. Mikhail Averyanich frequently failed to find him home, which had never happened before, and Darushka was very disturbed because the doctor no longer drank beer at the appointed time and sometimes was even late for dinner.

One day—it was already the end of June—Dr. Khobotov came to see Andrei Yefimich on some business or other; not finding him at home, he went to look for him in the courtyard; he was told that the old doctor had gone to visit the mentally ill. Entering the annex and stopping in the entry, Khobotov heard the following conversation: "We'll never be in accord and you'll never succeed in converting me to your belief," Ivan Dmitrich was saying with irritation. "You are completely unfamiliar with reality and you've never suffered, but just fed on others' sufferings like a leech; while I've suffered uninterruptedly from the day I was born till now. Therefore I tell you frankly, I consider myself above you and more competent in every respect. It's not for you to teach me."

"I haven't the slightest pretension of converting you to my belief," said Andrei Yefimich softly, regretting people's refusal to understand him. "And that's not the point, my friend. The point is that you've suffered and I haven't. Sufferings and joys are transitory; leave them; the devil with them. The point is that you and I think; we see in each other people capable of thinking and reasoning, and this gives us solidarity, no matter how dissimilar our views may be. If you only knew, my friend, how bored I am by the general senselessness, incapability, denseness, and with what pleasure I talk to you each time! You are an intelligent man and I find you delightful."

Khobotov opened the door an inch and glanced in the ward: Ivan Dmitrich in his nightcap and Dr. Andrei Yefimich were sitting side by side. The lunatic was grimacing, shuddering and feverishly wrapping himself in his bathrobe, while the doctor sat motionless with head lowered, and his face was red, helpless, and sad. Khobotov shrugged his shoulders, grinned, and exchanged glances with Nikita, who also shrugged his shoulders.

The next day, Khobotov came to the annex with the assistant physician. Both stood eavesdropping in the entry.

"Looks like our old man's gone completely cuckoo!" said Khobotov on leaving the annex.

"Lord, have mercy on us sinners!" sighed the pompous Sergei Sergeich, carefully walking around a puddle to avoid spotting his brightly polished boots. "I confess, honored Yevgeny Fedorich, I've been expecting this for a long time!"

□ XII □

Thereafter, Andrei Yefimich began to notice a kind of secrecy around him. On meeting him, the attendants, nurses, and patients would look at him inquiringly and then whisper to each other. Little Masha, the superintendent's daughter, whom he used to enjoy meeting in the hospital garden, now inexplicably dashed away when he went up to her with a smile to stroke her head. When listening to him, postmaster Mikhail Averyanich no longer said: "Absolutely true," but muttered in incomprehensible embarrassment: "Yes, yes, yes . . ." and looked at him thoughtfully and sadly. For some reason he began advising his friend to give up vodka and beer, but being a delicate man, he did not talk about this directly, but through hints, telling first about a certain battalion commander, an excellent man, then about a regimental priest, a splendid fellow, both of whom drank and fell ill, but completely recovered after giving up drink. Two or three times, Andrei Yefimich's colleague Khobotov visited him; he, too, advised giving up drinking, and for no apparent reason prescribed bromic drops.

In August Andrei Yefimich received a letter from the town mayor requesting his presence on a very important matter. Arriving at the town hall at the appointed time, Andrei Yefimich found the military commander, the district school superintendent, a member of the town council, Khobotov and also a fat, blond man who was introduced to him as a doctor. This doctor, who had a difficult Polish name, lived thirty versts away on a stud farm and was just passing through town.

"This concerns you, sir," the council member said to Andrei Yefimich after everyone had exchanged greetings and sat down at the table. "Yevgeny

Fedorich here says that the dispensary is crowded in inadequate space in the main building and should be moved into one of the annexes. That, of course, is no problem; it can be moved, but the main difficulty is the annex needs repair."

"Yes, it won't do without repairs," said Andrei Yefimich after some thought. "If, for example, the corner annex were to be used as a dispensary, I believe a minimum of five hundred rubles would be needed for that. An unproductive expenditure."

Everyone was silent a moment.

"I already had the honor of reporting ten years ago," Andrei Yefimich continued in a gentle voice, "that in its present form this hospital represents a luxury beyond the town's means. It was built in the forties, but of course the means were not the same then. The town spends too much on unnecessary buildings and superfluous personnel. I think it would be possible, with another system, to support two model hospitals for the same money."

"Well then, please give us another system," the council member said briskly.

"I have already had the honor of reporting on this: transfer the medical section to the jurisdiction of the village council."

"Yes, give the village council money and it will steal it," laughed the fair-haired doctor.

"That's how it goes," agreed the council member, and he also started laughing.

Andrei Yefimich looked languidly and dully at the fair-haired doctor and said: "One must be just."

Again they were silent. Tea was served. The military commander, very embarrassed for some reason, touched Andrei Yefimich's hand across the table and said: "You've completely forgotten us, Doctor. But then, you're a monk: you don't play cards, don't like women. You're bored with our kind."

Everyone began talking about how boring it was for a well-bred person to live in this town. No theater, no music, and at the last dance at the club, there were about twenty ladies and only two cavaliers. The young people don't dance, but crowd around the buffet or play cards the whole time. Slowly and gently, not looking at anyone, Andrei Yefimich began to talk about what a pity, what a great pity it was that the citizens squander their vital energy, hearts, and minds on cards and gossip, and neither can nor want to spend the time in interesting conversation and reading, and do not want to make use of the pleasures the mind offers. There was only one interesting and remarkable mind; all the rest were base and shallow. Khobotov listened to his colleague attentively and suddenly asked: "Andrei Yefimich, what date is it today?"

Having received an answer, he and the fair-haired doctor, in the tone of examiners conscious of their own incompetence, began asking Andrei Yefimich what day it was today, how many days there are in a year, and whether it was true that a remarkable prophet lived in Ward No. 6.

In response to the last question, Andrei Yefimich blushed and said: "Yes, he's sick, but an interesting young man."

They asked him no more questions.

When he was putting on his overcoat in the entry, the military commander put a hand on his shoulder and said with a sigh: "For us old men, it's time for a rest."

As he left the hall, Andrei Yefimich understood that this had been a commission appointed to examine the state of his mind. He remembered the questions put to him, blushed, and for the first time in his life, deplored medicine.

"My God," he thought, remembering how the doctors had just examined him, "but they just heard about psychiatry so recently, and they hold an examination—how can they be so utterly ignorant? They haven't the slightest understanding of psychiatry!"

And for the first time in his life, he felt insulted and infuriated.

That same day, Mikhail Averyanich came to his house in the evening. Without a greeting, the postmaster went up to him, took him by both hands and said with emotion: "My dear, my friend, show me you believe in my sincere good will and consider me your friend . . . My friend!" And preventing Andrei Yefimich from speaking, he continued in agitation: "I love you for your erudition and the nobility of your soul. Listen to me, my dear. The rules of science oblige the doctors to hide the truth from you, but like a soldier I'll tell you the plain facts boldly: you're unwell! Forgive me, my dear, but it's the truth, everyone around noticed it long ago. Just now Dr. Yevgeny Fedorich told me you must rest and have some distraction for the sake of your health. Absolutely true! Splendid! I'm taking a leave now and going away to breathe another atmosphere. Show you're my friend, let's go together! Let's go, let's recapture our youth."

"I feel completely well," said Andrei Yefimich after reflecting. "And I can't go. Let me show you my friendship in some other way."

To go somewhere, for no reason, without books, without Darushka, without beer; to abruptly break a pattern of life established for twenty years—an idea of this sort seemed wild and fantastic to him at first. Then he thought of the conversation in the town hall, and his depressed frame of mind on returning home from there, and the thought of leaving, for a short time, the town in which stupid people considered him insane pleased him very much.

"And where exactly do you intend to go?" he asked.

"To Moscow, to St. Petersburg, to Warsaw . . . I spent five of the happiest years of my life in Warsaw. What an extraordinary town! Let's go, my dear!"

□   XIII   □

A week later, Andrei Yefimich was offered a rest, that is, asked to hand in his resignation, to which he reacted with indifference, and in another week he and Mikhail Averyanich were setting off in the stagecoach for the nearest railroad station. The days were cool, clear, with a blue sky and transparent horizon. They drove the two hundred versts to the station in forty-eight hours, stopping for the night twice on the way. When they were given badly washed glasses or when it took too long to harness the horses in the posting stations, Mikhail Averyanich would turn purple and, shaking all over, shout: "Shut up! Don't argue!" Seated in the carriage, he recounted without a minute's pause his travels through the Caucasus and the Polish Kingdom. How many adventures there had been, what encounters! He spoke loudly and made such round eyes that it was easy to believe he was lying. Moreover, as he talked, he breathed in Andrei Yefimich's face and guffawed in his ear. This bothered the doctor and kept him from thinking and concentrating.

For economy's sake, they traveled third class on the train in a car for nonsmokers. Half the passengers were respectable. Mikhail Averyanich soon became acquainted with everyone and, going from bench to bench, said loudly that one should not travel on these shocking railways. A complete fraud! It isn't like being on horseback: you sweep over a hundred versts in a day and feel healthy and fresh. And we have unproductive crops because they drained the Pinsky marshes. In general, the disorder is terrible. He became heated, spoke loudly, and did not let anyone else talk. This continual chatter interspersed with loud guffaws and vigorous gestures irked Andrei Yefimich.

"Which of us is insane?" he thought with annoyance. "I, who try not to disturb the passengers in any way, or this eogist, who thinks he is more intelligent and more interesting than anyone else and therefore gives nobody any peace?"

In Moscow, Mikhail Averyanich put on a military jacket without insignia and trousers with red piping. He walked around the streets in a military forage cap and a greatcoat, and soldiers saluted him. He now appeared to Andrei Yefimich as a man who had dissipated all the good traits of his aristocracy and kept only the bad. He loved to be waited on, even when it was completely unnecessary. He would shout for the waiter to bring him matches when there were matches lying on the table in front of him in plain sight; he was unembarrassed to appear in his underwear in front of the chambermaid; he indiscriminately addressed all lackeys, even the old men, with condescension, and when irritated, dubbed them blockheads and fools. This, Andrei Yefimich thought, was lordly, but disgusting.

Mikhail Averyanich first took his friend to the Iversky Chapel. He prayed fervently, bowing to the ground and weeping, after which he sighed deeply and said: "Even though you don't believe, it's somehow more peaceful when you pray. Kiss the holy image, my dear."

Andrei Yefimich became flustered and kissed the image while Mikhail Averyanich prayed in a whisper, his lips protruding and his head nodding, and tears started again in his eyes. Then they went to the Kremlin where they saw the Tsar-cannon and the Tsar-bell and even touched them with their fingers, enjoyed the view of the river, and visited Saint Savior's and the Rumyantsev Museum.

They had dinner at Testov's. Mikhail Averyanich studied the menu for a long time, smoothing his whiskers, and said in the tone of a gourmet at home in restaurants: "We'll see what you'll feed us today, my lamb!"

☐ XIV ☐

The doctor walked, gawked, ate, drank, but had only one feeling: annoyance with Mikhail Averyanich. He longed to take a rest from his friend, to get away from him, to hide; but his friend considered it his duty not to let the doctor out of his sight and to provide him with as many distractions as possible. When there was nothing to look at, he entertained him with conversation. Andrei Yefimich stood it for two days, then on the third, informed his friend he was ill and wished to spend the whole day in his room. His friend said in that case he, too, would stay home. Indeed, one must rest or one's legs would never hold out. Andrei Yefimich lay down on the couch, his face to the wall, and clenching his teeth, listened while his friend heatedly assured him that France would sooner or later, inevitably, beat Germany, that there were a great many swindlers in Moscow, and that one should never judge a horse's merits by its appearance. The doctor's ears began to hum and his heart to pound, but he was unable to make up his mind to ask his friend to either leave or be silent. Fortunately, Mikhail Averyanich tired of sitting in a hotel room and went out for a walk after dinner.

Left alone, Andrei Yefimich succumbed to a feeling of relief. How pleasant to lie motionless on a couch and know you are alone in the room! True happiness is impossible without solitude. The fallen angel probably betrayed God because he wanted solitude, which is unknown to the angels. Andrei Yefimich wanted to concentrate on the things he had seen and heard in the last few days, but he could not get Mikhail Averyanich out of his mind.

"But here he took leave and went with me out of friendship, out of magnanimity," the doctor thought with irritation. "There's nothing worse than this friendly guardianship. There you are, he seems kind, magnanimous, a jolly fellow, but he's boring. Unbearably boring. There are people like that who say nothing but intelligent and good things, yet you feel that they're unbearably dense."

During the following days, Andrei Yefimich declared himself sick and did not leave the hotel room. He lay with his face to the wall and suffered while his friend distracted him with conversation, or rested when his friend was absent. He was annoyed with himself for having come, and with his friend, who became more garrulous and familiar every day; he was completely unsuccessful in organizing his thoughts on a serious, elevated plane.

"I must be experiencing the reality Ivan Dmitrich spoke of," he thought, growing angry at his own pettiness. "However, it's rubbish ... I'll get home—and everything will go on as before ..."

In St. Petersburg, too, it was exactly the same: he did not leave the hotel room for days, lay on the couch, and only got up to drink beer.

Mikhail Averyanich was constantly in a hurry to get to Warsaw.

"My dear, why should I go there?" said Andrei Yefimich in a pleading voice. "Go alone, but let me go home! I beg you!"

"Under no condition!" protested Mikhail Averyanich. "It's an extraordinary town. I spent five of the happiest years of my life in it! I beg you!"

Andrei Yefimich did not have enough character to insist on his way, and with a sinking heart, he went to Warsaw. There he did not leave the hotel room, lay on the couch, and raged at himself, his friend, and the lackeys, who stubbornly refused to understand Russian, while Mikhail Averyanich, as usual, was hale, hearty, and jolly, scouring the city from morning till night and looking for his old acquaintances. Several times he did not come home for the night. After one night, spent no one knows where, he returned home in the early morning in a state of violent agitation. Red and disheveled, he paced from corner to corner for a long time, muttering to himself, then stopped and said: "Honor above all!"

After pacing a bit more, he clutched his head and announced in a tragic voice: "Yes, honor above all! Curse the moment I first thought of going into that Babylon! My dear," he turned to the doctor, "despise me! I've ruined myself gambling! Give me five hundred rubles!"

Andrei Yefimich counted out five hundred rubles and silently handed them to his friend. The latter, still purple with shame and anger, incoherently uttered some superfluous oath, put on his forage cap, and went out. Returning about two hours later, he fell into an armchair, sighed loudly, and said: "My honor is saved! Let's go, my friend! I don't want to stay in this accursed town another minute. Swindlers! Austrian spies!"

When the two friends returned to their own town, it was already November and a deep snow lay on the streets. Dr. Khobotov had taken Andrei Yefimich's place; he was still living in his old lodgings, waiting for Andrei Yefimich to come and clear out the hospital apartment. The homely woman he called his cook was already living in one of the annexes.

New hospital gossip was going around town. It was said that the homely woman had quarreled with the superintendent and that he had crawled on his knees before her, begging forgiveness.

Andrei Yefimich was obliged to look for a new apartment the very day of his return.

"My friend," the postmaster said to him timidly, "forgive an indiscreet question: what means do you have at your disposal?"

Andrei Yefimich silently counted his money and said: "Eighty-six rubles."

"I didn't mean that," Mikhail Averyanich said in confusion, not understanding the doctor. "I meant: what means do you have in general?"

"That's what I'm telling you: eight-six rubles ... I have nothing else."

Mikhail Averyanich considered the doctor an honest and honorable man, but still suspected him of having put aside at least twenty thousand. On learning that Andrei Yefimich was a pauper and had nothing to live on, he for some reason suddenly burst into tears and embraced his friend.

□ XV □

Andrei Yefimich was now living in the three-windowed little house of the commoner Belova. There were only three rooms in the house, not counting the kitchen. Two of them, with windows on the street, were occupied by the doctor, while Darushka and Belova with her three children lived in the third room and the kitchen. Occasionally a lover, a drunken peasant who bellowed and filled Darushka and the children with terror, came to spend the night with the mistress of the house. When he arrived, sat down in the kitchen and began demanding vodka, everyone became very uncomfortable, and the doctor used to take in the crying children out of pity and put them to bed on his floor, and this gave him great satisfaction.

The doctor arose at eight o'clock as before, and after having tea, sat down to read his old books and magazines. He no longer had money for new ones. Because the books were old or, perhaps, because of the change of circumstances, reading no longer fascinated, but tired him. To avoid spending his time idly, he organized a detailed catalogue of his books and glued labels on the backs of their covers; this mechanical, tedious work seemed more interesting to him than reading. In some incomprehensible way, monotonous, tedious work lulled his mind; he no longer thought about anything, and time passed quickly. Even sitting in the kitchen and scrubbing potatoes with Darushka or sorting over buckwheat seemed entertaining to him. On Saturdays and Sundays he went to church. Standing close to the wall and blinking his eyes, he would listen to the choir and think about his father, his mother, the university, and about religion; he was peaceful, melancholy, and later, as he left the church, he would regret that the service had ended so quickly.

Twice he went to the hospital to talk to Ivan Dmitrich. But both times, Ivan Dmitrich was unusually agitated and spiteful; he asked to be left in peace because he had tired of empty chatter long ago, and said that for all his sufferings, he asked the cursed wretched people for only one reward—solitary confinement. Could they refuse him even this? Both times, when Andrei Yefimich took leave of him and wished him good night, he snarled and said: "Go to the devil!"

And Andrei Yefimich did not know whether to go a third time or not. However, he wanted to go.

Formerly, after dinner, Andrei Yefimich used to walk around the room and think; now, from dinnertime until evening tea, he lay on the couch with his face to its back and yielded to petty thoughts which he was completely unable to subdue. He felt offended that after his more than twenty-year service they had given him neither a pension nor a bonus. True, he had served dishonestly, but then all civil employees receive pensions without exception, honest or not. Contemporary justice lies precisely in the fact that ranks, medals, and pensions are issued to reward not moral qualities and ability, but service in general, whatever it was. Why should he alone be an exception? He had absolutely no money. He was ashamed to walk past the tavern and see the owner. There were already thirty-two rubles due for beer. Money was due Belova, too. Darushka quietly sold old clothes and books and lied to the landlady, saying the doctor would soon receive a great deal of money.

He was angry with himself for having consumed on the trip the thousand rubles he had saved. How useful that thousand would be now! It annoyed him that people did not leave him in peace. Khobotov considered himself obliged to call on his sick colleague from time to time. Everything about him repelled Andrei Yefimich: the sated face and ugly, condescending voice, the word "colleague" and the high boots; what was particularly repellent was that he considered it his duty to treat Andrei Yefimich and thought he was in fact doing so. He brought a vial of bromic drops and some rhubarb pills on every visit.

Mikhail Averyanich also considered it his duty to call on his friend and entertain him. On each visit he behaved with affected familiarity, guffawed constrainedly, and assured Andrei Yefimich that he looked splendid today and that, thank God, things were getting better, and from this one could conclude that he considered his friend's condition hopeless. He had not yet paid back his Warsaw debt and was oppressed by a heavy shame; feeling constrained, he strove to laugh louder and talk more amusingly. His anecdotes and stories now seemed endless, and were agonizing for both Andrei Yefimich and himself.

In his presence, Andrei Yefimich usually lay on the couch with his face to the wall and listened, clenching his teeth; layers of seething distaste weighed on his heart, and after each of his friend's visits, he felt this seething rise higher and higher as if it were going to choke him.

To still his petty feelings, he would quickly start thinking about how he, Khobotov, and Mikhail Averyanich were to die sooner or later without leaving a dint on nature. When he tried to picture some sort of spirit flying past the earth in space after a million years, he saw only clay and naked rocks. Everything—even culture and moral law—would vanish without giving growth to so much as a bur. What did shame before the tavernkeeper matter, or the inane Khobotov, or the heavy friendship of Mikhail Averyanich? All that was trivia and nonsense.

But such arguments no longer helped. Hardly had he pictured the globe after a million years, when out from the naked rock appeared Khobotov in high boots or Mikhail Averyanich, guffawing constrainedly, and he even heard a shamefaced whisper: "And the Warsaw debt, my dear, I'll pay you back in the next few days ... without fail."

□ XVI □

One day Mikhail Averyanich came after dinner when Andrei Yefimich was lying on the couch. Khobotov happened to appear with bromic drops at the same time. Andrei Yefimich painfully raised himself, sat down, and braced himself on the couch with both hands.

"And today, my dear," Mikhail Averyanich began, "your face has much better color than yesterday. Yes, you're a fine fellow! A fine fellow, by God!"

"It's time now, it's time to get well, colleague," said Khobotov, yawning. "Perhaps you're getting tired of this trumpery yourself."

"We'll get well!" Mikhail Averyanich said merrily. "We'll live another hundred years! Yes, yes!"

"A hundred or not, twenty will be enough," comforted Khobotov. "Never mind, never mind, colleague, don't give up . . . Don't cloud things over."

"We'll still show what we're made of!" guffawed Mikhail Averyanich, and he slapped his friend on the knee. "We'll show them! Next summer, God willing, we'll sweep over to the Caucasus and ride all over it on horseback—clop! clop! clop! When we come back from the Caucasus, I shouldn't be surprised if we'd be going to a wedding." Mikhail Averyanich winked slyly. "We'll marry you, dear friend . . . marry . . ."

Andrei Yefimich suddenly felt the seething reach his throat; his heart was pounding frightfully.

"That's vulgar!" he said, quickly getting up and walking over to the window. "Don't you realize that you're saying vulgarities?"

He wanted to continue softly and politely, but in spite of himself, he suddenly clenched his fists and raised them above his head.

"Leave me!" he shouted in a strange voice, turning purple and trembling all over. "Out! Both of you, out, both!"

Mikhail Averyanich and Khobotov got up and stared at him, first in bewilderment and then in fear.

"Out, both of you!" Andrei Yefimich kept shouting. "Dense people! Stupid people! I don't need friendship nor your medicines, dense man! Vulgarity! Filth!"

Khobotov and Mikhail Averyanich, exchanging distraught glances, retreated to the door and went out in the entrance. Andrei Yefimich seized the vial of bromic drops and flung it after them; the vial shattered on the threshold with a crash.

"Go to the devil!" he shouted in a tearful voice, running into the entrance. "To the devil!"

After his guests' departure, shaking as if with fever, Andrei Yefimich lay down on the couch and kept repeating for a long time: "Dense people! Stupid people!"

When he had calmed himself, the first thought that came to him was that poor Mikhail Averyanich must now be frightfully embarrassed and heavyhearted, and that all this was terrible. Nothing of the kind had ever happened before. Where was his intelligence and tact? His understanding of things and philosophical indifference?

All night the doctor was unable to sleep from shame and annoyance with himself, and in the morning, at ten o'clock, he set off for the post office to apologize to the postmaster.

"We won't recall what happened," said Mikhail Averyanich with a sigh, much moved, firmly pressing his friend's hand. "Let whoever remembers the past lose an eye. Lyubavkin!" he suddenly shouted so loudly that all the postal staff and visitors jumped. "Bring a chair. And you wait a bit!" he shouted at a peasant woman who was poking a registered letter toward him through the grill. "Don't you see I'm busy? We won't remember the past," he continued tenderly, turning to Andrei Yefimich. "Sit down, I humbly beg you, my dear."

For a minute he silently stroked his knee and then said: "It didn't even occur to me to be offended by you. Illness isn't easy to take, I understand. Your fit frightened the doctor and me yesterday and we talked about you for a long time after. My dear, why don't you want to take care of your illness seriously? Can this go on? Forgive me for my friendly frankness," Mikhail Averyanich began whispering; "you live under the most unfavorable conditions: it's crowded, dirty, there's no one to nurse you, no money for treatment . . . My dear friend, the doctor and I implore you with all our hearts to listen to our advice: go to the hospital! There there's wholesome food and nursing and treatment. Between us, although Yevgney Fedorovich is *mauvais ton,** he's still knowledgeable; you can fully depend on him. He gave me his word he'd take care of you."

Andrei Yefimich was moved by the frank sympathy and the tears suddenly glistening on the postmaster's cheeks.

"Honored friend, don't believe it!" he whispered, putting his hand over his heart. "Don't believe them. It's a trick. My illness is only that in twenty years I've found only one intelligent person in the whole town, and he's a lunatic. There's no illness whatsoever; I simply fell into a bewitched circle from which there's no exit. It's all the same to me, I'm ready for anything."

"Go to the hospital, my dear."

"It's all the same to me, even into a pit."

"Give me your word, my dear, that you'll listen to Yevgeny Fedorich in everything."

"If you like, I'll give you my word. But I repeat, respected friend, I've fallen into a bewitched circle. Now everything, even the sincere sympathy of my friends, is bent to the same end—my finish. I'm finished and have the manliness to recognize it."

"You'll get well, dear friend."

"Why do you say that?" Andrei Yefimich asked with irritation. "It's a rare man who, before the end of his life, doesn't go through what I'm undergoing now. When you are told you have something on the order of bad kidneys or an enlarged heart and you begin taking treatment, or when they say you're a lunatic or a criminal, that is, in short, when people suddenly pay at-

* Bad taste.

tention to you, then you know that you've fallen into a bewitched circle you'll never get out of. If you try to get out, you get still more lost. You'd better give up because no human efforts can save you. That's how it seems to me."

Meanwhile people were crowding around the window grill. To avoid being in the way, Andrei Yefimich stood up and began taking leave. Mikhail Averyanich once again asked for his word of honor, and escorted him to the door.

Before evening that same day, Khobotov unexpectedly appeared at Andrei Yefimich's in his short fur coat and high boots, and said as if nothing had happened the day before: "I came to see you on business, colleague. I came to ask you: wouldn't you like to come with me on a consultation, ah?"

Thinking Khobotov wanted to distract him with a stroll or actually to permit him to earn something, Andrei Yefimich put on a coat and went out in the street. He was glad to have an opportunity to smooth over yesterday's wrong and make peace, and in his heart, he thanked Khobotov, who had not even mentioned yesterday and was apparently sparing his feelings. Such delicacy was hardly to be expected from this uncouth man.

"And where is your patient?" asked Andrei Yefimich.

"In the hospital. I've been wanting to show you for a long time now . . . Most interesting case."

They went into the hospital courtyard, and skirting the main building, turned toward the annex where the insane were housed. And all this in silence, for some reason. When they came into the annex, Nikita, as usual, jumped up and drew himself to attention.

"One man here developed a complication in the lungs," Khobotov said in an undertone as he entered the ward with Andrei Yefimich. "Wait here a moment, I'll be right back. I'm just going for a stethoscope."

And he left.

□ XVII □

It was already dusk. Ivan Dmitrich lay on his bed, his face buried in his pillow; the paralytic sat motionless, crying softly and moving his lips. The fat peasant and the former mail sorter were asleep. It was quiet.

Andrei Yefimich sat on Ivan Dmitrich's bed and waited. But half an hour went by, and instead of Khobotov, into the ward came Nikita, carrying a bathrobe, some underclothes, and slippers.

"Please get dressed, Your Honor," he said quietly. "This is your little bed, if you please, here," he added, pointing to an empty, obviously recently acquired bed. "It's nothing, God granting, you'll get well."

Andrei Yefimich understood everything. Without a word, he walked over to the bed at which Nikita was pointing and sat down; noticing that Nikita was standing and waiting, he undressed completely, feeling ashamed. Then he put on the hospital clothing; the drawers were very short, the shirt long, and the bathrobe smelled of smoked fish.

"You'll get well, God granting," repeated Nikita.

He collected Andrei Yefimich's clothing in his arms and went out, shutting the door behind him.

"It's all the same ..." thought Andrei Yefimich, bashfully wrapping himself in his bathrobe and feeling that he looked like a convict in his new clothing. "It's all the same ... All the same: a frock coat, a uniform, this bathrobe ..."

But what about his watch? And the notebook which had been in his side pocket? And his cigarettes? Where had Nikita taken his clothes? Now, perhaps, he would never again put on trousers, a waistcoat, and boots for the rest of his life. All this was somehow strange and even incomprehensible at first. Andrei Yefimich was still convinced now that there was no difference whatsoever between Belova's house and Ward No. 6, that everything in this world is nonsense and hustle and bustle; but still, his hands were trembling, his legs were growing cold, and he was uneasy at the thought that Ivan Dmitrich would soon wake up and see him in a bathrobe. He stood up, walked across the room, and sat down again.

Here he had been sitting for a half an hour, an hour, and was bored to exhaustion; was it possible to live through a day here, a week, and even years like these people? Here, now, he had sat a while, walked across the room, and sat down again; you could go look out the window and walk from corner to corner again. And then what? Sit there all the time like a Buddha and think? No, it was hardly possible.

Andrei Yefimich lay down, but immediately got up, wiped the cold sweat off his forehead with his sleeve, and felt that his whole face smelled of smoked fish. He walked across again.

"It's some kind of misunderstanding ..." he said aloud, spreading his hands in bewilderment. "It must be cleared up, there's a misunderstanding ..."

At that moment Ivan Dmitrich awoke. He sat up and propped his cheeks on his fists. He spat. Then he lazily glanced at the doctor and apparently understood nothing for the first moment; but soon his sleepy face became spiteful and derisive.

"Aha, they've shut you up here too, darling!" he said in a hoarse, drowsy voice, winking. "I'm very glad. First you drank other people's blood and now they'll drink yours. Splendid!"

"It's some kind of misunderstanding ..." said Andrei Yefimich, frightened by Ivan Dmitrich's words; he shrugged his shoulders and repeated: "A misunderstanding of some kind ..."

Ivan Dmitrich spat again and lay down. "Cursed life!" he snarled. "And what's bitter and insulting, you see, is this life won't end with a reward for suffering or an apotheosis, as in opera, but with death; peasants will come and drag the corpse by the hands and feet to the cellar. Brr! Well, never mind ... In return, we'll have our holiday in the other world ... I'll come back here from that world as a ghost and scare these vermin. I'll make them turn gray."

Moiseika returned home from one of his walks, and held out his hand on seeing the doctor.

"Give a little kopeck!" he said.

□ **XVIII** □

Andrei Yefimich walked over to the window and looked at the fields. Darkness was already falling, and on the horizon to the right, a cold, livid moon was rising. Nor far from the hospital fence, at about two hundred yards, no more, stood a tall white house surrounded by a stone wall. This was the prison.

"So this is reality!" thought Andrei Yefimich, and he became terrified.

The moon was terrifying, and the prison and the nails on the fence, the distant flames in the bone-charring factory. Andrei Yefimich heard a sigh behind him. He glanced around and saw a man with glistening stars and medals on his chest who was smiling and slyly winking. This, too, seemed terrifying.

Andrei Yefimich assured himself that there was nothing special about the moon and the prison, that sane people wear medals too, and that with time everything will rot and turn into clay; but despair suddenly overwhelmed him; he seized the window bars with both hands and shook them with all his strength. The strong bars did not yield.

Then, to calm his terror, he went over to Ivan Dmitrich's bed and sat down.

"I've lost my heart, my dear," he murmured, trembling and wiping off cold sweat. "Lost heart."

"Then philosophize," Ivan Dmitrich said derisively.

"My God, my God ... Yes, yes ... You once said there was no philosophy in Russia, but that everyone philosophizes, even the nobodies. But you see, the philosophizing of the nobodies does no one any harm," said Andrei Yefimich in a voice as if longing to cry and complain. "Why this spiteful laugh, my friend? And how can these nobodies avoid philosophizing if they're discontented? For an intelligent, cultured, proud, freedom-loving man, in God's image, to have no alternative to becoming a doctor in a dirty, stupid little town with a whole lifetime of cupping glasses, leeches, and mustard plaster! Charlatanism, narrowness, vulgarity! Oh, my God!"

"You're babbling idiocies. If being a doctor repels you, be a minister instead."

"There's nothing, nothing to be done. We're weak, my dear ... I was indifferent once, reasoned boldly and soundly, but it took just one rough touch from life for me to lose heart ... Prostration ... We're weak, we're wretched ... And you, too, my friend. You're intelligent, well-born, you imbibed good impulses with your mother's milk, but hardly had you stepped out into life than you were worn out and fell ill ... Weak, weak!"

Aside from fear and a feeling of insult, something else harassed Andrei Yefimich constantly from the onset of evening. At last he realized it was a desire for beer and a smoke.

"I'm going out of here, my dear," he said. "I'll tell them to give us some light here ... I can't ... not up to ..."

Andrei Yefimich went to the door and opened it, but Nikita immediately jumped up and stood in his way.

"Where're you going? Forbidden, forbidden!" he said. "It's time to sleep!"

"But, just for a minute, to walk around the courtyard!" Andrei Yefimich became panic-stricken.

"Forbidden, forbidden, not allowed. You know yourself."

Nikita slammed the door and leaned his back against it.

"But what difference will it make to anyone if I go out?" asked Andrei Yefimich, shrugging his shoulders. "I don't understand! Nikita, I must go out!" he said in a trembling voice. "I have to!"

"Don't make disorders, it's not good!" said Nikita didactically.

"The devil knows what this is!" screamed Ivan Dmitrich suddenly, and he jumped up. "What right does he have not to let us out? How dare they hold us here? It's clearly stated in the law, I think that no one can be deprived of freedom without a trial! It's violence! Tyranny!"

"Of course it's tyranny!" said Andrei Yefimich, encouraged by Ivan Dmitrich's cry. "I must, I have to go out. He has no right. Give way, I tell you!"

"Do you hear, you dense brute?" cried Ivan Dmitrich and he rapped his fist on the door. "Open or I'll break down the door. Slaughterer!"

"Open!" cried Andrei Yefimich, his whole body trembling. "I insist!"

"Talk away!" answered Nikita behind the door. "Talk away!"

"At least go call Yevgney Fedorich here. Tell him I ask him to come . . . for a minute!"

"Tomorrow he'll come himself."

"They'll never let us out!" Ivan Dmitrich was saying meanwhile. "They'll let us rot here! O Lord, is there really no hell in the other world and will these scoundrels be forgiven? Where is justice then? Open, scoundrel, I'm suffocating!" he cried in a hoarse voice and charged the door. "I'll beat my brains out! Murderers!"

Nikita quickly opened the door, shoved Andrei Yefimich aside roughly with both hands and his knee, then swung and struck him in the face with his fist. Andrei Yefimich felt as though a huge salt wave had covered him from his head down and was dragging him to bed; it was, in fact, salty in his mouth: probably blood flowing from his teeth. As if trying to swim out, he waved his arms and seized at someone's bed, and at that moment felt Nikita strike him twice on the back.

A loud shriek came from Ivan Dmitrich. They must be beating him too.

Then everything grew still. Watery moonlight filtered through the bars, and on the floor lay a shadow like a snare. It was terrible. Andrei Yefimich lay holding his breath; he was waiting with terror to be struck again. It was as though someone had taken a sickle, thrust it in him, and turned it a few times in his chest and bowels. He bit the pillow and clenched his teeth with pain, and suddenly amid the chaos, the terrible unendurable thought flashed clearly in his mind that these people who now looked like black shadows in the moonlight must have experienced the same pain for years, day after day. How could it happen that throughout over twenty years he had not known and had not wanted to know that? He had not known, had had no understanding of pain, meaning he was not guilty, yet his conscience, as intractable and hard as Nikita, made him grow cold from the top of his head to his heels. He jumped up, wanted to cry out with all his strength and run as fast as possible to kill Nikita, then Khobotov, the superintendent, and the orderly, then himself, but not a sound came out of his chest and his legs would not obey; panting, he tore at the bathrobe and shirt over his chest, ripped them, and fell unconscious on the bed.

□ XIX □

The next morning his head ached, his ears hummed, and he felt unwell throughout his body. He was not ashamed to remember his weakness of yesterday. He had been fainthearted, afraid even of the moon, had frankly expressed feelings and thoughts he had not suspected in himself before. For example, his thoughts about the discontent of the philosophizing nobodies. But now it was all the same to him.

He did not eat, did not drink, lay motionless, and kept silent.

"It's all the same to me," he thought when they questioned him. "I won't answer . . . It's all the same."

After dinner Mikhail Averyanich came bringing a quarter-pound of tea and a pound of fruit candy. Darushka also came and stood by the bed for a whole hour with an expression of dense sorrow on her face. Dr. Khobotov visited him too. He brought a vial of bromic drops and ordered Nikita to fumigate the ward.

Toward evening Andrei Yefimich died of an apoplectic fit. At first he felt a violent chill and nausea; something horrid seemed to penetrate his whole body, even his fingers, stretch from his stomach to his head, and flood his eyes and ears. It turned green before his eyes. Andrei Yefimich understood that his end had come and remembered that Ivan Dmitrich, Mikhail Averyanich, and millions of people believe in immortality. If it should suddenly exist? But he did not want immortality, and thought of it only for an instant. A herd of unusually handsome and graceful deer he had been reading about yesterday ran past him; then a woman stretched a hand toward him with a registered letter . . . Mikhail Averyanich said something. Then everything disappeared and Andrei Yefimich lost consciousness forever.

The peasants came, took him by the hands and feet, and carried him off to the chapel. There he lay on a table with open eyes and the moon illuminated him through the night. In the morning, Sergei Sergeich came, prayed piously before the crucifix, and closed his former superior's eyes.

A day later they buried Andrei Yefimich. The funeral was attended only by Mikhail Averyanich and Darushka.

FYODOR DOSTOEVSKY

Notes from Underground

Part One

UNDERGROUND[1]

I

I am a sick man . . . I am a spiteful man. I am an unpleasant man. I think my liver is diseased. However, I don't know beans about my disease, and I am not sure what is bothering me. I don't treat it and never have, though I respect medicine and doctors. Besides, I am extremely superstitious, let's say sufficiently so to respect medicine. (I am educated enough not to be superstitious, but I am.) No, I refuse to treat it out of spite. You probably will not understand that. Well, but *I* understand it. Of course, I can't explain to you just whom I am annoying in this case by my spite. I am perfectly well aware that I cannot "get even" with the doctors by not consulting them. I know better than anyone that I thereby injure only myself and no one else. But still, if I don't treat it, it is out of spite. My liver is bad, well then—let it get even worse!

I have been living like that for a long time now—twenty years. I am forty now. I used to be in the civil service, but no longer am. I was a spiteful official. I was rude and took pleasure in being so. After all, I did not accept bribes, so I was bound to find a compensation in that, at least. (A bad joke but I will not cross it out. I wrote it thinking it would sound very witty; but now that I see myself that I only wanted to show off in a despicable way, I will purposely not cross it out!) When petitioners would come to my desk

[1] The author of these notes and the "Notes" themselves are, of course, imaginary. Nevertheless, such persons as the writer of these notes, not only may, but positively must, exist in our society, considering those circumstances under which our society was in general formed. I wanted to expose to the public more clearly than it is done usually, one of the characters of the recent past. He is one of the representatives of the current generation. In this excerpt, entitled "Underground," this person introduces himself, his views, and, as it were, tries to explain the reasons why he appeared and was bound to appear in our midst. In the following excerpt, the actual notes of this person about several events in his life, will appear. (*Fyodor Dostoevsky*)

for information I would gnash my teeth at them, and feel intense enjoyment when I succeeded in distressing someone. I was almost always successful. For the most part they were all timid people—of course, they were petitioners. But among the fops there was one officer in particular I could not endure. He simply would not be humble, and clanked his sword in a disgusting way. I carried on a war with him for eighteen months over that sword. At last I got the better of him. He left off clanking it. However, that happened when I was still young. But do you know, gentlemen, what the real point of my spite was? Why, the whole trick, the real vileness of it lay in the fact that continually, even in moments of the worst spleen, I was inwardly conscious with shame that I was not only not spiteful but not even an embittered man, that I was simply frightening sparrows at random and amusing myself by it. I might foam at the mouth, but bring me some kind of toy, give me a cup of tea with sugar, and I would be appeased. My heart might even be touched, though probably I would gnash my teeth at myself afterward and lie awake at night with shame for months after. That is the way I am.

I was lying when I said just now that I was a spiteful official. I was lying out of spite. I was simply indulging myself with the petitioners and with the officer, but I could never really become spiteful. Every moment I was conscious in myself of many, very many elements completely opposite to that. I felt them positively teeming in me, these opposite elements. I knew that they had been teeming in me all my life, begging to be let out, but I would not let them, would not let them, purposely would not let them out. They tormented me till I was ashamed; they drove me to convulsions, and finally, they bored me, how they bored me! Well, are you not imagining, gentlemen, that I am repenting for something now, that I am asking your forgiveness for something? I am sure you are imagining that. However, I assure you it does not matter to me if you are.

Not only could I not become spiteful, I could not even become anything: neither spiteful nor kind, neither a rascal nor an honest man, neither a hero nor an insect. Now, I am living out my life in my corner, taunting myself with the spiteful and useless consolation than an intelligent man cannot seriously become anything and that only a fool can become something. Yes, an intelligent man in the nineteenth century must and morally ought to be pre-eminently a characterless creature; a man of character, an active man, is pre-eminently a limited creature. That is the conviction of my forty years. I am forty years old now, and forty years, after all, is a whole lifetime; after all, that is extreme old age. To live longer than forty years is bad manners; it is vulgar, immoral. Who does live beyond forty? Answer that, sincerely and honestly. I will tell you who do: fools and worthless people do. I tell all old men that to their face, all those respectable old men, all those silver-haired and reverend old men! I tell the whole world that to its face. I have a right to say so, for I'll go on living to sixty myself. I'll live till seventy! Till eighty! Wait, let me catch my breath.

No doubt you think, gentlemen, that I want to amuse you. You are mistaken in that, too. I am not at all such a merry person as you imagine, or as you may imagine; however, if irritated by all this babble (and I can feel that you are irritated) you decide to ask me just who I am—then my answer is, I am a certain low-ranked civil servant. I was in the service in order to have something to eat (but only for that reason), and when last year a distant relation left me six thousand roubles in his will I immediately retired from the service and settled down in my corner. I used to live in this corner before, but now I have settled down in it. My room is a wretched, horrid one on the outskirts of town. My servant is an old country-woman, spiteful out of stupidity, and, moreover, she always smells bad. I am told that the Petersburg climate is bad for me, and that with my paltry means it is very expensive to live in Petersburg. I know all that better than all these sage and experienced counsellors and monitors. But I am going to stay in Petersburg. I will not leave Petersburg! I will not leave because . . . Bah, after all it does not matter in the least whether I leave or stay.

But incidentally, what can a decent man speak about with the greatest pleasure?

Answer: About himself.

Well, then, I will talk about myself.

□ **II** □

Now I want to tell you, gentlemen, whether you care to hear it or not, why I could not even become an insect. I tell you solemnly that I wanted to become an insect many times. But I was not even worthy of that. I swear to you, gentlemen, that to be hyperconscious is a disease, a real positive disease. Ordinary human consciousness would be too much for man's everyday needs, that is, half or a quarter of the amount which falls to the lot of a cultivated man of our unfortunate nineteenth century, especially one who has the particular misfortune to inhabit Petersburg, the most abstract and intentional city in the whole world. (There are intentional and unintentional cities.) It would have been quite enough, for instance, to have the consciousness by which all so-called straightforward persons and men of action live. I'll bet you think I am writing all this to show off, to be witty at the expense of men of action; and what is more, that out of ill-bred showing-off, I am clanking a sword, like my officer. But, gentlemen, whoever can pride himself on his diseases and even show off with them?

However, what am I talking about? Everyone does that. They do pride themselves on their diseases, and I, perhaps, more than anyone. There is no doubt about it: my objection was absurd. Yet just the same, I am firmly convinced not only that a great deal of consciousness, but that any consciousness is a disease. I insist on it. Let us drop that too, for a minute. Tell me this: why did it happen that at the very, yes, at the very moment when I was most capable of recognizing every refinement of "all the sublime and beautiful," as we used to say at one time, I would, as though purposely, not only feel but do such hideous things, such that—well, in short, such as everyone probably does but which, as though purposely, occurred to me at the very time when I was most conscious that they ought not to be done. The more conscious I was of goodness, and of all that "sublime and beautiful," the more deeply I sank into my mire and the more capable I became of sinking into it completely. But the main thing was that all this did not seem to occur in me accidentally, but as though it had to be so. As though it were my most normal condition, and not in the least disease or depravity, so that finally I even lost the desire to struggle against this depravity. It ended by my almost believing (perhaps actually believing) that probably this was really my normal condition. But at first, in the beginning, that is, what agonies I suffered in that struggle! I did not believe that others went through the same things, and therefore I hid this fact about myself as a secret all my life. I was ashamed (perhaps I am even ashamed now). I reached the point of feeling a sort of secret abnormal, despicable enjoyment in returning home to my corner on some disgusting Petersburg night, and being acutely conscious that that day I had again done something loathsome, that what was done could never be undone, and secretly, inwardly gnaw, gnaw at myself for it, nagging and consuming myself till at last the bitterness turned into a sort of shameful accursed sweetness, and finally into real positive enjoyment! Yes, into enjoyment, into enjoyment! I insist upon that. And that is why I have started to speak, because I keep wanting to know for a fact whether other people feel such an enjoyment. Let me explain: the enjoyment here consisted precisely in the hyperconsciousness of one's own degradation; it was from feeling oneself that one had reached the last barrier, that it was nasty, but that it could not be otherwise; that you no longer had an escape; that you could never become a different person; that even if there remained enough time and faith for you to change into something else you probably would not want to change; or if you did want to, even then you would do nothing; because perhaps in reality there was nothing for you to change into. And the worst of it, and the root of it all, was that it all proceeded according to the normal and fundamental laws of hyperconsciousness, and with the inertia that was the direct result of those laws, and that consequently one could not only not change but one could do absolutely nothing. Thus it would follow, as the result of hyper-consciousness, that one is not to blame for being a scoundrel, as though that were any consolation to the scoundrel once he himself has come to realize that he actually is a scoundrel. But enough. Bah, I have talked a lot of nonsense, but what have I explained? Can this enjoyment be explained? But I will explain it! I will get to the bottom of it! That is why I have taken up my pen.

To take an instance, I am terribly vain. I am as suspicious and touchy as a hunchback or a dwarf. But to tell the truth, there have been moments when if someone had happened to slap my face I would, perhaps, have even been glad of that. I say, very seriously, that I would probably have been able to discover a peculiar sort of enjoyment even in that—the enjoyment, of course, of despair; but in despair occur the most intense enjoyments, especially when one is very acutely conscious of one's hopeless position. As for the slap in the face—why then the consciousness of being beaten to a pulp would positively overwhelm one. The worst of it is, no matter how I tried, it still turned out that I was always the most to blame in everything, and what is most humiliating of all, to blame for no fault of my own but, so to say, through the laws of nature. In the first place, to blame because I am cleverer than any of the people surrounding me. (I have always considered myself cleverer than any of the people surrounding me, and sometimes, would you believe it, I have even been ashamed of that. At any rate, all my life, I have, as it were, looked away and I could never look people straight in the eye.) To blame, finally, because even if I were magnanimous, I would only have suffered more from the consciousness of all its uselessness. After all, I would probably never have been able to do anything with my magnanimity—neither to forgive, for my assailant may have slapped me because of the laws of nature, and one cannot forgive the laws of nature; nor to forget, for even if it were the laws of nature, it is insulting all the same. Finally, even if I had wanted to be anything but magnanimous, had desired on the contrary to revenge myself on the man who insulted me, I could not have revenged myself on anyone for anything because I would certainly never have made up my mind to do anything, even if I had been able to. Why would I not have made up my mind? I want to say a few words about that in particular.

□ **III** □

After all, people who know how to revenge themselves and to take care of themselves in general, how do they do it? After all, when they are possessed, let us suppose, by the feeling of revenge, then for the time there is nothing else but that feeling left in their whole being. Such a man simply rushes straight toward his object like an infuriated bull with its horns down, and nothing but a wall will stop him. (By the way: facing the wall, such people—that is, the straightforward persons and men of action—are genuinely nonplussed. For them a wall is not an evasion, as for example for us people who think and consequently do nothing; it is not an excuse for turning aside, an excuse for which our kind is always very glad, though we scarcely believe in it ourselves, usually. No, they are nonplussed in all sincerity. The wall has for them something tranquilizing, morally soothing, final—maybe even something mysterious . . . but of the wall later.) Well, such a direct person I regard as the real normal man, as his tender mother nature wished to see him when she graciously brought him into being on the earth. I envy such a man till I am green in the face. He is stupid. I am not disputing that, but perhaps the normal man should be stupid, how do you know? Perhaps it is very beautiful, in fact. And I am all the more convinced of that suspicion, if one can call it so, by the fact that if, for instance, you take the antithesis of the normal man, that is, the hyperconscious man, who has come, of course, not out of the lap of nature but out of a retort (this is almost mysticism, gentlemen, but I suspect this, too), this retort-made man is sometimes so nonplussed in the presence of his antithesis that with all his hyperconsciousness he genuinely thinks of himself as a mouse and not a man. It may be a hyperconscious mouse, yet it is a mouse, while the other is a man, and therefore, etc. And the worst is, he himself, his very own self, looks upon himself as a mouse. No one asks him to do so. And that is an important point. Now let us look at this mouse in action. Let us suppose, for instance, that it feels insulted, too (and it almost always does feel insulted), and wants to revenge itself too. There may even be a greater accumulation of spite in it than in *l'homme de la nature et de la vérité*. The base, nasty desire to repay with spite whoever has offended it, rankles perhaps even more nastily in it than in *l'homme de la nature et de la vérité*, because *l'homme de la nature et de la vérité* through his innate stupidity looks upon his revenge as justice pure and simple; while in consequence of his hyperconsciousness the mouse does not believe in the justice of it. To come at last to the deed itself, to the very act of revenge. Apart from the one fundamental nastiness the unfortunate mouse succeeds in creating around it so many other nastinesses in the form of doubts and questions, adds to the one question so many unsettled questions, that there inevitably works up around it a sort of fatal brew, a stinking mess, made up of its doubts, agitations and lastly of the contempt spat upon it by the straightforward men of action who stand solemnly about it as judges and arbitrators, laughing at it till their healthy sides ache. Of coure the only thing left for it is to dismiss all that with a wave of its paw, and, with a smile of assumed contempt in which it does not even believe itself, creep ignominiously into its mouse-hole. There, in its nasty, stinking, underground home our insulted, crushed and ridiculed mouse promptly becomes absorbed in cold, malignant and, above all, everlasting spite. For forty years together it will remember its injury down to the smallest, most shameful detail, and every time will add, of itself, details still more shameful, spitefully teasing and irritating itself with its own imagination. It will be ashamed of its own fancies, but yet it will recall everything, it will go over it again and again, it will invent lies against itself pretending that those things might have happened, and will forgive nothing. Maybe it will begin to revenge itself, too, but, as it were, piecemeal, in trivial ways, from behind the stove, incognito, without believing either in its own right to vengeance, or in the success of its revenge, knowing beforehand that from all its efforts at revenge it will suffer a hundred times more than he on whom it revenges itself, while he, probably will not even feel it. On its deathbed it will recall it all over again, with interest accumulated over all the years. But it is just in that cold, abominable half-despair, half-belief, in that conscious burying oneself alive for grief in the underworld for forty years, in that hyperconsciousness and yet to some extent doubtful hopelessness of one's position, in that hell of unsatisfied desires turned inward, in that fever of oscillations, of resolutions taken for ever and regretted again a minute later—that the savor of that strange enjoyment of which I have spoken lies. It is so subtle, sometimes so difficult to analyze consciously, that somewhat limited people, or simply people with strong nerves, will not understand anything at all in it. "Possibly," you will add on your own account with a grin, "people who have never received a slap in the face will not understand it either," and in that way you will politely hint to me that I, too, perhaps, have been slapped in the face in my life, and so I speak as an expert. I'll bet that you are thinking that. But set your minds at rest, gentlemen, I have not received a slap in the face, though it doesn't matter to me at all what you may think about it. Possibly, I even myself regret that I have given so few slaps in the face during my life. But enough, not another word on the subject of such extreme interest to you.

I will continue calmly about people with strong nerves who do not understand a certain refinement of enjoyment. Though in certain circumstances these gentlemen bellow their loudest like bulls, though this, let us suppose, does them the greatest honor, yet, as I have already said, confronted with the impossible they at once resign themselves. Does the impossible mean the stone wall? What stone wall? Why, of course, the laws of nature, the conclusions of natural science, of mathematics. As soon as they prove to you, for instance, that you are descended from a monkey, then it is no use scowling, accept it as a fact. When they prove to you that in reality one drop of your own fat must be dearer to you than a hundred thousand of your fellow creatures, and that this conclusion is the final solution of all so-called virtues and duties and all such ravings and prejudices, then you might as well accept it, you can't do anything about it, because two times two is a law of mathematics. Just try refuting it.

"But really," they will shout at you, "there is no use protesting; it is a case of two times two makes four! Nature does not ask your permission, your wishes, and whether you like or dislike her laws does not concern her. You are bound to accept her as she is, and consequently also all her conclusions. A wall, you see, is a wall—etc. etc." Good God! but what do I care about the laws of nature and arithmetic, when, for some reason, I dislike those laws and the fact that two times two makes four? Of course I cannot break through a wall by battering my head against it if I really do not have the strength to break through it, but I am not going to resign myself to it simply because it is a stone wall and I am not strong enough.

As though such a stone wall really were a consolation, and really did contain some word of conciliation, if only because it is as true as two times two makes four. Oh, absurdity of absurdities! How much better it is to understand it all, to be conscious of it all, all the impossibilities and the stone walls, not to resign yourself to a single one of those impossibilities and stone walls if it disgusts you to resign yourself; to reach, through the most inevitable, logical combinations, the most revolting conclusions on the everlasting theme that you are yourself somehow to blame even for the stone wall, though again it is as clear as day you are not to blame in the least, and therefore grinding your teeth in silent impotence sensuously to sink into inertia, brooding on the fact that it turns out that there is even no one for you to feel vindictive against, that you have not, and perhaps never will have, an object for your spite, that it is a sleight-of-hand, a bit of juggling, a card-sharper's trick, that it is simply a mess, no knowing what and no knowing who, but in spite of all these uncertainties, and jugglings, still there is an ache in you, and the more you do not know, the worse the ache.

☐ IV ☐

"Ha, ha, ha! Next you will find enjoyment in a toothache," you cry with a laugh.

"Well? So what? There is enjoyment even in a toothache," I answer. I had a toothache for a whole month and I know there is. In that case, of course, people are not spiteful in silence, they moan; but these are not sincere moans, they are malicious moans, and the maliciousness is the whole point. The sufferer's enjoyment finds expression in those moans; if he did not feel enjoyment in them he would not moan. It is a good example, gentlemen, and I will develop it. The moans express in the first place all the aimlessness of your pain, which is so humiliating to your consciousness; the whole legal system of Nature on which you spit disdainfully, of course, but from which you suffer all the same while she does not. They express the consciousness that you have no enemy, but that you do have a pain; the consciousness that in spite of all the dentists in the world you are in complete slavery to your teeth; that if someone wishes it, your teeth will leave off aching, and if he does not, they will go on aching another three months; and that finally if you still disagree and still protest, all that is left you for your own gratification is to thrash yourself or beat your wall with your fist as hard as you can, and absolutely nothing more. Well then, these mortal insults, these jeers on the part of someone unknown, end at least in an enjoyment which sometimes reaches the highest degree of sensuality. I beg you, gentlemen, to listen sometimes to the moans of an educated man of the nineteenth century who is suffering from a toothache, particularly on the second or third day of the attack, when he has already begun to moan not as he moaned on the first day, that is, not simply because he has a toothache, not just as any coarse peasant might moan, but as a man affected by progress and European civilization, a man who is "divorced from the soil and the national principles," as they call it these days. His moans become nasty, disgustingly spiteful, and go on for whole days and nights. And, after all, he himself knows that he does not benefit at all from his moans; he knows better than anyone that he is only lacerating and irritating himself and others in vain; he knows that even the audience for whom he is exerting himself and his whole family now listen to him with loathing, do not believe him for a second, and that deep down they understand that he could moan differently, more simply, without trills and flourishes, and that he is only indulging himself like that out of spite, out of malice. Well, sensuality exists precisely in all these consciousnesses and infamies. "It seems I am troubling you, I am lacerating your hearts, I am keeping everyone in the house awake. Well, stay awake then, you, too, feel every minute that I have a toothache. I am no longer the hero to you now that I tried to appear before, but simply a nasty person, a scoundrel. Well, let it be that way, then! I am very glad that you see through me. Is it nasty for you to hear my foul moans? Well, let it be nasty. Here I will let you have an even nastier flourish in a minute...." You still do not understand, gentlemen? No, it seems our development and our consciousness must go further to understand all the intricacies of this sensuality. You laugh? I am delighted. My jokes, gentlemen, are of course in bad taste, uneven, involved, lacking self-confidence. But of course that is because I do not respect myself. Can a man with consciousness respect himself at all?

◻ **V** ◻

Come, can a man who even attempts to find enjoyment in the very feeling of self-degradation really have any respect for himself at all? I am not saying this now from any insipid kind of remorse. And, indeed, I could never endure to say, "Forgive me, Daddy, I won't do it again," not because I was incapable of saying it, but, on the contrary, perhaps just because I was too capable of it, and in what a way, too! As though on purpose I used to get into trouble on occasions when I was not to blame in the faintest way. That was the nastiest part of it. At the same time I was genuinely touched and repentant, I used to shed tears and, of course, tricked even myself, though it was not acting in the least and there was a sick feeling in my heart at the time. For that one could not even blame the laws of nature, though the laws of nature have offended me continually all my life more than anything. It is loathsome to remember it all, but it was loathsome even then. Of course, in a minute or so I would realize with spite that it was all a lie, a lie, an affected, revolting lie, that is, all this repentance, all these emotions, these vows to reform. And if you ask why I worried and tortured myself that way, the answer is because it was very dull to twiddle one's thumbs, and so one began cutting capers. That is really it. Observe yourselves more carefully, gentlemen, then you will understand that that's right! I invented adventures for myself and made up a life, so as to live at least in some way. How many times it has happened to me—well, for instance, to take offence at nothing, simply on purpose; and one knows oneself, of course, that one is offended at nothing, that one is pretending, but yet one brings oneself, at last, to the point of really being offended. All my life I have had an impulse to play such pranks, so that in the end, I could not control it in myself. Another time, twice, in fact, I tried to force myself to fall in love. I even suffered, gentlemen, I assure you. In the depth of my heart I did not believe in my suffering, there was a stir of mockery, but yet I did suffer, and in the real, regular way I was jealous, I was beside myself, and it was all out of boredom, gentlemen, all out of boredom; inertia overcame me. After all, the direct, legitimate, immediate fruit of consciousness is inertia, that is, conscious thumb twiddling. I have referred to it already, I repeat, I repeat it emphatically: all straightforward persons and men of action are active just because they are stupid and limited. How can that be explained? This way: as a result of their limitation they take immediate and secondary causes for primary ones, and in that way persuade themselves more quickly and easily than other people do that they have found an infallible basis for their activity, and their minds are at ease and that, you know, is the most important thing. To begin to act, you know, you must first have your mind completely at ease and without a trace of doubt left in it. Well, how am I, for example, to set my

mind at rest? Where are the primary causes on which I am to build? Where
are my bases? Where am I to get them from? I exercise myself in the process
of thinking, and consequently with me every primary cause at once draws
after itself another still more primary, and so on to infinity. That is precisely
the essence of every sort of consciousness and thinking. It must be a case of
the laws of nature again. In what does it finally result? Why, just the same.
Remember I spoke just now of vengeance. (I am sure you did not grasp
that.) I said that a man revenges himself because he finds justice in it. Therefore he has found a primary cause, found a basis, to wit, justice. And so he is
completely set at rest, and consequently he carries out his revenge calmly and
successfully, as he is convinced that he is doing a just and honest thing. But,
after all, I see no justice in it, I find no sort of virtue in it either, and consequently if I attempt to revenge myself, it would only be out of spite. Spite, of
course, might overcome everything, all my doubts, and could consequently
serve quite successfully in a place of a primary cause, precisely because it is not
a cause. But what can be done if I do not even have spite (after all, I began
with that just now)? Again, in consequence of those accursed laws of consciousness, my spite is subject to chemical disintegration. You look into it,
the object flies off into air, your reasons evaporate, the criminal is not to be
found, the insult becomes fate rather than an insult, something like the
toothache, for which no one is to blame, and consequently there is only the
same outlet left again—that is, to beat the wall as hard as you can. So you
give it up as hopeless because you have not found a fundamental cause. And
try letting yourself be carried away by your feelings, blindly, without reflection, without a primary cause, repelling consciousness at least for a time; hate
or love, if only not to sit and twiddle your thumbs. The day after tomorrow,
at the latest, you will begin despising yourself for having knowingly deceived
yourself. The result—a soap-bubble and inertia. Oh, gentlemen, after all, perhaps I consider myself an intelligent man only because all my life I have been
able neither to begin nor to finish anything. Granted, granted I am a babbler,
a harmless annoying babbler, like all of us. But what is to be done if the direct and sole vocation of every intelligent man is babble, that is, the intentional pouring of water through a sieve?

□ **VI** □

Oh, if I had done nothing simply out of laziness! Heavens, how I would have
respected myself then. I would have respected myself because I would at least

have been capable of being lazy; there would at least have been in me one positive quality, as it were, in which I could have believed myself. Question: Who is he? Answer: A loafer. After all, it would have been pleasant to hear that about oneself! It would mean that I was positively defined, it would mean that there was something to be said about me. "Loafer"—why, after all, it is a calling and an appointment, it is a career, gentlemen. Do not joke, it is so. I would then, by rights, be a member of the best club, and would occupy myself only in continually respecting myself. I knew a gentleman who prided himself all his life on being a connoisseur of Lafitte. He considered this as his positive virtue, and never doubted himself. He died, not simply with a tranquil but with a triumphant conscience, and he was completely right. I should have chosen a career for myself then too: I would have been a loafer and a glutton, not a simple one, but, for instance, one in sympathy with everything good and beautiful. How do you like that? I have long had visions of it. That "sublime and beautiful" weighs heavily on my mind at forty. But that is when I am forty, while then—oh, then it would have been different! I would have found myself an appropriate occupation, namely, to drink to the health of everything sublime and beautiful. I would have seized every opportunity to drop a tear into my glass and then to drain it to all that is sublime and beautiful. I would then have turned everything into the sublime and the beautiful; I would have sought out the sublime and the beautiful in the nastiest, most unquestionable trash. I would have become as tearful as a wet sponge. An artist, for instance, paints Ge's picture.[2] At once I drink to the health of the artist who painted Ge's picture, because I love all that is "sublime and beautiful." An author writes "Whatever You Like"[3]; at once I drink to the health of "Whatever You Like" because I love all that is "sublime and beautiful." I would demand respect for doing so, I would persecute anyone who would not show me respect. I would live at ease, I would die triumphantly—why, after all, it is charming, perfectly charming! And what a belly I would have grown, what a triple chin I would have established, what a red nose I would have produced for myself, so that every passer-by would have said, looking at me: "Here is an asset! Here is something really positive!" And, after all, say what you like, it is very pleasant to hear such remarks about oneself in this negative age, gentlemen.

[2] N. N. Ge exhibited his "Last Supper" in 1863. Dostoevsky thought it a faulty conception. The sentence makes no grammatical sense and may refer to Shchedrin's article on the painting, wherein its meaning is further distorted so that, in a sense, "a new picture" is created.

[3] An article on improving man written by Shchedrin, in 1863.

□ VII □

But these are all golden dreams. Oh, tell me, who first declared, who first proclaimed, that man only does nasty things because he does not know his own real interests; and that if he were enlightened, if his eyes were opened to his real normal interests, man would at once cease to do nasty things, would at once become good and noble because, being enlightened and understanding his real advantage, he would see his own advantage in the good and nothing else, and we all know that not a single man can knowingly act to his own disadvantage. Consequently, so to say, he would begin doing good through necessity. Oh, the babe! Oh, the pure, innocent child! Why, in the first place, when in all these thousands of years has there ever been a time when man has acted only for his own advantage? What is to be done with the millions of facts that bear witness that men, *knowingly*, that is, fully understanding their real advantages, have left them in the background and have rushed headlong on another path, to risk, to chance, compelled to this course by nobody and by nothing, but, as it were, precisely because they did not want the beaten track, and stubbornly, willfully, went off on another difficult, absurd way seeking it almost in the darkness. After all, it means that this stubbornness and willfulness were more pleasant to them than any advantage. Advantage! What is advantage? And will you take it upon yourself to define with perfect accuracy in exactly what the advantage of man consists of? And what if it so happens that a man's advantage *sometimes* not only may, but even must, consist exactly in his desiring under certain conditions what is harmful to himself and not what is advantageous. And if so, if there can be such a condition then the whole principle becomes worthless. What do you think—are there such cases? You laugh; laugh away, gentlemen, so long as you answer me: have man's advantages been calculated with perfect certainty? Are there not some which not only have been included but cannot possibly be included under any classification? After all, you, gentlemen, so far as I know, have taken your whole register of human advantages from the average of statistical figures and scientific-economic formulas. After all, your advantages are prosperity, wealth, freedom, peace—and so on, and so on. So that a man who, for instance, would openly and knowingly oppose that whole list would, to your thinking, and indeed to mine too, of course, be an obscurantist or an absolute madman, would he not? But, after all, here is something amazing: why does it happen that all these statisticians, sages and lovers of humanity, when they calculate human advantages invariably leave one out? They don't even take it into their calculation in the form in which it should be taken, and the whole reckoning depends upon that. There would be no great harm to take it, this advantage, and to add it to the list. But the trouble is, that this strange advantage does not fall under any classification and does not figure in any list. For instance, I have a friend. Bah, gentlemen! But after all he is your friend, too; and indeed there is no one, no one, to whom he is not a friend! When he prepares for any undertaking this gentleman immediately explains to you, pompously and clearly, exactly how he must act in accordance with the laws of reason and truth. What is more, he will talk to you with excitement and passion of the real normal interests of man; with irony he will reproach the short-sighted fools who do not understand their own advantage, for the true significance of virtue; and, within a quarter of an hour, without any sudden outside provocation, but precisely through that something internal which is stronger than all his advantages, he will go off on quite a different tack—that is, act directly opposite to what he has just been saying himself, in opposition to the laws of reason, in opposition to his own advantage—in fact, in opposition to everything. I warn you that my friend is a compound personality, and therefore it is somehow difficult to blame him as an individual. The fact is, gentlemen, it seems that something that is dearer to almost every man than his greatest advantages must really exist, or (not to be illogical) there is one most advantageous advantage (the very one omitted of which we spoke just now) which is more important and more advantageous than all other advantages, for which, if necessary, a man is ready to act in opposition to all laws, that is, in opposition to reason, honor, peace, prosperity—in short, in opposition to all those wonderful and useful things if only he can attain that fundamental, most advantageous advantage which is dearer to him than all.

"Well, but it is still advantage just the same," you will retort. But excuse me, I'll make the point clear, and it is not a case of a play on words, but what really matters is that this advantage is remarkable from the very fact that it breaks down all our classifications, and continually shatters all the systems evolved by lovers of mankind for the happiness of mankind. In short, it interferes with everything. But before I mention this advantage to you, I want to compromise myself personally, and therefore I boldly declare that all these fine systems—all these theories for explaining to mankind its real normal interests, so that inevitably striving to obtain these interests, it may at once become good and noble—are, in my opinion, so far, mere logical exercises! Yes, logical exercises. After all, to maintain even this theory of the regeneration of mankind by means of its own advantage, is, after all, to my mind almost the same thing as—as to claim, for instance, with Buckle, that through civilization mankind becomes softer, and consequently less bloodthirsty, and less fitted for warfare. Logically it does not seem to follow from his arguments. But man is so fond of systems and abstract deductions that he is ready to distort the truth intentionally, he is ready to deny what he can see and hear just to justify his logic. I take this example because it is the most glaring instance of it. Only look about you: blood is being spilled in streams, and in the merriest way, as though it were champagne. Take the whole of the nineteenth century in which Buckle lived. Take Napoleon—both the Great and the present one. Take North America—the eternal union. Take farcical Schleswig-Holstein. And what is it that civilization softens in us? Civilization only produces a greater variety of sensations in man—and absolutely nothing more. And through the development of this variety, man may even come to find enjoyment in bloodshed. After all, it has already happened to him. Have you noticed that the subtlest slaughterers have almost always been the most civilized gentlemen, to whom the various Attilas and Stenka Razins could never hold a candle, and if they are not so conspicuous as the Attilas and Stenka Razins it is precisely because they are so often met with, are so ordinary and have become so familiar to us. In any case if civilization has not made man more bloodthirsty, it has at least made him more abominably, more loathsomely bloodthirsty than before. Formerly he saw justice in bloodshed and with his conscience at peace exterminated whomever he thought he should. And now while we consider bloodshed an abomination, we nevertheless engage in this abomination and even more than ever before. Which is worse? Decide that for yourselves. It is said that Cleopatra (pardon the example from Roman history) was fond of sticking gold pins into her slavegirls' breasts and derived enjoyment from their screams and writhing. You will say that that occurred in comparatively barbarous times; that these are barbarous times too, because (also comparatively speaking) pins are stuck in even now; that even though man has now learned to see more clearly occasionally than in barbarous times, he is still far from having *accustomed* himself to act as reason and science would dictate. But all the same you are fully convinced that he will inevitably accustom himself to it when he gets completely rid of certain old bad habits, and when common sense and science have completely re-educated human nature and turned it in a normal direction. You are confident that man will then refrain from erring *intentionally*, and will, so to say, willy-nilly, not want to set his will against his normal interests. More than that: then, you say, science itself will teach man (though to my mind that is a luxury) that he does not really have either caprice or will of his own and that he has never had it, and that he himself is something like a piano key or an organ stop, and that, moreover, laws of nature exist in this world, so that everything he does is not done by his will at all, but is done by itself, according to the laws of nature. Consequently we have only to discover these laws of nature, and man will no longer be responsible for his actions and life will become exceedingly easy for him. All human actions will then, of course, be tabulated according to these laws, mathematically, like tables of logarithms up to 108,000 and entered in a table; or, better still, there would be published certain edifying works like the present encyclopedic lexicons, in which everything will be so clearly calculated and designated that there will be no more incidents or adventures in the world.

Then—it is still you speaking—new economic relations will be established, all ready-made and computed with mathematical exactitude, so that every possible question will vanish in a twinkling, simply because every possible answer to it will be provided. Then the crystal palace will be built. Then—well, in short, those will be halcyon days. Of course there is no guaranteeing (this is my comment now) that it will not be, for instance, terribly boring then (for what will one have to do when everything is calculated according to the table?) but on the other hand everything will be extraordinarily rational. Of course boredom may lead you to anything. After all, boredom even sets one to sticking gold pins into people, but all that would not matter. What is bad (this is my comment again) is that for all I know people will be thankful for the gold pins then. After all, man is stupid, phenomenally stupid. Or rather he is not stupid at all, but he is so ungrateful that you could not find another like him in all creation. After all, it would not surprise me in the least, if, for instance, suddenly for no reason at all, general rationalism in the midst of the future, a gentleman with an ignoble, or rather with a reactionary and ironical, countenance were to arise and, putting his arms akimbo, say to us all: "What do you think, gentlemen, hadn't we better kick over all that rationalism at one blow, scatter it to the winds, just to send these logarithms to the devil, and to let us live once more according to our own foolish will!" That again would not matter; but what is annoying is that after all he would be sure to find followers—such is the nature of man. And all that for the most foolish reason, which, one would think, was hardly worth mentioning: that is, that man everywhere and always, whoever he may be, has preferred to act as he wished and not in the least as his reason and advantage dictated. Why, one may choose what is contrary to one's own interests, and sometimes one *positively ought* (that is my idea). One's own free unfettered choice, one's own fancy, however wild it may be, one's own fancy worked up at times to frenzy—why that is that very "most advantageous advantage" which we have overlooked, which comes under no classification and through which all systems and theories are continually being sent to the devil. And how do these sages know that man must necessarily need a rationally advantageous choice? What man needs is simply *independent* choice, whatever that independence may cost and wherever it may lead. Well, choice, after all, the devil only knows . . .

□   **VIII**   □

"Ha! ha! ha! But after all, if you like, in reality, there is no such thing as choice," you will interrupt with a laugh. "Science has even now succeeded in analyzing man to such an extent that we know already that choice and what is called freedom of will are nothing other than—"

Wait, gentlemen, I meant to begin with that myself. I admit that I was even frightened. I was just going to shout that after all the devil only knows what choice depends on, and that perhaps that was a very good thing, but I remembered the teaching of science—and pulled myself up. And here you have begun to speak. After all, really, well, if some day they truly discover a formula for all our desires and caprices—that is, an explanation of what they depend upon, by what laws they arise, just how they develop, what they are aiming at in one case or another and so on, and so on, that is, a real mathematical formula—then, after all, man would most likely at once stop to feel desire, indeed, he will be certain to. For who would want to choose by rule? Besides, he will at once be transformed from a human being into an organ stop or something of the sort; for what is a man without desire, without free will and without choice, if not a stop in an organ? What do you think? Let us consider the probability—can such a thing happen or not?

"H'm!" you decide. "Our choice is usually mistaken through a mistaken notion of our advantage. We sometimes choose absolute nonsense because in our stupidity we see in that nonsense the easiest means for attaining an advantage assumed beforehand. But when all that is explained and worked out on paper (which is perfectly possible, for it is contemptible and senseless to assume in advance that man will never understand some laws of nature), then, of course, so-called desires will not exist. After all, if desire should at any time come to terms completely with reason, we shall then, of course, reason and not desire, simply because, after all, it will be impossible to retain reason and *desire* something senseless, and in that way knowingly act against reason and desire to injure ourselves. And as all choice and reasoning can really be calculated, because some day they will discover the laws of our so-called free will—so joking aside, there may one day probably be something like a table of desires so that we really shall choose in accordance with it. After all, if, for instance, some day they calculate and prove to me that I stuck my tongue out at someone because I could not help sticking my tongue out at him and that I had to do it in that particular way, what sort of *freedom* is left me, especially if I am a learned man and have taken my degree somewhere? After all, then I would be able to calculate my whole life for thirty years in advance. In short, if that comes about, then, after all, we could do nothing about it. We would have to accept it just the same. And, in fact, we ought to repeat to ourselves incessantly that at such and such a time and under such and such circumstances, Nature does not ask our leave; that we must accept her as she is and not as we imagine her to be, and if we really aspire to tables and indices and well, even—well, let us say to the chemical retort, then it cannot be helped. We must accept the retort, too, or else it will be accepted without our consent."

Yes, but here I come to a stop! Gentlemen, you must excuse me for philosophizing; it's the result of forty years underground! Allow me to indulge my fancy for a minute. You see, gentlemen, reason, gentlemen, is an excellent thing, there is no disputing that, but reason is only reason and can only satisfy man's rational faculty, while will is a manifestation of all life, that is, of all human life including reason as well as all impulses. And although our life, in this manifestation of it, is often worthless, yet it is life nevertheless and not simply extracting square roots. After all, here I, for instance, quite naturally want to live, in order to satisfy all my faculties for life, and not simply my rational faculty, that is, not simply one-twentieth of all my faculties for life. What does reason know? Reason only knows what it has succeeded in learning (some things it will perhaps never learn; while this is nevertheless no comfort, why not say so frankly?) and human nature acts as a whole, with everything that is in it, consciously or unconsciously, and, even if it goes wrong, it lives. I suspect, gentlemen, that you are looking at me with compassion; you repeat to me that an enlightened and developed man, such, in short, as the future man will be, cannot knowingly desire anything disadvantageous to himself, that this can be proved mathematically. I thoroughly agree, it really can—by mathematics. But I repeat for the hundredth time, there is one case, one only, when man may purposely, consciously, desire what is injurious to himself, what is stupid, very stupid—simply in order *to have the right* to desire for himself even what is very stupid and not to be bound by an obligation to desire only what is rational. After all, this very stupid thing, after all, this caprice of ours, may really be more advantageous for us, gentlemen, than anything else on earth, especially in some cases. And in particular it may be more advantageous than any advantages even when it does us obvious harm, and contradicts the soundest conclusions of our reason about our advantage—because in any case it preserves for us what is most precious and most important—that is, our personality, our individuality. Some, you see, maintain that this really is the most precious thing for man; desire can, of course, if it desires, be in agreement with reason; particularly if it does not abuse this practice but does so in moderation, it is both useful and sometimes even praiseworthy. But very often, and even most often, desire completely and stubbornly opposes reason, and . . . and . . . and do you know that that, too, is useful and sometimes even praiseworthy? Gentlemen, let us suppose that man is not stupid. (Indeed, after all, one cannot say that about him anyway, if only for the one consideration that, if man is not stupid, then, after all, who is wise?) But if he is not stupid, he is just the same monstrously ungrateful! Phenomenally ungrateful. I even believe that the best definition of man is—a creature that walks on two legs and is ungrateful. But that is not all, that is not his worst defect; his worst defect is his perpetual immorality, perpetual—from the days of the Flood to the Schleswig-Holstein period of human destiny. Immorality, and consequently lack of good sense; for it has long been accepted that lack of good sense is due to no other cause than immorality. Try it, and cast a look upon the history of mankind. Well, what will you see? Is it a grand spectacle? All right, grand, if you like. The Colossus of Rhodes, for instance, that is worth something. Mr. Anaevsky may well testify that some say it is the work of human hands, while others maintain that it was created by Nature herself. Is it variegated? Very well, it may be variegated too. If one only took the dress uniforms, military and civilian, of all peoples in all ages—that alone is worth something, and if you take the undress uniforms you will never get to the end of it; no historian could keep up with it. Is it monotonous? Very well. It may be monotonous, too; they fight and fight; they are fighting now, they fought first and they fought last—you will admit that it is almost too monotonous. In short, one may say anything about the history of the world—anything that might enter the most disordered imagination. The only thing one cannot say is that it is rational. The very word sticks in one's throat. And, indeed, this is even the kind of thing that continually happens. After all, there are continually turning up in life moral and rational people, sages, and lovers of humanity, who make it their goal for life to live as morally and rationally as possible, to be, so to speak, a light to their neighbors, simply in order to show them that it is really possible to live morally and rationally in this world. And so what? We all know that those very people sooner or later toward the end of their lives have been false to themselves, playing some trick, often a most indecent one. Now I ask you: What can one expect from man since he is a creature endowed with such strange qualities? Shower upon him every earthly blessing, drown him in bliss so that nothing but bubbles would dance on the surface of his bliss, as on a sea; give him such economic prosperity that he would have nothing else to do but sleep, eat cakes and busy himself with ensuring the continuation of world history and even then man, out of sheer ingratitude, sheer libel, would play you some loathsome trick. He would even risk his cakes and would deliberately desire the most fatal rubbish, the most uneconomical absurdity, simply to introduce into all this positive rationality his fatal fantastic element. It is just his fantastic dreams, his vulgar folly, that he will desire to retain, simply in order to prove to himself (as though that were so necessary) that men still are men and not piano keys, which even if played by the laws of nature themselves threaten to be controlled so completely that soon one will be able to desire nothing but by the calendar. And, after all, that is not all: even if man really were nothing but a piano key, even if this were proved to him by natural science and mathematics, even then he would not become reasonable, but would purposely do something perverse out of sheer ingratitude, simply to have his own way. And if he does not find any means he will devise destruction and chaos, will devise suffering of all sorts, and will thereby have his own way. He will launch a curse upon the world, and, as only man can curse (it is his privilege, the primary distinction between him and other animals) then, after all, perhaps only by his curse will he attain his object, that is, really convince himself that he is a man and not a piano key! If you say that all this, too, can be calculated and tabulated, chaos and darkness and curses, so that the mere possibility of calculating it all beforehand would stop it all, and reason would reassert itself—then man would purposely go mad in order to be rid of reason and have his own way! I believe in that, I vouch for it, because, after all, the whole work of man seems really to consist in nothing but proving to himself continually that he is a man and not an organ stop. It may be at the cost of his skin! But he has proved it; he may become a caveman, but he will have proved it. And after that can one help sinning, rejoicing that it has not yet come, and that desire still depends on the devil knows what!

You will shout at me (that is, if you will still favor me with your shout) that, after all, no one is depriving me of my will, that all they are concerned with is that my will should somehow of itself, of its own free will, coincide with my own normal interests, with the laws of nature and arithmetic.

Bah, gentlemen, what sort of free will is left when we come to tables and arithmetic, when it will all be a case of two times two makes four? Two times two makes four even without my will. As if free will meant that!

□ **IX** □

Gentlemen, I am joking, of course, and I know myself that I'm joking badly, but after all you know, one can't take everything as a joke. I am, perhaps, joking with a heavy heart. Gentlemen, I am tormented by questions; answer them for me. Now you, for instance, want to cure men of their old habits and reform their will in accordance with science and common sense. But how do you know, not only that it is possible, but also that it is *desirable*, to reform man in that way? And what leads you to the conclusion that it is so *necessary* to reform man's desires? In short, how do you know that such a reformation will really be advantageous to man? And to go to the heart of the matter, why are you *so sure* of your conviction that not to act against his real normal advantages guaranteed by the conclusions of reason and arithmetic is always advantageous for man and must be a law for all mankind? After all, up to now it is only your supposition. Let us assume it to be a law of logic, but perhaps not a law of humanity at all. You gentlemen perhaps think that I am mad? Allow me to defend myself. I agree that man is pre-eminently a creative animal, predestined to strive consciously toward a goal, and to engage in engineering; that is, eternally and incessantly, to build new roads, *wherever they may lead.* But the reason why he sometimes wants to swerve aside may be precisely that he is *forced* to make that road, and perhaps, too, because however stupid the straightforward practical man may be in general, the thought nevertheless will sometimes occur to him that the road, it would seem, almost always does lead *somewhere,* and that the destination it leads to is less important than the process of making it, and that the chief thing is to save the well-behaved child from despising engineering, and so giving way to the fatal idleness, which, as we all know, is the mother of all vices. Man likes to create and build roads, that is beyond dispute. But why does he also have such a passionate love for destruction and chaos? Now tell me that! But on that point I want to say a few special words myself. May it not be that he loves chaos and destruction (after all, he sometimes unquestionably likes it very much, that is surely so) because he is instinctively afraid of attaining his goal and completing the edifice he is constructing? How do you know, perhaps he only likes that edifice from a distance, and not at all at close range, perhaps he only likes to build it and does not want to live in it, but will leave it, when completed, *aux animaux domestiques*—such as the ants, the sheep, and so on, and so on. Now the ants have quite a different taste. They have an amazing edifice of that type, that endures forever—the anthill.

With the anthill, the respectable race of ants began and with the anthill they will probably end, which does the greatest credit to their perseverance and staidness. But man is a frivolous and incongruous creature, and perhaps, like a chessplayer, loves only the process of the game, not the end of it. And who knows (one cannot swear to it), perhaps the only goal on earth to which mankind is striving lies in this incessant process of attaining, or in other words, in life itself, and not particularly in the goal which of course must always be two time two makes four, that is a formula, and after all, two times two makes four is no longer life, gentlemen, but is the beginning of death. Anyway, man has always been somehow afraid of this two times two makes four, and I am afraid of it even now. Granted that man does nothing but seek that two times two makes four, that he sails the oceans, sacrifices his life in the quest, but to succeed, really to find it—he is somehow afraid, I assure you. He feels that as soon as he has found it there will be nothing for him to look for. When workmen have finished their work they at least receive their pay, they go to the tavern, then they wind up at the police station—and there is an occupation for a week. But where can man go? Anyway, one can observe a certain awkwardness about him every time he attains such goals. He likes the process of attaining, but does not quite like to have attained, and that, of course, is terribly funny. In short, man is a comical creature; there seems to be a kind of pun in it all. But two times two makes four is, after all, something insufferable. Two times two makes four seems to me simply a piece of insolence. Two times two makes four is a fop standing with arms akimbo barring your path and spitting. I admit that two times two makes four is an excellent thing, but if we are going to praise everything, two times two makes five is sometimes also a very charming little thing.

And why are you so firmly, so triumphantly convinced that only the normal and the positive—in short, only prosperity—is to the advantage of man? Is not reason mistaken about advantage? After all, perhaps man likes something besides prosperity? Perhaps he likes suffering just as much? Perhaps suffering is just as great an advantage to him as prosperity? Man is sometimes fearfully, passionately in love with suffering and that is a fact. There is no need to appeal to universal history to prove that; only ask yourself, if only you are a man and have lived at all. As far as my own personal opinion is concerned, to care only for prosperity seems to me somehow even ill-bred. Whether it's good or bad, it is sometimes very pleasant to smash things, too. After all, I do not really insist on suffering or on prosperity either. I insist on my caprice, and its being guaranteed to me when necessary. Suffering would be out of place in vaudevilles, for instance; I know that. In the crystal palace it is even unthinkable; suffering means doubt, means negation, and what would be the good of a crystal palace if there could be any doubt about it? And yet I am sure man will never renounce real suffering, that is, destruction and chaos. Why, after all, suffering is the sole origin of consciousness. Though I stated at the beginning that consciousness, in my opinion, is the greatest misfortune for man, yet I know man loves it and would not give it up for any satisfaction. Consciousness, for instance, is infinitely superior to two times two makes four. Once you have two times two makes four, there is nothing left to do or to understand. There will be nothing left but to bottle up your five senses and plunge into contemplation. While if you stick to consciousness, even though you attain the same result, you can at least flog yourself at times, and that will, at any rate, liven you up. It may be reactionary, but corporal punishment is still better than nothing.

□ **X** □

You believe in a crystal edifice that can never be destroyed; that is, an edifice at which one would neither be able to stick out one's tongue nor thumb one's nose on the sly. And perhaps I am afraid of this edifice just because it is of crystal and can never be destroyed and that one could not even put one's tongue out at it even on the sly.

You see, if it were not a palace but a chicken coop and rain started, I might creep into the chicken coop to avoid getting wet, and yet I would not call the chicken coop a palace out of gratitude to it for sheltering me from the rain. You laugh, you even say that in such circumstances a chicken coop is as good as a mansion. Yes, I answer, if one had to live simply to avoid getting wet.

But what is to be done if I have taken it into my head that this is not the only object in life, and that if one must live one may as well live in a mansion. That is my choice, my desire. You will only eradicate it when you have changed my desire. Well, do change it, tempt me with something else, give me another ideal. But in the meantime, I will not take a chicken coop for a palace. Let the crystal edifice even be an idle dream, say it is inconsistent with the laws of nature and that I have invented it only through my own stupidity, through some old-fashioned irrational habits of my generation. But what do I care if it is inconsistent? Does it matter at all, since it exists in my desires, or rather exists as long as my desires exist? Perhaps you are laughing again? Laugh away; I will put up with all your laughter rather than pretend that I am satisfied when I am hungry. I know, anyway, that I will not be appeased with a compromise, with an endlessly recurring zero, simply because it is consistent with the laws of nature and *really* exists. I will not accept as the crown of my desires a block of buildings with apartments for the poor on a lease of a thousand years and, to take care of any contingency, a dentist's shingle hanging out. Destroy my desires, eradicate my ideals, show me something better, and I will follow you. You may say, perhaps, that it is not worth your getting involved in it; but in that case, after all, I can give you the same answer. We are discussing things seriously; but if you won't deign to give me your attention, then, after all, I won't speak to you, I do have my underground.

But while I am still alive and have desires I would rather my hand were withered than to let it bring one brick to such a building! Don't remind me that I have just rejected the crystal edifice for the sole reason that one cannot put out one's tongue at it. I did not say it at all because I am so fond of putting my tongue out. Perhaps the only thing I resented was that of all your edifices up to now, there has not been a single one at which one could not put out one's tongue. On the contrary, I would let my tongue be cut off out of sheer gratitude if things could be so arranged that I myself would lose all desire to put it out. What do I care that things cannot be so arranged, and that one must be satisfied with model apartments? Why then am I made with such desires? Can I have been made simply in order to come to the conclusion that the whole way I am made is a swindle? Can this be my whole purpose? I do not believe it.

But do you know what? I am convinced that we underground folk ought to be kept in tow. Though we may be able to sit underground forty years without speaking, when we do come out into the light of day and break out we talk and talk and talk.

□ **XI** □

The long and the short of it is, gentlemen, that it is better to do nothing! Better conscious inertia! And so hurrah for underground!

Though I have said that I envy the normal man to the point of exasperation, yet I would not care to be in his place as he is now (though I will not stop envying him. No, no; anyway the underground life is more advantageous!). There, at any rate, one can—Bah! But after all, even now I am lying! I am lying because I know myself as surely as two times two makes four, that it is not at all underground that is better, but something different, quite different, for which I long but which I cannot find! Damn underground!

I will tell you another thing that would be better, and that is, if I myself believed even an iota of what I have just written. I swear to you, gentlemen, that I do not really believe one thing, not even one word, of what I have just written. That is, I believe it, perhaps, but at the same time, I feel and suspect that I am lying myself blue in the face.

"Then why have you written all this?" you will say to me.

"I ought to put you underground for forty years without anything to do and then come to you to find out what stage you have reached! How can a man be left alone with nothing for forty years?"

"Isn't that shameful, isn't that humiliating?" you will say, perhaps, shaking your heads contemptuously. "You long for life and try to settle the problems of life by a logical tangle. And how tiresome, how insolent your outbursts are, and at the same time, how scared you are! You talk nonsense and are pleased with it; you say impudent things and are constantly afraid of them and apologizing for them. You declare that you are afraid of nothing and at the same time try to ingratiate yourself with us. You declare that you are gnashing your teeth and at the same time you try to be witty so as to amuse us. You know that your witticisms are not witty, but you are evidently well satisfied with their literary value. You may perhaps really have suffered, but you have no respect whatsoever for your own suffering. You may be truthful in what you have said but you have no modesty; out of the pettiest vanity you bring your truth to public exposure, to the market place, to ignominy. You doubtlessly mean to say something, but hide your real meaning for fear, because you lack the resolution to say it, and only have a cowardly impudence. You boast of consciousness, but you are unsure of your ground, for though your mind works, yet your heart is corrupted by depravity, and you cannot have a full, genuine consciousness without a pure heart. And how tiresome you are, how you thrust yourself on people and grimace! Lies, lies, lies!"

Of course I myself have made up just now all the things you say. That, too, is from underground. For forty years I have been listening to your words there through a crack under the floor. I have invented them myself. After all there was nothing else I could invent. It is no wonder that I have learned them by heart and that it has taken a literary form.

But can you really be so credulous as to think that I will print all this and give it to you to read too? And another problem; why do I really call you "gentlemen," why do I address you as though you really were my readers? Such declarations as I intend to make are never printed nor given to other people to read. Anyway, I am not strong-minded enough for that, and I don't see why I should be. But you see a fancy has occurred to me and I want to fulfill it at all costs. Let me explain.

Every man has some reminiscences which he would not tell to everyone, but only to his friends. He has others which he would not reveal even to his friends, but only to himself, and that in secret. But finally there are still others which a man is even afraid to tell himself, and every decent man has a considerable number of such things stored away. That is, one can even say that the more decent he is, the greater the number of such things in his mind. Anyway, I have only lately decided to remember some of my early adventures. Till now I have always avoided them, even with a certain uneasiness. Now, however, when I am not only recalling them, but have actually decided to write them down, I want to try the experiment whether one can be perfectly frank, even with oneself, and not take fright at the whole truth. I will observe, parenthetically, that Heine maintains that a true autobiography is almost an impossibility, and that man is bound to lie about himself. He considers that Rousseau certainly told lies about himself in his confessions, and even intentionally lied, out of vanity. I am convinced that Heine is right; I understand very well that sometimes one may, just out of sheer vanity, attribute regular crimes to oneself, and indeed I can very well conceive that kind of vanity. But Heine judged people who made their confessions to the public. I, however, am writing for myself, and wish to declare once and for all that if I write as though I were addressing readers, that is simply because it is easier for me to write in that way. It is merely a question of form, only an empty form—I shall never have readers. I have made this plain already.

I don't wish to be hampered by any restrictions in compiling my notes. I shall not attempt any system or method. I will jot things down as I remember them.

But here, perhaps, someone will take me at my word and ask me: if you really don't count on readers, why do you make such compacts with yourself—and on paper too—that is, that you won't attempt any system or method, that you will jot things down as you remember them, etc., etc.? Why do you keep explaining? Why do you keep apologizing?

Well, there it is, I answer.

Incidentally, there is a whole psychological system in this. Or, perhaps, I am simply a coward. And perhaps also, that I purposely imagine an audience before me in order to conduct myself in a more dignified manner while I am jotting things down. There are perhaps thousands of reasons.

And here is still something else. What precisely is my object in writing? If it is not for the public, then after all, why should I not simply recall these incidents in my own mind without putting them down on paper?

Quite so; but yet it is somehow more dignified on paper. There is something more impressive in it; I will be able to criticize myself better and improve my style. Besides perhaps I will really get relief from writing. Today, for instance, I am particularly oppressed by a certain memory from the distant past. It came back to my mind vividly a few days ago, and since then, has remained with me like an annoying tune that one cannot get rid of. And yet I must get rid of it. I have hundreds of such memories, but at times some single one stands out from the hundreds and oppresses me. For some reason I believe that if I write it down I will get rid of it. Why not try?

Besides, I am bored, and I never do anything. Writing will really be a sort of work. They say work makes man kindhearted and honest. Well, here is a chance for me, anyway.

It is snowing today. A wet, yellow, dingy snow. It fell yesterday too and a few days ago. I rather think that I remembered that incident which I cannot shake off now, apropos of the wet snow. And so let it be a story apropos of the wet snow.

Part Two

APROPOS OF THE WET SNOW

When from the gloom of corruption
I delivered your fallen soul
With the ardent speech of conviction;
And, full of profound torment,
Wringing your hands, you cursed
The vice that ensnared you;
When, with memories punishing
Forgetful conscience
You told me the tale
Of all that happened before me,
And suddenly, covering your face,
Full of shame and horror,
You tearfully resolved,
Outraged, shocked. . . .
Etc., etc., etc.

From the poetry of N. A. NEKRASOV.

I

At that time I was only twenty-four. My life was even then gloomy, disorganized, and solitary to the point of savagery. I made friends with no one and
even avoided talking, and hid myself in my corner more and more. At work
in the office I even tried never to look at anyone, and I was very well aware
that my colleagues looked upon me, not only as a crank, but looked upon
me—so I always thought—seemed to look upon me with a sort of loathing. I
sometimes wondered why no one except me thought that he was looked

upon with loathing. One of our clerks had a repulsive, pock-marked face, which even looked villainous. I believe I would not have dared to look at anyone with such an unsightly face. Another had a uniform so worn that there was an unpleasant smell near him. Yet not one of these gentlemen was disconcerted either by his clothes or his face or in some moral sense. Neither of them imagined that he was looked at with loathing, and even if he had imagined it, it would not have mattered to him, so long as his superiors did not look at him in that way. It is perfectly clear to me now that, owing to my unbounded vanity and, probably, to the high standard I set for myself, I very often looked at myself with furious discontent, which verged on loathing, and so I inwardly attributed the same view to everyone. For instance, I hated my face; I thought it disgusting, and even suspected that there was some-thing base in its expression and therefore every time I turned up at the office I painfully tried to behave as independently as possible so that I might not be suspected of being base, and to give my face as noble an expression as possi-ble. "Let my face even be ugly," I thought, "but let it be noble, expressive, and, above all, *extremely* intelligent." But I was absolutely and painfully cer-tain that my face could never express those perfections; but what was worst of all, I thought it positively stupid-looking. And I would have been quite satisfied if I could have looked intelligent. In fact, I would even have put up with looking base if, at the same time, my face could have been thought ter-ribly intelligent.

Of course, I hated all my fellow-clerks, one and all, and I despised them all, yet at the same time I was, as it were, afraid of them. It happened at times that I even thought more highly of them than of myself. It somehow hap-pened quite suddenly then that I alternated between despising them and thinking them superior to myself. A cultivated and decent man cannot be vain without setting an inordinately high standard for himself, and without despising himself at certain moments to the point of hatred. But whether I despised them or thought them superior I dropped my eyes almost every time I met anyone. I even made experiments whether I could face So-and-So's looking at me, and I was always the first to drop my eyes. This tormented me to the point of frenzy. I was also morbidly afraid of being ridiculous, and so I slavishly worshipped the conventional in everything external. I loved to fall into the common rut, and had a whole-hearted terror of any kind of eccen-tricity in myself. But how could I live up to it? I was morbidly cultivated as a cultivated man of our age should be. They were all dull, and as like one an-other as so many sheep. Perhaps I was the only one in the office who con-stantly thought that I was a coward and a slave, and I thought it precisely because I was cultivated. But I did not only think it, in actuality it was really so. I was a coward and a slave. I say this without the slightest embarrassment. Every decent man in our age must be a coward and a slave. That is his normal condition. I am profoundly convinced of that. He is made that way and is constructed for that very purpose. And not only at the present time owing to some casual circumstances, but always, at all times, a decent man must be a coward and a slave. That is the law of nature for all decent people on the earth. If any one of them happens to be brave about something, he need not be comforted or carried away by that; he will funk out just the same before something else. That is how it invariably and inevitably ends. Only asses and mules are brave, and even they are so only until they come up against the wall. It is not even worth while to pay attention to them. Because they don't mean anything at all.

Still another circumstance tormented me in those days: that no one resembled me and that I resembled no one else. "I am alone and they are *every one*," I thought—and pondered.

From that it can be seen that I was still an absolute child.

The very opposite sometimes happened. After all, how vile it sometimes seemed to have to go to the office; things reached such a point that I often came home ill. But all at once, for no rhyme or reason, there would come a phase of skepticism and indifference (everything happened to me in phases), and I would myself laugh at my intolerance and fastidiousness. I would reproach myself with being *romantic*. Sometimes I was unwilling to speak to anyone, while at other times I would not only talk, but even think of forming a friendship with them. All my fastidiousness would suddenly vanish for no rhyme or reason. Who knows, perhaps I never had really had it, and it had simply been affected, and gotten out of books. I have still not decided that question even now. Once I quite made friends with them, visited their homes, played preference, drank vodka, talked of promotions . . . But here let me make a digression.

We Russians, speaking generally, have never had those foolish transcendental German, and still more, French, romantics on whom nothing produces any effect; if there were an earthquake, if all France perished at the barricades, they would still be the same, they would not even change for decency's sake, but would still go on singing their transcendental songs, so to speak, to the hour of their death, because they are fools. We, in Russia, have no fools; that is well known. That is what distinguishes us from foreign lands. Consequently those transcendental natures do not exist among us in their pure form. We only think they do because our "positivistic" journalists and critics of that time, always on the hunt for Kostanzhoglos and Uncle Peter Ivaniches[1] and foolishly accepting them as our ideal, slandered our romantics, taking them for the same transcendental sort that exists in Germany or France. On the contrary, the characteristics of our romantics are absolutely and directly opposed to the transcendental European type, and not a single European standard can be applied to them. (Allow me to make use of this

[1] Characters in Part II of Gogol's *Dead Souls* and Goncharov's *The Same Old Story,* respectively.

word "romantic"—an old-fashioned and much-respected word which has done good service and is familiar to all.) The characteristics of our romantics are to understand everything, *to see everything and often to see it incomparably more clearly than our most positivistic minds see it;* to refuse to accept anyone or anything, but at the same time not to despise anything; to give way, to yield, from policy; never to lose sight of a useful practical goal (such as rent-free government quarters, pensions, decorations), to keep their eye on that object through all the enthusiasms and volumes of lyrical poems, and at the same time to preserve "the sublime and the beautiful" inviolate within them to the hour of their death, and also, incidentally, to preserve themselves wrapped in cotton, like some precious jewel if only for the benefit of "the sublime and the beautiful." Our romantic is a man of great breadth and the greatest rogue of all our rogues, I assure you. I can even assure you from experience. Of course all that occurs if he is intelligent. But what am I saying! The romantic is always intelligent, and I only meant to observe that although we have had foolish romantics they don't count, and they were only so because in the flower of their youth they degenerated completely into Germans, and to preserve their precious jewel more comfortably, settled somewhere out there—by preference in Weimar or the Black Forest. I, for instance, genuinely despised my official work and did not openly abuse it simply through necessity because I was in it myself and got a salary for it. And, as a result, take note, I did not openly abuse it. Our romantic would rather go out of his mind (which incidentally happened very rarely) than abuse it, unless he had some other career in view; and he is never kicked out, unless, of course, he is taken to the lunatic asylum as "the King of Spain" and then only if he went very mad. But after all, it is only the thin, fair people who go out of their minds in Russia. Innumerable romantics later in life rise to considerable rank in the service. Their versatility is remarkable! And what a faculty they have for the most contradictory sensations! I was comforted by those thoughts even in those days, and I am so still. That is why there are so many "broad natures" among us who never lose their ideal even in the depths of degradation; and though they never lift a finger for their ideal, though they are arrant thieves and robbers, yet they tearfully cherish their first ideal and are extraordinarily honest at heart. Yes, only among us can the most arrant rogue be absolutely and even loftily honest at heart without in the least ceasing to be a rogue. I repeat, our romantics, after all, frequently become such accomplished rascals (I use the term "rascals" affectionately), suddenly display such a sense of reality and practical knowledge, that their bewildered superiors and the public can only gape in amazement at them.

Their many-sidedness is really astounding, and goodness knows what it may turn itself into under future circumstances, and what lies in store for us later on. They are good stuff! I do not say this out of any foolish or boastful patriotism. But I feel sure that you are again imagining that I am joking. Or perhaps it's just the contrary, and you are convinced that I really think so. Anyway, gentlemen, I shall welcome both views as an honor and a special favor. And do forgive my digression.

I did not, of course, maintain a friendship with my comrades and soon was at loggerheads with them, and in my youthful inexperience I even gave up bowing to them, as though I had cut off all relations. That, however, only happened to me once. As a rule, I was always alone.

In the first place, at home, I spent most of my time reading. I tried to stifle all that was continually seething within me by means of external sensations. And the only source of external sensation possible for me was reading. Reading was a great help, of course, it excited, delighted and tormented me. But at times it bored me terribly. One longed for movement just the same, and I plunged all at once into dark, subterranean, loathsome—not vice but petty vice. My petty passions were acute, smarting, from my continual sickly irritability I had hysterical fits, with tears and convulsions. I had no resource except reading—that is, there was then nothing in my surroundings which I could respect and which attracted me. I was overwhelmed with depression, too; I had an hysterical craving for contradictions and for contrast, and so I took to vice. I have not said all this to justify myself, after all—but no, I am lying. I did want to justify myself. I make that little observation for my own benefit, gentlemen. I don't want to lie. I vowed to myself I would not.

I indulged my vice in solitude at night, furtively, timidly, filthily, with a feeling of shame which never deserted me, even at the most loathsome moments, and which at such moments drove me to curses. Even then I already had the underground in my soul. I was terribly afraid of being seen, of being met, of being recognized. I visited various completely obscure places.

One night as I was passing a tavern, I saw through a lighted window some gentlemen fighting with billiard cues, and saw one of them thrown out of the window. At another time I would have felt very much disgusted, but then I was suddenly in such a mood that I actually envied the gentleman thrown out of the window, and I envied him so much that I even went into the tavern and into the billiard-room, "Perhaps," I thought, "I'll have a fight, too, and they'll throw me out of the window."

I was not drunk, but what is one to do—after all, depression will drive a man to such a pitch of hysteria. But nothing happened. It seemed that I was not even equal to being thrown out of the window and I went away without having fought.

An officer put me in my place from the very first moment.

I was standing by the billiard-table and in my ignorance blocking up the way, and he wanted to pass; he took me by the shoulders and without a word—without a warning or an explanation—moved me from where I was standing to another spot and passed by as though he had not noticed me. I could even have forgiven blows, but I absolutely could not forgive his having moved me and so completely failing to notice me.

Devil knows what I would then have given for a real regular quarrel—a more decent, a more *literary* one, so to speak. I had been treated like a fly. This officer was over six feet, while I am short and thin. But the quarrel was in my hands. I had only to protest and I certainly would have been thrown out of the window. But I changed my mind and preferred to beat a resentful retreat.

I went out of the tavern straight home, confused and troubled, and the next night I continued with my petty vices, still more furtively, abjectly and miserably than before, as it were, with tears in my eyes—but still I did continue them. Don't imagine, though, that I funked out on the officer through cowardice. I have never been a coward at heart, though I have always been a coward in action. Don't be in a hurry to laugh. There is an explanation for it. I have an explanation for everything, you may be sure.

Oh, if only that officer had been one of the sort who would consent to fight a duel! But no, he was one of those gentlemen (alas, long extinct!) who preferred fighting with cues, or, like Gogol's Lieutenant Pirogov, appealing to the police. They did not fight duels and would have thought a duel with a civilian like me an utterly unseemly procedure in any case—and they looked upon the duel altogether as something impossible, something freethinking and French, but they were quite ready to insult people, especially when they were over six feet.

I did not funk out through cowardice here but through unbounded vanity. I was not afraid of his six feet, not of getting a sound thrashing and being thrown out of the window; I would probably have had sufficient physical courage; but I lacked sufficient moral courage. What I was afraid of was that everyone present, from the insolent marker down to the lowest little stinking pimply clerk hanging around in a greasy collar, would jeer at me and fail to understand when I began to protest and to address them in literary language. For even now we cannot, after all, speak of the point of honor— not of honor, but of the point of honor (*point d'honneur*)—except in literary language. You cannot allude to the "point of honor" in ordinary language. I was fully convinced (the sense of reality, in spite of all romanticism!) that they would all simply split their sides with laughter and that the officer would not simply, that is, not uninsultingly, beat me, but would certainly prod me in the back with his knee, kick me round the billiard-table that way and only then perhaps have pity and throw me out of the window. Of course, this trivial incident could not have ended like that with me. I often met that officer afterward in the street and observed him very carefully. I am not quite sure whether he recognized me. I imagine not; I judge from certain signs. But I—I stared at him with spite and hatred and so it went on—for several years! My resentment even grew deeper with the years. At first I began making stealthy inquiries about this officer. It was difficult for me to do so, for I knew no one. But one day I heard someone call him by his name in the street when I was following him at a distance, just as though I were tied to him—and so I learned his surname. Another time I followed him to his flat, and for a few pennies learned from the porter where he lived, on which floor, whether he lived alone or with others, and so on—in fact, everything one could learn from a porter. One morning, though I had never tried to write anything before, it suddenly occurred to me to describe this officer in the form of an exposé, in a satire, in a tale. I wrote the tale with relish. I did expose him. I slandered him; at first I so altered his name that it could easily be recognized but on second thought I changed it, and sent the story to the *Annals of the Fatherland*. But at that time such exposés were not yet the fashion and my story was not printed. That was a great vexation to me. Sometimes I was positively choked with resentment. At last I decided to challenge my enemy to a duel. I composed a splendid, charming letter to him, imploring him to apologize to me, and hinting rather plainly at a duel in case of refusal. The letter was so composed that if the officer had had the least understanding of the "sublime and the beautiful" he would certainly have rushed to me to fling himself on my neck and to offer me his friendship. And how fine that would have been! How we would have gotten along! How we would have gotten along! "He could have shielded me with his higher rank, while I could have improved his mind with my culture, and, well—my ideas, and all sorts of things might have happened." Just think, this was two years after his insult to me, and my challenge was the most ridiculous anachronism, in spite of all the ingenuity of my letter in disguising and explaining away the anachronism. But, thank God (to this day I thank the Almighty with tears in my eyes), I did not send the letter to him. Cold shivers run down my back when I think of what might have happened if I had sent it. And all at once I revenged myself in the simplest way, by a stroke of genius! A brilliant thought suddenly dawned upon me. Sometimes on holidays I used to stroll along the sunny side of the Nevsky between three and four in the afternoon. That is, I did not stroll so much as experience innumerable torments, humiliations and resentments; but no doubt that was just what I wanted. I used to wriggle like an eel among the passers-by in the most unbecoming fashion, continually moving aside to make way for generals, for officers of the Guards and the Hussars, or for ladies. In those minutes I used to feel a convulsive twinge at my heart, and hot all the way down my back at the mere thought of the wretchedness of my dress, of the wretchedness and vulgarity of my little wriggling figure. This was a regular martyrdom, a continual, intolerable humiliation at the thought, which passed into an incessant and direct sensation, that I was a fly in the eyes of this whole world, a nasty, disgusting fly—more intelligent, more cultured, more noble than any of them, of course, but a fly that was continually making way for everyone, insulted and humiliated by everyone. Why I inflicted this torment upon myself, why I went to the Nevsky, I don't know. I felt simply *drawn* there at every possible opportunity.

Already then I began to experience a rush of the enjoyment of which I spoke in the first chapter. After my affair with the officer I felt even more drawn there than before: it was on the Nevsky that I met him most frequently, it was *there* that I could admire him. He, too, went there chiefly on holidays. He, too, made way for generals and persons of high rank, and he, too, shifted among them like an eel; but people like me, or even neater than I, he simply walked over; he made straight for them as though there was nothing but empty space before him, and never, under any circumstances, moved aside. I gloated over my resentment watching him and—resentfully made way for him every time. It tormented me that even in the street I could not be on an even footing with him. "Why must you invariably be the first to move aside?" I kept asking myself in hysterical rage, waking up sometimes at three o'clock in the morning. "Why precisely you and not he? After all, there's no regulation about it; after all, there's no written law about it. Let the making way be equal as it usually is when refined people meet; he moves halfway and you move halfway; you pass with mutual respect." But that never happened, and I always made way, while he did not even notice I moved aside for him. And lo and behold the most astounding idea dawned upon me! "What," I thought, "if I meet him and—don't move aside? What if I don't move aside on purpose, even if I were to bump into him? How would that be?" This audacious idea little by little took such a hold on me that it gave me no peace. I dreamt of it continually, terribly, and I purposely went to the Nevsky more frequently in order to picture more vividly how I would do it when I did do it. I was delighted. This plan seemed to me more and more practical and possible. "Of course I will not really bump him," I thought, already more good-natured in my joy. "I will simply not turn aside, will bump against him, not very violently, but just shouldering each other— just as much as decency permits. I will bump him just as much as he bumps me." At last I made up my mind completely. But my preparations took a great deal of time. To begin with, when I carried out my plan I would have to look rather more decent, and I had to think of my clothes. "In any case, if, for instance, there were any sort of public scandal (and the public there is of the most *superflu:* the Countess walks there; Prince D. walks there; the whole literary world is there), I would have to be well dressed; that inspires respect and of itself puts us in some way on equal footing in the eyes of high society." With that in mind I asked for my salary in advance, and bought at Churkin's a pair of black gloves and a decent hat. Black gloves seemed to me both more dignified and *bon ton* than the lemon-colored ones which I had contemplated at first. "The color is too gaudy, it looks as though one were trying to be conspicuous," and I did not take the lemon-colored ones. I had gotten ready a good shirt, with the bone studs, long beforehand; but my overcoat very much delayed me. The coat in itself was a very good one, it kept me warm; but it was wadded and it had a raccoon collar which was the height of vulgarity. I had to change the collar at any sacrifice, and to have a beaver one like an officer's. For this purpose I began visiting the Gostiny Dvor and after several attempts I lit on a piece of cheap German beaver. Though these German beavers very soon wear out and look shabby, at first, when new, they look exceedingly well, and after all, I only needed it for one occasion. I asked the price; even so, it was too expensive. After thinking it over thoroughly I decided to sell my raccoon collar. The rest of the money—a considerable sum for me, I decided to borrow from Anton Antonich Sye- tochkin, my superior, an unassuming person, but grave and dependable. He never lent money to anyone, but I had, on entering the service, been specially recommended to him by an important personage who had got me my job. I was terribly worried. To borrow from Anton Antonich seemed to me mon- strous and shameful. I did not sleep for two or three nights, and indeed I did not sleep well in general at that time, I was in a fever; I had a vague sinking at my heart or suddenly it would start to throb, throb, throb! Anton Anton- ich was at first surprised, then he frowned, then he reflected, and did after all lend me the money, receiving from me a written authorization to take from my salary a fortnight later the sum that he had lent me. In this way every- thing was at last ready. The handsome beaver was established in place of the mean-looking raccoon, and I began by degrees to get to work. It would never have done to act offhand, at random; the plan had to be carried out skillfully, by degrees. But I must confess that after many efforts I almost even began to despair: we could not run into each other and that is all there was to it. I made every preparation, I was quite determined—it seemed as though we would run into one another directly—and before I knew what I was doing I had stepped aside for him again and he had passed without noticing me. I even prayed as I approached him that God would grant me determination. One time I had made up my mind thoroughly, but it ended in my stumbling and falling at his feet because at the very last instant when I was only some six inches from him my courage failed me. He very calmly stepped over me, while I flew to one side like a ball. That night I was ill again, feverish and delirious. And suddenly it ended most happily. The night before I had made up my mind not to carry out my fatal plan and to abandon it all, and with that goal in mind I went to the Nevsky for the last time, just to see how I would abandon it all. Suddenly, three paces from my enemy, I unexpectedly made up my mind—I closed my eyes, and we ran full tilt, shoulder to shoul- der into each other! I did not budge an inch and passed him on a perfectly equal footing! He did not even look round and pretended not to notice it; but he was only pretending, I am convinced of that. I am convinced of that

to this day! Of course, I got the worst of it—he was stronger, but that was
not the point. The point was that I had attained my goal, I had kept up my
dignity. I had not yielded a step, and had put myself publicly on an equal
social footing with him. I returned home feeling that I was perfectly avenged
for everything. I was delighted. I was triumphant and sang Italian arias. Of
course, I will not describe to you what happened to me three days later; if you
have read my first chapter "Underground," you can guess for yourself. The
officer was afterward transferred; I have not seen him now for fourteen years.
What is the dear fellow doing now? Whom is he walking over?

□　**II**　□

But the period of my dissipation would end and I always felt terribly sick afterward. It was followed by remorse—I tried to drive it away; I felt too sick.
By degrees, however, I grew used to that, too. I grew used to everything, that
is, I did not really grow used to it, but rather I voluntarily resigned myself to
enduring it. But I had a means of escape that reconciled everything—that was
to find refuge in "the sublime and the beautiful," in dreams. Of course I was
a terrible dreamer. I would dream for three months on end, tucked away in
my corner, and you may believe me that at those moments I had no resemblance to the gentleman who, in his chicken-hearted anxiety, put a German
beaver collar on his greatcoat. I suddenly became a hero. I would not have
received my six-foot lieutenant even if he had called on me. I could not even
picture him before me then. What were my dreams and how I could satisfy
myself with them, it is hard to say now, but at the time I did satisfy myself
with them, to some extent. Dreams were particularly sweet and vivid after a
little vice; they came with remorse and with tears, with curses and transports.
There were moments of such positive intoxication, of such happiness, that
there was not the faintest trace of irony within me, on my honor. I had faith,
hope, love. That is just it. I believed blindly at such times that by some miracle, through some external circumstance, all this would suddenly open out,
expand; that suddenly a vista of suitable activity—beneficial, good, and above
all, *ready-made* (what sort of activity I had no idea, but the great thing was
that it should be all ready for me)—would rise up before me, and I should
come out into the light of day, almost riding a white horse and crowned with
laurel. I could not conceive of a secondary role for myself, and for that reason
I quite contentedly played the lowest one in reality. Either to be a hero or to
grovel in the mud—there was nothing between. That was my ruin, for when

I was in the mud I comforted myself with the thought that at other times I was a hero, and I took refuge in this hero for the mud: for an ordinary man, say, it is shameful to defile himself, but a hero is too noble to be utterly defiled, and so he might defile himself. It was worth noting that these attacks of "the sublime and the beautiful" visited me even during the period of vice and just at the times when I had sunk to the very bottom. They came in separate spurts, as though reminding me of themselves, but did not banish the vice by their appearance. On the contrary, they seemed to add a zest to it by contrast, and were only sufficiently present to serve as an appetizing sauce. That sauce was made up of contradictions and sufferings, of agonizing inward analysis, and all these torments and pin-pricks lent my vice a certain piquancy, even a significance—in short, completely fulfilled the function of a good sauce. There was even a certain depth of meaning in it. And I could hardly have restrained myself to the simple, vulgar, direct clerk-like vice and have endured all the filthiness of it. What could have attracted me about it then and have driven me at night into the street? No, I had a noble loophole for everything.

And what love, oh Lord, what love I felt at times in those dreams of mine! In those "flights into the sublime and the beautiful"; though it was fantastic love, though it was never applied to anything human in reality, yet there was so much of this love that afterward one did not even feel the impulse to apply it in reality; that would have been a superfluous luxury. Everything, however, always passed satisfactorily by a lazy and fascinating transition into the sphere of art; that is, into the beautiful forms of life, ready made, violently stolen from the poets and novelists and adapted to all sorts of needs and uses. I, for instance, was triumphant over everyone; everyone, of course, lay in the dust and was forced to recognize my superiority spontaneously, and I forgave them all. I, a famous poet, and a courtier, fell in love; I inherited countless millions and immediately devoted them to humanity, and at the same time I confessed before all the people my shameful deeds, which, of course, were not merely shameful, but contained an enormous amount of "the sublime and the beautiful," something in the Manfred style. Everyone would weep and kiss me (what idiots they would be if they did not), while I would go barefoot and hungry preaching new ideas and fighting a victorious Austerlitz against the reactionaries. Then a march would sound, an amnesty would be declared, the Pope would agree to retire from Rome to Brazil; then there would be a ball for the whole of Italy at the Villa Borghese on the shores of Lake Como, Lake Como being for that purpose transferred to the neighborhood of Rome; then would come a scene in the bushes, etc., etc.—as though you did not know all about it! You will say that it is vulgar and base to drag all this into public after all the tears and raptures I have myself admitted. But why is it base? Can you imagine that I am ashamed of it all, and that it was stupider than anything in your life, gentlemen? And I can assure you that some of these fancies were by no means badly composed. Not every-

thing took place on the shores of Lake Como. And yet you are right—it really
is vulgar and base. And what is most base of all is that I have now started to
justify myself to you. And even more base than that is my making this remark now. But that's enough, or, after all, there will be no end to it; each
step will be more base than the last.

I could never stand more than three months of dreaming at a time without feeling an irresistible desire to plunge into society. To plunge into society
meant to visit my superior, Anton Antonich Syetochkin. He was the only
permanent acquaintance I have had in my life, and I even wonder at the fact
myself now. But I even went to see him only when that phase came over me,
and when my dreams had reached such a point of bliss that it became essential to embrace my fellows and all mankind immediately. And for that purpose I needed at least one human being at hand who actually existed. I had to
call on Anton Antonich, however, on Tuesday—his at-home day; so I always
had to adjust my passionate desire to embrace humanity so that it might fall
on a Tuesday. This Anton Antonich lived on the fourth floor in a house in
Five Corners, in four low-pitched rooms of a particularly frugal and sallow
appearance, one smaller than the next. He had two daughters and their aunt,
who used to pour out the tea. Of the daughters one was thirteen and another
fourteen, they both had snub noses, and I was terribly embarrassed by them
because they were always whispering and giggling together. The master of
the house usually sat in his study on a leather couch in front of the table,
with some gray-headed gentleman, usually a colleague from our office or even
some other department. I never saw more than two or three visitors there,
and those always the same. They talked about the excise duty, about business
in the senate, about salaries, about promotions, about His Excellency, and the
best means of pleasing him, and so on, and so on. I had the patience to sit
like a fool beside these people for four hours at a stretch, listening to them
without knowing what to say to them or venturing to say a word. I became
stupefied; several times I felt myself perspiring. I was overcome by a sort of
paralysis; but that was pleasant and useful for me. On returning home I de-
ferred for a time my desire to embrace all mankind.

I had, however, one other acquaintance of a sort, Simonov, who was an
old schoolfellow. Indeed I had a number of schoolfellows in Petersburg, but I
did not associate with them and had even given up nodding to them in the
street. Perhaps I even transferred into the department I was in simply to
avoid their company and to cut off at one stroke all connection with my hateful childhood. Curses on that school and all those terrible years of penal servitude! In short, I parted from my schoolfellows as soon as I got out into the
world. There were two or three left to whom I nodded in the street. One of
them was Simonov, who had been in no way distinguished at school, was of a
quiet and even disposition; but I discovered in him a certain independence of
character and even honesty. I don't even suppose that he was particularly lim-

ited. I had at one time spent some rather soulful moments with him, but these had not lasted long and had somehow been suddenly clouded over. He was evidently uncomfortable at these reminiscences, and was, it seemed, always afraid that I might take up the same tone again. I suspected that he had an aversion for me, but I still went on going to see him, not being completely certain of it.

And so on one occasion, on a Thursday, unable to endure my solitude and knowing that it was Thursday Anton Antonich's door would be closed, I thought of Simonov. Climbing up four floors to his place, I was thinking that I made the man uncomfortable and that it was a mistake to go to see him. But as it always happened that such reflections impelled me even more strongly, as though purposely, to put myself into a false position, I went in. It was almost a year since I had last seen Simonov.

□ **III** □

I found two more of my old schoolfellows with him. They seemed to be discussing an important matter. All of them scarcely took any notice of my entrance, which was strange, for I had not seen them for years. Evidently they looked upon me as something on the level of a common fly. I had not been treated like that even at school, although everybody hated me there. I knew, of course, that they must despise me now for my lack of success in the service, and for having let myself sink so low, going about badly dressed and so on which seemed to them a sign of my inaptitude and insignificance. But nevertheless I had not expected such contempt. Simonov even seemed surprised at my turning up. Even in the old days he had always seemed surprised at my coming. All this disconcerted me; I sat down, feeling rather miserable, and began listening to what they were saying.

They were engaged in an earnest and even heated discussion about a farewell dinner these gentlemen wanted to arrange together the very next day for their friend Zverkov, an officer in the army, who was going away to a distant province. Monsieur Zverkov had been all the time at school with me too. I had begun to hate him particularly in the upper classes. In the lower classes he had simply been a pretty, playful boy whom everybody liked. I had hated him, however, even in the lower classes, just because he was a pretty and playful boy. He was always consistently poor in his work, and got worse and worse as he went on; nevertheless he was successfully graduated as influence

FYODOR DOSTOEVSKY

was exerted on his behalf. During his last year at school he inherited an estate of two hundred serfs, and as almost all of us were poor he even started to boast before us. He was vulgar to the worst degree, but nevertheless he was a good-natured fellow, even when he boasted. In spite of superficial, fantastic and rhetorical notions of honor and dignity, all but a very few of us positively grovelled before Zverkov, and the more so the more he boasted. And they did not grovel for any advantage, but simply because he had been favored by the gifts of nature. Moreover, we came somehow to accept the idea that Zverkov was a specialist in regard to tact and good manners. That particularly infuriated me. I hated the sharp, self-confident tone of his voice, his admiration for his own witticisms, which were terribly stupid, though he was bold in his expressions; I hated his handsome but stupid face (for which I would, however, have gladly exchanged my *intelligent* one), and the free-and-easy military manners in fashion in the 'forties. I hated the way in which he used to talk of his future conquests of women (he did not venture to begin with women until he had officer's epaulettes and was looking forward to them with impatience), and boasted of the duels he would constantly be fighting. I remember how, I, invariably so taciturn, suddenly attacked Zverkov, when one day he talked at a leisure moment with his schoolfellows of the affairs he would have in the future and growing as sportive as a puppy in the sun, he all at once declared that he would not leave a single village girl on his estate unnoticed, that that was his *droit de seigneur,* and that if the peasants dared to protest he would have them all flogged and double their taxes, the bearded rascals. Our servile rabble applauded, but I attacked him, not at all out of compassion for the girls and their fathers, but simply because they were applauding such a beetle. I got the better of him on that occasion, but though Zverkov was stupid he was lively and impudent, and so laughed it off, and even in such a way that my victory was not really complete: the laugh was on his side. He got the better of me on several occasions afterward, but without malice, somehow just in jest, casually, in fun. I remained maliciously and contemptuously silent. When we left school he made advances to me: I did not rebuff them much, for I was flattered, but we soon parted naturally. Afterward I heard of his barrack-room success as a lieutenant, and of the *fast life* he was leading. Then there came other rumors—of his *successes* in the service. By then he no longer greeted me in the street, and I suspected that he was afraid of compromising himself by greeting a person as insignificant as I. I also saw him once in the theatre, in the third tier of boxes. By then he was a staff officer. He was twisting and twirling about, ingratiating himself with the daughters of an ancient general. In three years his looks had gotten considerably worse, though he was still rather handsome and smart. He had somehow swelled, started to put on weight. One could see that by the time he was thirty he would be completely fat. So it was, finally, to this Zverkov that my schoolfellows were going to give a dinner on his departure.

They had kept up with him for those three years, though privately they did not consider themselves on an equal footing with him, I am convinced of that.

Of Simonov's two visitors, one was Ferfichkin, a Russianized German—a little fellow with the face of a monkey, a blockhead who was always deriding everyone, a very bitter enemy of mine from our days in the lower classes—a vulgar, impudent, boastful fellow, who affected a most sensitive feeling of personal honor, though, of course, he was a wretched little coward at heart. He was one of those admirers of Zverkov who made up to the latter out of calculation, and often borrowed money from him. Simonov's other visitor, Trudolyubov, was a person in no way remarkable—a military lad, tall with a cold face, quite honest. But he worshipped success of every sort, and was only capable of thinking of promotion. He was some distant relation of Zverkov and this, foolish as it seems, gave him a certain importance among us. He never thought me of any consequence whatever; while his behavior to me was not quite courteous, it was tolerable.

"Well, then, with seven roubles each," said Trudolyubov, "twenty-one *roups* from the three of us, we can dine well. Zverkov, of course, won't pay."

"Of course not, since we are inviting him," Simonov decided.

"Can you imagine," Ferfichkin interrupted hotly and conceitedly, like some insolent flunky boasting of his master the general's decorations, "can you imagine that Zverkov will let us pay alone? He will accept from delicacy, but he will order *a half case* on his own."

"Why do we need half a case for the four of us?" observed Trudolyubov, taking notice only of the half case.

"So the three of us, with Zverkov for the fourth, twenty-one roubles, at the Hôtel de Paris at five o'clock tomorrow," Simonov, who had been asked to make the arrangements, concluded finally.

"How about twenty-one roubles?" I asked in some agitation, even offended, apparently; "if you count me it will be twenty-eight, not twenty-one roubles."

It seemed to me that to invite myself so suddenly and unexpectedly would be positively graceful, and that they would all be conquered at once and would look at me with respect.

"Do you want to join, too?" Simonov observed, with displeasure, and seemed to avoid looking at me. He knew me inside out.

It infuriated me that he knew me inside out.

"Why not? After all, I am an old schoolfellow of his too, I believe, and I must admit I feel offended that you have left me out," I said, boiling over again.

"And where were we to find you?" Ferfichkin put in roughly.

"You were never on good terms with Zverkov," Trudolyubov added, frowning. But I had already clutched at the idea and would not let go.

"I do not think that anyone has a right to judge that," I retorted in a shaking voice, as though God only knows what had happened. "Perhaps that is just my reason for wishing it now, that I have not always been on good terms with him."

"Oh, there's no making you out—with these refinements," Trudolyubov jeered.

"We'll put your name down," Simonov decided, addressing me. "To-morrow at five o'clock at the Hôtel de Paris."

"What about the money?" Ferfichkin began in an undertone, indicating me to Simonov, but he broke off, for even Simonov was embarrassed.

"That will do," said Trudolyubov, getting up. "If he wants to come so much, let him."

"But after all it's a private thing, between us friends," Ferfichkin said crossly, as he too picked up his hat. "It's not an official meeting. Perhaps we do not want you at all—"

They went away. Ferfichkin did not salute me in any way as he went out. Trudolyubov barely nodded. Simonov, with whom I remained alone, was in some state of vexed perplexity, and looked at me strangely. He did not sit down and did not ask me to.

"H'm—yes—tomorrow, then. Will you pay your share now? I just ask so as to know," he muttered in embarrassment.

I blazed up in anger but as I did so I remembered that I had owed Simonov fifteen roubles for ages—which I had, indeed, never forgotten, though I had not paid it.

"You will understand, Simonov, that I could have had no idea when I came here—I am very much vexed that I have forgotten—"

"All right, all right, it doesn't matter. You can pay tomorrow after the dinner. After all, I simply wanted to know—Please don't—"

He broke off and began pacing the room still more vexed. As he walked he began to thump with his heels and stomped even louder.

"Am I keeping you?" I asked, after two minutes of silence.

"Oh, no!" he said, starting, "that is—to be truthful—yes. I have to go and see someone—not far from here," he added in a sort of apologetic voice, somewhat ashamed.

"My goodness, but why didn't you say so?" I cried, seizing my cap with, incidentally, an astonishingly free-and-easy air, which was the last thing I would have expected of myself.

"After all, it's close by—not two paces away," Simonov repeated, accompanying me to the front door with a fussy air which did not suit him at all. "So five o'clock, punctually, tomorrow," he called down the stairs after me. He was very glad to get rid of me. I was in a fury.

"What possessed me, what possessed me to force myself upon them?" I gnashed my teeth, as I strode along the street. "For a scoundrel, a pig like that Zverkov! Of course, I had better not go; of course, I can just snap my fingers at them. I am not bound in any way. I'll send Simonov a note by to-morrow's post—"

But what made me furious was that I knew for certain that I would go, that I would purposely go; and the more tactless, the more ill-mannered my going would be, the more certainly I would go.

And there was even a positive obstacle to my going: I had no money. All I had altogether, was nine roubles. But I had to give seven of that to my servant, Apollon, for his monthly wages. That was all I paid him—he had to keep himself.

Not to pay him was impossible, considering his character. But I will talk about that fellow, about that plague of mine, another time.

However, I knew I would go after all and would not pay him his wages.

That night I had the most hideous dreams. No wonder; the whole evening I had been oppressed by memories of my days of penal servitude at school, and I could not shake them off. I was sent to the school by distant relations, upon whom I was dependent and of whom I have heard nothing since—they sent me there, a lonely, silent boy, already crushed by their re-proaches, already troubled by doubt, and looking savagely at everything around him. My schoolfellows met me with spiteful and merciless jibes be-cause I was not like any of them. But I could not endure their taunts; I could not give in to them as cheaply as they gave in to one another. I hated them from the first, and shut myself away from everyone in timid, wounded and disproportionate pride. Their coarseness revolted me. They laughed cynically at my face, at my clumsy figure; and yet what stupid faces they themselves had. In our school the boys' faces somehow degenerated and grew stupider particularly. How many fine-looking boys came to us? In a few years they be-came repulsive looking. Even at sixteen I wondered at them morosely; even then I was struck by the pettiness of their thoughts, the stupidity of their pursuits, their games, their conversations. They had no understanding of such essential things, they took no interest in such striking, impressive sub-jects, that I could not help considering them inferior to myself. It was not wounded vanity that drove me to it, and for God's sake do not thrust upon me your hackneyed remarks, repeated to nausea, that "I was only a dreamer, while they even then understood real life." They understood nothing, they had no idea of real life, and I swear that that was what made me most indig-nant with them. On the contrary, the most obvious, striking reality they ac-cepted with fantastic stupidity and even then had already begun to respect only success. Everything that was just, but oppressed and looked down upon, they laughed at cruelly and shamefully. They took rank for intelligence; even at sixteen they were already talking about a snug berth. Of course a great deal of it was due to their stupidity, to the bad examples that constantly sur-rounded them in their childhood and boyhood. They were monstrously de-

praved. Of course much of that, too, was superficial and much was only affected cynicism; of course there were glimpses of youth and freshness in them
even beneath their depravity; but even that freshness was not attractive in
them, and showed itself in a certain rakishness. I hated them terribly, though
perhaps I was worse than any of them. They repaid me in kind, and did not
conceal their aversion for me. But by then I did not want them to like me; on
the contrary, I continually longed for them to humiliate me. To escape from
their derision I purposely began to make all the progress I could with my
studies and forced my way to the very top. This impressed them. Moreover,
they all began to grasp slowly that I was already reading books none of them
could read, and understood things (not forming part of our school curricu-
lum) of which they had not even heard. They took a savage and sarcastic
view of it, but were morally impressed, especially as the teachers began to notice me on those grounds. The mockery ceased but the hostility remained,
and cold and strained relations were formed between us. In the end I could
not stand it myself; with years a craving for society, for friends, developed in
me. I attempted to get on friendly terms with some of my schoolfellows; but
somehow or other my intimacy with them was always strained and soon
ended of itself. Once, indeed, I did have a friend. But I was already a tyrant at
heart; I wanted to exercise unlimited power over him; I tried to instil into
him a contempt for his surroundings; I required of him a disdainful and
complete break with those surroundings. I frightened him with my passionate affection; I reduced him to tears, to convulsions. He was a simple and devoted soul; but when he submitted to me completely I began to hate him
immediately and rejected him—as though all I needed him for was to win a
victory over him, to subjugate him and nothing else. But I could not subjugate all of them; my friend was not at all like them either, he was, in fact, a
rare exception. The first thing I did on leaving school was to give up the special job for which I had been destined so as to break all ties, to curse my past
and scatter it to the winds— And goodness knows why, after all that, I
should drag myself to that Simonov!

Early next morning I roused myself and jumped out of bed with excitement, as though it were all about to happen at once. But I believed that some
radical change in my life was coming, and would inevitably come that day.
Owing to its rarity, perhaps, any external event, however trivial, always made
me feel as though some radical change in my life would occur immediately. I
went to the office as usual, however, but slipped away home two hours early
to get ready. The important thing, I thought, is not to be the first to arrive,
or they will think I was overjoyed at coming. But there were thousands of
such important points to consider, and they all agitated me to the point of
impotence. I polished my boots a second time with my own hands; nothing
in the world would have induced Apollon to clean them twice a day, as he
considered that it was more than his duties required of him. I stole the

brushes to clean them from the passage, so that he would not detect it and then start to despise me. Then I minutely examined my clothes, and found that everything looked old, worn and threadbare. I had let myself get too slovenly. My uniform, perhaps, was in good shape, but I could hardly go out to dinner in my uniform. And the worst thing was that on the knee of my trousers was a big yellow stain. I had a foreboding that that stain would in itself deprive me of nine-tenths of my personal dignity. I knew, too, that it was stooping very low to think so. "But this is no time for thinking: now the real thing is beginning," I thought, and my heart sank. I knew, too, perfectly well even then, that I was monstrously exaggerating the facts. But how could I help it? I could not control myself and I was already shaking with fever. With despair I pictured to myself how coldly and disdainfully that "scoundrel" Zverkov would greet me; with what dull-witted, absolutely profound contempt the blockhead Trudolyubov would look at me; with what nasty insolence the beetle Ferfichkin would snigger at me in order to curry favor with Zverkov; how completely Simonov would take it all in, and how he would despise me for the abjectness of my vanity and faint-heartedness, and worst of all how paltry, *unliterary,* commonplace it would all be. Of course the best thing would be not to go at all. But that was the most impossible of all: once I feel impelled to do anything, I am completely drawn into it, head first. I would have jeered at myself ever afterward: "So you funked it, you funked the *real thing,* you funked it!" On the contrary, I passionately longed to show all that "rabble" that I was not at all such a coward as I pictured myself. What is more, even in the acutest paroxysm of this cowardly fever, I dreamed of getting the upper hand, of overcoming them, carrying them away, making them like me—if only for my "elevation of thought and unmistakable wit." They would abandon Zverkov, he would sit on one side, silent and ashamed, while I would crush Zverkov. Then, perhaps, I would be reconciled to him and toast our camaraderie; but what was most spiteful and insulting for me was that I knew even then, knew completely and for certain that I needed nothing of all this really, that I did not really want to crush, to subdue, to attract them, and that I would be the first not to care a straw, really, for the result, even if I did achieve it. Oh, how I prayed to God for the day to pass quickly! In inexpressible anguish I went to the window, opened a pane and looked out into the turbid darkness of the thickly falling wet snow.

At last my wretched little wall clock hissed out five. I seized my hat trying not to look at Apollon, who had been all day expecting his month's wages, but in his pride was unwilling to be the first to speak about it. I slipped past him and out the door, and jumping into a high-class sledge, on which I spent my last half-rouble, I drove up in grand style to the Hôtel de Paris.

☐ IV ☐

I had already known the day before that I would be the first to arrive. But it was no longer a question of precedence.

Not only were they not there, but I even had difficulty finding our room. The table had still not been completely set. What did it mean? After a good many questions I finally ascertained from the waiters that the dinner had been ordered not for five, but for six o'clock. This was confirmed at the buffet too. I even felt ashamed to go on questioning them. It was still only twenty-five minutes past five. If they changed the dinner hour they ought in any case to have let me know—that is what the post is for, and not to have subjected me to "shame" both in my own eyes and—well, before the waiters. I sat down: the servant began to set the table; I felt even more insulted when he was present. Toward six o'clock they brought in candles, though there were lamps burning in the room. It had not occurred to the waiter, however, to bring them in at once when I arrived. In the next room, two gloomy, angry-looking persons were eating their dinners in silence at two different tables. There was a great deal of noise, even shouting, in a room farther away; one could hear the laughter of a crowd of people, and nasty little shrieks in French; there were ladies at the dinner. In short, it was sickening. I rarely passed a more unpleasant time, so much so that when they did arrive all together punctually at six I was for the first moment overjoyed to see them, as though they were my deliverers, and almost forgot it was incumbent upon me to look insulted.

Zverkov walked in at the head of them; evidently he was the leading spirit. He and all of them were laughing; but, seeing me, Zverkov drew himself up, walked up to me unhurriedly with a slight, rather jaunty bend from the waist, and shook hands with me in a friendly but not over-friendly fashion, with a sort of circumspect courtesy almost like a general's as though in giving me his hand he were warding off something. I had imagined, on the contrary, that as soon as he came in he would immediately break into his former thin, shrieking laugh and fall to making his insipid jokes and witticisms. I had been preparing for them ever since the previous day, but I had never expected such condescension, such high-official courtesy. So, then, he felt himself immeasurably superior to me in every respect! If he had only meant to insult me by that high-official tone, it would still not have mattered, I thought—I could pay him back for it one way or another. But what if, in reality, without the least desire to be offensive, that sheep's-head had seriously acquired the notion that he was immeasurably superior to me and could only look at me in a patronizing way? The very supposition made me gasp.

"I was surprised to hear of your desire to join us," he began, lisping and drawling, which was something new. "You and I seem to have seen nothing of one another. You fight shy of us. You shouldn't. We are not such terrible people as you think. Well, anyway, I am glad to renew our acquaintance."

And he turned carelessly to put down his hat on the window sill.

"Have you been waiting long?" Trudolyubov inquired.

"I arrived punctually at five o'clock as I was informed yesterday," I answered aloud, with an irritability that promised an imminent explosion.

"Didn't you let him know that we had changed the hour?" said Trudolyubov to Simonov.

"No, I didn't. I forgot," the latter replied, with no sign of regret, and without even apologizing to me he went off to order the *hors d'oeuvres*.

"So you've been here a whole hour? Oh, you poor fellow!" Zverkov cried ironically, for according to his notions this was bound to be extremely funny. That scoundrel Ferfichkin followed with his nasty little snigger like a puppy yapping. My position struck him, too, as extremely ludicrous and embarrassing.

"It isn't funny at all!" I cried to Ferfichkin, more and more irritated. "It wasn't my fault, but other people's. They neglected to let me know. It was—it was—it was simply absurd."

"It's not only absurd, but something else as well," muttered Trudolyubov, naïvely taking my part. "You are too complacent about it. It was simply rudeness—unintentional, of course. And how could Simonov—h'm!"

"If a trick like that had been played on me," observed Ferfichkin, "I would—"

"But you should have ordered yourself something," Zverkov interrupted, "or simply asked for dinner without waiting for us."

"You will allow that I might have done that without your permission," I rapped out. "If I waited, it was—"

"Let us sit down, gentlemen," cried Simonov, coming in. "Everything is ready; I can answer for the champagne; it is capitally chilled.—After all, I did not know your address. Where was I to look for you?" He suddenly turned to me, but again he seemed to avoid looking at me. Evidently he had something against me. He must have made up his mind after what happened yesterday.

Everybody sat down: I did the same. It was a round table. Trudolyubov was on my left, Simonov on my right. Zverkov was sitting opposite, Ferfichkin next to him, between him and Trudolyubov.

"Te-e-ell me, are you—in a government agency?" Zverkov went on, attending to me. Seeing that I was embarrassed, he seriously thought that he ought to be friendly to me, and, so to speak, cheer me up. "Does he want me to throw a bottle at his head or something?" I thought, in a fury. In my unaccustomed surroundings I was unnaturally quick to be irritated.

"In the N——office," I answered jerkily, with my eyes on my plate.

"And—ha-ave you a go-od berth? Te-e-ll me, what ma-a-de you leave your former job?"

"What ma-a-de me was that I wanted to leave my original job," I drawled twice as much as he, hardly able to control myself. Ferfichkin snorted. Simonov looked at me ironically. Trudolyubov stopped eating and began looking at me with curiosity.

Zverkov was jarred but he pretended not to notice it.

"A-a-and the remuneration?"

"What remuneration?"

"I mean, your sa-a-lary?"

"Why are you cross-examining me?"

However, I told him at once what my salary was. I blushed terribly.

"It is not very handsome," Zverkov observed majestically.

"Yes, you can't afford to dine in restaurants on that," Ferfichkin added insolently.

"I think it's very low," Trudolyubov observed gravely.

"And how thin you have grown! How you have changed!" added Zverkov, with a shade of venom in his voice, scanning me and my attire with a sort of insolent compassion.

"Oh, spare his blushes," cried Ferfichkin, sniggering.

"My dear sir, permit me to tell you I am not blushing," I broke out at last; "do you hear? I am dining here, at this restaurant, at my own expense, at mine, not at other people's—note that, Monsieur Ferfichkin."

"Wha-at do you mean? Isn't everyone here dining at his own expense? You seem to be—" Ferfichkin let fly at me, turning as red as a lobster, and looking me in the face with fury.

"Tha-at's what I mean," I answered, feeling I had gone too far, "and I imagine it would be better to talk of something more intelligent."

"You intend to show off your intelligence, I suppose?"

"Don't disturb yourself, that would be quite out of place here."

"What are you clacking away like that for, my good sir, eh? Have you gone out of your wits in your *dumb*partment?"

"Enough, gentlemen, enough!" Zverkov cried, authoritatively.

"How stupid it is," muttered Simonov.

"It really is stupid. We have met here, a company of friends, for a farewell dinner to a good comrade and you are settling old scores," said Trudolyubov, rudely addressing himself to me alone. "Yesterday you invited yourself to join us, so don't disturb the general harmony."

"Enough, enough!" cried Zverkov. "Stop it, gentlemen, it's out of place. Better let me tell you how I nearly got married the day before yesterday . . ."

And then followed a burlesque narrative of how this gentleman had almost been married two days before. There was not a word about marriage, however, but the story was adorned with generals, colonels and high courtiers while Zverkov practically took the lead among them. It was greeted with approving laughter; Ferfichkin even squealed.

No one paid any attention to me, and I sat crushed and humiliated.

"Good heavens, these are not the people for me!" I thought. "And what a fool I have made of myself before them! I let Ferfichkin go too far, though. The brutes imagine that it is an honor for me to sit down with them. They don't understand that I do them an honor. I to them and not they to me! I've grown thinner! My clothes! Oh, damn my trousers! Zverkov long ago noticed the yellow stain on the knee . . . But what's the use! I must get up at once, this very minute, take my hat and simply go without a word—out of contempt! And tomorrow I can send a challenge. The scoundrels! After all, I don't care about the seven roubles. They may think . . . Damn it! I don't care about the seven roubles. I'll go this minute!"

Of course I remained.

I drank sherry and Lafitte by the glassful in my distress. Being unaccustomed to it, I quickly became intoxicated and my annoyance increased with the intoxication. I longed all at once to insult them all in a most flagrant manner and then go away. To seize the moment and show what I could do, so that they would say, "Though he is absurd, he's clever," and—and—in short, damn them all!

I scanned them all insolently with my dulled eyes. But they seemed to have forgotten me altogether. *They* were noisy, vociferous, cheerful. Zverkov kept talking. I began to listen. Zverkov was talking about some sumptuous lady whom he had at last led on to declaring her love (of course, he was lying like a horse), and how he had been helped in this affair by an intimate friend of his, a Prince Kolya, an officer in the Hussars, who had three thousand serfs.

"And yet, this Kolya, who has three thousand serfs, has not put in an appearance here tonight at all to see you off," I cut in suddenly. For a minute everyone was silent.

"You are drunk already." Trudolyubov deigned to notice me at last, glancing contemptuously in my direction. Zverkov, without a word, examined me as though I were a little beetle. I dropped my eyes. Simonov made haste to fill up the glasses with champagne.

Trudolyubov raised his glass, as did everyone else but me.

"Your health and good luck on the journey!" he cried to Zverkov. "To old times, gentlemen, to our future, hurrah!"

They all tossed off their glasses, and crowded round Zverkov to kiss him. I did not move; my full glass stood untouched before me.

"Why, aren't you going to drink it?" roared Trudolyubov, losing patience and turning menacingly to me.

"I want to make a toast separately, on my own account . . . and then I'll drink it, Mr. Trudolyubov."

"Disgusting crank!" muttered Simonov.

I drew myself up in my chair and feverishly seized my glass, prepared for something extraordinary, though I did not know myself precisely what I was going to say.

"*Silence!*" cried Ferfichkin, in French. "Now for a display of wit!"

Zverkov waited very gravely, knowing what was coming.

"Lieutenant Zverkov," I began, "let me tell you that I hate phrases, phrasemongers and corseted waists—that's the first point, and there is a second one to follow it."

There was a general stir.

"The second point is: I hate dirty stories and people who tell dirty stories. Especially people who tell dirty stories!

"The third point: I love truth, sincerity and honesty," I went on almost mechanically, for I was beginning to shiver with horror and had no idea how I came to be talking like this. "I love thought, Monsieur Zverkov; I love true comradeship, on an equal footing and not—h'm—I love—but, however, why not? I will drink to your health, too, Monsieur Zverkov. Seduce the Circassian girls, shoot the enemies of the fatherland and—and—to your health, Monsieur Zverkov!"

Zverkov got up from his seat, bowed to me and said:

"I am very much obliged to you."

He was frightfully offended and even turned pale.

"Damn the fellow!" roared Trudolyubov, bringing his fist down on the table.

"Well, he ought to be punched in the nose for that," squealed Ferfichkin.

"We ought to turn him out," muttered Simonov.

"Not a word, gentlemen, not a movement!" cried Zverkov solemnly, checking the general indignation. "I thank you all, but I can show him for myself how much value I attach to his words."

"Mr. Ferfichkin, you will give me satisfaction tomorrow at the latest for your words just now!" I said aloud, turning with dignity to Ferfichkin.

"A duel, you mean? Certainly," he answered. But probably I was so ridiculous as I challenged him and it was so out of keeping with my appearance that everyone, including Ferfichkin, roared with laughter.

"Yes, let him alone, of course! After all, he is completely drunk," Trudolyubov said with disgust.

"I will never forgive myself for letting him join us," Simonov muttered again.

"Now is the time to throw a bottle at their heads," I thought to myself. I picked up the bottle . . . and poured myself a full glass.

"No, I had better sit on to the end," I went on thinking; "you would be pleased, my friends, if I left. Nothing will induce me to go. I'll go on sitting here, and drinking to the end, on purpose, as a sign that I don't attach the slightest importance to you. I will go on sitting and drinking because this is a public-house and I paid my entrance money. I'll sit here and drink, for I look upon you as so many pawns, as inanimate pawns. I'll sit here and drink—and sing if I want to—yes, sing, for I have the right to—to sing—h'm!"

But I did not sing. I simply tried not to look at any of them. I assumed most unconcerned attitudes and waited with impatience for them to speak *first,* of their own accord. But alas, they did not speak! And oh, how I wished, how I wished at that moment to be reconciled to them! It struck eight, at last nine. They moved from the table to the sofa. Zverkov stretched himself on a couch and put one foot on a round table. The wine was brought there. He did, as a matter of fact, order three bottles on his own account. He didn't, of course, invite me to join them. They all sat round him on the sofa. They listened to him, almost with reverence. It was evident that they were fond of him. "For what? For what?" I wondered. From time to time they were moved to drunken enthusiasm and kissed each other. They talked of the Caucasus, of the nature of true passion, of advantageous jobs in the service, of the income of a Hussar called Podkharzhevsky, whom none of them knew personally and rejoiced that he had a large income; of the extraordinary grace and beauty of a Princess D., whom none of them had ever seen; then it came to Shakespeare's being immortal.

I smiled contemptuously and walked up and down the other side of the room, opposite the sofa, along the wall, from the table to the stove and back again. I tried my very utmost to show them that I could do without them, and yet I purposely stomped with my boots, thumping with my heels. But it was all in vain. They paid no attention at all. I had the patience to walk up and down in front of them that way from eight o'clock till eleven, in one and the same place, from table to the stove and from the stove back again to the table. "I walk up and down to please myself and no one can prevent me." The waiter who came into the room several times stopped to look at me. I was somewhat giddy from turning round so often; at moments it seemed to me that I was in delirium. During those three hours I was three times soaked with sweat, and then dry again. At times, with an intense, acute pang, I was stabbed to the heart by the thought that ten years, twenty years, forty years would pass, and that even in forty years I would remember with loathing and humiliation those filthiest, most ludicrous, and most terrible moments of my life. No one could have gone out of his way to degrade himself more shamelessly and voluntarily, and I fully realized it, fully, and yet I went on pacing up and down from the table to the stove. "Oh, if you only knew what thoughts and feelings I am capable of, how cultured I am!" I thought at moments, mentally addressing the sofa on which my enemies were sitting. But my enemies behaved as though I did not exist in the room. Once—only once—they turned toward me, just when Zverkov was talking about Shake-speare, and I suddenly gave a contemptuous laugh. I snorted in such an affected and nasty way that they all at once broke off their conversation, and silently and gravely for two minutes watched me walking up and down from the table to the stove, *paying no attention whatsoever to them*. But nothing came of it; they said nothing, and two minutes later they ceased to notice me again. It struck eleven.

"Gentlemen," cried Zverkov, getting up from the sofa, "let us all go there *now!*"

"Of course, of course," the others said.

I turned sharply to Zverkov. I was so exhausted, so broken, that I would have cut my throat to put an end to it. I was in a fever; my hair, soaked with perspiration, stuck to my forehead and temples.

"Zverkov, I beg your pardon," I said abruptly and resolutely. "Ferfichkin, yours too, and everyone's, everyone's; I have insulted you all!"

"Aha! A duel is not in your line, old man," Ferfichkin hissed venomously.

It sent a deep pang to my heart.

"No, it's not the duel I am afraid of, Ferfichkin! I am ready to fight you tomorrow, after we are reconciled. I insist upon it, in fact, and you cannot refuse. I want to show you that I am not afraid of a duel. You will fire first and I will fire into the air."

"He is comforting himself," remarked Simonov.

"He's simply raving," declared Trudolyubov.

"But let us pass. Why are you barring our way? Well, what do you want?" Zverkov answered disdainfully. They were all flushed; their eyes were bright; they had been drinking heavily.

"I asked for your friendship, Zverkov; I insulted you, but—"

"Insulted? You-u insulted me-e-e! Permit me to tell you, sir, that you never, under any circumstances, could possibly insult *me.*"

"And that's enough of you. Out of the way!" concluded Trudolyubov. "Let's go."

"Olympia is mine, gentlemen, that's agreed!" cried Zverkov.

"We won't dispute your right, we won't dispute your right," the others answered, laughing.

I stood as though spat upon. The party went noisily out of the room. Trudolyubov struck up some stupid song. Simonov remained behind for a moment to tip the waiters. I suddenly went up to him.

"Simonov! give me six roubles!" I said, decisively and desperately.

He looked at me in extreme amazement, with dulled eyes. He, too, was drunk.

"You don't mean you are even coming with us *there?*"

"Yes."

"I've no money," he snapped out, and with a scornful laugh he went out of the room.

I clutched his overcoat. It was a nightmare.

"Simonov! I saw you had money, why do you refuse me? Am I a scoundrel? Beware of refusing me; if you knew, if you knew why I am asking! Everything depends upon it! My whole future, my whole plans!"

Simonov pulled out the money and almost flung it at me.

"Take it, if you have no sense of shame!" he pronounced pitilessly, and ran to overtake them.

I was left alone for a moment. Disorder, the remains of dinner, a broken wineglass on the floor, spilt wine, cigarette butts, intoxication and delirium in my brain, an agonizing misery in my heart and finally the waiter, who had seen and heard all and was looking inquisitively into my face.

"I am going *there!*" I shouted. "Either they will all fall down on their knees to beg for my friendship—or I will give Zverkov a slap in the face!"

□ V □

"So this is it, so this is it at last, a clash with reality," I muttered as I ran headlong downstairs. "This, it seems, is very different from the Pope's leaving Rome and going to Brazil; this, it seems, is very different from the ball on the shores of Lake Como!"

"You are a scoundrel," flashed through my mind, "if you laugh at this now."

"No matter!" I cried, answering myself. "Now everything is lost!"

There was no trace of them left, but that made no difference—I knew where they had gone.

At the steps was standing a solitary night sledge-driver in a rough peasant coat, powdered over with the wet, and, as it were, warm snow that was still falling thickly. It was sultry and warm. The little shaggy piebald horse was also powdered with snow and was coughing. I remember that very well. I made a rush for the roughly made sledge; but as soon as I raised my foot to get into it, the recollection of how Simonov had just given me six roubles seemed to double me up and I tumbled into the sledge like a sack.

"No, I must do a great deal to make up for all that," I cried. "But I will make up for it or perish on the spot this very night. Start!"

We set off. There was an absolute whirl in my head.

"They won't go down on their knees to beg for my friendship. That is a mirage, a cheap mirage, revolting, romantic and fantastical—that is another ball at Lake Como. And so I have to slap Zverkov's face! It is my duty to. And so it is settled; I am flying to give him a slap in the face. Hurry up!"

The cabby tugged at the reins.

"As soon as I go in I'll give it to him. Ought I to say a few words by way of preface before giving him the slap? No, I'll simply go in and give it to him. They will all be sitting in the drawing-room, and he with Olympia on the sofa. That damned Olympia! She laughed at my looks on one occasion and refused me. I'll pull Olympia's hair, pull Zverkov's ears! No, better one ear, and pull him by it round the room. Maybe they will all begin beating me and will kick me out. That is even very likely. No matter! Anyway, I will slap him first; the initiative will be mine; and according to the code of honor that is everything: he will be branded and no blows can wipe off the slap, nothing but a duel can. He will be forced to fight. And let them beat me then. Let them, the ungrateful wretches! Trudolyubov will beat me hardest, he is so strong; Ferfichkin is sure to catch hold from the side and tug at my hair. But no matter, no matter! That's what I am going for. The blockheads will be forced at last to see the tragedy of it all! When they drag me to the door I shall call out to them that in reality they are not worth my little finger." "Get on, driver, get on!" I cried to the driver. He started and flicked his whip, I shouted so savagely.

"We shall fight at daybreak, that's a settled thing. I am through with the Department. Ferfichkin called the Department 'Dumbpartment' before. But where can I get pistols? Nonsense! I'll call my salary in advance and buy them. And powder, and bullets? That's the second's business. And how can it all be done by daybreak? And where am I to get a second? I have no friends. Nonsense!" I cried, lashing myself more and more into a fury. "Nonsense! The first person I meet in the street is bound to be my second, just as he would be bound to pull a drowning man out of water. The strangest things may happen. Even if I were to ask the Director himself to be my second to-morrow, even he would be bound to consent, if only from a feeling of chivalry, and to keep the secret! Anton Antonich—"

The fact is that at that very minute the disgusting absurdity of my plans and the other side of the question were clearer and more vivid to my imagination than they could be to anyone on earth, but—

"Get on, driver, get on, you rascal, get on!"

"Ugh, sir!" said the son of toil.

Cold shivers suddenly ran down me.

"Wouldn't it be better . . . wouldn't it be better . . . to go straight home now? Oh, my God! Why, why did I invite myself to this dinner yesterday? But no, it's impossible. And my three hours' walk from the table to the stove? No, they, they and no one else must pay for my walking up and down! They must wipe out this dishonor! Drive on!

"And what if they hand me over to the police? They won't dare! They'll be afraid of the scandal. And what if Zverkov is so contemptuous that he refuses to fight a duel? That is even sure to happen, but in that case I'll show them—I will turn up at the posting station when he is setting off tomorrow—I'll catch him by the leg, I'll pull off his coat when he gets into the carriage. I'll get my teeth into his hand, I'll bite him. See to what lengths you can drive a desperate man! He may hit me on the head and they may pummel me from behind. I will shout to the whole crowd of spectators: 'Look at this young puppy who is driving off to captivate the Circassian girls after letting me spit in his face!'

"Of course, after that everything will be over! The Department will have vanished off the face of the earth. I will be arrested. I will be tried, I will be dismissed from the service, thrown in prison, sent to Siberia, deported. Never mind! In fifteen years when they let me out of prison I will trudge off to him, a beggar in rags, I shall find him in some provincial city. He will be married and happy. He will have a grown-up daughter ... I will say to him: 'Look, monster, at my hollow cheeks and my rags! I've lost everything—my career, my happiness, art, science, *the woman I loved,* and all through you. Here are pistols. I have come to discharge my pistol and—and I ... forgive you.' Then I will fire into the air and he will hear nothing more of me."

I was actually on the point of tears, though I knew perfectly well at that very moment that all this was out of Pushkin's *Silvio* and Lermontov's *Masquerade*. And all at once I felt terribly ashamed, so ashamed that I stopped the sledge, stepped out of it and stood still in the snow in the middle of the street. The driver sighed and gazed at me in astonishment.

What was I to do? I could not go on there—that was clearly absurd, and I could not leave things as they were, because that would seem as though— "Heavens, how could I leave things! And after such insults!" "No!" I cried, throwing myself into the sledge again. "It is ordained! It is fate! Drive on, drive on to that place!"

And in my impatience I punched the sledge-driver on the back of the neck.

"What are you up to? What are you hitting me for?" the poor man shouted, but he whipped up his nag so that it began to kick out.

The wet snow was falling in big flakes; I unbuttoned myself. I did not care about it. I forgot everything else, for I had finally decided on the slap, and felt with horror that after all it was going to happen *now, at once,* that it would happen immediately and that *no force could stop it.* The deserted street lamps gleamed sullenly in the snowy darkness like torches at a funeral. The snow drifted under my greatcoat, under my coat, under my necktie, and melted there. I did not cover myself up—after all, all was already lost, anyway. At last we arrived. I jumped out, almost fainting, ran up the steps and began knocking and kicking at the door. My legs, particularly at the knee, felt terribly weak. The door was opened quickly as though they knew I was coming. As a matter of fact, Simonov had warned them that perhaps another would arrive, and this was a place in which one had to give notice and to observe certain precautions. It was one of the "millinery establishments" which were abolished by the police a long time ago. By day it really was a shop; but at night, if one had an introduction, one might visit it for other purposes.

I walked rapidly through the dark shop into the familiar drawing-room, where there was only one candle burning, and stopped in amazement; there was no one there.

"Where are they?" I asked somebody.

But by now, of course, they had separated.

Before me stood a person with a stupid smile, the "madam" herself, who had seen me before. A minute later a door opened and another person came in.

Paying no attention to anything, I strode about the room, and, I believe, I talked to myself. I felt as though I had been saved from death and was conscious of it, joyfully, all over: after all, I would have given that slap. I would certainly, certainly have given it! But now they were not here and—everything had vanished and changed! I looked round. I could not realize my condition yet. I looked mechanically at the girl who had come in and had a glimpse of a fresh, young, rather pale face, with straight, dark eyebrows, and with a grave, as it were, amazed glance, eyes that attracted me at once. I would have hated her if she had been smiling. I began looking at her more intently and, as it were, with effort. I had not fully collected my thoughts. There was something simple and good-natured in her face, but something strangely serious. I am sure that this stood in her way here, and that not one of those fools had noticed her. She could not, however, have been called a beauty, though she was tall, strong-looking, and well built. She was very simply dressed. Something loathsome stirred in me. I went straight up to her—

I happened to look at myself in the mirror. My harassed face struck me as extremely revolting, pale, spiteful, nasty, with disheveled hair. "No matter, I am glad of it," I thought; "I am glad that I shall seem revolting to her; I like that."

□   VI   □

... Somewhere behind a screen a clock began wheezing, as though under some great pressure, as though someone were strangling it. After an unnaturally prolonged wheezing there followed a shrill, nasty and, as it were, unexpectedly rapid chime—as though someone were suddenly jumping forward. It struck two. I woke up, though I had not really been asleep but only lay semi-conscious.

It was almost completely dark in the narrow, cramped, low-pitched room, cluttered up with an enormous wardrobe and piles of cardboard boxes and all sorts of frippery and litter. The candle stump that had been burning on the table was going out and it gave a faint flicker from time to time. In a few minutes it would be completely dark.

I was not long in coming to myself; everything came back to my mind at once, without an effort, as though it had been in ambush to pounce upon me again. And, indeed, even while I was unconscious, a point continually seemed to remain in my memory that could not ever be forgotten, and around it my dreams moved drearily. But strange to say, everything that had happened to me during that day seemed to me now, on waking, to be in the far, far-away distant past, as though I had long, long ago lived all that down.

My head was heavy. Something seemed to be hovering over me, provoking me, rousing me and making me restless. Misery and gall seemed to surge up in me again and to seek an outlet. Suddenly I saw beside me two wide-open eyes scrutinizing me curiously and persistently. The look in those eyes was coldly detached, sullen, utterly detached, as it were; it weighed heavily on me.

A grim idea came into my brain and passed all over my body, like some nasty sensation, such as one feels when one goes into a damp and mouldy cellar. It was somehow unnatural that those two eyes only now thought of beginning to examine me. I recalled, too, that during those two hours I had not said a single word to this creature, and had, in fact considered it entirely unnecessary; it had even for some reason gratified me before. Now I suddenly realized vividly how absurd, revolting as a spider, was the idea of vice which, without love, grossly and shamelessly begins directly with that in which true love finds its consummation. For a long time we gazed at each other like that, but she did not drop her eyes before mine and did not change her expression, so that at last, somehow, I felt uncomfortable.

"What is your name?" I asked abruptly, to put an end to it quickly.

"Liza," she answered almost in a whisper, but somehow without any friendliness; she turned her eyes away.

I was silent.

"What weather today—the snow—it's abominable!" I said, almost to myself, putting my arm under my head despondently, and gazing at the ceiling.

She made no answer. This was all outrageous.

"Are you a local girl?" I asked a minute later, almost angrily, turning my head slightly toward her.

"No."

"Where do you come from?"

"From Riga," she answered reluctantly.

"Are you a German?"

"No, Russian."

"Have you been here long?"

"Where?"

"In this house?"

"A fortnight."

She spoke more and more jerkily. The candle went out: I could no longer distinguish her face.

"Have you a father and mother?"

"Yes—no—I have."

"Where are they?"

"There—in Riga."

"What are they?"

"Oh, nothing."

"Nothing? Why, what do they do?"

"Tradespeople."

"Have you always lived with them?"

"Yes."

"How old are you?"

"Twenty."

"Why did you leave them?"

"Oh, for no reason."

That answer meant "Let me alone; I feel wretched." We were silent.

God knows why I did not go away. I felt myself more and more wretched and dreary. The images of the previous day started to flit through my mind in confusion independently of my will. I suddenly recalled something I had seen that morning when, full of anxious thoughts, I was hurrying to the office.

"I saw them carrying a coffin out yesterday and they nearly dropped it," I suddenly said aloud with no desire at all to start a conversaion, but just so, almost by accident.

"A coffin?"

"Yes, in the Haymarket; they were bringing it up out of a cellar."

"From a cellar?"

"Not from a cellar, but from a basement. Oh, you know—down below—from a house of ill-fame. It was filthy all round—eggshells, litter—a stench. It was loathsome."

Silence.

"A nasty day to be buried," I began, simply to avoid being silent.

"Nasty, in what way?"

"The snow, the wet." (I yawned.)

"It doesn't matter," she said suddenly, after a brief silence.

"No, it's abominable." (I yawned again.) "The gravediggers must have sworn at getting drenched by the snow. And there must have been water in the grave."

"Why would there be water in the grave?" she asked, with a sort of curiosity, but speaking even more harshly and abruptly than before. I suddenly began to feel provoked.

"Why, there must have been water at the bottom a foot deep. You can't dig a dry grave in Volkovo Cemetery."

"Why?"

"Why? Why, the place is waterlogged. It's a regular marsh. So they bury them in water. I've seen it myself—many times."

(I had never seen it at all, and I had never even been in Volkovo, but had only heard stories of it.)

"Do you mean to say it doesn't matter to you whether you die?"

"But why should I die?" she answered, as though defending herself.

"Why, some day you will die, and you will die just the same as that dead woman. She was—a girl like you. She died of consumption."

"The wench would have died in a hospital, too . . ." (She knows all about it already; she said "wench," not "girl.")

"She was in debt to her madam," I retorted, more and more provoked by the discussion; "and went on earning money for her almost up to the very end, though she was in consumption. Some coachmen standing by were talking about her to some soldiers and telling them so. No doubt her former acquaintances. They were laughing. They were going to meet in a pot-house to drink to her memory." (I lied a great deal here.)

Silence followed, profound silence. She did not even stir.

"And is it better to die in a hospital?"

"Isn't it just the same? Besides, why should I die?" she added irritably.

"If not now, a little later."

"Why a little later?"

"Why, indeed? Now you are young, pretty, fresh, you fetch a high price. But after another year of this life you will be very different—you will fade."

"In a year?"

"Anyway, in a year you will be worth less," I continued malignantly. "You will go from here to something lower, another house; a year later—to a third, lower and lower, and in seven years you will come to a basement in the Haymarket. And that's if you are lucky. But it would be much worse if you got some disease, consumption, say—and caught a chill, or something or other. It's not easy to get over an illness in your way of life. If you catch anything you may not get rid of it. And so you would die."

"Oh, well, then I will die," she answered, quite vindictively, and she made a quick movement.

"But after all, it's a pity."

"For whom?"

"Pity for life."

Silence.

"Were you engaged? Eh?"

"What's that to you?"

"Oh, I am not cross-examining you. It's nothing to me. Why are you so cross? Of course you may have had your own troubles. What is it to me? I simply felt sorry."

"For whom?"

"Sorry for you."

"No need," she whispered hardly audibly, and again made a faint movement.

That incensed me at once. What! I was so gentle with her, and she—

"Why, what do you think? Are you on the right path, ah?"

"I don't think anything."

"That's what's wrong, that you don't think. Wake up while there is still time. And there is still time. You are still young, good-looking; you might love, be married, be happy—"

"Not all married women are happy," she snapped out in the rude, fast way she had spoken before.

"Not all, of course, but anyway it is much better than the life here. Infinitely better. Besides, with love one can live even without happiness. Even in sorrow life is sweet; life is sweet, however one lives. But here you have nothing except foulness. Phew!"

I turned away with disgust; I was no longer reasoning coldly. I began to feel myself what I was saying and warmed to the subject. I was already longing to expound the cherished *little ideas* I had brooded over in my corner. Something suddenly flared up in me. An object had "appeared" before me.

"Never mind my being here. I am not an example for you. I am, perhaps, even worse than you are. I was drunk when I came here, though," I hastened, however, to say in self-defense. "Besides, a man is no example for a woman. It's a different thing. I may degrade and defile myself, but I am not anyone's slave. I come and go, and there's an end to it. I shake it off, and I am a different man. But you are a slave from the start. Yes, a slave! You give up everything, your whole freedom. If you want to break your chains afterward, you won't be able to; you will be caught more and more in the snares. It is an accursed bondage. I know it. I won't mention anything else, maybe you won't understand it, but tell me: after all, surely you are in debt to your madam already? There, you see," I added, though she made no answer, but only listened in silence, entirely absorbed, "that's bondage for you! You will never buy your freedom. They will see to that. It's like selling your soul to the devil—

"And besides—perhaps I, too, am just as unfortunate, how do you know—and wallow in the mud on purpose, also out of misery? After all, men take to drink out of grief; well, maybe I am here out of grief. Come, tell me, what good is there here? Here you and I—were intimate—just now and did not say one word to one another all the time, and it was only afterward you began staring at me like a wild creature, and I at you. Is that loving? Is that how human beings are intimate? It's hideous, that's what it is!"

"Yes!" she assented sharply and hurriedly.

I was even amazed by the eagerness of this "yes." So the same thought may have been straying through her mind when she was staring at me just before. So she, too, was capable of certain thoughts? "Damn it all, this was curious, this was *kinship?*" I thought, almost rubbing my hands. And indeed how can one fail to manage a young soul like that?

The sport in it attracted me most.

She turned her head nearer to me, and it seemed to me in the darkness that she propped herself on her arm. Perhaps she was scrutinizing me. How I regretted that I could not see her eyes. I heard her deep breathing.

"Why did you come here?" I asked her, with a note of authority already in my voice.

"Oh, I don't know."

"But after all how nice it would be to be living in your own father's house! It's warm and free; you have a nest of your own."

"But what if it's worse than this?"

"I must take the right tone," flashed through my mind. "I may not get far with sentimentality."

But it was only a momentary thought. I swear she really did interest me. Besides, I was exhausted and moody. And after all, cunning so easily goes hand in hand with feeling.

"Who denies it?" I hastened to answer. "Anything may happen. I am, after all, convinced that someone has wronged you and is guiltier toward you than you toward them. After all, I know nothing of your story, but it's not likely a girl like you has come here of her own inclination—"

"What kind of girl am I?" she whispered, hardly audible, but I heard it.

Damn it all, I was flattering her. That was abominable. But perhaps it was a good thing— She was silent.

"See, Liza, I will tell you about myself. If I had had a home from childhood, I shouldn't be what I am now. I often think about that. After all, no matter how bad it may be at home, at least they are your father and mother, and not enemies, strangers. Once a year, at least, they'll show their love for you. Anyway, you know you are at home. I grew up without a home; and perhaps that's why I've turned so—unfeeling."

I waited again.

"Perhaps she doesn't understand," I thought, "and, indeed, it is absurd, this moralizing."

"If I were a father and had a daughter, I believe I should love my daughter more than my sons, really," I began indirectly, as though talking of something else, in order to distract her attention. I confess I blushed.

"Why so?" she asked.

Ah! so she was listening!

"I don't know, Liza. I knew a father who was a stern, strict man, but he used to go down on his knees to his daughter, used to kiss her hands and feet, he couldn't make enough of her, really. When she danced at parties he used to stand for five hours at a stretch without taking his eyes off her. He was mad about her; I understand that! She would fall asleep tired at night, and he would get up to kiss her in her sleep and make the sign of the cross over her. He would go about in a dirty old coat, he was stingy to everyone else, but would spend his last penny for her, giving her expensive presents, and it was a delight to him when she was pleased with what he gave her. Fathers always love their daughters more than mothers do. Some girls live happily at home! And I believe I would never let my daughter marry."

"What next?" she said with a faint smile.

"I would be jealous, I really would. To think that she should kiss anyone else! That she should love a stranger more than her father! It's painful to imagine it. Of course, that's all nonsense, of course every father would be reasonable at last. But I believe before I would let her marry, I would worry myself to death; I would find fault with all her suitors. But I would end by letting her marry whom she herself loved. After all, the one whom the daughter loves always seems the worst to the father. That is always so. So many families get into trouble with that."

"Some are glad to sell their daughters, rather than to marry them honorably."

Ah! So that was it!

"Such a thing, Liza, happened in those accursed families in which there is neither love nor God," I retorted warmly, "and where there is no love, there is no sense either. There are such families, it's true, but I am not speaking of them. You must have seen wickedness in your own family, if you talk like that. You must have been genuinely unlucky. H'm!—that sort of thing mostly comes about through poverty."

"And is it any better among the rich? Even among the poor, honest people live happily."

"H'm—yes. Perhaps. Another thing, Liza, man only likes to count his troubles, but he does not count his joys. If he counted them up as he ought, he would see that every lot has enough happiness provided for it. And what if all goes well with the family, if the blessing of God is upon it, if the husband is a good one, loves you, cherishes you, never leaves you! There is happiness in such a family! Sometimes there is happiness even in the midst of sorrow; and indeed sorrow is everywhere. If you marry *you will find out for yourself.* But think of the first years of married life with one you love: what happiness, what happiness there sometimes is in it! And indeed it's the ordinary thing. In those early days even quarrels with one's husband end happily. Some women get up more quarrels with their husbands the more they love them. Indeed, I knew a woman like that: she seemed to say that because she loved him deeply, she would torment him out of love so that he'd feel it. Did you know that you may torment a man on purpose out of love? Women are particularly given to that, thinking to themselves, 'I will love him so much afterward, I will make so much of him, that it's no sin to torment him a little now.' And everyone in the house rejoices in the sight of you, and you are happy and gay and peaceful and honorable. Then there are some women who are jealous. If the husband goes off someplace—I knew one such woman, she couldn't restrain herself, but would jump up at night and would run off on the sly to find out where he was, whether he was with some other woman. That's already bad. And the woman knows herself it's wrong, and her heart fails her and she suffers, but, after all, she loves—it's all through love. And how sweet it is to make up after quarrels, to admit she was wrong, or to forgive him! And they are both so happy, all at once they become so happy, as though they had met anew, been married over again; as though their love had begun anew. And no one, no one should know what passes between husband and wife if they love one another. And no matter how their quarrels ended they ought not to call in even their own mothers to judge between them and tell tales of one another. They are their own judges. Love is a holy mystery and ought to be hidden from all other eyes, no matter what happens. That makes it holier and better. They respect one another more, and much is built on respect. And if once there has been love, if they have been married for love, why should love pass away? Surely one can keep it! It is rare that one cannot keep it. And if the husband is kind and straightforward, why should not love last? The first phase of married love will pass, it is true, but then there will come a love that is better still. Then there will be the union of souls, they will have everything in common, there will be no secrets between them. And once they have children, the most difficult times will seem to them happy, so long as there is love and courage. Even toil will be a joy, you may deny yourself bread for your children and even that will be a joy. After all, they will love you for it afterward; so you are laying by for your future. As the children grow up you feel that you are an example, a support for them; that even after you die your children will always cherish your thoughts and feelings, because they have received them from you, they will take on your semblance and likeness. So you see it is a great duty. How can it fail to draw the father and mother closer? People say it's a trial to have children. Who says that? It is heavenly joy! Are you fond of little children, Liza? I am awfully fond of them. You know—a little rosy baby boy at your bosom, and what husband's heart is not touched, seeing his wife nursing his child! A plump little rosy baby, sprawling and snuggling, chubby little hands and feet, clean tiny little nails, so tiny that it makes one laugh to look at them; eyes that look as if they understand everything. And while it sucks it clutches at your bosom with its little hand, plays. When its father comes up, the child tears itself away from the bosom, flings itself back, looks at its father, laughs, as though it were God knows how funny, and falls to sucking again. Or it will bite its mother's breast when it is cutting its little teeth while it looks sideways at her with its little eyes as though to say, 'Look, I am biting!' Is not all that a joy when they are all three together, husband, wife and child? One can forgive a great deal for the sake of such moments. Yes, Liza, one must first learn to live oneself before one blames others!"

"It's by pictures, pictures like that one must get at you," I thought to myself, though I did not speak with real feeling, and all at once I flushed crimson. "What if she were suddenly to burst out laughing, what would I do then?" That idea drove me to fury. Toward the end of my speech I really was excited, and now my vanity was somehow wounded. The silence continued. I almost wanted to nudge her.

"Why are you . . ." she began, and stopped. But I understood: there was a quiver of something different in her voice, not abrupt, harsh and unyielding as before, but something soft and shamefaced, so shamefaced that I suddenly felt ashamed and guilty.

"What?" I asked with tender curiosity.

"Why, you . . ."

"What?"

"Why you—speak exactly like a book," she said, and something sarcastic was heard in her voice.

That remark sent a pang to my heart. It wsa not what I was expecting.

I did not understand that she was hiding her feelings by sarcasm and that this is usually the last refuge of modest and chaste-souled people when the privacy of their soul is coarsely and intrusively invaded, and that their pride makes them refuse to surrender till the last moment and shrink from expressing their feelings to you. I ought to have guessed the truth for the timidity with which she had a number of times attempted her sarcasm, only bringing herself to utter it at last with an effort. But I did not guess, and a spiteful feeling took possession of me.

"Wait a bit!" I thought.

□ VII □

"Oh, hush, Liza! How can you talk about my speaking like a book when it makes even me, an outsider, feel sick? Though I don't look at it as an outsider, for, indeed, all that has touched me to the heart. Is it possible, is it possible that you do not feel sick at being here yourself? Evidently habit does wonders! God knows what habit can do with anyone. Can you really and seriously think that you will never grow old, that you will always be good-looking, and that they will keep you here forever and ever? I say nothing of the filth here. Though let me tell you this about it; about your present life, I mean; even though you are young now, attractive, nice, with soul and feeling, yet you know, as soon as I came to myself just now, I felt at once sick at being here with you! After all, one can only come here when one is drunk. But if you were anywhere else, living as decent people live, I would perhaps be more than attracted by you, I would fall in love with you, would be glad of a look from you, let alone a word. I would hang about your door, would go down on my knees to you, we would become engaged and I would even consider it an honor to do so. I would not dare to have an impure thought about you. But here, after all, I know that I have only to whistle and you have to come with me whether you like it or not. I don't consult your wishes, but you mine. The lowest laborer hires himself as a workman but he doesn't make a slave of himself altogether; besides, he knows that he will be free again. But when will you be free? Only think what you are giving up here! What is it you are making a slave of? It is your soul, together with your body; you are selling your soul which you have no right to dispose of! You give your love to be outraged by every drunkard! Love! But after all, that's everything, but after all, it's a jewel, it's a maiden's treasure, love—why, after all a man would be ready to give his soul, to face death to gain that love. But how much is your love worth now? You can be bought, all of you, body and soul, and there is no need to strive for love when you can have everything without love. And after all, there is no greater insult for a girl than that, do you understand? To be sure, I have heard that they comfort you, poor fools, they let you have lovers of your own here. But after all, that's simply a farce, that's simply a sham, it's just laughing at you, and you are taken in by it! Why, do you suppose he really loves you, that lover of yours? I don't believe it. How can he love you when he knows that you may be called away from him any minute? He would be a vile fellow if he did! Would he have a grain of respect for you? What have you in common with him? He laughs at you and robs you—that is all his love amounts to! You are lucky if he does not beat you. Very likely he does beat you, too. Ask him, if you have one, whether he will marry you. He will laugh in your face, if he doesn't spit in it

or give you a blow—yet he may not be worth a plugged nickel himself. And
for what have you ruined your life, if you come to think of it? For the coffee
they give you to drink and the plentiful meals? But after all, why do they feed
you? An honest girl couldn't swallow the food, she would know why she was
being fed. You are in debt here, and, of course, you will always be in debt,
and you will go on in debt to the end, till the visitors here begin to scorn
you. And that will soon happen, don't rely upon your youth—all that flies
by, like an express train here, after all. You will be kicked out. And not simply kicked out; long before that they will begin to nag you, scold you, abuse
you, as though you had not sacrificed your health for her, had not ruined
your youth and your soul for her benefit, but as though you had ruined her,
ravaged her, robbed her. And don't expect anyone to take your part; the
others, your companions, will attack you, too, to win her favor, for all are in
slavery here, and have lost all conscience and pity long ago. They have become utterly vile, and nothing on earth is viler, more loathsome and more
insulting than their abuse. And you are laying down everything here, everything unconditionally, youth and health and beauty and hope, and at
twenty-two you will look like a woman of thirty-five, and you will be lucky if
you are not diseased, pray to God for that! No doubt you are thinking now
after all that you have a lark and no work to do! Yet there is no harder or
more dreadful work in the world or ever has been. One would think that the
heart alone would be worn out with tears. And you won't dare to say a word,
not half a word, when they drive you away from here: you will go away as
though you were to blame. You will change to another house, then to a
third, then somewhere else, till you come down at last to the Haymarket.
There you will be beaten at every turn; that is a courtesy there, the visitors
there don't know how to be friendly without beating you. You don't believe
that it is so hateful there? Go and look for yourself some time, you can see
with your own eyes. Once, one New Year's Day, I saw a woman at a door.
Her own kind had turned her out as a joke, to give her a taste of the frost
because she had been howling too much, and they shut the door behind her.
At nine o'clock in the morning she was already completely drunk, dishevelled, half-naked, covered with bruises, her face was powdered, but she had a
black eye, blood was trickling from her nose and her teeth; some cabman had
just beaten her. She was sitting on the stone steps, a salt fish of some sort was
in her hand; she was howling, wailing something about her 'fate' and beating
with the fish on the steps, and cabmen and drunken soldiers were crowding
in the doorway taunting her. You don't believe that you will ever be like
that? I would not like to believe it, either, but how do you know, maybe ten
years, eight years ago that very woman with that salt fish came here fresh as a
little cherub, innocent, pure, knowing no evil, blushing at every word. Perhaps she was like you, proud, ready to take offence, not like the others; perhaps she looked like a queen, and knew what happiness was in store for the

man who would love her and whom she would love. Do you see how it ended? And what if at that very minute when she was beating on the filthy steps with that fish, drunken and dishevelled—what if at that very minute she recalled the pure early days in her father's house, when she used to go to school and the neighbor's son watched for her on the way, declaring that he would love her as long as he lived, that he would devote his life to her, and when they vowed to love one another for ever and be married as soon as they were grown up. No, Liza, it would be a joy for you, a joy if you were to die soon of consumption in some corner, in some cellar like that woman just now. In the hospital, do you say? You will be lucky if they take you, but what if you are still of use to the madam here? Consumption is a queer disease, it is not like fever. The patient goes on hoping till the last minute and says he is all right. He deludes himself. And that's just advantageous for your madam. Don't doubt it, that's how it is; you have sold your soul, and what is more you owe money, so you don't even dare to say a word. But when you are dying, everyone will abandon you, everyone will turn away from you, for there will be nothing to get from you. What's more, they will reproach you for taking up space, for taking so long to die. You won't even be able to beg for a drink of water without getting abuse. 'Aren't you going to die, you foul wench; you won't let us sleep with your moaning, you make the gentlemen sick.' That's true. I have heard such things said myself. When you are really dying they will push you into the filthiest corner in the cellar; in the damp and darkness; what will your thoughts be, lying there alone? When you die, strange hands will lay you out, with grumbling and impatience; no one will bless you, no one will sigh for you, they will only want to get rid of you as soon as possible; they will buy a coffin, take you to the grave as they did that poor woman today, and celebrate your memory at the tavern. There is slush, filth, wet snow in the grave—no need to put themselves out for you: 'Let her down, Vanyukha; it's just like her "fate" after all, here she goes in, head first, the wench. Shorten the cord, you rascal.' 'It's all right as it is.' 'All right, is it? Why, she's on her side! Wasn't she a human being, too? Well, never mind, cover her up.' And they won't care to waste much time quarreling over you. They will scatter the wet blue clay as quickly as they can and go off to the tavern—and there your memory on earth will end; other women have children who visit their graves, fathers, husbands. While for you there will be neither tear, nor sigh, nor remembrance; no one, no one in the whole wide world will ever come to you; your name will vanish from the face of the earth as though you had never existed, had never been born at all! Nothing but filth and mud, no matter how much you knock on your coffin lid at night, when the dead arise, however you cry: 'Let me out, kind people, to live in the light of day! My life was no life at all; my life has been thrown away like a dirty rag; it was drunk away in the tavern at the Haymarket; let me out, kind people, to live in the world again!' "

And I worked myself up to such a pitch that I began to have a lump in my throat myself and—and suddenly I stopped, sat up in dismay, and bending over apprehensively, began to listen with a beating heart. I had reason to be worried.

I felt for some time that I was turning her soul upside down and breaking her heart, and the more I was convinced of it, the more I wanted to gain my end as quickly and as effectively as possible. The sport, the sport attracted me; yet it was not merely the sport.

I knew I was speaking stiffly, artificially, even bookishly, in short I did not know how to speak except "just like a book." But that did not bother me: after all I knew, I felt, that I would be understood and that this very bookishness would perhaps even be a help. But now, having achieved my effect, I was suddenly panic-stricken. No, I had never, never before witnessed such despair! She was lying face down, pressing her face deep into the pillow and clutching it in both hands. Her heart was being torn. Her youthful body was shuddering all over as though in convulsions. Suppressed sobs rent her bosom and suddenly burst out in weeping and wailing, then she pressed even deeper into the pillow: she did not want anyone here, not a single living soul, to know of her anguish and her tears. She bit the pillow, bit her hand till it bled (I saw that afterward), or, thrusting her fingers into her dishevelled hair, seemed rigid with the effort to restrain herself, holding her breath and clenching her teeth. I began to say something to her, to beg her to calm herself, but felt that I did not dare; and suddenly, all in a sort of chill, almost in terror, began fumbling in the dark, trying hurriedly to get dressed to go. It was dark: try as I would, I could not finish dressing quickly. Suddenly I felt a box of matches and a candlestick with a whole new candle in it. As soon as the room was lighted up, Liza sprang up, sat up in bed, and with a contorted face, with a half-insane smile, looked at me almost senselessly. I sat down beside her and took her hands; she came to herself, made a movement toward me, would have clasped me, but did not dare, and slowly bowed her head before me.

"Liza, my dear, I was wrong to— Forgive me," I began but she squeezed my hand in her fingers so tightly that I felt I was saying the wrong thing and stopped.

"This is my address, Liza, come to me."

"I will come," she whispered resolutely, her head still bowed.

"But now I am going, good-by—till we meet again."

I got up; she, too, stood up and suddenly flushed all over, shuddered, snatched up a shawl that was lying on a chair and muffled herself in it to her chin. As she did this she gave another sickly smile, blushed and looked at me strangely. I felt wretched; I was in haste to get away—to disappear.

"Wait a minute," she said suddenly, in the passage just at the doorway, stopping me with her hand on my overcoat. She put down the candle hastily

and ran off; evidently she had thought of something or wanted to show me
something. As she ran away she flushed, her eyes shone, and a smile appeared
on her lips—what was the meaning of it? Against my will I waited; she came
back a minute later with an expression that seemed to ask forgiveness for
something. In fact, it was not the same face, nor the same look it had been
before: sullen, mistrustful and obstinate. Her look was now imploring, soft,
and at the same time trustful, caressing, timid. Children look that way at
people they are very fond of, of whom they are asking a favor. Her eyes were a
light hazel, they were lovely eyes, full of life, capable of expressing love as
well as sullen hatred.

Making no explanation, as though I, as a sort of higher being, must understand everything without explanations, she held out a piece of paper to
me. Her whole face was positively beaming at that instant with naïve, almost
childish, triumph. I unfolded it. It was a letter to her from a medical student
or someone of that sort—a very high-flown and flowery, but extremely respectful, declaration of love. I don't recall the words now, but I remember
well enough that through the high-flown phrases there was apparent a genuine feeling, which cannot be feigned. When I had finished reading it I met
her glowing, questioning, and childishly impatient eyes fixed upon me. She
fastened her eyes upon my face and waited impatiently for what I would say.
In a few words, hurriedly, but with a sort of joy and pride, she explained to
me that she had been to a dance somewhere, in a private house, at some
"very, very nice people's house, a *family* who *still know nothing,* absolutely
nothing," for she had only come here so lately and it had all happened—and
she hadn't made up her mind to stay and was certainly going away as soon as
she had paid her debt—"and at that party there had been that student who
had danced with her the whole evening, had talked to her, and it turned out
that he had known her in the old days at Riga when he was a child, they had
played together, but a very long time ago—and he knew her parents, but
about this he knew nothing, nothing, nothing whatever, and had no suspicion! And the day after the dance (three days ago) he had sent her that letter
through the friend with whom she had gone to the party—and—well, that
was all."

She dropped her shining eyes with a sort of bashfulness as she finished.

The poor girl was keeping that student's letter as a treasure and had run
to fetch it, her only treasure, because she did not want me to go away without knowing that she, too, was honestly and genuinely loved; that she, too,
was addressed respectfully. No doubt that letter was destined to lie in her box
and lead to nothing. But it doesn't matter, I am certain that she would guard
it as a treasure all her life, as her pride and justification, and now at such a
minute she had thought of that letter and brought it with naïve pride to raise
herself in my eyes that I might see, that I, too, might think well of her. I said
nothing, pressed her hand and went out. I so longed to get away. I walked

home all the way in spite of the fact that the wet snow was still falling in large flakes. I was exhausted, shattered, in bewilderment. But behind the bewilderment the truth was already gleaming. The loathsome truth!

□ VIII □

It was some time, however, before I consented to recognize that truth. Waking up in the morning after some hours of heavy, leaden sleep, and immediately realizing all that had happened on the previous days, I was positively amazed at my last night's *sentimentality* with Liza, at all those "horrors and pity of yesterday." After all, to have such an attack of womanish hysteria, pah! I concluded. "And why did I force my address upon her? What if she comes? Let her come, though; it is all right—" But *obviously* that was not now the chief and the most important matter: I had to make haste and at all costs save my reputation in the eyes of Zverkov and Simonov as quickly as possible; that was the chief business. And I was so taken up that morning that I actually forgot all about Liza.

First of all I had to repay at once what I had borrowed the day before from Simonov. I resolved on a desperate course: to borrow fifteen roubles from Anton Antonich. As luck would have it he was in the best of humors that morning, and gave it to me at once, as soon as I asked. I was so delighted at this that, as I signed the I O U with a swaggering air, I told him *casually* that the night before "I had been making merry with some friends at the Hôtel de Paris; we were giving a farewell party to a comrade, in fact, I might say a friend of my childhood, and you know—a desperate rake, spoilt—of course, he belongs to a good family, and has considerable means, a brilliant career; he is witty, charming, carries on affairs with certain ladies, you understand; we drank an extra 'half-a-case' and—" And after all it went off all right; all this was said very lightly, unconstrainedly and complacently.

On reaching home I promptly wrote to Simonov.

To this hour I am lost in admiration when I recall the truly gentlemanly, good-humored, candid tone of my letter. With tact and good taste, and, above all, entirely without superfluous words, I blamed myself for all that had happened. I defended myself, "if only I may still be allowed to defend myself," by alleging that being utterly unaccustomed to wine, I had been intoxicated by the first glass which (I claimed) I had drunk before they arrived, while I was waiting for them at the Hôtel de Paris between five and six o'clock. I particularly begged Simonov's pardon; I asked him also to convey my explanations to all the others, especially to Zverkov whom "I remember as though in a dream" I seem to have insulted. I added that I would have called upon all of them myself, but that my head ached, and that besides, I was rather ashamed. I was especially pleased with that "certain lightness," almost carelessness (strictly within the bounds of politeness, however), which was suddenly reflected in my style, and better than any possible arguments, gave them at once to understand that I took rather an independent view of "all that unpleasantness last night"; that I was by no means so utterly crushed as you, gentlemen, probably imagine; but on the contrary that I looked at it as a gentleman serenely respecting himself should. "On a young hero's past no censure is cast!"

"There is, after all, even an aristocratic playfulness about it!" I thought admiringly, as I read over the letter. "And it's all because I am a cultured and educated man! Others in my place would not have known how to extricate themselves, but here I have gotten out of it and am as gay as ever again, and all because I am a cultured and educated man of our day." And, indeed, perhaps, everything really was due to the wine yesterday. H'm!—well, no, it was not the wine. I drank nothing at all between five and six while I was waiting for them. I had lied to Simonov; lied shamelessly; and even now I wasn't ashamed—

Hang it all, though! The important thing was that I was rid of it.

I put six roubles in the letter, sealed it up, and asked Apollon to take it to Simonov. When he learned that there was money in the letter, Apollon became more respectful and agreed to take it. Toward evening I went out for a walk. My head was still aching and giddy, after yesterday. But as evening came on and the twilight grew thicker, my impressions changed and grew more and more confused and, after them, my thoughts. Something was not dead within me, in the depths of my heart and conscience it would not die, and it expressed itself as a burning anguish. For the most part I jostled my way through the most crowded business streets, along Meshchansky Street, along Sadovy Street and in the Yusupov Garden. I always particularly liked to stroll along these streets at dusk just when they become more crowded with people of all sorts, merchants and artisans going home from their day's work, with faces looking malicious out of anxiety. What I liked was just that cheap bustle, that bare, humdrum prosaic quality. On this occasion all that bustling in the streets irritated me more than ever. I could not make out what was wrong with me, I could not find the clue. Something was rising up, rising up continually in my soul, painfully, and refusing to be appeased. I returned home completely upset; it was just as though some crime were lying on my conscience.

The thought that Liza was coming worried me continually. It seemed queer to me that of all yesterday's memories, the memory of her tormented me as it were, particularly, quite separately, as it were. I had succeeded in forgetting everything else by evening time. I dismissed it all and was still perfectly satisfied with my letter to Simonov. But on this point I was not satisfied at all. It was as though I were worried only by Liza. "What if she comes," I thought incessantly. "Well, so what, it's all right, let her come! H'm! it's horrid that she should see how I live for instance. Yesterday I seemed such a—hero to her, while now, h'm! It's horrid, though, that I have let myself sink so low, the room looks like a beggar's. And I brought myself to go out to dinner in such a suit! And my oilcloth sofa with the stuffing sticking out. And my robe, which will not cover me! What tatters. And she will see all this and she will see Apollon. That beast is certain to insult her. He will fasten upon her in order to be rude to me. And I, of course, will be panic-stricken as usual. I will begin to bow and scrape before her and to pull my robe around me, I will begin to smile, to lie. Oh, how foul! And it isn't the foulness of it that matters most! There is something more important, more loathsome, viler! Yes, viler! And to put on that dishonest lying mask again!"

When I reached that thought I flared up all at once.

"Why dishonest? How dishonest? I was speaking sincerely last night. I remember there was real feeling in me, too. What I wanted was to awake noble feelings in her. Her crying was a good thing, it will have a good effect."

Yet I could not feel at ease.

All that evening even when I had come back home, even after nine o'clock, when I calculated that Liza could not possibly come, she still haunted me, and what was worse, she always came back to my mind in the same position. One moment out of all that had happened last night presented itself before me vividly: the moment when I struck a match and saw her pale, distorted face, with its tortured look. And what a pitiful, what an unnatural, what a distorted smile she had at that moment! But I did not know then that even fifteen years later I would still always picture Liza to myself with that pitiful, distorted, inappropriate smile which was on her face at that minute.

Next day I was ready again to look upon it all as nonsense, due to overexcited nerves, and, above all, as *exaggerated.* I always recognized that as a weak point of mine, and was sometimes very much afraid of it. "I exaggerate everything, that is where I go wrong," I repeated to myself every hour. But, nevertheless, Liza will very likely come still, nevertheless, was the refrain with which all my reflections ended then. I was so uneasy that I sometimes flew into a fury. "She'll come, she is certain to come!" I cried, running about the room, "if not today, she will come tomorrow; she'll seek me out! The damnable romanticism of these *pure hearts!* Oh, the vileness—oh, the silliness—oh, the stupidity of these 'wretched sentimental souls'! Why, how could one fail to understand? How could one possibly fail to understand?"

But at this point I stopped short, and even in great confusion.

"And how few, how few words," I thought, in passing, "were needed; how little of the idyllic (and affectedly, bookishly, artificially idyllic too) had sufficed to turn a whole human life at once according to my will. That's innocence for you! That's virgin soil for you!"

At times the thought occurred to me to go to her, "to tell her all" and beg her not to come to me. But this thought stirred such wrath in me that I believed I would have crushed that "damned" Liza if she had happened to be near me at the time. I would have insulted her, have spat at her, have turned her out, have struck her!

One day passed, however, a second and a third; she did not come and I began to grow calmer, I felt particularly bold and cheerful after nine o'clock, I even began sometimes to dream, and rather sweetly: I, for instance, became the salvation of Liza, simply through her coming to me and my talking to her. I develop her, educate her. Finally, I notice that she loves me, loves me passionately. I pretend not to understand (I don't know, however, why I pretend, just for effect, perhaps). At last all confusion, beautiful, trembling and sobbing, she flings herself at my feet and tells me that I am her savior, and that she loves me better than anything in the world. I am amazed, but —"Liza," I say, "can you really believe that I have noticed your love? I saw it all, I divined it, but I did not dare to approach you first, because I had an influence over you and was afraid that you would force yourself, out of gratitude, to respond to my love, would try to rouse in your heart a feeling which was perhaps absent, and I did not wish that because it would be—tyranny. It would be indelicate (in short, I launch off at that point into European, inexplicably lofty subtleties, à la George Sand), but now, now you are mine, you are my creation, you are pure, you are beautiful, you are my beautiful wife.

> "And into my house come bold and free,
> Its rightful mistress there to be."

Then we begin to live together happily, go abroad, etc., etc. In short, in the end it seemed vulgar to me myself, and I began to put out my tongue at myself.

Besides, they won't let her out, "the hussy!" I thought. After all, they don't let them go out very readily especially in the evening (for some reason I fancied she would have to come in the evening, and precisely at seven o'clock). Though she did say she was not altogether a slave there yet, and had certain rights; so, h'm! Damn it all, she will come, she is sure to come!

It was a good thing, in fact, that Apollon distracted my attention at that time by his rudeness. He drove me beyond all patience! He was the bane of my life, the curse laid upon me by Providence. We had been squabbling continually for years, and I hated him. My God, how I hated him! I believe I had never hated anyone in my life as I hated him, especially at some moments. He was an elderly, dignified man, who worked part of his time as a tailor. But for some unknown reason, he despised me beyond all measure, and looked down upon me insufferably. Though indeed, he looked down upon everyone. Simply to glance at that flaxen, smoothly brushed head, at the tuft of hair he combed up on his forehead and oiled with sunflower oil, at that dignified mouth, always pursed, made one feel one was confronting a man who never doubted himself. He was an insufferable pedant, the greatest pedant I had met on earth, and with that had a vanity only befitting Alexander the Great. He was in love with every button on his coat, every nail on his fingers—absolutely in love with them, and he looked it! In his behavior to me he was an absolute tyrant, spoke very little to me, and if he chanced to glance at me he gave me a firm, majestically self-confident and invariably ironical look that sometimes drove me to fury. He did his work with the air of doing me the greatest favor. Though he did scarcely anything for me, and did not, indeed, consider himself obliged to do anything, there could be no doubt that he looked upon me as the greatest fool on earth, and that the reason he did not "get rid of me" was simply that he could get wages from me every month. He consented "to do nothing" for me for seven roubles a month. Many sins should be forgiven me for what I suffered from him. My hatred reached such a point that sometimes his very walk almost threw me into convulsions. What I loathed particularly was his lisp. His tongue must have been a little too long or something of that sort, for he continually lisped, and seemed to be very proud of it, imagining that it greatly added to his dignity. He spoke in a slow, measured tone, with his hands behind his back and his eyes fixed on the ground. He maddened me particularly when he read the Psalms aloud to himself behind his partition. I waged many a battle over that reading! But he was awfully fond of reading aloud in the evenings, in a slow, even, chanting voice, as though over the dead. It is interesting that he has ended up that way. He hires himself out to read the Psalms over the dead, and at the same time he kills rats and makes shoe polish. But at that time I could not get rid of him, it was as though he were chemically combined with my existence. Besides, nothing would have induced him to consent to leave me. I could not live in a furnished room: my apartment was my privacy, my shell, my cave, in which I concealed myself from all mankind, and Apollon seemed to me, God only knows why, an integral part of that apartment, and for seven whole years I could not get rid of him.

For example, to be two or three days late with his wages was impossible. He would have made such a fuss, I would not have known where to hide my head. But I was so exasperated with everyone during that period, that I made up my mind for some reason and with some object to *punish* Apollon and not to pay him for a fortnight the wages I owed him. I had intended to do this for a long time, for the last two years, simply in order to teach him not to give himself airs with me, and to show him that if I liked I could withhold his wages. I decided to say nothing to him about it, and even to be silent purposely in order to conquer his pride and force him to be the first to speak of his wages. Then I would take the seven roubles out of a drawer, show him I have the money and have put it aside purposely, but that I don't want, I don't want, I simply don't want to pay his wages, I don't want to just because that is *what I want,* because "I am master and it is for me to decide," because he has been disrespectful, because he is a ruffian; but if he were to ask respectfully I might be softened and give it to him, otherwise he might wait another fortnight, another three weeks, a whole month . . .

But no matter how angry I was, he always got the better of me. I could not even hold out for four days. He began as he always did begin such cases, for there had been such cases already, there had been attempts (and it may be observed I knew all this beforehand, I knew his nasty tactics by heart), to wit: he would begin by fixing upon me an exceedingly severe stare, keeping it up for several minutes at a time, particularly upon meeting me or seeing me out of the house. If I held out and pretended not to notice these stares, he would, still in silence, proceed to further tortures. All at once, for no reason at all, he would softly and smoothly walk into my room when I was pacing up and down, or reading, stand at the door, one hand behind his back and one foot forward, and fix upon me a stare more than severe, utterly contemptuous. If I suddenly asked him what he wanted, he would not answer, but continue to stare at me persistently for some seconds longer, then, with a peculiar compression of his lips and a very significant air, deliberately turn round and deliberately go back to his room. Two hours later he would come out again and again present himself before me in the same way. It has happened that in my fury I did not even ask him what he wanted, but simply raised my head sharply and imperiously and began staring back at him. So we stared at one another for two minutes; at last he turned with deliberation and dignity and went back again for two hours.

If I were still not brought to reason by all this, but persisted in my revolt, he would suddenly begin sighing while he looked at me, long, deep sighs as though measuring by them the depths of my moral degradation, and, of course, it ended at last by his triumphing completely: I raged and shouted, but was still forced to do what he wanted.

This time the usual maneuvers of "severe staring" had scarcely begun when I lost my temper and flew at him in a fury. I was irritated beyond endurance even without him.

"Wait," I shouted in a frenzy, as he was slowly and silently turning with one hand behind his back, to go to his room. "Wait! Come back, come back, I tell you!" and I must have bawled so unnaturally, that he turned round and even looked at me with a certain amazement. However, he persisted in saying nothing, and that infuriated me.

"How dare you come and look at me like that without being sent for? Answer!"

After looking at me calmly for half a minute, he began turning round again.

"Wait!" I roared, running up to him. "Don't stir! There. Answer, now: what did you come in to look at?"

"If you have any order to give me at the moment, it is my duty to carry it out," he answered, after another silent pause, with a slow, measured lisp, raising his eyebrows and calmly twisting his head from one side to another, all this with exasperating composure.

"That's not it, that is not what I am asking you about, you torturer!" I shouted, shaking with anger. "I'll tell you myself, you torturer, why you came here: you see, I don't give you your wages, you are so proud you don't want to bow down and ask for it, and so you have come to punish me with your stupid stares, to torture me, and you have no sus-pic-ion, you torturer, how stupid it is—stupid, stupid, stupid, stupid!"

He would have turned round again without a word, but I seized him.

"Listen," I shouted to him. "Here's the money, do you see, here it is" (I took it out of the table drawer) "here's the whole seven roubles but you are not going to have it, you . . . are . . . not . . . going . . . to . . . have it until you come respectfully with bowed head to beg my pardon. Do you hear?"

"That cannot be," he answered, with the most unnatural self-confidence.

"It will be so," I said. "I give you my word of honor, it will be!"

"And there's nothing for me to beg your pardon for," he went on, as though he had not noticed my exclamations at all. "Why, besides, you called me a 'torturer,' for which I can summon you at the police station at any time for insulting behavior."

"Go, summon me," I roared, "go at once, this very minute, this very second! You are a torturer all the same! A torturer! A torturer!" But he merely looked at me, then turned, and regardless of my loud calls to him, he walked to his room with an even step and without looking round.

"If it had not been for Liza nothing of this would have happened," I decided inwardly. Then, after waiting a minute, I myself went behind the screen with a dignified and solemn air, though my heart was beating slowly and violently.

"Apollon," I said quietly and emphatically, though I was breathless, "go at once without a minute's delay and fetch the police officer."

He had meanwhile settled himself at his table, put on his spectacles and taken up something to tailor. But, hearing my order, he burst into a guffaw.

"At once, go this minute! Go on, or else you can't imagine what will happen."

"You are certainly not in your right mind," he observed, without even raising his head, lisping as deliberately as ever and threading his needle.

"Whoever heard of a man sending for the police against himself? And as for being frightened—you are upsetting yourself about nothing for nothing will come
of it."

"Go!" I shrieked, grabbing him by the shoulder. I felt that in another minute I would hit him.

But I did not notice that suddenly the door from the passage softly and slowly opened at that instant and a figure came in, stopped short, and began staring at us in amazement. I glanced, nearly died with shame, and rushed back to my room. There, clutching at my hair with both hands, I leaned my head against the wall and stood motionless in that position.

Two minutes later I heard Apollon's deliberate footsteps.

"There is *some woman* asking for you," he said, looking at me with peculiar severity. Then he stood aside and let in—Liza. He would not go away, but stared at us sarcastically.

"Go away, go away," I commanded in desperation. At that moment my clock began whirring and wheezing and struck seven.

□ IX □

And into my house came bold and free,
Its rightful mistress there to be.
From the same poetic work

I stood before her crushed, crestfallen, revoltingly embarrassed, and I believe I smiled as I did my utmost to wrap myself in the skirts of my ragged wadded robe—just exactly as I had imagined the scene not long before in a fit of depression. After standing over us for a couple of minutes Apollon went away, but that did not make me more comfortable. What made it worse was that suddenly, she, too, became embarrassed, more so, in fact, than I would have expected. At the sight of me, of course.

"Sit down," I said mechanically, moving a chair up to the table, and I sat down on the sofa. She obediently sat down at once and gazed at me open-eyed, evidently expecting something from me at once. This naïveté of expectation drove me to fury, but I restrained myself.

She ought to have tried not to notice, as though everything had been as usual, while instead she . . . and I dimly felt that I would make her pay dearly for *all this.*

"You have found me in a strange position, Liza," I began, stammering and knowing that this was the wrong way to begin.

"No, no, don't imagine anything," I cried, seeing that she had suddenly flushed. "I am not ashamed of my poverty. On the contrary, I look on my poverty with pride. I am poor but honorable. One can be poor and honorable," I muttered. "However—would you like tea?"

"No—" she was beginning.

"Wait a minute."

I leapt up and ran to Apollon. I had to get out of the room somehow.

"Apollon," I whispered in feverish haste, flinging down before him the seven roubles which had remained all the time in my clenched fist, "here are your wages. You see I give them to you; but for that you must come to my rescue: bring me tea and a dozen rusks from the restaurant. If you won't go, you'll make a man miserable! You don't know what this woman is. This is—everything! You may be imagining something, but you don't know what a woman she is!"

Apollon, who had already sat down to his work and put on his spectacles again, at first glanced askance at the money without speaking or putting down his needle; then, without paying the slightest attention to me, or making any answer, he went on busying himself with his needle, which he had not yet threaded. I waited before him for several minutes with my arms crossed *à la Napoléon*. My temples were moist with sweat. I was pale, I felt it. But, thank God, he must have been moved to pity, looking at me. Having threaded his needle, he deliberately got up from his seat, deliberately moved back his chair, deliberately took off his spectacles, deliberately counted the money, and finally asking me over his shoulder: "Shall I get a whole pot?" deliberately walked out of the room. As I was going back to Liza, the thought occurred to me on the way: shouldn't I run away just as I was in my robe, no matter where, and let come what may?

I sat down again. She looked at me uneasily. For some minutes we were silent.

"I will kill him," I shouted suddenly, striking the table with my fist so that the ink spurted out of the inkstand.

"What are you saying!" she cried, starting.

"I will kill him! kill him!" I shrieked, suddenly striking the table in absolute frenzy, and at the same time fully understanding how stupid it was to be in such a frenzy

"You don't know, Liza, what that torturer is to me. He is my torturer. He has gone now to fetch some rusks; he—"

And suddenly I burst into tears. It was an hysterical attack. How ashamed I felt in the midst of my sobs; but still I could not restrain them.

She was frightened. "What is the matter? What is wrong?" she shrieked, fussing around me.

"Water, give me water, over there!" I muttered in a faint voice, though I was inwardly conscious that I could easily have done without water and without muttering in a faint voice. But I was what is called *putting it on,* to save appearances, though the attack was a genuine one.

She gave me water, looking at me in bewilderment. At that moment Apollon brought in the tea. It suddenly seemed to me that this commonplace and prosaic tea was terribly undignified and paltry after all that had happened, and I blushed. Liza even looked at Apollon with alarm. He went out without a glance at us.

"Liza, do you despise me?" I asked, looking at her fixedly, trembling with impatience to know what she was thinking.

She was embarrassed and did not know what to answer.

"Drink your tea," I said to her angrily. I was angry with myself, but, of course, it was she who would have to pay for it. A horrible spite against her suddenly surged up in my heart; I believe I could have killed her. To revenge myself on her I swore inwardly not to say a word to her all the time. "She is the cause of it all," I thought.

Our silence lasted for five minutes. The tea stood on the table; we did not touch it. I had got to the point of purposely refraining from beginning to drink in order to embarrass her further; it was awkward for her to begin alone. Several times she glanced at me with mournful perplexity. I was obstinately silent. I was, of course, myself the chief sufferer, because I was fully conscious of the disgusting meanness of my spiteful stupidity, and yet at the same time I absolutely could not restrain myself.

"I want to—get away—from there altogether," she began, to break the silence in some way, but, poor girl, that was just what she ought not to have spoken about at such a moment, stupid enough even without that to a man so stupid as I was. My heart positively ached with pity for her tactless and unnecessary straightforwardness. But something hideous at once stifled all compassion in me: it even provoked me to greater venom. Let the whole world go to pot. Another five minutes passed.

"Perhaps I am in your way?" she began timidly, hardly audibly, and was getting up.

But as soon as I saw this first impulse of wounded dignity I positively trembled with spite, and at once burst out.

"Why did you come to me, tell me that, please?" I began, gasping for breath and regardless of all logical connection in my words. I longed to have it all out at once, at one burst: I did not even trouble how to begin.

"Why did you come? Answer, answer," I cried, hardly knowing what I was doing. "I'll tell you, my good girl, why you came. You came because I talked *fine sentiments* to you then. So now you are soft as butter and longing for fine sentiments again. So you may as well know, know that I was laughing at you then. And I am laughing at you now. Why are you shuddering? Yes, I was laughing at you! I had been insulted just before, at dinner, by the fellows who came that evening before me. I came to you, meaning to thrash one of them, an officer; but I didn't succeed. I didn't find him; I had to avenge the insult on someone to get my own back again; you turned up, I vented my spleen on you and laughed at you. I had been humiliated, so I wanted to humiliate; I had been treated like a rag, so I wanted to show my power. That's what it was, and you imagined I had come there on purpose to save you, didn't you? Did you imagine that? Did you imagine that?"

I knew that she would perhaps get muddled and not grasp all the details, but I knew, too, that she would grasp the gist of it very well. And, so, indeed, she did. She turned white as a handkerchief, tried to say something, and distorted her mouth painfully but she sank on a chair as though she had been felled by an ax. And all the time afterward she listened to me with her lips parted and her eyes wide open, shuddering with awful terror. The cynicism, the cynicism of my words overwhelmed her—

"Save you!" I went on, jumping up from my chair and running up and down the room before her. "Save you from what? But perhaps I am worse than you myself. Why didn't you throw it in my teeth when I was giving you that sermon: 'But you, what did you come here for yourself? Was it to read us a sermon?' Power, power was what I wanted then, sport was what I wanted, I wanted to wring out your tears, your humiliation, your hysteria— that was what I wanted then! After all, I couldn't keep it up then, because I am a wretch, I was frightened, and, the devil knows why, gave you my address in my folly. Afterward, before I got home, I was cursing and swearing at you because of that address. I hated you already because of the lies I had told you. Because I only like to play with words, to dream in my mind, but, do you know, what I really want is that you would all go to hell, that is what I want. I want peace; yes, I'd sell the whole world for a farthing right now, so long as I was left in peace. Is the world to go to pot, or am I to go without my tea? I say let the world go to pot as long as I get my tea every time. Did you know that, or not? Well, anyway, I know that I am a blackguard, a scoundrel, an egotist, a sluggard. Here I have been shuddering for the last three days at the thought of your coming. And do you know what has worried me particularly for these three days? That I posed as such a hero to you then, and now you would see me in a wretched torn robe, a beggar, an abomination. I told you just now that I was not ashamed of my poverty; you may as well know that I am ashamed of it; I am more ashamed of it than of anything, more afraid of it than of being found out if I were a thief, because I am as vain as though I had been skinned and the very air blowing on me hurt. Surely by now even you must have realized that I will never forgive you for having found me in this wretched robe, just as I was flying at Apollon like a spiteful sheep-dog at his lackey, and the lackey was jeering at him! And I shall never forgive you for the tears I could not help shedding before you just now, like some silly woman put to shame! And for what I am confessing to you now, I shall never forgive *you*, either! Yes—you must answer for it all because you turned up like this, because I am a blackguard, because I am the nastiest, stupidest, pettiest, absurdest and most envious of all worms on earth, none of whom is a bit better than I am, but who, the devil only knows why, are never embarrassed; while I will always be insulted by every louse, that is my doom! And what is it to me that you don't understand a word of this! And what do I care, what do I care about you, and whether you go to ruin there or not? Do you understand how I will hate you now after saying this, for having been here and listening? After all, a man speaks out like this once in a life-time and then it is in hysterics! What more do you want? Why, after all, do you still stand there in front of me? Why do you torment me? Why don't you go?"

But at this point a strange thing happened.

I was so accustomed to think and imagine everything from books, and to picture everything in the world to myself just as I had made it up in my dreams beforehand, that I could not even take in this strange circumstance all at once. What happened was this: Liza, wounded and crushed by me, under-stood a great deal more than I imagined. She understood from all this what a woman understands first of all, if she feels genuine love, that is, that I was myself unhappy.

The frightened and wounded expression on her face was followed first by a look of sorrowful perplexity. When I began to call myself a scoundrel and a blackguard and my tears flowed (that tirade was accompanied throughout by tears) her whole face worked convulsively. She was on the point of getting up and stopping me; when I finished she took no notice of my shouting: "Why are you here, why don't you go away?" but realized only that it must have been very bitter to me to say all this. Besides, she was so crushed, poor girl; she considered herself infinitely beneath me; how could she feel anger or resentment? Suddenly she leapt up from her chair with an irresistible impulse and held out her hands, yearning toward me, though still timid and not dar-ing to stir. At this point there was an upheaval in my heart too. Then she suddenly rushed to me, threw her arms round me and burst into tears. I, too, could not restrain myself, and sobbed as I never had before.

"They won't let me—I can't be—good!" I managed to say, then I went to the sofa, fell on it, face downward, and sobbed on it for a quarter of an hour in genuine hysterics. She knelt near me, put her arms round me and stayed motionless in that position.

But the trouble was that the hysterics could not go on for ever. And (after all, I am writing this loathsome truth) lying face downward on the sofa with my face thrust into my nasty leather pillow, I began by degrees to be aware of a far-away, involuntary but irresistible feeling that after all it would be awkward for me to raise my head now and look Liza straight in the face. Why was I ashamed? I don't know, but I was ashamed. In my over-wrought brain the thought also occurred that our parts were after all com-

pletely reversed now, that she was now the heroine, while I was just a crushed
and humiliated creature as she had been before me that night—four days before . . . And all this came into my mind during the minutes I was lying face
down on the sofa!

My God! surely I was not envious of her then?

I don't know, to this day I cannot decide, and at the time, of course, I
was still less able to understand what I was feeling than now. I cannot get on
without domineering and tyrannizing over someone, after all, but—but, after
all, there is no explaining anything by reasoning and consequently it is useless to reason.

I conquered myself, however, and raised my head—I had to do so sooner
or later—and I am convinced to this day that it was just because I was
ashamed to look at her that another feeling was suddenly kindled and flamed
up in my heart—a feeling of mastery and possession. My eyes gleamed with
passion, and I gripped her hands tightly. How I hated her and how I was
drawn to her at that minute! The one feeling intensified the other. It was almost like an act of vengeance! At first there was a look of amazement, even of
terror, on her face, but only for one instant. She warmly and rapturously embraced me.

□ X □

A quarter of an hour later I was rushing up and down the room in frenzied
impatience, from minute to minute I went up to the screen and peeped
through the crack at Liza. She was sitting on the floor with her head leaning
against the bed, and must have been crying. But she did not go away, and
that irritated me. This time she understood it all. I had insulted her once and
for all, but—there's no need to describe it. She realized that my outburst of
passion had been simply revenge, a new humiliation for her and that to my
earlier, almost generalized hatred was added now a *personal, envious* hatred—
though I do not maintain positively that she understood all this distinctly;
but she certainly did fully understand that I was a despicable man, and what
was worse, incapable of loving her.

I know I shall be told that this is incredible; that it is incredible to be as
spiteful and stupid as I was; it may be added it was strange that I would not
love her, or at any rate, appreciate her love. Why is it strange? In the first
place, by then I was incapable of love, for, I repeat, with me loving meant
tyrannizing and showing my moral superiority. I have never in my life ever

been able to imagine any other sort of love, and have nowadays come to the point of sometimes thinking that love really consists in the right—freely given of the beloved object—to be tyrannized over. Even in my underground dreams I did not imagine love in any form except as a struggle. I always began it with hatred and ended it with moral subjugation, and afterward I could never imagine what to do with the subjugated object. And what is there incredible in that, since I had so succeeded in corrupting myself morally, since I was so out of touch with "real life," that I had just thought of reproaching her and putting her to shame for having come to me to hear "fine sentiments," and I did not even guess that she had come not at all to hear fine sentiments, but to love me, because to a woman true resurrection, true salvation from any sort of ruin, and true moral regeneration is contained in love and can only show itself in that form. I no longer hated her so much, however, when I was running about the room peeping through the crack in the screen. I was only insufferably oppressed by her being here. I wanted her to disappear. I wanted "peace," I wanted to be left alone in my underground world. "Real life" oppressed me with its novelty so much that I could hardly breathe.

But several minutes passed and she still remained without stirring, as though she were unconscious. I had the shamelessness to tap softly at the screen as though to remind her. She started, sprang up, and flew to seek her shawl, her hat, her coat, just as though she were making her escape from me. Two minutes later she came from behind the screen and looked with heavy eyes at me. I gave a spiteful grin, which was forced, however, to *keep up appearances,* and I turned away from her look.

"Good-by," she said, going toward the door.

I ran up to her, seized her hand, opened it, thrust something in it—and closed it again. Then I turned immediately and hurriedly rushed to the other corner of the room, to avoid seeing, anyway—

I meant to lie a moment ago—to write that I did this accidentally, not knowing what I was doing, through foolishness, through losing my head. But I don't want to lie, and so I will say straight out that I opened her hand and put the money in it—from spite. It came into my head to do so while I was running up and down the room and she was sitting behind the screen. But I can say this for certain: though I did that cruel thing purposely, it was not an impulse from the heart, but came from my evil brain. This cruelty was so affected, so purposely made up, so completely a product of the brain, of *books,* that I could not even keep it up for a minute—first I rushed to the corner to avoid seeing her, and then in shame and despair rushed after Liza. I opened the door in the passage and began listening.

"Liza! Liza!" I cried on the stairs, but in a low voice, not boldly.

There was no answer, but it seemed to me I heard her footsteps, lower down on the stairs.

"Liza!" I cried, more loudly.

No answer. But at that minute I heard the stiff outer glass door open heavily with a creak and slam violently. The roar echoed up the stairs.

She had gone. I went back to my room in hesitation. I felt horribly oppressed.

I stood still at the table beside the chair on which she had sat and looked aimlessly before me. A minute passed. Suddenly I started; straight before me on the table I saw—in short, I saw a crumpled blue five-rouble note, the one I had thrust into her hand a minute before. It was the same note; it could be no other, there was no other in the apartment. So she had managed to fling it from her hand on the table at the moment when I had rushed into the farther corner.

So what? I might have expected that she would do that. Might I have expected it? No, I was such an egotist, I was so lacking in respect for people in actuality, that I could not even imagine she would do so. I could not endure it. A moment later I flew like a madman to get dressed, flinging on what I could at random and ran headlong after her. She could not have got two hundred paces away when I ran out into the street.

It was a still night, and the snow was coming down in masses and falling almost perpendicularly, blanketing the pavement and the empty street. There was no one in the street, no sound was to be heard. The street lamps gave a disconsolate and useless glimmer. I ran two hundred paces to the intersection and stopped short. Where had she gone? And why was I running after her?

Why? To fall down before, to sob with remorse, to kiss her feet, to beg her forgiveness! I longed for that. My whole heart was being rent to pieces, and never, never will I recall that minute with indifference. But—what for? I thought. Would I not begin to hate her, perhaps, even tomorrow, just because I had kissed her feet today? Would I give her happiness? Had I not again recognized that day, for the hundredth time, what I was worth? Would I not torment her?

I stood in the snow, gazing into the troubled darkness and pondered this.

"And will it not be better? *Will it not be better?*" I fantasied afterward at home, stifling the living pang of my heart with fantastic dreams. "Will it not be better that she carry the outrage with her forever? Outrage—why, after all, that is purification: it is the most stinging and painful consciousness! Tomorrow I would have defiled her soul and have exhausted her heart, while now the feeling of humiliation will never die in her, and however loathsome the filth awaiting her, that outrage will elevate and purify her—by hatred—h'm!—perhaps by forgiveness also. But will all that make things easier for her, though? . . ."

And, indeed, I will at this point ask an idle question on my own account: which is better—cheap happiness or exalted sufferings? Well, which is better?

So I dreamed as I sat at home that evening, almost dead with the pain in my soul. Never yet had I endured such suffering and remorse, but could there possibly have been the faintest doubt when I ran out from my lodging that I would turn back halfway? I never met Liza again and I have heard nothing about her. I will add, too, that for a long time afterward I remained pleased with the *phrase* about the utility of outrage and hatred, in spite of the fact that I almost fell ill from misery.

Even now, many years later, I somehow remember all this as very bad. I have many bad memories now, but—hadn't I better end my "Notes" here? I believe I made a mistake in beginning to write this *story;* so it's hardly literature so much as corrective punishment. After all, to tell long stories, for example, showing how I have ruined my life by morally rotting in my corner, through lack of fitting environment, through divorce from reality, and vainglorious spite in my underground world, would certainly not be interesting; a novel needs a hero, and all the traits of an anti-hero are *expressly* gathered together here, and what matters most, it all produces an unpleasant impression, for we are all divorced from life, we are all cripples, every one of us, more or less. We are so far divorced from it that we immediately feel a sort of loathing for actual "real life," and so cannot even stand to be reminded of it. After all, we have reached the point of almost looking at actual "real life" as an effort, almost as hard work, and we are all privately agreed, that it is better in books. And why do we sometimes fret, why are we perverse and ask for something else? We don't know why ourselves. It would be worse for us if our capricious requests were granted. Come, try, come give anyone of us, for instance, a little more independence, untie our hands, widen the spheres of our activity, relax the controls and we—yes, I assure you—we would immediately beg to be under control again. I know that you will very likely be angry with me for that, and will begin to shout and stamp your feet. "Speak for yourself," you will say, "and for your miseries in your underground holes, but don't dare to say 'all of us.'" Excuse me, gentlemen, after all I do not mean to justify myself with that "all of us." As for what concerns me in particular I have only, after all, in my life carried to an extreme what you have not dared to carry halfway, and what's more, you have taken your cowardice for good sense, and have found comfort in deceiving yourselves. So that perhaps, after all, there is more "life" in me than in you. Look into it more carefully! After all, we don't even know where living exists now, what it is, and what it is called! Leave us alone without books and we will be lost and in a confusion at once—we will not know what to join, what to cling to, what to love and what to hate, what to respect and what to despise. We are even oppressed by being men—men with real *individual* body and blood. We are ashamed of it, we think it a disgrace and try to contrive to be some sort of impossible generalized man. We are still-born, and for many years we have not been begotten by living fathers, and that suits us better and better. We are developing a taste for it. Soon we shall somehow contrive to be born from an idea. But enough; I don't want to write more from "underground" . . .

The "notes" of this paradoxalist do not end here, however. He could not resist and continued them. But it also seems to me that we may stop here.

ALBERT CAMUS

The Fall

May I, *monsieur,* offer my services without running the risk of intruding? I fear you may not be able to make yourself understood by the worthy ape who presides over the fate of this establishment. In fact, he speaks nothing but Dutch. Unless you authorize me to plead your case, he will not guess that you want gin. There, I dare hope he understood me; that nod must mean that he yields to my arguments. He is taking steps; indeed, he is making haste with prudent deliberation. You are lucky; he didn't grunt. When he refuses to serve someone, he merely grunts. No one insists. Being master of one's moods is the privilege of the larger animals. Now I shall withdraw, *monsieur,* happy to have been of help to you. Thank you; I'd accept if I were sure of not being a nuisance. You are too kind. Then I shall bring my glass over beside yours.

You are right. His silence is deafening. It's the silence of the primeval forest, heavy with threats. At times I am amazed by his obstinacy in snubbing civilized languages. His business consists in entertaining sailors of all nationalities in this Amsterdam bar, which for that matter he named—no one knows why—*Mexico City*. With such duties wouldn't you think there might be some fear that his ignorance would be awkward? Fancy the Cro-Magnon man lodged in the Tower of Babel! He would certainly feel out of his element. Yet this one is not aware of his exile; he goes his own sweet way and nothing touches him. One of the rare sentences I have ever heard from his mouth proclaimed that you could take it or leave it. What did one have to take or leave? Doubtless our friend himself. I confess I am drawn by such creatures who are all of a piece. Anyone who has considerably meditated on man, by profession or vocation, is led to feel nostalgia for the primates. They at least don't have any ulterior motives.

Our host, to tell the truth, has some, although he harbors them deep within him. As a result of not understanding what is said in his presence, he has adopted a distrustful disposition. Whence that look of touchy dignity as if he at least suspected that all is not perfect among men. That disposition makes it less easy to discuss anything with him that does not concern his business. Notice, for instance, on the back wall above his head that empty rectangle marking the place where a picture has been taken down. Indeed, there *was* a picture there, and a particularly interesting one, a real masterpiece. Well, I was present when the master of the house received it and when he gave it up. In both cases he did so with the same distrust, after weeks of rumination. In that regard you must admit that society has somewhat spoiled the frank simplicity of his nature.

Mind you, I am not judging him. I consider his distrust justified and should be inclined to share it if, as you see, my communicative nature were not opposed to this. I am talkative, alas, and make friends easily. Although I know how to keep my distance, I seize any and every opportunity. When I used to live in France, were I to meet an intelligent man I immediately sought his company. If that be foolish ... Ah, I see you smile at that use of the subjunctive. I confess my weakness for that mood and for fine speech in general. A weakness that I criticize in myself, believe me. I am well aware that an addiction to silk underwear does not necessarily imply that one's feet are dirty. Nonetheless, style, like sheer silk, too often hides eczema. My consolation is to tell myself that, after all, those who murder the language are not pure either. Why yes, let's have another gin.

Are you staying long in Amsterdam? A beautiful city, isn't it? Fascinating? There's an adjective I haven't heard in some time. Not since leaving Paris, in fact, years ago. But the heart has its own memory and I have forgotten nothing of our beautiful capital, nor of its quays. Paris is a real *trompe-l'oeil,* a magnificent stage-setting inhabited by four million silhouettes. Nearly five million at the last census? Why, they must have multiplied. And that wouldn't surprise me. It always seemed to me that our fellow citizens had two passions: ideas and fornication. Without rhyme or reason, so to speak. Still, let us take care not to condemn them; they are not the only ones, for all Europe is in the same boat. I sometimes think of what future historians will say of us. A single sentence will suffice for modern man: he fornicated and read the papers. After that vigorous definition, the subject will be, if I may say so, exhausted.

Oh, not the Dutch; they are much less modern! They have time—just look at them. What do they do? Well, these gentlemen over here live off the labors of those ladies over there. All of them, moreover, both male and female, are very middle-class creatures who have come here, as usual, out of mythomania or stupidity. Through too much or too little imagination, in short. From time to time, these gentlemen indulge in a little knife or revolver play, but don't get the idea that they're keen on it. Their role calls for it, that's all, and they are dying of fright as they shoot it out. Nevertheless, I find them more moral than the others, those who kill in the bosom of the family by attrition. Haven't you noticed that our society is organized for this kind of liquidation? You have heard, of course, of those tiny fish in the rivers of Brazil that attack the unwary swimmer by thousands and with swift little nibbles clean him up in a few minutes, leaving only an immaculate skeleton? Well, that's what their organization is. "Do you want a good clean life? Like everybody else?" You say yes, of course. How can one say no? "O.K. You'll be cleaned up. Here's a job, a family, and organized leisure activities." And the little teeth attack the flesh, right down to the bone. But I am unjust. I shouldn't say *their* organization. It is *ours,* after all: it's a question of which will clean up the other.

Here is our gin at last. To your prosperity. Yes, the ape opened his mouth to call me doctor. In these countries everyone is a doctor, or a professor. They like showing respect, out of kindness and out of modesty. Among them, at least, spitefulness is not a national institution. Besides, I am not a doctor. If you want to know, I was a lawyer before coming here. Now, I am a judge-penitent.

But allow me to introduce myself: Jean-Baptiste Clamence, at your service. Pleased to know you. You are in business, no doubt? In a way? Excellent reply! Judicious too: in all things we are merely "in a way." Now, allow me to play the detective. You are my age in a way, with the sophisticated eye of the man in his forties who has seen everything, in a way; you are well dressed in a way, that is as people are in our country; and your hands are smooth. Hence a bourgeois, in a way! But a cultured bourgeois! Smiling at the use of the subjunctive, in fact, proves your culture twice over because you recognize it to begin with and then because you feel superior to it. Lastly, I amuse you. And be it said without vanity, this implies in you a certain open-mindedness. Consequently you are in a way ... But no matter. Professions interest me less than sects. Allow me to ask you two questions and don't answer if you consider them indiscreet. Do you have any possessions? Some? Good. Have you shared them with the poor? No? Then you are what I call a Sadducee. If you are not familiar with the Scriptures, I admit that this won't help you. But it does help you? So you know the Scriptures? Decidedly, you interest me.

As for me ... Well, judge for yourself. By my stature, my shoulders, and this face that I have often been told was shy, I rather look like a rugby player, don't I? But if I am judged by my conversation I have to be granted a little subtlety. The camel that provided the hair for my overcoat was probably mangy; yet my nails are manicured. I, too, am sophisticated, and yet I confide in you without caution on the sole basis of your looks. Finally, despite my good manners and my fine speech, I frequent sailors' bars in the Zeedijk. Come on, give up. My profession is double, that's all, like the human being. I have already told you, I am a judge-penitent. Only one thing is simple in my case: I possess nothing. Yes, I was rich. No, I shared nothing with the poor. What does that prove? That I, too, was a Sadducee ... Oh, do you hear the foghorns in the harbor? There'll be fog tonight on the Zuider Zee.

You're leaving already? Forgive me for having perhaps detained you. No, I beg you; I won't let you pay. I am at home at *Mexico City* and have been particularly pleased to receive you here. I shall certainly be here tomorrow, as I am every evening, and I shall be pleased to accept your invitation. Your way back? ... Well ... But if you don't have any objection, the easiest thing would be for me to accompany you as far as the harbor. Thence, by going around the Jewish quarter you'll find those fine avenues with their parade of streetcars full of flowers and thundering sounds. Your hotel is on one of them, the Damrak. You first, please. I live in the Jewish quarter or what was called so until our Hitlerian brethren made room. What a cleanup! Seventy-five thousand Jews deported or assassinated; that's real vacuum-cleaning. I admire that diligence, that methodical patience! When one has no character one *has* to apply a method. Here it did wonders incontrovertibly, and I am living on the site of one of the greatest crimes in history. Perhaps that's what helps me to understand the ape and his distrust. Thus I can struggle against my natural inclination carrying me toward fraternizing. When I see a new face, something in me sounds the alarm. "Slow! Danger!" Even when the attraction is strongest, I am on my guard.

Do you know that in my little village, during a punitive operation, a German officer courteously asked an old woman to please choose which of her two sons would be shot as a hostage? Choose!—can you imagine that? That one? No, this one. And see him go. Let's not dwell on it, but believe me, *monsieur,* any surprise is possible. I knew a pure heart who rejected distrust. He was a pacifist and libertarian and loved all humanity and the animals with an equal love. An exceptional soul, that's certain. Well, during the last wars of religion in Europe he had retired to the country. He had written on his threshold: "Wherever you come from, come in and be welcome." Who do you think answered that noble invitation? The militia, who made themselves at home and disemboweled him.

Oh, pardon, *madame!* But she didn't understand a word of it anyway. All these people, eh? out so late despite this rain which hasn't let up for days. Fortunately there is gin, the sole glimmer of light in this darkness. Do you feel the golden, copper-colored light it kindles in you? I like walking through the city of an evening in the warmth of gin. I walk for nights on end, I dream or talk to myself interminably. Yes, like this evening—and I fear making your head swim somewhat. Thank you, you are most courteous. But it's the overflow; as soon as I open my mouth, sentences start to flow. Besides, this country inspires me. I like these people swarming on the sidewalks, wedged into a little space of houses and canals, hemmed in by fogs, cold lands, and the sea steaming like a wet wash. I like them, for they are double. They are here and elsewhere.

Yes, indeed! From hearing their heavy tread on the damp pavement, from seeing them move heavily between their shops full of gilded herrings and jewels the color of dead leaves, you probably think they are here this evening? You are like everybody else; you take these good people for a tribe of syndics and merchants counting their gold crowns with their chances of eternal life, whose only lyricism consists in occasionally, without doffing their broad-brimmed hats, taking anatomy lessons? You are wrong. They walk along with us, to be sure, and yet see where their heads are: in that fog compounded of neon, gin, and mint emanating from the shop signs above them. Holland is a dream, *monsieur,* a dream of gold and smoke—smokier by day, more gilded by night. And night and day that dream is peopled with Lohengrins like these, dreamily riding their black bicycles with high handle-bars, funereal swans constantly drifting throughout the whole land, around the seas, along the canals. Their heads in their copper-colored clouds, they dream; they cycle in circles; they pray, somnambulists in the fog's gilded incense; they have ceased to be here. They have gone thousands of miles away, toward Java, the distant isle. They pray to those grimacing gods of Indonesia with which they have decorated all their shopwindows and which at this moment are floating aimlessly above us before alighting, like sumptuous monkeys, on the signs and stepped roofs to remind these homesick colonials that Holland is not only the Europe of merchants but also the sea, the sea that leads to Cipango and to those islands where men die mad and happy.

But I am letting myself go! I am pleading a case! Forgive me. Habit, *monsieur,* vocation, also the desire to make you fully understand this city, and the heart of things! For we are at the heart of things here. Have you noticed that Amsterdam's concentric canals resemble the circles of hell? The middle-class hell, of course, peopled with bad dreams. When one comes from the outside, as one gradually goes through those circles, life—and hence its crimes—becomes denser, darker. Here, we are in the last circle. The circle of the ... Ah, you know that? By heaven, you become harder to classify. But you understand then why I can say that the center of things is here, although we stand at the tip of the continent. A sensitive man grasps such oddities. In any case, the newspaper readers and the fornicators can go no further. They come from the four corners of Europe and stop facing the inner sea, on the drab strand. They listen to the foghorns, vainly try to make out the silhouettes of boats in the fog, then turn back over the canals and go home through the rain. Chilled to the bone, they come and ask in all languages for gin at *Mexico City.* There I wait for them.

Till tomorrow, then, *monsieur et cher compatriote.* No, you will easily find your way now: I'll leave you near this bridge. I never cross a bridge at night. It's the result of a vow. Suppose, after all, that someone should jump in the water. One of two things—either you do likewise to fish him out and, in cold weather, you run a great risk! Or you forsake him there and suppressed dives sometimes leave one strangely aching. Good night. What? Those ladies behind those windows? Dream, *monsieur,* cheap dream, a trip to the Indies! Those persons perfume themselves with spices. You go in, they draw the curtains, and the navigation begins. The gods come down onto the naked bodies and the islands are set adrift, lost souls crowned with the tousled hair of palm trees in the wind. Try it.

What is a judge-penitent? Ah, I intrigued you with that business. I meant no harm by it, believe me, and I can explain myself more clearly. In a way, that even belongs to my official duties. But first I must set forth a certain number of facts that will help you to understand my story.

A few years ago I was a lawyer in Paris and, indeed, a rather well-known lawyer. Of course, I didn't tell you my real name. I had a specialty: noble cases. Widows and orphans, as the saying goes—I don't know why, because there are improper widows and ferocious orphans. Yet it was enough for me to sniff the slightest scent of victim on a defendant for me to swing into action. And what action! A real tornado! My heart was on my sleeve. You would really have thought that justice slept with me every night. I am sure you would have admired the rightness of my tone, the appropriateness of my emotion, the persuasion and warmth, the restrained indignation of my speeches before the court. Nature favored me as to my physique, and the noble attitude comes effortlessly. Furthermore, I was buoyed up by two sincere feelings: the satisfaction of being on the right side of the bar and an instinctive scorn for judges in general. That scorn, after all, wasn't perhaps so instinctive. I know now that it had its reasons. But, seen from the outside, it looked rather like a passion. It can't be denied that, for the moment at least, we have to have judges, don't we? However, I could not understand how a man could offer himself to perform such a surprising function. I accepted the fact because I saw it, but rather as I accepted locusts. With this difference: that the invasions of those Orthoptera never brought me a sou whereas I earned my living by carrying on a dialogue with people I scorned.

But, after all, I was on the right side; that was enough to satisfy my conscience. The feeling of the law, the satisfaction of being right, the joy of self-esteem, *cher monsieur,* are powerful incentives for keeping us upright or keeping us moving forward. On the other hand, if you deprive men of them, you transform them into dogs frothing with rage. How many crimes committed merely because their authors could not endure being wrong! I once knew a manufacturer who had a perfect wife, admired by all, and yet he deceived her. That man was literally furious to be in the wrong, to be blocked from receiving, or granting himself, a certificate of virtue. The more virtues his wife manifested, the more vexed he became. Eventually, living in the wrong became unbearable to him. What do you think he did then? He gave up deceiving her? Not at all. He killed her. That is how I entered into relations with him.

My situation was more enviable. Not only did I run no risk of joining the criminal camp (in particular I had no chance of killing my wife, being a bachelor), but I even took up their defense, on the sole condition that they should be noble murderers, as others are noble savages. The very manner in which I conducted that defense gave me great satisfactions. I was truly above reproach in my professional life. I never accepted a bribe, it goes without saying, and I never stooped either to any shady proceedings. And—this is even rarer—I never deigned to flatter any journalist to get him on my side, nor any civil servant whose friendship might be useful to me. I even had the luck of seeing the Legion of Honor offered to me two or three times and of being able to refuse it with a discreet dignity in which I found my true reward. Finally, I never charged the poor a fee and never boasted of it. Don't think for a moment, *cher monsieur,* that I am bragging. I take no credit for this. The avidity which in our society substitutes for ambition has always made me laugh. I was aiming higher; you will see that the expression is exact in my case.

But you can already imagine my satisfaction. I enjoyed my own nature to the fullest, and we all know that there lies happiness, although, to soothe one another mutually, we occasionally pretend to condemn such joys as selfishness. At least I enjoyed that part of my nature which reacted so appropriately to the widow and orphan that eventually, through exercise, it came to dominate my whole life. For instance, I loved to help blind people cross streets. From as far away as I could see a cane hesitating on the edge of a sidewalk, I would rush forward, sometimes only a second ahead of another charitable hand already outstretched, snatch the blind person from any solicitude but mine, and lead him gently but firmly along the crosswalk among the traffic obstacles toward the refuge of the other sidewalk, where we would separate with a mutual emotion. In the same way, I always enjoyed giving directions in the street, obliging with a light, lending a hand to heavy pushcarts, pushing a stranded car, buying a paper from the Salvation Army lass or flowers from the old peddler, though I knew she stole them from the Montparnasse cemetery. I also liked—and this is harder to say—I liked to give alms. A very Christian friend of mine admitted that one's initial feeling on seeing a beggar approach one's house is unpleasant. Well, with me it was worse: I used to exult. But let's not dwell on this.

Let us speak rather of my courtesy. It was famous and unquestionable. Indeed, good manners provided me with great delights. If I had the luck, certain mornings, to give up my seat in the bus or subway to someone who obviously deserved it, to pick up some object an old lady had dropped and return it to her with a smile I knew well, or merely to forfeit my taxi to someone in a greater hurry than I, it was a red-letter day. I even rejoiced, I must admit, those days when the transport system being on strike I had a chance to load into my car at the bus stops some of my unfortunate fellow citizens unable to get home. Giving up my seat in the theater to allow a couple to sit together, hoisting a girl's suitcases onto the rack in a train—these were all deeds I performed more often than others because I paid more attention to the opportunities and was better able to relish the pleasure they give.

Consequently I was considered generous, and so I was. I gave a great deal in public and in private. But far from suffering when I had to give up an object or a sum of money, I derived constant pleasures from this—among them a sort of melancholy which occasionally rose within me at the thought of the sterility of those gifts and the probable ingratitude that would follow. I even took such pleasure in giving that I hated to be obliged to do so. Exactitude in money matters bored me to death and I conformed ungraciously. I had to be the master of my liberalities.

These are just little touches but they will help you grasp the constant delights I experienced in my life, and especially in my profession. Being stopped in the corridor of the law courts by the wife of a defendant you represented out of justice or pity alone—I mean without charge—hearing that woman whisper that nothing, no, nothing could ever repay what you had done for them, replying that it was quite natural, that anyone would have done as much, even offering some financial help to tide over the bad days ahead, then—in order to cut the effusions short and preserve their proper resonance—kissing the hand of a poor woman and breaking away—believe me, *cher monsieur,* this is achieving more than the vulgar ambitious man and rising to that supreme summit where virtue is its own reward.

Let's pause on these heights. Now you understand what I meant when I spoke of aiming higher. I was talking, it so happens, of those supreme summits, the only places I can really live. Yes, I have never felt comfortable except in lofty places. Even in the details of daily life, I needed to feel *above.* I preferred the bus to the subway, open carriages to taxis, terraces to closed-in places. An enthusiast for sport planes in which one's head is in the open, on boats I was the eternal pacer of the top deck. In the mountains I used to flee the deep valleys for the passes and plateaus; I was the man of the mesas at least. If fate had forced me to choose between work at a lathe or as a roofer, don't worry, I'd have chosen the roofs and become acquainted with dizziness. Coalbins, ships' holds, undergrounds, grottoes, pits were repulsive to me. I had even developed a special loathing for speleologists, who had the nerve to fill the front page of our newspapers, and whose records nauseated me. Striving to reach elevation minus eight hundred at the risk of getting one's head caught in a rocky funnel (a siphon, as those fools say!) seemed to me the exploit of perverted or traumatized characters. There was something criminal underlying it.

A natural balcony fifteen hundred feet above a sea still visible bathed in sunlight, on the other hand, was the place where I could breathe most freely, especially if I were alone, well above the human ants. I could readily understand why sermons, decisive preachings, and fire miracles took place on accessible heights. In my opinion no one meditated in cellars or prison cells (unless they were situated in a tower with a broad view); one just became moldy. And I could understand that man who, having entered holy orders, gave up the frock because his cell, instead of overlooking a vast landscape as he expected, looked out on a wall. Rest assured that as far as I was concerned I did not grow moldy. At every hour of the day, within myself and among others, I would scale the heights and light conspicuous fires, and a joyful greeting would rise toward me. Thus at least I took pleasure in life and in my own excellence.

My profession satisfied most happily that vocation for summits. It cleansed me of all bitterness toward my neighbor, whom I always obligated without ever owing him anything. It set me above the judge whom I judged in turn, above the defendant whom I forced to gratitude. Just weigh this, *cher monsieur,* I lived with impunity. I was concerned in no judgment; I was not on the floor of the courtroom, but somewhere in the flies like those gods that are brought down by machinery from time to time to transfigure the action and give it its meaning. After all, living aloft is still the only way of being seen and hailed by the largest number.

Besides, some of my good criminals had killed in obedience to the same feeling. Reading the newspapers afterward, in the sorry condition in which they then were, doubtless brought them a sort of unhappy compensation. Like many men, they had no longer been able to endure anonymity, and that impatience had contributed to leading them to unfortunate extremities. To achieve notoriety it is enough, after all, to kill one's concierge. Unhappily, this is usually an ephemeral reputation, so many concierges are there who deserve and receive the knife. Crime constantly monopolizes the headlines, but the criminal appears there only fugitively, to be replaced at once. In short, such brief triumphs cost too dear. Defending our unfortunate aspirants after a reputation amounted, on the other hand, to becoming really well known, at the same time and in the same places, but by more economical means. Consequently this encouraged me to making more meritorious efforts so that they would pay as little as possible. What they were paying they were doing so to some extent in my place. The indignation, talent, and emotion I expended on them washed away, in return, any debt I might feel toward them. The judges punished and the defendants expiated, while I, free of any duty, shielded from judgment as from penalty, I freely held sway bathed in a light as of Eden.

Indeed, wasn't that Eden, *cher monsieur:* no intermediary between life and me? Such was my life. I never had to learn how to live. In that regard, I already knew everything at birth. Some people's problem is to protect themselves from men or at least to come to terms with them. In my case, the understanding was already established. Familiar when it was appropriate, silent when necessary, capable of a free and easy manner as readily as of dignity, I was always in harmony. Hence my popularity was great and my successes in society innumerable. I was acceptable in appearance; I revealed myself to be both a tireless dancer and an unobtrusively learned man; I managed to love simultaneously—and this is not easy—women and justice; I indulged in sports and the fine arts—in short, I'll not go on for fear you might suspect me of self-flattery. But just imagine, I beg you, a man at the height of his powers, in perfect health, generously gifted, skilled in bodily exercises as in those of the mind, neither rich nor poor, sleeping well, and fundamentally pleased with himself without showing this otherwise than by a felicitous sociability. You will readily see how I can speak, without immodesty, of a successful life.

Yes, few creatures were more natural than I. I was altogether in harmony with life, fitting into it from top to bottom without rejecting any of its ironies, its grandeur, or its servitude. In particular the flesh, matter, the physical in short, which disconcerts or discourages so many men in love or in solitude, without enslaving me, brought me steady joys. I was made to have a body. Whence that harmony in me, that relaxed mastery that people felt, even to telling me sometimes that it helped them in life. Hence my company was in demand. Often, for instance, people thought they had met me before. Life, its creatures and its gifts, offered themselves to me, and I accepted such marks of homage with a kindly pride. To tell the truth, just from being so fully and simply a man, I looked upon myself as something of a superman.

I was of respectable but humble birth (my father was an officer), and yet, certain mornings, let me confess it humbly, I felt like a king's son, or a burning bush. It was not a matter, mind you, of the certainty I had of being more intelligent than everyone else. Besides, such certainty is of no consequence because so many imbeciles share it. No, as a result of being showered with blessings, I felt, I hesitate to admit, marked out. Personally marked out, among all, for that long and uninterrupted success. This, after all, was a result of my modesty. I refused to attribute that success to my own merits and could not believe that the conjunction in a single person of such different and such extreme virtues was the result of chance alone. This is why in my happy life I felt somehow that that happiness was authorized by some higher decree. When I add that I had no religion you can see even better how extraordinary that conviction was. Whether ordinary or not, it served for some time to raise me above the daily routine and I literally soared for a period of years, for which, to tell the truth, I still long in my heart of hearts. I soared until the evening when ... But no, that's another matter and it must be forgotten. Anyway, I am perhaps exaggerating. I was at ease in everything, to be sure, but at the same time satisfied with nothing. Each joy made me desire another. I went from festivity to festivity. On occasion I danced for nights on end, ever madder about people and life. At times, late on those nights when the dancing, the slight intoxication, my wild enthusiasm, everyone's violent unrestraint would fill me with a tired and overwhelmed rapture, it would seem to me—at the breaking point of fatigue and for a second's flash—that at last I understood the secret of creatures and of the world. But my fatigue would disappear the next day, and with it the secret; I would rush forth anew. I ran on like that, always heaped with favors, never satiated, without knowing where to stop, until the day—until the evening rather when the music stopped and the lights went out. The gay party at which I had been so happy ... But allow me to call on our friend the primate. Nod your head to thank him and, above all, drink up with me, I need your understanding.

I see that that declaration amazes you. Have you never suddenly needed understanding, help, friendship? Yes, of course. I have learned to be satisfied with understanding. It is found more readily and, besides, it's not binding. "I beg you to believe in my sympathetic understanding" in the inner discourse always precedes immediately "and now, let's turn to other matters." It's a board chairman's emotion; it comes cheap, after catastrophes. Friendship is less simple. It is long and hard to obtain, but when one has it there's no getting rid of it; one simply has to cope with it. Don't think for a minute that your friends will telephone you every evening, as they ought to, in order to find out if this doesn't happen to be the evening when you are deciding to commit suicide, or simply whether you don't need company, whether you are not in a mood to go out. No, don't worry, they'll ring up the evening you are not alone, when life is beautiful. As for suicide, they would be more likely to push you to it, by virtue of what you owe to yourself, according to them. May heaven protect us, *cher monsieur,* from being set on a pedestal by our friends! Those whose duty is to love us—I mean relatives and connections (what an expression!)—are another matter. They find the right word, all right, and it hits the bull's-eye; they telephone as if shooting a rifle. And they know how to aim. Oh, the Bazaines!

What? What evening? I'll get to it, be patient with me. In a certain way I *am* sticking to my subject with all that about friends and connections. You see, I've heard of a man whose friend had been imprisoned and who slept on the floor of his room every night in order not to enjoy a comfort of which his friend had been deprived. Who, *cher monsieur,* will sleep on the floor for us? Whether I am capable of it myself? Look, I'd like to be and I shall be. Yes, we shall all be capable of it one day, and that will be salvation. But it's not easy, for friendship is absent-minded or at least unavailing. It is incapable of achieving what it wants. Maybe, after all, it doesn't want it enough? Maybe we don't love life enough? Have you noticed that death alone awakens our feelings? How we love the friends who have just left us? How we admire those of our teachers who have ceased to speak, their mouths filled with earth! Then the expression of admiration springs forth naturally, that admiration they were perhaps expecting from us all their lives. But do you know why we are always more just and more generous toward the dead? The reason is simple. With them there is no obligation. They leave us free and we can take our time, fit the testimonial in between a cocktail party and a nice little mistress, in our spare time, in short. If they forced us to anything, it would be to remembering, and we have a short memory. No, it is the recently dead we love among our friends, the painful dead, our emotion, ourselves after all!

For instance, I had a friend I generally avoided. He rather bored me, and, besides, he was something of a moralist. But when he was on his deathbed, I was there—don't worry. I never missed a day. He died satisfied with me, holding both my hands. A woman who used to chase after me, and in vain, had the good sense to die young. What room in my heart at once! And when, in addition, it's a suicide! Lord, what a delightful commotion! One's telephone rings, one's heart overflows, and the intentionally short sentences yet heavy with implications, one's restrained suffering and even, yes, a bit of self-accusation!

That's the way man is, *cher monsieur.* He has two faces: he can't love without self-love. Notice your neighbors if perchance a death takes place in the building. They were asleep in their little routine and suddenly, for example, the concierge dies. At once they awake, bestir themselves, get the details, commiserate. A newly dead man and the show begins at last. They need tragedy, don't you know; it's their little transcendence, their *apéritif.* Moreover, is it mere chance that I should speak of a concierge? I had one, really ill favored, malice incarnate, a monster of insignificance and rancor, who would have discouraged a Franciscan. I had even given up speaking to him, but by his mere existence he compromised my customary contentedness. He died and I went to his funeral. Can you tell me why?

Anyway, the two days preceding the ceremony were full of interest. The concierge's wife was ill, lying in the single room, and near her the coffin had been set on sawhorses. Everyone had to get his mail himself. You opened the

door, said *"Bonjour, madame,"* listened to her praise of the dear departed as
she pointed to him, and took your mail. Nothing very amusing about that.
And yet the whole building passed through her room, which stank of carbo-
lic acid. And the tenants didn't send their servants either; they came themselves to take advantage of the unexpected attraction. The servants did too, of
course, but on the sly. The day of the funeral, the coffin was too big for the
door. "Oh my dearie," the wife said from her bed with a surprise at once delighted and grieved, "how big he was!" "Don't worry, *madame,"* replied the
funeral director, "we'll get him through edgewise, and upright." He was got
through upright and then laid down again, and I was the only one (with a
former cabaret doorman who, I gathered, used to drink his Pernod every evening with the departed) to go as far as the cemetery and strew flowers on a
coffin of astounding luxury. Then I paid a visit to the concierge's wife to receive her thanks expressed as by a great tragedienne. Tell me, what was the
reason for all that? None, except the *apéritif.*

I likewise buried an old fellow member of the Lawyers' Guild. A clerk to
whom no one paid attention, but I always shook his hand. Where I worked I
used to shake everyone's hand, moreover, being doubly sure to miss no one.
Without much effort, such cordial simplicity won me the popularity so necessary to my contentment. For the funeral of our clerk the President of the
Guild had not gone out of his way. But I did, and on the eve of a trip, as was
amply pointed out. It so happened that I knew my presence would be noticed
and favorably commented on. Hence, you see, not even the snow that was
falling that day made me withdraw.

What? I'm getting to it, never fear; besides, I have never left it. But let
me first point out that my concierge's wife, who had gone to such an outlay
for the crucifix, heavy oak, and silver handles in order to get the most out of
her emotion, had shacked up a month later with an overdressed yokel proud
of his singing voice. He used to beat her; frightful screams could be heard
and immediately afterward he would open the window and give forth with
his favorite song: "Women, how pretty you are!" "All the *same!"* the neighbors would say. All the same what? I ask you. All right, appearances were
against the baritone, and against the concierge's wife, too. But nothing
proves that they were not in love. And nothing proves either that she did not
love her husband. Moreover, when the yokel took flight, his voice and arm
exhausted, she—that faithful wife—resumed her praises of the departed. After
all, I know of others who have appearances on their side and are no more
faithful or sincere. I knew a man who gave twenty years of his life to a scat-
terbrained woman, sacrificing everything to her, his friendships, his work, the
very respectability of his life, and who one evening recognized that he had
never loved her. He had been bored, that's all, bored like most people. Hence
he had made himself out of whole cloth a life full of complications and

drama. Something must happen—and that explains most human commitments. Something must happen, even loveless slavery, even war or death.
Hurray then for funerals!

But I at least didn't have that excuse. I was not bored because I was riding on the crest of the wave. On the evening I am speaking about I can say
that I was even less bored than ever. And yet . . . You see, *cher monsieur,* it was
a fine autumn evening, still warm in town and already damp over the Seine.
Night was falling; the sky, still bright in the west, was darkening; the street
lamps were glowing dimly. I was walking up the quays of the Left Bank toward the Pont des Arts. The river was gleaming between the stalls of the secondhand booksellers. There were but few people on the quays; Paris was
already at dinner. I was treading on the dusty yellow leaves that still recalled
summer. Gradually the sky was filling with stars that could be seen for a moment after leaving one street lamp and heading toward another. I enjoyed the
return of silence, the evening's mildness, the emptiness of Paris. I was happy.
The day had been good: a blind man, the reduced sentence I had hoped for, a
cordial handclasp from my client, a few liberalities, and in the afternoon, a
brilliant improvisation in the company of several friends on the hardhearted-
ness of our governing class and the hypocrisy of our leaders.

I had gone up on the Pont des Arts, deserted at that hour, to look at the
river that could hardly be made out now night had come. Facing the statue of
the Vert-Galant, I dominated the island. I felt rising within me a vast feeling
of power and—I don't know how to express it—of completion, which
cheered my heart. I straightened up and was about to light a cigarette, the
cigarette of satisfaction, when, at that very moment, a laugh burst out behind
me. Taken by surprise, I suddenly wheeled around; there was no one there. I
stepped to the railing; no barge or boat. I turned back toward the island and,
again, heard the laughter behind me, a little farther off as if it were going
downstream. I stood there motionless. The sound of the laughter was de-
creasing, but I could still hear it distinctly behind me, come from nowhere
unless from the water. At the same time I was aware of the rapid beating of
my heart. Please don't misunderstand me; there was nothing mysterious
about that laugh; it was a good, hearty, almost friendly laugh, which re-es-
tablished the proper proportions. Soon I heard nothing more, anyway. I returned to the quays, went up the rue Dauphine, bought some cigarettes I
didn't need at all. I was dazed and had trouble breathing. That evening I rang
up a friend, who wasn't at home. I was hesitating about going out when,
suddenly, I heard laughter under my windows. I opened them. On the sidewalk, in fact, some youths were loudly saying good night. I shrugged my
shoulders as I closed the windows; after all, I had a brief to study. I went into
the bathroom to drink a glass of water. My reflection was smiling in the mirror, but it seemed to me that my smile was double . . .

What? Forgive me, I was thinking of something else. I'll see you again tomorrow, probably. Tomorrow, yes, that's right. No, no, I can't stay. Besides, I am called in consultation by that brown bear of a man you see over there. A decent fellow, for sure, whom the police are meanly persecuting out of sheer perversity. You think he looks like a killer? Rest assured that his actions conform to his looks. He burgles likewise, and you will be surprised to learn that that cave man is specialized in the art trade. In Holland everyone is a specialist in paintings and in tulips. This one, with his modest mien, is the author of the most famous theft of a painting. Which one? I may tell you. Don't be surprised at my knowledge. Although I am a judge-penitent, I have my side line here: I am the legal counselor of these good people. I studied the laws of the country and built up a clientele in this quarter where diplomas are not required. It wasn't easy, but I inspire confidence, don't I? I have a good, hearty laugh and an energetic handshake, and those are trump cards. Besides, I settled a few difficult cases, out of self-interest to begin with and later out of conviction. If pimps and thieves were invariably sentenced, all decent people would get to thinking they themselves were constantly innocent, *cher monsieur*. And in my opinion—all right, all right, I'm coming!—that's what must be avoided above all. Otherwise, everything would be just a joke.

Really, *mon cher compatriote,* I am grateful to you for your curiosity. However, there is nothing extraordinary about my story. Since you are interested, I'll tell you that I thought a little about that laugh, for a few days, then forgot about it. Once in a great while, I seemed to hear it within me. But most of the time, without making any effort, I thought of other things.

Yet I must admit that I ceased to walk along the Paris quays. When I would ride along them in a car or bus, a sort of silence would descend on me. I was waiting, I believe. But I would cross the Seine, nothing would happen, and I would breathe again. I also had some health problems at that time. Nothing definite, a dejection perhaps, a sort of difficulty in recovering my good spirits. I saw doctors, who gave me stimulants. I was alternately stimulated and depressed. Life became less easy for me: when the body is sad the heart languishes. It seemed to me that I was half unlearning what I had never learned and yet knew so well—how to live. Yes, I think it was probably then that everything began.

But this evening I don't feel quite up to snuff either. I even find trouble expressing myself. I'm not talking so well, it seems to me, and my words are less assured. Probably the weather. It's hard to breathe; the air is so heavy it weighs on one's chest. Would you object, *mon cher compatriote,* to going out and walking in the town a little? Thank you.

How beautiful the canals are this evening! I like the breath of stagnant waters, the smell of dead leaves soaking in the canal and the funereal scent rising from the barges loaded with flowers. No, no, there's nothing morbid about such a taste, I assure you. On the contrary, it's deliberate with me. The truth is that I force myself to admire these canals. What I like most in the world in Sicily, you see, and especially from the top of Etna, in the sunlight, provided I dominate the island and the sea. Java, too, but at the time of the trade winds. Yes, I went there in my youth. In a general way, I like all islands. It is easier to dominate them.

Charming house, isn't it? The two heads you see up there are heads of Negro slaves. A shop sign. The house belonged to a slave dealer. Oh, they weren't squeamish in those days! They had assurance; they announced: "You see, I'm a man of substance; I'm in the slave trade; I deal in black flesh." Can you imagine anyone today making it known publicly that such is his business? What a scandal! I can hear my Parisian colleagues right now. They are adamant on the subject; they wouldn't hesitate to launch two or three manifestoes, maybe even more! And on reflection, I'd add my signature to theirs. Slavery?—certainly not, we are against it! That we should be forced to establish it at home or in our factories—well, that's natural; but boasting about it, that's the limit!

I am well aware that one can't get along without domineering or being served. Every man needs slaves as he needs fresh air. Commanding is breathing—you agree with me? And even the most destitute manage to breathe. The lowest man in the social scale still has his wife or his child. If he's unmarried, a dog. The essential thing, after all, is being able to get angry with someone who has no right to talk back. "One doesn't talk back to one's father"—you know the expression? In one way it is very odd. To whom should one talk back in this world if not to what one loves? In another way, it is convincing. Somebody has to have the last word. Otherwise, every reason can be answered with another one and there would never be an end to it. Power, on the other hand, settles everything. It took time, but we finally realized that. For instance, you must have noticed that our old Europe at last philosophizes in the right way. We no longer say as in simple times: "This is the way I think. What are your objections?" We have become lucid. For the dialogue we have substituted the communiqué: "This is the truth," we say. "You can discuss it as much as you want; we aren't interested. But in a few years there'll be the police who will show you we are right."

Ah, this dear old planet! All is clear now. We know ourselves; we now know of what we are capable. Just take me, to change examples if not subjects, I have always wanted to be served with a smile. If the maid looked sad, she poisoned my days. She had a right not to be cheerful, to be sure. But I told myself that it was better for her to perform her service with a laugh than with tears. In fact, it was better for me. Yet, without boasting, my reasoning was not altogether idiotic. Likewise, I always refused to eat in Chinese restaurants. Why? Because Orientals when they are silent and in the presence of whites often look scornful. Naturally they keep that look when serving. How then can you enjoy the glazed chicken? And, above all, how can you look at them and think you are right?

Just between us, slavery, preferably with a smile, is inevitable then. But we must not admit it. Isn't it better that whoever cannot do without having slaves should call them free men? For the principle to begin with, and, secondly, not to drive them to despair. We owe them that compensation, don't we? In that way, they will continue to smile and we shall maintain our good conscience. Otherwise, we'd be obliged to reconsider our opinion of ourselves; we'd go mad with suffering, or even become modest—for everything would be possible. Consequently, no shop signs, and this one is shocking. Besides, if everyone told all, displayed his true profession and identity, we shouldn't know which way to turn! Imagine the visiting cards: Dupont, jittery philosopher, or Christian landowner, or adulterous humanist—indeed, there's a wide choice. But it would be hell! Yes, hell must be like that: streets filled with shop signs and no way of explaining oneself. One is classified once and for all.

You, for instance, *mon cher compatriote,* stop and think of what your sign would be. You are silent? Well, you'll tell me later on. I know mine in any case: a double face, a charming Janus, and above it the motto of the house: "Don't rely on it." On my cards: "Jean-Baptiste Clamence, play actor." Why, shortly after the evening I told you about, I discovered something. When I would leave a blind man on the sidewalk to which I had convoyed him, I used to tip my hat to him. Obviously the hat tipping wasn't intended for him, since he couldn't see it. To whom was it addressed? To the public. After playing my part, I would take the bow. Not bad, eh? Another day during the same period, to a motorist who was thanking me for helping him, I replied that no one would have done as much. I meant, of course, anyone. But that unfortunate slip weighed heavy on me. For modesty, really, I took the cake.

I have to admit it humbly, *mon cher compatriote,* I was always bursting with vanity. I, I, I is the refrain of my whole life, which could be heard in everything I said. I could never talk without boasting, especially if I did so with that shattering discretion that was my specialty. It is quite true that I always lived free and powerful. I simply felt released in regard to all for the excellent reason that I recognized no equals. I always considered myself more intelligent than everyone else, as I've told you, but also more sensitive and more skillful, a crack shot, an incomparable driver, a better lover. Even in the fields in which it was easy for me to verify my inferiority—like tennis, for instance, in which I was but a passable partner—it was hard for me not to think that, with a little time for practice, I would surpass the best players. I admitted only superiorities in me and this explained my good will and serenity. When I was concerned with others, I was so out of pure condescension, in utter freedom, and all the credit went to me: my self-esteem would go up a degree.

Along with a few other truths, I discovered these facts little by little in the period following the evening I told you about. Not all at once nor very clearly. First I had to recover my memory. By gradual degrees I saw more clearly, I learned a little of what I knew. Until then I had always been aided by an extraordinary ability to forget. I used to forget everything, beginning with my resolutions. Fundamentally, nothing mattered. War, suicide, love, poverty got my attention, of course, when circumstances forced me, but a courteous, superficial attention. At times, I would pretend to get excited about some cause foreign to my daily life. But basically I didn't really take part in it except, of course, when my freedom was thwarted. How can I express it? Everything slid off—yes, just rolled off me.

In the interest of fairness, it should be said that sometimes my forgetfulness was praiseworthy. You have noticed that there are people whose religion consists in forgiving all offenses, and who do in fact forgive them but never forget them? I wasn't good enough to forgive offenses, but eventually I always forgot them. And the man who thought I hated him couldn't get over seeing me tip my hat to him with a smile. According to his nature, he would then admire my nobility of character or scorn my ill breeding without realizing that my reason was simpler: I had forgotten his very name. The same infirmity that often made me indifferent or ungrateful in such cases made me magnanimous.

I lived consequently without any other continuity than that, from day to day, of I, I, I. From day to day women, from day to day virtue or vice, from day to day, like dogs—but every day myself secure at my post. Thus I progressed on the surface of life, in the realm of words as it were, never in reality. All those books barely read, those friends barely loved, those cities barely visited, those women barely possessed! I went through the gestures out of boredom or absent-mindedness. Then came human beings; they wanted to cling, but there was nothing to cling to, and that was unfortunate—for them. As for me, I forgot. I never remembered anything but myself.

Gradually, however, my memory returned. Or rather, I returned to it, and in it I found the recollection that was awaiting me. But before telling you of it, allow me, *mon cher compatriote,* to give you a few examples (they will be useful to you, I am sure) of what I discovered in the course of my exploration.

One day in my car when I was slow in making a getaway at the green light while our patient fellow citizens immediately began honking furiously behind me, I suddenly remembered another occasion set in similar circumstances. A motorcycle ridden by a spare little man wearing spectacles and plus fours had gone around me and planted itself in front of me at the red light. As he came to a stop the little man had stalled his motor and was vainly striving to revive it. When the light changed, I asked him with my usual courtesy to take his motorcycle out of my way so I might pass. The little man was getting irritable over his wheezy motor. Hence he replied, according to the rules of Parisian courtesy, that I could go climb a tree. I insisted, still polite, but with a slight shade of impatience in my voice. I was immediately told that in any case I could go straight to hell. Meanwhile several horns began to be heard behind me. With greater firmness I begged my interlocutor to be polite and to realize that he was blocking traffic. The irascible character, probably exasperated by the now evident ill will of his motor, informed me that if I wanted what he called a thorough dusting off he would gladly give it to me. Such cynicism filled me with a healthy rage and I got out of my car with the intention of thrashing this coarse individual. I don't think I am cowardly (but what doesn't one think!); I was a head taller than my adversary and my muscles have always been reliable. I still believe the dusting off would have been received rather than given. But I had hardly set foot on the pavement when from the gathering crowd a man stepped forth, rushed at me, assured me that I was the lowest of the low and that he would not allow me to strike a man who had a motorcycle between his legs and hence was at a disadvantage. I turned toward this musketeer and, in truth, didn't even see him. Indeed, hardly had I turned my head when, almost simultaneously, I heard the motorcycle begin popping again and received a violent blow on the ear. Before I had the time to register what had happened, the motorcycle rode away. Dazed, I mechanically walked toward d'Artagnan when, at the same moment, an exasperated concert of horns rose from the now considerable line of vehicles. The light was changing to green. Then, still somewhat bewildered, instead of giving a drubbing to the idiot who had addressed me, I docilely returned to my car and drove off. As I passed, the idiot greeted me with a "poor dope" that I still recall.

A totally insignificant story, in your opinion? Probably. Still it took me some time to forget it, and that's what counts. Yet I had excuses. I had let myself be beaten without replying, but I could not be accused of cowardice. Taken by surprise, addressed from both sides, I had mixed everything up and the horns had put the finishing touch to my embarrassment. Yet I was unhappy about this as if I had violated the code of honor. I could see myself getting back into my car without a reaction, under the ironic gaze of a crowd especially delighted because, as I recall, I was wearing a very elegant blue suit. I could hear the "poor dope" which, in spite of everything, struck me as justified. In short, I had collapsed in public. As a result of a series of circumstances, to be sure, but there are always circumstances. As an afterthought I clearly saw what I should have done. I saw myself felling d'Artagnan with a good hook to the jaw, getting back into my car, pursuing the monkey who had struck me, overtaking him, jamming his machine against the curb, taking him aside, and giving him the licking he had fully deserved. With a few variants, I ran off this little film a hundred times in my imagination. But it was too late, and for several days I chewed a bitter resentment.

Why, it's raining again. Let's stop, shall we, under this portico? Good. Where was I? Oh, yes, honor! Well, when I recovered the recollection of that episode, I realized what it meant. After all, my dream had not stood up to facts. I had dreamed—this was now clear—of being a complete man who managed to make himself respected in his person as well as in his profession. Half Cerdan, half de Gaulle, if you will. In short, I wanted to dominate in all things. This is why I assumed the manner, made a particular point of displaying my physical skill rather than my intellectual gifts. But after having been struck in public without reacting, it was no longer possible for me to cherish that fine picture of myself. If I had been the friend of truth and intelligence I claimed to be, what would that episode have mattered to me? It was already forgotten by those who had witnessed it. I'd have barely accused myself of having got angry over nothing and also, having got angry, of not having managed to face up to the consequences of my anger, for want of presence of mind. Instead of that, I was eager to get my revenge, to strike and conquer. As if my true desire were not to be the most intelligent or most generous creature on earth, but only to beat anyone I wanted, to be the stronger, in short, and in the most elementary way. The truth is that every intelligent man, as you know, dreams of being a gangster and of ruling over society by force alone. As it is not so easy as the detective novels might lead one to believe, one generally relies on politics and joins the cruelest party. What does it matter, after all, if by humiliating one's mind one succeeds in dominating everyone? I discovered in myself sweet dreams of oppression.

I learned at least that I was on the side of the guilty, the accused, only in exactly so far as their crime caused me no harm. Their guilt made me eloquent because I was not its victim. When I was threatened, I became not only a judge in turn but even more: an irascible master who wanted, regardless of all laws, to strike down the offender and get him on his knees. After that, *mon cher compatriote,* it is very hard to continue seriously believing one has a vocation for justice and is the predestined defender of the widow and orphan.

Since the rain is coming down harder and we have the time, may I impart to you another discovery I made, soon after, in my memory? Let's sit down on this bench out of the rain. For centuries pipe smokers have been watching the same rain falling on the same canal. What I have to tell you is a bit more difficult. This time it concerns a woman. To begin with, you must know that I always succeeded with women—and without much effort. I don't say succeed in making them happy or even in making myself happy through them. No, simply succeed. I used to achieve my ends just about whenever I wanted. I was considered to have charm. Fancy that! You know what charm is: a way of getting the answer yes without having asked any clear question. And that was true of me at the time. Does that surprise you? Come now, don't deny it. With the face I now have, that's quite natural. Alas, after a certain age every man is responsible for his face. Mine ... But what matter? It's a fact—I was considered to have charm and I took advantage of it.

Without calculation, however; I was in good faith, or almost. My relationship with women was natural, free, easy, as the saying goes. No guile in it except that obvious guile which they look upon as a homage. I loved them, according to the hallowed expression, which amounts to saying that I never loved any of them. I always considered misogyny vulgar and stupid, and almost all the women I have known seemed to me better than I. Nevertheless, setting them so high, I made use of them more often than I served them. How can one make it out?

Of course, true love is exceptional—two or three times a century, more or less. The rest of the time there is vanity or boredom. As for me, in any case I was not the Portuguese Nun. I am not hardhearted; far from it—full of pity on the contrary and with a ready tear to boot. Only, my emotional impulses always turn toward me, my feelings of pity concern me. It is not true, after all, that I never loved. I conceived at least one great love in my life, of which I was always the object. From that point of view, after the inevitable hardships of youth, I was early focused: sensuality alone dominated my love life. I looked merely for objects of pleasure and conquest. Moreover, I was aided in this by my constitution: nature had been generous with me. I was considerably proud of this and derived many satisfactions therefrom—without my knowing now whether they were physical or based on prestige. Of course you will say that I am boasting again. I shan't deny it and I am hardly proud of doing so, for here I am boasting of what is true.

In any case, my sensuality (to limit myself to it) was so real that even for a ten-minute adventure I'd have disowned father and mother, even were I to regret it bitterly. Indeed—*especially* for a ten-minute adventure and even more so if I were sure it was to have no sequel. I had principles, to be sure, such as that the wife of a friend is sacred. But I simply ceased quite sincerely, a few days before, to feel any friendship for the husband. Maybe I ought not to call this sensuality? Sensuality is not repulsive. Let's be indulgent and use the word "infirmity," a sort of congenital inability to see in love anything but the physical. That infirmity, after all, was convenient. Combined with my faculty for forgetting, it favored my freedom. At the same time, through a certain appearance of inaccessibility and unshakable independence it gave me, it provided the opportunity for new successes. As a result of not being romantic, I

ALBERT CAMUS

gave romance something to work on. Our feminine friends have in common with Bonaparte the belief that they can succeed where everyone else has failed.

In this exchange, moreover, I satisfied something in addition to my sensuality: my passion for gambling. I loved in women my partners in a certain game, which had at least the taste of innocence. You see, I can't endure being bored and appreciate only diversions in life. Any society, however brilliant, soon crushes me, whereas I have never been bored with the women I liked. It hurts me to confess it, but I'd have given ten conversations with Einstein for an initial rendezvous with a pretty chorus girl. It's true that at the tenth rendezvous I was longing for Einstein or a serious book. In short, I was never concerned with the major problems except in the intervals between my little excesses. And how often, standing on the sidewalk involved in a passionate discussion with friends, I lost the thread of the argument being developed because a devastating woman was crossing the street at that very moment.

Hence I played the game. I knew they didn't like one to reveal one's purpose too quickly. First, there had to be conversation, fond attentions, as they say. I wasn't worried about speeches, being a lawyer, nor about glances, having been an amateur actor during my military service. I often changed parts, but it was always the same play. For instance, the scene of the incomprehensible attraction, of the "mysterious something," of the "it's unreasonable, I certainly didn't want to be attracted, I was even tired of love, etc. . . ." always worked, though it is one of the oldest in the repertory. There was also the gambit of the mysterious happiness no other woman has ever given you; it may be a blind alley—indeed, it surely is (for one cannot protect oneself too much)—but it just happens to be unique. Above all, I had perfected a little speech which was always well received and which, I am sure, you will applaud. The essential part of that act lay in the assertion, painful and resigned, that I was nothing, that it was not worth getting involved with me, that my life was elsewhere and not related to everyday happiness—a happiness that maybe I should have preferred to anything, but there you were, it was too late. As to the reasons behind this decisive lateness, I maintained secrecy, knowing that it is always better to go to bed with a mystery. In a way, moreover, I believed what I said; I was living my part. It is not surprising that my partners likewise began to "tread the boards" enthusiastically. The most sensitive among them tried to understand me, and that effort led them to melancholy surrenders. The others, satisfied to note that I was respecting the rules of the game and had the tactfulness to talk before acting, progressed without delay to the realities. This meant I had won—and twice over, since, besides the desire I felt for them, I was satisfying the love I bore myself by verifying each time my special powers.

This is so true that even if some among them provided but slight pleasure, I nevertheless tried to resume relations with them, at long intervals, helped doubtless by that strange desire kindled by absence and a suddenly re-covered complicity, but also to verify the fact that our ties still held and that it was my privilege alone to tighten them. Sometimes I went so far as to make them swear not to give themselves to any other man, in order to quiet my worries once and for all on that score. My heart, however, played no part in that worry, nor even my imagination. A certain type of pretension was in fact so personified in me that it was hard for me to imagine, despite the facts, that a woman who had once been mine could ever belong to another. But the oath they swore to me liberated me while it bound them. As soon as I knew they would never belong to anyone, I could make up my mind to break off—which otherwise was almost always impossible for me. As far as they were concerned, I had proved my point once and for all and assured my power for a long time. Strange, isn't it? But that's the way it was, *mon cher compatriote.* Some cry: "Love me!" Others: "Don't love me!" But a certain genus, the worst and most unhappy, cries: "Don't love me and be faithful to me!"

Except that the proof is never definitive, after all; one has to begin again with each new person. As a result of beginning over and over again, one gets in the habit. Soon the speech comes without thinking and the reflex follows; and one day you find yourself taking without really desiring. Believe me, for certain men at least, not taking what one doesn't desire is the hardest thing in the world.

This is what happened eventually and there's no point in telling you who she was except that, without really stirring me, she had attracted me by her passive, avid manner. Frankly, it was a shabby experience, as I should have expected. But I never had any complexes and soon forgot the person, whom I didn't see again. I thought she hadn't noticed anything and didn't even imagine she could have an opinion. Besides, in my eyes her passive manner cut her off from the world. A few weeks later, however, I learned that she had related my deficiencies to a third person. At once I felt as if I had been somewhat deceived; she wasn't so passive as I had thought and she didn't lack judg-ment. Then I shrugged my shoulders and pretended to laugh. I even laughed outright; clearly the incident was unimportant. If there is any realm in which modesty ought to be the rule, isn't it sex with all the unforeseeable there is in it? But no, each of us tries to show up to advantage, even in solitude. Despite having shrugged my shoulders, what was my behavior in fact? I saw that woman again a little later and did everything necessary to charm her and really take her back. It was not very difficult, for *they* don't like either to end on a failure. From that moment onward, without really intending it, I began, in fact, to mortify her in every way. I would give her up and take her back, force her to give herself at inappropriate times and in inappropriate places, treat her so brutally, in every regard, that eventually I attached myself to her as I imagine the jailer is bound to his prisoner. And this kept up till the day when, in the violent disorder of painful and constrained pleasure, she paid a tribute aloud to what was enslaving her. That very day I began to move away from her. I have forgotten her since.

I'll agree with you, despite your polite silence, that that adventure is not very pretty. But just think of your life, *mon cher compatriote!* Search your memory and perhaps you will find some similar story that you'll tell me later on. In my case, when that business came to mind, I again began to laugh. But it was another kind of laugh, rather like the one I had heard on the Pont des Arts. I was laughing at my speeches and my pleadings in court. Even more at my court pleading than at my speeches to women. To them, at least, I did not lie much. Instinct spoke clearly, without subterfuges, in my attitude. The act of love, for instance, is a confession. Selfishness screams aloud, vanity shows off, or else true generosity reveals itself. Ultimately in that regrettable story, even more than in my other affairs, I had been more outspoken than I thought; I had declared who I was and how I could live. Despite appearances, I was therefore more worthy in my private life—even when (one might say: especially when) I behaved as I have told you—than in my great professional flights about innocence and justice. At least, seeing myself act with others, I couldn't deceive myself as to the truth of my nature. No man is a hypocrite in his pleasures—have I read that or did I think it myself, *mon cher compatriote?*

When I examined thus the trouble I had in separating definitively from a woman—a trouble which used to involve me in so many simultaneous liaisons—I didn't blame my softheartedness. That was not what impelled me when one of my mistresses tired of waiting for the Austerlitz of our passion and spoke of leaving me. At once I was the one who made a step forward, who yielded, who became eloquent. As for affection and softheartedness, I aroused them in women, experiencing merely the appearance of them myself—simply a little excited by this refusal, alarmed also by the possible loss of someone's affection. At times I truly thought I was suffering, to be sure. But the rebellious female had merely to leave in fact for me to forget her without effort, as I forgot her presence when, on the contrary, she had decided to return. No, it was not love or generosity that awakened me when I was in danger of being forsaken, but merely the desire to be loved and to receive what in my opinion was due me. The moment I was loved and my partner again forgotten, I shone, I was at the top of my form, I became likable.

Be it said, moreover, that as soon as I had re-won that affection I became aware of its weight. In my moments of irritation I told myself that the ideal solution would have been the death of the person I was interested in. Her death would, on the one hand, have definitively fixed our relationship and, on the other, removed its compulsion. But one cannot long for the death of everyone or, in the extreme, depopulate the planet in order to enjoy a freedom that cannot be imagined otherwise. My sensibility was opposed to this, and my love of mankind.

The only deep emotion I occasionally felt in these affairs was gratitude, when all was going well and I was left, not only peace, but freedom to come and go—never kinder and gayer with one woman than when I had just left another's bed, as if I extended to all others the debt I had just contracted toward one of them. In any case, however apparently confused my feelings were, the result I achieved was clear: I kept all my affections within reach to make use of them when I wanted. On my own admission, I could live happily only on condition that all the individuals on earth, or the greatest possible number, were turned toward me, eternally in suspense, devoid of independent life and ready to answer my call at any moment, doomed in short to sterility until the day I should deign to favor them. In short, for me to live happily it was essential for the creatures I chose not to live at all. They must receive their life, sporadically, only at my bidding.

Oh, I don't feel any self-satisfaction, believe me, in telling you this. Upon thinking of that time when I used to ask for everything without paying anything myself, when I used to mobilize so many people in my service, when I used to put them in the refrigerator, so to speak, in order to have them at hand some day when it would suit me, I don't know how to name the odd feeling that comes over me. Isn't it shame, perhaps? Tell me, *mon cher compatriote,* doesn't shame sting a little? It does? Well, it's probably shame, then, or one of those silly emotions that have to do with honor. It seems to me in any case that that feeling has never left me since the adventure I found at the heart of my memory, which I cannot any longer put off relating, despite my digresssions and the inventive efforts for which, I hope, you give me credit.

Look, the rain has stopped! Be kind enough to walk home with me. I am strangely tired, not from having talked so much but at the mere thought of what I still have to say. Oh, well, a few words will suffice to relate my essential discovery. What's the use of saying more, anyway? For the statue to stand bare, the fine speeches must take flight like pigeons. So here goes. That particular night in November, two or three years before the evening when I thought I heard laughter behind me, I was returning to the Left Bank and my home by way of the Pont Royal. It was an hour past midnight, a fine rain was falling, a drizzle rather, that scattered the few people on the streets. I had just left a mistress, who was surely already asleep. I was enjoying that walk, a little numbed, my body calmed and irrigated by a flow of blood gentle as the falling rain. On the bridge I passed behind a figure leaning over the railing and seeming to stare at the river. On closer view, I made out a slim young woman dressed in black. The back of her neck, cool and damp between her dark hair and coat collar, stirred me. But I went on after a moment's hesitation. At the end of the bridge I followed the guys toward Saint-Michel, where I lived. I had already gone some fifty yards when I heard the sound—which, despite the distance, seemed dreadfully loud in the midnight silence—of a body striking the water. I stopped short, but without turning around. Almost at once I heard a cry, repeated several times, which was going downstream; then it suddenly ceased. The silence that followed, as the night suddenly stood still, seemed interminable. I wanted to run and yet didn't stir. I was trembling, I believe from cold and shock. I told myself that I had to be quick and I felt an irresistible weakness steal over me. I have forgotten what I thought then. "Too late, too far . . ." or something of the sort. I was still listening as I stood motionless. Then, slowly under the rain, I went away. I informed no one.

But here we are; here's my house, my shelter! Tomorrow? Yes, if you wish. I'd like to take you to the island of Marken so you can see the Zuider Zee. Let's meet at eleven at *Mexico City*. What? That woman? Oh, I don't know. Really I don't know. The next day, and the days following, I didn't read the papers.

A doll's village, isn't it? No shortage of quaintness here! But I didn't bring you to this island for quaintness, *cher ami*. Anyone can show you peasant headdresses, wooden shoes, and ornamented houses with fishermen smoking choice tobacco surrounded by the smell of furniture wax. I am one of the few people, on the other hand, who can show you what really matters here.

We are reaching the dike. We'll have to follow it to get as far as possible from these too charming houses. Please, let's sit down. Well, what do you think of it? Isn't it the most beautiful negative landscape? Just see on the left that pile of ashes they call a dune here, the gray dike on the right, the livid beach at our feet, and in front of us, the sea the color of a weak lye-solution with the vast sky reflecting the colorless waters. A soggy hell, indeed! Everything horizontal, no relief; space is colorless, and life dead. Is it not universal obliteration, everlasting nothingness made visible? No human beings, above all, no human beings! You and I alone facing the planet at last deserted! The sky is alive? You are right, *cher ami*. It thickens, becomes concave, opens up air shafts and closes cloudy doors. Those are the doves. Haven't you noticed that the sky of Holland is filled with millions of doves, invisible because of their altitude, which flap their wings, rise or fall in unison, filling the heavenly space with dense multitudes of grayish feathers carried hither and thither by the wind? The doves wait up there all year round. They wheel above the earth, look down, and would like to come down. But there is nothing but the sea and the canals, roofs covered with shop signs, and never a head on which to light.

You don't understand what I mean? I'll admit my fatigue. I lose the thread of what I am saying; I've lost that lucidity to which my friends used to enjoy paying respects. I say "my friends," moreover, as a convention. I have no more friends; I have nothing but accomplices. To make up for this, their number has increased; they are the whole human race. And within the human race, you first of all. Whoever is at hand is always the first. How do I know I have no friends? It's very easy: I discovered it the day I thought of killing myself to play a trick on them, to punish them, in a way. But punish whom? Some would be surprised, and no one would feel punished. I realized I had no friends. Besides, even if I had had, I shouldn't be any better off. If I had been able to commit suicide and then see their reaction, why, then the game would have been worth the candle. But the earth is dark, *cher ami,* the coffin thick, and the shroud opaque. The eyes of the soul—to be sure—if there is a soul and it has eyes! But you see, we're not sure, we can't be sure. Otherwise, there would be a solution; at least one could get oneself taken seriously. Men are never convinced of your reasons, of your sincerity, of the seriousness of your sufferings, except by your death. So long as you are alive, your case is doubtful; you have a right only to their skepticism. So if there were the least certainty that one could enjoy the show, it would be worth proving to them what they are unwilling to believe and thus amazing them. But you kill yourself and what does it matter whether or not they believe you? You are not there to see their amazement and their contrition (fleeting at best), to witness, according to every man's dream, your own funeral. In order to cease being a doubtful case, one has to cease being, that's all.

Besides, isn't it better thus? We'd suffer too much from their indifference. "You'll pay for this!" a daughter said to her father who had prevented her from marrying a too well groomed suitor. And she killed herself. But the father paid for nothing. He loved fly-casting. Three Sundays later he went back to the river—to forget, as he said. He was right; he forgot. To tell the truth, the contrary would have been surprising. You think you are dying to punish your wife and actually you are freeing her. It's better not to see that. Besides the fact that you might hear the reasons they give for your action. As far as I am concerned, I can hear them now: "He killed himself because he couldn't bear . . ." Ah, *cher ami,* how poor in invention men are! They always think one commits suicide for a reason. But it's quite possible to commit suicide for two reasons. No, that never occurs to them. So what's the good of dying intentionally, of sacrificing yourself to the idea you want people to have of you? Once you are dead, they will take advantage of it to attribute idiotic or vulgar motives to your action. Martyrs, *cher ami,* must choose between being forgotten, mocked, or made use of. As for being understood—never!

Besides, let's not beat about the bush; I love life—that's my real weakness. I love it so much that I am incapable of imagining what is not life. Such avidity has something plebeian about it, don't you think? Aristocracy cannot imagine itself without a little distance surrounding itself and its life. One dies if necessary, one breaks rather than bending. But I bend, because I continue to love myself. For example, after all I have told you, what do you think I developed? An aversion for myself? Come, come, it was especially with others that I was fed up. To be sure, I knew my failings and regretted them. Yet I continued to forget them with a rather meritorious obstinacy. The prosecution of others, on the contrary, went on constantly in my heart. Of course—does that shock you? Maybe you think it's not logical? But the question is not to remain logical. The question is to slip through and, above all—yes, above all, the question is to elude judgment. I'm not saying to avoid punishment, for punishment without judgment is bearable. It has a name, besides, that guarantees our innocence: it is called misfortune. No, on the contrary, it's a matter of dodging judgment, of avoiding being forever judged without ever having a sentence pronounced.

But one can't dodge it so easily. Today we are always ready to judge as we are to fornicate. With this difference, that there are no inadequacies to fear. If you doubt this, just listen to the table conversation during August in those summer hotels where our charitable fellow citizens take the boredom cure. If you still hesitate to conclude, read the writings of our great men of the moment. Or else observe your own family and you will be edified. *Mon cher ami,* let's not give them any pretext, no matter how small, for judging us! Otherwise, we'll be left in shreds. We are forced to take the same precautions as the animal tamer. If, before going into the cage, he has the misfortune to cut himself while shaving, what a feast for the wild animals! I realized this all at once the moment I had the suspicion that maybe I wasn't so admirable. From then on, I became distrustful. Since I was bleeding slightly, there was no escape for me; they would devour me.

My relations with my contemporaries were apparently the same and yet subtly out of tune. My friends hadn't changed. On occasion, they still extolled the harmony and security they found in my company. But I was aware only of the dissonances and disorder that filled me; I felt vulnerable and open to public accusation. In my eyes my fellows ceased to be the respectful public to which I was accustomed. The circle of which I was the center broke and they lined up in a row as on the judge's bench. In short, the moment I grasped that there was something to judge in me, I realized that there was in them an irresistible vocation for judgment. Yes, they were there as before, but they were laughing. Or rather it seemed to me that everyone I encountered was looking at me with a hidden smile. I even had the impression, at that time, that people were tripping me up. Two or three times, in fact, I stumbled as I entered public places. Once, even, I went sprawling on the floor. The Cartesian Frenchman in me didn't take long to catch hold of himself and attribute those accidents to the only reasonable divinity—that is, chance. Nonetheless, my distrust remained.

Once my attention was aroused, it was not hard for me to discover that I had enemies. In my profession, to begin with, and also in my social life. Some among them I had obliged. Others I should have obliged. All that, after all, was natural, and I discovered it without too much grief. It was harder and more painful, on the other hand, to admit that I had enemies among people I hardly knew or didn't know at all. I had always thought, with the ingenuousness I have already illustrated to you, that those who didn't know me couldn't resist liking me if they came to know me. Not at all! I encountered hostility especially among those who knew me only at a distance without my knowing them myself. Doubtless they suspected me of living fully, given up completely to happiness; and that cannot be forgiven. The look of success, when it is worn in a certain way, would infuriate a jackass. Then again, my life was full to bursting, and for lack of time, I used to refuse many advances. Then I would forget my refusals, for the same reason. But those advances had been made me by people whose lives were not full and who, for that very reason, would remember my refusals.

Thus it is that in the end, to take but one example, women cost me dear. The time I used to devote to them I couldn't give to men, who didn't always forgive me this. Is there any way out? Your successes and happiness are forgiven you only if you generously consent to share them. But to be happy it is essential not to be too concerned with others. Consequently, there is no escape. Happy and judged, or absolved and wretched. As for me, the injustice was even greater: I was condemned for past successes. For a long time I had lived in the illusion of a general agreement, whereas, from all sides, judgments, arrows, mockeries rained upon me, inattentive and smiling. The day I was alerted I became lucid; I received all the wounds at the same time and lost my strength all at once. The whole universe then began to laugh at me.

That is what no man (except those who are not really alive—in other words, wise men) can endure. Spitefulness is the only possible ostentation. People hasten to judge in order not to be judged themselves. What do you expect? The idea that comes most naturally to man, as if from his very nature, is the idea of his innocence. From this point of view, we are all like that little Frenchman at Buchenwald who insisted on registering a complaint with the clerk, himself a prisoner, who was recording his arrival. A complaint? The clerk and his comrades laughed: "Useless, old man. You don't lodge a com-

plaint here." "But you see, sir," said the little Frenchman, "my case is exceptional. I am innocent!"

We are all exceptional cases. We all want to appeal against something!
Each of us insists on being innocent at all cost, even if he has to accuse the
whole human race and heaven itself. You won't delight a man by compli-
menting him on the efforts by which he has become intelligent or generous.
On the other hand, he will beam if you admire his natural generosity. In-
versely, if you tell a criminal that his crime is not due to his nature or his
character but to unfortunate circumstances, he will be extravagantly grateful
to you. During the counsel's speech, this is the moment he will choose to
weep. Yet there is no credit in being honest or intelligent by birth. Just as
one is surely no more responsible for being a criminal by nature than for
being a criminal by circumstance. But those rascals want grace, that is, irre-
sponsibility, and they shamelessly allege the justifications of nature or the excuses of circumstances, even if they are contradictory. The essential thing is
that they should be innocent, that their virtues, by grace of birth, should not
be questioned and that their misdeeds, born of a momentary misfortune,
should never be more than provisional. As I told you, it's a matter of dodging
judgment. Since it is hard to dodge it, tricky to get one's nature simultaneously admired and excused, they all strive to be rich. Why? Did you ever ask
yourself? For power, of course. But especially because wealth shields from immediate judgment, takes you out of the subway crowd to enclose you in a
chromium-plated automobile, isolates you in huge protected lawns, Pull-
mans, first-class cabins. Wealth, *cher ami,* is not quite acquittal, but reprieve,
and that's always worth taking.

Above all, don't believe your friends when they ask you to be sincere
with them. They merely hope you will encourage them in the good opinion
they have of themselves by providing them with the additional assurance
they will find in your promise of sincerity. How could sincerity be a condition of friendship? A liking for truth at any cost is a passion that spares
nothing and that nothing resists. It's a vice, at times a comfort, or a selfishness. Therefore, if you are in that situation, don't hesitate: promise to tell the
truth and then lie as best you can. You will satisfy their hidden desire and
doubly prove your affection.

This is so true that we rarely confide in those who are better than we.
Rather, we are more inclined to flee their society. Most often, on the other
hand, we confess to those who are like us and who share our weaknesses.
Hence we don't want to improve ourselves or be bettered, for we should first
have to be judged in default. We merely wish to be pitied and encouraged in
the course we have chosen. In short, we should like, at the same time, to
cease being guilty and yet not to make the effort of cleansing ourselves. Not
enough cynicism and not enough virtue. We lack the energy of evil as well as
the energy of good. Do you know Dante? Really? The devil you say! Then

you know that Dante accepts the idea of neutral angels in the quarrel between God and Satan. And he puts them in Limbo, a sort of vestibule of his Hell. We are in the vestibule, *cher ami.*

Patience? You are probably right. It would take patience to wait for the Last Judgment. But that's it, we're in a hurry. So much in a hurry, indeed, that I was obliged to make myself a judge-penitent. However, I first had to make shift with my discoveries and put myself right with my contemporaries' laughter. From the evening when I was called—for I was really called—I had to answer or at least seek an answer. It wasn't easy; for some time I floundered. To begin with, that perpetual laugh and the laughers had to teach me to see clearly within me and to discover at last that I was not simple. Don't smile; that truth is not so basic as it seems. What we call basic truths are simply the ones we discover after all the others.

However that may be, after prolonged research on myself, I brought out the fundamental duplicity of the human being. Then I realized, as a result of delving in my memory, that modesty helped me to shine, humility to conquer, and virtue to oppress. I used to wage war by peaceful means and eventually used to achieve, through disinterested means, everything I desired. For instance, I never complained that my birthday was overlooked; people were even surprised, with a touch of admiration, by my discretion on this subject. But the reason for my disinterestedness was even more discreet: I longed to be forgotten in order to be able to complain to myself. Several days before the famous date (which I knew very well) I was on the alert, eager to let nothing slip that might arouse the attention and memory of those on whose lapse I was counting (didn't I once go so far as to contemplate falsifying a friend's calendar?). Once my solitude was thoroughly proved, I could surrender to the charms of a virile self-pity.

Thus the surface of all my virtues had a less imposing reverse side. It is true that, in another sense, my shortcomings turned to my advantage. For example, the obligation I felt to conceal the vicious part of my life gave me a cold look that was confused with the look of virtue; my indifference made me loved; my selfishness wound up in my generosities. I stop there, for too great a symmetry would upset my argument. But after all, I presented a harsh exterior and yet could never resist the offer of a glass or of a woman! I was considered active, energetic, and my kingdom was the bed. I used to advertise my loyalty and I don't believe there is a single person I loved that I didn't eventually betray. Of course, my betrayals didn't stand in the way of my fidelity; I used to knock off a considerable pile of work through successive periods of idleness; and I had never ceased aiding my neighbor, thanks to my enjoyment in doing so. But however much I repeated such facts to myself, they gave me but superficial consolations. Certain mornings, I would get up the case against myself most thoroughly, coming to the conclusion that I excelled above all in scorn. The very people I helped most often were the most scorned. Courteously, with a solidarity charged with emotion, I used to spit daily in the face of all the blind.

Tell me frankly, is there any excuse for that? There is one, but so wretched that I cannot dream of advancing it. In any case, here it is: I have never been really able to believe that human affairs were serious matters. I had no idea where the serious might lie, except that it was not in all this I saw around me—which seemed to me merely an amusing game, or tiresome. There are really efforts and convictions I have never been able to understand. I always looked with amazement, and a certain suspicion, on those strange creatures who died for money, fell into despair over the loss of a "position," or sacrificed themselves with a high and mighty manner for the prosperity of their family. I could better understand that friend who had made up his mind to stop smoking and through sheer will power had succeeded. One morning he opened the paper, read that the first H-bomb had been exploded, learned about its wonderful effects, and hastened to a tobacco shop.

To be sure, I occasionally pretended to take life seriously. But very soon the frivolity of seriousness struck me and I merely went on playing my role as well as I could. I played at being efficient, intelligent, virtuous, civic-minded, shocked, indulgent, fellow-spirited, edifying . . . In short, there's no need of going on, you have already grasped that I was like my Dutchmen who are here without being here: I was absent at the moment when I took up the most space. I have never been really sincere and enthusiastic except when I used to indulge in sports, and in the army, when I used to act in plays we put on for our own amusement. In both cases there was a rule of the game, which was not serious but which we enjoyed taking as if it were. Even now, the Sunday matches in an overflowing stadium, and the theater, which I loved with the greatest passion, are the only places in the world where I feel innocent.

But who would consider such an attitude legitimate in the face of love, death, and the wages of the poor? Yet what can be done about it? I could imagine the love of Isolde only in novels or on the stage. At times people on their deathbed seemed to me convinced of their roles. The lines spoken by my poor clients always struck me as fitting the same pattern. Whence, living among men without sharing their interests, I could not manage to believe in the commitments I made. I was courteous and indolent enough to live up to what was expected of me in my profession, my family, or my civic life, but each time with a sort of indifference that spoiled everything. I lived my whole life under a double code, and my most serious acts were often the ones in which I was the least involved. Wasn't that after all the reason that, added to my blunders, I could not forgive myself, that made me revolt most violently against the judgment I felt forming, in me and around me, and that forced me to seek an escape?

For some time, my life continued outwardly as if nothing had changed. I was on rails and speeding ahead. As if purposely, people's praises increased. And that's just where the trouble came from. You remember the remark: "Woe to you when all men speak well of you!" Ah, the one who said that spoke words of wisdom! Woe to me! Consequently, the engine began to have whims, inexplicable breakdowns.

Then it was that the thought of death burst into my daily life. I would measure the years separating me from my end. I would look for examples of men of my age who were already dead. And I was tormented by the thought that I might not have time to accomplish my task. What task? I had no idea. Frankly, was what I was doing worth continuing? But that was not quite it. A ridiculous fear pursued me, in fact: one could not die without having confessed all one's lies. Not to God or to one of his representatives; I was above that, as you well imagine. No, it was a matter of confessing to men, to a friend, to a beloved woman, for example. Otherwise, were there but one lie hidden in a life, death made it definitive. No one, ever again, would know the truth on this point, since the only one to know it was precisely the dead man sleeping on his secret. That absolute murder of a truth used to make me dizzy. Today, let me interject, it would cause me, instead, subtle joys. The idea, for instance, that I am the only one to know what everyone is looking for and that I have at home an object which kept the police of three countries on the run is a sheer delight. But let's not go into that. At the time, I had not yet found the recipe and I was fretting.

I pulled myself together, of course. What did one man's lie matter in the history of generations? And what pretension to want to drag out into the full light of truth a paltry fraud, lost in the sea of ages like a grain of sand in the ocean! I also told myself that the body's death, to judge from those I had seen, was in itself sufficient punishment that absolved all. Salvation was won (that is, the right to disappear definitively) in the sweat of the death agony. Nonetheless the discomfort grew; death was faithful at my bedside; I used to get up with it every morning, and compliments became more and more unbearable to me. It seemed to me that the falsehood increased with them so inordinately that never again could I put myself right.

A day came when I could bear it no longer. My first reaction was excessive. Since I was a liar, I would reveal this and hurl my duplicity in the face of all those imbeciles, even before they discovered it. Provoked to truth, I would accept the challenge. In order to forestall the laughter, I dreamed of hurling myself into the general derision. In short, it was still a question of dodging judgment. I wanted to put the laughers on my side, or at least to put myself on their side. I contemplated, for instance, jostling the blind on the street; and from the secret, unexpected joy this gave me I recognized how much a part of my soul loathed them; I planned to puncture the tires of invalids' vehicles, to go and shout "Lousy proletarian" under the scaffoldings on which laborers were working, to slap infants in the subway. I dreamed of all that and did none of it, or if I did something of the sort, I have forgotten it. In any case, the very word "justice" gave me strange fits of rage. I continued, of necessity, to use it in my speeches to the court. But I took my revenge by publicly inveighing against the humanitarian spirit; I announced the publication of a manifesto exposing the oppression that the oppressed inflict on decent people. One day while I was eating lobster at a sidewalk restaurant and a beggar bothered me, I called the proprietor to drive him away and loudly approved the words of that administrator of justice: "You are embarrassing people," he said. "Just put yourself in the place of these ladies and gents, after all!" Finally, I used to express, to whoever would listen, my regret that it was no longer possible to act like a certain Russian landowner whose character I admired. He would have a beating administered both to his peasants who bowed to him and to those who didn't bow to him in order to punish a boldness he considered equally impudent in both cases.

However, I recall more serious excesses. I began to write an "Ode to the Police" and an "Apotheosis of the Guillotine." Above all, I used to force myself to visit regularly the special cafés where our professional humanitarian free thinkers gathered. My good past record assured me of a welcome. There, without seeming to, I would let fly a forbidden expression: "Thank God ..." I would say, or more simply: "My God ..." You know what shy little children our café atheists are. A moment of amazement would follow that outrageous expression, they would look at one another dumbfounded, then the tumult would burst forth. Some would flee the café, others would gabble indignantly without listening to anything, and all would writhe in convulsions like the devil in holy water.

You must look on that as childish. Yet maybe there was a more serious reason for those little jokes. I wanted to upset the game and above all to destroy that flattering reputation, the thought of which threw me into a rage. "A man like you ..." people would say sweetly, and I would blanch. I didn't want their esteem because it wasn't general, and how could it be general, since I couldn't share it? Hence it was better to cover everything, judgment and esteem, with a cloak of ridicule. I had to liberate at all cost the feeling that was stifling me. In order to reveal to all eyes what he was made of, I wanted to break open the handsome wax-figure I presented everywhere. For instance, I recall an informal lecture I had to give to a group of young fledgling lawyers. Irritated by the fantastic praises of the president of the bar, who had introduced me, I couldn't resist long. I had begun with the enthusiasm and emotion expected of me, which I had no trouble summoning up on order. But I suddenly began to advise alliance as a system of defense. Not, I said, that alliance perfected by modern inquisitions which judge simultaneously a thief and an honest man in order to crush the second under the crimes of the first. On the contrary, I meant to defend the thief by exposing the crimes of the honest man, the lawyer in this instance. I explained myself very clearly on this point:

"Let us suppose that I have accepted the defense of some touching citizen, a murderer through jealousy. Gentlemen of the jury, consider, I should say, how venial it is to get angry when one sees one's natural goodness put to the test by the malignity of the fair sex. Is it not more serious, on the contrary, to be by chance on this side of the bar, on my own bench, without ever having been good or suffered from being duped? I am free, shielded from your severities, yet who am I? A Louis XIV in pride, a billy goat for lust, a Pharaoh for wrath, a king of laziness. I haven't killed anyone? Not yet, to be sure! But have I not let deserving creatures die? Maybe. And maybe I am ready to do so again. Whereas this man—just look at him—will not do so again. He is still quite amazed to have accomplished what he has." This speech rather upset my young colleagues. After a moment, they made up their minds to laugh at it. They became completely reassured when I got to my conclusion, in which I invoked the human individual and his supposed rights. That day, habit won out.

By repeating these pleasant indiscretions, I merely succeeded in disconcerting opinion somewhat. Not in disarming it, or above all in disarming myself. The amazement I generally encountered in my listeners, their rather reticent embarrassment, somewhat like what you are showing—no, don't protest—did not calm me at all. You see, it is not enough to accuse yourself in order to clear yourself; otherwise, I'd be as innocent as a lamb. One must accuse oneself in a certain way, which it took me considerable time to perfect. I did not discover it until I fell into the most utterly forlorn state. Until then, the laughter continued to drift my way, without my random efforts succeeding in divesting it of its benevolent, almost tender quality that hurt me.

But the sea is rising, it seems to me. It won't be long before our boat leaves; the day is ending. Look, the doves are gathering up there. They are crowding against one another, hardly stirring, and the light is waning. Don't you think we should be silent to enjoy this rather sinister moment? No, I interest you? You are very polite. Moreover, I now run the risk of really interesting you. Before explaining myself on the subject of judges-penitent, I must talk to you of debauchery and of the little-ease.

You are wrong, *cher,* the boat is going at top speed. But the Zuider Zee is a dead sea, or almost. With its flat shores, lost in the fog, there's no saying where it begins or ends. So we are steaming along without any landmark; we can't gauge our speed. We are making progress and yet nothing is changing. It's not navigation but dreaming.

In the Greek archipelago I had the contrary feeling. Constantly new islands would appear on the horizon. Their treeless backbone marked the limit of the sky and their rocky shore contrasted sharply with the sea. No confusion possible; in the sharp light everything was a landmark. And from one island to another, ceaselessly on our little boat, which was nevertheless dawdling, I felt as if we were scudding along, night and day, on the crest of the short, cool waves in a race full of spray and laughter. Since then, Greece itself drifts somewhere within me, on the edge of my memory, tirelessly ... Hold on, I, too, am drifting; I am becoming lyrical! Stop me, *cher,* I beg you.

By the way, do you know Greece? No? So much the better. What should we do there, I ask you? There one has to be pure in heart. Do you know that there male friends walk along the street in pairs holding hands? Yes, the women stay home and you often see a middle-aged, respectable man, sporting mustaches, gravely striding along the sidewalks, his fingers locked in those of his friend. In the Orient likewise, at times? All right. But tell me, would you take my hand in the streets of Paris? Oh, I'm joking. *We* have a sense of decorum; scum makes us stilted. Before appearing in the Greek islands, we should have to wash at length. There the air is chaste and sensual enjoyment as transparent as the sea. And we ...

Let's sit down on these steamer chairs. What a fog! I interrupted myself, I believe, on the way to the little-ease. Yes, I'll tell you what I mean. After having struggled, after having used up all my insolent airs, discouraged by the uselessness of my efforts, I made up my mind to leave the society of men. No, no, I didn't look for a desert island; there *are* no more. I simply took refuge among women. As you know, they don't really condemn any weakness; they would be more inclined to try to humiliate or disarm our strength. This is why woman is the reward, not of the warrior, but of the criminal. She is his harbor, his haven; it is in a woman's bed that he is generally arrested. Is she not all that remains to us of earthly paradise? In distress, I hastened to my natural harbor. But I no longer indulged in pretty speeches. I still gambled a little, out of habit; but invention was lacking. I hesitate to admit it for fear of using a few more naughty words: it seems to me that at that time I felt the need of love. Obscene, isn't it? In any case, I experienced a secret suffering, a sort of privation that made me emptier and allowed me, partly through obligation and partly out of curiosity, to make a few commitments. Inasmuch as I needed to love and be loved, I thought I was in love. In other words, I acted the fool.

I often caught myself asking a question which, as a man of experience, I had always previously avoided. I would hear myself asking: "Do you love me?" You know that it is customary to answer in such cases: "And you?" If I answered yes, I found myself committed beyond my real feelings. If I dared to say no, I ran the risk of ceasing to be loved, and I would suffer therefor. The greater the threat to the feeling in which I had hoped to find calm, the more I demanded that feeling of my partner. Hence I was led to ever more explicit promises and came to expect of my heart an ever more sweeping feeling. Thus I developed a deceptive passion for a charming fool of a woman who had so thoroughly read "true love" stories that she spoke of love with the assurance and conviction of an intellectual announcing the classless society. Such conviction, as you must know, is contagious. I tried myself out at talking likewise of love and eventually convinced myself. At least until she became my mistress and I realized that the "true love" stories, though they taught how to talk of love, did not teach how to make love. After having loved a parrot, I had to go to bed with a serpent. So I looked elsewhere for the love promised by books, which I had never encountered in life.

But I lacked practice. For more than thirty years I had been in love exclusively with myself. What hope was there of losing such a habit? I didn't lose it and remained a trifler in passion. I multiplied the promises. I contracted simultaneous loves as, at an earlier period, I had multiple liaisons. In this way I piled up more misfortunes, for others, than at the time of my fine indifference. Have I told you that in despair my parrot wanted to let herself die of hunger? Fortunately I arrived in time and submitted to holding her hand until she met, on his return from a journey to Bali, the engineer with graying temples who had already been described to her by her favorite weekly. In any case, far from finding myself transported and absolved in the whirlwind—as the saying goes—of passion, I added even more to the weight of my crimes and to my deviation from virtue. As a result, I conceived such a loathing for love that for years I could not hear *"La Vie en rose"* or the *"Liebestod"* without gritting my teeth. I tried accordingly to give up women, in a certain way, and to live in a state of chastity. After all, their friendship ought to satisfy me. But this was tantamount to giving up gambling. Without desire, women bored me beyond all expectation, and obviously I bored them too. No more gambling and no more theater—I was probably in the realm of truth. But truth, *cher ami,* is a colossal bore.

Despairing of love and of chastity, I at last bethought myself of debauchery, a substitute for love, which quiets the laughter, restores silence, and above all, confers immortality. At a certain degree of lucid intoxication, lying late at night between two prostitutes and drained of all desire, hope ceases to be a torture, you see; the mind dominates the whole past, and the pain of living is over forever. In a sense, I had always lived in debauchery, never having ceased wanting to be immortal. Wasn't this the key to my nature and also a result of the great self-love I have told you about? Yes, I was bursting with a longing to be immortal. I was too much in love with myself not to want the precious object of my love never to disappear. Since, in the waking state and with a little self-knowledge, one can see no reason why immortality should be conferred on a salacious monkey, one has to obtain substitutes for that immortality. Because I longed for eternal life, I went to bed with harlots and drank for nights on end. In the morning, to be sure, my mouth was filled with the bitter taste of the mortal state. But, for hours on end, I had soared in bliss. Dare I admit it to you? I still remember with affection certain nights when I used to go to a sordid nightclub to meet a quick-change dancer who honored me with her favors and for whose reputation I even fought one evening with a bearded braggart. Every night I would strut at the bar, in the red light and dust of that earthly paradise, lying fantastically and drinking at length. I would wait for dawn and at last end up in the always unmade bed of my princess, who would indulge mechanically in sex and then sleep without transition. Day would come softly to throw light on this disaster and I would get up and stand motionless in a dawn of glory.

Alcohol and women provided me, I admit, the only solace of which I was worthy. I'll reveal this secret to you, *cher ami,* don't fear to make use of it. Then you'll see that true debauchery is liberating because it creates no obligations. In it you possess only yourself; hence it remains the favorite pastime of the great lovers of their own person. It is a jungle without past or future, without any promise above all, nor any immediate penalty. The places where it is practiced are separated from the world. On entering, one leaves behind fear and hope. Conversation is not obligatory there; what one comes for can be had without words, and often indeed without money. Ah, I beg you, let me pay honor to the unknown and forgotten women who helped me then! Even today, my recollection of them contains something resembling respect.

In any case, I freely took advantage of that liberation. I was even seen in a hotel dedicated to what is called sin, living simultaneously with a mature prostitute and an unmarried girl of the best society. I played the gallant with the first and gave the second an opportunity to learn the realities. Unfortunately the prostitute had a most middle-class nature; she since consented to write her memoirs for a confessions magazine quite open to modern ideas. The girl, for her part, got married to satisfy her unbridled instincts and make use of her remarkable gifts. I am not a little proud likewise to have been admitted as an equal, at that time, by a masculine guild too often reviled. But I'll not insist on that: you know that even very intelligent people glory in being able to empty one bottle more than the next man. I might ultimately have found peace and release in that happy dissipation. But, there too, I encountered an obstacle in myself. This time it was my liver, and a fatigue so dreadful that it hasn't yet left me. One plays at being immortal and after a few weeks one doesn't even know whether or not one can hang on till the next day.

The sole benefit of that experience, when I had given up my nocturnal

exploits, was that life became less painful for me. The fatigue that was gnawing at my body had simultaneously cauterized many raw spots in me. Each
excess decreases vitality, hence suffering. There is nothing frenzied about debauchery, contrary to what is thought. It is but a long sleep. You must have
noticed that men who really suffer from jealousy have no more urgent desire
than to go to bed with the woman they nevertheless think has betrayed them.
Of course, they want to assure themselves once more that their dear treasure
still belongs to them. They want to possess it, as the saying goes. But there is
also the fact that immediately afterward they are less jealous. Physical jealousy
is a result of the imagination at the same time that it is a self-judgment. One
attributes to the rival the nasty thoughts one had oneself in the same circumstances. Fortunately excess of sensual satisfaction weakens both imagination
and judgment. The suffering then lies dormant as long as virility does. For
the same reasons adolescents lose their metaphysical unrest with their first
mistress; and certain marriages, which are merely formalized debauches, become the monotonous hearses of daring and invention. Yes, *cher ami,* bourgeois marriage has put our country into slippers and will soon lead it to the
gates of death.

I am exaggerating? No, but I am straying from the subject. I merely
wanted to tell you the advantage I derived from those months of orgy. I lived
in a sort of fog in which the laughter became so muffled that eventually I
ceased to notice it. The indifference that already had such a hold over me now
encountered no resistance and extended its sclerosis. No more emotions! And
even temper, or rather no temper at all. Tubercular lungs are cured by drying
up and gradually asphyxiate their happy owner. So it was with me as I peacefully died of my cure. I was still living on my work, although my reputation
was seriously damaged by my flights of language and the regular exercise of
my profession compromised by the disorder of my life. It is noteworthy, however, that I aroused less resentment by my nocturnal excesses than by my
verbal provocations. The reference, purely verbal, that I often made to God in
my speeches before the court awakened mistrust in my clients. They probably
feared that heaven could not represent their interests as well as a lawyer invincible when it came to the code of law. Whence it was but a step to conclude that I invoked the divinity in proportion to my ignorance. My clients
took that step and became scarce. Now and then I still argued a case. At
times even, forgetting that I no longer believed in what I was saying, I was a
good advocate. My own voice would lead me on and I would follow it; without really soaring, as I once did, I at least got off the ground and did a lttle
hedgehopping. Outside of my profession, I saw but few people and painfully
kept alive one or two tired liaisons. It even happened that I would spend
purely friendly evenings, without any element of desire, yet with the difference that, resigned to boredom, I scarcely listened to what was being said. I

became a little fatter and at last was able to believe that the crisis was over. Nothing remained but to grow older.

One day, however, during a trip to which I was treating a friend without telling her I was doing so to celebrate my cure, I was aboard an ocean liner— on the upper deck, of course. Suddenly, far off at sea, I perceived a black speck on the steel-gray ocean. I turned away at once and my heart began to beat wildly. When I forced myself to look, the black speck had disappeared. I was on the point of shouting, of stupidly calling for help, when I saw it again. It was one of those bits of refuse that ships leave behind them. Yet I had not been able to endure watching it; for I had thought at once of a drowning person. Then I realized, calmly as you resign yourself to an idea the truth of which you have long known, that that cry which had sounded over the Seine behind me years before had never ceased, carried by the river to the waters of the Channel, to travel throughout the world, across the limitless expanse of the ocean, and that it had waited for me there until the day I had encountered it. I realized likewise that it would continue to await me on seas and rivers, everywhere, in short, where lies the bitter water of my baptism. Here, too, by the way, aren't we on the water? On this flat, monotonous, interminable water whose limits are indistinguishable from those of the land? Is it credible that we shall ever reach Amsterdam? We shall never get out of this immense holy-water fount. Listen. Don't you hear the cries of invisible gulls? If they are crying in our direction, to what are they calling us?

But they are the same gulls that were crying, that were already calling over the Atlantic the day I realized definitively that I was not cured, that I was still cornered and that I had to make shift with it. Ended the glorious life, but ended also the frenzy and the convulsions. I had to submit and admit my guilt. I had to live in the little-ease. To be sure, you are not familiar with that dungeon cell that was called the little-ease in the Middle Ages. In general, one was forgotten there for life. That cell was distinguished from others by ingenious dimensions. It was not high enough to stand up in nor yet wide enough to lie down in. One had to take on an awkward manner and live on the diagonal; sleep was a collapse, and waking a squatting. *Mon cher,* there was genius—and I am weighing my words—in that so simple invention. Every day through the unchanging restriction that stiffened his body, the condemned man learned that he was guilty and that innocence consists in stretching joyously. Can you imagine in that cell a frequenter of summits and upper decks? What? One could live in those cells and still be innocent? Improbable! Highly improbable! Or else my reasoning would collapse. That innocence should be reduced to living hunchbacked—I refuse to entertain for a second such a hypothesis. Moreover, we cannot assert the innocence of anyone, whereas we can state with certainty the guilt of all. Every man testifies to the crime of all the others—that is my faith and my hope.

Believe me, religions are on the wrong track the moment they moralize and fulminate commandments. God is not needed to create guilt or to punish. Our fellow men suffice, aided by ourselves. You were speaking of the Last Judgment. Allow me to laugh respectfully. I shall wait for it resolutely, for I have known what is worse, the judgment of men. For them, no extenuating circumstances; even the good intention is ascribed to crime. Have you at least heard of the spitting-cell, which a nation recently thought up to prove itself the greatest on earth? A walled-up box in which the prisoner can stand without moving. The solid door that locks him in his cement shell stops at chin level. Hence only his face is visible, and every passing jailer spits copiously on it. The prisoner, wedged into his cell, cannot wipe his face, though he is allowed, it is true, to close his eyes. Well, that, *mon cher,* is a human invention. They didn't need God for that little masterpiece.

What of it? Well, God's sole usefulness would be to guarantee innocence, and I am inclined to see religion rather as a huge laundering venture—as it was once but briefly, for exactly three years, and it wasn't called religion. Since then, soap has been lacking, our faces are dirty, and we wipe one another's noses. All dunces, all punished, let's all spit on one another and—hurry! to the little-ease! Each tries to spit first, that's all. I'll tell you a big secret, *mon cher.* Don't wait for the Last Judgment. It takes place every day.

No, it's nothing; I'm merely shivering a little in this damned humidity. We're landing anyway. Here we are. After you. But stay a little, I beg you, and walk home with me. I haven't finished; I must go on. Continuing is what is hard. Say, do you know why he was crucified—the one you are perhaps thinking of at this moment? Well, there were heaps of reasons for that. There are always reasons for murdering a man. On the contrary, it is impossible to justify his living. That's why crime always finds lawyers, and innocence only rarely. But, beside the reasons that have been very well explained to us for the past two thousand years, there was a major one for that terrible agony, and I don't know why it has been so carefully hidden. The real reason is that *he* knew he was not altogether innocent. If he did not bear the weight of the crime he was accused of, he had committed others—even though he didn't know which ones. Did he really not know them? He was at the source, after all; he must have heard of a certain Slaughter of the Innocents. The children of Judea massacred while his parents were taking him to a safe place—why did they die if not because of him? Those blood-spattered soldiers, those infants cut in two filled him with horror. But given the man he was, I am sure he could not forget them. And as for that sadness that can be felt in his every act, wasn't it the incurable melancholy of a man who heard night after night the voice of Rachel weeping for her children and refusing all comfort? The lamentation would rend the night, Rachel would call her children who had been killed for him, and he was still alive!

Knowing what he knew, familiar with everything about man—ah, who would have believed that crime consists less in making others die than in not dying onself!—brought face to face day and night with his innocent crime, he found it too hard for him to hold on and continue. It was better to have done with it, not to defend himself, to die, in order not to be the only one to live, and to go elsewhere where perhaps he would be upheld. He was not upheld, he complained, and as a last straw, he was censored. Yes, it was the third evangelist, I believe, who first suppressed his complaint. "Why hast thou forsaken me?"—it was a seditious cry, wasn't it? Well, then, the scissors! Mind you, if Luke had suppressed nothing, the matter would hardly have been noticed; in any case, it would not have assumed such importance. Thus the censor shouts aloud what he proscribes. The world's order likewise is ambiguous.

Nonetheless, the censored one was unable to carry on. And I know, *cher,* whereof I speak. There was a time when I didn't at any minute have the slightest idea how I could reach the next one. Yes, one can wage war in this world, ape love, torture one's fellow man, or merely say evil of one's neighbor while knitting. But, in certain cases, carrying on, merely continuing, is superhuman. And he was not superhuman, you can take my word for it. He cried aloud his agony and that's why I love him, my friend who died without knowing.

The unfortunate thing is that he left us alone, to carry on, whatever happens, even when we are lodged in the little-ease, knowing in turn what he knew, but incapable of doing what he did and of dying like him. People naturally tried to get some help from his death. After all, it was a stroke of genius to tell us: "You're not a very pretty sight, that's certain! Well, we won't go into the details! We'll just liquidate it all at once, on the cross!" But too many people now climb onto the cross merely to be seen from a greater distance, even if they have to trample somewhat on the one who has been there so long. Too many people have decided to do without generosity in order to practice charity. Oh, the injustice, the rank injustice that has been done him! It wrings my heart!

Good heavens, the habit has seized me again and I'm on the point of making a speech to the court. Forgive me and realize that I have my reasons. Why, a few streets from here there is a museum called Our Lord in the Attic. At the time, they had the catacombs in the attic. After all, the cellars are flooded here. But today—set your mind at rest—their Lord is neither in the attic nor in the cellar. They have hoisted him onto a judge's bench, in the secret of their hearts, and they smite, they judge above all, they judge in his name. He spoke softly to the adulteress: "Neither do I condemn thee!" but that doesn't matter; they condemn without absolving anyone. In the name of the Lord, here is what you deserve. Lord? He, my friend, didn't expect so much. He simply wanted to be loved, nothing more. Of course, there are those who love him, even among Christians. But they are not numerous. He had foreseen that too; he had a sense of humor. Peter, you know, the coward,

Peter denied him: "I know not the man . . . I know not what thou sayest . . . etc." Really, he went too far! And my friend makes a play on words: "Thou art Peter, and upon this rock I will build my church." Irony could go no further, don't you think? But no, they still triumph! "You see, he had said it!" He had said it indeed; he knew the question thoroughly. And then he left forever, leaving them to judge and condemn, with pardon on their lips and the sentence in their hearts.

For it cannot be said there is no more pity; no, good Lord, we never stop talking of it. Simply, no one is ever acquitted any more. On dead innocence the judges swarm, the judges of all species, those of Christ and those of the Antichrist, who are the same anyway, reconciled in the little-ease. For one mustn't blame everything exclusively on the Christians. The others are involved too. Do you know what has become of one of the houses in this city that sheltered Descartes? A lunatic asylum. Yes, general delirium and persecution. We, too, naturally, are obliged to come to it. You have had a chance to observe that I spare nothing, and as for you, I know that you agree in thought. Wherefor, since we are all judges, we are all guilty before one another, all Christs in our mean manner, one by one crucified, always without knowing. We should be at least if I, Clamence, had not found a way out, the only solution, truth at last . . .

No, I am stopping, *cher ami,* fear nothing! Besides, I'm going to leave you, for we are at my door. In solitude and when fatigued, one is after all inclined to take oneself for a prophet. When all is said and done, that's really what I am, having taken refuge in a desert of stones, fogs, and stagnant waters—an empty prophet for shabby times, Elijah without a messiah, choked with fever and alcohol, my back up against this moldy door, my finger raised toward a threatening sky, showering imprecations on lawless men who cannot endure any judgment. For they can't endure it, *très cher,* and that's the whole question. He who clings to a law does not fear the judgment that reinstates him in an order he believes in. But the keenest of human torments is to be judged without a law. Yet we are in that torment. Deprived of their natural curb, the judges, loosed at random, are racing through their job. Hence we have to try to go faster than they, don't we? And it's a real madhouse. Prophets and quacks multiply; they hasten to get there with a good law or a flawless organization before the world is deserted. Fortunately, *I* arrived! I am the end and the beginning; I announce the law. In short, I am a judge-penitent.

Yes, yes, I'll tell you tomorrow what this noble profession consists of. You are leaving the day after tomorrow, so we are in a hurry. Come to my place, will you? Just ring three times. You are going back to Paris? Paris is far; Paris is beautiful; I haven't forgotten it. I remember its twilights at about this same season. Evening falls, dry and rustling, over the roofs blue with smoke, the city rumbles, the river seems to flow backward. Then I used to

wander in the streets. They wander now too, I know! They wander, pretending to hasten toward the tired wife, the forbidding home ... Ah, *mon ami,* do
you know what the solitary creature is like as he wanders in big cities? ...

I'm embarrassed to be in bed when you arrive. It's nothing, just a little fever
that I'm treating with gin. I'm accustomed to these attacks. Malaria, I think,
that I caught at the time I was pope. No, I'm only half joking. I know what
you're thinking: it's very hard to disentangle the true from the false in what
I'm saying. I admit you are right. I myself ... You see, a person I knew used
to divide human beings into three categories: those who prefer having nothing to hide rather than being obliged to lie, those who prefer lying to having
nothing to hide, and finally those who like both lying and the hidden. I'll let
you choose the pigeonhole that suits me.

But what do I care? Don't lies eventually lead to the truth? And don't
all my stories, true or false, tend toward the same conclusion? Don't they all
have the same meaning? So what does it matter whether they are true or false
if, in both cases, they are significant of what I have been and of what I am?
Sometimes it is easier to see clearly into the liar than into the man who tells
the truth. Truth, like light, blinds. Falsehood, on the contrary, is a beautiful
twilight that enhances every object. Well, make of it what you will, but I was
named pope in a prison camp. Sit down, please. You are examining this
room. Bare, to be sure, but clean. A Vermeer, without furniture or copper
pots. Without books either, for I gave up reading some time ago. At one
time, my house was full of half-read books. That's just as disgusting as those
people who cut a piece off a *foie gras* and have the rest thrown out. Anyway, I
have ceased to like anything but confessions, and authors of confessions write
especially to avoid confessing, to tell nothing of what they know. When they
claim to get to the painful admissions, you have to watch out, for they are
about to dress the corpse. Believe me, I know what I'm talking about. So I
put a stop to it. No more books, no more useless objects either; the bare ne-
cessities, clean and polished like a coffin. Besides, these Dutch beds, so hard
and with their immaculate sheets—one dies in them as if already wrapped in a
shroud, embalmed in purity.

You are curious to know my pontifical adventures? Nothing out of the
ordinary, you know. Shall I have the strength to tell you of them? Yes, the
fever is going down. It was all so long ago. It was in Africa where, thanks to

a certain Rommel, war was raging. I wasn't involved in it—no, don't worry. I had already dodged the one in Europe. Mobilized, of course, but I never saw action. In a way, I regret it. Maybe that would have changed many things? The French army didn't need me on the front; it merely asked me to take part in the retreat. A little later I got back to Paris, and the Germans. I was tempted by the Resistance, about which people were beginning to talk just about the time I discovered that I was patriotic. You are smiling? You are wrong. I made my discovery on a subway platform, at the Châtelet station. A dog had strayed into the labyrinth of passageways. Big, wiry-haired, one ear cocked, eyes laughing, he was cavorting and sniffing the passing legs. I have a very old and very faithful attachment for dogs. I like them because they always forgive. I called this one, who hesitated, obviously won over, wagging his tail enthusiastically a few yards ahead of me. Just then, a young German soldier, who was walking briskly, passed me. Having reached the dog, he caressed the shaggy head. Without hesitating, the animal fell in step with the same enthusiasm and disappeared with him. From the resentment and the sort of rage I felt against the German soldier, it was clear to me that my reaction was patriotic. If the dog had followed a French civilian, I'd not even have thought of it. But, on the contrary, I imagined that friendly dog as the mascot of a German regiment and that made me fly into a rage. Hence the test was convincing.

I reached the Southern Zone with the intention of finding out about the Resistance. But once there and having found out, I hesitated. The undertaking struck me as a little mad and, in a word, romantic. I think especially that underground action suited neither my temperament nor my preference for exposed heights. It seemed to me that I was being asked to do some weaving in a cellar, for days and nights on end, until some brutes should come to haul me from hiding, undo my weaving, and then drag me to another cellar to beat me to death. I admired those who indulged in such heroism of the depths, but couldn't imitate them.

So I crossed over to North Africa with the vague intention of getting to London. But in Africa the situation was not clear; the opposing parties seemed to be equally right and I stood aloof. I can see from your manner that I am skipping rather fast, in your opinion, over these details which have a certain significance. Well, let's say that, having judged you at your true value, I am skipping over them so that you will notice them the better. In any case, I eventually reached Tunisia, where a fond friend gave me work. That friend was a very intelligent woman who was involved in the movies. I followed her to Tunis and didn't discover her real business until the days following the Allied landing in Algeria. She was arrested that day by the Germans and I, too, but without having intended it. I don't know what became of her. As for me, no harm was done me and I realized, after considerable anguish, that it was chiefly as a security measure. I was interned near Tripoli in a camp where we suffered from thirst and destitution more than from brutality. I'll not describe it to you. We children of the mid-century don't need a diagram to imagine such places. A hundred and fifty years ago, people became sentimental about lakes and forests. Today we have the lyricism of the prison cell. Hence, I'll leave it to you. You need add but a few details: the heat, the vertical sun, the flies, the sand, the lack of water.

There was a young Frenchman with me who had faith. Yes, it's decidedly a fairy tale! The Du Guesclin type, if you will. He had crossed over from France into Spain to go and fight. The Catholic general had interned him, and having seen that in the Franco camps the chick-peas were, if I may say so, blessed by Rome, he had developed a profound melancholy. Neither the sky of Africa, where he had next landed, nor the leisures of the camp had distracted him from that melancholy. But his reflections, and the sun, too, had somewhat unhinged him. One day when, under a tent that seemed to drip molten lead, the ten or so of us were panting among the flies, he repeated his diatribes against the Roman, as he called him. He looked at us with a wild stare, his face unshaven for days. Bare to the waist and covered with sweat, he drummed with his hands on the visible keyboard of his ribs. He declared to us the need for a new pope who should live among the wretched instead of praying on a throne, and the sooner the better. He stared with wild eyes as he shook his head. "Yes," he repeated, "as soon as possible!" Then he calmed down suddenly and in a dull voice said that we must choose him among us, pick a complete man with his vices and virtues and swear allegiance to him, on the sole condition that he should agree to keep alive, in himself and in others, the community of our sufferings. "Who among us," he asked, "has the most failings?" As a joke, I raised my hand and was the only one to do so. "O.K., Jean-Baptiste will do." No, he didn't say just that because I had another name then. He declared at least that nominating oneself as I had done presupposed also the greatest virtue and proposed electing me. The others agreed, in fun, but with a trace of seriousness all the same. The truth is that Du Guesclin had impressed us. It seems to me that even I was not altogether laughing. To begin with, I considered that my little prophet was right; and then with the sun, the exhausting labor, the struggle for water, we were not up to snuff. In any case, I exercised my pontificate for several weeks, with increasing seriousness.

Of what did it consist? Well, I was something like a group leader or the secretary of a cell. The others, in any case, and even those who lacked faith, got into the habit of obeying me. Du Guesclin was suffering; I administered his suffering. I discovered then that it was not so easy as I thought to be a pope, and I remembered this just yesterday after having given you such a scornful speech on judges, our brothers. The big problem in the camp was the water allotment. Other groups, political or sectarian, had formed, and each prisoner favored his comrades. I was consequently led to favor mine, and this was a little concession to begin with. Even among us, I could not maintain complete equality. According to my comrades' condition, or the work they had to do, I gave an advantage to this or that one. Such distinctions are far-reaching, you can take my word for it. But decidedly I am tired and no longer want to think of that period. Let's just say that I closed the circle the day I drank the water of a dying comrade. No, no, it wasn't Du Guesclin; he was already dead, I believe, for he stinted himself too much. Besides, had he been there, out of love for him I'd have resisted longer, for I loved him—yes, I loved him, or so it seems to me. But I drank the water, that's certain, while convincing myself that the others needed me more than this fellow who was going to die anyway and that I had a duty to keep myself alive for them. Thus, *cher,* empires and churches are born under the sun of death. And in order to correct somewhat what I said yesterday, I am going to tell you the great idea that has come to me while telling all this, which—I'm not sure now—I may have lived or only dreamed. My great idea is that one must forgive the pope. To begin with, he needs it more than anyone else. Secondly, that's the only way to set oneself above him . . .

Did you close the door thoroughly? Yes? Make sure, please. Forgive me, I have the bolt complex. On the point of going to sleep, I can never remember whether or not I pushed the bolt. And every night I must get up to verify. One can be sure of nothing, as I've told you. Don't think that this worry about the bolt is the reaction of a frightened possessor. Formerly I didn't lock my apartment or my car. I didn't lock up my money; I didn't cling to what I owned. To tell the truth, I was a little ashamed to own anything. Didn't I occasionally, in my social remarks, exclaim with conviction: "Property, gentlemen, is murder!" Not being sufficiently big-hearted to share my wealth with a deserving poor man, I left it at the disposal of possible thieves, hoping thus to correct injustice by chance. Today, moreover, I possess nothing. Hence I am not worried about my safety, but about myself and my presence of mind. I am also eager to block the door of the closed little universe of which I am the king, the pope, and the judge.

By the way, will you please open that cupboard? Yes, look at that painting. Don't you recognize it? It is "The Just Judges." That doesn't make you jump? Can it be that your culture has gaps? Yet if you read the papers, you would recall the theft in 1934 in the St. Bavon Cathedral of Ghent, of one of the panels of the famous van Eyck altarpiece, "The Adoration of the Lamb." That panel was called "The Just Judges." It represented judges on horseback coming to adore the sacred animal. It was replaced by an excellent copy, for the original was never found. Well, here it is. No, I had nothing to do with it. A frequenter of *Mexico City*—you had a glimpse of him the other evening—sold it to the ape for a bottle, one drunken evening. I first advised our friend to hang it in a place of honor, and for a long time, while they were being looked for throughout the world, our devout judges sat enthroned at

Mexico City above the drunks and pimps. Then the ape, at my request, put it in custody here. He balked a little at doing so, but he got a fright when I explained the matter to him. Since then, these estimable magistrates form my sole company. At *Mexico City,* above the bar, you saw what a void they left.

Why I did not return the panel? Ah! Ah! You have a policeman's reflex, you do! Well, I'll answer you as I would the state's attorney, if it could ever occur to anyone that this painting had wound up in my room. First, because it belongs not to me but to the proprietor of *Mexico City,* who deserves it as much as the Archbishop of Ghent. Secondly, because among all those who file by "The Adoration of the Lamb" no one could distinguish the copy from the original and hence no one is wronged by my misconduct. Thirdly, because in this way I dominate. False judges are held up to the world's admiration and I alone know the true ones. Fourth, because I thus have a chance of being sent to prison—an attractive idea in a way. Fifth, because those judges are on their way to meet the Lamb, because there is no more lamb or innocence, and because the clever rascal who stole the panel was an instrument of the unknown justice that one ought not to thwart. Finally, because this way everything is in harmony. Justice being definitively separated from innocence—the latter on the cross and the former in the cupboard—I have the way clear to work according to my convictions. With a clear conscience I can practice the difficult profession of judge-penitent, in which I have set myself up after so many blighted hopes and contradictions; and now it is time, since you are leaving, for me to tell you what it is.

Allow me first to sit up so I can breathe more easily. Oh, how weak I am! Lock up my judges, please. As for the profession of judge-penitent, I am practicing it at present. Ordinarily, my offices are at *Mexico City.* But real vocations are carried beyond the place of work. Even in bed, even with a fever, I am functioning. Besides, one doesn't practice this profession, one breathes it constantly. Don't get the idea that I have talked to you at such length for five days just for the fun of it. No, I used to talk through my hat quite enough in the past. Now my words have a purpose. They have the purpose, obviously, of silencing the laughter, of avoiding judgment personally, though there is apparently no escape. Is not the great thing that stands in the way of our escaping it the fact that we are the first to condemn ourselves? Therefore it is essential to begin by extending the condemnation to all, without distinction, in order to thin it out at the start.

No excuses ever, for anyone; that's my principle at the outset. I deny the good intention, the respectable mistake, the indiscretion, the extenuating circumstance. With me there is no giving of absolution or blessing. Everything is simply totted up, and then: "It comes to so much. You are an evildoer, a satyr, a congenital liar, a homosexual, an artist, etc." Just like that. Just as flatly. In philosophy as in politics, I am for any theory that refuses to grant man innocence and for any practice that treats him as guilty. You see in me, *très cher,* an enlightened advocate of slavery.

Without slavery, as a matter of fact, there is no definitive solution. I very soon realized that. Once upon a time, I was always talking of freedom. At breakfast I used to spread it on my toast, I used to chew it all day long, and in company my breath was delightfully redolent of freedom. With that key word I would bludgeon whoever contradicted me; I made it serve my desires and my power. I used to whisper it in bed in the ear of my sleeping mates and it helped me to drop them. I would slip it . . . Tchk! Tchk! I am getting excited and losing all sense of proportion. After all, I did on occasion make a more disinterested use of freedom and even—just imagine my naïveté—defended it two or three times without of course going so far as to die for it, but nevertheless taking a few risks. I must be forgiven such rash acts; I didn't know what I was doing. I didn't know that freedom is not a reward or a decoration that is celebrated with champagne. Nor yet a gift, a box of dainties designed to make you lick your chops. Oh, no! It's a chore, on the contrary, and a long-distance race, quite solitary and very exhausting. No champagne, no friends raising their glasses as they look at you affectionately. Alone in a forbidding room, alone in the prisoner's box before the judges, and alone to decide in face of oneself or in the face of others' judgment. At the end of all freedom is a court sentence; that's why freedom is too heavy to bear, especially when you're down with a fever, or are distressed, or love nobody.

Ah, *mon cher,* for anyone who is alone, without God and without a master, the weight of days is dreadful. Hence one must choose a master, God being out of style. Besides, that word has lost its meaning; it's not worth the risk of shocking anyone. Take our moral philosophers, for instance, so serious, loving their neighbor and all the rest—nothing distinguishes them from Christians, except that they don't preach in churches. What, in your opinion, keeps them from becoming converted? Respect perhaps, respect for men; yes, human respect. They don't want to start a scandal, so they keep their feelings to themselves. For example, I knew an atheistic novelist who used to pray every night. That didn't stop anything: how he gave it to God in his books! What a dusting off, as someone or other would say. A militant freethinker to whom I spoke of this raised his hands—with no evil intention, I assure you—to heaven: "You're telling me nothing new," that apostle sighed, "they are all like that." According to him, eighty per cent of our writers, if only they could avoid signing, would write and hail the name of God. But they sign, according to him, because they love themselves, and they hail nothing at all because they loathe themselves. Since, nevertheless, they cannot keep themselves from judging, they make up for it by moralizing. In short, their satanism is virtuous. An odd epoch, indeed! It's not at all surprising that minds are confused and that one of my friends, an atheist when he was a model husband, got converted when he became an adulterer!

Ah, the little sneaks, play actors, hypocrites—and yet so touching! Believe me, they all are, even when they set fire to heaven. Whether they are atheists or churchgoers, Muscovites or Bostonians, all Christians from father to son. But it so happens that there is no more father, no more rule! They are free and hence have to shift for themselves; and since they don't want freedom or its judgments, they ask to be rapped on the knuckles, they invent dreadful rules, they rush out to build piles of faggots to replace churches. Savonarolas, I tell you. But they believe solely in sin, never in grace. They think of it, to be sure. Grace is what they want—acceptance, surrender, happiness, and maybe, for they are sentimental too, betrothal, the virginal bride, the upright man, the organ music. Take me, for example, and I am not sentimental—do you know what I used to dream of? A total love of the whole heart and body, day and night, in an uninterrupted embrace, sensual enjoyment and mental excitement—all lasting five years and ending in death. Alas!

So, after all, for want of betrothal or uninterrupted love, it will be marriage, brutal marriage, with power and the whip. The essential is that everything should become simple, as for the child, that every act should be ordered, that good and evil should be arbitrarily, hence obviously, pointed out. And I agree, however Sicilian and Javanese I may be and not at all Christian, though I feel friendship for the first Christian of all. But on the bridges of Paris I, too, learned that I was afraid of freedom. So hurray for the master, whoever he may be, to take the place of heaven's law. "Our Father who art provisionally here . . . Our guides, our delightfully severe masters, O cruel and beloved leaders . . ." In short, you see, the essential is to cease being free and to obey, in repentance, a greater rogue than oneself. When we are all guilty, that will be democracy. Without counting, *cher ami,* that we must take revenge for having to die alone. Death is solitary, whereas slavery is collective. The others get theirs, too, and at the same time as we—that's what counts. All together at last, but on our knees and heads bowed.

Isn't it good likewise to live like the rest of the world, and for that doesn't the rest of the world have to be like me? Threat, dishonor, police are the sacraments of that resemblance. Scorned, hunted down, compelled, I can then show what I am worth, enjoy what I am, be natural at last. This is why, *très cher,* after having solemnly paid my respects to freedom, I decided on the sly that it had to be handed over without delay to anyone who comes along. And every time I can, I preach in my church of *Mexico City,* I invite the good people to submit to authority and humbly to solicit the comforts of slavery, even if I have to present it as true freedom.

But I'm not being crazy; I'm well aware that slavery is not immediately realizable. It will be one of the blessings of the future, that's all. In the meantime, I must get along with the present and seek at least a provisional solution. Hence I had to find another means of extending judgment to everybody in order to make it weigh less heavily on my own shoulders. I found the means. Open the window a little, please; it's frightfully hot. Not too much, for I am cold also. My idea is both simple and fertile. How to get everyone involved in order to have the right to sit calmly on the outside myself? Should I climb up to the pulpit, like many of my illustrious contemporaries, and curse humanity? Very dangerous, that is! One day, or one night, laughter bursts out without a warning. The judgment you are passing on others eventually snaps back in your face, causing some damage. And so what? you ask. Well, here's the stroke of genius. I discovered that while waiting for the masters with their rods, we should, like Copernicus, reverse the reasoning to win out. Inasmuch as one couldn't condemn others without immediately judging oneself, one had to overwhelm oneself to have the right to judge others. Inasmuch as every judge some day ends up as a penitent, one had to travel the road in the opposite direction and practice the profession of penitent to be able to end up as a judge. You follow me? Good. But to make myself even clearer, I'll tell you how I operate.

First I closed my law office, left Paris, traveled. I aimed to set up under another name in some place where I shouldn't lack for a practice. There are many in the world, but chance, convenience, irony, and also the necessity for a certain mortification made me choose a capital of waters and fogs, girdled by canals, particularly crowded, and visited by men from all corners of the earth. I set up my office in a bar in the sailors' quarter. The clientele of a port-town is varied. The poor don't go into the luxury districts, whereas eventually the gentlefolk always wind up at least once, as you have seen, in the disreputable places. I lie in wait particularly for the bourgeois, and the straying bourgeois at that; it's with him that I get my best results. Like a virtuoso with a rare violin, I draw my subtlest sounds from him.

So I have been practicing my useful profession at *Mexico City* for some time. It consists to begin with, as you know from experience, in indulging in public confession as often as possible. I accuse myself up and down. It's not hard, for I now have acquired a memory. But let me point out that I don't accuse myself crudely, beating my breast. No, I navigate skillfully, multiplying distinctions and digressions, too—in short, I adapt my words to my listener and lead him to go me one better. I mingle what concerns me and what concerns others. I choose the features we have in common, the experiences we have endured together, the failings we share—good form, in other words, the man of the hour as he is rife in me and in others. With all that I construct a portrait which is the image of all and of no one. A mask, in short, rather like those carnival masks which are both lifelike and stylized, so that they make people say: "Why, surely I've met him!" When the portrait is finished, as it is this evening, I show it with great sorrow: "This, alas, is what I am!" The prosecutor's charge is finished. But at the same time the portrait I hold out to my contemporaries becomes a mirror.

Covered with ashes, tearing my hair, my face scored by clawing, but with piercing eyes, I stand before all humanity recapitulating my shames without losing sight of the effect I am producing, and saying: "I was the lowest of the low." Then imperceptibly I pass from the "I" to the "we." When I get to "This is what we are," the trick has been played and I can tell them off. I am like them, to be sure; we are in the soup together. However, I have a superiority in that I know it and this gives me the right to speak. You see the advantage, I am sure. The more I accuse myself, the more I have a right to judge you. Even better, I provoke you into judging yourself, and this relieves me of that much of the burden. Ah, *mon cher,* we are odd, wretched creatures, and if we merely look back over our lives, there's no lack of occasions to amaze and horrify ourselves. Just try. I shall listen, you may be sure, to your own confession with a great feeling of fraternity.

Don't laugh! Yes, you are a difficult client; I saw that at once. But you'll come to it inevitably. Most of the others are more sentimental than intelligent; they are disconcerted at once. With the intelligent ones it takes time. It is enough to explain the method fully to them. They don't forget it; they reflect. Sooner or later, half as a game and half out of emotional upset, they give up and tell all. *You* are not only intelligent, you look polished by use. Admit, however, that today you feel less pleased with yourself than you felt five days ago? Now I shall wait for you to write me or come back. For you will come back, I am sure! You'll find me unchanged. And why should I change, since I have found the happiness that suits me? I have accepted duplicity instead of being upset about it. On the contrary, I have settled into it and found there the comfort I was looking for throughout life. I was wrong, after all, to tell you that the essential was to avoid judgment. The essential is being able to permit oneself everything, even if, from time to time, one has to profess vociferously one's own infamy. I permit myself everything again, and without the laughter this time. I haven't changed my way of life; I continue to love myself and to make use of others. Only, the confession of my crimes allows me to begin again lighter in heart and to taste a double enjoyment, first of my nature and secondly of a charming repentance.

Since finding my solution, I yield to everything, to women, to pride, to boredom, to resentment, and even to the fever that I feel delightfully rising at this moment. I dominate at last, but forever. Once more I have found a height to which I am the only one to climb and from which I can judge everybody. At long intervals, on a really beautiful night I occasionally hear a distant laugh and again I doubt. But quickly I crush everything, people and things, under the weight of my own infirmity, and at once I perk up.

So I shall await your respects at *Mexico City* as long as necessary. But remove this blanket; I want to breathe. You will come, won't you? I'll show you the details of my technique, for I feel a sort of affection for you. You will see me teaching them night after night that they are vile. This very evening, moreover, I shall resume. I can't do without it or deny myself those moments when one of them collapses, with the help of alcohol, and beats his breast. Then I grow taller, *très cher,* I grow taller, I breathe freely, I am on the mountain, the plain stretches before my eyes. How intoxicating to feel like God the Father and to hand out definitive testimonials of bad character and habits. I sit enthroned among my bad angels at the summit of the Dutch heaven and I watch ascending toward me, as they issue from the fogs and the water, the multitude of the Last Judgment. They rise slowly; I already see the first of them arriving. On his bewildered face, half hidden by his hand, I read the melancholy of the common condition and the despair of not being able to escape it. And as for me, I pity without absolving, I understand without forgiving, and above all, I feel at last that I am being adored!

Yes, I am moving about. How could I remain in bed like a good patient? I must be higher than you, and my thoughts lift me up. Such nights, or such mornings rather (for the fall occurs at dawn), I go out and walk briskly along the canals. In the livid sky the layers of feathers become thinner, the doves move a little higher, and above the roofs a rosy light announces a new day of my creation. On the Damrak the first streetcar sounds its bell in the damp air and marks the awakening of life at the extremity of this Europe where, at the same moment, hundreds of millions of men, my subjects, painfully slip out of bed, a bitter taste in their mouths, to go to a joyless work. Then, soaring over this whole continent which is under my sway without knowing it, drinking in the absinthe-colored light of breaking day, intoxicated with evil words, I am happy—I am happy, I tell you, I won't let you think I'm not happy, I am happy unto death! Oh, sun, beaches, and the islands in the path of the trade winds, youth whose memory drives one to despair!

I'm going back to bed; forgive me. I fear I got worked up; yet I'm not weeping. At times one wanders, doubting the facts, even when one has discovered the secrets of the good life. To be sure, my solution is not the ideal. But when you don't like your own life, when you know that you must change lives, you don't have any choice, do you? What can one do to become another? Impossible. One would have to cease being anyone, forget oneself for someone else, at least once. But how? Don't bear down too hard on me. I'm like that old beggar who wouldn't let go of my hand one day on a café terrace: "Oh, sir," he said, "it's not just that I'm no good, but you lose track of the light." Yes, we have lost track of the light, the mornings, the holy innocence of those who forgive themselves.

Look, it's snowing! Oh, I must go out! Amsterdam asleep in the white night, the dark jade canals under the little snow-covered bridges, the empty streets, my muffled steps—there will be purity, even if fleeting, before tomorrow's mud. See the huge flakes drifting against the windowpanes. It must be the doves, surely. They finally make up their minds to come down, the little dears; they are covering the waters and the roofs with a thick layer of feathers;

they are fluttering at every window. What an invasion! Let's hope they are bringing good news. Everyone will be saved, eh?—and not only the elect. Possessions and hardships will be shared and you, for example, from today on you will sleep every night on the ground for me. The whole shooting match, eh? Come now, admit that you would be flabbergasted if a chariot came down from heaven to carry me off, or if the snow suddenly caught fire. You don't believe it? Nor do I. But still I must go out.

All right, all right, I'll be quiet; don't get upset! Don't take my emotional outbursts or my ravings too seriously. They are controlled. Say, now that you are going to talk to me about yourself, I shall find out whether or not one of the objectives of my absorbing confession is achieved. I always hope, in fact, that my interlocutor will be a policeman and that he will arrest me for the theft of "The Just Judges." For the rest—am I right?—no one can arrest me. But as for that theft, it falls within the provisions of the law and I have arranged everything so as to make myself an accomplice: I am harboring that painting and showing it to whoever wants to see it. You would arrest me then; that would be a good beginning. Perhaps the rest would be taken care of subsequently; I would be decapitated, for instance, and I'd have no more fear of death; I'd be saved. Above the gathered crowd, you would hold up my still warm head, so that they could recognize themselves in it and I could again dominate—an exemplar. All would be consummated; I should have brought to a close, unseen and unknown, my career as a false prophet crying in the wilderness and refusing to come forth.

But of course you are not a policeman; that would be too easy. What? Ah, I suspected as much, you see. That strange affection I felt for you had sense to it then. In Paris you practice the noble profession of lawyer! I sensed that we were of the same species. Are we not all alike, constantly talking and to no one, forever up against the same questions although we know the answers in advance? Then please tell me what happened to you one night on the quays of the Seine and how you managed never to risk your life. You yourself utter the words that for years have never ceased echoing through my nights and that I shall at last say through your mouth: "O young woman, throw yourself into the water again so that I may a second time have the chance of saving both of us!" A second time, eh, what a risky suggestion! Just suppose, *cher maître*, that we should be taken literally? We'd have to go through with it. Brr . . . ! The water's so cold! But let's not worry! It's too late now. It will always be too late. Fortunately!

WILLIAM FAULKNER

Old Man

Once (it was in Mississippi, in May, in the flood year 1927) there were two convicts. One of them was about twenty-five, tall, lean, flat-stomached, with a sunburned face and Indian-black hair and pale, china-colored outraged eyes— an outrage directed not at the men who had foiled his crime, not even at the lawyers and judges who had sent him here, but at the writers, the uncorporeal names attached to the stories, the paper novels—the Diamond Dicks and Jesse Jameses and such—whom he believed had led him into his present predicament through their own ignorance and gullibility regarding the medium in which they dealt and took money for, in accepting information on which they placed the stamp of verisimilitude and authenticity (this so much the more criminal since there was no sworn notarised statement attached and hence so much the quicker would the information be accepted by one who expected the same unspoken good faith, demanding, asking, expecting no certification, which he extended along with the dime or fifteen cents to pay for it) and retailed for money and which on actual application proved to be impractical and (to the convict) criminally false; there would be times when he would halt his mule and plow in midfurrow (there is no walled penitentiary in Mississippi; it is a cotton plantation which the convicts work under the rifles and shotguns of guards and trusties) and muse with a kind of enraged impotence, fumbling among the rubbish left him by his one and only experience with courts and law, fumbling until the meaningless and verbose shibboleth took form at last (himself seeking justice at the same blind fount where he had met justice and been hurled back and down): Using the mails to defraud: who felt that he had been defrauded by the third-class mail system not of crass and stupid money which he did not particularly want anyway, but of liberty and honor and pride.

He was in for fifteen years (he had arrived shortly after his nineteenth birthday) for attempted train robbery. He had laid his plans in advance, he had followed his printed (and false) authority to the letter; he had saved the paper-backs for two years, reading and re-reading them, memorising them, comparing and weighing story and method against story and method, taking the good from each and discarding the dross as his workable plan emerged, keeping his mind open to make the subtle last-minute changes, without haste and without impatience, as the newer pamphlets appeared on their appointed days as a conscientious dressmaker makes the subtle alterations in a court presentation costume as the newer bulletins appear. And then when the day came, he did not even have a chance to go through the coaches and collect the watches and the rings, the brooches and the hidden money-belts, because he had been captured as soon as he entered the express car where the safe and the gold would be. He had shot no one because the pistol which they took away from him was not that kind of a pistol although it was loaded; later he admitted to the District Attorney that he had got it, as well as the dark lantern in which a candle burned and the black handkerchief to wear over the face, by peddling among his pinehill neighbors subscriptions to the *Detectives' Gazette.* So now from time to time (he had ample leisure for it) he mused with that raging impotence, because there was something else he could not tell them at the trial, did not know how to tell them. It was not the money he had wanted. It was not riches, not the crass loot; that would have been merely a bangle to wear upon the breast of his pride like the Olympic runner's amateur medal—a symbol, a badge to show that he too was the best at his chosen gambit in the living and fluid world of his time. So that at times as he trod the richly shearing black earth behind his plow or with a hoe thinned the sprouting cotton and corn or lay on his sullen back in his bunk after supper, he cursed in a harsh steady unrepetitive stream, not at the living men who had put him where he was but at what he did not even know were pen-names, did not even know were not actual men but merely the designations of shades who had written about shades.

The second convict was short and plump. Almost hairless, he was quite white. He looked like something exposed to light by turning over rotting logs or planks and he too carried (though not in his eyes like the first convict) a sense of burning and impotent outrage. So it did not show on him and hence none knew it was there. But then nobody knew very much about him, including the people who had sent him here. His outrage was directed at no printed word but at the paradoxical fact that he had been forced to come here of his own free choice and will. He had been forced to choose between the Mississippi State penal farm and the Federal Penitentiary at Atlanta, and the fact that he, who resembled a hairless and pallid slug, had chosen the out-of-doors and the sunlight was merely another manifestation of the close-guarded and solitary enigma of his character, as something recognisable roils momentarily into view from beneath stagnant and opaque water, then sinks again. None of his fellow prisoners knew what his crime had been, save that he was in for a hundred and ninety-nine years—this incredible and impossible period of punishment or restraint itself carrying a vicious and fabulous quality which indicated that his reason for being here was such that the very men, the paladins and pillars of justice and equity who had sent him here had during that moment become blind apostles not of mere justice but of all human decency, blind instruments not of equity but of all human outrage and vengeance, acting in a savage personal concert, judge, lawyer and jury, which certainly abrogated justice and possibly even law. Possibly only the Federal and State's Attorneys knew what the crime actually was. There had been a woman in it and a stolen automobile transported across a State line, a filling station robbed and the attendant shot to death. There had been a second man in the car at the time and anyone could have looked once at the convict (as the two attorneys did) and known he would not even have had the synthetic courage of alcohol to pull trigger on anyone. But he and the woman and the stolen car had been captured while the second man, doubtless the actual murderer, had escaped, so that, brought to bay at last in the State's Attorney's office, harried, dishevelled and snarling, the two grimly implacable and viciously gleeful attorneys in his front and the now raging woman held by two policemen in the anteroom in his rear, he was given his choice. He could be tried in Federal Court under the Mann Act and for the automobile, that is, by electing to pass through the anteroom where the woman raged he could take his chances on the lesser crime in Federal Court, or by accepting a sentence for manslaughter in the State Court he would be permitted to quit the room by a back entrance, without having to pass the woman. He had chosen; he stood at the bar and heard a judge (who looked down at him as if the District Attorney actually had turned over a rotten plank with his toe and exposed him) sentence him to a hundred and ninety-nine years at the State Farm. Thus (he had ample leisure too; they had tried to teach him to plow and had failed, they had put him in the blacksmith shop and the foreman trusty himself had asked to have him removed: so that now, in a long apron like a woman, he cooked and swept and dusted in the deputy wardens' barracks) he too mused at times with that sense of impotence and outrage though it did not show on him as on the first convict since he leaned on no halted broom to do it and so none knew it was there.

It was this second convict who, toward the end of April, began to read aloud to the others from the daily newspapers when, chained ankle to ankle and herded by armed guards, they had come up from the fields and had eaten supper and were gathered in the bunkhouse. It was the Memphis newspaper which the deputy wardens had read at breakfast; the convict read aloud from it to his companions who could have had but little active interest in the outside world, some of whom could not have read it for themselves at all and did not even know where the Ohio and Missouri river basins were, some of whom had never seen the Mississippi River although for past periods ranging from a few days to ten and twenty and thirty years (and for future periods ranging from a few months to life) they had plowed and planted and eaten and slept beneath the shadow of the levee itself, knowing only that there was water beyond it from hearsay and because now and then they heard the whistles of steamboats from beyond it and, during the last week or so had seen the stacks and pilot houses moving along the sky sixty feet above their heads.

But they listened, and soon even those who like the taller convict had probably never before seen more water than a horse pond would hold knew what thirty feet on a river gauge at Cairo or Memphis meant and could (and did) talk glibly of sandboils. Perhaps what actually moved them were the accounts of the conscripted levee gangs, mixed blacks and whites working in double shifts against the steadily rising water; stories of men, even though they were negroes, being forced like themselves to do work for which they received no other pay than coarse food and a place in a mudfloored tent to sleep on—stories, pictures, which emerged from the shorter convict's reading voice: the mudsplashed white men with the inevitable shotguns, the antlike lines of negroes carrying sandbags, slipping and crawling up the steep face of the revetment to hurl their futile ammunition into the face of a flood and return for more. Or perhaps it was more than this. Perhaps they watched the approach of the disaster with that same amazed and incredulous hope of the slaves—the lions and bears and elephants, the grooms and bathmen and pastrycooks—who watched the mounting flames of Rome from Ahenobarbus' gardens. But listen they did and presently it was May and the wardens' newspaper began to talk in headlines two inches tall—those black staccato slashes of ink which, it would amost seem, even the illiterate should be able to read: *Crest Passes Memphis at Midnight 4000 Homeless in White River Basin Governor Calls out National Guard Martial Law Declared in Following Counties Red Cross Train with President Hoover Leaves Washington Tonight;* then, three evenings later (It had been raining all day—not the vivid brief thunderous downpours of April and May, but the slow steady gray rain of November and December before a cold north wind. The men had not gone to the fields at all during the day, and the very second-hand optimism of the almost twenty-four-hour-old news seemed to contain its own refutation.): *Crest Now Below Memphis 22,000 Refugees Safe at Vicksburg Army Engineers Say Levees Will Hold.*

"I reckon that means it will bust tonight," one convict said.

"Well, maybe this rain will hold on until the water gets here," a second said. They all agreed to this because what they meant, the living unspoken thought among them, was that if the weather cleared, even though the levees broke and the flood moved in upon the Farm itself, they would have to return to the fields and work, which they would have had to do. There was nothing paradoxical in this, although they could not have expressed the reason for it which they instinctively perceived: that the land they farmed and the substance they produced from it belonged neither to them who worked it nor to those who forced them at guns' point to do so, that as far as either—convicts or guards—were concerned, it could have been pebbles they put into the ground and papier-mâché cotton- and corn-sprouts which they thinned. So it was that, what between the sudden wild hoping and the idle day and the evening's headlines, they were sleeping restlessly beneath the sound of the rain on the tin roof when at midnight the sudden glare of the electric bulbs and the guards' voices waked them and they heard the throbbing of the waiting trucks.

"Turn out of there!" the deputy shouted. He was fully dressed—rubber boots, slicker and shotgun. "The levee went out at Mound's Landing an hour ago. Get up out of it!"

When the belated and streaming dawn broke the two convicts, along with twenty others, were in a truck. A trusty drove, two armed guards sat in the cab with him. Inside the high, stall-like topless body the convicts stood, packed like matches in an upright box or like the pencil-shaped ranks of cordite in a shell, shackled by the ankles to a single chain which wove among the motionless feet and swaying legs and a clutter of picks and shovels among which they stood, and was riveted by both ends to the steel body of the truck.

Then and without warning they saw the flood about which the plump convict had been reading and they listening for two weeks or more. The road ran south. It was built on a raised levee, known locally as a dump, about eight feet above the flat surrounding land, bordered on both sides by the barrow pits from which the earth of the levee had been excavated. These barrow pits had held water all winter from the fall rains, not to speak of the rain of yesterday, but now they saw that the pit on either side of the road had vanished and instead there lay a flat still sheet of brown water which extended into the fields beyond the pits, ravelled out into long motionless shreds in the bottom of the plow furrows and gleaming faintly in the gray light like the bars of a prone and enormous grating. And then (the truck was moving at good speed) as they watched quietly (they had not been talking much anyway but now they were all silent and quite grave, shifting and craning as one to look soberly off to the west side of the road) the crests of the furrows vanished too and they now looked at a single perfectly flat and motionless steel-colored sheet in which the telephone poles and the straight hedgerows which marked section lines seemed to be fixed and rigid as though set in concrete.

It was perfectly motionless, perfectly flat. It looked, not innocent, but bland. It looked almost demure. It looked as if you could walk on it. It looked so still that they did not realise it possessed motion until they came to the first bridge. There was a ditch under the bridge, a small stream, but ditch and stream were both invisible now, indicated only by the rows of cypress and bramble which marked its course. Here they both saw and heard movement—the slow profound eastward and upstream ("It's running backward," one convict said quietly.) set of the still rigid surface, from beneath which came a deep faint subaquean rumble which (though none in the truck could have made the comparison) sounded like a subway train passing far beneath the street and which inferred a terrific and secret speed. It was as if the water itself were in three strata, separate and distinct, the bland and unhurried surface bearing a frothy scum and a miniature flotsam of twigs and screening as though by vicious calculation the rush and fury of the flood itself, and beneath this in turn the original stream, trickle, murmuring along in the opposite direction, following undisturbed and unaware its appointed course and serving its Lilliputian end, like a thread of ants between the rails on which an express train passes, they (the ants) as unaware of the power and fury as if it were a cyclone crossing Saturn.

Now there was water on both sides of the road and now, as if once they had become aware of movement in the water the water seemed to have given over deception and concealment, they seemed to be able to watch it rising up the flanks of the dump; trees which a few miles back had stood on tall trunks above the water now seemed to burst from the surface at the level of the lower branches like decorative shrubs on barbered lawns. The truck passed a negro cabin. The water was up to the window ledges. A woman clutching two children squtted on the ridgepole, a man and a halfgrown youth, standing waist-deep, were hoisting a squealing pig onto the slanting roof of a barn, on the ridgepole of which sat a row of chickens and a turkey. Near the barn was a haystack on which a cow stood tied by a rope to the center pole and bawling steadily; a yelling negro boy on a saddleless mule which he flogged steadily, his legs clutching the mule's barrel and his body leaned to the drag of a rope attached to a second mule, approached the haystack, splashing and floundering. The woman on the housetop began to shriek at the passing truck, her voice carrying faint and melodious across the brown water, becoming fainter and fainter as the truck passed and went on, ceasing at last, whether because of distance or because she had stopped screaming those in the truck did not know.

Then the road vanished. There was no perceptible slant to it yet it had slipped abruptly beneath the brown surface with no ripple, no ridgy demarcation, like a flat thin blade slipped obliquely into flesh by a delicate hand, annealed into the water without disturbance, as if it had existed so for years, had been built that way. The truck stopped. The trusty descended from the cab and came back and dragged two shovels from among their feet, the blades clashing against the serpentining of the chain about their ankles. "What is it?" one said. "What are you fixing to do?" The trusty didn't answer. He returned to the cab, from which one of the guards had descended, without his shotgun. He and the trusty, both in hip boots and each carrying a shovel, advanced into the water, gingerly, probing and feeling ahead with the shovel handles. The same convict spoke again. He was a middle-aged man with a wild thatch of iron-gray hair and a slightly mad face. "What the hell are they doing?" he said. Again nobody answered him. The truck moved, on into the water, behind the guard and the trusty, beginning to push ahead of itself a thick slow viscid ridge of chocolate water. Then the gray-haired convict began to scream. "God damn it, unlock the chain!" He began to struggle, thrashing violently about him, striking at the men nearest him until he reached the cab, the roof of which he now hammered on with his fists, screaming. "God damn it, unlock us! Unlock us! Son of a bitch!" he screamed, addressing no one. "They're going to drown us! Unlock the chain!" But for all the answer he got the men within radius of his voice might have been dead. The truck crawled on, the guard and the trusty feeling out the road ahead with the reversed shovels, the second guard at the wheel, the twenty-two convicts packed like sardines into the truck bed and padlocked by the ankles to the body of the truck itself. They crossed another bridge—two delicate and paradoxical iron railings slanting out of the water, travelling parallel to it for a distance, then slanting down into it again with an outrageous quality almost significant yet apparently meaningless like something in a dream not quite nightmare. The truck crawled on.

Along toward noon they came to a town, their destination. The streets were paved; now the wheels of the truck made a sound like tearing silk. Moving faster now, the guard and the trusty in the cab again, the truck even had a slight bone in its teeth, its bow-wave spreading beyond the submerged sidewalks and across the adjacent lawns, lapping against the stoops and porches of houses where people stood among piles of furniture. They passed through the business district; a man in hip boots emerged knee-deep in water from a store, dragging a flat-bottomed skiff containing a steel safe.

At last they reached the railroad. It crossed the street at right angles, cutting the town in two. It was on a dump, a levee, also, eight or ten feet above the town itself; the street ran blankly into it and turned at right angles beside a cotton compress and a loading platform on stilts at the level of a freight car door. On this platform was a khaki army tent and a uniformed National Guard sentry with a rifle and bandolier.

The truck turned and crawled out of the water and up the ramp which cotton wagons used and where trucks and private cars filled with household goods came and unloaded onto the platform. They were unlocked from the chain in the truck and shackled ankle to ankle in pairs they mounted the platform and into an apparently inextricable jumble of beds and trunks, gas and electric stoves, radios and tables and chairs and framed pictures which a chain of negroes under the eye of an unshaven white man in muddy corduroy and hip boots carried piece by piece into the compress, at the door of which another guardsman stood with his rifle, they (the convicts) not stopping here but herded on by the two guards with their shotguns, into the dim and cavernous building where among the piled heterogeneous furniture the ends of cotton bales and the mirrors on dressers and sideboards gleamed with an identical mute and unreflecting concentration of pallid light.

They passed on through, onto the loading platform where the army tent and the first sentry were. They waited here. Nobody told them for what nor why. While the two guards talked with the sentry before the tent the convicts sat in a line along the edge of the platform like buzzards on a fence, their shackled feet dangling above the brown motionless flood out of which the railroad embankment rose, pristine and intact, in a kind of paradoxical denial and repudiation of change and portent, not talking, just looking quietly across the track to where the other half of the amputated town seemed to float, house shrub and tree, ordered and pageant-like and without motion, upon the limitless liquid plain beneath the thick gray sky.

After a while the other four trucks from the Farm arrived. They came up, bunched closely, radiator to tail light, with their four separate sounds of tearing silk and vanished beyond the compress. Presently the ones on the platform heard the feet, the mute clashing of the shackles, the first truckload emerged from the compress, the second, the third; there were more than a hundred of them now in their bed-ticking overalls and jumpers and fifteen or twenty guards with rifles and shotguns. The first lot rose and they mingled, paired, twinned by their clanking and clashing umbilicals; then it began to rain, a slow steady gray drizzle like November instead of May. Yet not one of them made any move toward the open door of the compress. They did not even look toward it, with longing or hope or without it. If they thought at all, they doubtless knew that the available space in it would be needed for furniture, even if it were not already filled. Or perhaps they knew that, even if there were room in it, it would not be for them, not that the guards would wish them to get wet but that the guards would not think about getting them out of the rain. So they just stopped talking and with their jumper collars turned up and shackled in braces like dogs at a field trial they stood, immobile, patient, almost ruminant, their backs turned to the rain as sheep and cattle do.

After another while they became aware that the number of soldiers had increased to a dozen or more, warm and dry beneath rubberised ponchos, there was an officer with a pistol at his belt, then and without making any move toward it, they began to smell food and, turning to look, saw an army field kitchen set up just inside the compress door. But they made no move, they waited until they were herded into line, they inched forward, their heads lowered and patient in the rain, and received each a bowl of stew, a mug of coffee, two slices of bread. They ate this in the rain. They did not sit down because the platform was wet, they squatted on their heels as country men do, hunching forward, trying to shield the bowls and mugs into which nevertheless the rain splashed steadily as into miniature ponds and soaked, invisible and soundless, into the bread.

After they had stood on the platform for three hours, a train came for them. Those nearest the edge saw it, watched it—a passenger coach apparently running under its own power and trailing a cloud of smoke from no visible stack, a cloud which did not rise but instead shifted slowly and heavily aside and lay upon the surface of the aqueous earth with a quality at once weightless and completely spent. It came up and stopped, a single old fashioned open-ended wooden car coupled to the nose of a pushing switch engine considerably smaller. They were herded into it, crowding forward to the other end where there was a small cast iron stove. There was no fire in it, nevertheless they crowded about it—the cold and voiceless lump of iron stained with fading tobacco and hovered about by the ghosts of a thousand Sunday excursions to Memphis or Moorhead and return—the peanuts, the bananas, the soiled garments of infants—huddling, shoving for places near it. "Come on, come on," one of the guards shouted. "Sit down, now." At last three of the guards, laying aside their guns, came among them and broke up the huddle, driving them back and into seats.

There were not enough seats for all. The others stood in the aisle, they stood braced, they heard the air hiss out of the released brakes, the engine whistled four blasts, the car came into motion with a snapping jerk; the platform, the compress fled violently as the train seemed to transpose from immobility to full speed with that same quality of unreality with which it had appeared, running backward now though with the engine in front where before it had moved forward but with the engine behind.

When the railroad in its turn ran beneath the surface of the water, the convicts did not even know it. They felt the train stop, they heard the engine blow a long blast which wailed away unechoed across the waste, wild and forlorn, and they were not even curious; they sat or stood behind the rain-streaming windows as the train crawled on again, feeling its way as the truck had while the brown water swirled between the trucks and among the spokes of the driving wheels and lapped in cloudy steam against the dragging fire-filled belly of the engine; again it blew four short harsh blasts filled with the wild triumph and defiance yet also with repudiation and even farewell, as if the articulated steel itself knew it did not dare stop and would not be able to return. Two hours later in the twilight they saw through the streaming windows a burning plantation house. Juxtaposed to nowhere and neighbored by nothing it stood, a clear steady pyre-like flame rigidly fleeing its own reflection, burning in the dusk above the watery desolation with a quality paradoxical, outrageous and bizarre.

Sometime after dark the train stopped. The convicts did not know where they were. They did not ask. They would no more have thought of asking where they were than they would have asked why and what for. They couldn't even see, since the car was unlighted and the windows fogged on the outside by rain and on the inside by the engendered heat of the packed bodies. All they could see was a milky and sourceless flick and glare of flash-lights. They could hear shouts and commands, then the guards inside the car began to shout; they were herded to their feet and toward the exit, the ankle chains clashing and clanking. They descended into a fierce hissing of steam, through ragged wisps of it blowing past the car. Laid-to alongside the train and resembling a train itself was a thick blunt motor launch to which was attached a string of skiffs and flat boats. There were more soldiers; the flash-lights played on the rifle barrels and bandolier buckles and flicked and glinted on the ankle chains of the convicts as they stepped gingerly down into knee-deep water and entered the boats; now car and engine both vanished com-pletely in steam as the crew began dumping the fire from the firebox.

After another hour they began to see lights ahead—a faint wavering row of red pin-pricks extending along the horizon and apparently hanging low in the sky. But it took almost another hour to reach them while the convicts squatted in the skiffs, huddled into the soaked garments (they no longer felt the rain any more at all as separate drops) and watched the lights draw nearer and nearer until at last the crest of the levee defined itself; now they could discern a row of army tents stretching along it and people squatting about the fires, the wavering reflections from which, stretching across the water, revealed an involved mass of other skiffs tied against the flank of the levee which now stood high and dark overhead. Flashlights glared and winked along the base, among the tethered skiffs; the launch, silent now, drifted in.

When they reached the top of the levee they could see the long line of khaki tents, interspersed with fires about which people—men, women and children, negro and white—crouched or stood among shapeless bales of clothing, their heads turning, their eyeballs glinting in the firelight as they looked quietly at the striped garments and the chains; further down the levee, huddled together too though untethered, was a drove of mules and two or three cows. Then the taller convict became conscious of another sound. He did not begin to hear it all at once, he suddenly became aware that he had been hearing it all the time, a sound so much beyond all his experience and his powers of assimilation that up to this point he had been as oblivious of it as an ant or flea might be of the sound of the avalanche on which it rides; he had been travelling upon water since early afternoon and for seven years now he had run his plow and harrow and planter within the very shadow of the levee on which he now stood, but this profound deep whisper which came from the further side of it he did not at once recognise. He stopped. The line of convicts behind jolted into him like a line of freight cars stopping, with an iron clashing like cars. "Get on!" a guard shouted.

"What's that?" the convict said. A negro man squatting before the nearest fire answered him:

"Dat's him. Dat's de Ole Man."

"The old man?" the convict said.

"Get on! Get on up there!" the guard shouted. They went on; they passed another huddle of mules, the eyeballs rolling too, the long morose faces turning into and out of the firelight; they passed them and reached a section of empty tents, the light pup tents of a military campaign, made to hold two men. The guards herded the convicts into them, three brace of shackled men to each tent.

They crawled in on all fours, like dogs into cramped kennels, and settled down. Presently the tent became warm from their bodies. Then they became quiet and then all of them could hear it, they lay listening to the bass whisper deep, strong and powerful. "The old man?" the train-robber convict said.

"Yah," another said. "He dont have to brag."

At dawn the guards waked them by kicking the soles of the projecting feet. Opposite the muddy landing and the huddle of skiffs an army field kitchen was set up, already they could smell the coffee. But the taller convict at least, even though he had had but one meal yesterday and that at noon in the rain, did not move at once toward the food. Instead and for the first time he looked at the River within whose shadow he had spent the last seven years of his life but had never seen before; he stood in quiet and amazed surmise and looked at the rigid steel-colored surface not broken into waves but merely slightly undulant. It stretched from the levee on which he stood, further than he could see—a slowly and heavily roiling chocolate-frothy expanse broken ony by a thin line a mile away as fragile in appearance as a single hair, which after a moment he recognised. *It's another levee,* he thought quietly. *That's what we look like from there. That's what I am standing on looks like from there.* He was prodded from the rear; a guard's voice carried forward: "Go on! Go on! You'll have plenty of time to look at that!"

They received the same stew and coffee and bread as the day before; they squatted again with their bowls and mugs as yesterday, though it was not raining yet. During the night an intact wooden barn had floated up. It now lay jammed by the current against the levee while a crowd of negroes swarmed over it, ripping off the shingles and planks and carrying them up the bank; eating steadily and without haste, the taller convict watched the barn dissolve rapidly down to the very water-line exactly as a dead fly vanished beneath the moiling industry of a swarm of ants.

They finished eating. Then it began to rain again, as upon a signal, while they stood or squatted in their harsh garments which had not dried out during the night but had merely become slightly warmer than the air. Presently they were haled to their feet and told off into two groups, one of which was armed from a stack of mud-clogged picks and shovels nearby, and marched away up the levee. A little later the motor launch with its train of skiffs came up across what was, fifteen feet beneath its keel, probably a cotton field, the skiffs loaded to the gunwales with negroes and a scattering of white poeple nursing bundles on their laps. When the engine shut off the faint plinking of a guitar came across the water. The skiffs warped in and unloaded; the convicts watched the men and women and children struggle up the muddy slope, carrying heavy towsacks and bundles wrapped in quilts. The sound of the guitar had not ceased and now the convicts saw him—a young, black, lean-hipped man, the guitar slung by a piece of cotton plow line about his neck. He mounted the levee, still picking it. He carried nothing else, no food, no change of clothes, not even a coat.

The taller convict was so busy watching this that he did not hear the guard until the guard stood directly beside him shouting his name. "Wake up!" the guard shouted. "Can you fellows paddle a boat?"

"Paddle a boat where?" the taller convict said.

"In the water," the guard said. "Where in hell do you think?"

"I aint going to paddle no boat nowhere out yonder," the tall convict said, jerking his head toward the invisible river beyond the levee behind him.

"No, it's on this side," the guard said. He stooped swiftly and unlocked the chain which joined the tall convict and the plump hairless one. "It's just down the road a piece." He rose. The two convicts followed him down to the boats. "Follow them telephone poles until you come to a filling station. You can tell it, the roof is still above water. It's on a bayou and you can tell the bayou because the tops of the trees are sticking up. Follow the bayou until you come to a cypress snag with a woman in it. Pick her up and then cut straight back west until you come to a cotton house with a fellow sitting on the ridgepole—" He turned, looking at the two convicts, who stood perfectly still, looking first at the skiff and then at the water with intense sobriety. "Well? What are you waiting for?"

"I cant row a boat," the plump convict said.

"Then it's high time you learned," the guard said. "Get in."

The tall convict shoved the other forward. "Get in," he said. "That water aint going to hurt you. Aint nobody going to make you take a bath."

As, the plump one in the bow and the other in the stern, they shoved away from the levee, they saw other pairs being unshackled and manning the other skiffs. "I wonder how many more of them fellows are seeing this much water for the first time in their lives too," the tall convict said. The other did not answer. He knelt in the bottom of the skiff, pecking gingerly at the water now and then with his paddle. The very shape of his thick soft back seemed to wear that expression of wary and tense concern.

Some time after midnight a rescue boat filled to the guard rail with homeless men and women and children docked at Vicksburg. It was a steamer, shallow of draft; all day long it had poked up and down cypress- and gum-choked bayous and across cotton fields (where at times instead of swimming it waded) gathering its sorry cargo from the tops of houses and barns and even out of trees, and now it warped into that mushroom city of the forlorn and despairing where kerosene flares smoked in the drizzle and hurriedly strung electrics glared upon the bayonets of martial policemen and the Red Cross brassards of doctors and nurses and canteen-workers. The bluff overhead was almost solid with tents, yet still there were more people than shelter for them; they sat or lay, single and by whole families, under what shelter they could find or sometimes under the rain itself, in the little death of profound exhaustion while the doctors and the nurses and the soldiers stepped over and around and among them.

Among the first to disembark was one of the penitentiary deputy wardens, followed closely by the plump convict and another white man—a small man with a gaunt unshaven wan face still wearing an expression of incredulous outrage. The deputy warden seemed to know exactly where he wished to go. Followed closely by his two companions he threaded his way swiftly among the piled furniture and the sleeping bodies and stood presently in a fiercely lighted and hastily established temporary office, almost a military post of command in fact, where the Warden of the Penitentiary sat with two army officers wearing majors' leaves. The deputy warden spoke without preamble. "We lost a man," he said. He called the tall convict's name.

"Lost him?" the Warden said.

"Yah. Drowned." Without turning his head he spoke to the plump convict. "Tell him," he said.

"He was the one that said he could row a boat," the plump convict said. "I never. I told him myself—" he indicated the deputy warden with a jerk of his head "—I couldn't. So when we got to the bayou—"

"What's this?" the Warden said.

"The launch brought word in," the deputy warden said. "Woman in a cypress snag on the bayou, then this fellow—" he indicated the third man; the Warden and the two officers looked at the third man "—on a cottonhouse. Never had room in the launch to pick them up. Go on."

"So we come to where the bayou was," the plump convict continued in a voice perfectly flat, without any inflection whatever. "Then the boat got away from him. I dont know what happened. I was just sitting there because he was so positive he could row a boat. I never saw any current. Just all of a sudden the boat whirled clean around and begun to run fast backward like it was hitched to a train and it whirled around again and I happened to look up and there was a limb right over my head and I grabbed it just in time and that boat was snatched out from under me like you'd snatch off a sock and I saw it one time more upside down and that fellow that said he knew all about rowing holding to it with one hand and still holding the paddle in the other—" He ceased. There was no dying fall to his voice, it just ceased and the convict stood looking quietly at a half-full quart of whiskey sitting on the table.

"How do you know he's drowned?" the Warden said to the deputy. "How do you know he didn't just see his chance to escape, and took it?"

"Escape where?" the other said. "The whole Delta's flooded. There's fifteen foot of water for fifty miles, clean back to the hills. And that boat was upside down."

"That fellow's drowned," the plump convict said. "You dont need to worry about him. He's got his pardon; it wont cramp nobody's hand signing it, neither."

"And nobody else saw him?" the Warden said. "What about the woman in the tree?"

"I don't know," the deputy said. "I aint found her yet. I reckon some other boat picked her up. But this is the fellow on the cotton house."

Again the Warden and the two officers looked at the third man, at the gaunt, unshaven wild face in which an old terror, an old blending of fear and impotence and rage still lingered. "He never came for you?" the Warden said. "You never saw him?"

"Never nobody came for me," the refugee said. He began to tremble though at first he spoke quietly enough. "I set there on that sonabitching cottonhouse, expecting hit to go any minute. I saw that launch and them boats come up and they never had no room for me. Full of bastard niggers and one of them setting there playing a guitar but there wasn't no room for me. A guitar!" he cried; now he began to scream, trembling, slavering, his face twitching and jerking. "Room for a bastard nigger guitar but not for me—"

"Steady now," the Warden said. "Steady now."

"Give him a drink," one of the officers said. The Warden poured the drink. The deputy handed it to the refugee, who took the glass in both jerking hands and tried to raise it to his mouth. They watched him for perhaps twenty seconds, then the deputy took the glass from him and held it to his lips while he gulped, though even then a thin trickle ran from each corner of his mouth, into the stubble on his chin.

"So we picked him and—" the deputy called the plump convict's name now "—both up just before dark and come on in. But that other fellow is gone."

"Yes," the Warden said. "Well. Here I haven't lost a prisoner in ten years, and now, like this—I'm sending you back to the Farm tomorrow. Have his family notified, and his discharge papers filled out at once."

"All right," the deputy said. "And listen, chief. He wasn't a bad fellow and maybe he never had no business in that boat. Only he did say he could paddle one. Listen. Suppose I write on his discharge, Drowned while trying to save lives in the great flood of nineteen twenty-seven, and send it down for the Governor to sign it. It will be something nice for his folks to have, to hang on the wall when neighbors come in or something. Maybe they will even give his folks a cash bonus because after all they sent him to the Farm to raise cotton, not to fool around in a boat in a flood."

"All right," the Warden said. "I'll see about it. The main thing is to get his name off the books as dead before some politician tries to collect his food allowance."

"All right," the deputy said. He turned and herded his companions out. In the drizzling darkness again he said to the plump convict: "Well, your partner beat you. He's free. He's done served his time out but you've got a right far piece to go yet."

"Yah," the plump convict said. "Free. He can have it."

As the short convict had testified, the tall one, when he returned to the surface, still retained what the short one called the paddle. He clung to it, not instinctively against the time when he would be back inside the boat and would need it, because for a time he did not believe he would ever regain the skiff or anything else that would support him, but because he did not have time to think about turning it loose. Things had moved too fast for him. He had not been warned, he had felt the first snatching tug of the current, he had seen the skiff begin to spin and his companion vanish violently upward like in a translation out of Isaiah, then he himself was in the water, struggling against the drag of the paddle which he did not know he still held each time he fought back to the surface and grasped at the spinning skiff which at one instant was ten feet away and the next poised above his head as though about to brain him, until at last he grasped the stern, the drag of his body becoming a rudder to the skiff, the two of them, man and boat and with the paddle perpendicular above them like a jackstaff, vanishing from the view of the short convict (who had vanished from that of the tall one with the same celerity though in a vertical direction) like a tableau snatched offstage intact with violent and incredible speed.

He was now in the channel of a slough, a bayou, in which until today no current had run probably since the old subterranean outrage which had created the country. There was plenty of current in it now though; from his trough behind the stern he seemed to see the trees and sky rushing past with vertiginous speed, looking down at him between the gouts of cold yellow in lugubrious and mournful amazement. But they were fixed and secure in something; he thought of that, he remembered in an instant of despairing rage the firm earth fixed and founded strong and cemented fast and stable forever by the generations of laborious sweat, somewhere beneath him, beyond the reach of his feet, when, and again without warning, the stern of the skiff struck him a stunning blow across the bridge of his nose. The instinct which had caused him to cling to it now caused him to fling the paddle into the boat in order to grasp the gunwale with both hands just as the skiff pivoted and spun away again. With both hands free he now dragged himself over the stern and lay prone on his face, streaming with blood and water and panting, not with exhaustion but with that furious rage which is terror's aftermath.

But he had to get up at once because he believed he had come much faster (and so farther) than he had. So he rose, out of the watery scarlet puddle in which he had lain, streaming, the soaked denim heavy as iron on his limbs, the black hair plastered to his skull, the blood-infused water streaking his jumper, and dragged his forearm gingerly and hurriedly across his lower face and glanced at it then grasped the paddle and began to try to swing the skiff back upstream. It did not even occur to him that he did not know where his companion was, in which tree among all which he had passed or might pass. He did not even speculate on that for the reason that he knew so incontestably that the other was upstream from him, and after his recent experience the mere connotation of the term upstream carried a sense of such violence and force and speed that the conception of it as other than a straight line was something which the intelligence, reason, simply refused to harbor, like the notion of a rifle bullet the width of a cotton field.

The bow began to swing back upstream. It turned readily, it outpaced the aghast and outraged instant in which he realised it was swinging far too easily, it had swung on over the arc and lay broadside to the current and began again that vicious spinning while he sat, his teeth bared in his bloody streaming face while his spent arms flailed the impotent paddle at the water, that innocent-appearing medium which at one time had held him in iron-like and shifting convolutions like an anaconda yet which now seemed to offer no more resistance to the thrust of his urge and need than so much air, like air; the boat which had threatened him and at last actually struck him in the face with the shocking violence of a mule's hoof now seemed to poise weightless upon it like a thistle bloom, spinning like a wind vane while he flailed at the water and thought of, envisioned, his companion safe, inactive and at ease in the tree with nothing to do but wait, musing with impotent and terrified fury upon that arbitrariness of human affairs which had abrogated to the one the secure tree and to the other the hysterical and unmanageable boat for the very reason that it knew that he alone of the two of them would make any attempt to return and rescue his companion.

The skiff had paid off and now ran with the current again. It seemed again to spring from immobility into incredible speed, and he thought he must already be miles away from where his companion had quitted him, though actually he had merely described a big circle since getting back into the skiff, and the object (a clump of cypress trees choked by floating logs and debris) which the skiff was now about to strike was the same one it had careened into before when the stern had struck him. He didn't know this because he had not yet ever looked higher than the bow of the boat. He didn't look higher now, he just saw that he was going to strike; he seemed to feel run through the very insentient fabric of the skiff a current of eager gleeful vicious incorrigible wilfulness; and he who had never ceased to flail at the bland treacherous water with what he had believed to be the limit of his strength now from somewhere, some ultimate absolute reserve, produced a final measure of endurance, will to endure which adumbrated mere muscle and nerves, continuing to flail the paddle right up to the instant of striking, completing one last reach thrust and recover out of pure desperate reflex, as a man slipping on ice reaches for his hat and money-pocket, as the skiff struck and hurled him once more flat on his face in the bottom of it.

This time he did not get up at once. He lay flat on his face, slightly spread-eagled and in an attitude almost peaceful, a kind of abject meditation. He would have to get up sometime, he knew that, just as all life consists of having to get up sooner or later and then having to lie down again sooner or later after a while. And he was not exactly exhausted and he was not particularly without hope and he did not especially dread getting up. It merely seemed to him that he had accidentally been caught in a situation in which time and environment, not himself, was mesmerised; he was being toyed with by a current of water going nowhere, beneath a day which would wane toward no evening; when it was done with him it would spew him back into the comparatively safe world he had been snatched violently out of and in the meantime it did not much matter just what he did or did not do. So he lay on his face, now not only feeling but hearing the strong quiet rustling of the current on the underside of the planks, for a while longer. Then he raised his head and this time touched his palm gingerly to his face and looked at the blood again, then he sat up onto his heels and leaning over the gunwale he pinched his nostrils between thumb and finger and expelled a gout of blood and was in the act of wiping his fingers on his thigh when a voice slightly above his line of sight said quietly, "It's taken you a while," and he who up to this moment had had neither reason nor time to raise his eyes higher than the bows looked up and saw, sitting in a tree and looking at him, a woman. She was not ten feet away. She sat on the lowest limb of one of the trees holding the jam he had grounded on, in a calico wrapper and an army private's tunic and a sunbonnet, a woman whom he did not even bother to examine since that first startled glance had been ample to reveal to him all the generations of her life and background, who could have been his sister if he had a sister, his wife if he had not entered the penitentiary at an age scarcely out of adolescence and some years younger than that at which even his prolific and monogamous kind married—a woman who sat clutching the trunk of the tree, her stockingless feet in a pair of man's unlaced brogans less than a yard from the water, who was very probably somebody's sister and quite certainly (or certainly should have been) somebody's wife, though this too he had entered the penitentiary too young to have had more than mere theoretical female experience to discover yet. "I thought for a minute you wasn't aiming to come back."

"Come back?"

"After the first time. After you run into this brush pile the first time and got into the boat and went on." He looked about, touching his face tenderly again; it could very well be the same place where the boat had hit him in the face.

"Yah," he said. "I'm here now though."

"Could you maybe get the boat a little closer? I taken a right sharp strain getting up here; maybe I better . . ." He was not listening; he had just discovered that the paddle was gone; this time when the skiff hurled him forward he had flung the paddle not into it but beyond it. "It's right there in them brush tops," the woman said. "You can get it. Here. Catch a holt of this." It was a grapevine. It had grown up into the tree and the flood had torn the roots loose. She had taken a turn with it about her upper body; she now loosed it and swung it out until he could grasp it. Holding to the end of the vine he warped the skiff around the end of the jam, picking up the paddle, and warped the skiff on beneath the limb and held it and now he watched her move, gather herself heavily and carefully to descend—that heaviness which was not painful but just excruciatingly careful, that profound and almost lethargic awkwardness which added nothing to the sum of that first aghast amazement which had served already for the catafalque of invincible dream since even in durance he had continued (and even with the old avidity, even though they had caused his downfall) to consume the impossible pulp-printed fables carefully censored and as carefully smuggled into the penitentiary; and who to say what Helen, what living Garbo, he had not dreamed of rescuing from what craggy pinnacle or dragoned keep when he and his companion embarked in the skiff. He watched her, he made no further effort to help her beyond holding the skiff savagely steady while she lowered herself from the limb—the entire body, the deformed swell of belly bulging the calico, suspended by its arms, thinking, *And this is what I get. This, out of all the female meat that walks, is what I have to be caught in a runaway boat with.*

"Where's that cottonhouse?" he said.

"Cottonhouse?"

"With that fellow on it. The other one."

"I dont know. It's a right smart of cottonhouses around here. With folks on them too, I reckon." She was examining him. "You're bloody as a hog," she said. "You look like a convict."

"Yah," he said, snarled. "I feel like I done already been hung. Well, I got to pick up my pardner and then find that cottonhouse." He cast off. That is, he released his hold on the vine. That was all he had to do, for even while the bow of the skiff hung high on the log jam and even while he held it by the vine in the comparatively dead water behind the jam, he felt steadily and constantly the whisper, the strong purring power of the water just one inch beyond the frail planks on which he squatted and which, as soon as he released the vine, took charge of the skiff not with one powerful clutch but in a series of touches light, tentative, and catlike; he realised now that he had entertained a sort of foundationless hope that the added weight might make the skiff more controllable. During the first moment or two he had a wild (and still foundationless) belief that it had; he had got the head upstream and managed to hold it so by terrific exertion continued even after he discovered that they were travelling straight enough but stern-first and continued somehow even after the bow began to wear away and swing: the old irresistible movement which he knew well by now, too well to fight against it, so that he let the bow swing on downstream with the hope of utilising the skiff's own momentum to bring it through the full circle and so upstream again, the skiff travelling broadside then bow-first then broadside again, diagonally across the channel, toward the other wall of submerged trees; it began to flee beneath him with terrific speed, they were in an eddy but did not know it; he had no time to draw conclusions or even wonder; he crouched, his teeth bared in his blood-caked and swollen face, his lungs bursting, flailing at the water while the trees stooped hugely down at him. The skiff struck, spun, struck again; the woman half lay in the bow, clutching the gunwales, as if she were trying to crouch behind her own pregnancy; he banged now not at the water but at the living sapblooded wood with the paddle, his desire now not to go anywhere, reach any destination, but just to keep the skiff from beating itself to fragments against the tree trunks. Then something exploded, this time against the back of his head, and stooping trees and dizzy water, the woman's face and all, fled together and vanished in bright soundless flash and glare.

An hour later the skiff came slowly up an old logging road and so out of the bottom, the forest, and into (or onto) a cottonfield—a gray and limitless desolation now free of turmoil, broken only by a thin line of telephone poles like a wading millipede. The woman was now paddling, steadily and deliberately, with that curious lethargic care, while the convict squatted, his head between his knees, trying to stanch the fresh and apparently inexhaustible flow of blood from his nose with handfuls of water. The woman ceased paddling, the skiff drifted on, slowing, while she looked about. "We're done out," she said.

The convict raised his head and also looked about. "Out where?"

"I thought maybe you might know."

"I don't even know where I used to be. Even if I knowed which way was north, I wouldn't know if that was where I wanted to go." He cupped another handful of water to his face and lowered his hand and regarded the resulting crimson marbling on his palm, not with dejection, not with concern, but with a kind of sardonic and vicious bemusement. The woman watched the back of his head.

"We got to get somewhere."

"Don't I know it? A fellow on a cottonhouse. Another in a tree. And now that thing in your lap."

"It wasn't due yet. Maybe it was having to climb that tree quick yesterday, and having to set in it all night. I'm doing the best I can. But we better get somewhere soon."

"Yah," the convict said. "I thought I wanted to get somewhere too and I aint had no luck at it. You pick out a place to get to now and we'll try yours. Gimme that oar." The woman passed him the paddle. The boat was a double-ender; he had only to turn around.

"Which way you fixing to go?" the woman said.

"Never you mind that. You just keep on holding on." He began to paddle, on across the cottonfield. It began to rain again, though not hard at first. "Yah," he said. "Ask the boat. I been in it since breakfast and I aint never knowed, where I aimed to go or where I was going either."

That was about one oclock. Toward the end of the afternoon the skiff (they were in a channel of some sort again, they had been in it for some time; they had got into it before they knew it and too late to get out again, granted there had been any reason to get out, as, to the convict anyway, there was certainly none and the fact that their speed had increased again was reason enough to stay in it) shot out upon a broad expanse of debris-filled water which the convict recognised as a river and, from its size, the Yazoo River though it was little enough he had seen of this country which he had not quitted for so much as one single day in the last seven years of his life. What he did not know was that it was now running backward. So as soon as the drift of the skiff indicated the set of the current, he began to paddle in that direction which he believed to be downstream, where he knew there were towns—Yazoo City, and as a last resort, Vicksburg, if his luck was that bad, if not, smaller towns whose names he did not know but where there would be people, houses, something, anything he might reach and surrender his charge to and turn his back on her forever, on all pregnant and female life forever and return to that monastic existence of shotguns and shackles where he would be secure from it. Now, with the imminence of habitations, release from her, he did not even hate her. When he looked upon the swelling and unmanageable body before him it seemed to him that it was not the woman at all but rather a separate demanding threatening inert yet living mass of which both he and she were equally victims; thinking, as he had been for the last three or four hours, of that minute's—nay, second's—aberration of eye or hand which would suffice to precipitate her into the water to be dragged down to death by that senseless millstone which in its turn would not even have to feel agony, he no longer felt any glow of revenge toward her as its custodian, he felt sorry for her as he would for the living timber in a barn which had to be burned to rid itself of vermin.

He paddled on, helping the current, steadily and strongly, with a calculated husbandry of effort, toward what he believed was downstream, towns, people, something to stand upon, while from time to time the woman raised herself to bail the accumulated rain from the skiff. It was raining steadily now though still not hard, still without passion, the sky, the day itself dissolving without grief; the skiff moved in a nimbus, an aura of gray gauze which merged almost without demarcation with the roiling spittle-frothed debris-choked water. Now the day, the light, definitely began to end and the convict permitted himself an extra notch or two of effort because it suddenly seemed to him that the speed of the skiff had lessened. This was actually the case though the convict did not know it. He merely took it as a phenomenon of the increasing obfuscation, or at most as a result of the long day's continuous effort with no food, complicated by the ebbing and fluxing phases of anxiety and impotent rage at his absolutely gratuitous predicament. So he stepped up his stroke a beat or so, not from alarm but on the contrary, since he too had received that lift from the mere presence of a known stream, a river known by its ineradicable name to generations of men who had been drawn to live beside it as man always has been drawn to dwell beside water, even before he had a name for water and fire, drawn to the living water, the course of his destiny and his actual physical appearance rigidly coerced and postulated by it. So he was not alarmed. He paddled on, upstream without knowing it, unaware that all the water which for forty hours now had been pouring through the levee break to the north was somewhere ahead of him, on its way back to the River.

It was full dark now. That is, night had completely come, the gray dissolving sky had vanished, yet as though in perverse ratio surface visibility had sharpened, as though the light which the rain of the afternoon had washed out of the air had gathered upon the water as the rain itself had done, so that the yellow flood spread on before him now with a quality almost phosphorescent, right up to the instant where vision ceased. The darkness in fact had its advantages; he could now stop seeing the rain. He and his garments had been wet for more than twenty-four hours now so he had long since stopped feeling it, and now that he could no longer see it either it had in a certain sense ceased for him. Also, he now had to make no effort even not to see the swell of his passenger's belly. So he was paddling on, strongly and steadily, not alarmed and not concerned but just exasperated because he had not yet begun to see any reflection on the clouds which would indicate the city or cities which he believed he was approaching but which were actually now miles behind him, when he heard a sound. He did not know what it was because he had never heard it before and he would never be expected to hear such again since it is not given to every man to hear such at all and to none to hear it more than once in his life. And he was not alarmed now either because there was not time, for although the visibility ahead, for all its clarity, did not extend very far, yet in the next instant to the hearing he was also seeing something such as he had never seen before. This was that the sharp line where the phosphorescent water met the darkness was now about ten feet higher than it had been an instant before and that it was curled forward upon itself like a sheet of dough being rolled out for a pudding. It reared, stooping; the crest of it swirled like the mane of a galloping horse and, phosphorescent too, fretted and flickered like fire. And while the woman huddled in the bows, aware or not aware the convict did not know which, he (the convict), his swollen and blood-streaked face gaped in an expression of aghast and incredulous amazement, continued to paddle directly into it. Again he simply had not had time to order his rhythm-hypnotised muscles to cease. He continued to paddle though the skiff had ceased to move forward at all but seemed to be hanging in space while the paddle still reached thrust recovered and reached again; now instead of space the skiff became abruptly surrounded by a welter of fleeing debris—planks, small buildings, the bodies of drowned yet antic animals, entire trees leaping and diving like porpoises above which the skiff seemed to hover in weightless and airy indecision like a bird above a fleeing countryside, undecided where to light or whether to light at all, while the convict squatted in it still going through the motions of paddling, waiting for an opportunity to scream. He never found it. For an instant the skiff seemed to stand erect on its stern and then shoot scrabbling and scrambling up the curling wall of water like a cat, and soared on above the licking crest itself and hung cradled into the high actual air in the limbs of a tree, from which bower of new-leafed boughs and branches the convict, like a bird in its nest and still waiting his chance to scream and still going through the motions of paddling though he no longer even had the paddle now, looked down upon a world turned to furious motion and in incredible retrograde.

Some time about midnight, accompanied by a rolling cannonade of thunder and lightning like a battery going into action, as though some forty hours' constipation of the elements, the firmament itself, were discharging in clapping and glaring salute to the ultimate acquiescence to desperate and furious motion, and still leading its charging welter of dead cows and mules and outhouses and cabins and hencoops, the skiff passed Vicksburg. The convict didn't know it. He wasn't looking high enough above the water; he still squatted, clutching the gunwales and glaring at the yellow turmoil about him out of which entire trees, the sharp gables of houses, the long mournful heads of mules which he fended off with a splintered length of plank snatched from he knew not where in passing (and which seemed to glare reproachfully back at him with sightless eyes, in limber-lipped and incredulous amazement) rolled up and then down again, the skiff now travelling forward now sideways now sternward, sometimes in the water, sometimes riding for yards upon the roofs of houses and trees and even upon the backs of the mules as though even in death they were not to escape that burden-bearing doom with which their eunuch race was cursed. But he didn't see Vicksburg; the skiff, travelling at express speed, was in a seething gut between soaring and dizzy banks with a glare of light above them but he did not see it; he saw the flotsam ahead of him divide violently and begin to climb upon itself, mounting, and he was sucked through the resulting gap too fast to recognise it as the trestling of a railroad bridge; for a horrible moment the skiff seemed to hang in static indecision before the looming flank of a steamboat as though undecided whether to climb over it or dive under it, then a hard icy wind filled with the smell and taste and sense of wet and boundless desolation blew upon him; the skiff made one long bounding lunge as the convict's native state, in a final paroxysm, regurgitated him onto the wild bosom of the Father of Waters.

This is how he told about it seven weeks later, sitting in new bed-ticking garments, shaved and with his hair cut again, on his bunk in the barracks:

During the next three or four hours after the thunder and lightning had spent itself the skiff ran in pitch streaming darkness upon a roiling expanse which, even if he could have seen, apparently had no boundaries. Wild and invisible, it tossed and heaved about and beneath the boat, ridged with dirty phosphorescent foam and filled with a debris of destruction—objects nameless and enormous and invisible which struck and slashed at the skiff and whirled on. He did not know he was now upon the River. At that time he would have refused to believe it, even if he had known. Yesterday he had known he was in a channel by the regularity of the spacing between the bordering trees. Now, since even by daylight he could have seen no boundaries, the last place under the sun (or the streaming sky rather) he would have suspected himself to be would have been a river; if he had pondered at all about his present whereabouts, about the geography beneath him, he would merely have taken himself to be travelling at dizzy and inexplicable speed above the largest cottonfield in the world; if he who yesterday had known he was in a river, had accepted that fact in good faith and earnest, then had seen that river turn without warning and rush back upon him with furious and deadly intent like a frenzied stallion in a lane—if he had suspected for one second that the wild and limitless expanse on which he now found himself was a river, consciousness would simply have refused; he would have fainted.

When daylight—a gray and ragged dawn filled with driving scud between icy rain-squalls—came and he could see again, he knew he was in no cottonfield. He knew that the wild water on which the skiff tossed and fled flowed above no soil tamely trod by man, behind the straining and surging buttocks of a mule. That was when it occurred to him that its present condition was no phenomenon of a decade, but that the intervening years during which it consented to bear upon its placid and sleepy bosom the frail mechanicals of man's clumsy contriving was the phenomenon and this the norm and the river was now doing what it liked to do, had waited patiently the ten years in order to do, as a mule will work for you ten years for the privilege of kicking you once. And he also learned something else about fear too, something he had even failed to discover on that other occasion when he was really afraid—that three or four seconds of that night in his youth while he looked down the twice-flashing pistol barrel of the terrified mail clerk before the clerk could be persuaded that his (the convict's) pistol would not shoot: that if you just held on long enough a time would come in fear after which it would no longer be agony at all but merely a kind of horrible outrageous itching, as after you have been burned bad.

He did not have to paddle now, he just steered (who had been without food for twenty-four hours now and without any sleep to speak of for fifty) while the skiff sped on across that boiling desolation where he had long since begun to not dare believe he could possibly be where he could not doubt he was, trying with his fragment of splintered plank merely to keep the skiff intact and afloat among the houses and trees and dead animals (the entire towns, stores, residences, parks and farmyards, which leaped and played about him like fish), not trying to reach any destination, just trying to keep the skiff afloat until he did. He wanted so little. He wanted nothing for himself. He just wanted to get rid of the woman, the belly, and he was trying to do that in the right way, not for himself, but for her. He could have put her back into another tree at any time—

"Or you could have jumped out of the boat and let her and it drown," the plump convict said. "Then they could have given you the ten years for escaping and then hung you for the murder and charged the boat to your folks."

"Yah," the tall convict said.—But he had not done that. He wanted to do it the right way, find somebody, anybody he could surrender her to, something solid he could set her down on and then jump back into the river, if that would please anyone. That was all he wanted—just to come to something, anything. That didn't seem like a great deal to ask. And he couldn't do it. He told how the skiff fled on—

"Didn't you pass nobody?" the plump convict said. "No steamboat, nothing?"

"I dont know," the tall one said.—while he tried merely to keep it afloat, until the darkness thinned and lifted and revealed—

"Darkness?" the plump convict said. "I thought you said it was already daylight."

"Yah," the tall one said. He was rolling a cigarette, pouring the tobacco carefully from a new sack, into the creased paper. "This was another one. They had several while I was gone."—the skiff to be moving still rapidly up a winding corridor bordered by drowned trees which the convict recognised again to be a river running again in the direction that, until two days ago, had been upstream. He was not exactly warned through instinct that this one, like that of two days ago, was in reverse. He would not say that he now believed himself to be in the same river, though he would not have been surprised to find that he did believe this, existing now, as he did and had and apparently was to continue for an unnamed period, in a state in which he was toy and pawn on a vicious and inflammable geography. He merely realised that he was in a river again, with all the subsequent inferences of a comprehensible, even if not familiar, portion of the earth's surface. Now he believed that all he had to do would be to paddle far enough and he would come to something horizontal and above water even if not dry and perhaps even populated; and, if fast enough, in time, and that his only other crying urgency was to refrain from looking at the woman who, as vision, the incontrovertible and apparently inescapable presence of his passenger, returned with dawn, had ceased to be a human being and (you could add twenty-four more hours to the first twenty-four and the first fifty now, even counting the hen. It was dead, drowned, caught by one wing under a shingle on a roof which had rolled momentarily up beside the skiff yesterday and he had eaten some of it raw though the woman would not) had become instead one single inert monstrous sentient womb from which, he now believed, if he could only turn his gaze away and keep it away, would disappear, and if he could only keep his gaze from pausing again at the spot it had occupied, would not return. That's what he was doing this time when he discovered the wave was coming.

He didn't know how he discovered it was coming back. He heard no sound, it was nothing felt nor seen. He did not even believe that finding the skiff to be now in slack water—that is, that the motion of the current which, whether right or wrong, had at least been horizontal, had now stopped that and assumed a vertical direction—was sufficient to warn him. Perhaps it was just an invincible and almost fanatic faith in the inventiveness and innate viciousness of that medium on which his destiny was now cast, apparently forever; a sudden conviction far beyond either horror or surprise that now was none too soon for it to prepare to do whatever it was it intended doing. So he whirled the skiff, spun it on its heel like a running horse, whereupon, reversed, he could not even distinguish the very channel he had come up. He did not know whether he simply could not see it or if it had vanished some time ago and he not aware at the time; whether the river had become lost in a drowned world or if the world had become drowned in one limitless river. So now he could not tell if he were running directly before the wave or quartering across its line of charge; all he could do was keep that sense of swiftly accumulating ferocity behind him and paddle as fast as his spent and now numb muscles could be driven, and try not to look at the woman, to wrench his gaze from her and keep it away until he reached something flat and above water. So, gaunt, hollow-eyed, striving and wrenching almost physically at his eyes as if they were two of those suction-tipped rubber arrows shot from the toy gun of a child, his spent muscles obeying not will now but that attenuation beyond mere exhaustion which, mesmeric, can continue easier than cease, he once more drove the skiff full tilt into something it could not pass and, once more hurled violently forward onto his hands and knees, crouching, he glared with his wild swollen face up at the man with the shotgun and said in a harsh, croaking voice: "Vicksburg? Where's Vicksburg?"

Even when he tried to tell it, even after the seven weeks and he safe, secure, riveted warranted and doubly guaranteed by the ten years they had added to his sentence for attempted escape, something of the old hysteric incredulous outrage came back into his face, his voice, his speech. He never did even get on the other boat. He told how he clung to a strake (it was a dirty unpainted shanty boat with a drunken rake of tin stove pipe, it had been moving when he struck it and apparently it had not even changed course even though the three people on it must have been watching him all the while—a second man, barefoot and with matted hair and beard also at the steering sweep, and then—he did not know how long—a woman leaning in the door, in a filthy assortment of men's garments, watching him too with the same cold speculation) being dragged violently along, trying to state and explain his simple (and to him at least) reasonable desire and need; telling it, trying to tell it, he could feel again the old unforgettable affronting like an ague fit as he watched the abortive tobacco rain steadily and faintly from between his shaking hands and then the paper itself part with a thin dry snapping report:

"Burn my clothes?" the convict cried. "Burn them?"

"How in hell do you expect to escape in them billboards?" the man with the shotgun said. He (the convict) tried to tell it, tried to explain as he had tried to explain not to the three people on the boat alone but to the entire circumambience—desolate water and forlorn trees and sky—not for justification because he neded none and knew that his hearers, the other convicts, required none from him, but rather as, on the point of exhaustion, he might have picked dreamily and incredulously at a suffocation. He told the man with the gun how he and his partner had been given the boat and told to pick up a man and a woman, how he had lost his partner and failed to find the man, and now all in the world he wanted was something flat to leave the woman on until he could find an officer, a sheriff. He thought of home, the place where he had lived almost since childhood, his friends of years whose ways he knew and who knew his ways, the familiar fields where he did work he had learned to do well and to like, the mules with characters he knew and respected as he knew and respected the characters of certain men; he thought of the barracks at night, with screens against the bugs in summer and good stoves in winter and someone to supply the fuel and the food too; the Sunday ball games and the picture shows—things which, with the exception of the ball games, he had never known before. But most of all, his own character (Two years ago they had offered to make a trusty of him. He would no longer need to plow or feed stock, he would only follow those who did with a loaded gun, but he declined. "I reckon I'll stick to plowing," he said, absolutely without humor. "I done already tried to use a gun one time too many.") his good name, his responsibility not only toward those who were responsible toward him but to himself, his own honor of doing what was asked of him, his pride in being able to do it, no matter what it was. He thought of this and listened to the man with the gun talking about escape and it seemed to him that, hanging there, being dragged violently along (it was here he said that he first noticed the goats' beards of moss in the trees, though it could have been there for several days so far as he knew. It just happened that he first noticed it here.) that he would simply burst.

"Cant you get it into your head that the last thing I want to do is run away?" he cried. "You can set there with that gun and watch me; I give you fair lief. All I want is to put this woman—"

"And I told you she could come aboard," the man with the gun said in his level voice. "But there aint no room on no boat of mine for nobody hunting a sheriff in no kind of clothes, let alone a penitentiary suit."

"When he steps aboard, knock him in the head with the gun barrel," the man at the sweep said. "He's drunk."

"He aint coming aboard," the man with the gun said. "He's crazy."

Then the woman spoke. She didn't move, leaning in the door, in a pair of faded and patched and filthy overalls like the two men: "Give them some grub and tell them to get out of here." She moved, she crossed the deck and looked down at the convict's companion with her cold sullen face. "How much more time have you got?"

"It wasn't due till next month," the woman in the boat said. "But I—" The woman in overalls turned to the man with the gun.

"Give them some grub," she said. But the man with the gun was still looking down at the woman in the boat.

"Come on," he said to the convict. "Put her aboard, and beat it."

"And what'll happen to you," the woman in overalls said, "when you try to turn her over to an officer. When you lay alongside a sheriff and the sheriff asks you who you are?" Still the man with the gun didn't even look at her. He hardly even shifted the gun across his arm as he struck the woman across the face with the back of his other hand, hard. "You son of a bitch," she said. Still the man with the gun did not even look at her.

"Well?" he said to the convict.

"Dont you see I cant?" the convict cried. "Cant you see that?"

Now, he said, he gave up. He was doomed. That is, he knew now that he had been doomed from the very start never to get rid of her, just as the ones who sent him out with the skiff knew that he never would actually give up; when he recognised one of the objects which the woman in overalls was hurling into the skiff to be a can of condensed milk, he believed it to be a presage, gratuitous and irrevocable as a death-notice over the telegraph, that he was not even to find a flat stationary surface in time for the child to be born on it. So he told how he held the skiff alongside the shanty boat while the first tentative toying of the second wave made up beneath him, while the woman in overalls passed back and forth between house and rail, flinging the food—the hunk of salt meat, the ragged and filthy quilt, the scorched lumps of cold bread which she poured into the skiff from a heaped dishpan like so much garbage—while he clung to the strake against the mounting pull of the current, the new wave which for the moment he had forgotten because he was still trying to state the incredible simplicity of his desire and need until the man with the gun (the only one of the three who wore shoes) began to stamp at his hands, he snatching his hands away one at a time to avoid the heavy shoes, then grasping the rail again until the man with the gun kicked at his face, he flinging himself sideways to avoid the shoe and so breaking his hold on the rail, his weight canting the skiff off at a tangent on the increasing current so that it began to leave the shanty boat behind and he paddling again now, violently, as a man hurries toward the precipice for which he knows at last he is doomed, looking back at the other boat, the three faces sullen derisive and grim and rapidly diminishing across the widening water and at last, apoplectic, suffocating with the intolerable fact not that he had been refused but that he had been refused so little, had wanted so little, asked for so little, yet there had been demanded of him in return the one price out of all breath which (they must have known) if he could have paid it, he would not have been where he was, asking what he asked, raising the paddle and shaking it and screaming curses back at them even after the shotgun flashed and the charge went scuttering past along the water to one side.

So he hung there, he said, shaking the paddle and howling, when suddenly he remembered that other wave, the second wall of water full of houses and dead mules building up behind him back in the swamp. So he quit yelling then and went back to paddling. He was not trying to outrun it. He just knew from experience that when it overtook him, he would have to travel in the same direction it was moving in anyway, whether he wanted to or not, and when it did overtake him, he would begin to move too fast to stop, no matter what places he might come to where he could leave the woman, land her in time. Time: that was his itch now, so his only chance was to stay ahead of it as long as he could and hope to reach something before it struck. So he went on, driving the skiff with muscles which had been too tired so long they had quit feeling it, as when a man has had bad luck for so long that he ceases to believe it is even bad, let alone luck. Even when he ate—the scorched lumps the size of baseballs and the weight and durability of cannel coal even after having lain in the skiff's bilge where the shanty boat woman had thrown them—the iron-like lead-heavy objects which no man would have called bread outside of the crusted and scorched pan in which they had cooked—it was with one hand, begrudging even that from the paddle.

He tried to tell that too—that day while the skiff fled on among the bearded trees while every now and then small quiet tentative exploratory feelers would come up from the wave behind and toy for a moment at the skiff, light and curious, then go on with a faint hissing sighing, almost a chuckling, sound, the skiff going on, driving on with nothing to see but trees and water and solitude: until after a while it no longer seemed to him that he was trying to put space and distance behind him or shorten space and distance ahead but that both he and the wave were now hanging suspended simultaneous and unprogressing in pure time, upon a dreamy desolation in which he paddled on not from any hope even to reach anything at all but merely to keep intact what little of distance the length of the skiff provided between himself and the inert and inescapable mass of female meat before him; then night and the skiff rushing on, fast since any speed over anything unknown and invisible is too fast, with nothing before him and behind him the outrageous idea of a volume of moving water toppling forward, its crest frothed and shredded like fangs, and then dawn again (another of those dreamlike alterations day to dark then back to day again with that quality truncated, anachronic and unreal as the waxing and waning of lights in a theatre scene) and the skiff emerging now with the woman no longer supine beneath the shrunken soaked private's coat but sitting bolt upright, gripping the gunwales with both hands, her eyes closed and her lower lip caught between her teeth and he driving the splintered board furiously now, glaring at her out of his wild swollen sleepless face and crying, croaking, "Hold on! For God's sake hold on!"

"I'm trying to," she said. "But hurry! Hurry!" He told it, the unbelievable: hurry, hasten: the man falling from a cliff being told to catch onto something and save himself; the very telling of it emerging shadowy and burlesque, ludicrous, comic and mad, from the ague of unbearable forgetting with a quality more dreamily furious than any fable behind proscenium lights:

He was in a basin now— "A basin?" the plump convict said. "That's what you wash in."

"All right," the tall one said, harshly, above his hands. "I did." With a supreme effort he stilled them long enough to release the two bits of cigarette paper and watched them waft in light fluttering indecision to the floor between his feet, holding his hands motionless even for a moment longer—a basin, a broad peaceful yellow sea which had an abruptly and curiously ordered air, giving him, even at that moment, the impression that it was accustomed to water even if not total submersion; he even remembered the name of it, told to him two or three weeks later by someone: Atchafalaya—

"Louisiana?" the plump convict said. "You mean you were clean out of Mississippi? Hell fire." He stared at the tall one. "Shucks," he said. "That aint but just across from Vicksburg."

"They never named any Vicksburg across from where I was," the tall one said. "It was Baton Rouge they named." And now he began to talk about a town, a little neat white portrait town nestling among enormous very green trees, appearing suddenly in the telling as it probably appeared in actuality, abrupt and airy and miragelike and incredibly serene before him behind a scattering of boats moored to a line of freight cars standing flush to the doors in water. And now he tried to tell that too: how he stood waist-deep in water for a moment looking back and down at the skiff in which the woman half lay, her eyes still closed, her knuckles white on the gunwales and a tiny thread of blood creeping down her chin from her chewed lip, and he looking down at her in a kind of furious desperation.

"How far will I have to walk?" she said.

"I don't know, I tell you!" he cried. "But it's land somewhere yonder! It's land, houses."

"If I try to move, it wont even be born inside a boat," she said. "You'll have to get closer."

"Yes," he cried, wild, desperate, incredulous. "Wait. I'll go and surrender, then they will have—" He didn't finish, wait to finish; he told that too: himself splashing, stumbling, trying to run, sobbing and gasping; now he saw it—another loading platform standing above the yellow flood, the khaki figures on it as before, identical, the same; he said how the intervening days since that first innocent morning telescoped, vanished as if they had never been, the two contiguous succeeding instants (succeeding? simultaneous) and he transported across no intervening space but merely turned in his own footsteps, plunging, splashing, his arms raised, croaking harshly. He heard the startled shout, "There's one of them!", the command, the clash of equipment, the alarmed cry: "There he goes! There he goes!"

"Yes!" he cried, running, plunging, "here I am! Here! Here!" running on, into the first scattered volley, stopping among the bullets, waving his arms, shrieking, "I want to surrender! I want to surrender!" watching not in terror but in amazed and absolutely unbearable outrage as a squatting clump of the khaki figures parted and he saw the machine gun, the blunt thick muzzle slant and drop and probe toward him and he still screaming in his hoarse crow's voice, "I want to surrender! Cant you hear me?" continuing to scream even as he whirled and plunged splashing, ducking, went completly under and heard the bullets going thuck-thuck-thuck on the water above him and he scrabbling still on the bottom, still trying to scream even before he regained his feet and still all submerged save his plunging unmistakable buttocks, the outraged screaming bubbling from his mouth and about his face since he merely wanted to surrender. Then he was comparatively screened, out of range, though not for long. That is (he didn't tell how nor where) there was a moment in which he paused, breathed for a second before running again, the course back to the skiff open for the time being though he could still hear the shouts behind him and now and then a shot, and he panting, sobbing, a long savage tear in the flesh of one hand, got when and how he did not know, and he wasting precious breath, speaking to no one now any more than the scream of the dying rabbit is addressed to any mortal ear but rather an indictment of all breath and its folly and suffering, its infinite capacity for folly and pain, which seems to be its only immortality: "All in the world I want is just to surrender."

He returned to the skiff and got in and took up his splintered plank. And now when he told this, despite the fury of element which climaxed it, it (the telling) became quite simple; he now even creased another cigarette paper between fingers which did not tremble at all and filled the paper from the tobacco sack without spilling a flake, as though he had passed from the machine gun's barrage into a bourne beyond any more amazement: so that the subsequent part of his narrative seemed to reach his listeners as though from beyond a sheet of slightly milky though still transparent glass, as something not heard but seen—a series of shadows, edgeless yet distinct, and smoothly flowing, logical and unfrantic and making no sound: They were in the skiff, in the center of the broad placid trough which had no boundaries and down which the tiny forlorn skiff flew to the irresistible coercion of a current going once more he knew not where, the neat small liveoak-bowered towns unattainable and miragelike and apparently attached to nothing upon the airy and unchanging horizon. He did not believe them, they did not matter, he was doomed; they were less than the figments of smoke or of delirium, and he driving his unceasing paddle without destination or even hope now, looking now and then at the woman sitting with her knees drawn up and locked and her entire body one terrific clench while the threads of bloody saliva crept from her teeth-clenched lower lip. He was going nowhere and fleeing from nothing, he merely continued to paddle because he had paddled so long now that he believed if he stopped his muscles would scream in agony. So when it happened he was not surprised. He heard the sound which he knew well (he had heard it but once before, true enough, but no man needed hear it but once) and he had been expecting it; he looked back, still driving the paddle, and saw it, curled, crested with its strawlike flotsam of trees and debris and dead beasts and he glared over his shoulder at it for a full minute out of that attenuation far beyond the point of outragement where even suffering, the capability of being further affronted, had ceased, from which he now contemplated with savage and invulnerable curiosity the further extent to which his now anesthetised nerves could bear, what next could be invented for them to bear, until the wave actually began to rear above his head into its thunderous climax. Then only did he turn his head. His stroke did not falter, it neither slowed nor increased; still paddling with that spent hypnotic steadiness, he saw the swimming deer. He did not know what it was nor that he had altered the skiff's course to follow it, he just watched the swimming head before him as the wave boiled down and the skiff rose bodily in the old familiar fashion on a welter of tossing trees and houses and bridges and fences, he still paddling even while the paddle found no purchase save air and still paddled even as he and the deer shot forward side by side at arm's length, he watching the deer now, watching the deer begin to rise out of the water bodily until it was actually running along upon the surface, rising still, soaring clear of the water altogether, vanishing upward in a dying crescendo of splashings and snapping branches, its damp scut flashing upward, the entire animal vanishing upward as smoke vanishes. And now the skiff struck and canted and he was out of it too, standing knee-deep, springing out and falling to his knees, scrambling up, glaring after the vanished deer. "Land!" he croaked. "Land! Hold on! Just hold on!" He caught the woman beneath the arms, dragging her out of the boat, plunging and panting after the vanished deer. Now earth actually appeared—an acclivity smooth and swift and steep, bizarre, solid and unbelievable; an Indian mound, and he plunging at the muddy slope, slipping back, the woman struggling in his muddy hands.

"Let me down!" she cried. "Let me down!" But he held her, panting, sobbing, and rushed again at the muddy slope; he had almost reached the flat crest with his now violently unmanageable burden when a stick under his foot gathered itself with thick convulsive speed. *It was a snake,* he thought as his feet fled beneath him and with the indubitable last of his strength he half pushed and half flung the woman up the bank as he shot feet first and face down back into that medium upon which he had lived for more days and nights than he could remember and from which he himself had never completely emerged, as if his own failed and spent flesh were attempting to carry out his furious unflagging will for severance at any price, even that of drowning, from the burden with which, unwitting and without choice, he had been doomed. Later it seemed to him that he had carried back beneath the surface with him the sound of the infant's first mewling cry.

When the woman asked him if he had a knife, standing there in the streaming bedticking garments which had got him shot at, the second time by a machine gun, on the two occasions when he had seen any human life after leaving the levee four days ago, the convict felt exactly as he had in the fleeing skiff when the woman suggested that they had better hurry. He felt the same outrageous affronting of a condition purely moral, the same raging impotence to find any answer to it; so that, standing above her, spent suffocating and inarticulate, it was a full minute before he comprehended that she was now crying. "The can! The can in the boat!" He did not anticipate what she could want with it; he did not even wonder nor stop to ask. He turned running; this time he thought, *It's another moccasin* as the thick body truncated in that awkward reflex which had nothing of alarm in it but only alertness, he not even shifting his stride though he knew his running foot would fall within a yard of the flat head. The bow of the skiff was well up the slope now where the wave had set it and there was another snake just crawling over the stern into it and as he stooped for the bailing can he saw something else swimming toward the mound, he didn't know what—a head, a face at the apex of a vee of ripples. He snatched up the can; by pure juxtaposition of it and water he scooped it full, already turning. He saw the deer again, or another one. That is, he saw a deer—a side glance, the light smoke-colored phantom in a cypress vista then gone, vanished, he not pausing to look after it, galloping back to the woman and kneeling with the can to her lips until she told him better.

It had contained a pint of beans or tomatoes, something, hermetically sealed and opened by four blows of an axe heel, the metal flap turned back, the jagged edges razor-sharp. She told him how, and he used this in lieu of a knife, he removed one of his shoelaces and cut it in two with the sharp tin. Then she wanted warm water—"If I just had a little hot water," she said in a weak serene voice without particular hope; only when he thought of matches it was again a good deal like when she had asked him if he had a knife, until she fumbled in the pocket of the shrunken tunic (it had a darker double vee on one cuff and a darker blotch on the shoulder where service stripes and a divisional emblem had been ripped off but this meant nothing to him) and produced a match-box contrived by telescoping two shotgun shells. So he drew her back a little from the water and went to hunt wood dry enough to burn, thinking this time, *It's just another snake,* only, he said, he should have thought *ten thousand other snakes;* and now he knew it was not the same deer because he saw three at one time, does or bucks he did not know which since they were all antlerless in May and besides he had never seen one of any kind anywhere before except on a Christmas card; and then the rabbit, drowned, dead anyway, already torn open, the bird, the hawk, standing upon it—the erected crest, the hard vicious patrician nose, the intolerant omnivorous yellow eye—and he kicking at it, kicking it lurching and broadwinged into the actual air.

When he returned with the wood and the dead rabbit, the baby, wrapped in the tunic, lay wedged between two cypress-knees and the woman was not in sight, though while the convict knelt in the mud, blowing and nursing his meagre flame, she came slowly and weakly from the direction of the water, Then, the water heated at last and there produced from some where he was never to know, she herself perhaps never to know until the need comes, no woman perhaps ever to know, only no woman will even wonder, that square of something somewhere between sackcloth and silk—squatting, his own wet garments steaming in the fire's heat, he watched her bathe the child with a savage curiosity and interest that became amazed unbelief, so that at last he stood above them both, looking down at the tiny terra-cotta colored creature resembling nothing, and thought, *And this is all. This is what severed me violently from all I ever knew and did not wish to leave and cast me upon a medium I was born to fear, to fetch up at last in a place I never saw before and where I do not even know where I am.*

Then he returned to the water and refilled the bailing can. It was drawing toward sunset now (or what would have been sunset save for the high prevailing overcast) of this day whose beginning he could not even remember; when he returned to where the fire burned in the interlaced gloom of the cypresses, even after this short absence, evening had definitely come, as though darkness too had taken refuge upon that quarter-acre mound, that earthen Ark out of Genesis, that dim wet cypress-choked life-teeming constricted desolation in what direction and how far from what and where he had no more idea than of the day of the month, and had now with the setting of the sun crept forth again to spread upon the waters. He stewed the rabbit in sections while the fire burned redder and redder in the darkness where the shy wild eyes of small animals—once the tall mild almost plate-sized stare of one of the deer—glowed and vanished and glowed again, the broth hot and rank after the four days; he seemed to hear the roar of his own saliva as he watched the woman sip the first canful. Then he drank too; they ate the other fragments which had been charring and scorching on willow twigs; it was full night now. "You and him better sleep in the boat," the convict said. "We want to get an early start tomorrow." He shoved the bow of the skiff off the land so it would lie level, he lengthened the painter with a piece of grapevine and returned to the fire and tied the grapevine about his wrist and lay down. It was mud he lay upon, but it was solid underneath, it was earth, it did not move; if you fell upon it you broke your bones against its incontrovertible passivity sometimes but it did not accept you substanceless and enveloping and suffocating, down and down and down; it was hard at times to drive a plow through, it sent you spent, weary, and cursing its light-long insatiable demands back to your bunk at sunset at times but it did not snatch you violently out of all familiar knowing and sweep you thrall and impotent for days against any returning. *I dont know where I am and I dont reckon I know the way back to where I want to go,* he thought. *But at least the boat has stopped long enough to give me a chance to turn it around.*

He waked at dawn, the light faint, the sky jonquil-colored; the day would be fine. The fire had burned out; on the opposite side of the cold ashes lay three snakes motionless and parallel as underscoring, and in the swiftly making light others seemed to materialise: earth which an instant before had been mere earth broke up into motionless coils and loops, branches which a moment before had been mere branches now become immobile ophidian festoons even as the convict stood thinking about food, about something hot before they started. But he decided against this, against wasting this much time, since there still remained in the skiff quite a few of the rocklike objects which the shanty woman had flung into it, besides (thinking this) no matter how fast nor successfully he hunted, he would never be able to lay up enough food to get them back to where they wanted to go. So he returned to the skiff, paying himself back to it by his vine-spliced painter, back to the water on which a low mist thick as cotton batting (though apparently not very tall, deep) lay, into which the stern of the skiff was already beginning to disappear although it lay with its prow almost touching the mound. The woman waked, stirred. "We fixing to start now?" she said.

"Yah," the convict said. "You aint aiming to have another one this morning, are you?" He got in and shoved the skiff clear of the land, which immediately began to dissolve into the mist. "Hand me the oar," he said over his shoulder, not turning yet.

"The oar?"

He turned his head. "The oar. You're laying on it." But she was not, and for an instant during which the mound, the island continued to fade slowly into the mist which seemed to enclose the skiff in weightless and impalpable wool like a precious or fragile bauble or jewel, the convict squatted not in dismay but in that frantic and astonished outrage of a man who, having just escaped a falling safe, is struck by the following two-ounce paper weight which was sitting on it: this the more unbearable because he knew that never in his life had he less time to give way to it. He did not hesitate. Grasping the grapevine end he sprang into the water, vanishing in the violent action of climbing and reappeared still climbing and (who had never learned to swim) plunged and threshed on toward the almost-vanished mound, moving through the water then upon it as the deer had done yesterday and scrabbled up the muddy slope and lay gasping and panting, still clutching the grapevine end.

Now the first thing he did was to choose what he believed to be the most suitable tree (for an instant in which he knew he was insane he thought of trying to saw it down with the flange of the bailing can) and build a fire against the butt of it. Then he went to seek food. He spent the next six days seeking it while the tree burned through and fell and burned through again at the proper length and he nursing little constant cunning flames along the flanks of the log to make it paddle-shaped, nursing them at night too while the woman and baby (it was eating, nursing now, he turning his back or even returning into the woods each time she prepared to open the faded tunic) slept in the skiff. He learned to watch for stooping hawks and so found more rabbits and twice possums; they ate some drowned fish which gave them both a rash and then a violent flux and one snake which the woman thought was turtle and which did them no harm, and one night it rained and he got up and dragged brush, shaking the snakes (he no longer thought, *It aint nothing but another moccasin,* he just stepped aside for them as they, when there was time, telescoped sullenly aside for him) out of it with the old former feeling of personal invulnerability and built a shelter and the rain stopped at once and did not recommence and the woman went back to the skiff.

Then one night—the slow tedious charring log was almost a paddle now—one night and he was in bed, in his bed in the bunkhouse and it was cold, he was trying to pull the covers up only his mule wouldn't let him, prodding and bumping heavily at him, trying to get into the narrow bed with him and now the bed was cold too and wet and he was trying to get out of it only the mule would not let him, holding him by his belt in its teeth, jerking and bumping him back into the cold wet bed and, leaning, gave him a long swipe across the face with its cold limber musculated tongue and he waked to no fire, no coal even beneath where the almost-finished paddle had been charring and something else prolonged and coldly limber passed swiftly across his body where he lay in four inches of water while the nose of the skiff alternately tugged at the grapevine tied about his waist and bumped and shoved him back into the water again. Then something else came up and began to nudge at his ankle (the log, the oar, it was) even as he groped frantically for the skiff, hearing the swift rustling going to and fro inside the hull as the woman began to thrash about and scream. "Rats!" she cried. "It's full of rats!"

"Lay still!" he cried. "It's just snakes. Cant you hold still long enough for me to find the boat?" Then he found it, he got into it with the unfinished paddle; again the thick muscular body convulsed under his foot; it did not strike; he would not have cared, glaring astern where he could see a little—the faint outer luminosity of the open water. He poled toward it, thrusting aside the snake-looped branches, the bottom of the skiff resounding faintly to thick solid plops, the woman shrieking steadily. Then the skiff was clear of the trees, the mound, and now he could feel the bodies whipping about his ankles and hear the rasp of them as they went over the gunwale. He drew the log in and scooped it forward along the bottom of the boat and up and out; against the pallid water he could see three more of them in lashing convolutions before they vanished. "Shut up!" he cried. "Hush! I wish I was a snake so I could get out too!"

When once more the pale and heatless wafer disc of the early sun stared down at the skiff (whether they were moving or not the convict did not know) in its nimbus of fine cotton batting, the convict was hearing again that sound which he had heard twice before and would never forget—that sound of deliberate and irresistible and monstrously disturbed water. But this time he could not tell from what direction it came. It seemed to be everywhere, waxing and fading; it was like a phantom behind the mist, at one instant miles away, the next on the point of overwhelming the skiff within the next second; suddenly, in the instant he would believe (his whole weary body would spring and scream) that he was about to drive the skiff point-blank into it and with the unfinished paddle of the color and texture of sooty bricks, like something gnawed out of an old chimney by beavers and weighing twenty-five pounds, he would whirl the skiff frantically and find the sound dead ahead of him again. Then something bellowed tremendously above his head, he heard human voices, a bell jangled and the sound ceased and the mist vanished as when you draw your hand across a frosted pane, and the skiff now lay upon a sunny glitter of brown water flank to flank with, and about thirty yards away from him, a steamboat. The decks were crowded and packed with men women and children sitting or standing beside and among a homely conglomeration of hurried furniture, who looked mournfully and silently down into the skiff while the convict and the man with a megaphone in the pilot house talked to each other in alternate puny shouts and roars above the chuffing of the reversed engines:

"What in hell are you trying to do? Commit suicide?"

"Which is the way to Vicksburg?"

"Vicksburg? Vicksburg? Lay alongside and come aboard."

"Will you take the boat too?"

"Boat? Boat?" Now the megaphone cursed, the roaring waves of blasphemy and biological supposition empty cavernous and bodiless in turn, as if the water, the air, the mist had spoken it, roaring the words then taking them back to itself and no harm done, no scar, no insult left anywhere. "If I took aboard every floating sardine can you sonabitchin mushrats want me to I wouldn't even have room forward for a leadsman. Come aboard! Do you expect me to hang here on stern engines till hell freezes?"

"I aint coming without the boat," the convict said. Now another voice spoke, so calm and mild and sensible that for a moment it sounded more foreign and out of place than even the megaphone's bellowing and bodiless profanity:

"Where is it you are trying to go?"

"I aint trying," the convict said. "I'm going. Parchman." The man who had spoken last turned and appeared to converse with a third man in the pilot house. Then he looked down at the skiff again.

"Carnarvon?"

"What?" the convict said. "Parchman?"

"All right. We're going that way. We'll put you off where you can get home. Come aboard."

"The boat too?"

"Yes, yes. Come along. We're burning coal just to talk to you." So the convict came alongside then and watched them help the woman and baby over the rail and he came aboard himself, though he still held to the end of the vine-spliced painter until the skiff was hoisted onto the boiler deck. "My God," the man, the gentle one, said, "is that what you have been using for a paddle?"

"Yah," the convict said. "I lost the plank."

"The plank," the mild man (the convict told how he seemed to whisper it), "the plank. Well. Come along and get something to eat. Your boat is all right now."

"I reckon I'll wait here," the convict said. Because now, he told them, he began to notice for the first time that the other people, the other refugees who crowded the deck, who had gathered in a quiet circle about the up-turned skiff on which he and the woman sat, the grapevine painter wrapped several times about his wrist and clutched in his hand, staring at him and the woman with queer hot mournful intensity, were not white people—

"You mean niggers?" the plump convict said.

"No. Not Americans."

"Not Americans? You was clean out of *America* even?"

"I don't know," the tall one said. "They call it Atchafalaya."—Because after a while he said, "What?" to the man and the man did it again, gobble-gobble—

"Gobble-gobble?" the plump convict said.

"That's the way they talked," the tall one said. "Gobble-gobble, whang, caw-caw-to-to."—And he sat there and watched them gobbling at one an-other and then looking at him again, then they fell back and the mild man (he wore a Red Cross brassard) entered, followed by a waiter with a tray of food. The mild man carried two glasses of whiskey.

"Drink this," the mild man said. "This will warm you." The woman took hers and drank it but the convict told how he looked at his and thought, *I aint tasted whiskey in seven years.* He had not tasted it but once be-fore that; it was at the still itself back in a pine hollow; he was seventeen, he had gone there with four companions, two of whom were grown men, one of twenty-two or -three, the other about forty; he remembered it. That is, he re-membered perhaps a third of that evening—a fierce turmoil in the hell-colored firelight, the shock and shock of blows about his head (and likewise of his own fists on other hard bone), then the waking to a splitting and blinding sun in a place, a cowshed, he had never seen before and which later turned out to be twenty miles from his home. He said he thought of this and he looked about at the faces watching him and he said,

"I reckon not."

"Come, come," the mild man said. "Drink it."

"I dont want it."

"Nonsense," the mild man said. "I'm a doctor. Here. Then you can eat."
So he took the glass and even then he hesitated but again the mild man said,
"Come along, down with it; you're still holding us up," in that voice still
calm and sensible but a little sharp too—the voice of a man who could keep
calm and affable because he wasn't used to being crossed—and he drank the
whiskey and even in the second between the sweet full fire in his belly and
when it began to happen he was trying to say, "I tried to tell you! I tried to!"
But it was too late now in the pallid sun-glare of the tenth day of terror and
hopelessness and despair and impotence and rage and outrage and it was
himself and the mule, his mule (they had let him name it—John Henry)
which no man save he had plowed for five years now and whose ways and
habits he knew and respected and who knew his ways and habits so well that
each of them could anticipate the other's very movements and intentions; it
was himself and the mule, the little gobbling faces flying before them, the
familiar hard skull-bones shocking against his fists, his voice shouting,
"Come on, John Henry! Plow them down! Gobble them down, boy!" even as
the bright hot red wave turned back, meeting it joyously, happily, lifted,
poised, then hurling through space, triumphant and yelling, then again the
old shocking blow at the back of his head: he lay on the deck, flat on his back
and pinned arm and leg and cold sober again, his nostrils gushing again, the
mild man stooping over him with behind the thin rimless glasses the coldest
eyes the convict had ever seen—eyes which the convict said were not looking
at him but at the gushing blood with nothing in the world in them but
complete impersonal interest.

"Good man," the mild man said. "Plenty of life in the old carcass yet,
eh? Plenty of good red blood too. Anyone ever suggest to you that you were
hemophilic?" ("What?" the plump convict said. "Hemophilic? You know
what that means?" The tall convict had his cigarette going now, his body
jackknifed backward into the coffinlike space between the upper and lower
bunks, lean, clean, motionless, the blue smoke wreathing across his lean dark
aquiline shaven face. "That's a calf that's a bull and a cow at the same time."

"No, it aint," a third convict said. "It's a calf or a colt that aint neither
one."

"Hell fire," the plump one said. "He's got to be one or the other to keep
from drounding." He had never ceased to look at the tall one in the bunk;
now he spoke to him again: "You let him call you that?") The tall one had
done so. He did not answer the doctor (this was where he stopped thinking
of him as the mild man) at all. He could not move either, though he felt
fine, he felt better than he had in ten days. So they helped him to his feet and
steadied him over and lowered him onto the upturned skiff beside the
woman, where he sat bent forward, elbows on knees in the immemorial attitude, watching his own bright crimson staining the mud-trodden deck, until
the doctor's clean clipped hand appeared under his nose with a phial.

"Smell," the doctor said. "Deep." The convict inhaled, the sharp ammoniac sensation burned up his nostrils and into his throat. "Again," the doctor said. The convict inhaled obediently. This time he choked and spat a gout of blood, his nose now had no more feeling than a toenail, other than it felt about the size of a ten-inch shovel, and as cold.

"I ask you to excuse me," he said. "I never meant—"

"Why?" the doctor said. "You put up as pretty a scrap against forty or fifty men as I ever saw. You lasted a good two seconds. Now you can eat something. Or do you think that will send you haywire again?"

They both ate, sitting on the skiff, the gobbling faces no longer watching them now, the convict gnawing slowly and painfully at the thick sandwich, hunched, his face laid sideways to the food and parallel to the earth as a dog chews; the steamboat went on. At noon there were bowls of hot soup and bread and more coffee; they ate this too, sitting side by side on the skiff, the grapevine still wrapped about the convict's wrist. The baby waked and nursed and slept again and they talked quietly:

"Was it Parchman he said he was going to take us?"

"That's where I told him I wanted to go."

"It never sounded exactly like Parchman to me. It sounded like he said something else." The convict had thought that too. He had been thinking about that fairly soberly ever since they boarded the steamboat and soberly indeed ever since he had remarked the nature of the other passengers, those men and women definitely a little shorter than he and with skin a little different in pigmentation from any sunburn, even though the eyes were sometimes blue or gray, who talked to one another in a tongue he had never heard before and who apparently did not understand his own, people the like of whom he had never seen about Parchman nor anywhere else and whom he did not believe were going there or beyond there either. But after his hillbilly country fashion and kind he would not ask, because to his raising asking information was asking a favor and you did not ask favors of strangers; if they offered them perhaps you accepted and you expressed gratitude almost tediously recapitulant, but you did not ask. So he would watch and wait, as he had done before, and do or try to do to the best of his ability what the best of his judgment dictated.

So he waited, and in midafternoon the steamboat chuffed and thrust through a willow-choked gorge and emerged from it, and now the convict knew it was the River. He could believe it now—the tremendous reach, yellow and sleepy in the afternoon—("Because it's too big," he told them soberly. "Aint no flood in the world big enough to make it do more than stand a little higher so it can look back and see just where the flea is, just exactly where to scratch. It's the little ones, the little piddling creeks that run backward one day and forward the next and come busting down on a man full of dead mules and hen houses.")—and the steamboat moving up this now (*like a ant crossing a plate,* the convict thought, sitting beside the woman on the upturned skiff, the baby nursing again, apparently looking too out across the water where, a mile away on either hand, the twin lines of levee resembled parallel unbroken floating thread) and then it was nearing sunset and he began to hear, to notice, the voices of the doctor and of the man who had first bawled at him through the megaphone now bawling again from the pilot house overhead:

"Stop? Stop? Am I running a street car?"

"Stop for the novelty then," the doctor's pleasant voice said. "I dont know how many trips back and forth you have made in yonder nor how many of what you call mushrats you have fetched out. But this is the first time you ever had two people—no, three—who not only knew the name of some place they wished to go to but were actually trying to go there." So the convict waited while the sun slanted more and more and the steamboat-ant crawled steadily on across its vacant and gigantic plate turning more and more to copper. But he did not ask, he just waited. *Maybe it was Carrollton he said,* he thought. *It began with a C.* But he did not believe that either. He did not know where he was, but he did know that this was not anywhere near the Carrollton he remembered from that day seven years ago when, shackled wrist to wrist with the deputy sheriff, he had passed through it on the train—the slow spaced repeated shattering banging of trucks where two railroads crossed, a random scattering of white houses tranquil among trees on green hills lush with summer, a pointing spire, the finger of the hand of God. But there was no river there. *And you aint never close to this river without knowing it,* he thought. *I dont care who you are nor where you have been all your life.* Then the head of the steamboat began to swing across the stream, its shadow swinging too, travelling long before it across the water, toward the vacant ridge of willow-massed earth empty of all life. There was nothing there at all, the convict could not even see either earth or water beyond it; it was as though the steamboat were about to crash slowly through the thin low frail willow barrier and embark into space, or lacking this, slow and back and fill and disembark him into space, granted it was about to disembark him, granted this was that place which was not near Parchman and was not Carrollton either, even though it did begin with C. Then he turned his head and saw the doctor stooping over the woman, pushing the baby's eyelid up with his forefinger, peering at it.

"Who else was there when he came?" the doctor said.

"Nobody," the convict said.

"Did it all yourselves, eh?"

"Yes," the convict said. Now the doctor stood up and looked at the convict.

"This is Carnarvon," he said.

"Carnarvon?" the convict said. "That aint—" Then he stopped, ceased.

And now he told about that—the intent eyes as dispassionate as ice behind the rimless glasses, the clipped quick-tempered face that was not accustomed to being crossed or lied to either. ("Yes," the plump convict said. "That's what I was aiming to ask. Them clothes. Anybody would know them. How if this doctor was as smart as you claim he was—"

"I had slept in them for ten nights, mostly in the mud," the tall one said. "I had been rowing since midnight with that sapling oar I had tried to burn out that I never had time to scrape the soot off. But it's being scared and worried and then scared and then worried again in clothes for days and days and days that changes the way they look. I dont mean just your pants." He did not laugh. "Your face too. That doctor knowed."

"All right," the plump one said. "Go on.")

"I know it," the doctor said. "I discovered that while you were lying on the deck yonder sobering up again. Now dont lie to me. I dont like lying. This boat is going to New Orleans."

"No," the convict said immediately, quietly, with absolute finality. He could hear them again—the thuck-thuck-thuck on the water where an instant before he had been. But he was not thinking of the bullets. He had forgotten them, forgiven them. He was thinking of himself crouching, sobbing, panting, before running again—the voice, the indictment, the cry of final and irrevocable repudiation of the old primal faithless Manipulator of all the lust and folly and injustice: *All in the world I wanted was just to surrender;* thinking of it, remembering it but without heat now, without passion now and briefer than an epitaph: *No. I tried that once. They shot at me.*

"So you don't want to go to New Orleans. And you didn't exactly plan to go to Carnarvon. But you will take Carnarvon in preference to New Orleans." The convict said nothing. The doctor looked at him, the magnified pupils like the heads of two bridge nails. "What were you in for? Hit him harder than you thought, eh?"

"No. I tried to rob a train."

"Say that again." The convict said it again. "Well? Go on. You dont say that in the year 1927 and just stop, man." So the convict told it, dispassionately too—about the magazines, the pistol which would not shoot, the mask and the dark lantern in which no draft had been arranged to keep the candle burning so that it died almost with the match but even then left the metal too hot to carry, won with subscriptions. *Only it aint my eyes or my mouth either he's watching,* he thought. *It's like he is watching the way my hair grows on my head.* "I see," the doctor said. "But something went wrong. But you've had plenty of time to think about it since. To decide what was wrong, what you failed to do."

"Yes," the convict said. "I've thought about it a right smart since."

"So next time you are not going to make that mistake."

"I don't know," the convict said. "There aint going to be a next time."

"Why? If you know what you did wrong, they wont catch you next time."

The convict looked at the doctor steadily. They looked at each other steadily; the two sets of eyes were not so different after all. "I reckon I see what you mean," the convict said presently. "I was eighteen then. I'm twenty-five now."

"Oh," the doctor said. Now (the convict tried to tell it) the doctor did not move, he just simply quit looking at the convict. He produced a pack of cheap cigarettes from his coat. "Smoke?" he said.

I wouldn't care for none," the convict said.

"Quite," the doctor said in that affable clipped voice. He put the cigarettes away. "There has been conferred upon my race (the Medical race) also the power to bind and to loose, if not by Jehovah perhaps, certainly by the American Medical Association—on which incidentally, in this day of Our Lord, I would put my money, at any odds, at any amount, at any time. I dont know just how far out of bounds I am on this specific occasion but I think we'll put it to the touch." He cupped his hands to his mouth, toward the pilot house overhead. "Captain!" he shouted. "We'll put these three passengers ashore here." He turned to the convict again. "Yes," he said. "I think I shall let your native State lick its own vomit. Here." Again his hand emerged from his pocket, this time with a bill in it.

"No," the convict said.

"Come, come; I dont like to be disputed either."

"No," the convict said. "I aint got any way to pay it back."

"Did I ask you to pay it back?"

"No," the convict said. "I never asked to borrow it either."

So once more he stood on dry land, who had already been toyed with twice by that risible and concentrated power of water, once more than should have fallen to the lot of any one man, any one lifetime, yet for whom there was reserved still another unbelievable recapitulation, he and the woman standing on the empty levee, the sleeping child wrapped in the faded tunic and the grapevine painter still wrapped about the convict's wrist, watching the steamboat back away and turn and once more crawl onward up the platter-like reach of vacant water burnished more and more to copper, its trailing smoke rolling in slow copper-edged gouts, thinning out along the water, fading, stinking away across the vast serene desolation, the boat growing smaller and smaller until it did not seem to crawl at all but to hang stationary in the airy substanceless sunset, dissolving into nothing like a pellet of floating mud.

Then he turned and for the first time looked about him, behind him, recoiling, not through fear but through pure reflex and not physically but the soul, the spirit, that profound sober alert attentiveness of the hillman who will not ask anything of strangers, not even information, thinking quietly,

No. This aint Carrollton neither. Because he now looked down the almost perpendicular landward slope of the levee through sixty feet of absolute space,
upon a surface, a terrain flat as a waffle and of the color of a waffle or perhaps
of the summer coat of a claybank horse and possessing that same piled density of a rug or peltry, spreading away without undulation yet with that curious appearance of imponderable solidity like fluid, broken here and there by
thick lumps of arsenical green which nevertheless still seemed to possess no
height and by writhen veins of the color of ink which he began to suspect to
be actual water but with judgment reserved, with judgment still reserved
even when presently he was walking in it. That's what he said, told: So they
went on. He didn't tell how he got the skiff singlehanded up the revetment
and across the crown and down the opposite sixty foot drop, he just said he
went on, in a swirling cloud of mosquitoes like hot cinders, thrusting and
plunging through the saw-edged grass which grew taller than his head and
which whipped back at his arms and face like limber knives, dragging by the
vine-spliced painter the skiff in which the woman sat, slogging and stumbling knee-deep in something less of earth than water, along one of those
black winding channels less of water than earth: and then (he was in the skiff
too now, paddling with the charred log, what footing there had been having
given away beneath him without warning thirty minutes ago, leaving only
the air-filled bubble of his jumper-back ballooning lightly on the twilit water
until he rose to the surface and scrambled into the skiff) the house,
the cabin a little larger than a horse-box, of cypress boards and an iron roof,
rising on ten-foot stilts slender as spiders' legs, like a shabby and death-
stricken (and probably poisonous) wading creature which had got that far
into that flat waste and died with nothing nowhere in reach or sight to lie
down upon, a pirogue tied to the foot of a crude ladder, a man standing in
the open door holding a lantern (it was that dark now) above his head, gobbling down at them.

   He told it—of the next eight or nine or ten days, he did not remember
which, while the four of them—himself and the woman and baby and the
little wiry man with rotting teeth and soft wild bright eyes like a rat or a
chipmunk, whose language neither of them could understand—lived in the
room and a half. He did not tell it that way, just as he apparently did not
consider it worth the breath to tell how he had got the hundred-and-sixty-
pound skiff singlehanded up and across and down the sixty-foot levee. He
just said, "After a while we come to a house and we stayed there eight or nine
days then they blew up the levee with dynamite so we had to leave." That
was all. But he remembered it, but quietly now, with the cigar now, the good
one the Warden had given him (though not lighted yet) in his peaceful and
steadfast hand, remembering that first morning when he waked on the thin
pallet beside his host (the woman and baby had the one bed) with the fierce
sun already latticed through the warped rough planking of the wall, and

stood on the rickety porch looking out upon that flat fecund waste neither earth nor water, where even the senses doubted which was which, which rich and massy air and which mazy and impalpable vegetation, and thought quietly, *He must do something here to eat and live. But I dont know what. And until I can go on again, until I can find where I am and how to pass that town without them seeing me I will have to help him do it so we can eat and live too, and I dont know what.* And he had a change of clothing too, almost at once on that first morning, not telling any more than he had about the skiff and the levee who he had begged borrowed or bought from the man whom he had not laid eyes on twelve hours ago and with whom on the day he saw him for the last time he still could exchange no word, the pair of dungaree pants which even the Cajan had discarded as no longer wearable, filthy, buttonless, the legs slashed and frayed into fringe like that on an 1890 hammock, in which he stood naked from the waist up and holding out to her the mud-caked and soot-stained jumper and overall when the woman waked on that first morning in the crude bunk nailed into one corner and filled with dried grass, saying, "Wash them. Good. I want all them stains out. All of them."

"But the jumper," she said. "Aint he got ere old shirt too? That sun and them mosquitoes—" But he did not even answer, and she said no more either, though when he and the Cajan returned at dark the garments were clean, stained a little still with the old mud and soot, but clean, resembling again what they were supposed to resemble as (his arms and back already a fiery red which would be blisters by tomorrow) he spread the garments out and examined them and then rolled them up carefully in a six-months-old New Orleans paper and thrust the bundle behind a rafter, where it remained while day followed day and the blisters on his back broke and suppurated and he would sit with his face expressionless as a wooden mask beneath the sweat while the Cajan doped his back with something on a filthy rag from a filthy saucer, she still saying nothing since she too doubtless knew what his reason was, not from that rapport of the wedded conferred upon her by the two weeks during which they had jointly suffered all the crises emotional social economic and even moral which do not always occur even in the ordinary fifty married years (the old married: you have seen them, the electroplate reproductions, the thousand identical coupled faces with only a collarless stud or a fichu out of Louisa Alcott to denote the sex, looking in pairs like the winning braces of dogs after a field trial, out from among the packed columns of disaster and alarm and baseless assurance and hope and incredible insensitivity and insulation from tomorrow propped by a thousand morning sugar bowls or coffee urns; or singly, rocking on porches or sitting in the sun beneath the tobacco-stained porticoes of a thousand county courthouses, as though with the death of the other having inherited a sort of rejuvenescence, immortality; relict, they take a new lease on breath and seem to live forever, as though that flesh which the old ceremony or ritual had morally purified and made legally one had actually become so with long tedious habit and he or she who entered the ground first took all of it with him or her, leaving only the old permanent enduring bone, free and trammelless)—not because of this but because she too had stemmed at some point from the same dim hill-bred Abraham.

So the bundle remained behind the rafter and day followed day while he and his partner (he was in partnership now with his host, hunting alligators on shares, on the halvers he called it—"Halvers?" the plump convict said. "How could you make a business agreement with a man you claim you couldn't even talk to?"

"I never had to talk to him," the tall one said. "Money aint got but one language.") departed at dawn each day, at first together in the pirogue but later singly, the one in the pirogue and the other in the skiff, the one with the battered and pitted rifle, the other with the knife and a piece of knotted rope and a lightwood club the size and weight and shape of a Thuringian mace, stalking their pleistocene nightmares up and down the secret inky channels which writhed the flat brass-colored land. He remembered that too: that first morning when turning in the sunrise from the rickety platform he saw the hide nailed drying to the wall and stopped dead, looking at it quietly, thinking quietly and soberly, So *that's it. That's what he does in order to eat and live,* knowing it was a hide, a skin, but from what animal, by association, ratiocination or even memory of any picture out of his dead youth, he did not know but knowing that it was the reason, the explanation, for the little lost spider-legged house (which had already begun to die, to rot from the legs upward almost before the roof was nailed on) set in that teeming and myriad desolation, enclosed and lost within the furious embrace of flowing mare earth and stallion sun, divining through pure rapport of kind for kind, hillbilly and bayou-rat, the two one and identical because of the same grudged dispensation and niggard fate of hard and unceasing travail not to gain future security, a balance in the bank or even in a buried soda can for slothful and easy old age, but just permission to endure and endure to buy air to feel and sun to drink for each's little while, thinking (the convict), *Well, anyway I am going to find out what it is sooner than I expected to,* and did so, re-entered the house where the woman was just waking in the one sorry built-in straw-filled bunk which the Cajan had surrendered to her, and ate the breakfast (the rice, a semi-liquid mess violent with pepper and mostly fish considerably high, the chicory-thickened coffee) and, shirtless, followed the little scuttling bobbing bright-eyed rotten-toothed man down the crude ladder and into the pirogue. He had never seen a pirogue either and he believed that it would not remain upright—not that it was light and precariously balanced with its open side upward but that there was inherent in the wood, the very log, some dynamic and unsleeping natural law, almost will, which its present position outraged and violated—yet accepting this too as he had the fact that that hide had belonged to something larger than any calf or hog and that anything which looked like that on the outside would be more than likely to have teeth and claws too, accepting this, squatting in the pirogue, clutching both gunwales, rigidly immobile as though he had an egg filled with nitroglycerin in his mouth and scarcely breathing, thinking, *If that's it, then I can do it too and even if he cant tell me how I reckon I can watch him and find out.* And he did this too, he remembered it, quietly even yet, thinking, *I thought that was how to do it and I reckon I would still think that even if I had it to do again now for the first time*—the brazen day already fierce upon his naked back, the crooked channel like a voluted thread of ink, the pirogue moving steadily to the paddle which both entered and left the water without a sound; then the sudden cessation of the paddle behind him and the fierce hissing gobble of the Cajan at his back and he squatting bate-breathed and with that intense immobility of complete sobriety of a blind man listening while the frail wooden shell stole on at the dying apex of its own parted water. Afterward he remembered the rifle too—the rust-pitted single-shot weapon with a clumsily wired stock and a muzzle you could have driven a whiskey cork into, which the Cajan had brought into the boat—but not now; now he just squatted, crouched, immobile, breathing with infinitesimal care, his sober unceasing gaze going here and there constantly as he thought, *What? What? I not only dont know what I am looking for, I dont even know where to look for it.* Then he felt the motion of the pirogue as the Cajan moved and then the tense gobbling hissing actually, hot rapid and repressed, against his neck and ear, and glancing downward saw projecting between his own arm and body from behind the Cajan's hand holding the knife, and glaring up again saw the flat thick spit of mud which as he looked at it divided and became a thick mud-colored log which in turn seemed, still immobile, to leap suddenly against his retinae in three—no, four—dimensions: volume, solidity, shape, and another: not fear but pure and intense speculation and he looking at the scaled motionless shape, thinking not, *It looks dangerous* but *It looks big,* thinking, *Well, maybe a mule standing in a lot looks big to a man that never walked up to one with a halter before,* thinking, *Only if he could just tell me what to do it would save time,* the pirogue drawing nearer now, creeping now, with no ripple now even and it seemed to him that he could even hear his companion's held breath and he taking the knife from the other's hand now and not even thinking this since it was too fast, a flash; it was not a surrender, not a resignation, it was too calm, it was a part of him, he had drunk it with his mother's milk and lived with it all his life: *After all a man cant only do what he has to do, with what he has to do it with, with what he has learned, to the best of his judgment. And I reckon a hog is still a hog, no matter what it looks like. So here goes,* sitting still for an instant longer until the bow of the pirogue grounded lighter than the falling of a leaf and stepped out of it and paused just for one instant while the words *It does look big* stood for just a second, unemphatic and trivial, somewhere

where some fragment of his attention could see them and vanished, and stooped straddling, the knife driving even as he grasped the near foreleg, this all in the same instant when the lashing tail struck him a terrific blow upon the back. But the knife was home, he knew that even on his back in the mud, the weight of the thrashing beast longwise upon him, its ridged back clutched to his stomach, his arm about its throat, the hissing head clamped against his jaw, the furious tail lashing and flailing, the knife in his other hand probing for the life and finding it, the hot fierce gush: and now sitting beside the profound up-bellied carcass, his head again between his knees in the old attitude while his own blood freshened the other which drenched him, thinking, *It's my durn nose again.*

So he sat there, his head, his streaming face, bowed between his knees in an attitude not of dejection but profoundly bemused, contemplative, while the shrill voice of the Cajan seemed to buzz at him from an enormous distance; after a time he even looked up at the antic wiry figure bouncing hysterically about him, the face wild and grimacing, the voice gobbling and high; while the convict, holding his face carefully slanted so the blood would run free, looked at him with the cold intentness of a curator or custodian paused before one of his own glass cases, the Cajan threw up the rifle, cried "Boom-boom-boom!" flung it down and in pantomime re-enacted the recent scene then whirled his hands again, crying "Magnifique! Magnifique! Cent d'argent! Mille d'argent! Tout l'argent sous le ciel de Dieu!" But the convict was already looking down again, cupping the coffee-colored water to his face, watching the constant bright carmine marble it, thinking, *It's a little late to be telling me that now,* and not even thinking this long because presently they were in the pirogue again, the convict squatting again with that unbreathing rigidity as though he were trying by holding his breath to decrease his very weight, the bloody skin in the bows before him and he looking at it, thinking, *And I cant even ask him how much my half will be.*

But this not for long either, because as he was to tell the plump convict later, money has but one language. He remembered that too (they were at home now, the skin spread on the platform, where for the woman's benefit now the Cajan once more went through the pantomime—the gun which was not used, the hand-to-hand battle; for the second time the invisible alligator was slain amid cries, the victor rose and found this time that not even the woman was watching him. She was looking at the once more swollen and inflamed face of the convict. "You mean it kicked you right in the face?" she said.

"Nah," the convict said harshly, savagely. "It never had to. I done seem to got to where if that boy was to shoot me in the tail with a bean blower my nose would bleed.")—remembered that too but he did not try to tell it. Perhaps he could not have—how two people who could not even talk to one another made an agreement which both not only understood but which each knew the other would hold true and protect (perhaps for this reason) better than any written and witnessed contract. They even discussed and agreed somehow that they should hunt separately, each in his own vessel, to double the chances of finding prey. But this was easy: the convict could almost understand the words in which the Cajan said, "You do not need me and the rifle; we will only hinder you, be in your way." And more than this, they even agreed about the second rifle: that there was someone, it did not matter who—friend, neighbor, perhaps one in business in that line—from whom they could rent a second rifle; in their two patois, the one bastard English, the other bastard French—the one volatile, with his wild bright eyes and his voluble mouth full of stumps of teeth, the other sober, almost grim, swollen-faced and with his naked back blistered and scoriated like so much beef—they discussed this, squatting on either side of the pegged-out hide like two members of a corporation facing each other across a mahogany board table, and decided against it, the convict deciding: "I reckon not," he said. "I reckon if I had knowed enough to wait to start out with a gun, I still would. But since I done already started out without one, I dont reckon I'll change." Because it was a question of the money in terms of time, days. (Strange to say, that was the one thing which the Cajan could not tell him: how much the half would be. But the convict knew it was half.) He had so little of them. He would have to move on soon, thinking (the convict), *All this durn foolishness will stop soon and I can get on back,* and then suddenly he found that he was thinking, *Will have to get on back,* and he became quite still and looked about at the rich strange desert which surrounded him, in which he was temporarily lost in peace and hope and into which the last seven years had sunk like so many trivial pebbles into a pool, leaving no ripple, and he thought quietly, with a kind of bemused amazement, *Yes. I reckon I had done forgot how good making money was. Being let to make it.*

So he used no gun, his the knotted rope and the Thuringian mace, and each morning he and the Cajan took their separate ways in the two boats to comb and creep the secret channels about the lost land from (or out of) which now and then still other pint-sized dark men appeared gobbling, abruptly and as though by magic from nowhere, in other hollowed logs, to follow quietly and watch him at his single combats—men named Tine and Toto and Theule, who were not much larger than and looked a good deal like the muskrats which the Cajan (the host did this too, supplied the kitchen too, he expressed this too like the rifle business, in his own tongue, the convict comprehending this too as though it had been English: "Do not concern yourself about food, O Hercules. Catch alligators: I will supply the pot.") took now and then from traps as you take a shoat pig at need from a pen, and varied the eternal rice and fish (the convict did tell this: how at night, in the cabin, the door and one sashless window battened against mosquitoes—a form, a ritual, as empty as crossing the fingers or knocking on wood—sitting beside the bug-swirled lantern on the plank table in a temperature close to blood heat he would look down at the swimming segment of meat on his sweating plate and think, *It must be Theule. He was the fat one.*)—day following day, unemphatic and identical, each like the one before and the one which would follow while his theoretical half of a sum to be reckoned in pennies, dollars, or tens of dollars he did not know, mounted—the mornings when he set forth to find waiting for him like the *matador* his *aficionados* the small clump of constant and deferential pirogues, the hard noons when ringed half about by little motionless shells he fought his solitary combats, the evenings, the return, the pirogues departing one by one into inlets and passages which during the first few days he could not even distinguish, then the platform in the twilight where before the static woman and the usually nursing infant and the one or two bloody hides of the day's take the Cajan would perform his ritualistic victorious pantomime before the two growing rows of knifemarks in one of the boards of the wall; then the nights when, the woman and child in the single bunk and the Cajan already snoring on the pallet and the reeking lantern set close, he (the convict) would sit on his naked heels, sweating steadily, his face worn and calm, immersed and indomitable, his bowed back raw and savage as beef beneath the suppurant old blisters and the fierce welts of tails, and scrape and chip at the charred sapling which was almost a paddle now, pausing now and then to raise his head while the cloud of mosquitoes about it whined and whirled, to stare at the wall before him until after a while the crude boards themselves must have dissolved away and let his blank unseeing gaze go on and on unhampered, through the rich oblivious darkness, beyond it even perhaps, even perhaps beyond the seven wasted years during which, so he had just realised, he had been permitted to toil but not to work. Then he would retire himself, he would take a last look at the rolled bundle behind the rafter and blow out the lantern and lie down as he was beside his snoring partner, to lie sweating (on his stomach, he could not bear the touch of anything to his back) in the whining ovenlike darkness filled with the forlorn bellowing of alligators, thinking not, *They never gave me time to learn* but *I had forgot how good it is to work.*

Then on the tenth day it happened. It happened for the third time. At first he refused to believe it, not that he felt that now he had served out and discharged his apprenticeship to mischance, had with the birth of the child reached and crossed the crest of his Golgotha and would now be, possibly not permitted so much as ignored, to descend the opposite slope free-wheeling. That was not his feeling at all. What he declined to accept was the fact that a power, a force such as that which had been consistent enough to concentrate upon him with deadly undeviation for weeks, should with all the wealth of cosmic violence and disaster to draw from, have been so barren of invention and imagination, so lacking in pride of artistry and craftsmanship, as to repeat itself twice. Once he had accepted, twice he even forgave, but three times he simply declined to believe, particularly when he was at last persuaded to realise that this third time was to be instigated not by the blind potency of volume and motion but by human direction and hands: that now the cosmic joker, foiled twice, had stooped in its vindictive concentration to the employing of dynamite.

He did not tell that. Doubtless he did not know himself how it happened, what was happening. But he doubtless remembered it (but quietly above the thick rich-colored pristine cigar in his clean steady hand), what he knew, divined of it. It would be evening, the ninth evening, he and the woman on either side of their host's empty place at the evening meal, he hearing the voices from without but not ceasing to eat, still chewing steadily, because it would be the same as though he were seeing them anyway—the two or three or four pirogues floating on the dark water beneath the platform on which the host stood, the voices gobbling and jabbering, incomprehensible and filled not with alarm and not exactly with rage or ever perhaps absolute surprise but rather just cacophony like those of disturbed marsh fowl, he (the convict) not ceasing to chew but just looking up quietly and maybe without a great deal of interrogation or surprise too as the Cajan burst in and stood before them, wild-faced, glaring, his blackened teeth gaped against the inky orifice of his distended mouth, watching (the convict) while the Cajan went through his violent pantomime of violent evacuation, ejection, scooping something invisible into his arms and hurling it out and downward and in the instant of completing the gesture changing from instigator to victim of that which he had set into pantomimic motion, clasping his head and, bowed over and not otherwise moving, seeming to be swept on and away before it, crying "Boom! Boom! Boom!", the convict watching him, his jaw not chewing now, though for just that moment, thinking, *What? What is it he is trying to tell me?* thinking (this a flash too, since he could not have expressed this, and hence did not even know that he had ever thought it) that though his life had been cast here, circumscribed by this environment, accepted by this environment and accepting it in turn (and he had done well here—this quietly, soberly indeed, if he had been able to phrase it, think it instead of merely knowing it—better than he had ever done, who had not even known until now how good work, making money, could be) yet it was not his life, he still and would ever be no more than the water bug upon the surface of the pond, the plumbless and lurking depths of which he would never know, his only actual contact with it being the instants when on lonely and glaring mud-spits under the pitiless sun and amphitheatred by his motionless and riveted semicircle of watching pirogues, he accepted the gambit which he had not elected, entered the lashing radius of the armed tail and beat at the thrashing and hissing head with his lightwood club, or this failing, embraced without hesitation the armored body itself with the frail web of flesh and bone in which he walked and lived and sought the raging life with an eight-inch knife-blade.

So he and the woman merely watched the Cajan as he acted out the whole charade of eviction—the little wiry man gesticulant and wild, his hysterical shadow leaping and falling upon the rough wall as he went through the pantomime of abandoning the cabin, gathering in pantomime his meagre belongings from the walls and corners—objects which no other man would want and only some power or force like blind water or earthquake or fire would ever dispossess him of, the woman watching too, her mouth slightly open upon a mass of chewed food, on her face an expression of placid astonishment, saying, "What? What's he saying?"

"I don't know," the convict said. "But I reckon if it's something we ought to know we will find it out when it's ready for us to." Because he was not alarmed, though by now he had read the other's meaning plainly enough. *He's fixing to leave,* he thought. *He's telling me to leave too*—this later, after they had quitted the table and the Cajan and the woman had gone to bed and the Cajan had risen from the pallet and approached the convict and once more went through the pantomime of abandoning the cabin, this time as one repeats a speech which may have been misunderstood, tediously, carefully repetitional as to a child, seeming to hold the convict with one hand while he gestured, talked, with the other, gesturing as though in single syllables, the convict (squatting, the knife open and the almost-finished paddle across his lap) watching, nodding his head, even speaking in English: "Yah; sure. You bet. I got you."—trimming again at the paddle but no faster, with no more haste than on any other night, serene in his belief that when the time came for him to know whatever it was, that would take care of itself, having already and without even knowing it, even before the possibility, the question, ever arose, declined, refused to accept even the thought of moving also, thinking about the hides, thinking, *If there was just some way he could tell me where to carry my share to get the money* but thinking this only for an instant between two delicate strokes of the blade because almost at once he thought, *I reckon as long as I can catch them I wont have no big trouble finding whoever it is that will buy them.*

So the next morning he helped the Cajan load his few belongings—the pitted rifle, a small bundle of clothing (again they traded, who could not even converse with one another, this time the few cooking vessels, a few rusty traps by definite allocation, and something embracing and abstractional which included the stove, the crude bunk, the house or its occupancy—something—in exchange for one alligator hide)—into the pirogue, then, squatting and as two children divide sticks they divided the hides, separating them into two piles, one-for-me-and-one-for-you, two-for-me-and-two-for-you, and the Cajan loaded his share and shoved away from the platform and paused again, though this time he only put the paddle down, gathered something invisibly into his two hands and flung it violently upward, crying "Boom? Boom?" on a rising inflection, nodding violently to the half-naked and savagely scoriated man on the platform who stared with a sort of grim equability back at him and said, "Sure. Boom. Boom." Then the Cajan went on. He did not look back. They watched him, already paddling rapidly, or the woman did; the convict had already turned.

"Maybe he was trying to tell us to leave too," she said.

"Yah," the convict said. "I thought of that last night. Hand me the paddle." She fetched it to him—the sapling, the one he had been trimming at nightly, not quite finished yet though one more evening would do it (he had been using a spare one of the Cajan's. The other had offered to let him keep it, to include it perhaps with the stove and the bunk and the cabin's freehold, but the convict had declined. Perhaps he had computed it by volume against so much alligator hide, this weighed against one more evening with the tedious and careful blade.) and he departed too with his knotted rope and mace, in the opposite direction, as though not only not content with refusing to quit the place he had been warned against, he must establish and affirm the irrevocable finality of his refusal by penetrating even further and deeper into it. And then and without warning the high fierce drowsing of his solitude gathered itself and struck at him.

He could not have told this if he had tried—this not yet midmorning and he going on, alone for the first time, no pirogue emerging anywhere to fall in behind him, but he had not expected this anyway, he knew that the others would have departed too; it was not this, it was his very solitude, his desolation which was now his alone and in full since he had elected to remain; the sudden cessation of the paddle, the skiff shooting on for a moment yet while he thought, *What? What?* Then, *No. No. No,* as the silence and solitude and emptiness roared down upon him in a jeering bellow: and now reversed, the skiff spun violently on its heel, he the betrayed driving furiously back toward the platform where he knew it was already too late, that citadel where the very crux and dear breath of his life—the being allowed to work and earn money, that right and privilege which he believed he had earned to himself unaided, asking no favor of anyone or anything save the right to be let alone to pit his will and strength against the sauric protagonist of a land, a region, which he had not asked to be projected into—was being threatened, driving the home-made paddle in grim fury, coming in sight of the platform at last and seeing the motor launch lying alongside it with no surprise at all but actually with a kind of pleasure as though at a visible justification of his outrage and fear, the privilege of saying *I told you so* to his own affronting, driving on toward it in a dreamlike state in which there seemed to be no progress at all, in which, unimpeded and suffocating, he strove dreamily with a weightless oar, with muscles without strength or resiliency, at a medium without resistance, seeming to watch the skiff creep infinitesimally across the sunny water and up to the platform while a man in the launch (there were five of them in all) gobbled at him in that same tongue he had been hearing constantly now for ten days and still knew no word of, just as a second man, followed by the woman carrying the baby and dressed again for departure in the faded tunic and the sunbonnet, emerged from the house, carrying (the man carried several other things but the convict saw nothing else) the paper-wrapped bundle which the convict had put behind the rafter ten days ago and no other hand had touched since, he (the convict) on the platform too now, holding the skiff's painter in one hand and the bludgeonlike paddle in the other, contriving to speak to the woman at last in a voice dreamy and suffo-cating and incredibly calm: "Take it away from him and carry it back into the house."

"So you can talk English, can you?" the man in the launch said. "Why didn't you come out like they told you to last night?"

"Out?" the convict said. Again he even looked, glared, at the man in the launch, contriving even again to control his voice: "I aint got time to take trips. I'm busy," already turning to the woman again, his mouth already open to repeat as the dreamy buzzing voice of the man came to him and he turning once more, in a terrific and absolutely unbearable exasperation, crying, "Flood? What flood? Hell a mile, it's done passed me twice months ago! It's gone! What flood?" and then (he did not think this in actual words either but he knew it, suffered that flashing insight into his own character or des-tiny: how there was a peculiar quality of repetitiveness about his present fate, how not only the almost seminal crises recurred with a certain monotony, but the very physical circumstances followed a stupidly unimaginative pat-tern) the man in the launch said, "Take him" and he was on his feet for a few minutes yet, lashing and striking in panting fury, then once more on his back on hard unyielding planks while the four men swarmed over him in a fierce wave of hard bones and panting curses and at last the thin dry vicious snap-ping of handcuffs.

"Damn it, are you mad?" the man in the launch said. "Cant you under-stand they are going to dynamite that levee at noon today?—Come on," he said to the others. "Get him aboard. Let's get out of here."

"I want my hides and boat," the convict said.

"Damn your hides," the man in the launch said. "If they dont get that levee blowed pretty soon you can hunt plenty more of them on the capitol steps at Baton Rouge. And this is all the boat you will need and you can say your prayers about it."

"I aint going without my boat," the convict said. He said it calmly and with complete finality, so calm, so final that for almost a minute nobody an-swered him, they just stood looking quietly down at him as he lay, half-naked, blistered and scarred, helpless and manacled hand and foot, on his back, delivering his ultimatum in a voice peaceful and quiet as that in which you talk to your bedfellow before going to sleep. Then the man in the launch moved; he spat quietly over the side and said in a voice as calm and quiet as the convict's:

"All right. Bring his boat." They helped the woman, carrying the baby and the paper-wrapped parcel, into the launch. Then they helped the convict to his feet and into the launch too, the shackles on his wrists and ankles clashing. "I'd unlock you if you'd promise to behave yourself," the man said. The convict did not answer this at all.

"I want to hold the rope," he said.

"The rope?"

"Yes," the convict said. "The rope." So they lowered him into the stern and gave him the end of the painter after it had passed the towing cleat, and they went on. The convict did not look back. But then, he did not look forward either, he lay half sprawled, his shackled legs before him, the end of the skiff's painter in one shackled hand. The launch made two other stops; when the hazy wafer of the intolerable sun began to stand once more directly overhead there were fifteen people in the launch; and then the convict, sprawled and motionless, saw the flat brazen land begin to rise and become a greenish-black mass of swamp, bearded and convoluted, this in turn stopping short off and there spread before him an expanse of water embraced by a blue dissolution of shoreline and glittering thinly under the noon, larger than he had ever seen before, the sound of the launch's engine ceasing, the hull sliding on behind its fading bow-wave. "What are you doing?" the leader said.

"It's noon," the helmsman said. "I thought we might hear the dynamite." So they all listened, the launch lost of all forward motion, rocking slightly, the glitter-broken small waves slapping and whispering at the hull, but no sound, no tremble even, came anywhere under the fierce hazy sky; the long moment gathered itself and turned on and noon was past. "All right," the leader said. "Let's go." The engine started again, the hull began to gather speed. The leader came aft and stooped over the convict, key in hand. "I guess you'll have to behave now, whether you want to or not," he said, unlocking the manacles. "Wont you?"

"Yes," the convict said. They went on; after a time the shore vanished completely and a little sea got up. The convict was free now but he lay as before, the end of the skiff's painter in his hand, bent now with three or four turns about his wrist; he turned his head now and then to look back at the towing skiff as it slewed and bounced in the launch's wake; now and then he even looked out over the lake, the eyes alone moving, the face grave and expressionless, thinking, *This is a great immensity of water, of waste and desolation, than I have ever seen before;* perhaps not; thinking three or four hours later, the shoreline raised again and broken into a clutter of sailing sloops and power cruisers, *These are more boats than I believed existed, a maritime race of which*

I also had no cognizance or perhaps not thinking it but just watching as the launch opened the shored gut of the ship canal, the low smoke of the city beyond it, then a wharf, the launch slowing in; a quiet crowd of people watching with that same forlorn passivity he had seen before and whose race he did recognise even though he had not seen Vicksburg when he passed it—the brand, the unmistakable hallmark of the violently homeless, he more so than any, who would have permitted no man to call him one of them.

"All right," the leader said to him. "Here you are."

"The boat," the convict said.

"You've got it. What do you want me to do—give you a receipt for it?"

"No," the convict said. "I just want the boat."

"Take it. Only you ought to have a bookstrap or something to carry it in." ("Carry it in?" the plump convict said. "Carry it where? Where would you have to carry it?")

He (the tall one) told that: how he and the woman disembarked and how one of the men helped him haul the skiff up out of the water and how he stood there with the end of the painter wrapped around his wrist and the man bustled up, saying, "All right. Next load! Next load!" and how he told this man too about the boat and the man cried, "Boat? Boat?" and how he (the convict) went with them when they carried the skiff over and racked, berthed, it with the others and how he lined himself up by a coca-cola sign and the arch of a draw bridge so he could find the skiff again quick when he returned, and how he and the woman (he carrying the paper-wrapped parcel) were herded into a truck and after a while the truck began to run in traffic, between close houses, then there was a big building, an armory—

"Armory?" the plump one said. "You mean a jail."

"No. It was a kind of warehouse, with people with bundles laying on the floor." And how he thought maybe his partner might be there and how he even looked about for the Cajan while waiting for a chance to get back to the door again, where the soldier was and how he got back to the door at last, the woman behind him and his chest actually against the dropped rifle.

"Gwan, gwan," the soldier said. "Get back. They'll give you some clothes in a minute. You cant walk around the streets that way. And something to eat too. Maybe your kinfolks will come for you by that time." And he told that too: how the woman said,

"Maybe if you told him you had some kinfolks here he would let us out." And how he did not; he could not have expressed this either, it too deep, too ingrained; he had never yet had to think it into words through all the long generations of himself—his hill-man's sober and jealous respect not for truth but for the power, the strength, of lying—not to be niggard with lying but rather to use it with respect and even care, delicate quick and strong, like a fine and fatal blade. And how they fetched him clothes—a blue jumper and overalls, and then food too (a brisk starched young woman saying, "But the baby must be bathed, cleaned. It will die if you dont" and the woman saying, "Yessum. He might holler some, he aint never been bathed before. But he's a good baby.") and now it was night, the unshaded bulbs harsh and savage and forlorn above the snorers and he rising, gripping the woman awake, and then the window. He told that: how there were doors in plenty, leading he did not know where, but he had a hard time finding a window they could use but he found one at last, he carrying the parcel and the baby too while he climbed through first—"You ought to tore up a sheet and slid down it," the plump convict said. But he needed no sheet, there were cobbles under his feet now, in the rich darkness. The city was there too but he had not seen it yet and would not—the low constant glare; Bienville had stood there too, it had been the figment of an emasculate also calling himself Napoleon but no more, Andrew Jackson had found it one step from Pennsylvania Avenue. But the convict found it considerably further than one step back to the ship canal and the skiff, the coca-cola sign dim now, the draw bridge arching spidery against the jonquil sky at dawn: nor did he tell, any more than about the sixty-foot levee, how he got the skiff back into the water. The lake was behind him now; there was but one direction he could go. When he saw the River again he knew it at once. He should have; it was now ineradicably a part of his past, his life; it would be a part of what he would bequeath, if that were in store for him. But four weeks later it would look different from what it did now, and did: he (the Old Man) had recovered from his debauch, back in banks again, the Old Man, rippling placidly toward the sea, brown and rich as chocolate between levees whose inner faces were wrinkled as though in a frozen and aghast amazement, crowned with the rich green of summer in the willows; beyond them, sixty feet below, slick mules squatted against the broad pull of middle-busters in the richened soil which would not need to be planted, which would need only to be shown a cotton seed to sprout and make; there would be the symmetric miles of strong stalks by July, purple bloom in August, in September the black fields snowed over, spilled, the middles dragged smooth by the long sacks, the long black limber hands plucking, the hot air filled with the whine of gins, the September air then but now June air heavy with locust and (the towns) the smell of new paint and the sour smell of the paste which holds wall paper— the towns, the villages, the little lost wood landings on stilts on the inner face of the levee, the lower storeys bright and rank under the new paint and paper and even the marks on spile and post and tree of May's raging water- height fading beneath each bright silver gust of summer's loud and incon- stant rain; there was a store at the levee's lip, a few saddled and rope-bridled mules in the sleepy dust, a few dogs, a handful of negroes sitting on the steps beneath the chewing tobacco and malaria medicine signs, and three white men, one of them a deputy sheriff canvassing for votes to beat his superior (who had given him his job) in the August primary, all pausing to watch the skiff emerge from the glitter-glare of the afternoon water and approach and land, a woman carrying a child stepping out, then a man, a tall man who, approaching, proved to be dressed in a faded but recently washed and quite clean suit of penitentiary clothing, stopping in the dust where the mules dozed and watching with pale cold humorless eyes while the deputy sheriff was still making toward his armpit that gesture which everyone present realised was to have produced a pistol in one flashing motion for a considerable time while still nothing came of it. It was apparently enough for the newcomer, however.

"You a officer?" he said.

"You damn right I am," the deputy said. "Just let me get this damn gun—"

"All right," the other said. "Yonder's your boat, and here's the woman. But I never did find that bastard on the cottonhouse."

One of the Governor's young men arrived at the Penitentiary the next morning. That is, he was fairly young (he would not see thirty again though without doubt he did not want to, there being that about him which indicated a character which never had and never would want anything it did not, or was not about to, possess), a Phi Beta Kappa out of an Eastern university, a colonel on the Governor's staff who did not buy it with a campaign contribution, who had stood in his negligent Eastern-cut clothes and his arched nose and lazy contemptuous eyes on the galleries of any number of little lost backwoods stores and told his stories and received the guffaws of his overalled and spitting hearers and with the same look in his eyes fondled infants named in memory of the last administration and in honor (or hope) of the next, and (it was said of him and doubtless not true) by lazy accident the behinds of some who were not infants any longer though still not old enough to vote. He was in the Warden's office with a briefcase, and presently the deputy warden of the levee was there too. He would have been sent for presently though not yet, but he came anyhow, without knocking, with his hat on, calling the Governor's young man loudly by a nickname and striking him with a flat hand on the back and lifted one thigh to the Warden's desk, almost between the Warden and the caller, the emissary. Or the vizier with the command, the knotted cord, as began to appear immediately.

"Well," the Governor's young man said, "you've played the devil, haven't you?" The Warden had a cigar. He had offered the caller one. It had been refused, though presently, while the Warden looked at the back of his neck with hard immobility even a little grim, the deputy leaned and reached back and opened the desk drawer and took one.

"Seems straight enough to me," the Warden said. "He got swept away against his will. He came back as soon as he could and surrendered."

"He even brought that damn boat back," the deputy said. "If he'd a throwed the boat away he could a walked back in three days. But no sir. He's got to bring the boat back. 'Here's your boat and here's the woman but I never found no bastard on no cottonhouse.' " He slapped his knee, guffawing. "Them convicts. A mule's got twice as much sense."

"A mule's got twice as much sense as anything except a rat," the emissary said in his pleasant voice. "But that's not the trouble."

"What is the trouble?" the Warden said.

"This man is dead."

"Hell fire, he aint dead," the deputy said. "He's up yonder in that bunkhouse right now, lying his head off probly. I'll take you up there and you can see him." The Warden was looking at the deputy.

"Look," he said. "Bledsoe was trying to tell me something about that Kate mule's leg. You better go up to the stable and—"

"I done tended to it," the deputy said. He didn't even look at the Warden. He was watching, talking to, the emissary. "No sir. He aint—"

"But he has received an official discharge as being dead. Not a pardon nor a parole either: a discharge. He's either dead, or free. In either case he doesn't belong here." Now both the Warden and the deputy looked at the emissary, the deputy's mouth open a little, the cigar poised in his hand to have its tip bitten off. The emissary spoke pleasantly, extremely distinctly: "On a report of death forwarded to the Governor by the Warden of the Penitentiary." The deputy closed his mouth, though otherwise he didn't move. "On the official evidence of the officer delegated at the time to the charge and returning of the body of the prisoner to the Penitentiary." Now the deputy put the cigar into his mouth and got slowly off the desk, the cigar rolling across his lip as he spoke:

"So that's it. I'm to be it, am I?" He laughed shortly, a stage laugh, two notes. "When I done been right three times running through three separate administrations? That's on a book somewhere too. Somebody in Jackson can find that too. And if they cant, I can show—"

"Three administrations?" the emissary said. "Well, well. That's pretty good."

"You damn right it's good," the deputy said. "The woods are full of folks that didn't." The Warden was again watching the back of the deputy's neck.

"Look," he said. "Why dont you step up to my house and get that bottle of whiskey out of the sideboard and bring it down here?"

"All right," the deputy said. "But I think we better settle this first. I'll tell you what we'll do—"

"We can settle it quicker with a drink or two," the Warden said. "You better step on up to your place and get a coat so the bottle—"

"That'll take too long," the deputy said. "I wont need no coat." He moved to the door, where he stopped and turned. "I'll tell you what to do.

Just call twelve men in here and tell him it's a jury—he never seen but one before and he wont know no better—and try him over for robbing that train. Hamp can be the judge."

"You cant try a man twice for the same crime," the emissary said. "He might know that even if he doesn't know a jury when he sees one."

"Look," the Warden said.

"All right. Just call it a new train robbery. Tell him it happened yesterday, tell him he robbed another train while he was gone and just forgot it. He couldn't help himself. Besides, he wont care. He'd just as lief be here as out. He wouldn't have nowhere to go if he was out. None of them do. Turn one loose and be damned if he aint right back here by Christmas like it was a reunion or something, for doing the very same thing they caught him at before." He guffawed again. "Them convicts."

"Look," the Warden said. "While you're there, why dont you open the bottle and see if the liquor's any good. Take a drink or two. Give yourself time to feel it. If it's not good, no use in bringing it."

"O. K.," the deputy said. He went out this time.

"Couldn't you lock the door?" the emissary said. The Warden squirmed faintly. That is, he shifted his position in his chair.

"After all, he's right," he said. "He's guessed right three times now. And he's kin to all the folks in Pittman County except the niggers."

"Maybe we can work fast then." The emissary opened the briefcase and took out a sheaf of papers. "So there you are," he said.

"There what are?"

"He escaped."

"But he came back voluntarily and surrendered."

"But he escaped."

"All right," the Warden said. "He escaped. Then what?" Now the emissary said look. That is, he said,

"Listen, I'm on per diem. That's tax-payers, votes. And if there's any possible chance for it to occur to anyone to hold an investigation about this, there'll be ten senators and twenty-five representatives here on a special train maybe. On per diem. And it will be mighty hard to keep some of them from going back to Jackson by way of Memphis or New Orleans—on per diem."

"All right," the Warden said. "What does he say to do?"

"This. The man left here in charge of one specific officer. But he was delivered back here by a different one."

"But he surren—" This time the Warden stopped of his own accord. He looked, stared almost, at the emissary. "All right. Go on."

"In specific charge of an appointed and delegated officer, who returned here and reported that the body of the prisoner was no longer in his possession; that, in fact, he did not know where the prisoner was. That's correct, isn't it?" The Warden said nothing. "Isn't that correct?" the emissary said, pleasantly, insistently.

"But you cant do that to him. I tell you he's kin to half the—"

"That's taken care of. The Chief has made a place for him on the high-way patrol."

"Hell," the Warden said. "He cant ride a motorcycle. I dont even let him try to drive a truck."

"He wont have to. Surely an amazed and grateful State can supply the man who guessed right three times in succession in Mississippi general elections with a car to ride in and somebody to run it if necessary. He wont even have to stay in it all the time. Just so he's near enough so when an inspector sees the car and stops and blows the horn of it he can hear it and come out."

"I still dont like it," the Warden said.

"Neither do I. Your man could have saved all of this if he had just gone on and drowned himself, as he seems to have led everybody to believe he had. But he didn't. And the Chief says do. Can you think of anything better?" The Warden sighed.

"No," he said.

"All right." The emissary opened the papers and uncapped a pen and began to write. "Attempted escape from the Penitentiary, ten years' additional sentence," he said. "Deputy Warden Buckworth transferred to Highway Patrol. Call it for meritorious service even if you want to. It wont matter now. Done?"

"Done," the Warden said.

"Then suppose you send for him. Get it over with." So the Warden sent for the tall convict and he arrived presently, saturnine and grave, in his new bed-ticking, his jowls blue and close under the sunburn, his hair recently cut and neatly parted and smelling faintly of the prison barber's (the barber was in for life, for murdering his wife, still a barber) pomade. The Warden called him by name.

"You had bad luck, didn't you?" The convict said nothing. "They are going to have to add ten years to your time."

"All right," the convict said.

"It's hard luck. I'm sorry."

"All right," the convict said. "If that's the rule." So they gave him the ten years more and the Warden gave him the cigar and now he sat, jack-knifed backward into the space between the upper and lower bunks, the unlighted cigar in his hand while the plump convict and four others listened to him. Or questioned him, that is, since it was all done, finished, now and he was safe again, so maybe it wasn't even worth talking about any more.

"All right," the plump one said. "So you come back into the River. Then what?"

622   WILLIAM FAULKNER

"Nothing. I rowed."

"Wasn't it pretty hard rowing coming back?"

"The water was still high. It was running pretty hard still. I never made much speed for the first week or two. After that it got better." Then, suddenly and quietly, something—the inarticulateness, the innate and inherited reluctance for speech, dissolved and he found himself, listened to himself, telling it quietly, the words coming not fast but easily to the tongue as he required them: How he paddled on (he found out by trying it that he could make better speed, if you could call it speed, next the bank—this after he had been carried suddenly and violently out to midstream before he could prevent it and found himself, the skiff, travelling back toward the region from which he had just escaped and he spent the better part of the morning getting back inshore and up to the canal again from which he had emerged at dawn) until night came and they tied up to the bank and ate some of the food he had secreted in his jumper before leaving the armory in New Orleans and the woman and the infant slept in the boat as usual and when daylight came they went on and tied up again that night too and the next day the food gave out and he came to a landing, a town, he didn't notice the name of it, and he got a job. It was a cane farm—

"Cane?" one of the other convicts said. "What does anybody want to raise cane for? You cut cane. You have to fight it where I come from. You burn it just to get shut of it."

"It was sorghum," the tall convict said.

"Sorghum?" another said. "A whole farm just raising sorghum? *Sorghum?* What did they do with it?" The tall one didn't know. He didn't ask, he just came up the levee and there was a truck waiting full of niggers and a white man said, "You there. Can you run a shovel plow?" and the convict said, "Yes," and the man said, "Jump in then," and the convict said, "Only I've got a—"

"Yes," the plump one said. "That's what I been aiming to ask. What did—" The tall convict's face was grave, his voice was calm, just a little short:

"They had tents for the folks to live in. They were behind." The plump one blinked at him.

"Did they think she was your wife?"

"I don't know. I reckon so." The plump one blinked at him.

"Wasn't she your wife? Just from time to time kind of, you might say?" The tall one didn't answer at all. After a moment he raised the cigar and appeared to examine a loosening of the wrapper because after another moment he licked the cigar carefully near the end. "All right," the plump one said. "Then what?" So he worked there four days. He didn't like it. Maybe that was why: that he too could not quite put credence in that much of what he believed to be sorghum. So when they told him it was Saturday and paid him and the white man told him about somebody who was going to Baton

Rouge the next day in a motor boat, he went to see the man and took the six dollars he had earned and bought food with it and tied the skiff behind the motor boat and went to Baton Rouge. It didn't take long and even after they left the motor boat at Baton Rouge and he was paddling again it seemed to the convict that the River was lower and the current not so fast, so hard, so they made fair speed, tying up to the bank at night among the willows, the woman and baby sleeping in the skiff as of old. Then the food gave out again. This time it was a wood landing, the wood stacked and waiting, a wagon and team being unladen of another load. The men with the wagon told him about the sawmill and helped him drag the skiff up the levee; they wanted to leave it there but he would not so they loaded it onto the wagon too and he and the woman got on the wagon too and they went to the sawmill. They gave them one room in a house to live in here. They paid two dollars a day and furnish. The work was hard. He liked it. He stayed there eight days.

"If you liked it so well, why did you quit?" the plump one said. The tall convict examined the cigar again, holding it up where the light fell upon the rich chocolate-colored flank.

"I got in trouble," he said.

"What trouble?"

"Woman. It was a fellow's wife."

"You mean you had been toting one piece up and down the country day and night for over a month, and now the first time you have a chance to stop and catch your breath almost you got to get in trouble over another one?" The tall convict had thought of that. He remembered it: how there were times, seconds, at first when if it had not been for the baby he might have, might have tried. But they were just seconds because in the next instant his whole being would seem to flee the very idea in a kind of savage and horrified revulsion; he would find himself looking from a distance at this millstone which the force and power of blind and risible Motion had fastened upon him, thinking, saying aloud actually, with harsh and savage outrage even though it had been two years since he had had a woman and that a nameless and not young negress, a casual, a straggler whom he had caught more or less by chance on one of the fifth-Sunday visiting days, the man—husband or sweetheart—whom she had come to see having been shot by a trusty a week or so previous and she had not heard about it: "She aint even no good to me for that."

"But you got this one, didn't you?" the plump convict said.

"Yah," the tall one said. The plump one blinked at him.

"Was it good?"

"It's all good," one of the others said. "Well? Go on. How many more did you have on the way back? Sometimes when a fellow starts getting it it looks like he just cant miss even if—" That was all, the convict told them. They left the sawmill fast, he had no time to buy food until they reached the next landing. There he spent the whole sixteen dollars he had earned and they went on. The River was lower now, there was no doubt of it, and sixteen dollars' worth looked like a lot of food and he thought maybe it would do, would be enough. But maybe there was more current in the River still than it looked like. But this time it was Mississippi, it was cotton; the plow handles felt right to his palms again, the strain and squat of the slick buttocks against the middle buster's blade was what he knew, even though they paid but a dollar a day here. But that did it. He told it: they told him it was Saturday again and paid him and he told about it—night, a smoked lantern in a disc of worn and barren earth as smooth as silver, a circle of crouching figures, the importunate murmurs and ejaculations, the meagre piles of worn bills beneath the crouching knees, the dotted cubes clicking and scuttering in the dust; that did it. "How much did you win?" the second convict said.

"Enough," the tall one said.

"But how much?"

"Enough," the tall one said. It was enough exactly; he gave it all to the man who owned the second motor boat (he would not need food now), he and the woman in the launch now and the skiff towing behind, the woman with the baby and the paper-wrapped parcel beneath his peaceful hand, on his lap; almost at once he recognised, not Vicksburg because he had never seen Vicksburg, but the trestle beneath which on his roaring wave of trees and houses and dead animals he had shot, accompanied by thunder and lightning, a month and three weeks ago; he looked at it once without heat, even without interest as the launch went on. But now he began to watch the bank, the levee. He didn't know how he would know but he knew he would, and then it was early afternoon and sure enough the moment came and he said to the launch owner: "I reckon this will do."

"Here?" the launch owner said. "This dont look like anywhere to me."

"I reckon this is it," the convict said. So the launch put inshore, the engine ceased, it drifted up and lay against the levee and the owner cast the skiff loose.

"You better let me take you on until we come to something," he said. "That was what I promised."

"I reckon this will do," the convict said. So they got out and he stood with the grapevine painter in his hand while the launch purred again and drew away, already curving; he did not watch it. He laid the bundle down and made the painter fast to a willow root and picked up the bundle and turned. He said no word, he mounted the levee, passing the mark, the tide-line of the old raging, dry now and lined, traversed by shallow and empty cracks like foolish and deprecatory senile grins, and entered a willow clump and removed the overalls and shirt they had given him in New Orleans and dropped them without even looking to see where they fell and opened the parcel and took out the other, the known, the desired, faded a little, stained and worn, but clean, recognisable, and put them on and returned to the skiff and took up the paddle. The woman was already in it.

The plump convict stood blinking at him. "So you come back," he said. "Well well." Now they all watched the tall convict as he bit the end from the cigar neatly and with complete deliberation and spat it out and licked the bite smooth and damp and took a match from his pocket and examined the match for a moment as though to be sure it was a good one, worthy of the cigar perhaps, and raked it up his thigh with the same deliberation—a motion almost too slow to set fire to it, it would seem—and held it until the flame burned clear and free of sulphur, then put it to the cigar. The plump one watched him, blinking rapidly and steadily. "And they give you ten years more for running. That's bad. A fellow can get used to what they give him at first, to start off with, I dont care how much it is, even a hundred and ninety-nine years. But ten more years. Ten years more, on top of that. When you never expected it. Ten more years to have to do without no society, no female companionship—" He blinked steadily at the tall convict. But he (the tall convict) had thought of that too. He had had a sweetheart. That is, he had gone to church singings and picnics with her—a girl a year or so younger than he, short-legged, with ripe breasts and a heavy mouth and dull eyes like ripe muscadines, who owned a baking-powder can almost full of ear-rings and brooches and rings bought (or presented at suggestion) from ten-cent stores. Presently he had divulged his plan to her, and there were times later when, musing, the thought occurred to him that possibly if it had not been for her he would not actually have attempted it—this a mere feeling, unworded, since he could not have phrased this either: that who to know what Capone's uncandled bridehood she might not have dreamed to be her destiny and fate, what fast car filled with authentic colored glass and machine guns, running traffic lights. But that was all past and done when the notion first occurred to him, and in the third month of his incarceration she came to see him. She wore ear-rings and a bracelet or so which he had never seen before and it never became quite clear how she had got that far from home, and she cried violently for the first three minutes though presently (and without his ever knowing either exactly how they had got separated or how she had made the acquaintance) he saw her in animated conversation with one of the guards. But she kissed him before she left that evening and said she would return the first chance she got, clinging to him, sweating a little, smelling of scent and soft young female flesh, slightly pneumatic. But she didn't come back though he continued to write to her, and seven months later he got an answer. It was a postcard, a colored lithograph of a Birmingham hotel, a childish X inked heavily across one window, the heavy writing on the reverse slanted and primer-like too: *This is where were honnymonning at. Your friend (Mrs.) Vernon Waldrip*

The plump convict stood blinking at the tall one, rapidly and steadily.

"Yes, sir," he said. "It's them ten more years that hurt. Ten more years to do without a woman, no woman a tall a fellow wants—" He blinked steadily and rapidly, watching the tall one. The other did not move, jackknifed backward between the two bunks, grave and clean, the cigar burning smoothly and richly in his clean steady hand, the smoke wreathing upward across his face saturnine, humorless, and calm. "Ten more years—"

"Women—!" the tall convict said.

JOSEPH CONRAD

Youth

This could have occurred nowhere but in England, where men and sea interpenetrate, so to speak—the sea entering into the life of most men, and the men knowing something or everything about the sea, in the way of amusement, of travel, or of breadwinning.

We were sitting round a mahogany table that reflected the bottle, the claret-glasses, and our faces as we leaned on our elbows. There was a director of companies, an accountant, a lawyer, Marlow, and myself. The director had been a *Conway* boy, the accountant had served four years at sea, the lawyer—a fine crusted Tory, High Churchman, the best of old fellows, the soul of honour—had been chief officer in the P. & O. service in the good old days when the mail-boats were square-rigged at least on two masts, and used to come down the China Sea before a fair monsoon with stun'sails set alow and aloft. We all began life in the merchant service. Between the five of us there was the strong bond of the sea, and also the fellowship of the craft, which no amount of enthusiasm for yachting, cruising, and so on can give, since one is only the amusement of life and the other is life itself.

Marlow (at least I think that is how he spelt his name) told the story, or rather the chronicle, of a voyage:

"Yes, I have seen a little of the Eastern seas; but what I remember best is my first voyage there. You fellows know there are those voyages that seem ordered for the illustration of life, that might stand for a symbol of existence. You fight, work, sweat, nearly kill yourself, sometimes do kill yourself, trying to accomplish something—and you can't. Not from any fault of yours. You simply can do nothing, neither great nor little—not a thing in the world—not even marry an old maid, or get a wretched 600-ton cargo of coal to its port of destination.

"It was altogether a memorable affair. It was my first voyage to the East, and my first voyage as second mate; it was also my skipper's first command. You'll admit it was time. He was sixty if a day; a little man, with a broad, not very straight back, with bowed shoulders and one leg more bandy than the other, he had that queer twisted-about appearance you see so often in men who work in the fields. He had a nut-cracker face—chin and nose trying to come together over a sunken mouth—and it was framed in iron-grey fluffy hair, that looked like a chin-strap of cotton-wool sprinkled with coal-dust. And he had blue eyes in that old face of his, which were amazingly like a boy's, with that candid expression some quite common men preserve to the end of their days by a rare internal gift of simplicity of heart and rectitude of soul. What induced him to accept me was a wonder. I had come out of a crack Australian clipper, where I had been third officer, and he seemed to have a prejudice against crack clippers as aristocratic and high-toned. He said to me, 'You know, in this ship you will have to work.' I said I had to work in every ship I had ever been in. 'Ah, but this is different, and you gentlemen out of them big ships; . . . but there! I dare say you will do. Join tomorrow.'

"I joined tomorrow. It was twenty-two years ago; and I was just twenty. How time passes! It was one of the happiest days of my life. Fancy! Second mate for the first time—a really responsible officer! I wouldn't have thrown up my new billet for a fortune. The mate looked me over carefully. He was also an old chap, but of another stamp. He had a Roman nose, a snow-white, long beard, and his name was Mahon, but he insisted that it should be pronounced Mann. He was well connected; yet there was something wrong with his luck, and he had never got on.

"As to the captain, he had been for years in coasters, then in the Mediterranean, and last in the West Indian trade. He had never been round the Capes. He could just write a kind of sketchy hand, and didn't care for writing at all. Both were thorough good seamen of course, and between those two old chaps I felt like a small boy between two grandfathers.

"The ship also was old. Her name was the *Judea*. Queer name, isn't it? She belonged to a man Wilmer, Wilcox—some name like that; but he has been bankrupt and dead these twenty years or more, and his name don't matter. She had been laid up in Shadwell basin for ever so long. You may imagine her state. She was all rust, dust, grime—soot aloft, dirt on deck. To me it was like coming out of a palace into a ruined cottage. She was about 400 tons, had a primitive windlass, wooden latches to the doors, not a bit of brass about her, and a big square stern. There was on it, below her name in big letters, a lot of scroll-work, with the gilt off, and some sort of a coat of arms, with the motto 'Do or Die' underneath. I remember it took my fancy immensely. There was a touch of romance in it, something that made me love the old thing—something that appealed to my youth!

"We left London in ballast—sand ballast—to load a cargo of coal in a northern port for Bankok. Bankok! I thrilled. I had been six years at sea, but had only seen Melbourne and Sydney, very good places, charming places in their way—but Bankok!

"We worked out of the Thames under canvas, with a North Sea pilot on board. His name was Jermyn, and he dodged all day long about the galley drying his handkerchief before the stove. Apparently he never slept. He was a dismal man, with a perpetual tear sparkling at the end of his nose, who either had been in trouble, or was in trouble, or expected to be in trouble—couldn't be happy unless something went wrong. He mistrusted my youth, my common sense, and my seamanship, and made a point of showing it in a hundred little ways. I dare say he was right. It seems to me I knew very little then, and I know not much more now; but I cherish a hate for that Jermyn to this day.

"We were a week working up as far as Yarmouth Roads, and then we got into a gale—the famous October gale of twenty-two years ago. It was wind, lightning, sleet, snow, and a terrific sea. We were flying light, and you may imagine how bad it was when I tell you we had smashed bulwarks and a flooded deck. On the second night she shifted her ballast into the lee bow, and by that time we had been blown off somewhere on the Dogger Bank. There was nothing for it but go below with shovels and try to right her, and there we were in that vast hold, gloomy like a cavern, the tallow dips stuck and flickering on the beams, the gale howling above, the ship tossing about like mad on her side; there we all were, Jermyn, the captain, every one, hardly able to keep our feet, engaged on that gravedigger's work, and trying to toss shovelfuls of wet sand up to windward. At every tumble of the ship you could see vaguely in the dim light men falling down with a great flourish of shovels. One of the ship's boys (we had two), impressed by the weirdness of the scene, wept as if his heart would break. We could hear him blubbering somewhere in the shadows.

"On the third day the gale died out, and by-and-by a north country tug picked us up. We took sixteen days in all to get from London to the Tyne! When we got into dock we had lost our turn for loading, and they hauled us off to a tier where we remained for a month. Mrs. Beard (the captain's name was Beard) came from Colchester to see the old man. She lived on board. The crew of runners had left, and there remained only the officers, one boy and the steward, a mulatto who answered to the name of Abraham. Mrs. Beard was an old woman, with a face all wrinkled and ruddy like a winter apple, and the figure of a young girl. She caught sight of me once, sewing on a button, and insisted on having my shirts to repair. This was something different from the captains' wives I had known on board crack clippers. When I brought her the shirts, she said: 'And the socks? They want mending, I am sure, and John's—Captain Beard's—things are all in order now. I would be glad of something to do.' Bless the old woman. She overhauled my outfit for me, and meantime I read for the first time *Sartor Resartus* and Burnaby's *Ride to Khiva*.

I didn't understand much of the first then; but I remember I preferred the soldier to the philosopher at the time; a preference which life has only confirmed. One was a man, and the other was either more—or less. However, they are both dead and Mrs. Beard is dead, and youth, strength, genius, thoughts, achievements, simple hearts—all dies. . . . No matter.

"They loaded us at last. We shipped a crew. Eight able seamen and two boys. We hauled off one evening to the buoys at the dock-gates, ready to go out, and with a fair prospect of beginning the voyage next day. Mrs. Beard was to start for home by a late train. When the ship was fast we went to tea. We sat rather silent through the meal—Mahon, the old couple, and I. I finished first, and slipped away for a smoke, my cabin being in a deck-house just against the poop. It was high water, blowing fresh with a drizzle; the double dock-gates were opened, and the steam-colliers were going in and out in the darkness with their lights burning bright, a great plashing of propellers, rattling of winches, and a lot of hailing on the pier-heads. I watched the procession of head-lights gliding high and of green lights gliding low in the night, when suddenly a red gleam flashed at me, vanished, came into view again, and remained. The fore-end of a steamer loomed up close. I shouted down the cabin, 'Come up, quick!' and then heard a startled voice saying afar in the dark. 'Stop her, sir.' A bell jingled. Another voice cried warningly. 'We are going right into that barque, sir.' The answer to this was a gruff 'All right,' and the next thing was a heavy crash as the steamer struck a glancing blow with the bluff of her bow about our fore-rigging. There was a moment of confusion, yelling, and running about. Steam roared. Then somebody was heard saying, 'All clear, sir.' . . . 'Are you all right?' asked the gruff voice. I had jumped forward to see the damage, and hailed back, 'I think so.' 'Easy astern,' said the gruff voice. A bell jingled. 'What steamer is that?' screamed Mahon. By that time she was no more to us than a bulky shadow manoeuvring a little way off. They shouted at us some name—a woman's name. Miranda or Melissa—or some such thing. 'This means another month in this beastly hole,' said Mahon to me, as we peered with lamps about the splintered bulwarks and broken braces. 'But where's the captain?'

"We had not heard or seen anything of him all that time. We went aft to look. A doleful voice arose hailing somewhere in the middle of the dock, '*Judea* ahoy!' . . . How the devil did he get there? . . . 'Hallo!' we shouted. 'I am adrift in our boat without oars,' he cried. A belated water-man offered his services, and Mahon struck a bargain with him for half-a-crown to tow our skipper alongside; but it was Mrs. Beard that came up the ladder first. They had been floating about the dock in that mizzly cold rain for nearly an hour. I was never so surprised in my life.

"It appears that when he heard my shout 'Come up' he understood at once what was the matter, caught up his wife, ran on deck, and across, and down into our boat, which was fast to the ladder. Not bad for a sixty-year-old. Just imagine that old fellow saving heroically in his arms that old woman—the woman of his life. He set her down on a thwart, and was ready to climb back on board when the painter came adrift somehow, and away they went together. Of course in the confusion we did not hear him shouting. He looked abashed. She said cheerfully, 'I suppose it does not matter my losing the train now?' 'No, Jenny—you go below and get warm,' he growled. Then to us: 'A sailor has no business with a wife—I say. There I was, out of the ship. Well, no harm done this time. Let's go and look at what that fool of a steamer smashed.'

"It wasn't much, but it delayed us three weeks. At the end of that time, the captain being engaged with his agents, I carried Mrs. Beard's bag to the railway-station and put her all comfy into a third-class carriage. She lowered the window to say, 'You are a good young man. If you see John—Captain Beard—without his muffler at night, just remind him from me to keep his throat well wrapped up.' 'Certainly, Mrs. Beard,' I said. 'You are a good young man; I noticed how attentive you are to John—to Captain—' The train pulled out suddenly; I took my cap off to the old woman: I never saw her again. . . . Pass the bottle.

"We went to sea next day. When we made that start for Bankok we had been already three months out of London. We had expected to be a fortnight or so—at the outside.

"It was January, and the weather was beautiful—the beautiful sunny winter weather that has more charm than in the summer-time, because it is unexpected, and crisp, and you know it won't, it can't, last long. It's like a windfall, like a godsend, like an unexpected piece of luck.

"It lasted all down the North Sea, all down Channel; and it lasted till we were three hundred miles or so to the westward of the Lizards: then the wind went round to the sou'west and began to pipe up. In two days it blew a gale. The *Judea,* hove to, wallowed on the Atlantic like an old candle-box. It blew day after day: it blew with spite, without interval, without mercy, without rest. The world was nothing but an immensity of great foaming waves rushing at us, under a sky low enough to touch with the hand and dirty like a smoked ceiling. In the stormy space surrounding us there was as much flying spray as air. Day after day and night after night there was nothing round the ship but the howl of the wind, the tumult of the sea, the noise of water pouring over her deck. There was no rest for her and no rest for us. She tossed, she pitched, she stood on her head, she sat on her tail, she rolled, she groaned, and we had to hold on while on deck and cling to our bunks when below, in a constant effort of body and worry of mind.

"One night Mahon spoke through the small window of my berth. It opened right into my very bed, and I was lying there sleepless, in my boots, feeling as though I had not slept for years, and could not if I tried. He said excitedly—

" 'You got the sounding-rod in here, Marlow? I can't get the pumps to suck. By God; it's no child's play.'

"I gave him the sounding-rod and lay down again, trying to think of various things—but I thought only of the pumps. When I came on deck they were still at it, and my watch relieved at the pumps. By the light of the lantern brought on deck to examine the sounding-rod I caught a glimpse of their weary, serious faces. We pumped all the four hours. We pumped all night, all day, all the week—watch and watch. She was working herself loose, and leaked badly—not enough to drown us at once, but enough to kill us with the work at the pumps. And while we pumped the ship was going from us piecemeal: the bulwarks went, the stanchions were torn out, the ventilators smashed, the cabin-door burst in. There was not a dry spot in the ship. She was being gutted bit by bit. The long-boat changed, as if by magic, into matchwood where she stood in her gripes. I had lashed her myself, and was rather proud of my handiwork, which had withstood so long the malice of the sea. And we pumped. And there was no break in the weather. The sea was white like a sheet of foam, like a caldron of boiling milk; there was not a break in the clouds, no—not the size of a man's hand—no, not for so much as ten seconds. There was for us no sky, there were for us no stars, no sun, no universe—nothing but angry clouds and an infuriated sea. We pumped watch and watch, for dear life; and it seemed to last for months, for years, for all eternity, as though we had been dead and gone to a hell for sailors. We forgot the day of the week, the name of the month, what year it was, and whether we had ever been ashore. The sails blew away, she lay broadside on under a weather-cloth, the ocean poured over her, and we did not care. We turned those handles, and had the eyes of idiots. As soon as we had crawled on deck I used to take a round turn with a rope about the men, the pumps, and the mainmast, and we turned, we turned incessantly, with the water to our waists, to our necks, over our heads. It was all one. We had forgotten how it felt to be dry.

"And there was somewhere in me the thought: By Jove! this is the deuce of an adventure—something you read about; and it is my first voyage as second mate—and I am only twenty—and here I am lasting it out as well as any of these men, and keeping my chaps up to the mark. I was pleased. I would not have given up the experience for worlds. I had moments of exultation. Whenever the old dismantled craft pitched heavily with her counter high in the air, she seemed to me to throw up, like an appeal, like a defiance, like a cry to the clouds without mercy, the words written on her stern: '*Judea*, London. Do or Die.'

"O youth! The strength of it, the faith of it, the imagination of it! To me she was not an old rattletrap carting about the world a lot of coal for a freight—to me she was the endeavour, the test, the trial of life. I think of her with pleasure, with affection, with regret—as you would think of someone dead you have loved. I shall never forget her. . . . Pass the bottle.

"One night when tied to the mast, as I explained, we were pumping on, deafened with the wind, and without spirit enough in us to wish ourselves dead, a heavy sea crashed aboard and swept clean over us. As soon as I got my breath I shouted, as in duty bound. 'Keep on, boys!' when suddenly I felt something hard floating on deck strike the calf of my leg. I made a grab at it and missed. It was so dark we could not see each other's faces within a foot—you understand.

"After the thump the ship kept quiet for a while, and the thing, whatever it was, struck my leg again. This time I caught it—and it was a saucepan. At first, being stupid with fatigue and thinking of nothing but the pumps, I did not understand what I had in my hand. Suddenly it dawned upon me, and I shouted, 'Boys, the house on deck is gone. Leave this, and let's look for the cook.'

"There was a deck-house forward, which contained the galley, the cook's berth, and the quarters of the crew. As we had expected for days to see it swept away, the hands had been ordered to sleep in the cabin—the only safe place in the ship. The steward, Abraham, however, persisted in clinging to his berth, stupidly, like a mule—from sheer fright I believe, like an animal that won't leave a stable falling in an earthquake. So we went to look for him. It was chancing death, since once out of our lashings we were as exposed as if on a raft. But we went. The house was shattered as if a shell had exploded inside. Most of it had gone overboard—stove, men's quarters and their property, all was gone; but two posts, holding a portion of the bulkhead to which Abraham's bunk was attached, remained as if by a miracle. We groped in the ruins and came upon this, and there he was, sitting in his bunk, surrounded by foam and wreckage, jabbering cheerfully to himself. He was out of his mind; completely and for ever mad, with this sudden shock coming upon the fag-end of his endurance. We snatched him up, lugged him aft, and pitched him head-first down the cabin companion. You understand there was no time to carry him down with infinite precautions and wait to see how he got on. Those below would pick him up at the bottom of the stairs all right. We were in a hurry to go back to the pumps. That business could not wait. A bad leak is an inhuman thing.

"One would think that the sole purpose of that fiendish gale had been to make a lunatic of that poor devil of a mulatto. It eased before morning, and next day the sky cleared, and as the sea went down the leak took up. When it came to bending a fresh set of sails the crew demanded to put back—and really there was nothing else to do. Boats gone, decks swept clean, cabin gutted, men without a stitch but what they stood in, stores spoiled, ship strained. We put her head for home, and—would you believe it? The wind came east right in our teeth. It blew fresh, it blew continuously. We had to beat up every inch of the way, but she did not leak so badly, the water keeping comparatively smooth. Two hours' pumping in every four is no joke—but it kept her afloat as far as Falmouth.

"The good people there live on casualties of the sea, and no doubt were glad to see us. A hungry crowd of shipwrights sharpened their chisels at the sight of that carcass of a ship. And, by Jove! they had pretty pickings off us before they were done. I fancy the owner was already in a tight place. There were delays. Then it was decided to take part of the cargo out and caulk her topsides. This was done, the repairs finished, cargo reshipped; a new crew came on board, and we went out—for Bankok. At the end of a week we were back again. The crew said they weren't going to Bankok—a hundred and fifty days' passage—in a something hooker that wanted pumping eight hours out of the twenty-four; and the nautical papers inserted again the little paragraph: 'Judea. Barque. Tyne to Bankok; coals; put back to Falmouth leaky and with crew refusing duty.'

"There were more delays—more tinkering. The owner came down for a day, and said she was as right as a little fiddle. Poor old Captain Beard looked like the ghost of a Geordie skipper—through the worry and humiliation of it. Remember he was sixty, and it was his first command. Mahon said it was a foolish business, and would end badly. I loved the ship more than ever, and wanted awfully to get to Bankok. To Bankok! Magic name, blessed name. Mesopotamia wasn't a patch on it. Remember I was twenty, and it was my first second-mate's billet, and the East was waiting for me.

"We went out and anchored in the outer roads with a fresh crew—the third. She leaked worse than ever. It was as if those confounded shipwrights had actually made a hole in her. This time we did not even go outside. The crew simply refused to man the windlass.

"They towed us back to the inner harbour, and we became a fixture, a feature, an institution of the place. People pointed us out to visitors as 'That 'ere barque that's going to Bankok—has been here six months—put back three times.' On holidays the small boys pulling about in boats would hail 'Judea, ahoy!' and if a head showed above the rail shouted, 'Where you bound to?—Bankok?' and jeered. We were only three on board. The poor old skipper mooned in the cabin. Mahon undertook the cooking, and unexpectedly developed all a Frenchman's genius for preparing nice little messes. I looked languidly after the rigging. We became citizens of Falmouth. Every shopkeeper knew us. At the barber's or tobacconist's they asked familiarly, 'Do you think you will ever get to Bankok?' Meantime the owner, the underwriters, and the charterers squabbled amongst themselves in London, and our pay went on. . . . Pass the bottle.

"It was horrid. Morally it was worse than pumping for life. It seemed as though we had been forgotten by the world, belonged to nobody, would get nowhere; it seemed that, as if bewitched, we would have to live for ever and ever in that inner harbour, a derision and a byword to generations of long-shore loafers and dishonest boatmen. I obtained three months' pay and a five days' leave, and made a rush for London. It took me a day to get there and pretty well another to come back—but three months' pay went all the same. I don't know what I did with it. I went to a music-hall, I believe, lunched, dined, and supped in a swell place in Regent Street, and was back to time, with nothing but a complete set of Byron's works and a new railway rug to show for three months' work. The boat-man who pulled me off to the ship said, 'Hallo! I thought you had left the old thing. *She* will never get to Bankok.' 'That's all you know about it.' I said, scornfully—but I didn't like that prophecy at all.

"Suddenly a man, some kind of agent to somebody, appeared with full powers. He had grog-blossoms all over his face, an indomitable energy, and was a jolly soul. We leaped into life again. A hulk came alongside, took our cargo, and then we went into dry dock to get our copper stripped. No wonder she leaked. The poor thing, strained beyond endurance by the gale, had, as if in disgust, spat out all the oakum of her lower seams. She was recaulked, new coppered, and made as tight as a bottle. We went back to the hulk and reshipped our cargo.

"Then, on a fine moonlight night, all the rats left the ship.

"We had been infested with them. They had destroyed our sails, consumed more stores than the crew, affably shared our beds and our dangers, and now, when the ship was made seaworthy, concluded to clear out. I called Mahon to enjoy the spectacle. Rat after rat appeared on our rail, took a last look over his shoulder, and leaped with a hollow thud into the empty hulk. We tried to count them, but soon lost the tale. Mahon said: 'Well, well! don't talk to me about the intelligence of rats. They ought to have left before, when we had that narrow squeak from foundering. There you have the proof how silly is the superstition about them. They leave a good ship for an old rotten hulk, where there is nothing to eat, too, the fools! . . . I don't believe they know what is safe or what is good for them, any more than you or I.'

"And after some more talk we agreed that the wisdom of rats had been grossly overrated, being in fact no greater than that of men.

"The story of the ship was known, by this, all up the Channel from Land's End to the Forelands, and we could get no crew on the south coast. They sent us one all complete from Liverpool, and we left once more—for Bankok.

"We had fair breezes, smooth water right into the tropics, and the old *Judea* lumbered along in the sunshine. When she went eight knots everything cracked aloft, and we tied our caps to our heads; but mostly she strolled on at the rate of three miles an hour. What could you expect? She was tired—that old ship. Her youth was where mine is—where yours is—you fellows who listen to this yarn; and what friend would throw your years and your weariness in your face? We didn't grumble at her. To us aft, at least, it seemed as though we had been born in her, reared in her, had lived in her for ages, had never known any other ship. I would just as soon have abused the old village church at home for not being a cathedral.

"And for me there was also my youth to make me patient. There was all the East before me, and all life, and the thought that I had been tried in that ship and had come out pretty well. And I thought of men of old who, centuries ago, went that road in ships that sailed no better, to the land of palms, and spices, and yellow sands, and of brown nations ruled by kings more cruel than Nero the Roman, and more splendid than Solomon the Jew. The old bark lumbered on, heavy with her age and the burden of her cargo, while I lived the life of youth in ignorance and hope. She lumbered on through an interminable procession of days; and the fresh gilding flashed back at the setting sun, seemed to cry out over the darkening sea the words painted on her stern, '*Judea,* London. Do or Die.'

"Then we entered the Indian Ocean and steered northerly for Java Head. The winds were light. Weeks slipped by. She crawled on, do or die, the people at home began to think of posting us as overdue.

"One Saturday evening, I being off duty, the men asked me to give them an extra bucket of water or so—for washing clothes. As I did not wish to screw on the fresh-water pump so late, I went forward whistling, and with a key in my hand to unlock the forepeak scuttle, intending to serve the water out of a spare tank we kept there.

"The smell down below was as unexpected as it was frightful. One would have thought hundreds of paraffin-lamps had been flaring and smoking in that hole for days. I was glad to get out. The man with me coughed and said, 'Funny smell, sir.' I answered negligently, 'It's good for the health they say,' and walked aft.

"The first thing I did was to put my head down the square of the midship ventilator. As I lifted the lid a visible breath, something like a thin fog, a puff of faint haze, rose from the opening. The ascending air was hot, and had a heavy, sooty, paraffiny smell. I gave one sniff, and put down the lid gently. It was no use choking myself. The cargo was on fire.

"Next day she began to smoke in earnest. You see it was to be expected, for though the coal was of a safe kind, that cargo had been so handled, so broken up with handling, that it looked more like smithy coal than anything else. Then it had been wetted—more than once. It rained all the time we were taking it back from the hulk, and now with this long passage it got heated, and there was another case of spontaneous combustion.

"The captain called us into the cabin. He had a chart spread on the table, and looked unhappy. He said, 'The coast of West Australia is near, but I mean to proceed to our destination. It is the hurricane month, too; but we will just keep her head for Bankok, and fight the fire. No more putting back anywhere, if we all get roasted. We will try first to stifle this 'ere damned combustion by want of air.'

"We tried. We battened down everything, and still she smoked. The smoke kept coming out through imperceptible crevices; it forced itself through bulkheads and covers; it oozed here and there and everywhere in slender threads, in an invisible film, in an incomprehensible manner. It made its way into the cabin, into the forecastle; it poisoned the sheltered places on the deck, it could be sniffed as high as the mainyard. It was clear that if the smoke came out the air came in. This was disheartening. This combustion refused to be stifled.

"We resolved to try water, and took the hatches off. Enormous volumes of smoke, whitish, yellowish, thick, greasy, misty, choking, ascended as high as the trucks. All hands cleared out aft. Then the poisonous cloud blew away, and we went back to work in a smoke that was no thicker now than that of an ordinary factory chimney.

"We rigged the force-pump, got the hose along, and by-and-by it burst. Well, it was as old as the ship—a prehistoric hose, and past repair. Then we pumped with the feeble head-pump, drew water with buckets, and in this way managed in time to pour lots of Indian Ocean into the main hatch. The bright stream flashed in sunshine, fell into a layer of white crawling smoke, and vanished on the black surface of coal. Steam ascended mingling with the smoke. We poured salt water as into a barrel without a bottom. It was our fate to pump in that ship, to pump out of her, to pump into her; and after keeping water out of her to save ourselves from being drowned, we frantically poured water into her to save ourselves from being burnt.

"And she crawled on, do or die, in the serene weather. The sky was a miracle of purity, a miracle of azure. The sea was polished, was blue, was pellucid, was sparkling like a precious stone, extending on all sides, all round to the horizon—as if the whole terrestrial globe had been one jewel, one colossal sapphire, a single gem fashioned into a planet. And on the lustre of the great calm waters the *Judea* glided imperceptibly, enveloped in languid and unclean vapours, in a lazy cloud that drifted to leeward, light and slow; a pestiferous cloud defiling the splendour of sea and sky.

"All this time of course we saw no fire. The cargo smouldered at the bottom somewhere. Once Mahon, as we were working side by side, said to me with a queer smile: 'Now, if only she would spring a tidy leak—like that time when we first left the Channel—it would put a stopper on this fire. Wouldn't it?' I remarked irrelevantly, 'Do you remember the rats?'

"We fought the fire and sailed the ship too as carefully as though nothing had been the matter. The steward cooked and attended on us. Of the other twelve men, eight worked while four rested. Everyone took his turn, captain included. There was equality, and if not exactly fraternity, then a deal of good feeling. Sometimes a man, as he dashed a bucketful of water down the hatchway, would yell out, 'Hurrah for Bankok!' and the rest laughed. But generally we were taciturn and serious—and thirsty. Oh! how thirsty! And we had to be careful with the water. Strict allowance. The ship smoked, the sun blazed. . . . Pass the bottle.

"We tried everything. We even made an attempt to dig down to the fire. No good, of course. No man could remain more than a minute below. Mahon, who went first, fainted there, and the man who went to fetch him out did likewise. We lugged them out on deck. Then I leaped down to show how easily it could be done. They had learned wisdom by that time, and contented themselves by fishing for me with a chain-hook tied to a broom-handle, I believe. I did not offer to go and fetch up my shovel, which was left down below.

"Things began to look bad. We put the long-boat into the water. The second boat was ready to swing out. We had also another, a 14-foot thing, on davits aft, where it was quite safe.

"Then, behold, the smoke suddenly decreased. We redoubled our efforts to flood the bottom of the ship. In two days there was no smoke at all. Everybody was on the broad grin. This was on a Friday. On Saturday no work, but sailing the ship of course, was done. The men washed their clothes and their faces for the first time in a fortnight, and had a special dinner given them. They spoke of spontaneous combustion with contempt, and implied *they* were the boys to put out combustions. Somehow we all felt as though we each had inherited a large fortune. But a beastly smell of burning hung about the ship. Captain Beard had hollow eyes and sunken cheeks. I had never noticed so much before how twisted and bowed he was. He and Mahon prowled soberly about hatches and ventilators, sniffing. It struck me suddenly poor Mahon was a very, very old chap. As to me, I was as pleased and proud as though I had helped to win a great naval battle. O! Youth!

"The night was fine. In the morning a homeward-bound ship passed us hull down—the first we had seen for months; but we were nearing the land at last, Java Head being about 190 miles off, and nearly due north.

"Next day it was my watch on deck from eight to twelve. At breakfast the captain observed. 'It's wonderful how that smell hangs about the cabin.' About ten, the mate being on the poop, I stepped down on the main-deck for a moment. The carpenter's bench stood abaft the mainmast: I leaned against it sucking at my pipe, and the carpenter, a young chap, came to talk to me. He remarked, 'I think we have done very well, haven't we?' and then I perceived with annoyance the fool was trying to tilt the bench. I said curtly, 'Don't, Chips,' and immediately became aware of a queer sensation, of an absurd delusion—I seemed somehow to be in the air. I heard all round me like a pent-up breath released—as if a thousand giants simultaneously had said

Phoo!—and felt a dull concussion which made my ribs ache suddenly. No doubt about it—I was in the air, and my body was describing a short parabola. But short as it was, I had the time to think several thoughts in, as far as I can remember, the following order: 'This can't be the carpenter—What is it?—Some accident—Submarine volcano?—Coals, gas!—By Jove! we are being blown up—Everybody's dead—I am falling into the after-hatch—I see fire in it.'

"The coal-dust suspended in the air of the hold had glowed dull-red at the moment of the explosion. In the twinkling of an eye, in an infinitesimal fraction of a second since the first tilt of the bench, I was sprawling full length on the cargo. I picked myself up and scrambled out. It was quick like a rebound. The deck was a wilderness of smashed timber, lying crosswise like trees in a wood after a hurricane; an immense curtain of soiled rags waved gently before me—it was the main-sail blown to strips. I thought, The masts will be toppling over directly; and to get out of the way bolted on all-fours towards the poop-ladder. The first person I saw was Mahon, with eyes like saucers, his mouth open, and the long white hair standing straight on end round his head like a silver halo. He was just about to go down when the sight of the main-deck stirring, heaving up, and changing into splinters before his eyes, petrified him on the top step. I stared at him in unbelief, and he stared at me with a queer kind of shocked curiosity. I did not know that I had no hair, no eye-brows, no eyelashes, that my young moustache was burnt off, that my face was black, one cheek laid open, my nose cut, and my chin bleeding. I had lost my cap, one of my slippers, and my shirt was torn to rags. Of all this I was not aware. I was amazed to see the ship still afloat, the poop-deck whole—and, most of all, to see anybody alive. Also the peace of the sky and the serenity of the sea were distinctly surprising. I suppose I expected to see them convulsed with horror. . . . Pass the bottle.

"There was a voice hailing the ship from somewhere—in the air, in the sky—I couldn't tell. Presently I saw the captain—and he was mad. He asked me eagerly, 'Where's the cabin-table?' and to hear such a question was a frightful shock. I had just been blown up, you understand, and vibrated with that experience,—I wasn't quite sure whether I was alive. Mahon began to stamp with both feet and yelled at him. 'Good God! don't you see the deck's blown out of her?' I found my voice, and stammered out as if conscious of some gross neglect of duty, 'I don't know where the cabin-table is.' It was like an absurd dream.

"Do you know what he wanted next? Well, he wanted to trim the yards. Very placidly, and as if lost in thought, he insisted on having the foreyard squared. 'I don't know if there's anybody alive,' said Mahon, almost tearfully. 'Surely,' he said, gently, 'there will be enough left to square the foreyard.'

"The old chap, it seems, was in his own berth winding up the chronometers, when the shock sent him spinning. Immediately it occurred to him—as he said afterwards—that the ship had struck something, and he ran out into the cabin. There, he saw, the cabin-table had vanished somewhere. The deck being blown up, it had fallen down into the lazarette of course. Where we had our breakfast that morning he saw only a great hole in the floor. This appeared to him so awfully mysterious, and impressed him so immensely, that what he saw and heard after he got on deck were mere trifles in comparison. And, mark, he noticed directly the wheel deserted and his barque off her course—and his only thought was to get that miserable, stripped, un-decked, smouldering shell of a ship back again with her head pointing at her port of destination. Bankok! That's what he was after. I tell you this quiet, bowed, bandy-legged, almost deformed little man was immense in the single-ness of his idea and in his placid ignorance of our agitation. He motioned us forward with a commanding gesture, and went to take the wheel himself.

"Yes; that was the first thing we did—trim the yards of that wreck! No one was killed, or even disabled, but everyone was more or less hurt. You should have seen them! Some were in rags, with black faces, like coal-heavers, like sweeps, and had bullet heads that seemed closely cropped, but were in fact singed to the skin. Others, of the watch below, awakened by being shot out from their collapsing bunks, shivered incessantly, and kept on groaning even as we went about our work. But they all worked. That crew of Liverpool hard cases had in them the right stuff. It's my experience they always have. It is the sea that gives it—the vastness, the loneliness surrounding their dark stolid souls. Ah! Well! we stumbled, we crept, we fell, we barked our shins on the wreckage, we hauled. The masts stood, but we did not know how much they might be charred down below. It was nearly calm, but a long swell ran from the west and made her roll. They might go at any moment. We looked at them with apprehension. One could not foresee which way they would fall.

"Then we retreated aft and looked about us. The deck was a tangle of planks on edge, of planks on end, of splinters, of ruined woodwork. The masts rose from that chaos like big trees above a matted undergrowth. The interstices of that mass of wreckage were full of something whitish, sluggish, stirring—of something that was like a greasy fog. The smoke of the invisible fire was coming up again, was trailing, like a poisonous thick mist in some valley choked with dead wood. Already lazy wisps were beginning to curl up-wards amongst the mass of splinters. Here and there a piece of timber, stuck upright, resembled a post. Half of a fife-rail had been shot through the fore-sail, and the sky made a patch of glorious blue in the ignobly soiled canvas. A portion of several boards holding together had fallen across the rail, and one end protruded overboard, like a gangway leading upon nothing, like a gang-way leading over the deep sea, leading to death—as if inviting us to walk the plank at once and be done with our ridiculous troubles. And still the air, the sky—a ghost, something invisible was hailing the ship.

"Someone had the sense to look over, and there was the helmsman, who had impulsively jumped overboard, anxious to come back. He yelled and swam lustily like a merman, keeping up with the ship. We threw him a rope, and presently he stood amongst us streaming with water and very crestfallen. The captain had surrendered the wheel, and apart, elbow on rail and chin in hand, gazed at the sea wistfully. We asked ourselves, What next? I thought, Now, this is something like. This is great. I wonder what will happen. O youth!

"Suddenly Mahon sighted a steamer far astern. Captain Beard said, 'We may do something with her yet.' We hoisted two flags, which said in the international language of the sea, 'On fire. Want immediate assistance.' The steamer grew bigger rapidly, and by-and-by spoke with two flags on her foremast, 'I am coming to your assistance.'

"In half an hour she was abreast, to windward, within hail, and rolling slightly, with her engines stopped. We lost our composure, and yelled all together with excitement, 'We've been blown up.' A man in a white helmet, on the bridge, cried, 'Yes! All right! All right!' and he nodded his head, and smiled, and made soothing motions with his hand as though at a lot of frightened children. One of the boats dropped in the water, and walked towards us upon the sea with her long oars. Four Calashes pulled a swinging stroke. This was my first sight of Malay seamen. I've known them since, but what struck me then was their unconcern: they came alongside, and even the bowman standing up and holding to our main-chains with the boat-hook did not deign to lift his head for a glance. I thought people who had been blown up deserved more attention.

"A little man, dry like a chip and agile like a monkey, clambered up. It was the mate of the steamer. He gave one look, and cried, 'O boys—you had better quit.'

"We were silent. He talked apart with the captain for a time,—seemed to argue with him. Then they went away together to the steamer.

"When our skipper came back we learned that the steamer was the *Somerville,* Captain Nash, from West Australia to Singapore *via* Batavia with mails, and that the agreement was she should tow us to Anjer or Batavia, if possible, where we could extinguish the fire by scuttling, and then proceed on our voyage—to Bankok! The old man seemed excited. 'We will do it yet,' he said to Mahon, fiercely. He shook his fist at the sky. Nobody else said a word.

"At noon the steamer began to tow. She went ahead slim and high, and what was left of the *Judea* followed at the end of seventy fathom of tow rope—followed her swiftly like a cloud of smoke with mast-heads protruding above. We went aloft to furl the sails. We coughed on the yards, and were careful about the bunts. Do you see the lot of us there, putting a neat furl on the sails of that ship doomed to arrive nowhere? There was not a man who didn't think that at any moment the masts would topple over. From aloft we could not see the ship for smoke, and they worked carefully, passing the gaskets with even turns. 'Harbour furl—aloft there!' cried Mahon from below.

"You understand this? I don't think one of those chaps expected to get down in the usual way. When we did I heard them saying to each other, 'Well, I thought we would come down overboard, in a lump—sticks and all—blame me if I didn't.' 'That's what I was thinking to myself,' would answer wearily another battered and bandaged scarecrow. And, mind, these were men without the drilled-in habit of obedience. To an onlooker they would be a lot of profane scallywags without a redeeming point. What made them do it—what made them obey me when I, thinking consciously how fine it was, made them drop the bunt of the foresail twice to try and do it better? What? They had no professional reputation—no examples, no praise. It wasn't a sense of duty; they all knew well enough how to shirk, and laze, and dodge—when they had a mind to it—and mostly they had. Was it the two pounds ten a month that sent them there? They didn't think their pay half good enough. No; it was something in them, something inborn and subtle and everlasting. I don't say positively that the crew of a French or German merchantman wouldn't have done it, but I doubt whether it would have been done in the same way. There was a completeness in it, something solid like a principle, and masterful like an instinct—a disclosure of something secret—of that hidden something, that gift of good or evil that makes racial difference, that shapes the fate of nations.

"It was that night at ten that, for the first time since we had been fighting it, we saw the fire. The speed of the towing had fanned the smouldering destruction. A blue gleam appeared forward, shining below the wreck of the deck. It wavered in patches, it seemed to stir and creep like the light of a glow-worm. I saw it first, and told Mahon. 'Then the game's up,' he said. 'We had better stop this towing, or she will burst out suddenly fore and aft before we can clear out.' We set up a yell; rang bells to attract their attention; they towed on. At last Mahon and I had to crawl forward and cut the rope with an axe. There was no time to cast off the lashings. Red tongues could be seen licking the wilderness of splinters under our feet as we made our way back to the poop.

"Of course they very soon found out in the steamer that the rope was gone. She gave a loud blast of her whistle, her lights were seen sweeping in a wide circle, she came up ranging close alongside, and stopped. We were in a tight group on the poop looking at her. Every man had saved a little bundle or a bag. Suddenly a conical flame with a twisted top shot up forward and threw upon the black sea a circle of light, with the two vessels side by side and heaving gently in its centre. Captain Beard had been sitting on the gratings still and mute for hours, but now he rose slowly and advanced in front of us, to the mizzen-shrouds. Captain Nash hailed: 'Come along! Look sharp. I have mail-bags on board. I will take you and your boats to Singapore.'

" 'Thank you! No!' said our skipper. 'We must see the last of the ship.'

" 'I can't stand by any longer,' shouted the other. 'Mails—you know.'

" 'Ay! ay! We are all right.'

" 'Very well! I'll report you in Singapore. . . . Goodbye!'

"He waved his hand. Our men dropped their bundles quietly. The steamer moved ahead, and passing out of the circle of light, vanished at once from our sight, dazzled by the fire which burned fiercely. And then I knew that I would see the East first as commander of a small boat. I thought it fine; and the fidelity to the old ship was fine. We should see the last of her. Oh, the glamour of youth! Oh, the fire of it, more dazzling than the flames of the burning ship, throwing a magic light on the wide earth, leaping audaciously to the sky, presently to be quenched by time, more cruel, more pitiless, more bitter than the sea—and like the flames of the burning ship surrounded by an impenetrable night.

*

"The old man warned us in his gentle and inflexible way that it was part of our duty to save for the underwriters as much as we could of the ship's gear. Accordingly we went to work aft, while she blazed forward to give us plenty of light. We lugged out a lot of rubbish. What didn't we save? An old barometer fixed with an absurd quantity of screws nearly cost me my life: a sudden rush of smoke came upon me, and I just got away in time. There were various stores, bolts of canvas, coils of rope; the poop looked like a marine bazaar, and the boats were lumbered to the gunwales. One would have thought the old man wanted to take as much as he could of his first command with him. He was very, very quiet, but off his balance evidently. Would you believe it? He wanted to take a length of old stream-cable and a kedge-anchor with him in the long-boat. We said, 'Aye, aye, sir,' deferentially, and on the quiet let the things slip overboard. The heavy medicine-chest went that way, two bags of green coffee, tins of paint—fancy, paint!—a whole lot of things. Then I was ordered with two hands into the boats to make a stowage and get them ready against the time it would be proper for us to leave the ship.

"We put everything straight, stepped the long-boat's mast for our skipper, who was to take charge of her, and I was not sorry to sit down for a moment. My face felt raw, every limb ached as if broken. I was aware of all my ribs, and would have sworn to a twist in the backbone. The boats, fast astern, lay in a deep shadow, and all around I could see the circle of the sea lighted by the fire. A gigantic flame arose forward straight and clear. It flared fierce, with noises like the whirr of wings, with rumbles as of thunder. There were cracks, detonations, and from the cone of flame the sparks flew upwards, as man is born to trouble, to leaky ships, and to ships that burn.

"What bothered me was that the ship, lying broadside to the swell and to such wind as there was—a mere breath—the boats would not keep astern where they were safe, but persisted, in a pig-headed way boats have, in getting under the counter and then swinging alongside. They were knocking about dangerously and coming near the flame, while the ship rolled on them, and, of course, there was always the danger of the masts going over the side at any moment. I and my two boat-keepers kept them off as best as we could, with oars and boat-hooks; but to be constantly at it became exasperating, since there was no reason why we should not leave at once. We could not see those on board, nor could we imagine what caused the delay. The boat-keepers were swearing feebly, and I had not only my share of the work but also had to keep at it two men who showed a constant inclination to lay themselves down and let things slide.

"At last I hailed, 'On deck there,' and someone looked over. 'We're ready here,' I said. The head disappeared, and very soon popped up again. 'The captain says, All right, sir, and to keep the boats well clear of the ship.'

"Half an hour passed. Suddenly there was a frightful racket, rattle, clanking of chain, hiss of water, and millions of sparks flew up into the shivering column of smoke that stood leaning slightly above the ship. The catheads had burned away, and the two red-hot anchors had gone to the bottom, tearing out after them two hundred fathom of red-hot chain. The ship trembled, the mass of flame swayed as if ready to collapse, and the fore topgallant-mast fell. It darted down like an arrow of fire, shot under, and instantly leaping up within an oar's-length of the boats, floated quietly, very black on the luminous sea. I hailed the deck again. After some time a man in an unexpectedly cheerful but also muffled tone, as though he had been trying to speak with his mouth shut, informed me, 'Coming directly, sir,' and vanished. For a long time I heard nothing but the whirr and roar of the fire. There were also whistling sounds. The boats jumped, tugged at the painters, ran at each other playfully, knocked their sides together, or, do what we would, swung in a bunch against the ship's side. I couldn't stand it any longer, and swarming up a rope, clambered aboard over the stern.

"It was as bright as day. Coming up like this, the sheet of fire facing me was a terrifying sight, and the heat seemed hardly bearable at first. On a settee cushion dragged out of the cabin Captain Beard, his legs drawn up and one arm under his head, slept with the light playing on him. Do you know what the rest were busy about? They were sitting on deck right aft, round an open case, eating bread and cheese and drinking bottled stout.

"On the background of flames twisting in fierce tongues above their heads they seemed at home like salamanders, and looked like a band of desperate pirates. The fire sparkled in the whites of their eyes, gleamed on patches of white skin seen through the torn shirts. Each had the marks as of a battle about him—bandaged heads, tied-up arms, a strip of dirty rag round a knee—and each man had a bottle between his legs and a chunk of cheese in his hand. Mahon got up. With his handsome and disreputable head, his hooked profile, his long white beard, and with an uncorked bottle in his hand, he resembled one of those reckless sea-robbers of old making merry amidst violence and disaster. 'The last meal on board,' he explained solemnly. 'We had nothing to eat all day, and it was no use leaving all this.' He flourished the bottle and indicated the sleeping skipper. 'He said he couldn't swallow anything, so I got him to lie down,' he went on; and as I stared, 'I don't know whether you are aware, young fellow, the man had no sleep to speak of for days—and there will be dam' little sleep in the boats.' 'There will be no boats by-and-by if you fool about much longer,' I said, indignantly. I walked up to the skipper and shook him by the shoulder. At last he opened his eyes, but did not move. 'Time to leave her, sir,' I said quietly.

"He got up painfully, looked at the flames, at the sea sparkling round the ship, and black, black as ink farther away; he looked at the stars shining dim through a thin veil of smoke in a sky black, black as Erebus.

" 'Youngest first,' he said.

"And the ordinary seaman, wiping his mouth with the back of his hand, got up, clambered over the taffrail, and vanished. Others followed. One, on the point of going over, stopped short to drain his bottle, and with a great swing of his arm flung it at the fire. 'Take this!' he cried.

"The skipper lingered disconsolately, and we left him to commune alone for a while with his first command. Then I went up again and brought him away at last. It was time. The ironwork on the poop was hot to the touch.

"Then the painter of the long-boat was cut, and the three boats, tied together, drifted clear of the ship. It was just sixteen hours after the explosion when we abandoned her. Mahon had charge of the second boat, and I had the smallest—the 14-foot thing. The long-boat would have taken the lot of us; but the skipper said we must save as much property as we could—for the underwriters—and so I got my first command. I had two men with me, a bag of biscuits, a few tins of meat, and a breaker of water. I was ordered to keep close to the long-boat, that in case of bad weather we might be taken into her.

"And do you know what I thought? I thought I would part company as soon as I could. I wanted to have my first command all to myself. I wasn't going to sail in a squadron if there were a chance for independent cruising. I would make land by myself. I would beat the other boats. Youth! All youth! The silly, charming, beautiful youth.

"But we did not make a start at once. We must see the last of the ship. And so the boats drifted about that night, heaving and setting on the swell. The men dozed, waked, sighed, groaned. I looked at the burning ship.

"Between the darkness of earth and heaven she was burning fiercely upon a disc of purple sea shot by the blood-red play of gleams; upon a disc of water glittering and sinister. A high, clear flame, an immense and lonely flame, ascended from the ocean, and from its summit the black smoke poured continuously at the sky. She burned furiously; mournful and imposing like a funeral pile kindled in the night, surrounded by the sea, watched over by the stars. A magnificent death had come like a grace, like a gift, like a reward to that old ship at the end of her laborious days. The surrender of her weary ghost to the keeping of stars and sea was stirring like the sight of a glorious triumph. The masts fell just before daybreak, and for a moment there was a burst and turmoil of sparks that seemed to fill with flying fire the night patient and watchful, the vast night lying silent upon the sea. At daylight she was only a charred shell, floating still under a cloud of smoke and bearing a glowing mass of coal within.

"Then the oars were got out, and the boats forming in a line moved round her remains as if in procession—the long-boat leading. As we pulled across her stern a slim dart of fire shot out viciously at us, and suddenly she went down, head first, in a great hiss of steam. The unconsumed stern was the last to sink; but the paint had gone, had cracked, had peeled off, and there were no letters, there was no word, no stubborn device that was like her soul, to flash at the rising sun her creed and her name.

"We made our way north. A breeze sprang up, and about noon all the boats came together for the last time. I had no mast or sail in mine, but I made a mast out of a spare oar and hoisted a boat-awning for a sail, with a boat-hook for a yard. She was certainly over-masted, but I had the satisfaction of knowing that with the wind aft I could beat the other two. I had to wait for them. Then we all had a look at the captain's chart, and, after a sociable meal of hard bread and water, got our last instructions. These were simple: steer north, and keep together as much as possible. 'Be careful with that jury-rig, Marlow,' said the captain; and Mahon, as I sailed proudly past his boat, wrinkled his curved nose and hailed, 'You will sail that ship of yours under water, if you don't look out, young fellow.' He was a malicious old man— and may the deep sea where he sleeps now rock him gently, rock him tenderly to the end of time!

"Before sunset a thick rain-squall passed over the two boats, which were far astern, and that was the last I saw of them for a time. Next day I sat steering my cockle-shell—my first command—with nothing but water and sky around me. I did sight in the afternoon the upper sails of a ship far away, but said nothing, and my men did not notice her. You see I was afraid she might be homeward bound, and I had no mind to turn back from the portals of the East. I was steering for Java—another blessed name—like Bankok, you know. I steered many days.

"I need not tell you what it is to be knocking about in an open boat. I remember nights and days of calm, when we pulled, we pulled, and the boat seemed to stand still, as if bewitched within the circle of the sea horizon. I remember the heat, the deluge of rain-squalls that kept us baling for dear life (but filled our water-cask), and I remember sixteen hours on end with a mouth dry as a cinder and a steering-oar over the stern to keep my first command head on to a breaking sea. I did not know how good a man I was till then. I remember the drawn faces, the dejected figures of my two men, and I remember my youth and the feeling that will never come back any more—the feeling that I could last for ever, outlast the sea, the earth, and all men; the deceitful feeling that lures us on to joys, to perils, to love, to vain effort—to death; the triumphant conviction of strength, the heat of life in the handful of dust, the glow in the heart that with every year grows dim, grows cold, grows small, and expires—and expires, too soon, too soon—before life itself.

"And this is how I see the East. I have seen its secret places and have looked into its very soul; but now I see it always from a small boat, a high outline of mountains, blue and afar in the morning; like faint mist at noon; a jagged wall of purple at sunset. I have the feel of the oar in my hand, the vision of a scorching blue sea in my eyes. And I see a bay, a wide bay, smooth as glass and polished like ice, shimmering in the dark. A red light burns far off upon the gloom of the land, and the night is soft and warm. We drag at the oars with aching arms, and suddenly a puff of wind, a puff faint and tepid and laden with strange odours of blossoms, of aromatic wood, comes out of the still night—the first sigh of the East on my face. That I can never forget. It was impalpable and enslaving, like a charm, like a whispered promise of mysterious delight.

"We had been pulling this finishing spell for eleven hours. Two pulled, and he whose turn it was to rest sat at the tiller. We had made out the red light in that bay and steered for it, guessing it must mark some small coasting port. We passed two vessels, outlandish and high-sterned, sleeping at anchor, and, approaching the light, now very dim, ran the boat's nose against the end of a jutting wharf. We were blind with fatigue. My men dropped the oars and fell off the thwarts as if dead. I made fast to a pile. A current rippled softly. The scented obscurity of the shore was grouped into vast masses, a density of colossal clumps of vegetation, probably—mute and fantastic shapes. And at their foot the semicircle of a beach gleamed faintly, like an illusion. There was not a light, not a stir, not a sound. The mysterious East faced me, perfumed like a flower, silent like death, dark like a grave.

"And I sat weary beyond expression, exulting like a conqueror, sleepless and entranced as if before a profound, a fateful enigma.

"A splashing of oars, a measured dip reverberating on the level of water, intensified by the silence of the shore into loud claps, made me jump up. A boat, a European boat, was coming in. I invoked the name of the dead: I hailed *Judea* ahoy! A thin shout answered.

"It was the captain. I had beaten the flagship by three hours, and I was glad to hear the old man's voice again, tremulous and tired. 'Is it you, Marlow?' 'Mind the end of that jetty, sir,' I cried.

"He approached cautiously, and brought up with the deep-sea lead-line which we had saved—for the underwriters. I eased my painter and fell alongside. He sat, a broken figure at the stern, wet with dew, his hands clasped in his lap. His men were asleep already. 'I had a terrible time of it,' he murmured. 'Mahon is behind—not very far.' We conversed in whispers, in low whispers, as if afraid to wake up the land. Guns, thunder, earthquakes would not have awakened the men just then.

"Looking round as we talked, I saw away at sea a bright light travelling in the night. 'There's a steamer passing the bay,' I said. She was not passing, she was entering, and she even came close and anchored. 'I wish,' said the old man, 'you would find out whether she is English. Perhaps they could give us a passage somewhere.' He seemed nervously anxious. So by dint of punching and kicking I started one of my men into a state of somnambulism, and giving him an oar, took another and pulled towards the lights of the steamer.

"There was a murmur of voices in her, metallic hollow clangs of the engine-room, footsteps on the deck. Her ports shone, round like dilated eyes. Shapes moved about, and there was a shadowy man high up on the bridge. He heard my oars.

"And then, before I could open my lips, the East spoke to me, but it was a Western voice. A torrent of words was poured into the enigmatical, the fateful silence; outlandish, angry words, mixed with words and even whole sentences of good English, less strange but even more surprising. The voice swore and cursed violently; it riddled the solemn peace of the bay by a volley of abuse. It began by calling me Pig, and from that went crescendo into unmentionable adjectives—in English. The man up there raged aloud in two languages, and with a sincerity in his fury that almost convinced me I had, in some way, sinned against the harmony of the universe. I could hardly see him, but began to think he would work himself into a fit.

"Suddenly he ceased, and I could hear him snorting and blowing like a porpoise. I said—

" 'What steamer is this, pray?'

" 'Eh? What's this? And who are you?'

" 'Castaway crew of an English barque burnt at sea. We came here to-night. I am the second mate. The captain is in the long-boat, and wishes to know if you would give us a passage somewhere.'

" 'Oh, my goodness! I say. . . . This is the *Celestial* from Singapore on her return trip. I'll arrange with your captain in the morning, . . . and, . . . I say, . . . did you hear me just now?'

" 'I should think the whole bay heard you.'

" 'I thought you were a shore-boat. Now, look here—this infernal lazy scoundrel of a caretaker has gone to sleep again—curse him. The light is out, and I nearly ran foul of the end of this damned jetty. This is the third time he plays me this trick. Now, I ask you, can anybody stand this kind of thing? It's enough to drive a man out of his mind. I'll report him. . . . I'll get the Assistant Resident to give him the sack, by . . . ! See—there's no light. It's out, isn't it? I take you to witness the light's out. There should be a light, you know. A red light on the—'

" 'There was a light,' I said, mildly.

" 'But it's out, man! What's the use of talking like this? You can see for yourself it's out—don't you? If you had to take a valuable steamer along this Godforsaken coast you would want a light, too. I'll kick him from end to end of his miserable wharf. You'll see if I don't. I will—'

" 'So I may tell my captain you'll take us?' I broke in.

" 'Yes, I'll take you. Goodnight,' he said, brusquely.

"I pulled back, made fast again to the jetty, and then went to sleep at last. I had faced the silence of the East. I had heard some of its language. But when I opened my eyes again the silence was as complete as though it had never been broken. I was lying in a flood of light, and the sky had never looked so far, so high, before. I opened my eyes and lay without moving.

"And then I saw the men of the East—they were looking at me. The whole length of the jetty was full of people. I saw brown, bronze, yellow faces, the black eyes, the glitter, the colour of an Eastern crowd. And all these beings stared without a murmur, without a sigh, without a movement. They stared down at the boats, at the sleeping men who at night had come to them from the sea. Nothing moved. The fronds of palms stood still against the sky. Not a branch stirred along the shore, and the brown roofs of hidden houses peeped through the green foliage, through the big leaves that hung shining and still like leaves forged of heavy metal. This was the East of the ancient navigators, so old, so mysterious, resplendent and sombre, living and unchanged, full of danger and promise. And these were the men. I sat up suddenly. A wave of movement passed through the crowd from end to end, passed along the heads, swayed the bodies, ran along the jetty like a ripple on the water, like a breath of wind on a field—and all was still again. I see it now—the wide sweep of the bay, the glittering sands, the wealth of green infinite and varied, the sea blue like the sea of a dream, the crowd of attentive faces, the blaze of vivid colour—the water reflecting it all, the curve of the shore, the jetty, the high-sterned outlandish craft floating still, and the three boats with the tired men from the West sleeping, unconscious of the land and the people and of the violence of sunshine. They slept thrown across the thwarts, curled on bottom-boards, in the careless attitudes of death. The head of the old skipper, leaning back in the stern of the long-boat, had fallen on his breast, and he looked as though he would never wake. Farther out old Mahon's face was upturned to the sky, with the long white beard spread out on his breast, as though he had been shot where he sat at the tiller; and a man, all in a heap in the bows of the boat, slept with both arms embracing the stem-head and with his cheek laid on the gunwale. The East looked at them without a sound.

"I have known its fascination since; I have seen the mysterious shores, the still water, the lands of brown nations, where a stealthy Nemesis lies in wait, pursues, overtakes so many of the conquering race, who are proud of their wisdom, of their knowledge, of their strength. But for me all the East is contained in that vision of my youth. It is all in that moment when I opened my young eyes on it. I came upon it from a tussle with the sea—and I was young—and I saw it looking at me. And this is all that is left of it! Only a moment; a moment of strength, of romance, of glamour—of youth! ... A flick of sunshine, upon a strange shore, the time to remember, the time for a sigh, and—goodbye!—Night—Goodbye ...!"

He drank.

"Ah! The good old time—the good old time. Youth and the sea. Glamour and the sea! The good, strong sea, the salt, bitter sea, that could whisper to you and roar at you and knock your breath out of you."

He drank again.

"By all that's wonderful it is the sea, I believe, the sea itself—or is it youth alone? Who can tell? But you here—you all had something out of life: money, love—whatever one gets on shore—and, tell me, wasn't that the best time, that time when we were young at sea; young and had nothing, on the sea that gives nothing, except hard knocks—and sometimes a chance to feel your strength—that only—what you all regret?"

And we all nodded at him: the man of finance, the man of accounts, the man of law, we all nodded at him over the polished table that like a still sheet of brown water reflected our faces, lined, wrinkled; our faces marked by toil, by deceptions, by success, by love; our weary eyes looking still, looking always, looking anxiously for something out of life, that while it is expected is already gone—has passed unseen, in a sigh, in a flash—together with the youth, with the strength, with the romance of illusions.

HENRY JAMES

The Lesson of the Master

He had been told the ladies were at church, but this was corrected by what he saw from the top of the steps—they descended from a great height in two arms, with a circular sweep of the most charming effect—at the threshold of the door which, from the long bright gallery, overlooked the immense lawn. Three gentlemen, on the grass, at a distance, sat under the great trees, while the fourth figure showed a crimson dress that told as a "bit of colour" amid the fresh rich green. The servant had so far accompanied Paul Overt as to introduce him to this view, after asking him if he wished first to go to his room. The young man declined that privilege conscious of no disrepair from so short and easy a journey and always liking to take at once a general perceptive possession of a new scene. He stood there a little with his eyes on the group and on the admirable picture, the wide grounds of an old country house near London—that only made it better—on a splendid Sunday in June. "But that lady, who's *she?*" he said to the servant before the man left him.

"I think she's Mrs. St. George, sir."

"Mrs. St. George, the wife of the distinguished—" Then Paul Overt checked himself, doubting if a footman would know.

"Yes, sir—probably, sir," said his guide, who appeared to wish to intimate that a person staying at Summersoft would naturally be, if only by alliance, distinguished. His tone, however, made poor Overt himself feel for the moment scantly so.

"And the gentlemen?" Overt went on.

"Well, sir, one of them's General Fancourt."

"Ah yes, I know; thank you." General Fancourt was distinguished, there was no doubt of that, for something he had done, or perhaps even hadn't done—the young man couldn't remember which—some years before in India. The servant went away, leaving the glass doors open into the gallery, and Paul Overt remained at the head of the wide double staircase, saying to himself that the place was sweet and promised a pleasant visit, while he leaned on the balustrade of fine old ironwork which, like all the other details, was of the same period as the house. It all went together and spoke in one voice—a rich English voice of the early part of the eighteenth century. It might have been church-time on a summer's day in the reign of Queen Anne; the stillness was too perfect to be modern, the nearness counted so as distance, and there was something so fresh and sound in the originality of the large smooth house, the expanse of beautiful brickwork that showed for pink rather than red and that had been kept clear of messy creepers by the law under which a woman with a rare complexion disdains a veil. When Paul Overt became aware that the people under the trees had noticed him he turned back through the open doors into the great gallery which was the pride of the place. It marched across from end to end and seemed—with its bright colours, its high panelled windows, its faded flowered chintzes, its quickly-recognized portraits and pictures, the blue-and-white china of its cabinets and the attenuated festoons and rosettes of its ceiling—a cheerful upholstered avenue into the other century.

Our friend was slightly nervous; that went with his character as a student of fine prose, went with the artist's general disposition to vibrate; and there was a particular thrill in the idea that Henry St. George might be a member of the party. For the young aspirant he had remained a high literary figure, in spite of the lower range of production to which he had fallen after his first three great successes, the comparative absence of quality in his later work. There had been moments when Paul Overt almost shed tears for this; but now that he was near him—he had never met him—he was conscious only of the fine original source and of his own immense debt. After he had taken a turn or two up and down the gallery he came out again and descended the steps. He was but slenderly supplied with a certain social boldness—it was really a weakness in him—so that, conscious of a want of acquaintance with the four persons in the distance, he gave way to motions recommended by their not committing him to a positive approach. There was a fine English awkwardness in this—he felt that too as he sauntered vaguely and obliquely across the lawn, taking an independent line. Fortunately there was an equally fine English directness in the way one of the gentlemen presently rose and made as if to 'stalk' him, though with an air of conciliation and reassurance. To this demonstration Paul Overt instantly responded, even if the gentleman were not his host. He was tall, straight, and elderly and had, like the great house itself, a pink smiling face, and into the bargain a white moustache. Our young man met him half-way while he laughed and said: "Er—Lady Watermouth told us you were coming; she asked me just to look after you." Paul Overt thanked him, liking him on the spot, and turned round with him to walk toward the others. "They've all gone to church—all except us," the stranger continued as they went; "we're just sitting here—it's so jolly." Overt pronounced it jolly indeed: it was such a lovely place. He mentioned that he was having the charming impression for the first time.

"Ah, you've not been here before?" said his companion. "It's a nice little place—not much to *do,* you know." Overt wondered what he wanted to "do"—he felt that he himself was doing so much. By the time they came to where the others sat he had recognized his initiator for a military man and—such was the turn of Overt's imagination—had found him thus still more sympathetic. He would naturally have a need for action, for deeds at variance with the pacific pastoral scene. He was evidently so good-natured, however, that he accepted the inglorious hour for what it was worth. Paul Overt shared it with him and with his companions for the next twenty minutes; the latter looked at him and he looked at them without knowing much who they were, while the talk went on without much telling him even what it meant. It seemed indeed to mean nothing in particular; it wandered, with casual pointless pauses and short terrestrial flights, amid names of persons and places—names which, for our friend, had no great power of evocation. It was all sociable and slow, as was right and natural of a warm Sunday morning.

His first attention was given to the question, privately considered, of whether one of the two younger men would be Henry St. George. He knew many of his distinguished contemporaries by their photographs, but had never, as happened, seen a portrait of the great misguided novelist. One of the gentlemen was unimaginable—he was too young; and the other scarcely looked clever enough, with such mild undiscriminating eyes. If those eyes were St. George's the problem presented by the ill-matched parts of his genius would be still more difficult of solution. Besides, the deportment of their proprietor was not, as regards the lady in the red dress, such as could be natural, toward the wife of his bosom, even to a writer accused by several critics of sacrificing too much to manner. Lastly Paul Overt had a vague sense that if the gentleman with the expressionless eyes bore the name that had set his heart beating faster (he also had contradictory conventional whiskers—the young admirer of the celebrity had never in a mental vision seen *his* face in so vulgar a frame) he would have given him a sign of recognition or of friendliness, would have heard of him a little, would know something about *Ginistrella,* would have an impression of how that fresh fiction had caught the eye of real criticism. Paul Overt had a dread of being grossly proud, but even morbid modesty might view the authorship of *Ginistrella* as constituting a degree of identity. His soldierly friend became clear enough: he was 'Fancourt', but was also 'the General'; and he mentioned to the new visitor in the course of a few moments that he had but lately returned from twenty years' service abroad.

"And now you remain in England?" the young man asked.

"Oh yes; I've bought a small house in London."

"And I hope you like it," said Overt, looking at Mrs. St. George.

"Well, a little house in Manchester Square—there's a limit to the enthusiasm *that* inspires."

"Oh I meant being at home again—being back in Piccadilly."

"My daughter likes Piccadilly—that's the main thing. She's very fond of art and music and literature and all that kind of thing. She missed it in India and she finds it in London, or she hopes she'll find it. Mr. St. George has promised to help her—he has been awfully kind to her. She has gone to church—she's fond of that too—but they'll all be back in a quarter of an hour. You must let me introduce you to her—she'll be so glad to know you. I dare say she has read every blest world you've written."

"I shall be delighted—I haven't written so very many," Overt pleaded, feeling, and without resentment, that the General at least was vagueness itself about that. But he wondered a little why, expressing this friendly disposition, it didn't occur to the doubtless eminent soldier to pronounce the word that would put him in relation with Mrs. St. George. If it was a quesiton of introductions Miss Fancourt—apparently as yet unmarried—was far away, while the wife of his illustrious confrère was almost between them. This lady struck Paul Overt as altogether pretty, with a surprising juvenility and a high smartness of aspect, something that—he could scarcely have said why—served for mystification. St. George certainly had every right to a charming wife, but he himself would never have imagined the important little woman in the aggressively Parisian dress the partner for life, the *alter ego,* of a man of letters. That partner in general, he knew, that second self, was far from presenting herself in a single type: observation had taught him that she was not inveterately, not necessarily plain. But he had never before seen her look so much as if her prosperity had deeper foundations than an ink-spotted study-table littered with proof-sheets. Mrs. St. George might have been the wife of a gentleman who 'kept' books rather than wrote them, who carried on great affairs in the City and made better bargains than those that poets mostly make with publishers. With this she hinted at a success more personal—a success peculiarly stamping the age in which society, the world of conversation, is a great drawing-room with the City for its ante-chamber. Overt numbered her years at first as some thirty, and then ended by believing that she might approach her fiftieth. But she somehow in this case juggled away the excess and the difference—you only saw them in a rare glimpse, like the rabbit in the conjurer's sleeve. She was extraordinarily white, and her every element and item was pretty; her eyes, her ears, her hair, her voice, her hands, her feet—to which her relaxed attitude in her wicker chair gave a great publicity—and the numerous ribbons and trinkets with which she was bedecked. She looked as if she had put on her best clothes to go to church and then had decided they were too good for that and had stayed at home. She told a story of some length about the shabby way Lady Jane had treated the Duchess, as well as an anecdote in relation to a purchase she had made in Paris—on her way back from Cannes; made for Lady Egbert, who had never refunded the money. Paul Overt suspected her of a tendency to figure great people as larger than life, until he noticed the manner in which she handled Lady Egbert, which was so sharply mutinous that it reassured him. He felt he should have understood her better if he might have met her eye; but she scarcely so much as glanced at him. "Ah here they come—all the good ones!" she said at last; and Paul Overt admired at his distance the return of the churchgoers—several persons, in couples and threes, advancing in a flicker of sun and shade at the end of a large green vista formed by the level grass and the overarching boughs.

"If you mean to imply that *we're* bad, I protest," said one of the gentlemen—"after making one's self agreeable all the morning!"

"Ah, if they've found you agreeable—!" Mrs. St. George gaily cried. "But if we're good the others are better."

"They must be angels then," said the amused General.

"Your husband was an angel, the way he went off at your bidding," the gentleman who had first spoken declared to Mrs. St. George.

"At my bidding?"

"Didn't you make him go to church?"

"I never made him do anything in my life but once—when I made him burn up a bad book. That's all!" At her "That's all!" our young friend broke into an irrepressible laugh; it lasted only a second, but it drew her eyes to him. His own met them, though not long enough to help him to understand her; unless it were a step towards this that he saw on the instant how the burnt book—the way she alluded to it!—would have been one of her husband's finest things.

"A bad book?" her interlocutor repeated.

"I didn't like it. He went to church because your daughter went," she continued to General Fancourt. "I think it my duty to call your attention to his extraordinary demonstrations to your daughter."

"Well, if you don't mind them I don't," the General laughed.

"*Il s'attache à ses pas.* But I don't wonder—she's so charming."

"I hope she won't make him burn any books!" Paul Overt ventured to exclaim.

"If she'd make him write a few it would be more to the purpose," said Mrs. St. George. "He has been of a laziness of late—!"

Our young man stared—he was so struck with the lady's phraseology. Her "write a few" seemed to him almost as good as her "That's all." Didn't she, as the wife of a rare artist, know what it was to produce *one* perfect work of art? How in the world did she think they were turned off? His private conviction was that, admirably as Henry St. George wrote, he had written for the last ten years, and especially for the last five, only too much, and there was an instant during which he felt inwardly solicited to make this public. But before he had spoken a diversion was effected by the return of the absentees. They strolled up dispersedly—there were eight or ten of them—and the circle under the trees rearranged itself as they took their place in it. They made it much larger, so that Paul Overt could feel—he was always feeling that sort of thing, as he said to himself—that if the company had already been interesting to watch the interest would now become intense. He shook hands with his hostess, who welcomed him without many words, in the manner of a woman able to trust him to understand and conscious that so pleasant an occasion would in every way speak for itself. She offered him no particular facility for sitting by her, and when they had all subsided again he found himself still next General Fancourt, with an unknown lady on his other flank.

"That's my daughter—that one opposite," the General said to him without loss of time. Overt saw a tall girl, with magnificent red hair, in a dress of a pretty grey-green tint and of a limp silken texture, a garment that clearly shirked every modern effect. It had therefore somehow the stamp of the latest thing, so that our beholder quickly took her for nothing if not contemporaneous.

"She's very handsome—very handsome," he repeated while he considered her. There was something noble in her head, and she appeared fresh and strong.

Her good father surveyed her with complacency, remarking soon: "She looks too hot—that's her walk. But she'll be all right presently. Then I'll make her come over and speak to you."

"I should be sorry to give you that trouble. If you were to take me over there—!" the young man murmured.

"My dear sir, do you suppose I put myself out that way? I don't mean for you, but for Marian," the General added.

"I would put myself out for her soon enough," Overt replied; after which he went on: "Will you be so good as to tell me which of those gentlemen is Henry St. George?"

"The fellow talking to my girl. By Jove, he is making up to her—they're going off for another walk."

"Ah, is that he—really?" Our friend felt a certain surprise, for the personage before him seemed to trouble a vision which had been vague only while not confronted with the reality. As soon as the reality dawned the mental image, retiring with a sigh, became substantial enough to suffer a slight wrong. Overt, who had spent a considerable part of his short life in foreign lands, made now, but not for the first time, the reflection that whereas in those countries he had almost always recognized the artist and the man of letters by his personal 'type', the mould on his face, the character of his head, the expression of his figure, and even the indications of his dress, so in England this identification was as little as possible a matter of course, thanks to the greater conformity, the habit of sinking the profession instead of advertising it, the general diffusion of the air of the gentleman—the gentleman committed to no particular set of ideas. More than once, on returning to his own country, he had said to himself about the people met in society: "One sees them in this place and that, and one even talks with them; but to find out what they *do* one would really have to be a detective." In respect to several individuals whose work he was the opposite of "drawn to"—perhaps he was wrong—he found himself adding "No wonder they conceal it—when it's so bad!" He noted that oftener than in France and in Germany his artist looked like a gentleman—that is like an English one—while, certainly outside a few exceptions, his gentleman didn't look like an artist. St. George was not one of the exceptions; that circumstance he definitely apprehended before the great man had turned his back to walk off with Miss Fancourt. He certainly looked better behind than any foreign man of letters—showed for beautifully correct in his tall black hat and his superior frock coat. Somehow, all the same, these very garments—he wouldn't have minded them so much on a week-day—were disconcerting to Paul Overt, who forgot for the moment that the head of the profession was not a bit better dressed than himself. He had caught a glimpse of a regular face, a fresh colour, a brown moustache, and a pair of eyes surely never visited by a fine frenzy, and he promised himself to study these denotements on the first occasion. His superficial sense was that their owner might have passed for a lucky stockbroker—a gentleman driving eastward every morning from a sanitary suburb in a smart dog-cart. That carried out the impression already derived from his wife. Paul's glance, after a moment, travelled back to this lady, and he saw how her own had followed her husband as he moved off with Miss Fancourt. Overt permitted himself to wonder a little if she were jealous when another woman took him away. Then he made out that Mrs. St. George wasn't glaring at the indifferent maiden. Her eyes rested but on her husband, and with unmistakable serenity. That was the way she wanted him to be—she liked his conventional uniform. Overt longed to hear more about the book she had induced him to destroy.

□ **II** □

As they all came out from luncheon General Fancourt took hold of him with an "I say, I want you to know my girl!" as if the idea had just occurred to him and he hadn't spoken of it before. With the other hand he possessed himself all paternally of the young lady. "You know all about him. I've seen you with his books. She reads everything—everything!" he went on to Paul. The girl smiled at him and then laughed at her father. The General turned away and his daughter spoke—"Isn't papa delightful?"

"He is indeed, Miss Fancourt."

"As if I read you because I read 'everything'!"

"Oh I don't mean for saying that," said Paul Overt. "I liked him from the moment he began to be kind to me. Then he promised me this privilege."

"It isn't for you he means it—it's for me. If you flatter yourself that he thinks of anything in life but me you'll find you're mistaken. He introduces everyone. He thinks me insatiable."

"You speak just like him," laughed our youth.

"Ah but sometimes I want to"—and the girl coloured. "I don't read everything—I read very little. But I *have* read you."

"Suppose we go into the gallery," said Paul Overt. She pleased him greatly, not so much because of this last remark—though that of course was not too disconcerting—as because, seated opposite to him at luncheon, she had given him for half an hour the impression of her beautiful face. Something else had come with it—a sense of generosity, of an enthusiasm which, unlike many enthusiasms, was not all manner. That was not spoiled for him by his seeing that the repast had placed her again in familiar contact with Henry St. George. Sitting next her this celebrity was also opposite our young man, who had been able to note that he multiplied the attentions lately brought by his wife to the General's notice. Paul Overt had gathered as well that this lady was not in the least discomposed by these fond excesses and that she gave every sign of an unclouded spirit. She had Lord Masham on one side of her and on the other the accomplished Mr. Mulliner, editor of the new high-class lively evening paper which was expected to meet a want felt in circles increasingly conscious that Conservatism must be made amusing, and unconvinced when assured by those of another political colour that it was already amusing enough. At the end of an hour spent in her company Paul Overt thought her still prettier than at the first radiation, and if her profane allusions to her husband's work had not still rung in his ears he should have liked her—so far as it could be a question of that in connexion with a woman to whom he had not yet spoken and to whom probably he should never speak if it were left to her. Pretty women were a clear need to this genius, and for the hour it was Miss Fancourt who supplied the want. If Overt had promised himself a closer view the occasion was now of the best, and it brought consequences felt by the young man as important. He saw more in St. George's face, which he liked the better for its not having told its whole story in the first three minutes. That story came out as one read, in short instalments—it was excusable that one's analogies should be somewhat professional—and the text was a style considerably involved, a language not easy to translate at sight. There were shades of meaning in it and a vague perspective of history which receded as you advanced. Two facts Paul had particularly heeded. The first of these was that he liked the measured mask much better at inscrutable rest than in social agitation; its almost convulsive smile above all displeased him (as much as any impression from that source could), whereas the quiet face had a charm that grew in proportion as stillness settled again. The change to the expression of gaiety excited, he made out, very much the private protest of a person sitting gratefully in the twilight when the lamp is brought in too soon. His second reflection was that, though generally averse to the flagrant use of ingratiating arts by a man of age 'making up' to a pretty girl, he was not in this case too painfully affected: which seemed to prove either that St. George had a light hand or the air of being younger than he was, or else that Miss Fancourt's own manner somehow made everything right.

Overt walked with her into the gallery, and they strolled to the end of it, looking at the pictures, the cabinets, the charming vista, which harmonized with the prospect of the summer afternoon, resembling it by a long brightness, with great divans and old chairs that figured hours of rest. Such a place as that had the added merit of giving those who came into it plenty to talk about. Miss Fancourt sat down with her new acquaintance on a flowered sofa, the cushions of which, very numerous, were tight ancient cubes of many sizes, and presently said: "I'm so glad to have a chance to thank you."

"To thank me—?" He had to wonder.

"I liked your book so much. I think it splendid."

She sat there smiling at him, and he never asked himself which book she meant; for after all he had written three or four. That seemed a vulgar detail, and he wasn't even gratified by the idea of the pleasure she told him—her handsome bright face told him—he had given her. The feeling she appealed to, or at any rate the feeling she excited, was something larger, something that had little to do with any quickened pulsation of his own vanity. It was responsive admiration of the life she embodied, the young purity and richness of which appeared to imply that real success was to resemble *that,* to live, to bloom, to present the perfection of a fine type, not to have hammered out headachy fancies with a bent back at an ink-stained table. While her grey eyes rested on him—there was a widish space between these, and the division of her rich-coloured hair, so thick that it ventured to be smooth, made a free arch above them—he was almost ashamed of that exercise of the pen which it was her present inclination to commend. He was conscious he should have liked better to please her in some other way. The lines of her face were those of a woman grown, but the child lingered on in her complexion and in the sweetness of her mouth. Above all she was natural—that was indubitable now; more natural than he had supposed at first, perhaps on account of her aesthetic toggery, which was conventionally unconventional, suggesting what he might have called a tortuous spontaneity. He had feared that sort of thing in other cases, and his fears had been justified; for, though he was an aritst to the essence, the modern reactionary nymph, with the brambles of the woodland caught in her folds and a look as if the satyrs had toyed with her hair, made him shrink not as a man of starch and patent leather, but as a man potentially himself a poet or even a faun. The girl was really more candid than her costume, and the best proof of it was her supposing her liberal character suited by any uniform. This was a fallacy, since if she was draped as a pessimist he was sure she liked the taste of life. He thanked her for her appreciation—aware at the same time that he didn't appear to thank her enough and that she might think him ungracious. He was afraid she would ask him to explain something he had written, and he always winced at that—perhaps too timidly—for to his own ear the explanation of a work of art sounded fatuous. But he liked her so much as to feel a confidence that in the long run he should be able to show her he wasn't rudely evasive. Moreover she surely wasn't quick to take offence, wasn't irritable; she could be trusted to wait. So when he said to her, "Ah, don't talk of anything I've done, don't talk of it *here;* there's another man in the house who's the actuality!"—when he uttered this short sincere protest it was with the sense that she would see in the words neither mock humility nor the impatience of a successful man bored with praise.

"You mean Mr. St. George—isn't he delightful?"

Paul Overt met her eyes, which had a cool morning light that would have half broken his heart if he hadn't been so young. "Alas I don't know him. I only admire him at a distance."

"Oh you *must* know him—he wants so to talk to you," returned Miss Fancourt, who evidently had the habit of saying the things that, by her quick calculation, would give people pleasure. Paul saw how she would always calculate on everything's being simple between others.

"I shouldn't have supposed he knew anything about me," he professed.

"He does then—everything. And if he didn't I should be able to tell him."

"To tell him everything?" our friend smiled.

"You talk just like the people in your book!" she answered.

"Then they must all talk alike."

She thought a moment, not a bit disconcerted. "Well, it must be so difficult. Mr. St. George tells me it *is*—terribly. I've tried too—and I find it so. I've tried to write a novel."

"Mr. St. George oughtn't to discourage you," Paul went so far as to say.

"You do much more—when you wear that expression."

"Well, after all, why try to be an artist?" the young man pursued. "It's so poor—so poor!"

"I don't know what you mean," said Miss Fancourt, who looked grave.

"I mean as compared with being a person of action—as living your works."

"But what's art but an intense life—if it be real?" she asked. "I think it's the only one—everything else is so clumsy!" Her companion laughed and she brought out with her charming serenity what next struck her. "It's so interesting to meet so many celebrated people."

"So I should think—but surely it isn't new to you."

"Why I've never seen anyone—anyone: living always in Asia."

The way she talked of Asia somehow enchanted him. "But doesn't that continent swarm with great figures? Haven't you administered provinces in India and had captive rajahs and tributary princes chained to your car?"

It was as if she didn't care even *should* he amuse himself at her cost. "I was with my father after I left school to go out there. It was delightful being with him—we're alone together in the world he and I—but there was none of the society I like best. One never heard of a picture—never of a book except bad ones."

"Never of a picture? Why, wasn't all life a picture?"

She looked over the delightful place where they sat. "Nothing to compare to this. I adore England!" she cried.

It fairly stirred in him the sacred chord. "Ah of course I don't deny that we must do something with her, poor old dear, yet."

"She hasn't been touched, really," said the girl.

"Did Mr. St. George say that?"

There was a small, as he felt, harmless spark of irony in his question; which, however, she answered very simply, not noticing the insinuation. "Yes, he says England hasn't been touched—not considering all there is," she went on eagerly. "He's so interesting about our country. To listen to him makes one want so to do something."

"It would make *me* want to," said Paul Overt, feeling strongly, on the instant, the suggestion of what she said and that of the emotion with which she said it, and well aware of what an incentive, on St. George's lips, such a speech might be.

"Oh you—as if you hadn't! I should like so to hear you talk together," she added ardently.

"That's very genial of you; but he'd have it all his own way. I'm prostrate before him."

She had an air of earnestness. "Do you think then he's so perfect?"

"Far from it. Some of his later books seem to me of a queerness—!"

"Yes, yes—he knows that."

Paul Overt stared. "That they seem to me of a queerness—!"

"Well yes, or at any rate that they're not what they should be. He told me he didn't esteem them. He has told me such wonderful things—he's so interesting."

There was a certain shock for Paul Overt in the knowledge that the fine genius they were talking of had been reduced to so explicit a confession and had made it, in his misery, to the first comer; for though Miss Fancourt was charming what was she after all but an immature girl encountered at a country house? Yet precisely this was part of the sentiment he himself had just expressed; he would make way completely for the poor peccable great man not because he didn't read him clear, but altogether because he did. His consideration was half composed of tenderness for superficialities which he was sure their perpetrator judged privately, judged more ferociously than anyone, and which represented some tragic intellectual secret. He would have his reasons for his psychology *à fleur de peau,* and these reasons could only be cruel ones, such as would make him dearer to those who already were fond of him. "You excite my envy. I have my reserves, I discriminate—but I love him," Paul said in a moment. "And seeing him for the first time this way is a great event for me."

"How momentous—how magnificent!" cried the girl. "How delicious to bring you together!"

"*Your* doing it—that makes it perfect," our friend returned.

"He's as eager as you," she went on. "But it's so odd you shouldn't have met."

"It's not really so odd as it strikes you. I've been out of England so much—made repeated absences all these last years."

She took this in with interest. "And yet you write of it as well as if you were always here."

"It's just the being away perhaps. At any rate the best bits, I suspect, are those that were done in dreary places abroad."

"And why were they dreary?"

"Because they were health resorts—where my poor mother was dying."

"Your poor mother?"—she was all sweet wonder.

"We went from place to place to help her to get better. But she never did. To the deadly Riviera (I hate it!), to the high Alps, to Algiers, and far away—a hideous journey—to Colorado."

"And she isn't better?" Miss Fancourt went on.

"She died a year ago."

"Really? like mine! Only that's years since. Some day you must tell me about your mother," she added.

He could at first, on this, only gaze at her. "What right things you say! If you say them to St. George I don't wonder he's in bondage."

It pulled her up for a moment. "I don't know what you mean. He doesn't make speeches and professions at all—he isn't ridiculous."

"I'm afraid you consider then that I am."

"No, I don't"—she spoke it rather shortly. And then she added: "He understands—understands everything."

The young man was on the point of saying jocosely: "And I don't—is that it?" But these words, in time, changed themselves to others slightly less trivial: "Do you suppose he understands his wife?"

Miss Fancourt made no direct answer, but after a moment's hesitation put it: "Isn't she charming?"

"Not in the least!"

"Here he comes. Now you must know him," she went on. A small group of visitors had gathered at the other end of the gallery and had been there overtaken by Henry St. George, who strolled in from a neighbouring room. He stood near them a moment, not falling into the talk but taking up an old miniature from a table and vaguely regarding it. At the end of a minute he became aware of Miss Fancourt and her companion in the distance; whereupon, laying down his miniature, he approached them with the same proscrastinating air, his hands in his pockets and his eyes turned, right and left, to the pictures. The gallery was so long that this transit took some little time, especially as there was a moment when he stopped to admire the fine Gainsborough. "He says Mrs. St. George has been the making of him," the girl continued in a voice slightly lowered.

"Ah, he's often obscure!" Paul laughed.

"Obscure?" she repeated as if she heard it for the first time. Her eyes rested on her other friend, and it wasn't lost upon Paul that they appeared to send out great shafts of softness. "He's going to speak to us!" she fondly breathed. There was a sort of rapture in her voice, and our friend was startled. "Bless my soul, does she care for him like *that?*—is she in love with him?" he mentally inquired. "Didn't I tell you he was eager?" she had meanwhile asked of him.

"It's eagerness dissimulated," the young man returned as the subject of their observation lingered before his Gainsborough.

"He edges towards us shyly. Does he mean that she saved him by burning that book?"

"That book? what book did she burn?" The girl quickly turned her face to him.

"Hasn't he told you then?"

"Not a word."

"Then he doesn't tell you everything!" Paul had guessed that she pretty much supposed he did. The great man had now resumed his course and come nearer; in spite of which his more qualified admirer risked a profane observation: "St. George and the Dragon is what the anecdote suggests!"

His companion, however, didn't hear it: she smiled at the dragon's adversary. "He *is* eager— he is!" she insisted.

"Eager for you—yes."

But meanwhile she had called out: "I'm sure you want to know Mr. Overt. You'll be great friends and it will always be delightful to me to remember I was here when you first met and that I had something to do with it."

There was a freshness of intention in the words that carried them off; nevertheless our young man was sorry for Henry St. George, as he was sorry at any time for any person publicly invited to be responsive and delightful. He would have been so touched to believe that a man he deeply admired should care a straw for him that he wouldn't play with such a presumption if it were possibly vain. In a single glance of the eye of the pardonable Master he read—having the sort of divination that belonged to his talent—that this personage had ever a store of friendly patience, which was part of his rich outfit, but was versed in no printed page of a rising scribbler. There was even a relief, a simplification, in that: liking him so much already for what he had done, how could one have liked him any more for a perception which must at the best have been vague? Paul Overt got up, trying to show his compassion, but at the same instant he found himself encompassed by St. George's happy personal art—a manner of which it was the essence to conjure away false positions. It all took place in a moment. Paul was conscious that he knew him now, conscious of his handshake and of the very quality of his hand; of his face, seen nearer and consequently seen better, of a general fraternizing assurance, and in particular of the circumstance that St. George didn't dislike him (as yet at least) for being imposed by a charming but too gushing girl, attractive enough without such danglers. No irritation at any rate was reflected in the voice with which he questioned Miss Fancourt as to some project of a walk—a general walk of the company round the park. He had soon said something to Paul about a talk—'We must have a tremendous lot of talk; there are so many things, aren't there?'—but our friend could see this idea wouldn't in the present case take very immediate effect. All the same he was extremely happy, even after the matter of the walk had been settled— the three presently passed back to the other part of the gallery, where it was discussed with several members of the party; even when, after they had all gone out together, he found himself for half an hour conjoined with Mrs. St. George. Her husband had taken the advance with Miss Fancourt, and this pair were quite out of sight. It was the prettiest of rambles for a summer afternoon—a grassy circuit, of immense extent, skirting the limit of the park within. The park was completely surrounded by its old mottled but pefect red wall, which, all the way on their left, constituted in itself an object of interest. Mrs. St. George mentioned to him the surprising number of acres thus enclosed, together with numerous other facts relating to the property and the family, and the family's other properties: she couldn't too strongly urge on him the importance of seeing their other houses. She ran over the

names of these and rang the changes on them with the facility of practice,
making them appear an almost endless list. She had received Paul Overt very
amiably on his breaking ground with her by the mention of his joy in having
just made her husband's acquaintance, and struck him as so alert and so ac-
commodating a little woman that he was rather ashamed of his *mot* about her
to Miss Fancourt; though he reflected that a hundred other people, on a hundred occasions, would have been sure to make it. He got on with Mrs. St.
George, in short, better than he expected; but this didn't prevent her suddenly becoming aware that she was faint with fatigue and must take her way
back to the house by the shortest cut. She professed that she hadn't the
strength of a kitten and was a miserable wreck; a character he had been too
preoccupied to discern in her while he wondered in what sense she could be
held to have been the making of her husband. He had arrived at a glimmer-
ing of the answer when she announced that she must leave him, though this
perception was of course provisional. While he was in the very act of placing
himself at her disposal for the return the situation underwent a change; Lord
Masham had suddenly turned up, coming back to them, overtaking them,
emerging from the shrubbery—Overt could scarcely have said how he appeared—and Mrs. St. George had protested that she wanted to be left alone
and not to break up the party. A moment later she was walking off with Lord
Masham. Our friend fell back and joined Lady Watermouth, to whom he
presently mentioned that Mrs. St. George had been obliged to renounce the
attempt to go further.

"She oughtn't to have come out at all," her ladyship rather grumpily remarked.

"Is she so very much of an invalid?"

"Very bad indeed." And his hostess added with still greater austerity:
"She oughtn't really to come to one!" He wondered what was implied by
this, and presently gathered that it was not a reflection on the lady's conduct
or her moral nature: it only represented that her strength was not equal to her
aspirations.

□   III   □

The smoking-room at Summersoft was on the scale of the rest of the place;
high, light, commodious, and decorated with such refined old carvings and
mouldings that it seemed rather a bower for ladies who should sit at work at
fading crewels than a parliament of gentlemen smoking strong cigars. The

gentlemen mustered there in considerable force on the Sunday evening, collecting mainly at one end, in front of one of the cool fair fireplaces of white marble, the entablature of which was adorned with a delicate little Italian "subject". There was another in the wall that faced it, and, thanks to the mild summer night, a fire in neither; but a nucleus for aggregation was furnished on one side by a table in the chimney-corner laden with bottles, decanters, and tall tumblers. Paul Overt was a faithless smoker; he would puff a cigarette for reasons with which tobacco had nothing to do. This was particularly the case on the occasion of which I speak; his motive was the vision of a little direct talk with Henry St. George. The "tremendous" communion of which the great man had held out hopes to him earlier in the day had not yet come off, and this saddened him considerably, for the party was to go its several ways immediately after breakfast on the morrow. He had, however, the disappointment of finding that apparently the author of *Shadowmere* was not disposed to prolong his vigil. He wasn't among the gentlemen assembled when Paul entered, nor was he one of those who turned up, in bright habiliments, during the next ten minutes. The young man waited a little, wondering if he had only gone to put on something extraordinary; this would account for his delay as well as contribute further to Overt's impression of his tendency to do the approved superficial thing. But he didn't arrive—he must have been putting on something more extraordinary than was probable. Our hero gave him up, feeling a little injured, a little wounded, at this loss of twenty coveted words. He wasn't angry, but he puffed his cigarette sighingly, with the sense of something rare possibly missed. He wandered away with his regret and moved slowly round the room, looking at the old prints on the walls. In this attitude he presently felt a hand on his shoulder and a friendly voice in his ear. "This is good. I hoped I should find you. I came down on purpose." St. George was there without a change of dress and with a fine face—his graver one—to which our young man all in a flutter responded. He explained that it was only for the Master—the idea of a little talk—that he had sat up, and that, not finding him, he had been on the point of going to bed.

"Well, you know, I don't smoke—my wife doesn't let me," said St. George, looking for a place to sit down. "It's very good for me—very good for me. Let us take that sofa."

"Do you mean smoking's good for you?"

"No, no—her not letting me. It's a great thing to have a wife who's so sure of all the things one can do without. One might never find them out one's self. She doesn't allow me to touch a cigarette." They took possession of a sofa at a distance from the group of smokers, and St. George went on: "Have you got one yourself?"

"Do you mean a cigarette?"

"Dear no—a wife."

"No; and yet I'd give up my cigarette for one."

"You'd give up a good deal more than that," St. George returned. "However, you'd get a great deal in return. There's a something to be said for wives," he added, folding his arms and crossing his outstretched legs. He declined tobacco altogether and sat there without returning fire. His companion stopped smoking, touched by his courtesy; and after all they were out of the fumes, their sofa was in a far-away corner. It would have been a mistake, St. George went on, a great mistake for them to have separated without a little chat; "for I know all about you," he said. "I know you're very remarkable. You've written a very distinguished book."

"And how do you know it?" Paul asked.

"Why, my dear fellow, it's in the air, it's in the papers, it's everywhere." St. George spoke with the immediate familiarity of a confrère—a tone that seemed to his neighbour the very rustle of the laurel. "You're on all men's lips and, what's better, on all women's. And I've just been reading your book."

"Just? You hadn't read it this afternoon," said Overt.

"How do you know that?"

"I think you should know how I know it," the young man laughed.

"I suppose Miss Fancourt told you."

"No indeed—she led me rather to suppose you had."

"Yes—that's much more what she'd do. Doesn't she shed a rosy glow over life? But you didn't believe her?" asked St. George.

"No, not when you came to us there."

"Did I pretend? Did I pretend badly?" But without waiting for an answer to this St. George went on: "You ought always to believe such a girl as that—always, always. Some women are meant to be taken with allowances and reserves; but you must take *her* just as she is."

"I like her very much," said Paul Overt.

Something in his tone appeared to excite on his companion's part a momentary sense of the absurd; perhaps it was the air of deliberation attending this judgement. St. George broke into a laugh to reply. "It's the best thing you can do with her. She's a rare young lady! In point of fact, however, I confess I hadn't read you this afternoon."

"Then you see how right I was in this particular case not to believe Miss Fancourt."

"How right? how can I agree to that when I lost credit by it?"

"Do you wish to pass exactly for what she represents you? Certainly you needn't be afraid," Paul said.

"Ah, my dear young man, don't talk about passing—for the likes of me! I'm passing away—nothing else than that. She has a better use for her young imagination (isn't it fine?) than in 'representing' in any way such a weary wasted used-up animal!" The Master spoke with a sudden sadness that produced a protest on Paul's part; but before the protest could be uttered he went on, reverting to the latter's striking novel: "I had no idea you were so good—one hears of so many things. But you're surprisingly good."

"I'm going to be surprisingly better," Overt made bold to reply.

"I see that, and it's what fetches me. I don't see so much else—as one looks about—that's going to be surprisingly better. They're going to be consistently worse—most of the things. It's so much easier to be worse—heaven knows I've found it so. I'm not in a great glow, you know, about what's breaking out all over the place. But you *must* be better—you really must keep it up. I haven't of course. It's very difficult—that's the devil of the whole thing, keeping it up. But I see you'll be able to. It will be a great disgrace if you don't."

"It's very interesting to hear you speak of yourself; but I don't know what you mean by your allusions to your having fallen off," Paul Overt observed with pardonable hypocrisy. He liked his companion so much that the fact of any decline of talent or of care had ceased for the moment to be vivid to him.

"Don't say that—don't say that," St. George returned gravely, his head resting on the top of the sofa-back and his eyes on the ceiling. "You know perfectly what I mean. I haven't read twenty pages of your book without seeing that you can't help it."

"You make me very miserable," Paul ecstatically breathed.

"I'm glad of that, for it may serve as a kind of warning. Shocking enough it must be, especially to a young fresh mind, full of faith—the spectacle of a man meant for better things sunk at my age in such dishonour." St. George, in the same contemplative attitude, spoke softly but deliberately, and without perceptible emotion. His tone indeed suggested an impersonal lucidity that was practically cruel—cruel to himself—and made his young friend lay an argumentative hand on his arm. But he went on while his eyes seemed to follow the graces of the eighteenth-century ceiling: "Look at me well, take my lesson to heart—for it *is* a lesson. Let that good come of it at least that you shudder with your pitiful impression, and that this may help to keep you straight in the future. Don't become in your old age what I have in mine—the depressing, the deplorable illustration of the worship of false gods!"

"What do you mean by your old age?" the young man asked.

"It has made me old. But I like your youth."

Paul answered nothing—they sat for a minute in silence. They heard the others going on about the governmental majority. Then "What do you mean by false gods?" he inquired.

His companion had no difficulty whatever in saying, "The idols of the market; money and luxury and 'the world'; placing one's children and dressing one's wife; everything that drives one to the short and easy way. Ah the vile things they make one do!"

"But surely one's right to want to place one's children."

"One has no business to have any children," St. George placidly declared. "I mean of course if one wants to do anything good."

"But aren't they an inspiration—an incentive?"

"An incentive to damnation, artistically speaking."

"You touch on very deep things—things I should like to discuss with you," Paul said. "I should like you to tell me volumes about yourself. This is a great feast for *me*!"

"Of course it is, cruel youth. But to show you I'm still not incapable, degraded as I am, of an act of faith, I'll tie my vanity to the stake for you and burn it to ashes. You must come and see me—you must come and see us," the Master quickly substituted. "Mrs. St. George is charming; I don't know whether you've had any opportunity to talk with her. She'll be delighted to see you; she likes great celebrities, whether incipient or predominant. You must come and dine—my wife will write to you. Where are you to be found?"

"This is my little address"—and Overt drew out his pocket-book and extracted a visiting-card. On second thoughts, however, he kept it back, remarking that he wouldn't trouble his friend to take charge of it but would come and see him straightway in London and leave it at his door if he should fail to obtain entrance.

"Ah you'll probably fail; my wife's always out—or when she isn't out is knocked up from having *been* out. You must come and dine—though that won't do much good either, for my wife insists on big dinners." St. George turned it over further, but then went on: "You must come down and see us in the country, that's the best way; we've plenty of room, and it isn't bad."

"You've a house in the country?" Paul asked enviously.

"Ah not like this! But we have a sort of place we go to—an hour from Euston. That's one of the reasons."

"One of the reasons?"

"Why my books are so bad."

"You must tell me all the others!" Paul longingly laughed.

His friend made no direct rejoinder to this, but spoke again abruptly. "Why have I never seen you before?"

The tone of the question was singularly flattering to our hero, who felt it to imply the great man's now perceiving he had for years missed something. "Partly, I suppose, because there has been no particular reason why you should see me. I haven't lived in the world—in your world. I've spent many years out of England, in different places abroad."

"Well, please don't do it any more. You must do England—there's such a lot of it."

"Do you mean I must write about it?" and Paul struck the note of the listening candour of a child.

"Of course you must. And tremendously well, do you mind? That takes off a little of my esteem for this thing of yours—that it goes on abroad. Hang 'abroad'! Stay at home and do things here—do subjects we can measure."

"I'll do whatever you tell me," Overt said, deeply attentive. "But pardon me if I say I don't understand how you've been reading my book," he added. "I've had you before me all the afternoon, first in that long walk, then at tea on the lawn, till we went to dress for dinner, and all the evening at dinner and in this place."

St. George turned his face about with a smile. "I gave it but a quarter of an hour."

"A quarter of an hour's immense, but I don't understand where you put it in. In the drawing-room after dinner you weren't reading—you were talking to Miss Fancourt."

"It comes to the same thing, because we talked about *Ginistrella*. She described it to me—she lent me her copy."

"Lent it to you?"

"She travels with it."

"It's incredible," Paul blushed.

"It's glorious for you, but it also turned out very well for me. When the ladies went off to bed she kindly offered to send the book down to me. Her maid brought it to me in the hall and I went to my room with it. I hadn't thought of coming here, I do that so little. But I don't sleep early, I always have to read an hour or two. I sat down to your novel on the spot, without undressing, without taking off anything but my coat. I think that's a sign my curiosity had been strongly roused about it. I read a quarter of an hour, as I tell you, and even in a quarter of an hour I was greatly struck."

"Ah the beginning isn't very good—it's the whole thing!" said Overt, who had listened to this recital with extreme interest. "And you laid down the book and came after me?" he asked.

"That's the way it moved me. I said to myself, 'I see it's off his own bat, and he's there, by the way, and the day's over and I haven't said twenty words to him.' It occurred to me that you'd probably be in the smoking-room and that it wouldn't be too late to repair my omission. I wanted to do something civil to you, so I put on my coat and came down. I shall read your book again when I go up."

Our friend faced round in his place—he was touched as he had scarce ever been by the picture of such a demonstration in his favour. "You're really the kindest of men. *Cela s'est passé comme ça?*—and I've been sitting here with you all this time and never apprehended it and never thanked you!"

"Thank Miss Fancourt—it was she who wound me up. She has made me feel as if I had read your novel."

"She's an angel from heaven!" Paul declared.

"She is indeed. I've never seen anyone like her. Her interest in literature's touching—something quite peculiar to herself; she takes it all so seriously. She feels the arts and she wants to feel them more. To those who practise them it's almost humiliating—her curiosity, her sympathy, her good faith. How can anything be as fine as she supposes it?"

"She's a rare organization," the younger man sighed.

"The richest I've ever seen—an artistic intelligence really of the first order. And lodged in such a form!" St. George exclaimed.

"One would like to represent such a girl as that." Paul continued.

"Ah, there it is—there's nothing like life!" said his companion. "When you're finished, squeezed dry and used up and you think the sack's empty, you're still appealed to, you still get touches and thrills, the idea springs up—out of the lap of the actual—and shows you there's always something to be done. But I shan't do it—she's not for me!"

"How do you mean, not for you?"

"Oh, it's all over—she's for you, if you like."

"Ah, much less!" said Paul. "She's not for a dingy little man of letters; she's for the world, the bright rich world of bribes and rewards. And the world will take hold of her—it will carry her away."

"It will try—but it's just a case in which there may be a fight. It would be worth fighting, for a man who had it in him, with youth and talent on his side."

These words rang not a little in Paul Overt's consciousness—they held him briefly silent. "It's a wonder she has remained, as she is; giving herself away so—with so much to give away."

"Remaining, you mean, so ingenuous—so natural? Oh, she doesn't care a straw—she gives away because she overflows. She has her own feelings, her own standards; she doesn't keep remembering that she must be proud. And then she hasn't been here long enough to be spoiled; she has picked up a fashion or two, but only the amusing ones. She's a provincial—a provincial of genius," St. George went on; "her very blunders are charming, her mistakes are interesting. She has come back from Asia with all sorts of excited curiosities and unappeased appetites. She's first-rate herself and she expends herself on the second-rate. She's life herself and she takes a rare interest in imitations. She mixes all things up, but there are none in regard to which she hasn't perceptions. She sees things in a perspective—as if from the top of the Himalayas—and she enlarges everything she touches. Above all she exaggerates—to herself, I mean. She exaggerates you and me!"

There was nothing in that description to allay the agitation caused in our younger friend by such a sketch of a fine subject. It seemed to him to show the art of St. George's admired hand, and he lost himself in gazing at the vision—this hovered there before him—of a woman's figure which should be part of the glory of a novel. But at the end of a moment the thing had turned into smoke, and out of the smoke—the last puff of a big cigar—proceeded the voice of General Fancourt, who had left the others, and come and planted himself before the gentlemen on the sofa. "I suppose that when you fellows get talking you sit up half the night."

"Half the night?—*jamais de la vie!* I follow a hygiene!"—and St. George rose to his feet.

"I see—you're hothouse plants," laughed the General. "That's the way you produce your flowers."

"I produce mine between ten and one every morning—I bloom with a regularity!" St. George went on.

"And with a splendour!" added the polite General, while Paul noted how little the author of *Shadowmere* minded, as he phrased it to himself, when addressed as a celebrated story-teller. The young man had an idea *he* should never get used to that; it would always make him uncomfortable—from the suspicion that people would think they had to—and he would want to prevent it. Evidently his great colleague had toughened and hardened—had made himself a surface. The group of men had finished their cigars and taken up their bedroom candlesticks; but before they all passed out Lord Watermouth invited the pair of guests who had been so absorbed together to "have" something. It happened that they both declined; upon which General Fancourt said: "Is that the hygiene? You don't water the flowers?"

"Oh, I should drown them!" St. George replied; but, leaving the room still at his young friend's side, he added whimsically, for the latter's benefit, in a lower tone: "My wife doesn't let me."

"Well, I'm glad I'm not one of you fellows!" the General richly concluded.

The nearness of Summersoft to London had this consequence, chilling to a person who had had a vision of sociability in a railway carriage, that most of the company, after breakfast, drove back to town, entering their own vehicles, which had come out to fetch them, while their servants returned by train with their luggage. Three or four young men, among whom was Paul Overt, also availed themselves of the common convenience; but they stood in the portico of the house and saw the others roll away. Miss Fancourt got into a victoria with her father after she had shaken hands with our hero and said, smiling in the frankest way in the world. "I *must* see you more. Mrs. St. George is so nice: she has promised to ask us both to dinner together." This lady and her husband took their places in a perfectly appointed brougham—she required a closed carriage—and as our young man waved his hat to them in response to their nods and flourishes he reflected that, taken together, they were an honourable image of success, of the material rewards and the social credit of literature. Such things were not the full measure, but he nevertheless felt a little proud for literature.

Before a week had elapsed he met Miss Fancourt in Bond Street, at a private view of the works of a young artist in "black-and-white" who had been so good as to invite him to the stuffy scene. The drawings were admirable, but the crowd in the one little room was so dense that he felt himself up to his neck in a sack of wool. A fringe of people at the outer edge endeavoured by curving forward their backs and presenting, below them, a still more convex surface of resistance to the pressure of the mass, to preserve an interval between their noses and the glazed mounts of the pictures; while the central body, in the comparative gloom projected by a wide horizontal screen hung under the skylight and allowing only a margin for the day, remained upright, dense and vague, lost in the contemplation of its own ingredients. This contemplation sat especially in the sad eyes of certain female heads, surmounted with hats of strange convolution and plumage, which rose on long necks above the others. One of the heads, Paul perceived, was much the most beautiful of the collection, and his next discovery was that it belonged to Miss Fancourt. Its beauty was enhanced by the glad smile she sent him across surrounding obstructions, a smile that drew him to her as fast as he could make his way. He had seen for himself at Summersoft that the last thing her nature contained was an affectation of indifference; yet even with this circumspection he took a fresh satisfaction in her not having pretended to await his arrival with composure. She smiled as radiantly as if she wished to make him hurry, and as soon as he came within earshot she broke out in her voice of joy: "He's here—he's here—he's coming back in a moment!"

"Ah, your father?" Paul returned as she offered him her hand.

"Oh dear no, this isn't my poor father's line. I mean Mr. St. George. He has just left me to speak to someone—he's coming back. It's he who brought me—wasn't it charming?"

"Ah, that gives him a pull over me—I couldn't have 'brought' you, could I?"

"If you had been so kind as to propose it—why not you as well as he?" the girl returned with a face that, expressing no cheap coquetry, simply affirmed a happy fact.

"Why he's a *père de famille*. They've privileges," Paul explained. And then quickly: "Will you go to see places with *me?*" he asked.

"Anything you like!" she smiled. "I know what you mean, that girls have to have a lot of people—" Then she broke off: "I don't know; I'm free. I've always been like that—I can go about with anyone. I'm so glad to meet you," she added with a sweet distinctness that made those near her turn round.

"Let me at least repay that speech by taking you out of this squash," her friend said. "Surely people aren't happy here!"

"No, they're awfully *mornes*, aren't they? But I'm very happy indeed and I promised Mr. St. George to remain in this spot till he comes back. He's going to take me away. They send him invitations for things of this sort—more than he wants. It was so kind of him to think of me."

"They also send me invitations of this kind—more than *I* want. And if thinking of *you* will do it—!" Paul went on.

"Oh, I delight in them—everything that's life—everything that's London!"

"They don't have private views in Asia, I suppose," he laughed. "But what a pity that for this year, even in this gorged city, they're pretty well over."

"Well, next year will do, for I hope you believe we're going to be friends always. Here he comes!" Miss Fancourt continued before Paul had time to respond.

He made out St. George in the gaps of the crowd, and this perhaps led to his hurrying a little to say: "I hope that doesn't mean I'm to wait till next year to see you."

"No, no—aren't we to meet at dinner on the twenty-fifth?" she panted with an eagerness as happy as his own.

"That's almost next year. Is there no means of seeing you before?"

She stared with all her brightness. "Do you mean you'd *come?*"

"Like a shot, if you'll be so good as to ask me!"

"On Sunday then—this next Sunday?"

"What have I done that you should doubt it?" the young man asked with delight.

Miss Fancourt turned instantly to St. George, who had now joined them, and announced triumphantly: "He's coming on Sunday—this next Sunday!"

"Ah, my day—my day too!" said the famous novelist, laughng, to their companion.

"Yes, but not yours only. You shall meet in Manchester Square; you shall talk—you shall be wonderful!"

"We don't meet often enough," St. George allowed, shaking hands with his disciple. "Too many things—ah too many things! But we must make it up in the country in September. You won't forget you've promised me that?"

"Why he's coming on the twenty-fifth—you'll see him then," said the girl.

"On the twenty-fifth?" St. George asked vaguely.

"We dine with you; I hope you haven't forgotten. He's dining out that day," she added gaily to Paul.

"Oh bless me, yes—that's charming! And you're coming? My wife didn't tell me," St. George said to him. "Too many things—too many things!" he repeated.

"Too many people—too many people!" Paul exclaimed, giving ground before the penetration of an elbow.

"You oughtn't to say that. They all read you."

"Me? I should like to see them! Only two or three at most," the young man returned.

"Did you ever hear anything like that? He knows, haughtily, how good he is!" St. George declared, laughing to Miss Fancourt. "They read *me*, but that doesn't make me like them any better. Come away from them, come away!" And he led the way out of the exhibition.

"He's going to take me to the Park," Miss Fancourt observed to Overt with elation as they passed along the corridor that led to the street.

"Ah, does he go there?" Paul asked, taking the fact for a somewhat unexpected illustration of St. George's *moeurs*.

"It's a beautiful day—there'll be a great crowd. We're going to look at the people, to look at types," the girl went on. "We shall sit under the trees; we shall walk by the Row."

"I go once a year—on business," said St. George, who had overheard Paul's question.

"Or with a country cousin, didn't you tell me? I'm the country cousin!" she continued over her shoulder to Paul as their friend drew her toward a hansom to which he had signalled. The young man watched them get in; he returned, as he stood there, the friendly wave of the hand with which, ensconced in the vehicle beside her, St. George took leave of him. He even lingered to see the vehicle start away and lose itself in the confusion of Bond Street. He followed it with his eyes; it put to him embarrassing things. "She's not for *me*!" the great novelist had said emphatically at Summersoft; but his manner of conducting himself toward her appeared not quite in harmony with such a conviction. How could he have behaved differently if she *had* been for him? An indefinite envy rose in Paul Overt's heart as he took his way on foot alone; a feeling addressed alike, strangely enough, to each of the occupants of the hansom. How much he should like to rattle about London with such a girl! How much he should like to go and look at "types" with St. George.

The next Sunday at four o'clock he called in Manchester Square, where his secret wish was gratified by his finding Miss Fancourt alone. She was in a large bright friendly occupied room, which was painted red all over, draped with the quaint cheap florid stuffs that are represented as coming from southern and eastern countries, where they are fabled to serve as the counterpanes of the peasantry, and bedecked with pottery of vivid hues, ranged on casual shelves, and with many water-colour drawings from the hand (as the visitor learned) of the young lady herself, commemorating with a brave breadth the sunsets, the mountains, the temples and palaces of India. He sat an hour—more than an hour, two hours—and all the while no one came in. His hostess was so good as to remark, with her liberal humanity, that it was delightful they weren't interrupted; it was so rare in London, especially at that season, that people got a good talk. But luckily now, of a fine Sunday, half the world went out of town, and that made it better for those who didn't go, when these others were in sympathy. It was the defect of London—one of two or three, the very short list of those she recognized in the teeming world-city she adored—that there were too few good chances for talk; you never had time to carry anything far.

"Too many things—too many things!" Paul said, quoting St. George's exclamation of a few days before.

"Ah yes, for him there are too many—his life's too complicated."

"Have you seen it *near*? That's what I should like to do; it might explain some mysteries," her visitor went on. She asked him what mysteries he meant, and he said: "Oh peculiarities of his work, inequalities, superficialities. For one who looks at it from the artistic point of view it contains a bottomless ambiguity."

She became at this, on the spot, all intensity. "Ah do describe that more—it's so interesting. There are no such suggestive questions. I'm so fond of them. He thinks he's a failure—fancy!" she beautifully wailed.

"That depends on what his ideal may have been. With his gifts it ought to have been high. But till one knows what he really proposed to himself—? Do *you* know by chance?" the young man broke off.

"Oh he doesn't talk to me about himself. I can't make him. It's too provoking."

Paul was on the point of asking what then he did talk about, but discretion checked it and he said instead: "Do you think he's unhappy at home?"

She seemed to wonder. "At home?"

"I mean in his relations with his wife. He has a mystifying little way of alluding to her."

"Not to me," said Marian Fancourt with her clear eyes. "That wouldn't be right, would it?" she asked gravely.

"Not particularly; so I'm glad he doesn't mention her to you. To praise her might bore you, and he has no business to do anything else. Yet he knows you better than me."

"Ah but he respects *you*!" the girl cried as with envy.

Her visitor stared a moment, then broke into a laugh. "Doesn't he respect you?"

"Of course, but not in the same way. He respects what you've done—he told me so, the other day."

Paul drank it in, but retained his faculties. "When you went to look at types?"

"Yes—we found so many: he has such an observation of them! He talked a great deal about your book. He says it's really important."

"Important! Ah the grand creature!"—and the author of the work in question groaned for joy.

"He was wonderfully amusing, he was inexpressibly droll, while we walked about. He sees everything; he has so many comparisons and images, and they're always exactly right. *C'est d'un trouvé,* as they say."

"Yes, with his gifts, such things as he ought to have done!" Paul sighed.

"And don't you think he *has* done them?"

Ah it was just the point. "A part of them, and of course even that part's immense. But he might have been one of the greatest. However, let us not make this an hour of qualifications. Even as they stand," our friend earnestly concluded, "his writings are a mine of gold."

To this proposition she ardently responded, and for half an hour the pair talked over the Master's principal productions. She knew them well—she knew them even better than her visitor, who was struck with her critical intelligence and with something large and bold in the movement in her mind. She said things that startled him and that evidently had come to her directly; they weren't picked-up phrases—she placed them too well. St. George had been right about her being first-rate, about her not being afraid to gush, not remembering that she must be proud. Suddenly something came back to her, and she said: "I recollect that he did speak of Mrs. St. George to me once. He said, apropos of something or other, that she didn't care for perfection."

"That's a great crime in an artist's wife," Paul returned.

"Yes, poor thing!" and the girl sighed with a suggestion of many reflections, some of them mitigating. But she presently added: "Ah perfection, perfection—how one ought to go in for it! I wish *I* could."

"Everyone can in his way," her companion opined.

"In *his* way, yes—but not in hers. Women are so hampered—so condemned! Yet it's a kind of dishonour if you don't, when you want to *do* something, isn't it?" Miss Fancourt pursued, dropping one train in her quickness to take up another, an accident that was common with her. So these two young persons sat discussing high themes in their eclectic drawing-room in their London "season"—discussing, with extreme seriousness, the high theme of perfection. It must be said in extenuation of this eccentricity that they were interested in the business. Their tone had truth and their emotion beauty; they weren't posturing for each other or for someone else.

The subject was so wide that they found themselves reducing it; the perfection to which, for the moment, they agreed to confine their speculations was that of the valid, the exemplary work of art. Our young woman's imagination, it appeared, had wandered far in that direction, and her guest had the rare delight of feeling in their conversation a full interchange. This episode will have lived for years in his memory and even in his wonder; it had the

quality that fortune distils in a single drop at a time—the quality that lubri-
cates many ensuing frictions. He still, whenever he likes, has a vision of the
room, the bright red sociable talkative room with the curtains that, by a
stroke of successful audacity, had the note of vivid blue. He remembers where
certain things stood, the particular book open on the table and the almost
intense odour of the flowers placed, at the left, somewhere behind him. These
facts were the fringe, as it were, of a fine special agitation which had its birth
in those two hours and of which perhaps the main sign was in its leading
him inwardly and repeatedly to breathe, "I had no idea there was anyone like
this—I had no idea there was anyone like this!" Her freedom amazed him and
charmed him—it seemed so to simplify the practical question. She was on the
footing of an independent personage—a motherless girl who had passed out
of her teens and had a position and responsibilities, who wasn't held down to
the limitations of a little miss. She came and went with no dragged duenna,
she received people alone, and, though she was totally without hardness, the
question of protection or patronage had no relevancy in regard to her. She
gave such an impression of the clear and the noble combined with the easy
and the natural that in spite of her eminent modern situation she suggested
no sort of sisterhood with the "fast" girl. Modern she was indeed, and made
Paul Overt, who loved old colour, the golden glaze of time, think with some
alarm of the muddled palette of the future. He couldn't get used to her interest in the arts he cared for; it seemed too good to be real—it was so unlikely
an adventure to tumble into such a well of sympathy. One might stray into
the desert easily—that was on the cards and that was the law of life; but it
was too rare an accident to stumble on a crystal well. Yet if her aspirations
seemed at one moment too extravagant to be real they struck him at the next
as too intelligent to be false. They were both high and lame, and, whims for
whims, he preferred them to any he had met in a like relation. It was probable enough she would leave them behind—exchange them for politics or
"smartness" or mere prolific maternity, as was the custom of scribbling daub-
ing educated flattered girls in an age of luxury and a society of leisure. He
noted that the water-colours on the walls of the room she sat in had mainly
the quality of being naive, and reflected that naïveté in art is like a zero in
number: its importance depends on the figure it is united with. Meanwhile,
however, he had fallen in love with her. Before he went away, at any rate, he
said to her: "I thought St. George was coming to see you today, but he
doesn't turn up."

For a moment he supposed she was going to cry *"Comment donc?* Did you
come here only to meet him?" But the next he became aware of how little
such a speech would have fallen in with any note of flirtation he had as yet
perceived in her. She only replied: "Ah yes, but I don't think he'll come. He
recommended me not to expect him." Then she gaily but all gently added:
"He said it wasn't fair to you. But I think I could manage two."

"So could I," Paul Overt returned, stretching the point a little to meet her. In reality his appreciation of the occasion was so completely an appreciation of the woman before him that another figure in the scene, even so esteemed a one as St. George, might for the hour have appealed to him vainly. He left the house wondering what the great man had meant by its not being fair to him; and, still more than that, whether he had actually stayed away from the force of that idea. As he took his course through the Sunday solitude of Manchester Square, swinging his stick and with a good deal of emotion fermenting in his soul, it appeared to him he was living in a world strangely magnanimous. Miss Fancourt had told him it was possible she should be away, and that her father should be, on the following Sunday, but that she had the hope of a visit from him in the other event. She promised to let him know should their absence fail, and then he might act accordingly. After he had passed into one of the streets that open from the Square, he stopped, without definite intentions, looking sceptically for a cab. In a moment he saw a hansom roll through the place from the other side and come a part of the way toward him. He was on the point of hailing the driver when he noticed a "fare" within; then he waited, seeing the man prepare to deposit his passenger by pulling up at one of the houses. The house was apparently the one he himself had just quitted; at least he drew that inference as he recognized Henry St. George in the person who stepped out of the hansom. Paul turned off as quickly as if he had been caught in the act of spying. He gave up his cab—he preferred to walk; he would go nowhere else. He was glad St. George hadn't renounced his visit altogether—that would have been too absurd. Yes, the world was magnanimous, and even he himself felt so as, on looking at his watch, he noted but six o'clock, so that he could mentally congratulate his successor on having an hour still to sit in Miss Fancourt's drawing-room. He himself might use that hour for another visit, but by the time he reached the Marble Arch the idea of such a course had become incongruous to him. He passed beneath that architectural effort and walked into the Park till he got upon the spreading grass. Here he continued to walk; he took his way across the elastic turf and came out by the Serpentine. He watched with a friendly eye the diversions of the London people, he bent a glance almost encouraging on the young ladies paddling their sweethearts about the lake and the guardsmen tickling tenderly with their bearskins the artificial flowers in the Sunday hats of their partners. He prolonged his meditative walk; he went into Kensington Gardens, he sat upon the penny chairs, he looked at the little sail-boats launched upon the round pond and was glad he had no engagement to dine. He repaired for this purpose, very late, to his club, where he found himself unable to order a repast and told the waiter to bring whatever there was. He didn't even observe what he was served with, and he spent the evening in the library of the establishment, pretending to read an article in an American magazine. He failed to discover what it was about; it appeared in a dim way to be about Marian Fancourt.

Quite late in the week she wrote to him that she was not to go into the country—it had only just been settled. Her father, she added, would never settle anything, but put it all on her. She felt her responsibility—she had to—and since she was forced this was the way she had decided. She mentioned no reasons, which gave our friend all the clearer field for bold conjecture about them. In Manchester Square on this second Sunday he esteemed his fortune less good, for she had three or four other visitors. But there were three or four compensations; perhaps the greatest of which was that, learning how her father had after all, at the last hour, gone out of town alone, the bold conjecture I just now spoke of found itself becoming a shade more bold. And then her presence was her presence, and the personal red room was there and was full of it, whatever phantoms passed and vanished, emitting incomprehensible sounds. Lastly, he had the resource of staying till everyone had come and gone and of believing this grateful to her, though she gave no particular sign. When they were alone together he came to his point. "But St. George did come—last Sunday. I saw him as I looked back."

"Yes; but it was the last time."

"The last time?"

"He said he would never come again."

Paul Overt stared. "Does he mean he wishes to cease to see you?"

"I don't know what he means," the girl bravely smiled. "He won't at any rate see me here."

"And pray why not?"

"I haven't the least idea," said Marian Fancourt, whose visitor found her more perversely sublime than ever yet as she professed this clear helplessness.

□ V □

"Oh I say, I want you to stop a little," Henry St. George said to him at eleven o'clock the night he dined with the head of the profession. The company—none of it indeed *of* the profession—had been numerous and was taking its leave; our young man, after bidding good night to his hostess, had put out his hand in farewell to the master of the house. Besides drawing from the latter the protest I have cited this movement provoked a further priceless word about their chance now to have a talk, their going into his room, his having still everything to say. Paul Overt was all delight at this kindness; nevertheless he mentioned in weak jocose qualification the bare fact that he had promised to go to another place which was at a considerable distance.

"Well then you'll break your promise, that's all. You quite awful humbug!" St. George added in a tone that confirmed our young man's ease.

"Certainly I'll break it—but it was a real promise."

"Do you mean to Miss Fancourt? You're following her?" his friend asked.

He answered by a question. "Oh is *she* going?"

"Base imposter!" his ironic host went on. "I've treated you handsomely on the article of that young lady: I won't make another concession. Wait three minutes—I'll be with you." He gave himself to his departing guests, accompanied the long-trained ladies to the door. It was a hot night, the windows were open, the sound of the quick carriages and of the linkmen's call came into the house. The affair had rather glittered; a sense of festal things was in the heavy air: not only the influence of that particular entertainment, but the suggestion of the wide hurry of pleasure which in London on summer nights fills so many of the happier quarters of the complicated town. Gradually Mrs. St. George's drawing-room emptied itself; Paul was left alone with his hostess, to whom he explained the motive of his waiting. "Ah yes, some intellectual, some *professional,* talk," she leered; "at this season doesn't one miss it? Poor dear Henry, I'm so glad!" The young man looked out of the window a moment, at the called hansoms that lurched up, at the smooth broughams that rolled away. When he turned round Mrs. St. George had disappeared; her husband's voice rose to him from below—he was laughing and talking, in the portico, with some lady who awaited her carriage. Paul had solitary possession, for some minutes, of the warm deserted rooms where the covered tinted lamplight was soft, the seats had been pushed about and the odour of flowers lingered. They were large, they were pretty, they contained objects of value; everything in the picture told of a "good house." At the end of five minutes a servant came in with a request from the Master that he would join him downstairs; upon which, descending, he followed his conductor through a long passage to an apartment thrown out, in the rear of the habitation, for the special requirements, as he guessed, of a busy man of letters.

St. George was in his shirt-sleeves in the middle of a large high room—a room without windows, but with a wide skylight at the top, that of a place of exhibition. It was furnished as a library, and the serried bookshelves rose to the ceiling, a surface of incomparable tone produced by dimly-gilt "backs" interrupted here and there by the suspension of old prints and drawings. At the end farthest from the door of admission was a tall desk, of great extent, at which the person using it could write only in the erect posture of a clerk in a counting-house; and stretched from the entrance to this structure was a wide plain band of crimson cloth, as straight as a garden-path and almost as long,

where, in his mind's eye, Paul at once beheld the Master pace to and fro during vexed hours—hours, that is, of admirable composition. The servant gave
him a coat, an old jacket with a hang of experience, from a cupboard in the
wall, retiring afterwards with the garment he had taken off. Paul Overt welcomed the coat; it was a coat for talk, it promised confidences—having visibly
received so many—and had tragic literary elbows. "Ah we're practical—we're
practical!" St. George said as he saw his visitor look the place over. "Isn't it a
good big cage for going round and round? My wife invented it and she locks
me up here every morning."

Our young man breathed—by way of tribute—with a certain oppression.
"You don't miss a window—a place to look out?"

"I did at first awfully; but her calculation was just. It saves time, it has
saved me many months in these ten years. Here I stand, under the eye of
day—in London of course, very often, it's rather a bleared old eye—walled in
to my trade. I can't get away—so the room's a fine lesson in concentration.
I've learnt the lesson. I think; look at that big bundle of proofs and acknowl-
edge it." He pointed to a fat roll of papers, on one of the tables, which had
not been undone.

"Are you bringing out another—?" Paul asked in a tone the fond deficiencies of which he didn't recognize till his companion burst out laughing,
and indeed scarce even then.

"You humbug, you humbug!"—St. George appeared to enjoy caressing
him, as it were, with that opprobrium. "Don't I know what you think of
them?" he asked, standing there with his hands in his pockets and with a new
kind of smile. It was as if he were going to let his young votary see him all
now.

"Upon my word in that case you know more than I do!" the latter ventured to respond, revealing a part of the torment of being able neither clearly
to esteem nor distinctly to renounce him.

"My dear fellow," said the more and more interesting Master, "don't
imagine I talk about my books specifically; they're not a decent subject—*il ne
manquerait plus que ça!* I'm not so bad as you may apprehend! About myself,
yes, a little, if you like; though it wasn't for that I brought you down here. I
want to ask you something—very much indeed; I value this chance. Therefore sit down. We're practical, but there *is* a sofa, you see—for she does humour my poor bones so far. Like all really great administrators and
disciplinarians she knows when wisely to relax." Paul sank into the corner of
a deep leathern couch, but his friend remained standing and explanatory. "If
you don't mind, in this room, this is my habit. From the door to the desk and
from the desk to the door. That shakes up my imagination gently; and don't
you see what a good thing it is that there's no window for her to fly out of?
The eternal standing as I write (I stop at that bureau and put it down, when
anything comes, and so we go on) was rather wearisome at first, but we

adopted it with an eye to the long run; you're in better order—if your legs
don't break down!—and you can keep it up for more years. Oh we're practical—we're practical!" St. George repeated, going to the table and taking up
all mechanically the bundle of proofs. But, pulling off the wrapper, he had a
change of attention that appealed afresh to our hero. He lost himself a moment, examining the sheets of his new book, while the younger man's eyes
wandered over the room again.

"Lord, what good things I should do if I had such a charming place as
this to do them in!" Paul reflected. The outer world, the world of accident
and ugliness, was so successfully excluded, and within the rich protecting
square, beneath the patronizing sky, the dream-figures, the summoned company, could hold their particular revel. It was a fond prevision of Overt's
rather than an observation on actual data, for which occasions had been too
few, that the Master thus more closely viewed would have the quality, the
charming gift, of flashing out, all surprisingly, in personal intercourse and at
moments of suspended or perhaps even of diminished expectation. A happy
relation with him would be a thing proceeding by jumps, not by traceable
stages.

"Do you read them—really?" he asked, laying down the proofs on Paul's
inquiring of him how soon the work would be published. And when the
young man answered "Oh yes, always," he was moved to mirth again by
something he caught in his manner of saying that. "You go to see your
grandmother on her birthday—and very proper it is, especially as she won't
last for ever. She has lost every faculty and every sense; she neither sees, nor
hears, nor speaks; but all customary pieties and kindly habits are respectable.
Only you're strong if you *do* read 'em! *I* couldn't, my dear fellow. You *are*
strong, I know; and that's just a part of what I wanted to say to you. You're
very strong indeed. I've been going into your other things—they've interested me immensely. Someone ought to have told me about them before—someone I could believe. But whom can one believe? You're
wonderfully on the right road—it's awfully decent work. Now do you mean
to keep it up?—that's what I want to ask you."

"Do I mean to do others?" Paul asked, looking up from his sofa at his
erect inquisitor and feeling partly like a happy little boy when the schoolmaster is gay, and partly like some pilgrim of old who might have consulted a
world-famous oracle. St. George's own performance had been infirm, but as
an adviser he would be infallible.

"Others—others? Ah the number won't matter; one other would do, if
it were really a further step—a throb of the same effort. What I mean is have
you it in your heart to go in for some sort of decent perfection?"

"Ah decency, ah perfection—!" the young man sincerely sighed. "I
talked of them the other Sunday with Miss Fancourt."

It produced on the Master's part a laugh of odd acrimony. "Yes, they'll 'talk' of them as much as you like! But they'll do little to help one to them. There's no obigation of course; only you strike me as capable," he went on. "You must have thought it all over. I can't believe you're without a plan. That's the sensation you give me, and it's so rare that it really stirs one up—it makes you remarkable. If you haven't a plan, if you *don't* mean to keep it up, surely you're within your rights; it's nobody's business, no one can force you, and not more than two or three people will notice you don't go straight. The others—*all* the rest, every blest soul in England, will think you do—will think you *are* keeping it up; upon my honour they will! I shall be one of the two or three who know better. Now the question is whether you can do it for two or three. Is that the stuff you're made of?"

It locked his guest a minute as in closed throbbing arms. "I could do it for one, if you were the one."

"Don't say that; I don't deserve it; it scorches me," he protested with eyes suddenly grave and glowing. "The 'one' is of course one's self, one's conscience, one's idea, the singleness of one's aim. I think of that pure spirit as a man thinks of a woman he has in some detested hour of his youth loved and forsaken. She haunts him with reproachful eyes, she lives for ever before him. As an artist, you know, I've married for money." Paul stared and even blushed a little, confounded by this avowal; whereupon his host, observing the expression of his face, dropped a quick laugh and pursued: "You don't follow my figure. I'm not speaking of my dear wife, who had a small fortune—which, however, was not my bribe. I fell in love with her, as many other people have done. I refer to the mercenary muse whom I led to the altar of literature. Don't, my boy, put your nose into *that* yoke. The awful jade will lead you a life!"

Our hero watched him, wondering and deeply touched. "Haven't you been happy?"

"Happy? It's a kind of hell."

"There are things I should like to ask you," Paul said after a pause.

"Ask me anything in all the world. I'd turn myself inside out to save you."

"To 'save' me?" he quavered.

"To make you stick to it—to make you see it through. As I said to you the other night at Summersoft, let my example be vivid to you."

"Why your books are not so bad as that," said Paul, fairly laughing and feeling that if ever a fellow had breathed the air of art—!

"So bad as what?"

"Your talent's so great that it's in everything you do, in what's less good as well as in what's best. You've some forty volumes to show for it—forty volumes of wonderful life, of rare observation, of magnificent ability."

"I'm very clever, of course I know that"—but it was a thing, in fine, this author made nothing of. "Lord, what rot they'd all be if I hadn't been! I'm a successful charlatan," he went on—"I've been able to pass off my system. But do you know what it is? It's *carton-pierre.*"

"*Carton-pierre?*" Paul was struck, and gaped.

"Lincrusta-Walton!"

"Ah don't say such things—you make me bleed!" the younger man protested, "I see you in a beautiful fortunate home, living in comfort and honour."

"Do you call it honour?"—his host took him up with an intonation that often comes back to him. "That's what I want *you* to go in for. I mean the real thing. This is brummagem."

"Brummagen?" Paul ejaculated while his eyes wandered, by a movement natural at the moment, over the luxurious room.

"Ah they make it so well today—it's wonderfully deceptive!"

Our friend thrilled with the interest and perhaps even more with the pity of it. Yet he wasn't afraid to seem to patronize when he could still so far envy. "Is it deceptive that I find you living with every appearance of domestic felicity—blest with a devoted, accomplished wife, with children whose acquaintance I haven't yet had the pleasure of making, but who *must* be delightful young people, from what I know of their parents?"

St. George smiled as for the candour of his question. "It's all excellent, my dear fellow—heaven forbid I should deny it. I've made a great deal of money; my wife has known how to take care of it, to use it without wasting it, to put a good bit of it by, to make it fructify. I've got a loaf on the shelf; I've got everything in fact but the great thing."

"The great thing?" Paul kept echoing.

"The sense of having done the best—the sense which is the real life of the artist and the absence of which is his death, of having drawn from his intellectual instrument the finest music that nature had hidden in it, of having played it as it should be played. He either does that or he doesn't—and if he doesn't he isn't worth speaking of. Therefore, precisely, those who really know *don't* speak of him. He may still hear a great chatter, but what he hears most is the incorruptible silence of Fame. I've squared her, you may say, for my little hour—but what's my little hour? Don't imagine for a moment," the Master pursued, "that I'm such a cad as to have brought you down here to abuse or to complain of my wife to you. She's a woman of distinguished qualities, to whom my obligations are immense; so that, if you please, we'll say nothing about her. My boys—my children are all boys—are straight and strong, thank God, and have no poverty of growth about them, no penury of needs. I receive periodically the most satisfactory attestation from Harrow, from Oxford, from Sandhurst—oh we've done the best for them!—of their eminence as living thriving consuming organisms."

"It must be delightful to feel that the son of one's loins is at Sandhurst," Paul remarked enthusiastically.

"It is—it's charming. Oh I'm a patriot!"

The young man then could but have the greater tribute of questions to pay. "Then what did you mean—the other night at Summersoft—by saying that children are a curse?"

"My dear youth, on what basis are we talking?" and St. George dropped upon the sofa at a short distance from him. Sitting a little sideways he leaned back against the opposite arm with his hands raised and interlocked behind his head. "On the supposition that a certain perfection's possible and even desirable—isn't it so? Well, all I say is that one's children interfere with perfection. One's wife interferes. Marriage interferes."

"You think then the artist shouldn't marry?"

"He does so at his peril—he does so at his cost."

"Not even when his wife's in sympathy with his work?"

"She never is—she can't be! Women haven't a conception of such things."

"Surely they on occasion work themselves," Paul objected.

"Yes, very badly indeed. Oh, of course, often they think they understand, they think they sympathize. Then it is they're most dangerous. Their idea is that you shall do a great lot and get a great lot of money. Their great nobleness and virtue, their exemplary conscientiousness as British females, is in keeping you up to that. My wife makes all my bargains with my publishers for me, and has done so for twenty years. She does it consummately well— that's why I'm really pretty well off. Aren't you the father of their innocent babes, and will you withhold from them their natural sustenance? You asked me the other night if they're not an immense incentive. Of course they are— there's no doubt of that!"

Paul turned it over: it took, from eyes he had never felt open so wide, so much looking at. "For myself I've an idea I need incentives."

"Ah well then, *n'en parlons plus!*" his companion handsomely smiled.

"*You* are an incentive, I maintain," the young man went on. "You don't affect me in the way you'd apparently like to. Your great success is what I see—the pomp of Ennismore Gardens!"

"Success?"—St. George's eyes had a cold fine light. "Do you call it success to be spoken of as you'd speak of me if you were sitting here with another artist—a young man intelligent and sincere like yourself? Do you call it success to make you blush—as you *would* blush!—if some foreign critic (some fellow, of course I mean, who should know what he was talking about and should have shown you he did, as foreign critics like to show it) were to say to you: 'He's the one, in this country, whom they consider the most perfect, isn't he?' Is it success to be the occasion of a young Englishman's having to stammer as you would have to stammer at such a moment for old England? No, no; success is to have made people wriggle to another tune. Do try it!"

Paul continued all gravely to glow. "Try what?"

"Try to do some really good work."

"Oh I want to, heaven knows!"

"Well, you can't do it without sacrifices—don't believe that for a moment," the Master said. "I've made none. I've had everything. In other words I've missed everything."

"You've had the full rich masculine human general life, with all the responsibilities and duties and burdens and sorrows and joys—all the domestic and social initiations and complications. They must be immensely suggestive, immensely amusing," Paul anxiously submitted.

"Amusing?"

"For a strong man—yes."

"They've given me subjects without number, if that's what you mean; but they've taken away at the same time the power to use them. I've touched a thousand things, but which one of them have I turned into gold? The artist has to do only with that—he knows nothing of any baser metal. I've led the life of the world, with my wife and my progeny; the clumsy coventional expensive materialized vulgarized brutalized life of London. We've got everything handsome, even a carriage—we're perfect Philistines and prosperous hospitable eminent people. But, my dear fellow, don't try to stultify yourself and pretend you don't know what we *haven't* got. It's bigger than all the rest. Between artists—come!" the Master wound up. "You know as well as you sit there that you'd put a pistol-ball into your brain if you had written my books!"

It struck his listener that the tremendous talk promised by him at Summersoft had indeed come off, and with a promptitude, a fulness, with which the latter's young imagination had scarcely reckoned. His impression fairly shook him and he throbbed with the excitement of such deep soundings and such strange confidences. He throbbed indeed with the conflict of his feelings—bewilderment and recognition and alarm, enjoyment and protest and assent, all commingled with tenderness (and a kind of shame in the participation) for the sores and bruises exhibited by so fine a creature, and with a sense of the tragic secret nursed under his trappings. The idea of *his,* Paul Overt's becoming the occasion of such an act of humility made him flush and pant, at the same time that his consciousness was in certain directions too much alive not to swallow—and not intensely to taste—every offered spoonful of the revelation. It had been his odd fortune to blow upon the deep waters, to make them surge and break in waves of strange eloquence. But how couldn't he give out a passionate contradiction of his host's last extravagance, how couldn't he enumerate to him the parts of his work he loved, the splendid things he had found in it, beyond the compass of any other writer of the day? St. George listened a while, courteously; then he said, laying his hand on his visitor's: "That's all very well; and if your idea's to do nothing better there's

no reason you shouldn't have as many good things as I—as many human and
material appendages, as many sons or daughters, a wife with as many gowns,
a house with as many servants, a stable with as many horses, a heart with as
many aches." The Master got up when he had spoken thus—he stood a moment—near the sofa looking down on his agitated pupil. "Are you possessed
of any property?" it occurred to him to ask.

"None to speak of."

"Oh well then there's no reason why you shouldn't make a goodish income—if you set about it the right way. Study *me* for that—study me well.
You may really have horses."

Paul sat there some minutes without speaking. He looked straight before him—he turned over many things. His friend had wandered away, taking
up a parcel of letters from the table where the roll of proofs had lain. "What
was the book Mrs. St. George made you burn—the one she didn't like?" our
young man brought out.

"The book she made me burn—how did you know that?" The Master
looked up from his letters quite without the facial convulsion the pupil had
feared.

"I heard her speak of it at Summersoft."

"Ah yes—she's proud of it. I don't know—it was rather good."

"What was it about?"

"Let me see." And he seemed to make an effort to remember. "Oh yes—
it was about myself." Paul gave an irrepressible groan for the disappearance of
such a production, and the elder man went on: "Oh but *you* should write
it—*you* should do me." And he pulled up—from the restless motion that had
come upon him; his fine smile a generous glare. "There's a subject, my boy;
no end of stuff in it!"

Again Paul was silent, but it was all tormenting. "Are there no women
who really understand—who can take part in a sacrifice?"

"How can they take part? They themselves are the sacrifice. They're the
idol and the altar and the flame."

"Isn't there even *one* who sees farther?" Paul continued.

For a moment St. George made no answer; after which, having torn up
his letters, he came back to the point all ironic. "Of course I know the one
you mean. But not even Miss Fancourt."

"I thought you admired her so much."

"It's impossible to admire her more. Are you in love with her?" St.
George asked.

"Yes," Paul Overt presently said.

"Well then give it up."

Paul stared. "Give up my 'love'?"

"Bless me, no. Your idea." And then as our hero but still gazed: "The
one you talked with her about. The idea of a decent perfection."

"She'd help it—she'd help it!" the young man cried.

"For about a year—the first year, yes. After that she'd be as a millstone round its neck."

Paul frankly wondered. "Why she has a passion for the real thing, for good work—for everything you and I care for most."

" 'You and I' is charming, my dear fellow!" his friend laughed. "She has it indeed, but she'd have a still greater passion for her children—and very proper too. She'd insist on everything's being made comfortable, advantageous, propitious for them. That isn't the artist's business."

"The artist—the artist! Isn't he a man all the same?"

St. George had a grand grimace. "I mostly think not. You know as well as I what he has to do: the concentration, the finish, the independence he must strive for from the moment he begins to wish his work really decent. Ah my young friend, his relation to women, and especially to the one he's most intimately concerned with, is at the mercy of the damning fact that whereas he can in the nature of things have but one standard, they have about fifty. That's what makes them so superior," St. George amusingly added. "Fancy an artist with a change of standards as you'd have a change of shirts or of dinner-plates. To *do* it—to do it and make it divine—is the only thing he has to think about. 'Is it done or not?' is his only question. Not 'Is it done as well as a proper solicitude for my dear little family will allow?' He has nothing to do with the relative—he has only to do with the absolute; and a dear little family may represent a dozen relatives."

"Then you don't allow him the common passions and affections of men?" Paul asked.

"Hasn't he a passion, an affection, which includes all the rest? Besides, let him have all the passions he likes—if he only keeps his independence. He must be able to be poor."

Paul slowly got up. "Why then did you advise me to make up to her?"

St. George laid his hand on his shoulder. "Because she'd make a splendid wife! And I hadn't read you then."

The young man had a strained smile. "I wish you had left me alone!"

"I didn't know that that wasn't good enough for you," his host returned.

"What a false position, what a condemnation of the artist, that he's a mere disfranchised monk and can produce his effect only by giving up personal happiness. What an arraignment of art!" Paul went on with a trembling voice.

"Ah you don't imagine by chance that I'm defending art? 'Arraignment'—I should think so! Happy the societies in which it hasn't made its appearance, for from the moment it comes they have a consuming ache, they have an incurable corruption, in their breast. Most assuredly is the artist in a

false position! But I thought we were taking him for granted. Pardon me,"
St. George continued: *"Ginistrella* made me!"

Paul stood looking at the floor—one o'clock struck, in the stillness, from
a neighbouring church tower. "Do you think she'd ever look at me?" he put
to his friend at last.

"Miss Fancourt—as a suitor? Why should I think it? That's why I've
tried to favour you—I've had a little chance or two of bettering your opportunity."

"Forgive me asking you, but do you mean by keeping away yourself?"
Paul said with a blush.

"I'm an old idiot—my place isn't there," St. George stated gravely.

"I'm nothing yet, I've no fortune; and there must be so many others,"
his companion pursued.

The Master took this considerably in, but made little of it. "You're a
gentleman and a man of genius. I think you might do something."

"But if I must give that up—the genius?"

"Lots of people, you know, think I've kept mine," St. George wonderfully grinned.

"You've a genius for mystification!" Paul declared; but grasping his
hand gratefully in attenuation of this judgement.

"Poor dear boy, I do worry you! But try, try, all the same. I think your
chances are good and you'll win a great prize."

Paul held fast the other's hand a minute; he looked into the strange deep
face. "No, I *am* an artist—I can't help it!"

"Ah show it then!" St. George pleadingly broke out. "Let me see before
I die the thing I most want, the thing I yearn for: a life in which the passion—ours—is really intense. If you can be rare don't fail of it! Think what it
is—how it counts—how it lives!"

They had moved to the door and he had closed both his hands over his
companion's. Here they paused again and our hero breathed deep. "I want to
live!"

"In what sense?"

"In the greatest."

"Well then stick to it—see it through."

"With your sympathy—your help?"

"Count on that—you'll be a great figure to me. Count on my highest
appreciation, my devotion. You'll give me satisfaction—if that has any
weight with you." After which, as Paul appeared still to waver, his host
added: "Do you remember what you said to me at Summersoft?"

"Something infatuated, no doubt!"

" 'I'll do anything in the world you tell me.' You said that."

"And you hold me to it?"

"Ah what am I?" the Master expressively sighed.

"Lord what things I shall have to do!" Paul almost moaned as he departed.

□   VI   □

"It goes on too much abroad—hang abroad!" These or something like them had been the Master's remarkable words in relation to the action of *Ginistrella;* and yet, though they had made a sharp impression on the author of that work, like almost all spoken words from the same source, he a week after the conversation I have noted left England for a long absence and full of brave intentions. It is not a perversion of the truth to pronounce that encounter the direct cause of his departure. If the oral utterance of the eminent writer had the privilege of moving him deeply it was especially on his turning it over at leisure, hours and days later, that it appeared to yield him its full meaning and exhibit its extreme importance. He spent the summer in Switzerland and, having in September begun a new task, determined not to cross the Alps till he should have made a good start. To this end he returned to a quiet corner he knew well, on the edge of the Lake of Geneva and within sight of the towers of Chillon: a region and a view for which he had an affection that sprang from old associations and was capable of mysterious revivals and refreshments. Here he lingered late, till the snow was on the nearer hills, almost down to the limit to which he could climb when his stint, on the shortening afternoons, was performed. The autumn was fine, the lake was blue, and his book took form and direction. These felicities, for the time embroidered his life, which he suffered to cover him with its mantle. At the end of six weeks he felt he had learnt St. George's lesson by heart, had tasted and proved its doctrine. Nevertheless he did a very inconsistent thing: before crossing the Alps he wrote to Marian Fancourt. He was aware of the perversity of this act, and it was only as a luxury, an amusement, the reward of a strenuous autumn, that he justified it. She had asked of him no such favour when, shortly before he left London, three days after their dinner in Ennismore Gardens, he went to take leave of her. It was true she had had no ground—he hadn't named his intention of absence. He had kept his counsel for want of due assurance: it was that particular visit that was, the next thing, to settle the matter. He had paid the visit to see how much he really cared for her, and quick departure, without so much as an explicit farewell, was the sequel to this inquiry, the answer to which had created within him a deep yearning. When he wrote her from Clarens he noted that he owed her an explanation (more than three months after) for not having told her what he was doing.

She replied now briefly but promptly, and gave him a striking piece of news: that of the death, a week before, of Mrs. St. George. This exemplary woman had succumbed, in the country, to a violent attack of inflammation of the lungs—he would remember that for a long time she had been delicate. Miss Fancourt added that she believed her husband overwhelmed by the blow; he would miss her too terribly—she had been everything in life to him. Paul Overt, on this, immediately wrote to St. George. He would from the day of their parting have been glad to remain in communication with him, but had hitherto lacked the right excuse for troubling so busy a man. Their long nocturnal talk came back to him in every detail, but this was no bar to an expression of proper sympathy with the head of the profession, for hadn't that very talk made it clear that the late accomplished lady was the influence that ruled his life? What catastrophe could be more cruel than the extinction of such an influence? This was to be exactly the tone taken by St. George in answering his young friend upwards of a month later. He made no allusion of course to their important discussion. He spoke of his wife as frankly and generously as if he had quite forgotten that occasion, and the feeling of deep bereavement was visible in his words. "She took everything off my hands— off my mind. She carried on our life with the greatest art, the rarest devotion, and I was free, as few men can have been, to drive my pen, to shut myself up with my trade. This was a rare service—the highest she could have rendered me. Would I could have acknowledged it more fitly!"

A certain bewilderment, for our hero, disengaged itself from these remarks: they struck him as a contradiction, a retraction, strange on the part of a man who hadn't the excuse of witlessness. He had certainly not expected his correspondent to rejoice in the death of his wife, and it was perfectly in order that the rupture of a tie of more than twenty years should have left him sore. But if she had been so clear a blessing what in the name of consistency had the dear man meant by turning *him* upside down that night—by dosing him to that degree, at the most sensitive hour of his life, with the doctrine of renunciation? If Mrs. St. George was an irreparable loss, then her husband's inspired advice had been a bad joke and renunciation was a mistake. Overt was on the point of rushing back to London to show that, for his part, he was perfectly willing to consider it so, and he went so far as to take the manuscript of the first chapters of his new book out of his table drawer, to insert it into a pocket of his portmanteau. This led to his catching a glimpse of certain pages he hadn't looked at for months, and that accident, in turn, to his being struck with the high promise they revealed—a rare result of such retrospections, which it was his habit to avoid as much as possible: they usually brought home to him that the glow of composition might be a purely subjective and misleading emotion. On this occasion a certain belief in himself disengaged itself whimsically from the serried erasures of his first draft, making him think it best after all to pursue his present trial to the end. If he could write as well under the rigour of privation it might be a mistake to change the conditions before that spell had spent itself. He would go back to London, of course, but he would go back only when he should have finished his book. This was the vow he privately made, restoring his manuscript to the table drawer. It may be added that it took him a long time to finish his book, for the subject was as difficult as it was fine, and he was literally embarrassed by the fulness of his notes. Something within him warned him that he must make it supremely good—otherwise he should lack, as regards his private behaviour, a handsome excuse. He had a horror of this deficiency and found himself as firm as need be on the question of the lamp and the file. He crossed the Alps at last and spent the winter, the spring, the ensuing summer, in Italy, where still, at the end of a twelvemonth, his task was unachieved. "Stick to it—see it through": this general injunction of St. George's was good also for the particular case. He applied it to the utmost, with the result that when in its slow order the summer had come round again he felt he had given all that was in him. This time he put his papers into his portmanteau, with the address of his publisher attached, and took his way northward.

He had been absent from London for two years—two years which, seeming to count as more, had made such a difference in his own life—through the production of a novel far stronger, he believed, than *Ginistrella*—that he turned out into Piccadilly, the morning after his arrival, with a vague expectation of changes, of finding great things had happened. But there were few transformations in Piccadilly—only three or four big red houses where there had been low black ones—and the brightness of the end of June peeped through the rusty railings of the Green Park and glittered in the varnish of the rolling carriages as he had seen it in other, more cursory Junes. It was a greeting he appreciated; it seemed friendly and pointed, added to the exhilaration of his finished book, of his having his own country and the huge oppressive amusing city that suggested everything, that contained everything, under his hand again. "Stay at home and do things here—do subjects we can measure," St. George had said; and now it struck him he should ask nothing better than to stay at home for ever. Late in the afternoon he took his way to Manchester Square, looking out for a number he hadn't forgotten. Miss Fancourt, however, was not at home, so that he turned rather dejectedly from the door. His movement brought him face to face with a gentleman just approaching it and recognized on another glance as Miss Fancourt's father. Paul saluted this personage, and the General returned the greeting with his customary good manner—a manner so good, however, that you could never tell whether it meant he placed you. The disappointed caller felt the impulse to address him; then, hesitating, became both aware of having no particular remark to make, and convinced that though the old soldier remembered him he remembered him wrong. He therefore went his way without computing the irresistible effect his own evident recognition would have on the General, who ever neglected a chance to gossip. Our young man's face was expressive, and observation seldom let it pass. He hadn't taken ten steps before he heard himself called after with a friendly semi-articulate "Er—I beg your pardon!" He turned round and the General, smiling at him from the porch, said: "Won't you come in? I won't leave you the advantage of me!" Paul declined to come in, and then felt regret, for Miss Fancourt, so late in the afternoon, might return at any moment. But her father gave him no second chance; he appeared mainly to wish not to have struck him as ungracious. A further look at the visitor had recalled something, enough at least to enable him to say: "You've come back, you've come back?" Paul was on the point of replying that he had come back the night before, but he suppressed, the next instant, this strong light on the immediacy of his visit and, giving merely a general assent, alluded to the young lady he deplored not having found. He had come late in the hope she would be in. "I'll tell her—I'll tell her," said the old man; and then he added quickly, gallantly: "You'll be giving us something new? It's a long time, isn't it?" Now he remembered him right.

"Rather long. I'm very slow," Paul explained. "I met you at Summersoft a long time ago."

"Oh yes—with Henry St. George. I remember very well. Before his poor wife—" General Fancourt paused a moment, smiling a little less. "I dare say you know."

"About Mrs. St. George's death? Certainly—I heard at the time."

"Oh no, I mean—I mean he's to be married."

"Ah I've not heard that!" But just as Paul was about to add "To whom?" the General crossed his intention.

"When did you come back? I know you've been away—by my daughter. She was very sorry. You ought to give her something new."

"I came back last night," said our young man, to whom something had occurred which made his speech for the moment a little thick.

"Ah most kind of you to come so soon. Couldn't you turn up at dinner?"

"At dinner!" Paul just mechanically repeated, not liking to ask whom St. George was going to marry, but thinking only of that.

"There are several people, I believe. Certainly St. George. Or afterwards if you like better. I believe my daughter expects—" He appeared to notice something in the visitor's raised face (on his steps he stood higher) which led him to interrupt himself and the interruption gave him a momentary sense of awkwardness, from which he sought a quick issue. "Perhaps then you haven't heard she's to be married."

Paul gaped again. "To be married?"

"To Mr. St. George—it has just been settled. Odd marriage isn't it?"

Our listener uttered no opinion on this point: he only continued to stare. "But I dare say it will do—she's so awfully literary!" said the General.

Paul had turned very red. "Oh it's a surprise—very interesting, very charming! I'm afraid I can't dine—so many thanks!"

"Well, you must come to the wedding!" cried the General. "Oh I remember that day at Summersoft. He's a great man, you know."

"Charming—charming!" Paul stammered for retreat. He shook hands with the General and got off. His face was red and he had the sense of its growing more and more crimson. All the evening at home—he went straight to his rooms and remained there dinnerless—his cheek burned at intervals as if it had been smitten. He didn't understand what had happened to him, what trick had been played him, what treachery practised. "None, none," he said to himself. "I've nothing to do with it. I'm out of it—it's none of my business." But that bewildered murmur was followed again and again by the incongruous ejaculations: "Was it a plan—was it a plan?" Sometimes he cried to himself, breathless. "Have I been duped, sold, swindled?" If at all, he was an absurd, an abject victim. It was as if he hadn't lost her till now. He had renounced her, yes; but that was another affair—that was a closed but not a locked door. Now he seemed to see the door quite slammed in his face. Did he expect her to wait—was she to give him his time like that: two years at a stretch? He didn't know what he had expected—he only knew what he hadn't. It wasn't this—it wasn't this. Mystification, bitterness, and wrath rose and boiled in him when he thought of the deference, the devotion, the credulity with which he had listened to St. George. The evening wore on and the light was long; but even when it had darkened he remained without a lamp. He had flung himself on the sofa, where he lay through the hours with his eyes either closed or gazing at the gloom, in the attitude of a man teaching himself to bear something, to bear having been made a fool of. He had made it too easy—that idea passed over him like a hot wave. Suddenly, as he heard eleven o'clock strike, he jumped up, remembering what General Fancourt had said about his coming after dinner. He'd go—he'd see her at least; perhaps he should see what it meant. He felt as if some of the elements of a hard sum had been given him and the others were wanting: he couldn't do his sum till he had got all his figures.

He dressed and drove quickly, so that by half past eleven he was at Manchester Square. There were a good many carriages at the door—a party was going on; a circumstance which at the last gave him a slight relief, for now he would rather see her in a crowd. People passed him on the staircase; they were going away, going "on" with the hunted herdlike movement of London society at night. But sundry groups remained in the drawing-room, and it was some minutes, as she didn't hear him announced, before he discovered and spoke to her. In this short interval he had seen St. George talking to a lady before the fireplace; but he at once looked away, feeling unready for an encounter, and therefore couldn't be sure the author of *Shadowmere* noticed him. At all events he didn't come over; though Miss Fancourt did as soon as she saw him—she almost rushed at him, smiling rustling radiant beautiful. He had forgotten what her head, what her face offered to the sight; she was in white, there were gold figures on her dress, and her hair was a casque of gold. He saw in a single moment that she was happy, happy with an aggressive splendour. But she wouldn't speak to him of that, she would speak only of himself.

"I'm so delighted; my father told me. How kind of you to come!" She struck him as so fresh and brave, while his eyes moved over her, that he said to himself irresistibly: "Why to *him,* why not to youth, to strength, to ambition, to a future? Why, in her rich young force, to failure, to abdication, to superannuation?" In his thought at that sharp moment he blasphemed even against all that had been left of his faith in the peccable Master. "I'm so sorry I missed you," she went on. "My father told me. How charming of you to have come so soon!"

"Does that surprise you?" Paul Overt asked.

"The first day? No, from you—nothing that's nice." She was interrupted by a lady who bade her good night, and he seemed to read that it cost her nothing to speak to him in that tone; it was her old liberal lavish way, with a certain added amplitude that time had brought; and if this manner began to operate on the spot, at such a juncture in her history, perhaps in the other days too it had meant just as little or as much—a mere mechanical charity, with the difference now that she was satisfied, ready to give but in want of nothing. Oh she was satisfied—and why shouldn't she be? Why shouldn't she have been surprised at his coming the first day—for all the good she had ever got from him? As the lady continued to hold her attention Paul turned from her with a strange irritation in his complicated artistic soul and a sort of disinterested disappointment. She was so happy that it was almost stupid—a disproof of the extraordinary intelligence he had formerly found in her. Didn't she know how bad St. George could be, hadn't she recognized the awful thinness—? If she didn't she was nothing, and if she did why such an insolence of serenity? This question expired as our young man's eyes settled at last on the genius who had advised him in a great crisis. St. George was still before the chimney-piece, but now he was alone—fixed, waiting, as if he meant to stop after everyone—and he met the clouded gaze of the young friend so troubled as to the degree of his right (the right his resentment would have enjoyed) to regard himself as a victim. Somehow the ravage of the question was checked by the Master's radiance. It was as fine in its way as Marian Fancourt's, it denoted the happy human being; but also it represented to Paul Overt that the author of *Shadowmere* had now definitely ceased to count—ceased to count as a writer. As he smiled a welcome across the place he was almost banal, was almost smug. Paul fancied that for a moment he hesitated to make a movement, as if for all the world he *had* his bad conscience; then they had already met in the middle of the room and had shaken hands—expressively, cordially on St. George's part. With which they had passed back together to where the elder man had been standing, while St. George said: "I hope you're never going away again. I've been dining here; the General told me." He was handsome, he was young, he looked as if he had still a great fund of life. He bent the friendliest, most unconfessing eyes on his disciple of a couple of years before; asked him about everything, his health, his plans, his late occupations, the new book. "When will it be out—soon, soon, I hope? Splendid, eh? That's right; you're a comfort, you're a luxury! I've read you all over again these last six months." Paul waited to see if he would tell him what the General had told him in the afternoon and what Miss Fancourt, verbally at least, of course hadn't. But as it didn't come out he at last put the question.

"Is it true, the great news I hear—that you're to be married?"

"Ah you *have* heard it then?"

"Didn't the General tell you?" Paul asked.

The Master's face was wonderful. "Tell me what?"

"That he mentioned it to me this afternoon?"

"My dear fellow, I don't remember. We've been in the midst of people. I'm sorry, in that case, that I lose the pleasure, myself, of announcing to you a fact that touches me so nearly. It *is* a fact, strange as it may appear. It has only just become one. Isn't it ridiculous?" St. George made this speech without confusion, but on the other hand, so far as our friend could judge, without latent impudence. It struck his interlocutor that, to talk so comfortably and coolly, he must simply have forgotten what had passed between them. His next words, however, showed he hadn't, and they produced, as an appeal to Paul's own memory, an effect which would have been ludicrous if it hadn't been cruel. "Do you recall the talk we had at my house that night, into which Miss Fancourt's name entered? I've often thought of it since."

"Yes; no wonder you said what you did"—Paul was careful to meet his eyes.

"In the light of the present occasion? Ah but there was no light then. How could I have foreseen this hour?"

"Didn't you think it probable?"

"Upon my honour, no," said Henry St. George. "Certainly I owe you that assurance. Think how my situation has changed."

"I see—I see," our young man murmured.

His companion went on as if, now that the subject had been broached, he was, as a person of imagination and tact, quite ready to give every satisfaction—being both by his genius and his method so able to enter into everything another might feel. "But it's not only that; for honestly, at my age, I never dreamed—a widower with big boys and with so little else! It has turned

out differently from anything one could have dreamed, and I'm fortunate beyond all measure. She has been so free, and yet she consents. Better than anyone else perhaps—for I remember how you liked her before you went away,
and how she liked you—you can intelligently congratulate me."

"She has been so free!" Those words made a great impression on Paul
Overt, and he almost writhed under that irony in them as to which it so little
mattered whether it was designed or casual. Of course she had been free, and
appreciably perhaps by his own act; for wasn't the Master's allusion to her
having liked him a part of the irony too? "I thought that by your theory you
disapproved of a writer's marrying."

"Surely—surely. But you don't call me a writer?"

"You ought to be ashamed," said Paul.

"Ashamed of marrying again?"

"I won't say that—but ashamed of your reasons."

The elder man beautifully smiled. "You must let me judge of them, my
good friend."

"Yes, why not? For you judged wonderfully of mine."

The tone of these words appeared suddenly, for St. George, to suggest
the unsuspected. He stared as if divining a bitterness. "Don't you think I've
been straight?"

"You might have told me at the time perhaps."

"My dear fellow, when I say I couldn't pierce futurity—!"

"I mean afterwards."

The Master wondered. "After my wife's death?"

"When this idea came to you."

"Ah never, never! I wanted to save you, rare and precious as you are."

Poor Overt looked hard at him. "Are you marrying Miss Fancourt to
save me?"

"Not absolutely, but it adds to the pleasure. I shall be the making of
you," St. George smiled. "I was greatly struck, after our talk, with the brave
devoted way you quitted the country, and still more perhaps with your force
of character in remaining abroad. You're very strong—you're wonderfully
strong."

Paul tried to sound his shining eyes; the strange thing was that he
seemed sincere—not a mocking fiend. He turned away, and as he did so heard
the Master say something about his giving them all the proof, being the joy
of his old age. He faced him again, taking another look. "Do you mean to say
you've stopped writing?"

"My dear fellow, of course I have. It's too late. Didn't I tell you?"

"I can't believe it!"

"Of course you can't—with your own talent! No, no; for the rest of my
life I shall only read *you.*"

"Does she know that—Miss Fancourt?"

"She will—she will." Did he mean this, our young man wondered, as a covert intimation that the assistance he should derive from that young lady's fortune, moderate as it was, would make the difference of putting it in his power to cease to work ungratefuly an exhausted vein? Somehow, standing there in the ripeness of his successful manhood, he didn't suggest that any of his veins were exhausted. "Don't you remember the moral I offered myself to you that night as pointing?" St. George continued. "Consider at any rate the warning I am at present."

This was too much—he *was* the mocking fiend. Paul turned from him with a mere nod for good night and the sense in a sore heart that he might come back to him and his easy grace, his fine way of arranging things, some time in the far future, but couldn't fraternize with him now. It was necessary to his soreness to believe for the hour in the intensity of his grievance—all the more cruel for its not being a legal one. It was doubtless in the attitude of hugging this wrong that he descended the stairs without taking leave of Miss Fancourt, who hadn't been in view at the moment he quitted the room. He was glad to get out into the honest dusky unsophisticating night, to move fast, to take his way home on foot. He walked a long time, going astray, paying no attention. He was thinking of too many other things. His steps recovered their direction, however, and at the end of an hour he found himself before his door in the small inexpensive empty street. He lingered, questioning himself still before going in, with nothing around and above him but moonless blackness, a bad lamp or two and a few far-away dim stars. To these last faint creatures he raised his eyes; he had been saying to himself that he should have been "sold" indeed, diabolically sold, if now, on his new foundation, at the end of a year, St. George were to put forth something of his prime quality—something of the type of *Shadowmere* and finer than his finest. Greatly as he admired his talent Paul literally hoped such an incident wouldn't occur; it seemed to him just then that he shouldn't be able to bear it. His late adviser's words were still in his ears—"You're very strong, wonderfully strong." Was he really? Certainly he would have to be, and it might a little serve for revenge. *Is* he? the reader may ask in turn, if his interest has followed the perplexed young man so far. The best answer to that perhaps is that he's doing his best, but that it's too soon to say. When the new book came out in the autumn Mr. and Mrs. St. George found it really magnificent. The former still has published nothing but Paul doesn't even yet feel safe. I may say for him, however, that if this event were to occur he would really be the very first to appreciate it: which is perhaps a proof that the Master was essentially right and that Nature had dedicated him to intellectual, not to personal passion.

WILLA CATHER

*My Mortal
Enemy*

Part One

I

I first met Myra Henshawe when I was fifteen, but I had known about her ever since I could remember anything at all. She and her runaway marriage were the theme of the most interesting, indeed the only interesting, stories that were told in our family, on holidays or at family dinners. My mother and aunts still heard from Myra Driscoll, as they called her, and Aunt Lydia occasionally went to New York to visit her. She had been the brilliant and attractive figure among the friends of their girlhood, and her life had been as exciting and varied as ours was monotonous.

Though she had grown up in our town, Parthia, in southern Illinois, Myra Henshawe never, after her elopement, came back but once. It was in the year when I was finishing High School, and she must then have been a woman of forty-five. She came in the early autumn, with brief notice by telegraph. Her husband, who had a position in the New York offices of an Eastern railroad, was coming West on business, and they were going to stop over for two days in Parthia. He was to stay at the Parthian, as our new hotel was called, and Mrs. Henshawe would stay with Aunt Lydia.

I was a favourite with my Aunt Lydia. She had three big sons, but no daughter, and she thought my mother scarcely appreciated me. She was always, therefore, giving me what she called "advantages," on the side. My mother and sister were asked to dinner at Aunt Lydia's on the night of the Henshawes' arrival, but she had whispered to me: "I want you to come in early, an hour or so before the others, and get acquainted with Myra."

That evening I slipped quietly in at my aunt's front door, and while I was taking off my wraps in the hall I could see, at the far end of the parlour, a short, plump woman in a black velvet dress, seated upon the sofa and softly playing on Cousin Bert's guitar. She must have heard me, and, glancing up, she saw my reflection in a mirror; she put down the guitar, rose, and stood to await my approach. She stood markedly and pointedly still, with her shoulders back and her head lifted, as if to remind me that it was my business to get to her as quickly as possible and present myself as best I could. I was not accustomed to formality of any sort, but by her attitude she succeeded in conveying this idea to me.

I hastened across the room with so much bewilderment and concern in my face that she gave a short, commiserating laugh as she held out to me her plump, charming little hand.

"Certainly this must be Lydia's dear Nellie, of whom I have heard so much! And you must be fifteen now, by my mournful arithmetic—am I right?"

What a beautiful voice, bright and gay and carelessly kind—but she continued to hold her head up haughtily. She always did this on meeting people—partly, I think, because she was beginning to have a double chin and was sensitive about it. Her deep-set, flashing grey eyes seemed to be taking me in altogether—estimating me. For all that she was no taller than I, I felt quite overpowered by her—and stupid, hopelessly clumsy and stupid. Her black hair was done high on her head, *à la* Pompadour, and there were curious, zigzag, curly streaks of glistening white in it, which made it look like the fleece of a Persian goat or some animal that bore silky fur. I could not meet the playful curiosity of her eyes at all, so I fastened my gaze upon a necklace of carved amethysts she wore inside the square-cut neck of her dress. I suppose I stared, for she said suddenly: "Does this necklace annoy you? I'll take it off if it does."

I was utterly speechless. I could feel my cheeks burning. Seeing that she had hurt me, she was sorry, threw her arm impulsively about me, drew me into the corner of the sofa and sat down beside me.

"Oh, we'll get used to each other! You see, I prod you because I'm certain that Lydia and your mother have spoiled you a little. You've been over-praised to me. It's all very well to be clever, my dear, but you mustn't be solemn about it—nothing is more tiresome. Now, let us get acquainted. Tell me about the things you like best; that's the short cut to friendship. What do you like best in Parthia? The old Driscoll place? I knew it!"

By the time her husband came in I had begun to think she was going to like me. I wanted her to, but I felt I didn't have half a chance with her; her charming, fluent voice, her clear light enunciation bewildered me. And I was never sure whether she was making fun of me or the thing we were talking about. Her sarcasm was so quick, so fine at the point—it was like being touched by a metal so cold that one doesn't know whether one is burned or chilled. I was fascinated, but very ill at ease, and I was glad when Oswald Henshawe arrived from the hotel.

He came into the room without taking off his overcoat and went directly up to his wife, who rose and kissed him. Again I was some time in catching up with the situation; I wondered for a moment whether they might have come down from Chicago on different trains; for she was clearly glad to see him—glad not merely that he was safe and had got round on time, but because his presence gave her lively personal pleasure. I was not accustomed to that kind of feeling in people long married.

Mr. Henshawe was less perplexing than his wife, and he looked more as I had expected him to look. The prominent bones of his face gave him a rather military air; a broad, rugged forehead, high cheek-bones, a high nose, slightly arched. His eyes, however, were dark and soft, curious in shape—exactly like half-moons—and he wore a limp, drooping moustache, like an Englishman. There was something about him that suggested personal bravery, magnanimity, and a fine, generous way of doing things.

"I am late," he explained, "because I had some difficulty in dressing. I couldn't find my things."

His wife looked concerned for a moment, and then began to laugh softly. "Poor Oswald! You were looking for your new dress shirts that bulge in front. Well, you needn't! I gave them to the janitor's son."

"The janitor's son?"

"Yes. To Willy Bunch, at home. He's probably wearing one to an Iroquois ball to-night, and that's the right place for it."

Mr. Henshawe passed his hand quickly over his smooth, iron-grey hair. "You gave away my six new shirts?"

"Be sure I did. You shan't wear shirts that give you a bosom, not if we go to the poorhouse. You know I can't bear you in ill-fitting things."

Oswald looked at her with amusement, incredulity, and bitterness. He turned away from us with a shrug and pulled up a chair. "Well, all I can say is, what a windfall for Willy!"

"That's the way to look at it," said his wife teasingly. "And now try to talk about something that might conceivably interest Lydia's niece. I promised Liddy to make a salad dressing."

I was left alone with Mr. Henshawe. He had a pleasant way of giving his whole attention to a young person. He "drew one out" better than his wife had done, because he did not frighten one so much. I liked to watch his face, with its outstanding bones and languid, friendly eyes—that perplexing combination of something hard and something soft. Soon my mother and uncle and my boy cousins arrived. When the party was complete I could watch and enjoy the visitors without having to think of what I was going to say next. The dinner was much gayer than family parties usually are. Mrs. Henshawe seemed to remember all the old stories and the old jokes that had been asleep for twenty years.

"How good it is," my mother exlcaimed, "to hear Myra laugh again!"

Yes, it was good. It was sometimes terrible, too, as I was to find out later. She had an angry laugh, for instance, that I still shiver to remember. Any stupidity made Myra laugh—I was destined to hear that one very often! Untoward circumstances, accidents, even disasters, provoked her mirth. And it was always mirth, not hysteria; there was a spark of zest and wild humour in it.

□   **II**   □

The big stone house, in its ten-acre park of trees and surrounded by a high, wrought-iron fence, in which Myra Driscoll grew up, was still, in my time, the finest property in Parthia. At John Driscoll's death it went to the Sisters of the Sacred Heart, and I could remember it only as a convent. Myra was an orphan, and had been taken into this house as a very little girl and brought up by her great-uncle.

John Driscoll made his fortune employing contract labour in the Missouri swamps. He retired from business early, returned to the town where he had been a poor boy, and built a fine house in which he took great pride. He lived in what was considered great splendour in those days. He kept fast horses, and bred a trotter that made a national record. He bought silver instruments for the town band, and paid the salary of the bandmaster. When the band went up to serenade him on his birthday and on holidays, he called the boys in and treated them to his best whisky. If Myra gave a ball or a garden-party, the band furnished the music. It was, indeed, John Driscoll's band.

Myra, as my aunt often said, had everything: dresses and jewels, a fine riding horse, a Steinway piano. Her uncle took her back to Ireland with him, one summer, and had her painted by a famous painter. When they were at home, in Parthia, his house was always open to the young people of the town. Myra's good looks and high spirits gratified the old man's pride. Her wit was of the kind that he could understand, native and racy, and none too squeamish. She was very fond of him, and he knew it. He was a coarse old codger, so unlettered that he made a poor showing with a pen. It was always told of him that when he became president of our national bank, he burned a lot of the treasury notes sent up to his house for him to sign, becuase he had "spoiled the sig-nay-ture." But he knew a great deal about men and their motives. In his own way he was picturesque, and Myra appreciated it—not many girls would have done so. Indeed, she was a good deal like him; the blood tie was very strong. There was never a serious disagreement between them until it came to young Henshawe.

Oswald Henshawe was the son of a German girl of good family, and an Ulster Protestant whom Driscoll detested; there was an old grudge of some kind between the two men. This Ulsterman was poor and impractical, a wandering schoolmaster, who had charge for a while of the High School in Parthia, and afterwards taught in smaller towns about. Oswald put himself through Harvard with very little help from his parents. He was not taken account of in our town until he came home from college, a handsome and promising young man. He and Myra met as if for the first time, and fell in love with each other. When old Driscoll found that Oswald was calling on his niece, he forbade him the house. They continued to meet at my grandfather's, however, under the protection of my Aunt Lydia. Driscoll so persecuted the boy that he felt there was no chance for him in Parthia. He roused himself and went to New York. He stayed there two years without coming home, sending his letters to Myra through my aunt.

All Myra's friends were drawn into the web of her romance; half a dozen young men understudied for Oswald so assiduously that her uncle might have thought she was going to marry any one of them. Oswald, meanwhile, was pegging away in New York, at a time when salaries were small and advancement was slow. But he managed to get on, and in two years he was in a position to marry. He wrote to John Driscoll, telling him his resources and prospects, and asked him for his niece's hand. It was then that Driscoll had it out with Myra. He did not come at her in a tantrum, as he had done before, but confronted her with a cold, business proposition. If she married young Henshawe, he would cut her off without a penny. He could do so, because he had never adopted her. If she did not, she would inherit two-thirds of his property—the remaining third was to go to the church. "And I advise ye to think well," he told her. "It's better to be a stray dog in this world than a man without money. I've tried both ways, and I know. A poor man stinks, and God hates him."

Some months after this conversation, Myra went out with a sleighing party. They drove her to a neighbouring town where Oswald's father had a school, and where Oswald himself had quietly arrived the day before. There, in the presence of his parents and of Myra's friends, they were married by the civil authority, and they went away on the Chicago express, which came through at two in the morning.

When I was a little girl my Aunt Lydia used to take me for a walk along the broad stone flagging that ran all the way around the old Driscoll grounds. Through the high iron fence we could see the Sisters, out for recreation, pacing two and two under the apple-trees. My aunt would tell me again about that thrilling night (probably the most exciting in her life), when Myra Driscoll came down that path from the house, and out of those big iron gates, for the last time. She had wanted to leave without taking anything but the clothes she wore—and indeed she walked out of the house with nothing but her muff and her *porte-monnaie* in her hands. My prudent aunt, however, had put her toilet articles and some linen into a travelling-bag, and thrown it out of the back window to one of the boys stationed under an apple-tree.

"I'll never forget the sight of her, coming down that walk and leaving a great fortune behind her," said Aunt Lydia. "I had gone out to join the others before she came—she preferred to leave the house alone. We girls were all in the sleighs and the boys stood in the snow holding the horses. We had begun to think she had weakened, or maybe gone to the old man to try to move him. But we saw by the lights behind when the front door opened and shut, and here she came, with her head high, and that quick little bouncing step of hers. Your Uncle Rob lifted her into the sleigh, and off we went. And that hard old man was as good as his word. Her name wasn't mentioned in his will. He left it all to the Catholic Church and to institutions."

"But they've been happy, anyhow?" I sometimes asked her.

"Happy? Oh, yes! As happy as most people."

That answer was disheartening; the very point of their story was that they should be much happier than other people.

When I was older I used to walk around the Driscoll place alone very often, especially on spring days, after school, and watch the nuns pacing so mildly and measuredly among the blossoming trees where Myra used to give garden-parties and have the band to play for her. I thought of the place as being under a spell, like the Sleeping Beauty's palace; it had been in a trance, or lain in its flowers like a beautiful corpse, ever since that winter night when Love went out of the gates and gave the dare to Fate. Since then, chanting and devotions and disicpline, and the tinkle of little bells that seemed forever calling the Sisters in to prayers.

I knew that this was not literally true; old John Driscoll had lived on there for rnany years after the flight of his niece. I myself could remember his funeral—remember it very vividly—though I was not more than six years old when it happened. I sat with my parents in the front of the gallery, at the back of the church that the old man had enlarged and enriched during the latter days of his life. The high altar blazed with hundreds of candles, the choir was entirely filled by the masses of flowers. The bishop was there, and a flock of priests in gorgeous vestments. When the pall-bearers arrived, Driscoll did not come to the church; the church went to him. The bishop and clergy went down the nave and met that great black coffin at the door, preceded by the cross and boys swinging cloudy censers, followed by the choir chanting to the organ. They surrounded, they received, they seemed to assimilate into the body of the church, the body of old John Driscoll. They bore it up to the high altar on a river of colour and incense and organ-tone; they claimed it and enclosed it.

In after years, when I went to other funerals, stark and grim enough, I thought of John Driscoll as having escaped the end of all flesh; it was as if he had been translated, with no dark conclusion to the pageant, no "night of the grave" about which our Protestant preachers talked. From the freshness of roses and lilies, from the glory of the high altar, he had gone straight to the greater glory, through smoking censers and candles and stars.

After I went home from that first glimpse of the real Myra Henshawe, twenty-five years older than I had always imagined her, I could not help feeling a little disappointed. John Driscoll and his niece had suddenly changed places in my mind, and he had got, after all, the more romantic part. Was it not better to get out of the world with such pomp and dramatic splendour than to linger on in it, having to take account of shirts and railway trains, and getting a double chin into the bargain?

The Henshawes were in Parthia three days, and when they left, it was settled that I was to go on to New York with Aunt Lydia for the Christmas holidays. We were to stay at the old Fifth Avenue Hotel, which, as Myra said, was only a stone's throw from their apartment, "if at any time a body was to feel disposed to throw one, Liddy!"

☐ III ☐

My aunt Lydia and I arrived at the Jersey City station on the day before Christmas—a soft, grey December morning, with a little snow falling. Myra Henshawe was there to meet us; very handsome, I thought, as she came walking rapidly up the platform, her plump figure swathed in furs—a fur hat on her head, with a single narrow garnet feather sticking out behind, like the pages' caps in old story-books. She was not alone. She was attended by a tall, elegant young man in a blue-grey ulster. He had one arm through hers, and in the other hand he carried a walking-stick.

"This is Ewan Gray," said Mrs. Henshawe, after she had embraced us. "Doubtless you have seen him play in Chicago. He is meeting an early train, too, so we planned to salute the morn together, and left Oswald to breakfast alone."

The young man took our hand-luggage and walked beside me to the ferry-boat, asking polite questions about our trip. He was a Scotchman, of an old

theatrical family, a handsome fellow, with a broad, fair-skinned face, sand-col-
oured hair and moustache, and fine grey eyes, deep-set and melancholy, with
black lashes. He took us up to the deck of the ferry, and then Mrs. Henshawe
told him he had better leave us. "You must be there when Esther's train gets
in—and remember, you are to bring her to dine with us to-morrow night.
There will be no one else."

"Thank you, Myra." He stood looking down at her with a grateful, almost humble expression, holding his soft hat against his breast, while the
snow-flakes fell about his head. "And may I call in for a few moments tonight, to show you something?"

She laughed as if his request pleased her. "Something for her, I expect?
Can't you trust your own judgment?"

"You know I never do," he said, as if that were an old story.

She gave him a little push. "Do put your hat on, or you'll greet Esther
with a sneeze. Run along."

She watched him anxiously as he walked away, and groaned: "Oh, the
deliberation of him! If I could only make him hurry once. You'll hear all
about him later, Nellie. You'll have to see a good deal of him, but you won't
find it a hardship, I trust!"

The boat was pulling out, and I was straining my eyes to catch, through
the fine, reluctant snow, my first glimpse of the city we were approaching.
We passed the *Wilhelm der Grosse* coming up the river under tug, her sides
covered with ice after a stormy crossing, a flock of sea gulls in her wake. The
snow blurred everything a little, and the buildings on the Battery all ran together—looked like an enormous fortress with a thousand windows. From
the mass, the dull gold dome of the *World* building emerged like a ruddy autumn moon at twilight.

From the Twenty-third Street station we took the crosstown car—people
were economical in those days—to the Fifth Avenue Hotel. After we had unpacked and settled our things, we went across the Square to lunch at Pur-
cell's, and there Mrs. Henshawe told us about Ewan Gray. He was in love
with one of her dearest friends, Esther Sinclair, whose company was coming
into New York for the holidays. Though he was so young, he had, she said,
"a rather spotty past," and Miss Sinclair, who was the daughter of an old
New England family and had been properly brought up, couldn't make up
her mind whether he was stable enough to marry. "I don't dare advise her,
though I'm so fond of him. You can see; he's just the sort of boy that women
pick up and run off into the jungle with. But he's never wanted to marry before; it might be the making of him. He's distractedly in love—goes about
like a sleep-walker. Still, I couldn't bear it if anything cruel happened to
Esther."

Aunt Lydia and Myra were going to do some shopping. When we went
out into Madison Square again, Mrs. Henshawe must have seen my wistful

gaze, for she stopped short and said: "How would Nellie like it if we left her here, and picked her up as we come back? That's our house, over there, second floor—so you won't be far from home. To me this is the real heart of the city; that's why I love living here." She waved to me and hurried my aunt away.

Madison Square was then at the parting of the ways; had a double personality, half commercial, half social, with shops to the south and residences on the north. It seemed to me so neat, after the raggedness of our Western cities; so protected by good manners and courtesy—like an open-air drawing-room. I could well imagine a winter dancing party being given there, or a reception for some distinguished European visitor.

The snow fell lightly all the afternoon, and friendly old men with brooms kept sweeping the paths—very ready to talk to a girl from the country, and to brush off a bench so that she could sit down. The trees and shrubbery seemed well-groomed and sociable, like pleasant people. The snow lay in clinging folds on the bushes, and outlined every twig of every tree—a line of white upon a line of black. Madison Square Garden, new and spacious then, looked to me so light and fanciful, and Saint Gaudens' Diana, of which Mrs. Henshawe had told me, stepped out freely and fearlessly into the grey air. I lingered long by the intermittent fountain. Its rhythmical splash was like the voice of the place. It rose and fell like something taking deep, happy breaths; and the sound was musical, seemed to come from the throat of spring. Not far away, on the corner, was an old man selling English violets, each bunch wrapped in oiled paper to protect them from the snow. Here, I felt, winter brought no desolation; it was tamed, like a polar bear led on a leash by a beautiful lady.

About the Square the pale blue shadows grew denser and drew closer. The street lamps flashed out all along the Avenue, and soft lights began to twinkle in the tall buildings while it was yet day—violet buildings, just a little denser in substance and colour than the violet sky. While I was gazing up at them I heard a laugh close beside me, and Mrs. Henshawe's arm slipped through mine.

"Why, you're fair moon-struck, Nellie! I've seen the messenger boys dodging all about you!" It was true, droves of people were going through the Square now, and boys carrying potted plants and big wreaths. "Don't you like to watch them? But we can't stay. We're going home to Oswald. Oh, hear the penny whistle! They always find me out." She stopped a thin lad with a cap and yarn comforter but no overcoat, who was playing *The Irish Washerwoman* on a little pipe, and rummaged in her bag for a coin.

The Henshawes' apartment was the second floor of an old brownstone house on the north side of the Square. I loved it from the moment I entered it; such solidly built, high-ceiled rooms, with snug fire-places and wide doors and deep windows. The long, heavy velvet curtains and the velvet chairs were a wonderful plum-colour, like ripe purple fruit. The curtains were lined with that rich cream-colour that lies under the blue skin of ripe figs.

Oswald was standing by the fire, drinking a whisky and soda while he waited for us. He put his glass down on the mantel as we opened the door, and forgot all about it. He pushed chairs up to the hearth for my aunt and me, and stood talking to us while his wife went to change her dress and to have a word with the Irish maid before dinner.

"By the way, Myra," he said, as she left us, "I've put a bottle of champagne on ice; it's Christmas eve."

Everything in their little apartment seemed to me absolutely individual and unique, even the dinner service; the thick grey plates and the soup tureen painted with birds and big, bright flowers—I was sure there were no others like them in the world.

As we were finishing dinner the maid announced Mr. Gray. Henshawe went into the parlour to greet him, and we followed a moment later. The young man was in evening clothes, with a few sprays of white hyacinth in his coat. He stood by the fire, his arm on the mantel. His clean, fair skin and melancholy eyes, his very correct clothes, and something about the shape of his hands, made one conscious of a cool, deliberate fastidiousness in him. In spite of his spotty past he looked, that night, as fresh and undamaged as the flowers he wore. Henshawe took on a slightly bantering tone with him, and seemed to be trying to cheer him up. Mr. Gray would not sit down. After an interval of polite conversation he said to his host: "Will you excuse me if I take Myra away for a few moments? She has promised to do something kind for me."

They went into Henshawe's little study, off the parlour, and shut the door. We could hear a low murmur of voices. When they came back to us Mrs. Henshawe stood beside Gray while he put on his caped cloak, talking encouragingly. "The opals are beautiful, but I'm afraid of them, Ewan. Oswald would laugh at me, but all the same they have a bad history. Love itself draws on a woman nearly all the bad luck in the world; why, for mercy's sake, add opals? He brought two bracelets for me to decide between them, Oswald, both lovely. However did they let you carry off two, Ewan?"

"They know me there. I always pay my bills, Myra. I don't know why, but I do. I suppose it's the Scotch in me."

He wished us all good-night.

"Give a kiss to Esther for me," said Mrs. Henshawe merrily at the door. He made no reply, but bent over her hand and vanished.

"What he really wanted was to show me some verses he's made for her," said Mrs. Henshawe, as she came back to the fire. "And very pretty ones they are, for sweet-heart poetry."

Mr. Henshawe smiled. "Maybe you obliged him with a rhyme or two, my dear? Lydia—" he sat down by my aunt and put his hand on hers—"I'd never feel sure that I did my own courting, if it weren't that I was a long way off at the time. Myra is so fond of helping young men along. We nearly always have a love affair on hand."

She put her hand over his lips. "Hush! I hate old women who egg on courtships."

When Oswald had finished his cigar we were taken out for a walk. This was primarily for the good of her "figger," Myra said, and incidentally we were to look for a green bush to send to Madame Modjeska. "She's spending the holidays in town, and it will be dismal at her hotel."

At the florist's we found, among all the little trees and potted plants, a glistening holly-tree, full of red berries and pointed like a spire, easily the queen of its companions. "That is naturally hers," said Mrs. Myra.

Her husband shrugged. "It's naturally the most extravagant."

Mrs. Myra threw up her head. "Don't be petty, Oswald. It's not a woollen petticoat or warm mittens that Madame is needing." She gave careful instructions to the florist's man, who was to take the tree to the Savoy; he was to carry with it a box of cakes, "of my baking," she said proudly. He was to ask for Mrs. Hewes, the housekeeper, and under her guidance he was to carry the tree up to Madame Modjeska's rooms himself. The man showed a sympathetic interest, and promised to follow instructions. Then Mrs. Henshawe gave him a silver dollar and wished him a Merry Christmas.

As we walked home she slipped her arm through mine, and we fell a little behind the other two. "See the moon coming out, Nellie—behind the tower. It wakens the guilt in me. No playing with love; and I'd sworn a great oath never to meddle again. You send a handsome fellow like Ewan Gray to a fine girl like Esther, and it's Christmas eve, and they rise above us and the white world around us, and there isn't anybody, not a tramp on the park benches, that wouldn't wish them well—and very likely hell will come of it!"

□ **IV** □

The next morning, Oswald Henshawe, in a frock-coat and top-hat, called to take Aunt Lydia and me to church. The weather had cleared before we went to bed, and as we stepped out of our hotel that morning, the sun shone blindingly on the snow-covered park, the gold Diana flashed against a green-blue sky. We were going to Grace Church, and the morning was so beautiful that we decided to walk.

"Lydia," said Henshawe, as he took us each by an arm, "I want you to give me a Christmas present."

"Why, Oswald," she stammered.

"Oh, I have it ready! You've only to present it." He took a little flat package from his pocket and slipped it into her muff. He drew both of us closer to him. "Listen, it's nothing. It's some sleeve-buttons, given me by a young woman who means no harm, but doesn't know the ways of the world very well. She's from a breezy Western city, where a rich girl can give a present whenever she wants to and nobody questions it. She sent these to my office yesterday. If I send them back to her it will hurt her feelings; she would think I had misunderstood her. She'll get hard knocks here, of course, but I don't want to give her any. On the other hand—well, you know Myra; nobody better. She would punish herself and everybody else for this young woman's questionable taste. So I want you to give them to me, Lydia."

"Oh, Oswald," cried my aunt, "Myra is so keen! I'm not clever enough to fool Myra. Can't you just put them away in your office?"

"Not very well. Besides," he gave a slightly embarrassed laugh, "I'd like to wear them. They are very pretty."

"Now, Oswald . . ."

"Oh, it's all right, Lydia, I give you my word it is. But you know how a little thing of that sort can upset my wife. I thought you might give them to me when you come over to dine with us to-morrow night. She wouldn't be jealous of you. But if you don't like the idea . . . why, just take them home with you and give them to some nice boy who would appreciate them."

All through the Christmas service I could see that Aunt Lydia was distracted and perplexed. As soon as we got back to the hotel and were safe in our rooms she took the brown leather case from her muff and opened it. The sleeve-buttons were topazes, winy-yellow, lightly set in crinkly gold. I believe she was seduced by their beauty. "I really think he ought to have them, if he wants them. Everything is always for Myra. He never gets anything for himself. And all the admiration is for her; why shouldn't he have a little? He has been devoted to a fault. It isn't good for any woman to be humoured and pampered as he has humoured her. And she's often most unreasonable with him—most unreasonable!"

The next evening, as we were walking across the Square to the Henshawes, we glanced up and saw them standing together in one of their deep front windows, framed by the plum-coloured curtains. They were looking out, but did not see us. I noticed that she was really quite a head shorter than he, and she leaned a little towards him. When she was peaceful, she was like a dove with its wings folded. There was something about them, as they stood in the lighted window, that would have discouraged me from meddling, but it did not shake my aunt.

As soon as we were in the parlour, before we had taken off our coats, she said resolutely: "Myra, I want to give Oswald a Christmas present. Once an old friend left with me some cuff-links he couldn't keep—unpleasant associations, I suppose. I thought of giving them to one of my own boys, but I brought them for Oswald. I'd rather he would have them than anybody."

Aunt Lydia spoke with an ease and conviction which compelled my admiration. She took the buttons out of her muff, without the box, of course, and laid them in Mrs. Henshawe's hand.

Mrs. Henshawe was delighted. "How clever of you to think of it, Liddy, dear! Yes, they're exactly right for him. There's hardly any other stone I would like, but these are exactly right. Look, Oswald, they're the colour of a fine Moselle." It was Oswald himself who seemed disturbed, and not overpleased. He grew red, was confused in his remarks, and was genuinely reluctant when his wife insisted upon taking the gold buttons out of his cuffs and putting in the new ones. "I can't get over your canniness, Liddy," she said as she fitted them.

"It's not like me, is it, Myra?" retorted my aunt; "not like me at all to choose the right sort of thing. But did it never occur to you that anyone besides yourself might know what is appropriate for Oswald? No, I'm sure it never did!"

Mrs. Myra took the laugh so heartily to herself that I felt it was a shame to deceive her. So, I am sure, did Oswald. During dinner he talked more than usual, but he was ill at ease. Afterwards, at the opera, when the lights were down, I noticed that he was not listening to the music, but was looking listlessly off into the gloom of the house, with something almost sorrowful in his strange, half-moon eyes. During an *entr'acte* a door at the back was opened, and a draught blew in. As he put his arm back to pull up the cloak which had slipped down from his wife's bare shoulders, she laughed and said: "Oh, Oswald, I love to see your jewels flash!"

He dropped his hand quickly and frowned so darkly that I thought he would have liked to put the topazes under his heel and grind them up. I thought him properly served then, but often since I have wondered at his gentle heart.

□ V □

During the week between Christmas and New Year's day I was with Mrs. Henshawe a great deal, but we were seldom alone. It was the season of calls and visits, and she said that meeting so many people would certainly improve my manners and my English. She hated my careless, slangy, Western speech. Her friends, I found, were of two kinds: artistic people—actors, musicians, literary men—with whom she was always at her best because she admired them; and another group whom she called her "moneyed" friends (she seemed to like the word), and these she cultivated, she told me, on Oswald's account. "He is the sort of man who does well in business only if he has the incentive of friendships. He doesn't properly belong in business. We never speak of it, but I'm sure he hates it. He went into an office only because we were young and terribly in love, and had to be married."

The business friends seemed to be nearly all Germans. On Sunday we called at half-a-dozen or more big houses. I remember very large rooms, much upholstered and furnished, walls hung with large paintings in massive frames, and many stiff, dumpy little sofas, in which the women sat two-and-two, while the men stood about the refreshment tables, drinking champagne and coffee and smoking fat black cigars. Among these people Mrs. Myra took on her loftiest and most challenging manner. I could see that some of the women were quite afraid of her. They were in great haste to rush refreshments to her, and looked troubled when she refused anything. They addressed her in German and profusely complimented her upon the way she spoke it. We had a carriage that afternoon, and Myra was dressed in her best—making an especial effort on Oswald's account; but the rich and powerful irritated her. Their solemnity was too much for her sense of humour; there was a biting edge to her sarcasm, a curl about the corners of her mouth that was never there when she was with people whose personality charmed her.

I had one long, delightful afternoon alone with Mrs. Henshawe in Central Park. We walked for miles, stopped to watch the skating, and finally had tea at the Casino, where she told me about some of the singers and actors I would meet at her apartment on New Year's eve. Her account of her friends was often more interesting to me than the people themselves. After tea she hailed a hansom and asked the man to drive us about the park a little, as a fine sunset was coming on. We were jogging happily along under the elms, watching the light change on the crusted snow, when a carriage passed from which a handsome woman leaned out and waved to us. Mrs. Henshawe bowed stiffly, with a condescending smile. "There, Nellie," she exclaimed, "that's the last woman I'd care to have splashing past me, and me in a hansom cab!"

I glimpsed what seemed to me insane ambition. My aunt was always thanking God that the Henshawes got along as well as they did, and worrying because she felt sure Oswald wasn't saving anything. And here Mrs. Myra was wishing for a carriage—with stables and a house and servants, and all that went with a carriage! All the way home she kept her scornful expression, holding her head high and sniffing the purple air from side to side as we drove down Fifth Avenue. When we alighted before her door she paid the driver, and gave him such a large fee that he snatched off his hat and said twice: "Thank you, thank you, my lady!" She dismissed him with a smile and a nod. "All the same," she whispered to me as she fitted her latchkey, "it's very nasty, being poor!"

That week Mrs. Henshawe took me to see a dear friend of hers, Anne Aylward, the poet. She was a girl who had come to New York only a few years before, had won the admiration of men of letters, and was now dying of tuberculosis in her early twenties. Mrs. Henshawe had given me a book of her poems to read, saying: "I want you to see her so that you can remember her in after years, and I want her to see you so that we can talk you over."

Miss Aylward lived with her mother in a small flat overlooking the East River, and we found her in a bathchair, lying in the sun and watching the river boats go by. Her study was a delightful place that morning, full of flowers and plants and baskets of fruit that had been sent her for Christmas. But it was Myra Henshawe herself who made that visit so memorably gay. Never had I seen her so brilliant and strangely charming as she was in that sunlit study up under the roofs. Their talk quite took my breath away; they said such exciting, such fantastic things about people, books, music—anything; they seemed to speak together a kind of highly flavoured special language.

As we were walking home she tried to tell me more about Miss Aylward, but tenderness for her friend and bitter rebellion at her fate choked her voice. She suffered physical anguish for that poor girl. My aunt often said that Myra was incorrigibly extravagant; but I saw that her chief extravagance was in caring for so many people and in caring for them so much. When she but mentioned the name of someone whom she admired, one got an instant impression that the person must be wonderful, her voice invested the name with a sort of grace. When she liked people she always called them by name a great many times in talking to them, and she enunciated the name, no matter how commonplace, in a penetrating way, without hurrying over it or slurring it; and this, accompanied by her singularly direct glance, had a curious effect. When she addressed Aunt Lydia, for instance, she seemed to be speaking to a person deeper down than the blurred, taken-for-granted image of my aunt that I saw every day, and for a moment my aunt became more individual, less matter-of-fact to me. I had noticed this peculiar effect of Myra's look and vocative when I first met her, in Parthia, where her manner of addressing my relatives had made them all seem a little more attractive to me.

One afternoon when we were at a matinée I noticed in a loge a young man who looked very much like the photographs of a story-writer popular at that time. I asked Mrs. Henshawe whether it could be he. She looked in the direction I indicated, then looked quickly away again.

"Yes, it's he. He used to be a friend of mine. That's a sad phrase, isn't it? But there was a time when he could have stood by Oswald in a difficulty—and he didn't. He passed it up. Wasn't there. I've never forgiven him."

I regretted having noticed the man in the loge, for all the rest of the afternoon I could feel the bitterness working in her. I knew that she was suffering. The scene on the stage was obliterated for her; the drama was in her mind. She was going over it all again; arguing, accusing, denouncing.

As we left the theatre she sighed: "Oh, Nellie, I wish you hadn't seen him! It's all very well to tell us to forgive our enemies; our enemies can never hurt us very much. But oh, what about forgiving our friends?"—she beat on her fur collar with her two gloved hands—"that's where the rub comes!"

The Henshawes always gave a party on New Year's eve. That year most of the guests were stage people. Some of them, in order to get there before midnight, came with traces of make-up still on their faces. I remember old Jefferson de Angelais arrived in his last-act wig, carrying his plumed hat—during the supper his painted eyebrows spread and came down over his eyes like a veil. Most of them are dead now, but it was a fine group that stood about the table to drink the New Year in. By far the handsomest and most distinguished of that company was a woman no longer young, but beautiful in age, Helena Modjeska. She looked a woman of another race and another period, no less queenly than when I had seen her in Chicago as Marie Stuart, and as Katharine in *Henry VIII.* I remember how, when Oswald asked her to propose a toast, she put out her long arm, lifted her glass, and looking into the blur of the candlelight with a grave face, said: "To my coun-n-try!"

As she was not playing, she had come early, some time before the others, bringing with her a young Polish woman who was singing at the Opera that winter. I had an opportunity to watch Modjeska as she sat talking to Myra and Esther Sinclair—Miss Sinclair had once played in her company. When the other guests began to arrive, and Myra was called away, she sat by the fire in a high-backed chair, her head resting lightly on her hand, her beautiful face half in shadow. How well I remember those long, beautifully modelled hands, with so much humanity in them. They were worldly, indeed, but fashioned for a nobler worldliness than ours; hands to hold a sceptre, or a chalice—or, by courtesy, a sword.

The party did not last long, but it was a whirl of high spirits. Everybody was hungry and thirsty. There was a great deal of talk about Sarah Bernhardt's *Hamlet,* which had been running all week and had aroused hot controversy; and about Jean de Reszke's return to the Metropolitan that night, after a long illness in London.

By two o'clock everyone had gone but the two Polish ladies. Modjeska, after she put on her long cloak, went to the window, drew back the plum-coloured curtains, and looked out. "See, Myra," she said with that Slav accent she never lost, though she read English verse so beautifully, "the Square is quite white with moonlight. And how still all the ci-ty is, how still!" She turned to her friend; "Emelia, I think you must sing something. Something old . . . yes, from *Norma*." She hummed a familiar air under her breath, and looked about for a chair. Oswald brought one. "Thank you. And we might have less light, might we not?" He turned off the lights.

She sat by the window, half draped in her cloak, the moonlight falling across her knees. Her friend went to the piano and commenced the *Casta Diva* aria, which begins so like the quivering of moonbeams on the water. It was the first air on our old music-box at home, but I had never heard it sung—and I have never heard it sung so beautifully since. I remember Oswald, standing like a statue behind Madame Modjeska's chair, and Myra, crouching low beside the singer, her head in both hands, while the song grew and blossomed like a great emotion.

When it stopped, nobody said anything beyond a low good-bye. Modjeska again drew her cloak around her, and Oswald took them down to their carriage. Aunt Lydia and I followed, and as we crossed the Square we saw their cab going up the Avenue. For many years I associated Mrs. Henshawe with that music, thought of that aria as being mysteriously related to something in her nature that one rarely saw, but nearly always felt; a compelling, passionate, overmastering something for which I had no name, but which was audible, visible in the air that night, as she sat crouching in the shadow. When I wanted to recall powerfully that hidden richness in her, I had only to close my eyes and sing to myself: *"Casta diva, casta diva!"*

□ VI □

On Saturday I was to lunch at the Henshawes' and go alone with Oswald to hear Bernhardt and Coquelin. As I opened the door into the entry hall, the first thing that greeted me was Mrs. Henshawe's angry laugh, and a burst of rapid words that stung like cold water from a spray.

"I tell you, I will know the truth about this key, and I will go through any door your keys open. Is that clear?"

Oswald answered with a distinctly malicious chuckle: "My dear, you'd have a hard time getting through that door. The key happens to open a safety deposit box."

Her voice rose an octave in pitch. "How dare you lie to me, Oswald? How dare you? They told me at your bank that this wasn't a bank key, though it looks like one. I stopped and showed it to them—the day you forgot your keys and telephoned me to bring them down to your office."

"The hell you did!"

I coughed and rapped at the door . . . they took no notice of me. I heard Oswald push back a chair. "Then it was you who took my keys out of my pocket? I might have known it! I never forget to change them. And you went to the bank and made me and yourself ridiculous. I can imagine their amusement."

"Well, you needn't! I know how to get information without giving any. Here is Nellie Birdseye, rapping at the gates. Come in, Nellie. You and Oswald are going over to Martin's for lunch. He and I are quarrelling about a key ring. There will be no luncheon here to-day."

She went away, and I stood bewildered. This delightful room had seemed to me a place where light-heartedness and charming manners lived—housed there just as the purple curtains and the Kiva rugs and the gay water-colours were. And now everything was in ruins. The air was still and cold like the air in a refrigerating-room. What I felt was fear; I was afraid to look or speak or move. Everything about me seemed evil. When kindness has left people, even for a few moments, we become afraid of them, as if their reason had left them. When it has left a place where we have always found it, it is like shipwreck; we drop from security into something malevolent and bottomless.

"It's all right, Nellie." Oswald recovered himself and put a hand on my shoulder. "Myra isn't half so furious with me as she pretends. I'll get my hat and we'll be off." He was in his smoking-jacket, and had been sitting at his desk, writing. His inkwell was uncovered, and on the blotter lay a half-written sheet of note paper.

I was glad to get out into the sunlight with him. The city seemed safe and friendly and smiling. The air in that room had been like poison. Oswald tried to make it up to me. We walked round and round the Square, and at Martin's he made me drink a glass of sherry, and pointed out the interesting people in the dining-room and told me stories about them. But without his hat, his head against the bright window, he looked tired and troubled. I wondered, as on the first time I saw him, in my own town, at the contradiction in his face: the strong bones, and the curiously shaped eyes without any fire in them. I felt that his life had not suited him; that he possessed some kind of courage and force which slept, which in another sort of world might have asserted themselves brilliantly. I thought he ought to have been a soldier or an explorer. I have since seen those half-moon eyes in other people, and they were always inscrutable, like his; fronted the world with courtesy and kindness, but one never got behind them.

We went to the theatre, but I remember very little of the performance except a dull heartache, and a conviction that I should never like Mrs. Myra so well again. That was on Saturday. On Monday Aunt Lydia and I were to start for home. We positively did not see the Henshawes again. Sunday morning the maid came with some flowers and a note from Myra, saying that her friend Anne Aylward was having a bad day and had sent for her.

On Monday we took an early boat across the ferry, in order to breakfast in the Jersey station before our train started. We had got settled in our places in the Pullman, the moment of departure was near, when we heard an amused laugh, and there was Myra Henshawe, coming into the car in her fur hat, followed by a porter who carried her bags.

"I didn't plot anything so neat as this, Liddy," she laughed, a little out of breath, "though I knew we'd be on the same train. But we won't quarrel, will we? I'm only going as far as Pittsburgh. I've some old friends there. Oswald and I have had a disagreement, and I've left him to think it over. If he needs me, he can quite well come after me."

All day Mrs. Myra was jolly and agreeable, though she treated us with light formality, as if we were new acquaintances. We lunched together, and I noticed, sitting opposite her, that when she was in this mood of high scorn, her mouth, which could be so tender—which cherished the names of her friends and spoke them delicately—was entirely different. It seemed to curl and twist about like a little snake. Letting herself think harm of anyone she loved seemed to change her nature, even her features.

It was dark when we got into Pittsburgh. The Pullman porter took Myra's luggage to the end of the car. She bade us good-bye, started to leave us, then turned back with an icy little smile. "Oh, Liddy dear, you needn't have perjured yourself for those yellow cuff-buttons. I was sure to find out, I always do. I don't hold it against you, but it's disgusting in a man to lie for personal decorations. A woman might do it, now, . . . for pearls!" With a bright nod she turned away and swept out of the car, her head high, the long garnet feather drooping behind.

Aunt Lydia was very angry. "I'm sick of Myra's dramatics," she declared. "I've done with them. A man never *is* justified, but if ever a man was . . ."

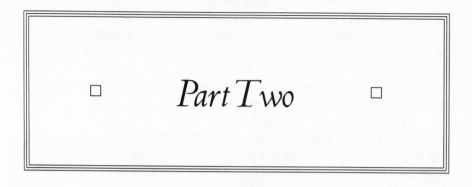

Part Two

I

Ten years after that visit to New York I happened to be in a sprawling over-grown West-coast city which was in the throes of rapid development—it ran about the shore, stumbling all over itself and finally tumbled untidily into the sea. Every hotel and boarding-house was overcrowded, and I was very poor. Things had gone badly with my family and with me. I had come West in the middle of the year to take a position in a college—a college that was as experimental and unsubstantial as everything else in the place. I found lodg-ings in an apartment-hotel, wretchedly built and already falling to pieces, al-though it was new. I moved in on a Sunday morning, and while I was unpacking my trunk, I heard, through the thin walls, my neighbour stirring about; a man, and, from the huskiness of his cough and something measured in his movements, not a young man. The caution of his step, the guarded consideration of his activities, let me know that he did not wish to thrust the details of his housekeeping upon other people any more than he could help.

Presently I detected the ugly smell of gasolene in the air, I heard a sound of silk being snapped and shaken, and then a voice humming very low an old German air—yes, Schubert's *Frühlingsglaube;* ta ta te-ta / ta-ta ta-ta ta-ta / ta. In a moment I saw the ends of dark neckties fluttering out of the window next mine.

All this made me melancholy—more than the dreariness of my own case. I was young, and it didn't matter so much about me; for youth there is al-ways the hope, the certainty, of better things. But an old man, a gentleman, living in this shabby, comfortless place, cleaning his neckties of a Sunday morning and humming to himself . . . it depressed me unreasonably. I was glad when his outer door shut softly and I heard no more of him.

There was an indifferent restaurant on the ground floor of the hotel. As I was going down to my dinner that evening, I met, at the head of the stairs, a man coming up and carrying a large black tin tray. His head was bent, and his eyes were lowered. As he drew aside to let me pass, in spite of his thin white hair and stooped shoulders, I recognised Oswald Henshawe, whom I had not seen for so many years—not, indeed, since that afternoon when he took me to see Sarah Bernhardt play *Hamlet*.

When I called his name he started, looked at me, and rested the tray on the sill of the blindless window that lighted the naked stairway.

"Nellie! Nellie Birdseye! Can it be?"

His voice was quite uncertain. He seemed deeply shaken, and pulled out a handkerchief to wipe his forehead. "But, Nellie, you have grown up! I would not know you. What good fortune for Myra! She will hardly believe it when I tell her. She is ill, my poor Myra. Oh, very ill! But we must not speak of that, nor seem to know it. What it will mean to her to see you again! Her friends always were so much to her, you remember? Will you stop and see us as you come up? Her room is thirty-two; rap gently, and I'll be waiting for you. Now I must take her dinner. Oh, I hope for her sake you are staying some time. She has no one here."

He took up the tray and went softly along the uncarpeted hall. I felt little zest for the canned vegetables and hard meat the waitress put before me. I had known that the Henshawes had come on evil days, and were wandering about among the cities of the Pacific coast. But Myra had stopped writing to Aunt Lydia, beyond a word of greeting at Christmas and on her birthday. She had ceased to give us any information about their way of life. We knew that several years after my memorable visit in New York, the railroad to whose president Oswald had long been private secretary, was put into the hands of a receiver, and the retiring president went abroad to live. Henshawe had remained with the new management, but very soon the road was taken over by one of the great trunk lines, and the office staff was cut in two. In the reorganisation Henshawe was offered a small position, which he indignantly refused—his wife wouldn't let him think of accepting it. He went to San Francisco as manager of a commission house; the business failed, and what had happened to them since I did not know.

I lingered long over my dismal dinner. I had not the courage to go upstairs. Henshawe was not more than sixty, but he looked much older. He had the tired, tired face of one who has utterly lost hope.

Oswald had got his wife up out of bed to receive me. When I entered she was sitting in a wheel-chair by an open window, wrapped in a Chinese dressing-gown, with a bright shawl over her feet. She threw out both arms to me, and as she hugged me, flashed into her old gay laugh.

"Now wasn't it clever of you to find us, Nellie? And we so safely hidden—in earth, like a pair of old foxes! But it was in the cards that we should meet again. Now I understand; a wise woman has been coming to read my fortune for me, and the queen of hearts has been coming up out of the pack when she had no business to; a beloved friend coming out of the past. Well, Nellie, dear, I couldn't think of any old friends that weren't better away, for one reason or another, while we are in temporary eclipse. I gain strength faster if I haven't people on my mind. But you, Nellie . . . that's different." She put my two hands to her cheeks, making a frame for her face. "That's different. Somebody young, and clear-eyed, chock-full of opinions, and without a past. But you may have a past, already? The darkest ones come early."

I was delighted. She was . . . she was herself, Myra Henshawe! I hadn't expected anything so good. The electric bulbs in the room were shrouded and muffled with coloured scarfs, and in that light she looked much less changed than Oswald. The corners of her mouth had relaxed a little, but they could still curl very scornfully upon occasion; her nose was the same sniffy little nose, with its restless, arched nostrils, and her double chin, though softer, was no fuller. A strong cable of grey-black hair was wound on the top of her head, which, as she once remarked, "was no head for a woman at all, but would have graced one of the wickedest of the Roman emperors."

Her bed was in the alcove behind her. In the shadowy dimness of the room I recognised some of the rugs from their New York apartment, some of the old pictures, with frames peeling and glass cracked. Here was Myra's little inlaid tea-table, and the desk at which Oswald had been writing that day when I dropped in upon their quarrel. At the windows were the dear, plum-coloured curtains, their cream lining streaked and faded—but the sight of them rejoiced me more than I could tell the Henshawes.

"And where did you come from, Nellie? What are you doing here, in heaven's name?"

While I explained myself she listened intently, holding my wrist with one of her beautiful little hands, which were so inexplicably mischievous in their outline, and which, I noticed, were still white and well cared for.

"Ah, but teaching, Nellie! I don't like that, not even for a temporary expedient. It's a cul-de-sac. Generous young people use themselves all up at it; they have no sense. Only the stupid and the phlegmatic should teach."

"But won't you allow me, too, a temporary eclipse?"

She laughed and squeezed my hand. "Ah, we wouldn't be hiding in the shadow, if we were five-and-twenty! We were throwing off sparks like a pair of shooting stars, weren't we, Oswald? No, I can't bear teaching for you, Nellie. Why not journalism? You could always make your way easily there."

"Because I hate journalism. I know what I want to do, and I'll work my way out yet, if only you'll give me time."

"Very well, dear." She sighed. "But I'm ambitious for you. I've no patience with young people when they drift. I wish I could live their lives for them; I'd know how! But there it is; by the time you've learned the short cuts, your feet puff up so that you can't take the road at all. Now tell me about your mother and my Lydia."

I had hardly begun when she lifted one finger and sniffed the air. "Do you get it? That bitter smell of the sea? It's apt to come in on the night wind. I live on it. Sometimes I can still take a drive along the shore. Go on; you say that Lydia and your mother are at present in disputation about the possession of your late grandfather's portrait. Why don't you cut it in two for them, Nellie? I remember it perfectly, and half of it would be enough for anybody!"

While I told her any amusing gossip I could remember about my family, she sat crippled but powerful in her brilliant wrappings. She looked strong and broken, generous and tyrannical, a witty and rather wicked old woman, who hated life for its defeats, and loved it for its absurdities. I recalled her angry laugh, and how she had always greeted shock or sorrow with that dry, exultant chuckle which seemed to say, "Ah-ha, I have one more piece of evidence, one more, against the hideous injustice God permits in this world!"

While we were talking, the silence of the strangely balmy February evening was rudely disturbed by the sound of doors slamming and heavy tramping overhead. Mrs. Henshawe winced, a look of apprehension and helplessness, a tortured expression, came over her face. She turned sharply to her husband, who was resting peacefully in one of their old, deep chairs, over by the muffled light. "There they are, those animals!"

He sat up. "They have just come back from church," he said in a troubled voice.

"Why should I have to know when they come back from church? Why should I have the details of their stupid, messy existence thrust upon me all day long, and half the night?" she broke out bitterly. Her features became tense, as from an attack of pain, and I realised how unable she was to bear things.

"We are unfortunate in the people who live over us," Oswald explained. "They annoy us a great deal. These new houses are poorly built, and every sound carries."

"Couldn't you ask them to walk more quietly?" I suggested.

He smiled and shook his head. "We have, but it seems to make them worse. They are that kind of people."

His wife broke in. "The palavery kind of Southerners; all that slushy gush on the surface, and no sensibilities whatever—a race without consonants and without delicacy. They tramp up there all day long like cattle. The stalled ox would have trod softer. Their energy isn't worth anything, so they use it up gabbling and running about, beating my brains ito a jelly."

She had scarcely stopped for breath when I heard a telephone ring overhead, then shrieks of laughter, and two people ran across the floor as if they were running a foot-race.

"You hear?" Mrs. Henshawe looked at me triumphantly. "Those two silly old hens race each other to the telephone as if they had a sweetheart at the other end of it. While I could still climb stairs, I hobbled up to that woman and implored her, and she began gushing about 'mah sistah' and 'mah son,' and what 'rahfined' people they were. . . . Oh, that's the cruelty of being poor; it leaves you at the mercy of such pigs! Money is a protection, a cloak; it can buy one quiet, and some sort of dignity." She leaned back, exhausted, and shut her eyes.

"Come, Nellie," said Oswald, softly. He walked down the hall to my door with me. "I'm sorry the disturbance began while you were there. Sometimes they go to the movies, and stay out later," he said mournfuly. "I've talked to that woman and to her son, but they are very unfeeling people."

"But wouldn't the management interfere in a case of sickness?"

Again he shook his head. "No, they pay a higher rent than we do—occupy more rooms. And we are somewhat under obligation to the management."

□ **II** □

I soon discovered the facts about the Henshawes' present existence. Oswald had a humble position, poorly paid, with the city traction company. He had to be at his desk at nine o'clock every day except Sunday. He rose at five in the morning, put on an old duck suit (it happened to be a very smart one, with frogs and a military collar, left over from prosperous times), went to his wife's room and gave her her bath, made her bed, arranged her things, and then got their breakfast. He made the coffee on a spirit lamp, the toast on an electric toaster. This was the only meal of the day they could have together, and as they had it long before the ruthless Poindexters overhead began to tramp, it was usually a cheerful occasion.

After breakfast Oswald washed the dishes. Their one luxury was a private bath, with a large cupboard, which he called his kitchen. Everything else done, he went back to his own room, put it in order, and then dressed for the office. He still dressed very neatly, though how he managed to do it with the few clothes he had, I could not see. He was the only man staying in that shabby hotel who looked well-groomed. As a special favour from his company he was allowed to take two hours at noon, on account of his sick wife. He came home, brought her her lunch from below, then hurried back to his office.

Myra made her own tea every afternoon, getting about in her wheel-chair or with the aid of a cane. I found that one of the kindest things I could do for her was to bring her some little sandwiches or cakes from the Swedish bakery to vary her tinned biscuit. She took great pains to get her tea nicely; it made her feel less shabby to use her own silver tea things and the three glossy English cups she had carried about with her in her trunk. I used often to go in and join her, and we spent some of our pleasantest hours at that time of the day, when the people overhead were usually out. When they were in, and active, it was too painful to witness Mrs. Henshawe's suffering. She was acutely sensitive to sound and light, and the Poindexters did tramp like cattle—except that their brutal thumping hadn't the measured dignity which the step of animals always has. Mrs. Henshawe got great pleasure from flowers, too, and during the late winter months my chief extravagance and my chief pleasure was in taking them to her.

One warm Saturday afternoon, early in April, we went for a drive along the shore. I had hired a low carriage with a kindly Negro driver. Supported on his arm and mine, Mrs. Henshawe managed to get downstairs. She looked much older and more ill in her black broadcloth coat and a black taffeta hat that had once been smart. We took with us her furs and an old steamer blanket. It was a beautiful, soft spring day. The road, unfortunately, kept winding away from the sea. At last we came out on a bare headland, with only one old twisted tree upon it, and the sea beneath.

"Why, Nellie!" she exclaimed, "it's like the cliff in *Lear,* Gloucester's cliff, so it is! Can't we stay here? I believe this nice darky man would fix me up under the tree there and come back for us later."

We wrapped her in the rug, and she declared that the trunk of the old cedar, bending away from the sea, made a comfortable back for her. The Negro drove away, and I went for a walk up the shore because I knew she wanted to be alone. From a distance I could see her leaning against her tree and looking off to sea, as if she were waiting for something. A few steamers passed below her, and the gulls dipped and darted about the headland, the soft shine of the sun on their wings. The afternoon light, at first wide and watery-pale, grew stronger and yellower, and when I went back to Myra it was beating from the west on her cliff as if thrown by a burning-glass.

She looked up at me with a soft smile—her face could still be very lovely in a tender moment. "I've had such a beautiful hour, dear; or has it been longer? Light and silence: they heal all one's wounds—all but one, and that is healed by dark and silence. I find I don't miss clever talk, the kind I always used to have about me, when I can have silence. It's like cold water poured over fever."

I sat down beside her, and we watched the sun dropping lower toward his final plunge into the Pacific. "I'd love to see this place at dawn," Myra said suddenly. "That is always such a forgiving time. When that first cold, bright streak comes over the water, it's as if all our sins were pardoned; as if the sky leaned over the earth and kissed it and gave it absolution. You know how the great sinners always come home to die in some religious house, and the abbot or the abbess went out and received them with a kiss?"

When we got home she was, of course, very tired. Oswald was waiting for us, and he and the driver carried her upstairs. While we were getting her into bed, the noise overhead broke out—tramp, tramp, bang! Myra began to cry.

"Oh, I've come back to it, to be tormented again! I've two fatal maladies, but it's those coarse creatures I shall die of. Why didn't you leave me out there, Nellie, in the wind and night? You ought to get me away from this, Oswald. If I were on my feet, and you laid low, I wouldn't let you be despised and trampled upon."

"I'll go up and see those people to-morrow, Mrs. Henshawe," I promised. "I'm sure I can do something."

"Oh, don't, Nellie!" She looked up at me in affright. "She'd turn a deaf ear to you. You know the Bible says the wicked are deaf like the adder. And, Nellie, she has the wrinkled, white throat of an adder, that woman, and the hard eyes of one. Don't go near her!"

(I went to see Mrs. Poindexter the next day, and she had just such a throat and just such eyes. She smiled, and said that the sick woman underneath was an old story, and she ought to have been sent to a sanatorium long ago.)

"Never mind, Myra. I'll get you away from it yet. I'll manage," Oswald promised as he settled the pillows under her.

She smoothed his hair. "No, my poor Oswald, you'll never stagger far under the bulk of me. Oh, if youth but knew!" She closed her eyes and pressed her hands over them. "It's been the ruin of us both. We've destroyed each other. I should have stayed with my uncle. It was money I needed. We've thrown our lives away."

"Come, Myra, don't talk so before Nellie. You don't mean it. Remember the long time we were happy. That was reality, just as much as this."

"We were never really happy. I am a greedy, selfish, worldly woman; I wanted success and a place in the world. Now I'm old and ill and a fright, but among my own kind I'd still have my circle; I'd have courtesy from people of gentle manners, and not have my brains beaten out by hoodlums. Go away, please, both of you, and leave me!" She turned her face to the wall and covered her head.

We stepped into the hall, and the moment we closed the door we heard the bolt slip behind us. She must have sprung up very quickly. Oswald walked with me to my room. "It's apt to be like this, when she has enjoyed something and gone beyond her strength. There are times when she can't have anyone near her. It was worse before you came."

I persuaded him to come into my room and sit down and drink a glass of cordial.

"Sometimes she has locked me out for days together," he said. "It seems strange—a woman of such generous friendships. It's as if she had used up that part of herself. It's a great strain on me when she shuts herself up like that. I'm afraid she'll harm herself in some way."

"But people don't do things like that," I said hopelessly.

He smiled and straightened his shoulders. "Ah, but she isn't people! She's Myra Driscoll, and there was never anybody else like her. She can't endure, but she has enough desperate courage for a regiment."

□ III □

The next morning I saw Henshawe breakfasting in the restaurant, against his custom, so I judged that his wife was still in retreat. I was glad to see that he was not alone, but was talking, with evident pleasure, to a young girl who lived with her mother at this hotel. I had noticed her respectful admiration for Henshawe on other occasions. She worked on a newspaper, was intelligent and, Oswald thought, promising. We enjoyed talking with her at lunch or dinner. She was perhaps eighteen, overgrown and awkward, with short hair and a rather heavy face; but there was something unusual about her clear, honest eyes that made one wonder. She was always on the watch to catch a moment with Oswald, to get him to talk to her about music, or German poetry, or about the actors and writers he had known. He called her his little chum, and her admiration was undoubtedly a help to him. It was very pretty and naïve. Perhaps that was one of the things that kept him up to the mark in his dress and manner. Among people he never looked apologetic or crushed. He still wore his topaz sleeve-buttons.

On Monday, as I came home from school, I saw that the door of Mrs. Henshawe's room was slightly ajar. She knew my step and called to me: "Can you come in, Nellie?"

She was staying in bed that afternoon, but she had on her best dressing-gown, and she was manicuring her neat little hands—a good sign, I thought.

"Could you stop and have tea with me, and talk? I'll be good to-day, I promise you. I wakened up in the night crying, and it did me good. You see, I was crying about things I never feel now; I'd been dreaming I was young, and the sorrows of youth had set me crying!" She took my hand as I sat down beside her. "Do you know that poem of Heine's, about how he found in his eye a tear that was not of the present, an old one, left over from the kind he used to weep? A tear that belonged to a long dead time of his life and was an anachronism. He couldn't account for it, yet there it was, and he addresses it so prettily: 'Thou old, lonesome tear!' Would you read it for me? There's my little Heine, on the shelf over the sofa. You can easily find the verse, *Du alte, einsame Thräne!*"

I ran through the volume, reading a poem here and there where a leaf had been turned down, or where I saw a line I knew well. It was a fat old book, with yellow pages, bound in tooled leather, and on the fly-leaf, in faint violet ink, was an inscription, "To Myra Driscoll from Oswald," dated 1876.

My friend lay still, with her eyes closed, and occasionally one of those anachronistic tears gathered on her lashes and fell on the pillow, making a little grey spot. Often she took the verse out of my mouth and finished it herself.

"Look for a little short one, about the flower that grows on the suicide's grave, *die Armesünderblum',* the poor-sinner's-flower. Oh, that's the flower for me, Nellie; *die Arme—sünder—blum'!*" She drew the word out until it was a poem in itself.

"Come, dear," she said presently, when I put down the book, "you don't really like this new verse that's going round, ugly lines about ugly people and common feelings—you don't really?"

When I reminded her that she liked Walt Whitman, she chuckled slyly. "Does that save me? Can I get into your new Parnassus on that dirty old man? I suppose I ought to be glad of any sort of ticket at my age! I like naughty rhymes, when they don't try to be pompous. I like the kind bad boys write on fences. My uncle had a rare collection of such rhymes in his head that he'd picked off fences and out-buildings. I wish I'd taken them down; I might become a poet of note! My uncle was a very unusual man. Did they ever tell you much about him at home? Yes, he had violent prejudices; but that's rather good to remember in these days when so few people have any real passions, either of love or hate. He would help a friend, no matter what it cost him, and over and over again he risked ruining himself to crush an enemy. But he never did ruin himself. Men who hate like that usually have the fist-power to back it up, you'll notice. He gave me fair warning, and then he kept his word. I knew he would; we were enough alike for that. He left his money wisely; part of it went to establish a home for aged and destitute women in Chicago, where it was needed."

While we were talking about this institution and some of the refugees it sheltered, Myra said suddenly: "I wonder if you know about a clause concerning me in that foundation? It states that at any time the founder's niece, Myra Driscoll Henshawe, is to be received into the institution, kept without charge, and paid an allowance of ten dollars a week for pocket money until

the time of her death. How like the old Satan that was! Be sure when he dictated that provision to his lawyer, he thought to himself: 'She'd roll herself
into the river first, the brach!' And then he probably thought better of me,
and maybe died with some decent feeling for me in his heart. We were very
proud of each other, and if he'd lived till now, I'd go back to him and ask his
pardon; because I know what it is to be old and lonely and disappointed. Yes,
and because as we grow old we become more and more the stuff our forebears
put into us. I can feel his savagery strengthen in me. We think we are so individual and so misunderstood when we are young; but the nature our strain of
blood carries is inside there, waiting, like our skeleton."

It had grown quite dusk while we talked. When I rose and turned on
one of the shrouded lights, Mrs. Henshawe looked up at me and smiled
drolly. "We've had a fine afternoon, and Biddy forgetting her ails. How the
great poets do shine on, Nellie! Into all the dark corners of the world. They
have no night."

They shone for her, certainly. Miss Stirling, "a nice young person from
the library," as Myra called her, ran in occasionally with new books, but
Myra's eyes tired quickly, and she used to shut a new book and lie back and
repeat the old ones she knew by heart, the long declamations from *Richard II*
or *King John*. As I passed her door I would hear her murmuring at the very
bottom of her rich Irish voice:

Old John of Gaunt, time-honoured Lan-cas-ter . . .

□ **IV** □

One afternoon when I got home from school I found a note from Mrs. Henshawe under my door, and went to her at once. She greeted me and kissed me
with unusual gravity.

"Nellie, dear, will you do a very special favour for me to-morrow? It is
the fifteenth of April, the anniversary of Madame Modjeska's death." She
gave me a key and asked me to open an old trunk in the corner. "Lift the tray,
and in the bottom, at one end, you will find an old pair of long kid gloves,
tied up like sacks. Please give them to me."

I burrowed down under old evening wraps and dinner dresses and came
upon the gloves, yellow with age and tied at both ends with corset lacings;
they contained something heavy that jingled. Myra was watching my face

and chuckled. "Is she thinking they are my wedding gloves, piously preserved? No, my dear; I went before a justice of the peace, and married without gloves, so to speak!" Untying the string, she shook out a little rain of ten-
and twenty-dollar gold pieces.

"All old Irish women hide away a bit of money." She took up a coin and
gave it to me. "Will you go to St. Joseph's Church and inquire for Father
Fay; tell him you are from me, and ask him to celebrate a mass to-morrow for
the repose of the soul of Helena Modjeska, Countess Bozenta-Chlapowska.
He will remember; last year I hobbled there myself. You are surprised, Nellie?
Yes, I broke with the Church when I broke with everything else and ran
away with a German free-thinker; but I believe in holy words and holy rites
all the same. It is a solace to me to know that to-morrow a mass will will be
said here in heathendom for the spirit of that noble artist, that beautiful and
gracious woman."

When I put the gold back into the trunk and started making the tea, she
said: "Oswald, of course, doesn't know the extent of my resources. We've
often needed a hundred dollars or two so bitter bad; he wouldn't understand.
But that is money I keep for unearthly purposes; the needs of this world
don't touch it."

As I was leaving she called me back: "Oh, Nelllie, can't we go to Gloucester's cliff on Saturday, if it's fine? I do long to!"

We went again, and again. Nothing else seemed to give her so much
pleasure. But the third time I stopped for her, she declared she was not equal
to it. I found her sitting in her chair, trying to write to an old friend, an Irish
actress I had met at her apartment in New York, one of the guests at that
New Year's Eve party. Her son, a young actor, had shot himself in Chicago
because of some sordid love affair. I had seen an account of it in the morning
paper.

"It touches me very nearly," Mrs. Henshawe told me. "Why, I used to
keep Billy with me for weeks together when his mother was off on tour. He
was the most truthful, noble-hearted little fellow. I had so hoped he would be
happy. You remember his mother?"

I remembered her very well—large and jovial and hearty she was. Myra
began telling me about her, and the son, whom she had not seen since he was
sixteen.

"To throw his youth away like that, and shoot himself at twenty-three!
People are always talking about the joys of youth—but, oh, how youth can
suffer! I've not forgotten; those hot southern Illinois nights, when Oswald
was in New York, and I had no word from him except through Liddy, and I
used to lie on the floor all night and listen to the express trains go by. I've
not forgotten."

"Then I wonder why you are sometimes so hard on him now," I murmured.

Mrs. Henshawe did not reply to me at once. The corners of her mouth trembled, then drew tight, and she sat with eyes closed as if she were gathering herself for something.

At last she sighed, and looked at me wistfully. "It's a great pity, isn't it, Nellie, to reach out a grudging hand and try to spoil the past for anyone? Yes, it's a great cruelty. But I can't help it. He's a sentimentalist, always was; he can look back on the best of those days when we were young and loved each other, and make himself believe it was all like that. It wasn't. I was always a grasping, worldly woman; I was never satisfied. All the same, in age, when the flowers are so few, it's a great unkindness to destroy any that are left in a man's heart." The tears rolled down her cheeks, she leaned back, looking up at the ceiling. She had stopped speaking because her voice broke. Presently she began again resolutely. "But I'm made so. People can be lovers and enemies at the same time, you know. We were. . . . A man and woman draw apart from that long embrace, and see what they have done to each other. Perhaps I can't forgive him for the harm I did him. Perhaps that's it. When there are children, that feeling goes through natural changes. But when it remains so personal . . . something gives way in one. In age we lose everything; even the power to love."

"He hasn't," I suggested.

"He has asked you to speak for him, my dear? Then we have destroyed each other indeed!"

"Certainly he hasn't, Mrs. Myra! But you are hard on him, you know, and when there are so many hard things, it seems a pity."

"Yes, it's a great pity." She drew herself up in her chair. "And I'd rather you didn't come any more for the time being, Nellie. I've been thinking the tea made me nervous." She was smiling, but her mouth curled like a little snake, as I had seen it do long ago. "Will you be pleased to take your things and go, Mrs. Casey?" She said it with a laugh, but a very meaning one.

As I rose I watched for some sign of relenting, and I said humbly enough: "Forgive me, if I've said anything I shouldn't. You know I love you very dearly."

She mockingly bowed her tyrant's head. "It's owing to me infirmities, dear Mrs. Casey, that I'll not be able to go as far as me door wid ye."

□ V □

For days after that episode I did not see Mrs. Henshawe at all. I saw Oswald at dinner in the restaurant every night, and he reported her condition to me as if nothing had happened. The short-haired newspaper girl often came to our table, and the three of us talked together. I could see that he got great refreshment from her. Her questions woke pleasant trains of recollection, and her straightforward affection was dear to him. Once Myra, in telling me that it was a pleasure to him to have me come into their lives again thus, had remarked: "He was always a man to feel women, you know, in every way." It was true. That crude little girl made all the difference in the world to him. He was generous enough to become quite light-hearted in directing her inexperience and her groping hunger for life. He even read her poor little "specials" and showed her what was worst in them and what was good. She took correction well, he told me.

Early in June Mrs. Henshawe began to grow worse. Her doctors told us a malignant growth in her body had taken hold of a vital organ, and that she would hardly live through the month. She suffered intense pain from pressure on the nerves in her back, and they gave her opiates freely. At first we had two nurses, but Myra hated the night nurse so intensely that we dismissed her, and, as my school was closed for the summer, I took turns with Oswald in watching over her at night. She needed little attention except renewed doses of codeine. She slept deeply for a few hours, and the rest of the night lay awake, murmuring to herself long passages from her old poets.

Myra kept beside her now an ebony crucifix with an ivory Christ. It used to hang on the wall, and I had supposed she carried it about because some friend had given it to her. I felt now that she had it by her for a different reason. Once when I picked it up from her bed to straighten her sheet, she put out her hand quickly and said: "Give it to me. It means nothing to people who haven't suffered."

She talked very little after this last stage of her illness began; she no longer complained or lamented, but toward Oswald her manner became strange and dark. She had certain illusions; the noise overhead she now attributed entirely to her husband. "Ah, there, he's beginning it again," she would say. "He'll wear me down in the end. Oh, let me be buried in the king's highway!"

When Oswald lifted her, or did anything for her now, she was careful to thank him in a guarded, sometimes a cringing tone. "It's bitter enough that I should have to take service from you—you whom I have loved so well," I heard her say to him.

When she asked us to use candles for light during our watches, and to have no more of the electric light she hated, she said accusingly, at him rather than to him: "At least let me die by candlelight; that is not too much to ask."

Father Fay came to see her almost daily now. His visits were long, and she looked forward to them. I was, of course, not in her room when he was there, but if he met me in the corridor he stopped to speak to me, and once he walked down the street with me talking of her. He was a young man, with a fresh face and pleasant eyes, and he was deeply interested in Myra. "She's a most unusual woman, Mrs. Henshawe," he said when he was walking down the street beside me. Then he added, smiling quite boyishly: "I wonder whether some of the saints of the early Church weren't a good deal like her. She's not at all modern in her make-up, is she?"

During those days and nights when she talked so little, one felt that Myra's mind was busy all the while—that it was even abnormally active, and occasionally one got a clue to what occupied it. One night when I was giving her her codeine she asked me a question.

"Why is it, do you suppose, Nellie, that candles are in themselves religious? Not when they are covered by shades, of course—I mean the flame of a candle. Is it because the Church began in the catacombs, perhaps?"

At another time, when she had been lying like a marble figure for a long while, she said in a gentle, reasonable voice:

"Ah, Father Fay, that isn't the reason! Religion is different from everything else; *because in religion seeking is finding.*"

She accented the word "seeking" very strongly, very deeply. She seemed to say that in other searchings it might be the object of the quest that brought satisfaction, or it might be something incidental that one got on the way; but in religion, desire was fulfillment, it was the seeking itself that rewarded.

One of those nights of watching stands out in my memory as embracing them all, as being the burden and telling the tale of them all. Myra had had a very bad day, so both Oswald and I were sitting up with her. After midnight she was quiet. The candles were burning as usual, one in her alcove. From my chair by the open window I could see her bed. She had been motionless for more than an hour, lying on her back, her eyes closed. I thought she was asleep. The city outside was as still as the room in which we sat. The sick woman began to talk to herself, scarcely above a whisper, but with perfect distinctness; a voice that was hardly more than a soft, passionate breath. I seemed to hear a soul talking.

"I could bear to suffer . . . so many have suffered. But why must it be like this? I have not deserved it. I have been true in friendship; I have faithfully nursed others in sickness. . . . Why must I die like this, alone with my mortal enemy?"

Oswald was sitting on the sofa, his face shaded by his hand. I looked at him in affright, but he did not move or shudder. I felt my hands grow cold and my forehead grow moist with dread. I had never heard a human voice utter such a terrible judgment upon all one hopes for. As I sat on through the night, after Oswald had gone to catch a few hours of sleep, I grew calmer; I began to understand a little what she meant, to sense how it was with her. Violent natures like hers sometimes turn against themselves . . . against themselves and all their idolatries.

□ VI □

On the following day Mrs. Henshawe asked to be given the Sacrament. After
she had taken it she seemed easier in mind and body. In the afternoon she
told Henshawe to go to his office and begged me to leave her and let her
sleep. The nurse we had sent away that day at her urgent request. She wanted
to be cared for by one of the nursing Sisters from the convent from now on,
and Father Fay was to bring one to-morrow.

I went to my room, meaning to go back to her in an hour, but once on
my bed I slept without waking. It was dark when I heard Henshawe knocking on my door and calling to me. As I opened it, he said in a despairing
tone: "She's gone, Nellie, she's gone!"

I thought he meant she had died. I hurried after him down the corridor
and into her room. It was empty. He pointed to her empty bed. "Don't you
see? She has gone. God knows where!"

"But how could she? A woman so ill? She must be somewhere in the
building."

"I've been all over the house. You don't know her, Nellie. She can do
anything she wills. Look at this."

On the desk lay a sheet of note paper scribbled in lead pencil: *"Dear
Oswald: my hour has come. Don't follow me. I wish to be alone. Nellie knows where
there is money for masses."* That was all. There was no signature.

We hurried to the police station. The chief sent a messenger out to the
men on the beat to warn them to be on the watch for a distraught woman
who had wandered out in delirium. Then we went to Father Fay. "The
Church has been on her mind for a long while," said Henshawe. "It is one of
her delusions that I separated her from the Church. I never meant to."

The young priest knew nothing. He was distressed, and offered to help
us in our search, but we thought he had better stay at home on the chance
that she might come to him.

When we got back to the hotel it was after eleven o'clock. Oswald said
he could not stay indoors; I must be there within call, but he would go back
to help the police.

After he left I began to search Mrs. Henshawe's room. She had worn her
heavy coat and her furs, though the night was warm. When I found that the
pair of Austrian blankets was missing, I felt I knew where she had gone.
Should I try to get Oswald at the police station? I sat down to think it over.
It seemed to me that she ought to be allowed to meet the inevitable end in
the way she chose. A yearning strong enough to lift that ailing body and drag
it out into the world again should have its way.

At five o'clock in the morning Henshawe came back with an officer and a Negro cabman. The driver had come to the station and reported that at six last night a lady, with her arms full of wraps, had signalled him at the side door of the hotel, and told him to drive her to the boat landing. When they were nearing the landing, she said she did not mean to stop there, but wanted to go farther up the shore, giving him clear directions. They reached the cliff she had indicated. He helped her out of the cab, put her rugs under the tree for her, and she gave him a ten-dollar gold piece and dismissed him. He protested that the fare was too much, and that he was afraid of getting into trouble if he left her there. But she told him a friend was going to meet her, and that it would be all right. The lady had, he said, a very kind, coaxing way with her. When he went to the stable to put up his horse, he heard that the police were looking for a woman who was out of her head, and he was frightened. He went home and talked it over with his wife, who sent him to report at headquarters.

The cabman drove us out to the headland, and the officer insisted upon going along. We found her wrapped in her blankets, leaning against the cedar trunk, facing the sea. Her head had fallen forward; the ebony crucifix was in her hands. She must have died peacefully and painlessly. There was every reason to believe she had lived to see the dawn. While we watched beside her, waiting for the undertaker and Father Fay to come, I told Oswald what she had said to me about longing to behold the morning break over the sea, and it comforted him.

□ **VII** □

Although she had returned so ardently to the faith of her childhood, Myra Henshawe never changed the clause in her will, which requested that her body should be cremated, and her ashes buried "in some lonely and unfrequented place in the mountains, or in the sea."

After it was all over, and her ashes sealed up in a little steel box, Henshawe called me into her room one morning, where he was packing her things, and told me he was going to Alaska.

"Oh, not to seek my fortune," he said, smiling. "That is for young men. But the steamship company have a place for me in their office there. I have always wanted to go, and now there is nothing to hold me. This poor little box goes with me; I shall scatter her ashes somewhere in those vast waters. And this I want you to keep for remembrance." He dropped into my hands the necklace of carved amethysts she had worn on the night I first saw her.

"And Nellie—" He paused before me with his arms folded, standing exactly as he stood behind Modjeska's chair in the moonlight on that New Year's night; standing like a statue, or a sentinel, I had said then, not knowing what it was I felt in his attitude; but now I knew it meant indestructible constancy . . . almost indestructible youth. "Nellie," he said, "I don't want you to remember her as she was here. Remember her as she was when you were with us on Madison Square, when she was herself, and we were happy. Yes, happier than it falls to the lot of most mortals to be. After she was stricken, her recollection of those things darkened. Life was hard for her, but it was glorious, too; she had such beautiful friendships. Of course, she was absolutely unreasonable when she was jealous. Her suspicions were sometimes—almost fantastic." He smiled and brushed his forehead with the tips of his fingers, as if the memory of her jealousy was pleasant still, and perplexing still. "But that was just Molly Driscoll! I'd rather have been clawed by her, as she used to say, than petted by any other woman I've ever known. These last years it's seemed to me that I was nursing the mother of the girl who ran away with me. Nothing ever took that girl from me. She was a wild, lovely creature, Nellie. I wish you could have seen her then."

Several years after I said good-bye to him, Oswald Henshawe died in Alaska. I have still the string of amethysts, but they are unlucky. If I take them out of their box and wear them, I feel all evening a chill over my heart. Sometimes, when I have watched the bright beginning of a love story, when I have seen a common feeling exalted into beauty by imagination, generosity, and the flaming courage of youth, I have heard again that strange complaint breathed by a dying woman into the stillness of night, like a confession of the soul: "Why must I die like this, alone with my mortal enemy!"

PHILIP ROTH

The Ghost Writer

□ I □

MAESTRO

It was the last daylight hour of a December afternoon more than twenty years ago—I was twenty-three, writing and publishing my first short stories, and like many a *Bildungsroman* hero before me, already contemplating my own massive *Bildungsroman*—when I arrived at his hideaway to meet the great man. The clapboard farmhouse was at the end of an unpaved road twelve hundred feet up in the Berkshires, yet the figure who emerged from the study to bestow a ceremonious greeting wore a gabardine suit, a knitted blue tie clipped to a white shirt by an unadorned silver clasp, and well-brushed ministerial black shoes that made me think of him stepping down from a shoeshine stand rather than from the high altar of art. Before I had composure enough to notice the commanding, autocratic angle at which he held his chin, or the regal, meticulous, rather dainty care he took to arrange his clothes before sitting—to notice anything, really, other than that I had miraculously made it from my unliterary origins to here, to him—my impression was that E. I. Lonoff looked more like the local superintendent of schools than the region's most original storyteller since Melville and Hawthorne.

Not that the New York gossip about him should have led me to expect anything more grand. When I had recently raised his name before the jury at my first Manhattan publishing party—I'd arrived, excited as a starlet, on the arm of an elderly editor—Lonoff was almost immediately disposed of by the wits on hand as though it were comical that a Jew of his generation, an immigrant child to begin with, should have married the scion of an old New England family and lived all these years "in the country"—that is to say, in the *goyish* wilderness of birds and trees where America began and long ago had ended. However, since everybody else of renown I mentioned at the party also seemed slightly amusing to those in the know, I had been skeptical about their satiric description of the famous rural recluse. In fact, from what I saw at that party, I could begin to understand why hiding out twelve hundred feet up in the mountains with just the birds and the trees might not be a bad idea for a writer, Jewish or not.

The living room he took me into was neat, cozy, and plain: a large circular hooked rug, some slipcovered easy chairs, a worn sofa, a long wall of books, a piano, a phonograph, an oak library table systematically stacked with journals and magazines. Above the white wainscoting, the pale-yellow walls were bare but for half a dozen amateur watercolors of the old farmhouse in different seasons. Beyond the cushioned windowseats and the colorless cotton curtains tied primly back I could see the bare limbs of big dark maple trees and fields of driven snow. Purity. Serenity. Simplicity. Seclusion. All one's concentration and flamboyance and originality reserved for the grueling, exalted, transcendent calling. I looked around and I thought, This is how I will live.

After directing me to one of a pair of easy chairs beside the fireplace, Lonoff removed the fire screen and peered in to be sure the draft was open. With a wooden match he lighted the kindling that apparently had been laid there in anticipation of our meeting. Then he placed the fire screen back into position as precisely as though it were being fitted into a groove in the hearth. Certain that the logs had caught—satisfied that he had successfully ignited a fire without endangering the two-hundred-year-old house or its inhabitants—he was ready at last to join me. With hands that were almost ladylike in the swiftness and delicacy of their movements, he hiked the crease in each trouser leg and took his seat. He moved with a notable lightness for such a large, heavyset man.

"How would you prefer to be addressed?" asked Emanuel Isidore Lonoff. "As Nathan, Nate, or Nat? Or have you another preference entirely?" Friends and acquaintances called him Manny, he informed me, and I should do the same. "That will make conversation easier."

I doubted that, but I smiled to indicate that no matter how light-headed it was bound to leave me, I would obey. The master then proceeded to undo me further by asking to hear something from me about my life. Needless to say, there wasn't much to report about my life in 1956—certainly not, as I saw it, to someone so knowing and deep. I had been raised by doting parents in a Newark neighborhood neither rich nor poor; I had a younger brother who was said to idolize me; at a good local high school and an excellent college I had performed as generations of my forebears had expected me to; subsequently I had served in the Army, stationed just an hour from home, writing public-information handouts for a Fort Dix major, even while the massacre for which my carcass had been drafted was being bloodily concluded in Korea. Since my discharge I had been living and writing in a five-flight walk-up off lower Broadway, characterized by my girl friend, when she came to share the place and fix it up a little, as the home of an unchaste monk.

To support myself I crossed the river to New Jersey three days a week to a job I'd held on and off since my first summer in college, when I'd answered an ad promising high commissions to aggressive salesmen. At eight each morning our crew was driven to some New Jersey mill town to sell magazine subscriptions door-to-door, and at six we were picked up outside a designated saloon and driven back to downtown Newark by the overseer, McElroy. He was a spiffy rummy with a hairline mustache who never tired of warning us—two high-minded boys who were putting away their earnings for an education, and three listless old-timers, pale puffy men wrecked by every conceivable misfortune—not to fool with the housewives we found alone at home in their curlers: you could get your neck broken by an irate husband, you could be set up for walloping blackmail, you could catch any one of fifty leprous varieties of clap, and what was more, there were only so many hours in the day. "Either get laid," he coldly advised us, "or sell *Silver Screen*. Take your pick." "Mammon's Moses" we two college boys called him. Since no housewife ever indicated a desire to invite me into the hallway to so much as rest my feet—and I was vigilantly on the lookout for lasciviousness flaring up in any woman of any age who seemed even half willing to listen to me from behind her screen door—I of necessity chose perfection in the work rather than the life, and by the end of each long day of canvassing had ten to twenty dollars in commissions to my credit and an unblemished future still before me. It was only a matter of weeks since I had relinquished this unhallowed life—and the girl friend in the five-flight walk-up, whom I no longer loved—and, with the help of the distinguished New York editor, had been welcomed for the winter months as a communicant at the Quahsay Colony, the rural artists' retreat across the state line from Lonoff's mountain.

From Quahsay I had sent Lonoff the literary quarterlies that had published my stories—four so far—along with a letter telling him how much he had meant to me when I came upon his work "some years ago" in college. In the same breath I mentioned coming upon his "kinsmen" Chekhov and Gogol, and went on to reveal in other unmistakable ways just how serious a literary fellow I was—and, hand in hand with that, how young. But then nothing I had ever written put me in such a sweat as that letter. Everything undeniably true struck me as transparently false as soon as I wrote it down, and the greater the effort to be sincere, the worse it went. I finally sent him the tenth draft and then tried to stick my arm down the throat of the mailbox to extract it.

I wasn't doing any better in the plain and cozy living room with my autobiography. Because I could not bring myself to utter even the mildest obscenity in front of Lonoff's early American mantelpiece, my imitation of Mr. McElroy—a great favorite among my friends—didn't really have much to recommend it. Nor could I speak easily of all McElroy had warned us against, or begin to mention how tempted I would have been to yield, if opportunity had only knocked. You would have thought, listening to my bowdlerized version of what was a tepid enough little life history, that rather than having received a warm and gracious letter from the famous writer inviting me to come and spend a pleasant evening in his house, I had made this journey to plead a matter of utmost personal urgency before the most stringent of inquisitors, and that if I made one wrong move, something of immeasurable value to me would be lost forever.

Which was pretty much the case, even if I didn't completely understand as yet how desperate I was for his recognition, and why. Far from being nonplused by my bashful, breathless delivery—out of character though it was for me in those confident years—I should have been surprised to find that I wasn't down on the hooked rug, supplicating at his feet. For I had come, you see, to submit myself for candidacy as nothing less than E. I. Lonoff's spiritual son, to petition for his moral sponsorship and to win, if I could, the magical protection of his advocacy and his love. Of course, I had a loving father of my own, whom I could ask the world of any day of the week, but my father was a foot doctor and not an artist, and lately we had been having serious trouble in the family because of a new story of mine. He was so bewildered by what I had written that he had gone running to *his* moral mentor, a certain Judge Leopold Wapter, to get the judge to get his son to see the light. As a result, after two decades of a more or less unbroken amiable conversation, we had not been speaking for nearly five weeks now, and I was off and away seeking patriarchal validation elsewhere.

And not just from a father who was an artist instead of a foot doctor, but from the most famous literary ascetic in America, that giant of patience and fortitude and selflessness who, in the twenty-five years between his first book and his sixth (for which he was given a National Book Award that he quietly declined to accept), had virtually no readership or recognition, and invariably would be dismissed, if and when he was even mentioned, as some quaint remnant of the Old World ghetto, an out-of-step folklorist pathetically oblivious of the major currents of literature and society. Hardly anyone knew who he was or where actually he lived, and for a quarter of a century almost nobody cared. Even among his readers there had been some who thought that E. I. Lonoff's fantasies about Americans had been written in Yiddish somewhere inside czarist Russia before he supposedly died there (as, in fact, his father had nearly perished) from injuries suffered in a pogrom. What was so admirable to me was not only the tenacity that had kept him writing his own kind of stories all that time but that having been "discovered" and popularized, he refused all awards and degrees, declined membership in all honorary institutions, granted no public interviews, and chose not to be photographed, as though to associate his face with his fiction were a ridiculous irrelevancy.

The only photograph anyone in the reading public had ever seen was the watery sepia portrait which had appeared in 1927 on an inside jacket flap of *It's Your Funeral:* the handsome young artist with the lyrical almond eyes and the dark prow of a paramour's pompadour and the kissable, expressive under-lip. So different was he now, not just because of jowls and a belly and the white-fringed, bald cranium but as a human type altogether, that I thought (once I began to be able to think) it had to be something more ruthless than time that accounted for the metamorphosis: it would have to be Lonoff himself. Other than the full, glossy eyebrows and the vaguely heavenward tilt of the willful chin, there was really nothing at all to identify him, at fifty-six, with the photo of the passionate, forlorn, shy Valentino who, in the decade lorded over by the young Hemingway and Fitzgerald, had written a collection of short stories about wandering Jews unlike anything written before by any Jew who had wandered into America.

In fact, my own first reading through Lonoff's canon—as an orthodox college atheist and highbrow-in-training—had done more to make me realize how much I was still my family's Jewish offspring than anything I had carried forward to the University of Chicago from childhood Hebrew lessons, or mother's kitchen, or the discussions I used to hear among my parents and our relatives about the perils of intermarriage, the problem of Santa Claus, and the injustice of medical-school quotas (quotas that, as I understood early on, accounted for my father's career in chiropody and his ardent lifelong support of the B'nai B'rith Anti-Defamation League). As a grade-school kid I could already debate these intricate issues with anyone (and did, when called upon); by the time I left for Chicago, however, my passion had been pretty well spent and I was as ready as an adolescent could be to fall headlong for Robert Hutchins' Humanities One. But then, along with tens of thousands of others, I discovered E. I. Lonoff, whose fiction seemed to me a response to the same burden of exclusion and confinement that still weighed upon the lives of those who had raised me, and that had informed our relentless household obsession with the status of the Jews. The pride inspired in my parents by the establishment in 1948 of a homeland in Palestine that would gather in the unmurdered remnant of European Jewry was, in fact, not so unlike what welled up in me when I first came upon Lonoff's thwarted, secretive, imprisoned souls, and realized that out of everything humbling from which my own striving, troubled father had labored to elevate us all, a literature of such dour wit and poignancy could be shamelessly conceived. To me it was as though the hallucinatory strains in Gogol had been filtered through the humane skepticism of Chekhov to nourish the country's first "Russian" writer. Or so I argued in the college essay where I "analyzed" Lonoff's style but kept to myself an explication of the feelings of kinship that his stories had revived in me for our own largely Americanized clan, moneyless immigrant shop-keepers to begin with, who'd carried on a shtetl life ten minutes' walk from the pillared banks and gargoyled insurance cathedrals of downtown Newark; and what is more, feelings of kinship for our pious, unknown ancestors, whose Galician tribulations had been only a little less foreign to me, while growing up securely in New Jersey, than Abraham's in the Land of Canaan. With his vaudevillian's feel for legend and landscape (a Chaplin, I said of Lonoff in my senior paper, who seized upon just the right prop to bring an entire society and its outlook to life); with his "translated" English to lend a mildly ironic flavor to even the most commonplace expression; with his cryptic, muted, dreamy resonance, the sense given by such little stories of saying so much—well, I had proclaimed, who in American literature was like him?

The typical hero of a Lonoff story—the hero who came to mean so much to bookish Americans in the mid-fifties, the hero who, some ten years after Hitler, seemed to say something new and wrenching to Gentiles about Jews, and to Jews about themselves, and to readers and writers of that recuperative decade generally about the ambiguities of prudence and the anxieties of disorder, about life-hunger, life-bargains, and life-terror in their most elementary manifestations—Lonoff's hero is more often than not a nobody from nowhere, away from a home where he is not missed, yet to which he must return without delay. His celebrated blend of sympathy and pitilessness (monumentalized as "Lonovian" by *Time*—after decades of ignoring him completely) is nowhere more stunning than in the stories where the bemused isolate steels himself to be carried away, only to discover that his meticulous thoughtfulness has caused him to wait a little too long to do anyone any good, or that acting with bold and uncharacteristic impetuosity, he has totally misjudged what had somehow managed to entice him out of his manageable existence, and as a result has made everything worse.

The grimmest, funniest, and most unsettling stories of all, where the pitiless author seems to me to teeter just at the edge of self-impalement, were written during the brief period of his literary glory (for he died in 1961 of a bone-marrow disease; and when Oswald shot Kennedy and the straitlaced bulwark gave way to the Gargantuan banana republic, his fiction, and the authority it granted to all that is prohibitive in life, began rapidly losing "relevance" for a new generation of readers). Rather than cheering him up, Lonoff's eminence seemed to strengthen his dourest imaginings, confirming for him visions of terminal restraint that might have seemed insufficiently supported by personal experience had the world denied him its rewards right down to the end. Only when a little of the coveted bounty was finally his for the asking—only when it became altogether clear just how stupefyingly unsuited he was to have and to hold anything other than his art—was he inspired to write that brilliant cycle of comic parables (the stories "Revenge," "Lice," "Indiana," "Eppes Essen," and "Adman") in which the tantalized hero does not move to act *at all*—the tiniest impulse toward amplitude or self-surrender, let alone intrigue or adventure, peremptorily extinguished by the ruling triumvirate of Sanity, Responsibility, and Self-Respect, assisted handily by their devoted underlings: the timetable, the rainstorm, the headache, the busy signal, the traffic jam, and, most loyal of all, the last-minute doubt.

Did I sell any magazines other than *Photoplay* and *Silver Screen?* Did I use the same line at every door or adapt my sales pitch to the customer? How did I account for my success as a salesman? What did I think people were after who subscribed to these insipid magazines? Was the work boring? Did anything unusual ever happen while I was prowling neighborhoods I knew nothing about? How many crews like Mr. McElroy's were there in New Jersey? How could the company afford to pay me three dollars for each subscription I sold? Had I ever been to Hackensack? What was it like?

It was difficult to believe that what I was doing merely to support myself until I might begin to live as he did could possibly be of interest to E. I. Lonoff. He was a courteous man, obviously, and he was trying his best to put me at ease, but I was thinking, even as I gave my all to his cross-examination, that it wasn't going to be long before he came up with a way of getting rid of me before dinner.

"I wish I knew that much about selling magazines," he said.

To indicate that it was all right with me if I was being condescended to and that I would understand if I was soon asked to leave, I went red.

"I wish," he said, "I knew that much about anything. I've written fantasy for thirty years. Nothing happens to me."

It was here that the striking girl-woman appeared before me—just as he had aired, in faintly discernible tones of self-disgust, this incredible lament and I was trying to grasp it. Nothing happened to him? Why, genius had happened to him, art had happened to him, the man was a visionary!

Lonoff's wife, the white-haired woman who had instantly removed herself after letting me into the house, had pushed open the door of the study across the foyer from the living room, and there she was, hair dark and profuse, eyes pale—gray or green—and with a high prominent oval forehead that looked like Shakespeare's. She was seated on the carpet amid a pile of papers and folders, swathed in a "New Look" tweed skirt—by now a very old, outmoded look in Manhattan—and a large, loose-fitting, white wool sweater; her legs were drawn demurely up beneath the expanse of skirt and her gaze was fixed on something that was clearly elsewhere. Where had I seen the severe dark beauty before? Where but in a portrait by Velázquez? I remembered the 1927 photograph of Lonoff—"Spanish" too in its way—and immediately I assumed that she was his daughter. Immediately I assumed more than that. Mrs. Lonoff had not even set the tray down on the carpet beside her before I saw myself married to the *infanta* and living in a little farmhouse of our own not that far away. Only how old was she if Mama was feeding her cookies while she finished her homework on Daddy's floor? With that face, whose strong bones looked to me to have been worked into alignment by a less guileless sculptor than nature—with that face she *must* be more than twelve. Though if not, I could wait. That idea appealed to me even more than the prospect of a marriage here in the living room in spring. Showed strength of character, I thought. But what would the famous father think? He of course wouldn't need to be reminded of the solid Old Testament precedent for waiting seven years before making Miss Lonoff my bride; on the other hand, how would he take it when he saw me hanging around outside her high school in my car?

Meanwhile, he was saying to me, "I turn sentences around. That's my life. I write a sentence and then I turn it around. Then I look at it and I turn it around again. Then I have lunch. Then I come back in and write another sentence. Then I have tea and turn the new sentence around. Then I read the two sentences over and turn them both around. Then I lie down on my sofa and think. Then I get up and throw them out and start from the beginning. And if I knock off from this routine for as long as a day, I'm frantic with boredom and a sense of waste. Sundays I have breakfast late and read the papers with Hope. Then we go for a walk in the hills, and I'm haunted by the loss of all that good time. I wake up Sunday mornings and I'm nearly crazy at the prospect of all those unusable hours. I'm restless, I'm bad-tempered, but she's a human being too, you see, so I go. To avoid trouble she makes me leave my watch at home. The result is that I look at my wrist instead. We're walking, she's talking, then I look at my wrist—and that generally does it, if my foul mood hasn't already. She throws in the sponge and we come home. And at home what is there to distinguish Sunday from Thursday? I sit back down at my little Olivetti and start looking at sentences and turning them around. And I ask myself, Why is there no way but this for me to fill my hours?"

By now Hope Lonoff had closed the study door and returned to her chores. Together Lonoff and I listened to her Mixmaster whirling in the kitchen. I didn't know what to say. The life he described sounded like paradise to me; that he could think to do nothing better with his time than turn sentences around seemed to me a blessing bestowed not only upon him but upon world literature. I wondered if perhaps I was supposed to be laughing, despite the deadpan delivery, at his description of his day, if it wasn't intended as mordant Lonovian comedy; though then again, if he meant it and was as depressed as he sounded, oughtn't I to remind him just who he was and how much he mattered to literate mankind? But how could he not know that?

The Mixmaster whirled and the fire popped and the wind blew and the trees groaned while I tried, at twenty-three, to think of how to dispel his gloom. His openness about himself, so at odds with his formal attire and his pedantic manner, had me as unnerved as anything else; it was hardly what I was accustomed to getting from people more than twice my age, even if what he said about himself was tinged with self-satire. Especially if it was tinged with self-satire.

"I wouldn't even try to write after my tea any more if I knew what to do with myself for the rest of the afternoon." He explained to me that by three o'clock he no longer had the strength or the determination or even the desire to go on. But what else was there? If he played the violin or the piano, then he might have had some serious activity other than reading to occupy him when he was not writing. The problem with just listening to music was that if he sat alone with a record in the afternoon, he soon found himself turning the sentences around in his head and eventually wound up back at his desk again, skeptically looking at his day's work. Of course, to his great good fortune, there was Athene College. He spoke with devotion of the students in the two classes that he taught there. The little Stockbridge school had made a place for him on the faculty some twenty years before the rest of the academic world suddenly became interested, and for that he would always be grateful. But in truth, after so many years of teaching these bright and lively young women, both he and they, he found, had begun to repeat themselves a little.

"Why not take a sabbatical?" I was not a little thrilled, after all I had been through in my first fifteen minutes, to hear myself telling E. I. Lonoff how to live.

"I took a sabbatical. It was worse. We rented a flat in London for a year. Then I had every day to write. Plus Hope being miserable because I wouldn't stop to go around with her to look at the buildings. No—no more sabbaticals. This way, at least two afternoons a week I have to stop, no questions asked. Besides, going to the college is the high point of my week. I carry a briefcase. I wear a hat. I nod hello to people on the stairway. I use a public toilet. Ask Hope. I come home reeling from the pandemonium."

"Are there no children—of your own?"

The phone began ringing in the kitchen. Ignoring it, he informed me that the youngest of their three children had graduated from Wellesley several years before; he and his wife had been alone together now for more than six years.

So the girl isn't his daughter. Who is she then, being served snacks by his wife on the floor of his study? His concubine? Ridiculous, the word, the very idea, but there it was obscuring all other reasonable and worthy thoughts. Among the rewards you got for being a great artist was the concubinage of Velázquez princesses and the awe of young men like me. I felt at a loss again, having such ignoble expectations in the presence of my literary conscience—though weren't they just the kind of ignoble expectations that troubled the masters of renunciation in so many of Lonoff's short stories?

Really, who knew better than E. I. Lonoff that it is not our high purposes alone that make us moving creatures, but our humble needs and cravings? Nonetheless, it seemed to me a good idea to keep my humble needs and cravings to myself.

The kitchen door opened a few inches and his wife said softly, "For you."

"Who is it? Not the genius again."

"Would I have said you were here?"

"You have to learn to tell people no. People like that make fifty calls a day. Inspiration strikes and they go for the phone."

"It's not him."

"He has the right wrong opinion on everything. A head full of ideas, every one of them stupid. Why does he hit me when he talks? Why must he understand everything? Stop fixing me up with intellectuals. I don't think fast enough."

"I've said I was sorry. And it's not him."

"Who is it?"

"Willis."

"Hope, I'm talking to Nathan here."

"I'm sorry. I'll tell him you're working."

"Don't use work as an excuse. I don't buy that."

"I can tell him you have a guest."

"Please," I said, meaning I was no one, not even a guest.

"All that wonder," said Lonoff to his wife. "Always so greatly moved. Always on the brink of tears. What is he so compassionate about all the time?"

"You," she said.

"All that sensitivity. Why does anybody want to be so sensitive?"

"He admires you," she said.

Buttoning his jacket, Lanoff rose to take the unwanted call. "Either it's the professional innocents," he explained to me, "or the deep thinkers."

I extended my sympathy with a shrug, wondering, of course, if my letter hadn't qualified me in both categories. Then I wondered again about the girl behind the study door. Does she live at the college or is she here with the Lonoffs on a visit from Spain? Would she ever be coming out of that study? If not, how do I go in? If not, how can I arrange to see her again by myself?

I *must see you again.*

I opened a magazine, the better to dispel my insidious daydreams and wait there like a thoughtful man of letters. Leafing through the pages, I came across an article about the Algerian political situation and another about the television industry, both of which had been underlined throughout. Read in sequence, the underlinings formed a perfect precis of each piece and would have served a schoolchild as excellent preparation for a report to his current-events class.

When Lonoff emerged—in under a minute—from the kitchen, he immediately undertook to explain about the *Harper's* in my hand. "My mind strays," he told me, rather as though I were a physician who had stopped by to ask about his strange and troubling new symptoms. "At the end of the page I try to summarize to myself what I've read and my mind is a blank—I've been sitting in my chair doing nothing. Of course, I have always read books with pen in hand, but now I find that if I don't, even while reading magazines, my attention is not on what's in front of me."

Here she appeared again. But what had seemed from a distance like beauty, pure and severe and simple, was more of a puzzle up close. When she crossed the foyer into the living room—entering just as Lonoff had ended his fastidious description of the disquieting affliction that came over him when he read magazines—I saw that the striking head had been conceived on a much grander and more ambitious scale than the torso. The bulky sweater and the pounds and pounds of tweed skirt did much, of course, to obscure the little of her there was, but mostly it was the drama of that face, combined with the softness and intelligence in her large pale eyes, that rendered all other physical attributes (excluding the heavy, curling hair) blurry and inconsequential. Admittedly, the rich calm of those eyes would have been enough to make me wilt with shyness, but that I couldn't return her gaze directly had also to do with this unharmonious relation between body and skull, and its implication, to me, of some early misfortune, of something vital lost or beaten down, and, by way of compensation, something vastly overdone. I thought of a trapped chick that could not get more than its beaked skull out of the encircling shell. I thought of those macrocephalic boulders the Easter Island heads. I thought of febrile patients on the verandas of Swiss sanatoria imbibing the magic-mountain air. But let me not exaggerate the pathos and originality of my impressions, especially as they were subsumed soon enough in my unoriginal and irrepressible preoccupation: mostly I thought of the triumph it would be to kiss that face, and the excitement of her kissing me back.

"Done," she announced to Lonoff, "for now."

His look of wistful solicitude made me wonder if she could be his *grand*daughter. All at once he seemed the most approachable of men, relieved of every care and burden. Perhaps, I thought—still trying to explain some oddness in her that I couldn't identify—she is the child of a daughter of his own who is dead.

"This is Mr. Zuckerman, the short-story writer," he said, teasing sweetly, like *my* grandfather now. "I gave you his collected works to read."

I rose and shook her hand.

"This is Miss Bellette. She was once a student here. She has been staying with us for a few days, and has taken it upon herself to begin sorting through my manuscripts. There is a movement afoot to persuade me to deposit with Harvard University the pieces of paper on which I turn my sentences around. Amy works for the Harvard library. The Athene library has just extended her an exceptional offer, but she tells us she is tied to her life in Cambridge. Meanwhile, she has cunningly been using the visit to try to persuade me—"

"No, no, no," she said emphatically. "If you see it that way, my cause is doomed." As if she hadn't charm enough, Miss Bellette's speech was made melodious by a faint foreign accent. "The maestro," she explained, turning my way, "is by temperament counter-suggestible."

"And counter that," he moaned, registering a mild protest against the psychological lingo.

"I've just found twenty-seven drafts of a single short story," she told me.

"Which story?" I asked eagerly.

" 'Life Is Embarrassing.' "

"To get it wrong," said Lonoff, "so many times."

"They ought to construct a monument to your patience," she told him.

He gestured vaguely toward the crescent of plumpness buttoned in beneath his jacket. "They have."

"In class," she said, "he used to tell the writing students, 'There is no life without patience.' None of us knew what he was talking about."

"You knew. You had to know. My dear young lady, I learned that from watching you."

"But I can't wait for anything," she said.

"But you do."

"Bursting with frustration all the while."

"If you weren't bursting," her teacher informed her, "you wouldn't need patience."

At the hall closet she stepped out of the loafers she'd worn into the living room and slipped on white woolen socks and a pair of red snow boots. Then from a hanger she took down a plaid hooded jacket, into whose sleeve was tucked a white wool cap with a long tassel that ended in a fluffy white ball. Having seen her only seconds before banter so easily with the celebrated writer—having myself felt ever so slightly drawn into the inner circle by her easy, confident way with him—I was surprised by the childish hat. The costume, now that she had it on, seemed like a little girl's. That she could act so wise and dress up so young mystified me.

Along with Lonoff I stood in the open doorway waving goodbye. I was now in awe of two people in this house.

There was still more wind than snow, but in Lonoff's orchard the light had all but seeped away, and the sound of what was on its way was menacing. Two dozen wild old apple trees stood as first barrier between the bleak un-

paved road and the farmhouse. Next came a thick green growth of rhodo-
dendron, then a wide stone wall fallen in like a worn molar at the center,
then some fifty feet of snow-crusted lawn, and finally, drawn up close to the
house and protectively overhanging the shingles, three maples that looked
from their size to be as old as New England. In back, the house gave way to
unprotected fields, drifted over since the first December blizzards. From there
the wooded hills began their impressive rise, undulating forest swells that
just kept climbing into the next state. My guess was that it would take even
the fiercest Hun the better part of a winter to cross the glacial waterfalls and
wind-blasted woods of those mountain wilds before he was able to reach the
open edge of Lonoff's hayfields, rush the rear storm door of the house, crash
through into the study, and, with spiked bludgeon wheeling high in the air
above the little Olivetti, cry out in a roaring voice to the writer tapping out
his twenty-seventh draft, "You must change your life!" And even he might
lose heart and turn back to the bosom of his barbarian family should he approach those black Massachusetts hills on a night like this, with the cocktail
hour at hand and yet another snowstorm arriving from Ultima Thule. No,
for the moment, at least, Lonoff seemed really to have nothing to worry
about from the outside world.

We watched from the front step until Lonoff was sure that she had
cleared both the windshield and rear window; snow had already begun adher-
ing to the icy glass. "Drive very slowly," he called. To get into the diminu-
tive green Renault she had to hike up a handful of long skirt. Above the
snow boots I saw an inch of flesh, and quickly looked elsewhere so as not to
be found out.

"Yes, be careful," I called to her, in the guise of Mr. Zuckerman the
short-story writer. "It's slippery, it's deceptive."

"She has a remarkable prose style," Lonoff said to me when we were back
inside the house. "The best student writing I've ever read. Wonderful clarity.
Wonderful comedy. Tremendous intelligence. She wrote stories about the
college which capture the place in a sentence. Everything she sees, she takes
hold of. And a lovely pianist. She can play Chopin with great charm. She
used to practice on our daughter's piano when she first came to Athene. That
was something I looked forward to at the end of the day."

"She seems to be quite a girl," I said thoughtfully. "Where is she from
originally?"

"She came to us from England."

"But the accent . . . ?"

"That," he allowed, "is from the country of Fetching."

"I agree," I dared to say, and thought: Enough shyness then, enough
boyish uncertainty and tongue-tied deference. This, after all, is the author of
"Life Is Embarrassing"—if he doesn't know the score, who does?

Standing by the fire, the two of us warming ourselves, I turned to Lonoff and said, "I don't think I could keep my wits about me, teaching at a school with such beautiful and gifted and fetching girls."

To which he replied flatly, "Then you shouldn't do it."

A surprise—yes, yet another—awaited me when we sat down to dinner. Lonoff uncorked a bottle of Chianti that had been waiting for us on the table and proposed a toast. Signaling his wife to raise her glass along with his, he said, "To a wonderful new writer."

Well, *that* loosened me up. Excitedly, I began talking about my month at Quahsay, how much I loved the serenity and beauty of the place, how I loved walking the trails there at the end of the day and reading in my room at night—rereading Lonoff of late, but that I kept to myself. From his toast it was obvious that I had not lost as much ground as I feared by confessing to the lure of clever, pretty college girls, and I did not want to risk offending him anew by seeming to fawn. The fawning, supersensitive Willis, I remembered, had been given less than sixty seconds on the phone.

I told the Lonoffs about the joy of awakening each morning knowing there were all those empty hours ahead to be filled only with work. Never as a student or a soldier or a door-to-door salesman did I have regular stretches of uninterrupted time to devote to writing, nor had I ever lived before in such quiet and seclusion, or with my few basic needs so unobtrusively satisfied as they were by the Quahsay housekeeping staff. It all seemed to me a marvelous, a miraculous gift. Just a few evenings before, after a day-long snowstorm, I had accompanied the Colony handyman when he set out after dinner on the snowplow to clear the trails that twisted for miles through the Quahsay woods. I described for the Lonoffs my exhilaration at watching the snow crest in the headlights of the truck and then fall away into the forest; the bite of the cold and the smack of the tire chains had seemed to me all I could ever want at the end of a long day at *my* Olivetti. I supposed I was being professionally innocent despite myself, but I couldn't stop going on about my hours on the snowplow after the hours at my desk: it wasn't just that I wanted to convince Lonoff of my pure and incorruptible spirit—my problem was that I wanted to believe it myself. My problem was that I wanted to be wholly worthy of his thrilling toast. "I could live like that forever," I announced.

"Don't try it," he said. "If your life consists of reading and writing and looking at the snow, you'll wind up like me. Fantasy for thirty years."

Lonoff made "Fantasy" sound like a breakfast cereal.

Here for the first time his wife spoke up—though given the self-effacing delivery, "spoke down" would be more exact. She was a smallish woman with gentle gray eyes and soft white hair and a multitude of fine lines crisscrossing her pale skin. Though she could well have been, as the amused literati had it, Lonoff's "high-born Yankee heiress"—and an excellent example of the species at its most maidenly—what she looked like now was some frontier survivor, the wife of a New England farmer who long ago rode out of these mountains to make a new start in the West. To me the lined face and the shadowy, timorous manner bore witness to a grinding history of agonized childbearing and escapes from the Indians, of famine and fevers and wagon-train austerities—I just couldn't believe that she could look so worn down from living alongside E. I. Lonoff while he wrote short stories for thirty years. I was to learn later that aside from two terms at a Boston art school and a few months in New York—and the year in London trying to get Lonoff to Westminster Abbey—Hope had strayed no farther than had the locally prominent lawyers and clergymen who were her forebears, and whose legacy by now came to nothing more tangible than one of the Berkshires' "best" names and the house that went with it.

She had met Lonoff when he came at the age of seventeen to work for a chicken farmer in Lenox. He himself had been raised just outside Boston, though until he was five lived in Russia. After his father, a jeweler, nearly died from injuries suffered in the Zhitomir pogrom, Lonoff's parents emigrated to primitive Palestine. There typhus carried them both away, and their son was cared for by family friends in a Jewish farming settlement. At seven he was shipped alone from Jaffa to wealthy relatives of his father's in Brookline; at seventeen he chose vagabondage over college at the relatives' expense; and then at twenty he chose Hope—the rootless Levantine Valentino taking as his mate a cultivated young provincial woman, bound to the finer things by breeding and temperament, and to a settled place by old granite gravestones, church-meetinghouse plaques, and a long mountain road bearing the name Whittlesey: somebody from somewhere, for all the good that was to do him.

Despite everything that gave Hope Lonoff the obedient air of an aging geisha when she dared to speak or to move, I still wondered if she was not going to remind him that his life had consisted of something more than reading and writing and looking at snow: it had also consisted of her and the children. But there was not the hint of a reprimand in her unchallenging voice when she said, "You shouldn't express such a low opinion of your achievement. It's not becoming." Even more delicately, she added, "And it's not true."

Lonoff lifted his chin. "I was not measuring my achievement. I have neither too high nor too low an estimate of my work. I believe I know exactly wherein my value and originality lie. I know where I can go and just how far, without making a mockery of the thing we all love. I was only suggesting—surmising is more like it—that an unruly personal life will probably better serve a writer like Nathan than walking in the woods and startling the deer. His work has turbulence—that should be nourished, and not in the woods. All I was trying to say is that he oughtn't to stifle what is clearly his gift."

"I'm sorry," replied his wife. "I didn't understand. I thought you were expressing distaste for your own work." "Work" she pronounced in the accent of her region, without the "r."

"I was expressing distaste," said Lonoff, employing that pedantic tone he'd taken with Amy on the subject of her patience, and with me, describing his light-reading problem, "but not for the work. I was expressing distaste for the range of my imagination."

With a self-effacing smile designed to atone on the spot for her audacity, Hope said, "Your imagination or your experience?"

"I long ago gave up illusions about myself and experience."

She pretended to be brushing the crumbs from around the bread board, that and no more—while with unforeseen, somewhat inexplicable insistence, she softly confessed, "I never quite know what that means."

"It means I know who I am. I know the kind of man I am and the kind of writer. I have my own kind of bravery, and please, let's leave it at that."

She decided to. I remembered my food and began to eat again.

"Do you have a girl friend?" Lonoff asked me.

I explained the situation—to the extent that I was willing to.

Betsy had found out about me and a girl she had known since ballet school. The two of us had kissed over a glass of Gallo in the kitchen, playfully she had shown me the tip of her wine-stained tongue, and I, quick to take heart, had pulled her out of her chair and down beside the sink. This took place one evening when Betsy was off dancing at the City Center and the friend had stopped by to pick up a record and investigate a flirtation we'd begun some months earlier, when Betsy was away touring with the company. On my knees, I struggled to unclothe her; not resisting all that strenuously, she, on her knees, told me what a bastard I was to be doing this to Betsy. I refrained from suggesting that she might be less than honorable herself; trading insults while in heat wasn't my brand of aphrodisia, and I was afraid of a fiasco if I should try it and get carried away. So, shouldering the burden of perfidy for two, I pinned her pelvis to the kitchen linoleum, while she continued, through moist smiling lips, to inform me of my character flaws. I was then at the stage of my erotic development when nothing excited *me* as much as having intercourse on the floor.

Betsy was a romantic, excitable, high-strung girl who could be left quivering by the backfire of a car—so when the friend intimated over the phone to her a few days later that I wasn't to be trusted, it nearly destroyed her. It was a bad time for her, anyway. Yet another of her rivals had been cast as a cygnet in *Swan Lake,* and so, four years after having been enlisted by Balanchine as a seventeen-year-old of great promise, she had yet to rise out of the corps and it didn't look to her now as though she ever would. And how she worked to be the best! Her art was everything, a point of view no less beguiling to me than the large painted gypsy-girl eyes and the small unpainted she-monkey face, and those elegant, charming tableaux she could achieve, even when engaged in something so aesthetically unpromising as, half asleep in the middle of the night, taking a lonely pee in my bathroom. When we were first introduced in New York, I knew nothing about ballet and had never seen a real dancer on the stage, let alone off. An Army friend who'd grown up next door to Betsy in Riverdale had gotten us tickets for a Tchaikovsky extravaganza and then arranged for a girl who was dancing in it to have coffee with us around the corner from the City Center that afternoon. Fresh from rehearsal and enchantingly full of herself, Betsy amused us by recounting the horrors of her self-sacrificing vocation—a cross, as she described it, between the life of a boxer and the life of a nun. And the worrying! She had begun studying at the age of eight and had been worrying ever since about her height and her weight and her ears and her rivals and her injuries and her chances—right now she was in absolute terror about tonight. I myself couldn't see that she had reason to be anxious about anything (least of all those ears), so entranced was I already by the dedication and the glamour. At the theater I unfortunately couldn't remember—once the music had begun and dozens of dancers rushed on stage—whether earlier she had told us that she was one of the girls in lavender with a pink flower in their hair or one of the girls in pink with a lavender flower in their hair, and so I spent most of the evening just trying to find her. Each time I thought that the legs and arms I was watching were Betsy's, I became so elated I wanted to cheer—but then another pack of ten came streaking across the stage and I thought, No, there, *that's* her.

"You were wonderful," I told her afterward. "Yes? Did you like my little solo? It's not actually a solo—it lasts only about fifteen seconds. But I do think it's awfully charming." "Oh, I thought it was terrific," I said, "it seemed like more than fifteen seconds to me."

A year later our artistic and amatory alliance came to an end when I confessed that the mutual friend had not been the first girl to be dragged onto the floor while Betsy was safely off dancing her heart out and I had nighttime hours with nothing to do and nobody to stop me. I had been at this for some time now and, I admitted, it was no way to be treating her. Bold honesty, of course, produced far more terrible results than if I had only confessed to seducing the wily seductress and left it at that; nobody had asked me about anybody else. But carried away by the idea that if I were a perfidious brute, I at least would be a truthful perfidious brute, I was crueler than was either necessary or intended. In a fit of penitential gloom, I fled from New York to Quahsay, where eventually I managed to absolve myself of the sin of lust and the crime of betrayal by watching from behind the blade of the snowplow as it cleared the Colony roads for my solitary and euphoric walks—walks during which I did not hesitate to embrace trees and kneel down and kiss the glistening snow, so bursting was I with a sense of gratitude and freedom and renewal.

Of all this, I told the Lonoffs only the charming part about how we had met and also that now, sadly, my girl friend and I were trying a temporary separation. Otherwise, I portrayed her in such uxorious detail that, along with the unnerving sense that I might be laying it on a little thick for this old married couple, I wound up in wonder at the idiot I had been to relinquish her love. Describing all her sterling qualities, I had, in fact, brought myself nearly to the point of grief, as though instead of wailing with pain and telling me to leave and never come back, the unhappy dancer had died in my arms on our wedding day.

Hope Lonoff said, "I knew that she was a dancer from the *Saturday Review*."

The *Saturday Review* had published an article on America's young, unknown writers, photographers and thumbnail sketches of "A Dozen to Keep Your Eye On," selected by the editors of the major literary quarterlies. I had been photographed playing with Nijinsky, our cat. I had confessed to the interviewer that my "friend" was with the New York City Ballet, and when asked to name the three living writers I admired most, I had listed E. I. Lonoff first.

I was disturbed now to think that this must have been the first Lonoff had heard of me—though, admittedly, while answering the interviewer's impossible questions, I had been hoping that my comment might bring my work to his attention. The morning the magazine apeared on the newsstands I must have read the bit about "N. Zuckerman" fifty times over. I tried to put in my self-prescribed six hours at the typewriter but got nowhere, what with picking up the article and looking at my picture every five minutes. I don't know what I expected to see revealed there—the future probably, the titles of my first ten books—but I do remember thinking that this photograph of an intense and serious young writer playing so gently with a kitty cat, and said to be living in a five-flight Village walk-up with a young ballerina, might inspire any number of thrilling women to want to try to take her place.

"I would never have allowed that to appear," I said, "if I had realized how it was all going to come out. They interviewed me for an hour and then what they used of what I said was nonsense."

"Don't apologize," said Lonoff.

"Don't indeed," said his wife, smiling at me. "What's wrong with having your picture in the paper?"

"I didn't mean the picture—though that, too. I never knew they were going to use the one of me with the cat. I expected they'd use the one at the typewriter. I should have realized they couldn't show everybody at a typewriter. The girl who came around to take the pictures"—and whom I had tried unsuccessfully to throw onto the floor—"said she'd just take the picture of the cat for Betsy and me."

"Don't apologize," Lonoff repeated, "unless you know for sure you're not going to do it again next time. Otherwise, just do it and forget it. Don't make a production out of it."

Hope said, "He only means he understands, Nathan. He has the highest respect for what you are. We don't have visitors unless they're people Manny respects. He has no tolerance for people without substance."

"Enough," said Lonoff.

"I just don't want Nathan to resent you for superiority feelings you don't have."

"My wife would have been happier with a less exacting companion."

"But you *are* less exacting," she said, "with everyone but yourself. Nathan, you don't have to defend yourself. Why shouldn't you enjoy your first bit of recognition? Who deserves it more than a gifted young man like yourself? Think of all the worthless people held up for our esteem every day: movie stars, politicians, athletes. Because you can happen to be a writer doesn't mean you have to deny yourself the ordinary human pleasure of being praised and applauded."

"Ordinary human pleasures have nothing to do with it. Ordinary human pleasures be damned. The young man wants to be an artist."

"Sweetheart," she replied, "you must sound to Nathan so—so unyielding. And you're really not that way at all. You're the most forgiving and understanding and modest person I have ever known. Too modest."

"Let's forget how I sound and have dessert."

"But you are the kindest person. He is, Nathan. You've met Amy, haven't you?"

"Miss Bellette?"

"Do you know all he's done for her? She wrote him a letter when she was sixteen years old. In care of his publisher. The most charming, lively letter—so daring, so brash. She told him her story, and instead of forgetting it, he wrote her back. He has always written people back—a polite note even to the fools."

"What was her story?" I asked.

"Displaced," said Lonoff. "Refugee." That seemed to him to suffice, though not to the wagon-train wife, who surprised me now by the way that she pressed on. Was it the little bit of wine that had gone to her head? Or was there not something seething in her?

"She said she was a highly intelligent, creative, and charming sixteen-year-old who was now living with a not very intelligent, creative, or charming family in Bristol, England. She even included her IQ," Hope said. "No, no, that was the second letter. Anyway, she said she wanted a new start in life and she thought the man whose wonderful story she'd read in her school anthology—"

"It wasn't an anthology, but you might as well keep going."

Hope tried her luck with a self-effacing smile, but the wattage was awfully dim. "I think I can talk about this without help. I'm only relating the facts, and calmly enough, I had thought. Because the story was in a magazine, and not in an anthology, doesn't mean that I have lost control of myself. Furthermore, Amy is not the subject, not by any means. The subject is your extraordinary kindness and charity. Your concern for anyone in need—anyone except yourself, and your needs."

"Only my 'self,' as you like to call it, happens not to exist in the everyday sense of the word. Consequently, you may stop lavishing praise upon it. And worrying about its 'needs.' "

"But your self *does* exist. It has a perfect *right* to exist—and in the everyday sense!"

"Enough," he suggested again.

With that, she rose to begin to clear the dishes for dessert, and all at once a wineglass struck the wall. Hope had thrown it. "Chuck me out," she cried, "I want you to chuck me out. Don't tell me you can't, because you must! I want you to! I'll finish the dishes, then chuck me out, tonight! I beg of you—I'd rather live and die alone, I'd rather endure that than another moment of your bravery! I cannot take any more moral fiber in the face of life's disappointments! Not yours and not mine! I cannot bear having a loyal, dignified husband who has no illusions about himself *one second more!*"

My heart, of course, was pounding away, though not entirely because the sound of glass breaking and the sight of a disappointed woman, miserably weeping, was new to me. It was about a month old. On our last morning together Betsy had broken every dish of the pretty little Bloomingdale's set that we owned in common, and then, while I hesitated about leaving my apartment without making my position clear, she started in on the glassware. The hatred for me I had inspired by telling the whole truth had me particularly confused. If only I had lied, I thought—if only I had said that the friend who had intimated I might not be trustworthy was a troublemaking bitch, jealous of Betsy's success and not a little crazy, none of this would be happening. But then, if I had lied to her, I would have *lied* to her. Except that what I would have said about the friend would in essence have been true! I didn't get it. Nor did Betsy when I tried to calm her down and explain what a swell fellow I actually was to have been so candid about it all. It was here, in fact, that she set about destroying the slender drinking glasses, a set of six from Sweden that we had bought to replace the jelly jars on a joyous quasi-connubial outing some months earlier at Bonniers (bought along with the handsome Scandinavian throw rug onto which, in due course, I had tried to drag the photographer from the *Saturday Review*).

Hope Lonoff had now slumped back into her chair, the better to plead with her husband across the table. Her face was patched with blotches where she had been digging at the soft, creased skin in a fit of self-abasement. The frantic, agitated movement of her fingers alarmed me more even than the misery of her voice, and I wondered if I shouldn't reach over and pick up the serving fork from the table before she turned the prongs into her bosom and gave Lonoff's "self" the freedom to pursue what she thought it needed. But as I was only a guest—as I was "only" just about anything you could think of—I left all cutlery where it was and waited for the worst.

"Take her, Manny. If you want her, take her," she cried, "and then you won't be so miserable, and everything in the world won't be so bleak. She's not a student any more—she's a woman! You are *entitled* to her—you rescued her from oblivion, you are more than entitled: it's the only thing that makes sense! Tell her to accept that job, tell her to stay! She should! And I'll move away! Because I cannot live another moment as your jailer! Your nobility is eating away the last thing that is left! You are a monument and can take it and take it—but I'm down to nothing, darling, and I can't. Chuck me out! Please, now, before your goodness and your wisdom kill us both!"

Lonoff and I sat talking together in the living room after dinner, each sipping with admirable temperance at the tablespoonful of cognac he had divided between two large snifters. I had so far experienced brandy only as a stopgap household remedy for toothache: a piece of absorbent cotton, soaked in the stuff, would be pressed against my throbbing gum until my parents could get me to the dentist. I accepted Lonoff's offer, however, as though it accorded with my oldest post-prandial custom. The comedy thickened when my host, another big drinker, went to look for the right glasses. After a systematic search he finally found them at the rear of the bottom cabinet in the foyer breakfront. "A gift," he explained, "I thought they were still in the box," and took two into the kitchen to wash away dust that seemed to have been accumulating since the time of Napoleon, whose name was on the sealed brandy bottle. While he was at it he decided to wash the four other glasses in the set, and put them back in hiding in the breakfront before rejoining me to begin our merrymaking at the hearth.

Not much later—in all, maybe twenty minutes after he had refused to respond in any way to her plea to be replaced by Amy Bellette—Hope could be heard in the kitchen, washing the dishes that Lonoff and I had silently cleared from the table following her departure. She seemed to have gotten down from their bedroom by a back stairway—probably so as not to disturb our conversation.

While helping him to clear up, I had not known what to do about her broken wineglass or about the saucer she inadvertently had knocked to the floor when she rushed from the table. My duty as ingenue was clearly to spare

the stout man in the business suit from bending over, especially as he was
E. I. Lonoff; on the other hand, I was still trying to get through by pretending that nothing shocking had happened in my presence. To keep the tantrum
in perspective, he might even prefer that the broken bits be left where they
were for Hope to clean up later, provided she did not first commit suicide in
their room.

Even as my sense of moral niceties and my youthful cowardice battled it
out with my naïveté, Lonoff, groaning slightly from the effort, brushed the
glass into a dustpan and retrieved the saucer from beneath the dining table. It
had broken neatly in two, and after inspecting the edges he observed, "She
can glue it."

In the kitchen he left the dish for her to repair on a long wooden
counter where pink and white geraniums were growing in clay pots beneath
the windows. The kitchen was a bright, pretty room, a little cheerier and livelier looking than the rest of the house. Besides the geraniums flowering
abundantly here even in winter, tall reeds and dried flowers were stuck all
about in pitchers and vases and little odd-shaped bottles. The windowed wall
cupboards were bright and homey and reassuring: food staples labeled with
unimpeachable brand names—enough Bumble Bee tuna for an Eskimo family to survive on in their igloo till spring—and jars of tomatoes, beans, pears,
crabapples, and the like, which seemed to have been put up by Hope herself.
Pots and pans with shining copper bottoms hung in rows from a pegboard
beside the stove, and along the wall above the breakfast table were half a
dozen pictures in plain wooden frames, which turned out to be short nature
poems signed "H.L.," copied in delicate calligraphy and decorated with watercolor designs. It did indeed look to be the headquarters of a woman who,
in her own unostentatious way, could glue anything and do anything, except
figure out how to make her husband happy.

We talked about literature and I was in heaven—also in a sweat from the
spotlight he was giving me to bask in. Every book new to me I was sure he
must have annotated with his reading pen long ago, yet his interest was
pointedly in hearing my thoughts, not his own. The effect of his concentrated attention was to make me heap insight onto precocious insight, and
then to hang upon his every sigh and grimace, investing what was only a little bout of after-dinner dyspepsia with the direst implications about my taste
and my intelligence. Though I worried that I was trying too hard to sound
like the kind of deep thinker for whom he had no love, I still couldn't stop
myself, under the spell now not just of the man and his accomplishment but
of the warm wood fire, of the brandy snifter balanced in my hand (if not yet
the brandy), and of the snow falling heavily beyond the cushioned windowseats, as dependably beautiful and mystifying as ever. Then there were the
great novelists, whose spellbinding names I chanted as I laid my cross-cul-
tural comparisons and brand-new eclectic enthusiasms at his feet—Zucker-

man, with Lonoff, discussing Kafka: I couldn't quite get it, let alone get over it. And then there was his dinner-table toast. It still gave me a temperature of a hundred and five each time I remembered it. To myself I swore that I would struggle for the rest of my life to deserve it. And wasn't that why he'd proposed it, this pitiless new master of mine?

"I've just finished reading Isaac Babel," I told him.

He considered this, impassively.

"I was thinking, for sport more or less, that he is the missing link; those stories are what connect you, if you don't mind my mentioning your work—"

He crossed his hands on his belly and rested them there, movement enough to make me say, "I'm sorry."

"Go ahead. Connected to Babel. How?"

"Well, 'connected' of course isn't the right word. Neither is 'influence.' It's family resemblance that I'm talking about. It's as though, as I see it, you are Babel's American cousin—and Felix Abravanel is the other. You through 'The Sin of Jesus' and something in *Red Cavalry,* through the ironical dreaming and the blunt reporting, and, of course, through the writing itself. Do you see what I mean? There's a sentence in one of his war stories: 'Voroshilov combed his horse's mane with his Mauser.' Well, that's just the kind of thing that you do, a stunning little picture in every line. Babel said that if he ever wrote his autobiography he'd call it *The Story of an Adjective.* Well, if it were possible to imagine you writing your autobiography—if such a thing were even imaginable—you might come up with that title too. No?"

"And Abravanel?"

"Oh, with Abravanel it's Benya Krik and the Odessa mob: the gloating, the gangsters, all those gigantic types. It isn't that he throws in his sympathy with the brutes—it isn't that in Babel, either. It's their awe of them. Even when they're appalled, they're in awe. Deep reflective Jews a little lovesick at the sound of all that un-Talmudic bone crunching. Sensitive Jewish sages, as Babel says, dying to climb trees."

" 'In my childhood I led the life of a sage, when I grew up I started climbing trees.' "

"Yes, that's the line," said I, expecting no less but still impressed. On I went. "Look at Abravanel's *Properly Scalded.* Movie moguls, union moguls, racketeer moguls, women who are moguls just with their breasts—even the down and out bums who used to be moguls, talking like moguls of the down and out. It's Babel's fascination with big-time Jews, with conscienceless Cossacks, with everybody who has it his own way. The Will as the Big Idea. Except Babel doesn't come off so lovable and enormous himself. That's not how he sees things. He is a sort of Abravanel with the self-absorption drained away. And if you drain away enough, well, in the end you arrive at Lonoff."

"And what about you?"

"Me?"

"Yes. You haven't finished. Aren't you a New World cousin in the Babel clan, too? What is Zuckerman in all of this?"

"Why—nothing. I've only published the four stories that I sent you. My relationship is nonexistent. I think I'm still at the point where my relationship to my *own* work is practically nonexistent."

So I said, and quickly reached for my glass so as to duck my disingenuous face and take a bitter drop of brandy on my tongue. But Lonoff had read my designing mind, all right; for when I came upon Babel's description of the Jewish writer as a man with autumn in his heart and spectacles on his nose, I had been inspired to add, "and blood in his penis," and had then recorded the words like a challenge—a flaming Dedalian formula to ignite *my* soul's smithy.

"What else?" Lonoff asked. "Come on, don't get bashful. This is enjoyable. Talk, please."

"About—?"

"All these books you read."

"Your books included or excluded?" I asked him.

"Suit yourself."

I said, "I think of you as the Jew who got away."

"And does that help?"

"There's *some* truth in it, isn't there? You got away from Russia and the pogroms. You got away from the purges—and Babel didn't. You got away from Palestine and the homeland. You got away from Brookline and the relatives. You got away from New York—"

"And all of this is recorded where? Hedda Hopper?"

"Some there. The rest I pieced together myself."

"To what end?"

"When you admire a writer you become curious. You look for his secret. The clues to his puzzle."

"But New York—I was there for three months over twenty years ago. Who told you I got away from New York?"

"Some of the Jews down there you got away from."

"I was there for three months and I think I got a word in only once. What word I don't remember, but suddenly I belonged to a faction."

"That's why you left?"

"Also, there was the girl I'd fallen in love with and married. She wasn't happy."

"Why not?"

"Same as me. Those were terrifying intellectual personalities even back then. Real ideological Benya Kriks, even in their diapers. I didn't have enough strong opinions to last me down there through a year. My Hope had even fewer."

"So you came back here, you got away for good."

"From Jews? Not altogether. The game warden tells me there are some more up in these woods besides me. But you're more or less right. It's the deer in their fields that drive the farmers crazy, not the few of us they see around here in caftans. But where's the secret, Nathan? What's the puzzle?"

"Away from all Jews, and a story by you without a Jew in it is unthinkable. The deer, the farmers, the game warden—"

"And don't forget Hope. And my fair-haired children."

"And still all you write about are Jews."

"Proving what?"

"That," I said, cautiously, "is what I'd like to ask you."

He thought about it for a moment. "It proves why the young rabbi in Pittsfield can't live with the idea that I won't be 'active.' "

I waited for more, but in vain.

"Do you know Abravanel?" I asked.

"Nathan, surely by now you get the picture."

"What picture?"

"I don't know anybody. I turn sentences around, and that's it. Why would Abravanel want to know me? I put him to sleep. He spoke at Amherst last spring. An invitation arrived so we drove over to hear him. But that's the only time we've ever met. Before the lecture he came down the aisle to where I was sitting and introduced himself. He was very flattering. My respectful younger colleague. Afterward we had a drink with him and his actress. A very polished fellow. The satirist you don't really see till you catch the commedia dell'arte profile. There's where the derision lives. Head-on he's something of a heartthrob. Bombay black eyes, and so on. And the young Israeli wife is like lava. The Gentile dream of the melon-breasted Jewess. And the black head of coarse, curly hair—the long female version of his. You could polish a pot with it. They tell me that when she played in the big movie of the Bible she stole the show from the Creation. So there were those two, and there was I with Hope. And with this," he said, once more lightly laying his hands on his belly. "I understand he does a humorous imitation of me for his friends. No harm intended. One of my former students ran into him in Paris. He'd just addressed a full house at the Sorbonne. I'm told that upon hearing my name he referred to me as 'the complete man—as unimpressive as he is unimpressed.' "

"You don't like him much."

"I'm not in the business. 'Liking people' is often just another racket. But you're right to think well of his books. Not up my alley maybe, all that vanity face to face, but when he writes he's not just a little Houyhnhnm tapping out his superiority with his hooves. More like a Dr. Johnson eating opium— the disease of his life makes Abravanel fly. I admire the man, actually. I admire what he puts his nervous system through. I admire his passion for the front-row seat. Beautiful wives, beautiful mistresses, alimony the size of the national debt, polar expeditions, war-front reportage, famous friends, famous enemies, breakdowns, public lectures, five-hundred-page novels every third year, and still, as you said before, time and energy left over for all that self-absorption. The gigantic types in the books *have* to be that big to give him something to think about to rival himself. Like him? No. But impressed, oh yes. Absolutely. It's no picnic up there in the egosphere. I don't know when the man sleeps, or if he has ever slept, aside from those few minutes when he had that drink with me."

Outside, it was like a silent-film studio, where they made snowstorms by hurling mattress wadding into a wind machine. Large, ragged snowclots raced across the window, and when I heard their icy edges nicking at the glass—and the sounds of someone puttering in the kitchen—I remembered Lonoff's wife begging to be discarded, and wondered if the plea would have been quite so thoroughgoing on a sunny spring day. "I think I better get the taxi," I said, pointing to my watch, "so as to catch the last bus back."

Of course, I wanted never to leave. True, while Hope was falling apart at the dinner table I had momentarily found myself wishing for my cabin at Quahsay; now, however, the way the crisis seemed magically to have resolved itself served only to intensify my awe of Lonoff, particularly for what he unblushingly had called *my own kind of bravery*. If only I had thought to take his approach when *Betsy* had gone wild; if only I had kept my mouth shut until she finished berating me, then swept up the broken crockery and settled into my chair to read another book! Now, why didn't I? Because I was twenty-three and he was fifty-six? Or because I was guilty and he was innocent? Yes, his authority, and the rapid restoration of household sanity and order, might well owe something to that. "Take her! It's the only thing that makes sense!" cried Hope, and Lonoff's easy victory seemed to reside in never even having wanted to.

I also hated calling a taxi because of Amy Bellette. I was hoping, a little crazily, that when she came back from dinner with the college librarian, she would offer to drive me through the storm to my bus. Earlier, while Lonoff was measuring out the brandy—concentrating like a bartender who'd trained at Los Alamos with fissionable fifths—I had asked where she went. I hadn't the nerve to inquire about her status as a displaced person. But at the table, when he'd said that she had come to Athene as a refugee, I was reminded of "the children starving in Europe" whom we had heard so much about when we were children eating in New Jersey. If Amy had been one of them, perhaps that explained the something in her that seemed to me thwarted and underdeveloped, despite the dazzling maturity and severe good looks. I wondered if the dark refugee girl with the curious name Bellette could be Jewish, and in Europe had suffered from worse than starvation.

"Yes," said Lonoff, "you'd better call the taxi."

Reluctantly I stood to go.

"Or, if you like," he said, "you can stay over and sleep in the study."

"No, I think I really have to be off," I said, and cursed the upbringing that had taught me never to be greedy about second helpings, How much better if I had been raised in the gutter! Only how would I have gotten from the gutter to here?

"Suit yourself," Lonoff told me.

"I wouldn't want to inconvenience your wife."

"I think it will disturb her more if you leave than if you stay. She might hold herself responsible. I'm certain she would."

I pretended I had taken my dinner on the moon. "But why?"

"Sit down. Stay for breakfast, Nathan."

"I'd better not. I shouldn't."

"You know who Jimmy Durante is?"

"Of course."

"Do you know the old Durante number 'Did you ever have the feeling that you wanted to go, still have the feeling that you wanted to stay'?"

"Yes."

"Sit."

I sat—suiting myself, as the man said.

"Besides," he told me, "if you go now, you'll leave most of your cognac."

"If I go, so will you."

"Well, the Jew who got away didn't get away altogether." He smiled at me. "You don't have to finish it, just because you're staying. That's not part of the deal."

"No, no, I want to," I said, and took my biggest sip of the night. Saluting me with his glass, he followed suit.

"Hope will be pleased," he said. "She misses people. She misses the children and their friends. She went to art school in Boston before I brought her back here, sixteen versts to the nearest railway station. Manhattan terrified her, but Boston's her Moscow, she'd move there tomorrow. She thinks I would enjoy it in Cambridge. But all I need are those dinner parties. I'd rather talk to the horse."

"You have a horse?"

"No."

I loved him! Yes, nothing less than love for this man with no illusions: love for the bluntness, the scrupulosity, the severity, the estrangement; love for the relentless winnowing out of the babyish, preening, insatiable self; love for the artistic mulishness and the suspicion of nearly everything else; and love for the buried charm, of which he'd just given me a glimpse. Yes, all Lonoff had to say was that he did not even have the horse to talk to and somehow that did it, released in me a son's girlish love for the man of splen-

did virtue and high achievement who understands life, and who understands
the son, and who approves.

I should mention here that some three years earlier, after several hours in the
presence of Felix Abravanel, I had been no less overcome. But if I did not fall
at his feet straightaway, it was because even a college senior as writer-wor-
shipping as myself could see that with Abravanel such boundless adoration—
at least if offered up by a youthful male admirer—was doomed to go unre-
quited. The ardor of those books, composed in the sunny stillness of his
California canyon and seething with unbuttoned and aggressive innocence,
seemed to have little to do with the author himself when he came coolly out
into the fallen world he'd been so ardent about down in the canyon. In fact,
the writer who found irresistible all vital and dubious types, not excluding
the swindlers of both sexes who trampled upon the large hearts of his opti-
mistic, undone heroes; the writer who could locate the hypnotic core in the
most devious American self-seeker and lead him to disclose, in spirited locu-
tions all his own, the depths of his conniving soul; the writer whose absorption with "the grand human discord" made his every paragraph a little novel
in itself, every page packed as tight as Dickens or Dostoevsky with the latest
news of manias, temptations, passions, and dreams, with mankind aflame
with feeling—well, in the flesh he gave the impression of being out to lunch.
    Which isn't to suggest that Felix Abravanel lacked charm. On the con-
trary, the charm was like a moat so oceanic that you could not even see the
great turreted and buttressed thing it had been dug to protect. You couldn't
even find the drawbridge. He was like California itself—to get there you had
to take a plane. There were moments during his public lecture—this was at
Chicago, my last year there—when Abravanel had to pause at the lectern,
seemingly to suppress saying something off the cuff that would have been
just too charming for his audience to bear. And he was right. We might have
charged the stage to eat him up alive if he had been any more sly and enchanting and wise. Poor marvelous Abravanel (I mean this without satire)—even what was intended to guard the great rose window of his inner
brilliance was itself so damn beautiful that the ungifted multitudes and art
lovers of the world could not but find him all the more alluring. On the
other hand, maybe he wanted it that way. There is obviously no simple way
to be great, or so I was beginning to find out.
    After the lecture I had been invited to come along to a faculty-club re-
ception by the professor whose protégé I was. When we were able at last to
break through the rings of admirers, I was introduced as the student whose
story would be discussed the next morning in the class Abravanel had consented to visit. From the dash of imperiousness in the photographed face I
had never envisioned him quite so guarded-looking, or with a head a good
size and a half too small for the six-foot plank that supported it. He reminded

me, amid all those who would flatter and adore him, of a radio tower with its tiny red light burning high up to warn off low-flying aircraft. He wore a five-hundred-dollar shantung suit, a burgundy silk tie, and gleaming narrow black tasseled loafers, but everything that counted, all that made for the charm and the laughs and the books and the breakdowns, was stored compactly right up there at the top—at the edge of a precipice. It was a head that the Japanese technicians, with their ingenuity for miniaturizing, might have designed, and then given over to the Jews to adorn with the rug dealer's thinning dark hair, the guarded appraising black eyes, and a tropical bird's curving bill. A fully Semiticized little transistor on top, terrific clothes down below—and still the overall impression was of somebody's stand-in.

I thought, In the novels nothing ever seems to get by him, so how come when he's here, he's not? Perhaps so much assails him that he has to close down ninety percent of himself to phenomena in order not to explode. Though then again, I thought, maybe he's just out to lunch.

Abravanel shook my hand obligingly and was about to turn away to shake another obligingly when the professor repeated my name. "Of course," said Abravanel, "N. Zuckerman." He had read a mimeographed copy of my story on the plane from the Coast; so had Andrea read it. "Sweetheart," he said, "this is Zuckerman."

Well, where to begin? Andrea had maybe only five years on me, but five years put to good use. After graduating from Sarah Lawrence, she had evidently continued her education at Elizabeth Arden and Henri Bendel. As we all knew—her fame having preceded her—Andrea's father had been a dollar-a-year man in the first Roosevelt Administration, and Mother was Carla Peterson Rumbough, the loquacious liberal congresswoman from Oregon. While still a college student she had written the first of her portraits of "Men in Power" for *The Saturday Evening Post,* the series eventually collected in her best-selling book. Undoubtedly (as the envious were quick enough to point out), family contacts had got her going, but clearly what encouraged those busy and powerful men to keep on talking was the proximity of Andrea herself, for Andrea was a most juicy girl. Truly, you felt that if you pressed her, you could drink a glassful of refreshing, healthy Andrea for breakfast.

At the time, she was in residence with Abravanel at his Pacific Palisades retreat, a few miles from the home of his friend and mentor, Thomas Mann. ("The grand human discord" was how Mann had perceived Abravanel's subject in the elevating preface with which he had consecrated the German edition of *Properly Scalded.*) After Abravanel's latest divorce (and rumored emotional collapse), Andrea had come to interview him for the *Post* series and, as transcontinental literary legend had it, had never left. Legend also had it that Abravanel was not only the first man of letters to be named a man of power in America but the first man of power to whose advances Andrea had yielded. I myself wondered if maybe Andrea wasn't the first journalist to whose advances Abravanel had yielded. He looked more like the one who would have had to be seduced.

"How terrific finally to meet you," Andrea said, briskly shaking my hand. The briskness of the handshake was in disarming contrast with the soft voluptuous appearance. The face was heart-shaped and gentle, but the handshake said, "Have no doubts, I am the girl who has everything." Not that I was about to argue. I was already convinced a month before laying eyes on her, when we had exchanged letters about hotel accommodations. As student representative of the University Lecture Committee, I had, per her instructions, reserved a room in their two names at the Windermere, the closest the neighborhood had to a grand hotel. "Mr. Abravanel and Miss Rumbough?" the desk clerk had asked. "Are they husband and wife, sir?" This question was put to me, mind you, in March of 1953, and so when I answered with the lie that I had devised to shelter a hero from scandal—"Mrs. Abravanel is the well-known journalist; that of course is her professional name"—I was sure that the end result of Miss A. Rumbough's bohemian daring would be my expulsion from college without a degree.

"I loved your story," she said. "It's *so* funny."

Grimly I acknowledged the compliment tendered my wit by the bosomy girl with the heart-shaped face and the milkmaid complexion and the soldierly self-assured grip. In the meantime, having passed me on to Andrea to dispose of, Abravanel found himself being exhibited by another of our professors to a huddle of graduate students waiting shyly beside their teacher to ask the writer serious questions. "Oh, well," I heard him say, with a light annihilating laugh, "I don't have the time these days to think about 'influences'—Andrea keeps me pretty much on the run." "Felix," she was telling me, "is nuts about the story, too. You should have seen him on the plane. He just kept throwing back his head and laughing. Where are you going to publish it? Maybe Felix ought to talk to—" She mentioned a name. It was Knebel, but for one whose stories had appeared previously only in the college literary quarterly, the effect would have been no more stunning if she had said, "After the reception I have to get back to the hotel to interview Marshal Tito in the bar—but while I do, Felix can rise unto Heaven from the lobby and discuss your funny little mimeographed story with the author of *The Brothers Karamazov*. We all met in Siberia when Felix and I did the prison tour." Somewhere behind me I heard Abravanel applying himself to another serious question from the graduate division. "Alienation? Oh," he said, with that light laugh, "let the other guy be alienated." Simultaneously Andrea informed me, "He's seeing Sy tomorrow night in New York—" (Sy being Knebel, the editor for twenty years of the New York intellectual quarterly that I had been devouring for the past two).

The next day Abravanel visited our advanced-writing class, accompanied—to the surprise of those ready to live only for art—by the bold Andrea.

Her luminous, shameless presence in the very front row (and her white jersey dress; and her golden hair, out of some rustic paradise) led me to recall October afternoons half a lifetime ago when I sat like a seething prisoner, practicing my penmanship at my sloping school desk while the World Series was being broadcast live to dinky radios in every gas station in America. It was then that I learned what tore at the hearts of the delinquents and the dummies who loathed the classroom and the teacher and wished the whole place would burn down.

Hands plunged ito his pockets, and angled casually against the professor's desk, Abravanel spoke of my story with oblique admiration, defending it, largely with his laugh, from criticism brought by the orthodox Forsterites that my narrator was "two-dimensional" instead of being "round" like the characters they'd read about in *Aspects of the Novel*. But that day to all carping I was immune. *Andrea,* I thought, whenever one of those fools said "round."

Afterward I was invited by Abravanel for a cup of coffee at a local luncheonette, along with Andrea, my professor, and a member of the sociology department, an old friend from Abravanel's youth who had been waiting outside the classroom door to give Abravanel a nostalgic hug (which the author managed graciously to accept even while backing away). Abravanel had extended the invitation personally (as I was to write my parents) and with what sounded for the first time like real sympathy: "They're a rough bunch, Zuckerman. You better come along for a transfusion." I figured he would tell me over the cup of coffee that he was taking his copy of my story to New York to show to Seymour Knebel. For a hundred reasons I was in ecstasy. When he told me to come along for my transfusion, I could not remember having *myself* ever felt like such a round character before. What Mann had done for him he was about to do for me. Literary history in the making. Good thing Andrea was there to get it all down for posterity.

But over his coffee Abravanel said not a word: just leaned his long demi-emaciated frame back in his chair, looking smooth and strokable as a cat in his teaching attire of soft gray flannel slacks, a light mauve pullover, and a cashmere sports coat. With hands and ankles elegantly crossed, he left it to his buoyant young companion to do the talking—lively, funny stories, mostly, about Felix's old father, an L.A. housepainter, and the winning remarks he made to her in his homely mix of two languages. Even the sociology professor was bowled over, though from campus gossip I knew he was a dear friend of Abravanel's litigious first wife and disapproved of the writer's treatment of her, first in the flesh, then in fiction. Moreover, he was said to disapprove of Abravanel's way with women generally and, on top of that, believed that a novelist of his stature oughtn't to have articles about himself in *The Saturday Evening Post*. Yet now the sociology professor began lifting his voice so as to get Andrea to hear him. As a boy, he also had been a great fan of Felix's father's malapropisms, and he wanted it known. " 'That fellow,' " shouted the sociologist, imitating the elder Abravanel, " 'he ain't here no more—poor guy committed suitcase.' " If Abravanel thought the retired housepainter was so impressive for speaking cockeyed English all his life, he didn't let on. So genteel and assured and courtly was the posture he'd assumed to listen to Andrea tell her stories that I found myself doubting it. Out in the open, Abravanel's cup did not spill over with sentiment for the old days in L.A.; such effusions he left to readers of his novels who had come to love the super-charged emotional world of his childhood as though it had been their own. He himself seemed to prefer to look down at us from a long way off, like a llama or a camel.

"Good luck" was what he said to me when they got up to catch the New York train—and Andrea said even less. This time, because we knew each other, she took my hand in five soft fingers, but the touch of the fairy princess seemed to mean much the same to me as the garrison handshake at the faculty-club reception. She's forgotten, I thought, about Knebel. Or maybe she's told Abravanel and figured he'd take care of it, and he's forgotten. Or maybe she's told him and he said, "Forget it." Watching her leave the luncheonette on Abravanel's arm—seeing her hair brush his shoulder as out on the street she rose on her toes to whisper something into his ear—I realized that they'd had other things than my story to think about when they got back to the Windermere the night before.

All of this was why, from Quahsay, I had mailed my four published stories to Lonoff. Felix Abravanel was clearly not in the market for a twenty-three-year-old son.

Just before nine, having checked the time on his watch, Lonoff drank up his last drop of brandy, which had sat thirty minutes at the bottom of the glass. He said that though he must be off, I might stay in the living room and listen to music, or, if I preferred, I could retire to his study, where I would be sleeping. Beneath the corduroy cover I would find that the study daybed was already made up with fresh linen. Blankets and an extra pillow were in the closet there, on the bottom shelf, and fresh towels were in the downstairs-bathroom cupboard—please, I mustn't hesitate to use the striped ones, they were the least worn and best for a shower—and also in the cupboard, at the rear of the second shelf, I would find a toothbrush in its original unopened plastic case, and a small new tube of Ipana. Any questions?

"No."

Was there anything else that I would need?

"Thank you, this is all perfect."

He winced when he stood—lumbago, he explained, from turning one too many sentences around that day—and said that he still had his evening's reading. He did not do justice to a writer unless he read him on consecutive days and for no less than three hours at a sitting. Otherwise, despite his note-taking and underlining, he lost touch with a book's inner life and might as well not have begun. Sometimes, when he unavoidably had to miss a day, he would go back and begin all over again, rather than be nagged by his sense that he was wronging a serious author.

He told me all this in the same fastidious way he had described the location of the toothpaste and towels: a blunt, colloquial, pointedly ungrandiloquent Lonoff seemed to take turns with a finicky floorwalker Lonoff as official representative to the unwritten world.

"My wife considers this a grave affliction," he added. "I don't know how to relax. Soon she'll be telling me to go out and have a good time."

"Not that soon," I said.

"It's only as it should be," he said, "for somebody else to think I'm a fool. But I can't afford the luxury myself. How else am I supposed to read a book of real depth? For 'enjoyment'? For the hell of it—to put me to sleep?" Wearily—more ready for bed, I would have thought from the tired, irascible tone, than for one hundred and eighty minutes concentrating on the inner life of a deep book by a serious author—he asked, "How else am I to conduct my life?"

"How else would you like to?"

Well, I had done it, escaped at last from wooden self-consciousness and egregious overearnestness—and sporadic attempts to be witty in the Lonovian mode—and put to him a direct, simple question, the answer to which I wanted very much to hear.

"How else might I like to?"

It thrilled me to see him standing there taking altogether seriously what I had asked. "Yes. How would you live now, if you had your way?"

Rubbing at the small of his back, he replied, "I would live in a villa outside Florence."

"Yes? With whom?"

"A woman, of course." He answered without hesitation, as though I were another grown man.

So, as though I were one, I went ahead and asked, "How old would she be, this woman?"

He smiled down at me. "We have both had too much to drink."

I showed him that there was brandy enough still to swirl around in my snifter.

"For us," he added, and not bothering this time to catch the trouser crease in his fingers, sat back down somewhat gracelessly in his chair.

"Please," I said, "I don't mean to keep you from reading. I'll be fine alone."

"Sometimes," he said, "I like to imagine I've read my last book. And looked for the last time at my watch. How old would you think she should be?" he asked. "The woman in Florence. As a writer, what would be your guess?"

"I think you'll have to ask me to guess that thirty years from now. I don't know."

"I say thirty-five. How does that strike you?"

"As right, if you say so."

"She would be thirty-five and she would make life beautiful for me. She would make life comfortable and beautiful and new. She would drive me in the afternoon to San Gimignano, to the Uffizi, to Siena. In Siena we would visit the cathedral and drink coffee in the square. At the breakfast table she would wear long feminine nightgowns under her pretty robe. They would be things I had bought for her in a shop by the Ponte Vecchio. I would work in a cool stone room with French windows. There would be flowers in a vase. She would cut them and put them there. And so on, Nathan, in this vein."

Most men want to be children again, or kings, or quarterbacks, or multimillionaires. All Lonoff seemed to want was a thirty-five-year-old woman and a year abroad. I thought of Abravanel, that fruit gatherer, and the Israeli actress—"like lava"—who was Abravanel's third wife. And of that rounded character Andrea Rumbough. In whose sea did Andrea bob now? "If that's all . . ." I said.

"Go on. We're having drunken conversation."

"If that's all, it doesn't sound too hard to arrange," I heard myself telling him.

"Oh, yes? What young woman that you know is out looking for a fifty-six-year-old bald man to accompany to Italy?"

"You're not the stereotypical bald man of fifty-six. Italy with you wouldn't be Italy with anyone."

"What does that mean? I'm supposed to cash in the seven books for a piece of ass?"

The unforeseen plunge into street talk made *me* feel momentarily like the boutonniered floorwalker. "That isn't what I meant. Though of course that happens, such things are done. . . ."

"Yes, in New York you must see a lot of it."

"No one with seven books in New York City settles for one piece of ass. That's what you get for a couplet." I had spoken as though I knew what I was talking about. "All I meant was that you're not exactly asking for a harem."

"Like the fat lady said about the polka-dot dress, 'It's nice, but it's not Lonoff.' "

"Why not?"

"Why not?" he repeated, a little scornfully.

"I meant—why couldn't it be?"

"Why should it be?"

"Because—you want it."

His answer: "Not a good enough reason."

I lacked the courage to ask "Why not?" again. If drunk, still only drunk Jews. So far and no further, I was sure. And I was right.

"No," he said, "you don't chuck a woman out after thirty-five years because you'd prefer to see a new face over your fruit juice."

Thinking of his fiction, I had to wonder if he had ever let her in, or the children either, who, he had told me earlier, had provided him with diversion and brought a certain gaiety into his world for so long as they lived at home. In his seven volumes of stories I could not think of a single hero who was not a bachelor, a widower, an orphan, a foundling, or a reluctant fiancé.

"But there's more to it than that," I said. "More to it than the new face . . . isn't there?"

"What, the bed? I had the bed. I know my singularity," said Lonoff, "and what I owe to it." Here, abruptly, he concluded our drunken conversation. "I've got my reading. Let me show you before I go how to work the phonograph. We have an excellent classical record collection. You know about wiping the records? There is a cloth—"

He came heavily to his feet; slowly and heavily, like an elephant. All the obstinacy seemed to have gone out of him, whether owing to our exchange or to the pain in his back—or exhaustion with his singularity—I didn't know. Maybe every day ended like this.

"Mr. Lonoff—Manny," I said, "may I ask you something before you go, while we're alone—about my stories? I don't know if I entirely understood what you meant by 'turbulence.' At dinner. I don't mean to hang on to one word, but any word from you—well, I'd like to be sure I understand it. That is, I'm thrilled just that you read them, and I'm still amazed even to have been invited, and now staying over—all that should be enough. It is enough. And the toast you made"—I felt my emotions getting out of hand, as I had, to my astonishment, while receiving my college diploma with my parents looking on—"I hope I can live up to it. I don't take those words lightly. But about the stories themselves, what I'd like to know is what you think is wrong with them, what you think I might do—to be better?"

How benign was his smile! Even while kneading the lumbago. "Wrong?"

"Yes."

"Look, I told Hope this morning: Zuckerman has the most compelling voice I've encountered in years, certainly for somebody starting out."

"Do I?"

"I don't mean style"—raising a finger to make the distinction. "I mean voice: something that begins at around the back of the knees and reaches well above the head. Don't worry too much about 'wrong.' Just keep going. You'll get there."

There. I tried to envision it, but couldn't. It was more than I could take being *here*.

I told Hope this morning.

Meanwhile, buttoning his jacket and smoothing down his tie—and checking his watch with the glance that ruined his wife's every Sunday—he attended to the last item of business on the agenda. Working the record player. I had interrupted his train of thought.

"I want to show you what happens if the arm doesn't go all the way back at the end of the record."

"Sure," I said, "absolutely."

"It's been acting up lately and nobody is able to fix it. Some days it somehow fixes itself, and then out of the blue it's on the blink again."

I followed him over to the turntable, thinking less about his classical record collection than about my voice starting back of my knees.

"This is the volume, of course. This is the start button. This is the reject, you push it—"

And this, I realized, is the excruciating scrupulosity, the same maddening, meticulous attention to every last detail that makes you great, that keeps you going and got you through and now is dragging you down. Standing with E. I. Lonoff over the disobedient arm of his record player, I understood the celebrated phenomenon for the first time: a man, his destiny, and his work—all one. What a terrible triumph!

"And," he reminded me, "it would be best for the records, and for your own pleasure, if you remember to wipe them first."

Oh, the fussiness, the fastidiousness! The floorwalker incarnate! To wrestle the blessing of his fiction out of that misfortune—"triumph" didn't begin to describe it.

Suddenly I wanted to kiss him. I know this happens to men more often than is reported, but I was new to manhood (about five minutes into it, actually) and was bewildered by the strength of a feeling that I had rarely had toward my own father once I'd begun to shave. It seemed, at the moment, even stronger than what invariably came over me when I was left alone with those long-necked aerial friends of Betsy's, who walked with their feet turned charmingly outward and looked (just like Betsy!) so appetizingly wan and light and liftable. But in this house of forbearance I was better at suppressing my amorous impulses than I had been lately, unchained in Manhattan.

◻ **II** ◻

NATHAN DEDALUS

Who could sleep after that? I didn't even turn the lamp off to try. For the longest time I just stared at E. I. Lonoff's tidy desk: neat piles of typing paper, each stack a different pale color—for different drafts, I assumed. Finally I got up and, sacrilege though it surely was, sat on his typing chair in my undershorts. No wonder his back hurt. It wasn't a chair made for relaxing in, not if you were his size. Lightly I touched my fingers to his portable typewriter keys. Why a portable for a man who went nowhere? Why not a machine on the order of a cannonball, black and big and built to write for all time? Why not a comfortable padded executive's chair to lean back in and think? Why not indeed.

Pinned to the bulletin board beside his desk—the cell's only real embellishments—were a little wall calendar from the local bank and two annotated index cards. One card bore a fragmentary sentence ascribed to "Schumann, on Chopin's Scherzo No. 2 in B flat minor, Op. 31." It read, "... so overflowing with tenderness, boldness, love, and contempt that it may be compared, not inappropriately, to a poem by Byron." I didn't know what to make of it there, or rather, what Lonoff made of it, until I remembered that Amy Bellette could play Chopin with great charm. Maybe it was she who had typed it out for him, scrupulous attribution and all—enclosing it, perhaps, with the gift of a record so that in the late afternoons he could listen to Chopin even when she was no longer around. Perhaps it was this very line she'd been musing upon when I first saw her on the study floor: musing because the description seemed as pertinent to herself as to the music ...

If displaced, what had become of her family? Murdered? Did that explain her "contempt"? But for whom the overflowing love, then? Him? If so, the contempt might well be for Hope. If so, if so.

It required no ingenuity to guess the appeal of the quotation typed on the other card. After what Lonoff had been telling me all evening, I could understand why he might want these sentences hanging over his head while beneath them he sat turning his own sentences around. "We work in the dark—we do what we can—we give what we have. Our doubt is our passion and our passion is our task. The rest is the madness of art." Sentiments ascribed to a story I did not know by Henry James called "The Middle Years." But "the madness of art"? I would have thought the madness of everything but art. The art was what was sane, no? Or was I missing something? Before the night was over I was to read "The Middle Years" twice through, as though preparing to be examined on it in the morning. But that was canon law to me then: ready to write a thousand words on "What does Henry James mean by 'the madness of art'?" if the question should happen to turn up on my paper napkin at breakfast.

Photographs of Lonoff's children were set out on a bookshelf behind the typing chair: one male, two females, not a trace of the paternal genes in any of their bones. One of the girls, a fair, freckled maiden in horn-rimmed glasses, looked, in fact, much as her shy, studious mother probably did back in her art-school days. Beside her photo in the twin frame was a postcard that had been mailed from Scotland to Massachusetts one August day nine years earlier, addressed to the writer alone. This perhaps accounted for its status as a memento to be preserved under glass. Much about his life indicated that communicating with his children had been no easier for him than having enough opinions for Manhattan in the thirties. "Dear Pop, We are now in Banffshire (Highlands) and I am standing amidst the wreck of Balvenie Castle, Dufftown, where Mary Stuart once stayed. Yesterday we biked to Cawdor (Thane of Cawdor, *ca.* 1050, Shakespeare's Macbeth), where Duncan was murdered. See you soon, Love, Becky."

Also directly behind his desk were several shelves of his works in foreign translation. Seating myself on the floor I tried translating from French and German sentences that I had read first in Lonoff's English. With the more exotic tongues the most I could do was try to spot his characters' names in the hundreds of indecipherable pages. Pechter. Marcus. Littman. Winkler. There they were, surrounded on all sides by Finnish.

And which language was hers? Portuguese? Italian? Hungarian? In which did she overflow like a poem by Byron?

On a large lined pad that I took from my briefcase, a bulging *Bildungsroman* briefcase—ten pounds of books, five obscure magazines, and easily enough paper to write the whole of my first novel if it should happen to come to me while riding back and forth on the bus—I began methodically to list everything on his bookshelves I had not read. There was more German philosophy than I had been expecting, and only halfway down the page I already seemed to have sentenced myself to a lifetime at hard labor. But, worthily, I kept going—to the accompaniment of the words with which he had commended me before going up to his reading. That, and the toast, had been echoing in my head for an hour. On a clean sheet of paper I finally wrote down what he'd said so as to see exactly what he'd meant. All he'd meant.

As it turned out, I wanted someone else to see as well, for soon I had forgotten the forthcoming ordeal with Heidegger and Wittgenstein, and was seated with my pad at Lonoff's desk, struggling to explain to my father—the foot-doctor father, the first of my fathers—the "voice" that, according to no less a vocalist than E. I. Lonoff, started back of my knees and reached above my head. The letter was overdue. Three weeks now he had been waiting for some enlightened sign of contrition for the offenses I had begun to commit against my greatest supporters. And for three weeks I had let him stew, if that is how you describe being yourself unable to think of little else upon awakening from bad dreams at 4 A.M.

Our trouble had begun when I gave my father the manuscript of a story based on an old family feud in which he had played peacemaker for nearly two years before the opponents ended up shouting in court. The story was the most ambitious I had written—some fifteen thousand words—and, as I saw it, my motives for sending it to him were no less benign than those I'd had in college, when I mailed home poems for the family to read even before they appeared in the student verse magazine. It wasn't trouble I was looking for but admiration and praise. Out of the oldest and most ingrained of habits, I wanted to please them and make them proud.

That wasn't hard either. For years I had been making him proud just by sending along clippings for his "files," a voluminous accumulation of magazine and newspaper articles—including an unbroken series of transcripts of "America's Town Meeting of the Air"—on what he called "vital issues." Whenever I was home on a visit, my mother, who could repeat herself, would invariably remind me—with her own deeply satisfied look—of the thrill it gave him to say to his patients (after working them around to the vital issue on his mind), "I just got something in the mail this morning on that subject. My son Nathan saw it at college. He's out at the University of Chicago. Straight A's in everything. Went out there when he was sixteen—special program. Well, he saw it in one of the Chicago papers and sent it on for my files."

Oh, what sitting ducks I had for parents! A son of theirs would have had to be a half-wit or a sadist *not* to make them proud. And I was neither; I was dutiful and thoughtful, and too excited with myself in flight to be ungrateful for the boost I'd begun with. Despite the flaming wrangles of my adolescence—weekend night hours, fashions in footwear, the unhygienic high-school hangout, my alleged but ceaselessly disavowed penchant for the last word—we had emerged from our fifty textbook scenes of domestic schism much the same close family bound by the same strong feelings. I'd slammed a lot of doors and declared a few wars, but still I loved them like their child. And whether or not I wholly knew just how extensive the addiction, I was much in need of their love for me, of which I assumed there was an inexhaustible supply. That I couldn't—wouldn't?—assume otherwise goes a long way toward explaining why I was naïve enough to expect nothing more than the usual encouragement for a story that borrowed from our family history instances of what my exemplary father took to be the most shameful and disreputable transgressions of family decency and trust.

The facts I had begun my story with were these:

A great-aunt of mine, Meema Chaya, had left for the education of two fatherless grandsons the pot of money she had diligently hoarded away as a seamstress to Newark's upper crust. When Essie, the widowed mother of the twin boys, attempted to invade the trust to send them from college to medical school, her younger brother, Sidney, who was to inherit the money remaining in Meema Chaya's estate upon conclusion of the boys' higher education, had sued to stop her. For four years Sidney had been waiting for Richard and Robert to graduate from Rutgers—waiting mostly in pool rooms and saloons, to hear the family tell it—so he could buy a downtown parking lot with his legacy. Loudly—his way—Sidney proclaimed that he was not about to postpone the good life just so there could be two more fancy doctors driving Caddies around South Orange. Those in the family who detested Sidney's womanizing and his shady friends immediately lined up in support of the boys and their dignified aspirations, leaving Sidney with a phalanx consisting of his ill-used, timid wife Jenny, and his mysterious Polish tootsie Annie, whose scandalously florid *shmatas* were much discussed, if never once seen, at family weddings, funerals, etc. Also in the phalanx, for all it was worth to him, was me. My admiration was long-standing, dating back to Sidney's Navy days, when he had won four thousand dollars on the homeward journey of the battleship *Kansas,* and was said to have thrown into the South Pacific, for the sharks to dispose of, a Mississippi sore loser who at the end of an all-night poker game had referred to the big winner as a dirty Jew. The lawsuit, whose outcome hinged on how exhaustive Meema Chaya had meant to be in her will with the ringing words "higher education," was eventually decided by the judge—a *goy*—in Sidney's favor, though within only a few years the Raymond Boulevard parking lot bought with his inheritance became such a hot piece of real estate that it was nationalized out from under him by the Mob. For his trouble they gave Sidney a tenth of what it was worth, and shortly thereafter his heart broke like a balloon in the bed of yet another overdressed bimbo not of our persuasion. My cousins Richard and Robert were meanwhile being put through medical school by their iron-willed mother. After she lost the lawsuit, Essie quit her job at a downtown department store and for the next ten years went to work on the road selling shingles and siding. So iron-willed was she that by the time she had finally bought carpeting and venetians for the new offices leased for Richard and Robert in suburban North Jersey, there was hardly a working-class neighborhood in the state that she hadn't left encased in asphalt. Out canvassing one hot afternoon during the twins' internship, Essie had decided to spend an hour in an air-cooled Passaic movie theater. In her thousands of days and nights finding leads and closing deals, this was said to be the first time ever that she stopped to do anything other than eat and call the boys. But now residencies in orthopedics and dermatology were only just around the corner, and the thought of their advent, combined with the August heat, made her just a little light-headed. In the dark movie theater, however, Essie hadn't even time to mop her brow before a fellow in the next seat put his hand on her knee. He must have been a very lonely fellow—it was a very stout knee; nonetheless, she broke the hand for him, at the wrist, with the hammer carried in her purse all these years to protect herself and the future of two fatherless sons. My story, entitled "Higher Education," concluded with Essie taking aim.

"Well, you certainly didn't leave anything out, did you?"

Thus began my father's critique on the Sunday I'd come to say goodbye before leaving for the winter at Quahsay. Earlier in the day, along with a favorite aunt and uncle and a childless neighbor couple—also called "Aunt" and "Uncle" by me since the cradle—I had partaken of our family's traditional Sunday brunch. Fifty-two Sundays a year, for most of my lifetime, my father went out to the corner for the smoked fish and the warm rolls, my brother and I set the table and squeezed the juice, and for three hours my mother was unemployed in her own house. "Like a queen" was how she described the predicament. Then, after my parents had read the Newark Sunday papers and listened on the radio to "The Eternal Light"—great moments from Jewish history in weekly half-hour dramatizations—we two boys were rounded up and the four of us set off in the car to visit relatives. My father, long in contention with an opinionated older brother for the vacant position of family patriarch, generally delivered a hortatory sermon somewhere along the way to somebody who seemed to him to need it, and then we drove home. And always at dusk, before we reassembled around the kitchen table to observe the Sunday-evening rites—to partake of the sacred delicatessen supper, washed down with sacramental soda pop; to await together the visitation from heaven of Jack Benny, Rochester, and Phil Harris—the "men," as my mother called us, went off for their brisk walk to the nearby park. "Hi, Doc—how are you?" So the neighbors we passed along the way always greeted my popular and talkative father, and though he seemed never to be bothered by it, for a time his class-conscious little boy used to think that if only there had been no quotas and he'd become a *real* physician, they would have greeted him as "Doctor Zuckerman." "Doc" was what they called the pharmacist who made milk shakes and sold cough drops.

"Well, Nathan," began my father, "you certainly didn't leave anything out, did you?"

I was by then a little weary from doing my duty and anxious to leave for New York to pack for Quahsay. My brunch-time visit had now lasted the entire day and, to my surprise, had been marked by the comings and goings of numerous relatives and old family friends dropping by seemingly just to see me. Kibitzing, reminiscing, swapping dialect jokes, and munching too much fruit, I had hung around until the company began to leave, and then had stayed on, at my father's request, so that he could give me his thoughts on my story. Portentously he said he wanted an hour with me alone.

At four that afternoon, in our coats and scarves, the two of us set out for the park. Every half hour a New York bus stopped just by the park gateway on Elizabeth Avenue, and my plan was to catch one after he'd had his say.

"I left a lot of things out." I pretended to be innocent of what he meant—as innocent as when I'd sent him the story, though the moment he'd spoken in the house of giving me his "thoughts" (rather than his pat on the head), I realized immediately how mindless I had been. Why hadn't I waited to see if I could even get it published, and then shown him the story already in print? Or would that only have made it worse? "Things had to be left out—it's only fifty pages."

"I mean," he said sadly, "you didn't leave anything disgusting out."

"Did I? Didn't I? I wasn't thinking along those lines, exactly."

"You make everybody seem awfully greedy, Nathan."

"But everybody was."

"That's one way of looking at it, of course."

"That's the way you looked at it yourself. That's why you were so upset that they wouldn't compromise."

"The point is, there is far more to our family than this. And you know that. I hope that today reminded you of the kind of people we are. In case in New York you've forgotten."

"Dad, I had a good time seeing everybody. But you didn't have to give me a refresher course in the family's charms."

But on he went. "And people who are crazy about you. Is there anybody who came into the house today whose face didn't light up when they laid eyes on you? And you couldn't have been kinder, you couldn't have been a sweeter boy. I watched you with your family and with all our old dear friends, and I thought to myself, Then what is this story all about? Why is he going on like this about ancient history?"

"It wasn't ancient history when it happened."

"No, then it was nonsense."

"You didn't seem to think so. You were running from Essie to Sidney for over a year."

"The fact remains, son, there is more to the family, much much more, than is in this story. Your great-aunt was as kind and loving and hard-working a woman as you could ever meet in this world. Your grandmother and all her sisters were, every last one of them. They were women who thought only of others."

"But the story is not about them."

"But they are *part* of the story. They are the *whole* story as far as I'm concerned. Without them there would be no story at all! Who the hell was

Sidney? Does anybody in his right mind even think about him any longer? To you, as a boy, I suppose he was an amusing character, somebody to get a kick out of, who came and went. I can understand how that would be: a big six-foot ape in bell-bottom trousers, clanking his I.D. bracelet and talking a mile a minute as though he was Admiral Nimitz and not just the nobody who swabbed the deck. Which is all he ever was, of course. I remember how he came to the house and got down on the floor and taught you and your little brother to roll dice. As a joke. I wanted to throw the lummox out on his ear."

"I don't even remember that."

"Well, I do. I remember plenty. I remember it all. To Meema Chaya, Sidney was never anything but heartache. Little children don't realize that underneath the big blowhard who rolls on the floor and makes them laugh there can be somebody who makes other people cry. And he made your great-aunt cry plenty, and from the time he was old enough to go into the street, looking for grief to give her. And still, *still,* that woman left him that chunk of her hard-earned dough, and prayed that somehow it would help. She rose above all the misery and the shame he had caused her—just like the wonderful woman that she was. 'Chaya' means life, and that is what she had in her to give to everybody. But that you leave out."

"I didn't leave it out. I suggest as much about her on the first page. But you're right—I don't go into Meema Chaya's life."

"Well, that would be some story."

"Well, that isn't this story."

"And do you fully understand what a story like this story, when it's published, will mean to people who don't know us?"

We had by now descended the long incline of our street and reached Elizabeth Avenue. No lawn we passed, no driveway, no garage, no lamppost, no little brick stoop was without its power over me. Here I had practiced my sidearm curve, here on my sled I'd broken a tooth, here I had copped my first feel, here for teasing a friend I had been slapped by my mother, here I had learned that my grandfather was dead. There was no end to all I could re-member happening to me on this street of one-family brick houses more or less like ours, owned by Jews more or less like us, to whom six rooms with a "finished" basement and a screened-in porch on a street with shade trees was something never to be taken for granted, given the side of the city where they'd started out.

Across the wide thoroughfare was the entrance to the park. There my father used to seat himself—each Sunday the same bench—to watch my brother and me play tag, yelling our heads off after hours of good behavior with grandparents, great-aunts and great-uncles, ordinary aunts and uncles—sometimes it seemed to me that there were more Zuckermans in Newark than Negroes. I wouldn't see as many of them in a year as I saw cousins on an ordinary Sunday driving around the city with my father. "Oh," he used to say, "how you boys love to shout," and with one hand for each son's head would smooth back our damp hair as we started out of the park and back up the familiar hill where we lived. "Any game with shouting in it," he would tell our mother, "and these two are in seventh heaven." Now my younger brother was knuckling under to the tedium of a pre-dental course, having surrendered (to my father's better judgment) a halfhearted dream of a career as an actor, and I—? I apparently was shouting again.

I said, "I think maybe I'll just get the bus. Maybe we should skip the park. It's been a long day, and I have to go home and get ready to leave for Quahsay tomorrow."

"You haven't answered my question."

"It wouldn't be useful, Dad. The best thing now is to put the story in the mail and send it back to me—and try to forget it."

My suggestion triggered a light sardonic laugh from my father.

"All right," I said sharply, "then don't forget it."

"Calm down," he replied. "I'll walk you to the bus. I'll wait with you."

"You really ought to go home. It's getting cold."

"I'm plenty warm," he informed me.

We waited in silence at the bus stop.

"They take their time on Sundays," he finally said. "Maybe you should come home and have dinner. You could catch one first thing in the morning."

"I've got to go to Quahsay first thing in the morning."

"They can't wait?"

"I can't," I said.

I stepped out into the street to watch for the bus.

"You're going to get yourself killed out there."

"Perhaps."

"So," he said, when at last, in my own sweet time, I came back up on the curb, "what do you do with the story now? Send it to a magazine?"

"It's long for a magazine. Probably no magazine will publish it."

"Oh, they'll publish it. The *Saturday Review* has put you on the map. That was a wonderful write-up, a terrific honor to be chosen like that at your age."

"Well, we'll see."

"No, no. You're on your way. The *Saturday Review* never sold so many copies in North Jersey as when your picture was in it. Why do you think everybody came by today, Frieda and Dave, Aunt Tessie, Birdie, Murray, the Edelmans? Because they saw your picture and they're proud."

"They all told me."

"Look, Nathan, let me have my say. Then you can go, and up there at the artists' colony maybe you'll think over in peace and quiet what I'm trying to get you to understand. If you were going to turn out to be nobody, I wouldn't be taking this seriously. But I do take you seriously—and you have to take yourself seriously, and what you are doing. Stop looking for that goddam bus and listen to me, *please.* You can catch the *next* bus! Nathan, you are not in school any more. You are the older brother and you are out in the world and I am treating you accordingly."

"I understand that. But that doesn't mean that we can't disagree. That's what it *does* mean."

"But from a lifetime of experience I happen to know what ordinary people will think when they read something like this story. And you don't. You can't. You have been sheltered from it all your life. You were raised here in this neighborhood where you went to school with Jewish children. When we went to the shore and had the house with the Edelmans, you were always among Jews, even in the summertime. At Chicago your best friends who you brought home were Jewish boys, always. It's not your fault that you don't know what Gentiles think when they read something like this. But I can tell you. They don't think about how it's a great work of art. They don't know about art. Maybe I don't know about art myself. Maybe none of our family does, not the way that you do. But that's my point. People don't read art—they read about *people.* And they judge them as such. And how do you think they will judge the people in your story, what conclusions do you think they will reach? Have you thought about that?"

"Yes."

"And what have you concluded?"

"Oh, I can't put it into one word, not out here in the street. I didn't write fifteen thousand words so as now to put it into one word."

"Well, I can. And the street isn't a bad place for it. Because I know the word. I wonder if you fully understand just how very little love there is in this world for Jewish people. I don't mean in Germany, either, under the Nazis. I mean in run-of-the-mill Americans, Mr. and Mrs. Nice Guy, who otherwise you and I consider perfectly harmless. Nathan, it is there. I guarantee you it is there. I *know* it is there. I have seen it, I have felt it, even when they do not express it in so many words."

"But I'm not *denying* that. Why did Sidney throw that redneck off his ship—?"

"Sidney," he said furiously, "never threw any redneck off any ship! Sidney threw the bull, Nathan! Sidney was a petty hoodlum who cared about nobody and nothing in this world but the good of Sidney!"

"And who actually existed, Dad—and no better than I depict him!"

"Better? He was worse! How rotten he was you don't *begin* to know. I could tell you stories about that bastard that would make your hair stand on end."

"Then where *are* we? If he was *worse*—Oh, look, we're not getting anywhere. Please, it's getting dark, it's going to snow—*go home*. I'll write when I get up there. But there is no more to say on this subject. We just disagree, period."

"All right!" he said crisply, "all right!" But only, I knew, to defuse me for the moment.

"Dad, go home, please."

"It won't hurt if I wait with you. I don't like you waiting out here by yourself."

"I can manage perfectly well out here by myself. I have for years now."

Some five minutes later, blocks away, we saw what looked like the lights of the New York bus.

"Well," I said, "I'll be back down in a few months. I'll keep in touch— I'll phone—"

"Nathan, your story, as far as Gentiles are concerned, is about one thing and one thing only. Listen to me, before you go. It is about kikes. Kikes and their love of money. That is all your good Christian friends will see, I guarantee you. It is not about the scientists and teachers and lawyers they become and the things such people accomplish for others. It is not about the immigrants like Chaya who worked and saved and sacrificed to get a decent footing in America. It is not about the wonderful peaceful days and nights you spent growing up in our house. It is not about the lovely friends you always had. No, it's about Essie and her hammer, and Sidney and his chorus girls, and that shyster of Essie's and his filthy mouth, and, as best I can see, about what a jerk I was begging them to reach a decent compromise before the whole family had to be dragged up in front of a *goyisher* judge."

"I didn't depict you as a jerk. Christ, far from it. I thought," I said angrily, "I was administering a bear hug, to tell you the truth."

"Oh, did you? Well, it didn't come out that way. Look, son, maybe I *was* a jerk, trying to talk sense to such people. I don't mind being made a little fun of—that couldn't bother me less. I've been around in life. But what I can't accept is what you don't see—what you don't *want* to see. This story isn't us, and what is worse, it isn't even *you*. You are a loving boy. I watched you like a hawk all day. I've watched you all your life. You are a good and kind and considerate young man. You are not somebody who writes this kind of story and then pretends it's the truth."

"But I *did* write it." The light changed, the New York bus started toward us across the intersection—and he threw his arms onto my shoulders. Making me all the more belligerent. "I *am* the kind of person who writes this kind of story!"

"You're not," he pleaded, shaking me just a little.

But I hopped up onto the bus, and then behind me the pneumatic door, with its hard rubber edge, swung shut with what I took to be an overly appropriate thump, a symbol of the kind you leave out of fiction. It was a sound that suddenly brought back to me the prize fights at the Laurel Garden, where once a year my brother and I used to wager our pennies with one another, each of us alternately backing the white fighter or the colored fighter, while Doc Zuckerman waved hello to his few acquaintances in the sporting crowd, among them, on one occasion, Meyer Ellenstein, the dentist who became the city's first Jewish mayor. What I heard was the heartrending thud that follows the roundhouse knockout punch, the sound of the stupefied heaveweight hitting the canvas floor. And what I saw, when I looked out to wave good-bye for the winter, was my smallish, smartly dressed father—turned out for my visit in a new "fingertip" car coat that matched the coffee-toned slacks and the checkered peaked cap, and wearing, of course, the same silver-rimmed spectacles, the same trim little mustache that I had grabbed at from the crib; what I saw was my bewildered father, alone on the darkening street-corner by the park that used to be our paradise, thinking himself and all of Jewry gratuitously disgraced and jeopardized by my inexplicable betrayal.

Nor was that the end. So troubled was he that several days later, against the counsel of my mother, and after an unpleasant phone conversation with my younger brother, who warned him from Ithaca that I wasn't going to like it when I found out, he decided to seek an audience with Judge Leopold Wapter, after Ellenstein and Rabbi Joachim Prinz perhaps the city's most admired Jew.

Wapter had been born of Galician Jews in the slums adjacent to the city's sweatshops and mills some ten years before our family arrived there from Eastern Europe in 1900. My father still remembered having been rescued by one of the Wapter brothers—it could have been the future jurist himself—when a gang of Irish hooligans were having some fun throwing the seven-year-old mocky up into the air in a game of catch. I had heard this story more than once in my childhood, usually when we drove by the landscaped gardens and turreted stone house on Clinton Avenue where Wapter lived with a spinster daughter—one of the first Jewish students at Vassar College to earn the esteem of her Christian teachers—and his wife, the department-store heiress, whose philanthropic activities had given her family name the renown among the Jews of Essex County that it was said to have in her native Charleston. Because the Wapters occupied a position of prestige and authority rather like that accorded in our household to President and Mrs. Roosevelt, I used to imagine her, when I was a small boy, going around wearing Mrs. Roosevelt's dowager hats and dresses, and, oddly for a Jewish woman, speaking in the First Lady's awesome Anglified tones. It did not seem to me that, coming from South Carolina, she could really *be* Jewish. Which was exactly what she thought about me, after reading my story.

To approach the judge, my father had first to contact a lofty cousin of ours—an attorney, a suburbanite, and a former Army colonel who had been president for several years of the judge's Newark temple. Cousin Teddy had already helped him to the judge once before, back when my father had gotten it into his head that I should be one of the five youngsters for whom each year Wapter wrote letters of recommendation to college-admissions officers which—it was said—never failed to do the trick. To go up before Judge Wapter I had to wear a blue suit on a bus in broad daylight and then, from where the bus left me off at the Four Corners (our Times Square), to walk all the way up Market Street through throngs of shoppers, whom I imagined dropping in their tracks at the sight of me out in my only dress suit at that hour. I was to be interviewed at the Essex County Courthouse, in his "chambers," a word that had been intoned to relatives on the phone so frequently and with such reverence by my mother during the preceding week that it may well have accounted for the seven visits I made to our bathroom before I could get myself buttoned for good into the blue suit.

Teddy had telephoned the night before to give me some tips on how to conduct myself. This explained the suit and my father's black silk socks, which I was wearing held up with a pair of his garters, and also the initialed briefcase, a grade-school graduation present that I had never removed from the back of my closet. In the gleaming briefcase I carried ten typewritten pages I had written for International Relations the year before on the Balfour Declaration.

As instructed, I "spoke up" right away and offered to show the judge the essay. To my relief, his chambers had turned out to be one room, not ten— and a room no more grand than the principal's office in our high school. Nor did the tanned, plumpish, cheery judge have the shock of white hair I had been expecting. And though not as small as my father, he still was easily a foot shorter than Abraham Lincoln, whose bronze statue you pass coming into the courthouse. He actually looked years younger than my own anxious father, and not half as serious. Reputedly an excellent golfer, he was probably either on his way to or from a game; that's how I later came to terms with his argyle socks. But when I first noticed them—as he leaned back in his leather chair to flip through my essay—I was shocked. It was as though he were the callow, unworldly applicant, and I, with my father's garters pulled tight as a tourniquet, were the judge. "May I keep this for now, Nathan?" he asked, turning with a smile through my pages of *op. cits* and *ibids*. "I'd like to take it home for my wife to see." Then began the inquiry. I had prepared myself the night before (at Teddy's suggestion) by reading through the Constitution of the United States, the Declaration of Independence, and the editorial page of the Newark *Evening News*. The members of Truman's Cabinet and the majority and minority leaders of both Houses of Congress I of course knew already by heart, though before bed I had gone over them out loud with my mother just to help her relax.

To the judge's questions I gave the following answers:

Journalist. The University of Chicago. Ernie Pyle. One brother, younger. Reading—and sports. The Giants in the National League and the Tigers in the American. Mel Ott and Hank Greenberg. Li'l Abner. Thomas Wolfe. Canada; Washington, D.C.; Rye, New York; New York City itself; Philadelphia; and the Jersey shore. No, sir, never to Florida.

When the judge's secretary made public the names of Newark's five Jewish boys and girls whose college applications Wapter would endorse, mine was one.

I never saw the judge again, though to please my father I had sent my sponsor a letter from the University of Chicago during orientation week of my freshman year, thanking him again for all he had done on my behalf. The letter I received from Wapter some seven years later, during my second week as a guest at Quahsay, was the first I knew of their meeting to talk about "Higher Education."

Dear Nathan:

My familiarity with your fine family goes back, as you must know, to the turn of the century on Prince Street, where we were all poor people in a new land, struggling for our basic needs, our social and civil rights, and our spiritual dignity. I still remember you as one of the outstanding Jewish graduates of our Newark public-school system. I was most pleased to hear from your father that your college record was at the same high level of achievement that you had maintained throughout your school career here, and that you are already beginning to gain recognition in the field of short-story writing. Since there is nothing a judge likes better than to be right from time to time, I was delighted to know that my confidence in you as a high-school senior has already been substantiated in the larger world. I expect that your family and your community can look forward to great achievements from you in the not too distant future.

Your father, knowing of my interest in the development of our outstanding young people, recently asked if I would take time out from my judicial duties to write you with my candid opinion of one of your short stories. He informed me that you are soon to submit the short story entitled "Higher Education" to a leading national magazine, and he wanted to know whether I thought the story contained material suitable for such publication.

In our lengthy and interesting conversation here in my chambers, I informed him that classically, down through the ages and in all countries, the artist has always considered himself beyond the mores of the community in which he lived. Great artists, as history reveals, have been harshly persecuted time and again by the

frightened and ill-educated, who do not understand that the artist
is a special individual with a unique contribution to make to
mankind. Socrates was considered an enemy of the people and a
corrupter of the young. The Norwegian playwright and Nobel
Prize winner, Henrik Ibsen, was forced into exile because his countrymen failed to understand the profound truth of his great
dramas. I explained to your father that I for one would never want
to be allied with the intolerance shown by the Greeks towards Socrates, or by the Norwegians towards Ibsen. On the other hand, I
do believe that, like all men, the artist has a responsibility to his
fellow man, to the society in which he lives, and to the cause of
truth and justice. With that responsibility and that alone as my
criterion, I would attempt to give him an opinion on the suitability for publication in a national magazine of your latest fictional
effort.

Attached you will find a questionnaire about your story, prepared jointly by my wife and myself. Because of Mrs. Wapter's interest in literature and the arts—and because I did not think it fair
to rely solely upon my reading—I have taken the liberty of secur-
ing her opinion. These are serious and difficult questions to which
Mrs. Wapter and I would like you to give just one hour of your
time. We don't want you to answer them to our satisfaction—we
want you to answer them to your own. You are a young man of
great promise and, we all think, of potentially great talent. But
with great talent come great responsibilities, and an obligation to
those who have stood behind you in the early days so that your
talent might come to fruition. I would like to think that if and
when the day should dawn that you receive *your* invitation to
Stockholm to accept a Nobel Prize, we will have had some small
share in awakening your conscience to the responsibilities of your
calling.

Sincerely yours,
Leopold Wapter

P.S. If you have not yet seen the Broadway production of *The
Diary of Anne Frank,* I strongly advise that you do so. Mrs. Wapter
and I were in the audience on opening night; we wish that
Nathan Zuckerman could have been with us to benefit from that
unforgettable experience.

The sheet of questions prepared for me by the Wapters read as follows:

TEN QUESTIONS FOR NATHAN ZUCKERMAN

1. If you had been living in Nazi Germany in the thirties, would
   you have written such a story?

2. Do you believe Shakespeare's Shylock and Dickens's Fagin have been of no use to anti-Semites?

3. Do you practice Judaism? If so, how? If not, what credentials qualify you for writing about Jewish life for national magazines?

4. Would you claim that the characters in your story represent a fair sample of the kinds of people that make up a typical contemporary community of Jews?

5. In a story with a Jewish background, what reason is there for a description of physical intimacy between a married Jewish man and an unmarried Christian woman? Why in a story with a Jewish background must there be (a) adultery; (b) incessant fighting within a family over money; (c) warped human behavior in general?

6. What set of aesthetic values makes you think that the cheap is more valid than the noble and the slimy is more truthful than the sublime?

7. What in your character makes you associate so much of life's ugliness with Jewish people?

8. Can you explain why in your story, in which a rabbi appears, there is nowhere the grandeur of oratory with which Stephen S. Wise and Abba Hillel Silver and Zvi Masliansky have stirred and touched their audiences?

9. Aside from the financial gain to yourself, what benefit do you think publishing this story in a national magazine will have for (a) your family; (b) your community; (c) the Jewish religion; (d) the well-being of the Jewish people?

10. Can you honestly say that there is anything in your short story that would not warm the heart of a Julius Streicher or a Joseph Goebbels?

Three weeks after hearing from the judge and Mrs. Wapter, and only days before my visit to Lonoff, I was interrupted around noon by the Colony secretary. She had come out to my cabin in her coat, apologizing for the disturbance, but saying that I had a long-distance phone call that had been described by the other party as an emergency.

When my mother heard my voice she began to cry. "I know it's wrong to bother you," she said, "but I can't take any more. I can't take another night of it. I can't sit through another meal."

"What is it? What's the matter?"

"Nathan, did you or didn't you get a letter from Judge Wapter?"

"Oh, I got it all right."

"But"—she was flabbergasted—"then why didn't you answer it?"

"He should not have gone to Wapter with that story, Mother."

"Oh, darling, maybe he shouldn't. But he did. He did because he knows you respect the judge—"

"I don't even *know* the judge."

"That's not *true*. He did so much for you when you were ready for college. He gave you such a wonderful boost. It turns out that in his files he still had the essay you wrote on the Balfour Declaration in high school. His secretary took out the files and there it was. Daddy saw it, right in his chambers. Why you haven't given him the courtesy of a reply . . . Daddy is beside himself. He can't believe it."

"He'll have to."

"But all he wanted was for you not to bring yourself harm. You know that."

"I thought it was the harm I was going to do the Jews that you're all worried about."

"Darling, please, for my sake, why won't you answer Judge Wapter? Why won't you give him the hour he asks for? Surely you have an hour where you are to write a letter. Because you cannot, at the age of twenty-three, ignore such a person. You cannot make enemies at twenty-three of people who are so admired and loved, and by Gentiles, too."

"Is that what my father says?"

"He says so much, Nathan. It's been three *weeks* now."

"And how does he even know I haven't answered?"

"From Teddy. He didn't hear from you, so finally he called him. You can well imagine. Teddy is a little fit to be tied. He's not used to this treatment, either. After all, he also extended himself on our behalf when you wanted to go to Chicago."

"Ma, I hate to suggest this, but it could be that the judge's famous letter, procured after great ass-kissing all around, had about as much effect on the University of Chicago as a letter about my qualifications from Rocky Graziano."

"Oh, Nathan, where's your humility, where's your modesty—where's the courtesy you have always had?"

"Where are my father's *brains!*"

"He only wants to *save* you."

"From what?"

"*Mistakes.*"

"Too late, Mother. Didn't you read the Ten Questions for Nathan Zuckerman?"

"Dear, I did. He sent us a copy—and the letter, too."

"The Big Three, Mama! Streicher, Goebbels, and your son! What about the *judge's* humility? Where's *his* modesty?"

"He only meant that what happened to the Jews—"

"In Europe—not in Newark! We are not the wretched of Belsen! We were not the victims of that crime!"

"But we *could* be—in their place we *would* be. Nathan, violence is nothing new to Jews, you *know* that!"

"Ma, you want to see physical violence done to the Jews of Newark, go to the office of the plastic surgeon where the girls get their noses fixed. That's where the Jewish blood flows in Essex County, that's where the blow is delivered—with a mallet! To their bones—and to their pride!"

"Please don't shout at me. I'm not up to all of this, please—that's why I'm calling. Judge Wapter did not mean *you* were Goebbels. God forbid. He was only a little shocked still from reading your story. We all were, you can understand that."

"Oh, maybe then you all shock a little too easily. Jews are heirs to greater shocks than I can possibly deliver with a story that has a sharpie in it like Sidney. Or Essie's hammer. Or Essie's lawyer. You know as much yourself. You just *said* as much."

"Oh, darling, then tell the judge that. Just tell him that, the way you told it to me, and that'll do it. Your father will be happy. Write him *something*. You can write such wonderful and beautiful letters. When Grandma was dying, you wrote her a letter that was like a poem. It was like—like listening to French, it was so beautiful. What you wrote about the Balfour Declaration was so beautiful when you were only fifteen years old. The judge gave it back to Daddy and said he still remembered how much it had impressed him. He's not against you, Nathan. But if you get your back up and show disrespect, then he will be. And Teddy too, who could be such a help."

"Nothing I could write Wapter would convince him of anything. Or his wife."

"You could tell him you went to see *The Diary of Anne Frank*. You could at least do that."

"I didn't see it. I read the book. *Everybody* read the book."

"But you liked it, didn't you?"

"That's not the issue. How can you *dis*like it? Mother, I will not prate in platitudes to please the adults!"

"But if you just said that, about reading the book, and liking it . . . Because Teddy told Daddy—well, Nathan, is this true?—that to him it looks like you don't really like Jews very much."

"No, Teddy's got it confused. It's him I don't like very much."

"Oh, darling, don't be clever. Don't start that last-word business, please. Just answer me, I'm so confused in the middle of all this. Nathan, tell me something."

"What?"

"I'm only quoting Teddy. Darling . . ."

"What is it, Ma?"

"Are you really anti-Semitic?"

"I'll leave it to you. What do you think?"

"Me? I never heard of such a thing. But Teddy . . ."

"I know, he's a college graduate and lives with wall-to-wall carpeting in Millburn. But they come pretty stupid too."

"Nathan!"

"Sorry, but that's my opinion."

"Oh, I don't know anything any more—all this from that story! Please, if you will not do anything else I ask, at least phone your father. He's been waiting for something for three whole weeks now. And he's a doer, your father, he's not a man who knows how to wait. Darling, phone him at his office. Phone him now. For me."

"No."

"I beg of you."

"No."

"Oh, I can't believe this is you."

"It *is* me!"

"But—what about your father's love?"

"I am on my own!"

In Lonoff's study that night I began letter after letter explaining myself to my father, but each time I got to the point of repeating E. I. Lonoff's praise for my work, I tore the thing up in a rage. I owed no explanations, and he wouldn't buy those I offered anyway, if he even understood them. Because my voice started back of my knees and reached above my head wasn't going to make him any happier about my informing on those unsavory family miscreants who were nobody's business but our own. Nor would it help to argue that Essie wielding her hammer came off in my story as something more impressive than an embarassment; that wasn't what other people were going to say about a woman who behaved like that, and then expressed herself in a court of law like a man in a barroom brawl. Nor would a spin through the waxworks of my literary museum—from Babel's Odessa gangsters to Abravanel's Los Angeles worldlings—convince him that I was upholding the responsibilities placed on me by his hero, the judge. Odessa? Why not Mars? He was talking about what people would say when they read that story in North Jersey, where we happened to come from. He was talking about the *goyim,* who looked down on us with enough unearned contempt already, and who would be only too pleased to call us all kikes because of what I had written for the whole world to read about Jews fighting over money. It was not for me to leak the news that such a thing could possibly happen. That was worse than informing—that was collaborating.

Oh, this is useless, I thought, this is idiotic—and tore up yet another half-finished letter in my defense. That the situation between us had deteriorated so rapidly—by his going to Wapter with my story, and by my refusal to justify myself to my elders—was as it had to be, sooner or later. Hadn't Joyce, hadn't Flaubert, hadn't Thomas Wolfe, the romantic genius of my high-school reading list, all been condemned for disloyalty or treachery or immorality by those who saw themselves as slandered in their works? As even the judge knew, literary history was in part the history of novelists infuriating fellow countrymen, family, and friends. To be sure, our dispute hadn't achieved the luster of literary history quite yet, but still, writers weren't writers, I told myself, if they didn't have the strength to face the insolubility of that conflict and go on.

But what about sons? It wasn't Flaubert's father or Joyce's father who had impugned me for my recklessness—it was my own. Nor was it the Irish he claimed I had maligned and misrepresented, but the Jews. Of which I was one. Of which, only some five thousand days past, there had been millions more.

Yet each time I tried again to explain my motives, the angrier with him I became. It's you who humiliated yourself—now live with it, you moralizing ass! Wapter, that know-nothing windbag! That dopey pillar! And the pious belle with her love for the arts! Worth ten million and she chides *me* about "financial gain"! And Abba Hillel Silver on top of that! Oh, don't waste time on prodigal me about Rabbi Silver's grandeur, lady, tell my late cousin Sidney and his friends in the Mob—quote Zvi Masliansky to them, like you do at the country club on the eighteenth hole!

At around eleven I heard the town snowplow clearing the unpaved road beyond the apple orchard. Later a pickup truck with a snowblade clamped to the front end charged into the driveway and shoved the evening's snowfall into the orchard atop the snowfall of the previous thirty nights. The little Renault arrived last, swerving slowly into the driveway about half an hour later, one beam on high, the other dim, and with half-dead windshield wipers.

At the first sound of her car returning, I had flipped off all my lights and crawled to the study window on my knees so as to watch her make her way toward the house. For I had not stayed awake simply because I couldn't forget my father's disapproval or E. I. Lonoff's toast—I also had no intention of being unconscious when the enchanting and mysterious houseguest (all the more alluring, of course, as Hope's imagined erotic rival) got back to change into her nightdress on the floor above me. What I would be able to do about this, I had no idea. However, just to be awake and unclothed in one bed while she was awake and nearly unclothed in another was better than nothing. It was a start.

But predictably, it was worse than nothing and the start of little that was new. The lantern on the half-buried lamppost between the house and the car shed went dark, and then, from where I was kneeling beside the study door, I heard her enter the house. She moved through the hallway and up the carpeted stairs—and that was the last of her that I saw or heard until about an hour later, when I was privileged to audit another astounding course, this one in the adult evening division of the Lonoff School of the Arts. The rest of what I'd been waiting up for I had, of course, to imagine. But that is easier work by far than making things up at the typewriter. For that kind of imagining you don't have to have your picture in the *Saturday Review*. You don't even have to know the alphabet. Being young will usually get a fellow through with flying colors. You don't even have to be young. You don't have to be anything.

Virtuous reader, if you think that after intercourse all animals are sad, try masturbating on the daybed in E. I. Lonoff's study and see how you feel when it's over. To expiate my sense of utter shabbiness, I immediately took to the high road and drew from Lonoff's bookshelves the volume of Henry James stories containing "The Middle Years," the source of one of the two quotations pinned to the bulletin board. And there where I had indulged myself in this most un-Jamesian lapse from the amenities, I read the story two times through, looking to discover what I could about the doubt that's the writer's passion, the passion that's his task, and the madness of—of all things—art.

Dencombe, a novelist "who had a reputation," is convalescing from a debilitating ailment at an English health resort when a copy of his latest book, *The Middle Years,* arrives from his publisher. Seated alone on a bench looking out to sea, Dencombe reluctantly opens the book—to discover what he believes is the artistic distinction that had always evaded him. His genius has flowered, however, just when he no longer has the strength to develop a " 'last manner' . . . to which his real treasure would be gathered." That would require a second existence, and everything tells him that the first one is nearly over.

While fearfully contemplating the end of his life, Dencombe is joined on the bench by a garrulous young stranger carrying his own copy of *The Middle Years.* He begins to speak ardently of Dencombe's achievement to the mild gentleman who he finds has also been reading the new novel. The admirer—"the greatest admirer . . . whom it was supposable he might boast"—is Dr. Hugh, physician to a rich, eccentric English countess who is at the hotel, like Dencombe, to recover from some grave illness. Inflamed with passion for *The Middle Years,* Dr. Hugh opens the book to read aloud a particularly beautiful passage; but, having mistakenly seized Dencombe's copy rather than his own, he discovers that the printed text has been altered in a dozen places by a pencil. With this, the anonymous and ailing author on the brink of being discovered—"a passionate corrector" never able to arrive at a final form—feels his sickness sweeping over him and loses consciousness.

In the days that follow, Dencombe, bedridden, hopes that some remedy miraculously concocted by the attentive young physician will restore his strength. However, when he learns that the countess plans to disinherit Dr. Hugh of a magnificent fortune if he continues to neglect her for the novelist, Dencombe encourages Dr. Hugh to follow her to London. But Dr. Hugh cannot overcome his passionate idolatry, and by the time he acts on Dencombe's advice to hurry to his employer, he has already suffered "a terrible injury" for which Dencombe almost believes himself to be responsible: the countess has died, in a relapse brought on by her jealousy, bequeathing to the young physician not a penny. Says Dr. Hugh, returning from her grave to the dying soul whom he adores, "I had to choose."

"You chose to let a fortune go?"

"I chose to accept, whatever they might be, the consequences of my infatuation," smiled Doctor Hugh. Then, as a larger pleasantry: "The fortune be hanged! It's your own fault if I can't get your things out of my head."

A thin black line had been drawn beneath the "pleasantry" in Lonoff's book. In script so tiny it was almost unreadable, the writer had noted beside it a droll pleasantry of his own: "And also your fault if I can."

From there on, down both margins of the final page describing Dencombe's death, Lonoff had penned three vertical lines. Nothing resembling drollery here. Rather, the six surgically precise black lines seemed to simulate the succession of fine impressions that James's insidious narrative about the novelist's dubious wizardry had scored upon Lonoff's undeluded brain.

After Dencombe has learned the consequences of the young man's infatuation—consequences so utterly irreconcilable with his own honorable convictions that, upon hearing of his place in it all, Dencombe utters, "a long bewildered moan"—he lies "for many hours, many days . . . motionless and absent."

At the last he signed to Doctor Hugh to listen and, when he was down on his knees by the pillow, brought him very near. "You've made me think it all a delusion."

"Not your glory, my dear friend," stammered the young man.

"Not my glory—what there is of it! It *is* glory—to have been tested, to have had our little quality and cast our little spell. The thing is to have made somebody care. You happen to be crazy of course, but that doesn't affect the law."

"You're a great success!" said Doctor Hugh, putting into his young voice the ring of a marriage-bell.

Dencombe lay taking this in; then he gathered strength to speak once more. "A second chance—*that's* the delusion. There never was to be but one. We work in the dark—we do what we can—we give what we have. Our doubt is our passion and our passion is our task. The rest is the madness of art."

"If you've doubted, if you've despaired, you've always 'done' it," his visitor subtly argued.

"We've done something or other," Dencombe conceded.

"Something or other is everything. It's the feasible. It's *you!*"

"Comforter!" poor Dencombe ironically sighed.

"But it's true," insisted his friend.

"It's true. It's frustration that doesn't count."

"Frustration's only life," said Doctor Hugh.

"Yes, it's what passes." Poor Dencombe was barely audible, but he had marked with the words the virtual end of his first and only chance.

Within moments of hearing muffled voices coming from above my head, I stood up on the daybed—my finger still holding my place in the book—and, stretching to my full height, tried to make out what was being said up there and by whom. When that didn't help, I thought of climbing onto Lonoff's desk; it was easily a foot or so higher than the daybed and would put my ear only inches from the room's low ceiling. But if I should fall, if I should alter by a millimeter the placement of his typing paper, if somehow I should leave footprints—no, I couldn't risk it and shouldn't even have been thinking of it. I had gone far enough already by expropriating the corner of the desk to compose my half dozen unfinished letters home. My sense of propriety, not to mention the author's gracious hospitality, required me to restrain myself from committing such a sordid, callow little indecency.

But in the meantime I had done it.

A woman was crying. Which one, over what, who was there comforting her—or causing the tears? Just a little higher and maybe I could find out. A thick dictionary would have been perfect, but Lonoff's Webster's was down on a shelf of fat reference books level with the typing chair, and the best I could manage under pressure was to gain another couple of inches by kneeling to insert between the desk and my feet the volume of stories by Henry James.

Ah, the unreckoned consequences, the unaccountable uses of art! Dencombe would understand. James would understand. But would Lonoff? *Don't fall.*

"Now you're being sensible." Lonoff was the speaker. "You had to see for yourself, and so you saw."

A light thud directly overhead. Someone had dropped into a chair. The weary writer? In his bathrobe now, or still in suit and tie and polished shoes?

Then I heard Amy Bellette. And what was *she* wearing at this hour? "I saw nothing—only more misery either way. Of course I can't live here—but I can't keep living there, either. I can't live anywhere. I can't *live*."

"Quiet down. She's had it for today. Let her rest, now that she's asleep."

"She's ruining everyone's life."

"Don't blame her for what you hold against me. I'm the one who says no around here. Now *you* go to sleep."

"I can't. I don't want to. We can talk."

"We've talked."

Silence. Were they down on their knees listening through the old floorboards for *me*? Then they had long since heard my drumming heart.

Bedsprings! Lonoff climbing in beside her!

But it was Amy getting out of bed I heard, not Lonoff climbing in. Her feet lightly crossed the floor only inches above my lips.

"I love you. I love you so, Dad-da. There's no one else like you. They're all such dopes."

"You're a good girl."

"Let me sit on your lap. Just hold me a little and I'll be fine."

"You're fine now. You're always fine in the end. You're the great survivor."

"No, just the world's strongest weakling. Oh, tell me a story. Sing me a song. Oh, imitate the great Durante, I really need it tonight."

At first it sounded like somebody coughing. But then I could hear that, yes, he was singing to her, very quietly, in the manner of Jimmy Durante—"So I ups to him, and he ups to me"—I could catch just the one line, but that was enough for me to recall the song itself being sung by Durante on his radio show, in the celebrated raffish voice, and with the hoarse, endearing simplehearted delivery that the famous author was now impersonating overhead.

"More," said Amy.

Was she now on his lap? Amy in her nightie and Lonoff in his suit?

"You go to sleep," he told her.

"More. Sing 'I Can Do Without Broadway.' "

" 'Oh, I know don well I can do widout Broadway—*but* . . . can Broadway do widout meeeee? . . . ' "

"Oh, Manny, we could be so happy—in Florence, my sweetest, we could come out of hiding."

"We're not in hiding. We never have been."

"No, not when it's like this. But otherwise it's all so false and wrong and lonely. We could make each other so happy. I wouldn't be your little girl over there. I would when we played, but otherwise I'd be your wife."

"We'd be what we've always been. Stop dreaming."

"No, not so. Without her—"

"You want a corpse on your conscience? She would be dead in a year."

"But I have a corpse on my conscience." The floor creaked where her two feet had suddenly landed. So she *had* been on his lap! "Look!"

"Cover yourself."

"My corpse."

Scuffling on the floorboards. The heavy tread of Lonoff on the move.

"Good night."

"Look at it."

"Melodrama, Amy. Cover up."

"You prefer tragedy?"

"Don't wallow. You're not convincing. Decide not to lose hold—and then don't."

"But I'm going crazy! I cannot live apart from you! I don't know how. Oh, why didn't I take that job—and move back! And the hell with her!"

"You did the right thing. You know just what to do."

"Yes, give things up!"

"Dreamy things, correct."

"Oh, Manny, would it kill you just to kiss my breasts? Is that dreamy, too? Would it cause the death of anyone if you just did that?"

"You cover yourself now."

"Dad-da, *please.*"

But next I heard Lonoff's carpet slippers—yes, he was out of his suit, dressed for bed—padding through the upstairs corridor. Soundlessly as I could, I slipped down from the desk and made my way on my toes to the daybed, where, from the sheer physical effort that had gone into my acrobatic eavesdropping, I collapsed. My astonishment at what I'd overheard, my shame at the unpardonable breach of his trust, my relief at having escaped undiscovered—all that turned out to be nothing, really, beside the frustration I soon began to feel over the thinness of my imagination and what that promised for the future. Dad-da, Florence, the great Durante; her babyishness and desire, his mad, heroic restraint—Oh, if only I could have imagined the scene I'd overheard! If only I could invent as presumptuously as real life! If one day I could just *approach* the originality and excitement of what actually goes on! But if I ever did, what then would they think of me, my father and his judge? How would my elders hold up against that? And if they couldn't, if the blow to their sentiments was finally too wounding, just how well would I hold up against being hated and reviled and disowned?

□ III □

FEMME FATALE

It was only a year earlier that Amy had told Lonoff her whole story. Weeping hysterically, she had phoned him one night from the Biltmore Hotel in New York; as best he could understand, that morning she had come down alone on a train from Boston to see the matinee performance of a play, intending to return home again by train in the evening. Instead, after coming out of the theater she had taken a hotel room, where ever since she had been "in hiding."

At midnight, having only just finished his evening's reading and gone up to bed, Lonoff got into his car and drove south. By four he had reached the city, by six she had told him that it was the dramatization of Anne Frank's diary she had come to New York to see, but it was midmorning before she could explain even somewhat coherently her connection with this new Broadway play.

"It wasn't the play—I could have watched that easily enough if I had been alone. It was the people watching with me. Carloads of women kept pulling up to the theater, women wearing fur coats, with expensive shoes and handbags. I thought, This isn't for me. The billboards, the photographs, the marquee, I could take all that. But it was the women who frightened me— and their families and their children and their homes. Go to a movie, I told myself, go instead to a museum. But I showed my ticket, I went in with them, and of course it happened. It had to happen. It's what happens there. The women cried. Everyone around me was in tears. Then at the end, in the row behind me, a woman screamed, 'Oh, no.' That's why I came running here. I wanted a room with a telephone in it where I could stay until I'd found my father. But all I did once I was here was sit in the bathroom thinking that if he knew, if I told him, then they would have to come out on the stage after each performance and announce, 'But she is really alive. You needn't worry, she survived, she is twenty-six now, and doing very well.' I would say to him, 'You must keep this our secret—no one but you must ever know.' But suppose he was found out? What if we both were? Manny, I couldn't call him. And I knew I couldn't when I heard that woman scream 'Oh, no.' I knew then what's been true all along: I'll never see him again. I have to be dead to everyone."

Amy lay on the rumpled bed, wrapped tightly in a blanket, while Lonoff listened in silence from a chair by the window. Upon entering the unlocked room, he had found her sitting in the empty bathtub, still wearing her best dress and her best coat: the coat because she could not stop trembling, in the tub because it was the farthest she could get from the window, which was twenty floors above the street.

"How pathetic, you must think. What a joke," she said.

"A joke? On whom? I don't see the joke."

"My telling this to you."

"I still don't get it."

"Because it's like one of your stories. An E. I. Lonoff story ... called ... oh, you'd know what to call it. You'd know how to tell it in three pages. A homeless girl comes from Europe, sits in the professor's class being clever, listens to his records, plays his daughter's piano, virtually grows up in his house, and then one day, when the waif is a woman and out on her own, one fine day in the Biltmore Hotel, she casually announces ... "

He left his chair and came to sit beside her on the bed while she went to pieces again. "Yes," he said, "quite casually."

"Manny, I'm not a lunatic, I'm not a crackpot, I'm not some girl—you must believe me—trying to be interesting and imitate your art!"

"My dear friend," he replied, his arms around her now and rocking her like a child, "if this is all so—"

"Oh, Dad-da, I'm afraid it really is."

"Well, then, you have left my poor art far behind."

This is the tale that Amy told the morning after she had gone alone to the Cort Theatre to sit amid the weeping and inconsolable audience at the famous New York production of *The Diary of Anne Frank*. This is the story that the twenty-six-year-old young woman with the striking face and the fetching accent and the felicitous prose style and the patience, according to Lonoff, of a Lonoff, expected him to believe was true.

After the war she had become Amy Bellette. She had not taken the new name to disguise her identity—as yet there was no need—but, as she imagined at the time, to forget her life. She had been in a coma for weeks, first in the filthy barracks with the other ailing and starving inmates, and then in the squalid makeshift "infirmary." A dozen dying children had been rounded up by the SS and placed beneath blankets in a room with twelve beds in order to impress the Allied armies advancing upon Belsen with the amenities of concentration-camp living. Those of the twelve still alive when the British got there had been moved to an army field hospital. It was here that she finally came around. She understood sometimes less and sometimes more than the nurses explained to her, but she would not speak. Instead, without howling or hallucinating, she tried to find a way to believe that she was somewhere in Germany, that she was not yet sixteen, and that her family was dead. Those were the facts; now to grasp them.

"Little Beauty" the nurses called her—a silent, dark, emaciated girl—and so, one morning, ready to talk, she told them that the surname was Bellette. Amy she got from an American book she had sobbed over as a child, *Little Women*. She had decided, during her long silence, to finish growing up in America now that there was nobody left to live with in Amsterdam. After Belsen she figured it might be best to put an ocean the size of the Atlantic between herself and what she needed to forget.

She learned of her father's survival while waiting to get her teeth examined by the Lonoff's family dentist in Stockbridge. She had been three years with foster families in England, and almost a year as a freshman at Athene College, when she picked an old copy of *Time* out of the pile in the waiting room and, just turning pages, saw a photograph of a Jewish businessman named Otto Frank. In July of 1942, some two years after the beginning of the Nazi occupation, he had taken his wife and his two young daughters into hiding. Along with another Jewish family, the Franks lived safely for twenty-five months in a rear upper story of the Amsterdam building where he used to have his business offices. Then, in August 1944, their whereabouts were apparently betrayed by one of the workers in the warehouse below, and the hideout was uncovered by the police. Of the eight who'd been together in the sealed-off attic rooms, only Otto Frank survived the concentration camps. When he came back to Amsterdam after the war, the Dutch family who had been their protectors gave him the notebooks that had been kept in hiding by his younger daughter, a girl of fifteen when she died in Belsen: a diary, some ledgers she wrote in, and a sheaf of papers emptied out of her briefcase when the Nazis were ransacking the place for valuables. Frank printed and circulated the diary only privately at first, as a memorial to his family, but in 1947 it was published in a regular edition under the title *Het Achterhuis*—"The House Behind." Dutch readers, *Time* said, were greatly affected by the young teenager's record of how the hunted Jews tried to carry on a civilized life despite their deprivations and the terror of discovery.

Alongside the article—"A Survivor's Sorrows"—was the photograph of the diarist's father, "now sixty." He stood alone in his coat and hat in front of the building on the Prinsengracht Canal where his late family had improvised a last home.

Next came the part of her story that Lonoff was bound to think improbable. She herself, however, could not consider it all that strange that she should be thought dead when in fact she was alive; nobody who knew the chaos of those final months—the Allies bombing everywhere, the SS in flight—would call that improbable. Whoever claimed to have seen her dead of typhus in Belsen had either confused her with her older sister, Margot, or had figured that she was dead after seeing her so long in a coma, or had watched her being carted away, as good as dead, by the Kapos.

"Belsen was the third camp," Amy told him. "We were sent first to Westerbork, north of Amsterdam. There were other children around to talk to, we were back in the open air—aside from being frightened it really wasn't that awful. Daddy lived in the men's barracks, but when I got sick he managed somehow to get into the women's camp at night and to come to my bed and hold my hand. We were there a month, then we were shipped to Auschwitz. Three days and three nights in the freight cars. Then they opened the doors and that was the last I saw of him. The men were pushed in one direction, we were pushed in the other. That was early September. I saw my mother last at the end of October. She could hardly speak by then. When Margot and I were shipped from Auschwitz, I don't even know if she understood."

She told him about Belsen. Those who had survived the cattle cars lived at first in tents on the heath. They slept on the bare ground in rags. Days went by without food or fresh water, and after the autumn storms tore the tents from their moorings, they slept exposed to the wind and rain. When at last they were being moved into barracks, they saw ditches beyond the camp enclosure piled high with bodies—the people who had died on the heath from typhus and starvation. By the time winter came, it seemed as if everyone still alive was either sick or half mad. And then, while watching her sister slowly dying, she grew sick herself. After Margot's death, she could hardly remember the women in the barracks who had helped her, and knew nothing of what happened to them.

It was not so improbable either that after her long hospital convalescence she had not made her way to the address in Switzerland where the family had agreed to meet if they should ever lose touch with one another. Would a weak sixteen-year-old girl undertake a journey requiring money, visas—requiring hope—only to learn at the other end that she was as lost and alone as she feared?

No, no, the improbable part was this: that instead of telephoning *Time* and saying, "I'm the one who wrote the diary—find Otto Frank!" she jotted down in her notebook the date on the magazine's cover and, after a tooth had been filled, went off with her school books to the library. What was improbable—inexplicable, indefensible, a torment still to her conscience—was that, calm and studious as ever, she checked *The New York Times Index* and the *Readers' Guide to Periodical Literature* for "Frank, Anne" and "Frank, Otto" and *"Het Achterhuis,"* and, when she found nothing, went down to the library's lowest stacks, where the periodicals were shelved. There she spent the remaining hour before dinner rereading the article in *Time*. She read it until she knew it by heart. She studied her father's photograph. Now sixty. And those were the words that did it—made of her once again the daughter who cut his hair for him in the attic, the daughter who did her lessons there with him as her tutor, the daughter who would run to his bed and cling to him under the covers when she heard the Allied bombers flying over Amsterdam:

suddenly she was the daughter for whom he had taken the place of everything she could no longer have. She cried for a very long time. But when she went to dinner in the dormitory, she pretended that nothing catastrophic had once again happened to Otto Frank's Anne.

But then right from the beginning she had resolved not to speak about what she had been through. Resolutions were her strong point as a young girl on her own. How else could she have lasted on her own? One of the thousand reasons she could not bear Uncle Daniel, the first of her foster fathers in England, was that sooner or later he wound up telling whoever walked into the house about all that had happened to Amy during the war. And then there was Miss Giddings, the young teacher in the school north of London who was always giving the orphaned little Jewess tender glances during history class. One day after school Miss Giddings took her for a lemon-curd tart at the local tearoom and asked her questions about the concentration camps. Her eyes filled with tears as Amy, who felt obliged to answer, confirmed the stories she had heard but could never quite believe. "Terrible," Miss Giddings said, "so terrible." Amy silently drank her tea and ate her lovely tart, while Miss Giddings, like one of her own history students, tried in vain to understand the past. "Why is it," the unhappy teacher finally asked, "that for centuries people have hated Jews?" Amy rose to her feet. She was stunned. "Don't ask me that!" the girl said—"ask the madmen who hate us!" And she had nothing further to do with Miss Giddings as a friend—or with anyone else who asked her anything about what they couldn't possibly understand.

One Saturday only a few months after her arrival in England, vowing that if she heard another plaintive "Belsen" out of Uncle Daniel's mouth she would run off to Southampton and stow away on an American ship—and having had about enough of the snooty brand of sympathy the pure-bred English teachers offered at school—she burned her arm while ironing a blouse. The neighbors came running at the sound of her screams and rushed her to the hospital emergency room. When the bandage was removed, there was a patch of purple scar tissue about half the size of an egg instead of her camp number.

After the accident, as her foster parents called it, Uncle Daniel informed the Jewish Welfare Board that his wife's ill health made it impossible for them to continue to have Amy in their home. The foster child moved on to another family—and then another. She told whoever asked that she had been evacuated from Holland with a group of Jewish schoolchildren the week before the Nazis invaded. Sometimes she did not even say that the schoolchildren were Jewish, an omission for which she was mildly rebuked by the Jewish families who had accepted responsibility for her and were troubled by her lying. But she could not bear them all laying their helpful hands upon her shoulders because of Auschwitz and Belsen. If she was going to be thought exceptional, it would not be because of Auschwitz and Belsen but because of what she had made of herself since.

They were kind and thoughtful people, and they tried to get her to understand that she was not in danger in England. "You needn't feel frightened or threatened in any way," they assured her. "Or ashamed of anything." "I'm not ashamed. That's the point." "Well, that isn't always the point when young people try to hide their Jewish origins." "Maybe it isn't with others," she told them, "but it is with me."

On the Saturday after discovering her father's photograph in *Time,* she took the morning bus to Boston, and in every foreign bookstore looked in vain for a copy of *Het Achterhuis.* Two weeks later she traveled the three hours to Boston again, this time to the main post office to rent a box. She paid for it in cash, then mailed the letter she was carrying in her handbag, along with a money order for fifteen dollars, to Contact Publishers in Amsterdam, requesting them to send, postage paid, to Pilgrim International Bookshop, P.O. Box 152, Boston, Mass., U.S.A., as many copies as fifteen dollars would buy of *Het Achterhuis* by Anne Frank.

She had been dead for him some four years; believing her dead for another month or two would not really hurt much more. Curiously she did not hurt more either, except in bed at night when she cried and begged forgiveness for the cruelty she was practicing on her perfect father, now sixty.

Nearly three months after she had sent the order off to her Amsterdam publisher, on a warm, sunny day at the beginning of August, there was a package too large for the Pilgrim Bookshop post-office box waiting to be picked up in Boston. She was wearing a beige linen skirt and a fresh white cotton blouse, both ironed the night before. Her hair, cut in pageboy style that spring, had been washed and set the previous night, and her skin was evenly tanned. She was swimming a mile every morning and playing tennis every afternoon and, all in all, was as fit and energetic as a twenty-year-old could be. Maybe that was why, when the postal clerk handed her the parcel, she did not tear at the string with her teeth or faint straightaway onto the marble floor. Instead, she walked over to the Common—the package mailed from Holland swinging idly from one hand—and wandered along until she found an unoccupied bench. She sat first on a bench in the shade, but then got up and walked on until she found a perfect spot in the sunshine.

After thoroughly studying the Dutch stamps—postwar issues new to her—and contemplating the postmark, she set about to see how carefully she could undo the package. It was a preposterous display of unruffled patience and she meant it to be. She was feeling at once triumphant and giddy. Forbearance, she thought. Patience. Without patience there is no life. When she had finally untied the string and unfolded, without tearing, the layers of thick brown paper, it seemed to her that what she had so meticulously removed from the wrappings and placed onto the lap of her clean and pretty American girl's beige linen skirt was her survival itself.

Van Anne Frank. Her book. Hers.

She had begun keeping a diary less than three weeks before Pim told her that they were going into hiding. Until she ran out of pages and had to carry over onto office ledgers, she made the entries in a cardboard-covered notebook that he'd given her for her thirteenth birthday. She still remembered most of what happened to her in the achterhuis, some of it down to the most minute detail, but of the fifty thousand words recording it all, she couldn't remember writing one. Nor could she remember anything much of what she'd confided there about her personal problems to the phantom confidante she'd named Kitty—whole pages of her tribulations as new and strange to her as her native tongue.

Perhaps because *Het Achterhuis* was the first Dutch book she'd read since she'd written it, her first thought when she finished was of her childhood friends in Amsterdam, the boys and girls from the Montessori school where she'd learned to read and write. She tried to remember the names of the Christian children, who would have survived the war. She tried to recall the names of her teachers, going all the way back to kindergarten. She pictured the faces of the shopkeepers, the postman, the milk deliveryman who had known her as a child. She imagined their neighbors in the houses on Merwedeplein. And when she had, she saw each of them closing her book and thinking, Who realized she was so gifted? Who realized we had such a writer in our midst?

The first passage she reread was dated over a year before the birth of Amy Bellette. The first time round she'd bent back the corner of the page; the second time, with a pen from her purse, she drew a dark meaningful line in the margin and beside it wrote—in English, of course—"uncanny." (Everything she marked she was marking for him, or made the mark actually pretending to be him.) *I have an odd way of sometimes, as it were, being able to see myself through someone else's eyes. Then I view the affairs of a certain "Anne" at my ease, and browse through the pages of her life as if she were a stranger. Before we came here, when I didn't think about things as much as I do now, I used at times to have the feeling that I didn't belong to Mansa, Pim, and Margot, and that I would always be a bit of an outsider. Sometimes I used to pretend I was an orphan . . .*

Then she read the whole thing from the start again, making a small marginal notation—and a small grimace—whenever she came upon anything she was sure he would consider "decorative" or "imprecise" or "unclear." But mostly she marked passages she couldn't believe that she had written as little more than a child. Why, what eloquence, Anne—it gave her gooseflesh, whispering her own name in Boston—what deftness, what wit! How nice, she thought, if I could write like this for Mr. Lonoff's English 12. "It's good," she heard him saying, "it's the best thing you've ever done, Miss Bellette."

But of course it was—she'd had a "great subject," as the girls said in English class. Her family's affinity with what families were suffering everywhere had been clear to her right from the beginning. *There is nothing we can do but wait as calmly as we can till the misery comes to an end. Jews and Christians wait, the whole earth waits; and there are many who wait for death.* But while writing these lines ("Quiet, emphatic feeling—that's the idea. E.I.L.") she had had no grandiose delusions about her little achterhuis diary's ever standing as part of the record of the misery. It wasn't to educate anybody other than herself—out of her great expectations—that she kept track of how trying it all was. Recording it was enduring it; the diary kept her company and it kept her sane, and whenever being her parents' child seemed to her as harrowing as the war itself, it was where she went to confess. Only to Kitty was she able to speak freely about the hopelessness of trying to satisfy her mother the way Margot did; only to Kitty could she openly bewail her inability even to pronounce the word "Mumsie" to her aloud—and to concede the depth of her feeling for Pim, a father she wanted to want her to the exclusion of all others, *not only as his child, but for me—Anne, myself.*

Of course it had eventually to occur to any child so *mad on books and reading* that for all she knew she was writing a book of her own. But most of the time it was her morale that she was sustaining not, at fourteen, literary ambition. As for developing into a writer—she owed that not to any decision to sit down each day and try to be one but to their stifling life. That, of all things, seemed to have nurtured her talent! Truly, without the terror and the claustrophobia of the achterhuis, as a *chatterbox* surrounded by friends and *rollicking with laughter,* free to come and go, free to clown around, free to pursue her every last expectation, would she ever have written sentences so deft and so eloquent and so witty? She thought, Now maybe that's the problem in English 12—not the absence of the great subject but the presence of the lake and the tennis courts and Tanglewood. The perfect tan, the linen skirts, my emerging reputation as the Pallas Athene of Athene College— maybe that's what's doing me in. Maybe if I were locked up again in a room somewhere and fed on rotten potatoes and clothed in rags and terrified out of my wits, maybe then I could write a decent story for Mr. Lonoff!

It was only with the euphoria of *invasion fever,* with the prospect of the Allied landings and the German collapse and the coming of that golden age known around the achterhuis as *after the war,* that she was able to announce to Kitty that the diary had perhaps done more than just assuage her adolescent loneliness. After two years of honing her prose, she felt herself ready for the great undertaking: *my greatest wish is to become a journalist someday and later on a famous writer.* But that was in May of 1944, when to be famous someday seemed to her no more or less extraordinary than to be going back to school in September. Oh, that May of marvelous expectations! Never again another winter in the achterhuis. Another winter and she would have gone crazy.

The first year there it hadn't been that bad; they'd all been so busy settling in that she didn't have time to feel desperate. In fact, so diligently had they all worked to transform the attic into a *superpractical* home that her father had gotten everybody to agree to subdivide the space still further and take in another Jew. But once the Allied bombing started, the superpractical home became her torture chamber. During the day the two families squabbled over everything, and then at night she couldn't sleep, sure that the Gestapo was going to come in the dark to take them away. In bed she began to have horrifying visions of Lies, her schoolfriend, reproaching her for being safe in bed in Amsterdam and not in a concentration camp, like all her Jewish friends: *"Oh, Anne, why have you deserted me? Help, oh, help me, rescue me from this hell!"* She would see herself *in a dungeon, without Mummy and Daddy*—and worse. Right down to the final hours of 1943 she was dreaming and thinking *the most terrible things*. But then all at once it was over. Miraculously. "And what did it, Professor Lonoff? See *Anna Karenina*. See *Madame Bovary*. See half the literature of the Western world." The miracle: desire. She would be back to school in September, but she would not be returning to class the same girl. She was no longer a girl. Tears would roll down her cheeks at the thought of a naked woman. Her unpleasant menstrual periods became a source of the strangest pleasure. At night in bed she was excited by her breasts. Just these sensations—but all at once forebodings of her miserable death were replaced with a craze for life. One day she was completely recovered, and the next she was, of course, in love. Their troubles had made her her own woman, at fourteen. She began going off on private visits to the secluded corner of the topmost floor, which was occupied exclusively by Peter, the Van Daans' seventeen-year-old son. That she might be stealing him away from Margot didn't stop her, and neither did her scandalized parents: first just teatime visits, then evening assignations—then the defiant letter to the disappointed father. On May 3rd of that marvelous May: *I am young and I possess many buried qualities; I am young and strong and am living a great adventure.* And two days later, to the father who had saved her from the hell that had swallowed up Lies, to the Pim whose favorite living creature she had always longed to be, a declaration of her independence, *in mind and body,* as she bluntly put it: *I have now reached the stage that I can live entirely on my own, without Mummy's support or anyone else's for that matter . . . I don't feel in the least bit responsible to any of you . . . I don't have to give an account of my deeds to anyone but myself . . .*

Well, the strength of a woman on her own wasn't all she'd imagined it to be. Neither was the strength of a loving father. He told her it was the most unpleasant letter he'd ever received, and when she began to cry with

shame for having been *too low for words,* he wept along with her. He burned
the letter in the fire, the weeks passed, and she found herself growing disen-
chanted with Peter. In fact, by July she was wondering how it would be possible, in their circumstances, to *shake him off,* a problem resolved for her on a
sunny August Friday, when in the middle of the morning, as Pim was helping Peter with his English lessons and she was off studying by herself, the
Dutch Green Police arrived and dissolved forever the secret household still
heedful of propriety, obedience, discretion, self-improvement, and mutual respect. The Franks, as a family, came to an end, and, fittingly enough, thought
the diarist, so did her chronicle of their effort to go sensibly on as themselves,
in spite of everything.

The third time she read the book through was on the way back to Stockbridge that evening. Would she ever read another book again? How, if she
couldn't put this one down? On the bus she began to speculate in the most
immodest way about what she had written—had "wrought." Perhaps what
got her going was the rumbling, boundless, electrified, indigo sky that had
been stalking the bus down the highway since Boston: outside the window
the most outlandish El Greco stage effects, outside a Biblical thunderstorm
complete with baroque trimmings, and inside Amy curled up with her
book—and with the lingering sense of tragic grandeur she'd soaked up from
the real El Grecos that afternoon in the Boston Museum of Fine Arts. And
she was exhausted, which probably doesn't hurt fantastical thinking, either.
Still spellbound by her first two readings of *Het Achterhuis,* she had rushed on
to the Gardner and the Fogg, where, to top off the day, the self-intoxicated
girl with the deep tan and the animated walk had been followed by easily a
dozen Harvard Summer School students eager to learn her name. Three museums because back at Athene she preferred to tell everyone the truth, more
or less, about the big day in Boston. To Mr. Lonoff she planned to speak at
length about all the new exhibitions she'd gone to see at his wife's suggestion.

The storm, the paintings, her exhaustion—none of it was really necessary, however, to inspire the sort of expectations that resulted from reading
her published diary three times through in the same day. Towering egotism
would probably have been sufficient. Perhaps she was only a very young
writer on a bus dreaming a very young writer's dreams.

All her reasoning, all her fantastical thinking about the ordained mission of
her book followed from this: neither she nor her parents came through in the
diary as anything like representative of religious or observant Jews. Her
mother lit candles on Friday night and that was about the extent of it. As for

celebrations, she found St. Nicholas's Day, once she'd been introduced to it in hiding, much more fun than Chanukah, and along with Pim made all kinds of clever gifts and even written a Santa Claus poem to enliven the festivities. When Pim settled upon a children's Bible as her present for the holiday—so she might learn something about the New Testament—Margot hadn't approved. Margot's ambition was to be a midwife in Palestine. She was the only one of them who seemed to have given serious thought to religion. The diary that Margot kept, had it ever been found, would not have been quite so sparing as hers in curiosity about Judaism, or plans for leading a Jewish life. Certainly it was impossible for her to imagine Margot thinking, let alone writing with longing in her diary, *the time will come when we are people again, and not just Jews.*

She had written these words, to be sure, still suffering the aftereffects of a nighttime burglary in the downstairs warehouse. The burglary had seemed certain to precipitate their discovery by the police, and for days afterward everyone was weak with terror. And for her, along with the residue of fear and the dubious sense of relief, there was, of course, the guilt-tinged bafflement when she realized that, unlike Lies, she had again been spared. In the aftermath of that gruesome night, she went around and around trying to understand the meaning of their persecution, one moment writing about the misery of being Jews and only Jews to their enemies, and then in the next airily wondering if *it might even be our religion from which the world and all peoples learn good. . . . We can never become just Netherlanders,* she reminded Kitty, *we will always remain Jews, but we want to, too*—only to close out the argument with an announcement one most assuredly would not have come upon in "The Diary of Margot Frank": *I've been saved again, now my first wish after the war is that I may become Dutch! I love the Dutch, I love this country, I love the language and want to work here. And even if I have to write to the Queen myself, I will not give up until I have reached my goal.*

No, that wasn't mother's Margot talking, that was father's Anne. To London to learn English, to Paris to look at clothes and study art, to Hollywood, California, to interview the stars as someone named "Anne Franklin"—while self-sacrificing Margot delivered babies in the desert. To be truthful, while Margot was thinking about God and the homeland, the only deities she ever seemed to contemplate at any length were to be found in the mythology of Greece and Rome, which she studied all the time in hiding, and adored. To be truthful, the young girl of her diary was, compared to Margot, only dimly Jewish, though in that entirely the daughter of the father who calmed her fears by reading aloud to her at night not the Bible but Goethe in German and Dickens in English.

But that was the point—that was what gave her diary the power to make the nightmare real. To expect the great callous and indifferent world to care about the child of a pious, bearded father living under the sway of the rabbis and the rituals—that was pure folly. To the ordinary person with no great gift for tolerating even the smallest of differences the plight of that family wouldn't mean a thing. To ordinary people it probably would seem that they had invited disaster by stubbornly repudiating everything modern and European—not to say Christian. But the family of Otto Frank, that would be another matter! How could even the most obtuse of the ordinary ignore what had been done to the Jews *just for being Jews,* how could even the most benighted of the Gentiles fail to get the idea when they read in *Het Achterhuis* that once a year the Franks sang a harmless Chanukah song, said some Hebrew words, lighted some candles, exchanged some presents—a ceremony lasting about ten minutes—and that was all it took to make them the enemy. It did not even take that much. It took nothing—that was the horror. And that was truth. And that was the power of her book. The Franks could gather together by the radio to listen to concerts of Mozart, Brahms, and Beethoven; they could entertain themselves with Goethe and Dickens and Schiller; she could look night after night through the genealogical tables of all of Europe's royal families for suitable mates for Princess Elizabeth and Princess Margaret Rose; she could write passionately in her diary of her love for Queen Wilhelmina and her desire for Holland to be her fatherland—and none of it made any difference. Europe was not theirs nor were they Europe's, not even her Europeanized family. Instead, three flights up from a pretty Amsterdam canal, they lived crammed into a hundred square feet with the Van Daans, as isolated and despised as any ghetto Jews. First expulsion, next confinement, and then, in cattle cars and camps and ovens, obliteration. And why? Because the Jewish problem to be solved, the degenerates whose contamination civilized people could no longer abide, were they themselves, Otto and Edith Frank, and their daughters, Margot and Anne.

This was the lesson that on the journey home she came to believe she had the power to teach. But only if she were believed to be dead. Were *Het Achterhuis* known to be the work of a living writer, it would never be more than it was: a young teenager's diary of her trying years in hiding during the German occupation of Holland, something boys and girls could read in bed at night along with the adventures of the Swiss Family Robinson. But dead she had something more to offer than amusement for ages 10–15; dead she had written, without meaning to or trying to, a book with the force of a masterpiece to make people finally see.

And when people had finally seen? When they had learned what she had the power to teach them, what then? Would suffering come to mean something new to them? Could she actually make them humane creatures for any longer than the few hours it would take to read her diary through? In her room at Athene—after hiding in her dresser the three copies of *Het Achterhuis*—she thought more calmly about her readers-to-be than she had while pretending to be one of them on the stirring bus ride through the lightning storm. She was not, after all, the fifteen-year-old who could, while hiding from a holocaust, tell Kitty, *I still believe that people are really good at heart.* Her youthful ideals had suffered no less than she had in the windowless freight car from Westerbork and in the barracks at Auschwitz and on the Belsen heath. She had not come to hate the human race for what it was—what could it be but what it was?—but she did not feel seemly any more singing its praises.

What would happen when people had finally seen? The only realistic answer was Nothing. To believe anything else was only to yield to longings which even she, the great longer, had a right to question by now. To keep her existence a secret from her father so as to help improve mankind . . . no, not at this late date. The improvement of the living was their business, not hers; they could improve themselves, if they should ever be so disposed; and if not, not. Her responsibility was to the dead, if to anyone—to her sister, to her mother, to all the slaughtered schoolchildren who had been her friends. There was her diary's purpose, there was her ordained mission: to restore in print their status as flesh and blood . . . for all the good that would do them. An ax was what she really wanted, not print. On the stairwell at the end of her corridor in the dormitory there was a large ax with an enormous red handle, to be used in case of fire. But what about in case of hatred—what about murderous rage? She stared at it often enough, but never found the nerve to take it down from the wall. Besides, once she had it in her hands, whose head would she split open? Whom could she kill in Stockbridge to avenge the ashes and the skulls? If she even could wield it. No, what she had been given to wield was *Het Achterhuis, van Anne Frank.* And to draw blood with it she would have to vanish again into another achterhuis, this time fatherless and all on her own.

So she renewed her belief in the power of her less than three hundred pages, and with it the resolve to keep from her father, sixty, the secret of her survival. "For them," she cried, "for them," meaning all who had met the fate that she had been spared and was now pretending to. "For Margot, for my mother, for Lies."

Now every day she went to the library to read *The New York Times.* Each week she read carefully through the newsmagazines. On Sundays she read about all the new books being published in America: novels said to be "notable" and "significant," none of which could possibly be more notable and more significant than her posthumously published diary; insipid best-sellers from which real people learned about fake people who could not exist and would not matter if they did. She read praise for historians and biographers whose books, whatever their merit, couldn't possibly be as worthy of recognition as hers. And in every column in every periodical she found in the library—American, French, German, English—she looked for her own real name. It could not end with just a few thousand Dutch readers shaking their heads and going about their business—it was too important for that! "For them, for them"—over and over, week after week, "for them"—until at last she began to wonder if having survived in the achterhuis, if having outlived the death camps, if masquerading here in New England as somebody other than herself did not make something very suspect—and a little mad—of this seething passion to "come back" as the avenging ghost. She began to fear that she was succumbing to having not succumbed.

And why should she! Who was she pretending to be but who she would have been anyway if no achterhuis and no death camps had intervened? Amy was not somebody else. The Amy who had rescued her from her memories and restored her to life—beguiling, commonsensical, brave, and realistic Amy—was herself. Who she had every right to be! Responsibility to the dead? Rhetoric for the pious! There was nothing to give the dead—they were dead. "Exactly. The importance, so-called, of this book is a morbid illusion. And playing dead is melodramatic and disgusting. And hiding from Daddy is worse. No atonement is required," said Amy to Anne. "Just get on the phone and tell Pim you're alive. He is sixty."

Her longing for him now exceeded even what it had been in childhood, when she wanted more than anything to be his only love. But she was young and strong and she was living a great adventure, and she did nothing to inform him or anyone that she was still alive; and then one day it was just too late. No one would have believed her; no one other than her father would have wanted to. Now people came every day to visit their secret hideaway and to look at the photographs of the movie stars that she'd pinned to the wall beside her bed. They came to see the tub she had bathed in and the table where she'd studied. They looked out of the loft window where Peter and she had cuddled together watching the stars. They stared at the cupboard camouflaging the door the police had come through to take them away. They looked at the open pages of her secret diary. That was her handwriting, they whispered, those are her words. They stayed to look at everything in the achterhuis that she had ever touched. The plain passageways and serviceable little rooms that she had, like a good composition student, dutifully laid out for Kitty in orderly, accurate, workaday Dutch—the super-practical achterhuis was now a holy shrine, a Wailing Wall. They went away from it in silence, as bereft as though she had been their own.

But it was they who were hers. "They wept for me," said Amy; "they pitied me; they prayed for me; they begged my forgiveness. I was the incarnation of the millions of unlived years robbed from the murdered Jews. It was too late to be alive now. I was a saint."

That was her story. And what did Lonoff think of it when she was finished? That she meant every word and that not a word was true.

After Amy had showered and dressed, she checked out of the hotel and he took her to eat some lunch. He phoned Hope from the restaurant and explained that he was bringing Amy home. She could walk in the woods, look at the foliage, sleep safely in Becky's bed; over a few days' time she would be able to collect herself, and then she could return to Cambridge. All he explained about her collapse was that she appeared to him to be suffering from exhaustion. He had promised Amy that he would say no more.

On the ride back to the Berkshires, while Amy told him what it had been like for her during the years when she was being read in twenty different languages by twenty million people, he made plans to consult Dr. Boyce. Boyce was at Riggs, the Stockbridge psychiatric hospital. Whenever a new book appeared, Dr. Boyce would send a charming note asking the author if he would kindly sign the doctor's copy, and once a year the Lonoffs were invited to the Boyces' big barbecue. At Dr. Boyce's request, Lonoff once relectantly consented to meet with a staff study group from the hospital to discuss "the creative personality." He didn't want to offend the psychiatrist, and it might for a while pacify his wife, who liked to believe that if he got out and mixed more with people things would be better at home.

The study group turned out to have ideas about writing that were too imaginative for his taste, but he made no effort to tell them they were wrong. Nor did he think that he was necessarily right. They saw it their way, he saw it like Lonoff. Period. He had no desire to change anyone's mind. Fiction made people say all kinds of strange things—so be it.

The meeting with the psychiatrists had been underway for only an hour when Lonoff said it had been an enjoyable evening but he had to be getting home. "I have the evening's reading still ahead of me. Without my reading I'm not myself. However, you must feel free to talk about my personality when I'm gone." Boyce, smiling warmly, replied, "I hope we've amused you at least a little with our naïve speculations." "I would have liked to amuse *you*. I apologize for being boring." "No, no," said Boyce, "passivity in a man of stature has a charm and mystery all its own." "Yes?" said Lonoff. "I must tell my wife."

But an hour wasted some five years ago was hardly to the point. He trusted Boyce and knew that the psychiatrist would not betray his confidence when he went the next day to talk with him about his former student and quasi daughter, a young woman of twenty-six, who had disclosed to him that of all the Jewish writers, from Franz Kafka to E. I. Lonoff, she was the most famous. As for his own betrayal of the quasi daughter's confidence, it did not count for much as Amy elaborated further upon her consuming delusion.

"Do you know why I took this sweet name? It wasn't to protect me from my memories. I wasn't hiding the past from myself or myself from the past. I was hiding from hatred, from hating people the way people hate spiders and rats. Manny, I felt flayed. I felt as though the skin had been peeled away from half my body. Half my face had been peeled away, and everybody would stare in horror for the rest of my life. Or they would stare at the other half, at the half still intact; I could see them smiling, pretending that the flayed half wasn't there, and talking to the half that was. And I could hear myself screaming at them, I could see myself thrusting my hideous side right up into their unmarred faces to make them properly horrified. 'I was pretty! I was whole! I was a sunny, lively little girl! Look, look at what they did to me!' But whatever side they looked at, I would always be screaming, 'Look at the other! Why don't you look at the other!' That's what I thought about in the hospital at night. However they look at me, however they talk to me, however they try to comfort me, I will always be this half-flayed thing. I will never be young, I will never be kind or at peace or in love, and I will hate them all my life.

"So I took the sweet name—to impersonate everything that I wasn't. And a very good pretender I was, too. After a while I could imagine that I wasn't pretending at all, that I had become what I would have been anyway. Until the book. The package came from Amsterdam, I opened it, and there it was: my past, myself, my name, *my face intact*—and all I wanted was revenge. It wasn't for the dead—it had nothing to do with bringing back the dead or scourging the living. It wasn't corpses I was avenging—it was the motherless, fatherless, sisterless, venge-filled, hate-filled, shame-filled, half-flayed, seething thing. It was myself. I wanted tears, I wanted their Christian tears to run like Jewish blood, for me. I wanted their pity—and in the most pitiless way. And I wanted love, to be loved mercilessly and endlessly, just the way I'd been debased. I wanted my fresh life and my fresh body, cleansed and unpolluted. And it needed twenty million people for that. Twenty million ten times over.

"Oh, Manny, I want to live with you! That's what I need! The millions won't do it—it's you! I want to go home to Europe with you. Listen to me, don't say no, not yet. This summer I saw a small house for rent, a stone villa up on a hillside. It was outside Florence. It had a pink tile roof and a garden. I got the phone number and I wrote it down. I still have it. Oh, everything beautiful that I saw in Italy made me think of how happy you could be there—how happy I would be there, looking after you I thought of the trips we'd take. I thought of the afternoons in the museums and having coffee later by the river. I thought of listening to music together at night. I thought of making your meals. I thought of wearing lovely nightgowns to bed. Oh, Manny, their Anne Frank is theirs; I want to be *your* Anne Frank. I'd like at last to be my own. Child Martyr and Holy Saint isn't a position I'm really qualified for any more. They wouldn't even have me, not as I am, longing for somebody else's husband, begging him to leave his loyal wife to run off with a girl half his age. Manny, does it matter that I'm your daughter's age and you're my father's? Of course I love the Dad-da in you, how could I not? And if you love the child in me, why shouldn't you? There's nothing strange in that—so does half the world. Love has to start somewhere, and that's where it starts in us. And as for who I am—well," said Amy, in a voice as sweet and winning as any he'd ever heard, "you've got to be somebody, don't you? There's no way around that."

At home they put her to bed. In the kitchen Lonoff sat with his wife drinking the coffee she'd made him. Every time he pictured Amy at the dentist's office reading about Otto Frank in *Time* magazine, or in the library stacks searching for her "real" name, every time he imagined her on Boston Common addressing to her writing teacher an intimate disquisition on "her" book, he wanted to let go and cry. He had never suffered so over the suffering of another human being.

Of course he told Hope nothing about who Amy thought she was. But he didn't have to, he could guess what she would say if he did: it was for him, the great writer, that Amy had chosen to become Anne Frank; that explained it all, no psychiatrist required. For him, as a consequence of her infatuation: to enchant him, to bewitch him, to break through the scrupulosity and the wisdom and the virtue into his imagination, and there, as Anne Frank, to become E. I. Lonoff's *femme fatale*.

□ **IV** □

MARRIED TO TOLSTOY

The next morning we all ate breakfast together like a happy family of four. The woman whom Lonoff could not throw out after thirty years just because he might prefer to see a new face over his fruit juice proudly told us—over our fruit juice—of the accomplishments of the children whose chairs Amy and I occupied. She showed us recent photographs of them, all with their own children. Lonoff had not mentioned to me the night before that he was a grandfather several times over. But why would he?

Hope seemed overnight to have been transformed from his aging, aggrieved, lonely wife into somebody rather more like the happy author of the sweet nature poems framed on the kitchen wall, the tender of the geraniums, the woman of whom Lonoff had said over the broken saucer, "She can glue it." Nor did Lonoff seem quite the same man; whether deliberately or not, he was humming "My Blue Heaven" when he came to the breakfast table. And almost immediately began the mordant clowning, also designed to make Hope all the happier.

And why the change? Because Amy would return to Cambridge after breakfast.

But I could not really think of her as Amy any longer. Instead I was continually drawn back into the fiction I had evolved about her and the Lonoffs while I lay in the dark study, transported by his praise and throbbing with resentment of my disapproving father—and, of course, overcome by what had passed between my idol and the marvelous young woman before he had manfully gone back to bed with his wife.

Throughout breakfast, my father, my mother, the judge and Mrs. Wapter were never out of my thoughts. I'd gone the whole night without sleep, and now I couldn't think straight about them or myself, or about Amy, as she was called. I kept seeing myself coming back to New Jersey and saying to my family, "I met a marvelous young woman while I was up in New England. I love her and she loves me. We are going to be married." "Married? But so fast? Nathan, is she Jewish?" "Yes, she is." "But who is she?" "Anne Frank."

"I eat too much," said Lonoff, as Hope poured the water for his tea.

"It's exercise you need," Hope said. "It's more walking. You gave up your afternoon walk and so you began to gain weight. You actually eat almost nothing. Certainly nothing that's fattening. It's sitting at the desk that does it. And staying in the house."

"I can't face another walk. I can't face those trees again."

"Then walk in the other direction."

"For ten years I walked in the other direction. That's why I started walking in this direction. Besides, I'm not even walking when I'm walking. The truth is, I don't even see the trees."

"That's not so," Hope said. "He loves nature," she informed me. "He knows the name of everything that grows."

"I'm cutting down on my food," said Lonoff. "Who wants to split an egg with me?"

Hope said, happily, "You can treat yourself to a whole egg this morning."

"Amy, you want to split an egg with me?"

His invitation for her to speak gave me my first opportunity to turn her way without embarrassment. It was so. It *could* be. The same look of unarmored and unimpaired intelligence, the same musing look of serene anticipation . . . The forehead wasn't Shakespeare's—it was *hers*.

She was smiling, as though she too were in the best of spirits and his refusal to kiss her breasts the night before had never happened. "Couldn't do it," she said to him.

"Not even half?" asked Lonoff.

"Not even a sixteenth."

This is my Aunt Tessie, this is Frieda and Dave, this is Birdie, this is Murray

. . . as you see, we are an enormous family. This is my wife, everyone. She is all I have ever wanted. If you doubt me, just look at her smile, listen to her laugh. Remember the shadowed eyes innocently uplifted in the clever little face? Remember the dark hair clipped back with a barrette? Well, this is she . . . Anne, says my father—the Anne? Oh, how I have misunderstood my son. How mistaken we have been!

"Scramble an egg, Hope," said Lonoff. "I'll eat half if you'll eat half."

"You can eat the whole thing," she replied. "Just start taking your walks again."

He looked at me, imploringly. "Nathan, eat half."

"No, no," said his wife and, turning to the stove, announced triumphantly, "You'll eat the whole egg!"

Beaten, Lonoff said, "And to top things off, I threw out my razor blade this morning."

"And why," said Amy, pretending still to be in her blue heaven too, "did you do a thing like that?"

"I thought it through. My children are finished with college. My house is paid for. I have Blue Cross and Major Medical protection. I have a '56 Ford. Yesterday I got a check for forty-five dollars in royalties from Brazil—money out of the blue. Throw it out, I told myself, and have a fresh shave with a new blade. Then I thought: No, there's at least one shave left in this blade, maybe even two. Why be wasteful? But then I thought it through further: I have seen books on the paperback racks, I have publishers in twenty countries, there's a new shingle roof on the house, there's a quiet new furnace in the basement, there's brand-new plumbing in Hope's little bathroom. The bills are all paid, and what is more, there is money left over in the bank that is earning three percent interest for our old age. The hell with it, I thought, enough thinking—and I put in a new blade. And look how I butchered myself. I almost took my ear off."

Amy: "Proves you shouldn't be impulsive."

"I only wanted to see what it was like living like everybody else."

"And?" asked Hope, back at the table now, frying pan in hand.

"I told you. I almost took my ear off."

"Here's your egg."

"I only want half."

"Darling, feast for once," said Hope, kissing his head.

Dear Mom and Dad: We have been with Anne's father for three days now. They have both been in the most moving state of exaltation since our arrival . . .

"And here's your mail," said Hope.

"I never used to look at this stuff until the end of the day," he explained to me.

"He wouldn't even look at the newspaper headlines," said Hope. "He wouldn't even eat breakfast with us until a few years ago. But when the children were all gone, I refused to sit here by myself."

"But I wouldn't let you talk to me, would I? That's new."

"Let me make you another egg," she said.

He pushed aside his empty plate. "No, darling, no. I'm full."

Dear Folks: Anne is pregnant, and happier, she says, than she ever thought possible again . . .

He was sorting now through the half dozen letters in his hand. He said to me, "This is what gets forwarded from a publisher. One in a hundred is worth opening. In five hundred."

"What about a secretary to open them?" I asked.

"He's too conscientious," Hope explained. "He can't do it that way. Besides, a secretary is another person. We can't turn the house into Grand Central Station."

"A secretary is six other people," he informed her.

"What is it this time?" she asked Lonoff as he turned over the penciled sheets in his hand. "Read it, Manny."

"You read it." He handed the letter across to his wife. "Let Nathan see what it is to be lifted from obscurity. Let him not come hammering at our door to tell us that he wasn't warned."

She wiped her hands on her apron and took the letter. It was quite a morning she was having, a new life altogether. And why? Because Amy was on her way.

" 'Dear Mr. Lonoff,' " she read. " 'I suggest that you with your talent write a story with the following plot. A non-Jew comes from the West to New York City and meets Jews for the first time. Being a good-natured person he does them favors. When he gives up part of his lunch hour at work to help them, they act like pigs in getting as much of his time as possible. When he helps his co-workers by getting them ball-point pens wholesale, the same happens. They try to get him to buy some for strangers by saying, "A man I know wants to buy a dozen pens," and saying later, "I didn't tell you to, I didn't ask you to buy them for him, I only told you I wanted two dozen and you can't tell me I told you to buy him two dozen." Consequently he develops a dislike for Jews. Later he finds out that non-Jews who don't try to impose are trying to put him out of a job while the Jews take his side when the boss wants to fire him. When he gets sick, the Jews donate blood for him. At the end he has a conversation with a person in which he learns how the history of the Jews led to their habit of opportunism. Yours truly, Ray W. Oliver. P.S. I am also a writer of short stories. I am willing to collaborate with you on a story using that plot.' "

"Me too," said Amy.

"The consequences of his infatuation," I said. A line out of "The Middle Years," but not even Lonoff seemed to remember it. "From Henry James," I added, flushing. " 'The rest is the madness of art.' "

"Aha," said Lonoff.

Ass! Idiot! I had been caught—while showing off my erudition! *Aha.* He knew everything.

But rather than asking me to get up and go because of the way I had behaved in his study, he opened a second letter and removed the small index card inside. He read it and handed it to Hope.

"Oh, these," she said. "They make me so angry."

"Has style, however," said Lonoff. "I like the absence of the salutation. Just puts out the line and hangs up the wash. Read it, Hopie."

"I hate these so."

"Go on. For Nathan's edification."

Then he *didn't* know. Or knew and forgave me.

" 'I have just finished your brilliant story, "Indiana," ' " Hope read. "What do you know about the Middle West, you little Jewish shit? Your Jew omniscience is about as agreeable to the average person as is your kike sense of "art." Sally M., Fort Wayne.' "

Lonoff, meanwhile, had been carefully slicing open a blue overseas air letter.

"New Delhi," he announced.

"You've been made a Brahman," said Amy.

Hope smiled at the girl who would be gone now in less than an hour. "He won't accept."

"Well," replied Amy, "maybe he's in luck and they made him an Untouchable."

"Or less," said Lonoff, and handed the letter to Hope.

"You can't have everything," Amy told him.

Hope read, this time without being prompted. " 'Dear Sir, I am a twenty-two-year-old youth from India. I introduce myself as there is no other way to make your acquaintance. Perhaps you may not relish the idea of being acquainted with a stranger who is bent on exploiting you.' " Here, suddenly, her confidence seemed shaken, and she looked up at Lonoff, confused as to what to do next.

He told her. "Go on."

"—'bent on exploiting you. I beg your assistance fully aware of the barriers like caste, creed, etc., that divide us. As I am just a beggar in different garb I will put forward my request rather impetuously. My desire is to settle down in America. Will you please take me out of my country by some means? If my educational qualification disqualifies me from entering America as a student, and if all other means fail, will you just adopt me as the last resort? I am quite ashamed to write such a request for I am so old and I have parents who depend upon me to provide for them during their old age. I shall do any kind of work and I will try my best to be of some use to you. Sir, by now you would have formed in your mind the unimpressive figure of a short, dark, ambitious Indian guy whose character is sprinkled with a generous amount of jealousy. If you have thought in the above manner you are in for a surprise. For the above description suits me to the core. I want to escape from the harsh realities and live with some peace and pursue part-time education. Sir, please let me know whether it is possible for you to assist your humble servant—' "

Hope brought the letter to her chest—she saw that Amy had pushed back her chair and was standing. "I'm sorry," Hope said to her.

"Why?" asked Amy, forcing a smile.

Hope's hands began to tremble.

I glanced toward Lonoff, but he was saying nothing.

With just a tinge of exasperation, Amy said, "I don't understand why you should be so sorry."

Hope undertook to fold the letter from India, though not with any method I could discern. Her eyes went to the geraniums when she said, "I didn't mean to embarrass you."

"But I'm not embarrassed," said Amy, innocently.

"I didn't *say* you were," Hope conceded. "I said I didn't *mean* to."

Amy didn't follow—that was the act. She waited for Hope to explain herself further.

"Forget it, please," said Hope.

"It's forgotten," Lonoff said softly.

"I'm going now," Amy said to him.

"Must you," asked Lonoff, "without finishing the coffee?"

"You're half an hour behind schedule already," Amy said. "What with all this promiscuous socializing over your egg, it could take you the rest of the morning to recover."

"Yes," I said, jumping up, "and I have to be off, too."

"There's no bus this early," Lonoff informed me. "The first bus north arrives at eleven-twenty."

"Still, if she could drop me in town, I'll just walk around—if that's not out of your way," I added, and looked as shyly as I had the day before at the girl I had veiled in so many imaginings, and whom *still* I couldn't see plain.

"Suit yourself," said Lonoff.

He rose and came around the table to kiss Amy on her cheek. "Stay in touch," he told her. "And thanks for the help."

"I think I at least got each of the books separated out. At least that's in order."

"Fine. The rest I have to see to myself. And think about. I'm not sure it's for me, my friend."

"Please," she said, "I beseech you, don't destroy anything."

A charade it may have been, but still I understood her to be entreating him about the worksheets of his old stories that she had been sorting for the Harvard manuscript collection. But to Hope the girl's request clearly had a

less innocent intention. Before either of them could speak another double en-
tendre in her presence, Hope was out of the room.

We heard her mount the stairs, and then the bedroom door slammed
shut overhead.

"Excuse me one moment," said Lonoff, and buttoning his jacket, he followed after his wife.

Silently Amy and I took our things from the hall closet and got dressed
for the snow. Then we stood there trying to decide what to do next. I had all
I could do not to say, "Did you ever have the feeling that you wanted to go,
still have the feeling that you wanted to stay?"

What I came up with was not much better. "Last night at dinner he told
me about the letter that you sent him from England."

She took this in and went back to waiting. On her head was the white
wool cap with the long tassel that ended in a fluffy white ball. Of course! He
had given it to her, her first winter here in the Berkshires; and now she could
not part with it, no more than she could part with him, her second Pim.

"When was that?" I asked. "When were you living in England?"

"Oh, my." She closed her eyes and pressed one hand to her forehead. I
saw then how very tired she was. Neither of us had slept the night before, she
thinking of who she might become living in Florence with Lonoff, and I
thinking of who she might have been. When the sleeve of her coat fell back,
I of course saw that there was no scar on her forearm. No scar; no book; no
Pim. No, the loving father who must be relinquished for the sake of his
child's art was not hers; he was mine. "I was short, dark, ambitious—and sixteen. Eleven years ago," she said.

Making her Anne Frank's age exactly, had she survived.

"Where had you been before England?"

"That's a long story."

"You'd been through the war?"

"I missed the war."

"How so?"

She smiled politely. I was getting on her nerves. "Luck."

"I suppose that's how I missed it too," I replied.

"And what did you have instead?" she asked me.

"My childhood. What did *you* have instead?"

Dryly, she said, "Somebody else's. I think perhaps we should go, Mr.
Zuckerman. I have to be off. It's a long drive."

"I'd rather not leave without saying goodbye."

"I'd rather not, either, but we better."

"I'm sure he wanted us to wait."

"Oh, did he?" she said strangely, and I followed her into the living
room, where we sat in the easy chairs beside the fireplace. She had taken Lonoff's chair and I took my place in the other. Angrily she removed the hat.

"He's been awfully generous to me," I explained. "It's been quite a visit. For me," I added.

"He's a generous man."

"He helped you to come to America."

"Yes."

"From England."

She picked up the magazine that I'd leafed through the evening before while Lonoff spoke on the phone.

I said, "Pardon me, for insisting . . ."

She smiled vaguely at me and began turning pages.

"It's just—that you bear some resemblance to Anne Frank."

A shiver went down my body when she replied, "I've been told that before."

"You *have?*"

"But," she said, bringing her intelligent eyes directly up to mine, "I'm afraid I'm not she."

Silence.

"You've read her book, however."

"Not really," she said. "I looked at it."

"Oh, but it's quite a book."

"Is it?"

"Oh, yes. She was a marvelous young writer. She was something for thirteen. It's like watching an accelerated film of a fetus sprouting a face, watching her mastering things. You must read it. Suddenly she's discovering reflection, suddenly there's portraiture, character sketches, suddenly there's a long intricate eventful happening so beautifully recounted it seems to have gone through a dozen drafts. And no poisonous notion of being *interesting* or *serious.* She just *is.*" My whole body was damp from the effort of compressing my thoughts and presenting them to her before Lonoff returned to inhibit me. "The ardor in her, the spirit in her—always on the move, always starting things, being boring as unbearable to her as being bored—a terrific writer, really. And an enormously appealing child. I was thinking"—the thought had only just occurred to me, of course, in the rapture of praising Anne Frank to one who might even be her—"she's like some impassioned little sister of Kafka's, his lost little daughter—a kinship is even there in the face. I think. Kafka's garrets and closets, the hidden attics where they hand down the indictments, the camouflaged doors—everything he dreamed in Prague was, to her, real Amsterdam life. What he invented, she suffered. Do you remember the first sentence of *The Trial?* We were talking about it last night, Mr. Lonoff and myself. It could be the epigraph for her book. 'Someone must have falsely traduced Anne F., because one morning without having done anything wrong, she was placed under arrest.' "

However, despite *my* ardor, Amy's mind was elsewhere. But then so was mine, really—back in New Jersey, where the lucky childhood had been spent. To be wed somehow to you, I thought, my unassailable advocate, my invulnerable ally, my shield against their charges of defection and betrayal and reckless, heinous informing! Oh, marry me, Anne Frank, exonerate me before my outraged elders of this idiotic indictment! Heedless of Jewish feeling? Indifferent to Jewish survival? Brutish about their well-being? Who dares to accuse of such unthinking crimes the husband of Anne Frank!

But, alas, I could not lift her out of her sacred book and make her a character in this life. Instead, I was confronted by Amy Bellette (whoever *she* might be), turning the pages of Lonoff's magazine, and, while she savored his every underlining, waiting to see if at the last minute he would not change his life, and hers with it. The rest was so much fiction, the unchallengeable answer to their questionnaire that I proposed to offer the Wapters. And far from being unchallengeable, far from acquitting me of their charges and restoring to me my cherished blamelessness, a fiction that of course would seem to them a desecration even more vile than the one they had read.

Hope was coming down the stairs, dressed for the outdoors in a hooded green loden coat and wearing snow boots pulled over her wool trousers. She held firmly to the banister with one hand—to prevent herself from falling—and in the other carried a small overnight bag.

Lonoff spoke to her from the top of the stairs. "This won't do," he said softly. "This is pure—"

"Let's all have what we want, please." She spoke without looking back at him; in her emotional state she had all she could do to negotiate the stairs.

"This is hardly what you want."

She stopped—"It is what I have wanted for *years*"—then proceeded once more with leaving home.

"Come back up here. You don't know what you're saying."

"You're just frightened," she said, from between her teeth, "of losing your boredom."

"I can't hear you, Hope."

Safely now at the bottom landing, the little woman turned and looked up the stairs. "You're just worried about how you will get all your writing done and all your reading done and all your brooding done without the boredom of me. Well, let someone else be boring for you from now on! Let someone else be no trouble!"

"Please come back up here."

Rather than doing as he asked, she picked up her bag and came into the living room. I alone stood to receive her.

"Take off your coat," she said to Amy. "Now *you're* going to have thirty-five years of it!" And with that she began to shake with sobs.

Lonoff was now making the cautious trek down the stairs. "Hope, this is playacting. And pure indulgence."

"*I am going,*" she told him.

"You're not going anywhere. Put the bag down."

"No! I am going to Boston! But don't worry—she knows where everything is. It's practically home to her already. No precious time will be lost. She can hang her things back in the closet and be ready to begin boring you as soon as I'm out the door. You won't even notice the difference."

Amy, unable to watch any longer, looked down into her lap, prompting Hope to say, "Oh, she thinks otherwise. Of course she does. I've seen her fondling each sheet of each draft of each story. She thinks with her it will all be the religion of art up here. Oh, will it ever! Let her try to please you, Manny! Let her serve as the backdrop for your thoughts for thirty-five years. Let her see how noble and heroic you are by the twenty-seventh draft. Let her cook you wonderful meals and light candles for your dinner. Let her get everything ready to make you happy and then see the look on your stone face when you come in at night and sit down at the table. A surprise for dinner? Oh, my dear girl, that is merely his due for a miserable day of bad writing. *That* gets no rise out of him. And candles in the old pewter holders? Candles, after all these years? How poignant of her, he thinks, how vulgar, what a wistful souvenir of yesterday's tearooms. Yes, have her run hot baths for your poor back twice a day, and then go a week without being talked to—let alone being touched in bed. Ask him in bed, 'What is it, dear, what's the matter?' But of course you know all too well what the matter is—you know why he won't hold you, why he doesn't even know you're *there*. The fiftieth draft!"

"That is enough," said Lonoff. "Quite thorough, very accurate, and enough."

"Fondling those papers of yours! Oh, she'll see! I got fondled more by strangers on the rush-hour subway during two months in 1935 than I have up here in the last twenty years! Take off your coat, Amy—you're staying. The classroom daydream has come true! You get the creative writer—and I get to go!"

"She's not staying," Lonoff said, softly again. "You're staying."

"Not for thirty-five more years of this!"

"Oh, Hopie." He put a hand out to her face, where the tears were still falling.

"I'm going to Boston! I'm going to Europe! It's too late to touch me now! I'm taking a trip around the world and never coming back! And you," she said, looking down at Amy in her chair, "*you* won't go anywhere. *You* won't see anything. If you even go out to dinner, if once in six months you get him to accept an invitation to somebody's home, then it'll be even worse—then for the hour before you go your life will be misery from his kvetching about what it's going to be like when those people start in with their *ideas*. If you dare to change the *pepper* mill, he'll ask what's the matter, what was wrong with the old one? It takes three months for him just to get used to a new brand of *soap.* Change the soap and he goes around the house *sniffing,* as though something dead is on the bathroom sink instead of just a bar of Palmolive. Nothing can be touched, nothing can be changed, everybody must be quiet, the children must shut up, their friends must stay away until four— There is his religion of art, my young successor: rejecting life! *Not* living is what he makes his beautiful fiction *out* of! And you will now be the person he is not living with!"

Amy pushed herself up out of her chair and put on the childish hat with the ball on the end of the tassel. Looking past Hope, she said to Lonoff, "I'm going."

"*I'm* going," Hope cried.

To me Amy said, "I'm leaving now, if you'd like a ride to town."

"*I'm* leaving now," Hope told her. "Take that silly hat off! School is over! You are twenty-seven! This is officially your house!"

"It's not, Hope," Amy said, beginning at last to cry. "It's yours."

And so broken and pathetic did she seem in that moment of capitulation that I thought, But of course last night is not the first time she's sat cuddled up in his lap—but of course he's seen her unclothed before. They have been lovers! Yet when I tried to imagine E. I. Lonoff stripped of his suit and on his back, and Amy naked and astride his belly, I couldn't, no more than any son can.

I don't think I could keep my wits about me, teaching such beautiful and gifted and fetching girls.

Then you shouldn't do it.

Oh, Father, is this so, were you the lover of this lovesick, worshipful, displaced daughter half your age? Knowing full well you'd never leave Hope? You succumbed too? Can that be? *You?*

The bed? I had the bed.

Convinced now that that wasn't so—that nobody, nobody, has ever really *had* the bed—I persisted nonetheless in believing that it was.

"You do as I say!" Hope again, ordering Amy. "You stay and look after him! He cannot stay here alone!"

"But I won't be alone," Lonoff explained to her. "You know that I won't be alone. Enough, enough now, for your sake, too. This is all because we've had visitors. This is all because somebody new stayed the night. There was company, we all had breakfast, and you got excited. Now everybody's going away—and this came over you. You got lonely. You got frightened. Everybody understands."

"Look, Manny, *she* is the child—don't you treat *me* like the child! She is now the child-bride here—"

But before Hope could describe her in further detail, Amy was past her and out the front door.

"Oh, the little bitch!" cried Hope.

"Hope," said Lonoff. "Don't. Not that routine."

But he did not move to stop her as she too ran from the house, carrying her bag.

I said, "Do you want me—to do anything?"

"No, no. Let it run its course."

"Okay."

"Calm down, Nathan. One at a time we are about to calm down."

Then we heard Hope scream.

I followed him to the front window, expecting to see blood on the snow. Instead, there was Hope, seated in a drift only a few feet from the house, while Amy's car was slowly backing out of the car shed. But for the billowing exhaust fumes everything out of doors was gleaming. It was as though not one but two suns had risen that morning.

Hope watched, we watched. The car turned in the driveway. Then it was out onto the road and gone.

"Mrs. Lonoff's fallen down."

"I see that," he said sadly.

We watched her struggle to her feet. Lonoff rapped on the frosted window with his knuckles. Without bothering to look back up to the house, Hope retrieved the overnight bag from where it lay on the path and proceeded with cautious tiny steps to the car shed, where she got into the Lonoffs' Ford. But the car only whined when she tried to start it; effort after effort produced only that most disheartening of winter sounds.

"The battery," he explained.

"Maybe she flooded it."

Again she tried: same results.

"No, the battery," he said. "It's been happening all month. You charge it up and it makes no difference."

"You may need a new one," I said, since that was what he wanted to talk about.

"I shouldn't. The car is practically brand-new. Where does it go but into town?"

We waited, and finally Hope got out of the car.

"Well, good thing you got a lemon," I said.

"Perhaps." He walked around to the hallway and opened the front door. I continued to watch from the window.

"Hope," he called. "Come in now. That's it."

"No!"

"But how can I live alone?"

"The boy can live with you."

"Don't be silly. The boy is going. Come inside now. If you slip again, you're going to get hurt. Darling, it's slippery, it's cold as hell—"

"I'm going to Boston."

"How will you do that?"

"I'll walk if I have to."

"Hope, it's twenty degrees. Come back in and get warm and calm down. Have some tea with me. Then we'll talk about moving to Boston."

Here, with her two hands, she hurled the overnight bag into the snow at her feet. "Oh, Manny, you wouldn't move into Stockbridge because the streets are paved, so how could I ever get you to Boston? And what difference would it be in Boston anyway? You'd be just the same—you'd be worse. How could you concentrate in Boston, with all those people swarming around? There, somebody might even ask you something about your work!"

"Then maybe the best bet is to stay here."

"Even here you can't think if I so much as make toast in the kitchen—I have to catch my toast before it pops up so you won't be disturbed in the study!"

"Oh, Hopie," he said, laughing a little, "that's overdoing things. For the next thirty-five years just make your toast and forget about me."

"I *can't*."

"Learn," he said sternly.

"No!" Picking up the bag, she turned and started down the driveway. Lonoff closed the door. I watched from the window to see that she stayed on her feet. The snow had been banked so high by the town plow the night before that when she turned into the road she immediately passed out of sight. But then, of course, she wasn't very big to begin with.

Lonoff was at the hall closet, wrestling with his overshoes.

"Would you like me to come along? To help?" I asked.

"No, no. I can use the exercise after that egg." He stamped his feet on the floor in an attempt to save himself from having to bend over again to get the boots on right. "And you must have things to write down. There's paper on my desk."

"Paper for what?"

"Your feverish notes." He pulled a large, dark, belted coat—not *quite* a caftan—from the closet and I helped him into it. Pressing a dark hat over his bald head, he completed the picture of the chief rabbi, the archdeacon, the magisterial high priest of perpetual sorrows. I handed him his scarf, which had fallen out of a coat sleeve onto the floor. "You had an earful this morning."

I shrugged. "It wasn't so much."

"So much as what, last night?"

"Last night?" Then does he know all I know? But what *do* I know, other than what I can imagine?

"I'll be curious to see how we all come out someday. It could be an interesting story. You're not so nice and polite in your fiction," he said. "You're a different person."

"Am I?"

"I should hope so." Then, as though having concluded administering my rites of confirmation, he gravely shook my hand. "Which way did she go on the road? To the left?"

"Yes. Down the mountain."

He found his gloves in his pocket and after a quick glance at his watch opened the front door. "It's like being married to Tolstoy," he said, and left me to make my feverish notes while he started off after the runaway spouse, some five minutes now into her doomed journey in search of a less noble calling.

JOHN FOWLES

The Ebony Tower

David arrived at Coëtminais the afternoon after the one he had landed at Cherbourg and driven down to Avranches, where he had spent the intervening Tuesday night. That had allowed an enjoyable meander over the remaining distance; a distant view of the spectacular spired dream of Mont-Saint-Michel, strolls around Saint-Malo and Dinan, then south in the splendid September weather and through the new countryside. He took at once to the quiet landscapes, orcharded and harvested, precise and pollarded, self-concentrated, exhaling a spent fertility. Twice he stopped and noted down particularly pleasing conjucntions of tone and depth—parallel stripes of watercolor with penciled notes of amplification in his neat hand. Though there was some indication of the formal origin in these verbal notes—that a stripe of color was associated with a field, a sunlit wall, a distant hill—he drew nothing. He also wrote down the date, the time of day and the weather, before he drove on.

He felt a little guilty to be enjoying himself so much, to be here so unexpectedly alone, without Beth, and after he had made such a fuss; but the day, the sense of discovery, and of course the object of the whole exercise looming formidably and yet agreeably just ahead, everything conspired to give a pleasant illusion of bachelor freedom. Then the final few miles through the forest of Paimpont, one of the last large remnants of the old wooded Brittany, were deliciously right: green and shaded minor roads, with occasional sunshot vistas down the narrow rides cut through the endless trees. Things about the old man's most recent and celebrated period fell into place at once. No amount of reading and intelligent deduction could supplant the direct experience. Well before he arrived, David new he had not wasted his journey.

He turned off down an even smaller forest road, a deserted *voie communale* and a mile or so along that he came on the promised sign. *Manoir de Coëtminais. Chemin privé.* There was a white gate, which he had to open and shut. Half a mile on again through the forest he found his way barred, just before the trees gave way to sunlight and a grassy orchard, by yet another gate. There was a signboard nailed to the top bar. Its words made him smile inwardly, since beneath the heading *Chien méchant* they were in English: *Strictly no visitors except by prior arrangement.* But as if to confirm that the sign was not to be taken lightly, he found the gate padlocked on the inner side. It must have been forgotten that he was arriving that afternoon. He felt momentarily discomfited; as long as the old devil hadn't forgotten his coming completely. He stood in the deep shade staring at the sunlight beyond. He couldn't have forgotten; David had sent a brief note of reminder and grateful anticipation only the previous week. Somewhere close in the trees behind him a bird gave a curious trisyllabic call, like a badly played tin flute. He glanced around, but could not see it. It wasn't English; and in some obscure way this reminded David that he was. Guard-dog or not, one couldn't . . . he went back to his car, switched off, locked the doors, then returned to the gate and climbed over.

He walked along the drive through the orchard, whose aged trees were clustered with codlings and red cider-apples. There was no sign of a dog, no barking. The *manoir,* islanded and sundrenched in its clearing among the sea of huge oaks and beeches, was not quite what he had expected, perhaps because he spoke very little French—hardly knew the country outside Paris— and had translated the word visually as well as verbally in terms of an English manor house. In fact it had more the appearance of a once substantial farm; nothing very aristocratic about the facade of pale ochre plaster broadly latticed by reddish beams and counterpointed by dark brown shutters. To the east there was a little wing at right angles, apparently of more recent date. But the ensemble had charm; old and compact, a warm face of character, a good solid feel. He had simply anticipated something grander.

There was a graveled courtyard opposite the southward of the house. Geraniums by the foot of the wall, two old climbing roses, a scatter of white doves on the roof; all the shutters were in use, the place asleep. But the main door, with a heraldic stone shield above, its details effaced by time and placed eccentrically toward the west end of the house, was lodged open. David walked cautiously across the gravel to it. There was no knocker, no sign of a bell; nor, mercifully, of the threatened dog. He saw a stone-flagged hall, an oak table beside an ancient wooden staircase with worn and warped medieval-looking banisters that led upward. Beyond, on the far side of the house, another open door framed a sunlit garden. He hesitated, aware that he had arrived sooner than suggested; then tapped on the masive main door with his knuckles. A few seconds later, realizing the futility of the weak sound, he stepped over the threshold. To his right stretched a long gallery-like living room. Ancient partitions must have been knocked down, but some of the major black uprights had been retained and stood out against the white walls with a skeletal bravura. The effect was faintly Tudor, much more English than the exterior. A very handsome piece of dense but airy space, antique carved-wood furniture, bowls of flowers, a group of armchairs and two sofas farther down; old pink and red carpets; and inevitably, the art ... no surprise—except that one could walk in on it like this—since David knew there was a distinguished little collection besides the old man's own work. Famous names were already announced. Ensor, Marquet, that landscape at the end must be a "cool" Derain, and over the fireplace ...

But he had to announce himself. He walked across the stone floor beside the staircase to the doorway on the farside of the room. A wide lawn stretched away, flower beds, banks of shrubs, some ornamental trees. It was protected from the north by a high wall, and David saw another line back there of lower buildings, hidden from the front of the house; barns and byres when the place was a farm. In midlawn there was a catalpa pruned into a huge green mushroom; in its shade sat, as if posed, conversing, a garden table and three wicker chairs. Beyond, in a close pool of heat, two naked girls lay side by side on the grass. The further, half hidden, was on her back, as if asleep. The nearer was on her stomach, chin propped on her hands, reading a book. She wore a wide-brimmed straw hat, its crown loosely sashed with some deep red material. Both bodies were very brown, uniformly brown, and apparently oblivious of the stranger in the shadowed doorway thirty yards away. He could not understand that they had not heard his car in the forest silence. But he really was earlier than the "teatime" he had proposed in his letter; or perhaps there had after all been a bell at the door, a servant who should have heard. For a brief few seconds he registered the warm tones of the two indolent female figures, the catalpa-shade green and the grass green, the intense carmine of the hat-sash, the pink wall beyond with its ancient espalier fruit trees. Then he turned and went back to the main door, feeling more amused than embarrassed. He thought of Beth again: how she would have adored this being plunged straight into the legend ... the wicked old faun and his famous afternoons.

Where he had first intruded he saw at once what he had, in his curiosity, previously missed. A bronze hand-bell sat on the stone floor behind one of the doorjambs. He picked it up and rang—then wished he hadn't the sharp schoolyard jangle assaulted the silent house, its sunlit peace. And nothing happened; no footsteps upstairs, no door opening at the far end of the long room he stood in. He waited on the threshold. Perhaps half a minute passed. Then one of the girls, he didn't know which, appeared in the garden door and came toward him. She now wore a plain white cotton *galabiya;* a slim girl of slightly less than medium height and in her early twenties; brown and gold hair and regular features; level-eyed, rather wide eyes, and barefooted.

She was unmistakably English. She stopped some twenty feet away, by the bottom of the stairs.

"David Williams?"

He made an apologetic gesture. "You were expecting me?"

"Yes."

She did not offer to shake hands.

"Sorry to steal in like this. Your gate out there's locked."

She shook her head. "Just pull on it. The padlock. I'm sorry." She did not seem it; and at a loss. She said, "Henry's asleep."

"Then don't wake him, for God's sake." He smiled. "I'm a bit early. I thought it would be harder to find."

She surveyed him a moment: his asking to be welcomed.

"He's such a bastard if he doesn't get his siesta."

He grinned. "Look, I took his letter at its word—about putting me up?—but if . . ."

She glanced beyond him, through the door; then back at his face, with an indifferent little tilt of query.

"Your wife?"

He explained about Sandy's chicken pox, the last-minute crisis. "She's flying to Paris on Friday. If my daughter's over the worst. I'll pick her up there."

The level eyes appraised him again.

"Then I'll show you where you are?"

"If you're sure . . ."

"No problems."

She made a vague gesture for him to follow her, and turned to the stairs; simple, white, bizarrely modest and handmaidenly after that first glimpse.

He said, "Marvelous room."

She touched the age-blackened handrail that mounted beside them. "This is fifteenth century. They say." But she looked neither at him nor the room; and asked nothing, as if he had driven a mere five miles to get there.

At the top of the stairs she turned to the right down a corridor. A long rush mat ran down the center of it. She opened the second door they came to and went a step in, holding the handle, watching him, uncannily like the *patronne* at the hotel where he had stayed the previous night. He almost expected to hear a price.

"The bathroom's next door."

"Lovely. I'll just go and fetch my car."

"As you wish."

She closed the door. There was something preternaturally grave about her, almost Victorian, despite the *galabiya*. He smiled encouragingly as they went back down the corridor to the stairs.

"And you're . . . ?"

"Henry calls me the Mouse."

At last a tiny dryness in her face; or a challenge, he wasn't sure.

"You've known him long?"

"Since spring."

He tried to evoke some sympathy.

"I know he's not mad about this sort of thing."

She shrugged minutely.

"As long as you stand up to him. It's mostly bark."

She was trying to tell him something, very plainly; perhaps just that if he *had* seen her in the garden, this was the real distance she kept from visitors. She was apparently some kind of equivalent of his hostess and yet she behaved as if the house had nothing very much to do with her. They came to the bottom of the stairs, and she turned toward the garden.

"Out here? Half an hour? I get him up at four."

He grinned again, the nurselike tone in her voice, so dismissive of all that the outside world might think of the man she called "Henry" and "him"

"Fine."

"Make *comme chez vous*. Right?"

She hesitated a moment, as if she knew she was being too cool and sibylline. There was even a faint hint of diffidence, a final poor shadow of a welcoming smile. Then she looked down and turned away and padded silently back toward the garden; as she went out through the door the *galabiya* momentarily lost its opacity against the sunlight beyond; a fleeting naked shadow. He remembered he had forgotten to ask about the dog; but presumably she would have thought of it and tried to recall when he had been less warmly received into a strange house ... as if he had taken too much, when he taken nothing, for granted—and certainly not her presence. He had understood the old man had put all that behind him.

He walked back through the orchard to the gate. At least she hadn't misled him there. The hasp came away from the body of the padlock as soon as he pulled. He drove back and parked in the shade of a chestnut opposite the front of the house, got out his overnight bag and breifcase, then an informal jeans suit on a hanger. He glanced through the doorway out into the garden at the back as he went upstairs; but the two girls seemed to have disappeared. In the corridor above he stopped to look at two paintings he had noticed when she first showed him up and failed to put a name to ... but now, of course, Maximilien Luce. Lucky old man, to have bought before art became a branch of greed, of shrewd investment. David forgot his cold reception.

His room was simply furnished, a double bed in some rather clumsy rural attempt at an Empire style, a walnut wardrobe riddled with worm, a chair, an old chaise longue with tired green upholstery; a gilt mirror, stains on the mercury. The room smelled faintly musty, seldom used; furnished out

of local auctions. The one incongruity was the signed Laurencin over the bed.
David tried to lift it off its hook, to see the picture in a better light. But the
frame was screwed to the wall. He smiled and shook his head; if only poor
old Beth were there.

David had been warned by the London publishing house—by the senior
member of it who had set the project up—of the reefs, far more formidable
than locked gates, that surrounded any visit to Coëtminais. The touchiness,
the names one must not mention, the coarse language, the baiting: no doubt
had been left that this particular "great man" could also be the most frightful
old bastard. He could also, it seemed, be quite charming—if he like you.
Naïve as a child in some ways, had said the publisher. Then, Don't argue
with him about England and the English, just accept he's a lifelong exile and
can't bear to be reminded of what he might have missed. Finally: he desperately wants us to do the book. David was not to let himself be duped into
thinking the subject of it didn't care a fig for home opinion.

In many ways his journey was not strictly necessary. He had already
drafted the introduction, he knew pretty well what he was going to say; there
were the major catalogue essays, especially that for the 1969 Tate Retrospective . . . the British art establishment's belated olive branch; those for the two
recent Paris shows, and the New York; Myra Levey's little monograph in the
Modern Masters series, and the correspondence with Matthew Smith; a scatter
of usable magazine interviews. A few biographical details remained to be
cleared up, though even they could have been done by letter. There were of
course any number of artistic queries one could have asked—or would have
liked to; but the old man had never shown himself very helpful there, indeed
rather more likely on past record to be hopelessly cryptic, maliciously misleading or just downright rude. So it was essentially the opportunity of meeting a man one had spent time on and whose work one did, with reservations,
genuinely admire . . . the fun of it, to say one had met him. And after all, he
was now indisputably major, one had to put him with the Bacons and Suth-
erlands. It could even be argued that he was the most interesting of that select band, though he would probably himself say that he was simply the least
bloody English.

Born in 1896, a student at the Slade in the great days of the Steers-Tonks
regime, a characteristically militant pacifist when cards had to be declared in
1916, in Paris (and spirtually out of England for good) by 1920, then ten
years and more in the queasy—Russia itself having turned to socialist realism—no-man's-land between surrealism and communism, Henry Breasley had
still another decade to wait before any sort of serious recognition at home—
the revelation, during his five years of "exile from exile" in Wales during the
Second World War, of the Spanish Civil War drawings. Like most artists,

Breasley had been well ahead of the politicians. To the British the 1942 exhibition in London of his work from 1937–38 suddenly made sense; they too had learned what war was about, of the bitter folly of giving the benefit of the doubt to international fascism. The more intelligent knew that there was nothing very prescient about his record of the Spanish agony; indeed in spirit it went straight back to Goya. But its power and skill, the superbly incisive draftsmanship, were undeniable. The mark was made; so, if more in private, was the reputation of Breasley's "difficulty" as an individual. The legend of his black bile for everything English and conventionally middle-class—especially if it had anything to do with official views on art, or its public administration—was well established by the time he returned to Paris in 1946.

Then for another decade nothing very much happened to his name in popular terms. But he had become collectible, and there was a growing band of influential admirers in both Paris and London, though like every other European painter he suffered from the rocketing ascendancy of New York as world arbiter of painting values. In England he never quite capitalized on the savage impact, the famous "black sarcasm" of the Spanish drawings; yet he showed a growing authority, a maturity in his work. Most of great nudes and interiors came from this period; the long-buried humanist had begun to surface, though as always the public was more interested in the bohemian side of it—the stories of his drinking and his women, as transmitted in the spasmodic hounding he got from the yellower and more chauvinistic side of Fleet Street. But by the late 1950s this way of life had already become a quaintly historical thing. The rumors and realities of his unregenerate life-style, like his contempt for his homeland, became amusing . . . and even pleasingly authentic to the vulgar mind, with its propensity for confusing serious creation with colorful biography, for allowing van Gogh's ear to obscure any attempt to regard art as a supreme sanity instead of a chocolate-sucking melodrama. It must be confessed that Breasley himself did not noticeably refuse the role offered; if people wanted to be shocked, he generally obliged. But his closer friends knew that beneath the continuing occasional bouts of exhibitionism he had changed considerably.

In 1963 he bought the old *manoir* at Coëtminais and forsook his beloved Paris. A year later appeared his illustrations to Rabelais, his last fling as a pure draftsman, in a limited edition that has already become one of the most valuable books of its kind in this century; and in the same year he painted the first of the pictures in the last-period series that was to establish his international reputation beyond any doubt. Though he had always rejected the notion of a mystical interpretation—and enough of the old left-winger remained for any religious intention to be dismissed out of court—the great, both literally and metaphorically, canvases with their dominant greens and blues that began to flow out of his new studio had roots in a Henry Breasley the outer world had not hitherto guessed at. In a sense it was as if he had discovered who he really was much later than most artists of his basic technical ability and experience. If he did not quite become a recluse, he ceased to be a professional *enfant terrible*. He himself had once termed the paintings "dreams"; there was certainly a surrealist component from his twenties past, a fondness for anachronistic juxtapositions. Another time he had called them tapestries, and indeed the Aubusson *atelier* had done related work to his designs. There was a feeling— "an improbable marriage of Samuel Palmer and Chagell," as one critic had put it in reviewing the Tate Retrospective—of a fully absorbed eclecticism, something that had been evidenced all through his career, but not really come to terms with before Coëtminais; a hint of Nolan, though the subject matter was far less explicit, more mysterious and archetypal . . . "Celtic" had been a word frequently used, with the recurrence of the forest motif, the enigmatic figures and confrontations.

Breasley himself had partly confirmed this, when someone had had the successful temerity to ask him for a central source—and for once received a partly honest answer: Pisanello and Diaz de la Peña. The reference to Diaz and the Barbizon School was a self-sarcasm, needless to say. But pressed on Pisanello, Breasley had cited a painting in the National Gallery in London, *The Vision of St. Eustace;* and confessed it had haunted him all his life. If the reference at first sight seemed distinctly remote, it was soon pointed out that Pisanello and his early fifteenth-century patrons had been besotted by the Arthurian cycle.

What had brought young David Williams (born that same year of Breasley's first English success, 1942) to Coëtminais in the September of 1973 was precisely this last aspect of the old man's work. He had felt no special interest in Breasley before the Tate Retrospective, but he was forcibly struck then by certain correspondences with an art, or rather a style, the International Gothic, that had always interested the scholarly side of him. Two years later he had formulated the parallels he saw in an article. A complimentary copy had been sent to Breasley, but it was not acknowledged. A year passed, David had almost forgotten the whole thing, and certainly had not pursued any particular interest in the old man's work. The invitation from the publishers to write the biographical and critical introduction to *The Art of Henry Breasley* (with the added information that the offer was made with the painter's approval) had come very much out of the blue.

It was not quite a case of a young unknown visiting an old master. David Williams's parents were both architects, a still practicing husband-and-wife team of some renown. Their son had shown natural aptitude very young, an acute color sense, and he was born into the kind of environment where he received nothing but encouragement. In the course of time he went to art college, and settled finally for painting. He was a star student in his third year, already producing salable work. He was not only *rara avis* in that; unlike the majority of his fellow students, he was highly articulate as well.

Brought up in a household where contemporary art and all its questions were followed and discussed constantly and coherently, he could both talk and write well. He had some real knowledge of art history, helped by many stays in his parents' converted farmhouse in Tuscany, as distinct from mere personal enthusiasms. He was aware of his luck in all this, and of the envy it might provoke in his socially and naturally less gifted peers. Always rather fond of being liked, he developed a manner carefully blended of honesty and tact. Perhaps the most remarkable thing about him as a student was that he was on the whole quite popular; just as he was to be popular later as a teacher and lecturer—and even not wholly detested by his victims as an art critic. At least he never panned for panning's sake. He very rarely indeed found nothing at all to praise in an artist or an exhibition.

At his own choice he had gone for a year to the Courtauld Institute after college. Then for two years he combined the teaching of painting and general appreciation lectures. His own work came under the influence of Op Art and Bridget Riley, and benefited from her star. He became one of the passable young substitutes those who could not afford Riley herself tended to buy. Then (this was in 1967) he had had an affair with one of his third-year students that had rapidly become the real thing. They married and bought, with parental help, a house in Blackheath. David decided to try his luck at living by his own painting alone. But the arrival of Alexandra, the first of his two small daughters, and various other things—one of which was a small crisis of doubt about his own work, now shifting away from the Riley influence— drove him to look for extra income. He did not want to return to studio teaching, but he went back to lecturing part-time. A chance meeting led to an invitation to do some reviewing; and a year later still that had become lucrative enough for him to drop the lecturing. That had been his life since.

His own work began to get enough reputation as it moved from beneath the Op Art umbrella to guarantee plenty of red stars at his exhibitions. Though he remained a fully abstract artist in the common sense of the adjective (a color painter, in the current jargon), he knew he was tending toward nature and away from the high artifice of his "Riley" phase. His paintings had a technical precision, a sound architectonic quality inherited from his parents' predilections, and a marked subtlety of tone. To put it crudely, they went well on walls that had to be lived with, which was one good reason (one he knew and accepted) that he sold; another was that he had always worked to a smaller scale than most nonfigurative painters. This again was probably something he acquired from his mother and father; he was dubious about transatlantic monumentality, painting direct for the vast rooms of museums of modern art. Nor was he the kind of person who was ashamed to think of his work in flats and homes, enjoyed privately, on his own chosen scale.

If he disliked pretention, he was not on the other hand devoid of ambition. He still earned more by his painting than his writing, and that meant a very great deal to him; as did what one might call the state of his status among his own generation of painters. He would have despised the notion of a race, yet he kept a sharp eye on rivals and the public mention they received. He was not unaware of this; in the public mention constituted by his own reviewing, he knew he erred on the generous side with those he feared most.

His marriage had been very successful, except for one brief bad period when Beth had rebelled against "constant motherhood" and flown the banner of Women's Liberation; but now she had two sets of illustrations for children's books to her credit, another commissioned and a fourth in prospect. David had always admired his parents' marriage. His own had begun to assume that same easy camaraderie and cooperation. When he was approached about the Breasley introduction, he took it as one more sign that things in general were shaping up well.

He came to Coëtminais with only one small fear: that Breasley had not realized that he was a painter—to be precise, what kind of painter he was—as well as a writer on art. According to the publisher, the old man had asked no questions there. He had seen the article and thought it "read well"; and shown himself much more concerned about the quality of the color reproduction in the proposed book. Breasley's view that full abstraction had been the wrong road was widely known, and on the face of it he could have no time for David's own work. But perhaps he had softened on that subject— though he had had coals of fire to spare, when he was in London in 1969, for Victor Pasmore's head; more probably, since he lived so far from the London art scene, he was genuinely unaware of the partial snake he had taken to his bosom. David hoped the matter could be avoided; and if it couldn't, then he would have to play it by ear—and try to show the old man that the world had moved from such narrow-mindedness. His accepting the commission was proof of it. Breasley "worked"—and that he worked emotionally and stylistically in totally different, or distant, ways from one's own preferred line of descent (De Stijl, Ben Nicholson and the rest—including the arch-renegade Pasmore) in twentieth-century art was immaterial.

David was a young man who was above all tolerant, fair-minded and inquisitive.

He took advantage of the half hour or so before "Henry" was awakened to have a look at the art downstairs. Occasionally he glanced out of windows behind the house. The lawn remained empty, the silence of the house as when he had come. Inside the long room there was only one example of Breasley's own work, but plenty else to admire. The landscape was indeed a Derain, as David had guessed. Three very fine Permeke drawings. The Ensor and the Marquet. An early Bonnard. A characteristically febrile pencil sketch, unsigned, but unmistakably Dufy. Then a splendid Jawlensky (how on earth had he got his hands on that?), an Otto Dix signed proof nicely juxtaposed with a Nevinson drawing. Two Matthew Smiths, a Picabia, a little flower painting that must be an early Matisse, though it didn't look quite right ... there were those, and they were outnumbered by the paintings and drawings David couldn't assign. If one accepted the absence of the more extreme movements, one had a room of early twentieth-century art many smaller museums would have cut throats to lay their hands on. Breasley had collected pre-war, of course, and he had apparently always had a private income of sorts. An only child, he must have inherited quite a substantial sum when his mother died in 1925. His father, one of those Victorian gentlemen who appear to have lived comfortbly on doing nothing, had died in a hotel fire in 1907. According to Myra Levey, he too had dabbled with art collecting in a dilettante way.

Breasley had granted himself pride of place—and space—over the old stone fireplace in the center of the room. There hung the huge *Moon-hunt*, perhaps the best-known of the Coëtminais *oeuvre,* a painting David was going to discuss at some length and that he badly wanted to study at leisure again ... perhaps not least to confirm to himself that he wasn't overrating his subject. He felt faintly relieved that the picture stood up well to renewed acquaintance—he hadn't seen it in the flesh since the Tate exhibtion of four years previously—and even announced itself as better than memory and reproductions had rated it. As with so much of Breasley's work there was an obvious previous iconography—in this case, Uccello's *Night Hunt* and its spawn down through the centuries; which was in turn a challenged comparison, a deliberate risk ... just as the Spanish drawings had defied the great shadow of Goya by accepting its presence, even using and parodying it, so the memory of the Ashmolean Uccello somehow deepened and buttressed the painting before which Davis sat. It gave an essential tension, in fact: behind the mysteriousness and ambiguity (no hounds, no horses, no prey ... nocturnal figures among trees, but the title was needed), behind the modernity of so many of the surface elements there stood both a homage and a kind of thumbed nose to a very old tradition. One couldn't be quite sure it was a msterpiece, there was a clotted quality in some passages, a distinctly brusque use of impasto on closer examination; something faintly too static in the whole, a lack of tonal relief (but that again was perhaps just the memory of the Uccello). Yet it remained safely considerable, had presence—could stand very nicely, thank you, up against anything else in British painting since the war. Perhaps its most real mystery, as with the whole series, was that it could have been done at all by a man of Breasley's age. The *Moon-hunt* had been painted in 1965, in his sixty-ninth year. And that was eight years ago now.

Then suddenly, as if to solve the enigma, the living painter himself appeared from the garden door and came down toward David.

"Williams, my dear fellow."

He advanced, hand outstretched, in pale blue trousers and a dark blue shirt, an unexpected flash of Oxford and Cambridge, a red silk square. He was white-haired, though the eyebrows were still faintly gray; the bulbous nose, the misleadingly fastidious mouth, the pouched gray-blue eyes in a hale face. He moved almost briskly, as if aware that he had been remiss in some way; smaller and trimmer than David had visualized from the photographs.

"It's a great honor to be here, sir."

"Nonsense. Nonsense." And David's elbow was chucked, the smile and the quiz under the eyebrows and white relic of a forelock both searching and dismissive. "You've been looked after?"

"Yes. Splendid."

"Don't be put off by the Mouse. She's slightly gaga." The old man stood with his hands on his hips, an impression of someone trying to seem young, alert, David's age. "Thinks she's Lizzie Siddal. Which makes me that ghastly little Italian fudger . . . damn' insulting, what?"

David laughed. "I did notice a certain . . ."

Breasley raised his eyes to the ceiling.

"My dear man. You've no idea. Still. Gels that age. Well, how about some tea? Yes? We're out in the garden."

David gestured back at the *Moon-hunt* as they moved toward the west end of the room. "It's marvelous to see that again. I just pray the printers can rise to it."

Breasley shrugged, as if he didn't care; or was proof to the too direct compliment. Then he darted another quizzing look at David.

"And you? You're quite the cat's pajamas, I hear."

"Hardly that."

"Read your piece. All those fellows I've never heard of. Good stuff."

"But wrong?"

Breasley put a hand on his arm.

"I'm not a scholar, dear boy. Ignorance of things you probably know as well as your mother's tit would astound you. Never mind. Put up with me, what?"

They went out into the garden. The girl nicknamed the Mouse, still barefooted and in her white Arab garb, came obliquely across the lawn from the far end of the house, carrying a tray of tea things. She took no notice of the two men.

"See what I mean," muttered Breasley. "Needs her bloody arse tanned."

David bit his lips. As they came to the table under the catalpa, he saw the second girl stand from a little bay of the lawn that was hidden by a bank of shrubs from the house. She must have been reading all the time; he saw the straw hat with the red sash on the grass behind her as she came toward them, book still in hand. If the Mouse was odd, this creature was preposterous. She was even smaller, very thin, a slightly pinched face under a mop of frizzed-out hair that had been reddened with henna. Her concession to modesty had been to pull on a singlet, a man's or a boy's by the look of it, dyed black. It reached just, but only just, below her loins. The eyelids had also been blackened. She had the look of a rag doll, a neurotic golliwog, a figure from the wilder end of the King's Road.

"This is Anne," said the Mouse.

"Alias the Freak," said Breasley.

Breasley sat, and waved to David to sit beside him. He hesitated, since there was a chair short, but the Freak sat rather gauchely on the grass beside her friend's place. A pair of red briefs became visible, or conspicuous, beneath the black singlet. The Mouse began to pour the tea.

"First visit to these parts, Williams?"

That allowed David to be polite; sincerely so, about his newfound enthusiasm for Brittany and its landscapes. The old man seemed to approve; he began to talk about the house, how he had found it, its history, why he had turned his back on Paris. He handsomely belied his rogue reputation; it was almost as if he were delighted to have another man to talk to. He sat turned away from the girls, completely ignoring them, and David had a growing sense that they resented his presence; whether it was because of the attention he distracted, the formality he introduced, or that they must have heard all the old man was telling him before, he wasn't sure. Breasley wandered off— again belying his reputation—to Welsh landscapes, his early childhood, before 1914. David knew his mother had been Welsh, of the wartime spell in Breconshire, but not that he retained memories and affections for the place; missed its hills.

The old fellow spoke in a quirky staccato manner, half assetive, half tentative; weirdly antiquated slang, a constant lacing of obscenity; not intellectually or feelingly at all, but much more like some eccentric retired (it occurred to David with secret amusement) admiral. They were so breathtakingly inappropriate, all the out-of-date British upper-class mannerisms in the mouth of a man who had spent his life comprehensively denying all those same upper classes stood for. A similar pardox was seen in the straight white hair, brushed across the forehead in a style that Breasley must have retained since his youth—and which Hitler had long put out of fashion with younger men. It gave him a boyishness; but the ruddy, incipiently choleric face and the pale eyes suggested something much older and more dangerous. He chose transparently to come on as much more of a genial old fool than he was; and must know he deceived no one.

However, if the two girls had not been so silent—the Freak had even shifted her back to rest against the front of the other girl's chair, reached for her book and begun reading again—David would have felt comparatively at ease. The Mouse sat in white elegance and listened, but as if her mind were somewhere else—in a Millais set-piece, perhaps. If David sought her eyes, she would discompose her rather pretty features into the faintest semblance of a formal confirmation that she was still there; which gave the clear impression that she wasn't. He grew curious to know what the truth was, beyond the obvious. He had not come prepared for this, having gathered from the publisher that the old man now lived alone—that is, with only an elderly French housekeeper. During that tea the relationship seemed more daughterly than anything else. There was only one showing of the lion's claws.

David had mentioned Pisanello, knowing it was safe ground—and the recently discovered frescoes at Mantua. Breasley had seen them in reproduction, seemed genuinely interested to hear a firsthand account of them and genuinely ignorant—David had not taken his warning very seriously—of the techniques involved. But David had hardly launched into the complexities, of *arricciato, intonaco, sinopie* and the rest before Breasley interrupted.

"Freak dear gel, for God's sake stop reading that fucking book and listen."

She looked up, then put the paperback down and folded her arms. "Sorry."

It was said to David, ignoring the old man—and with an unconcealed boredom: you're a drag, but if he insists.

"And if you use that word, for Christ's sake sound as if you mean it."

"Didn't realize we were included."

"Balls."

"I was listening, anyway."

She had a faint Cockney accent, tired and brutalized.

"Don't be so bloody insolent."

"I was."

"Balls."

She pulled a grimace, glanced back up at the Mouse. "Hen-*ree.*"

David smiled. "What's the book?"

"Dear boy, keep out of this. If you don't mind." He leaned forward, pointing a finger at the girl. "Now no more. Learn something."

"Yes, Henry."

"My dear fellow, I'm so sorry. Do go on."

The little incident produced an unexpected reaction from the Mouse. She gave a surreptitious nod at David behind Breasley's back: whether to tell him that this was normal or to suggest he got on with it before a full-scale row developed was not clear. But as he did go on, he had the impression that she was listening with slightly more interest. She even asked a question, she evidently knew something about Pisanello. The old man must have talked about him.

Soon afterwrd Breaseley stood up and invited David to come and see his "workroom" in the buildings behind the garden. The girls did not move. As he followed Breasley out through an arched gate in the wall, David looked back and saw the thin brown figure in her black singlet pick up her book again. The old man winked at him as they strolled over the gravel toward the line of buildings to their left.

"Always the same. Have the little bitches into your bed. Lose all sense of proportion."

"They're students?"

"The Mouse. God knows what the other thinks she is."

But he clearly did not want to talk about them; as if they were mere moths around his candle, a pair of high-class groupies. He began explaining the conversions and changes he had made, what the buildings once were. They went through a doorway into the main studio, a barn whose upper floor had been removed. A long table littered with sketches and paper by the wide modern window looking north over the graveled yard; a paints table, the familiar smells and paraphernalia; and dominating the space, at its far end, another of the Coëtminais series, about three quarters completed—a twelve-by-six-foot canvas on a specially carpentered stand, with a set of movable steps in front to reach the top of the painting. It was a forest setting again, but with a central clearing, much more peopled than usual, less of the suba-queous feeling, under a first-class blue, almost a black, that managed to suggest both night and day, both heat and storm, a looming threat over the human component. There was this time an immediate echo (because one had learned to look for them) of the Brueghel family; and even a faint self-echo, of the *Moon-hunt* in the main house. David smiled at the painter.

"Are any clues being offered?"

"*Kermesse?* Perhaps. Not sure yet." The old man stared at his picture. "She's playing coy. Waiting, don't you know."

"She seems very good indeed to me. Already."

"Why I have to have women around me. Sense of timing. Bleeding and all that. Learning when not to work. Nine parts of the game." He looked at David. "But you know all this. Painter yourself, what?"

David took an inward breath and skated hastily over the thin ice; explaining about Beth, her sharing his studio at home, he knew what Breasley meant. The old man opened his hands, as if in agreement; and seemed amiably not interested in pursuing the matter of David's own work. He turned and sat on a stool by the bench at the window, then reached for a still life, a pencil drawing of some wild flowers: teaselheads and thistles lying scattered on a table. They were drawn with an impressive, if rather lifeless, accuracy.

"The Mouse. Beginning of a hand, don't you think?"

"Nice line."

Breasley nodded down toward the huge canvas. "I let her help. The donkey-work."

David murmured, "On that scale . . ."

"Clever girl, Williams. Don't let her fool you. Shouldn't make fun of her." The old man stared down at the drawing. "Deserves better." Then, "Couldn't do without her, really."

"I'm sure she's learning a lot."

"Know what people say. Old rake and all that. Man my age."

David smiled. "Not anymore."

But Breasley seemed not to hear.

"Don't care a fart about that, never have. When you start using their minds."

And he began to talk about age, turned back toward the painting with David standing beside him, staring at it; how the imagination, the ability to conceive, didn't after all, as one had supposed in one's younger days, atrophy. What declined was the physical and psychological stamina—"like one's poor old John Thomas"—to execute. One had to have help there. He seemed ashamed to have to confess it.

"Roman Charity. Know that thing? Old geezer sucking milk from some young biddy's tit. Often think of that."

"I can't believe it's so one-way as you suggest." David pointed at the drawing of the flowers. "You should see the kind of art education most of the kids are getting at home now."

"You think?"

"I'm sure. Most of them can't even draw."

Breasley stroked his white hair; again he seemed almost touchingly boyish, lacking in confidence. And David felt himself being seduced by this shyer yet franker being behind the language and the outward manner; who apparently had decided to trust him.

"Ought to send her packing. Haven't the guts."

"Isn't that up to her?"

"She didn't say anything? When you came?"

"She gave a very good imitation of a guardian angel."

"Come home to roost."

It was said with a hint of sardonic gloom; and remained cryptic, for the old man stood up with a sudden return of energy and brief touch, as if of apology, on David's arm.

"To hell with it. Come to grill me, what?"

David asked about the preliminary stages to the painting.

"Trial and error. Draw a lot. See."

He led David to the far end of the bench. The work-sketches were produced with the same odd mixture of timidity and assertiveness he had shown in talking about the girl—as if he both feared criticism and would suspect its absence.

This new painting, it seemed, had sprung from a very dim recollection of early childhood; of a visit to a fair, he was no longer sure where, he had been five or six, had been longing for the treat, had taken an intense pleasure in it, could still recall this overwhelming wanting—the memory seemed dense with desire—to experience each tent and stall, see everything, taste everything. And then a thunderstorm, which must have been apparent before to all the adults, but which for some reason came to him as a shock and a surprise, a dreadful disappointment. All the outward indications of the fair theme had progressively disappeared through the working sketches, much more elaborate and varied than David had expected, and were completely exorcised from the final *imago*. It was rather a clumsy literalness, a conceptual correlative of the way the old man spoke, had to be slowly exterminated by constant recomposition and refinement away from the verbal. But the story explained the strange inwardness, the lighted oblivion of the central scene of the painting. The metaphysical parallels, small planets of light in infinite nights and all the rest, had remained perhaps a fraction too obvious. It was all a shade too darkly Olympian; put in words, something of a pessimistic truism about the human condition. But the tone, the mood, the force of the statement carried conviction—and more than enough to overcome any personal prejudice David felt against overt literary content in paintings.

The talk broadened out; David managed to lead the old fellow back further into his past, to this life in France in the twenties, his friendships with Braque and Matthew Smith. Breasley's veneration for the former was long on the record, but he apparently had to make sure that David knew it. The difference between Braque and Picasso, Matisse "and crew" was between a great man and great boys.

"They knew it. He knew it. Everyone but the bloody world in general knows it."

David did not argue. Picasso's name had been actually pronounced as "pick-arshole." But in general the obscenities were reduced as they talked. The disingenuous mask of ignorance slipped, and the face of the old cosmopolitan that lay beneath began to show. David began to suspect he was dealing with a paper tiger; or certainly with one still living in a world before he himself was born. The occasional hint of aggression was based on such ludicrously old-fashioned notions of what shocked people, what red rags could infuriate them; to reverse the simile, it was rather like playing matador to a blind bull. Only the pompous fool could let himself be caught on such obvious horns.

They strolled back to the house just before six. Once again the two girls had disappeared. Breasley took him around the ground-floor room to look at the work there. There were anecdotes, some peremptory declarations of affection. One famous name got a black mark for being slick, "too damn' easy."

"Dozen-a-day man, don't you know. Bone lazy. That's what saved him. Fastidious my arse."

And there was more frankness when David asked what he looked for when he bought.

"Value for money, dear boy. Insurance. Never thought my own stuff would come to much. Now how about this fellow?"

They had stopped before the little flower painting David had tentatively ascribed to Matisse. David shook his head.

"Painted rubbish ever since."

It was hardly a clue, in present company. David smiled.

"I'm stumped."

"Miró. Done in 1915."

"Good God."

"Sad."

And he shook his head, as over the grave of someone who had died on the flower of his youth.

There were other small treasures David had failed to identify: a Sérusier, a remarkable Gauguinesque landscape by Filiger . . . but when they got to the far corner of the room, Breasley opened a door.

"Got a greater artist out here, Williams. You'll see. Dinner tonight."

The door led into a kitchen: a lantern-jawed gray-haired man sitting at a table and peeling vegetables, an elderly woman who turned from a modern cooking range and smiled. David was introduced: Jean-Pierre and Mathilde, who ran the house and garden. There was also a large Alsatian, which the man quietened as it stood. It was called Macmillan, to rhyme with Villon; because, Breasley explained with a sniff, it was an "old impostor." He spoke French for the first time, a strangely different voice, completely fluent and native-sounding to David's ears; but English was probably more the foreign language now. He gathered the dinner menu was being discussed. Breasley lifted potlids on the stove and sniffed, like some officer doing mess rounds. Then a pike was produced and examined, some story was being told by the man, apparently he had caught it that afternoon, the dog had been with him and tried to attack it when the fish was landed. Breasley bent and wagged a finger over the dog's head, he was to save his teeth for thieves; David was glad he had chanced to arrive when the animal was off the premises. He had the impression that this evening visit to the kitchen was something of a ritual. Its domesticity and familiarity, the tranquil French couple, made a reassuring contrast with the vaguely perverse note the presence of the two girls had introduced into his visit.

Back in the long room, Breasley told David to make himself at home. He had some letters to write. They would meet there again for an *apéritif* at half past seven.

"You're not too formal, I hope?"

"Freedom House, dear boy. Stark naked, if you like." He winked. "Gels won't mind."

David grinned. "Right."

The old man raised a hand and walked to the stairs. Halfway up he turned and spoke back down the room.

"World isn't all bare buds, eh what?"

A discreet minute or two later David also went upstairs. He sat on the chaise longue, writing notes. It was a shame one couldn't quote the old boy direct; but those first two hours had proved very useful; and there must be more to come. After a while he went and lay on the bed, hands behind his head, staring up at the ceiling. It was very warm, airless, though he had opened the shutters. Strange, he had experienced a little tinge of personal disappointment, finally, with Breasley; a little too much posing and wicked old sham for the end product, too great a dissonance between the man and his art; and illogically there loitered, even though David had wanted to keep off the subject, a tiny hurtness that he had been asked nothing about his own work. It was absurd, of course; merely a reaction to so blatant a monomania; and not without an element of envy ... this rather gorgeous old house, the studio setup, the collection, the faintly gamy ambiguity that permeated the place after predictable old Beth and the kids at home; the remoteness of it, the foreignness, the curious flashes of honesty, a patina ... fecundity, his whole day through that countryside, so many ripening apples

But he was being unfair to Beth, who after all had been more responsible than himself in the frantic last-hour discussions on Monday morning, when Sandy's chicken pox had removed from threatened to certain. Her mother was already there with them, ready to take over when they left, and perfectly able to cope ... and willing to do so; she took David's side. It was just Beth's conscience, that old streak of obstinacy in her—and a little hangover of guilt, he suspected, from her brief mutiny against the tyranny of children, soon after Louise was born. Even if there weren't complications, she insisted, she wouldn't be happy not knowing; and David must go, after all it was his work. Their intended week in the Ardèche, after Brittany, could still take place. They had finally agreed, when he set off for Southampton on the Monday evening, that unless there was a telegram at Coëtminais to the contrary on Thursday, she would be in Paris the next day. He had rushed out and booked the flight before he left; and brought flowers and a bottle of champagne home with the ticket. That had gained him a good mark from his mother-in-law. Beth had been drier. In his first frustration he had rather too obviously put his hatred of traveling alone, especially on this journey, above responsible parenthood. But her last words had been, "I'll forgive you in Paris."

A door by the top of the staircase, the one Breasley had gone into, opened briefly and he heard the sound of music, a radio or a record, it seemed like Vivaldi. Then silence again. He felt like a visitor; peripheral, not really wanted. His mind drifted back to the two girls. Of course one wasn't shocked that they went to bed with the old man; whatever one did with old men. Presumably they were well paid for their services, both literally and figuratively; they must know the kind of prices his work fetched now, let alone what the collection would be worth at auction. In some nagging way their presence irritated David. They must be after something, exploiting the old man's weaknesses. They were like a screen. He sensed a secret they did not want him to know.

He wished Beth were there. She was always less afraid of offending people, more immediate; and she could have got so much more out of the girls than he ever would.

He was glad he had finally decided to dress up a little—the jean suit, a shirt and scarf—when he went downstairs. The Mouse was in a creamy high-necked blouse and a long russet skirt, laying the long wooden table at the far end of the room. There were lamps on, the first dusk outside. David saw the back of Breasley's white head in a sofa by the fireplace; and then, as he came down the room, the Freak's frizzed mop leaning against his shoulder. She was slumped back, her feet on a stool, reading aloud in French from some magazine. She wore a bare-shouldered black satin dress with a flounced bottom, a Spanish line about it. The hand of the old man's encircling arm had slipped beneath the fabric and lay on the girl's left breast. He did not move it away when he saw David, merely raised his free hand and pointed down the room toward the Mouse.

"Have a drink, dear boy."

He too had changed; a pale summer coat, a white shirt, a purple bow tie. The girl twisted her head and slipped David a look up, charcoal eyes, intense red mouth, a thin grimace, then began slowly translating what she had read into English. David smiled, hesitated an awkward moment, then went on to where the Mouse moved around the table. She looked coolly up from her work.

"What can I get you?"

"Whatever you're having."

"Noilly Prat?"

"Lovely."

She went to an old carved *armoire* beside the door through to the kitchen; glasses, an array of bottles, a bowl of ice.

"Lemon?"

"Please."

He took his glass, and watched her pour a similar one for herself; then some frizzy fruit drink and finally a whisky ... poured with care, dispensed, she even held the glass up and lined two fingers to check the level of the ration before topping it with an equal amount of soda. Her blouse, made of some loose-woven fabric the color of old lace that allowed minute interstices of bare flesh, was long-sleeved and tight-wristed, high-necked, Edwardian in style; rather prim and demure except, as he soon realized, that nothing was worn underneath it. He watched her face in profile as she served the drinks; its quiet composure. Her movements were deft, at home in this domestic role. David wondered why the old man had to make fun of her; taste and intelligence seemed after all much more plausible than silliness. Nor did there seem anything Pre-Raphaelite about her now; she was simply a rather attractive bit of seventies bird . . . and a good deal easier to relate to than the absurd sex doll on the sofa, who was reading French again. Now and then the old man would correct her pronunciation and she would repeat a word. The Mouse took the drinks down to them, then came back to where David waited. He passed her her glass, and was aware of a very straight pair of eyes; suspiciously as if she had half read his thoughts. Then she silently raised the glass to him and sipped. One hand went to hold an elbow. And at last she smiled.

"Did we behave ourselves?"

"Absolutely. Very helpful."

"Give him time."

He grinned. Definitely, he began to take to her. She had fine features, very regular and well-proportioned; a good mouth; and the very clear eyes, blue-gray eyes set more intense by her tanned complexion, had lost their afternoon abstraction. They were made up a little now, a faintly Slavonic oblongness about them accentuated; and they had a directness he liked. One of his theories began to crumble. It was hard to believe they were exploiting the old man in any mercenary way.

"He showed me one of your drawings. The teasels? I was impressed."

She looked down a moment at her glass; a very deliberate hesitation; then up into his eyes again.

"And I liked your exhibition at the Redfern last autumn."

He gave a not entirely mock start of surprise; another smile.

"I didn't realize."

"I even went twice."

He said, "Where were you?"

"Leeds. For my Dip AD. Then two terms at the RCA."

He looked duly impressed. "Well, good God, you mustn't . . ."

"I'm learning more here."

He looked down, it wasn't his business, but he managed to suggest that even so, postgraduate acceptance by the fiercely selective Royal College of Art was not something one jacked in lightly.

"It's all right. Henry knows he's lucky to have me."

She said it with another smile, but it was meant neither ironically nor vainly, and David revised his opinion of the girl a step further. She had given

herself a reference; and she gained an immediate stature in his eyes, a seriousness. He had obviously got things badly wrong; been in some obscure way
teased on his first arrival. He saw at once the very real studio help she must be
giving the old man; and made a guess—the sexual services were provided by
the other girl alone.

"The new painting's remarkable. I don't know how he keeps on pulling
them out."

"Never thinking of anyone but himself. Mainly."

"And that's what you're learning?"

"Watching."

"He said he was very grateful to you."

"He's a child, really. He needs toys. Like affection. So he can try and
smash it to bits."

"But yours has remained whole?"

She shrugged. "We have to play up to him a little. Pretend we're in awe
of his wicked old reputation. The harem bit."

He smiled and looked down.

"I confess I was wondering what the reality was there."

"Our last visitor was told—within ten minutes of arrival—that we'd
both been ravished three times the previous night. You mustn't look as if
you doubt his word. In that area."

He laughed. "Right."

"He knows nobody believes him, but that's not the point."

"Understood."

She sipped her vermouth.

"And just to clear up any remaining illusions. Anne and I don't deny
him the little bit of sex life he can still manage."

Her eyes were on his. There was a defensiveness behind the frankness,
some kind of warning. They both looked down; David momentarily at the
line of the bare breasts beneath the blouse, then away. She seemed devoid of
coquetry, of any trace of the flagrant sexiness of her friend. Her self-possession
was so strong that it denied her good looks, that repeated undertone of nakedness, any significance; and yet it secretly drew attention to them.

She went on. "He's not verbal at all. As you must have realized. It's
partly having lived abroad so long. But something much deeper. He has to
see and to feel. Quite literally. The shadow of young girls in flower isn't
enough."

"I begin to realize just how lucky he is."

"I'm only giving you the debit side."

"I realize that as well."

She glanced secretively to where the old man sat, then back at David. "If
he turns nasty, you mustn't get rattled. It's no good backing down, he hates

that. Just stick to your guns. Keep cool." She smiled. "Sorry. If I'm sounding all-wise. But I do know him."

He swirled the lemon in the bottom of his glass. "I'm actually not quite sure why I'm allowed here. If he knows my work."

"That's why I'm warning you. He asked me, I had to tell him. In case he found out anyway."

"Oh Christ."

"Don't worry. He'll probably be satisfied with one or two mean digs. Which you needn't rise to."

He gave her a rueful look. "I suspect I'm being a bloody nuisance. For you."

She was smiling, and he smiled back.

"Since you mention it."

"We're delighted you've come. But it wouldn't do to show that too obviously in front of Henry."

"As I now completely understand."

There was suddenly a grain of mischief in her eyes.

"Now you have to learn Anne. She's more difficult than me."

But they never got on to Anne. The door from the kitchen opened and the gray head of the French housekeeper looked into the room.

"Je peux servir, mademoiselle?"

"Oui, Mathilde. Je viens vous aider."

She went into the kitchen. The other girl was on her feet, pulling Breasley to his. She was barebacked, the dress cut absurdly low. They came hand-in-hand down the room to where David waited. One had to grant her some kind of style. She had a little self-guying mince as she walked, something monkeyish, or repressed gaiety, provokingly artificial beside her white-haired companion's quiet walk. David doubted whether he would ever "learn" her.

Only one end of the long table was laid. Breasley stood at the head, the girl took the seat to his right. The old man gestured.

"Williams, dear boy."

He was to sit on the Freak's right. Mathilde and the Mouse appeared: a small soup tureen, a platter of *crudités,* another of variously pink rings of sausage, a butter dish. The soup was for Breasley. He remained standing, waiting with an old-fashioned courtesy to see the Mouse into her chair. When she sat, he bent over and lightly kissed the crown of her head. The two girls exchanged a neutral look. In spite of their seemingly disparate looks and intelligences there was evidently a closeness between them, a rapport that did not need words. The Mouse ladled soup into the dish before the old man. He tucked a large napkin between two buttons halfway down his shirtfront and spread it over his lap. The Freak silently insisted that David help himself first. The housekeeper went to a corner of the room and lighted an oil lamp, then brought it back and set it down in the empty space opposite David. On her way out to the kitchen she reached for a switch and the electric lights around them died. At the far end of the room a hidden lamp in the corridor upstairs remained on, silhouetting the handsome diagonal of the medievel staircase. At last pale phosphorescence in the evening light outside, over the trees; the faces bathed in the quiet lambency from the milky diffuser; the Mouse poured red wine from a bottle without a label for David, the old man and herself. The Freak, it seemed, did not drink; and hardly ate. She sat with the elbows of her bare brown arms on the table, picking up little bits of raw vegetable and nibbling at them, staring across at the Mouse with her dark eyes. She did not look at David. There was a little silence as they all set to; as if one waited for Breasley to declare conversation open. David was hungry, anyway, and feeling much more at home now that the girl opposite had cleared the air so completely. The lamplight made the scene like a Chardin, a Georges de la Tour; very peaceful. Then the Freak choked without warning. David flashed her a look—not food, it had been a stifled giggle.

The Mouse murmured, "Idiot."

"Sorry."

She made an absurd attempt, mouth pressed tight and down, leaning back, to control her nervousness; then abruptly clutched her white napkin to ther face and twisted up away from her chair. She stood five or six feet away, her back to them. Breasley went on calmly eating his soup. The Mouse smiled across at David.

"Not you."

"Needs her bloody bum tanned," murmured Breasley.

Still the girl stood, long bare spine to them, fuzz of dark red shadow perched over the scarecrow neck. Then she moved farther away, toward the fireplace, into the darkness.

"Mouse is a fan of yours, Williams. She tell you that?"

"Yes, we've already established a mutual admiration society."

"Very pernickety creature, our Mouse."

David smiled.

"Footsteps of Pythagoras, that right?"

The old man stayed intent on his soup. David glanced for help at the girl opposite.

"Henry's asking if you paint abstracts."

Eyes on his laden spoon, the old man muttered quickly, "Obstructs."

"Well yes. I'm . . . afraid I do."

He knew it was a mistake even before the Mouse's quick glance. The old man smiled up.

"And why are we afraid, dear boy?"

David said lightly, "Just a figure of speech."

"Very brainy stuff, I hear. Much admired, Mouse says."

David murmured, " '*Als ich kann.*' "

Breasley loked up a second time. "Come again?"

But suddenly the Freak was behind her chair. She held three pink chrysanthemum heads, removed from a pot David has seen in the fireplace. She put one by his hand; one by the old man's and the third by the Mouse's. Then she sat down with her hands on her lap, like a self-punished child. Breasley reached out and patted her arm in avuncular fashion.

"You were saying, Williams?"

"As sound as I can make them." He went quickly on. "I'd rather hoped humbly in the footsteps of . . ." but he saw too late he was heading for another mistake.

"Of whom, dear boy?"

"Braque?"

It was a mistake. David held his breath.

"Mean that synthetic cubist nonsense?"

"It makes sense to me, sir."

The old man did not answer for a moment. He ate more soup.

"All spawn bastards when we're young." David smiled, and stopped his tongue. "Saw a lot of atrocities in Spain. Unspeakable things. Happens in war. Not just them. Our side as well." He took another mouthful of soup, then laid the spoon down and leaned back and surveyed David. "Battle's over, dear man. doing it in cold blood, you with me? Don't go for that."

"As I've been warned, Mr. Breasley."

The old man suddenly relaxed a little; there was even a faint glint of amusement in his eyes.

"Long as you know, my boy."

David opened his hands: he knew. The Mouse spoke.

"Henry, do you want more soup?"

"Too much garlic."

"It's exactly the same as last night."

The old man grunted, then reached for the wine bottle. The Freak raised her hands and ran her splayed fingers through her hair, as if she were afraid it might be lying flat; then turned a little to David, her arms still high.

"You like my tattoo?"

In the hollow of the shaven armpit was a dark blue daisy.

Through the rest of the meal David managed, in tacit alliance with the Mouse, to keep the conversation off art. The food itself helped; the *quenelles* of pike in a *beurre blanc* sauce that was a new gastronomic experience to him, the *pré salé* lamb. They talked French cooking and love of food, then about Brittany, the Breton character. This was Haute Bretagne, David learned, as opposed to the Basse, or Bretagne Bretonnante farther west, where the lan-

guage was still spoken. *Coët* meant wood, or forest: *-minais,* of the monks. The
surrounding forest had once been abbatial land. Among themselves they
dropped that part, one spoke simply of Coët. Most of the talk was between
the Mouse and David, though she turned to Breasley from time to time for
confirmation or for further details. The Freak said next to nothing. David
sensed a difference of license accorded the two girls. The Mouse was allowed
to be herself; the other was there slightly on tolerance. She too, it emerged
at one point, had been an art student; but graphics, not fine arts. They had
first met at Leeds. But she gave the impression that she did not take her
qualifications very seriously; she was out of her class in her present company.

The old man, having drawn his drop of blood, seemed satisfied, prepared
to revert at least part of the way back to his predinner self. But if the Mouse
was successful in maintaining an innocuous conversation, she was less so in
keeping the wine from him. She drank very little herself, and David gave up
trying to keep pace with his host. A second bottle had been produced from
the *armoire.* By the time the meal was finished that was empty, too, and there
was a glaze in Breasley's eyes. He did not seem drunk, there was no fumbling
after his glass; just that ocular symptom of possession by an old demon. His
answers became increasingly brief; he hardly seemed to be listening anymore.
The Mouse had complained that they never saw any films, and the talk have
moved to that; what David had seen recently in London. Then the old man
broke in abruptly.

"Another bottle, Mouse."

She looked at him, but he avoided her eyes.

"In our guest's honor."

Still she hesitated. The old man stared at his empty glass, then raised a
hand and brought it down on the table. It was without force or anger, only a
vague impatience. But she got up and went to the *armoire.* They were apparently at a point where giving way was better than remonstrating. Breasley
leaned back in his chair, staring at David under the white quiff, almost benevolent, a kind of fixed smile. The Freak spoke to the table in front of her.

"Henry, can I get down?"

He remained staring at David. "Why?"

"I want to read my book."

"You're a fucking little ninny."

"Please."

"Bugger off then."

He had not looked at her. The Mouse came back with the third bottle,
and the Freak looked nervously up at her, as if her permission was needed as
well. There was a little nod, then David felt his thigh being briefly squeezed.
The Freak's hand had reached along beneath the table, apparently to give him
courage. She stood up and went down the room and up the stairs. Breasley

pushed the bottle toward David. It was not a politeness, but a challenge.

"Not for me, thanks I've had enough."

"Cognac? Calvados?

"No thanks."

The old man poured himself another full glass of wine.

"This pot stuff?" He nodded sideways down the room. "That's the book she wants to read."

The Mouse said quietly, "She's given it up. You know that perfectly well."

He took a mouthful of wine.

"Thought all the young whiz-kids indulged."

David said lightly, "Not personally."

"Interferes with the slide-rule stuff, does it?"

"I imagine. But I'm not a mathematician."

"What do you call it then?"

The Mouse waited, eyes down. Evidently she could not help him now, except as a silent witness. It was not worth pretending one did not know what the "it" meant. David met the old man's stare.

"Mr. Breasley, most of us feel abstraction has become a meaningless term. Since our conception of reality has changed so much this last fifty years."

The old man seemed to have to turn it over in his mind; then dismiss it.

"I call it betrayal. Greatest betrayal in the history of art."

The wine had gone to his cheeks and nose, and his eyes seemed almost opaque. He was less leaned than forced back against his armed chair, which he had shifted a little to face David. It also brought him a little closer to the girl beside him. David had talked too much to her during dinner, shown to much interest . . . he saw that now, and that the old man must have watched them talking before the meal. In some way he had to repossess her.

"Triumph of the bloody eunuch."

In that way.

"At least better than the triumph of the bloody dictator?"

"Balls. Spunk. Any spunk. Even Hitler's spunk. Or nothing."

Without looking at David, the Mouse said, "Henry feels that full abstraction represents a flight from human and social responsibility." He thought for one moment she was taking Breasley's side; then realized she had now set up as interpreter.

"But if philosophy needs logic? If applied mathematics needs the pure form? Surely there's a case for fundamentals in art, too?"

"Cock. Not fundamentals. Fundaments." He nodded at the girl beside him. "Pair of tits and a cunt. All that goes with them. That's reality. Not your piddling little theorems and pansy colors. I know what you people are after, Williams."

Once again the Mouse interpreted, in an absolutely neutral voice. "You're afraid of the human body."

"Perhaps simply more interested in the mind than the genitals."

"God help your bloody wife then."

David said evenly, "I thought we were talking about painting."

"How many women you slept with, Williams?"

"That's not your business, Mr. Breasley."

It was disconcerting, the fixity of the stare in the pause before an answer could be framed; like fencing in slow motion.

"Castrate. That's your game. Destroy."

"There are worse destroyers around than nonrepresentational art."

"Cock."

"You'd better tell that to Hiroshima. Or to someone who's been napalmed."

The old man snorted. There was another silence.

"Science hasn't got a soul. Can't help itself. Rat in a maze."

He swallowed the last of his glass and gestured impatiently at the Mouse to refill it. David waited, though he was tempted to jump in and ask why he had been invited to Coëtminais in the first place. He felt rattled, in spite of being forewarned. It was the violently personal nature of the assault, the realization that any rational defense, or discussion, would simply add fuel to the flames.

"What you people . . ." the old man stared at the filled glass, jumped words. "Betrayed the fort. Sold out. Call yourself avant-garde. Experimental. My arse. High treason, that's all. Mess of scientific pottage. Sold the whole bloody shoot down the river."

"Abstract painting is no longer avant-garde. And isn't the best propaganda for humanism based on the freedom to create as you like?"

Again the pause.

"Wishwash."

David forced a smile. "Then one's back with socialist realism? State control?"

"What controls you then, Wilson?"

"Williams," said the Mouse.

"Don't give me that liberal cant. Had to live with the stench of it all my life. *Le fairplay.* Sheer yellowbelly." Suddenly he pointed a finger at David. "Too old for it, my lad. Seen too much. Too many people die for decency. Tolerance. Keeping their arses clean."

He finished his wine in one contemptuous gulp, then reached for the bottle again. Its neck rattled against the rim of the glass and he poured too long, some spilled over. The Mouse lifted the glass and poured off a little into her own; then quietly wiped the spilled liquid from the table in front of the old man. David said nothing. He felt cool again now; but embarrassed.

"Good wines, know what they do? Piss on them. Piss in the vat." He rather shakily got the glass to his mouth, then set it down. The pauses grew longer between each burst of speech. "Fit ten Englishmen into a Frenchman's little finger." Another hiatus. "Not oil. Pigment. All shit. If it's any good. *Merde.* Human excrement. *Excrementum.* That which grows out. That's your fundamental. Not your goddam prissy little bits of abstract good taste." He paused again, as if he sought a way forward, and had finally to go back. "Wouldn't even wipe my arse with them."

There was a heavy silence. Somewhere outside an owl quavered. The girl sat, her chair pushed back a little from the table, her hands folded on her lap, eyes down, apparently prepared to wait for eternity for the old man's ramblings to finish. David wondered how often she had to suffer this monstrous bohemian travesty that the alcohol had released. All those ancient battles that had to be refought; when the matter was so tatally, both *de facto* and *de jure,* decided, and long before David was born. All form was not natural; and color had a nonrepresentational function . . . you could not more argue any longer about that than about Einstein's famous equation. Fission had taken place. One could dispute application, but not principle. So David thought; and some of it must have appeared on his face. He had also drunk more than usual.

"Disappointing you, Williams? Think I'm pissed? *In vino* bollocks?"

David shook his head. "Just overstating your case."

More silence.

"You really a painter, Williams? Or just a gutless bloody word-twister?"

David did not answer. There was another silence. The old man drank more wine.

"Say something."

"Hatred and anger are not luxuries we can afford anymore. At any level."

"Then God help you."

David smiled faintly. "He's also a nonoption."

The Mouse reached forward and poured more wine.

"Know what turning the cheek meant when I was young? Fellow who turned his cheek?"

"No."

"Bumboy. You a bumboy, Wilson?"

This time the Mouse did not bother to correct him; or David, to answer.

"On your knees and trousers down. Solves all, does it?"

"No. But then nor does fear."

"Does which?"

"Being afraid of losing . . . what isn't in question."

The old man stared at him.

"What the hell's he talking about?"

The Mouse said quietly, "He means your work and your views of art aren't in any danger. Henry. There's room for everyone."

She did not look at David, but shifted a little, forward and away from the old man; put an elbow on the table, then her hand to her chin. A finger rose momentarily to her lips. David was not to answer back anymore. Outside, Macmillan suddenly began barking; wild paroxysms of suspicion. A voice, the housekeeper's husband's, shouted. Neither the old man nor the girl took any notice; to them it must have been a familiar night sound. To David it was intensely symbolic, fraught, echoing the tension inside the old man.

"That's the line now, is it?"

The girl looked across at David. There was a faint smile in her eyes.

"Henry thinks one shouldn't show toleration for things one believes are bad."

"Same old story. Sit on the bloody English fence. Vote for Adolf."

There was more silence, but then suddenly she spoke.

"Henry, you can't stop totalitarian ideas by totalitarian methods. That way you only help breed them."

Perhaps some dim realization percolated through that she was now taking David's side. The old man's eyes wandered away into the shadows at the end of the table. When she had last refilled his glass, she had put the bottle back to her left, out of his reach.

He said slowly, "Trying to tell you something."

It wasn't clear whether he meant, I didn't mean to insult you personally; or, I've forgotten what it was.

David murmured, "Yes, I realize."

The old man's stare came back to him. He had difficulty in focusing. "What's your name?"

"Williams. David Williams."

The Mouse said, "Finish your wine."

But he ignored her.

"Not good with words. Never my line."

"I understand what you're saying."

"Don't hate, can't love. Can't love, can't paint."

"I understand."

"Bloody geometry. No good. Won't work. All tried it. Down the hole." His staring at David now had a desperate concentration, almost a clinging. He seemed to lose all train.

The Mouse prompted him. "Making is speaking."

"Can't write without words. Lines."

The girl stared down the room. She spoke very quietly.

"Art is a form of speech. Speech must be based on human needs, not abstract theories of grammar. Or anything but the spoken word. The real word."

"Other things. Ideas. Can't care."

David nodded gravely.

The Mouse went on. "Ideas are inherently dangerous because they deny human facts. The only answer to fascism is the human fact."

"Machine. What's it, computer thing."

David said, "I do understand."

"Tachiste. Fautrier. Wols fellow. Like frightened bloody sheep. Drip, drip." He stopped, a silence. "Yank, what's his name?"

David and the girl said it together, and he missed it. The Mouse repeated the name.

"Jackson Bollock." Once again he stared off into the darkness. "Better the bloody bomb than Jackson Bollock."

They said nothing. David stared at the ancient surface of the table in front of him; blackened oak, scarred and rubbed, the patina of centuries' use; centuries of aged voices, ordering back some threatening, remorseless tide. As if time knew ebb.

Then the old man spoke, with a strange lucidity, as if he had only been pretending to be drunk, and now summerized with one final inconsequence.

"Ebony tower. That's what I call it."

David glanced across at the girl, but she did not meet his look. Foreclosing had apparently become more important than interpreting. It was very clear that Breasley was not really pretending; David watched his eyes, how they searched hazily for the glass, or several glasses, in front of him. He reached, a last effort to seem positive and sober. The Mouse caught his hand and gently set the stem of the glass between the fingers. The old man had difficulty in getting it to his mouth, then tried to down the wine on one brave swallow. It dribbled down his chin, then splashed on his white shirt-front. The Mouse leaned forward and dabbed with her serviette.

She said gently, "Bed now."

"One more."

"No." She took the half-empty bottle and put it beside her chair on the floor. "All gone."

The old man's eyes found David.

"Qu'est-ce qu'il fout ici?"

The girl stood and put a hand under his elbow to urge him up.

He said, "Bed."

"Yes Henry."

But still he sat, slightly bowed, a very old man in a stupor. The girl waited patiently. Her downward eyes met David's, a curious gravity, as if she were frightened she might see contempt in his for this role she had to play. He pointed at himself—could he help? She nodded, but raised a finger; not yet. A moment later she bent and kissed the old man on the temple.

"Come on. Try and stand."

And now, like an obedient but vaguely timid small boy, he pressed his hands on the table. He was unsteady as he came to his feet, and lurched forward against the table-edge. David went quickly to his other side. Suddenly he collapsed down again into the chair. This time they pulled him up. How drunk he really was did not become apparent until they started to walk him down the room toward the stairs. He was in a seeming coma, his eyes closed; only his legs, by some ancient instinct, or long practice, managed to go through the motions of shuffling forward. The Mouse pulled at the bow tie, then unbottoned the top of the shirt. Somehow they got him up the stairs and into the large room at the west end of the house.

David saw a double and single bed, the Freak standing off the latter. She still wore the black dress, but now with a white jumper over it. He had a glimpse of more paintings and drawings on the walls, a table by the window that faced out west with jars of crayons and drawing pencils.

"Oh Henry. You wicked old thing."

The Mouse spoke across the old man's bowed head to David.

"We can manage now."

"Are you sure?"

Breasley muttered, "Pee."

The two girls led him around the beds and to a door beyond. They got him in and all three disappeared. David stood undecided, at a loss; and then suddenly he registered the painting over the bed. It was a Braque, one he knew he had seen somewhere in reproduction. It must have been listed as "private collection," he had never associated it with Breasley. He thought wrily back: the jejune folly of throwing such a name, such a relationship, at the old man in his own self-defense. The Freak came out of the bathroom and closed the door behind her. The additional irony of it struck him ... that painting, a certain six figures at any auction—and the gewgawish, unreliable-looking little creature who stood facing him across the room. There was the sound of vomiting.

"Is he like this every night?"

"Just sometimes." She had a thin smile. "It's not you. Just other people."

"I can't help undress him?"

She shook her head. "Don't worry. Really. We're used to it." He stood there in doubt. She said again, "Really."

He wanted to say that he admired them both for what they were doing; and found himself at an unusual loss for words.

"Well ... say good night to ... I don't actually know her real name."

"Di. Diana. Sleep well."

"And you."

She pressed her lips drily together and gave a little single nod. He left.

Back in his room, in pajamas, in bed, he lay propped on an elbow staring at a thriller he had brought. He felt he ought to stay at least potentially on hand for a while in case they did need further help; and though he felt tired, sleep was out of the question. He couldn't even read, the adrenaline had to calm down. It had been an extraordinary evening; and for the first time he was glad that Beth hadn't been there. She would have found it too much, flown off the handle probably; though the baiting had been so crude, so revealing of all the old man's weaknesses. Essentially one was dealing with a cantankerous child. And the Mouse, Diana, how staggeringly well she had handled him; quite a girl, quite a pair, there must be something better than was apparent in the other, a fidelity, a kind of courage. One took the Mouse's word now, the accuracy of her judgments; had needed her coolness; was curious to know if one had satisfied it. He recalled a certain amount of skeptical joking between Beth and himself: about the old man living up to his reputation. Beth's expecting to be groped at least twice or asking for her money back ... that at least was taken care of. The stories to tell in private back home. He tried to settle to his thriller.

Perhaps twenty minutes had passed since he had left the girls to their tyrant. The house had fallen silent. But now he heard someone come out of Breasley's bedroom, then light footsteps, the creak of a floorboard outside his room. There was a hesitation, then a gentle tap on his door.

"Come in."

The Mouse's head appeared around the door.

"I saw your light on. It's all right. He's asleep."

"I didn't realize how far gone he was."

"We have to let him do it sometimes. You did very well."

"I'm jolly glad you warned me."

"He'll be all contrite tomorrow. Meek as a lamb." She smiled. "Breakfast around nine? But you know. Sleep as long as you like."

She drew back to go, but he stopped her. "What on earth did that last thing he said mean? The ebony tower?"

"Oh," She smiled. "Nothing. Just one of the bats in his belfry." She tilted her head. "What he thinks has taken the place of the ivory tower?"

"Abstraction?"

She shook her head. "Anything he doesn't like about modern art. That he thinks is obscure because the artist is scared to be clear ... you know. Somewhere you dump everything you're too old to dig? You mustn't take it personally. He can only explain what he thinks by insulting people." She smiled again, her body still hidden by the door. "Okay?"

He smiled back, and nodded.

And she was gone, not back to the old man's room, but farther down the corridor. A door clicked quietly to. David would have liked to talk a little longer. The old teaching world—students you fancied, who fancied you a little, in some way the atmosphere of Coët reminded him of the days before

Beth had entered his life; not that he had even gone in much for having if off with students. He was a crypto-husband long before he married.

He read a little, then switched out the light and sank, in his usual way, almost immediately into sleep.

Once again the Mouse was proved right. Contrition was flagrant from the moment David appeared, punctually at nine, downstairs again. Breasley himself came in from the garden as David stood at the foot of the stairs uncertain of where breakfast took place. To one unversed in the recuperative powers of lifelong heavy drinkers, he seemed surprisingly spry, and newly dapper, in light trousers and a dark blue sports shirt.

"My *dear* man. So un*speak*ably sorry about last night. Gels tell me most ap*pall*ingly rude."

"Not at all. Honestly."

"Absolutely pissed. Very bad form."

David grinned. "Forgotten."

"Curse of my life, don't you know. Never learned when to stop."

"Please don't worry."

He took the abruptly extended hand.

"Very white of you, dear boy." The hand was retained, his eyes quizzed. "Say I must call you David. Surnames terribly square these days. That right?"

He used "square" as if it wre some daring new piece of slang.

"Please do."

"Splendid. Well. I'm Henry then. Yes? Now come and have some breakfast. We pig it in the kitchen in the mornings."

One the way down the room, Breasley said, "Gels suggest a little *déjeuner sur l'herbe*. Good idea, what? Picnic?" There was sunshine outside, a faint haze over the trees. "Rather proud of my forest. Worth a dekko."

"I'd love to."

The two girls, it seemed, were already up and out—to Plélan, the nearest village, to shop for food . . . and incidentally, or so David guessed, to allow the old man time to prove his penitence. He was taken on a stroll around the domain after breakfast. Breasley revealed a pride in his garden, a little vanity over what must have been a comparatively recently acquired knowledge of names and cultivation methods. They came on Jean-Pierre hoeing in the vegetable garden behind the east end of the house; and as he listened to the old man and the housekeeper's husband discussing an ailing young tulip tree and what could be done for it, David had again that pleasing sense of a much more dominant key in Breasley's life than the previous night's "recessive" exhibition of spleen. He had very evidently learned to live in Coët and its seasons; and a little later, when they were out in the orchard beyond the vegetables, there was an old water pear already ripe, David was to taste one, they must be eaten straight from the tree, the old man began to say as much—to confess he was a fool to have spent so much of his life in a city; to have left himself so little time to enjoy this. Between bites at his pear David asked why it had taken so long to find that out. Breasley gave a little sniff of self-contempt, then poked at a windfall with the end of his walking stick.

"The bitch Paris, dear boy. Know that bit of rhyme? Earl of Rochester, isn't it? 'Where man may live in direst need, but ne'er lack land to set his seed.' Neat. Says it all."

David smiled. They strolled on.

"Should have married. Damn' sight less expensive."

"But you'd have missed a lot?"

Another sniff of self-reproach. "One's the same as fifty, what?"

He seemed unawre of the irony: that he still had not managed to make do with one; and as if on cue a small white Renault came down the private lane from the outer world. The Mouse was driving. She waved through the window to where they stood, but did not stop. David and Breasley turned back toward the house. The old man pointed his stick after the car.

"Envy you chaps. Weren't like that when I was young."

"I thought the girls of the twenties were rather dazzling."

The stick was raised in genially outraged contradiction.

"Absolute piffle, my dear man. No idea. Spent half your life getting their legs open. Other half wishing you hadn't. Either that. Catching the clap off some tart. Dog's life. Don't know how we stood it."

But David was unconvinced, and knew he was meant to be. The old man regretted nothing at heart; or only the impossible, another life. Somehow something of the former sexual bantam clung physically around his old frame; he could never have been particularly good-looking, but there must have been an attack, a devil about him, a standing challenge to the monogamous. One could imagine him countlessly rebuffed, and indifferent to it; enormously selfish, both in bed and out; impossible, so one believed in him. And now even those many who must have refused to believe had been confounded: he had come through to this, reputation, wealth, the girls, freedom to be exactly as he always had been, a halo around his selfishness, a world at his every whim, every other world shut out, remote behind the arboreal sea. To someone like David, always inclined to see his own life (like his painting) in terms of logical process, its future advances dependent on intelligent present choices, it seemed not quite fair. Of course one knew that the way to the peak was never by the book, that hazard and all the rest must play its part, just as action and aleatory painting formed an at least theoretically important sector in the modern art spectrum. But some such mountaineering image drifted through his mind. One had acquired the best equipment one could afford—and one looked up. There on the summit stood a smirking old satyr in carpet slippers, delightedly damning all common sense and calculation.

By eleven they were *en route.* The girls walked ahead with baskets, down a long forest ride; and David walked behind with the old man, carrying a folding blue recliner on an aluminum frame—portable sofa for the senile, as Breasley disparagingy called it, but the Mouse had insisted on its being brought. He walked with a coat folded over his arm, a raffish old wide-brimmed panama on his head; engagingly seigneurial, pointing at shadows with his walking stick; lights, special perspetive qualities of "his" forest. The visit had been allowed to return to its proper purpose. The silence, the rather strange lack of birds; how did one get silence into paint? The theater now, didn't David notice the quality of empty stage?

David was rather more noticing that all this could be used in his introduction. *Anyone who has had the good fortune to walk with the master,* no, *with Henry Breasley in his beloved forest of Paimpont, that still potent evocation* ... the haze had gone, it was surprisingly warm, more like August than September, a peerless day; one couldn't actually write like that. But he was still basking—realizing his baptism of fire had been a blessing in disguise—in the old man's determined good graces. The importance, pervasive in the mood if tenuous in the actual symbolism, of Breton medieval literature in the Coëtminais series was generally accepted now, though David had not been able to trace much public clarification from Breasley himself on the real extent of the influence. He had read the subject up cursorily before coming, but now he played a little ignorant; and discovered Breasley to be rather more learned and lettered than his briskly laconic manner at first sound suggested. The old man explained in his offhand way the sudden twelfth- and thirteenth-century mania for romantic legends, the mystery of island Britain ("sort of Wild Northern, what, knights for cowboys") filtering all over Europe *via* its French namesake; the sudden preoccupation with love and adventure and the magical, the importance of the once endless forest—of which the actual one they were walking in, Paimpont now, but the Brocéliande of the *lais* of Chrétien de Troyes, was an example—as the matrix for all these goings-on; the breaking-out of the closed formal garden of other medieval art, the extraordinary yearning symbolized in these wandering horsemen and lost damsels and dragons and wizards, Tristan and Merlin and Lancelot ...

"All damn' nonsense," said Breasley. "Just here and there, don't you know, David. What one needs. Suggestive. Stimulating, that's the word." Then he went off on Marie de France and *Eliduc.* "Damn' good tale. Read it several times. What's that old Swiss bamboozler's name. Jung, yes? His sort of stuff. Archetypal and all that."

Ahead, the two girls turned off on a diagonal and narrower ride, more shady. Breasley and David followed some forty yards behind. The old man waved his stick.

"Those two gels now. Two gels in *Eliduc.*"

He began to tell its story. But consciously or unconsciously his distinctly shorthand manner of narration was more reminiscent of a Noel Coward farce than a noble medieval tale of crossed love, and once or twice David had to bite his lips. Nor did the actual figures of the two girls, the Freak in a red shirt, black dungarees and wellingtons, the Mouse in a dark green jersey (all bras were not burnt, David had noted) and pale trousers, help. More and more he realized the truth of what the latter had said: the old man's problem was an almost total inadequacy with words. If he didn't always cheapen, he certainly misrepresented everything he talked about. One had to keep remembering the way he could express himself in paint; and the gap was enormous. The art predicated a sensitive and complex man; and almost everything outward in him denied it. Though he would have loathed the comparison he was not unlike a certain kind of outdated Royal Academician—much more anxious to appear a stylish pillar of a dead society than to be anything that serious art was about. That was very probably one good reason for the continued exile: the old man must know his persona would never wash in the Britain of the 1970s. Only here could he still preserve it. Of course these were all things one could not put in the introduction, but David found them fascinating. Like the forest itself, the old man had his antique mysteries.

They came up to the two girls, who had stopped. It was a question of the point to leave the path and strike away through the trees to the forest pool that was the promised picnic place. Thre was a marker oak, a trunk with a dab of red paint. The Mouse thought they had missed it, but the old man made them go on; and rightly. In another hundred yards or so they arrived at the oak, and began to walk down a faint incline among the trees. The undergrowth became denser, they glimpsed the first water ahead: and a few minutes later they emerged on the grassy edge of the *étang*. It was much more a small lake than a pool, four hundred yards or more across at the point where they came to it and curving away on both sides. A dozen or so wild duck roosted in the middle. The forest stood all around its shores, not a house in sight; the water a delicate blue in the September sunlight, smooth as a mirror. The place had featured in two of the last-period paintings and David had a sense of familiarity, of *déjà vu*. It was very charming, miraculously unspoiled. They installed themselves in the thin shade of a solitary fir tree. The reclining chair was set for Breasley. He seemed grateful for it now, sat down at once and put his legs up; then made them adjust the back to a more upright position.

"Come on, you two. Off with your knickers and have your bathe."

The Freak slid a look at David, then away.

"We're shy."

"You'll swim, won't you, David? Keep 'em company?"

David looked for guidance from the Mouse, but she was bent over one of the baskets. He felt grossly unforewarned this time. Swimming had not been mentioned.

"Well . . . perhaps later?"

"You see," said the Freak.

"Not bleeding or anything, are you?"

"Oh Henry. For God's sake."

"Married man, m'dear. Seen pussy before."

The Mouse straightened and gave David a little glance, half apologetic, half wry.

"Costumes are considered unethical. Wearing them makes us even more impossible than usual."

But she lightened the taunt with a smile down at the old man.

David murmured, "Of course."

She looked at the Freak. "Let's go out on the spit, Anne. The bottom's harder there." She picked up a towel and began to walk away, but the Freak seemed now the more shy. She glanced resentfully at the two men.

"And easier for all the other dirty old birdwatchers."

The old man chuckled, and she put out her tongue at him. But then she too picked up a towel and followed her friend.

"Sit down, dear boy. Only codding you. Shy my arse."

David sat on the needled grass. He supposed that this had been sprung on him as a little demonstration of what they had to go through, though the previous night had seemed a conclusive enough witness to that. He felt teased, faintly conspired against: now it's our turn to shock you. The spit, a narrow little grass-topped promontory, ran out some sixty yards away. As the girls walked down it, the wild duck splashed off the middle of the lake and flew in a long curve up over the trees and away. The girls stopped near the end, and the Mouse began to peel off her jersey. When it was off she turned it ouside out again, then dropped it and unhooked her bra. The Freak cast a little look back across the glassy water to where David and the old man sat, then kicked out of her wellingtons and slipped off one shoulder strap of her dungarees. The Mouse reached down her jeans and briefs together, separated them, put them beside the rest of her clothes. She walked to the water and waded straight in. The other girl let her dungarees fall, then pulled off her shirt. She was wearing nothing else. As she too walked down to the water, she turned sideways to face the two men in the distance and gave a ridiculous flaunting sidestep, a strip-dancer's routine, arms out. The old man gave another throaty little chuckle and tapped David's arm with the side of his stick. He sat enthroned, like a sultan, watching his two young slaves, the two naked figures, warm backs against the azure water, as they waded out toward the center of the lake. Apparently the bottom shelved slowly. But then the Mouse plunged forward and began to swim away; a crawl, neatly, rather well. The Freak was more cautious, wading deeper, keeping her precious frizzed hair above the water; when she finally fell cautiously forward she did a timid breast-stroke.

"Pity you're married," said Breasley. "They need a good fuck."

By the time they were halfway through lunch, David felt a good deal more at his ease. It had all been rather stupid, his first embarrassment. If Beth had been there, for instance . . . they often swam like that on holidays themselves, even deliberately looked for deserted beaches, she would have joined the girls like a shot.

His recovery was partly due to the old man, who had started, once the two girls were swimming, talking again; or rather, at last, his ultimate proof of contrition, he aked David something about himself. The question of how and what he painted was avoided, but Breasley seemed interested to know how he had "come into the game," his life and background about Beth and the children. He even came out with an invitation: bring your wife and kids one day, like to meet 'em, like little gels . . . and David was vain enough to feel pleased. What had happened after the dinner had been, rather in the medieval context they had discussed on the walk, a kind of ordeal. Very evidently he had passed the test; which left him wondering how much, besides the direct advice, he owed to the Mouse. She must have told the old man a few home truths when he woke up; and perhaps reminded him that his reputation was at least temporarily a little in David's hands.

Meanwhile the girls had come out of the water, dried themselves, and lay side by side in the sun on the spit. The ordeal had indeed been like a reef; and now David was through, after the buffeting, to the calm inner lagoon. Another echo, this time of Gauguin; brown breasts and the garden of Eden. Strange, how Coët and its way of life seemed to compose itself so naturally into such moments, into the faintly mythic and timeless. The uncontemporary. And then yet another such moment had come. The girls had stood. They must have come to some decision about modesty, or the cost of it before the old man's tongue, because they walked back as they were, carrying their clothes; without outward self-consciousness now, but with something of that studied and improbable indifference of people in a nudist colony.

"Hey, we're hungry," said the Freak.

The pubic was dyed the same red as her other hair. Naked, she looked even more waiflike. The girls began to unpack the baskets, kneeling in the sun, while David helped Breasley move nearer to the edge of the shade. Gauguin disappeared; and Manet took his place.

Soon, during the eating, the girls' bare bodies seemed natural. They seemed to still something in the old man as well. There were no more obscenities, but a kind of quiet pagan contentment. The lovely French bread, the little cartons of goodies the girls had brought back from Plélan . . . no

wine, the old man drank Vichy water, the girls milk; a bottle of beer for
David. The Freak sat cross-legged. Something about her, perhaps just the exotic hair and darkness of her tan, was faintly negroid, aboriginal, androgy-
nous. Psychologically she still repelled something in David, he couldn't quite
say ... but what began to seem very distinctly a kind of intelligent charity in
the Mouse was shadowed in her by a fecklessness, a perversity. Though she
made no cracks, one had the impression that the sexual implications of their
behavior both excited and amused her. It might be "civilized" to the others;
with her, and her not wholly concealed little air of knowingness, it was something else—not a moral inhibition, of course, but a hint that she knew David
was getting something for nothing; which went with his feeling that he had
yet to prove himslf with her. She still vaguely resented his presence. What he
had to learn about her, beyond a little ability to debunk, a trendily shallow
narcissism, a life-style that patently hid a life-failure, he could not imagine.
She seemed so much a mere parasite on the other girl's poise and honesty; her
only apparent virtue, that she was tolerated.

And perhaps she repelled him also by physical contrast. The Mouse, despite her slightness, had a much more feminine figure, long-legged, attractively firm small breasts. She sat up on one arm opposite David, her legs
curled away. He watched her body when she turned to pass something, when
he knew the direction of his eyes would not be caught. They talked banally
enough; and once again the ghost of infidelity stalked through David's
mind—not any consideration of its actuality, but if he hadn't been married, if
Beth ... that is to say, if Beth didn't sometimes have certain faults, an occasional brisk lack of understanding of him, an overmundane practicality,
which this attractively cool and honest young mistress of a situation would
be too intelligent (for he saw in her something that he aimed at in his own
painting, a detachment and at the same time a matter-of-factness) to show or
at any rate to abuse. It wasn't that one didn't still find Beth desirable, that the
idea of a spell together in France without the kids after Coët (hovering in it
Beth's tacit reacceptance of motherhood, a third child, the son they both
wanted) ... just that one was tempted. One might, if one wasn't what one
was; and if it were offered—that is, it was a safe impossibility and a very remote probability away.

The lights of the Mouse's skin were bronzed where the sun caught it,
duller yet softer in the shadows. The nipples, the lines of the armpits. A
healed scar on one of her toes. The way her wheaty hair was drying, slightly
tangled, careless; and a smallness, a Quattrocento delicacy, the clothes and
long skirts she wore were misleading; contrasted with an animality, the nest
of hair between her legs. She sat sideways, facing the lake, and peeled an
apple; passed a quarter back to the old man, then offered another to David. It
was antiseptic; and disturbing.

Henry had to have his siesta. The Freak stood and let down the back of the recliner. Then she knelt beside the old man and whispered something in his ear. He reached out a hand to her waist and ran it slowly up to the arm, then drew her forward; and she leaned over and touched his mouth with her own. He patted her bare bottom. Then he folded his hands across his stomach, while she arranged a purple handkerchief across his eyes. The fine mouth, the pink bulb of the nose. The girl stood and stared down at him for a moment, then grimaced back at the other two.

The Mouse smiled at David and murmured, "Free period. We'd better go out of hearing."

They stood. The two girls picked up their towels, and the Freak fished in one of the baskets and found her book. Then they walked back toward the spit, some thirty yards away, just out of earshot. The towels were spread, the girls both stretched out on their stomachs, feet toward the lake, chins propped on hands. David sat, then lay on an elbow, five or six feet away on the landward side. He had a brief and much more absurd recall of a painting: two little boys listening to an Eizabethan sailor. He could read the title of the Freak's book: *The Magus*. He guessed at astrology, she would be into all that nonsense. But now she suddenly grinned at him.

"Wish you hadn't come then?"

"Good lord no."

"Di told me. Last night. I'm sorry. I knew I just couldn't face it."

He smiled. "I'd have asked to get down myself if I'd realized."

The Freak touched two fingers to her mouth and transferred the kiss to the Mouse's shoulder.

"Poor old Di. I always leave it to her."

Poor old Di smiled and looked down.

David said, "How long do you think you'll last out?"

The Freak made a dry little gesture at the Mouse: for her to answer. She shook her head.

"I don't think about the future."

"As an ex-art tutor . . ."

"I know."

The Freak pulled another of her faces at David.

"Common sense will get you nowhere."

The Mouse said, "It's not that."

"Just hard to leave?"

"Chance, I suppose. You know. It brought one here in the first place. And somehow it's got to take one away."

"How did it bring you here?"

She glanced at the Freak: some secret irony.

"Go on. Tell him."

"It's so stupid." She avoided David's eyes.

He murmured, "I'm all ears."

She reached a hand down from her chin and picked at the grass; the shadowed breasts; shrugged.

"Last summer. August. I was here, in France, with a friend. Another art student, a sculptor. He was on a Neolithic kick and we were hitching down to Carnac." She looked up at David. "The megalithic avenues? By pure chance we got a lift on the N24 out of Rennes from a schoolteacher at Ploërmel. Just down the road. We told him we were English art students and he told us about Henry. Of course we knew his name and everything. I even knew he lived somewhere in Brittany." She raised the bottom of one of her legs in the air. The hollowed back, the delicate brown cheeks. She shook her head. "It was just one of those absurd things. Let's be mad and knock on his door. So we camped at Paimpoint. Turned up at Henry's about eleven the next morning. Pretending we hadn't seen the sign on the gate. Expecting the boot and nearly getting it. But we gushed like crazy. How much we loved his work. Inspiration to all our generation. All that. Suddenly he fell for it, we'd got a bloody nerve . . . you know. All this was at the door. So we got in and he showed us around a bit. The things in the long room. Most of the time we were trying not to laugh. That way he talks, he seemed such an old phony." She stretched her hands out on the grass, comtemplated them. "Then the studio. I saw what he was doing. Perhaps you felt it yesterday. Bump. You're in a different world." She propped her chin again, and stared into the trees behind them. "You've spent three years getting all the right attitudes to painting. Knowing even less what you're doing at the end than you did at the beginning. Then you meet this ridiculous old ragbag of all the wrong attitudes. And he's there. All your own clever little triumphs and progresses are suddenly cut down to scale." She said quickly, "I'm sorry, I don't mean that you should have felt that. But I did."

"No, I know exactly what you mean."

She smiled. "Then you shouldn't. You're much, much better than that."

"I doubt it, but never mind."

"That's all really. Oh except at the end, Tom had gone away to fetch his camera, we'd left our rucksacks outside. Henry tells me I'm a very attractive 'gel,' he wishes he was younger. I laughed, said I wished I was older. And suddenly he took my hands. Kissed one. All rather corny. It happened so quickly. Tom came back, took some photos. Then Henry suddenly asked if we'd like to stay to lunch. But we felt it was just a nice gesture—one was meant to refuse. Silly. He never makes nice gestures. Without a reason. Perhaps I sensed that already, something in his eyes. And I knew Tom wanted to get on. Anyway, it sort of ruined everything. You know how it is, when you turn someone down because you don't think it matters and realize too late that it does." She glanced sideways down at the fir tree. "I suppose we left the impression that we'd been doing it just for jokes. That we weren't really interested in him. Which was true in a way. He was just a famous name. It was so stupid. Just celebrity hunting." She paused a moment. "It was strange. Even as we walked away, I felt bad. I wanted to go back."

She said nothing for a moment. The Freak had spread her elbows out on the ground and lay with her face couched and turned toward the Mouse.

"Two terms, nine months later, I'm not happy in London. It's all over with Tom. I feel I'm getting nowhere at the College. It's not their fault. Just the way I am." She picked at the grass again. "You meet someone famous, you start seeing their work in a different way. Noticing it. I kept remembering that day in August. How mean we'd been to what was basically just a poor old tongue-tied rather lonely man. Oh and . . . all sorts of other things. To do with my own work. One day I just sat down and wrote him a letter. About myself. Saying I wished we'd stayed to lunch. Not walked out like that. And if by any chance he needed domestic help. A paint mixer. Anything."

"He remembered who you were?"

"I sent him one of the photos Tom took. Henry and me standing together." She smiled to herself. "It was the sort of letter that starts sending shivers of embarrassment down your spine the moment you've posted it. I knew he wouldn't answer."

"But he did."

"A telegram. 'Can always use a pretty girl. When?' "

The Freak said, "Dear old him. Straight to the bloody point."

The Mouse pulled a face at David. "I came very innocently. Of course I knew about his past. His reputation. But I thought I could handle it. Keep a strictly granddaughterly sort of role. Or just walk out, if it got impossible." She looked down. "But Henry's got one rather extraordinary quality. A kind of magic. Apart from his painting. The way he can . . . dissolve things in you. Make them not seem to matter. Like this, I suppose. Learning not to be ashamed of one's body. And to be ashamed of one's conventions. He put it rather well once. He said exceptions don't prove rules, they're just exceptions to rules." She evidently felt herself at a loss for words. She smiled up. "We can't explain it to anyone. You have to be us to understand."

The Freak said, "Anyway, it's more like nursing."

There was a little silence. David said, "And how did you come here, Anne?"

The Mouse answered. "It began to get a bit much for me. No one to talk to. We shared a flat in Leeds. Kept in touch; I knew Anne wasn't very happy doing her ATD. So as soon as she finished that."

"I came for one week. Ha ha."

David grinned at the girl's couched face.

"At least more interesting than teaching?"

"And better paid."

"He can afford it."

The Mouse said, "I have to give it back to him. There's no arrangement. He just throws bundles of money at us. A hundred pounds. Two. If we go into Rennes with him, we hardly dare look at clothes. He always wants to buy them."

"He's sweet really," said the Freak. She turned on her back. The dark-ended boy's breasts, the tuft of reddened hair; she raised a knee and scratched just above it, then let it fall.

The Mouse said, "Working with him's very strange. He never loses patience with a painting. Even a drawing. You know, I'll hate what I've done sometimes. You rip it up? Henry'll throw things away. But always with a sort of regret. He gives work a kind of sacrosanct quality. Even when it's not going well. Everything he isn't with people." She paused, then shook her head. "And he hardly talks in the studio. Almost as if he's dumb, as if words would spoil everything."

The Freak spoke to the sky. "Well the way he uses them." She mimicked the old man's voice. " 'Are you bleeding or something?' I ask you." And she reached a hand skyward as if to push the memory away.

"He has to compensate."

The Freak clicked her tongue in agreement. "Oh, I know. Poor old bastard. Must be terrible, really." She turned sideways on an elbow, looked at the Mouse. "It's strange isn't it, Di? He's still quite sexy, in his funny old way." She looked at David. "You know, when I first . . . you think of blokes your own age and all that. But he must have been sensational. When he was young . . . and oh Christ, you ought to hear his stories." She pulled another clown's face at David. "On the good old days. What was that thing the other night, Di?"

"Don't be silly. They're just fantasies."

"I bloody well hope so."

The Mouse said, "It's contact. Not sex. Memories. The human thing. What he was trying to say last night."

David detected a difference between the two girls. One wanted to play down the sexual side, the other to admit it. He had a sudden intuition that the Freak was using his presence to air a disagreement between them and that in this context he was on her side.

"That housekeeper and her husband must have broad minds."

The Mouse looked down at the grass. "You mustn't tell anyone, but do you know how Jean-Pierre spent the late forties and fifties?" David shook his head. "In prison. For murder."

"Good grief."

"He killed his father. Some family quarrel about land. French peasants. Mathilde housekept for Henry when he came back to Paris in 1946. He knew all about Jean-Pierre. I've got all this from Mathilde, actually. Henry can do no wrong. He stood by them."

The Freak sniffed. "And more. With Mathilde."

The Mouse queried David. "That rather heavy model he used in some of the first postwar nudes?"

"My God. I never realized."

"Even Mathilde doesn't talk about that side of it. Just that 'Monsieur Henri' gave her faith to live. To wait, she says. She's also the one person Henry never but never loses his temper with. The other day he flew off the handle at dinner with Anne about something. Marched out into the kitchen. Five minutes later I go in. There he is. Eating with Mathilde at the table, listening to her read out a letter from her sister. Just like a vicar with his favorite parishioner." She had a small smile. "One could be jealous."

"Does he draw you two?"

"His hand's too shaky now. There are one or two of Anne. A lovely joke one. You know that famous Lautrec poster of Yvette Guilbert? A parody of that."

The Freak ran fingers up through her friz and toward the sky. "And he did it so *fast*. Can't have been thirty seconds. Minute at most, wasn't it, Di? Fantastic. Honestly."

She turned back on her stomach, chin on hands. Deep scarlet nails.

The Mouse eyed David again. "Has he discussed your article with you?"

"Only to claim he's never heard their names. Beyond Pisanello."

"Don't believe him. He's got an incredible memory for paintings. I've kept some of the sketches he does. He's trying to tell you about some picture and you don't quite know which one he means—and then sometimes he'll draw them. Like Anne says. Like lightning. Almost total recall."

"That restores my morale a bit."

"He'd never have agreed to your doing the book if you hadn't been reasonably near the truth."

"I was beginning to wonder."

"He's always so much more aware of what he's doing than you think. Even at his most outrageous. I took him into Rennes one day, before Anne came, to see *Death in Venice*. I had some dotty idea the real Henry would rather like it. The visual part of it, anyway. He was good as gold for the first twenty minutes. Then that heavenly looking boy appears. Next time he's on the screen Henry says, 'Pretty gel, that—done many pictures, has she?'"

David laughed; and her eyes were full of light, laughter. She was suddenly her age, not grave at all.

"Impossible, you can't imagine. He starts arguing about whether it's a girl or a boy. In a loud voice. In English, of course. Then we're on bumboys and modern decadence. The people around us start telling him to shut up. Then he's off with them in French. He didn't know there were so many queers in Rennes, and . . ." she put an imaginary pistol to her head. "There was nearly a riot. I had to drag him out before the *flics* were called in. All the way home he told me that what he calls the *k*inema began and ended with Douglas Fairbanks Senior and Mary Pickford. Totally obtuse. He hasn't seen ten films in the last twenty years. But he knows all about it. Like you last night. The more reasonable you are, the less he hears."

"But it's an act?"

"In a curious way, it's a sense of style. There's even something honest in it. You know, he's sort of saying I'm not going to be your age. I'm old, I am what I am, I don't want to understand."

The Freak said, "Like the way he talks. He keeps telling me I behave like a flapper. And you laugh, you say, *Henry,* flappers went out with lace-up corsets and camiknickers. For Gawd's sake. But it just makes him worse, doesn't it, Di?"

"But it's not as stupid as it sounds. He knows we've got to have something to laugh at. To hate in him, really."

"To forgive in him."

The Mouse opened her hands.

There was a little silence. The autumnal sun beat down. A butterfly, a Red Admiral, glided past and fluttered momentarily above the chamber of the Mouse's back. David knew what had happened; a sudden nostalgia for the old art-college relationship. That need for frankness, chewing the fat; testing one's tutor for general humanity, seeing how far he was prepared to come off it; not just confessing, but using confession.

The Mouse spoke to the grass. "I hope all this isn't shocking you."

"I'm delighted you're both so intelligent about him."

"We sometimes wonder about that." She added, "Whether we aren't what he's nicknamed us."

He smiled. "You don't seem very timid to me."

"Except I ran out."

"But you said you were learning more."

"About life. But . . ."

"Not your work?"

"I'm trying to start from the beginning again. I don't know yet."

"That's not mouselike."

The Freak said, "Anyway, who cares. I'd rather fight old Henry than forty bloody kids."

The Mouse smiled, and the Freak pushed her shoulder.

"It's all right for you." She looked at David. "Honestly. I was a bloody mess. As a student. The drug thing. Not the hard stuff. You know. Sleeping around. Di knows, I got involved with so many rotten bastards. Honestly." She pushed the other girl's leg with a foot. "Didn't I, Di?" The Mouse nodded. The Freak looked past David to where the old man slept. "I mean at least with him it's not being just laid and where's the next chick. Least he's grateful. I'll never forget one bloke. He'd just . . . you know, big deal. You

know what he says?" David shook his head. " 'Why you so bloody skinny?' "
She hit her head. "I mean, honest to God, I think of what I used to put up
with. And poor old Henry with tears in his eyes when he finally makes it."
She looked down then, as if she knew she had said too much, then suddenly
grinned up at David. "Make your fortune with *News of the World.*"

"I think the rights are yours."

For a long moment she gave him a look: both questing and quizzing.
She had brown eyes, the most attractive things in her small face. They also
had a directness, a kind of gentleness if you looked closely at them; and
David realized that he had in that forty minutes since lunch begun to learn
her. He guessed at an affectionateness beneath the flip language, and an honesty—not the Mouse's kind of honesty, which was an emancipated middle-
class one based on a good mind and proven talent, but something much
more working-class, something that had been got the hard way, by living the
"bloody mess." The friendship, the rapport became comprehensible; there
was both an identity and a complementarity. It must have been something to
do with their nakedness, the sun and water and low voices, the silent lostness
of the lake behind; but he felt drawn on into a closer and closer mesh with
these three unknown lives, as if he had known them much longer, or the
lives he did know had somehow mysteriously faded and receded in the last
twenty-four hours. Now was acutely itself; yesterday and tomorrow became
the myths. There was a sense of privilege too; almost metaphysical, that he
had been born into an environment and an age that permitted such swift process—and more banal, that career should grant opportunities. One's friends,
if they could see one now. He did then think of Beth.

He had looked down from the Freak's eyes, and there had been a little
silence. And then the Mouse glanced around (but not quite casually enough,
as if confession had got too near the bone) at the water and then at her
friend.

"I'm going to swim again."

"Okay."

The Mouse turned and sat up, back to David. The Freak smiled at him.

"Be our guest."

He had foreseen this; and decided what to do. He glanced back at where
the old man lay.

"If I shan't provoke anything."

She raised her eyebrows, Groucho Marx style; a little wriggle.

"Only us."

The Mouse reached out and smacked her bottom lightly. Then she stood
and walked down toward the water. A silence, the Freak lay on, staring at the
grass. Finally she spoke in a lower voice.

"Waste, isn't it?"

"She seems to know what she's doing."

She gave a dry little smile. "You're joking."

He watched the Mouse wading into the water; Diana, slim-backed and small-rumped; something underfoot, she stepped sideways before going deeper.

"You think you should leave?"

"I'm only here because she is." She looked down."In a funny sort of way Di's the odd one out. Old Henry and me, we kind of live from day to day. Know what I mean. We couldn't be innocent if we tried. Di's the other way around."

The girl in the water plunged and began to swim away.

"And she doesn't realize?"

"Not really. She's stupid. The way clever girls are sometimes. Okay, she sees through old Henry. The person she can't see through is herself." The Freak was avoiding his eyes now; there was almost a shyness about her. "If you could try and get her to talk. Maybe this evening. We'll get Henry off to bed early. She needs someone from outside."

"Well of course . . . I'll try."

"Okay." She was silent a moment, then she pushed abruptly up and knelt back on her heels. A grin. "She likes you. She thinks your work's sensational. It was all an act. Yesterday afternoon."

"She told me."

She appraised him a moment, then stood; for a second guyed the modest Venus, one hand over her loins, the other over her breasts.

"We shan't look."

She went to the water. David stood and got out of his clothes. He came alongside the Freak when the peaty water was around his waist. She flashed a smile at him, then swanned forward with a little scream. A moment later he dived in himself and swam out after the distant head.

Five hours later the same head faced him across the dinner table, and he was beginning to find it difficult to think of anything else. She had appeared only briefly before dinner, she was busy in the kitchen with the Freak; and now she had changed into a black shirt and another long skirt, striped browns and a burnt orange; night and autumn; and done her hair up in a way that managed to seem both classically elegant and faintly disheveled. There was just a tiny air that she was out to kill; and she was succeeding. The more he learned her, the more he watched her, the more he liked her; as temperament, as system of tastes and feelings, as female object. He knew it, and concealed it . . . not only to her, partly also to himself; that is, he analyzed what he had so rapidly begun to find attractive about her—why that precise blend of the physical and the psychological, the reserved and the open, the controlled and the (for he had also begun to believe what the Freak had said) uncertain, called so strongly to something in his own nature. Strange, how these things hit you out of the blue, were somehow inside you almost before you could see them approaching. He felt a little bewitched, possessed; and decided it must be mainly the effect of being without Beth. They lived so close, one had forgotten what the old male freedom was like; and perhaps it was most of all a matter of having to have some personal outlet for his feelings about the whole day. He had enjoyed it enormously, when he looked back. It had been so densely woven and yet simple; so crowded with new experience and at the same time primitive, atavistic, time-escaped. Above all he felt accepted, almost one of the household now.

With the girls his credentials had been established by his swimming with them; he had realized afterward that that had been needed—to prove he was a sport, on the Freak's level; that he condoned a choice at the Mouse's more thinking one. He had caught up with her some hundred yards from the shore. They had chatted a little about the lake, the temperature, the niceness of it, as they trod water some ten feet apart. He saw the Freak go back on shore. Breasley seemed still asleep under the fir tree. They had swum slowly back together, toward the thin figure drying herself. He came out of the water beside the Mouse, and the Freak had handed him her damp towel. The sunlight, the trees, the intuition of watching eyes; what faint shadows of embarrassment he still felt had very little to do with the girls . . . or only with the whiteness of his skin beside theirs.

He had not dressed at once, but sat propped back on his arms beside his clothes, drying off a little more in the sun. The two girls lay on their backs, their head toward him as before, feet to the water. The deep peace of the lake, the serene isolation; or not quite, at the end of the farthest vista there was a tiny movement, an angler, a line being cast, a speck of peasant blue. He said nothing. He felt a kind of mental—an abstract?—randiness; a sinuous wave of the primeval male longing for the licitly promiscuous, the polygamous, the caress of two bodies, sheikdom. That wickedly casual remark from the old man about what the two girls needed bred daydreams; time out of responsibility . . . such a shiftingness of perception, what one was, what one suppressed. Not much more than twelve hours ago he had very nearly dismissed and condemned them as beneath his notice; and now what had been lazily hypothetical during lunch had grown, even then, so much closer, more precise in its potentialities, more imaginable. It was like the days or weeks one might have spent on a painting, bringing it up, refining it, all compressed into a few hours. One knew why, of course. The hurtling pressure of time, prosaic reality—that long drive to Paris, he had to be there, or almost there, by this same hour the next day. Perhaps it constituted the old man's real stroke of genius, to take an old need to escape from the city, for a mysterious remoteness, and to see its ancient solution, the Celtic green source, was still viable; fortunate old man, to stay both percipient and profoundly amoral, to buy this last warm solitude and dry affection with his fame. David glanced back. Still he slept, as if dead. The way the two silent girls lay meant nothing prevented his long survey up and down the lines of their bodies; as perhaps they knew. Their tacitly sparing his modesty—more talk would have meant facing him—was also their secret advantage. He had a knowledge of a brutality totally alien to his nature; how men could rape. Something both tender and provocative in that defenselessness stirred him deeply.

He stood up and put on his clothes. He would tell Beth, because sooner or later he told her everything; but not till they had made love again.

Then the slow walk home through the forest, a sudden mania in the girls—they had taken a slightly different route, to show him a picturesquely ruined farm in an overgrown clearing—for blackberries, a good old-fashioned English blackberry-and-apple pie. The old man claimed to despise "the damn' things," but played an amiably grumbling part, even pulling down some of the high sprays with the crook of his walking stick. For fifteen minutes or so they were all childishly absorbed in it. Another moment of prospective nostalgia for David—he would not be there to enjoy the eating; which was wrong, that was why they'd been in the kitchen. The Mouse had made the pastry, Anne done the fruit. Specially for him, they said, as if to atone for something emasculating in the situation, something unfair. He was touched.

For part of the way home after the blackberrying he had walked beside the Mouse, ahead of the other girl and the old man. Rather unexpectedly she had been a little shy, as if she knew that the Freak had said something—she both wanted to talk, he felt, and was on her guard against revealing too much. They had discussed the Royal College, why she had left it, but in a rather neutral, general sort of way. Apparently she had felt a kind of claustrophobia, too many elite talents cooped up in too small a space, she had become too self-conscious, too aware of what other people were doing; it had all been her fault. He glimpsed a different girl beneath the present one: rather highly strung, fiercely self-critical, over-conscientious—as the one piece of work of hers that he had seen suggested. She was also anxious not to make too much of it, her artistic future; or at any rate to bore him with it. They slid away to art education in general. He was warned she was a different person on her own, much more difficult to dissolve without the catalyst of the Freak. She had even stopped and turned, and waited to let the others catch up. He was fairly sure it hadn't been merely to give Henry no cause for jealousy. In a way the conversation was a failure. But it did not make her less attractive to him.

Perhaps nothing had better summed up his mood as they returned than the mater of the telegram from Beth that might or might not be waiting back at the house. It was no good pretending. He had unreservedly hoped, not of course that Sandy was seriously ill, but that something else delayed Beth's journey to Paris. They had even foreseen that, that she might have to put it off for a day or two more. That was all he wanted, just one day more. The wish had not been granted: there was no telegram.

As some compensation, he did have one last very useful *tête-à-tête* with Breasley. Most of his remaining questions of a biographical kind were answered—in the old man's fashion, but David sensed that he was not being seriously misled. At times there was even a convincing honesty. David had asked about the apparent paradox of the old man's pacifism in 1916 and his serving as medical orderly with the International Brigade during the Spanish Civil War.

"White feather, dear boy. Quite literal, you know. Had a collection of the damn' things. Didn't care, all a joke. Russell, he converted me. Hearing him talk, public lecture he gave. Best brain, best heart. Unique. Never met it again." They were up at the window table in his bedroom, with the two beds behind them. David had asked to be shown the Braque—and heard the story of the other Breasley once owned but had had to sell to pay for Coët and its conversion. The old man smiled at him. "Years go by. Keep thinking, don't you know. Whether it wasn't all just yellowbelly. Have to find out in the end. Get it out of your system. Know what I mean?"

"I can imagine."

The old man stared out of the window; the setting sun on the trees.

"Scared stiff. The whole time. Hated it. Had to draw. Only way I got through." He smiled. "Not death. You prayed for death. Still hear the pain. Relive it. Wanted to pin it. Kill it. Couldn't draw it well enough."

"Perhaps not for yourself. You did for the rest of us."

The old man shook his head.

"Salt on the sparrow's tail. Mug's game."

David had led him into less traumatic areas of his life; and even risked, toward the end, giving the old man some of his own medicine. If he pretended ignorance of the parallels David had drawn in his article, how was it that the girls so admired his memory for paintings? Breasley cast him a wry look and pulled his nose.

"Little bitches gave the game away, did they?"

"I twisted their arms when you were asleep."

The old man looked down and smoothed the edge of the table.

"Never forgot a good picture in my life, David." He looked out over the garden again. "The names, yes. But what's a name. Bit of fiddle in a corner. That's all." He cocked a cryptic thumb back at the Braque and winked. "The image survives; is all that matters."

"So I won't have to leave myself out of the bibliography?"

"Hanged man. Not the Verona thing. Foxe I think. Can't remember now."

He was talking about a detail in the background of the Pisanello *St. George and the Princess* and an echo in one of the most somber of the

Coëtminais series, untitled, but *Desolation* would have done; a wood of hanged figures and of living ones who seemed as if they wished they were hanged.

"Foxe escapes me."

"*Book of Martyrs.* Woodcuts. Old copy at home. Terrified me. Aged six, seven. Far worse than the real thing. Spain."

David risked a further step.

"Why are you so reluctant to reveal sources?"

The question visibly pleased the old man; as if David had fallen into a trap.

"My dear boy. Painted to paint. All my life. Not to give clever young buggers like you a chance to show off. Like shitting, yes? You ask why you do it. How you do it. You die of blocked arsehole. Don't care a fart in hell where my ideas come from. Never have. Let it happen. That's all. Couldn't even tell you how it starts. What half it means. Don't want to know." He nodded back at the Braque. "Old George had a phrase. *Trop de racine.* Yes? Too much root. Origin. Past. Not the flower. That no. Thing on the wall. *Faut couper la racine.* Cut the roof off. He used to say that."

"Painters shouldn't be intellectuals?"

The old man smiled.

"Bastard. Never knew a good one who wasn't. Old Pickbum. Appalling fellow. Flashing his gnashers at you. Sooner trust a man-eating shark."

"But he was reasonably articulate about what he was doing?"

The old man puffed in violent disagreement. "Eyewash. My dear boy. *Fumisterie.* All the way." He added, "Very fast worker. Overproduced all his life. Had to cod people."

"*Guernica?*"

"Good gravestone. Lets all the scum who didn't care a damn at the time show off their fine feelings."

There was a flash of bitterness; a tiny red light suddenly; something still raw. David knew they were back with abstraction and realism and the old man's own record of Spain. The grudge against Picasso was explained. But Breasley himself drew back from that brink.

"*Si jeunesse savait* ... know that?"

"Of course."

"That's all. Just paint. That's my advice. Leave the clever talk to the poor sods who can't."

David had smiled and looked down. Some time later he had stood to go, but the old man stopped him before he could move away.

"Glad you've hit it off with the gels, David. Wanted to say. Gives 'em a break."

"They're a nice pair of kids."

"Seem happy, do they?"

"I've had no complaints."

"Not much to offer now. Bit of pocket money." He sought confirmation on something. "Never much good at wages. That sort of thing."

"I'm quite sure they're not here for that."

"Something regular. Might be better, don't you think?"

"Why don't you ask the Mouse?"

The old man was staring out of the window. "Very sensitive gel. Money."

"Would you like me to sound them out?"

Breasley raised a hand. "No, no, my dear fellow. Just your advice. Man to man, don't you know." Then he suddenly looked up at David. "Know why I call her the Mouse?"

"I did rather wonder."

"Not the animal."

The old man hesitated, then reached and took a sheet of notepaper from a drawer beside him. Standing at his shoulder, David watched him address himself to the paper as if to some formal document; but all he did was to print in pencil the letter M and then, after a space, the letters U, S, E. In the space between the M and the U the wrinkled hand drew, in five or six quick strokes, an O-shaped vulva. Then Breasley glanced dryly back up at David; a wink, the tip of his tongue slipped out like a lizard's. Almost before David had grasped the double meaning the piece of paper was crumpled up.

"Mustn't tell her."

"Of course not."

"Dread losing her. Try to hide it."

"I think she understands that."

The old man nodded, then gave a little shrug, as if age and fate must win in the end; and there was no more to be said.

All of which David had meditated on, as he lay in his bath soon afterward: how the relationship worked because of its distances, its incomprehensions, the reticences behind its facade of frankness ... as a contemporary arrangement, a *ménage à trois* of beautiful young uninhibited people, it would very probably fail. There would be jealousies, preferences, rifts in the lute ... and its being so locked away, islanded, out of David's own real and daily world, Blackheath and the rush-hour traffic, parties, friends, exhibitions, the kids. Saturday shopping, parents ... London, getting and spending. How desperately one could long for ... for this, suitably translated. Beth and he must definitely attempt it; perhaps Wales, or the West Country, which couldn't be all St. Ives, a cloud of postures around two or three serious names.

The poor sods who can't. Yes.

What he would finally remember about the old man was his wildness, in the natural history sense. The surface wildness, in language and behavior, was ultimately misleading—like the aggressive display of some animals, its deeper motive was really peace and space, territory, not a gratuitous show of virility. The grotesque faces the old fellow displayed were simply to allow his real self to run free. He did not really live at the *manoir;* but in the forest outside. All his life he must have had this craving for a place to hide; a profound shyness, a timidity; and forced himself to behave in an exactly contrary fashion. It would have driven him out of England in the beginning; but once in France he would have used his Englishness—for it was remarkable, when one thought, how much of a native persona he had retained through his long exile—to hide from whatever in French culture threatened to encroach. The fundamental Englishness of the Coëtminais series was already argued in a paragraph of the draft introduction, but David made a mental resolution to expand and strengthen it. It began to seem almost the essential clue; the wild old outlaw, hiding behind the flamboyant screen of his outrageous behavior and his cosmopolitan influences, was perhaps as simply and inalienably native as Robin Hood.

The distance aspect of the relationship was in fact predominant during that dinner. Though he had had his whisky before, Henry drank two glasses of wine with it, and even then cut heavily with water. He seemed tired, withdrawn, in a state of delayed hangover. Every year of his age showed, and David felt that the two girls and himself were in collusion, almost, to emphasize the abyss. The Freak was in a talkative mood, telling David about the agonies of her teacher training course in her own brand of slang and elliptic English. The old man watched her as if slightly puzzled by this sudden vivacity . . . and out of his depth. Half the time he was not very sure what she was getting at: micro-teaching, systems art, psychotherapy, they came from another planet. David could guess the enigma, to one who still lived the titanic battlefield of early twentieth-century art, of all this reduction of passionate theory and revolutionary practice to a technique of mass education, an "activity" you fitted in between English and maths. *Les Demoiselles d'Avignon,* and a billion tins of poster paint.

They had coffee, and the old man was now very nearly silent. The Mouse urged him to bed.

"Nonsense. Like to hear you young things talk."

She said gently, "Stop pretending. You're very tired."

He grumbled on a bit, sought male support from David, and received none. In the end the Mouse took him upstairs. As soon as they had disappeared, the Freak moved into the old man's chair at the head of the table. She poured David more coffee. She was less exotically dressed that evening—a black Kate Greenaway dress sprigged with little pink and green flowers. Its cottage simplicity somehow suited her better; or better what David had begun to like in her.

She said, "We'll go upstairs when Di comes back. You ought to see her work."

"I'd like to."

"She's silly about it. Shy."

He stirred his coffee. "What happened to her boyfriend?"

"Tom?" She shrugged. "Oh, the usual. He couldn't take it, really. When she got accepted by the Royal College. He was the one who was supposed to get in."

"That happens."

"He was one of those boys who thinks he knows it all. Public school and all that. I couldn't stand him, personally. He was always so bloody sure of himself. Only Di could never see it."

"She took it badly?"

She nodded. "What I was saying. She's so innocent. In some ways." There was a little pause, then she stopped fiddling with her coffee spoon and surveyed him in the lamplight: her frankest eyes.

"Can I tell you a great secret, David?"

He smiled. "Of course."

"What I was trying to say this afternoon." She looked down the room to the stairs, then back to him, and lowered her voice. "He wants her to marry him."

"Oh God."

"It's so bloody daft, I . . ."

"You don't mean she's . . ."

She shook her head. "But you don't know her. So many ways she's much brighter than I am, but honestly she makes some daft decisions. I mean this whole scene." She grinned without humor. "Two smashing girls like us. We must be out of our tiny minds." She said, "We don't even joke about it anymore. Okay, with you this afternoon. But that's the first time in weeks."

"She's said no?"

"She says. But she's still here, isn't she? I mean, its like she's got a father fixation or something." She sought his eyes again. "She's such a smashing girl, David. Honestly, you've no idea. My Mum and Dad, they're Jehovah's Witnesses. Absolutely barmy. I've had such fucking awful problems at home. I mean, I haven't *got* a home. I couldn't have survived without Di. Even this last year. Being able to write to her." She went on before he could speak. "And she's so inconsistent." She waved around the room. "She even turns all this into a reason for not marrying him. Crazy. Screw you whole life. Just as long as you don't get anything out of it."

"She's not going to meet anyone of her own age here."

"What I mean." She sprawled on a elbow facing David across the table. They were still talking in low voices. "She won't even look at what there is. Frinstance last week we went into Rennes to do some shopping. A couple of

French boys picked us up. In a café. Students. You know, it was all a gas. Fun. They were all right. So they chat us up. Di says we're staying on our *vacances* with a friend of her family's." She grimaced. "Then they want to drive out one day and see us." The fingers combed up through her hair. "Fantastic. You wouldn't believe it. Di's suddenly like a bloody security officer or something. The way she gave those boys the chop. Then straight back home and off with her clothes because old Henry's been lonely and wants a feel." She said, "And I mean *that*. You know, what . . . it's not the physical thing. He can hardly do it anymore, it's just . . . you know, David, sex, honest to God, I've seen it all. Much sicker scenes than this. But it's not the same with Di. She's just had that one twit at Leeds. For serious. That's why I'm so bad for her. She thinks it's either like it is with Henry or the way I used to go on. She just doesn't know what it's about. What it can be about."

"Have you—"

But he was not to learn whether she had thought of leaving on her own. A door closed quietly upstairs. The Freak sat back in her chair, and David turned to see the subject of their conversation coming down the shadowed stairs. She waved toward them, the pool of light they sat in, then came down the room; slim and cool and composed, belying what had been said. She sat down again opposite David, with a little air of relief

"He's been good today."

"As you predicted."

She raised crossed fingers. "And what have we been talking about?"

"You."

David added, "Whether you'd let me see your work."

She look down. "There's so little to see."

"What there is."

"It's mostly drawing. I've done hardly any painting."

The two girls eyed each other a moment; a challenge and a reluctance, a ghost of some previous argument in private. But then the reluctant one smiled and stood.

David followed the girls upstairs, then down the corridor past his own room to a door at the east end of the house. It was another large room, there was a bed, but it had more the feel of a sitting-room; a student's room, if the art on the walls had not been original and distinguished, instead of homemade or in reproduction. The Freak went to a record player in one corner, began to sort through a pile of records. The girl beside him said, "Over here."

There was a long worktable, inks, watercolors, a tilted drawing board with a half-finished sketch pinned to it. The table was scrupulously neat, in contrast to the one in the old man's studio . . . very much the way David liked to have his own "bench" at home. The Mouse reached up a portfolio and put it on the table, but kept it closed in front of her for a moment.

"I'd gone completely nonrepresentational by the end of Leeds. I got into the RCA on that. So these are going backward really." She gave him a shy little smile. "What I began to feel I'd missed out."

Technically the drawing was impressive, if rather lacking in individuality. The coolness that was pleasant in her personality became a kind of coldness on paper, something too painstaking and *voulu*. There was rather surprisingly a complete absence of the quick freedom of the old man's line, its firmness and vigor—a comparison David did not have to make from memory, since the drawing that had been mentioned, his tossed-off little parody of the Freak in the Lautrec style, turned up in the portfolio. Its haste showed; and the instinctive mastery of living line. David was complimentary, of course; asked the standard questions, what she was trying to do, where she felt she was getting near it. The Freak now stood at his other side. He had expected pop music; but it was Chopin, turned low, mere background.

They came to a batch of drawings with additional watercolor washes, not representational, but color records that were something of the kind that David used himself. He liked them better, one or two tones, contrasts, the rather tentative workshop feel after the over-meticulous essays in pure draftsmanship. The Mouse went to a cupboard across the room and came back with four canvases.

"I have to keep them hidden from Henry. And I'm sorry if they look like bad David Williamses."

She looked for a place to hang them, then took a pencil drawing off the wall and handed it to David. Gwen John. He belatedly realized who the sitter was; Henry, he must have been about David's present age, Sitting bolt upright, in a wooden chair, a little stagy, self-important in spite of the informality of his clothes: a fierce young modernist of the late twenties. The Mouse tilted an angle lamp to light the place she had chosen. David put the ousted drawing down.

The canvases she showed bore no obvious similarity to his own work, beyond being delicately precise abstracts and on a smaller scale (like his own preferred working-size) than most such pictures in the manner. He very probably would not have noticed an influence if she hadn't mentioned it. But their quality, and this was a field where he was thoroughly at home—its problems, the viability of the solutions, was not something he had to pretend to see.

"Now I know why the College took you."

"One day they work. The next they don't."

"Normal. They work."

The Freak said, "Go on. Tell her they're bloody marvelous."

"I can't do that. I'm too envious."

"She's only asking five hundred each."

"Anne, stop being a fool."

David said, "Let's see that last one beside the sketch."

The sketch had been of a climbing rose against a wall; the painting was a trellis of pinks and grays and creams, a palette of dangers—which had been avoided. He would have been afraid of it himself, the inherent sentiment, the lack of accent. The ruling quarters of his own zodiac were more those of the colors of the clothes the Mouse wore: autumn and winter.

For twenty minutes or more they talked painting: his own work methods, media, a renewed interest he had in lithography, how he "grew" his ideas . . . all in a way he had done often enough when he taught, but had rather lost the habit of. Beth lived too near to him to need explanation, took all that for granted; and anyway, there had never been a similarity of stylistic purpose. He understood both critically and intuitively what this girl was trying to do. It did bear an analogy with his own development; in a more feminine, decorative kind of way—more concerned with textures and correspondences than form—she was abstracting from natural rather than artificial color ranges. She said Henry had influenced her in one way, by claiming that color could be drawn; she had learned a lot by forcing herself to prove that it couldn't.

They sat down, David in an armchair, the two girls opposite on a sofa. He discovered more about them, their home backgrounds, their friendship; Henry and the present were tacitly barred for a while. Again the Freak talked most, she was funny about her hair-raisingly bigoted parents, her variously rebellious brothers and a younger sister, the hell of a childhood and adolescence in the back streets of Acton. The Mouse was more reserved about her family. She was an only child, it seemed; her father owned and ran a small engineering works at Swindon. Her mother had "artistic" tastes, kept an antique shop as a kind of hobby in Hungerford. They had a smashing house there, the Freak put in. Georgian. Ever so posh. David had an impression of some wealth; of parents too intelligent to be stock provincial; and that she did not want to talk about them.

There came a little silence; and just as David was searching for some not too obvious way of getting them back to the present and future, the Freak was on her feet and standing over his chair.

"I'm going to bed, David. You mustn't. Di's a night bird."

She blew him a kiss, she was gone. She had done it too suddenly, too blatantly, and he was caught off balance. The girl he was left with would not look at him; she too knew it had been stage-managed.

He said, "Are you tired?"

"Not unless you are." There was an awkward moment. She murmured, "Henry gets nightmares. One of us always sleeps in his room."

He relaxed back in his chair.

"How on earth did he survive before you came?"

"His last lady friend left him two years ago. She was Swedish. She betrayed him in some way. Money. I don't know, he never talks about her. Mathilde says money."

"So he managed on his own for a bit?"

She took his point; and answered it with a faint smile.

"He didn't paint very much last year. He really does need help in the studio now."

"And I gather he's going to go on getting it?" It was more a statement than a question, and she looked down.

"Anne's been talking."

"A little. But if . . ."

"No, it's . . ."

She turned and put her bare feet up on the sofa, resting her back against one of its arms. She fiddled with a button on the black shirt. It was wild silk, faintly glossy; around each cuff, and the collar, a delicate edge of gold.

"How much did she say?"

"Just that she was worried."

She was silent a long moment; then spoke in a lower voice.

"About Henry wanting to marry me?"

"Yes."

"Did it shock you?"

He hesitated. "A bit."

"I haven't made up my mind." She shrugged. "I suppose it's just that when one's doing everything a wife would do . . ."

"Is the reverse true?"

"He needs me."

"I didn't quite mean that."

Again she was silent. He sensed that same struggle between wanting to talk and being afraid to that he had noticed after the blackberrying. But now she gave way.

"It's very difficult to explain, David. What's happened. Of course, I can't love him physically. And I know perfectly well that at least half his love for me is sheer selfishness. Having his life run for him. But he really doesn't swallow his own myth anymore. The gay old dog thing is strictly for strangers. Deep down he's just a rather lonely and frightened old man. I don't think he'd paint anymore if I left. It would kill him. Perhaps even literally."

"Why are the alternatives marriage or leaving him?"

"They're not. It's just that I feel I can't walk out on him now. So what's it matter. If it makes him happier."

Still she fiddled with the button, her head slightly bent; a faint air of a guilty child. The sophisticated little crown of hair, the bare ankles and feet. She sat with her knees cocked up.

"Anne also said you were worried about seeming to be after his money."

"Not what people might say. What it might do to me." She said, "It's not as if he doesn't know what the collection's worth. The Braque's going to the Maeght when he dies. But even without that. I mean it's ludicrously out of scale. As a reward. But he does know that."

"What might it do to you?"

She smiled wryly. "I want to be a painter. Not a loaded widow." She said softly, "Get thee behind me, Coët."

"The garret theory is out of date."

"No struggle at all?"

"I'm not quite sure which side I'm supposed to be arguing for."

She smiled again, without looking at him.

"I'm only twenty-three years old. It seems rather early to be sure you'll never want to live anywhere else. In any other way."

"But you're tempted?"

She was slow to answer.

"The whole ouside world. I don't even want to go into Rennes anymore. All those cars. People. Things happening. My parents, I've simply got to go home and see them. I keep putting it off. It's absurd. As if I'm under a spell. I even dreaded your coming. I really did love your show. Yet I made up my mind I wouldn't like you. Just because you come from out there and I thought you'd upset me and . . . you know."

She had left one of her own paintings on the wall behind the sofa. He knew it was not out of vanity. What last remaining doubts he had had about Diane's judgment were gone; the cool self-confidence of that first evening had been a pose, like the indifference of their first encounter. But the painting hung there as a kind of reminder of an identity between them; which grew. The silences no longer mattered.

"You parents know what's happening?"

"Not the whole . . . but they're not like Anne's. I could made them understand." She shrugged. "It's not that. Just the thought of leaving my little forest womb. Somehow here, everything remains possible. I'm just scared of making a decision. Either way." There was a tiny pattering sound, a moth banging against the lampshade behind the sofa. She glanced at it, then back at her lap. "And then I wonder whether there's any connection between becoming a decent painter and . . . being normal."

"You're not going to paint any better by forcing yourself to be abnormal."

"Doing what everyone expects."

"Surely what you ought to do is what you feel you need. And to hell with everyone."

"I don't know how to give up. That's my trouble. I always have to stick thing out to the bitter end."

"You gave up the College."

"It was totally against my nature. You've no idea. Trying to prove I wasn't what I am. And anyway, it was only out of the frying pan. I'm even worse now than I was before."

She had subsided a little, her knees still up. The one light in the room was on the floor behind her. David's eyes hardly moved now from the shadowed profile of her face. There was a deep nocturnal silence, both inside the house and out; as if they were alone in it, and in the world. He felt he had traveled much farther than he expected, into the haunted and unpredicted; and yet in some strange way it seemed always immanent. It had had to come, it had had causes, too small, too manifold to have been detected in the past or to be analyzed now.

"This . . . affair you had ended badly?"

"Yes."

"His fault?"

"Not really. I expected too much. He's jealous about my getting into the College.

"Yes, Anne told me."

There was another little silence.

He said, "I'm not being very helpful."

"Yes you are."

"Platitudes."

"No."

And more silence, as if they were quite literally in the forest; the way hidden birds sing, spasmodically, secretly shifting position between utterances.

She said, "Anne's got this marvelous ability to give herself. To keep hoping. One day someone nice will realize what she is. Behind all the nonsense."

"What would happen if she left you here on your own?"

"That's something I try not to think about."

"Why?"

Again she was slow to answer.

"I feel she's my last hold on . . . the real world?" She added, "I know I'm using her. Her affection. A kind of messiness in her. The eternal student." She smoothed a hand along the back of the sofa. "Sometimes I wonder if I'm not bent or something."

She had touched on what had also touched David's mind once or twice during that day. He guessed that dubbing herself the freak of the two hid a truth. The physical side of her life with Henry must be deeply against the grain of her "innocent" self. She was in that sense much more perverse than Anne. Yet the real repression must be of a normal sexuality, a femaleness that cried out for . . .

He said gently, "Not a hope. If I'm a judge."

"I'm not serious. We've even discussed it. We . . ." but she didn't finish.

"It seems to me that this remarkable honesty you have about yourself is a kind of danger. You know. There's something to be said for instinct."

"I don't have much faith in my instincts."

"Why not?"

"Being an only child. Having no comparisons to go by. You can get your own age group so wrong. I had it with Anne in the beginning. We lived in the same house, but for months I didn't like her. I thought she was just a little tramp. Then one day I went to her room to borrow something. And she was crying—her sister, some upset at home. We began to talk. She told me all about herself. And we never looked back." She said nothing for a moment. "The same thing happened with Tom, in reverse. I started feeling sorry for him. He was terribly insecure underneath. So one moment you're turning up your nose at a heart of gold, the next you're giving body and soul to someone who's not worth it." She said, "I did try. After Tom. At the college. With another first-year boy. He was nice, but . . . it was just bed. Feeling lonely."

"Perhaps you expect too much."

"Someone who can see what I am?"

"That's rather difficult. If you're hidden away."

She shook her head. "Perhaps I don't want it to happen. I don't know anymore."

There was another silence. She stared at her skirt. He watched her present metaphorical nakedness, and thought of the previous literal one; and knew that words were swiftly becoming unnecessary; were becoming, however frank or sympathetic, not what the situation asked. The moth battered minutely again at the lampshade. There were others loosely constellated on the glass outside the window over her worktable, pale fawn specks of delicate, foolish organism yearning for the impossible. Psyches. The cruelty of glass: as transparent as air, as divisive as steel. She spoke again.

"I've got so frightened by strangers. It's ridiculous, the other day Anne and I were picked up by two law students in Rennes—did she tell you?"

She looked across at him then; and he shook his head.

"I was panic-stricken that they'd find out about Coët. Want to come here. As if I was a virgin or something. A nun. It's the effort of getting to know people. All the crossed wires. Or the ones I seem to produce."

He could have smiled then: the statement denied itself. Perhaps she sensed it.

She murmured, "Present company excepted."

He said softly, "Not that rare a species."

She nodded, once, but said nothing. She seemed almost frozen now on the sofa, hypnotized by her hands, by the need not to look at him.

"I wanted to meet you. Last November. After the show. To come and talk about my work."

He leaned forward. "Why on earth ... it would have been so easy to fix." They had discovered that afternoon that David knew her tutor at the Royal College.

She gave a faint smile. "For the same reasons I wait till now to tell you?" She added, "And my one previous experience of inviting myself unwanted into a successful painter's life."

He had a sudden perception of the strange hazardousness of existence; of how little, a word from her, a raised 'phone, it would have taken for such a meeting to have been. Then what, he wondered; the same chemistry, in London? He didn't know; only that the now seemed more pregnant, more isolated, and somehow more inevitable. And he guessed, he began to know her so well, why the world had not been spoken: less a shyness than a kind of pride. There had been a photograph of him in the catalogue, a mention that he was married and had children. Perhaps that as well; already a flight from potential crossed wires. One way of not experiencing them was never to use the instrument.

"Do you wish you had?"

"It's too late for wishing."

Again neither of them spoke. Then she bent forward and touched her forehead against her knees. For a few moments he had both a fear and a wanting that she was about to cry. But with a sudden change of mood, or reaction to whatever she was thinking, she put her feet down off the couch and stood. He watched her walk to the worktable. She stared down at her portfolio a second, then looked up through the window at the night.

"I'm sorry. You didn't come here for all this."

"I wish desperately that I could help."

She began to tie up the portfolio. "You have. More than you know."

"It doesn't feel like it."

She said nothing for a moment or two.

"What do you think I should do?"

He hesitated, then smiled. "Find someone like me? Who isn't married? If that doesn't sound too impossibly vain."

She tied a final bow in the tags of black ribbon.

"And Henry?"

"Not even a Rembrandt has the right to ruin somene else's life."

"I'm not sure it isn't ruined already."

"That's self-pity. Not the real you."

"Cowardice."

"Also not the real you." He watched her staring out into the night again. "I know he dreads losing you. He told me. Before dinner. But he's lost

women all his life. I think he's more inured to it than you imagine." He
added, "And perhaps we could do something to make it easy. At least find
him help in the studio."

He felt a traitor, then; but in a good cause. She lifted the portfolio and
slippped it down beside the table, then shifted a wooden chair back to its center. But she remained with her hands on its back, turned away.

"It wouldn't be vain, David. But where do I find him?"

"You know the answer to that."

"I rather doubt if the College would take me back."

"I could very easily find out. When I return."

She moved and came behind the sofa, looking down across it at him.
"Can I get in touch? If I . . .?"

"Henry has my address. Any time. Very seriously."

She dropped her eyes. He knew he ought to stand, the tying-up of the
portfolio had been a hint that the evening was at an end, it was late, she
hadn't sat down again. Yet he was aware that she did not want him to go and
that he did not want to go himelf, that more than ever now, behind all the
honesty and the advice, tutor and student, a truth remained unsaid. A pretense, the undeclared knowledge of a shared imagination, hung in the air; in
her half-hidden figure against the light on the floor behind, in the silence, the
bed in the corner, the thousand ghosts of old rooms. One was stunned, perhaps; that knowledge could come so quickly . . . as if it was in the place, not
oneself. How impatient it was of barriers and obstacles, how it melted truth
and desire of all their conventional coats; one desired truth, one truthed desire, one read minds, jumped bridges, wanted so sharply, both physically and
psychologically. And the closeness of tomorrow, the end of this, was intolerable. One had to cling to it, even though one felt embarrassed, that some obscure loss of face was involved, the Dutch uncle being swiftly proved the
emperor with no clothes.

He murmured, "It's time I went."

She smile up at him much more normally, as if he had been supposing
things.

"I've taken to walking in the garden. Like Maud. Before I go to sleep."

"Is that an invitation?"

"I promise not to talk about myself anymore."

The secret tension broke. She went across the room to a painted tallboy
and took out a cardigan, then returned, pulling on the sleeves, freeing a
strand of hair from the back; smiling, almost brisk.

"Are your shoes all right? The dew's so heavy now."

"Not to worry."

They went silently downstairs and to the garden door. They couldn't go
out the front, Macmillan made such a racket. He watied while she slipped on
some wellingtons, then they left the house. There was a rising moon above

the long roof, slightly gibbous in the haze, faint stars, one bright planet. One lighted window, the lamp in the corridor outside Henry's room. They strolled over the grass and then through the courtyard past the studio. A gate on its far side led to another small orchard. There was a kind of central walk between the trees, kept mown; in the background, the black wall of the forest. The dew was heavy and pearled. But it was warm, very still, a last summer night. The ghostly apple trees, drained of color; a cheeping of crickets. David glanced secretly at the girl beside him; the way she watched the ground as she walked, was so silent now, strict to her promise. But he had not imagined. It was here, now, the unsaid. He knew it in every nerve and premonitory fiber. His move: he drew back into speech.

"I feel as if I've been here for a month."

"Part of the spell."

"You think?"

"All those legends. I don't laugh at them anymore."

They spoke almost in whispers; like thieves; the ears of the invisible dog. He wanted to reach out and take her hand.

The last effort to distance. "He will turn up. The knight errant."

"For two days. Then leave."

It was said. And they walked on, as if it had not been said, for a least another five seconds.

"Diana, I daren't answer that."

"I didn't expect you to."

He had his hands in his coat pockets, forced forward.

"If one only had two existences."

She murmured, "Glimpses." Then, "It's just Coët."

"Where everything is not possible." He added, "Alas."

"I imagined so much about you. When I knew you were coming. Everything except not wanting you to leave."

"It's the same for me."

"If only you hadn't come alone."

"Yes."

Once more he had that uncanny sense of melted time and normal process; of an impulsion that was indeed spell-like and legendary. One kept finding oneself ahead of where one was; where one should have been.

And he thought of Beth, probably in bed now in Blackheath, in another world, asleep; of his absolute certainty that there could not be another man beside her. His real fear was losing that certainty. Childish: if he was unfaithful, then she could be. No logic. They didn't deny themselves the sole enjoyment of any other pleasure: a good meal, buying clothes, a visit to an exhibition. They were not even against sexual liberation in other people, in some of their freinds; if they were against anything, it was having a general opinion on such matters, judging them morally. Fidelity was a mater of taste and theirs happened simply to conform to it; like certain habits over eating or shared views on curtain fabrics. What one happened to like to live on and with. So why make an exception of this? Why deny experience, his artistic soul's sake, why ignore the burden of the old man's entire life? Take what you can. And so little: a warmth, a clinging, a brief entry into another body. One small releasing act. And the terror of it, the enormity of destroying what one had so carefully built.

They stopped before another gate at the far end of the orchard. Beyond there was a dim ride through the forest.

She said, "It's my fault. I . . ."

"You?"

"Fairy tales. About sleeping princesses."

"They could live together. Afterward."

But he thought: would any decent prince have refused, just because they couldn't? When she waited, she said nothing—or everything. No strings now. If you want.

He had meant it to be very brief. But once he found her mouth and felt her body, her arms come around him, it had no hope of being brief. It very soon lost all hope of being anything but erotic. He was wanted physically, as well as emotionally; and he wanted desperately in both ways himself. They leaned back against the gate, her body was crushed against his. He felt the pressure of her hips, her tongue and all it offered in imitation, and did not resist. She was the one who brought it to an end, pulling her mouth abruptly away and turning her head against her neck. Their bodies stayed and clung together. He kissed the top of her head. They stood there like that, in silence, for perhaps a minute. Once or twice he patted her back gently; and stared into the night and the trees; saw himself standing there, someone else, in another life. In the end she pulled gently away and turned against the gate, her back to him, with bowed head. He put an arm around her shoulders and moved her a little toward him, then kissed her hair again.

"I'm sorry."

"I wanted you to."

"Not just that. Everything."

She said, "It's all a lie, isn't it? It does exist."

"Yes."

There was a silence.

"All the time we were talking I was thinking, if he wants to go to bed with me I'll say yes and it'll solve everything. I'll know. It was all going to be so simple."

"If only it could be."

"So many if only's." He contracted his arm, held her a little closer. "It's so ironic. You read about Tristan and Yseult. Lying in the forest with a sword between them. Those dotty old medieval people. All that nonsense about chastity. And then . . ."

She pulled away and stood by the gatepost, four or five feet from him. "Please don't cry."

"It's all right, David. Just let me be a second." She said, "And please don't say anything. I understand."

He searched for words, but found none; or none that explained him. Once again, he felt hurtled forward—beyond the sex, the fancying, to where—her word—one glimpsed . . . and against that there rose a confrontation he had once analyzed, the focus of that same Pisanello masterpiece, not the greatest but perhaps the most haunting and mysterious in all European art, that had come casually up with the old man earlier that evening: the extraordinary averted and lost eyes of the patron saint of chivalry, the implacably resentful stare of the sacrifical and to-be-saved princess of Trebizond. She had Beth's face now. He read meanings he had never seen before.

The slight figure of the girl cast as dragon turned, a small smile on her face. She held out a hand.

"Shall we pretend this never happened?"

He took the hand and they began to walk back toward the house.

He murmured, "I could say so much."

"I know."

She pressed his hand: but please don't. After a step or two their fingers interlaced and squeezed; and did not relax, as if they were being pulled apart, must not be severed; and also as if hands knew what fools these mortals, or at least mortal intentions and mortal words, were. He saw her naked again, all the angles and curves of her body on the grass; he felt her mouth, the surrender in it. The trap of marriage, when the physical has turned to affection, familiar postures, familiar games, a safe mutual art and science; one had forgotten the desperate ignorance, the wild desire to know. To give. To be given to.

He had to let go of her hand to open and close the gate from the orchard into the courtyard. The catch made a little metallic sound, and Macmillan began to bark from somewhere in front of the house. He took her hand again. They silently passed the studio, he saw through the north window the long black shadow of the incomplete *Kermesse* canvas sleeping on its stand. The garden, the neurotically suspicious dog still barking. They came to the house, still without having said a word, and went in. She let go of his hand, bent and took off her wellingtons. A faint light reached back to them from the lamp in the corridor upstairs. She straightened and he sought her eyes in the shadows.

He said, "It can't solve anything. But please let me take you to bed."

She stared at him a long moment, then looked down and shook her head.

"Why not?"

"Knights errant mustn't lose their armor."

"With all its phony shine?"

"I don't want it exorcised."

He had only made explicit what had seemed implicit ouside on the way back; that tense interlacing of the fingers, that silence. Bodies mean more than words; now, more than all tomorrows.

He said, "You know it's not just ..."

"That's also why."

Still he sought for loopholes; reasons.

"Because I hung back?"

She shook her head, then looked into his eyes. "I shan't ever forget you. These two days."

She took a sudden step and caught his arms to prevent them reaching up toward her. He felt the quick press of her mouth against his, then she was walking toward the stairs. She turned to climb them, hesitated a fraction as she saw he was following, went on up. Past the door to Henry's room, then along the corridor. She did not look around, but she must have heard him close behind. She stopped with her back to him, outside his bedroom door.

"Just let me hold you for a little."

"It would only make it worse."

"But if an hour ago you ..."

"That was with someone else. And I was someone else."

"Perhaps they were right."

She looked down the corridor at her own door.

"Where will you be this time tomorrow, David?"

"I still want to go to bed with you."

"Out of charity."

"Wanting you."

"Fuck and forget?"

He left a hurt silence. "Why the brutality?"

"Because we're not brutes."

"Then it wouldn't be like that."

"But worse. We wouldn't forget."

He moved behind her and put his hands on her shoulders.

"Look, the crossed wires are mainly words. I just want to undress you and ..."

For one fleeting moment he thought he had found the answer. Something in her was still undecided. The maddening closeness, the silent complicity of everything around them—a few steps, a frantic tearing-off of clothes in the darkness, a sinking, knowing, possessing, release.

Without turning she reached up and caught his right hand on her shoulder in the briefest convulsive grip. Then she was walking away. He whispered her name in a kind of incredulous despair. But she did not stop; and he felt frozen, fatally unable to move. He watched her go into her room, the door close; and he was left with all the agonized and agonizing deflation of a man who has come to a momentous decision, only to have it cursorily dismissed. He turned into his room and stood in its blackness in a rage of lost chance; made out his faint shape there in the old gilt-framed mirror. A ghost, a no-man. The horror was that he was still being plunged forward, still melt-ing, still realizing; as there are rare psychic phenomena read of, imagined, yet missed when they finally happen. To one part of him—already desperate to diminish, to devalue—it was merely a perverse refusal; and to another, an acute and overwhelming sense of loss, of being cleft, struck down, endlessly deprived . . . and deceived. He wanted with all his being—now it was too late; was seared unendurably by something that did not exist, racked by an emotion as extinct as the dodo. Even as he stood there he knew is was a far more than sexual experience, but a fragment of one that reversed all logic, process, that struck new suns, new evolutions, new universes out of nothingness. It was metaphysical: something far beyond the girl; an anguish, a being bereft of a freedom whose true nature he had only just seen.

For the first time in his life he knew more than the fact of being; but the passion to exist.

Meanwhile, in the here and now, he felt a violet desire to punish—him-self, the girl so close, Beth far away in the London night. Tht word she had used . . . he saw her sitting on the sofa, her bowed head by the gate, her al-most still-present face in the shadows downstairs . . . intolerable, intolerable, intolerable.

He went back out in the corridor and looked down toward Henry's room; then walked to the door at the other end. He did not knock. But nei-ther did the door open. He tried the handle again, stood a few seconds. Then he did tap. There was no reply.

He was awakened by his own and unlocked door opening. It was a quarter past eight. The Freak came across to his bed with a glass of orange juice and handed it to him as he sat up. For a moment he had forgotten; and then he remembered.

"Your early call. Monsewer."

"Thanks."

He took a mouthful of the orange juice. She was wearing a polo-neck jumper, a knee-length skirt, which gave her an unwonted practical look. She stared down at him a moment, then without warning turned and sat on the end of his bed. She read from a sheet of message-pad paper in her hand.

" 'Tell Henry I've gone shopping. Back after lunch.' "

She looked up at the wall by the door, studiously avoiding David's eyes; and studiously waiting for his explanation.

"She's gone out?"

"Well it looks like it, doesn't it?" He said nothing; she waited. "So what happened?"

He hesitated. "We had a sort of misunderstanding."

"Okay. So what about?"

"I'd rather she told you."

She was apparently not to be put off by a mere curt tone of voice. She took a breath.

"You talked?" He said nothing. "I'd just like to know why she's gone off like this."

"Obviously. She doesn't want to see me."

"Well *why*, for Christ's sake?" She threw him a sharp little stare of accusation. "All yesterday. I'm not blind." She looked away. "Di doesn't talk with strangers. Has to be something fantastic to break that block."

"I haven't not realized that."

"But you just talked." She gave him another stab of a look. "Honest to God, I think you're so mean. You know it's not the sex. Just she needs a nice bloke. Just one. To tell her she's okay, she's normal, she turns men on."

"I think she knows that."

"Then why's she gone out?"

"Because there's nothing more to say."

"And you couldn't forget your bloody principles for just one night."

He spoke to the glass in his hand. "You've got it all rather wrong."

She stared at him, then struck her forehad. "Oh Christ. No, She didn't . . .?"

He murmured, "Wouldn't."

She leaned forward, holding her mop of red hair.

"I give up."

"Well you mustn't. She needs you. More than ever at the moment."

After a second she leaned back and glanced at him with a wry grin, then touched his foot under the bedclothes.

"Sorry. I ought to have guessed."

She got off the bed and went to the window; opened the shutters then remained there staring down at something outside. She spoked without turning.

"Old Henry?"

"Just the way we are." He felt embarrassed, in all sense undressed; and at the same time knew a need to be more naked still.

"I didn't imagine it, then?"

He was leaning on an elbow, staring down at the bedclothes.

"I didn't think things like this could happen."

"It's this place. You think, fantastic. When you first come. Then you realize it's the original bad trip."

There was a silence. She said, "Christ, it's such a bloody mess, isn't it?" She looked up into the blue morning sky outside. "That sadistic old shit up there. You know, you sort of seemed to fit. Really need each other." She gave him a fierce little look back across the room. "You should have made it, David. Just once. Just to spite the old bastard. Just for me."

"We lack your guts, Anne. That's all really."

"Oh sure. My famous loose knickers."

He said gently, "Balls."

She returned beside the foot of the bed, watching him.

"Didn't like me when you came, did you?"

"That's just a fading memory now."

She examined the smile and his eyes for authenticity; then abruptly bit her lips and twitched up a side of her jumper. There was a flash of bare brown waist above the skirt.

"How about me instead? Time for a quickie?"

He grinned. "You're impossible."

She cocked a knee onto the end of the bed, crossed her arms as if to tear off her jumper, leaned toward him; only the eyes teased.

"I know all sorts of tricks."

He held out the empty glass.

"I'll try to imagine them. While I'm shaving."

She clasped her hands over her heart and threw her eyes up. Then she moved and took the glass. She stood over him a moment.

"I think old Di's crazy." She reached out a finger and dabbed his nose. "You're almost dishy. For a born square."

And there was a second Parthian shot. Her head poked back around the door.

"Oh, and I couldn't help noticing. Quite well hung, too."

Her kindness, frankness; God bless the poor in taste. But that little touch of warmth and affection faded so fast, almost before her footsteps died away. David lay back in his bed, staring at the ceiling, trying to understand what had happened, where he had gone wrong, whey she had condemned him to this. He felt drowned in disillusion, intolerably depressed and shaken. The unendurable day ahead. Her body, her face, her psyche, her calling: she was out there somewhere in the trees, waiting for him. It was impossible, but he had fallen in love; if not with her wholly, at least wholly with the idea of love. If she had stood in the door that moment, begged him not to leave, to take her away . . . he didn't know. Perhaps if they had gone to bed together, if he had just had her naked through the brief night, the sense of failure, of eternally missed chance, would have been less brutal.

But he knew even that was an illusion. A final separation then would have been impossible. Even if he had gone away to Paris, as he must now; perhaps from anywhere else he could have gone away for good, but here . . . they would have had to meet again. Somehow, somewhere.

He had escaped that. But it felt like a sentence, not a pardon.

By midday, when he had driven a third or so of the two hundred and fifty miles to Paris, he had still not recovered. All but the automaton who drove down the endless miles of *route nationale* remained at Coët. The old man had continued at his most affable over breakfast, David really must come again and bring his wife, must forgive him his faults, his age, his "maundering on" . . . he was even wished well in his own painting; but that did not compensate for the bitter knowledge that the token acceptance of the invitation was a farce. He was banned for life now, he could never bring Beth here. They shook hands as he stood by the car. He kissed Anne on both cheeks, and managed to whisper a last message.

"Tell her . . . what we said?" She nodded. "And kiss her for me."

The ghost of a dry grimace. "Hey, we're not *that* desperate." But her brown eyes belied the flipness; and it was the last time he had felt like smiling.

The journey had begun badly: not three hundred yards after he had closed the gate on the private road to Coët, something orange-brown, a mouse, but too big for a mouse, and oddly sinuous, almost like a snake, but too small for a snake, ran across the road just in front of his car. It seemed to disappear under the wheels. David slowed and glanced back; and saw a minute blemish on the dark tarmac of the deserted forest lane. Something, a faint curiousity, a masochism, a not wanting to leave, any excuse, made him stop and walk back. It was a weasel. One of his wheels must have run straight over it. It was dead, crushed. Only the head had escaped. A tiny malevolent eye still stared up, and a trickle of blood, like a red flower, had split from the gaping mouth. He stared down at it for a moment, then turned and went back to the car. The key of the day had been set.

All along the road to Rennes he looked for a figure by a parked white Renault. He did not completely lose hope until he got on the *autoroute* that bypassed the city to the south. Then he knew the agony of never seeing her again. It seemed almost immediately like a punishment. Her disappearance that morning proved it: he had the blame. His crime had been realizing too late; at the orchard gate, when she had broken away; and he had let her, fatal indecision. Even back in the house, something in him as she had known, had asked not to be taken at his word. He had failed both in the contemporary and the medieval sense; as someone who wanted sex, as someone who renounced it.

His mind slid away to imaginary scenarios. Beth's plane would crash. He had never married. He had, but Diana had been Beth. She married Henry, who promptly died. She appeared in London, she could not live without him, he left Beth. In all these fantasies they ended in Coët, in a total harmony of work and love and moonlit orchard.

Futile, they would have disgraced an adolescent; and they compounded his bleakness, for it was also a kind of shock, though the reality of those first few minutes after she had left him had already sunk into his unconsciousness, that this could happen to him, could disturb and upset him so deeply; and what it said of a past complacency. It defined so well what he lacked. His inadequacy was that he did not believe in sin. Henry knew sin was a challenge to life; not an unreason, but an act of courage and imagination. He sinned out of need and instinct; David did not, out of fear. What Anne had said: just to spite the old bastard. He was obsessed with means, not ends; with what people thought of him, not what he thought of himself. His terror of vanity, selfishness, the Id, which he had to conceal under qualities he called "honesty" and fairmindedness" . . . that was why he secretly so enjoyed reviewing, the activity pandered to that side of him. The ultimate vanity (and folly, in an artist) was not to seem vain. That explained the high value he put in his own painting on understatement, technical decency, fitting the demands of his own critical-verbal vocabulary—the absurd way he always reviewed his own work in his imagination as he painted it. It all added up to the same thing: a fear of challenge.

And that was precisely what had happened to him: a challenge, and well beyond the moral and sexual. It had been like a trap, he saw this now as well. One sailed past that preposterously obvious reef represented by the first evening with the old man, and one's self-blindness, priggishness, so-called urbanity, love of being liked, did the rest. The real rock of truth had lain well past the blue lagoon.

The farther he drove, the less inclined he felt to excuse himself. There was a kind of superficial relief at being able to face Beth more or less openly—but even that seemed a consolation prize awarded the wrong man. He had finally stayed faithful by benefit of a turned key. And even that, the being technically innocent, that it should still mean something to him, betrayed his real crime: to dodge, escape, avert.

Coët had been a mirror, and the existence he was returning to sat mercilessly reflected and dissected in its surface . . . and how shabby it now looked, how insipid and anodyne, how safe. Riskless, that was the essence of it: was why, for instance, he was driving much faster than usual. Between the towns the roads were comparatively empty, he was making ample time, the wretched plane didn't land till after seven. One killed all risk, one refused all challenge, and so one became an artificial man. The old man's secret, not letting anything stand between self and expression; which wasn't a question of outward artistic aims, mere styles and techniques and themes. But how you did it; how wholly, how bravely you faced up to the constant recasting of yourself.

Slowly and inexorably it came to David that his failure that previous night was merely the symbol, not the crux of the matter. He remembered the old man's crude and outlandish pun on the word Mouse; if one wanted signs as to the nature of the rejection. Bungling the adventure of the body was trivial, part of the sexual comedy. But he had never really had, or even attempted to give himself, the far greater existential chance. He had had doubts about his work before; but not about his own fundamental nature, or at any rate that there was not in it the potential wherewithal to lay the rhost that profoundly haunts every artist: his lastingness. He had a dreadful vision of being in a dead end, born into a period of art history future ages would dismiss as a desert; as Constable and Turner and the Norwich School had degenerated into the barren academicism of the midcentury and later. Art had always gone in waves. Who knew if the late twentieth century might not be one of its most cavernous troughs? He knew the old man's answer: it was. Or it was unless you fought bloody tooth and fucking nail aginst some of its most cherished values and supposed victories.

Perhaps abstraction, the very word, gave the game away. You did not want how you lived to be reflected in your painting; or because it was so compromised, so settled-for-the-safe, you could only try to camouflage its hollow reality under craftsmanship and good taste. Geometry. Safety hid nothingness.

What the old man still had was an umbilical cord to the past; a step back, he stood by Pisanello's side. In spirit, anyway. While David was encapsulated in book knowledge, art as social institution, science, subject, matter for grants and committee discussion. That was the real kernel of his wildness. David and his generation, and all those to come, could only look back, through bars, like caged animals, born in captivity, at the old green freedom. That described exactly the experience of those last two days: the laboratory monkey allowed a glimpse of his lost true self. One was misled by the excess in vogue, the officially blessed indiscipline, the surface liberties of contemporary art; which all sprang from a profound frustration, a buried but not yet quite extinquished awareness of nonfreedom. It ran through the whole recent history of art education in Britain. That notorious diploma show where the fine arts students had shown nothing but blank canvases—what truer comment on the stale hypocrisy of the teaching and the helpless bankruptcy of the taught? One could not live by one's art, therefore one taught, a travesty of its basic principles; pretending that genius, making it, is arrived at by overnight experiment, histrionics, instead of endless years of solitary obstinacy; that the production of the odd instant success, like a white rabbit out of a hat, excuses the vicious misleading of thousands of innocents; that the maw of the teaching cesspit, the endless compounding of the whole charade, does not underpin the entire system. When schools lie . . .

Perhaps it was happening in the other arts—in writing, music. David did not know. All he felt was a distess, a nausea at his own. Castration. The triumph of the eunuch. He saw, who well he saw behind the clumsiness of the old man's attack; the sneer at *Guernica*. Turning away from nature and reality had atrociously distorted the relationship between painter and audience; now one painted for intellects and theories. Not people; and worst of all, not for oneself. Of course it paid dividends, in economic and vogue terms, but what had really been set up by this jettisoning of the human body and its natural physical perceptions was a vicious spiral, a vortex, a drain to nothingness, to a painter and a critic agreed on only one thing: that only they exist and have value. A good gravestone; for all the scum who didn't care a damn.

One sheltered behind notions of staying "open" to contemporary currents; forgetting the enormously increased velocity of progess and acceptance, how quickly now the avant-garde became *art pompier;* the daring, platitudinous. It was not just his own brand of abstraction that was at fault, but the whole headlong postwar chain, abstract expressionism, neoprimitivism Op Art and pop art, conceptualism, photorealism . . . *il faut couper la racine,* all right. But such rootlessness, orbiting in frozen outer space, cannot have been meant. They were like lemmings, at the mercy of a suicidal drive, seeking *Lebensraum* in an arctic sea; in a bottomless night, blind to everything but their own illusion.

The ebony tower.

As if to echo his inner gloom, the sky clouded over as he aproached the Ile de France, and the dull, stubbled plains around Chartres. Summer had died, autumn was. His life was one year only; and end now to all green growth. Ridiculous, as told himself at once. And yet the acute depression remained.

He came at last to the outskirts of Paris. The business of finding where he needed distracted him a little from all this soul-searching. Soon after five he booked into a likely looking hotel near Orly. They were giving Paris a miss, the destination in the Ardèche was a friend's cottage, another long day's driving. But they might stop somewhere. He dreaded the tomorrow, either way.

He had a shower and forced himself to reread his draft introduction to *The Art of Henry Breasley;* while his impressions were still fresh, to see what needed changing, expansion, more emphasis. It was hopeless. Phrases and judgments that only a few days previously had pleased him . . . ashes, botch. The banality, the jargon, the pretense of authority. The reality of Coët rose again behind the tawdry words. He lay back on the hotel bed and closed his eyes. A little later he was on his feet and staring out of the window. For the first time in many years he had felt the sting of imminent tears. Absurd, absurd. He would die if he never saw her again. He searched for writing paper, but there wasn't any in the room, it wasn't that kind of hotel, an endless one-nighter. He took out his notepad; but could only sit and stare at it. Too much. Like messing on with a painting one knew was no good; that one could only walk away from, without looking back, to one's separate door in the night.

Underlying all this there stood the knowledge that he would not change; he would go on painting as before, he would forget this day, he would find reasons to interpret everything differently, as a transient losing his head, a self-indulgent folly. A scar would grow over it, then fall away, and the skin would be as if there had never been a wound. He was crippled by common sense, he had no ultimate belief in chance and its exploitation, the missed opportunity would become the finally sensible decision, the decent thing; the flame of deep fire that had singed him a dream, a moment's illusion; her reality just one more unpursued idea kept among old sketchbooks at the back of a studio cupboard.

But till then, he knew: he had refused (and even if he had never seen her again) a chance of a new existence, and the ultimate quality and enduringness of his work had rested on acceptance. He felt a delayed but bitter envy of the old man. In the end it all came down to what one was born with: one either had the temperament for excess and a ruthless egocentricity, for keeping thought and feeling in different compartments, or one didn't; and David didn't. The abominable and vindictive injustice was that art is fundamentally amoral. However hard one tried, one was hopelessly handicapped: all to the pigs, none to the deserving. Coët had remorselessly demonstrated what he was born, still was, and always would be: a decent man and eternal also-ran.

That last was the label that seemed to have been lurking for hours when it finally came to him. He was left staring at the petered rise, which he saw almost literally above the dreary sea of roofs, wet now in a drizzle, outside the hotel; the collapsed parallel of what he was beside the soaring line of all that he might have been.

He got to Orly to find the flight was delayed for half an hour. There was fog at Heathrow. David hated airports at the best of times, the impersonality, herding, sense of anonymous passage; the insecurity. He stood by the window of the visitors' lounge, staring out into the flat distances. Dusk. Coët was in another universe; one and an eternal day's drive away. He tried to imagine what they were doing. Diana laying the table. Anne having her French lesson. The silence, the forest, the old man's voice. Macmillan barking. He suffered the most intense pang of the most terrible of all human deprivations; which is not of possession, but of knowledge. What she said; what she felt; what she thought. It pierced deeper than all questionings about art, or his art, his personal destiny. For a few terrible moments he saw himself, and all mankind, quite clear. Something in him, a last hope of redemption, of free will, burnt every boat; turned; ran for salvation. But the boats proof to all flame, the ultimate old masters, kept the tall shadow of him where he was; static and onward, returning home, a young Englishman staring at a distant row of frozen runway lights.

The flight arrival was announced and he went down to where he could watch for Beth. He had brought her holiday luggage in the car, and she came out with the first passengers. A wave. He raised his hand: a new coat, surprise for him, a little flounce and jiggle to show it off. Gay Paree. Free woman. Look, no children.

She comes with the relentless face of the present tense; with a dry delight, small miracle that he is actually here. He composes his face into an equal certainty.

She stops a few feet short of him.

"Hi."

She bites her lips.

"I thought for one ghastly moment."

She pauses.

"You were my husband."

Rehearsed. He smiles.

He kisses her mouth.

They walk away together, talking about their children.

He has a sense of retarded waking, as if in a postoperational state of consciousness some hours returned but not till now fully credited; a numbed sense of something beginning to slip inexorably away. A shadow of a face, hair streaked with gold, a closing door. *I wanted you to.* One knows one dreamed, yet cannot remember. The drowning cry, jackbooted day.

She says, "And you, darling?"

He surrenders to what is left: to abstraction.

"I survived."

BRIAN MOORE

Catholics

Part One

The fog lifted. The island was there. The visitor walked to the end of the disused pier and saw it across three miles of ocean, riding the sea like an overturned fishing boat. Morning sunlight moved along a keel of mountain, above valleys black as tarred boatsides.

He thought of Rome. Surprisingly, the Order itself had little descriptive information. In the Lungotevere Vaticano he had been handed an out-of-print book: *Weir's Guide to Religious Monuments.*

> MUCK ABBEY, Kerry, Ireland. On a small island off the rocky panoramic coastline of the Atlantic ocean known as "The ring of Kerry." The Monastery (Albanesian Order), founded 1216, rebuilt 1400–70, has a dependency, or cell, on the mainland, the priory of Holy Cross, at Mount Coom near the village of Cahirciveen. This priory, sacked by Cromwellian troops, was, in Penal times, a site for clandestine mass, conducted in the open air on a "Mass rock" altar. The Abbey itself (on Muck Island) escaped Cromwellian despoliation and sits on the western slope of the island overlooking a splendour of sea. From the abbey tower the visitor looks down on grey waves which curl on barren rock. The monks fish and gather kelp.

He had telephoned again before breakfast. The pretty girl at the desk in his hotel cranked up an incredibly old-fashioned device to call Exchange. "We're wanting Muck Island. No, Sheilagh, it's all right, it's for that priest who spoke to the island last night."

"There now, Father." He took the receiver. A bell rang and rang.

"Muck Island One," said a crackly voice, out in the Atlantic.

The visitor gave his name. He said he had been asked to call and check on the weather.

"What was your name again, now?"

"Kinsella. *Father* James Kinsella." He had learned his lesson.

"Ah, Father Kinsella. We'll send a boat for you, to be sure. Go down to the pier now, and Padraig will be along shortly."

Gulls, searching the remains of fish, skimmed overhead, dipped to the brackish waters beneath. Behind him, at the end of the road which led to the pier, were three roofless concrete boat sheds, floored with weeds, smelling of urine and sheep droppings. A very old car, which he had thought abandoned, sat in one of the sheds. Yesterday, when he first drove down here searching the fog for a sight of the island, he had looked in at the car. A purple silk stole lay on the front seat. At the hotel, after dinner, he asked who had built this pier. No, the monks had not built it, the Irish government built it, years ago, before the fishing became polluted. At that time, there were some twenty families living on the island. "They've nearly all come out since. Scattered now, to the four ends of the world."

"Polluted. Does that mean the monks don't fish any more?"

"Ah, no, the fishing is grand again. The water was cleaned up, a while back. The trouble is, it was done too late for the people of Muck. There do be only four families left on the island. And the monks."

The old car he had seen in the boat shed, was it the monastery car?

"It is, indeed. The monks do use it to drive to Cahirciveen of a Sunday. It's twenty miles, Father."

"But, what if the sea is rough, or if there's a fog, and a boat can't come over from the island?"

"Then no Mass is said at Cahirciveen."

No Mass? Yesterday's sights filled his mind; the streets of this Kerry village, grey nineteenth-century facades, market square, grey Gothic church, streets built before, and impassable to, today's traffic. Now existing in permanent confusion, cars, buses, trucks, campers, vans, moving in an endless clogged procession in and out of the narrow streets, while on the outskirts more vehicles were bogged in the muddy confusion of improvised car parks and tent villages. And everywhere in Cahirciveen, jammed into the shops and pubs, herded into the main square like beasts on a fair day, the pilgrims. No one knew how many there were on any given weekend, but for months there had not been a room or a bed to rent for fifty miles around. They were Irish, of course, but there seemed an almost equal number from England and Scotland. Others came by car ferry and charter plane from the continent; an emphasis of French, but also many Germans and even some pilgrims from Rome itself. The Americans had flown in two charter groups, many of them old souls who had never crossed the Atlantic before. They came, it seemed, simply to hear at least one Mass, say the rosary, and leave. The uncomfortable local accommodations did not encourage a long stay. It was a phenomenon, even in the history of pilgrimage. There were no miracles, there was no hysteria, there was not even a special fervor. The mood was nostalgic. The pilgrims rose early on Sunday, went in buses and cars to the foot of Mount Coom, five miles from the village. There, they ascended the mountain, on foot, to kneel on muddied grassy slopes, or on shelves of rock, often in the unyielding Irish rain. Most could see the Mass rock and the priest only from a distance, but all heard the Latin, thundering from loudspeakers rigged up by the townsfolk. Latin. The communion bell. Monks as altarboys saying the Latin responses. Incense. The old way.

"No Mass?" he said to the hotelkeeper. "But when they've come all this way, what do they do if there's no Mass?"

"Ah, now, Father, that's a grand thing to see. The pilgrims just stay there, kneeling and saying the rosary. They stay all day, waiting and praying."

"But don't some of them try to go out to the island itself?"

The hotelkeeper laughed, showing gap teeth. "No fear! No boat can land on Muck that doesn't know the trick of it. And the island boats will land nobody without the Abbot's permission. Besides," the hotelkeeper said, serious again, "these pilgrims do be good people. When the Abbot put up a sign in the church here in Cahirciveen saying 'Parishioners Only For Confession,' most of the pilgrims stopped bothering the monks. Mind you, the lines are still long. After Mass, on a Sunday, there do be three monks, hard at it in the church until it's time for them to take the boat back."

"But why do the confessions take so long?"

"We still have private confessions. One person at a time in the box."

Private confessions. *This* was not known in Rome. "What about public confessions?"

"Public confessions, Father?"

"Where the whole congregation stands before Mass and says an act of contrition?"

"Ah, that never took here."

Anger, sudden and cold, made Kinsella say: "It took everywhere else!" Ashamed, he saw the hotelkeeper bob his head, obedient, rebuked but unconvinced.

Yesterday when he first arrived by car from Shannon, Kinsella had carried a paramilitary dispatch case, a musette bag, and was wearing grey-green denim fatigues. At the desk of Hern's Hotel, the girl was curt. The hotel was full, there was a two-month waiting list, no reservations had been made for days. "But you took my reservation," he said. "You confirmed it, and the confirmation was telexed from Dublin to Amsterdam Ecumenical Center. This *is* Hern's Hotel, isn't it?"

"What was your name again, sir?"

"James Kinsella. Catholic priest," he said, in the Ecumenical manner.

"Oh, Father Kinsella. Oh, excuse me, Father. We have a room for you, certainly."

Father. In the crowded hotel lobby, every available seat was occupied. Standees circled disconsolately around racks of seaside postcards and shelves of paperback books. *Father.* Sun-reddened faces turned to stare, supercilious of his American accent, his ecumenical clothes. Most of these pilgrims were older than he, old enough to remember the Latin Mass. But there were young ones too, former Catholic Pentecostals, now eager for experience as the *penitentes* of the day. Their scorn towards him, his own scorn in reverse, met him as he went towards the stairs and the privileged bedroom. His friend Visher, a behaviorist, had made a study of current Catholic attitudes towards their clergy. "People are sheep," Visher said. "They haven't changed. They want those old parish priests and those old family doctors. Sheep need authoritarian sheepdogs nipping at their heels from birth to funeral. People don't want truth or social justice, they don't want this ecumenical tolerance. They want certainties. The old parish priest promised that. You can't, Jim."

Waves lapped the slimed boat steps. A new sound entered Kinsella's ear, the pulse of an engine. He looked at the sea but saw no boat. Sound, preceding vision, carrying clear over the whitecapped waves. Pulsing. Coming, coming; the painful confrontation. He and the Abbott of Muck.

"This will not be your first visit to Ireland," Father General said, looking up from the file. It was a statement, not a question, but he felt he should answer it.

"No sir. In my last year at Harvard, I went over there to attend a summer school. The Yeats school, in Sligo. My ancestors were Irish. They came from County Mayo, I believe. It's in the West, where this abbey is."

"William Butler Yeats." The General smiled his faint, Prussian smile. " 'What rough beast, its hour come round at last.' Appropriate. I want you to bury this beast. And I think the way to do that is for me to give you plenipotentiary status. Emissaries who must report back to headquarters, especially young ones, would seem to these old mastodons to be mere novices. I will make clear to this Abbot that you are me. What you decide will be the Order's final edict."

"What about the Father Provincial in Dublin, sir?"

The General sighed. "It seems that he and the Abbot of Muck have a disagreement going back as far as the Pauline papacy. As you know, since Vatican IV, bishops are no longer bound by the orders of provincials. These Irish Abbots are mitred and of episcopal rank. Each is a prelatus nullius, belonging to no one. This one has chosen to ignore the provincial's recommendations. However, he cannot ignore mine." Father General picked up a xerox sheet, a facsimile of an old chapter house record book, microfilmed, its original now destroyed. "The recalcitrant Abbot of Muck," the General said. "Let's see. He is one Tomás O'Malley, now in his sixty-ninth year, the son of a greengrocer. What is a greengrocer, I wonder?"

"A seller of vegetables, sir."

"Ah. The Abbot is the product of an Irish seminary, a place called Kilcoole. Prizewinner, Latin, oh, lala! Doctorate in—can't read this script, must be uncial—doesn't matter. Four years at Buckmore Abbey in Kent. Then, Ireland, Dublin, hmm, hmm, and appointed Abbot of Muck. Cast down on some remote little island and abandoned at a relatively early age, it would seem the Order had no great hopes of him. Subsequent life of poverty, thirty monks, fishermen all, income from kelp and dulse, whatever that is, and manure sales—well, that's quite enough of that. You can look this over at your leisure." The General picked up an Order Fact Form. "Now, this gives the age of the abbey, details of grants, etcetera. I think I see why the media people are interested, sick as we all are nowadays of a past we never knew. The monastery was founded in 1216." The General lolled in his Eames chair and looked out of the tall windows of his office. Below was the new pedestrian mall of the Lungotevere Vaticano and, beyond it, the dull, muddy flow of the Tiber. The General's eye moved left to fix on the roofs of the Vatican, and the dome of St. Peter's, immense, even at a distance. "The year twelve hundred and sixteen. Think of it. The fourth Lateran council had just closed. Innocent the Third was in the chair of Peter. And that great monstrosity down the road there, was three hundred years away from being built."

He looked again at the Fact Form. "In the beginning the abbey was not ours. It was founded by some local king, at the behest of Patrick, an Irish bishop saint. The Albanesians petitioned to take over in 1406. Within a couple of hundred years they owned half the lands of Kerry, which is why they have this priory on the mainland. The Abbot of Muck has always had the right to appoint the prior of the cell of Holy Cross at Cahirciveen."

"I believe there is no prior there now, sir."

"That's right, yes." The General consulted the Fact Form. "There are nearby parishes, of course, but the monks still cross to the mainland to say Mass and perform sacerdotal duties. And the changes that have taken place elsewhere in our time have simply been bypassed at Cahirciveen. Our Irish Provincial has made 'suggestions' on four differing occasions, but this Abbot remains blind and dumb. I wonder how long it would have gone on, if it had not been for the tourists? Anyway, it was a B.B.C. crew which did the damage. Latin Mass. Imagine that," the General said, and smiled. "I'd rather like to see one again, wouldn't you?"

"I don't really remember it, sir."

"Backs to the congregation, vestments, *introibo ad altare dei*. And the bell! The Sanctus! Oh, lala, how one forgets. And now it's packing them in. Listen to this. Ferry tours from Liverpool and Fishguard, charter flights from Leeds, Boston, New York—pilgrimage from France—even *bella Italia."* The General's amusement turned to a fit of sneezing. He used a nasal inhaler, then stared again at the brownish waters of the Tiber. "It is cliché to say it was to be expected. Even Vatican IV can't bury two thousand years in a few decades. But, I'd have thought Spain. Or, perhaps, some former Portuguese possession." The General sighed. "We are so infallibly fallible, aren't we? Wasn't it Chesterton who said something about a thing being too big to be seen? Ireland. Of course! Well, here you are. Take the file. Let my secretary have your itinerary. I'd suggest you hop a supersonic tonight and go straight to Amsterdam. It's a formality, of course, but in an affair of this kind everything should be strictly kosher." He smiled. "I'll alert the council that you are my plenipotentiary. After Amsterdam, get straight over to Ireland. Remember, I want this settled by the end of the month."

"Yes, sir."

"Get that old fool down off that mountain, James. And if he gives you any trouble—bite him!"

A fishing boat was instantly in sight, bashing through the tops of the white-caps, as though in the moment Kinsella had looked away, some Brobdingnagian hand had painted it into the seascape. A diesel-engined ten-tonner, it was built to scramble up and over these grey walls for waves. The wind force increased, sending a great slap of water over the edge of the pier. A black storm cloud filled the edge of the horizon. As the fishing boat approached across the strait, Kinsella picked up his dispatch case which contained the General's letter and an Order Plenipotentiary, signed in Amsterdam by the four current members of the World Ecumen Council. He walked to the stone steps as the boat cut its engines and drifted outside the bar. A man in a tweed hat appeared and moved about in the bow. Another stood in the wheelhouse, a stout young fellow in a white turtleneck sweater. Not monks, as he had expected, but islanders, the few fisher families still living on the Abbot's domain. The man in the tweed hat untied a black curragh, which floated light in a mussel shell at the stern of the ten-tonner. Pulling it close, he jumped in, raised long oars and rowed strongly towards the pier, the curragh swinging up like an amusement park gondola to hang on the whitetipped peaks, then fall, dizzyingly, into the trough of waves. The mother boat heeled. With a rattle, an anchor spilled like entrails from its bow, falling deep into the sea. The stout youth came out of the wheelhouse and stood at the side, staring across the water at Kinsella. With his curling red hair, freckled skin, snub nose and white fisherman's sweater he looked like Dylan Thomas.

The curragh, stroked easily now that it had passed into the shelter of the pier, came towards the steps where Kinsella waited. The rower had his back to the steps. Skilful, he shipped the oars as he glided alongside, his hand, with the blind touch of practice, finding the solitary iron bollard at the foot of the steps.

As the tweed-hatted rower turned to look back at the pier, a smile rose on Kinsella's face, an American smile, the currency of greeting. But the rower's eyes moved past him as though he were some idle seabird come to rest on the pier. Eyes swept the pier, the sheds, the road beyond, then, reluctantly, came back to him. "Morning," the boatman said.

"Hello there." Kinsella, smiling, moved confidently down the last slimed steps towards the curragh. But the boatman shook his head, warning him not to board. The boatman was young, vulpine, with a wild cub's grace. His grey eyes stared, as the eyes of an animal stare from a zoo cage.

"I'm James Kinsella, Catholic priest," Kinsella said, from Ecumenical habit.

The boatman's tongue appeared, round as a teat between his teeth. Its owner sucked on it, staring, silent.

"*Father* Kinsella," Kinsella corrected himself.

"Ah, come off it," the boatman said, in a soft island brogue.

"I'm sorry?"

"I come for a priest. I can't take nobody else. Sorry, now."

"But I'm the man you came for. I *am* a priest."

The boatman, sucking his tongue again, looked past Kinsella, again searching the pier, the sheds, the road beyond. Then turned to look out at the fishing boat anchored at the bar. On deck, Dylan Thomas raised his head in query.

"Not here yit," the boatman called.

The boy on deck turned and looked back at the distant mass of the island. The fat black cloud was now immense, moving like a dark lens across the sky. The boatman also stared up at the sky.

"Storm coming up?" Kinsella asked.

" 'Tis."

"Well, let's go, then. Do you want to see my papers, or something?"

"Come off it," the boatman said, again. He turned away as though Kinsella had already disappeared. Sat in the long, light curragh, gripping the bollard, steadying the craft which bobbed, on the lapping pier waves. Sucked his round tongue for a moment, then yelled across the water. "There's no-o car--aaaa-ar!"

On deck the white-sweatered boy pointed to the sky. "Let's go--o b--aack, Padraig," he called, syllables of sound separated in their transit across the waves.

The boatman abruptly let go of the bollard and took up his oars. Kinsella, irritated, reached down and caught hold of the curragh's stern.

"Let go of that."

"I tell you, I am Father Kinsella. The Abbot is expecting me."

Padraig, the boatman, let go of one oar, seized up a steel rowlock from beneath it and, swift as a biting dog, struck the knuckles which held the curragh's stern. With a gasp of pain, Kinsella drew his hand back. The rowlock snapped into its hole, the oar in it, and, with two swift strokes, the boatman swung the curragh out of reach.

"You don't look like a priest, I just can't imagine you as one." His mother said that, long ago, when in his second year at college he decided to study with Hartmann. Agnostic herself, his mother had continued her son's religious education after her Catholic husband died. She was one for keeping promises. Futures were another matter, as her son found when he told her he intended to become a Catholic priest. Useless to instance that his new hero, Gustav Hartmann, had taken Holy Orders as an Albanesian monk, much as Malraux had become a Minister of State in the Fifth Republic, not for the obvious condition, but as a means towards social action. Which, in Hartmann's case, had made him a twentieth-century Bolívar to this generation of South American revolutionary priests and nuns. The Church, Hartmann taught, despite its history and its dependence on myth and miracle, exists today as the quintessential structure through which social revolution can be brought to certain areas of the globe. The Kinsella's mother, a Liberal, born in the nineteen thirties, did not believe in the combination of Holy Orders and revolutionary theory. She, like that fisherman rowing away from him now, could not see things as they really were.

The curragh tied up beside the fishing boat. The fishing boat's engine came to life, the anchor growled up from the sea. As the fishing boat, turning, churning, headed back towards open waters, Kinsella found himself running, up the pier towards his rented car. Jumped in, went breakneck towards Cahirciveen and a telephone. He was a priest and they had not known he was a priest because the priests they knew wore black suits, or the clothes of old women, long brown habits, sandals, thick belts knotted about with big rosary beads, and he must telephone and order them to turn that boat around and send it back for him at once.

Four miles from the pier, driving through the flat trench landscape of a turf bog, he came, unexpectedly, to a crossroads. A whitewashed cottage stood on one corner, and what seemed to be a larger cottage, also whitewashed, but with a big barn behind it, faced on the opposite corner. On the doorway of the larger cottage was a sign.

P. MCGINN: LICENSED TO SELL WINES & SPIRITS

And a smaller sign in Gaelic. TELEFON.

Hens rose in fright as he swerved into the cobbled yard. A rooster ran past, wattles loose, one skelly eye fixed on the car in wild alarm. Inside the pub it was dark as evening. Two Irish laborers, wearing greasy old black suits, once their Sunday best, now their daily dungarees, white shirts open at the neck, and knee-length rubber Wellington boots. Faces the color of strawberry jam looked up from large glasses of black porter. Behind the small bar, a man, broad as a rainbarrel, wearing a white turtleneck sweater, wiped glasses with a linen cloth. "G'day," said he, to Kinsella. " 'Twill rain, I would say."

"I want to telephone Muck Island."

"You won't get them."

"I'm a priest. They're expecting me."

Strawberry faces of the laborers bobbed uniformly in greeting, as though Kinsella had just entered the pub. "G'day, Father," in unison, they sang. From beneath the bar the proprietor took up a receiver on a hand-crank stand, cranked it up, spoke in a language which Kinsella assumed to be Gaelic. Then: "There, Father. There you are, so."

The crackly island voice. "What? What...? Padraig didn't get you? Ah, sure that's a disaster." And, over the wire, wheezing laughter. "Didn't know you were a priest? Oh, God love us! I'm sorry, Father, but do you see that weather out there, I'm afraid we'll not get you in today.... What? What?"

He had to shout. Three faces watched him in that small, hop-stinking room. "Send the boat back! I have to get there today. It's urgent."

"Well now, Father, the minute the we-----eeee---ather clears, do you heeeee-- do you heeeee--aa-arr?"

Static crackles. Silence. Then a girl's voice. "You were cut off, Father. It's a bad connection at the best of times. I could try them later, if you like?"

"I'll call you," he said, and put the phone down.

Three faces turned to him. Unlike people from more civilised places they did not pretend that they had not overheard. Strawberry cheeks bunched in grins. "So, Padraig refused you," the proprietor said. "Isn't that a good one!"

They laughed. It was.

"Those boys on the island, you see," the proprietor explained. "They never come out, they have no notion that the priests out here do be just like the rest of us, nowadays. Begging your pardon, Father. Are you an American?"

"Yes."

"A grand country, so. You'll get out tomorrow. I'd say 'twill clear."

" 'Twill clear," one of the laborers promised.

"How much do I owe you for the phone?"

"Ah, not at all."

"Well, thank you. Thank you very much."

"G'day. Father."

"G'day. Father."

"Thank you again," Kinsella said.

Outside, in the cobbled yard, hens tacked cautiously around his feet. He looked at the crossroads and there, blurring its outlines, was a rainbow's end. The rainbow arched up and away from this place to disappear behind a brow of mountain. Raindrops spat warnings. Hens stalked to cover. Rain came, wetting to a thick flow. As Kinsella retreated into the shelter of the pub doorway, thunder banged above him. Thunderclouds, massing over the far mountain, advanced to take possession of the sky.

He felt cold. He thought of Hartmann in the rain forests of Brazil. He looked again for the rainbow, but it had vanished, shimmering, in that sudden rain. It had appeared, then disappeared, in this lonely place, a place which now, in its noon darkness, made him think of a Beckett landscape, that place in which Vladimir and Estragon might have waited for Godot. The rainbow had seemed to end, down there, in the center of the white cross formed by two concrete ribbons of road. In such phenomena people once read signs of God's hand. He turned and went back into the pub.

Part Two

The helicopter drifted over the crossroads, the pub, the yard, then, tilting slightly forward, moved downwind to land in a field on the edge of the bog. The rotor blades still turned at take-off speed as Kinsella hurried towards the machine in the afternoon's continuing drizzle, ducking under the great propellers as the pilot slid the door aside and held out a hand to take him up. He sat, buckling his seat belt. The door shut. The green-and-white helicopter, the wind from its rotor blades flattening the whin bushes of the field, rose like some huge dragonfly, its legs, which had bent on hinges under it, stiffening and retracting as it rose in flight. It poised, then, tilting forward, moved up and out. Away.

Below, three faces mooned up, the laborers and the publican. Like children they waved as the helicopter lurched over them. And were gone. Kinsella looked at the pilot, a young man of his own age, dark haired and smiling, staring ahead into the fog and rain. The pilot wore a uniform of black coveralls, but with showy encrustation of gold braid at wrists and shoulders, and, on the peak of his cap, a gold crest. Caparisoned like some admiral of former days, he seemed a personage of importance. Kinsella reflected on the times; cardinals went shabby in mufti; hirelings of all kinds had increased their false panoply of rank.

"Have you ever been on the island?" he shouted at the pilot.

"No, but I've flown over it."

Thunder. Lightning sheeted the sky. Within three minutes, they were over the ocean, a rough sea pitted by rainsqualls, but ahead, towards the west, a shaft of sunlight like a stage flood. The pilot pointed to it, grinning and winking to show this was good news. Kinsella nodded. He had waited three hours for the helicopter, fretting, worrying that it would not find the lonely crossroads. In action once more, airborne, travelling at speed, his confidence returned. He would be diplomatic, but firm. With luck, he could have agreement before nightfall.

Now they were over the island, chopping along above a deserted strand, fine grey sand, green grassy dunes, and, at the edge of the sweep of beach, a harbor with a stone pier and two fishing boats tied up at it. One was the ten-tonner which had refused him that morning. Beyond the pier was a ruined medieval castle, built strategically on a green headland, commanding the sea approach. He pointed at it and the pilot, nodding, flew up and hovered the helicopter over the roofless castle maw.

"The fort of Granuaile," the pilot shouted.
"What?"
"Very old. Grace O'Malley built it and lived in it."
"Who?"
"Grace O'Malley. The Sea Queen. Granuaile."

Circling the headland, the helicopter moved down the spine of the island, flying over the village adjoining the fort. The village was a street of a dozen whitewashed cottages, with hen-littered backyards in which were rough stone sheds housing animals and tools. As Kinsella peered down, two small children ran out, stared, then waved. Four of the dozen houses in the street were abandoned, windows broken, holes in the roofs. The helicopter bucked into stormy wind, lurched up and away over tiny fields divided into jagged squares by walls of roughly piled boulders. A road, never paved, led off to two other farms, long abandoned. The helicopter, using the road as a marker, curved across the bay, climbed a hillside to a mountain pass, dipped into the pass, was surrounded by walls of grey Gothic rocks, then came out to beauty, on the western slope of the island, to the abbey, as the old guidebook had said, on a headland, *a splendour of sea. From the abbey tower, the visitor looks down on grey waves which curl on barren rock.* The helicopter, strange dragonfly, wheeled and went down on a field to the left of the monastery, rotor blades fanning the grasses, as it came to rest, its strange legs extending, bending to accommodate its weight as it touched ground. The plexiglass door slid open. The rotor blades became visible, whirling, slowing.

"Was it to be the blackberries in the glass jars and the redcurrants in the stone pots? Or was it the other way around, you told me?"
Brother Paul, filled with the demanding urgency which infects the deliberations of small minds, entered the Abbot's parlor, above the chancery of the abbey, without knock or by-your-leave. The Abbot, looking out through the

narrow aperture of a thirteenth-century window, did not answer at once. When he did, he said, "Blackberries. Jars."

"Ah, I was right, so I was! I thought it was the blackberries in the glass jars. Would you come down yourself now, and have a look at the fruit?"

"We have a visitor," the Abbot said.

"A visitor?" Brother Paul was alarmed. "Ah, no. Sure, didn't Padraig go out this morning and come back empty? And no other boat could come in, in this weather."

But the Abbot did not seem to hear. "His vorpal blade went snicker-snack," the Abbot said. "It would be a good description of that helicopter out there."

"A what?" Brother Paul bustled to the window. "Oh, that's that yoke from Dingle. I've seen it many's the time passing over here. Is he broke down, or what? Why did he land?"

The Abbot looked at Paul. "Did you not hear it come over, a minute ago?"

Paul blushed. He was deaf, ashamed of it, and a bad liar. "How would I hear it and I down in the calefactory room taking the stems off berries?"

"Go on back down, now," the Abbot said, suddenly weary of Paul. "I had better see to our visitor."

But Paul lingered, his head close to the Abbot's in the vise of the narrow medieval window. "That's not the priest from Rome, surely?"

"I would say it is."

"They'd have to wear special clothes to go up in one of them things," Brother Paul announced. He had not travelled to the mainland in a decade, and had never travelled by air.

"Yes." The Abbot turned from the window. "Go along now and tell Brother Martin to bring the visitor up directly. There is no sense in my climbing the stairs twice."

"I will do that, then," Brother Paul said.

The Abbot turned back to the window. The green-and-white helicopter increased its engine noise, the blades blurring to invisibility. *The frumious bandersnatch,* the Abbot said to himself. The words fuming and furious made frumious, and frumious it was now as it rose, levitating a few feet above the grass, hesitating as though looking for directions. Getting its bearings, it tilted forward, moving up and out to sea. He will stay the night, the Abbot decided. I will ask Father Manus to get us salmon from the pool. The sky was clearing, but, out there towards Slea Head, the wind force was building. There would be rain.

He heard steps, uncertain, coming up the winding stone staircase beneath his parlor, heard, predictably, Martin's warning. "The ninth step is longer than the others, Father. The trip step, they called it in the old days. Be careful, so."

"Thank you," said the visitor in his American voice, the voice the Abbot had heard on the telephone. Footsteps reached the top of the second flight. Good. It would not do to trip Rome up. "This way, Father," the Abbot called.

To Kinsella, turning and turning in that cold stone turret, to come out through the narrow door into the Abbot's parlor was dizzying, confusing, causing him, at first, to miss his host's welcoming hand.

"How are you, Father." The Abbot's voice was very soft.

"I'm sorry, excuse me, how are you. Good to meet you, Father Abbot."

"So Padraig left you standing on the pier. Oh, he's thick, that lad. I am sorry you had such a lot of trouble."

"It wasn't his fault. He didn't realize I was a priest."

"But you came on, anyway. Enterprising. Do you know, Father, that's the first flying machine of any description that has ever landed on Muck. You've brought us the symbol of the century. Just when I thought we'd be able to close the hundred years out, and say we missed our time."

"Would you have preferred that, Father Abbot?"

"Preferred what?"

"To have missed this century, to have been born in another time?"

"I should think not," the Abbot said. "If we had lived in the eighteenth century, for instance, our religion was under interdiction by the English. And the nineteenth century was not much better. Unless you had a lust for becoming a martyr, the past was not a time to be a Catholic priest here."

"Yes, of course. I forgot," Kinsella said. "By the way, I have a letter for you from Father General. And this is my Ecumenical Order of Mission. Perhaps you'd care to have a look at them?"

The Abbot would indeed. He stretched out his hand. "An Irish name, you have," he said, as Kinsella undid his dispatch case.

"Yes."

"That is a County Mayo name." The Abbot took the letters, shuffling them like a mailman as he went towards his desk. The Abbot sat, spreading the letters, opening them with a paper knife, reading with attention. As Kinsella tried to read him, noticing first, below the heavy brown woollen robe, black farmer's boots, with double leather soles, great hobnail cleats, and white woollen socks, their tops folded over the tops of these formidable boots. Of course the monks would not wear sandals in this cold. And, similarly, there were fisherman's black oilskins and a fisherman's sou'wester hat, hung up behind the Abbot's door. Those boots; that hat. A practical man. His hands, clumsy on the pages of the Ecumenical Order of Mission, were a workingman's hands, scaled with old cuts, the nails doubled thick, blue edged. Thin neck, large, glottal Adam's apple, moving in the socket of an oversize collar. The Abbot's grizzled hair was cut very short and, with grey eyes set far back in his skull, separated from his weathered face by a web of white frown lines, he had the look of a sea bird, a fisher hawk, perhaps. Yet, as he put the Ecumenical Order aside and began, attentively, to read the General's letter, Kinsella thought he saw something else. There was, in this humbly dressed old monk, a presence, a power, which recalled to his visitor a painting seen in Venice: Bastiani's portrait of Doge Francesco Foscari, mercantile noble, consummate politician. No, this would not be easy.

"A red-letter day," the Abbot said cheerfully, holding the General's letter up, the better to read it in the window light. "I have been an Albanesian monk for forty-five years, yet this is the first time I've ever held in my hand the signature of our Father General. A red-letter day, indeed. A pity it has to be a letter of censure."

"It is not meant as such, I can assure you."

"I agree. The tone is not unkind," the Abbot said. "But if you have attention paid to you from headquarters and you in a place like this, well, it's a fair guess that you're in hot water."

Kinsella laughed.

"Do you know what we call a place like this, in Ireland? The back of beyond. That's where you are now. The back of beyond."

"It's a great phrase."

"Mind you," the Abbot said. "A few hundred years ago, no place in Christendom was the back of beyond. The Pope, in those days, had a very long arm, indeed. I'll show you something that turned up out in the back there, twenty years ago, in a heap of stuff that was stored away and forgotten. It might amuse you. I mean, the container." The Abbot tugged at the side drawer of his desk. It opened with an unused squeal. Took from the drawer a flat tin on which was a colored picture of a bearded British sailor of former times. And a legend: *Player's Navy Cut Cigarettes.* "In the days when a lot of people smoked cigarettes—fags they called them in Ireland—we had an old lay brother, he was very fond of a smoke and so, when he found this, he thought he was made. 'Fifty fags, Father' said he to me, pleased as Punch with himself. And so,"—the Abbot opened the box—"when he opened it up, lo and behold, this was what was in it." The Abbot took out a something, wrapped in tissue paper. He unwrapped it, showing a wax seal. "Have a look at that."

Kinsella took the seal, handling it gently as a sand dollar. Traced in brown wax, the letters:

P I U S

P A P A

I I

"In fourteen sixty-three, that seal came here on a letter. We had someone look up the date for us in Rome. In that year Pope Pius the Second wrote to Walter Tobar, the Abbot of Muck, and told him there was a deanship in Kerry reported to be held by a man who had no canonical title. The Pope wanted the Abbot to jump on the man and teach him a lesson. And the Abbot did what he was told."

Laughter, which became a fit of coughing. "So, you see when the word comes this far down the line it usually means trouble for somebody or other. Eh, Father?"

Kinsella smiled and carefully handed back the seal. The Abbot shut it in the tin box. "Cup of tea?"

"Oh, no thanks."

Irishly, the Abbot appraised this, and, Irishly, decided the denial was mere politeness. "Ah, you will!" the Abbot said. He called downstairs. "Brother Martin?"

"Aye."

"Bring us a cup of tea, will you?"

"Two teas," Martin's voice rumbled from below. The Abbot, this settled, again picked up Father General's letter. "I am the sort of person who has to read everything important at least twice over."

"Go ahead."

As the Abbot reread, Kinsella stared about the room. The parlor was large, with a high ceiling, located somewhere over the abbey's sacristy. Three narrow windows gave onto the sea. The furniture, carved by monks, was serviceable, without style. The walls were shelved by books, hundreds of them, spilling onto tables and stacked in odd corners. Surprisingly, there was a special table covered with old green paperback Penguin mystery stories. On the wall, to the Abbot's right, were three storie panels, seventeenth-century Celtic, saints or apostles, figures of beauty, their simplicity emphasised by a horrid oil which took pride of place behind the Abbot's desk, a Victorian painting of a ship sailing in a storm-tossed sea, under heavens rent by the Virgin Mary, prayerful, in blue and white robes, imploring her Heavenly Son for the vessel's safety.

On a window ledge, five large, wooden games boxes, each labelled in Italic script.

> CHESS (I)
> CHESS (II)
> DRAUGHTS (2 Sets)
> DOMINOES (I)
> DOMINOES (incomplete)

"Do you have television here?"

The Abbot paused in his reading. "Sometimes when there is something big happening in the world, we draw lots and five of us bicycle across the island to Doran's shop on the strand. They have television there."

A pause.

"Not more than five of us, though. Doran's is a small place."

"You know, of course, Father Abbot, that the Mass on Mount Coom and the pilgrims who come to Cahirciveen were widely publicised on a B.B.C. television program, a couple of months ago."

"Indeed I do. Didn't we get hundreds of letters about it. I had no notion the Latin Mass was so popular. Do you know, it has given us a new penance. When one of us accuses himself of error before the chapter, he now has to answer some of those letters."

Footsteps. Stout, stertorous, Brother Martin emerged from the stairwell. On a wooden tray were two heavy china bowls, the size of soup bowls. They were filled with strong tea. Milk, sugar, a knife, a pot of blackberry jam. And two plates, each with a thick slice of white bread.

"Did you want an egg with that?" Brother Martin asked, putting the tray down on the Abbot's desk.

"No. We've having salmon with our supper, if Brother Manus can find a few in the pool."

"Salmon?"

"Yes, salmon. Father Kinsella has come all the way from Rome. This is an occasion, Martin."

Brother Martin turned to Kinsella. "That bread is our own baking. Irish soda bread." He went back downstairs.

"Poor Martin, he's getting on. We all are, here. I remember, last year, I said to Father Matthew, our master of novices, I said when you retire, we will retire your job with you. For not one recruit did I see coming along. But, do you know, after that television program, we had all sorts of enquiries. I tell you, I could recruit enough young men now to fill a regiment."

"I suppose that's a relief."

"A relief?" The Abbot paused, staring over the rim of his tea bowl. He held the bowl, his index finger cupped over its lip, in the eighteenth-century manner.

"I mean the prospect of being able to get recruits."

"It is not," the Abbot said, putting down his tea bowl and addressing himself to bread and jam.

"You are not anxious for new recruits?"

"I am not. It is a hard life on this island. Fishing, drying kelp, farming a few potatoes. It rains a lot. The monastery is a cold place, there is no way of heating it properly. And we are often hard put to make ends meet."

"But, isn't that the thing about hardship? I mean, men will accept it, if they feel it's for a worthwhile cause."

"Just so." The Abbot spread blackberry jam on his bread. "But the monastic life, as you know yourself, Father, is often something else. I'd break all clergy into two groups. Proselytisers, or prayers. Or, if you like, missionaries or monks."

"Monks can also be missionaries, surely?"

"Not on Muck Island. It takes a special vocation to live in a place like this. Not many have it. I do not have it myself, I sometimes think."

"But you have lived on this island most of your adult life?"

"That does not mean I like it."

"You'd prefer to be somewhere else?"

"I did not say that."

"I'm sorry. Of course not."

"This blackberry jam," the Abbot said, "is last year's. Brother Paul is down in the calefactory room now, bottling this year's jam. He is thinking of his jam. He is not thinking of anything else. I would say Brother Paul has a true vocation for this life."

Kinsella bit into his bread. "And it's delicious jam."

"It is."

"I suppose I am the missionary type," Kinsella said. "My great desire was to be sent to South America."

"Ah, Father Gustav Hartmann. A fine man he must be."

"He is."

"So you went to South America?"

"No, But I studied with Father Hartmann in his class in Boston. He's crippled now, you know."

"No. I did not know."

"He was tortured so many times. The *pau de arara*. Finally, the Brazilian *militares* broke his back."

"I would like to meet him," the Abbot said. "Tell me, does he talk much about God?"

"In what way do you mean, Father Abbot?"

"Ah, I don't know. Forget it. No, what I mean is," the Abbot paused, as though thinking. "Is it souls he's after? Or is it the good of mankind?"

"I would say the second."

The Abbot nodded. "I gathered as much. Of course, I'm not well up on such things. I never had the missionary impulse myself."

"But your zeal for the old mass, your continuance of the Latin ritual, surely that could be interpreted as missionary spirit?"

"I thought you'd get around to that," the Abbot said, and laughed. "Come on. Let's take a turn outside. The rain has stopped and I want to order up that salmon for our supper. You'll stay the night?"

Kinsella hesitated.

"Ah, you will! What did you tell the man with the helicopter?"

"I said I would telephone him when I'm ready to leave. He can get here in about an hour."

"Time enough, then, to ring him in the morning." The Abbot stood and took his oilskins and sou'wester from the hook behind the door. "Mind the step as you go down."

At the foot of the staircase, a door led to the sacristy. They went through and emerged in the cloister. The Abbot moved briskly, his hobnailed boots loud on the flags of the walk, turning up through a slype and into the refectory, a large bare room around the walls of which were rough refectory tables and benches. In the adjoining kitchen two old monks peeled potatoes from a huge pile. On the hearth hung an iron pot, big as a cartoon cannibal's cookpot. The turf fire gave off a pleasant scent.

One of the old monks looked up and smiled at the visitor. He had two upper teeth, it seemed. "G'day," said he. " 'Twill clear, I would say."

"Ah, yes," said the other old monk.

"Where is Father Manus?"

"I hear tell he's looking for a couple of fish," one old monk said. The other giggled.

"Right, then," the Abbot said. "We'll go and see what he's got."

A door, heavy and stiff on its iron hinges, swung open and they were outside, on a slope of field, looking down at those grey rocks, the splendour of sea. Below, a path led to a small cove. Four black curraghs lay upended on a shelf of rock. A man, in oilskins, carrying a fishing creel, could be seen trudging slowly along the strand. "Come on, down," the Abbot said to his guest. "I think that's our fish."

As they went down the path—"The man with that creel is Father Manus, a very good soul. He is the priest who said the Mass that Sunday when the television fellows came. The other monks make fun of him, now. The reporters tried to interview him on the television but he wouldn't speak." The Abbot kicked a stone clear of the path. "He will speak to you, never fear. He's dying to get a chance at you, I warn you. Still, that's what you're here for, I suppose. Explanations, wasn't that what Father General called them?"

"Yes."

"Maaaaa-nus! Did you get a fish?"

Shouting, his voice lifted and lost in the wind. Implacable, the loud sea on grey-green rocks. The man in oilskins heard, held up his creel.

"We have our fish," the Abbot said.

"Good."

"When Manus catches a salmon he puts it in an ocean pool and the next day, when the boat goes over, we sell on the mainland. Salmon gets a big price. So tonight is a special treat. Eating salmon ourselves. It's things like that—" the Abbot turned on the path and looked back up, his fisher hawk's eyes searching Kinsella's face—"it's the little things that keep us going, here. Like the jam I was talking about. Do you follow me? That is the jam in our lives."

Then turned and went on down, a heavy old man in black oilskins, his head hidden by the sou'wester hat.

While the needs of your particular congregation might seem to be served by retention of the Latin Mass, nevertheless, as Father Kinsella will explain to you, your actions in continuing to employ the older form are, at this time, particularly susceptible to misinterpretation elsewhere as a deliberate contravention of the spirit of aggiorna-mento. *Such an interpretation can and will be made, not only with the councils of the Church itself, but within the larger councils of the ecumenical movement. This is particularly distressful to us at this time, in view of the* apertura, *possibly the most significant historical event of our century, when interpenetration between Christian and Buddhist faiths is on the verge of reality.*

For all of these reasons, in conclusion, I will only say that, while Father Kinsella is with you to hear explanations, be it understood his decision is mine and, as such, is irrevocable.

English was not, of course, Father General's first language. *Explanations* was an unfortunate choice of word. Kinsella watched the Abbot jump from rock to shore, landing heavily but surely, striding across the rain-damp sand to meet the other monk whose habit hung down soaking beneath his black oil-skin coat. I would be angered by the tone of that last paragraph. And this is an Abbot who ignored his own Provincial for a dozen years. What if he ig-nores me? In Brazil, when the Bishop of Manáos denounced Hartmann as a false priest he was banished from the city and, upriver, the villagers refused him food. But he stayed, eating wild roots, waiting in the rain forest until he had sapped the bishop's power. What could *I* do in this godforsaken spot?

"Hey!"

The other monk, grinning, held open his creel as the Abbot drew close. Three large salmon, silver-scaled, on a bed of green moss. Grinning, arrested as though in some long-ago school snapshot, the old monk seemed, some-how, to have retained the awkward, boyish grace of his adolescent days.

"Well, Father Abbot, and how will these suit you?" he said, then turned to nod and grin at Kinsella, as though inviting him to share an enormous and obvious joke.

"They will do," the Abbot said, playing his part with great deliberation as he held the creel up. "Yes, I will say they will do nicely, Manus. And this is Father Kinsella, all the way from Rome. Father Manus, our champion fisher-man."

"Hello, there," Kinsella said.

"From Rome? So you're the man from Rome. I'd never have thought it."

"What were you expecting?"

"Well, somebody older. A real sergeant-major. And most likely an Italian, or something on that order. You're American, are you?"

"I am."

"Anyway, I'm delighted to see you. Oh, God forgive me, I'm not delighted at all. Sure we're all in fear and trembling of what you're going to do here."

"Manus!" The Abbot, amused, hit Father Manus a thump between the shoulderblades. "Hold your tongue, man. Aren't you the alpha and the omega. When Manus was a little boy they told him it was a sin to tell a lie. I do believe he has not committed that sin since."

"Ah, but seriously, Father Kinsella," Father Manus said. "I have to talk to you. I mean it is an astonishing thing that's happened here. I go over to the mainland every Sunday. And you should just see the way the people react."

"It's beginning to rain," the Abbot warned. "If you want to talk to Father Kinsella, I'd suggest we do it inside. Come along, now."

Setting a brisk pace, he turned and led them back up the path from the beach. The heavy monastery door shut stiffly behind them as they regained the cloister. First to the kitchen, where Father Manus handed over the fish to the old kitchen monks. Then, the Abbot beckoning, Father Manus and Kinsella were led into a small room furnished with draughtsman's tables and high stools. "All right," the Abbot said. "I'll be referee. Now, Manus, here's your chance. Have at him. What was it you were going to say?"

"What was it I wanted to tell him? What was it I wanted, ah, Lord, I do not know, I tell you, Father Kinsella, since I heard you were coming, I have lain awake at night arguing the toss with myself, saying this and saying that, and—look, it is as plain as the nose on your face, we did nothing to start all this, we went on saying the Mass over there in Cahirciveen the way it was always said, the way we had always said it, the way we had been brought up to say it. The Mass! The Mass in Latin, the priest with his back turned to the congregation because both he and the congregation faced the altar where God was. Offering up the daily sacrifice of the Mass *to God.* Changing bread and wine into the body and blood of Jesus Christ the way Jesus told his disciples to do it at the Last Supper. 'This is my body and this is my blood. Do ye this in commemoration of me.' God sent His Son to redeem us. His Son came down into the world and was crucified for our sins and the Mass is the commemoration of that crucifixion, of that sacrifice of the body and blood of Jesus Christ for our sins. It is priest and people praying to God, assisting in a miracle whereby Jesus Christ again comes down among us, body and blood in the form of the bread and wine there on the altar. And the Mass was said in Latin because Latin was the language of the Church and the Church was one and universal and a Catholic could go into any church in the world, here or in Timbuktu, or in China, and hear the same Mass, the only Mass there was, the Latin Mass. And if the Mass was in Latin and people did not speak Latin, that was part of the mystery of it, for the Mass was not talking to your neighbor, it was talking to God. Almighty God! And we did it that way for nearly two thousand years and, in all that time, the church was a place to be quiet in, and respectful, it was a hushed place because God was there, God on the altar, in the tabernacle in the form of a wafer of bread and a chalice of wine. It was God's house, where, every day, the daily miracle took place. God coming down among us. A mystery. Just as this new Mass isn't a mystery, it's a mockery, a singsong, it's not talking to God, it's talking to your neighbor, and that's why it's in English, or German or Chinese or whatever language the people in the church happen to speak. It's a symbol, they say, but a symbol of what? It's some entertainment show, that's what it is. And the people see through it. They do! That's why they come to Coom Mountain, that's why they come on planes and boats and the cars thick on the roads and the people camping out in the fields, God help them, and that's why they are there with the rain pouring down on them, and when the Sanctus bell is rung at the moment of Elevation, when the priest kneels and raises up the Host—aye, that little round piece of bread that is now the body of Our Blessed Saviour—holds it up—Almighty God—and the congregation is kneeling at the priest's back, bowed down to adore their God, aye, Father, if you saw those people, their heads bare, the rain pelting off their faces, when they see the Host raised up, that piece of unleavened bread that, through the mystery and the miracle of the Mass, is now the body and blood of Jesus Christ, Our Saviour, then you would be ashamed, Father, you would be ashamed to sweep all that away and put in its place what you *have* put there—singing and guitars and turning to touch your neighbor, playacting and nonsense, all to make the people come into church the way they used to go to the parish hall for a bingo game!"

Clear: the challenge. His eyes ragebright, a tiny froth of spittle on his cheek as, confused, he came full stop in his tirade. The Abbot stepped between adversaries. "I wish I had all that fire and conviction, Manus. As for you, Father Kinsella, you've just found out we have a lot of sermons in us, here at the back of beyond."

"I'm sorry." Father Manus stared at Kinsella as he would at a man he had, unexpectedly, punched in the mouth. "But, still and all, what I said is only God's truth. Father Abbot will bear me out."

"I don't know what God's truth is," the Abbot said. "Do any of us? If we did, there would be no arguments between us. But it *is* true that a lot of people seem to feel the way Manus does about the old Mass. You know that, of course. That is why you're here."

"Anyway," Father Manus said, his voice loud again. "I think it would be a crime against the people's faith, if we were forced to give up the old way here."

"Manus," the Abbot said, gently. "I wonder would you ask Father Colum to start benediction. I would like to show Father Kinsella around. Would you do that now, like a good man?"

"Yes, Father Abbot, I will do that directly."

"You'll see each other again, at suppertime," the Abbot promised.

Impulsively Father Manus caught hold of Kinsella's arm. "There was nothing personal, Father."

"I know. I appreciate hearing your point of view."

A very dirty monk, face and hands stained with earth, appeared at the door, unaware that he was interrupting. "We found the lamb!" he shouted, then stared slackmouthed at the visitor.

"Good man yourself," the Abbot said. "Where was it?"

"But that's the story of it. In an old byre, by the ruin where the Cullens used to live. And lying down, keeping warm, up against a wee pony."

"With a pony?"

"Right forenenst it. A wee pony of Taig Murtagh's."

"And the pony didn't mind?"

"Divil a bit."

"There's the power of prayer for you," Father Manus said, his good humor restored.

"It took more than prayer," said the dirty monk. "It took the whole day."

"Go along now," the Abbot ordered, and the dirty monk went off with Father Manus. "Are you interested in Romanesque?" the Abbot asked Kinsella.

"Very much."

"Well, I'll show you a couple of things, then. Coming from Rome you will be hard to impress. Oh, what grand sights! I was there at the time of Pope John, years ago, may he rest in peace."

"To study?"

"Ah, no. Just on a holiday. I had been sick and so I was sent off on a jaunt. I went to London, then to Rome and on to Lourdes, in France. My first and last visit to the continent, I expect."

"You enjoyed it."

"Oh, I had a grand time. It was grand to see England again. I served my novitiate there, in Buckmore Abbey in Kent."

"I know."

"Ah, yes, sure you probably know all about me. They make you do your homework well, there on the Lungotevere Vaticano?"

Kinsella, smiling, shook his head. Walking now between cloister arches, Abbot and stranger, the object of constant, covert curiosity. Monks, meditating or reading their office, paced the covered walk, in silence. A light drizzle of rain fell in the rectangular cloister garth. These monks; this place. Most of them would know no other. *Hartmann, in class, sitting in his specially built orthopedic chair, by the window overlooking the Charles River in Boston, his eyes peering down, shaded by thick-freckled fingers. There was a two-man skiff on the water below. "The key," Hartmann said, "was when we discovered that no one, or almost no one, in the entire hierarchy of Brazil, Chile, Argentina—no one was truly happy with his posting or his position—once we grasped that truth, we could unlock any door. See that skiff down there? I will bet that one of those two rowers believes that the other man has the better seat. I would bet my life on it. Sometimes to force an issue, you have to bet your life on things like that—things you know nothing about."*

"This way," the Abbot said, leading him into the church. Now, standing in the nave of the abbey, Kinsella felt again that sudden, vivid emotion, that elation in silence of the great bear church at Vézelay, most beautiful of all French Romanesque abbeys, greater even than Autun. Here, as in Vézelay, on this remote Irish island on the edge of the Gothic world, that hush, that bareness which contains all the beauty of belief. Above him, grey stone rose to arch in the Gothic symbol of hands joined in prayer. As in Vézelay, it was an edifice empty as silence, grave as grace. In the chancel, the altar, a bare stone slab on which stood a small tabernacle with a door of beaten Irish gold. Two wooden candlesticks were its only ornaments. No second altar, Kinsella noticed, nothing to conform with the liturgical change of 1966. In the south transept, a small shrine to the Virgin and, above the main altar, a Romanesque crucifix, high on the chancel wall, starveling stone Christ, hung on nails on cross of Irish bog oak.

The Abbot's boots were loud in the nave. "Twelfth century, most of it. But this doorway and these windows are thirteenth century, a transition from Irish Romanesque to Gothic. This cross motif is similar to that in the Monastery of Cong, a Cistercian house. But this one is finer. Probably the finest in Ireland, they tell us."

"It is beautiful."

"A big church this, when you think of the place it's in. Of course there used to be more families living on Muck. The main construction is the original structure. There used to be a holy well on the island, at the time those things were popular. People came over from the mainland by boat to visit it. Little rowboats, made of skin and wood frames, coracles they were called. *Those* people had faith."

"Buckmore is a beautiful abbey too, I hear?"

The Abbot twisted around, head cocked oddly to one side. "It is. Different, of course. This abbey is older and has never been burned. It's one of the few in Ireland that escaped both Henry the Eighth and Cromwell. There are advantages to being remote."

Before leaving Rome, remembering Hartmann's advice in class, Kinsella had mentioned to Father General the question of a transfer. "Sometimes a more rewarding posting brings about a great change of heart," Kinsella said. Father General agreed. "But, only as a last resort. Use it, if absolutely necessary."

"The other thing I wanted to show you, is up there in the south transept," the Abbot said. "Come this way." Genuflecting, moving past benches where four monks knelt in prayer, heads cowled, faces hidden. "All of the Abbots of Muck are buried under this wall. Every one. Can you imagine that? As far as we know, it goes back to the founding. According to the records there are fifty-one laid down there like bottles of wine. And, God willing, I'll be fifty-two. It's rare having Abbots laid down like that. Our abbey in Santiago de Compostela is the only other one I've heard of that has this sort of arrangement."

"If you were appointed Abbot elsewhere, would they not send your body back here to be buried?"

"No. The rule holds only if the Abbot dies here. I'd say my chance is very good. I hope so, anyway. It's an idiotic sort of ambition, but I have it. Funny. This island is not exactly a summer resort, but, do you know, if I go out on the mainland now, I'll not sleep one night over there, if I can get back in. I feel at home here. I am at home nowhere else."

Kinsella stared at his host. Transfer foreseen and forestalled. Did this Abbot leave nothing to chance? And now, as though continuing a guided tour, the Abbot led him away, as monks in twos and threes, cowled, came in at every door until, some twenty-five, they filled the two front benches. From the sacristy, a priest emerged in a cope, silk and gold cloth, richly embroidered by nuns long dead. Before him, a lay brother with censer and chain. *Benediction.* The Abbot, hurrying his guest from this scene of irregularity, pushed upon a heavy door in the side of the nave. They went out under rain-dark skies.

"We have a little guest house, it's not very grand, but there is a hot tub. We'll have our supper at seven. That will give us plenty of time afterwards, if you want to have a chat."

"Thank you."

Following the Abbot along a mud-edged path under the west wall of the monastery towards a building like a large outhouse alone in a field. "It's off on its own, as you can see." The Abbot turned a key in the door. Inside, a small hall, with an unlit turf fire set in the grate. A coat hanger, a visitor's book on a wooden table, and, on the whitewashed wall, a crucifix made of woven reeds. Off the hall was a bedroom with a narrow monk's bed, a wooden chair, a sheepskin rug on the foor. The bathroom, adjoining, was primitive but adequate; tub, washbasin, toilet, all in a tiny space.

"We will pick you up at six-fifteen. If you are cold, just put a match to that fire."

The door shut. Kinsella moved like a prisoner in the cell-like rooms, then, deciding, stripped off his clothes and ran water in the old-fashioned bathtub. Lay in the tub, the steamy water blurring mirror and windowpane, listening to the cry of gulls, mind idling as his body, gentled by the warm water, grew slack and at ease. The Abbot seemed to be in charge. Father Manus had, no doubt, been brought in early, to dispose of the emotional appeal. There were probably others of his persuasion here. The Abbot used Father Manus to say what he himself is too shrewd to say. Father General's letter is what really interests him, he read it at least three times. He is not angling for preferment or power. Reasonable in what he says; captain of his ship. If this letter from the owners tells him to dump a cargo of ritual, my guess is he will do as he is bid. Hartmann, looking down at the two-man skiff on the Charles River, saying one must be prepared to gamble everything on a hunch. Will I gamble on the Abbot if he gives me his word? Or is there a grey eminence here, a *Mann im Schatten* I have not yet faced?

Kinsella rose, dripping, from the tub. In the evening air, already cool, the room misted like a steam bath. The towel was rough on his skin. He thought of the confessions; no one had mentioned the confessions. They were, he knew, the greatest danger.

Forty minutes later, when the knock came on the door, he was waiting, dressed in his grey-green fatigues and his flying jacket. Old, grinning school-boy face, hand clasping his sou'wester, keeping it firm on long grey locks, Father Manus entered the hall, scraping mud clots from the soles of his boots. "Terrible wind! I asked if I could come for you. I am heartsick."

"What?"

"I offered up prayers at Benediction in penance for shouting at you like some wild man from Borneo. As Father Abbot pointed out, sure, I never gave you a chance to open your mouth."

"That's all right."

"It is not all right. It's a disgrace." Father Manus blushed from the neck up, turning to hide his embarrassment, peering out at the gusty rain. "Pelting down. We'll have to run for it. They are all waiting to meet you in the ref."

Slamming the guest house door, Kinsella kept close to his guide, half running, until they reached the monastery gate. Hurried along the cloister walk to the refectory where the community was assembled, clustered in twos and threes like conference delegates, all whispers and shy smiles as Father Manus led the visitor in. Coats were taken and hung up. The Abbot came forward, genial, linking Kinsella's arm, leading him around, introducing him.

"Father John, Father Colum, Brother Kevin. And Brother Sean. Father Kinsella, from Rome. An Irish name that is? Yes. It is true what we heard, that Padraig refused to take you on his boat this morning? It is? Oh, glory be! And Father Terence, Father Kinsella from Rome. Terence is in charge of our farm here. Father Alphonsus, Father Kinsella. Did you come all the way from Rome now in that whirligig that landed here today? All the way from Rome, oh, did you hear what Father Alphonsus wants to know! Ah, for goodness sake don't you know that's a helicopter, it could not fly all the way from Rome. Ah, so you came in a bigger aeroplane, did you? I see. From Amsterdam to Shannon and then from Shannon by car. And the helicopter was only because of Padraig. So that was the way of it. Do you know, Father Kinsella. I hear tell there is not a village in Ireland that does not have some class of an airfield near by. Isn't that amazing. Yes, yes.

"And this is Father Matthew, our master of novices. What novices are you talking about, Father Abbot, I think it would be better to introduce me as jack of all trades and master of none. Hardly so, Father Matthew. Anyway, I want you to meet Father Kinsella, from Rome. Indeed, I know he is from Rome. We all do. You are here because of the doings at Cahirciveen, isn't that so? Yes. It is wonderful the response of the people there on Mount Coom. Wonderful. It would do your heart good to see the piety of the ordinary people. Indeed it would. And I hope—by the way, have you met Father Daniel?—Father Daniel, Father Kinsella, Father Daniel is our business manager. Excuse me, Father Matthew, you were saying? I was saying I hope you are not planning to change our ways, Father Kinsella. In what way, Father Matthew? The Mass, Father. I will be honest and tell you I have been saving a novena for weeks now, hoping that we will be allowed to go with this holy work."

The Abbot, smooth, led his visitor from danger. "If Father Kinsella would sit here, on my right? And this is Father Walter, my deputy. Sit on Father Kinsella's right, will you, Father Walter, that way we'll have him surrounded by the Muck Island Establishment, haha." Great noise of refectory benches as twenty-six monks sat in to supper. All waited. The Abbot rang a handbell. At once all eyes went to the kitchen door as the two old cook brothers, faces full of triumphal smiles, brought the salmon in. Three fish on three white china platters. Then great bowls of steaming boiled potatoes. Salt and butter dishes. Three big pitchers of buttermilk. When the food was on the table, the Abbot stood. All stood. All prayed:

"Bless us, O Lord, and these Thy gifts, which, of Thy bounty, we are about to receive, through Christ, Our Lord, Amen." Not, Kinsella noted, the approved Ecumenical grace, standard in all other monasteries of the Order. Afterwards, in continuing anachronism, all made the Sign of the Cross. All sat. The Abbot served his guest, then himself. The platters were passed. All ate in silence, quickly, heads bowed to their food. It was the old rule. When the Abbot rose, all rose. "We give Thee thanks, O Lord, for all Thy benefits, Who livest and reignest, world without end. Amen. May the souls of the faithful departed, through the mercy of God, rest in peace. Amen."

Afterwards, the community hovered respectfully, hoping to engage the visitor in further conversation. But the Abbot did not linger. "We will go up now to my parlor for a cup of tea. We are early to bed and early to rise, here. Fishermen and farmers of a sort, as we are, we must use the light God gives us. So, if you will come this way, Father?"

"Goodnight. Goodnight. Off so soon? Goodnight, Father. Sleep well." They watched him go, cheated by this abrupt departure: they had few visitors. Their long-skirted lines parted in polite reluctance as the Abbot, purposeful, led Kinsella back through the cloister, into the sacristy, and up the winding stone staircase to the parlor.

On the Abbot's desk, Brother Martin had left a pot of tea and, incongruously, a plate of lemon puff biscuits. The Abbot took one of the biscuits, holding it up between forefinger and thumb. "Martin is trying to bribe you," he said. "Whenever he wants to soften somebody up, he parts with a few of these. His married sister sends them to him, all the way from Manchester." He munched the biscuit and, munching, moved to pick up the Ecumenical Order of Mission. Frowning, he read it once again. "Sit down, Father. Make yourself comfortable." The Ecumenical Order was tossed on the desk, discarded. Again the General's letter. Read, how many times now? Re-read again, then held up, as though in exhibit. "Is there something I could say that might change your, and our Father General's opinion of these events?"

"Well, I wouldn't know, would I? As you haven't said anything yet."

The Abbot laughed as though this were some extremely subtle joke. "Do you know what they are calling you, over there in the refectory, Father?"

Kinsella waited, smiling at his host.

"The inquisitor." The Abbot laughed. "I thought that was good."

"Hardly an inquisitor."

"Why not? Didn't the Inquisition come around to seek our doctrinal error and punish it?"

"My mission is not punitive."

"Not yet. But what if the heresy continues?"

"Look," Kinsella said, slightly irritated. "This is the end of the twentieth century, not the beginning of the thirteenth. How can we even define what heresy is today?"

"Yesterday's orthodoxy is today's heresy."

"I wouldn't say that, Father Abbot."

"Then what have you got against us saying the Mass in the old way?"

"We are trying to create a uniform posture within the Church. If everyone decides to worship in his own way—well, it's obvious, it would create a disunity."

"Exactly," the Abbot said. "Breakdown. The loss of control. Look, I agree. There must be discipline. Dish of tea?"

"Thank you, yes."

"Milk and sugar?"

"Black."

The Abbot poured and passed the bowl of tea to his guest. "Explanations," the Abbot said. "Father General seems to feel they would be in order. Very well. I will try to explain why we kept the old Mass here. Will I tell you why?"

"Yes, I would like it—yes, please do."

"Did you know that Ireland used to be the only country in Europe where every Catholic went to Mass of a Sunday? Everyone, even the men?"

"Yes. I was here some years ago. In Sligo."

"Were you, now? Well, anyway, when this new Mass came in, we tried it, we did what we were told. But we noticed that the men would come into Cahirciveen with their families and stand, smoking and talking, outside the church. When Mass was over, they took their women home. Now, I thought that was a bad sign. I mean, this is Ireland, after all. I wrote our Father Provincial about it. He wrote back that the new Mass was popular everywhere else. Well, I did not know what to do. We were losing our congregation, hand over fist. I said to myself, maybe the people here are different from the people in other places, maybe they will not stand for this change. After all, what are we doing, playing at being Sunday priests over there on the mainland, if it's not trying to keep the people's faith in Almighty God? I am not a holy man, but, maybe because I am not, I felt I had no right to interfere. I thought it was my duty, not to disturb the faith they have. So, I went back to the old way."

"Then what happened?"

"Nothing happened."

"But it must have been noticed. There must have been talk in the diocese?"

"I suppose there was. But people are not well informed on liturgical matters. I think the people thought because we are an old order we had some special dispensation to do things the old way. Anyway, the old way became very popular, after the word got around."

"And, soon, you had thousands coming to Mass every Sunday."

"That is not so," the Abbot said. "For a number of years we did not have many extra people. Some older people from parishes about. But it was just lately it caught on. It was the tourists. Ireland is choked with tourists now in the summer months. I blame those new planes, those Supers, or whatever you call them."

"So, it was only last summer that you moved out of the priory in Cahirciveen and began saying Mass on Mount Coom?"

"You are well informed. I am not surprised. Our Father Provincial, in Dublin, is not what you would call an admirer of mine."

"On Mount Coom," Kinsella said. "You decided to say Mass on the Mass rock. According to my reading, the Mass rock, in Penal times, was associated with rebellion. Mass was said there, by outlaw priests, in secret, with some member of the congregation on the lookout in case the English soldiers came."

"The Mass rock was a mistake," the Abbot said. "At the time I did not think of the connection. I was just trying to accommodate the crowds."

"You accepted a gift of loudspeakers from the merchants of Cahirciveen."

"It is customary to accept gifts which aim at enchancing worship."

"But, loudspeakers," Kinsella said. "Surely, it has occurred to you that Mount Coom has become a place of pilgrimage?"

"Do you mean a sort of Lourdes?"

"As Lourdes used to be. Lourdes is no longer in operation."

"We are not at all like Lourdes. There are no miracles. We just say Mass."

"And hear private confessions. Which is not known even now, in Rome. I only found it out by accident, myself, the other day in Cahirciveen. As you know, private confessions have been abolished, except in cases of special need where the sin is so grave that private counsel is necessary."

The Abbot frowned. "All mortal sins are mortal to the soul. I find these new rulings difficult to apply."

"To begin with, as you know, the category of mortal or venial sin is no longer in use."

"But what am I to do?" The Abbot seemed suddenly distraught. "The people here still think it is a special sin to molest a child, to steal a man's wife, to marry in sin—ah—a whole lot of things! What am I to do if the people still believe that sin is mortal?"

"I know it must be difficult. But the retention of private confessions would be a serious mistake. The idea of Catholics confessing their sins in private to a priest has been distasteful to other groups within the Ecumen brotherhood. Now that the easier form has been sanctioned by the Vatican IV—you have read the debates, surely?"

"I have, indeed," the Abbot said. "I know that I am not in step, in the matter of confessions. But, remember, I tried to limit the confessions to people from our parish. It was all part of the same thing. We did not want to disturb the faith of the local people. Still. . . ." The Abbot paused and looked searchingly at his visitor. "You said yourself that Rome did not know about the private confessions. You were not sent here because of that?"

"No."

"Why were you sent, Father Kinsella? What, in particular, caused this—?" The Abbot picked up Father General's letter.

"American television is planning to do a special one-hour program on what has happened here. Did you know that?"

"So that's it!" The Abbot made a fist of his right hand and hit the top of his desk. "The damned television! I did not want television here. I will ban them. I was dead against it from the start."

"Even the President of the United States can't ban American television. If the networks want to televise what's going on here, it will be done. And it will be seen all over the world."

"I warned our monks and I told the merchants at Cahirciveen the selfsame thing, I said don't have anything to do with those telly people, just tell them it's none of their concern. I refused them permission for any filming on Church property."

"It didn't do much good, did it? Don't you see that even your action in refusing to let these ceremonies be filmed can lend a significance to them that you never intended? A program in the wrong hands, about this subject, could be made to look like the first stirrings of a Catholic counter-revolution."

"Ah, now begging your pardon, Father Kinsella, I find that very farfetched."

"Far-fetched? To the enemies of the Church, won't it seem that you have acted in direct contradiction to the counsels of Vatican IV?"

The Abbot stared at the fire. In the reflected light of the flames, his features seemed grey as a plaster cast. "I didn't think of myself as contradicting Rome. God forbid."

"I am sure you didn't. And I have been sent here, simply, to clarify things. To explain Father General's concern. And to ask you, for the greater good, to stop this Mass, and these private confessions, at once."

The Abbot, hitching the skirts of his robe, leaned towards the fire, staring at the flames. Kinsella stood. He began to speak, a pulse trembling in his throat, his voice loud in the room, the voice of a believer, telling his true creed. "Father General, in his letter, mentioned the *apertura* with Buddhism, which, of course, you've read about. Perhaps it seems to you that this has nothing to do with life here on this island, but, believe me, it has. Father General is president of the special Ecumenical Council which will inaugurate the Bangkok talks next month. It is the first time an Order head has been so chosen and any scandal about the Albanesians at this time could, as you can guess, be extremely embarrassing to Father General at the talks. He was anxious that you understand he is in a very delicate stage of these negotiations. The *bonze* demonstrations at Kuala Lumpur are, we feel, only a beginning of the opposition tactics."

The Abbot swivelled in his chair, staring up at his visitor. He did not speak. Then, rising, he walked to the windows of his parlor. The faded light of an Irish summer's evening washed a late northern brightness into the room. Through narrow windowpanes, the Abbot stared at the sky. Grey storm clouds sailed west towards America. The sky, abandoned, was bled white by a hidden sun. "I envy you," the Abbot said. "I have been a priest for forty-odd years, but I have never been sure why. It must be very rewarding to feel that one's actions might actually change something in this world of ours. If I ask you a question, I hope you won't be offended. But, when a young fellow like you kneels down in church, do you pray? Do you actually say prayers, things like the Hail Mary, the Our Father, and so on?"

"Are you asking me what do I believe?"

"Yes, if you wish. There is a book by a Frenchman called Francis Jeanson, have ever you heard of it? *An Unbeliever's Faith,* it is called."

"I have not read it."

"It is interesting. He believes there can be a future for Christianity, provided it gets rid of God. Your friend, Father Hartmann, has mentioned Jeanson in his own writings. The idea is, a Christianity that keeps God can no longer stand up to Marxism. You have not heard of the book?"

"Yes, I have heard of it." Kinsella said. "But I have not read it."

"A pity. I wanted to ask you—the Mass, for instance. What is the Mass to you?"

Kinsella looked at the Abbot, as the Abbot stared out at the evening sky. Now was the time for truth, if only a cautious part of the truth. "I suppose, the Mass to me, as to most Catholics in the world today, is a symbolic act. I do not believe that the bread and wine on the altar is changed into the body and blood of Christ, except in a purely symbolic manner. Therefore, I do not, in the old sense, think of God as actually being present, there in the tabernacle."

* * *

The Abbot turned from the window, head cocked on one side, his hawk's features quizzical. "Isn't that remarkable," the Abbot said. "And yet you seem to be what I would call a very *dedicated* young man."

"In what way is it remarkable, Father Abbot? It's the standard belief, in this day and age."

"Or lack of belief," the Abbot said. "I think I was born before my time. A man doesn't have to have such a big dose of faith anymore, does he?"

Kinsella smiled. "Perhaps not." He had been about to add that today's best thinking saw the disappearance of the church building as a place of worship in favor of a more generalised community concept, a group gathered in a meeting to celebrate God-in-others. But decided that, perhaps, the Abbot was not ready for that step.

"Yes," the Abbot said. "I see now why the old Mass is *non grata*. And why you're here to tell us to cease and desist."

"My job is, primarily, to explain the situation—including the special problems facing the Order at present—and, of course, to help handle any transitional problems which might arise with tourists or press."

"You mean when we give up the old Mass?"

"Yes."

"And if I choose to retain it?"

"I hope that won't be the case."

"But you are the General's plenipotentiary," the Abbot said. "If it *is* the case, then you have the authority to act against me."

"Yes, I do."

"I don't know why I'm asking," the Abbot said. "The letter made that quite clear. I must be a glutton for punishment."

"On the contrary, you seem to me a very reasonable man. And as an Abbot, with episcopal powers, you realise better than I do the need for seniors in our Order to act in concert and set an example."

"Now, now, hold on, hold your horses," the Abbot said, smiling. "I've had a terrible lot of sermons thrown at me these last weeks. I know what you're going to say, and so on and so forth. But, right now, what I need to do is sit down and think about this letter from Father General. I believe I will do that. We can talk in the morning. Will that be all right?"

"Of course."

"We'll not keep you here for ever, don't worry. Padraig will take you back to the mainland any time you want to go."

"Fine. No hurry."

The Abbot picked up the poker from the grate and hammered on the flagstones. "Martin?"

Below, a voice: "Yes, Father Abbot."

"Will you take our visitor to his quarters?"

Turned to Kinsella, holding out his hand. "Sleep well, Father. And thank you for coming to Muck. I'll be along to take you to breakfast in the morning. Would eight suit you?"

"Fine."

"Martin?"

"Yes, Father Abbot." Brother Martin was now at the head of the stair-well.

"Put a light on the west wall. Father Kinsella is not, like yourself, some class of a night cat."

Brother Martin laughed, as at an old joke. "This way, Father."

Stertorous, a noise like a man blowing on a fire to redden coals, why must they pick this overweight monk for the heart-hurting job of ascending and descending these winding turret stairs? Down, down, behind Brother Martin, gazing at the shiny tonsure on the back of his skull. Through the musty camphor smell of the sacristy, into the cloister walk, Brother Martin, by now wheezing in a frightening manner. At the west entrance an unoiled door opened with a scream of hinges and a monk, wearing a heavy frayed overcoat over his robe, his face half hidden by a full red beard, came out, beckoning. "Father Kinsella?"

"Yes."

"There was a telephone call for you."

"This is Brother Kevin," Brother Martin said.

" 'Twas a call from Dingle. The helicopter company. Did you want to ring them?"

"Maybe I'd better."

"Go along then, Martin. I'll take Father Kinsella back." Gripping Kinsella's arm. "Come in, come in."

And shut the screaming door. The room was like a bunker, a narrow window twelve feet long by two feet wide stretched along one wall, giving on a view of mountains, and a cove where curraghs were drawn up on the strand. Papers, manila folders, a short-wave radio and a telephone were jumbled on a long wooden table. The walls were lined with red and white buoys, lobster creels, fishing tackle of various sorts.

"I admit it's a shambles," said the red-bearded monk and now Kinsella recognized the crackly, humorous voice he had spoken to from the pub and from Hern's Hotel. "Will I get you Dingle?"

"Yes. Western Helicopters. Dingle 402, I think."

"That's right. Dan Gavin runs that outfit. I know him." He cranked the handle. "Would you get us Dingle 402, Sheilagh? Thanks, Sheilagh."

He turned to look at Kinsella. "Do the priests in Rome not dress like priests any more?"

"Clerical dress is optional, except on special occasions."

"That's a grand outfit *you're* wearing. Dashing! You look like a soldier boy."

The phone rang. The red-bearded monk handed over the receiver. Kinsella's pilot was on the line. "Yes, I called earlier, Father. We have a report that the island will be socked in around noon. Bad storm off the coast of Spain, coming up fast."

"By noon?"

"Yes. Mightn't even be able to get off by boat after that. Gale-force winds forecast for all of Kerry."

"I see." Held the phone, stared at by the red-bearded monk as, furious, his mind raced through a scenario. "All right," he said. "See if you can come in at nine, okay?"

"Same spot?"

"Right."

"Nine o'clock, then. Will do."

"Goodnight. And thank you."

Redbeard's lips went wide in a grin. "So you're leaving us in the morning, then?"

Kinsella smiled, but did not answer.

"Well, I suppose you'll be wanting to get back to your quarters. I'll show you the road. This way."

The door screamed. They went across the cloister and out at the west gate. Pre-darkness, a failing of light, dimmed the summer sky above them. The wind was strong, blowing the grasses flat along the edges of their muddy path. The red-bearded monk unlocked the guest house door. "Good night, sleep tight and don't let the bugs bite," he said, and cackled childishly.

"Good night. Thank you."

"Don't worry, there are no bugs at all. Not even bedbugs."

Kinsella locked himself in: he did not know why. Suddenly, he felt tense. The helicopter might be a mistake; it might have been wiser to remain passive, allowing the element of chance, the weather, to lay its onus on the Abbot. Kinsella went into the bathroom and brushed his teeth, then shaved for the second time that day. He stripped and, putting on his one-piece sleeping suit, lay on the narrow bed. With a fanatic like Father Manus, or even that very tall old man, the master of novices, your opposition was in the open, and less dangerous. What *did* the Abbot think? The one argument which seemed to have some effect on him was when he stared at the fire and said, "I didn't think of myself as contradicting Rome. God forbid." Obedience: in the end it was the only card. *Tu es Petrus.* And on this rock I will build my church. And the gates of hell will not prevail against it.

The wind had set up a small rattle in the windowframe. Below on the rocky bluff, constant as a ticking clock, the sound of waves, washing on shore. And then, startling as any human sound in a wild place, Kinsella heard a voice, singing out a hymn.

"Faith of our fathers living still
In spite of dungeon fire and sword.
Oh, how our hearts beat high with joy
When'er we hear that glorious word.
Faith of our fathers, holy faith,
We will be true to thee till death,
We will be true to thee till death."

When the verse ended, he jumped from his bed and ran to the window. No one. Grassy slopes leading to rock-strewn shore. Yet the voice had been close. And now, it began again.

"Our fathers chained in prisons dark
Were still in heart and conscience free."

Ran to the front door, unlocked it and went out. The light on the west wall, requested by the Abbot, shone down, casting its beam all along the path and the shore. Where was the singer?

"How sweet would be our children's fate,
If they, like them, could die for Thee.
Faith of our fathers, holy faith,
We will be true to thee till death.
We will be true to thee till death."

Silence. He stared about him, wind whipping his light zycron sleeping suit, his hair blowing in thick curls about his face. What about the dungeons into which our father's faith put so many poor souls? he wanted to shout. Sing along, you bastard, sing along, it will take more than songs and tricks. I have the power to order, to alter. He went back into the guest house and locked the door. Lay down, reviewing the conversations, the Abbot's remarks, the options. Towards midnight, he set his mind to wake at seven. He turned on his right side. Obedient, his mind admitted sleep.

At midnight, the Abbot left his parlor and went down the winding stairs. He was aware that rules were being broken; certain monks were not in bed. He knew this, without evidence, but as surely as he knew most other details of life on Muck. In time of crisis such things were to be expected. But not permitted. As he went through the sacristy, putting out the lights behind him, he heard a noise in the church. He went in through the door at the south transept.

* * *

There were no lights in the church, save a candle before the small shrine to the Virgin, and the red sanctuary lamp over the main altar. In the chancel Father Walter and Father Manus knelt side by side, in semi-darkness, their arms outstretched in that painful posture of adoration which simulates the outstretched arms of the crucified Christ. Behind them, less spectacularly at prayer, were Brothers Sean, John and Michael, and, sitting on a bench, two of the oldest monks, Father Benedict and Brother Paul. The Abbot's entrance was not noticed, although he made no effort to walk softly. A sign, he knew, that others were expected.

"Father Walter," the Abbot said, in a loud voice.

All eyes sideshot to south transept. All saw the Abbot who saw all. Father Walter, lowering his praying arms, rose stiffly from his knees and marched to the rear of the church to confront his superior. Father Manus was at once joined in cruciform adoration by old Father Benedict.

The Abbot put his arm on Father Walter and drew him out into the night damp of the cloister walk.
    "So you are in on this?"
    "Have you good news for us, I hope, Tomás?"
    "I have no news. I asked you a question."
    "Yes. I am the ringleader."
    "You are not. Adding a lie to your sins will not help whatever foolish aim you have in mind."
    "You know very well what I have in mind. It is what we all have in mind."
    "Is it. Do you know *my* mind?"
    "Asking God's help is not a sin."
    "Breaking the rule of obedience is."
    "Tomás, you are not going to be vexed with us, are you?"
    "I am very disappointed. I want you to go in there and tell those others to get off to their beds at once."
    Father Walter's face went happily into a smile. "Our prayers are answered, so!"
    "They are nothing of the sort. There is work to be done in the fields and in the abbey. The boats will have to be out to the pots and back by noon. The mackerel are running off Slea Head and I want nets out. We live by work, as I have said a hundred times. We are not a contemplative order."
    "This is a case when only the power of prayer can help."
    "You can not run a monastic community like a holiday camp, Walter. People taking it into their heads to stay up all night without a by-your-leave

or a with-your-leave. I asked everybody to behave as usual, while this visitor
was in the house. I am disappointed in you, Walter."

"It was my fault, so it was, Father Abbot."

"I know who the ringleader is, there is not any sense in you pretending
you are he. What you are is my deputy. If I cannot trust you to carry out an
order, then where am I?"

"I am sorry, Tomás. I will get them off to bed."

"I do not want to see them ten minutes from now. And I want no holy
vigils in cells, do you hear? The holiest thing every man jack of you can do is
turn out fit to work in the morning. Goodnight, now."

"Goodnight and God bless you," Father Walter said.

The Abbot crossed the cloister to a bay where there was an ambry used for
storing wood. He checked the lock which Brother Kevin had reported as
broken. It was broken. He heard them in the cloister walk behind him, but
did not turn around until all was silence. Then he went back into the church.

A dark church: the flickering oil flame of the sanctuary light over the altar,
the gutter of one fat five-day candle beneath the small shrine to Our Lady.
The Abbot genuflected, from habit, as he faced the chancel, then sat down
heavily on one of the benches near Our Lady's shrine. Looked at the candle,
beneath the shrine. Father Donald lit that. Every year, Father Donald's old
mother sent him a little money to buy things like warm gloves and mufflers.
Every year, he spent it in candles lit, before Our Lady's shrine, in time of
trouble. Candles as at Lourdes. "Lourdes is no longer in operation," the
Abbot's visitor had said tonight. Lourdes, that sad and dreadful place; the
Abbot thought of his own visit to Lourdes, remembering the thousands on
thousands of banked candles in the grotto where the Virgin was supposed to
have appeared to an illiterate French girl. With four other priests he had arrived on a pilgrimage excursion and, on the first morning, visited the shrine
to see the myriad crutches and trusses hung on the grotto wall, the medical
bureau with its certifications of 'miraculous' cures, the tawdry religious su-
permarkets, crammed with rosaries and statuettes, the long lines of stretchers
and wheelchairs on which lay the desperate and the ill, the stinking waters of
the 'miraculous' bathing pool. At noon, the Abbot fled to his hotel room,
where, pleading dysentery, he shut himself up, seeing no one, until it was
time for the excursion train to leave. Two days in that room, trying not to
think of what he had seen, trying to say his prayers.

It was not the first time. There had been moments before, sometimes hours,
even days, where, back on Muck or in some church on the mainland, that bad
time had come on him, that time when, staring at the altar, he knew the hell

of the metaphysicians: the hell of those deprived of God. When it came on him, he could not pray, prayers seemed false or without any meaning all. Then his trembling began, that fear and trembling which was a sort of purgatory presaging the true hell to come, the hell of no feeling, that null, that void. A man wearing the habit of a religious, sitting in a building, staring at a table called an altar on which there is a box called a tabernacle and inside the tabernacle there is a chalice with a lid called a ciborium and inside the ciborium are twelve round wafers of unleavened bread made by the Sisters of Knock Convent, Knock, Co. Mayo. That is all that is there. That is all that is in the tabernacle in this building which is said to be the house of God. And the man who sits facing the tabernacle is a man with the apt title of *prelatus nullis,* nobody's prelate, belonging to nobody. Not God's Abbot, although sometimes he tries to say the words; "Our Father Who Art in Heaven," but there is no Father in heaven, His name is not hallowed by these words, His kingdom will not come to he who sits and stares at the tabernacle; who, when he tries to pray, enters null; who, when in it, must remain, from day to day, weeks becoming months, and, sometimes, as after Lourdes, a year.

Lourdes was the worst time: it was not the first and it would not be the last. If he prayed. So the Abbot avoided prayer. One could pretend to a preference for private devotions. One's Mass could be said alone. He no longer read his daily office. As for public prayers, in a community like this there were always others, greedy to lead, Sometimes, one had to say a grace. One said the words, but did not pray. If one did not risk involving God, one did not risk one's peace of mind. He was needed here. He did his work. He did his best. But did not pray. He had not prayed now for, well, he did not want to think. A long time, yes. Some years.

Tonight, he sat in the church, as a man sits in an empty waiting room. After some minutes, footsteps sounded in the nave. The Abbot did not turn around. He, whom he expected, had come.

Father Matthew, six feet five inches tall, the biggest man on Muck, marched up the center aisle of the church with a tread like an armored knight. Master of Novices with no novices to master, an authoritarian figure denied the command he might have graced, in Kilcoole, long ago, he and the Abbot had been seminary classmates, and rivals for the Latin prize. At that time, the world was at war, and Winston Churchill had to deal with a stubborn, righteous, very tall, young French general, who led the Free French Forces under the banner of the Cross of Lorraine. Then, as now, physically and in temperament, Father Matthew resembled General de Gaulle. And then, as now, the Abbot knew what Churchill meant when he said "the cross

I have to bear is the Cross of Lorraine." Unyielding in his scruples, militant in his devotions, Father Matthew, even in his age, was no man to cross. Now, his hoar-white hair and beard making him a ghost in the near-darkness, he marched towards the altar, his lips moving in muttered devotions.

"Father Matthew!"

Father Matthew stopped, as though brought up short by an invisible fence. His great head probed the shadows. "Ah, Father Abbot. And where are the others?"

"What others?"

"The vigil."

"*What* vigil?"

"It is a vigil of devotion to honor Our Lady, offered up for the purpose of preserving the Latin Mass on Mount Coom and here on Muck."

"The other monks are in bed. I sent them to bed."

"And why did you do that, Father Abbot?"

"Because I am in charge here."

Father Matthew sighed, audibly.

"Father Matthew, it is some years now since I have taken it upon myself to rebuke you. The last thing in the world I want is to reopen our disagreements of former days. There is work to be done tomorrow. You will please go to your bed."

"I have made a solemn promise to Our Lady to hold a vigil in her honor this night."

"When you were ordained as an Albanesian monk, you made a solemn promise to God to obey your superiors. Go to bed."

Father Matthew stood immobile, tall as a round stone tower. "May I ask, then, Father Abbot, what is your decision about Mount Coom?"

From his bench, the Abbot looked up coldly at the figure in the aisle. "I am informed by Rome that the Mass is now merely symbolic. Do you understand what I am saying?"

"That is heresy, pure and simple!"

"Why it is heresy, Father Matthew?"

"Because the Mass is the daily miracle of the Catholic Faith. The Mass, in which bread and wine are changed by the priest into the body and blood of Jesus Christ. Without that, what is the Church?"

"Then our belief in Jesus Christ and His Church depends on a belief in miracles. Is that it, Matthew?"

"Of course that is it! St. Augustine said, 'I should not be a Christian but for the miracles.' And Pascal said, 'Had it not been for the miracles, there would have been no sin in not believing in Jesus Christ,' Without a miracle, Christ did not rise from His tomb and ascend into heaven. And without that, there would be no Christian Church!"

"Our visitor brings an order from our Father General. Would you obey that order, Father Matthew, even if that order instructed you to consider the Mass not as a miracle, but, let's say, just a pious ritual?"

"Far be it from me to speak out against my superiors," Father Matthew thundered, "but I am ashamed to hear that talk coming from you—and under God's roof."

"Are you, now?" the Abbot said, suddenly weary. "But, on the other hand, it seems you are not ashamed to *act* against the orders of your superiors. Even to the point of disobedience."

"I do not consider that I have ever been disobedient to our rule."

"You were told there were to be no vigils or special observances to-night."

"I acted according to my conscience, Father Abbot."

"Did you, indeed? And was it your conscience that sent you down to the shore, a while ago, singing hymns to annoy our visitor?"

"I sang a hymn, yes. Is he the sort of heathen who would be offended by the singing of a Catholic hymn?"

"Hold your tongue!" the Abbot shouted. "Go to your cell. Tomorrow, at suppertime, I want you in front of the chapter with an apology for your behavior. I have had enough of you, Matthew, all these years. Insolence and insubordination is the opposite of every vow you took when you became a monk. Are you not ashamed!"

"Father Abbot, I humbly apologise to you, since you ask me to apologise," Father Matthew said. The Abbot, in twenty years, had never spoken to him in this tone of voice. Shaken, but anxious not to show it, Father Matthew turned and genuflected to the altar. Rising, he made the Sign of the Cross. "Since atou order me to retire, I obey your order." Turning, he walked with heavy steps back down the aisle whence he came. The door at the foot of the nave banged shut.

The Abbot sighed. Years ago, he would have knelt and offered up an act of contrition for his unruly temper. But, years ago, he had felt a certainty about so many things. *Aggiornamento,* was that when uncertainty had begun? Changes of Doctrine. Setting oneself up as ultimate authority. Insubordination. He looked at the tabernacle. Insubordination. The beginning of break-down. And, long ago, that righteous prig at Wittenberg nailing his defiance to the church door.

The Abbot rose. He did not genuflect. He went down the side aisle and out into the night.

Part Three

Kinsella woke at seven. In the rectangle of window above his bed, the sky was already light. Gulls rode that sky, kites held by invisible string. When, dressed and shaven, he opened the guest house door and stepped outside, he met the rush of breakers on shore, a long retreating roar of water. Obbligato of gull cries overhead, their harsh, despairing scream seeming to mourn a death. Winds whipped like penny tops, spinning the long grasses this way and that. The sky, immense, hurried, shifted its scenery of ragged clouds. From the cover below, four curraghs were putting out to sea. A fifth rode, far out, waiting for the others, as, bending to their oars, monks seal-wet in black oilskins pushed the curraghs stiffly over fence-like waves, moving towards the deeps. The day's work had begun. Kinsella turned back towards the land. He felt the loneliness of islands, the sense of being shut in here on a barren out-cropping of the edge of Europe, surrounded by this desolation of ocean. Above him now, on a sloping field, four monks, skirts hitched up, spaded heavy shovels full of black earth. From the monastery itself he smelled the delicate scent of turf fires. An old monk, waiting just inside the cloister en-trance, saw Kinsella standing outside the guest house, waved to him and began to hurry towards him along the muddy path beneath the west wall of the monastery. The monk was not the Abbot of Muck.

Came closer: Father Manus, tall, white-haired and boyish, with the wanting-to-please smile of the Irish countryside. "Ah, good morning to you, Father. You slept well, I hope?"

"Yes, thank you."

"Father Abbot asked me to find out if you would like to say Mass this morning? It would be easily arranged, so."

Kinsella said he thought not.

"Then we'll put some breakfast into you, will we?"

"The Abbot was supposed to meet here at eight. Perhaps I should wait?"

"Ah, well, he might be a bit delayed. He told me to look after you. He's trying to get through on the telephone to Galway. We shipped some dulse down there last week and it's still stuck in the railway sheds."

"Dulse?"

"Dried seaweed. It is good eating. They sell it abroad, too. Have you never heard of it?"

"I'm afraid not."

In the refectory, the breakfast plates had already been cleared away. The old kitchen monk put his head around the door. "Two boiled eggs or one?"

"One, thank you."

The second old monk now appeared with a pot of tea and slices of home-made bread.

"Butter, for our visitor. And jam, too," Father Manus said, anxiously.

"I am getting it, so." The old monk sounded cross.

"You see," Father Manus told Kinsella. "We don't eat jam except on special occasions."

"Feast days!" the old monk said, and chortled unexpectedly.

"I will leave you, so, to your breakfast," Father Manus said, withdrawing.

The second old monk approached, bearing a boiled egg on a plate. Kinsella, sensing it was expected, bowed his head and silently said an Ecumen grace. No one said private grace nowadays. Grace was public and used only in mixed Ecumenical groups. The old monk withdrew. The kitchen door shut. Kinsella was alone in the refectory.

It was ten past eight. The Abbot's absence might well be deliberate. *Hartmann, suspended in his back brace, not seeming to be seated, but rather hung in his orthopedic chair, his freckled fingers, knitting, and unknitting on the outer steerer wheels. "Almost always, the techniques were the same. When the bishops had decided to deny our requests, we were made to wait. Conferences were cancelled, interviews delayed. Excuses offered without conviction. You must show them that while you are the Revolution and they are Tradition, the Revolution is the established faith and will prevail. Power is the concept they have always understood. Use it, and use it from the beginning."* If this monastery was organised as others were, the Abbot would know the exact moment the helicopter was due, might even wait almost to the moment of departure to offer some delaying tactic, or bring a compromise offer into play. It would not do. Immediate compliance could be ordered under threat of transfer. An acting Abbot could be installed at once. There was, however, a complication. The Abbot might not know it, but,

under Ecumen Rules, he had the right of appeal to the Amsterdam World Council. He would lose, of course, but the case might drag on for months. And, meantime, he could not be deposed. Such a confrontation was to be avoided. For one thing, it would almost certainly inspire a media circus with the Abbot as martyr. If the Abbot knew these rights of his, Kinsella also knew the catch to them. By Ecumen rules, the Abbot must, before bringing his case to the Amsterdam World Council, first have had a direct confrontation with his Order Superior. That Superior, Father General Humbertus Von Kleist, of the Albanesian Order, Grand Chancellor of the Pontifical Atheneum of St. Vicente, would face the Abbot on his arrival in Rome. The Abbot would need to be strong. Very strong.

But Kinsella felt it would not come to that. There were ways of shading the options, ways of exploring one's adversary's intentions without actually making a committing move.

"Was that egg fresh?"

The Abbot had come into the refectory, without any sound. He stood behind his visitor, thumbs hooked in the broad leather belt in which his rosary was knotted, his face mild in a morning smile.

"Delicious."

"They are our hens. They were not laying last month, but they are usually quite co-operative. I hope you slept well?"

"Yes. And you?"

"I was late to bed," the Abbot said, swinging his leg over the refectory bench and sitting down opposite Kinsella. At once, as though he had been peering through a crack in the door, the old kitchen brother appeared. He set a bowl before the Abbot and poured black tea into it, then went further down the table, wiping the top off with a dishcloth. The Abbot looked at the bowl. "Sometimes I wish my insides were lined with tin, like one of those old tea chests. I have a terrible taste for tea." He looked down the long table. "Brother Pius, get back to your work, if you please!"

"I *am* working," the old brother said, crossly, but stopped wiping off the table, and went back into the kitchen.

"There is great curiosity," the Abbot said. "The walls not only have ears, they have tongues as well. They announced to me at first light this morning that a helicopter is due in here at nine. Is that right?"

"There is supposed to be a bad storm coming up at noon."

"There is a storm," the Abbot said. "I heard it on the wireless. It will be here some time today. That is sure. There will be rain, starting any time now. But that is nothing new. Rain is what we get most of here, you know."

Kinsella nodded, hoping to encourage further talk.

"So you are off," the Abbot said.

"I hope so."

"Yes," the Abbot said. "You are right to go. No sense hanging around. You delivered your letter and that's all that's necessary."

"Not quite all," Kinsella said, very carefully. There was a great silence in the dining hall.

"Brother Pius and Brother Malachy, who is in there with you?" the Abbot shouted, suddenly.

"Nobody at all, Father Abbot."

"Well, get on with your work, then. Let me hear some noise."

There was a sudden rattle of pots and the noise of running water. The Abbot listened to be sure it continued. Then, putting his head to one side in his quizzical fashion, he stared at Kinsella. "Not quite all, you said? Was there something else?"

"You haven't told me what you're going to do. I don't feel I should leave until I know that."

"Do?" the Abbot said. "I will do as I am bid. Father General's letter is perfectly clear. No more Latin Mass here or on Mount Coom. No more private confessions. That is his wish, is it not?"

Kinsella stared; the helicopter on its way now, the Abbot's late arrival, this sudden *volte face,* this suspicious obedience. What was the trap, he asked himself, even as he nodded, yes, yes, indeed, this was what Father General wanted.

"Then it will be done," the Abbot said. "I had no right to take upon myself decisions which belong to my superiors. I have written a letter of apology to Father General, which I would ask you to deliver for me."

"Yes, of course." What was the catch? There must be a catch.

The Abbot took an envelope from the inner pocket of his robe. "I have not sealed it. You may read it, if you wish."

Carefully, Kinsella put the letter, unread, in the inside pocket of his fatigues jacket. "Why?" he said.

"Why, what? Why read the letter?"

"No. Why have you acted as you did?"

"Because it is my duty to obey."

"Yes, but, earlier, you felt that it was your duty to disobey—to retain the old Mass and so on."

The Abbot turned and stared at the kitchen door. "They are very nosey," he said. "Let us go outside. You'll want to be getting your bag, won't you?"

"Yes, of course."

Through the cloister they went, and over to the west entrance. Spits of rain in the wind, as the Abbot and his visitor turned onto the muddy path leading to the guest house. The Abbot took Kinsella's arm. "I did not want to discuss it in front of them," he said, distractedly. "You see, that will be the important part, how I break it to them. Some of them are very devout. They will take it hard. No, it will not be easy at all. To tell you the truth I am a bit nervous about it."

"Perhaps you would like me to break it to them."

"Oh, no, no, no," the Abbot said. "I want you to go. I want you away before they know. Oh, believe me, they would bother the life out of you, if they knew what you and I know now."

Bent his head, and gripped his visitor's arm tightly as they faced into the wind. "You asked why I acted as I did. I do not want you to think it was from an excess of zeal. On the contrary, it was, rather, from a lack of it. However, that's neither here nor there, is it? That is of no interest to anyone but me."

"It interests me," Kinsella said.

"I am not a holy man," the Abbot said. "Far from it. I would not like to fly under false colors. There are some holy men here, I suppose. On Muck, I mean. But I am not one of them. I have become a very secular man. Do you know what I mean?"

"I don't think I do."

"I am a sort of foreman here, a sort of manager. It is not a lot different from a secular job. The monks work hard and my job is to keep them together and see that they make a go of it. It's a simple life, here. Little jokes, little triumphs, little disasters. We're like a bunch of children, we pass the days as if we had an endless supply of them. It's only when someone like yourself comes along that we ask ourselves what are we here for. What good do we do?"

The Abbot stopped outside the guest house door. He turned the key and pushed the door open. "Ah, you are a tidy man. Bag all packed. You travel light. It is the best way. I'll take your bag."

"No, please."

"Very well, so. Let us go along now to the field. It is nearly nine. I want to get you off, you see, and then I have to face up to it. Face the music. It is all in how you tell them. The thing about being in charge is, you must be firm. As Father General is firm. And yourself. What would you have done if I had said I wouldn't follow orders?"

Kinsella laughed but did not speak.

"You are right, better not ask. By the way, what do you want me to say to the press and the telly people if they call up here?"

"Refer all inquiries to me. James Kinsella, Ecumenical Center Information Office, Amsterdam."

"I will do that," the Abbot said. "Let us cut across the field. Do you see them up there, waiting?"

Ahead, in the field where Kinsella landed yesterday, some ten or fifteen monks were gathered, looking about them, oblivious to the rain, scanning the skies in every direction. "They should be at their work," the Abbot said. "Of course they will all be after me, the minute you go. By the way, if they ask you something, do not answer. Let me deal with them."

As they came up the field, the monks turned to look at them. At that moment, above, the sound of an engine. "Your machine is on the way," the Abbot said, looking up.

"I don't see it."

"I do. It is over there. Here he comes. Right on the dot."

Three monks detached themselves from the larger group. The oldest of them, very tall, with white hair and beard, stood straight in the Abbot's path. "Do you have any news for us, Father Abbot?"

"Are the horses brought up from that lower field to take the load of fertiliser over to Doran's?"

"Yes, they are. May I ask our visitor a question?"

"You may not!" the Abbot said. "Let us pass."

Reluctant, the tall monk drew aside. The Abbot, still gripping his visitor's arm, hurried him on. "A holy man that," he said. "But a tiresome one."

"You really *are* expecting trouble."

"Not trouble, no. It is just difficult. Ah! There he comes. The frumious bandersnatch."

Engine noise made all speech impossible until the helicopter had landed and throttled back its motor. "You have my letter, have you?"

"Yes, I have."

"Well, safe home to Rome. And good luck to you, Father Kinsella."

"Good luck to you, sir."

The rain was heavy now as the pilot slid open the plexiglass door. Kinsella shook hands with his host, then, bending low, ran to the machine. The pilot reached out to pull him up. The door shut. The monks, in a ragged circle, seemed to press close. But, at that point the helicopter rose, lurched forward and went out to sea.

Kinsella looked down. The Abbot, standing alone, waved, waved. The other monks bunched in a cluster, stared up at the helicopter as it passed over the abbey tower, out to that splendour of sea. Kinsella saw the old man, a tiny figure on the promontory of land, turn and walk back towards the monastery gate. The monks, moving as in a pack, followed him in.

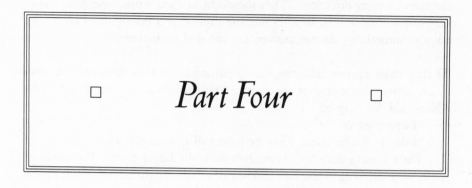

Part Four

Heard their shuffling feet, their voices, the whisperings as in church in the moment of talk at the end of the silence of a retreat, the mutterings increasing until, although he knew they were not more than twenty monks, they sounded as he imagined a mob might sound: knowing those who were and were not here, knowing that eight fishermen who always had the least to say in community disputes were out now in their curraghs, serving the sea, a master hard as eternity, but the land was a hard master too, yet all the monks from the farm were here, Terence's crew and Daniel's, who worked packing dulse and gathering kelp, yes, there were not more than nine men missing in the whole community, it would be what happened now that would decide it. What I say now. What I say to them now.

"Father Abbot?"

He turned in the cloister, saw all of them crowding in behind the triumvirate; Matthew, Manus, Walter. It was Walter who had called him.

"Yes, Father Walter?"

"Can you tell us, now? The man is gone."

Waited till they were all in, lined up in a long queue in the cloister walk. "Yes, I can tell you now. Father General, in Rome, has written me a letter of instruction. It will be obeyed. From now on, the new Mass will be said in English, here and at Cahirciveen. The altars will conform with liturgical changes and will face the congregation. There will be no further private confessions, except in the very special circumstances prescribed, where the nature of the confession warrants private consultation. That is all. We have our orders and it is up to all of us to carry them out to the very best of our ability. I am sure we will do that, won't we?"

He did not look at Matthew, or at Manus, but kept his eyes moving between Father Donald, who had a breakdown last year and was subject to sudden tears and Brother Kevin, whose hysteria was tight, reined in uncertain check. Something of that nature was what he feared, but the thing to do now was be firm, disperse them, reassert the rule of obedience. "And the first thing we will do," he said, attempting a smile, "is every man jack get back to work. That is all. Now, off you go."

"That is not all!" Father Matthew, angry as Isaiah, pointing an accusatory finger, rearing up in his great height. "Why have you not told the community, Father Abbot, what you told to me last night?"

"Last night I told you to go to bed. Now, I tell you to go to work." The laughter he had wanted, flickered, then stilled.

"You also told me that we are to consider the Mass from now on, not as a miracle, but as a 'pious ritual,' I believe you said."

"That is correct."

"How can a thing be a miracle one day and not a miracle the next day?"

"Maybe you are a greater theologian than the Pope or the Vatican Council, Father Matthew. I am not. I am a monk and I do as I am bid."

"No, no, no, no!" As the Abbot had feared, Father Donald had come to tears. "That is sacrilege, that is blasphemy. No, no, no, I can't be hearing that, no, no!"

The Abbot put his arm comfortingly on Father Donald's shoulders. "Now, Donald," the Abbot said. "You are not yourself, you mustn't be getting excited like this. Come along, everybody. Let's get to work."

"And *I* will not be put off like that," Father Matthew shouted. "I will not be ordered to believe something which I do not believe."

"No one can order belief," the Abbot said. "It is a gift from God." But even as he said this, said the only truth left to him, he saw in these faces that he was failing, that he was losing them, that he must do something he had never done, give something he had never given in these, his years as their Abbot. What had kept him in fear since Lourdes, must now be faced. What he feared most to do must be done. And if, in doing it, I enter null and never return, amen. My time has come.

Matthew, bent on trouble, began again. "You can all see what is being proposed here. It is a denial of everything the Mass stands for."

The Abbot held up his hands, commanding silence. There was silence. He turned and held open the door which led into the nave. "Please. Let us go into the church."

Stood, holding the door for them, as they moved past him, his eyes on their faces, these faces he knew better than his own, seeing every shade of wavering, from confusion, to doubt, to anger at him, to fear, to Father Donald's dangerous tears and Brother Kevin's hysterics, tight on snaffle, a horse ready to bolt. He entered behind them and shut the door. Moved past them in the aisle, going up into the great vault of the nave, moving in that silence, in the grey light of this place where he had spent the longest years of his life, this place where his body would lie, this place he feared most. He entered the chancel. He faced the altar.

"A miracle," he told them, "is when God is there in the tabernacle."

"But you said the opposite, you said that the sacrifice of the Mass is just ritual, that bread and wine remain bread and wine, that there are no miracles!"

Matthew, thundering: righteous, wronged. The Abbot, his back to all of them, heard their stiff intake of breath, the fear of their lives at these words, said in this place. He stared at the golden door of the tabernacle. His fear came. "Prayer is the only miracle," he said. "We pray. If our words become prayer, God will come."

Slowly, with the painful stiffness of age, he went down heavily on one knee, then on both. Knelt in the center of the aisle, facing the altar, the soles of his heavy farm boots showing from the hem of his robe. He trembled. He shut his eyes. "Let us pray."

He bent his head. "Our Father, Who art in Heaven," he said. His trembling increased. He entered null. He would never come back. In null.

He heard them kneel. "Our Father, Who art in Heaven." Relieved, their voices echoed his.

"Hallowed be Thy Name," the Abbot said.

"Hallowed be Thy Name."

WILFRID SHEED

The
Blacking Factory

AUTHOR'S NOTE

When Charles Dickens was twelve years old, he was abruptly removed from school and put to work in a blacking factory. The effect of this episode was such that he mentioned it to no one for twenty years and only broke down when somebody recognized him from those days and somebody else (his biographer, John Forster) asked him about it. In his subsequent account, Dickens wrote: "I have no idea how long it lasted; whether for a year or much more or less." In fact, it lasted for less than six months.

PROLOGUE

James Bannister III owns and operates two radio stations out of Salome, California, not far from Los Angeles. His audience consists mostly of old people who sit in the kitchen all day, drinking coffee and fussing with the dials. Ordinary radios do not seem to pick up these pinpoints of sound, the needle has to know its way; and even then it takes a deal of twiddling by a practiced hand to complete the mission.

Bannister talks on each of these stations for upwards of two hours a day. He is obviously an educated man and he knows that to many people small radio stations are a joke, like soapboxes. He also happens to believe in them. He says that radio listeners, for all their crotchets, are the only real listeners left, and he has the mail to prove it. Ardent, painstaking mail, wobbling above and below the lines, yet more carefully wrought, more soberly committed than anything in the whole lives of the TV watchers. "These are better people," he says simply. "Probably no less intelligent, and better, more serious."

Well, nobody wants to argue with Bannister, about that or anything else. He is a tireless arguer, fast on his feet and logical as a metronome. Every now and then, a fresh guest is gound up on his radio show—usually a guest who comes on believing that Bannister's politics are naïve. So unless you are very sure of yourself and very long-winded, you tend to concede him his point, along with his eyrie on the radio dial.

When not arguing, Bannister is on the shy side, given to sudden bursts of wit which sound harsher than they are because of his explosive delivery. At parties he is a notorious examiner of book jackets and stray magazines, if there are any about. Oddly enough he goes to a lot of parties, has never been known to turn down an invitation in fact, and has arrived at more than one with a high temperature and streaming eyes. He stands around patiently as if it were a church service, and is always among the last to leave.

He lives by himself in an old-fashioned apartment on the edge of town, keeping in excellent shape, with isometric exercises and a landlocked rowing machine. There is no visible girl friend, and you can never find an ashtray. His friendships tend to be decided for him on political lines, which he professes to deplore. He says that liberals are the intolerant ones—he likes them but they don't like him. He says he is sick of labels anyway.

The nastiest thing you can say about Bannister is that he has a slight English accent. (It all sounds the same in Salome, anyway.) This would be guaranteed to nettle Jim because he is actually the last of the great Anglophobes. It is his abiding belief that England has sold its soul in some particularly loathsome deal, and that Americans should keep clear of the stinking remains. "There is something sick there," he says. And again: "We're better *people* than they are."

His hatred of England flirts with being a fixation. When he gets within sniffing range of things British his voice ripens like a passion fruit. "Beatles," he'll say. "They're sending us their *beatles* now. Next they'll be sending us their maggots and their worms." "Latest word from the Funeral Home. Her Majesty gave an address today to the Royal Society of Perverts and Freeloaders. A gangrenous occasion, it was generally agreed" . . . Someone wrote in recently to say that the Redcoats, after all, were still some distance from Salome, and Bannister made a big thing of this on the air, saying that, what with the prime minister's hand in your pocket, who needed Redcoats—or perhaps the Redcoats were some new singing group? Robbing us blind that way. All in all, you have to think twice before you send a joke to Bannister.

Offstage, he is notable for a dogged sense of privacy. No matter how well you get to know him, he will not discuss his interior affairs with you. Nor does he care to hear *your* revelations. He seems to feel that there is something corrupt about all this self-exposure. Something dangerous to the Republic.

What is known is that he is the son of James Bannister II, the big New York real-estate man. Bannister II is a well-known ladies'-man, still active in his upper sixties: three times married and divorced, after a slow start (Hal Chester at the *Salome Sentinel* has the dates). The first Mrs. Bannister, Jim's mother, is rumored to spend most of her time in sanatoriums on some unspecified charge. If Bannister II has other children, the news hasn't reached Salome.

Jim never refers to either parent, but it is generally assumed that his America-first politics are not unpleasing to his father. At any rate, Bannister II is suspected of putting up some of the money for the radio stations. Mrs. Bannister is known only by her picture on Jim's piano, a curiously misty, old-fashioned one that looks as if it was taken before the First World War. Hal Chester's wife Clara believes that part of Jim still wanders the sanatoriums with his mother—but Clara Chester is another problem.

Jim Bannister's future is as clouded as his past. It seems unlikely that a man of his gifts will be content to keep his operation so small indefinitely. The local liberals consider him a real menace. They say that he is amassing contributions from the bless-you-son crowd and that he will break out any day now in a whole rash of radio stations, swamping the country in Bannister-style fascism. The local conservatives feel that there would be more chance of this (or its more favorably phrased equivalent) if he got off England for a while and turned his mind to local interests.

As a more or less liberal and a more or less friend, Hal Chester of the *Sentinel* spends a good deal of time defending Jim. He is not your usual crank, says Chester. He is a decent man, who deserves a hearing. Chester's friends say, "Nuts to you, Hal—that's the kind of thing people used to say about Mussolini! ... Suppose next you're going to say that he loves children." Chester: "Well, as a matter of fact ..." As one of the few people in Salome who is relatively unsolved, Jim comes in for a good deal of discussion. Most of it to little purpose.

So there he is, still young (some place in the late thirties by the look of him), rich, "nice"-looking, an uncertain quantity whose importance is what you make it. Some people feel he has the makings of greatness. Some who peg him a little lower than that are still happy to find a facsimile of a rational man on the right—compared with some of the others, Jim is a relatively civilizing influence, who helps to keep the yahoos in line. And still others say that's the most dangerous kind, the plausible kind. It is generally agreed that his broadcasts have been getting a little strident lately, but this can partly be put down to the medium. Jim is quite willing to discuss the phenomenon: he says that radio broadcasting has some of the effects of solitary confinement. He is manifestly not a common or garden nut.

Hear him on that for a moment: "This morning I got a letter from a man purporting to be a psychiatrist, offering me a free analysis. Very kind of him, I must say. A new concept in health service. He said that he was fascinated by the right-wing syndrome ... Now why do you suppose my learned friend has discovered a right-wing syndrome, but no left-wing syndrome? Could one of his eyes be missing? Why analyze me when he might be analyzing a big man like Walter Lippmann?" ... Well, maybe it's the setting. Lippmann appears in serious-looking newspapers, whereas you usually catch Bannister on your Aunt Minnie's baling-wire set right after Jack Mererdith's Hour of Faith or Doctor Price's attack on the cereal companies. There is a whirring and whining along the dial as Auntie gropes for inspiration; and the sound of bad acoustics in ramshackle studios. And finally Jim comes on.

"In this country," he might be saying, "and especially in the *West* of this country, Christendom has been given a second chance. People talk about Europe's wonderful postwar recovery, but to me this is no more than the last twitch of a corpse. No, I'm not talking about sex and I'm not talking about loose living. I'm talking about things like corruption of the heart; cynicism and snobbery and hypocrisy. I don't mind a girl in a bikini. But I don't want to hear that it's the Baroness Rotternburg. And I certainly don't want to hear that it's her *brother*. You have to apologize for even caring about these things any more. In the East, you are looked on as some kind of a yokel with straws in his hair. Yet what is more important than the quality of our national life? A little radio station in California may not be the ideal place to say it. But where else *can* you say it these days? Without being laughed at?"

Put like that, it is hard to disagree with. He takes you off guard by being literate. Bannister wins the arguments and loses the wars.

"The big Eastern magazines like to shed a tear now and then for the national morality. And you'll find that they usually shed it right next to a story about the latest pansy singing rage from England, or the latest trollop from Paris. You know, the one with the million-dollar death wish. What do they think they're doing? What do they think national morality is all about? ... Let me tell you some of the things I think it's about. I think it's the way we talk to each other in the street, the things we laugh at: I think it is a quality of heart. We're not ready for decadence yet. We're not ready for old families with chinless children, or limp wrists, or boys who look like girls ... Don't forget, there was a sweetness in this country once. There was joy in being a boy or girl in America at one time. You say to me, that's old-fashioned, and I can only say to you, is that bad? Is that really so terrible? It worked once. We liked it. Why this itch to change? Europe has changed and changed again. You can go over there if you like and see what change does for you. Look at the new houses outside Rome. Made of tin, chewing gum and adultery. They won't last as long as the Forum or the Coliseum. You can look at the stately homes of England. For fifty cents any pansy with hair down to his waist and a mind like a sewer can go and giggle at the past . . . I don't say we should have no change at all. But let us make our *own* changes. We're young. We don't need a senile old continent to show us how to do it. We don't have to learn tricks from a lecherous old duffer who has to find ways to stimulate his appetites"—your aunt purses her lips; but it is probably no better than those people deserve—"a clown with a painted face, a harlot that we fled four hundred years ago, and who is just beginning to catch up with us."

You listen to the country sounds through the window and the honest clack of the kitchen clock, and you think, yes, there is a sweetness here. Bannister may have something at that. It's silly prejudice not to give him a hearing: just because he talks at crank's length on a crank's medium.

"If I may be personal for a moment. You grow up in this country loving certain things. And you, as I say, grow up and people tell you, oh all that has changed—that was the twenties, or the thirties, or the war years, or the postwar years. You look around for the thing that you loved and it's gone.

"And in its place, what do you find? Some verminous import, some hybrid. Pop art—to show that we too can learn to hate beauty and life. 'Camp,' whatever that is. The 'jet set,' 'The Theatre of the Absurd.' I won't go through the whole list for you. You can get it from *Life* or *The Saturday Evening Post.*

"Anyway, when *I* grew up, I found I wasn't ready for this new country, this Lilliput. I wanted the thing I had loved, the freshness and joy of a young country, my country. And I came out here to the West. And here I stay."

And so on. At the end of it—after hearing him denounce cynicism and snobbery in that slightly affected accent (which he would probably give an arm to get rid of)—you can't help remembering that many country people consider him slightly Europeanized himself, hardly better than a limey. They may agree with him wholeheartedly, but there is a stubborn strain of mistrust—as if they would rather hear this stuff from one of their own. And that is, finally, the thing that may limit his effectiveness, and keep him, for all his gifts, in the minor leagues.

Hal Chester has been curious about Jim for some time, hoping some day to write a depth story for the paper, and he has done all the routine scratching around, trying to discover what makes Bannister tick. He managed to dig out an old profile of Jim's father in *The New Yorker* and from this morass of trivia was able to discover that Bannister II was, and presumably still is, a stout man with a long list of clubs, a chairman of many boards and a somewhat flashy dresser. Also, a self-made man, working off a middle-class base. The "II" after his name seems to be an afterthought. He made his big killing in the postwar boom—before that, he was a small, undistinguished operator in the New England area. Jim was mentioned only in passing, but whether this casualness was *The New Yorker's* or Mr. Bannister's, Hal could not make out.

Interestingly, Bannister II was quoted as taking no special interest in politics, either at home or abroad. Perhaps his son has been serving as his mouthpiece in this respect. The elder Bannister gave the investigator an over-all impression of shrewdness very well masked, clothed, as the writer put it, in coarse loud broadcloth. "I have never tried to run my son's life," was the only quote pertaining to Jim.

None of this has proved very helpful, at least to an amateur gumshoe like Hal Chester. Mr. Bannister II looks as if he might be a red herring alto-gether. Jim more or less follows the right-wing line on economics, which could be construed as a gesture to the old man, possibly even as part payment for the radio stations; but economic theory plays a comparatively small role in his rhetoric. He talks occasionally about the old village store balancing its books, etc., but this is filler material: he goes on about the smell of sawdust and the row of patent medicines and the salty old fellow bent over his ledger (*"balancing his books,* you'll notice")but has no time for statistics or economic *minutiae.*

Some people, including conservatives, say this is just talk anyway, that Bannister never saw a store like that in his life, "not where he came from." But some people will say anything to malign Bannister. Every time he carves up an opponent, they feel personally threatened, even if they happen to be on his side. And for all his charm, and his almost excessive politeness, there is this foreign thing about him that nags them. What does he want, what is he doing here? Although Jim has explained over and over that he is here because he believes in the West, etc., a lot of folk remain unconvinced. It doesn't sound like their idea of a reason at all.

Jim does seem to take this Western business quite seriously. He comes to Chester's office at least once a week (at first Hal had to go after him, but that has changed) and asks questions about local history, crop reports, real-estate developments ... He is unfailingly courteous, although, like other public speakers, not unfailingly attentive. Clara Chester reckons he thinks he ought to know this stuff, just as he thinks he ought to go to parties—but again, that's a typical Clara Chester opinion. In fact, he does use a good deal of Hal's lint-picking as flavoring matter for his broadcasts.

On evenings when he isn't working or socializing, he sometimes plays chess with Hal. Clara Chester, doubled up with theories and suspicions, watches him closely for signs of insanity. Her husband tries to use their re-laxed moments to ferret information. "What have you got against England?" he will ask casually. Jim shrugs, moves his pawn, suddenly asks for more cof-fee. Clara starts up as if from a trance: she has been staring at Jim for the last twenty minutes, baffled by his apparent normality.

Occasionally, Hal returns the calls. Jim's apartment is scrupulously neat, decorated with early American prints and lined with books on the Civil War, all as private and sealed off as himself. He does not drink alcohol, but offers some to his guest. They sit. Jim's voice is a little higher than it is on the airwaves. By God, it *does* sound English: Chester has a sudden crazy idea that it is meant to; that in some subterranean part of his mind Jim likes to be taken for an Englishman. This probably means that Hal has been talking to Clara too much lately. To change the subject he says, "I see you shaved your mustache, Jim." "Yes, I noticed it was the only one in Salome." "It looked, you'll pardon the expression, British?" "Yes, I guess it does out here. Although mustaches occur pretty frequently in American history, you'll find." Jim has an almost opulent sense of humor about himself. He pursues the joke like a terrier. "American mustaches have played their part on the world scene. Clark Gable's mustache, of course, was one of the great mustaches of all time. And Teddy Roosevelt, *there* was a mustache for you". . . . there is no fire and brimstone in these conversations, just rather conscientious small-talk. He is impenetrably unpretentious about his work, if it happens to come up. "These things have to be said by someone," he explains. "And I seem to be the one." This from the man who is feared by the local liberals.

As Jim closes the ledger on mustaches, Hal feels unaccountably a kind of wistfulness for his own past—an attic smelling of fresh laundry—and he thanks Jim for it. In Hal's private book Jim at his best is one of the pleasantest companions he knows: certainly the pleasantest he has ever encountered on the nut-wing of the far right, where the conversation usually proceeds (so Hal believes) in grunts. He believes that Jim is a gentleman.

Yet for all his private charm, he can be a tiger on the Salome airwaves; only recently he derided the mayor, an alleged friend, in language that ripped and hissed like a cat. And perhaps he *is* getting more ambitious. There is talk of a campaign for Congress. Of a newspaper merger. Of more radio stations. This may be just the liberals up to their old tricks, frightening themselves, but Frank Strange at the bank says, listen to his voice. It's more eager than it used to be. He's about to make his move.

Jim is most comfortable talking in lengthy set-pieces, and when you have had enough of these you leave. His farewells are the most excessively polite things he does. It occurs to Hal on the way out that Bannister may be trying to acquire political charm, which has an artificial effect at first on anybody, like a set of false teeth. Whatever it is, it has not lost Jim any fans. If anything, his audience is growing. And some of the local rich people have begun to take him up seriously, inviting him out for weekends, etc. God knows what he will be like in twenty years' time if he keeps this up.

The only really revealing thing that Hal Chester has on Jim is something that came out unexpectedly on a recent broadcast. Jim was interviewing a genuine Englishman who was passing through on a lecture tour, a novelist called Walters. Walters sounded just like the kind of arrogant, petty fellow who likes to tangle with small-town celebrities and remind them of their place. It was as if England itself had turned up, demanding an explanation. But Jim was totally unflustered by this. "I don't know why you pick on poor Europe. It seems to me quite the other way—that we are the simple wholesome people who have been corrupted by *you*."

"Yes," said Jim. "I know that argument. It's the conventional one, isn't it? Of course, I don't like the things we've sent you very much. But they come back much worse, don't they? Rock 'n' roll, for instance, was simply country music, until you got hold of it . . ."

"Oh, come now, Mr. er . . . Bannister—you're not going to blame us for *rock 'n' roll,* are you? This is really too much. England has been blamed for a number of things in her time, but really . . ."

Jim laughed good-naturedly. For a moment Hal almost forgot which of them was which. "It isn't just rock 'n' roll, of course," he said. "That was just a minor example. I'm talking about cultural decadence . . ."

"You mean the New York School of painting?"

"And amorality and cynicism and exploitation."

"You mean Hollywood. No, I'm sorry. Do go on."

"No, I don't mean Hollywood. A harmless, rather touching aberration, that's all Hollywood is or ever was—and long gone to its reward, you'll find if you keep up with these things. I'm told that the nastiest thing in Hollywood is the English colony, but I'm not talking about that either. No—I mean the English press, which is fifty times meaner and dirtier and more cynical than Hollywood ever was. I mean mods and rockers and sub-debs. The fungus that seems to accumulate on every fashion over there."

There was a pause. And then the condescending diagnosis. "Do you know what the trouble with you is, Bannister? I expect that some Englishman was beastly to you, at an impressionable age. We can be beastly, I don't deny it. It makes up for not having power, I suppose: And I've heard that some victims of English beastliness never recover from it."

"It isn't that simple," said Jim. There was a sudden harsh quality in his voice, as if he had been waiting for this man for years. "Apart from anything else, you people are not that effective. You think you've withered someone with an insult and he hasn't even understood what you've said."

"Oh? Then why do you hate England? If it isn't impolite of an Englishman to ask?"

Jim sounded almost surprised. "I don't hate England, Mr. Walters. I love it."

Fruitiest astonishment. "Excuse me—perhaps I'm on the wrong program? I hadn't gathered that at all. You *love* England, you say?"

"I don't love what it's become of course. And I don't want anything like that to happen here. But England itself . . ."

"I see. And how do you detach England itself from what England has become? You must be an extraordinarily subtle judge."

"I know England."

"Oh, indeed. Our films, I suppose. Our wonderful police."

"I was at school there."

"You were?" Lip-licking relish. "How extraordinarily interesting. How long, may I ask?"

"Long enough."

"Yes, but exactly *how* long?"

"One term and a bit, actually."

"I see." Sound of nodding. "What an acute boy you must have been. And what was the school, pray tell, that gave you this, mer-mer, microcosm of England?"

"Sopworth College."

"*No!* Not Sopworth College. I don't believe it." Sounds of gurgling amusement. Bannister is *right* about these people. "Well, of course. That explains everything! Sopworth College."

"What do you mean by that, Mr. Walters?"

"Well, of all the medieval institutions—no, *pre*-medieval institutions— Dark Ages institutions—no, *pre*-Dark Ages institutions—pre-Druidic, pre- Pleistocene, pre-creation . . . I hold no brief for any of the older public schools, but even among those—Sopworth *College,* oh dear, oh dear."

"Come now, Mr. Walters. Pull yourself together. Pull your rhetoric together, at least." Bannister sounded peeved, as if he cared about his old school.

"I exaggerate, of course. But you can't judge England by Sopworth College, old chap, honestly you can't. There's nothing else like it. I mean of all the creaking, middle-class, snobbish, imitation, mer-mer, pseudo . . . and of course I suppose you were there during the scruffy time just after the war. You poor blighter. You really have all my sympathy. On behalf of Her Majesty's government I should like to extend . . . Had I but world enough and time, I daresay . . ."

"It isn't that simple," said Jim in a bemused voice. "There are other things."

The Englishman had to rush and catch a boring plane after that, and the subject has not been referred to since on the Bannister programs. Hal keeps meaning to bring it up, but cannot quite bring himself to. Other people must feel the same way. There is something a little indecent about it, perhaps.

□ **I** □

In the spring of 1946 James Bannister III moved across the ocean to England, with all his possessions, including a baseball glove, a pair of ice skates and a Bix Beiderbecke record that got broken in transit. It had been a high-speed decision, which hit Jimmy so sharply that he didn't feel a thing at first: a swirl of arrangements, passport photos, purchase of suitcase, urgent trips downtown, several light showers of good wishes, and suddenly he and his father were up in the air talking to a stewardess and down again, in a gray, quiet country, eating water-cress sandwiches.

When Jimmy came to, he found his father having an exploratory interview with a cadaverous school official three days before term started. Consciousness came back in cautious waves. Jimmy became seriously aware of his clothes, item by item, of the sports coat with the comb sticking out of the breast pocket, of the two-tone shoes; the room began to fill up with real furniture—a leather armchair which creaked every time his father leaned forward to make a point, a hardwood chair for himself—and not that synthetic airplane stuff; and the official had thickness, although not much. The people Jimmy had seen in motion had no thickness at all. The official sat with the light behind him, forming a stark outline, like an old turkey, against the black bars on his window.

For the moment Jimmy was tied up with these perceptions and not too attentive to the talk. The official turned out to be the headmaster: naturally enough, but Jimmy hadn't grasped this at first, in his travel bemusement.

"Back home, Jimmy was asking if he could start using the car next year," Mr. Bannister said. "So I thought it was high time I brought him over here." Jimmy noted a false heartiness about his father, sitting there in his gray worsteds. Travel had unhinged the two of them.

The headmaster nodded. "The English boy matures somewhat more slowly than his American counterpart." His fingertips drummed viciously at each other. His voice was the wildest thing Jimmy had ever heard.

"Well, youth is our most precious possession, isn't it? No sense growing up before we have to."

"Quite," said the headmaster. Jimmy had an idea that this was probably the wrong way to talk to this man. But the right way might take some finding.

"Of course intellectually and culturally British boys are streets ahead of ours," Mr. Bannister said desperately, with a look of stark appeal at both of them.

"It's very kind of you to say so."

"Jimmy here is bright enough, but he could use some discipline. Don't be afraid to give him plenty of work."

Oh, this was ridiculous. Jimmy gazed at the window bars. Had anyone ever broken out of this place? he wondered. Or did the warden shoot them all down? The headmaster appeared to be smiling. "I think the boy will find his time sufficiently occupied."

Mr. Bannister talked with his son for a few minutes in the hall outside, in the same slightly hysterical way. "First-rate man that. Fine mind." He seemed to be trying to make a sale. "The British education is the finest in the world." Jimmy hoped his father would feel better when he got back to the hotel, or wherever he was going next.

They walked to the end of the quadrangle, where the hired car was waiting, and Mr. Bannister rather unexpectedly shook hands. Jimmy could not remember having touched his father's hand before. It had a pulpy feel to it. His father announced he was taking the next train back to London and clambered into the car, leaving Jimmy rather emphatically alone. As if some drawbridge had been retracted three thousand miles.

As he reviewed the data, Jimmy realized that in his fifteen and a half years he had had only a modest experience of being alone at all. He had been alone on a train to Florida two months ago, squatting among the GI's and their duffel bags, envying them their recent war. And he had been alone in a nightclub just last week with his friend Forrest Tuckerman trying to con the management into serving them rye and ginger ale. And of course he had been alone many times in the apartment while his father was out on his appointments. But this was aloneness on a new scale.

The best thing to do was to get moving. He decided to hang a left from the front door. The school was virtually deserted, and his feet crashed like wrecking balls as he moved off down a long, narrow hallway. "We are now in the death house in Sing Sing," he said, testing the echo. The walls were bare, except for an infinity of black doors with white numbers on them. He opened one of these at random and peeked in: desks and a blackboard facing each other in grim showdown. "This place spooks me, spooks me," he and the corridor said.

"Is that you, Bannister?" The headmaster's thin face and shining spectacles swiveted around the door at him. What was he doing in there? Would he have been behind any door that Jimmy happened to open? He spoke from the back of his long throat. An hour before, Jimmy had been introduced by his first name. But now it was the coldest of "Bannister's."

"I guess so."

"I guess so, sir."

"I guess so, sir."

"Getting the hang of things, are you?"

"Uh-huh."

"Did you speak?"

"Er—I mean yes sir, I am." The headmaster was making notations in a small black book. Numbering the desks, it looked like. There seemed no point in staying for this.

Out of doors all was gray and windy. But a change from the clammy old building. Jimmy rambled doggedly, to keep thinking at bay. Over cricket pitches, mildly wondering what the shaved parts in the middle were for (stomach operations, it looked like), past squash courts, into a genuine garden. The grass was dazzling, a shade of green he had never seen before.

He stepped over a flower bed as carefully as he could to avoid walking all the way round.

"Where are you going, you bloody young clot?"

A beefy boy in shorts (Jim didn't believe any of this for a moment) was lying on his stomach against a bank of tulips, clutching a pair of binoculars. He was of a shape Jimmy had never seen before.

"No place special. Just looking around."

"Well, you're not supposed to trample on the flower beds, like a bloody great elephant, and you're not supposed to go into the woods like a blasted young nymph. Otherwise feel free to come and go as you please." The boy drew a tired breath. "Until, that is to say, term time—at which point this becomes the master's garden and a prefect with a flaming sword and a busby hat stands guard over it. Any more questions?"

"No, your fatness," said Jimmy, whipping out a phrase Sam Pieper had once used on him, in his mysterious chubby period two years ago.

"And don't, I beseech you, try sarcasm. Your mouth is the wrong shape for it." Jimmy was puzzled: how did you answer a line like that? He groped for a riposte.

"Who are you, anyway?" He shot back finally.

"I just happen to be a prefect, that's *all*. Now buzz off and don't be tiresome."

"A prefect? Is that good?"

"Actually quite tremendous. Yes, oh indeed yes. If you fancy power, in ungovernable quantities."

"What can you do?"

"Just about anything, actually. What house are you in?"

"I don't know."

"What do you mean you don't know? Are you in Frisby, Upjohn, Cornwallis, or Farnsworth? Didn't Dr. Rabelais mumble anything to you about houses?"

"Who's Dr. Rabelais?" said Jimmy.

"Oh my God, impenetrable ignorance. Where does one begin?" He shook his head until the jowls rattled. "Buzz off now; be a *nice* little intellectual disaster area, won't you? Oh—and try to do something about that mouth, will you?"

"I don't have to take that stuff from you," said Jimmy.

"Oh, indeed you do, yes," said the fat boy, and he raised his binoculars to indicate dismissal. I could break him in two, thought Jimmy—but there was probably a rule against it. Some drops shook loose from the dark sky, and Jimmy returned to the gray building with his shoulders hunched, confused by the prevailing aimlessness and sorry his father had hurried off so quickly. He would have to find out from somebody whether he really had to take stuff from this guy. It seemed like a pretty obscene arrangement.

There were twelve boys in the dining hall that evening, bunched at the end of a long hardwood table: a table that cried out for a penknife. The meal was so bad that it had to be a mistake. Nobody could have planned all those potatoes. The fat boy sat at the far end chewing angrily.

"Who's that guy?" whispered Jimmy to a pale fellow next to him.

"That's the 'Brute,' otherwise known as 'Birdseed' and the 'Yellow-chested thrippet.' You have a fairly wide choice."

"Has he got a real name too? Or haven't they gotten around to that?"

"Wagstaff—funny enough by itself, you might say. But we leave nothing alone around here, all must be embroidered. Fuss, fuss, fuss."

"I found him lying on his gut in the flower bed. Could that be right?"

"Yes, that's quite normal in his case. He comes here early every term to glare at the birds. Poor little devils. You're American, I take it."

"Yes. Listen— He says he's a prefect. What does that mean?"

"It means he can flail you from morning to night, if he feels like it, with the headmaster's undisguised approval. This is a thoroughly medieval country, you understand. Light years behind the civilized world."

"And I can't flail him back?"

"Of course not. That would be anarchy, dash it."

"And is Wagstaff one of the worst?"

"Well, one doesn't call a man the 'Brute' for nothing I suppose. But he's not brawny enough to be the worst. The 'Basher' in Cornwallis, now, is a true gorilla, and not one of your impostors," said the pale boy. "I have scars that light up at night from the Basher." He didn't seem to want to talk any more, and Jimmy finished his starchy meal in silence.

That night Jimmy slept alone in a barracks-like dormitory belonging to Frisby house. The sheets were like cold sandpaper, and a harsh wind raked him all night. It was a comedown from his father's apartment on Eighty-fourth Street but no doubt it was better than the Army. Jimmy's thoughts had been preying much on the Army for the last year. In the morning, Wagstaff came and shook him awake and went away without a word. He appeared to be fairly boiling with anger and resentment: as if waking Jimmy was the last straw.

After the quietest of breakfasts, Jimmy went for yet another squishy walk on the grounds. He got as far as the woods, and sat on the wet grass that fringed the trees. There was nothing to see for miles, only the slate-gray buildings, and of course it was raining again. The school buildings did remind him of the state penitentiary, right down to the bars on the ground-floor windows. Sopworth College—even the name was wet. Well, it was all right if you liked a quiet life. The anesthesia of travel and novelty had worn off almost completely by now, and he tried to remember what the point was of his being here. "Fine education, first-rate mind." Was that all?

He pictured his father scurrying into the hired car and telling the driver to be off, before Jimmy came to and started asking questions. . . . It was really strange of his father to pull a thing like this without discussion. Usually he consulted Jimmy rather anxiously about decisions concerning himself. Yet there had been, Jim swore, no hint of this at the beginning of the winter. It had started out as an absolutely normal winter. His father had been working hard and nervously and staying out late, but there was certainly nothing strange about that. Jim was even working a little himself at that time. Wilbur de Forest was a mild private school that didn't expect much, but second-year high was a mite tougher than first.

To compensate, he really felt like a high-school boy for the first time, and not a displaced eighth-grader. He didn't know what he would feel like over here. Back at W. D. Junior High (two "rahs" and a Fig Newton), he had felt well and truly entrenched. It was the first time since infancy that he had stayed in the same school for two years. His clique had formed and hardened. And with the war over at last, he no longer belonged to a nothing age group. The too-young-to-fight, too-young-even-to-carry-a-ration-book crowd. The pin-prick shortages which his father was always carrying on about were being lifted one by one. A great new day was dawning.

Come to think of it, this was kind of a lousy time to be leaving the country. It hadn't struck him before that he would not be taking part in the postwar boom; that he would have to sit the whole thing out in this peculiar place. He began to feel sorry for himself, the dampness was soaking into his bones. But surely, he told himself quickly, they would have some kind of boom of their own over here. He didn't know anything about the place, but peacetime must include some kicks.

He had two more interviews to get through with management. The first was with the housemaster of Frisby, a pipe-and-brown-tweeds man. A heavy breather with whiskery nostrils.

"Ah, Bannister." He consulted his lists. "Angel, Appleby, here we are, *Ban*nister." He puffed his pipe and made a tick on his lists. "Settling in all right, are you, Bannister?"

"Sure."

"I think you'll find that the word 'sir' does wonders here."

"Yes, sir."

"It will probably take you a little time to get used to our ways. Come to me if you have any problems. That's what I'm here for, you know ... Oh, and we'll have to get you some respectable clothes. ..."

"Yes, sir." What kind of problem would you bring to this man? The housemaster was back at his lists again, making little marks. He looked up. "Well, that's all, Bannister."

"Er, thank you, er, sir." The housemaster nodded, and Jimmy tried to pull the door open. "Push," said the housemaster.

He simply didn't believe it.

The second interview was at the school infirmary. He had to register with the matron, a burly character in white starch, stiff as knight's armor. She tested his heart and his blood pressure.

"From Yankeeland, are you?" she asked in a low voice growl.

"Yes, ma'm."

"That's why you have all those pimples, I suppose."

"Don't English boys have pimples?"

"Not the way American boys have pimples, not pimples the size of gooseberries, not pimples the size of soccer balls. Petted and pampered and stuffed with rich food," she said, flaring suddenly. "I suppose you'll be having colds and flu all term long. Yanks always have shocking health."

He was nonplused. Were Americans especially unhealthy? What was going on here? "We did O.K. in the war," he said, and then felt very silly.

"Absolute rot," the matron flared again as she clamped his arm in the blood-pressure sleeve. "Came in when it was all over, and then swanked all over the place—I believe your people went utterly to pieces in the jungle, my nephew was in the jungle, you know, and the poor darlings had to be sent home to their mothers and their psychiatrists and I don't know what all, to be petted and pampered back to a state of 'normalcy'—ugh, what a word. And then, and *then*, you had the cheek to make a flick about Errol Flynn conquering Burma." She had unraveled the blood-pressure sleeve and grunted at the result of the test. Confirmed her worst fears, no doubt.

"You guys wouldn't have won without us," said Jimmy. Part of his problem was that he couldn't make out whether she was smart or stupid, kidding or serious. Burma? What was so great about Burma? He had thought that the main part of the war was fought on Okinawa and Iwo Jima. Anyhow, it didn't much matter. He was not a great war buff, and had rather lost interest in the details. The dismal thing was the way it excited the matron. He didn't feel like talking to a crazy woman at this particular time. "What about Guadalcanal?" he said. "What *about* it?" she said. She had him there.

At dinner (another mistaken meal) he asked the pale fellow what he thought of the matron.

"You mean Lady Hamilton? She's all right. Heart of gold under the revolting exterior is her line. If a chap pretends to be sick, she usually plays along. I mean to say if one faints on parade, you know military parade, she doesn't report the blotting paper she finds in one's socks."

"What blotting paper?"

"Blotting paper, you know, makes a chap faint. Gets one out of two hours of squalid drill. A definite jape."

"Sounds great."

"It's all right if you don't cut your head open when you hit the concrete. The chances of war, you know."

"I didn't think she was so hot."

"Who? Oh, you mean Eva Braun. Well, remember, she's the only woman you'll be seeing for three months, if you care for that sort of thing. Or do your interests run in other directions? Or are you too young to have any interests at all?"

"No, I'm not," said Jimmy quickly. What other directions? He decided to let that go.

"Well, then, better get on the right side of Eva."

"I thought you said she was called Lady Hamilton."

"Yes, you have the option, depending on which house you're in, what day it is and the color of your hair. As I say—fuss, fuss, fuss. She was named Lady Hamilton during the Napoleonic unpleasantness. You'll recall that, of course? Perhaps you'd prefer to call her, say, Dolly Madison. Feel perfectly free."

Nobody had talked to him so much since his arrival, if you could call it talking, and Jimmy felt that he might be making a possible friend.

"What are *you* doing here in the vacation?" he asked, trying to turn it into a real conversation and not one of these queer things.

"I'm one of those chaps who's all-brain," said the pale fellow. "They're preparing me for a scholarship to one of our ancient universities. Keeping me locked in a brightly lit room all day and all night, works wonders with chickens, so why not people? say they. If I win, I shall put the school on the map. The fees will rise like yeast. Dr. Rabelais will advertise in *The Times* for new succubae . . ."

"What are you talking about now?"

"Ah, I *thought* you were too young."

The pale fellow went silent, and Jimmy was left alone for the twentieth time that day with his thoughts and an unidentifiable green vegetable that tasted of wood. He had never found conversation so difficult. It must take years to make friends at this rate. And even if you made friends with someone like this, what would you have? The strain of watching him try to make every sentence clever would just wear you out.

He decided that in the vacation this place must function as a kind of funny farm, for misfits and basket cases. Tomorrow the normal guys, who weren't "all-brain," and who didn't watch birds, were due to arrive. There must be some among them who could talk more or less straight. The whole nation couldn't be like this, it was mathematically impossible. (And the food was mathematically impossible, too.) He went for a walk after supper and the air felt wet and gentle and moderately reassuring.

The next day the normal boys began to roll in. Jimmy stood in a corner under a staircase watching them come. A roaring horde swept past him down the main hallway. And this was the thing about them—they were all wearing *black coats and pinstriped trousers.* It was simply incredible: all scuttling toward the big staircase like a school of small bank-managers on the march, pink faces swimming along under a deafening roar. He had never in his life heard such a noise.

Jimmy began to cry. He hadn't planned it, or even considered the possibility. But that was what he seemed to be doing: wrapped as he was in his sports coat with the comb sticking out; watching two hundred or three hundred weird haircuts, odd shapes of skull, mild eyes. Realizing that no help was going to arrive. And those suits! So cry it was. He turned and ran up the stairs to the dormitory. There was nobody he could even discuss the situation with. The conversation around here was not for discussing situations in. "What did he think he was doing?" he said, being fully honest about it for just a moment. But his father could not have known about the black coats. He could not.

He lay on his bed trying to recapture his grip. To find yourself crying at his age was much worse than any particular thing you might be crying about. It simply wasn't possible for him to cry. It was like a blow in the back of the neck. The bank managers didn't seem to notice or care, as they pounded past him into the dormitory. They were probably used to people crying at this time of the year. But to Jimmy it opened some great abysm—all the things he hadn't cried about for years came roaring into it, saying "now! now!" and for a moment his body shook with the pressure; and then the tears were all gone, and he sat up emptily on his bed staring at the bank managers and listening to their high incredible voices and wondering how the human race had managed to diverge so violently as to form a country like this one.

□ II □

He went to bed right after supper, curiously exhausted, and only dimly sensed the bedding down of the others around him. A flashing of lights which his eyes resisted, and the jar of foreign voices—like trying to sleep on a train; then sufficient peace. He awoke several times during the night and was aware of a light, low-definition homesickness, like a sneeze in the back of the nose. If New York had such a thing as a decent season, it was spring, and he had gotten a first tantalizing smell of that just before leaving. Another thing about spring was that his father usually came to life around then and they bundled out of the apartment on weekends, and took ferry rides up to Bear Mountain and Poughkeepsie, or before that, drove up to Gloucester, where they planned the summer and fantasied the future. The back of the school year was broken, and the long vacation was just an arm's reach away. Here . . .

He pushed past this, back to pleasanter ground. He had had good times with his father; to get mad at him now was to cut off an important source of reassurance. For at least four years they had been very close friends indeed. Jimmy could picture the round pleasant face, the hand clutching the tickets. Tickets to Radio City, to ball games, to the ice show. When his mother left home, his father moved from the shadows and became the great ticket man. The braces came off Jim's teeth and his piano lessons were allowed to cease: gestures of friendship. They moved from Bridgeport to Boston to New York. This English thing was hard to understand in that context.

As he drifted off to sleep he thought fleetingly, as one might remember one's night prayers, about his mother. Her face was so pale in his mind that it was hardly a face at all. He was really thinking about the apartment on East Eighty-fourth Street and the one before that on West End, and the one before that . . . and when he came to her picture on the mantelpiece he flicked over it like a duster.

His mother was nothing but a piece of celluloid. When the piano lessons had stopped, he remembered thinking that you don't question a piece of luck like that. That was his last serious thought about her. He wondered now what she would make of this place—well, that was a silly question. Photographs don't have opinions. Neither should he just yet, until he had sampled a classroom or two; he went to sleep sharply, for the fourth and last time.

Classes began the following morning and Jimmy found himself staring into the English education system. The first class was geometry, which Jimmy had never done any of before. There was a dryness in the classroom air, like the taste of prison bread: something to do with everyone's wearing black. The master said a few cryptic words, then called out accusingly, "Smith," "Carruthers," "Thomson"; and they bawled back their answers, until just about everyone had spoken except Jimmy. He wondered dreamily what he would say when they got to him, but it all seemed so unreal; and then the bell chimed and that was the end of that. "Do exercise 35 for prep," said the geometry master, and the boys surged out of the room.

"Where am I supposed to go next?" Bannister asked the master.

"I don't know," said the master.

Jimmy went downstairs to reconnoiter the notice board. Room 12 Arithmetic. That shouldn't be too difficult. Arithmetic was something he thought he'd seen the last of two years ago. Win a few, lose a few. He puffed into room 12, to find the class already under way.

"Smedley, you horrible oaf"—this one wore a black gown with green mold on it—"do you realize that your parents are paying good money to send you here, when you might be doing useful work in the mines or the factories?"

"Yes, sir," said Smedley, in a funny accent, as the class tittered subserviently. Jimmy edged his way in quietly.

"Who are you? And what are you doing in those revolting clothes?" The master had spotted him anyway.

"Jim Bannister, sir."

"Well, Jimbannister, or whatever your bally name is, perhaps you've been sent by some Higher Agency to tell our backward friend Smedley what the logarithm of 312 is? One must never despair of Divine intervention, must one?"

"The *what*, sir?"

"Logarithm, logarithm, logarithm. Oh, another cruel joke!" He bounced around in his gown. "Providence has favored me with another oaf."

"What's a logarithm, sir?"

"Whaat?" the master howled. "Oh my God!" And he buried his face in his hands. "It's come to this, then."

"I'm sorry," said Jimmy. The master sat motionless in an attitude of comic shock and bereavement. Years of disappointment with boys and now this. "Why do they send them to *me*," he moaned softly.

"I'm sorry," Jimmy repeated. It was all too ridiculous. What kind of an act was this? The heavy, lined face told him that this was a grown-up; otherwise there was no way of knowing. The other boys continued to titter on cue, but without much spirit.

"Well, it's no use being sorry." The master was suddenly business-like. "But there isn't much I can do for you if you haven't even heard of logarithms. Have you done any problems in mensuration, you loathsome boy?"

"I don't think so."

"You don't *think* so, eh? I imagine you'd notice if you had. Well, I'm afraid you shouldn't be in this class at all in that case. Jones Minor, perhaps you can fill in for our untutored American cousin? What is the logarithm for 321, you benighted oaf?"

"Do you want me to stay here?" asked Jimmy.

"Suit yourself," said the master, already absorbed in his tilt with Jones

Minor. Jimmy sat in a diplomatic limbo, thinking of other classrooms he had
known, and wondering, furthermore, how this had ever come to be called
arithmetic.

As the class broke up, one of the boys sidled over to him: "Don't pay
attention to the 'Foghorn.' He's thoroughly uncivilized," and sidled away
again. Jimmy frowned: the boy looked young to be saying things like that.
But what was young and what was old in this country?

Outside in the corridor, boys were off and running again, this way and
that. Jimmy gathered, from a blur of bulletin board, that he had to get to the
other end of the school for his next class, and he joined a crowd which
seemed to be sprinting in that direction. They all chuffered into the classroom together, squeezing through the door somehow, and a moment later a
mild-looking man in a fuzzy brown suit was putting yet another tick next to
his name. "Ah yes, Bannister. *Here* we are, *I've* got you."

This time the class was Latin. Jimmy had already had a year of Latin. The
master seemed to be pretending to be shy—that was *his* routine. "What shall
we do today? Perhaps a few sentences from English into Latin." He opened
his book vaguely, and then looked up as if struck with a happy thought. "I
heard rather a good story last night. I don't suppose it would amuse you
chaps?"

"Oh please, sir," the cry went up, and the story was told. It was long,
and some of it was in Latin, but the boys laughed anyway. One of them went
into near paroxysms, flinging himself round like a dervish and slapping his
desk. Oh come on, thought Jimmy. You don't think you're going to get
away with that, do you? "That will do, Cornwallis," said the master: but he
smiled as he wiped his glasses. The gnomes looked at each other in surmise.

"Sir, do you think Yorkshire will win the championship this season?"
They probed at the loose tissue.

"Are they going to devalue the pound, sir?"

"Is socialized medicine really a good idea, sir?"

"Isn't it smashing to be able to travel again, sir? Where are you going to
go first, sir?"

"Sir, sir, *please,* sir . . ."

He answered their questions with gravity and foolish precision. Fifteen
minutes had gone already, only twenty-five remained. Maybe Jimmy would
avoid entanglements this time. But at some point the master straightened his
spectacles and summoned his woolly faculties. "That's enough now, you
chaps. We've wasted entirely too much time." He looked at them as severely
as he could and snapped his book open. "Why don't we try exercise 73? It
looks like an amusing one."

One of the boys handed out paper for the class to write on. Jimmy
searched through his Latin book for exercise 73. It consisted of five of the
stupidest sentences he had ever seen in his life. "Caesar decided that if he had

been told previously that the Gauls had encamped on the other side of the river he would certainly have moved his baggage back to the town from which he had departed at daybreak the day before." Jimmy chewed his pencil. "Regulus would have liked to disembark perhaps" . . . Yes, well. Very interesting. The other boys were already writing with beaverish determination, while the master appeared to be jotting down words on a crossword puzzle.

"Are you encountering difficulties, Bannister?" he said at last. Jimmy was sitting back with his hands in his pockets. He decided that this might be a good place to make a stand, before this madness went any further.

"Yes, sir. Great difficulties."

"Er, would you care to come up, Bannister? Perhaps we can solve them together."

Jimmy went up. The master looked at his paper closely, readjusting his spectacles. The paper started off "1. Caesar," and stopped. The master was profoundly disturbed.

"Is this all you've done?"

"Yes, sir."

The master peered at it again, and skewered his spectacles further into place. "This is distressing, Bannister." He squinted at the blank paper. Perhaps a closer look would turn up something, some words he hadn't noticed before . . . "Very distressing indeed." The master just sat and looked at the paper while Jimmy stood and looked at the floor. "Well, what are we going to do about it?" His face was close to agony.

"I don't know, sir."

"This isn't good enough, you know. Nothing like good enough."

He paused again. "Are you sure this is all you've done?" he asked. Invisible ink was a possibility. Jimmy couldn't make out what was the matter with this man: but he felt vaguely that it was up to himself to get them both out of the tangle.

"Maybe I should go see the headmaster," he suggested at last.

"Yes," the master grasped at the idea. "Perhaps that would be the best plan." He ran a hand through his thin sandy hair. "I'm afraid we can't be of much help to you here."

Jimmy strolled toward the door. He felt pretty good; the man had simply collapsed. Perhaps they all would.

"Sorry," said the master.

The headmaster, "Dr. Rabelais" (real name Smyth, but that was beside the point), sat shrouded in a great black gown, nursing a cup of tea. For ten minutes he worked away at his lists, giving Jimmy leisure to look around him. The room seemed less strange today, although strange enough. On the opposite wall hung six little dandified walking sticks, which, Jimmy conjectured, must be for making mean little furrows on your backside; the rest of the room was dull with bright patches. Among the forbidding books he spotted several funny ones which he had read himself. His thoughts futzed this way and that; summer days, lying on his back reading. Flinging aside his book, or his violin like the man in the ads, and charging into the sea. New images struggled against the protoplasm: dancing on some kind of bandstand in a white tuxedo, with, let's say, Marilyn Jenkins in pink chiffon with her teeth freshly liberated (Marilyn's scaffolding had kept them apart until recently), and driving home together in the roadster Forrest Tuckerman had talked of purchasing. After all, America was his country, and he had a right to be in it, for better or worse. This place might be all right for the people who belonged here; it was hard to tell. Maybe he could make the headmaster see all that. He was supposed to be a big brain.

"Infernal nuisance running a school these days"—Dr. Rabelais interrupted his thoughts—"ration books, identity cards, shortages, *et cetera*, *et cetera*. It's worse than the dashed civil service. Can I help you, Bannister?"

"Yes, sir." He gestured with his hands. "It's no good. I just can't seem to make it. I think I'd better just go home."

Dr. Rabelais looked uncomprehending. "Can't make what?"

"Anything. The school. The grade. Anything."

"Ah, I see. Don't you think you're judging the situation a trifle prematurely, Bannister?"

"No, I don't think so. Look, I went to three classes today, and I was made to look like a monkey in two of them. Now I don't mind looking like a monkey . . ."

"Excellent, the beginning of wisdom."

"If it's in a good cause. O.K., maybe I'm stupid, and can't help it. But don't you think it's a little bit unnecessary to spend a whole term proving it?"

"What exactly do you mean by that, Bannister?" The headmaster plunged deeper into his burrow of vagueness.

"Well, if I'm not mistaken, my father wrote you a letter last month describing my qualifications. Didn't you get the letter?"

"Yes, I think I have it here somewhere." The headmaster fished about on his desk.

"Well, then, how come you just throw me in over my head like that? You know I don't know any geometry . . ."

Dr. Rabelais looked terribly, terribly tired. On the evolutionary cycle, the human race had barely begun its journey. And now, here was this boy. "We must have patience," he said. "Rome wasn't built in a day, you know."

"Yes, so I've heard. The word gets around, about things like that."

"I don't believe that impertinence will help us materially in our quest. Restrain your native exuberance, I beg of you, or I may be required to restrain it for you. Now what was I saying?"

"That Rome wasn't built in a day, sir."

"Ah, yes. Now I agree that the analogy may seem remote in your particular case." His voice reminded Jim of old curtains. "Nevertheless it is not altogether without pertinence. We must make haste slowly, building slowly but surely. Labor omnia vincit, if you'll excuse a rather colorless paraphrase."

Jimmy could barely remember what he had come here to say. He was being woofed more and more tightly into the headmaster's endless tapestry: pinned by velvet threads, tenuous syllabic filaments.

"I just don't feel I belong here. I admit I'm stupid."

"Ah-hah." Dr. Rabelais wagged a much-wagged finger. "You can't get away with that, my boy. I've seen all your school reports from the age of five, and I've also had special recommendations from several old teachers. We know quite a bit about you, you know."

"I didn't think you cared."

"I warmly advise you to think very carefully before you venture another impertinence. Yes, we feel the utmost confidence that you can, as you say, 'make the grade.' Otherwise you would not be here, depend upon it. Now, as to your classwork, we can't very well put you in with boys of twelve and thirteen, can we? As it is, most of your colleagues are no more than fourteen, and backward to boot. There's a chap called Smedley in one of your classes who knows even less than you do if that be possible—another American as it happens, but that's neither here nor there. Now, it's simply up to you to make up the difference with stern applications of native wit. I believe you Americans call it 'Yankee ingenuity.' I knew some Americans during the war, you know."

"But the Latin teacher sent me in here because he didn't know what to do with me."

"Ah, Mr. Moore. Brilliant classicist, but not used to boys. I'll have a word with him. By the way, shouldn't you be somewhere at the moment?"

"I guess so, sir. I just don't know where."

"Well, out of respect for your frayed nerves, you might as well take the rest of the morning off. It must have been quite strenuous, settling in like this to a strange environment." He paused, hoping no doubt that Jimmy's hash was settled forever. "Morning off should fix things up."

"Thank you, sir."

A happy thought struck Dr. Rabelais.

"You may be a little daunted by the famous English reserve. Could that be it, do you suppose? I find it singularly relaxing myself, but my American acquaintances inform me that it tends to make them a trifle jumpy. If that's your trouble, I'm sure that time will take care of it. There are several quite pleasant chaps about the place, whom you will doubtless get to know in due course. Perhaps in the camaraderie of the cricket field . . ." His voice trailed off.

"Yes, sir."

"Is that all, Bannister?"

"Yes, sir, I guess so." He stumbled out of the room, assuming that his question must have been answered at some point, and that the answer was no, or yes, he was staying here, and continuing the farce. In his present state of brain fog, he was happy just to get out of the office.

That afternoon Jimmy was introduced to cricket. His fellow competitors in game number 16 were all playing against their wills. They were a squinting, shambling crowd, who detested cricket, and played it as badly as possible, partly as a protest, partly because they had no choice. Appropriately enough, Mr. Moore, the Latin master, was in charge of the game, and to him fell the gloomy task of preventing the players from fielding the ball with their boots, and heaving it willfully into the woods. ("Oh, I say chaps" was his formula for this.)

The game lumbered along, and Jimmy was glad to find that his own incompetence was lost in the general confusion. In fact, as a fielder he was somewhat above average, and he flung himself at the knobbly red ball with crazy abandon, because it seemed a nice straightforward thing to do.

Later he found that he was sitting next to Smedley while both awaited their brief turns at bat. Smedley was on the plump side and sluggish-looking, and easily the worst player of any game that Jimmy had ever seen: three reasons for slight contempt, as far as Jimmy was concerned.

"You had a bad time this morning, didn't you, Bannister?" Jimmy recognized Smedley's strange accent as simple American.

"I guess so," said Jimmy.

"Well, welcome to the club. I've been having a bad time all year."

"Gee, that long? How do you stand it?" He wouldn't have liked this guy back home, but here you took what you could get.

The fat boy gave him a long, solemn look. His face was American too: bulbous and open. Well, that was one kind of American face.

"Passive resistance," said Smedley at last. "The madder they act, the dumber I get. I'm trying to give them the impression that I'm too stupid to bother about. And I'm gaining."

"Don't they beat you?"

"Sometimes—when I overplay my hand. That's all they can do, though. And you get used to it. Especially with a figure like mine. Besides, there's a growing body of opinion that says I'm a real idiot, one of God's holy people, and maybe it's bad luck to push me around."

"But won't they kick you out someday?"

Smedley gave him the look. "And what do you think I've been waiting for?"

Jimmy thought this over for a second.

"Hey, Smedley, you're a great man." He'd need time to work this thing out in detail, but it looked, offhand, like a way to beat the system. Smedley gave no indication that it was meant to be a joke. It just seemed to be the way his mind worked.

Jim walked back to school with some of the old Bannister bounce. He figured that he might possibly try to do it the Uncle Tom way for a while, pay attention in class, and wait for the camaraderie of the cricket field, whatever that was. But if that didn't work, he would use the Smedley plan. Act dumb. Act obnoxiously dumb, swinishly dumb, and find himself on a boat to Marilyn Jenkins in no time.

He found himself for now just behind the headmaster, who was trudging up the slight incline to the dressing rooms and who looked unusually vulnerable in a pair of baggy tennis shorts. Rabelais was whacking his spider's legs absently with a squash racket, and Jimmy felt something like friendship, at least for his dilapidated back view. The front was something else. A slingshot aimed at the left calf would produce the most endearing little dance.

Jimmy pulled abreast, and smiled a greeting. Probably not the thing to do: but Rabelais let it go for now. "Settling in all right, are you, Bannister?" he said. "Not such a bad country, perhaps. I expect you'll find that we have our moments." And they both tunneled into the school, on a wave of rather freakish good cheer.

□ **III** □

The characters seemed to change. The boys he had seen in those first few days receded, dissolved; and new ones appeared. The pale fellow with the brain was nowhere to be seen. Wagstaff the bird watcher lorded it over another house, so was somebody else's problem. Jimmy was shuffled out of Mr. Moore's class (a clerical mistake in the first place, he gathered) and into the Latin equivalent of cricket game number 16. Dr. Rabelais clearly wanted as little to do with boys as possible once term had begun, and withdrew bit by bit into that all-purpose vagueness: his eyes empty as a blind man's, his legs seeming to whisper to each other, "I'll get you past these boys, never fear."

The boy in the bed next to Jimmy's had a Norman skull, which was depressing at first but later became a comfort like a tea cozy or an old piece of china. He didn't say anything to Jimmy for two whole weeks, but padded modestly to and fro with his tooth mug and his washcloth, and one night he cried in bed softly and politely, which came as quite a pleasant surprise for Jimmy.

Those first two weeks were incredible in a whole new way: Smedley plans, modified Smedley plans, were of no avail—because for that whole time nobody talked to him at all. It was like the first day of kindergarten prolonged indefinitely. Nobody looked at him or asked who he was. If they wanted the salt, they reached across him. If their arms weren't long enough, they went without salt. At night Jimmy was obliged to troop with them for their nightly wash, where they jostled him mutely to get at the basins. This was an awful scene. Flannel dressing gowns, the dismal swoop of slippers, and the boys rolling up their pajama legs and dunking their feet awkwardly in the washbasins—he didn't know why, but this was the low point of the day. Later in the sandpaper sheets he would lie grimly still, his hand between his thighs for comfort, like a drowning man clinging to driftwood. He felt he must be changing, losing his bearings, as men do in solitary confinement. He considered masturbating but was restrained by two thoughts: one being that it would induce the most violent melancholy in this setting and the other that any displacement of these impossible bedclothes would be noticeable for miles around. So he lay still like a knight on his coffin.

It was better in the morning. He could hear farm noises, the crunch of heavy boots on cobblestone and above that the shriek of the school crows. There was one man who always said, "Morning, Harry," and stopped to talk under Jimmy's window in a comfortable Midlands accent about weather prospects and such. Jimmy had never heard such a pleasant voice. Inside the dormitory the boys snored or muttered or went sniffing into the bathroom. When they were all in place they formed a line of gray mounds like a Druid graveyard. Jimmy lay there watching and listening to the voice through the window.

One evening, at the end of two weeks exactly, the boy with the Norman skull came and sat on his bed and said, "Do you like jazz, Bannister?"

"I guess so," said Jimmy, surprised at the sound of his own voice.

"I do too. Very much indeed. Do you know 'In the Mood'?"

"By Glenn Miller, you mean."

"Yes, that's it. I think it's super, don't you?"

"Yes, it's nice."

"Do you know 'Frenesí'?"

"I don't think so."

"It's Artie Shaw. Quite first-class." He hummed a few notes.

Jimmy was delighted to talk, on anyone's terms and this fellow, who had seemed so shy, went at it now with the utmost composure.

"We have a jazz club, you know. Your compatriot Smedley has furnished us with some of his records, and we also get speakers in from time to time. Last term we had a super talk on discography. By a Frenchman."

Discography? Jimmy didn't like to ask.

"Yes, several Glenn Millers. 'The Man I Love' by the Benny Goodman quartet—That man can really play the licorice stick, can't he? All in all, quite a good collection."

Jimmy stared at him solemnly; it wouldn't do to laugh.

"Anyhow, we were talking it over and we wondered"—there was a sock-picking pause and the fellow suddenly looked unspeakably embarrassed—"if you'd care to join us."

So Bannister joined the jazz club and listened that Thursday evening to the several Glenn Millers and to Benny Goodman's licorice stick. The whole Smedley collection, in fact. Smedley had changed his own *persona* for the occasion, slipping out of his banker's uniform and into a purple sports shirt and double-breasted suit, as one was allowed to do in the evenings. As the records spun, Smedley combed his wet hair into a lounge-lizard coif and snapped his fingers, while the others looked on with admiring interest.

It seemed that this deviant music room, with its bust of Elgar and illuminated manuscript of William Byrd, was the one place in the school where it was good to be an American; and Smedley had decided to be American to the hilt. It was obviously he who had taught them to say "licorice stick," and to nonchalant their smuggled cigarettes. "Gimme some skin, man," he said gravely as they entered. "Shake it but don't break it." "Tell you whut I'm gonna dew." His language seemed to have been purged of all but the most conspicuous Americanisms.

Jimmy felt a slight contempt for the records on principle—licorice stick indeed!—but they got to him after a few rounds. Glenn Miller, he thought. Billy Butterfield plays George Gershwin. Gershwin equals penthouse. Penthouse equals Fifth Avenue bus. Girls jumping on and climbing to the top deck with skirts swinging. Waiting for reviews at Sardi's. He missed it all so much. He didn't want to stay in this nuthouse another minute. "Frenesí" unraveled him completely. Play it again, Sam, he thought. Purple shadows and blue champagne. And outside, all those English boys. His throat seemed to constrict with some rich substance; but the sight of Smedley combing his hair steadied him.

He didn't like that. Americans don't behave like that. And he didn't like the way the other boys were looking at Smedley: a group of rich Romans inspecting the muscles of an African slave. It kept him from acting American himself. When they got to the end of the set, they played them all again, tapping their feet and scrutinizing Smedley. "What do you think, Bannister?" asked the boy with the Norman skull, whose name turned out to be Ryan. "It's very nice," said Bannister.

Several others looked around—let's hear from the other American chap. So Jimmy said, "Well, you can't really call this stuff jazz, can you? I mean I used to go down to Eddie Condon's and listen to Muggsy Spanier, and that was . . ."

"You went to Condon's? You heard Muggsy?" A clamor went up, chairs scraped forward. It was all so queer. "Tell us about Muggsy. Does Condon really drink two quarts of whiskey a night, or is that just propaganda? What about Peewee Russell?"

Something about the way they pronounced Muggsy—Jimmy felt as if he had played right into their hands. He had actually been to Condon's only that once, with Forrest Tuckerman, and had had to concentrate so hard on looking eighteen (squint, cigarette, flickering jaw muscle) that he hadn't noticed much else. He remembered that it was awfully smoky, and that, because the waiter had put him and Forrest maliciously close to the bandstand, the trombone had rent his skull in two.

"Hey, Jimmy, you been to Condon's, I hear," Smedley chimed in. "That Condon is a character, isn't he? And Peewee and Wild Bill ... I and my buddy used to go there on Sunday afternoons and buy them a few rounds, just to get them talking, you know ..."

No, no, no. Jimmy just couldn't cope with this. Jazz should have been his subject; yet these finely trained bank clerks were outflanking him even there. Two weeks of silence had rusted his tongue: so he left the exposition to Smedley, affirming with occasional grunts and looking as detached as he could. Ahead of him lay the long dark corridors back to Frisby house, the piping good nights ("Night, Smedley," "See you guys on the campus," "Right-oh, Smedley"). The boys teetering at their washbasins scrubbing their pale white feet.

On the way back to the Frisby dormitory with Ryan, he heartily denounced the records, and Ryan said meekly, "It's the best we can do, I'm afraid." Ryan, at least, accepted his authority in the field.

The corridor outside Frisby was dark enough to trip in. And as Jimmy edged along the wall, jangling with trumped-up outrage, he nearly stumbled into a dark pair of hands. A tall boy was standing there in dressing gown and pajamas, smiling apologetically and holding out his hands in a kind of supplication. "Are you all right, dear?" He reached for Jimmy's shoulders, and Jimmy twisted away.

He ran a few steps to keep up with Ryan. What had happened, nothing had happened. (*Dear?*) As he looked over his shoulder he saw that the boy was still standing there, still smiling. His face was quite luminous, fair and thin, but the rest was blacked out in shadows. That was the first friendly gesture Jim had encountered since coming here.

"Who was that?" he asked Ryan.

"That was Padgett," said Ryan. "He's a shocker, isn't he? Out there every night, rain or shine. I don't know why he hasn't been caught yet."

Jimmy honestly didn't know what Ryan was talking about. And he didn't much want to. He simply decided that he must leave this place as soon as possible.

*   *   *

On afternoons when he wasn't playing cricket, Jimmy went for long walks in the country. The other boys did military drill but as a representative of a foreign power he was excused from that, and he didn't much care to watch it. The shouting and the clump of boots presented the school at its bleakest, and he saw no point in punishing himself. So he took walks, along the exceptionally gentle paths that wound loosely round the school, and he got in the habit of composing imaginary letters to his father, all on the theme of "Get me out of here. A joke is a joke. *Now get me out of here.*" Sometimes he added, in his head, the words "before it's too late," although he had no idea what he meant by that. The other morning at breakfast, Ryan had said, "You just said 'actually.' Listen, chaps, Bannister said 'actually.' " But he didn't think it was that.

At fifteen I should be spending my time with my father, he thought theatrically. Time with Mr. Bannister. He'll be an old man when I get out of here, possibly dead. Certainly remarried. Remarried. To Gloria whatzit—that was the best he could hope for. The worst? . . . Jim had the uncanny feeling in the back of his mind that Padgett had been wearing make-up the other night, to make him glow so.

The imaginary letters lacked force, because he didn't feel so bad in the afternoons. The countryside was friendly, compared with the school corridors, and he was getting used to the hanging, motionless drizzle. He even liked the taste of the grass when he sat down on it to brood. He tried to remember how he would feel later in the day, and to borrow some of the night's agitation on credit, but the fields and the cows and the broken-down hedges left him hopelessly becalmed. There was a bowlegged farmer who rode a lady's bicycle down whichever path Jimmy happened to be taking and who always tipped his cap as he wobbled by, and Jimmy like him in the same way he liked the voice under his window in the morning.

After the misleading afternoon there were several more hours of classes to get through. By some mystery of scheduling, he kept landing in the Foghorn's class, where he felt he was being kept from learning arithmetic by sheer terror. Not just terror for himself, but terror for the Foghorn as well. For Jim had formed the idea that Mr. Withers was literally going crazy. His ranting seemed to get more and more absent-minded and hysterical as the term wore on: everyone was an oaf, everyone was a cause for despair. His eyes emptied out and he looked, in some curious way, like a man lost in a railroad station. Jim got a feeling that Mr. Withers had completely withdrawn from the scene and was railing at phantoms; private terrors.

After the Foghorn came geography presided over by a dwarf called Smiles, who paid close, ferret-like attention to everything and who made a stylish needlepoint thing of his bullying. He had decided from the first to make Jimmy a scapegoat because "Americans don't know the first thing about geography. You people have inherited much of Great Britain's power since the war and yet you haven't the remotest . . ." He seemed personally affronted by postwar developments and talked as if the shrinking red patches on the map were Jimmy's doing. "Bannister, come up here. I wonder if you could indicate to the class the whereabouts of the crown colony of Singapore. I suppose you know what *ocean* it's in, do you?" Titters. "You know, your president made us give a good deal of this away. I devoutly hope that his geography was better than yours." Jimmy hated standing up there, not only because he confirmed everything that Smiles said about America and geography, but also because Smiles seemed to be drenched in nicotine from head to foot. Even his rusty hair smelled of nicotine, and the fingers with which he seized Jimmy's arm impatiently, to guide him to Malaya and Borneo, werre outrageously long, yellow and fetid.

The last class of the day was possibly the worst of all. The French teacher posed a unique problem in that he took a rather florid liking to Jimmy, based on a notion that Jimmy was basically a first-rate student who had come upon bad times. "Ban-ees-tair—thees ees not op to you ol' standar," he would say sadly whenever Jimmy handed something in. He had been teaching a long time and had doubtless had a gifted pupil called Bannister in the old days. Now Bannister was back with his gifts gone.

Jimmy, of course, knew no French to speak of, and while he was getting reasonably inured to the steady diet of embarrassment in the other classes, he found Monsieur Necker's false hopes ever-freshly excruciating. He worked hard at French, but was so far below the original Bannister's standard that he continued to disappoint in about the same measure all the time he was in the class.

That was how the days went now—rounded off with godawful suppers and homework and the thwack of ping-pong balls in the Frisby common room; and then, trying to avoid Padgett on the way home. Padgett was, he now understood, a joke and nothing to be alarmed over. Old Padgett never actually did anything, but just stood there, smiling and whispering, "Good evening, dear," to anyone who would listen. "I think he's barmy," said Ryan. "If he wasn't a scholarship candidate, he wouldn't be here at all."

So much for Padgett. Still the Sopworth hallways at night seemed as strange as some underwater kingdom and Jim was happy to make it to his sandpaper bed without incident. The fact that Padgett was a joke was strange because he had never encountered a joke like that before. And how many other jokes lurked in the night? Even by daylight odd things could happen.

To wit, the Sprague caper, which showed him in a lightning flash how much he had changed since coming here. This was at the end of his first month, and he was so used by now to solitude that conversation seemed like a bizarre exception. He was on his way to Monday lunch, the culinary asshole of the universe, when Sprague happened. At first, all that registered was a distant cry of pain. "Hands out, you squalid little man. Hands *out . . .*" Jim looked around vaguely: he had just had forty minutes of the Foghorn, whose anonymous bellows had a dulling effect, like the guns on the Western front. "You—who are you, anyway? What's your miserable name? What's your unfortunate house?" Spam and boiled potatoes, Bannister was thinking. Thick flour on the spuds, bread pudding and custard. After such a morning, it wasn't much.

"Look here. You can't just walk past when I speak to you." A smallish boy stood now directly in Jimmy's path. "*Get* THOSE *hands out of* THOSE *pockets.*"

"Are you talking to me?"

"Who do you think I'm talking to, you verminous creature? President Roooosevelt? *Get* THOSE *hands—*"

One curious thing was that the boy's hands were wedged deep into his own pockets. It must be a local joke. "Look, I've had a hard morning," Jimmy said.

"This is plain, dumb insolence. You'll take those hands out of those pockets immediately, or I'll—" He stopped because Jimmy had already taken his hands out some moments before, without thinking, simply to make a despairing gesture. He continued to glare at Jimmy—quite meaninglessly as far as Jim was concerned. Two other boys had flung themselves against the wall, to watch in an agony of languor, their hands very much in their pockets. Jimmy squinted at his challenger. Two stringy blond whiskers corkscrewed from his chin, and his upper lip was a downy shambles. Five feet five or at the most six. I can take him, Jimmy thought. But why? "Look, if you don't mind—" Jimmy tried to edge round but found himself blocked again. "What is this?" He stared down at what seemed to be the gravitational focus: striped trousers stretched to bursting. Absently, Jimmy put his own hands back in his pockets.

"My God!" Jimmy took them out again, still without design. People who were late for lunch didn't get served. He tried sidestepping the other way, to get to his custard, but again his tormentor skipped with him and this time butted him lightly in the chest. The two friends against the wall looked suffocatingly bored. As if they had to contend with this sort of thing every day. The custard wasn't much, but suddenly Jim couldn't get it out of his mind.

"Look," he said. And he put his own hands inquiringly on the boy's chest. "I don't know if this is supposed to be a joke. I don't know who you are, or what you want—" He felt his stupid lip trembling. He couldn't think of anything to say, that was why. The lip gave a violent shudder: he hadn't cried for seven or eight years before coming to this crumby place. Here he never seemed to stop. To crown it all, the chest was harder to push than it looked. Embarrassment had weakened him. Jimmy tried one more quick breakthrough on the left and the little fellow darted across silently and blocked him against the school bulletin board. It was like a game in which use of the hands is illegal.

What Jimmy had forgotten about this kind of crying was that eventually it exploded on you like hiccups and you lost control of it. It was the *incredibility* that got him down. He thought of past fights—challenges he had met without enthusiasm, but met. But this wasn't even a challenge. He bent against the wall and tried to pull his nose and mouth together. If there were three people in the world he didn't want to cry in front of, it was, at the moment, these three snots.

"I ought to report you to your house prefect," said the boy, all business now. "However, perhaps I'll let it go this time. All I can tell you is, don't ever behave like this in front of a school prefect again. Here, try this on your nose." Reluctantly he pulled his hand out of its nest and thrust a huge handkerchief at Jimmy.

Jimmy handed the handkerchief back without using it. It would have been the final disgrace. The little man shrugged and went over and joined his friends, and they strolled together to the dining room, their hands still firmly entrenched. They were laughing, but Jimmy had a queer bad feeling that they were not talking about him at all, in fact that they would never refer to him again.

The best thing was to forget it. But Jimmy was too hungry for that. It festered on his empty stomach. Apparently it didn't matter when prefects got to the dining room, but it was certainly too late for him. He ran upstairs to the dormitory, ravening for the custard that might have been. He remembered seeing his father truckle to a traffic cop once, and feeling ashamed. But this was much worse. He had, in his quiet days and nights here, lost his ability to cope with a verbal crisis. He had just wanted to get out of there, at any cost. He took out his writing block and began a real letter to his father, imploring him to end this foolishness: but found that his grievances had suddenly become too delicate to mention. He sat on the bed chewing his pen, and in a moment the bank managers came pounding in again from lunch. Unless you locked yourself in the toilet, there was no question of privacy around here.

"I didn't see you at lunch, Bannister," said Ryan as he began to forage for cricket boots under his bed. "Didn't you feel well? Or were you devouring a food package from America, you greedy swine?" Ryan had chosen this moment to advance their friendship.

Jimmy looked up and without a moment of warning the tears came back. They didn't match his mood at all now—he was so angry that he wanted to belt someone. But the whole duct system was out of kilter. He hated to admit it but he was also moved by the fact that Ryan had spoken to him again.

"Do you know a little blond guy who goes around with his hands in his pockets? He wouldn't let me go in the dining room—" Jimmy sniffed this out somehow. "Wait till I catch up with that runt."

"What will you do to him?"

"We'll just see."

Ryan giggled. "I wouldn't make any positive plans if I were you. That sounds very much like Sprague, who only happens to be our beloved boxing captain—peerless lightweight and all that. He loves bashing people into the bulletin board. I don't know what he sees in it. You're lucky he kept his hands in his pockets."

Ryan's voice was surprisingly warm and sympathetic, as one of life's victims to another—they could be friends now. "You Yanks are headstrong, I'll give you that. Imagine tangling with a chap like Sprague. He plays soccer too, you know. He could have had you beaten to a jelly."

"I wouldn't have cared."

"You Yanks!" Ryan laughed again and said, "Have you seen my other boot?"

In Ryan's eyes he had behaved with headstrong dash, but in his own he knew better. He had wanted all the way to slug Sprague, but his nervous system had simply refused. It was like blowing a fuse. If someone else had described such a scene, he would have said, why didn't you just hit him? Well, you couldn't fight for the right to keep your hands in your pockets. That was the only answer he could think of. A fight required a cause. You couldn't race your motor over nothing.

That evening he saw Sprague again, patrolling the corridor with his two friends, like the Queen inspecting a new garbage-disposal unit. Jimmy thought once more of hitting him, but decided against. Who knew what crazy point of etiquette the scene would turn on this time? He could see himself blushing, stammering, unable to raise his hands—because he was *wearing the wrong color socks.* Good God, man. He wanted to slip past before his pants, shirt, garters caused comment. To miss another meal would be catastrophic. Sprague appeared to have forgotten him completely, looking round him and through as celebrities do; but as the blank eyes swivelled round, Jimmy whipped his hands from his pockets; and felt a smaller man for it.

So what with Padgett and Sprague, the terror by night and the arrow that flew in the day, the classrooms came to seem almost like sanctuaries. The school corridors were booby-trapped with embarrassment—could *that* be the secret of English education? To make your classwork the only sane part of the day? From the fourth to the eighth week of term Jimmy went through his educational period. The teachers were definitely more rational than the boys. They had to do their acts, it was expected of them, but they never departed from the script. Once you had gauged any particular master's sound and fury, had probed to the outer limits of his ferocity, you could set your panic quotient with confidence. Example, Mr. Quince, his new Latin teacher. "Bannister, you erk" —a typical Quince-ism, nothing to worry about there. "I wish you would give some thought to that glazed expression. It's getting on my nerves." Good. Humor. Sir? "Page 58, you clod. Unless you use a different system of numbering in your curious country." The storm would pass by today in the distance.

But other days Quince would seem really to care, and Jimmy would care too. "Bannister, this is a disgrace. Bannister, you're not trying." His features would fold over like a bloodhound's. And Jim would feel, please stop that, I'll try again.

Too late now for the Smedley stupidity plan. What a disaster that had been. He had tried it just once on Mr. Smiles in geography, a bad choice, and Mr. Smiles had almost broken his elbow with his fingers, while taunting American education at the same time. Since then Jim's nerve had deserted him. At the last second he would always shrink from acting stupider than he had to. It required a kind of verbal confidence, of a negative order. So he said, "I'm sorry, sir," to Mr. Quince, and meant it. Jimmy lived in the limbo of the half stupid and would never be one of God's holy people like Smedley.

Smedley, meanwhile, kept pursuing his own plan with a heavy-faced fanaticism. Jimmy sat near him in arithmetic and marveled at the way he never flinched or brightened up in face of the Foghorn's roars. As a result he became a dumping group for the Foghorn's excess bluster, and this had somehow worked itself into a privilege. Occasionally Mr. Withers would wing him fondly with a piece of chalk or a blackboard eraser. "Smedley, you *clown,* Smedley, you ineffable—no, don't bother to look it up. What would be the use? You would probably look it up under 'f.' You ineffable, as I say, transcen*den*tal oaf." There was actual warmth in his voice; he had reached with Smedley some empyrean of insult where they were alone in mystic union.

After that, Jimmy only got the Foghorn's second-best shot, joyless and mechanical and actually much harder to take. As term wore on, Smedley seemed to become the only boy worthy of the great man's powers; and then finally even Smedley roused him only rarely.

The only comfort about all this was that Smedley's plan did not seem to be getting him to America any quicker. On the other hand, his denseness had made him something of a culture hero among the boys. There was something grand and incorruptible about him, like a Western hero. His wooden expression could almost be construed as tough. And he was doggedly and systematically stupid. His ignorance was so intricately dovetailed and cross-referenced that he could never be caught out knowing something today that he hadn't known yesterday. And he presented his poverty so solemnly and with such reserves of dignity that even Jimmy was almost taken in by it. (He couldn't really *be* stupid, could he?) "What page was that? The green book, sir? I don't have any green book. Oh—you mean this one?" He fumbled at the very portal of the question. The Smedley plan had sounded so simple; but in practice it called for almost excruciating heroism. Jimmy felt that it was also, probably, the most honorable response to this place—but he just wasn't up to it himself.

A man wearies of ping-pong eventually, and Jimmy took to slipping out for short strolls after supper. As usual, he didn't find out that this was against the rules until too late: until yet another outraged prefect had pointed it out to him with a virtuoso display of sarcasm. But by then these discoveries were becoming a fact of life and Jimmy found that honor was satisfied by waving a cautious middle finger at the prefect after he had disappeared.

This was some weeks later, and by then Jimmy had already managed to put in a number of quite satisfactory walks. The cool night air on his face kept the spooks at bay, and the thickening twilight made for a richer texture of reverie than the gray afternoons. The gaunt school buildings looked impressive in shadow. The school chapel blew up to a cathedral and the gymnasium could have been the rear end of a fortress. Through the downstairs windows he could see boys playing ping-pong and chess. Not so bad.

One of those evenings he chanced to bump into someone who was making the tour counter-clockwise, and braced himself for the inevitable roar. He was bound to be doing something wrong. On closer view, it turned out to be Mr. Withers, the Foghorn, so he double-braced himself.

"Enjoying the night air, are you, Bannister?" said the Foghorn with treacherous pleasantness. Jimmy's hands were at least eighteen inches wide of his pockets on either side. Nothing to fear on that count.

"Yes, I guess so."

"It's nice at this time of year, isn't it? I believe we have longer evenings than you do in your country. But of course we pay for it in the winter." His voice and what Jimmy could see of his face were rather anxious, as if he had been working out some personal problem. "It's particularly nice in this part of the world," he said. "That's why I moved here, you know. The air has remarkable tonic qualities. And the earth is marvelously fertile if you go in, as I rather do, for gardening. You can grow absolutely anything down here. Which is why the school never wants for fresh vegetables, of course. Well, I won't be keeping you, Bannister. You'll want to be getting on." He began to drift away. "Evening, Bannister."

For a moment Jimmy had a curious feeling of sweetness. He was to remember this moment the next time the Foghorn wailed at him.

Another time he thought he saw the ghostly Padgett standing in his usual shadows. But Padgett, he reminded himself, was a joke. After that, when the prefect came out and told him he wasn't allowed to go outside by himself after supper, he wasn't all that sorry to hear it.

On Sunday afternoons there was a letter-writing period and Jimmy wrote his father: but not the wild letters that still shrieked through his mind like express trains during the week. He described the conditions at length, but found himself pulling his punches as if he was embarrassed to let his father know what a crazy school he went to. Mr. Bannister's letters usually arrived on Saturdays and, after Jimmy's heart had leaped at the first two, began to seem quite a bit flat. Jim wearied of being told that he "seemed to be settling in" and that the headmaster was a fine man. When his own turn came on Sunday, he would iron out his father's latest, and try to find something to respond to. But there was nothing there, his father seemed to be sending the same letter over and over.

This at least kept his homesickness in bounds. (Could that be the old man's strategy? Unlikely.) On those lank Sunday afternoons in the big blank study hall, his father almost seemed to join his mother on the piano—two old photos, peering at him under glass. He certainly didn't sound like the old friend on Bear Mountain; he didn't answer Jim's questions about the summer or how his business was going. He almost seemed to be copying the letters out of a letter book.

But then—his father didn't set up to be a man of letters, in any sense. He dictated whatever he could, and added a small uncertain signature at the bottom. He was a smart man, but most of his business was done through personal contact, and he took to his pen with reluctance and suspicion. There was no point drawing conclusions from his letters.

Without noticing how it happened or when, he suddenly found himself friends with the two boys on his left in the dormitory—Ryan and Philpott—and the one across the way—Samuelson. These three spent much time devising ways to sneak food out of the dining room and ruses for dodging Army drill, and Jim found himself first listening and then throwing in suggestions: and then suddenly his tongue snapped back into place, and he was their friend. Slight concessions were called for on all sides. For instance, they seldom talked about girls, but listened politely enough when the mood was upon Jimmy. Philpott usually giggled. "You Yanks are all oversexed," said Ryan. "Smedley's just the same. On and on he goes . . ."

"Don't you guys have any interest at all?"

"Well, some, I suppose. But it isn't the whole of life, you know."

"Worthington is interested, and Peters." Samuelson ticked them off solemnly, as if they were the boxing team. "Smedley is really the ringleader. He brings in all the new jokes."

"Do you know 'Roll me over in the clover'?" giggled Philpott. "I heard Smedley sing the whole thing the other night. An astonishing piece of work."

Jimmy almost had trouble remembering what girls looked like by now. You could scarcely reconstruct them from the matron, and she was the only woman he had seen lately. Hence he found it difficult to sustain any kind of erotic fantasy. The girls had a way of tuning into something else. He had lost his normal expectation about faces since coming here. His vision of Marilyn Jenkins, for instance, might suddenly turn quite fat like Winston Churchill, or thin like Dr. Rabelais. Or even grow a mustache. The picture-making faculty was disordered by this onrush of English faces.

So this was one more reason to curtail masturbation and hurl himself into whatever nighttime activities were going. This meant in effect a quite endless pilfering of food, and two pie-beds a week for a boy called Jamison. Jim got surprising pleasure from this latter. Jamison was the dormitory butt, a mild boy with thin hair and glasses, and the teasing of him was as orderly as a minuet. Every third night or so Jamison would shuffle the length of the dormitory to complain to Meredith, the resident prefect, about some fresh indignity. He and Meredith would then shuffle back together through the gloaming and there would be a brief interrogation, with Meredith trying to look stern and the witnesses embroidering hotly. "Now look here, you chaps, this has simply got to stop. You're not in the junior school any more." "I think it was a raid, sir. From one of the other dormitories." "Oh now, Philpott, come on." "No, honestly, sir." "Yes, I thought I saw a chap skulking. It wasn't one of our chaps, different sort of chap entirely," said Ryan. "I suppose he was wearing a mask, was he?" "Yes, that's right. A mask and a hat over his eyes, sir." Jim held his breath, shivering with amusement: he doubted if anyone found it as funny as he did. Afterwards Jamison would plod about repairing the damage: not upset, to all appearances, but seriously puzzled.

The dormitory came to life as term sank into its third month. Meredith had seemed at first as brutal as the other prefects, but he showed now a slack, gentle side. He allowed the boys to read books under the sheets, and even to get in a little furtive visiting. The Ryan–Philpott axis took to staging brief picnics of bread and jam: at first in whispers, but then, as Meredith failed to respond, more and more raucously. Ryan would sing a few bars from *H.M.S. Pinafore,* and everyone would shush him and Philpott would giggle as he shushed. Then Samuelson would start things up again with one of his huge burps (he had the gift of burping at will) and Philpott would begin to laugh helplessly, hysterically. "Wrap up, you chaps," someone would groan from the far corner, the end near Meredith's cubicle, and eventually Meredith himself would come out and shout "Silence!" and wave his flashlight about listlessly. Then Ryan would have a hand clamped over Philpott's mouth and

Jimmy would be shaking silently in his bed; laughing to himself over nothing, a burp and a snatch of song.

One day as he sat waiting in his cricket pads Jimmy found himself describing one of these affairs to Smedley. It really had seemed awfully funny, there was no doubt on that score, and Jimmy told it exuberantly. Samuelson's burp going off like a howitzer; Ryan yelling "ouch" as Philpott bit into his hand; Meredith's flashlight reluctantly playing on them and then swooping off again before it could get involved.

"I had the jam pot under my pillow. Ryan had the bread under his *sheets,* I think it was. Anyway he was halfway out of bed trying to keep Philpott quiet . . ."

Jimmy suddenly realized that Smedley wasn't even slightly amused. And he didn't have to be told why. Jam pots. "But still I'm called, burp, Butterfly." He looked at Smedley closely. There was no expression on the fat boy's face. By God, I'll get you, Smedley. For this I'll get you. Smedley shook his head slightly and didn't say anything. He wasn't mocking Jimmy, just being true to his own lights. He had a kind of integrity at that. He would never sell out to this place, as a lesser man might.

Smedley walked out to bat, his hips rolling suavely. A self-made man. An American. He missed the first ball bowled to him, with an imcompetence verging on grandeur, and began to walk back, unbuttoning his batting gloves.

Jimmy resolved then and there to cut out the dormitory capers. Pie-beds, for Godssake. At his time of life. That evening Ryan said, "What's the matter with Bannister?" "Bannister has a tummy ache. It's all that rich American food he gorges on secretly!" "Smile, there's a good chap." "Cut it out." Jimmy pushed Ryan's hand away—Ryan was actually squeezing at his cheeks. "There's no need to be ferocious, Bannister." (Murmur of "Yanks are so blooming violent" somewhere down the dormitory.) They backed off and left him alone. They had moods themselves sometimes and were quite considerate. He perched morosely on his pillows, deaf to the giggles and the snatch of *Pinafore.* Of course, he reasoned, Smedley wasn't grown up either: on the other hand, you had to pass through Smedley to get there.

The loneliness came back slowly, an inch at a time, on caterpillar treads: rolling from the back of his head and occupying his sinuses. He realized that the fooling around had at least kept that away—a pity it was childish. Just for the sake of someone to talk to, he had sold out completely. Smedley, on the other hand, was taking the trouble to keep himself American. Making little sacrifices. When he got home, he could say, "I kept the faith." Jimmy would have turned into an English schoolboy by then. He groaned and turned his back on the invitation. Imagine thinking that business was funny. He absolutely agreed with Smedley. Practical jokes in the dormitory—two months ago he would have said it was impossible. Almost sixteen, almost driving,

sipping his father's beer, narrowing his dates down from double to single—
and here he was, hiding jam under his pillow. What had happened to him?

The voices twittered like sparrows, with a swiss-swiss-swiss of whispered
s's. They were just as silly as Smedley said they were—but what else was
there? Without the foolishness, it went back to being an empty barracks,
damp, sniffling gloom, solitude, a druid graveyard, a waiting room—for
what? For nothing, for seeing his father again. He got out of bed. He dug for
his slippers without looking down. He felt instinctively that he must raise his
head. A strange wave of sweetness that absolutely must be ignored in this
place fanned across his loins, hardening his decision.

Now that he wasn't inside it, the laughter sounded harsh, exclusive.
There were boys farther down the dormitory who would have felt privileged
to join the picnics, as he could, at will; the laughter must sound to them like
laughter through the Colony Club window. In this kingdom of gnomes he
had social stature.

It was really the depth of shame. Worse than yielding ground to a blus-
tering prefect, worse than groping for logarithms that never came. But there
was really no choice, no other life around here. And maybe if you kept reminding yourself that you *knew* it was silly, kept part of yourself outside it . . .
He knotted the tassle on his dressing gown definitively. It was this or the
horrors again.

"Here comes Bannister. Everything all right now, Bannister? Have you
brought some lovely American Spam?" Jimmy bowed his head and submitted to the feast.

□ **IV** □

Toward the end of June there was a sharp change of air pressure all over. The
last month of the summer term was in fact a startlingly mellow experience.
One of the prefects stopped Jimmy in the corridor and asked him a serious
question about American horse racing. The masters seemed to slacken, doing
their various routines from memory (the Foghorn even got Jimmy's name
wrong on one occasion, and bawled out a fictitious boy called Manwairing in
his place). Half the boys seemed to be sitting for various public examinations, and this took the heat off the other half. Ryan explained that the masters had a professional stake in the pupils' performances and that they tended

to become pleasanter and more human as they watched and waited; as if when the Day of Judgment came they would be able to say, "At least I was a nice chap. For instance, I was kind to that dreadful American boy."

The classrooms were wheezingly jocular. Homework was assigned and then forgotten. Mr. Smiles, the geography teacher, seemed to make his peace with America and took to reminiscing instead about rock-climbing holidays in Scotland. Dwarfish scamperings. Some classes were canceled altogether in deference to the exam schedule; and the masters spent the long afternoons playing squash, stalking butterflies, grubbing for leaf mold.

Thus ended Jimmy's educational period. All his friends were sitting for the school certificate (an exam which seemed to be the watershed between the middle and upper school) except for Smedley. So the logic of the situation threw him toward Smedley; but Smedley made him nervous these days. As fellow Americans, they kept a diplomatic connection alive, with exchanges like "You guys should taste some real ice cream. Right, Bannister?" "Right!" but there was a basic mistrust. Jimmy's failure to pursue the Smedley plan had something to do with it. Jimmy's choice of friends had a lot to do with it.

His new circle of Ryan, Samuelson and Philpott was quite outside Smedley's world. Smedley obviously thought they were little twits, especially Philpott, and of course they were, by any normal standards. Jimmy felt Smedley's eyebrows going up every time their respective convoys clashed. Why didn't Bannister hang out with Worthington and Peters and Featherstone? These were the logical companions for a high-stepper from across the pond. When Smedley wasn't mooning around by himself, looking detached as hell, he was observed swapping prurient one-liners with these three. Worthington was reputed to be one of the reasons the school had stopped using maids in the kitchen a couple of terms back; Featherstone was said to keep a motorcycle in the neighboring village, which took him to parts of London where pimples were no handicap. Peters at least kept pictures.

Maybe if Jimmy had been aware of them sooner, he would have gone the same way as Smedley. But now he was used to his little friends and there was no combining the two groups. On afternoons when they weren't working, he hiked with his claque of twits to outlying teashops, or to farms which supplied real boiled eggs and homemade cider. Ryan trudged beside him in a monkish stoop, while Philpott would bound ahead and catch at leaves. Samuelson always wore a neat little raincoat with a belt. Their conversation was babyish in the main, full of nagging jokes and sexless chatter about the holidays. But then suddenly Ryan would say, "Do you believe in God, Bannister?" or "Do you think it was a ghastly mistake to nationalize steel?"

In general, Bannister found that he was treated as a man to respect in matters of experience, but as rather backward intellectually. It was understood, on the few occasions the question arose, that Jimmy had already lived a definitive sex life and was totally reliable on such matters. But when he was asked about politics and religion, less was expected. The question about God or nationalization was simply a polite introduction to the questioner's own thoughts.

Philpott, absurd, childish in every other walk of life, was deadly sober about his politics. "I am High Church in religion and Tory in politics," he would say, all seriously. Samuelson was also conservative. "One must have order" was his thought on this, and Ryan would jump up and down and say, "Yes, yes, yes. That's the whole point. That's why one must vote Labour." If they brought Jimmy in at all, it was only to say, "Of course, you Americans have a mad system, don't you?" Once they asked him to explain this system—the machinery of primaries, delegations, etc., and of course he couldn't; and Samuelson, who had never been west of Bath, had to explain for him.

He didn't really mind. He rather liked being considered the crude man from out of the West with little formal learning but much savvy; a chap who knew the right moves in a nightclub or the back of a movie theater. Compared with, say, Philpott, he was a shrine of experience. Compared with Smedley and Co., he was something else. With them such claims had to be proved and updated. Being American started him off with a certain amount of credit. He knew how to play seven-card stud, and the other variations that Smedley had brought over, and he had been to Eddie Condon's. But where was his motorcycle or his girl in London? And why did he go around with twits? Judgment seemed to be permanently suspended in his case, and he began to see these boys as a vague threat.

The evenings now were impossibly long, and boys played cricket patiently in the twilight after supper. Jimmy had learned more or less how to bowl a cricket ball and he liked the gentle plodding about in the half dark. He could not bring himself to miss a ball on purpose (another weakness of character) and so, inexorably, he moved within range of the under-sixteen cricket team; and then, on a day when half of the side was laid up with examinations, into the side itself. He scored three runs and almost made a running catch and was complimented on his keenness, which was in truth considerable. At one point he saw Smedley lounging past the boundary, stopping, gazing without expression like a Hereford cow, and he thought, Smedley, I've betrayed you again, here as elsewhere. And yet the funny thing was that Smedley never said anything disapproving, never looked anything worse than stolid. It's all in your mind, Bannister. He continued roaring after the ball and firing it back to the infield or whatever they called it.

As he trailed back to school, with his cricket boots scuffing to the seven o'clock chime of the church bells, he asked himself why he was still allowing the concept of Smedley to bother him. The answer was of course that Smedley stood for America in some way—rather as the matron stood for women. He had no very special personality of his own, only a great undifferentiated

Americanness. To lose touch with Smedley, to lose favor with Smedley, was to cut yourself off from the source.

Jim had in his pocket a fresh letter from his father and that seemed American too, which was odd. For your father to seem any nationality was odd. The voice that had always been neutral as water would probably have an accent the next time he heard it—a grotesque accent, if he didn't keep in tune with Smedley.

Anyway, there were only two weeks to go now. Ryan had begun to count off the actual hours till the end of term, 236–235 ... By the end of July, Jimmy would be back home, swimming, boating in the Sound with his father, smelling the fresh paint on the boats. He could picture the white sails, hundreds of them, bobbing under a flawless sky: an honest-to-john blue sky after three months of scattered showers, unsettled conditions, depressions in the Midlands.

When he got to the changing room, he took out the letter for the fifth time since breakfast and read it again, with the sailboats in mind, hoping to hear a friendly twang in his father's voice, some promise of a good summer ahead. But Mr. Bannister had nothing to say about the summer. His voice came through faintly, like the metallic sound of a long-distance phone call. He had been receiving still more satisfactory reports about Jimmy's progress; seemed to be getting the hang of things, popular with the boys. By next term he should—next *term?* Well, we'll see about that, buddy boy. He put the letter away and looked around at the empty shower stalls. Who was watching him getting the hang of things? Who saw him being popular with the boys? Nobody ever seemed to see him at all, nobody but his little cubicle of friends: and yet his father kept getting these wonderful reports ...

At supper Samuelson said, "I hear you distinguished yourself on the cricket pitch this afternoon?"

"I wouldn't say that."

"He was the absolute linchpin of the side," said Ryan. "Of course he kept dropping his bat and tearing over to mid-off and shouting, 'Let's get 'em, gang,' but apart from that ..."

"Yes, and spitting on the ball," said Philpott. "Wonderfully expressive people, Americans. Marvelous athletes, I hear."

"It's the food, of course. Limitless Spam." Samuelson flexed his bicep and belched. "Peanut butter, milk shakes, vitamin-enriched plastic meatballs, the lot! My father's been over there this year and he says you wouldn't believe it, my dear. He says Americans are all at least six foot six by this time, in their plastic socks, and weigh a minimum of twenty stone ..."

"Of course, take baseball," said Philpott suddenly. "It's just a form of rounders, isn't it? There's not much science to it, is there? You just slog the ball, don't you? It's not like cricket, is it?"

"My father says it's much more exciting than cricket," said Samuelson.

"Pooey on cricket," said a boy farther up the table, which started a familiar digression. Ryan leaned out of this to say, "Are you jazzing it tonight, Bannister?"

"I hadn't thought about it."

"We have a new record."

"That's nice. We could use one."

"It's by Duke. 'Take the A-Train.' Smashing." Now that he was attuned to finer distinctions, Jimmy found Ryan a somewhat incongruous figure at the jazz club. As term wore on, he seemed to become ever more bouncy and zestful, developing a tendency to roll his eyes and tap his foot ferociously, as if it had gone to sleep, whenever the music got the least bit hot. The others glanced at him from time to time with something like embarrassment: as if to say, "Please! Not in front of Smedley!"

But then everything had turned upside down. At the first meeting of the club Smedley had seemed almost like a comedian: using his Americanism as a clown would use a physical deformity, to raise a laugh and ward off disgust. But now Smedley seemed absolute master of the scene, poised, sure of his audience; the slang phrases sounded quite ingenious, even to Jimmy, who knew theoretically that they shouldn't be mixed half so thick. As for himself, he was now the other kind of American; the laconic, underplayed kind, trafficker in surly monosyllables. He wanted to explain that he had misled them about this, but he found that it was too late; he was stuck; with this particular group, he *was* laconic.

In some curious way this one room where it was good to be an American had become one of his worst rooms. He was expected to live up to something here; he was Bannister, the other American. A tone-setter. His facial expressions were studied covertly. Notice how Bannister does it, notice how he listens. Yet the music sounded a little foreign to him now, accustomed as he was to the dormitory voices, Philpott's selections from *Pinafore,* and the "Sir, sir, *please* sir!" of the classrooms.

The New York scenes that had hit him with such poignance two months ago had lost almost all their flavor. Had he really felt sentimental about a Fifth Avenue bus? Yes, and an IRT subway as well. He felt like a monk clutching a lost faith. The holy pictures meant nothing any more.

The twelve members of the jazz club came from all corners of the school. Jimmy didn't know any of them in real life except Ryan and Smedley. So he was slightly surprised when one of them wheeled on him and said, "Wasn't that you I saw playing for the Colts today?"

"Yes, you might have."

"I thought so," the fellow said. "Yes, I thought it was you."

"I didn't know that Yanks played cricket," said someone else.

"They don't," said Smedley.

"Oh."

Jimmy could still feel the tingle of the afternoon's game and of the cold shower afterwards. He would have liked more silly conversation about baseball and cricket, but this was hardly the place for it. This was Smoky Joe's saloon, the bust of Elgar notwithstanding, and Big Dwight Smedley had just dropped in to touch bases with a bunch of the boys. The A-train was off again and they were all tapping their feet rigorously. Smedley snapped his fingers softly and muttered, "Yeah, yeah. Well, all right then." The smoke from the mandatory cigarettes hung like fog. Why was he sitting in this stuffy room when he could be out practicing his cricket? He looked at Ryan with his cozy Norman skull: the only face he liked was the only face that didn't belong here. Ryan, grooving like a madman, because he was Bannister's friend and felt safe, under the wing of a real Yank. Ryan, stay the way you are. It's better than this.

Yet this was America, or a groping facsimile thereof, and Jim sensed that if he began enjoying cricket better than this, he would be in some kind of trouble when he got back.

Well, America wasn't just jazz, of course. There was also fishing with his father, and the like. The next day he began counting off the hours with Ryan, although this made them go more slowly of course. Which was perhaps the point. At night he got into the habit of conjuring American scenes just to keep them clear in his mind: Huckleberry Bannister afloat on his raft. Dead-End Bannister, swimming bare-ass off Pier 19, rustic Bannister and urban Bannister all combined and intermingled. America was a series of colored slides, dated 1935–45, deeply engrafted on his retina: some based on fact, for his life had contained equal parts of city and country and he came by both his wienie roasts and his sunsets over Manhattan legitimately—but some just things that he thought he had seen, and everything just a little too bright and sunlit in the un-nuanced Technicolor of the period. With his picture machine slightly on the fritz, he found it helpful to overexpose his fantasies. And since the slides were made in England, his American sky overcompensated by being a gross, undeviating blue. The light was so strong at times that he had to open his eyes and bathe them in the darkness of the dormitory.

One night when he was either awake or asleep he received a visitor. He had been trying to conjure up Marilyn Jenkins—or, if he couldn't get her, at least Paulette Goddard—when soft as a moonbeam, the ghostly Padgett slithered between his sheets. He knew it was Padgett without loking. It seemed quite inevitable, almost expected.

"How are you, my dear?" said Padgett.

Jimmy didn't turn round. He was too tired to scream. Too embarrassed for Padgett.

"You've been avoiding me. You've been very cruel, you know." Jimmy shut his eyes and blocked off the nerve ends. He was not going to think about this. He began to sense a restlessness behind him, a dry heaving of sheets. "Well, that's all I wanted to say."

When Jim looked round a moment later, Padgett was gone. Jim fell asleep, or perhaps had been asleep all along. He honestly never knew which. (There should be a rule about people like Padgett, he thought.) The memory bothered him for several nights after that, mainly the memory of his not screaming. But he managed at last to drive it away with American prints; and—perhaps the thing had been an exorcism—he never saw Padgett again. Ryan told him that Padgett had been sent home early, sick or something. So that was the end of that.

Dr. Rabelais suddenly came back to life in the last two weeks—as if his real life was lived in the vacation and he slept like a koala bear through the terms. He would be observed regaling knots of older boys in the corridors: the guffaw of the eighteen-year-old Englishman would probably echo in Jimmy's head forever. Dr. Rabelais arranged two-minute chats with every boy in the school, making up thus for three months of paralytic inattention. Jimmy must have been about 230th on the list, because he sensed a certain languor beyond the usual in the headmaster's style when the meeting finally eventuated.

"I hear you've been settling in very well, Bannister"— so that was where all that talk came from. "Mr. Worthing tells me that you're quite popular." If there was anybody Bannister had seen less of than the headmaster, it was Mr. Worthing, the housemaster of Frisby. All the petty house discipline was funneled through the prefects, and Mr. Worthing spent most of his time tinkering with his baby Austin, wiping his hands on oil rags, climbing in and puttering off through the gates.

"Scholastically, the picture is not quite as grim as it might once have appeared. Mr. Withers informs me that you have apparently mastered the mysteries of logarithms and should be prepared to sit for the school certificate a year from now; Monsieur Necker seems to feel"—Dr. Rabelais looked puzzled as he read this bit of the report—"that your French has gone off slightly? But that you are still one of his most satisfactory pupils. Well." Dr. Rabelais hurried on. "Mr. Smiles says that you have taken significant strides . . ."

There was simply no listening to this stuff. Jimmy gazed round, his eye pausing at the little white walking sticks. He wondered once more what they felt like. Bee stings? Razor cuts? They were part of the life of the place, very much so, and he was curious about them after listening to the veterans compare notes.

He had come within inches of finding out just two nights ago. Meredith, the dormitory prefect, had decided for some reason to reverse the general thaw in labor-management relations. Possibly wishing to make up for a lackluster performance through the balance of the term; possibly because

Ryan and the chaps had simply pushed him too far; possibly from some discontent of his own, about leaving school forever. In any event, he swung his torch flush onto the picnic for once, and then surprised everyone by not swinging it away again.

There was the usual ratlike scurry, for which Meredith seemed to allow sufficient time. But Jimmy was held for a second or two by a strange topor, mixed with a wish, perhaps, to test himself against an easier prefect than Sprague. What would happen if Meredith caught him? He hesitated, still on the edge of Ryan's bed, with a large coconut cake on his lap.

Someboy told him the next day that the cake possibly saved him from a charge of moral turpitude. But at the time it seemed to incriminate him further.

"Hello," he said to Meredith, who hovered a few feet away now, a dark lump of anxiety. Meredith waved the torch at him in a wild gesture. "Bannister! What the devil do you think you're doing?"

"Nothing."

"Devil do you think you're doing with that cake?"

"Nothing. Just sitting."

"Well, you don't just sit with a *cake*, Bannister. In the middle of the night! Do you?"

"Yes, Meredith. I mean, no, I guess not."

There was a breathless silence. Meredith had his torch beam leveled at the cake, lighting it up as if for a celebration. He, too, had face to save. His difficulty was obvious, and one could sense the other boys working it out quietly to themselves. Meredith did not lack for courage; as a rugby football player, it was said to be his strong suit. But this was a poser. Jimmy was close to the age where, by unwritten custom, beating stopped. Beyond that, he was an American. Did one beat Americans?

No one spoke. Meredith swung the torch around, and Jimmy half expected him to say, "Ryan! What would you do?" Jimmy sat and waited while the plate grew heavy on his knees. Meredith, he suddenly realized, had enjoyed the dormitory childishness as much as anyone, although he must be all of eighteen. He was now making a stern effort to grow up.

Finally Meredith spoke. "Put the damn thing away, will you?" And they heard him stomping slowly back to his eyrie at the far end of the dormitory. In its way, it almost made up for Sprague.

"I have been in correspondence with your father, and he quite agrees," Dr Rabelais droned, "that it would"—Jimmy was barely listening—"be beneficial"—it was like being in church—"for you to stay with us a bit longer and do some leisurely tutoring, tone you up, so to say, for the hard road that lies ahead . . ."

Jimmy's immediate reaction was one of only mild interest. He understood in a general way what the headmaster was getting at, but nothing said in that voice could have consequences in the real world. Besides, the thing was manifestly impossible. The words must have a different meaning over here.

"I have arranged for you to have a private room. You'll like that, I expect. And you will eat your meals . . ."

"You don't understand. I'm flying to America on the twenty-seventh. It's been fixed."

"Yes, the plans have been altered slightly. You're to stay here for the first two weeks . . ."

"No, it's impossible. Father told me himself the twenty-seventh."

"Perhaps a subsequent letter has gone astray. The mails have been in an infernal chaos since the war. I remember when you used to get a letter . . ."

"I don't believe it. It's a mistake. I'm flying on the twenty-seventh, you see."

The headmaster fished around for the blue air letter. "Very handy little things, these. Ingenious. American, I daresay. Yes, here we are." He handed it to Jimmy.

The typewriting, the tone were authentic. Mr. Bannister was delighted with his son's progress, concerned, fully cognizant, willing to leave it up to, eternally grateful . . . Jimmy looked at it blankly. At this point the thing that bothered him was his reservation on the twenty-seventh. It was all fixed, you see. He knew the ticket by heart, knew that his name was spelled wrong on it (Banester), knew that its powers were unchallengeable. It sat in his pocket right now, as solid as the crown jewels.

"It's only for two weeks," said the headmaster. "As you observe, your father has made a reservation for you on the"—he peered at the letter—"twelfth."

"The summer will be over by then."

"Surely not. In any event"—the headmaster became wearily stern—"it is absolutely imperative that you have the extra tuition, and two weeks is the absolute minimum if it's to do you any good at all. The school certificate is far from a certainty in your case, you know. By next summer you will be"—he shut his eyes and pondered—"sixteen . . ." He went on like this for several minutes, or perhaps it was hours, demonstrating in the course of it that Jimmy's "wonderful progress" was just a manner of speaking: that, in fact, if Jimmy had done any less well, he would have been out of the ball game altogether. "It will be quite a *coup* if we achieve the school certificate after such a very unpromising start."

Jimmy noticed that the office seemed to have become much darker, so perhaps he *had* been in there for hours; or perhaps it was the snuffing out of his ticket. The latter had become completely worthless. He could imagine a man in a blue uniform frowning and scratching the name Banester off his list, and then the steel door shutting without him, and the plane rising. The ticket was right here in his jacket *pocket!* Worthless—

"Here, here, don't do that." Dr. Rabelais moved clumsily, pulling out the inevitable white handkerchief. Jimmy shook his head. It had become a point of pride never to accept these things.

His mind was temporarily deflected by the crying problem. Leaky Jim. He had supposed, after the stupid, hands-in-pockets affair, that his crying days were really over this time. Not so. Just beginning. He truned his face from the headmaster and tried to wrestle with it privately. He could hear impatient voices through the door: a long line of boys were waiting to see the head-master and their voices had become shriller as the study had become darker. He would have to pass them on the way out.

"Well, Bannister." The headmaster was embarrassed now, tapping his finger. This seemed to be an aspect of the job he would never be able to cope with. He began to rise, and Jimmy had a strange feeling that he was going to swoop across the desk and pound his back. Jimmy made one last attempt to compose himself. He tried feeling angry, and the only result was a withering snort that startled both of them. He stood up and more or less bolted from the room.

He ran past the line of boys, trying to look determined and overdue somewhere else: but he was betrayed by another rending snort just as he had cleared the end man. He decided not to try the dormitory, which would be full of boys packing and skylarking, but veered off through a side door in the building, past another group of shrill, happy boys—the whole school reeked with happiness now—and out to one of the quiet lanes, where no one could bother him.

Another two weeks here wouldn't be so bad, he told himself. His father not telling him wasn't so bad. His father not telling him—he crouched down by an old stone wall in a last paroxysm: a lead weight squatted behind his eyes, in the bridge of his nose; and fresh tears were swimming around in his chest. The mails were, of course, a perfect chaos. But still.

He stopped crying, but stayed in the crouch for safety's sake. The talk about his progress had undoubtedly softened him up. That was one thing. Another thing was his . . . his . . . oh, this was ridiculous. He focused bleary eyes on the lane. The old man on the woman's bicycle would be by at any moment and one wouldn't want him to find one crying.

Look at it this way, Bannister—up till an hour ago, one had actually had mixed feelings about going home at all. One had actually . . . He must force himself to talk American. The stone wall across the way was supposed to be five hundred years old. How about that, sports fans. Behind that was a meadow with some stupid cows. Brown and white, which kind was that? Jerseys? Alderburies? The cows are taking over, men. Behind the cows a white farmhouse. Built by the Romans in 10,000 B.C. Utterly destroyed by the Vikings, restored, *ut*terly destroyed, restored . . . Only two weeks actually.

He saw now quite clearly that America was better than this stupid place would ever be. One aspect that hadn't occurred to him before came to mind now with the impact of something quite important. And that was that all the good ballplayers would be back from the war this year. Joe DiMaggio, Tommy Henrich, King Kong Keller. He had already missed more than half the season. He could see the bright grass of the Stadium, the white ball flying around like mercury; and hear the harsh mumble and smell the mustard as you went up the ramps. Cricket, for Pete's sake. Time out for tea, fellows. Effort, chaps.

Anger was good. He straightened up cautiously. He could probably stand now without crying. He had a grip on it. His crying days really were over. He suddenly knew it for a fact: but he wasn't going back to the dormitory to watch them pack. That was too much to ask. Instead he wandered farther into the country, raging at cricket and old farmhouses. Throwing stones at the trees or bouncing them along the road. Crumby old country.

Well, why didn't Father tell me? He looked at the thought with dry eyes, drying heart. Really, so what? It might bother him again later, but right now it didn't matter too much. His father wasn't that important. He had banked too heavily on that, that was why he was always crying. Two stupid weeks. He could survive it, he guessed. They wouldn't get much work out of him, that was for sure. After five hundred years they could use some new walls around here.

His feet got tired and he turned back. As he neared the school grounds he saw a dejected figure slumping toward the iron gates—from the other direction, as if he was coming out to meet himself. No, it was Smedley. Smedley, what ails you, boy? Smedley waved weakishly and sidled through the gates.

"I saw you crying outside Rabelais' office," he said.

"Yeah, I guess so."

"Things are tough all over. Whatsamatter, Jim—they keeping you another year?"

Uh-huh. And not only another year. Two weeks of the summer as well. Can you beat *that*, sports fans. They really love me around here."

"That's too bad. Just can't get enough of you, huh, kid?"

"That's right. Love that Bannister."

"Well"—Smedley kicked the ground—"you have my condolences. I'm only sorry I won't be around to watch you suffer."

"What do you mean?"

"I mean I went right in after you and got canned. It seems that in spite of all those good American dollars my father pays them to keep me they don't need the guy men call Dwight Smedley."

"Well—that's great, isn't it?"

"I guess *your* father will have to support the joint by himself." Smedley rambled. "One American to a school."

"It's great, though. Isn't it just what you wanted?"

"Yeah, I guess so." Smedley suddenly looked like a boy again, as he had the first time Jimmy had seen him. His face was round and gentle and desolate.

"Good luck, Jimmy," he said.

"You too, er, Dwight."

Smedley shuffled off to commune with the country lanes Smedley-fashion.

The packing seemed to last forever, and Jimmy got used to watching it eventually. There were jolly accusations of who's been pinching my this-and-that, and scuffles in the bathroom over unidentified soap and toothpastse. From being such a stiff place at first, the school had lapsed into feebleminded carnival. Even the matron conducted her final business in a pepper-and-salt suit, with a Tyrolean hat plainly visible on the rack outside.

"Going back to Yankeeland, are you?" she said.

"Yeah, any year now."

"I'm told it's rather lovely around Arizona," she conceded. "Is that where you're going?"

"No."

"Pity." She released the blood-pressure sleeve, which was sort of her trademark, and waved him on.

Seeing the school empty out was almost as bad as seeing it fill up. The boys chuffed along the main corridor lugging their outsize suitcases, with the cricket bats and the tennis racquets and even in one instance a pair of oars strapped to the sides: putting the whole mess down, breathing hard, and then heaving along again and out through the main door.

Outside, they piled into taxis and chartered buses, giggling and crowding. Jimmy strolled outside to say good-bye to his friends. Samuelson was rather abstracted, already halfway home in his mind. (A really nice little home for Samuelson, with a neat apple-pie bedroom, prints, boxes full of colored stones, sea shells.) Ryan gave a very warm handshake. "I'll see you in the autumn, I trust," he said. Philpott was running around the bags, trying to hide Ryan's under somebody else's mackintosh. All three were going to London to begin with, before heading their separate ways; and it would be a hysterical train ride if Philpott had anything to do with it.

In place of the crushing undifferentiated sadness he had become so used to, Jimmy experienced something new, which he called immediately by its right name—melancholy. The quadrangle was silent, except for the soft crunch of the matron's boots. "Cheerio, Bannister. Have a nice holiday." The door of Mr. Worthing's baby Austin clicked shut: "Crank-case" Worthing was giving the matron a lift to the station: they chatted together in the front seat like old friends. Again silence, except for the distant shriek of the crows. A curious sweetness flooded him, like a special sweet kind of blood. His bones felt light and there was even a sweet taste in his mouth. This feeling had approached him several times before, but he had shied away from it. The doorman at his apartment building was subject to fits of epilepsy. The man had told him of a strange, gorgeous elation that came on just before his attacks ... But nothing bad happened now. Jim circled the quadrangle twice, floating slowly like a soap bar, savoring the silence.

His drift was interrupted by a clatter at one of the side doors. A boy he didn't know came crashing out with suitcases under both arms. "Have they gone? *My God!*" cried the boy. "Have they actually left?"

Ha, ha, you're trapped! thought Jimmy, and it was all he could do not to laugh a sweet evil laugh at the way things were going.

It was arranged that he should have breakfast every day with Dr. Rabelais and his wife. The doctor read *The Times.* Jimmy read the *Telegraph,* and Mrs. Rabelais brought in cold toast and pungent, peel-ridden marmalade (strong enough to drown the taste of the margarine). The breakfasts were large and slow, and Jimmy got used to browsing through the pictures of King George and his daughters reviewing, inspecting, standing indefatigably by, and of the Queen Mother being handed things by small girls, the mellow endless court calendar. And when he had read almost every word of the *Telegraph,* he would squint at the pictures on the back page of the headmaster's *Times*—the Duchess of Kent assisting at the all-England croquet championships, the passing out at Aldershot (whatever that meant), the Queen Mother launching a new library.

Imperceptibly, he and th eDoctor would slide into the morning's work. The curious thing here was that Rabelais now treated him as an absolute equal, asking his opinion, deferring to his judgment. "What would be your rendering of this word? Chambers allows a third possible meaning, but his only reference is to Pliny, which is rather late for our purposes. What say you—shall we take a chance, or shall we follow the path of prudence?" "Let's take a chance, sir." "Very well, Bannister. A chance it shall be ..." Jimmy was getting to like this kind of talk.

They pottered their way through all the subjects in the syllabus, and although he couldn't see that it was getting him any closer to the school certificate, Jimmy did at least begin to understand the headmaster's musty enthusiasm for learning: and, just in this peculiar context, even to share it a little. Rabelais made it seem like an extension of *The Times.*

Jimmy had the afternoons pretty much to himself and was allowed to borrow Dr. Rabelais' barnacled bicycle for sorties to the nearby villages.

There he would dismount and, having parked his bike in whatever passed for a municipal center, cruise the streets slowly on foot, like an old man with nothing better to do, ruminating into shop windows, front parlors and even into back gardens. Nobody seemed to mind, or even to notice. At four o'clock he would seek out a stationer's and if there was a new issue of *Film Fun* or *Picture Post* to be had, he would carry it off to a café and read it over a large, solitary tea.

When he got back, the headmaster's wife would encourage him to take a bath, and he always made a business of it, stewing interminably and then drawing pictures on the steamed-up mirror and examining himself from various angles, keeping abreast of develoments. (Philpott had asked him one day if he thought he was handsome, and he had said yes, and Philpott had giggled. It had stuck in his mind.) He had reached the stage where he thought he needed to shave, but nobody else agreed. The pimples which the matron had sneered at had temporarily leveled off: but shaving would undoubtedly cause some confusion among them.

When the mirror had cleared all the way, it was his pleasure to stand in front of it swinging an imaginary bat in some indeterminate game, or to pitch, bowl, make faces, sometimes even to do a soft-shoe in his bare feet on the bath mat—until Mrs. Rabelais would knock on the door to ask if he was all right, and he would reach for his trousers in a reflex of embarrassment.

He always left the bathroom with regret, as one wakes from a good dream. But most evenings the headmaster would have him down afterwards for an orange squash or possibly a sip of sherry, so the prospect of evening was not as gloomy as it might have been. At dinner Dr. Rabelais had a tendency to make puns (surprising, because he never made them at any other time: it was like family prayers), after which he would retire to his study, leaving his wife and Jimmy to do the dishes and listen to the wireless.

So it turned out that the two weeks he had dreaded so much were among the happiest he had ever spent. Leaving the school at the end of them was not unlike leaving the warmth of the bathroom. He packed his ice skates and his baseball glove and jogged to the station in the headmaster's prewar Morris. The train ride to London was drafty and long, with no Philpott on hand to hide his suitcase and dash up and down the corridor. The only people who talk to fifteen-year-old boys in transit are people fifteen-year-old boys don't especially want to talk to. He liked the train itself, though, and enjoyed the lunch of sausage and mashed potatoes and the fields jogging alongside.

He was met at Paddington Station by a friend of his father's, a man called Soames, in a big American hat and a broad-shouldered topcoat which looked very strange. "Hiya, Jimmy," Mr. Soames said, although they had never met before. "Your dad told me"—his voice was as dissonant as his hat. He seemed friendly at first, but after a while Jimmy felt that he wasn't friendly at all. He paid no attention when Jimmy talked—and very little when he talked himself—but kept looking around and around to make sure that everything was going smoothly. "I bet you'll be glad to get home," he said.

"I guess so," said Jimmy. "I only wish I was going back for longer. *You* know, I'll just be getting used to things and then I'll have to turn round and come right back here."

Mr. Soames didn't answer: he apparently wasn't the man to discuss delicate points of sensibility with. He said, "Have you got your ticket? That's a mighty heavy suitcase, what have you got in there anyway? Bricks? Your dad will be glad to see you," etc. Driving in a taxi with this man through the dingy London streets lined with mustard-colored overcoats was one of the drearier things he'd done lately. Was Soames a typical American? He couldn't remember for the life of him.

It was probably possible to explain Mr. Soames, without dragging America into it. Mr. Soames worked in the embassy and saw thousands of people a day and he had developed a personality like a swinging door. Jimmy slumped back in the seat. There was no point in getting used to Mr. Soames, or even to London: he was flying away from both in the morning.

"You know you have a slight English accent, Jimmy?"

"I do?"

"Yes, you do. Your dad will be tickled."

The phrase "your dad" jarred more than anything Mr. Soames said. Of all the phrases he couldn't imagine Dr. or Mrs. Rabelais using, "your dad" surely came first. "Your father has been in touch with me, Bannister." The grave music came back to him, like the memory of a perfect croquet game or a really superb crossword clue. "Your father informs me that he fully concurs in my own view of the matter, which was not arrived at lightly, I assure you, where was I, Bannister—oh yes"—that was the way to talk. It was like a chapel at twilight with shafts of blue sunlight falling on the preacher's smock and the begats falling like rain—so I have an English accent, have I?

They had supper together in Jimmy's hotel, and Mrs. Soames, a listless blond woman who reminded Jimmy of a woman in a knitting pattern, made further comments on Jimmy's accent ("It's cute. Your dad will love it") and told him no, she didn't think he needed a shave, did he, Ted? He looked perfectly fine; and he went to bed early, glad to get away from the two of them. His memory could not have capsized completely: Americans were not all like that. He thought about his friends, Harry and Forrest and Vince; but as he dozed off, each of these friends seemed to take on a certain Soames-like quality, their clothes and voices and haircuts. "Your dad told us you'd be here, it's great to be back in the U.S.A., five'll get you ten, gimme some skin, man"—a grinning chorus of Smedleys and Soameses waited on the dock waving flags and frankfurters; he drifted by on his raft, in blinding sunlight; *rocketsredglare*, boom, *bombs bursting in air*, boom ... The P-49's flew overhead in endless volleys while the President talked total victory. Noise, war effort. Miss New Jersey drove her ten-millionth rivet while the bulbs popped and the new battleship slithered down the causeway. He twisted away from the racket and banged his head against the old brown cabinet that housed the porcelain chamber pot. Oh brother, this was going to be great.

As a result of his restless night, he slept a lot on the plane through the long day of a westward flight. When he wasn't asleep he read a detective story and chewed on the mints and bits of gum that the stewardess kept priming him with. (She had been especially asked to look after him, and this seemed to be the only thing she could think of: Jimmy in turn didn't like to refuse her.) The man next to him was contagiously shy, so that it was all very nice and quiet. Jimmy became uncomfortable just before the end, because he wanted to go to the bathroom, and this shy man next door had a way of jerking his knees nervously as Jimmy passed over and then half rising and getting pinned on the arm of the chair, and Jimmy was reluctant to set all this in motion. Then, when he could stand it no longer, the *fasten seat belts* sign went on and he was trapped for another twenty minutes or so. Outside of that, it was an uneventful trip.

□   V   □

Dad was the right word for him after all. To eyes accustomed to Dr. Rabelais, Jimmy's father seemed large, streamlined, all the bugs removed from the 1946 model. He had on a sky-blue summer suit and a broad silver necktie, a brown straw hat and two-toned shoes: not a single item that Rabelais could have worn to one's wildest dreams. Had he always dressed like that, or was it the postwar boom? The customs official was also very large and smooth, with manicured fingernails. He welcomed Jimmy back to the country and winked solemnly at Mr. Bannister, who unfortunately winked back.

"Which of these bags are yours, sonny?" asked the colored porter.

"These three, actually," said Jimmy.

The porter laughed, his father laughed. "Are you quite positive, old boy?" said the porter. His father laughed all the way into the cab. Jimmy felt a multiple embarrassment. Was this going to happen everywhere he went, and every time he opened his mouth? Tiresome, as Rabelais would say.

His father certainly shouldn't have laughed. It was all right for the porter, but his father had sent him to the darn school and shouldn't make fun of him. He found it preying on his mind as they drove into the city. It put him at temporary odds with his father, who was also fatter than he remembered.

"I have to go to the office this afternoon, Jimmy. I guess you could use some shut-eye."

"I slept on the plane."

"Oh, well, that's not like regular sleep, is it?"

"I guess not."

His father had been laughing to please the porter, not because he was really amused. Oh, well. Jimmy was glad to see him anyway. He was a nice comfortable man whom everyone had a slight urge to tease. Jimmy knew that the teasing was on sufferance; his father had a hard streak and would hit back if he felt he was being gotten at. Why am I telling myself all this? Jim was sleepy after all, and he faded off right there in the cab.

The plan was for Jimmy and his father to spend two nights together in town and drive out to Long Island the afternoon after tomorrow. This involved sharing a hotel room, because Mr. Bannister had given up apartments for good, now that he was living by himself. That evening Jimmy was seriously appalled at his father's large, slug-like belly, which flung out mountainous over his floral pajama pants. You would never have supposed that all this lurked under the smooth blue jacket. A gentleman's corset lay panting on the bag rack. Jimmy could hardly bear to look at it: although of course he could see nothing else in the room.

His father walked into the bathroom . . . Jimmy didn't want to think of him *as such.* He talked quickly, trying to sneak back into friendship that way.

"You know, when you travel from one place to another place you keep seeing things like it's for the first time."

Mr. Bannister was brushing his teeth already but gave a muffled sound of agreement, or anyway of interest.

"Like the cars. They really look crazy, don't they? You see one little guy in a great big car. What a waste of space, huh? And the food in the dining room tonight—I saw a lady leave a steak on her plate that would have fed four people in England." He got into bed and pulled up the sheet. "Did you ever eat powdered eggs? Take my advice. Don't." He felt his old voice coming back, forcing its way exultantly. "Powdered milk. That's even worse. They put it in your tea, and they say—now, I'll bet you can't tell the difference. Ach, ptui! *Can't tell the difference.*"

His father came out of the bathroom drying his ears.

"It's been an interesting experience for you, hasn't it, Jimmy?"

"Yeah, I guess so."

"I'll try to send you more food next term. Give you a change from those powdered eggs."

"Next term? Hey, I don't really have to go back next term, do I?"

"It's a wonderful cultural experience."

"Yeah, but enough cultural experience is enough."

"A fine educational system . . ."

"Very handy if you happen to find yourself in ancient Greece—" But the threat was still a long way away and he argued weakly. At the moment it was hardly even a threat; he rather liked the prospect of roaring along the drafty corridors again, with Ryan barking like a machine gun and Philpott crumpling against the bulletin board, or of drinking tea with Mrs. Rabelais, and reading the back of her husband's *Times,* and weaving into the village and bicycling home for more tea. He let the argument go for now. He could bring it up later if he felt like it.

His father sat on the side of Jim's bed, and told him how it was. "In years to come, you'll be thankful. A lot of the kids around here could use a taste of powdered eggs. Our kids are a lot too soft if you ask me."

What did he know about this man anyway? Jimmy shut his eyes and prayed for sleep. But he couldn't help thinking, just before he lost the thought in blackness, that Mr. Bannister sounded just like one of his own letters.

His wild remark to Rabelais, that he was getting back to America "too late for summer," had a certain truth to it. The summer had its own rhythm, and it had been pushing along all this time without waiting for him. Marilyn Jenkins, for instance, had left for Cape Cod. He called his other city friends the next afternoon and listened to the wrangle of telephones in empty apartments; or found himself talking to thick-voiced cleaning women, who always let the phone ring twenty times before answering. "He's out. They gone away, didn't say when they'd be back. O.K. You welcome." Strange, strange voices. The worst blow was getting no answer at Forrest Tuckerman's; he was really looking forward to gassing with Tuck.

His father worked late the next day and Jimmy finally fetched up at a movie: Cary Grant, neither English nor American, a way station or oasis . . . Jimmy was relieved to notice that some of the men sitting around the theater were dressed like his father. That was one embarrassment the fewer. In fact, Mr. Bannister looked a lot better by dinnertime: his face was creased and friendly, stamped with little red crow's-feet, and he had lost some of his accent. Jimmy almost asked about the two extra weeks in school and why his father hadn't written to warn him: but again he was suddenly *embarrassed* for his father, afraid for what silly thing he might say.

Instead he asked about the pennant races and what kind of year Phil Rizzuto was having for the Yankees, what it was like in general having all the prewar stars back from the Army. It occurred to him part way through the conversation that he didn't really care very much; and he wondered whether his father cared either. Well—it was something they could talk about.

His father's whale belly had lost most of its terrors this time around. Remind me never to let myself get fat, was all Jimmy thought about it. Mr. Bannister's night talk was more relaxed than it had been yesterday, reminding Jimmy of their previous bouts of summer friendship. He realized that he had indeed missed his father, it was just a matter of getting his land legs. He asked if his father had made any big sales lately, and Mr. Bannister began to describe one particular coup that had pleased him; and Jimmy suddenly felt a bone-crushing boredom, and decided then and there to keep this kind of talk to a minimum. His father sounded like a stockholder's report.

The next morning Jimmy went down to a drugstore for breakfast, with a crisp five-dollar bill in his pocket, and felt, as he slice through a pile of soggy, mottled pancakes, the first pure and delicate joy at being back. All this food—you couldn't stay mad at it for long. *The New York Times* was spread out on his left and the baseball information was suddenly as enthralling as it had ever been. He read every report of every game and then the box scores, noting how many hits Johnny Pesky had made (he liked the name Pesky) and how many chances Lou Boudreau had accepted. Five assists, three put-outs, no errors. How about *that,* you American mothers? He was so elated this morning he could have shouted.

His father left the office early that afternoon and, perhaps sensing that Jimmy was in a good mood, launched into a discussion of some girl he was seeing these days, Lorraine Somebody-or-other. Jimmy preferred to study the postwar cars through the side window. He didn't care to hear his father talk about girls.

"The Cadillac is the only car that looks any good," he said. "The new Chryslers stink."

"You'll be meeting Lorraine this evening and I hope you—I know you'll like her."

"I expect I will," Jimmy said politely. "I liked the last one: Gloria. The Studebaker looks kind of interesting in a morbid kind of way."

"Yes—Gloria was a fine girl, but she was never more than a friend. Lorraine is something special."

"Yeah?"

"I'm thinking of asking her to marry me."

"You are?" They passed a low-slung Mercury. A mustard-colored mess, in Jimmy's opinion. Mr. Bannister was gunning the car in his excitement, and Jimmy thought, oh for Pete's sake. Here we go again. A few months ago Mr. Bannister had been gunning his motor just as hard for Gloria. Then something had gone wrong in mid-winter, there was that sense of a mute scuffle, of voices late at night nicking at his sleep, and his father was free again. Right after that, Jim had been whisked off to England. He simply refused to take his father seriously in this area. The DeSoto was sort of point-less . . . he shut his eyes and opened them to the smell of fresh fish and the signs advertising fishing tackle and fried clams, and the stout men strolling the boards in T-shirts and peaked hats and sandals, details to be stored up for some winter or other.

They drove to the old summer house in Queequeg. His heart jumped a full inch at the sight of the dusty white clapboard. They went through the rooms opening the windows, expelling the must and letting in gray briny air. His father was still flushed and a bit absent-minded, and Jimmy had to face the fact that their last friendship, and the one before that too, had been abbreviated by girls. For several weeks each time he would see less of his father; and once he even wound up with his aunt in Brockton. But it always worked out. Meanwhile, he liked the stripped-down house. The bare floorboards and the empty closets with wire hangers dangling. Some of the best things about being back were odd things like this. A stack of old comic books stood by the bedside, looking wonderfully inviting, and having nothing better to do except unpack and make his bed, he squatted down on the mattress and began to leaf through *The Phantom.*

Thump, crunch, the clockwork collision of ill-drawn bones. About five comic books later he heard voices being piped through the floor, shrill cocktail-hour voices that pierced the planks like hot rivets, a woman with a wide mouth, a man showing off. He hoped this wasn't going to louse up the summer. He rammed through a couple more of the comics, although it was frankly an effort by now. More whirling capes and flashing feet than he had bargained for. He tossed *Flash Gordon* aside. Give me the Queen Mother any day—and went reluctantly downstairs.

His father was gently agitating the martinis, like holy water. Martinis usually meant a bad evening, worse than bourbon, much wild laughing and jokes that didn't make any sense, followed by midnight swims and mysterious excursions; and for him, the house to himself, a house that looked like an unmade bed, with ashtrays slopping over and glasses on the mantelpiece and even teetering on the back of the john—well, why go on? To the last giggle and door slam? It wouldn't be as bad now as it was a few years ago. During dinner he would at least be ignored. He was too old now to be haphazardly manhandled and flattered. ("Your're a fine boy, Willy." "Name is Jimmy.") Many dank evenings came back, just from watching his father's small hands on the martini pitcher. ("Willy here is going to be *all right.*")

The second thing he noticed was, my gosh, it's Mrs. Soames. There's been a terrible mistake. A stringy blonde with long heavy lids was drifting toward him, circling Mr. Bannister, and she was just like the woman in London. What a depressing development. Something had happened to women in his absence. She shook his hand and he felt long golden nails skimming against his palm. "I've heard so much about you," she said.

"You have?" he said—he had never worked out an answer to that one.

"Yes, your dad is always talking about you."

"He is?"

"Yes. He's very proud of you."

"Huh."

Having finally worked out how to talk to Englishmen, Jimmy had clean forgotten how to talk to Americans. No doubt it would come back in a day or two. But for now, "I'm very proud of *him*" was the only thing he could think of saying, and that was manifestly not the thing.

So he sat down quietly and listened to them instead. Their voices didn't sound quite so bad down here, but they were still awfully loud and scratching. Lorraine talked in a Seven Sisters drawl that sounded suspect to Jim (although he knew this accent sounded fake even when it was done right), and this brought out a trace of latent North Boston in Mr. Bannister's answers. It was like being able to look into people's skin through a microscope. "Can't you hear that she's a phony?" he wanted to tell his father at one point: and then: "Can't you hear that *he's* a phony?" to Lorraine. Can't you hear that we're all phonies? When Jimmy chimed in himself, his own voice sounded just as silly as theirs, and the thought of having to listen to the three of them all summer became really quite depressing.

The martinis went on and on, sizzling cold and smoky, and when dinner finally came along, Lorraine didn't eat any of it, but kept right on smoking and drinking and talking about the Wheeler estate, which had recently come on the market. As soon as he could, Jimmy slipped outside. They were getting affectionate, jamming two or three honeys into every sentence, and fumbling intermittently for each other's hands: the hairy arms of an out-of-shape tarantula groping for a daddy-longlegs. Jimmy also couldn't help wondering how his father disposed of his stomach during the act of love: and felt a bubble of nausea forming around the thought. He was happy to get out in the night air.

This summer was a big fat nothing so far. He hoped tomorrow to dig up some friends, but meanwhile he had to settle for this ugly, overtrained woman. She wasn't funny or interesting. She was an account executive, whatever that meant, and she had a niece about Jimmy's age—probably a junior account executive, another cross for him to bear. (Lorraine was dying to get the two of them together.) He just didn't like the feel of things—to tell you the truth, he could hardly wait to get back to England.

The next day he went to the Club with his father and Lorraine, and watched more martinis go down on the Club verandah. They had only joined the Club last summer, but already his father sat with the dullest people, which made him seem like an old member. "You remember Mrs. Vanderpatch, and Mrs. Fredericks. My son, Jimmy. He jus returned from England. He's in school there." Two flabby bathing-suited women, purple across the top of the chest, and startlingly white just below that. "Where's Dave?" he asked Mrs. Vanderpatch. "He's spending the summer in camp," she told him, thus eliminating one more friend from the running.

Rather than witness another scene of degeneration like last night's (Lorraine had finally kicked off her shoes and plunged into a South American dance with Mr. Bannister), he pulled out and went for a quick swim. The Club pool seemed to have been commandeered by the eighteen-year-old set, so he headed for the beach. He really didn't care for the basic American face as represented at the Club. Americans had never had faces before, of course, but they certainly had them now. Just look at the mouths on those women: huge red rings like the big end of a megaphone. Teeth like sharks. And the heavy stupid jowls on the men. He suddenly realized that he hadn't seen a single English person that you could seriously call fat. Here you hardly saw anything else.

"Hey, Jimmy." He looked around, and there was a human face at last. Forrest Tuckerman, dripping wet from the sea. Forrest! The guy he had been looking for, without much hope. Not just an American but a friend. The last time he had seen Forrest had been at his farewell party in March. They had each been allowed a beer for the occasion, and they had clinked the heavy glass bottles solemnly in a toast. So—here was Forrest.

"How you doing, Tuck?"

"Fine! I see you got back."

"Yeah."

"How was it?"

Jimmy shrugged. How was it? He shook his head. "They tell me I got an accent over there."

Forrest inclined his head and seemed to listen closely, although Jimmy had stopped talking. "Say something," Forrest said after a moment. "What do you want me to say?" "Anything." "It's a nice day." "You haven't got an accent," said Forrest.

Tuck was blonder than he remembered and his bones looked bigger. He was tanned through and through. Jimmy felt suddenly that he missed three crucial months of growth and sunlight.

"So how was it really?" said Forrest.

"Very queer, very strange. I couldn't describe it." They walked slowly to the beach. Jimmy remembered Forrest as being all dressed up for winter with an outsize overcoat and a long unwieldy scarf and a small, man's hat. It was hard to recognize this gawky stripped-down version, sniffling and dripping sea water, stepping from winter into summer. "Did anything happen when I was gone?" "Not much, I guess." "How's Sambo?" "Fine, far as I know. I didn't see much of Sambo lately." "How's Harry?" "I guess he's O.K. His family moved to Connecticut, you know."

The group at his party had seemed indissoluble, a scene he could rejoin at any moment. "See you fellows in three years," he had said on the way out. "See you, Jim," see you, see you ... And here they had fallen effortlessly apart. "Vince is changing schools next year. He didn't do too good in

English." Forrest smiled and his darn teeth had grown an inch. "You gotta do good in English, you know what I mean, *paisan?* You gotta talk it right."

Jimmy was still wearing his English clothes, a dark blue blazer and gray flannel pants. He felt funny standing on a beach like this, the sand lapping his trouser cuffs, as if he had arrived there in a dream. He said, "I'd better find a bathing hut."

"Yeah—well listen, see you, Jimmy."

Forrest had scented the sea and went loping toward it. Jimmy was relieved not to have to talk to him any more. Accent or no accent, they talked different.

He found a bathing hut and got changed very slowly, staring at the dry gray wood of the door and the wet sandy slats on the floor, not thinking about anything special. The sea air felt good anyway.

He stood outside the hut for a moment, squinting across the dunes. It was very stange being here. The roar of the breakers, the glare of the sun. For a moment he couldn't place where he was or how he had got here. In the middle distance stood Forrest, shivering from his latest dip, talking to a girl. Jimmy supposed he had better head in their direction, because Forrest was the only person he seemed to know around here. The unnerving thing was that, just like that, he felt he didn't much like Forrest. Friendship couldn't be like that, could it? Ah, he'd get used to Forrest again, by and by.

He tiptoed across the sand, finding it painfully hot. His eyes were on the girl now and she looked awfully pretty, but as he got close she moved away, leaving him with Forrest again.

"How's it going, Jimbo? You look as if you could use some sun."

"Yeah, I guess I could."

"They tell me it's always foggy in England." Forrest suddenly got excited. "You can't see where you're going or what you're doing, it's so foggy. Your candle goes out and you feel these slimy hands on your throat. Aargh! Oh, so sorry—I thought you were Carruthers. Is that right?"

"No."

"All the English movies I've seen take place in the fog. I guess they wait for a foggy day before they start shooting, right?"

"Maybe that's it."

"Playing cricket in the fog is what they do over there. 'I say, old boy, that's my wicket you're standing on'—" Jimmy wasn't getting used to this guy at all. He was forming a real loathing for him. Forrest must have sensed something was wrong. "Well, that's what they tell you. I don't really believe it. They make jokes like that about all the countries."

"It's a stupid custom," Jimmy said sharply.

"Yeah, I guess so." Forrest seemed embarrassed. His old friend had lost his sense of humor. Lost it in the fog. Jimmy wanted to explain—look, it isn't my sense of humor; I just wish I could show you how stupid all that stuff sounds, fog and cricket and the rest of it. He wasn't angry, just a little impatient. But Forrest didn't get it at all. His pale blue eyes blinked. "You coming in for a swim?" he said quickly. "All right." They started jogging the last few feet. "Oh, by the way—" Jimmy thought of a happier channel— "who was that girl you were talking to just now?"

"Her? That was Carol. Carol Fletcher."

"She looked nice."

"Yeah, you think so?" He sounded surprised.

"Well, I was pretty far away. Isn't she nice-looking?"

"I don't know. I thought she was kind of homely."

They stood uncertainly at the sea's edge, each willing to defer to the other's judgment about Carol Fletcher. Jimmy could have sworn she was good-looking, but he had made mistakes on this point before.

"Well, how *is* she? I mean, has she got a nice personality?"

"She's all right."

They looked at each other blankly. Jimmy's jaws were locked from the cold water round his shins. As for Forrest, the sea and the salt seemed to have washed his eyes away, the way the sea air bleached the trees and shrubs along the shore. Are we supposed to be friends? thought Jimmy. Is that why we're standing here

They ran together into the breakers and the first big one seemed to blow them apart. Forrest shot through it expertly. Jimmy was flipped backwards. He sat in the oozing sand and the sea came shouting at him again and hit him in the mouth and spun him half around. His mind was on Carol Fletcher. She was *his* idea of good-looking anyway. Forrest was not necessarily the last word.

He spent most of the rest of the morning looking for her, mainly to pass the time. Forrest had emerged from their joint plunge in a chillier mood. He must have been thinking it over in there and decided that he didn't much like Jimmy either. It was for the best. Jimmy sat on his towel in lonely grandeur, gazing at the horizon but with one eye out for Carol. Forrest encamped with some friends about fifty yards away. Jimmy didn't want to meet them. ("You have something in America called teenagers, I believe," Ryan had said. These boys looked like what Ryan had in mind.)

By lunch Carol Fletcher had become a second-degree obsession. He wasn't quite sure what she looked like any more, but he had a general impression of utter loveliness. He imagined walking quietly along the beach with her, throwing stones, laughing. Her in a white dress, him in a black tuxedo, her face a little vague in the twilight, and all the prettier for that. His difficulty in fantasying girls had righted itself—all it took was seeing one occasionally. Forrest and his friends got up to go and Forrest waved goodbye. He would have come over with a little encouragement, but Jimmy simply wasn't in the mood.

When he did see Carol again he had to be slightly disappointed. She was sitting in the Club lounge with a strange-looking mother, reading a movie magazine. Her hair was an ordinary brown, stiff with salt and pulled back tight. It took Jimmy a moment to readjust his feelings. But he had gone too far with her to turn back. He would love her now whatever she looked like.

He was sitting with his father again, and some other people he no longer bothered to register—more big mouths and flabby skin, creased red thighs, spongy, weaklooking arms—waiting for them all to finish their drinks and go into the dining room. Where they would undoubtedly have more drinks. This country was really one big pigsty, you know that. Slurp, slurp, slurp. His father had certainly made a lot of friends since last summer, but he hadn't been very choosy about it. Jim hoped nobody noticed the way he kept looking at Carol—he knew the kind of awful big-mouth kidding he would be in for if anyone did. But nobody noticed anything and finally Carol and her mother got up and left the lounge, and there was nothing to look at at all. Except the woman with the pendulous biceps scratching for a cigarette, and her husband's thin fingers drumming on the glass tabletop. (He said he was on the wagon, and he looked pretty desperate about it.)

At lunch Mr. Bannister asked Jimmy if he had had a good morning. "O.K., I guess. The water was colder than I remembered."

"Did you see any old friends?"

"Yeah. Forrest Tuckerman was around."

"I remember him. He was a nice boy. Fine manners."

"Yeah, he's all right."

Lorraine said, "I think Jimmy's losing his accent already. It's amazing how fast they pick things up at that age."

After lunch he went looking for Carol again and found her right away, sitting with her strange-looking mother on the verandah. He wasn't quite sure what to do next, so he just sat down on a rocking chair and looked at her, as long as he decently could. She didn't look round, so all he could see was a piece of one cheek. But it looked great. He watched her for half an hour, until she and her mother got up and stowed their stuff into beach baskets and left.

His father came out and asked him if he was having a good time and he said sure and his father ducked back in. He was playing bridge with his scaly-looking friends, so that was that for the afternoon.

Jimmy wandered back to the bathing hut and got into his wet trunks. He noticed that his chest was turning pink. By tonight his shoulder blades would be pillars of fire. Every year it happened, without fail. Whether it was worth going throuh this baptism of fire in mid-August was a question.

He draped a towel round the pink area and went back and sat on the sand. Carol had driven off somewhere with her mother, so there was no point in looking for her, although he did anyway, out of habit. It occurred to him that he should have brought a book: but to get one now he would have to change his clothes again, find the book, and get black into his bathing suit, and no book in the world was worth all that.

After a while the inevitable Forrest Tuckerman appeared again (he seemed to be everywhere, like an official greeter) with his little band of spear carriers. Forrest had obviously been reviewing the situation one more time—or possibly had discussed it with an older relative—and he came over with some determination and said, "Jimmy, I'd like you to meet my friends."

They squatted around him and Forrest called off the names. "Hi, Jimmy, hi, hello." They were all very tall. Jimmy had this feeling again of having been deprived of his summer's growth, his regulation three inches.

"Jimmy's been over in England."

"Yeah, how is it over there?"

"It rains a lot."

"I hear that."

Forrest was writing his name in the sand and making a big thing of the "T" in Tuckerman. "Jimmy says it isn't that foggy," he said diplomatically.

"Is that right?"

"I guess they wouldn't get anything done if it was, they'd keep bumping into each other, right?" Jimmy laughed politely this time. Fog jokes were something he would have to learn to live with.

"*You're* in enough fog already, Judson." Judson reached over and pushed the speaker out of his squat and onto his back. "Enough out of you, Pin-head," he said.

"Hey, they talk funny over there, don't they? Eh what, sniff sniff. Rip-ping, old boy."

"You get used to it."

"Yeah, I guess so. Say something in English, Jimmy. I mean in limey. 'Ow har you, old bean. Ain't it a nice die, old bean.' "

"I never heard anyone talk like that."

"How do they talk then?"

"Like me. I've got an English accent."

"Cut it out. *You* haven't got an English accent. You don't say 'Pip-pip, old chap!' " They all laughed.

"I *assure* you I have," said Jimmy—and they laughed again. "I guess you have at that," said the one called Pinhead. "That has real class—'I *assure* you.' Why can't *you* learn to talk like that, Judson? Your English is a disgrace to all of us. Ain't you got no education?"

"Duh," said Judson, scratching himself like an ape. "Whudjusay?"

It was like being hit methodically with a cushion. Jimmy hoped they would get onto something else in a minute. But Pinhead was still working the possibilities. "You really should teach Judson the King's English, Jimmy. Honestly, it's embarrassing. Any place you take this guy, it's a social catastrophe. He says Pop-pop when he ought to say Pip-pip; and when anyone else would say 'Beastly weather, what?' he says 'Lookada lousy rain.' "

"I guess you sound pretty funny to them too," said Jimmy. "I mean, to English people."

Again the effect was wrong. They looked down and around. "Yeah, I guess that's right," somebody murmured. Cheezt. Why didn't you tell us this guy had no sense of humor. That is a minimum expectation. Besides, it isn't like he was English himself. What does he care?

And Jimmy wanted to explain again: It's all so stupid. That's all I mind about. And he wanted to say, I've only been gone a few months, let's talk about the kind of stuff we would have talked about if I'd been here right along. But something had happened: there was no subject matter any more. Jimmy had never been exactly shy in his life, but you had to have subject matter.

"It looks like the Red Sox have a chance this year," he said tentatively.

"Yeah, I haven't looked at the standings lately," said Forrest. "Howie is a baseball nut."

"Not so much this year. I got more interested in tennis."

"Well, Judson is a baseall nut, and I mean *nut*," said Pinhead. "Aren't you, Judson? You just have to nod, don't try to say anything." Pinhead danced out of reach. "Judson is a typical Dodger fan—isn't that right, Judson? A dirty old bum." Judson jumped up and began to chase his tormentor toward the ocean. The others rose and joined the dance, pounding over the wet sand with wild eagerness, almost as if they wanted to get away. Jimmy ran after them, but again the sea scattered them, and when they came out he was alone again.

From an infinite distance Pinhead seemed to smile apologetically; we'd like to have you in the club, but you understand how it is—these things take time. Maybe we can process your application by Labor Day. The others toiled up the beach to the clubhouse, tugging at their bathing suits and sniffling. They had been making the awkward first moves of friendship back in June while Jimmy was still polishing his cricket. From behind they looked so much alike that they could have been brothers; that was from being together all summer. Jimmy felt that his own rear view had lagged behind and that he couldn't even *walk* with them any more.

He made a routine check on Carol Fletcher's whereabouts and was surprised to see her sitting up the beach a ways with her mother. Mrs. Fletcher was camped in a deck chair, in a gray print dress and sturdy stockings, as if it didn't make a bit of difference to her that this was a beach in summer. This reminded Jimmy of his own ripening skin and he pulled the towel round his neck, only to find that the grain of the terrycloth ran the wrong way wherever it touched down. His flesh had been burned raw.

The only thing to do then was to go inside. He was loath to leave Carol behind but he couldn't sit in the sun and he couldn't sit under the towel, so there was no choice. With so many rear glances that he was virtually walking backwards, he retreated to the bathing hut. One of the glances was picked up by Mrs. Fletcher, who looked annoyed, as if she was being spied upon through a knothole. She said something to Carol, who turned toward him and shrugged.

He spent a long time in the bathing hut, just diddling around. He thought of the bathroom at the headmaster's house, with the steamed-up mirrors and Dr. Rabelais' shaving brush and the tweezers Mrs. Rabelais used on her chin. And he remembered how he used to sit in the long thin tub (long and thin to fit the headmaster) and dream about America. And here he was in America dreaming about England. Making up color slides of it, the way he used to of America, only softening the light instead of hardening it. The pictures were straight from the tourist bureau—country walks, tea shoppes, cows everywhere, lots of greens and browns. He saw himself in a belted raincoat, strolling with Carol Fletcher, pausing to stare at a thatched cottage—but there *were* no thatched cottages near the school. He had never seen one in his life. He wondered where these pictures came from anyway.

He hated to leave the hut and go back to that wretched clubhouse, but there was no avoiding it. He found his father where he had left him, still playing bridge. "Are you having a good time, Jimmy?" said Mr. Bannister, a little uneasily.

"Uh-huh."

"That's good. There are some nice young people in the Club this year."

"A lot of families have bought houses out here just since the war," said his partner. "I'll bid three diamonds."

"Pass. That's *right*. This place used to be practically empty." It was hard to tell whether they were pleased or not with the expansion of the town. They seemed equally elated and depressed as they discussed it between bids. Recognition was sweet, bustle and boom were of the essence; yet they didn't enjoy losing their sanctuary. (What difference does it make, if you play cards all the time, thought Jimmy.) The new people were of course top quality, the very best available; they added a lot to the Club, took part in things; yet there was something dubious about them too, something faintly unpleasant. Being new was dirty and tasteless—he had had the same feeling himself with the boys this afternoon.

His father said nothing during this discussion, being not only new himself but also a real-estate man who was helping to bring these scoudrels in; and for a minute Jimmy thought, watch out, they're going to spot you . But then he saw that his father wasn't nervous. He was more confident than last year, no doubt about it. He knew that talk was cheap, but they all needed the real-estate man—along with the divorce lawyer and the kidney specialist. Jimmy had never supposed before coming here that real estate was anything to be ashamed of. But last year his father had been more diffident about it, showing his card reluctantly like a rubber-goods salesman.

The talk got more specific, and Jimmy realized that his father had indeed made some big sales out here recently. The Asbury estate was his master-piece—sold to Godfrey Farnes, the hotel magnate, a deplorable intruder and a valuable asset all in one. It was a funny conversation, because even Mr. Ban-nister seemed to have caught the elegiac note about what was happening to the place: he the literal agent of change. Oh, well.

Business never interested Jimmy for more than a few minutes. He began to wander off again and his father looked at him quickly and said, "Jimmy—how would you like to go sailing tomorrow?"

"Great!"

"You would?"

"Yes, I really mean that."

"Good." It might be agony tearing himself from the card table but he would do it. Jimmy felt that summer could now get into gear. The best dream of all, the white sailboat—surely nothing could go wrong with that one.

□ VI □

The sailing was O.K., although actually he spent the whole time thinking about Carol Fletcher. This obsession had developed feverishly during the night, along with his sunburn. He had filled the emptiness of drinks and dinner and Lorraine's chatter with thoughts of Carol; and then in bed he found that there was nothing else he *could* think about. His shoulders burned for her, and he even hallucinated her fitfully against the gray curtains of morning. By breakfast time, he was well and truly possessed. His father took him to church and he saw Carol there in person, and for a moment he was disappointed again, but by now he was even in love with his disappointment. Mrs. Fletcher sat next to her of course, looking just the same in church as she had on the beach, unsuited to any setting, and Jimmy began to fear that his dreams of Carol would soon start to include her mother, if he never saw them apart.

As he sat staring at Mrs. Fletcher he found himself thinking for the first time in his life about middle age as such. The stark ugliness of his father's friends, and let's face it, of his father too, had struck him the day before as simply a series of unfortunate accidents. But now as he gazed around he saw that it was no accident. The people in his pew were like a row of church gar-goyles, with scraggy skin and coarse, unhappy features. The minister's skull was red from modest sun-bathing, and his face was dry and bony, as if his skeleton had already begun to assert itself triumphantly against the flesh. The point was that this business was at work in everyone, even him and Carol. Even *Carol.*

So that was his meditation in church that day. Later he realized that he hadn't seen many older peole for the last three months and had lost his natu-ral link with them. If you excepted the masters at school, who were freaks and would have looked funny at any age, he had seen nothing but super young English complexions for three months. So this sudden onslaught of defective American flesh had simply overwhelmed him.

The vision nagged at him all day—gray skin, sagging, dripping off the bone—whipping his thoughts back to Carol from one more direction. His fa-ther and friends flubbered about the boat in striped T-shirts, trying to look like sportsmen: carrying bottles of beer and talking in loud pilot-to-navigator voices; Lorraine was wearing denim shorts and her thighs were blue in the back, a switchboard of worn-out veins. He thought, Carol doesn't have to get like that. Some movie stars don't get like that.

This was not the kind of thing he had expected to think about on his first yachting day. He tried for a while to concentrate on the mechanics of sailing, but he was past the age when people said, "Here, Sonny, you take a turn," and Mr. Ogilvy and Frank Small and Mr. Bannister plus the little guy in glasses were more than enough crew to keep the small sloop tacking along. He had been introduced all round, with what seemed like a mixture of pride and embarrassment, as "my son Jimmy—from England," after which he had been ignored in a manly sort of way. So he sat back and looked out to sea, tossed between two banks of thoughts: the physical and spiritual decay of middle age, and the antidote represented by a physically fit Carol.

He imagined taking Carol to meet Dr. and Mrs. Rabelais. All four sat in beaming silence—since Jimmy had not yet heard Carol speak, these sequences had to be silent. But Dr. Rabelais obviously approved of Carol, pouring her cups and cups of fresh tea, and later taking them both on a tour of the house, tromping cheerily about the attic, pointing things out. On the way down he clapped Jimmy on the shoulder in soundless approval. You've picked a winner, my boy.

The English style of not saying the obvious certainly had its points. As he listened to the hearty chat of his father's friends, he pictured Rabelais gri-macing slightly over, oh, a marmalade sandwich: raising his eyebrows, mur-muring, "Quite, oh yes, quite."

Unfortunately, when they spoke to Jimmy he found his jaw locking again. What was the answer to "How's it going, Jimmy?" anyway? He got so tired of saying "fine" to everything. "How's the boy. Your dad tells me you've been to England, how was it, how's the rationing. Your dad certainly picked a nice day." After each silly queston they waited politely for an answer, and would not be fobbed off with a mumble or a gesture. They looked right into his eyes until they had extorted yet another "Fine," or "He certainly did."

"You know something funny, Mr. Small?" he said when they had pushed off. "I was just thinking how many times people say 'How' in this country. 'How you doing?' 'How's tricks?' Isn't that what the Indians used to say too? How?"

"I guess it is," said Mr. Small.

"Do you think it might be something to do with the weather or what? that makes Americans say 'How'?"

Mr. Small chuckled uneasily. It did sound awfully silly, but it was the kind of theory that Dr. Rabelais used to throw out at breakfast, to start a whimsical discussion. "Maybe that's it," said Mr. Small. "I hadn't thought about it."

That was his last attempt at bright commentary. Mr. Small obviously thought he was some kind of pervert. He retired to a corner of the bow. Maybe they really preferred him just to say "fine." Or maybe there was a kind of clever talk that was acceptable from his age group which he had forgotten about. He could imagine Forrest Tuckerman and his friends doing it right. Diving off the boat with a final sally; and then the grown-ups could talk about wonderful kids, fine boys. "That boy of yours is going to be something, you must be proud of him." The speech patterns were unnaturally clear to Jim—he could see them in bright blocks, like subtitles in a movie. "Jimmy is quite a boy. We-'re ver-y proud. Proud of Jim-my. We-'re ver-y proud." If *he* dived off the boat, there would be a puzzled silence.

So he tried to keep himself unobtrusive, even eating lunch by himself. Making a neat pile of his cellophane wrappings. Contemplating the great American slurp. He gathered these men did not belong to the Club but were down here looking for houses or for better houses: beginning the slow climb to the Club. Real estate took over from navigation during the lunch hour. As for himself, there were, as everyone knew, two kinds of teenagers, glib ones and sullen ones: and although it wasn't his natural type, he would have to settle for sullen right now.

Behind his wall of plexiglass, he watched them spooning their potato salad, chewing it like horses. His father's associates had always been on the dumb side, hadn't they? Gloria, Mr. Bannister's previous companion, had teased him about it sometimes. "Really, James—those *truck* drivers." "I can't help it, dear. Those are the people I work with." His father himself was not dumb, but he had to pretend. Maybe they were all pretending. It was better to think about Carol, who was obviously highly intelligent in a quiet sort of way.

When they dismounted late in the afternoon, Jimmy noticed that a couple of the men affected a slight sailor's walk on the jetty. Honestly. It was too bad Gloria wasn't still around to make fun of them. *You should have piped them on shore, James.* He was parched for mockery.

"Did you have a good time, Jimmy?" his father asked. There was a slight anxiety in his eyes, as if he too had remembered Gloria. "I haven't had much time to talk to you—looking after the guests. And keeping us off the rocks."

"I had a great time."

"You did?"

"Yes, I really did." His tongue was loosed. "I used to dream about this at school, you know. Just sailing around and having lunch and sailing around some more."

"You weren't bored?" His father looked almost grateful.

"Oh, heck no. It was just the way I remembered it. Sailing around, taking it easy, wearing old clothes. This and going fishing were my two best memories."

"That's great. We'll have to fix up some fishing one of these days."

"You know, those are the things you miss in England, the old-clothes things." Saying made it so. "You know what I mean, lighting out for some place in an old car. With a gun or some fishing equipment—things you can do by yourself, or with just a friend. And cooking your own meals."

His father clutched his arm. "We'll fix up some fishing real soon," he said.

His father didn't have to go to work the next week, so they stayed out in the old house and Lorraine stayed with them. Jimmy had gotten used to her face and her voice by now but that was about all. She wasn't a friend and she wasn't an enemy. She was always saying, "What was that, Jimmy?" as if they literally spoke different languages. Well—none of that mattered. But his father wasn't himself in her company. He was more of a, well, banker, his humor was louder and slower, and the quotient of business talk was way up. As a by-product of their separation, Jimmy was plagued with all kinds of insights into his father this summer. He was forced to realize that the old man's character had actually been drifting about in strange ways for a long time, possibly since his wife had left him. Jimmy saw absolutely no point in thinking about his mother. He had no idea why she had left or why she had so lightly yielded his own custody. It didn't matter. But he found himself thinking about her anyway in relation to his father. While Mrs. Bannister was on hand, his father had been one of those fixed middle-aged men with a closetful of blue and brown suits and a repertoire of blue and brown jokes. Jimmy could see him perfectly; it was as if Mrs. B. had held him in place for all to behold.

Somehow all that had come unstuck with her departure. He and Jim had become friends, that was good, that was good: but then his father had begun courting these girls. Which got his *age* unstuck. He began behaving youthfully, but in fits and starts: thus putting Jimmy on a sort of sliding scale. When Mr. Bannister was in full caper, Jimmy was his old buddy; when he reverted to middle age, Jimmy was lowered into childhood with a swift thud.

Next his father's weight came unstuck. He began going on and off diets, in tune to some mysterious urgency, becoming now a jolly fat man, now a determined thin one. Even his clothes began to look confused. The girls all wanted different things, Jimmy supposed. Mr. Bannister's taste in women had been tentative from the first, as if he didn't really know what he was doing: one week it would be a loud-mouthed blonde, the next a language professor from N.Y.U. Now he had found a businesswoman from Radcliffe. There was no design to any of it. And with each girl his father's character would float loose again, and Jimmy would go shooting up and down the scale from small boy to young man to confederate. And his father's cheeds would go slack and hollow as he whipped his way through a new diet. The point about this summer was that Lorraine herself was a tentative sort of girl who didn't know what sort of Bannisters she wanted, father *or* son, so there was nothing to stabilize the old man at all, and every evening was a groping about.

With so much time to burn away, Jim now found himself remembering his mother a bit in her own right. After years of being content to be an old photograph, she began to move around a little. He remembered her saying, "There'll be plenty of time for girls later." That was one of her phrases. And "your father isn't feeling well this evening." She was taller than her husband, at least in high heels, and she had a tendency to walk around in her dressing gown. There was no point to these recollections, they just slipped in between thoughts of Carol, and sat there.

. . . As for Mr. Bannister, he would settle down presently. There was only so much to say about real estate. After all of the, say, 100,000 houses in Long Island had been discussed fully, he would get onto something else. Save us all from businesswomen, thought Jim. Lorraine was to blame for this sharp narrowing of focus. She managed to combine a snobbish interest in the holding families with a cold concern for the property itself: and the wretched Mr. Bannister fell in with her mood.

So the early part of the evenings at least was rather drippy. Jim wished he could play the piano. Those lessons he had been so happy to shuck off at the time of his mother's evaporation would have come in handy now. There was an upright in the summer cottage and stacks of withered sheet music in the seat, with pictures of forgotten singers and band leaders; and occasionally he tried to pick his way through a number or two. But there wasn't much to it. By the time he had mastered one of the wooden arrangements, he was usually sick of the tune. As the evening thickened, his father and Lorraine liked to play records, but then they wouldn't listen to them, which irritated him. (They insised they were listening, which made it that much worse.) He would crouch down next to the victrola to drown their voices. Eventually they left him in charge of the record selection, and then imperceptibly this became a form of duty. "How about putting a record on, Jimmy ... How about putting *another* record on, Jimmy?" They didn't care what he played, but they did notice the silence when he stopped.

The supply was only slightly larger than that of the jazz club at school, and the records were chipped and scratched, but there were some good ones. Jimmy Dorsey's "I'll never say never again again," brother Tommy's "I'm getting sentimental over you"; Bunny Berrigan, Claude Thornhill, the big boys of the late thirties. After his father and Lorraine had gone out to wherever they went, taking their voices with them, the records made a ripe background to the latest thoughts of Carol Fletcher—strolling through tall grass with Jim at her side, dabbling her feet in lily ponds (that was a weird one), staring at him with luminous eyes in darkened nightclubs: he had at last eliminated the episode with Dr. Rabelais. That was just silly.

Since there was no automatic record changer, he had to break off every few minutes and attend to the machine. Which kept him just busy enough to feel as if he were doing something. The spinning ten-inch records ground their way into his bones: he supposed he would never forget a word or even a bit of instrumental business on a single one of them as long as he lived. Sometimes he turned out the lights to heighten the effect, which led to some awkwardness with the record labels: he would peer at them by moonlight or, failing that, hold them against a splinter of light from the bathroom door. Once that was taken care of, he would fumble the record over the little knob and sit back for three minutes of meditation. He felt splendidly lonely in the dark, collar up against the world, Carol at his side—his father walked in and found him like this one evening, and a spooky exchange ensued. "Jimmy? Is that you? Are you all right? ... It's Jimmy, honey." Four large bewildered eyes when the lights went on. "I often listen to records in the dark." "You do?" Mr. Bannister looked as if he were about to seize Lorraine and shelter her against this madness. "You'd better get to bed, Jimmy." Jimmy ground out his cigarette and stumbled off.

The only snag concerning his idyll with Carol Fletcher was, of course, that he still hadn't met her and wasn't likely to. A year ago, even a few months ago, he would have gone up and blithely introduced himself to her—mother and all. At least, he thought he would have. But now as he edged closer to his sixteenth birthday he found a certain tendency to postponement, a not-today attitude. Mrs. Fletcher had taken a strong optical dislike to him—well, let's be frank about it, she obviously thought he was nuts, staring at them through the Club window as they rocked on the porch—and, in fact, it was really Mrs. Fletcher he shrank from meeting. Carol still showed no awareness of his existence, unless those occasional shrugs she gave her mother had something to do with him.

He supposesd he must be a premature victim of mother-in-law trouble. If he didn't make his move pretty soon, his nuttiness would be permanently established in both their minds and his cause would be hopeless. He had been here for ten days now, and already the summer was beginning to pack up and shift out. The boys were talking fall talk. Labor Day was the great watershed, and that was suddenly just a few days away. So—do something, Bannister. Stir yourself, you idle boy.

He tried the radical move of sitting in the next rocking chair and waiting for them to come out, but that only made things worse. He could see how he must look to them—that peculiar boy who comes out and sits in the next rocking chair. He thought of trying something through Forrest Tuckerman, but the lines were down with Forrest. He passed the gang every day on the beach and exchanged greetings: and they stopped courteously and chatted with him. But he might as well have been a diplomat from Africa. They talked as if he had never heard of football or high school or even girls: he almost began to wonder whether he had.

"I guess you'll be going back to England soon, huh, Jimmy?"

"Yeah, well, a couple of weeks, I guess."

"You go back later than we do."

"Yes, but our vacation begins a lot later too."

"That sounds like a good system."

"In a way. It depends."

Ever since he had discouraged their fog and accent jokes about England they had discussed it with this elaborate carefulness. They must have very interesting customs over there. Yes, indeed. Many in-ter-esting customs. Kids had changed since he left. He didn't remember all this politeness.

So they greeted and parted as swiftly as protocol allowed, and Jimmy wandered off with his books—*I, Claudius* this week: Carol would see from the title that he wasn't all idiot. He didn't like to ask Forrest about Carol in front of the others, and Forrest seemed to be cemented to his group, forever walking to and from the ocean with flippers or small surfboards, so Jimmy couldn't get at him.

Jimmy had just about given up: in fact, he was embarrassed even to dream aout Carol now, things had gotten so hopeless. He was rocking morosely next to Mrs. Fletcher one afternoon, thinking *this has got to stop*—Carol hadn't come out, so that Jimmy was feeling more than ordinarily futile: to go to all this trouble just to rock next to Mrs. Fletcher. He was startled by a friendly voice.

"What is that book you're reading, young man?"

He held it up. "A book," he said.

Mrs. Fletcher peered more closely. "Aren't you rather young to be reading *that* book?"

He shrugged.

"Well, you children seem to mature faster than we did." Her voice was much pleasanter than her face. "My daughter is so serious it almost frightens me."

"That so?"

"Yes. I often wish she was a little more playful. I'm always telling her that she should spend more time with people her own age." Mrs. Fletcher fanned herself with a trace of slyness. Jimmy had a feeling that she wasn't quite telling the truth. But maybe she was just intelligent. His father's friends said everything sstraight, without spin or guile. Mrs. Fletcher, he could see, might throw you a few knuckleballs.

"I've seen you sitting on the porch and I've suggested to Carol that you might be someone nice to talk to, but she just shrugs. She's a great shrugger, you know." Mrs. Fletcher sighed, but not as if she didn't understand: she understood all too well. "And what's your name, young man?"

"Bannister," he said, from English habit. "I mean Jim, James, Jim."

"My name is Lucy Fletcher. And my daughter's name is Carol." She smiled, as if to say—I expect you knew that? For a moment Jimmy wondered whether he really wanted to get in with these people: whether stupid friends weren't best after all. But just then Carol came through the screen door: the girl of a hundred goofy dreams, and it was too late to do anything but plunge in further.

She really didn't look so great from up close. But that was beside the point. Jimmy smiled uncontrollably.

"I see you've found a friend, Mother," said Carol.

"Yes. This is Jim Bannister."

"That's nice."

She looked at Jimmy without too much interest. His waves of devotion weren't getting through to her. "I think I'll go and play tennis in that case," she said.

Carol went back into the Club, clashing the screen door behind her. And Mrs. Fletcher said, "Which do you really prefer to be called, Jim or Jimmy or James?"

"It doesn't matter."

Fifteen minutes later Carol came out in tennis clothes, followed by Forrest and another couple. "Have a nice time, dear," said Mrs. Fletcher. "I will," said Carol. Jimmy watched the back of her legs as she walked down the road to the tennis courts. "I'm glad she's playing tennis again," said Mrs. Fletcher. "It's a very good game for the muscle tone. I'm sure that boy Forrest will make a very good structural engineer, or something, one of these days." She picked up her knitting and stared at it. "A witless occupation, knitting," she said. "I don't even know what this is going to be. Well, one can always call it a rug, I suppose. I was going to ask, do you knit? How silly of me."

Jimmy didn't know whether to wait for Carol to come back. Having got so close, it seemed a shame to give up. So he sat with Mrs. Fletcher, giving her half an ear, while he scanned the horizon for tennis players. At first he felt nervous that anyone should be so absolutely non-stop clever as Mrs. Fletcher, but after a while he stopped noticing it. He tried being clever himself and she was very nice about it, but that wasn't getting Carol back, so his conversation became vague, and finally so did Mrs. Fletcher's.

After three hours or so he gave up altogether. His neck hurt from nodding and chuckling and rocking and he had to go to the bathroom. When he got inside the Club the first thing he saw was Carol, playing cards with Forrest and the other two. She must have sneaked round the back, by way of the beach.

"Did you leaave Mother out there?" she asked him. He was grinning uncontrollably again. The unexpected result of dreaming about her so often. It was all he could do not to seize her arm and make off with her.

"I'd better go out," she said. "Here, do you want to play my hand?" She thrust the cards at Jimmy, who looked at them uncomprehendingly. They were canasta cards, Forrest explained, and Jimmy had to explain in turn that he had never heard of canasta. Carol was out on the porch in six (counted) strides and he had missed his connection again. He sat down glumly to learn this labyrinthine new game.

Once his disappoinment had been properly digested, Jimmy saw that he had in fact made progress. He had insinuated himself into the circle. Tomorrow he would try harder. The canasta game lasted till suppertime, by which time the Fletchers had left the porch for good. His father suggested a movie after supper. So that was it for the day. His father and Lorraine snuggled squelchingly in the balcony and Jimmy slumped next to them with his knees skewing out into the aisle, and felt once again the strangeness of being here at all: a smell of sea air had seeped into the movie house, where it mingled with the smell of popcorn and the smell of people who had been swimming all summer—well, it was pretty hard to sort out, but he could see that smells were what dislocated you more than anything. He tried not to watch his father. His cuddling was of the demurest, but Mr. Bannister looked so fat in that whole connection. Carol came to mind again, but he dismissed her sternly. The dreaming phase was behind him now.

The next day he hit the porch early, armed with his book. Still *I, Claudius*—weird afternoons with Tiberius on the isle of Capri, unforgettable nights with the Empress Julia. . . . The Fletchers didn't show up, so he made some feverish headway with the book. He was expecting some hearty man to ask him if he was glued to the porch, Sonny, but he got off unpestered and passed a lubricious morning with Claudius and his friends.

After lunch he was back at his post, and this time Mrs. Fletcher was waiting for him. "I think I'll call it a shroud," she said, holding up her knitting. Carol hadn't come out yet, and Jimmy was suddenly struck with a terrible foreboding. He started to rise and Mrs. Fletcher draped a light hand on his wrist. "A woolen shroud would be so much comfier, don't you think? than one of those starchy ones. So much more practical in a climate like ours."

He sank back, and the foreboding struck in all the way. Sure enough, Carol came out a few minutes later carrying her damn tennis racquet again. And behind her came that famous tennis player, Forrest Tuckerman.

"I saw you had company," said Carol. "So I thought I'd play tennis again."

"Yes, yes, I'm in good hands," said Mrs. Fletcher.

Carol waved goodbye and Jimmy watched her legs dwindling away next to Forrest's long, stupid ones—when did *he* become such a great tennis player? It was truly aggravating and Jimmy's first impulse was just to leave. But there seemed to be a rule that *somebody* had to sit with Mrs. Fletcher at all times. Otherwise she would capsize or catch fire. He hunched back in the rocking chair, almost too frustrated to speak.

It was a long afternoon. Mrs. Fletcher's chair made a clicking noise on the wooden floor which got on his nerves. The knitting needles sounded like castanets. This was not how he had planned to spend the summer.

At intervals he poked his head into the Club lounge to see if Carol had doubled back again the way she had yesterday. (If she had, maybe he could ask Forrest to sit with Mrs. Fletcher for a spell.) But the place was empty except for a waiter polishing glasses. It was one of those afternoons when everybody has a mission. You wach them leaving one by one, making plans, checking their lists and tickets, until there is nothing but you and your personal Mrs. Fletcher.

Mrs. Fletcher rocked mechanically like a blind woman, talking, talking, talking. Jimmy fantasized to kill the time. The waiter inside was a zombie, in the pay of Mrs. Fletcher: he would never hear a cry for help. Late at night he usually buried Mrs. Fletcher's victims in a bunker on the golf course. Rock, click, talked. Talked to death, poor devils. The noise was simply deafening. He still guessed that Mrs. Fletcher was O.K. but he didn't like this feeling that he couldn't leave her. He had an unfortunate side view of her face. There was something funny about it and he felt that if he walked away she might begin to scream.

No, not really. He could go away if he wanted to. There just wasn't any place to go. He picked up his book and Mrs. Fletcher politely stopped talking, but he couldn't concentrate. He stared at the book anyway, for a few minutes' peace. He found himself thinking about last summer when Gloria was here instead of Lorraine. What a step down in class *that* was, and he thought if all women were like Gloria there wouldn't be afternoons like this. Gloria was the type who didn't want to be appreciated, so he hadn't appreciated her, but she had made last summer better than he had realized at the time, most of the bright memories he had taken to school with him were Gloria's doing. A fat lot he'd take back from *this* summer. This summer that was already slipping away like an ice cube. He couldn't sit here another minute, he decided frantically, he couldn't spend the winter dreaming about Mrs. Fletcher.

But he did sit there, the balance of the lank afternnoon, until Carol and Forrest came back nibbling intimately on ice-cream cones. He felt like some sort of defective, obliged to sit with old ladies while the young people played tennis. He hoped that Carol would at least join them for a few minutes, but she went on in with Mrs. Fletcher, and the next thing he knew it was dinner and another day was gone.

By the next afternoon he realized that he was *expected* to sit with Mrs. Fletcher now. Carol had come to lunch in her tennis clothes and afterwards she stood with Forrest in the lounge. She looked at Jimmy hopefully as he came out of the dinning room. If he didn't volunteer, she would have to call off the tennis. He would be the villain.

"Look, Forrest," he wanted to say, "you don't even think she's good-looking, right? Let *me* play with her." Forrest was loking at him blankly, patting his racquet against his hand. No one could beat old Forrest at looking blank. "Look, Forrest. You'll enjoy Mrs. Fletcher. She's a fine woman. You'll learn something. Ah, forget it." He didn't say any of it, but trudged stoically out to the porch. Since it had never been officially stated that Mrs. Fletcher *needed* anyone to sit with her, he couldn't very well call for someone else to do it. A delicate situation.

This time at least, Carol favored him with a small grateful smile, a smile that bothered him the more he thought about it. She had doubtless been waiting all summer for someone to spring her from her mother's company; waiting, who knows, to get her hands on Forrest, who was waiting, who knows, to get his hands on her. This kind of thing happened every summer, to some poor mutt—a wild miscalculaion of some girl—and it wouldn't really matter if this summer wasn't so short and empty. It wouldn't matter at all.

Meanwhile he had Mrs. Fletcher as consolation prize. He could always make a hit with Mrs. Fletcher. Yesterday she had seemed like a criminal lunatic to whom he was chained. But today the roles were switched. She was chained to him, because somebody had to sit with Jim *Bannister* and she had been too slow to get away. What bothered him during the dusty vacant moments that followed was a feeling that he hadn't even had a chance with

Carol, hadn't even been a contender. Last year he would have been a contender.

"The last time I was in England was in 1938," said Mrs. Fletcher after a while. "A funny sort of year, with the war about to start, like the last night of a play, if you'll excuse the trite expression. You might try talking to Carol about England, although I don't suppose she remembers much about it."

"Were you in England? No kidding." He was pleased to hear that *somebody* else had been in England, that there was such a place—even if it was, of course, someone like Mrs. Fletcher. "What was it like when you were there? Did they always eat powdered eggs?"

"Gracious, no. They used to eat very well, of course they never knew how to cook, it's against their religion, I believe. Being uncomfortable is about all that's left of that."

She might look funny, but she was all right. Jimmy suddenly had a warm feeling about Mrs. Fletcher. "They certainly are uncomfortable," he said. "You should spend a night in our dormitory some time."

She laughed at that possibility ("I doubt if I shall, though") and went on to talk about lumbago and plumbing and the prevalence of rhubarb. Jimmy couldn't have enough of her now. "They have this vegetable called 'greens,' " he said. "That's all, just 'greens.' Well, what else could you call it? They have it at every meal."

"And don't forget kippers," she said. "Who but the English would eat kippers? Would even conceive kippers?"

"And jam. They're absolutely nuts about jam."

"Cold toast for breakfast," she said. She was getting excited too at this catalogue. "Cold toast for tea. I wonder how they *discovered* it?"

"And what gets me . . ." Jimmy wondered why nobody else wanted to talk to this fine woman. It must be some sort of curse that England put on you. She did have those funny eyes, of course—a little wall-eyed. That was why he had always thought she was watching him. It made her look a little crazy. But the real reason she looked funny was that she looked English. He saw that now.

His father came on the porch for a surprise visit. "I see you've found a friend, Jimmy."

"Yes. This is Mrs. Fletcher."

"Hello, Mrs. Fletcher."

Mr. Bannister sat down in Carol's rocking chair.

"Jimmy and I have been talking about England. I was condoling with him about the English diet."

"I guess it is pretty dull."

"We were waxing lyrical about kippers and marmalade."

"Is that so?"

Jimmy felt embarrassed. This was supposed to be funny talk, but Mr. Bannister wasn't getting it.

"Porridge and a really good cup of *tea*," she said.

"I guess things have been tough since the war."

Lorraine joined him and was introduced. She certainly wouldn't get it. Not with her own accent to worry about. Jimmy got up and went inside. He could hear Mrs. Fletcher through the window: "*Long* before the war, back at least as far as King Alfred" . . . He could suddenly see she was one of those silly people who couldn't change her way of talking to suit the company. She was a nut, after all. He was embarrassed for all three of them.

She was—the embarrassment deepened and shot out roots—worse than a nut: she was a freak, like him. His first impression was right. He went to the bathroom although he didn't need to, and decided then and there (a) that he didn't much like Carol anyway; she had a nasty expression; and (b) that he couldn't wait to get back to England.

□ **VII** □

After Labor Day the Country Club broke up and trooped back to the city. The roar of surf was switched off. Jimmy still had two and a half weeks to kill, and he decided to kill as much of them as possible at the movies. He didn't bother to look up any more old friends. Forrest Tuckerman had taught him what vicious changes summer made in people over here. Faces, interests were washed away, replaced: a sea change. And now they would be all pointed toward school and would have less than ever to say to him. The sight of boys lobbing a football in the park was a melancholy exit cue.

His father was back at work in the daytimes, and in the evenings Lorraine came over and the hum of business was resumed. Jimmy felt that Lorraine had given up on him—at least she seemed to find him unsuitable for her niece, who was never mentioned any more. O.K. with him. He didn't want to meet her lousy niece. Lorraine had been the worst possible thing that could have happened this summer. Jim blamed her for everything now— even, improbably, for the extra two weeks at Sopworth. He devoutly hoped his father would have found something better by Christmas, something that would divert him from mortgages and wealthy families. He didn't like to keep bringing up Gloria—he hadn't liked her that much—but she used to steer Mr. Bannister away from all those dull snobs at the Club. Come to think of it, he remembered some muffled arguments on the point. Meanwhile Jim himself was already deep in thoughts of England, those wonderful country scenes, swinging tavern signs, tea with friends—perhaps even tea with Dr. Rabelais now that they knew each other better. A lot of bad things—the shout scenes in class, the chronic discomfort—had been magically alchemized into pleasant memories. And Carol had been phased out and replaced by a totally faceless companion, who wore the same clothes but was a much better sport.

As the time drew to a close, he sensed that his father wanted a talk—a big talk to wrap up the summer. As soon as Jimmy felt this coming on, he found himself instinctively changing the subject. His father misunderstood the points at issue. He would say something unfortunate. About England, about the future. About himself and Lorraine. Several evenings were finessed successfully, and Jimmy began to feel that he might escape without a big talk at all. But his father caught up with him after supper, two nights before he was due to leave: there was a brief dispirited tussle—neither of them really wanted the damn talk. Jimmy looked pointedly at the TV and radio listings; his father gazed wistfully at the door. And they talked.

"Would you say that it's been a good summer, Jimmy?"

"Yes, definitely." They were sitting on the sofa facing the TV set so that they were talking to each other sideways, like people in a Catholic confessional. "Yes, I would."

"That's good. I've worried about it a little. You know—a boy of your age . . ."

"I know."

"I haven't seen as much of you as I hoped. We never did get to go fishing, did we?"

"That's all right."

"Well, a boy your age doesn't want to hang around with his father all the time, I guess."

Jimmy made a sound that could have meant yes, he does, or no, he doesn't, or the best elements of both. He didn't want his father to feel bad about this. He *had* had a good summer, in a screwy kind of way.

"How do you feel about going back to England?"

"I feel pretty good about it."

"You do?"

"Yes. I'm really looking forward to it."

His father looked at him doubtfully. Lorraine wasn't here tonight, and he looked thinner and more reflective. It occurred to Jimmy that he might be quite a shrewd man, when he wasn't fraternizing with his truck-driver friends (Gloria's phrase for them). It was funny the way Mr. Bannister went up and down, in and out.

"I sometimes wonder if I've done the right thing with you, Jimmy. I know it's a wonderful education over there, a wonderful opportunity." He rehearsed his old lines in a dry voice. "Socially, you may find it helpful—though that isn't the main reason, of course. But bouncing you around like this, I don't know. Are you sure you don't mind?"

"No, I don't mind."

"I don't know if I would have been so self-reliant. When I was your age, I went to prep school and I remember I was pretty homesick. And that was in *this* country. Maybe I should have settled for that in your case, do you think? A prep school in this country? What do you think, Jimmy?"

"If you're away from home, it doesn't matter how far you're away," said Jimmy untruthfully. "Away is away."

"Well, that's what *I* figured. Of course, your mother was very critical when she heard about it, but your mother is in no position ... well, we make these decisions, and then we hope we've done the right thing. I'm glad you're happy there."

"Definitely."

"I couldn't always tell from your letters. I worried about them."

"I guess there were some rough moments." Jimmy could hardly recall.

"Yes, of course." His father lowered his voice for a moment, to put a delicate question. "Were there any, you know, cruelties?"

Jimmy said no. This was one of those misunderstandings he had feared.

"It'll be even better next year," he added quickly.

Mr. Bannister rubbed the bridge of his nose for guidance. "It's funny the twists a man's life takes. A few years ago I could never have foreseen any of this. You don't mind my talking to you about it, Jimmy, you're old enough?" It was a genuine question, he really didn't know if Jimmy was old enough. Jimmy didn't know either, but nodded yes. "I haven't talked to you much about your mother, and I don't know how much you've guessed about her. She simply isn't capable of looking after you any more. Well, I'm sure you'd guessed that much."

Jimmy hadn't. He had guessed nothing. But he nodded again.

"Well, there it is. I don't know what *I'm* supposed to do. I don't know how *much* I'm supposed to do. There is such a thing as being too protective, too much of a father, don't you think?" He looked really troubled: how old is fifteen these days? He wouldn't be seeing his son for a while. Anything that didn't get said tonight might have to wait a long time. "Do you understand what I'm saying?"

Jimmy nodded once more. He had no idea what his father was saying.

"I want you to have the very best education going—that much I can see to. Beyond that I just don't know." He was making some kind of final appeal. Let me off the hook, he seemed to be saying. Confess that a good education is all you want or expect of me. He began talking quite incongruously about his damn business and the postwar boom. Jimmy was puzzled, couldn't quite grasp the point. "It's all right," he said. It wasn't the talk he'd expected at all.

Two days later they drove out to Idlewild with Lorraine sitting quietly between them. They shook hands—again that strange pulpy feeling—and parted. His father still wore a slightly petitionary expression. You're old enough, aren't you? I don't know what to do with a boy your age. As Jimmy boarded the plane, he felt more than old enough; he felt like one of the businessmen with the briefcases who lumbered up the gangway in front of him. After all, this was his third crossing. He waved encouragingly to his father, who waved back almost shyly. At his side Lorraine wigwagged with vigor. She had white golves on, he remembered.

The woman in the next seat was alternately thrilled and nauseated with this, her first flight. Jimmy found her amusing. Down below, Mrs. Fletcher and Carol and Forrest Tuckerman whirled away. The summer dwindled, vanished. Long Island became the size of a service-station map, and the motors roared toward the future. His face looked older in the washroom mirror. Surely he needed a shave now?

Mr. Soames, the ghostly ferryman, met him at the airport, and they went through the same process in reverse. There was something rather sad about Soames—he wasn't quite an American any more. Not one of the new models anyway. "You got your accent back," Soames said almost wistfully.

Jim spent what was left of this endless night at the neutral zone occupied by the Soameses. After a short day flying against the sun, sand the long comfortable evening, he felt alert and on top of things. Traveling east was much better than traveling west.

The railway station, the next day, had that pleasant rusty smell. Jimmy also approved of the chunks of soot on the glass roof and the empty slot machines. Clusters of boys with school caps or blazers, red, green, brown, sat on their suitcases and looked wretched, or stood up to greet each other, or wandered the lobby seaching for errant suitcases. Jimmy sought for traces of Sopworth, and finally found some fellows he didn't recognize, wearing the Sopworth cap.

"Hi," he said.

"Hello."

"Are you going to Sopworth?"

"Yes."

"So am I."

These must be new boys, just up from prep school. They were probably nervous about going to the Big Place. He understood too well. He dawdled with them a moment—an understanding older boy would have been a king-size help to him last year. But he only seemed to make them more uncomfortable. They stopped talking except to say, "I've finished my chocolate. None of the machines seem to work," "I've added three pounds since July, and I'm going to meet a dark stranger." "Ask it if it's got a friend," said Jimmy, but they didn't seem to see the point of this.

Mr. Soames had bought the train ticket and was looking around for him. A tragic, bewildered figure in his American topcoat. Jimmy strolled over to him, took the ticket, said goodbye. Soames wanted to see him right onto the train, but Jimmy didn't want to stand around with Soames. He wanted to look for friends. There was nothing he could do for Soames. The bags with the showy transatlantic labels had been mounted in the baggage car and there was nothing for it now but to wait.

So Mr. Soames left him, and he went on a buoyant prowl, He saw some more Sopworth boys at the newspaper stand, a little older than himself this time. He recognized them as belonging to Cornwallis house. He said hello, and they looked at him queerly. "I'm Bannister," he said. "Are you indeed?" said one of the boys. "He's Bannister," explained another suddenly. "Ah yes, of course he is," they all five nodded. "Bannister, yes, yes. Bannister, upon my soul."

He couldn't think of any way to join in their fun. He thought of dancing around, shouting, "Yes, yes, it's Bannister. Bannister is here." But that didn't seem quite to match. He decided to look for someone he knew. The Cornwallis crowd slightly jarred him. They had knocked a small chip off his confidence and he didn't want to lose any more. The sun, such as it was, had gone in, behind the dusky roof, and the station was becoming huge, noisy and dark. He made another slow circuit, but came up empty. He was half sorry to have released Mr. Soames. A companion gave you a look of purpose. He noticed that a line was beginning to form in front of his platform, so he joined it.

Schoolboys of all ages and sizes—he had never seen or imagined so many schoolboys—jostled and flapped around him. The train would take them en masse to some junction in the Midlands from which they would shoot out like spokes all over the country. Where, then, were Ryan and Samuelson and Philpott? Everyone else was grouped in by now. Jimmy should have made plans to meet his friends.

His ticket was clipped by a man with a white mustache, and Jim boarded the train. Ryan ad Philpott were not in the first compartment or the second or the third. He began to walk rapidly along the corridor, banging into people who were, mysteriously, already coming the other way. Everywhere he turned there were red-faced boys, chuffing along the aisle, or chaffering behind the compartment windows. He suddenly saw how strange they looked. Their features, the way their mouths worked. Their cheeks were as red as cricket balls after outdoorsy summers. No doubt about it, people did look different over here.

He gave up at last and came to roost in a compartment up near the engine. He had noticed people charging along the platform, and the train had filled up at blinding speed. Although he was one of the earlier arrivals, he was lucky to get a seat at all, crunched among four boys in yellow and blue caps, an Air Force officer, and two large schoolgirls, in a space designed presumably for six.

For sheer slowness and longness the journey set some sort of record. The boys struck up a conversation rather bravely with the Air Force man. He told them that he was stationed in Shropshire but had been stationed in Dorset up till a few weeks ago. One of the boys had, it seemed, spent the holidays in Dorset. What part? Do you know a town named Wobbles, it sounded like? Do I know a town called Wobbles? About ten miles outside Ketherington, isn't it? That's the place. On the A-something road. Oh yes, I know Wobbles all right.

Jimmy listened to the train for a while. When he tuned in again, one of the boys was asking if the Air Force man knew a town called Bumby, just outside Witchester. Is that anywhere near Flooding? Yes, just three villages away, actually. Humpletrimmer, humpletrimmer was the word from the train. It was carrying him farther into this alien countryside: where, if you didn't know Wobbles, couldn't even make a decent guess at Bumby, you were like a blind man. But at the other end of the tunnel lay Sopworth, and he knew all about Sopworth.

A porter looked in and told them that tea was served. They all stood up, after a round of "coming? coming? coming?" Jimmy decided to stay where he was. They would all be sitting in their groups, and he would have to find a vacant chair at someone else's table. Besides he remembered the terrible stuff they put in the cakes over here.

The Air Force man had left a small magazine to mark his seat. Jimmy crouched over it, and had a look. There was a picture in the center spread of a girl with naked breasts. Nothing new about that, of course—but he was suddenly scorched with lust. He couldn't take his eyes off the huge charcoal-gray nipples. He shut the magazine, and opened it again quickly. He wanted to bury his head in those paper breasts and leave it there. What *had* become of Mrs. Bannister anyway? He thought he could see for an instant two waxen breasts hanging dementedly out of a gold dressing gown ... but that was impossible. His mother's dressing gown was royal blue.

After about ten minutes he decided he had better put down the magazine and creep back to his place. He didn't want them all to troop back in and find him staring at the magazine: with red-eared ardor.

This freakish burst of excitement left him suddeny drained and weak. He could hardly face them when they got back from tea. The Air Force man picked up the magazine and glanced at it for a moment, as if checking for fingerprints, and then stuffed it casually into his pocket. He knows I've been reading it. It's written all over the cover. The signs of Jimmy's own helpless dwindling desire must be apparent to everyone—only it isn't desire, he wanted to explain. It's loneliness. The girl in the magazine looked a little like Gloria, he decided, his father's companion of last summer. And a little like who knows who else? Some valuable cockiness had seeped out, spent on that stupid picture.

They got to their junction, and had to stand about on another platform for half an hour. Jimmy couldn't wait to get to Sopworth now, to see some friendly faces. He strolled along the platform to set the blood flowing again: looked at the big hoardings advertising oxo, whatever that was. Bovril, Cadbury's chocolate: this wasn't the England he remembered. There were so many small things he hadn't accounted for. He read a playbill which announced the arrival of someone called Nervo and Knox for a limited engagement at the local Palladium, to be followed by Evelyn Laye in *Babes in the Wood,* our ever popular Christmas pantomime. He turned away. What he wanted was one token, one small sign that he was on the same globe he had been on yesterday.

There were certainly many more people with sandy hair than he remembered. The smell of the train conductors was a new development. The girls' legs were redder. More mustaches, hair in buns; bad teeth and tin spectacles. The people came in funny shapes too: high shoulders and short necks, round shoulders and furry ears; also faces like pug dogs, beetles, eagles, flamingos, weasels—and one actual pig, walking toward him now down the platform with a snout and a rolling gait. Stopping at the chocolate machine and jiggling the handle. Some crazy natural disaster had occurred during the summer, causing a biological jumble. He tried to think of it as funny, all these marvelous English characters, etc., but the effort made his throat dry. The odd thing was that he couldn't remember any of this from the last time.

He considered having some tea in the station tearoom, but it looked so dreary in there. A long line of schoolboys and adults in raincoats shuffled past a fat girl in a stained white uniform. They carried their cups to marble tables and lowered their faces into the tea. You would die of despair in there. Confidence, he was beginning to see, required a certain amount of strategy.

His heart lifted as his own train pulled in Once he was at Sopworth, he would know where he was. A number of Sopworth boys had converged on this train, and while he still didn't know any of them too well, they made a more familiar sound.

Traveling to Sopworth was like traveling to a warm spot—bosom was one word that came to mind. This wasn't just England any more, not just unadulterated foreignness, but something he could cope with. There were two other Sopworth boys in the compartment, and he could almost have hugged them. (Perhaps sensing this, they avoided his eye.)

The train arrived in chilly twilight. The station was the size of a postage stamp, good for maybe two trains a term. The Sopworth boys got off in a tumbling stream, and Jimmy was surprised, now that he saw them all together, at how few boys he knew to speak to. Ryan, Philpott, Samuelson, were definitely among the missing. He nodded at Peters and Featherstone, who nodded back. And that was about it.

The school had provided buses, and everyone went pounding toward those. This must be the runningest country in the world. He supposed he ought to look for his bags, but he couldn't find the baggage car; and finally someone told him—in a voice implying that he should have known this—that the baggage car had gone on to the depot at Greater Sopworth, where it would be unloaded in God's good time. The three minutes wasted on this quest deprived him of a seat on the bus, and he was obliged to stand jiggling in the aisle crisscrossed by four conversations, none of which made any sense. Words like devizes and assizes and scrum-half put him off the scent every time. There were no lights, and nothing much to look at except the backs of heads; but if he crouched low he could see the last shoals of bicycles lit like glowworms, passing through Sopworth's shopping center on the way home, and after that the darkening hedges and fields that he remembered so well—a little past their friendly best at this hour, abut still reassuring.

Ryan, Philpott, Samuelson, where are you? It was cold and dark, and the voices wouldn't stop their bird song: that bloody man Prothero called "leg-up" five minutes from time. Honestly, I could have scragged him . . . (Shyly) No, I shall be hooker, and you shall be prop. He remembered no such sounds as these. But Ryan, Philpott and Samuelson would speak properly and understandably. It was a rich diet of change that he'd been on today: but familiarity lay just ahead now.

Twilight had very nearly given in to night. (It certainly took its sweet time about it over here.) The bus pulled up at the school gates and the driver climbed irritably from his perch to open them. He reascended and the bus started chuffing up the dark drive. Without warning Jimmy's pulse began to race wantonly. Just a few yards to Philpott and company. The great black buildings (he swore they'd grown during the summer) came swinging round a bend in the drive. Grotesquely, feverishly desirable. Boys began to clamber from their seats, like animals from cages, trying to squeeze past Jimmy or push him out in front of them. Other buses had come up behind, teeming, suppurating with boys. Jimmy felt, incongruously, a little bus-sick. "Excuse me," he said, but found himself tottering down the steps under an implacable pressure of boys.

Nothing rude, nothing personal. One always gets off buses like that. They danced past him and ran toward the school. He began to run too. Eagerly. As toward home.

□ VIII □

Down the long main corridor they poured, wildly, as if someone had started a panic or, more likely, as if this part of term must be got through quickly—the settling in, the forgetting about home, all done on the double.

They swarmed at the bulletin boards, where their classrooms, sleeping quarters, rugby and soccer games (Sopworth was one of those rare schools that supported both sports—indifferently, to be sure) were allotted. Cries of "blast" and "wizard" rent the air. "I've got the Foghorn again." "Oh, good—Mr. Moore," and a groundswell of damns and bloodies.

Jimmy craned. Sopworth boys were slightly taller than the national average, and much ruder, but he managed to make out that he was back in the Frisby dormitory again. That was rather a blow. He had looked forward to a private room. He peered at the other names—Ryan and Samuelson had disappeared altogether. Dispositions made by stealth during the summer. He would have to make do with Philpott: the other boys on the dormitory roster were new to him.

He didn't really want to know what classes he was in but found himself shoved in that direction anyway. Here again he found that everyone had moved on except Bannister. Bannister was some sad relic, lost in the examination shuffle. More Foghorn, more Smiles. For a whole year. Ryan and Samuelson had presumably got their school certificates and had passed into the upper atmosphere where you specialized and the masters treated you like human beings. Philpott had been kept behind for general childishness, his character left to ripen in the Frisby dormitory. But even he had left Jimmy in the dust scholastically.

Jimmy had been pushed to the very end of the bulletin board by now, and it seemed to be time to resume running. The footsteps led now to the school dining room, where some kind of snack was in the works. Here surely he would find Ryan—the most food-minded man of his acquaintance: talking no doubt of lovely horsemeat from County Kildare, lovely toad-in-the-hole from County Mayo, ravishing bubble and squeak: "And now back to *this* muck." (Confirming belch from Samuelson.)

But again he was disappointed. None of his friends had arrived yet. The long Frisby table was runged with place cards, and he went on a reconnoiter. Samuelson had advanced a good twenty places during the summer: even the lowly Philpott had moved up about twelve. But Bannister was exactly where he had been. Surrounded by new names, just up from the junior school, presumably. Bannister, you're in the dustbin of history—a phrase from his summer reading. The school certificate seemed to be the great watershed.

He sat down at the place marked Bannister. A plate of jam sandwiches was being scrambled for in front of him and he plunged his hand into the scrum. Jam sandwiches. "Plums from fair South Africa. Whacko!" said a dismal twit. A too familiar brown teapot also was shimmying down the line, and he extracted some stewed tea from it. Bit into a jam sandwich, listened to the chatter of the boys around him—arrogant chatter of strangers, chatter he would be hearing all year, over his jam sandwiches and tea.

So far he had observed everything through a glaze of excitement and objectivity. There was this and then there was that. Movement and noise. All quite amusing and interesting. But now, as he sat still, a feeling that was not so good began very lightly to assert itself. Not so good at all. The roar of the dining room, the taste of the jam. Everyone was racing and shouting to avert some great tragedy.

He wolfed his sandwich and stood up. It was important for him to get moving again. He ran now, almost blindly, back along the main corridor. He had looked forward to finding his friends. He must find them now.

They were not in the Frisby recreation room. Some fellows that he knew only slightly were playing ping-pong. A couple of others were reading newspapers, like old men in a club, left over from the spring. They didn't look round as he burst upon them. There were no glad cries of "Bannister."

"Have you seen Ryan or Samuelson?" he said.

"What? (thunk) Ryan, you say? (thunk) I don't think he's here (thunk) any more." The ball scudded into the net. "No, I'm pretty sure he's somewhere else by now."

"That's not possible. I didn't hear anything."

"Oh well—if it's not possible, that's all right then. Whose serve is it?"

"It should be mine, actually. But since you've taken the last eight in a row, perhaps you'd care to continue . . ."

"Oh, sorry."

Their voices dimmed. "I mean to say some people *like* serving . . . like it very much indeed."

Jimmy went careening out again. If he stopped moving, his lungs would congest. Where were his darn friends? Well, there was always Philpott. Philpott at least would be up in the dormitory, unpacking his tooth mug, pinching things from other people's bags. Philpott would do for openers.

He felt himself running desperately like a man in a dream. All the other characters seemed to be going the other way. Some of them had no faces, others had too much. Jimmy was tireder than he thought and not too far from hysteria. This wasn't the place he remembered at all. He had never been here in his life. The geniality of last summer had been locked away. The prefects were already stiff and beady-eyed. The very walls and floors had hardened. And there was to be a whole year of this. A whole year.

He whizzed up the stairs. Philpott had better be in that dormitory.

There must be some satisfaction in the here and now. Last year he had kept in shape by dreaming about America; then he had dreamed about England; but now there was nothing left to dream about. Reality must deliver the goods.

To his amazement, Philpott was indeed in the dormitory, unpacking rather quietly and solemnly: folding things carefully and putting them in his cubicle.

"Hey, Philpott!" It was wildly elating to come across Philpott, at this juncture. "Man, it's good to see you."

Philpott looked up uncertainly. "Hello, Bannister." He was smaller than Jim remembered, and his features less pronounced; he was, as far as his face went, just a little boy. "What sort of holiday did you have, Bannister?" he asked solemnly.

"It was all right. How about yours?"

"We went to Brighton, actually," said Philpott. It was almost an apology. They sat silently. Jimmy had assumed they would just fall into coversation. "Do you always go to Brighton?" he gave a desperate prod.

"No. Sometimes we go to Keswick."

Sometimes to Keswick, indeed. He was worse than small. He was unformed. He also gave the impression that one mustn't get him too excited. He had turned pale at Jimmy's whooping introduction and remained slightly under-par.

"Where are the others?" Jim asked. "Where's Samuelson?"

"We won't be seeing much of Samuelson, I fear," said Philpott. "He's been given a room to himself in Dr. Rabelais' house."

"How'd he rate that?"

"He got seven distinctions in the school cert. They're hoping he'll get a scholarship."

Somebody else in the headmaster's house. He didn't want to hear about that. He didn't especially want to be told about Ryan either, but it was between that or asking, how was Brighton?

"Yes, it's true, he's been taken at Sandhurst."

Jimmy started to say something, but he noticed that Philpott's lips were trembling. He was the kind of boy who probably cried at the beginning of every term; he had come up here by himself to be ready for the first sad thought to strike.

The logical thing was to leave him alone. But he was the only friend Jimmy had left. So Jim sat awkwardly on Philpott's bed watching him cry, and then looking away, off down the dormitory, hoping he would stop soon. But Philpott wept on, quietly but insistently, in line with the Sopworth rubrics. At the far end of the room, another boy sat hunched over his locker, presumably sharing Philpott's unpretentious agony. By midnight this place would be a bawling, sniffing chaos.

Jimmy sat for several minutes, expecting Philpott to pull himself together for very pride. But Philpott treated his tears as if they were some simple allergy, to be endured patiently and without embarrassment.

His composure began to make Jimmy fidgety. He refused either to break
down or to pull himself together, but paddled along in the middle. Finally
the little fellow wiped his eyes in a business-like way, excused himself politely
and wandered to the bathroom. There goes my last friend. There isn't much
to him, is there? No, not too much.

Jimmy shut his eyes. Philpott gave the toilet the first of several flushings
as if each tear must be cleared away scrupulously to make room for the next.
The humorous side of Philpott was simply an invention of Ryan's, and now
Ryan was gone; leaving not one but two gaps, and possibly three, if you
counted Samuelson.

If I gave in to my feelings, it wouldn't help me to cry, thought Jimmy.
That was last year. His problem would not be solved by a trivial sprinkle
now. He didn't know exactly what his problem was, but he pictured it as
more a deep cracking kind of thing—much too dry to be helped by tears. A
Mohave Desert jeweled with cactus plants. If he masturbated tonight, disturbing the neighbors, it would be no more than the dry heaves: perhaps a
little sand and sawdust. Masturbation was out. Crying was out. But what was
his problem?

He went to his own bed and lay down. His mind went back to the picture in the magazine, but this did not produce the desired effect. There was
no warming spring in his loins. What had become of Mrs. Bannister anyway?
For all those years he had honestly not thought about it. He had, just three
days ago, evaded his father's hints very dextrously; but of course he knew. He
knew very well. Her last few months at home had been clear enough. "Wise
up, Bannister. You know she's crazy," he said out loud, and he couldn't tell
whether the voice that said it was American or English.

This frightened and sobered him. These last two days had been more
confusing than he realized. His heart still beat to American time, his nervous
system had gotten stuck somewhere over the Atlantic. To call him American,
or fifteen years old, or anything else, was quite meaningless. For a moment he
frankly hadn't known who he was.

He sat up and looked around. This was his home now, even if it didn't
look like it. The sound of Philpott sobbing and flushing had a homey ring to
it anyhow.

The new boys began to trickle in and get ready for bed. And Jimmy had
to endure again the sight of the rolled trouser leg and the foot dipped modestly in the basin. He would never know why that set his teeth on edge so.
The new boys in the dormitory were subdued by now, caught up in the
place's black spirit. Philpott had timed his collapse with some skill and left
the bathroom, fully composed, even bored, just as the others were entering.

He said good night to Jimmy in a rather stiff way: and Jimmy realized that he had minded very much about being watched at his evening tears.

Jimmy was terribly tired and thought he could escape into sleep without further fret. His fears of a wailing dormitory were not realized: outside of an occasional mutter that might have been protest, or sheer disbelief, and the usual grind of breathing and scratching and turning over, the place was practically silent.

After a few minutes a slight burbling hum asserted itself. Well, to be exact, one boy was burbling and another two were humming. A new group was forming at the far end of the dormitory, similar to his own group last summer. A Bannister-less group. They were quickly shushed by the new prefect, a fellow called Fingal: but the sound lingered sweetly on the air. When he shut his eyes he saw that things were still quite bad, very bad in fact. Luckily he knew how to handle such things now. It would not be like last term. He could not bear to go back to that. But there was no denying things were bad. Who was he kidding about this place being home? What kind of joke was that . . . ? Interesting, isn't it, that Mother opposed the whole thing? You bet she did. Poor old crazy Mother.

Battered all day by sights and sounds, he was now kept awake by this seeping rivulet of reflections. In a normal room he would have snapped on the light to chase the spooks, but here that would have caused a sensation. In the dark, he was stuck with his thoughts. He slipped a quarter-inch further into unconsciousness and found himself barreling along a gallery of some kind while his mother, hair flying out over her gold dressing gown, pleaded with Mr. Bannister not to send Jim to England. The combined noise of the roller skates was deafening. Finally Mr. Bannister scraped her off his legs, where she had flung herself, and left her face down on the floor. (that was a dream—no, it wasn't. That was the truth. That was exactly how it happened.)

He shook himself awake. It *was* a dream, or the grubby outskirts of one. He still had the taste of it in his mouth. The dry taste of fear. *"Could* you be quiet," mumbled someone from the next bed. *"Is* it asking too much?" You know, going crazy wasn't too impossible. A few dreams like that would get you there in no time. Having a mother like that helped show you the way.

For heaven's sake, Bannister, what a silly thing to say, in any accent. Going crazy probably takes years of preparation. The summer had been altogether mild and sane. He was miles away from insanity.

Again he addressed himself to sleep. But he now felt that in order to get there he must first say something—*anything*—out loud. It was a strange requirement, but absolutely inflexible. And if he met it, he would arouse the whole dormitory, and bring them, like the night animals in *Snow White,* blinking around his bed.

A dormitory would certainly be a heck of a place to go crazy in. You would have to do it without distrubing anybody. He lay with his eyes very wide open, wondering if he could somehow leap across the moat of viper-like dreams that surrounded real sleep. He tried various word and number games, but found he had to play them with his eyes open. The moment his eyes were shut, pictures of America began to form behind the lids, and he knew now that they were lies. Those sailboats, Huckleberry Bannister's raft, lazing away the summer with his friends—all terrible, terrible lies. If he gave in to them now, his whole mind would be a lie.

But the only alternative was to attend to the dormitory, with its callous night sounds. The snorers and scratchers knew, at worst, that they were snoring and scratching in their own country, so that their homesickness was superficial, verging on the smug. And closer to hand there were the rock hard sheets, insufficiently pulped, the better to build character. In his present fever, there was something really tragic about these sheets. If he cried over anything, it would be over that.

And if not the dormitory, the Bovril signs and the oxo signs. And if not the Bovril signs, the R.A.F. man talking about his billet in Nether Wobbles, or the stand-off half comparing notes with the wing three-quarters. And if none of these, the girl in the magazine, and, mysteriously Mrs. Bannister in her imaginary gold dressing gown.

Why did his mother have to pick tonight? And why did his head have to form pictures at all? He tried blanking out, and that brought him full circle to a total quivering consciousness of his sheets. It was as if the nation had lost all its good sheets in the war. The most daring part of Goering's plan. "Destroy a nation's sheets and you have *achtung schicklgruber sweinhund*" . . . He resented the way these ones touched him too firmly in places, missed him altogether in others. The stiffness formed tunnels along which the draft could winnow; so that, bad as the sheets were, he tried to wrap them tighter, stuffing them under his belly and pinning the harsh substance there.

He wished the American scenes were not lies. They had a kind of sickening attractiveness. He knew that he absolutely must not give in to them even for a second, but this made them all the more tempting. They promised, beyond everything else, sleep.

Very well—he would lie awake all night. Not so fatal. He would try to relax. . . . But even this was not vouchsafed him right away, for he kept slipping into the moat of waking dreams. Or getting locked in hopeless debate with his fluctuating consciousness.

You know that in real life there is no raft and no Huckleberry Bannister. The yachts in the Sound are manned by fat businessmen with big mouths and soft white arms. Fishing is what your father thinks he likes. To wish for these things is to wish for nothing.

Yes, yes, I know. But here comes the raft now. And who is yon gawky teenager playing the banjo? Why it's————. He turned over, dislodging the top sheet again. His skin would be covered in fever blisters by morning, and he would have a cold. Fine way to face the Foghorn. Well, forget *that*. Jim thought instead about baggage labels. No one else in the school could match his collection, except maybe that quiet boy from British Guiana, if he was back. And that was *all* he had, just baggage labels . . . poor devil. Which gave Jimmy a funny idea about traveling: namely that bits of you came off in various places and took time to reassemble. The boy from Guiana left his tongue at home. And parts of Jim Bannister still haunted his father's hotel room, reveling in the soft sheets and the air conditioning. A whole different Bannister, left hanging in the air.

Not only soft sheets, but so school tomorrow. The other Bannister had it made. Jimmy watched enviously as his transatlantic self dug his head into the pillow. A nice pillow without a single brick in it. Tomorrow this bum would start the day with ham and eggs and delicious box scores.

. . . Another myth, Bannister. Breakfast was never that good. The days that followed breakfast were usually long and boring. Admit it, Bannister. All right, I'll admit it. I won't think about the breakfasts. Or about lying in bed? That was pretty boring too, wasn't it? O.K. Or about lying in bed. Just let me sleep *now*.

Tomorrow's classrooms were beginning to weigh on his mind also. He knew from today's experience that anything pleasant he remembered about them would be missing tomorrow. It was a feature of reality to be unexpectedly lousy. He saw himself, too sleepy to think, being roasted alive by the Foghorn, and then on to another classroom to have his geography mocked by Mr. Smiles. (And *your* country, Bannister. Which direction is *that* in?) And then the *dernier* straw—M. Necker's gentle disappointment over his French.

He would want to go somewhere to rest up. But that was impossible. The day was a seamless nightmare. The din in the corridors unceasing, the legs churning, the feet how they pound; and in the afternnon, dropping with fatigue, he would be introduced to a new game. He supposed that all the talk about hookers and fly-halfs referred to that. A roaring, hostile game, with Bannister caught in the middle, being hooked and having his legs torn off like fly wings.

It didn't matter, he could take it. So long as he was *wide* awake, none of these thoughts were very terrible. No game could be as bad as that, they wouldn't allow it. Some society would step in. In general, things would not be half as bad as last term. He knew so much more. He was older, had two solo flights to his credit, had flashed a passport around.

—But I don't *know* any French. Whatever I learned last year is gone. Don't be disappointed, sir, please don't. Oh, my God, he's crying. Don't cry, sir. For pity's sake.

The picture in the magazine came round in its turn, as if his fantasies were on a revolving band. He flung himself between the breasts once more, almost breaking his pillow in half, trying to get there before it turned into Mrs. Bannister again. But it wasn't Mrs. Bannister at all, it was Carol Fletcher. No need to hurry. His heart rose for a moment. But she carefully picked him off her left breast and deposited him on the rug. She walked slowly away, swaying her hips about twenty feet to either side.

. . . It wasn't much of a dream, but he clung to it now, prostrate on the marble floor, trying to grip the smooth slabs. This was the closest he had gotten to sleep so far. He mustn't let it get away.

But he slipped back inexorably the other way. A dog was barking nearby, ordering him to his feet. Carol disappeared with a snap, like a cud of bubble gum, and there he was, face down on his pillow, which was hard as any marble. The boy in the next bed had pushed back his own crusty sheets and was having a coughing fit. Why, why did he have to pick that moment to cough? Another few seconds and Jimmy would have been out of reach.

"*Can't* you wrap up? said a voice in the dark. "*Is* it asking too much?"

"Sorry, I've got a tickle."

Oh, well, it didn't matter. Jimmy forced himself all the way awake, to resume his hold on things. He was, bear this in mind, older than last term, and more experienced. The masters would look smaller, if nothing else. He could give Smiles a thrashing, if worst came to worst.

Tomorrow, after lunch, he would sneak up here for a few minutes and have a nap. When he woke from that, he would be acclimatized. Two sleeping sessions was all it took. He knew how these things worked now. He had the strategies down cold.

. . . A nap in this place might be hard to come by, though. With no shades on the windows. And your head on a pillow that you're already sick of. You'll have a cauliflower ear, you'll have scars on your face . . . honestly, you ought to be here in this hotel room. The thing is, it's private. You know what will happen when you try resting in the dormitory, Bannister, don't you? Some darn fool will come in who can't find his hockey stick. He wonders if he might possibly have left it under your bed. There is no more depressing sound in the world than a man looking for his hockey stick under your bed.

Why were there no shades on the windows? He saw himself lying in streaming daylight, itching to yank at nonexistent shades. Pulling them down over his head finally, and sitting on the floor wrapped in brown paper . . . it didn't have to be someone looking for his hockey stick. It might be someone on the prowl for Brasso to clean his Army boots with or the button on his hat; or just the threat of someone coming to look for those things. Or just the big empty space—bedrooms are meant to be enclosed. That's nature's way, Bannister.

I suppose I shall skip Army drill again this year. That is not for the reason you think. It is not because I am an American, but because I have some hidden defect. I would crack in the jungle, for one thing. My pimples would give me away. Glowing like lightbulbs. Give the whole platoon away, in fact . . .

He tried quickly to make a dream of this, but it was just another waking-sleeping reverie. Perhaps he was really afraid to go to sleep. Perhaps it didn't take months to go crazy either, but could happen overnight, if you went to sleep with your head in the wrong position. Three hundred bad dreams in a row would splinter the strongest intelligence. And let us face it, Bannister, yours is not the strongest intelligence.

Several voices seemed to be at work in his skull now, old men and boys taking turns, Englishmen and Americans. Which one would win? Which would own the title to the Bannister estate? He wondered what time it was. He had no watch, and the chapel bells were dim and jumbled up. He could have been here for hours, or just minutes; he couldn't say for sure whether he had slept yet or not. Perhaps the summer had not been mild and sane at all, but a perfect preparation for the funny farm.

How had his mother known that *she* was going crazy? And how had she taken the news? There was a moment of heavy stillness in his mind, as if before a thunderstorm; he pictured his mother moving slowly around the kitchen, preparing a calming cup of tea. His father sat discreetly in the next room. It was very bad taste to mention her craziness at this particular point.

And then suddenly she began to scream like a frightened animal. His skull split with the noise. The only other sound was the front door banging, meaning his father had probably gone out. Without thinking, Jimmy sat up and reached for his slippers. He was going out too. He was halfway down the dormitory before he woke up fully. He had better talk to someone right away.

"Fingal, Fingal." He shook the prefect's thickly pajamaed shoulder.

"Who the devil are you, devil do you want?" Fingal, what could be seen of him, was a muffled ball of fear and rage.

"I had a bad dream," said Jim lamely.

"What? What dream?" Fingal was still asleep himself. That was what was so strange about him.

"I forget. I wanted to talk to someone. I think I'm going crazy."

"Who are you, anyway? What's your *name*?"

"Bannister, sir."

"And you think what?"

"That I'm going crazy."

Fingal grunted and turned onto his stomach. "You probably are," he said slyly. "You seem like that sort of boy." He lay like a beached whale; nothing would rouse him, now that he was warned. Jimmy wandered back toward his bed. He didn't really think he was going crazy—it was just that you needed a pretty good excuse to start a conversation at that time of night.

Someone returning from the bathroom slipped by like a ghost ship, trying not to wake himself up.

He, James Bannister III, could not face another dream like that last one, not for a while. It had shaken him, dislodged his insides, splintered the walls of his skull: like the caving in of some mineshaft. And yet he had spoken truth to Fingal. He could not remember anything about it.

Eventually the bell in the distance gave three distinct chimes. Three in the morning. He had just two things left up his sleeve to see him through the night. One was too fragile to contemplate—that was the thought of seeing Rabelais tomorrow. He sensed that it would be bad luck to invoke that right now; also it was too sweetly painful, like some oozing of bone marrow. Instead, there was this other thing. Simple damnation, you might call it.

Well, just this once, he whispered out loud to himself, just until he got acclimatized: he opened, slyly, lasciviously, his treasure chest of lies. The American slides, rivers, boardwalks, penthouses, the jabbering gaudy crew: picked out a Technicolor riverboat and lay himself sensuously down beside it, next to a phantom girl, both warmed, caressed by lies: a stiff, ruinous price to pay for sleep, and for avoiding nameless, faceless dreams. But a price that simply had to be paid.

☐ **IX** ☐

The next morning Rabelais addressed the whole school. It was a cold sharp morning. Mrs. Fletcher would have been amused by the breakfast. Wooden oatmeal, flannel toast. Everyone into the gym for a talk. Jimmy was so tired he hardly knew what he was doing. Great scrapings of sand in his eyes and temples lined with frost. He stumbled drunkenly behind the others. They shoved and gouged because they were too shy to express themselves any other way. They were really very decent chaps, guys, whatever.

The boys dragged their folded wooden chairs across the floor and banged them into place. Jimmy found himself sitting underneath the parallel bars. There was some mysterious gray padding on the wall behind him: Something that lunatics might fling themselves against. Three small boys, jabbering like monkeys, squeezed in behind him. Crazy as jaybirds. Rabelais would come in soon with a fireman's hose and quiet them.

Jim was waiting for Rabelais with a furious excitement. He wiped his mouth with the back of his hand. He had been banished from his own country, from his father's house, but this vague spindly man had taken him in and given hom a home of sorts. Rabelais would take care of things from here on in.

The headmaster was several minutes late, and a few venturesome souls began to stamp their feet: to be shushed furiously by the local prefect. Jimmy's eyes had gone stiff from weariness and were fixed in a stare. Rabelais would come through that door on the upper left. He would wander toward the lectern, rubbing his thin, kind hands. He would trip on the raised step, spread-eagling across the platform like a wounded bird.

The dear old man entered at last and did more or less as he was supposed to, although he didn't quite go down when he tripped on the step, and, grasping the frayed lapels of his great black gown, he began to talk. He welcomed them back, with a nasty cough. He told them they must all have haircuts within the next three days, or risk the usual caning. Something was a posititive disgrace, Jimmy didn't catch what it was. At any rate, one hoped that the baggage would all be collected by this evening. Positive disgrace. The back of the gym was already lined with trunks and suitcases relayed from Greater Sopworth. The thought that the bags hadn't even been *opened* yet was a sad one. A very sad one indeed.

A special word for the new boys. Expect take time grow accustomed to ways. Stop. Any difficulty come me. Stop. Jimmy yawned and looked around. All those faces. Just the noses alone. You will find your classrooms on the bulletin board, you will find the bulletin board ... Rabelais looked so nice and friendly after all those others: once we've all shaken hands with him, it will be all right.

Meanwhile he examined his conscience about last night, most specifically the wheatfield. The wheatfield had come with first light, a sheet of gold. Huge, far as the eye could see, none of your back-to-back houses and Bovril signs. Just a plain wheatfield. You didn't have to draw any conclusions about that. All you had to do was look at it. Gold. Blue. Uniform breeze combing it all back. No lie in that that he could see.

Will now read to you from this little blue book. School regulations, chapter 1, section I. What would be wrong, because untruthful, would be to imagine, say, a farmer in blue dungarees. At prayer with his wife. One must draw the line at that. Nothing wrong with plain scene. But no conclusions.

Walking on the grass. Expressly forbidden ... playing gramophones after supper, going out after dark ... *expressly* forbidden. An old-fashioned schoolhouse would also be a mistake at this point ... A flag on the blackboard. A teacher in a mother hubbard. There must be definite rules about that sort of thing.

The tone of the headmaster's speech had gotten spliced on somewhere. We will allow absolutely no freckle-faced kids into our schoolroom. We do not especially *like* freckle-faced kids, do we? Fishing is prohibited until further notice. You may sit quietly by the side of the stream, but that is all ...

Rabelais seemed slightly out of sorts, but that did not hide the fact that he was a thoroughly decent man. You could see the kindness in his eyes.

The headmaster came to a pause eventually and asked if there were any questions. A large earnest boy got up and asked for further refinements of regulation. Was one permitted, say, to keep one's bicycle in the Bywater area *after dark?* It was rather a fine point: Rabelais scratched his nose and said he had never considered it before. In a few days he would pin a ruling to the notice board.

Another question, then. Did the ukase pertaining to school lockers also apply to *desk drawers?* Jimmy's mind went spinning off again, into his own rule book. Military parades, for instance. What did they come under? Holidays, special events. See *firecrackers*. (Breasts? See under *dressing gown*.)

He had a notion that these were not the questions that Rabelais really wanted. The dry tonelessness of his answers could only mean profound disappointment. These people were not making contact with the real Dr. Rabelais at all.

Without any exact plan, Jimmy stood up himself and raised his hand. For a moment nobody noticed him and he reveled in the sense of standing up unseen. Then Rabelais caught his eye and said, "Yes, what is it?" Jim had no definite question in mind. He wanted to say, "Hello, sir. I got here all right. We're all very glad to see you." Things that needed saying. He looked at Rabelais with warmth and encouragement—somebody should say these things at the start of a school year.

"What is it, what do you want?" The glasses glinted like ice cubes. Contact had not been made yet. Perhaps Rabelais' eyesight was not too good. Incredibly, he didn't even seem to recognize Jimmy.

"It's me. I'm here." This place could still be saved by a simple gesture. He decided he had better get closer. He began to forge forward and politely a path was cleared for him. His eyes were fixed on Rabelais', waiting for the moment of recognition. The shy smile that could hardly be refused him. He felt that he was moving gracefully, not bumping into things.

Nobody interfered as he climbed the platform. They would give him a hearing. It was the English way. He was grinning uncontrollably at Rabelais as he had at Carol Fletcher. He even put out his hand—nothing could be fairer than that.

"What is it? What do you want? What are you doing up here?" It was almost a scream.

The scene froze. High on a lecure platform. Jimmy with his hand out. Rabelais' glasses glinting now like haw frost, concealing the great kindness of the man; the audience polite, curious.

Then everyone started to roar and bang their chairs. And the tension that had held him erect worked the other way and he pitched forward slightly into the great black arms of the headmaster, just too tired to stand. He said something but it was lost in the thick coarse folds. He was rather afraid he had made a fool of himself.

He heard a lot of quite distinct voices saying quite intelligent things. The one he liked best belonged to someone he took to be a very old, very fragile man, although he had noticed none such in the gym.

"This boy needs attention," the voice fluted. Jimmy tracked it down eventually to Rabelais himself and felt that although James Bannister III might have made a mistake in his approach to the headmaster, he had Rabelais on his side now. It was worth coming from America for that.

He turned to the crowd with a half smile. And he saw that what they were doing actually was laughing. The long strange faces were twisted. The big teeth stuck out viciously. The sound was like the shrieking in a stockyard.

The English way, indeed. He realized that he was clutching the headmaster's lapels—well, it wasn't that funny. And was it his imagination, or was the headmaster laughing too? Smirking anyway.

He wondered what happened next. Did he, as he fully intended to, hit the headmaster in the face? Did he grab the icy spectacles and twist them across the man's nose, and did he then volley his few obscenities into the crowd? Or did he do nothing but simply dream those things? For very shame, he could never remember what happened between that moment and his return to the United States, ticketed for a regular American prep school, a couple of weeks later.